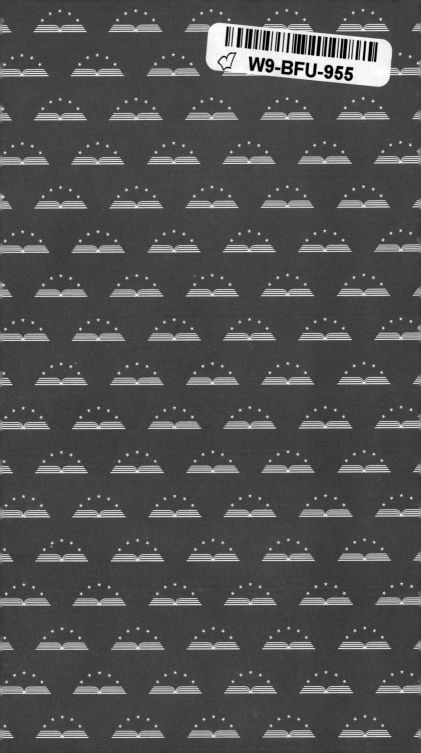

WILLIAM FAULKNER

WILLIAM FAULKNER

NOVELS 1926–1929

Soldiers' Pay
Mosquitoes
Flags in the Dust
The Sound and the Fury

THE LIBRARY OF AMERICA

The paper used in this publication meets the
minimum requirements of the American National Standard for
Information Sciences—Permanence of Paper for Printed
Library Materials, ANSI z39.48—1984.

Distributed to the trade
in the United States by Penguin Putnam Inc.
and in Canada by Penguin Books Canada Ltd.

Library of Congress Catalog Number: 2005049444
For cataloging information, see end of Notes.
ISBN 1—931082—89—8

First Printing
The Library of America—164

Manufactured in the United States of America

JOSEPH BLOTNER AND NOEL POLK
WROTE THE NOTES AND EDITED THE TEXTS
FOR THIS VOLUME

*The publishers wish to thank Mrs. Paul D. Summers, Jr.,
the Alderman Library of the University of Virginia, and
the Berg Collection of the New York Public Library
for the use of archival materials
and Mississippi State University
for technical assistance.*

The texts of
Soldiers' Pay, Mosquitoes, Flags in
the Dust, *and* The Sound and the Fury,
have been established by Noel Polk.

Chapter One.

Achilles— Did you shave this morning, Cadet?
Mercury— Yes, Sir.
Achilles— With what, Cadet?
Mercury— Issue, Sir.
Achilles— Carry on, Cadet.

——Old Play.
(about 19—?)

Lowe, Julian, number——, late a Flying Cadet, Umptieth Squadron, Air Service, known as "One Wing" by the other embryonic aces of his flight, regarded the world with a yellow and disgruntled eye. He suffered the same jaundice that many a more booted one than he did, from Flight Commanders through Generals to the ambrosial single-barred (not to mention that inexplicable beast of the field which the French so beautifully call an aspiring aviator): they had stopped the war on him.

So he sat in a smoldering of disgusted sorrow, not even enjoying his pullman prerogatives, spinning on his thumb his hat with its accursed white band.

"Had your nose in the wind, hey buddy?" said Yaphank going home and smelling to high heaven of bad whiskey.

"Ah, go to hell," he returned sourly and Yaphank doffed his tortured hat.

"Why, sure, General——or should I of said Lootenant? Excuse me, madam: I got gassed doing k.p. and my sight aint been the same since. On to Berlin! Yeh, sure, we're on to Berlin. I'm on to you, Berlin: I got your number. Number no thousand no hundred and naughty naught Private (very private) Joe Gilligan, late for parade, late for fatigue, late for breakfast when breakfast is late. The statue of liberty aint never seen me, and if she do, she'll have to 'bout face."

Cadet Lowe raised a sophisticated eye. "Say, whatcher drinking, anyway?"

"Brother, I dunno. Fellow that makes it was gave a Congressional medal last Chuesday because he has got a plan to

3

stop the war. Enlist all the Dutchmen in our army and make
'em drink so much of his stuff a day for forty days, see? Ruin
any war. Get the idea?"

"I'll say. Wont know whether its a war or a dance, huh?"

"Sure, they can tell. The women will all be dancing. Listen,
I had a swell jane and she said For Christ's sake, you cant
dance. And I said Like hell I cant. And we was dancing and
she said What are you, anyways? and I says What do you
wanta know for? I can dance as well as any general or major
or even a sergeant, because I just win four hundred in a poker
game and she said Oh, you did? and I said Sure, stick with
me, kid and she said Where is it? only I wouldn't show it to
her and then this fellow come up to her and said Are you dancing this one? and she said Sure I am. This bird dont dance.
Well, he was a sergeant, the biggest one I ever seen. Say, he
was like that fellow in Arkansaw that had some trouble with
a nigger and a friend said to him 'Well, I hear you killed a
nigger yesterday.' And he said 'Yes, weighed two hundred
pounds.' Like a bear." He took the lurching of the train lim-
berly and Cadet Lowe said For Christ's sake.

"Sure," agreed the other. "She wont hurt you, though. I
done tried it. My dog wont drink none of it of course, but
then he got bad ways hanging around Brigade H.Q. He's the
one trophy of the war I got: something that wasn't never
bawled out by a shave-tail for not saluting. Say, would you
kindly like to take a little something to keep off the sumnifer-
ous dews of this goddam country? The honor is all mine and
you wont mind it much after the first two drinks. Makes me
homesick: like a garage. Ever work in a garage?"

Sitting on the floor between two seats was Yaphank's travelling companion, trying to ignite a splayed and sodden cigar.
Like devastated France, thought Cadet Lowe, swimming his
memory through the adenoidal reminiscences of Captain
Bleyth, a R.A.F. pilot delegated to temporarily re-inforce their
democracy.

"Why, poor soldier," said his friend tearfully, "all alone in
no man's land and no matches. Aint war hell? I ask you." He
tried to push the other over with his leg, then he fell to kicking him, slowly. "Move over, you ancient marineer. Move
over, you goddam bastard. Alas, poor Jerks or something.

(I seen that in a play, see? Good line) Come on, come on; here's General Pershing come to have a drink with the poor soldiers." He addressed Cadet Lowe. "Look at him: aint he sodden in deprayvity?"

"Battle of Coonyak," the man on the floor muttered. "Ten men killed. Maybe fifteen. Maybe hundred. Poor children at home saying Alice where art thou?"

"Yeh, Alice. Where in hell are you? That other bottle. What'n'ell have you done with it? Keeping it to swim in when you get home?"

The man on the floor weeping said: "You wrong me as ever man wronged. Accuse me of hiding mortgage on house? Then take this soul and body: take all. Ravish me, big boy."

"Ravish a bottle of vinegar juice out of you, anyway," the other muttered busy beneath the seat. He rose triumphant, clutching a fresh bottle. "Hark! the sound of battle and the laughing horses draws near. But shall they dull this poor unworthy head? No! But I would like to of seen one of them laughing horses. Must of been lady horses all together. Your extreme highness," with ceremony, extending the bottle, "will you be kind enough to kindly condescend to honor these kind but unworthy strangers in a foreign land?"

Cadet Lowe accepted the bottle, drank briefly, gagged and spat his drink. The other supporting him massaged his back. "Come on, come on, they dont nothing taste that bad." Kindly cupping Lowe's opposite shoulder in his palm he forced the bottle mouthward again. Lowe released the bottle, defending himself. "Try again. I got you. Drink it, now."

"Jesus Christ," said Cadet Lowe, averting his head.

Passengers were interested and Yaphank soothed him. "Now, now. They wont nothing hurt you. You are among friends. Us soldiers got to stick together in a foreign country like this. Come on, drink her down. She aint worth nothing to no one, spit on his legs like that."

"Hell, man, I cant drink it."

"Why sure you can. Listen: think of flowers. Think of your poor gray-haired mother hanging on the front gate and sobbing her gray-haired heart out. Listen, think of having to go to work again when you get home. Aint war hell? I would of been a corporal at least, if she had just hung on another year."

"Hell, I cant."

"Why, you got to," his new friend told him kindly, pushing the bottle suddenly in his mouth and tilting it. To be flooded or to swallow were his choices so he drank and retained it. His belly rose and hung, then sank reluctant.

"There now, wasn't so bad, was it? Remember, this hurts me to see my good licker going more than it does you. But she do kind of smack of gasoline, dont she?"

Cadet Lowe's outraged stomach heaved at its muscular moorings like a captive balloon. He gaped and his vitals coiled coldly in a passionate ecstasy. His friend again thrust the bottle in his mouth.

"Drink, quick! You got to protect your investment, you know."

His private parts, flooded, washed back to his gulping and a sweet fire ran through him, and the pullman conductor came and regarded them in helpless disgust.

"Ten—shun" said Yaphank, springing to his feet. "Beware of officers! Rise, men, and salute the admiral here." He took the conductor's hand and held it. "Boys, this man commanded the navy," he said. "When the enemy tried to capture Coney Island he was there. Or somewhere between there and Chicago anyway, wasn't you, Colonel?"

"Look out, men, dont do that." But Yaphank had already kissed his hand.

"Now, run along, sergeant. And dont come back until dinner is ready."

"Listen, you must stop this. You will ruin my train."

"Bless your heart, captain, your train couldn't be no safer with us if it was your own daughter." The man sitting on the floor moved and Yaphank cursed him. "Sit still, cant you? Say, this fellow thinks its night. Suppose you have your hired man bed him down? He's just in the way here."

The conductor deciding Lowe was the sober one, addressed him.

"For God's sake, soldier, cant you do something with them?"

"Sure," said Cadet Lowe. "You run along: I'll look after them. They're all right."

"Well, do something with them. I cant bring a train into

Chicago with the whole army drunk on it. My God, Sherman was sure right."

Yaphank stared at him quietly. Then he turned to his companions. "Men," he said solemnly, "he dont want us here. And this is the reward we get for giving our flesh and blood to our country's need. Yes, sir, he dont want us here: he begrudges us riding on his train, even. Say, suppose we hadn't sprang to the nation's call, do you know what kind of a train you'd have? A train full of Germans. A train full of folks eating sausage and drinking beer, all going to Milwaukee, that's what you'd have."

"Couldn't be worse than a train full of you fellows not knowing where you're going," the conductor replied.

"All right," Yaphank answered. "If that's the way you feel, we'll get off your goddam train. Do you think this is the only train in the world?"

"No, no," the conductor said hastily, "not at all. I dont want you to get off. I just want you to straighten up and not disturb the other passengers."

The sitting man lurched clumsily and Cadet Lowe met interested stares.

"No," said Yaphank. "No! You have refused the hospitality of your train to the saviors of your country. We could have expected better treatment than this in Germany, even in Texas." He turned to Lowe. "Men, we will get off his train at the next station. Hey, General?"

"My God," repeated the conductor. "If we ever have another peace I dont know what the railroads will do. I thought war was bad, but My God."

"Run along," Yaphank told him, "run along. You probably wont stop for us, so I guess we'll have to jump off. Gratitude! Where is gratitude, when trains wont stop to let poor soldiers off? I know what it means. They'll fill trains with poor soldiers and run 'em off into Pacific ocean. Wont have to feed 'em any more. Poor soldiers! Woodrow, you wouldn't of treated me like this."

"Hey, what you doing?" But the man ignored him, tugging the window up and dragging a cheap paper suit-case across his companion's knees. Before either Lowe or the conductor could raise a hand he had pushed the suit-case out the window. "All out, men!"

His sodden companion heaved clawing from the floor. "Hey! That was mine you threw out!"

"Well, aint you going to get off with us? We are going to throw 'em all off, and when she slows down we'll jump ourselves."

"But you threw mine off first," the other said.

"Why sure. I was saving you the trouble, see? Now dont you feel bad about it: you can throw mine off if you want, and then Pershing here and the admiral can throw each other's off the same way. You got a bag, aint you?" he asked the conductor. "Get yours, quick, so we wont have so damn far to walk."

"Listen, soldiers," said the conductor, and Cadet Lowe, thinking of Elba, thinking of his coiling guts and a slow alcoholic fire in him, remarked the splayed official gold breaking the man's cap. New York swam flatly past: Buffalo was imminent, and sunset.

"Listen, soldiers," repeated the conductor. "I got a son in France: Sixth Marines he is. His mother aint heard from him since October. I'll do anything for you boys, see, but for God's sake act decent."

"No," replied the man, "you have refused us hospitality, so we get off. When does train stop? or have we got to jump?"

"No, no, you boys sit here. Sit here and behave and you'll be all right. No need to get off."

He moved swaying down the aisle and the sodden one removed his devastated cigar. "You threw my suit-case out," he repeated.

Yaphank took Cadet Lowe's arm. "Listen. Wouldn't that discourage you? God knows, I'm trying to help the fellow get a start in life, and what do I get? One complaint after another." He addressed his friend again. "Why sure, I threw your suit-case off. Whatcher wanta do? wait till we get to Buffalo and pay a quarter to have it took off for you?"

"But you threw my suit-case out," said the other again.

"All right: I did. Whatcher going to do about it?"

The other pawed himself erect, clinging to the window, and fell heavily over Lowe's feet. "For Christ's sake," his companion said, thrusting him into his seat. "Watch whatcher doing."

"Get off," the man mumbled wetly.

"Huh?"

"Get off, too," he explained, trying to rise again. He got onto his legs and lurching, bumping and sliding about the open window he thrust his head through it. Cadet Lowe caught him by the brief skirt of his blouse.

"Here, here, come back, you damn fool. You cant do that."

"Why sure he can," contradicted Yaphank, "let him jump off if he wants. He aint only going to Buffalo, anyways."

"Hell, he'll kill himself."

"My God," repeated the conductor returned at a heavy gallop. He leaned across Lowe's shoulder and caught the man's leg. The man with his head and torso through the window swayed lax and sodden as a meal sack. Yaphank pushed Lowe aside and tried to break the conductor's grip on the other's leg.

"Let him be: I dont believe he'll jump."

"But, good God, I cant take any chances. Look out, look out, soldier! Pull him back there!"

"Oh, for Christ's sake, let him go," said Lowe, giving up.

"Sure," the other amended, "let him jump. I'd kind of like to see him do it, since he suggested it himself. Besides, he aint the kind for young fellows like us to associate with. Good riddance. Lets help him off," he added shoving at the man's lumpy body. The would-be suicide's hat whipped from his head and the wind temporarily clearing his brain, he fought to draw himself in. He had changed his mind. His companion resisted, kindly.

"Come on, come on. Dont lose your nerve now. G'wan and jump."

"Help!" the man shrieked into the vain wind and "Help!" the conductor chorused, clinging to him, and two alarmed passengers and the porter came to his assistance. They overcame Yaphank and drew the now thoroughly alarmed man into the car. The conductor slammed shut the window.

"Gentlemen," he addressed the two passengers, "will you sit here and keep them from putting him out that window? I am going to put them all off as soon as we reach Buffalo. I'd stop the train and do it now, only they'll kill him as soon as they get him alone. Henry," to the porter, "call the train conductor and tell him to wire ahead to Buffalo we got two crazy men on board."

"Yeh, Henry," Yaphank amended to the negro, "tell 'em to have a band there and three bottles of whiskey. If they aint got a band of their own, tell 'em to hire one: I will pay for it." He dragged a blobby mass of bills from his pocket and stripping off one, gave it to the porter. "Do you want a band too?" he asked Lowe. "No," answering himself, "no, you dont need none. You can use mine. Run, now," he repeated.

"Yas suh, cap'm." White teeth were like a suddenly opened piano.

"Watch 'em, men," the conductor told his appointed guards. "You, Henry!" he shouted, following the vanishing white jacket.

Yaphank's companion sweating and pale, was about to become ill; Yaphank and Lowe sat easily respectively affable and belligerent. The new-comers touched shoulders for mutual support, alarmed but determined. Craned heads of other passengers became again smugly unconcerned over books and papers and the train rushed on along the sunset.

"Well, gentlemen," began Yaphank conversationally.

The two civilians sprang like plucked wires and one of them said Now, now soothingly, putting his hands on the soldier. "Just be quiet, soldier, and we'll look after you. Us Americans appreciates what you've done."

"Hank White," muttered the sodden one.

"Huh?" asked his companion.

"Hank White," he repeated.

The other turned to the civilian cordially. "Well, bless my soul, if here aint old Hank White in the flesh, that I was raised with! Why, Hank! We heard you was dead, or in the piano business or something. You aint been fired, have you? I notice you aint got no piano with you."

"No, no," the man answered in alarm, "you are mistaken: Schluss is my name. I got a swell line of ladies' underthings." He produced a card.

"Well, well, aint that nice. Say," he leaned confidentially toward the other, "you dont carry no women samples with you? No? I was afraid not. But never mind: I will get you one in Buffalo. Not buy you one, of course: just rent you one, you might say, for the time being. Horace," to Cadet Lowe, "where's that bottle?"

"Here she is, Major," responded Lowe taking the bottle from beneath his blouse. Yaphank offered it to the two civilians.

"Think of something far, far away, and drink fast," he advised.

"Why thanks," said the one called Schluss tendering the bottle formally to his companion. They stooped cautiously and drank. Yaphank and Cadet Lowe drank, not stooping.

"Be careful, soldiers," warned Schluss.

"Sure," said Cadet Lowe. They drank again.

"Wont the other one take nothing?" asked the here-to-fore silent one, indicating Yaphank's travelling companion. He was hunched awkwardly in the corner. His friend shook him and he slipped limply to the floor.

"That's the horror of the demon rum, boys," said Yaphank solemnly and he took another drink. And Cadet Lowe took another drink. He tendered the bottle.

"No, no," Schluss said with passion, "not no more right now."

"He dont mean that," Yaphank said, "he just aint thought." He and Lowe stared at the two civilians. "Give him time: he'll come to hisself."

After a while the one called Schluss took the bottle.

"That's right," Yaphank told Lowe confidentially. "For a while I thought he was going to insult the uniform. But you wasn't, was you?"

"No, no. They aint no one respects the uniform like I do. Listen, I would of liked to fought by your side, see? but someone got to look out for business while the boys are gone. Aint that right?" he appealed to Lowe.

"I dont know," said Lowe with courteous belligerence, "I never had time to work any."

"Come on, come on," Yaphank reprimanded him, "all of us wasn't young enough to be lucky as you."

"How was I lucky?" Lowe rejoined fiercely.

"Well, shut up about it, if you wasn't lucky. We got something else to worry about."

"Sure," Schluss added quickly, "we all got something to worry about." He tasted the bottle briefly and the other said:

"Come on, now, drink it."

"No, no, thanks, I got a plenty."

Yaphank's eye was like a snake's. "Take a drink, now. Do you want me to call the conductor and tell him you are worrying us to give you whiskey?"

The man gave him the bottle quickly. He turned to the other civilian. "What makes him act so funny?"

"No, no," said Schluss. "Listen, you soldiers drink if you want: we'll look after you."

The silent one added Like a brother and Yaphank said:

"They think we are trying to poison them. They think we are German spies, I guess."

"No, no! When I see a uniform, I respect it like it was my mother."

"Then, come on and drink."

Schluss gulped and passed the bottle. His companion drank also and sweat beaded them.

"Wont he take nothing?" repeated the silent one and Yaphank regarded the other soldier with compassion.

"Alas, poor Hank," he said, "poor boy's done for, I fear. The end of a long friendship, men." Cadet Lowe said Sure, seeing two distinct Hanks, and the other continued: "Look at that kind manly face. Children together we was, picking flowers in the flowery meadows; him and me made the middle-weight mule-wiper's battalion what she was; him and me devastated France together. And now look at him.

"Hank! Dont you recognise this weeping voice, this soft hand on your brow? General," he turned to Lowe, "will you be kind enough to take charge of the remains? I will deputize these kind strangers to stop at the first harness factory we pass and have a collar suitable for mules made of dog-wood with the initials H.W. in forget-me-nots."

Schluss in ready tears tried to put his arm about Yaphank's shoulders. "There, there, death aint only a parting. Brace up: take a little drink, then you'll feel better."

"Why, I believe I will," he replied, "you got a kind heart, buddy. Fall in when fire call blows, boys."

Schluss mopped his face with a soiled scented handkerchief and they drank again. New York in a rosy glow of alcohol and sunset streamed past breaking into Buffalo, and with fervent new fire in them they remarked the station. Poor Hank now slept peacefully in a spittoon.

Cadet Lowe and his friend being cold of stomach, rose and supported their companions. Schluss evinced a disinclination to get off: he said it couldn't possibly be Buffalo, that he had been to Buffalo too many times. Sure, they told him, holding him erect and the conductor glared at them briefly and vanished. Lowe and Yaphank got their hats and helped the civilians into the aisle.

"I'm certainly glad my boy wasn't old enough to be a soldier," remarked a woman passing them with difficulty and Lowe said to Yaphank:

"Say, what about him?"

"Him?" repeated the other, having attached Schluss to himself.

"That one back there," Lowe indicated the casual.

"Oh, him? You are welcome to him, if you want him."

"Why, aren't you together?"

Outside was the noise and smoke of the station: they saw through the windows hurrying people and porters and Yaphank moving down the aisle answered:

"Hell, no. I never seen him before. Let the porter sweep him out or keep him, which ever he likes."

They half dragged half carried the two civilians and with diabolical cunning Yaphank led the way through the train and dismounted from a day coach. On the platform Schluss put his arm around the soldier's neck.

"Listen, fellows," he said with passion, "y'know m'name, y'got addressh. Listen, I will show you 'Merica preshates what you done. Ol' Glory ever wave on land and sea. Listen, aint nothing I got soldier cant have, nothing. N'if you wasn't sholdiers I am still for you, one hundred pershent. I like you. I swear I like you."

"Why sure," the other agreed, supporting him. After a while he spied a policeman and he directed his companion's gait toward the officer. Lowe with his silent one followed. "Stand up, cant you?" he hissed but the man's eyes were filled with an inarticulate sadness, like a dog's. "Do the best you can, then," Cadet Lowe softened added and Yaphank stopping before the policeman was saying:

"Looking for two drunks, sergeant? These men were annoying a whole train-load of people. Cant nothing be done to protect soldiers from annoyance? If it aint top sergeants, its drunks."

"I'd like to see the man can annoy a soldier," answered the officer. "Beat it, now."

"But say, these men are dangerous. What are you good for, if you cant preserve the peace?"

"Beat it, I said. Do you want me to run all of you in?"

"You are making a mistake, sergeant. These are the ones you are looking for."

The policeman said Looking for? regarding him with interest.

"Sure. Didn't you get our wire? We wired ahead to have the train met."

"Oh, these are the crazy ones, are they? Where's the one they were trying to murder?"

"Sure, they are crazy. Do you think a sane man would get hisself into this state?"

The policeman looked at the four of them with a blasé eye. "G'wan, now. You're all drunk. Beat it, or I'll run you in."

"All right. Take us in. If we got to go to the station to get rid of these crazy ones, we'll have to."

"Where's the conductor of this train?"

"He's with a doctor, working on the wounded one."

"Say, you men better be careful. Whatcher trying to do—— kid me?"

Yaphank jerked his companion up. "Stand up," he said, shaking the man. "Love you like brother," the other muttered. "Look at him," he said, "look at both of 'em. And there's a man hurt on that train. Are you going to stand here and do nothing?"

"I thought you was kidding me. These are the ones, are they?" he raised his whistle and another policeman ran up. "Here they are, Ed. You watch 'em and I'll get aboard and see about that dead man. You soldiers stay here, see?"

"Sure, sergeant," Yaphank agreed. The officer ran heavily away and he turned to the civilians. "All right, boys. Here's the bell-hops come to carry you out where the parade starts. You go with them and me and this other officer will go back and get the conductor and the porter. They want to come, too."

Schluss again took him in his arms.

"Love you like brother. Anything got's yours. Ask me."

"Sure," he rejoined. "Watch 'em, cap, they're crazy as hell. Now, you run along with this nice man."

"Here," the policeman said, "you two wait here."

There came a shout from the train and the conductor's face was a bursting bellowing moon. "Like to wait and see it explode on him," Yaphank murmured. The policeman supporting the two men hurried toward the train. "Come on here," he shouted to Yaphank and Lowe.

As he drew away Yaphank spoke swiftly to Lowe.

"Come on, General," he said, "lets get going. So long, boys. Lets go, kid."

The policeman shouted Stop, there! but they disregarded him, hurrying down the long shed, leaving the excitement to clot about itself, for all of them.

Outside the station in the twilight the city broke sharply its sky-line against the winter evening and lights were shimmering birds on motionless golden wings, bell-notes in arrested flight: ugly everywhere beneath a rumored retreating magic of color.

Food for the belly, and winter, though spring was somewhere in the world, from the south blown up like a forgotten music. Caught both in the magic of change they stood feeling the spring in the cold air, as if they had but recently come into a new world, feeling their littleness and believing too that lying in wait for them was something new and strange. They were ashamed of this and silence was unbearable.

"Well, buddy," and Yaphank slapped Cadet Lowe smartly on the back, "that's one parade we'll sure be A.W.O.L. from, huh?"

2.

Who sprang to be his land's defence
And has been sorry ever since?
    Cadet!
Who cant date a single girl
Long as kee wees run the world?
    Kay—det!

With food in their bellies and a quart of whiskey snugly under Cadet Lowe's arm they boarded a train.

"Where are we going?" asked Lowe. "This train dont go to San Francisco, do she?"

"Listen," said Yaphank, "my name is Joe Gilligan. Gilligan, G-i-l-l-i-g-a-n, Gilligan, J-o-e, Joe; Joe Gilligan. My people captured Minneapolis from the Irish and taken a Dutch name, see? Did you ever know a man named Gilligan give you a bum steer? If you wanta go to San Francisco, all right. If you wanta go to St Paul or Omyhaw, its all right with me. And more than that, I'll see that you get there. I'll see that you go to all three of 'em if you want. But why'n hell do you wanta go so damn far as San Francisco?"

"I dont," replied Cadet Lowe. "I dont want to go anywhere specially. I like this train here——far as I am concerned I say, Lets fight this war out right here. But you see, my people live in San Francisco. That's why I am going there."

"Why, sure," Private Gilligan agreed readily. "Sometimes a man does wanta see his family—especially if he dont hafta live with 'em. I aint criticising you: I admire you for it, buddy. But say, you can go home any time. What I say is, Lets have a look at this glorious nation which we have fought for."

"Hell, I cant. My mother has wired me every day since the armistice to fly low and be careful and come home as soon as I am demobilized. I bet she wired the President to have me excused as soon as possible."

"Why sure. Of course she did. What can equal a mother's love? Except a good drink of whiskey. Where's that bottle? You aint betrayed a virgin, have you?"

"Here she is." Cadet Lowe produced it and Gilligan pressed the bell.

"Claude," he told a superior porter, "bring us two glasses and a bottle of sassperiller or something. We are among gentlemen today and we aim to act like gentlemen."

"Whatcher want glasses for?" asked Lowe. "Bottle was all right yesterday."

"You got to remember we are getting among strangers now. We dont want to offend no savage customs. Wait until you get to be a experienced traveller and you'll remember these things. Two glasses, Othello."

The porter in his starched jacket became a symbol of self sufficiency. "You cant drink in this car. Go to the buffet car."

"Ah, come on, Claude. Have a heart."

"We dont have no drinking in this car. Go to the buffet car if you want." He swung himself from seat to seat down the lurching car.

Private Gilligan turned to his companion. "Well! What do you know about that? Aint that one hell of a way to treat soldiers? I tell you, General, this is the worst run war I ever seen."

"Hell, lets drink out of the bottle."

"No, no. This thing has got to be a point of honor, now. Remember, we got to protect our uniforms from insult. You wait here and I'll see the conductor. We bought tickets, hey buddy?"

> With officers gone and officers' wives
> Having the grand old time of their lives—

an overcast sky, and earth dissolving monotonously into a gray mist, grayly. Occasional trees and houses marching through it; and towns like bubbles of ghostly sound beaded on a steel wire—

> Who's in the guard-room chewing the bars,
> Saying to hell with the government wars?
> Cadet!

And here was Gilligan returned, saying:

"Charles, at ease."

I might have known he would have gotten another one, thought Cadet Lowe looking up. He saw a belt and wings, he rose and met a young face with a dreadful scar across his brow. My God, he thought, turning sick. He saluted and the other peered at him with strained distraction. Gilligan holding his arm helped him into the seat. The man turned his puzzled gaze to Gilligan and murmured Thanks.

"Lootenant," said Gilligan, "you see here the pride of the nation. General, ring the bell for ice water. The lootenant here is sick."

Cadet Lowe pressed the bell, regarding with a re-birth of that old feud between American enlisted men and officers of all nations the man's insignia and wings and brass, not even wondering what a British officer in his condition could be doing travelling in America. Had I been old enough or lucky enough, this might have been me, he thought jealously.

The porter reappeared.

"No drinking in this car, I told you," he said. Gilligan produced a bill. "No, sir. Not in this car." Then he saw the third man. He leaned down to him quickly, then glanced suspiciously from Gilligan to Lowe.

"What youall doing with him?" he asked.

"Oh, he's just a lost foreigner I found back yonder. Now, Ernest——"

"Lost? He aint lost. He's from Gawgia. I'm looking after him. Cap'm," to the officer, "is these folks all right?"

Gilligan and Lowe looked at each other. "Christ, I thought he was a foreigner," Gilligan whispered.

The man raised his eyes to the porter's anxious face. "Yes," he said slowly, "they're all right."

"Does you want to stay here with them, or dont you want me to fix you up in your place?"

"Let him stay here," Gilligan said. "He wants a drink."

"But he aint got no business drinking. He's sick."

"Loot," Gilligan said, "do you want a drink?"

"Yes. I want a drink. Yes."

"But he oughtn't to have no whiskey, sir."

"I wont let him have too much. I am going to look after him. Come on, now, lets have some glasses, cant we?"

The porter began again "But he oughtn't—"

"Say, Loot," Gilligan interrupted, "cant you make your friend here get us some glasses to drink from?"

"Glasses?"

"Yeh: he dont want to bring us none."

"Does you want glasses, cap'm?"

"Yes, bring us some glasses, will you?"

"All right, cap'm." He stopped again. "You going to take care of him, aint you?" he asked Gilligan.

"Sure. Sure."

The porter gone, Gilligan regarded his guest with envy. "You sure got to be from Georgia to get service on this train. I showed him money but it never even shook him. Say, General," to Lowe, "we better keep the lootenant with us, huh? Might come in useful."

"Sure," agreed Lowe. "Say, sir, what kind of ships did you use?"

"Oh, for Christ's sake," interrupted Gilligan, "let him be. He's been devastating France, now he needs rest. Hey, Loot?"

Beneath his scarred and tortured brow the man's gaze was puzzled but kindly and the porter reappeared with glasses and a bottle of ginger ale. He produced a pillow which he placed carefully behind the officer's head, then he got two more pillows for the others, forcing them with ruthless kindness to relax. He was deftly officious, including them impartially in his activities, like Fate. Private Gilligan unused to this, became restive.

"Hey, ease up, George; lemme do my own pawing a while. I aim to paw this bottle if you'll gimme room."

He desisted, saying, "Is that all right, cap'm?"

"Yes, all right, thanks," the officer answered. Then: "Bring your glass and get a drink."

Gilligan solved the bottle and filled the glasses. Ginger ale hissed sweetly and pungently. "Up and at 'em, men."

The officer took his glass in his left hand and then Lowe noticed that his right hand was drawn and withered.

"Cheer-O," he said.

"Nose down," murmured Lowe. The man looked at him with poised glass. He looked at the hat on Lowe's knee and that groping puzzled thing behind his eyes became clear and sharp as with a mental process and Lowe thought that his lips had asked a question.

"Yes, sir. Cadet," he replied feeling warmly grateful, feeling again a youthful clean pride in his corps. But the effort had been too much and again the officer's gaze was puzzled and distracted.

Gilligan raised his glass, squinting at it. "Here's to peace," he said. "The first hundred years is the hardest."

Here was the porter again, with his own glass. " 'Nother nose in the trough," Gilligan complained, helping him.

The negro patted and re-arranged the pillow beneath the officer's head. "Excuse me, cap'm, but cant I get you something for your head?"

"No, no, thanks. Its all right."

"But you're sick, sir. Dont you drink too much."

"I'll be careful."

"Sure," Gilligan amended, "we'll watch him."

"Lemme pull the shade down: keep the light out of your eyes?"

"No, I dont mind the light. You run along. I'll call if I want anything."

With the instinct of his race the negro knew that his kindness was becoming untactful, yet he ventured again.

"I bet you haven't wired your folks to meet you. Whyn't you lemme wire 'em for you? I can look after you far as I go, but who's going to look after you then?"

"No, I'm all right, I tell you. You look after me as far as you go. I'll get along."

"All right. But I am going to tell your paw how you are acting some day. You ought to know better than that, cap'm." He said to Gilligan and Lowe: "You gentlemen call me if he gets sick."

"Yes, go on now, damn you. I'll call if I dont feel well."

Gilligan looked from his retreating back to the officer in admiration. "Loot, how do you do it?"

But the man only turned on them his puzzled gaze. He finished his drink and while Gilligan renewed them Cadet Lowe like a trailing hound repeated:

"Say, sir, what kind of ships did you use?"

The man looked at Lowe kindly, not replying and Gilligan said:

"Hush. Let him alone. Dont you see he dont remember himself? Do you reckon you would, with that scar? Let the war be. Hey, Lootenant?"

"I dont know. Another drink is better."

"Sure it is. Buck up, General. He dont mean no harm. He's just got to let her ride as she lays for a while. We all got horrible memories of the war: I lose eighty-nine dollars in a crap game once, besides losing, as that wop writer says, that an which thou knowest at Chatter Teary. So how about a little whiskey, men?"

"Cheer-O," said the officer again.

"What do you mean, Chateau Thierry?" said Lowe boyish in disappointment, feeling that he had been deliberately ignored by one to whom Fate had been kinder than to himself.

"You talking about Chatter Teary?"

"I'm talking about a place you were not at, anyway."

"I was there in spirit, sweetheart. That's what counts."

"You couldn't have been there any other way. There aint any such place."

"Hell there aint. Ask the Loot here if I aint right. How about it, Loot?"

But he was asleep. They looked at his face, young yet old as the world, beneath the dreadful scar. Even Gilligan's levity left him. "My God, it makes you sick at the stomach, dont it? I wonder if he knows how he looks? What do you reckon his folks will say when they see him? or his girl—if he has got one. And I'll bet he has."

New York flew away: it became noon within, by clock, but the gray imminent horizon had not changed. Gilligan said: "If he has got a girl, know what she'll say?"

Cadet Lowe knowing all the despair of abortive endeavor asked "What?"

New York passed on and Mahon beneath his martial harness slept. (Would I sleep? thought Lowe; had I wings, boots, would I sleep?) His wings indicated by a graceful sweep pointed sharply down above a ribbon: purple, white, purple, over his pocket, over his heart (supposedly). Lowe descried between the pinions a superimposed crown and three letters, then his gaze mounted to the sleeping scarred face. "What?" he repeated.

"She'll give him the air, buddy."

"Ah, come on. Of course she wont."

"Yes she will. You dont know women. Once the new has wore off it'll be some bird that stayed at home and made money, or some lad that wore shiny leggings and never got nowheres so he could get hurt, like you and me."

The porter came to hover over the sleeping man.

"He aint got sick, has he?" he whispered.

They told him No and the negro eased the position of the sleeping man's head. "You gentlemen look after him and be sure to call me if he wants anything. He's a sick man."

Gilligan and Lowe looking at the officer agreed and the porter lowered the shade. "You want some more ginger ale?"

"Yes," said Gilligan, assuming the porter's hushed tone and the negro withdrew. The two of them sat in a silent comradeship, the comradeship of those whose lives had become pointless through the sheer equivocation of events, of the sorry jade Circumstance. The porter brought ginger ale and they sat drinking while New York became Ohio.

Gilligan, that talkative unserious one, entered some dream within himself and Cadet Lowe young and dreadfully disappointed, knew all the old sorrows of the Jasons of the world who see their vessels sink ere the harbor is left behind. . . . Beneath his scar the officer slept in all the travesty of his wings and leather and brass, and a terrible old woman paused saying:

"Was he wounded?"

Gilligan waked from his dream. "Look at his face," he said fretfully, "he fell off of a chair onto an old woman he was talking to and done that."

"What insolence," said the woman glaring at Gilligan. "But cant something be done for him? He looks sick to me."

"Yes ma'am. Something can be done for him. What we are doing now—letting him alone."

She and Gilligan stared at each other, then she looked at Cadet Lowe young and belligerent and disappointed. She looked back to Gilligan. She said from the ruthless humanity of money:

"I shall report you to the conductor. That man is sick and needs attention."

"All right, ma'am. But you tell the conductor that if he bothers him now I'll knock his goddamn head off."

The old woman glared at Gilligan from beneath a quiet modish black hat and a girl's voice said:

"Let them alone, Mrs Henderson. They'll take care of him all right."

She was dark. Had Gilligan and Lowe ever seen an Aubrey Beardsley they would have known that Beardsley would have sickened for her: he had drawn her so often dressed in peacock hues, white and slim and depraved among meretricious trees and impossible marble fountains. Gilligan rose.

"That's right, miss. He is all right sleeping here with us. The porter is looking after him——" wondering why he should have to explain to her—— "and we are taking him home. Just leave him be. And thank you for your interest."

"But something ought to be done about it," the old woman repeated futilely. The girl led her away and the train ran swaying in afternoon. (Sure, it was afternoon. Cadet Lowe's wrist watch said so. It might be any state under the sun, but it was afternoon. Afternoon or evening or morning or night, far as the officer was concerned. He slept)

Damned old bitch, Gilligan muttered, careful not to wake him.

"Look how you've got his arm," the girl said returning. She moved his withered hand from his thigh. (His hand, too, seeing the scrofulous indication of his bones beneath the blistered skin) "Oh, his poor terrible face," she said, shifting the pillow under his head.

"Be quiet, ma'am," Gilligan said.

She ignored him. Gilligan expecting to see him wake, admitted defeat and she continued:

"Is he going far?"

"Lives in Georgia," Gilligan said. He and Cadet Lowe seeing that she was not merely passing their section, rose. Lowe remarking her pallid distinction, her black hair, the red scar of her mouth, her slim dark dress, knew an adolescent envy of the sleeper. She ignored Lowe with a brief glance. How impersonal she was, how self contained. Ignoring them.

"He cant get home alone," she stated with conviction. "Are you all going with him?"

"Sure," Gilligan assured her. Lowe wished to say something, something that would leave him fixed in her mind: something to reveal himself to her. But she glanced at the glasses, the bottle that Lowe feeling a fool yet clasped.

"You seem to be getting along pretty well, yourselves," she said.

"Snake medicine, miss. But wont you have some?"

Lowe envying Gilligan's boldness, his presence of mind, watched her mouth. She looked down the car.

"I believe I will, if you have another glass."

"Why, sure. General, ring the bell." She sat down beside Mahon and Gilligan and Lowe sat again. She seemed . . . she was young: she probably liked dancing yet at the same time she seemed not young——as if she knew everything. (She is married, and about twenty five, thought Gilligan) (She is about nineteen, and she is not in love, Lowe decided) She looked at Lowe.

"What's your outfit, soldier?"

"Flying Cadet," answered Lowe with slow patronage, "Air Service." She was a kid: she only looked old.

"Oh. Then of course you are looking after him. He's an aviator too, isn't he?"

"Look at his wings," Lowe answered. "British. Royal Air Force. Pretty good boys."

"Hell," said Gilligan, "he aint no foreigner."

"You dont have to be a foreigner to be with the British or French. Look at Lufbery. He was with the French until we come in."

The girl looked at him and Gilligan who had never heard of Lufbery said: "Whatever he is, he's all right. With us, any way. Let him be whatever he wants."

The girl said: "I am sure he is."

The porter appeared. "Cap'm's all right?" he whispered remarking her without surprise as is the custom of his race.

"Yes," she told him, "he's all right."

Cadet Lowe thought I bet she can dance and she added: "He couldn't be in better hands than these gentlemen." How keen she is! thought Gilligan. She has known disappointment. "I wonder if I could have a drink on your car?"

The porter examined her and then he said: "Yes, ma'am. I'll get some fresh ginger ale. You going to look after him?"

"Yes, for a while."

He leaned down to her. "I'm from Gawgia too. Long time ago."

"You were? I'm from Alabama."

"That's right. We got to look out for our own folks, aint we? I'll get you a glass right away."

The officer still slept and the porter returning hushed and anxious they sat drinking and talking with muted voices. New York was Ohio, and Ohio became a series of identical cheap houses with the same man entering gate after gate, smoking and spitting. Here was Cincinnati and under the blanched flash of her hand he waked easily.

"Are we in?" he asked. On her hand was a plain gold band. No engagement ring. (Pawned it, maybe, thought Gilligan. But she did not look poor)

"General, get the lootenant's hat."

Lowe climbed over Gilligan's knees and Gilligan said:

"Here's an old friend of ours, Loot. Meet Mrs Powers."

She took his hand, helping him to his feet and the porter appeared.

"Donald Mahon," he said, like a parrot. Cadet Lowe assisted by the porter returned with cap and stick and a trench coat and two kit bags. The porter helped him into the coat.

"I'll get yours, ma'am," said Gilligan but the porter circumvented him. Her coat was rough and heavy and light of color. She wore it carelessly and Gilligan and Cadet Lowe gathered up their "issued" impedimenta. The porter handed the officer his cap and stick, then he vanished with the luggage belonging to them. She glanced again down the length of the car.

"Where are my——"

"Yessum," the porter called from the door, across the coated shoulders of passengers, "I got your things, ma'am."

He had gotten them and his dark gentle hand lowered the officer carefully to the platform.

"Help the lootenant there," said the conductor officiously but he had already got the officer to the floor.

"You'll look after him, ma'am?"

"Yes. I'll look after him."

They moved down the shed and Cadet Lowe looked back. But the negro was efficient and skillful, busy with other passengers. He seemed to have forgotten them. And Cadet Lowe looked from the porter occupied with bags and the garnering of quarters and half dollars, to the officer in his coat and stick, remarking the set of his cap slanting backward bonelessly from his scarred brow, and he marvelled briefly upon his own kind.

But this was soon lost in the mellow death of evening in a street between stone buildings, among lights, and Gilligan in his awkward khaki and the girl in her rough coat, holding each an arm of Donald Mahon, silhouetted against it in the doorway.

3.

Mrs Powers lay in her bed aware of her long body beneath strange sheets, hearing the hushed night sounds of a hotel——muffled footfalls along mute carpeted corridors, discreet opening and shutting of doors, somewhere a murmurous pulse of machinery——all with that strange propensity which sounds anywhere else soothing have, when heard in a hotel, for keeping you awake. Her mind and body warming to the old familiarity of sleep became empty, then as she settled her body to the bed, shaping it for slumber, it filled with a remembered troubling sadness.

She thought of her husband youngly dead in France in a recurrence of fretful exasperation with having been tricked by a wanton Fate: a joke amusing to no one. Just when she had calmly decided that they had taken advantage of a universal hysteria for the purpose of getting of each other a brief ecstasy, just when she had decided calmly that they were better quit of each other with nothing to mar the memory of their three days together and had written him so, wishing him luck, she must be notified casually and impersonally that he had been killed in action. So casually, so impersonally; as if Richard Powers with whom she had spent three days were one man and Richard Powers commanding a platoon in the — Division were another.

And she being young must again know all the terror of parting, of that passionate desire to cling to something concrete in a dark world, in spite of war departments. He had not even got her letter! This in some way seemed the infidelity: having him die still believing in her bored though they both probably were.

She turned feeling sheets like water warmed by her bodily heat, upon her legs.

Oh, damn, damn. What a rotten trick you played on me. She recalled those nights during which they had tried to eradicate tomorrows from the world. Two rotten tricks, she thought. Anyway, I know what I'll do with the insurance, she added wondering what Dick thought about it—if he did know or care.

Her shoulder rounded upward, into her vision, the indication of her covered turning body swelled and died away toward the foot of the bed: she lay staring down the tunnel of her room, watching the impalpable angles of furniture, feeling through plastered smug walls a rumor of spring outside. The air-shaft was filled with a prophecy of April come again into the world. Like a heedless idiot into a world that had forgotten spring. The white connecting door took the vague indication of a transom and held it in a mute and luminous plane, and obeying an impulse she rose and slipped on a dressing gown.

The door opened quietly under her hand. The room, like hers, was a suggestion of furniture, identically vague. She could hear Mahon's breathing and she found a light switch with her fingers. Under his scarred brow he slept, the light full and sudden on his closed eyes did not disturb him. And she knew in an instinctive flash what was wrong with him, why his motions were hesitating, ineffectual.

He's going blind, she said bending over him. He slept and after a while there were sounds without the door. She straightened up swiftly and the noises ceased. Then the door opened to a blundering key and Gilligan entered supporting Cadet Lowe, glassy eyed and quite drunk.

Gilligan standing his lax companion upright said:

"Good afternoon, ma'am."

Lowe muttered wetly and Gilligan continued:

"Look at this lonely marineer I got here. Sail on, O proud and lonely," he told his attached and aimless burden. Cadet Lowe muttered again, not intelligible. His eyes were like two oysters.

"Huh?" asked Gilligan. "Come on, be a man: speak to the nice lady."

Cadet Lowe repeated himself liquidly and she whispered "Shhh: be quiet."

"Oh," said Gilligan with surprise, "Loot's asleep, huh? What's he want to sleep for, this time of day?"

Lowe with quenchless optimism essayed speech again and Gilligan comprehending said:

"That's what you want, is it? Why couldn't you come out like a man and say it? Wants to go to bed, for some reason," he explained to Mrs Powers.

"That's where he belongs," she said and Gilligan with alcoholic care led his companion to the other bed and with the exaggerated caution of the inebriate laid him upon it. Lowe drawing his knees up sighed and turned his back to them but Gilligan dragging at his legs removed his puttees and shoes, taking each shoe in both hands and placing it on a table. She leant against the foot of Mahon's bed fitting her long thigh to the hard rail, until he had finished.

At last Lowe freed of his shoes turned sighing to the wall and she said:

"How drunk are you, Joe?"

"Not very, ma'am. What's wrong? Loot need something?"

Mahon slept and Cadet Lowe immediately slept.

"I want to talk to you, Joe. About him," she added quickly feeling Gilligan's stare. "Can you listen or had you rather go to bed and talk it over in the morning?"

Gilligan focusing his eyes answered:

"Why, now suits me. Always oblige a lady."

Making her decision suddenly she said:

"Come in my room then."

"Sure: lemme get my bottle and I'm your man."

She returned to her room while he sought his bottle and when he joined her she was sitting on her bed clasping her knees, wrapped in a blanket. Gilligan drew up a chair.

"Joe, do you know he's going blind?" she said abruptly.

After a time her face became a human face and holding it in his vision he said:

"I know more than that. He's going to die."

"Die?"

"Yes, ma'am. If ever I seen death in a man's face, its in his. Goddamn this world," he burst out suddenly.

"Shhhh!" she whispered.

"That's right, I forgot," he said swiftly.

She clasped her knees, huddled beneath the blanket, changing the position of her body as it became cramped, feeling the wooden head-board of the bed, wondering why there were not iron beds, wondering why everything was as it was—— iron beds, why you deliberately took certain people to break your intimacy, why these people died, why you yet took others. . . . Will my death be like this: fretting and exasperating? Am I cold by nature, or have I spent all my emotional coppers, that I dont seem to feel things like others? Dick, Dick. Ugly and dead.

Gilligan sat brittlely in his chair, focusing his eyes with an effort, having those instruments of vision evade him, slimy as broken eggs. Lights completing a circle, an orbit; she with two faces sitting on two beds, clasping four arms around her knees. . . . Why cant a man be very happy or very unhappy? Its only a sort of pale mixture of the two. Like beer when you want a shot or a drink of water. Neither one nor other.

She moved and drew the blanket closer about her. Spring in an airshaft, the rumor of spring; but in the room steam heat suggested winter, dying away.

"Lets have a drink, Joe."

He rose careful and brittle and walking with meticulous deliberation he fetched a carafe and glasses. She drew a small table near them and Gilligan prepared two drinks. She drank and set the glass down. He lit a cigarette for her.

"Its a rotten old world, Joe."

"You damn right. And dying aint the half of it."

"Dying?"

"In his case, I mean. Trouble is, he probably wont die soon enough."

"Not die soon enough?"

Gilligan drained his glass. "I got the low down on him, see. He's got a girl at home: folks got 'em engaged when they was young, before he went off to war. And do you know what she's going to do when she sees his face?" he asked staring at her. At last her two faces became one face and her hair was black. Her mouth was like a scar.

"Oh, no, Joe. She wouldn't do that." She sat up. The blanket slipped from her shoulders and she replaced it, watching him intently.

Gilligan breaking the orbit of visible things by an effort of will said:

"Dont you kid yourself. I've seen her picture. And the last letter he had from her."

"He didn't show them to you!" she said quickly.

"That's all right about that. I seen 'em."

"Joe. You didn't go through his things?"

"Hell, ma'am, aint I and you trying to help him? Suppose I did do something that aint exactly according to holy Hoyle: you know damn well that I can help him——if I dont let a whole lot of donts stop me. And if I know I'm right there aint any donts or anything else going to stop me."

She looked at him and he hurried on:

"I mean, you and I know what to do for him, but if you are always letting A gentleman dont do this and A gentleman dont do that interfere, you cant help him. Do you see?"

"But what makes you so sure she will turn him down?"

"Why, I tell you I seen that letter: all the old bunk about knights of the air and the romance of battle, that even the fat crying ones outgrow soon as the excitement is over and uniforms and being wounded aint only not stylish no more, but it is troublesome."

"But aren't you taking a lot for granted, not to have seen her, even?"

"I've seen that photograph: one of them flighty looking pretty ones with lots of hair. Just the sort would have got herself engaged to him."

"How do you know it is still on? Perhaps she has forgotten him. And he probably doesn't remember her, you know."

"That aint it. If he dont remember her he's all right. But if he will know his folks he will want to believe that something in his world aint turned upside down."

They were silent a while, then Gilligan said: "I wish I could have knowed him before. He's the kind of a son I would have liked to have." He finished his drink.

"Joe, how old are you?"

"Thirty two, ma'am."

"How did you ever learn so much about us?" she asked with interest, watching him.

He grinned briefly. "It aint knowing, its just saying things. I think I done it through practice. By talking so much," he replied with sardonic humor. "I talk so much I got to say the right thing sooner or later. You dont talk much, yourself."

"Not much," she agreed. She moved carelessly and the blanket slipped entirely, exposing her thin night-dress; raising her arms and twisting her body to replace it her long shank was revealed and her turning ankle and her bare foot.

Gilligan without moving said: "Ma'am, lets get married."

She huddled quickly in the blanket again, already knowing a faint disgust with herself.

"Bless your heart, Joe. Dont you know my name is Mrs?"

"Sure. And I know too you aint got any husband. I dunno where he is or what you done with him, but you aint got a husband now."

"Goodness, I'm beginning to be afraid of you: you know too much. You are right: my husband was killed last year."

Gilligan looking at her said Rotten luck. And she tasting again a faint warm sorrow bowed her head to her arched clasped knees.

"Rotten luck. That's exactly what it was, what everything is. Even sorrow is a fake, now." She raised her face, her pallid face beneath her black hair, scarred with her mouth. "Joe, that was the only sincere word of condolence I ever had. Come here."

Gilligan went to her and she took his hand, holding it against her cheek. Then she removed it, shaking back her hair.

"You are a good fellow, Joe. If I felt like marrying anybody now, I'd take you. I'm sorry I played that trick, Joe."

"Trick?" repeated Gilligan gazing upon her black hair. Then he said Oh noncommittally.

"But we haven't decided what to do with that poor boy in there," she said with brisk energy, clasping her blanket. "That's what I wanted to talk to you about. Are you sleepy?"

"Not me," he answered. "I dont think I ever want to sleep again."

"Neither do I." She moved across the bed, propping her back against the head board. "Lie down here and lets decide on something."

"Sure," agreed Gilligan. "I better take off my shoes first. Ruin the hotel's bed."

"To hell with the hotel's bed," she told him. "Put your feet on it."

Gilligan lay down, shielding his eyes with his hand. After a time she said:

"Well, what's to be done?"

"We got to get him home first," Gilligan said. "I'll wire his folks tomorrow——his old man is a preacher, see. But its that damn girl bothers me. He sure ought to be let die in peace. But what else to do I dont know. I know about some things," he explained, "but after all women can guess and be nearer right than whatever I could decide on."

"I dont think anyone could do much more than you. I'd put my money on you every time."

He moved, shading his eyes again. "I dunno: I am good so far, but then you got to have more'n just sense. Say, why dont you come with the general and me?"

"I intend to, Joe." Her voice came from beyond his shielding hand. "I think I intended to all the time."

(She is in love with him) But he only said:

"Good for you. But I knowed you'd do the right thing. All right with your people, is it?"

"Yes. But what about money?"

"Money?"

"Well . . . for what he might need. You know. He might get sick any where."

"Lord, I cleaned up in a poker game and I aint had time to spend it. Money's all right. That aint any question," he said roughly.

"Yes, money's all right. You know I have my husband's insurance."

He lay silent, shielding his eyes. His khaki legs marring the bed ended in clumsy shoes. She nursed her knees, huddling in her blanket. After a space she said:

"Sleep, Joe?"

"Its a funny world, aint it?" he asked irrelevantly, not moving.

"Funny?"

"Sure. Soldier dies and leaves you money, and you spend the money helping another soldier die comfortable. Aint that funny?"

"I suppose so. . . . Everything is funny. Horribly funny."

"Anyway, its nice to have it all fixed," he said after a while. "He'll be glad you are coming along."

(Dear dead Dick) (Mahon under his scar, sleeping) (Dick, my dearest one)

She felt the head board against her head, through her hair, felt the bones of her long shanks against her arms clasping them, nursing them, saw the smug impersonal room like an appointed tomb (in which how many many discontents, desires, passions, had died?) high above a world of joy and sorrow and lust for living; high above impervious trees occupied solely with maternity and spring. (Dick, Dick. Dead ugly Dick. Once you were alive and young and passionate and ugly, after a time you were dead, dear Dick: that flesh, that body which I loved and did not love your beautiful young ugly body, dear Dick, become now a seething of worms, like new milk. Dear Dick)

Gilligan, Joseph, late a private, a democrat by enlistment and numbered like a convict, slept beside her, his boots (given him gratis by democrats of a higher rating among democrats) innocent and awkward upon a white spread of rented cloth immaculate and impersonal.

She evaded her blanket and reaching her arm swept the room with darkness. She slipped beneath the covers, settling her cheek on her palm. Gilligan undisturbed snored, filling the room with a homely comforting sound.

(Dick, dear ugly dead . . .)

4.

In the next room Cadet Lowe waked from a chaotic dream, opening his eyes and staring with detachment, impersonal as God, at lights burning about him. After a time he recalled his body, remembering where he was and by an effort he turned his head. In the other bed the man slept beneath his terrible face. (I am Julian Lowe. I eat, I digest, evacuate: I have flown. This man . . . this man here, sleeping beneath his scar. . . . Where do we touch? Oh, God, oh, God: knowing his own body, his stomach)

Raising his hand he felt his own undamaged brow. No scar there. Near him upon a chair was his hat severed by a white band, upon the table the other man's cap with its cloth crown sloping backward from a bronze initialled crest.

He tasted his sour mouth, knowing his troubled stomach. To have been him he moaned. Just to be him. Let him take this sound body of mine! Let him take it. To have got wings on my breast, to have got wings; and to have got his scar, too,

I would take death tomorrow. Upon a chair Mahon's tunic evinced above the left breast pocket wings breaking from an initialled circle beneath a crown, tipping downward in an arrested embroidered sweep; a symbolized desire.

To be him, to have gotten wings, but to have got his scar too! Cadet Lowe turned to the wall with passionate disappointment like a gnawing fox at his vitals. Slobbering and moaning Cadet Lowe too dreamed again, sleeping.

5.

> Achilles—— What preparation would you make for
>   a cross-country flight, Cadet?
> Mercury—— Empty your bladder and fill your
>   petrol tank, Sir.
> Achilles—— Carry on, Cadet.
>
> Old Play
(about 19—?)

Cadet Lowe waking remarked morning and Gilligan entering the room, dressed. Gilligan looking at him said:

"How you coming, ace?"

Mahon yet slept beneath his scar, upon a chair his tunic. Above the left pocket wings swept silkenly, breaking downward above a ribbon. Purple, white, purple.

"Oh, God," Lowe groaned.

Gilligan with the assurance of physical well-being stood in brisk arrested motion.

"As you were, fellow. I'm going out and have some breakfast sent up. You stay here until the loot wakes, huh?"

Cadet Lowe tasting his sour mouth groaned again. Gilligan regarded him.

"Oh, you'll stay all right, wont you? I'll be back soon."

The door closed after him and Lowe thinking of water rose and took his wavering way across the room to a water pitcher. Carafe. Like giraffe or like café? he wondered. The water was good, but lowering the vessel he felt immediately sick. After a while he recaptured the bed.

He dozed, forgetting his stomach, and remembering it he

dreamed and waked. He could feel his head like a dull constricted inflation, then he could distinguish the foot of his bed and thinking again of water he turned on a pillow and saw another identical bed and the suave indication of a dressing gown motionless beside it. Leaning over Mahon's scarred supineness she said "Dont get up."

Lowe said "I wont," closing his eyes tasting this mouth, seeing her long slim body against his red eyelids, opening his eyes to light and her thigh shaped and falling away into an impersonal fabric. With an effort he might have seen her ankles. Her feet will be there, he thought, unable to accomplish the effort and behind his closed eyes he thought of saying something which would leave his mouth on hers. Oh, God, he thought, feeling that no one had been so sick, imagining that she would say I love you, too. If I had wings, and a scar. . . . To hell with officers, he thought, sleeping again:

To hell with kee wees, anyway. I wouldn't be a goddamn kee wee. Rather be a sergeant. Rather be a mechanic. Crack up, Cadet. Hell, yes. Why not? War's over. Glad. Glad. Oh, God. His scar: his wings. Last time:

He was briefly in a Jenny again conscious of lubricating oil and a slow gracious restraint of braced plane surfaces, feeling an air blast and feeling the stick in his hand, watching bobbing rocker arms on the horizon, laying her nose on the horizon like a sighted rifle. Christ, what do I care? seeing her nose rise until the horizon was hidden, seeing the arc of a descending wing expose it again, seeing her become abruptly stationary while a mad world spinning vortexed about his seat. Sure, what do you care? asked a voice and waking he saw Gilligan beside him with a glass of whiskey.

"Drink her down, General," said Gilligan holding the glass under his nose.

"Oh, God, move it, move it."

"Come on, now; drink her down: you'll feel better. The loot is up and at 'em, and Mrs Powers. Whatcher get so drunk for, ace?"

"Oh, God, I dont know," answered Cadet Lowe, rolling his head in anguish. "Lemme alone."

Gilligan said "Come on, drink her, now." Cadet Lowe said "Go away" passionately.

"Lemme alone, I'll be all right."

"Sure you will. Soon as you drink this."

"I cant. Go away."

"You got to. You want I should break your neck?" asked Gilligan kindly, bringing his face up, kind and ruthless. Lowe eluded him and Gilligan reaching under his body, raised him.

"Lemme lie down," Lowe implored.

"And stay here forever? We got to go somewheres. We cant stay here."

"But I cant drink." Cadet Lowe's interior coiled passionately: an ecstasy. "For God's sake, let me alone."

"Ace," said Gilligan holding his head up, "you got to. You might just as well drink this yourself. If you dont, I'll put it down your throat, glass and all. Here, now."

The glass was between his lips so he drank, gulping, expecting to gag. But gulping, the stuff became immediately pleasant. It was like new life in him. He felt a kindly sweat and Gilligan removed the empty glass. Mahon dressed except for his belt sat beside a table. Gilligan vanished through a door and he rose, feeling shaky but quite fit. He took another drink. Water thundered in the bathroom and Gilligan returning said briskly: "Atta boy."

He pushed Lowe into the bathroom. "In you go, ace," he added.

Feeling the sweet bright needles of water burning his shoulders, watching his body slipping an endless silver sheathe of water, smelling soap: beyond that wall was her room, where she was, tall and red and white and black, beautiful. I'll tell her at once, he decided sawing his hard young body with a rough towel. Glowing he brushed his teeth and hair, then he had another drink under Mahon's quiet inverted stare and Gilligan's quizzical one. He dressed hearing her moving in her room. Maybe she's thinking of me, he told himself, swiftly donning his khaki.

He caught the officer's kind puzzled gaze and the man said: "How are you?"

"Never felt better after my solo," he answered wanting to sing. "Say, I left my hat in her room last night," he told Gilligan. "Guess I better get it."

"Here's your hat," Gilligan informed him unkindly, producing it.

"Well then, I want to talk to her. Whatcher going to say about that?" asked Cadet Lowe swept and garnished and belligerent.

"Why sure, General," Gilligan agreed readily. "She cant refuse one of the saviors of her country." He knocked on her door. "Mrs Powers?"

"Yes?" her voice was muffled.

"General Pershing here wants to talk to you. . . . Sure. . . . All right." He turned about, opening the door. "In you go, ace."

Lowe hating him ignored his wink, entering. She sat in bed with a breakfast tray upon her knees. She was not dressed and Lowe looked delicately away. But she said blandly:

"Cheerio, Cadet! How looks the air today?"

She indicated a chair and he drew it up to the bed, being so careful not to seem to stare that his carriage became noticeable. She looked at him quickly and kindly and offered him coffee. Courageous with whiskey on an empty stomach he knew hunger suddenly. He took the cup.

"Good morning," he said with belated courtesy, trying to be more than nineteen. (Why is nineteen ashamed of its age?) She treats me like a child, he thought, fretted and gaining courage, watching with increasing boldness her indicated shoulders and wondering with interest if she had stockings on.

Why didn't I say something as I came in? Something easy and intimate? Listen, when I first saw you my love for you was like——my love was like——my love for you——God, if I only hadn't drunk so much last night I could say it my love for you my love is love is like . . . and found himself watching her arms as she moved and her loose sleeves fell away from them, saying Yes he was glad the war was over and telling her that he had forty seven hours flying time and would have got wings in two weeks more and that his mother in San Francisco was expecting him.

She treats me like a child, he thought with exasperation, seeing the slope of her shoulders and the place where her breast was.

"How black your hair is," he said and she said:

"Lowe, when are you going home?"

"I dont know. Why should I go home? I think I'll have a look at the country first."

"But your mother!" She glanced at him.

"Oh, well," he said largely, "you know what women are—always worrying you."

"Lowe! How do you know so much about things? Women? You—aren't married, are you?"

"Me married?" repeated Lowe with ungrammatical zest, "me married? Not so's you know it. I have lots of girls, but married!" He brayed with brief unnecessary vigor. "What made you think so?" he asked with interest.

"Oh, I dont know. You look so—so mature, you see."

"Ah, that's flying does that. Look at him in there."

"Is that it? I had noticed something about you two . . . you would have been an ace too, if you'd seen any Germans, wouldn't you?"

He glanced at her quickly, like a struck dog. Here was his old dull despair again.

"I'm so sorry," she said with quick sincerity. "I didn't think: of course you would. Anyway, it wasn't your fault. You did your best, I know."

"Oh for Christ's sake," he said hurt, "what do you women want, anyway? I am as good a flyer as any ever was at the front—flying or any other way." He sat morose under her eyes. He rose suddenly. "Say, what's your name, anyway?"

"Margaret," she told him. He approached the bed where she sat and she said: "More coffee?" stopping him dead. "You've forgotten your cup. There it is, on the table."

Before he thought he had returned and fetched his cup, receiving coffee he did not want. He felt like a fool and being young he resented it. All right for you, he promised her and sat again in a dull rage. To hell with them all.

"I have offended you, haven't I?" she asked. "But, Lowe, I feel so bad, and you were about to make love to me."

"Why do you think that?" he asked hurt and dull.

"Oh, I dont know. But women can tell. And I dont want to be made love to. Gilligan has already done that."

"Gilligan? Why, I'll kill him if he has annoyed you."

"No, no: he didn't offend me, any more than you did. It was flattering. But why were you going to make love to me? You thought of it before you came in, didn't you?"

Lowe told her youngly: "I thought of it on the train when I first saw you. When I saw you I knew you were the woman for me. Tell me, you dont like him better than me because he has wings and a scar, do you?"

"Why, of course not." She looked at him a moment, calculating. Then she said: "Mr Gilligan says he is dying."

"Dying?" he repeated and "dying?" How the man managed to circumvent him at every turn! As if it were not enough to have wings and a scar. But to die. . . .

"Margaret," he said with such despair that she gazed at him in swift pity. (He was so young) "Margaret, are you in love with him?" (Knowing that if he were a woman, he would be)

"No, certainly not. I am not in love with any body. My husband was killed on the Aisne, you see," she told him gently.

"Oh, Margaret," he said with bitter sincerity, "I would have been killed there if I could, or wounded like him: dont you know it?"

"Of course, darling." She put the tray aside. "Come here."

Cadet Lowe rose again and went to her. "I would have been, if I'd had a chance," he repeated.

She drew him down beside her and he knew he was acting the child she supposed him to be, but he couldn't help it. His disappointment and despair were more than everything now. Here were her knees sweetly under his face and he put his arms around her legs.

"I wanted to be," he confessed more than he had ever believed, "I would take his scar and all."

"And be dead, like he is going to be?"

But what was death to Cadet Lowe, except something true and grand and sad? He saw a tomb, open, and himself in boots and belt and pilot's wings on his breast, a wound stripe. . . . What more could one ask of Fate?

"Yes, yes," he answered.

"Why, you have flown too," she told him, holding his face against her knees, "you might have been him, but you were lucky. Perhaps you would have flown too well to have been shot down as he was. Had you thought of that?"

"I dont know. I guess I would let them catch me, if I could have been him. You are in love with him."

"I swear I am not." She raised his head to see his face. "I would tell you if I were. Dont you believe me?" Her eyes were compelling: he believed her.

"Then, if you aren't, cant you promise to wait for me? I will be older soon and I'll work like hell and make money."

"What will your mother say?"

"Hell, I dont have to mind her like a kid for ever. I am nineteen, as old as you are, and if she dont like it, she can go to hell."

"Lowe!" she reproved him not telling him she was twenty four, "the idea! You go home and tell your mother——I will give you a note to her——and you can write what she says."

"But I had rather go with you."

"But, dear heart, what good will that do? We are going to take him home, and he is sick. Dont you see, darling, we cant do anything until we get him settled, and that you would only be in the way?"

"In the way?" he repeated in sharp pain.

"You know what I mean. We cant have anything to think about until we get him home, dont you see?"

"But you aren't in love with him?"

"I swear I'm not. Does that satisfy you?"

"Then, are you in love with me?"

She drew his face against her knees again. "You sweet child," she said, "of course I wont tell you—yet."

And he had to be satisfied with this. They held each other in silence for a time. "How good you smell," remarked Cadet Lowe at last.

She moved. "Come up here by me," she commanded and when he was beside her she took his face in her hands and kissed him. He put his arms around her and she drew his head between her breasts. After a while she stroked his hair and spoke.

"Now, are you going home at once?"

"Must I?" he asked vacuously.

"You must," she answered. "Today. Wire her at once. And I will give you a note to her."

"Oh hell, you know what she'll say."

"Of course I do. You haven't any sisters and brothers, have you?"

"No," he said in surprise. She moved and he sensed the fact that she desired to be released. He sat up. "How did you know?" he asked in surprise.

"I just guessed. But you will go, wont you? Promise."

"Well, I will then. But I will come back to you."

"Of course you will. I will expect you. Kiss me."

She offered her face coolly and he kissed her as she wished: coldly, remotely. She put her hands on his cheeks. "Dear boy," she said kissing him again, as his mother kissed him.

"Say, that's no way for engaged people to kiss," he objected.

"How do engaged people kiss?" she asked. He put his arms around her feeling her shoulder blades and drew her mouth against his with the technique he had learned. She suffered his kiss a moment, then thrust him away.

"Is that how engaged people kiss?" she asked laughing. "I like this better." She took his face in her palms and touched his mouth briefly and coolly. "Now, swear you'll wire your mother at once."

"But will you write to me?"

"Surely. But swear you will go today, in spite of what Gilligan may tell you."

"I swear," he answered looking at her mouth. "Cant I kiss you again?"

"When we are married," she said and he knew he was being dismissed. Thinking, knowing that she was watching him he crossed the room with an air, not looking back.

Here were yet Gilligan and the officer. Mahon said:

"Morning, old chap."

Gilligan looked at Lowe's belligerent front from a quizzical reserve of sardonic amusement.

"Made a conquest, hey ace?"

"Go to hell," replied Lowe. "Where's that bottle? I'm going home today."

"Here she is, General. Drink deep. Going home?" he repeated. "So are we, hey Loot?"

Chapter Two.

I.

JONES, Januarius Jones, born of whom he knew and cared not, becoming Jones alphabetically, January through a conjunction of calendar and biology, Januarius through the perverse conjunction of his own star and the compulsion of food and clothing——Januarius Jones baggy in gray tweed, being lately a fellow of Latin in a small college, leaned upon a gate of iron grill-work breaking a levee of green and embryonically starred honey-suckle, watching April busy in a hyacinth bed. Dew was on the grass and bees broke apple bloom in the morning sun while swallows were like plucked strings against a pale windy sky. A face regarded him across a suspended trowel and the metal clasps of crossed suspenders made a cheerful glittering.

The rector said: "Good morning, young man." His shining dome was friendly against an ivy covered wall above which the consummate grace of a spire and a gilded cross seemed to arc across motionless young clouds.

Januarius Jones caught in the spire's illusion of slow ruin murmured: "Watch it fall, sir." The sun was full on his round young face.

The horticulturist regarded him with benevolent curiosity.

"Fall? ah, you see an aeroplane," he stated. "My son was in that service during the war."

He became gigantic in black trousers and broken shoes. "A beautiful day for flying," he said from beneath his cupped hand. "Where do you see it?"

"No, sir," replied Jones, "no aeroplane, sir. I referred in a fit of unpardonable detachment to your spire. It was ever my childish delight to stand beneath a spire while clouds are moving overhead. The illusion of slow falling is perfect. Have you ever experienced this, sir?"

"To be sure I have, though it has been——let me see—— more years than I care to remember. But one of my cloth is prone to allow his own soul to atrophy in his zeal for the welfare of other souls that——"

42

"——that not only do not deserve salvation, but that do not particularly desire it," finished Jones.

The rector promptly rebuked him. Sparrows were delirious in ivy and the rambling façade of the rectory was a dream in jonquils and clipped sward. There should be children here, thought Jones. He said:

"I most humbly beg your pardon for my flippancy, doctor. I assure you that I—ah—took advantage of the situation without any ulterior motive whatever."

"I understand that, dear boy. My rebuke was tendered in the same spirit. There are certain conventions which we must observe in this world: one of them being an outward deference to the cloth which I unworthily perhaps, wear. And I have found this particularly incumbent upon we of the—— what shall I say——?"

"Integer vitae scelerisque purus
non eget Mauris iaculus neque arcu
nec venenatis sagittas,
Fusce, pharetra——" began Jones. The rector chimed in:
"——sive per Syrtis iter aestuosas
sive facturus per inhospitalem
Caucasum vel quae loac fabulosas
lambit Hydaspes." they concluded in galloping duet and stood in the ensuing silence regarding each other with genial enthusiasm.

"But come, come," cried the rector. His eyes were pleasant. "Shall I let the stranger languish without my gates?" The grilled iron swung open and his earthy hand was heavy on Jones' shoulder. "Come, let us try the spire."

The grass was good. A myriad bees vacillated between clover and apple bloom, apple bloom and clover and from the gothic mass of the church the spire rose: a prayer imperishable in bronze, immaculate in its illusion of slow ruin across motionless young clouds.

"My one sincere parishioner," murmured the divine. Sunlight was a windy golden plume about his bald head and Januarius Jones' face was a round mirror before which fauns and nymphs might have wantoned when the world was young. "Parishioner, did I say? It is more than that: it is by such as this that man may approach nearest to God. And how few will believe this! How few, how few." He stared unblinking into the sun-filled sky: drowned in his eyes was a despair long since grown cool and quiet.

"That is very true, sir. But we of this age believe that he who may be approached informally without the intercession of an office boy of some sort, is not worth approaching. We purchase our salvation as we do our real estate. Our God," continued Jones, "need not be compassionate, he need not be very intelligent. But he must have dignity."

The rector raised his great dirty hand.

"No, no, you do them injustice. But who has ever found justice in youth, or any of those tiresome virtues with which we coddle and cradle our hardening arteries and souls? Only the ageing need conventions and laws to aggregate to them-selves some of the beauty of this world. Without laws the young would rieve us of it as corsairs of old combed the blue seas."

The rector was silent a while. The intermittent shadows of young leaves were bird cries made visible and sparrows in ivy were flecks of sunlight become vocal. The rector continued:

"Had I the arranging of this world I should establish a certain point, say at about the age of thirty, upon reaching which a man would be automatically relegated to a plane where his mind would be no longer troubled with the futile recollection of temptations he had resisted and of the beauty he had failed to garner to himself. It is jealousy, I think, which makes us wish to prevent young people doing the things we had not the courage or the opportunity ourselves to accomplish once, and have not the power to do now."

Jones, wondering what temptations he had ever resisted and then recalling the women he might have seduced and hadn't, said:

"And then what? What would the people who have been unlucky enough to reach thirty do?"

"On this plane there would be no troubling physical things such as sunlight and space and birds in the trees——only unimportant things such as physical comfort: eating and sleeping and procreation."

What more could you want, thought Jones. Here was a swell place. A man could very well spend all his time eating and sleeping and procreating, Jones believed. He rather wished the rector (or any man who could imagine a world consisting solely of food and sleep and women) had had the creating of things and that he, Jones, could be forever thirty one years of age. The rector, though, seemed to hold different opinions.

"What would they do to pass the time?" asked Jones for the sake of argument, wondering what the others would do to pass the time, with eating and sleeping and fornication taken from them.

"Half of them would manufacture objects, and the other half would coin gold and silver with which to purchase the objects. Of course there would be storage places for the coins and objects, thus providing employment for some of the people. Others naturally would have to till the soil."

"But how would you finally dispose of the coins and objects? After a while you would have a single vast museum and a bank, both filled with useless and unnecessary things. And that is already the curse of our civilization—Things. Possessions, to which we are slaves, which require us to either labor honestly at least eight hours a day or do something illegal so as to keep them painted or dressed in the latest mode or filled with whiskey or gasoline."

"Quite true. And this would remind them too sorely of the world as it is. Needless to say, I have provided for both these contingencies. The coins would be reduced to bullion and coined over, and——" the reverend man looked at Jones in ecstasy—— "and the housewives could use the objects for fuel with which to cook food."

Old fool, thought Jones, saying:

"Marvellous, magnificent! You are a man after my own heart, doctor." (Why am I lying to him?)

The rector regarded Jones kindly. "Ah, boy, there is nothing after youth's own heart: youth has no heart."

"But, doctor. This borders on lese majesty. I thought we had declared truce regarding each other's cloth."

Shadows moved as the sun moved, a branch dappled the rector's brow: a laurelled Jove.

"What is your cloth?"

"Why——" began Jones.

"It is the diaper still, dear boy. But forgive me," he added quickly on seeing Jones' face. His arm was heavy and solid as an oak branch across Jones' shoulders. "Tell me, what do you consider the most admirable of virtues?"

Jones was placated. "Sincere arrogance," he returned promptly. The rector's great laugh boomed like bells in the sunlight, sent the sparrows like gusty leaves, whirling.

"Shall we be friends once more then? Come, I will make a concession: I will show you my flowers. You are young enough to appreciate them without feeling called upon to comment."

The garden was worth seeing. An avenue of roses bordered a gravelled path which passed out of the sunlight beneath two over-arching oaks. Beyond the oaks against a wall poplars in restless formal row were columns of a Greek temple, yet the poplars themselves in slim vague green were poised and vain as girls in a frieze. Against a privet hedge would be lilies soon like nuns in a cloister and blue hyacinths swung soundless bells, dreaming of Lesbos. Upon a lattice wall wistaria would soon burn in slow inverted lilac flame and following it they came lastly to a single rose-bush. The branches were huge and knotted with age, heavy and dark as a bronze pedestal, crowned with pale impermanent gold. The divine's hands lingered upon it with soft passion.

"Now this," he said, "is my son and my daughter, the wife of my bosom and the bread of my belly: it is my right hand and my left hand. Many is the night I have stood here beside it, after having removed the covering too soon, burning newspapers to keep the frost out. Once I recall, I was at a neighboring town attending a conference. The weather—it was March—had been most auspicious and I had removed the wrappings.

"The tips were already swelling. Ah, my boy, no young man ever awaited the coming of his mistress with more impatience than do I await the first bloom on this bush. (Who was the old pagan who kept his Byzantine goblet at his bed-side and slowly wore the rim away, kissing it? There is an analogy) . . . but what was I saying? —ah, yes. So I left this bush uncovered against my better judgment and repaired to the conference. The weather continued perfect until the last day, then the weather reports predicted a change. The bishop was to be present, I ascertained that I could not reach home by rail and return in time. At last I engaged a livery man to drive me home.

"The sky was becoming overcast, it was already turning colder. And then, three miles from home we came upon a stream and found the bridge gone. After some shouting I attracted the attention of a man plowing beyond the stream and he came over to us in a skiff. I engaged my driver to await me, was ferried across, walked home and covered my rose, walked back to the stream and returned in time. And that night—" the rector beamed upon Januarius Jones—— "Snow fell!"

Jones fatly supine on gracious grass, his eyes closed against the sun, stuffing his pipe: "This rose has almost made history. You have had the bush for some time, have you not? One does become attached to things one has long known." Januarius Jones was not particularly interested in flowers.

"I have a better reason than that. In this bush is prisoned a part of my youth, as wine is prisoned in a wine jar. But with this difference: my wine jar always renews itself."

"Oh," remarked Jones, despairing, "there is a story here, then."

"Yes, dear boy, rather a long story. But you are not comfortable lying there."

"Who ever is completely comfortable," Jones rushed into the breach, "unless he be asleep? It is the fatigue caused by man's inevitable contact with the earth which bears him be he standing sitting or lying, which keeps his mind in a continual fret over futilities. If a man, if a single man could be freed for a moment from the forces of gravity concentrating his weight upon that point of his body which touches earth, what would he not do? He would be a god, the lord of life, causing the high gods to tremble on their thrones: he would thunder at the very gates of infinity like a mailed knight. As it is, he must ever have behind his mind a dull wonder how anything composed of fire and air and water and omnipotence in equal parts can be so damn hard."

"That is true. Man cannot remain in one position long enough to really think. But about the rose bush——"

"Regard the buzzard," interrupted Jones with enthusiasm, fighting for time, "supported by air alone: what dignity! what singleness of purpose! What cares he whether or not Smith be governor? What cares he that the sovereign people annually commission comparative strangers about whom they know nothing save that these strangers have no inclination toward perspiration, to meddle with impunity in the affairs of the sovereign people?"

"But, my dear boy, this borders on anarchism."

"Anarchism? surely. The hand of Providence with money changing blisters. That is anarchism."

"At least you admit the hand of Providence."

"I dont know. Do I?" Jones his hat over his eyes and his pipe projecting beneath, heaved a box of matches from his jacket. He extracted one and scraped it on the box. It failed and he threw it weakly into a clump of violets. He tried another. He tried another. "Turn it around," murmured the rector. He did so and the match flared.

"How do you find the hand of Providence here?" he puffed around his pipe stem.

The rector gathered the dead matches from the clump of violets. "In this way: it enables man to rise and till the soil, so that he might eat. Would he, do you think, rise and labor if he could remain comfortably supine over long? Even that part of the body which the Creator designed for him to sit upon serves him for only a short period, then it rebels, it too gets his sullen bones up and hales them along. And there is no rest for him save in sleep."

"But he cannot sleep for more than a possible third of his time," Jones pointed out. "And soon it will not even be a third. The race is weakening, degenerating: we cannot stand nearly as much sleep as our comparatively recent (geologically speaking of course) fore-fathers could, not even as much as our more primitive contemporaries can. For we, the self-styled civilised peoples are now exercised over minds and arteries instead of stomachs and sex, as were our progenitors and our uncompelled contemporaries."

"Uncompelled?"

"Socially, of course. Doe believes that Doe and Smith should and must do this or that because Smith believes that Smith and Doe should and must do this or that."

"Ah yes." The divine again lifted his kind unblinking eyes

straight into the sun. The dew was off the grass and jonquils and narcissi were beginning to look drowsy, like girls after a ball. "It is drawing toward noon. Let us go in: I can offer you refreshment, and lunch if you are not engaged."

Jones rose. "No, no. Thank you a thousand times. But I shant trouble you."

The rector was hearty. "No trouble, no trouble at all. I am alone at present."

Jones demurred. He had a passion for food, and an instinct. He had only to pass a house for his instinct to inform him whether or not the food would be good. Jones did not react, gastronomically speaking, favorably to the rector.

The divine however overrode him with hearty affability: the rector would not take No. He attached Jones to himself and they trod their shadows across the lawn herding them beneath the subdued grace of a fanlight of dim-colored glass lovely with lack of washing. After the immaculate naked morning the interior of the hall vortexed with red fire. Jones temporarily blind stumbled violently over an object, and the handle of a pail clasped his ankle passionately. The rector bawling Emmy! dragged him, pail and all erect: he thanked his stars he had not been attached to the floor as he rose a sodden Venus, disengaging the pail. His dangling feet touched the floor and he felt his trouser leg with despair, fretfully. He's like a derrick, he thought with exasperation.

The rector bawled Emmy! again. There was an alarmed response from the depths of the house and one in gingham brushed them. The divine's great voice boomed like surf in the narrow confines and opening a door upon a flood of light he ushered the trickling Jones into his study.

"I shall not apologise," the rector began, "for the meagreness of the accommodations which I offer you. I am alone at present, you see. But, then, we philosophers want bread for the belly, not for the palate, eh? Come in, come in."

Jones despaired. A drenched trouser leg, and bread for the belly alone. And God only knew what this great lump of a divine meant by bread for the belly instead of the palate. Husks, probably. Regarding food, Jones was sybaritically rather than aesthetically inclined. Or even philosophically. He stood disconsolate, swinging his dripping leg.

"My dear boy, you are soaking!" exclaimed his host. "Come, off with your trousers."

Jones protested weakly.

"Emmy!" roared the rector again.

"All right, uncle Joe. Soon's I get this water up."

"Never mind the water right now. Run to my room and fetch me a pair of trousers."

"But the rug will be ruined!"

"Not irreparably, I hope. We'll take the risk. Fetch me the trousers. Now, dear boy, off with them. Emmy will dry them in the kitchen and then you will be right as rain."

Jones surrendered in dull despair. He had truly fallen among moral thieves. The rector assailed him with ruthless kindness and the gingham-clad one reappeared at the door with a twin of the rector's casual black nether coverings over her arm.

"Emmy, this is Mr——I do not recall having heard your name?——He will be with us at lunch. And Emmy, see if Miss Cecily wishes to come also."

This virgin shrieked at the spectacle of Jones ludicrous in his shirt and his pink fat legs and the trousers jerked solemn and lethargic into the room.

"Jones," supplied Januarius Jones, faintly. Emmy however was gone.

"Ah yes, Mr Jones." The rector fell upon him anew, doing clumsy and intricate things with the waist and bottoms of the trousers, and Jones decently if voluminously clad stood like a sheep in a gale while the divine pawed him heavily.

"Now," cried his host, "make yourself comfortable" (even Jones found irony in this) "while I find something that will quench thirst."

The guest regained his composure in a tidy shabby room. Upon a rag rug a desk bore a single white hyacinth in a handle-less teacup, above a mantel cluttered with pipes and twists of paper hung a single photograph. There were books every-where, on shelves, on window ledges, on chairs, on the floor: Jones saw the old testament in Greek in several volumes, a de-pressing huge book on international law, Jane Austen and Les Contes Drolatiques in dog-eared amity: a mutual supporting caress. The rector re-entered with milk in a pitcher of blue glass, and two mugs. From a drawer he extracted a bottle of Scotch whiskey.

"A sop to the powers," he said leering at Jones with innocent depravity. "Old dog and new tricks, my boy. But your pardon: perhaps you do not like this combination?"

Jones' morale rose balloon-like. "I will try any drink once," he said like Jurgen.

"Try it, anyway. If you do not like it you are perfectly at liberty to employ your own formula."

The beverage was more palatable than he would have thought. He sipped with relish. "Didn't you mention a son, sir?"

"That was Donald. He was shot down in Flanders last spring." The rector rose and took the photograph down from above the mantel. He handed it to his guest.

The boy was about eighteen, coatless: beneath unruly hair Jones saw a thin face with a delicate pointed chin and wild soft eyes. Jones' eyes were clear and yellow, obscene and old in sin as a goat's.

"There is death in his face," said Jones.

His host took the photograph and gazed at it. "There is always death in the faces of the young in spirit, the eternally young. Death for themselves or for others. And dishonor. But death, surely. And why not? why should death desire only those things which life has no more use for? Who gathers the withered rose?" The rector dreamed darkly in space for a while. After a time he added: "A companion sent back a few of his things." He propped the photograph upright on the desk and from a drawer he took a tin box. His great hand fumbled at the catch.

"Let me, sir," offered Jones knowing it was useless to volunteer, that the rector probably did this everyday. But the lid yielded as he spoke and the divine spread on the desk the sorry contents: a woman's chemise, a cheap papercovered 'Shropshire Lad,' a mummied hyacinth bulb. The rector picked up the bulb and it crumbled to dust in his hand.

"Tut, tut! How careless of me!" he ejaculated sweeping the dust carefully into an envelope. "I have often deplored the size of my hands. They should have been given to someone who could use them for something other than thumbing books or grubbing in flower beds. Donald's hands on the contrary were quite small, like his mother's: he was quite deft with his hands. What a surgeon he would have made."

He placed the things upon the desk before the photograph, like a ritual and propping his face in his earthy hands he took his ruined dream of his son into himself as one inhales tobacco smoke.

"Truly, there is life and death and dishonor in his face. Had you noticed Emmy? Years ago, about the time this picture was made. . . . But that is an old story. Even Emmy has probably forgotten it. . . . You will notice that he has neither coat nor cravat. How often has he appeared after his mother had seen him decently arrayed, on the street, in church, at formal gatherings carrying hat coat and collar in his hands. How often have I heard him say: Because it is too hot. Education in the bookish sense he had not: the schooling he got was because he wanted to go, the reading he did was because he wanted to read. Least of all did I teach him fortitude. What is fortitude? Emotional atrophy: gangrene. . . ."

He raised his face and looked at Jones. "What do you think? was I right? Or should I have made my son conform to a type?"

"Conform that face to a type? (So Emmy has already been dishonored, once, anyway) How could you? (I owe that dishonored one a grudge, too) Could you put a faun into formal clothes?"

The rector sighed. "Ah, Mr Jones, who can say?" He slowly returned the things to the tin box and sat clasping the box in his hand. "As I grow older, Mr Jones, I become more firmly convinced that we learn scarcely anything as we go through this world, and we learn nothing whatever which can ever help us or be of any particular benefit to us, even. However! . . ." He sighed again, heavily.

2.

Emmy, the dishonored virgin appeared saying: "What you want for dinner, uncle Joe? Ice cream or strawberry shortcake?" Blushing she avoided Jones' eye.

The rector looked at his guest, yearning. "What would you like, Mr Jones? But I know how young people are about ice cream. Would you prefer ice cream?"

But Jones was a tactful man in his generation and knowing about food himself he had an uncanny skill in anticipating other peoples' reactions to food. "If it is the same to you, Doctor, let it be short-cake."

"Short-cake, Emmy," the rector instructed with passion. Emmy withdrew. "Do you know," he continued with apologetic gratitude, "do you know, when a man becomes old, when instead of using his stomach his stomach uses him, and as his other physical compulsions become weaker and decline his predilections toward the food he likes obtrude themselves."

"Not at all, sir," Jones assured him. "I personally prefer a warm dessert to ice."

"Then you must return when there are peaches. I will give you a peach cobbler, with butter and cream. . . . But ah, my stomach has attained a sad ascendancy."

"Why shouldn't it, sir? Years reft us of sexual compulsions: why shouldn't we fill the interval with compulsions of food?"

The rector regarded him kindly and piercingly. "You are becoming specious. Man's life need not be always filled with compulsions of either sex or food, need it?"

But here came quick tapping feet down the bare hall and she entered saying "Good morning, uncle Joe," in her throaty voice, crossing the room with graceful effusion, not seeing Jones at once. Then she remarked him and paused like a bird in midflight, briefly. Jones rose and under his eyes she walked mincing and graceful, theatrical with body-consciousness to the desk. She bent sweetly as a young tree and the divine kissed her cheek. Jones' goat's eyes immersed her in yellow contemplation.

"Good morning, Cecily." The rector rose. "I had expected you earlier on such a day as this. But young girls must have their beauty sleep regardless of weather," he ended with elephantine joviality. "This is Mr Jones, Cecily. Miss Saunders, Mr Jones."

Jones bowed with obese incipient grace as she faced him, but at her expression of hushed delicate amazement he knew panic. Then he remembered the rector's cursed trousers and he felt his neck and ears slowly burn knowing that not only was he ridiculous but that she supposed he wore such things habitually. She was speechless and Jones damned the hearty oblivious rector slowly and completely. Curse the man: one moment it was Emmy and no trousers at all, next moment an attractive stranger and nether coverings like a tired balloon. The rector was saying bland as Fate:

"I had expected you earlier. I had decided to let you take some hyacinths."

"Uncle Joe! How won-derful!" Her voice was rough, like a tangle of golden wires. She dragged her fascinated gaze from Jones and hating them both Jones felt perspiration under his hair. "Why didn't I come sooner? But I am always doing the wrong thing as Mr——Mr Jones will know from my not coming in time to get hyacinths."

She looked at him again, as she might at a strange beast. Jones' confusion became anger and he found his tongue.

"Yes, it is too bad you didn't come earlier. You would have seen me more interestingly got up than this even. Emmy seemed to think so, at least."

"I beg your pardon?" she said.

The rector regarded him with puzzled affability. Then he understood. "Ah yes, Mr Jones suffered a slight accident and was forced to don a garment of mine."

"Thanks for saying 'was forced'," Jones said viciously. "Yes, stumbled over that pail of water the doctor keeps just inside the front door doubtless for the purpose of making his parishioners be sure they really require help from heaven, on their second visit," he explained, Greek-like giving his dignity its death-stroke with his own hand. "You I suppose are accustomed to it and can avoid it."

She looked from Jones' suffused angry face to the rector's kind puzzled one and screamed with laughter.

"Forgive me," she pleaded sobering as quickly. "I simply couldn't help it, Mr Jones. You'll forgive me, wont you?"

"Certainly. Even Emmy enjoyed it. Doctor, Emmy cannot have been so badly outraged after all, to suffer such a shock from seeing a man's bare——"

She covered up this gaucherie losing most of the speech in her own words.

"So you showed Mr Jones your flowers? Mr Jones should be quite flattered: that is quite a concession for uncle Joe to make," she said smoothly, turning to the divine, graceful and insincere as a French sonnet. "Is Mr Jones famous, then? You haven't told me you knew famous men."

The rector boomed his laugh.

"Well, Mr Jones, you seem to have concealed something from me (not as much as I would like to have, Jones thought) I didn't know I was entertaining a celebrity."

Jones' essential laziness of temper regained its ascendancy and he answered civilly: "Neither did I, sir."

"Ah, dont try to hide your light, Mr Jones. Women know these things. They see through us at once."

"Uncle Joe," she cautioned swiftly at this unfortunate remark watching Jones. But Jones was safe now.

"No, I dont agree with you. If they saw through us they would never marry us."

She was grateful and her glance showed a faint interest. (What color are her eyes?)

"Oh, that's what Mr Jones is! An authority on women."

Jones' vanity swelled and the rector saying Pardon me fetched a chair from the hall. She leaned her thigh against the desk and her eyes (Are they gray or blue or green?) met his yellow unabashed stare. She lowered her gaze and he remarked her pretty self-conscious mouth. This is going to be easy, he thought. The rector placed the chair for her and she sat and when the rector had taken his desk chair again Jones resumed his seat. How long her legs are, he thought, seeing her frail white dress shape to her short torso. She felt his bold examination and looked up.

"So Mr Jones is married," she remarked. She did something to her eyes and it seemed to Jones that she had touched him with her hands. I've got your number, he thought vulgarly.

He replied: "No, what makes you think so?" The rector filling his pipe regarded them kindly.

"Oh, I misunderstood you."

"That isn't why you thought so."

"No?"

"Its because you like married men," he told her boldly.

"Do I?" without interest. It seemed to Jones that he could see her interest ebb away from him, could feel it cool.

"Dont you?"

"You ought to know."

"I?" asked Jones. "How should I know?"

"Aren't you an authority on women?" she replied with sweet ingenuousness.

Speechless he could have strangled her. The divine applauded:

"Checkmate, Mr Jones!"

Just let me catch her eye again, he vowed, but she would not look at him. He sat silent and under his seething gaze she took the photograph from the desk and held it quietly for a time. Then she replaced it and reaching across the desk-top she laid her hand on the rector's.

"Miss Saunders was engaged to my son," the divine explained to Jones.

"Yes?" said Jones watching her profile, waiting for her to look at him again. Emmy, that unfortunate virgin, appeared at the door.

"All right, uncle Joe," she said vanishing immediately.

"Ah, lunch," the rector announced starting up.

They rose. "I cant stay," she demurred yielding to the divine's hand upon her back. Jones fell in behind. "I really shouldn't stay," she amended.

They moved down the dark hall and Jones watching her white dress flow indistinctly to her stride, imagining her kiss, cursed her. At a door she paused and stood aside courteously, as a man would. The rector stopped also as perforce did Jones and here was a French comedy regarding precedence. Jones with counterfeit awkwardness felt her soft corsetless thigh against the back of his hand and her sharp stare was like ice water. They entered the room. Made you look at me then, he muttered.

The rector remarking nothing said: "Sit here, Mr Jones" and the virgin Emmy gave him a haughty and antagonistic stare. He returned her a remote yellow one. I'll see about you later, he promised her soundlessly, sitting to immaculate linen. The rector drew the other guest's chair and sat himself at the head of the table.

"Cecily doesn't eat very much," he said carving a fowl, "so the burden will fall upon you and me. But I think we can be relied upon, eh, Mr Jones?"

She propped her elbows opposite him. And I'll attend to you, too, Jones promised her darkly. She still ignored his yellow gaze and he said: "Certainly, sir," employing upon her the old thought process he had used in school when he was prepared upon a certain passage but she ignored him with such thorough perfection that he knew a sudden qualm of unease, a faint doubt. I wonder if I am wrong? he pondered. I'll find out, he decided suddenly.

"You were saying, sir,"—still watching her oblivious shallow face—"as Miss Saunders so charmingly came in, that I am too specious. But one must always generalize about fornication. Only after——"

"Mr Jones!" the rector exclaimed heavily.

"——the fornication is committed should one talk about it at all, and then only to generalize, to become—in your words —specious. He who kisses and tells is not very much of a fellow, is he?"

"Mr Jones," the rector remonstrated.

"Mr Jones!" she echoed. "What a terrible man you are! Really, uncle Joe——"

Jones interrupted viciously: "As far as the kiss itself goes, women do not particularly care who does the kissing. All they are interested in is the kiss itself."

"Mr Jones!" she repeated, staring at him, then looking quickly away. She shuddered.

"Come, come, sir. There are ladies present." The rector achieved his aphorism.

Jones pushed his plate from him, Emmy's raw and formless hand removed it and here was a warm golden brow crowned with strawberries. Dam'f I look at her, he swore and so he did. Her gaze was remote and impersonal, green and cool as sea water, and Jones turned his eyes away first. She turned to the rector talking smoothly about flowers. He was politely ignored and he moodily engaged his spoon as Emmy appeared again.

Emmy emanated a thin hostility and staring from Jones to the girl she said:

"Lady to see you, uncle Joe."

The rector poised his spoon. "Who is it, Emmy?"

"I dunno. I never saw her before. She's waiting in your study."

"Has she had lunch? Ask her in here."

(She knows I am watching her. Jones knew exasperation and a puerile lust)

"She dont want anything to eat. She said not to disturb you till you had finished eating. You better go in and see what she wants," Emmy retreated.

The rector wiped his mouth and rose. "I suppose I must. You young people sit here until I return. Call Emmy if you want anything."

Jones sat in sullen silence turning his glass in his fingers. At last she looked at his bent ugly face.

"So you are unmarried as well as famous," she remarked.

"Famous because I'm unmarried," he replied darkly.

"And courteous because of which?"

"Either one you like."

"Well, frankly I prefer courtesy."

"Do you often get it?"

"Always . . . eventually."

He made no reply and she continued: "Dont you believe in marriage?"

"As long as there are no women in it."

She shrugged indifferently. Jones could not bear seeming a fool to anyone as shallow as he considered her and he blurted, wanting to kick himself:

"You dont like me, do you?"

"Oh, I like anyone who believes there may be something he doesn't know," she replied without interest.

"What do you mean by that?" (are they green or gray?) Jones a disciple of the cult of boldness with women rose and the table wheeled smoothly as he circled it: he wished faintly that he were more graceful. Those thrice unhappy trousers! You cant blame her, he thought with fairness, what would I think if she had appeared in one of her grandma's mother hubbards? He remarked her reddish dark hair and the delicate slope of her shoulder. (I'll put my hand on it and let it slide down her arm as she turns)

Without looking up she said suddenly: "Did uncle Joe tell

you about Donald?" (Oh, hell, thought Jones) "Isn't it funny," her chair scraped to her straightening knees, "we both thought of moving at the same time?"

She rose, her chair intervened woodenly and Jones stood ludicrous and foiled.

"You take mine and I'll take yours," she added moving around the table.

"You bitch," said Jones evenly and her green-blue eyes took him sweetly as water.

"What made you say that?" she asked quietly. Jones having to an extent eased his feelings thought he saw recurring interest in her expression. (I was right, he gloated)

"You know why I said it."

"Its funny how few men know that women like to be talked to that way," she remarked irrelevantly.

I wonder if she loves someone? I guess not—like a tiger loves meat. "I am not like other men," he told her.

He thought he saw derision in her brief glance but she merely yawned delicately. At last he had her classified in the animal kingdom: hamadryad, a slim jewelled one.

"Why doesn't George come for me!" she said as if in answer to his unspoken speculation, patting her mouth with the tips of petulant, delicate fingers. "Isn't it boring, waiting for someone?"

"Yes. Who is George, may I ask?"

"Certainly, you may ask."

"Well, who is he?" (I dont like her type, anyway) "I had gathered you were pining for the late lamented."

"The late lamented?"

"That fox-faced Henry or Oswald or something."

"Oh, Donald. Do you mean Donald?"

"Surely, let him be Donald then."

She regarded him impersonally. (I cant even make her angry, he thought fretfully) "Do you know, you are impossible."

"Alright, so I am," he answered with anger. "But then I wasn't engaged to Donald. And George is not calling for me."

"What makes you so angry? Because I wont let you put your hands on me?"

"My dear woman, if I had wanted to put my hands on you I would have done it."

"Yes?" Her rising inflection was a polite maddening derision.

"Certainly. Dont you believe it?" his own voice gave him courage.

"I dont know. . . . But what good would it do you?"

"No good at all. That's the reason I dont want to."

Her green eyes took him again. Sparse old silver on a buffet shadowed heavily under a high fanlight of colored glass identical with the one above the entrance, her fragile white dress across the table from him: he could imagine her long subtle legs, like Atalanta's reft of running. "Why do you tell yourself lies?" she asked with interest.

"Same reason you do."

"I?"

"Surely. You intend to kiss me and yet you are going to all this damn trouble about it."

"Do you know," she remarked with speculation, "I believe I hate you."

"I dont doubt it. I know damn well I hate you."

She moved in her chair, sloping the light now across her shoulders, releasing him, becoming completely another person. "Lets go to the study. Shall we?"

"Alright. Uncle Joe should be done with his caller by now." He rose and they faced each other across the broken meal. She did not rise.

"Well?" she said.

"After you, ma'am," he replied with mock deference.

"I have changed my mind. I think I'll wait here and talk to Emmy, if you dont object."

"Why Emmy?"

"Why not Emmy?"

"Ah, I see. You can feel fairly safe with Emmy: she probably wont want to put her hands on you. That's it, isn't it?" She glanced briefly at him. "What you mean is, that you will stay if I am going out of the room, dont you?"

"Suit yourself." She became oblivious of him, breaking a biscuit upon a plate and then dripping water upon it from a glass. Jones moved fatly in his borrowed trousers, circling the table again. As he approached she turned slightly in her chair extending her hand. He felt its slim bones in his fat moist palm, its nervous ineffectual flesh. Not good for anything.

Useless. But beautiful with lack of character. Beautiful hands. Its very fragility stopped him like a stone barrier.

"Oh, Emmy!" she called sweetly, "come here, darling. I have something to show you."

Emmy regarded them balefully from the door and Jones said quickly: "Will you fetch me my trousers, Miss Emmy?"

Emmy glanced from one to the other ignoring the girl's mute plea. (Oho, Emmy has fish of her own to fry, thought Jones) Emmy vanished and he put his hands on the girl's shoulders.

"Now what will you do? Call the doctor?"

She looked at him over her shoulder from beyond an inaccessible barrier. His anger grew and his hands wantonly crushed her dress.

"Dont ruin my clothes, please," she said icily. "Here, if you must."

She raised her face and Jones felt shame, but his boyish vanity would not let him stop now. Her face a prettiness of shallow characterless planes blurred into his, her mouth was motionless and impersonal, unresisting and cool. Her face from a blur became again a prettiness of characterless shallowness icy and remote and Jones ashamed of himself and angry with her therefore said with heavy irony: "Thanks."

"Not at all. If you got any pleasure from it you are quite welcome." She rose. "Let me pass, please."

He stood awkwardly aside. Her frigid polite indifference was unbearable. What a fool he had been! He had ruined everything.

"Miss Saunders," he blurted, "I—Forgive me: I dont usually act that way, I swear I dont."

She spoke over her shoulder. "You dont have to, I suppose? I imagine you are usually quite successful, usually?"

"I am very sorry. But I dont blame you. . . . One hates to convict oneself of stupidity."

After a while, hearing no further movement he looked up. She was like a flower stalk or a young tree relaxed against the table: there was something so fragile, so impermanent since robustness and strength were unnecessary yet strong withal as a poplar is strong through very absence of strength, about her; you knew that she lived, that her clear delicate being was nourished by sunlight and honey until even digestion was a beautiful function . . . as he watched something like a shadow came over her, somewhere between her eyes and her petulant pretty mouth, in the very clear relaxation of her body that caused him to go quickly to her. She stared into his unblinking goat's eyes as his hands sliding across her arms met at the small of her back and he did not know the door had opened until she jerked her mouth from his and twisted slimly from his clasp.

The rector loomed in the door staring into the room as if he did not recognise it. He has never seen us at all, Jones knew, then seeing the divine's face he said:

"He's ill."

The rector spoke. "Cecily——"

"What is it, uncle Joe?" she replied in sharp terror, going to him: "aren't you well?"

The divine balanced his huge body with a hand on either side of the doorway.

"Cecily, Donald's coming home," he said.

3.

There was that subtle effluvia of antagonism found inevitably in a room where two young "pretty" women are, and they sat examining each other with narrow care. Mrs Powers temporarily engaged in an unself-conscious accomplishment and being among strangers as well was rather oblivious of it, but Cecily never having been engaged in an unself-conscious action of any kind and being among people she knew examined the other closely with that attribute women have of gaining correct instinctive impressions of another's character, clothes, morals, etc. Jones' yellow stare took the newcomer at intervals, returning always however to Cecily who ignored him.

The rector tramped heavily back and forth. "Sick?" he boomed. "Sick? But we'll cure him. Get him home here with good food and rest and attention and we'll have him well in a week. Eh, Cecily?"

"Oh, uncle Joe! I cant believe it yet. That he is really safe." She rose as the rector passed her chair and sort of undulated into his arms, like a slim wave. It was beautiful.

"Here's the medicine for him, Mrs Powers," he said with heavy gallantry, embracing Cecily, speaking over her head to the contemplative pallor of the other woman's quiet watching face. "There, there, dont cry," he added kissing her. The audience watched this, Mrs Powers with speculative detached interest and Jones with morose speculation.

"Its because I am so happy——for you, dear uncle Joe," she answered. She turned against the rector's black bulk graceful as a flower stalk. "And we owe it all to Mrs—Mrs Powers," she continued in her slightly rough voice, like a tangle of golden wires, "she was so kind to bring him back to us." Her glance swept past Jones and flicked like a knife toward the other woman. (Damn little fool thinks I have tried to vamp him, Mrs Powers thought) Cecily moved toward her with studied impulse. "May I kiss you? do you mind?"

It was like kissing a silken smooth steel blade and Mrs Powers said brutally: "Not at all. I'd have done the same for anyone sick as he is, nigger or white. And you would too," she added with satisfying malice.

"Yes, it was so sweet of you," Cecily replied coolly noncommittal, exposing a slim leg from the arm of the caller's chair. Jones statically remote watched this comedy.

"Nonsense," the rector interposed. "Mrs Powers merely saw him fatigued with travel. I am sure he will be a different man tomorrow."

"I hope so," Mrs Powers answered with sudden weariness recalling his devastated face and that dreadful brow, his whole relaxed inertia of constant dull pain and ebbing morale. Its too late, she thought with instinctive perspicuity. Shall I tell them about that scar? she pondered. Prevent a scene when this—this creature (feeling the girl's body against her shoulder) sees it. But no I wont, she decided watching the tramping rector leonine in his temporary happiness. What a coward I am. Joe should have come: he might have known I'd bungle it someway.

The rector fetched his photograph. She took it: thin faced, with the serenity of a wild thing, the passionate serene alertness of a faun, and that girl leaning against the oaken branch of the rector's arm, believing that she is in love with the boy, or his illusion—pretending she is, anyway. No, no, I wont be catty. Perhaps she is—as much as she is capable of being in love with anyone. Its quite romantic, being reft of your love and then having him returned unexpectedly to your arms. And an aviator, too. What luck that girl has playing her parts. Even God helps her. . . . You cat! she's pretty and you are jealous. That's what's the matter with you, she thought in her bitter weariness. What makes me furious is her thinking that I am after him, am in love with him. Oh yes, I'm in love with him: I'd like to hold his poor ruined head against my breast and not let him wake again ever. . . . Oh hell, what a mess it all is. And that dull fat one yonder in somebody else's trousers watching her with his yellow unwinking eyes—like a goat's. I suppose she's been passing the time with him.

"——he was eighteen then," the rector was saying. "He would never wear hat nor tie: his mother could never make him. She saw him correctly dressed but it mattered not how formal the occasion, he invariably appeared without them."

Cecily rubbing herself like a cat on the rector's arm: "Oh, uncle Joe, I love him so!"

And Jones like another round and arrogant cat, blinking his yellow eyes muttered a shocking phrase. The rector was oblivious in speech and Cecily in her own graceful immersion but Mrs Powers half heard half saw and Jones looking up met her black stare. He tried to look her down but her gaze was as impersonal as a dissection so he averted his own and fumbled for his pipe.

There came a prolonged honking of a motor horn from without and Cecily sprang to her feet.

"Oh, there's—there's a friend of ours. I'll send him away and come straight back. Will you excuse me a moment, uncle Joe?"

"Eh?" the rector broke his speech. "Oh yes."

"And you, Mrs Powers?" She moved toward the door and her glance swept Jones again. "And you, Mr Jones?"

"George got a car, has he?" Jones said as she passed him, "bet you dont come back."

She gave him her cool stare and from beyond the study door she heard the rector's voice resume the story again—of Donald, of course. And now I'm engaged again, she thought complacently, enjoying George's face in anticipation when she would tell him. And that long black woman has been making love to him—or he to her. I guess its that, from what I know of Donald. Oh well, that's how men are, I guess. Perhaps he'll want to take us both. . . . She tripped down the steps into the sunlight: the sunlight caressed her with joy, as though she were a daughter of sunlight. How would I like to have a husband and a wife too, I wonder? Or two husbands? I wonder if I want one even, want to get married at all. . . . I guess its worth trying, once. I'd like to see that horrible fat one's face if he could hear me say that, she thought. Wonder why I let him kiss me? Ugh!

George leaned from his car watching her restricted swaying stride with faint lust. "Come on, come on," he called.

She did not increase her gait at all. He swung the door open, not bothering to dismount himself.

"My God, what took you so long?" he asked plaintively. "Dam'f I thought you were coming at all."

"I'm not," she told him laying her hand on the door. Her white dress in the nooning sun was unbearable to the eye, sloped to her pliant fragility. Behind her across the lawn was another pliant gesture, though this was only a tree, a poplar.

"Huh?"

"Not coming. My fiancé is arriving today."

"Ah hell, get in."

"Donald's coming today," she repeated watching him.

His face was ludicrous: blank as a plate, then shocked to slow amazement.

"Why, he's dead," he said vacuously.

"But he isn't dead," she told him sweetly. "A lady friend he's travelling with came on ahead and told us. Uncle Joe's like a balloon."

"Ah, come on, Cecily. You're kidding me."

"I swear I'm not. I'm telling you the God's truth."

His smooth empty face hung before her like a handsome moon, empty as a promise. Then it filled with an expression of a sort.

"Hell, you got a date with me tonight. Whatcher going to do about that?"

"What can I do? Donald will be here by then."

"Then its all off with us?"

She gazed at him, then looked quickly away. Funny how only an outsider had been able to bring home to her the significance of Donald's imminence, his return. She nodded dumbly beginning to feel miserable and lost.

He leaned from the car and caught her hand. "Get in here," he commanded.

"No, no, I cant," she protested trying to draw back. He held her wrist. "No, no, let me go. You are hurting me."

"I know it," he answered grimly. "Get in."

"Dont, George, dont! I must go back."

"Well, when can I see you?"

Her mouth trembled. "Oh, I dont know. Please, George. Dont you see how miserable I am?" Her eyes became blue, dark; the sunlight made bold the wrenched thrust of her body, her thin taut arm. "Please, George."

"Are you going to get in, or do you want me to pick you up and put you in?"

"I'm going to cry in a minute. You'd better let me go."

"Oh damn. Why, sugar, I didn't mean it that way. I just wanted to see you. We've got to see each other if it is going to be all off. Come on, I've been good to you."

She relaxed. "Well, but just around the block then. I've got to get back to them." She raised a foot to the running board. "Promise?" she insisted.

"Sure. Round the block it is. I wont run off with you if you say not."

She got in and as they drove off she looked quickly toward the house. There was a face in the window, a round face.

4.

George turned from the street and drove down a quiet lane bordered by trees, between walls covered with honeysuckle. He stopped the car and she said swiftly:

"No, no, George! Drive on."

But he cut the switch. "Please," she repeated. He turned in his seat.

"Cecily, you are kidding me, aren't you?"

She turned the switch and tried to reach the starter with her foot. He caught her hands, holding her.

"Look at me."

Her eyes grew blue again with foreboding.

"You are kidding me, aren't you?"

"I dont know. Oh, George, it all happened so suddenly! I dont know what to think. When we were in there talking about him it all seemed so grand for Donald to be coming back, in spite of that woman with him, and to be engaged to a man that will be famous when he gets here——oh, it seemed then that I did love him: it was exactly the thing to do. But now . . . I'm just not ready to be married yet. And he's been gone so long, and to take up with another woman on his way to me——I dont know what to do. I——I'm going to cry," she ended suddenly, putting her crooked arm on the seat-back and burying her face in her elbow. He put his arm around her shoulders and tried to draw her against him. She raised her hands between them straightening her arms.

"No, no, take me back."

"But, Cecily——"

"You mustn't! Dont you know I'm engaged to be married? He'll probably want to be married tomorrow, and I'll have to do it."

"But you cant do that. You aren't in love with him."

"But I've got to, I tell you!"

"Are you in love with him?"

"Take me back to uncle Joe's. Please."

He was the stronger and at last he held her close, feeling her small bones, her frail taut body beneath her dress.

"Are you in love with him?" he repeated.

She burrowed into his coat.

"Look at me." She refused to lift her face and he slipped his hand under her chin, raising it. "Are you?"

"Yes! Yes!" she said wildly staring at him. "Take me back."

"You are lying. You aren't going to marry him."

She was weeping. "Yes I am. I've got to. He expects it and uncle Joe expects it. I must, I tell you."

"Darling, you cant. Dont you love me? You know you do. You cant marry him." She stopped struggling and lay against him, crying. "Come on, say you wont marry him."

"George, I cant," she said hopelessly. "Dont you see I have got to marry him?"

Young and miserable they clung to each other. The slumberous afternoon lay about them in the empty lane. Even the sparrows seemed drowsy and from the spire of the church pigeons were remote and monotonous, unemphatic as sleep. She raised her face.

"Kiss me, George."

He tasted tears: their faces were coolly touching. She drew her head back, searching his face.

"That was the last time, George."

"No, no," he objected tightening his arms. She resisted a moment then kissed him passionately.

"Darling!"

"Darling!"

She straightened up dabbing at her eyes with his handkerchief. "There! I feel better now. Take me home, kind sir."

"But Cecily," he protested, trying to embrace her again. She put him aside coolly.

"Not any more, ever. Take me home, like a nice boy."

"But, Cecily——"

"Do you want me to get out and walk? I can, you know: it isn't far."

He started the engine and drove on in a dull youthful sorrow. She patted at her hair, her fingers bloomed slimly in it, and they turned onto the street again. As she descended at the gate he made a last despairing attempt.

"Cecily, for God's sake!"

She looked over her shoulder at his stricken face. "Dont be silly, George. Of course I'll see you again. I'm not married ——yet."

Her white dress in the sun was an unbearable shimmer sloping to her body's motion. She passed from sunlight to shadow mounting the steps. At the door she turned, flashed him a smile and waved her hand. Then her white dress faded beyond a fanlight of muted color dim with age and lovely with lack of washing leaving George to stare at the empty maw of the house in hope and despair and baffled youthful lust.

5.

Jones at the window saw them drive away. His round face was enigmatic as a god's, his clear obscene eyes showed no emotion. You are good you are, he thought in grudging unillusioned admiration. I hand it to you. He was still musing upon her when that mean looking black-haired woman interrupting the rector's endless reminiscences of his son's boyhood and youth, suggested that it was time to go to the station.

The divine became aware of the absence of Cecily who was at that moment sitting in a stationary motor car in an obscure lane, crying on the shoulder of a man whose name was not Donald. Jones the only one who had remarked the manner of her going was for some reason he could not have named, safely noncommittal. The rector stated fretfully that Cecily who was at that moment kissing a man whose name was not Donald, should not have gone away at that time. But the other woman (I bet she's mean as hell, thought Jones) interrupted again saying that it was better so.

"But she should have gone to the station to meet him," the rector stated with displeasure.

"No, no. Remember, he is sick. The less excitement the better for him. Besides it is better for them to meet privately."

"Ah yes, quite right, quite right. Trust a woman in these things, Mr Jones. And for that reason perhaps you had better wait also, dont you think?"

"By all means, sir. I will wait and tell Miss Saunders why you went without her. She will doubtless be anxious to know."

After the cab had come for them and gone Jones still standing stuffed his pipe with moody viciousness. He wandered aimlessly about the rooms staring out the windows in turn, puffing his pipe, then pausing to push a dead match beneath a rug with his toe he crossed deliberately to the rector's desk. He drew out and closed two drawers before finding the right one.

The bottle was squat and black, and tilted it took the light pleasantly. He replaced it wiping his mouth on the back of his hand. And just in time too, for her rapid brittle steps crossed the verandah and he heard a motor car retreating.

The door framed her fragile surprise.

She remarked "Oh. Where are the others?"

"What's the matter? have a puncture?" Jones countered nastily. Her eyes flew like birds and he continued: "The others? They went to the station, the railroad station. You know: where the trains come in. The doctor's son or something is coming home this afternoon. Fine news, isn't it? But come in, wont you?"

She entered hesitant, watching him.

"Oh, come on in, sister. I wont hurt you."

"But why didn't they wait for me?"

"They thought you didn't want to go, I suppose. Hadn't you left that impression?"

In the silence of the house was a clock like a measured respiration, and Emmy was faintly audible somewhere. These sounds reassured her. She entered a few steps.

"You saw me go. Didn't you tell them where I was?"

"Told them you went to the bathroom."

She looked at him curiously, knowing in some way that he was not lying. "Why did you do that?"

"It was your business where you were going, not mine. If you wanted them to know you should have told them yourself."

She sat down, alertly. "You're a funny sort of man, aren't you?"

Jones moved casually in no particular direction. "How funny?"

She rose. "Oh, I dont know exactly. . . . You dont like me and yet you told a lie for me."

"Hell, you dont think I mind telling a lie, do you?"

She said with speculation:

"I wouldn't put anything past you—if you thought you could get any fun out of it." Watching his eyes she moved toward the door.

The trousers hampered him but despite them his agility was amazing. But she was alert and her studied grace lent her muscular control and swiftness and so it was a bland rubbed panel of wood that he touched. Her dress whipped from sight and he heard a key and her muffled laughter, derisive.

"Damn your soul," he said in a quiet toneless emotion, "open the door."

The wood was bland and inscrutable: baffling, holding up

to him in its polished depths the fat white blur of his own face. Holding his breath he heard nothing beyond it save a clock somewhere.

"Open the door," he repeated but there was no sound. Has she gone away or not? He wondered, straining his ears, bending to the bulky tweeded Narcissus of himself in the polished wood. He thought of the windows and walking quietly he crossed the room, finding immovable gauze wire. He returned to the center of the room without trying to muffle his steps and stood in mounting anger, cursing her slowly. Then he saw the door handle move.

He sprang to it. "Open the door, you little slut, or I'll kick your screens out."

The lock clicked and he jerked the door open upon Emmy his trousers over her arm, meeting him with her frightened antagonistic eyes.

"Where——" began Jones and Cecily stepped from shadows, curtsying like a derisive flower.

"Welcome home, kind sir," she said. Like two dissimilar fish they swam in his yellow stare.

"Check-mate, Mr Jones." Jones paraphrased the rector in a reedy falsetto. "Do you know——"

"Yes," said Cecily quickly, taking Emmy's arm, "but tell us on the verandah." She led the way and Jones followed in reluctant admiration. She and the baleful speechless Emmy preceding him sat arm in arm in a porch swing while afternoon sought interstices in soon-to-be lilac wistaria: afternoon flowed and ebbed upon them as they swung and their respective silk and cotton shins took and released sunlight in running planes.

"Sit down, Mr Jones," she continued, gushing. "Do tell us about yourself. We are so interested, aren't we, Emmy dear?" Emmy was watchfully inarticulate, like an animal. "Emmy, dear Mr Jones, has missed all your conversation and admiring you as we all do—we simply cannot help it, Mr Jones—— she is naturally anxious to make up for it."

Jones cupped a match and there were two little flames in his eyes, leaping and sinking to pinpoints.

"You are silent, Mr Jones? Emmy and I both would like to hear some more of what you have learned about us from your extensive amatory career. Dont we, Emmy darling?"

"No, I wont spoil it for you," Jones replied heavily. "You are on the verge of getting some first hand information of your own. As for Miss Emmy, I'll teach her sometime in private."

Emmy continued to watch him with fierce dumb distrust. Cecily said: "At first hand?"

"Aren't you being married tomorrow? You can learn from Oswald. He should certainly be able to tell you, travelling as he seems to with a sparring partner. Got caught at last, didn't you?"

She shivered. She looked so delicate, so needing to be cared for that Jones becoming masculine and sentimental felt again like a cloddish brute. He lit his pipe again and Emmy convicting herself of the power of speech said:

"Yonder they come."

A cab had drawn up to the gate and Cecily sprang up running along the porch to the steps. Jones and Emmy rose and Emmy vanished somewhere as four people descended from the cab. So that's him, thought Jones ungrammatically, following Cecily, watching her as she stood poised on the top step like a bird, her hand to her breast. Trust her!

He looked again at the party coming through the gate, the rector looming above them all. There was something changed about the divine: age seemed to have suddenly overtaken him, unresisted, coming upon him like a highwayman. He's sure sick, Jones told himself. The woman, that Mrs Something-or-other left the party and hastened ahead. She mounted the steps to Cecily.

"Come, darling," she said taking the girl's arm, "come inside. He is not well and the light hurts his eyes. Come in and meet him there, hadn't you rather?"

"No, no: here. I have waited so long for him."

The other woman was kind but obdurate and she led the girl into the house. Cecily reluctant, with reverted head cried:

"Uncle Joe! his face! is he sick?"

The divine's face was gray and slack as dirty snow. At the steps he stumbled slightly and Jones sprang forward taking his arm. "Thanks, buddy," said the third man, in a private's uniform, whose hand was beneath Mahon's elbow. They mounted the steps and crossing the porch passed under the fanlight, into the dark hall.

"Take your cap, Loot," murmured the enlisted man.

The other removed it and handed it to him. They heard Cecily's tapping feet crossing the room and the study door opened letting a flood of light fall upon them and Cecily cried:

"Donald, Donald! She says your face is hu——ooooh," she ended, screaming as she saw him.

The light passing through her fine hair gave her a halo and lent her frail dress a fainting nimbus about her crumpling body like a stricken poplar. Mrs Powers moving quickly caught her but not before her head had struck the door jamb.

Chapter Three.

Mrs Saunders said: "You come away now, let your sister alone."

Young Robert Saunders fretted but optimistic, joining again that old battle between parent and child, hopeful in the face of invariable past defeat:

"But cant I ask her a civil question? I just want to know what his scar l——"

"Come on now, come with mamma."

"But I just want to know what his sc—"

"Robert."

"But mamma," he essayed again despairing.

His mother pushed him firmly doorward. "Run down to the garden and tell your father to come here. Run, now."

He left the room in exasperation. His mamma would have been shocked could she have read his thoughts. It wasn't her especially. They're all alike, he guessed largely, as has many a man before and since. He wasn't going to hurt the old 'fraid cat.

Cecily freed of her clothing lay crushed and pathetic between cool linen, surrounded by a mingled scent of cologne and ammonia, her fragile face coiffed in a towel. Her mother drew a chair to the side of the bed and examined her daughter's pretty shallow face, the sweep of her lashes upon her white cheek, her arms paralleling the shape of her body beneath the covers, her delicate blue-veined wrists and her long slender hands relaxed and palm-upward beside her. Then young Robert Saunders without knowing it had his revenge.

"Darling, what did his scar look like?"

Cecily shuddered turning her head on the pillow. "O o ooh, dont, dont, mamma! I c-cant bear to think of it."

(But I just want to ask you a civil question) "There, there. We wont talk about it until you feel better."

"Not ever, not ever. If I have to see him again I'll—I'll just die. I cant bear it, I cant bear it."

She was crying again frankly like a child, not even turning her head. Her mother rose and leaned over her. "There, there. Dont cry anymore. You'll be ill." She gently brushed the girl's hair from her temples, re-arranging the towel. She bent down and kissed her daughter's pale cheek. "Mamma's sorry, baby. Suppose you try to sleep. Shall I bring you a tray at supper time?"

"No, I couldn't eat. Just let me lie here alone and I'll feel better."

The older woman lingered, still curious. (I just want to ask her a civil question) The telephone rang and with a last ineffectual pat at the pillow she withdrew.

Lifting the receiver she remarked her husband closing the garden gate behind him.

"Yes? . . . Mrs Saunders. . . . Oh, George? . . . Quite well, thank you. How are you? . . . no, I am afraid not. . . . What? . . . Yes, but she is not feeling well . . . later, perhaps. . . . Not tonight. Call her tomorrow. . . . Yes, yes, quite well, thank you. Goodbye."

She passed through the cool darkened hall and onto the verandah letting her tightly corseted figure sink creaking into a rocking chair as her husband carrying a sprig of mint and his hat mounted the steps. Here was Cecily in the masculine and gone to flesh: the same slightly shallow good looks and somewhere an indicated laxness of moral fibre. He had once been precise and dapper but now he was clad slovenly in careless uncreased gray and earthy shoes. His hair still curled youthfully upon his head and he had Cecily's eyes. He was a Catholic which was almost as sinful as being a Republican, his fellow-townsmen while envying him his social and financial position in the community yet looked at him askance because he and his whole family were forced to make periodical trips to Atlanta, to attend church.

"Tobe," he bellowed taking a chair near his wife.

"Well, Robert," she began with zest, "Donald Mahon came home today."

"Government sent his body back, did they?"

"No, he came back himself. He got off the train this afternoon."

"Eh? Why, he's dead."

"But he isn't. Cecily was there and saw him. A strange fat young man brought her home in a cab—completely broken down. She said something about a scar on him. She fainted, poor child. I made her go to bed at once. I never did find who that strange young man was," she ended fretfully.

Tobe in a white jacket appeared with a tray containing ice, sugar, water, and a decanter. Mr Saunders sat staring at his wife. "Well, I'll be damned," he said at last. And again: "I'll be damned."

His wife rocked, complacent over her news. After a while Mr Saunders breaking his trance, stirred. He crushed his mint sprig between his fingers and taking a cube of ice he rubbed the mint over it then dropped both into a tall glass. Then he spooned sugar into the glass and dribbled whiskey into it, slowly, and slowly stirring he stared at his wife again.

"I'll be damned," he said for the third time.

Tobe filled the glass from a pitcher of water, and withdrew.

"So he came home. Well, well. I'm glad on the parson's account. Pretty decent feller."

"You must have forgotten what it means."

"Eh?"

"To us."

"To us?"

"Cecily was engaged to him, you know."

Mr Saunders sipped and setting his glass on the floor beside him he lit a cigar. "Well, we've given our consent, haven't we? I aint going to back out now." A thought occurred to him. "Does Sis still want to?"

"I dont know. It was such a shock to her, poor child, his coming home and the scar and all. But do you think it is a good thing?"

"I never did think it was a good thing. I never wanted it."

"Are you putting it off on me? Do you think I insisted on it?"

Mr Saunders from long experience said mildly: "She aint old enough to marry yet."

"Nonsense. How old was I when we married?"

He raised his glass again. "Seems to me you're the one insisting on it." Mrs Saunders rocking stared at him: he was made aware of his stupidity. "Why do you think it aint a good thing, then?"

"I declare, Robert. Sometimes . . ." she sighed and then as one explains to a child in fond exasperation at its stupidity:

"Well, an engagement in war-time and an engagement in peace-time are two different things. Really, I dont see how he can expect to hold her to it."

"Now look here, Minnie, if he went to war expecting her to wait for him and come back expecting her to take him, there's nothing else for them to do. And if she still wants to dont you go persuading her out of it. You hear?"

"Are you going to force your daughter into marriage? You just said yourself she is too young."

"Remember, I said if she still wants to. By the way, he aint lame or badly hurt, is he?" he added quickly.

"I dont know. Cecily cried when I tried to find out."

"Sis is a fool, sometimes. But dont you go monkeying with them, now, do you hear?"

He raised his glass and took a long draught, then he puffed at his cigar furiously, righteously.

"I declare, Robert, I dont understand you sometimes. The idea of driving your own daughter into marriage with a man that has nothing and who may be half dead and who probably wont work anyway. You know yourself what these soldiers are."

"You are the one wants her to get married. I dont. Who do you want her to take, then?"

"Well, there's Dr Gary. He likes her, and Harrison Maurier from Atlanta. Cecily likes him, I think."

Mr Saunders inelegantly snorted. "Who? That Maurier feller? I wouldn't have that damn feller around here at all. Slick hair and cigarettes all over the place. You better pick out another one."

"I'm not picking out anybody. I just dont want you to drive her into marrying that Mahon boy."

"I aint driving her, I tell you. You have already taught me better than to try to drive a woman to do anything. But I dont intend to interfere if she does want to marry Mahon."

She sat rocking and he finished his julep. The oaks became still with dusk and the branches of trees were as motionless as coral fathoms under seas. A tree frog took up his monotonous trilling and the west was a vast green lake, still as eternity. Tobe appeared silently.

"Supper served, Miss Minnie."

The cigar arced redly into a canna bed and they rose.

"Where is Bob, Tobe?"

"I dont know'm. I seed him gwine to'ds de garden a while back, but I aint seed him since."

"See if you can find him. And tell him to wash his face and hands."

"Yessum." He held the door for them and they passed into the house leaving the twilight behind them filled with Tobe's mellow voice, calling across the dusk.

2.

But young Robert Saunders could not hear him. He was at that moment climbing a high board fence which severed the dusk above his head. He conquered it at last and sliding downward his trousers evinced reluctance, then accepting the gambit accompanied him with a ripping sound. He sprawled in damp grass feeling a thin shallow fire across his young behind and said Damn, regaining his feet and disjointing his hip trying to see down his back.

Aint that hell, he remarked to the twilight. (I have rotten luck. Its all your fault too, for not telling me, he thought, gaining a vicarious revenge on all sisters) He picked up the object which had dropped from his pocket and crossed the rectory lawn through dew, toward the house. There was a light in a here-to-fore unused upper room and his heart sank. Had he gone to bed this early? Then he saw silhouetted feet on the balustrade and the red eye of a cigarette and he sighed with relief. That must be him.

He mounted the steps saying: "Hi, Donald."

"Hi, Colonel," answered the one sitting there. Approaching he discerned soldier clothes. That's him. Now I'll see, he thought exultantly snapping on a flash-light and throwing its beam full on the man's face. Aw, shucks. He was becoming thoroughly discouraged. Did anyone ever have such luck? There must be a cabal against him.

"You aint got no scar," he stated with dejection. "You aint even Donald, are you?"

"You guessed it, bub. I aint even Donald. But say, how about turning the search-light some other way?"

He snapped off the light in weary disillusion. He burst out: "They wont tell me nothing. I just want to know what his scar looks like but they wont tell me nothing about it. Say, has he gone to bed?"

"Yes, he's gone to bed. This aint a good time to see his scar."

"How about tomorrow morning?" hopefully. "Could I see it then?"

"I dunno. Better wait till then."

"Listen," he suggested with inspiration, "I tell you what: tomorrow about eight when I'm going to school you kind of get him to look out of the window and I'll be passing and I'll see it. I asked Sis, but she wouldn't tell me nothing."

"Who is Sis, bub?"

"She's just my sister. Gosh, she's mean. If I'd a seen his scar I'd a told her now, wouldn't I?"

"You bet. What's your sister's name?"

"Name's Cecily Saunders, like mine only mine's Robert Saunders. You'll do that, wont you?"

"Oh . . . Cecily. . . . Sure, you trust me, Colonel."

He sighed his relief yet still lingered. "Say, how many soldiers has he got here?"

"About one and a half, bub."

"One and a half? Are they alive?"

"Well, practically."

"How can you have one and a half soldiers if they are live ones?"

"Ask the war department. They can tell you."

He pondered briefly. "Gee, I wish we could get some soldiers at our house. Do you reckon we could?"

"Why, I expect you could."

"Could? how?" he asked eagerly.

"Ask your sister. She can tell you how."

"Aw, she wont tell me."

"Sure she will. You ask her."

"Well I'll try," he agreed without hope yet still optimistic. "Well, I guess I better be going. They might be kind of anxious about me," he explained descending the steps. "Goodbye, mister," he added politely.

"So long, Colonel."

I'll see his scar tomorrow, he thought with elation. I wonder if Sis does know how to get us a soldier? She dont know much but maybe she does know that. But girls dont never know nothing so I aint going to count on it. Anyway I'll see his scar tomorrow.

Tobe's white jacket looming around the corner of the house gleamed dully in the young night and as young Robert mounted the steps toward the yellow rectangle of the front door Tobe's voice said:

"Whyn't you come on to yo' supper? Yo' mommer gwine tear yo' and my hair bofe out if you late like this. She say fer you to clean up befo' you goes to de dinin' room: I done drawed you some nice water in de baff room. Run 'long now. I tell 'em you here."

He paused only to call through his sister's closed door: "I'm going to see it tomorrow. Yaaah!" then soaped and hungry he clattered into the dining room accomplishing an intricate field manoeuver lest his damaged rear be exposed. He ignored his mother's cold stare.

"Robert Saunders, where have you been?"

"Mamma, there's a soldier there says we can get one too."

"One what?" asked his father through his cigar smoke.

"A soldier."

"Soldier?"

"Yes sir, that one says we can."

"That one where?" asked his mother.

"Where Donald is. He says we can get one too."

"How get one?"

"He wouldn't tell me. But he says that Sis knows how."

Mr and Mrs Saunders looked at each other above young Robert's oblivious head as he bent over his plate spooning food into himself.

3.

On board the Frisco Limited,
Missouri, April 2, 1919

Dear Margaret—

I wonder if you miss me like I miss you. Well I never had much fun in St Louis I was there only a half a day. This is just a short note to remind you of waiting for me. Its to bad I had to leave you so soon after. I will see my mother and atend to a few business matters and I will come back pretty soon I will work like hell for you Margaret. This is just a short note to remind you of waiting for me. This dam train rocks so I can not write any way. Well give me reguards to Giligan tell him not to break his arm crooking it un til I get back. I will love you all ways.

With love
Julian.

"What is that child's name, Joe?" Mrs Powers in one of her straight dark dresses stood on the porch in the sun. The morning breeze was in her hair, beneath her clothing like water carrying sun with it: pigeons about the church spire leaned upon it like silver and slanting splashes of soft paint. The lawn sloping fence-ward was gray with dew and a negro informal in undershirt and overalls passed a lawn mower over the grass leaving behind his machine a darker green stripe like an unrolling carpet. Grass sprang from the whirling blades and clung wetly to his legs.

"What child?" Gilligan uncomfortable in new hard serge and a linen collar sat on the balustrade smoking moodily.

For reply she handed him the letter. With his cigarette in the tilted corner of his mouth he squinted through the smoke, reading.

"Oh, the ace. Name's Lowe."

"Of course: Lowe. I tried several times after he left us but I never could recall it."

Gilligan returned the letter to her. "Funny kid, aint he? So you scorned my affections and taken his, huh?"

Her windy dress molded her longly. "Lets go into the garden so I can have a cigarette."

"You could have it here. The padre wouldn't mind, I bet."

"I'm sure he wouldn't. I am considering his parishioners. What would they think to see a dark strange woman smoking a cigarette on the rectory porch at eight oclock in the morning?"

"They'll think you are one of them French what-do-you-call-'ems the loot brought back with him. Your good name wont be worth nothing after these folks get through with it."

"My good name is your trouble, not mine, Joe."

"My trouble? How you mean?"

"Men are the ones who worry about our good names, because they gave them to us. But we have other things to bother about, ourselves. What you mean by a good name is like a dress that's too flimsy to wear comfortably. Come on, lets go to the garden."

"You know you dont mean that," Gilligan told her. She smiled faintly, not turning her face to him.

"Come on," she repeated, descending the steps.

They left a delirium of sparrows and the sweet mown smell of fresh grass behind them and were in a gravelled path between rose bushes. The path ran on between two formal arching oaks, lesser roses rambling upon a wall paralleled them and Gilligan following her long stride trod brittle and careful. Whenever he was among flowers he always felt as if he had entered a room full of women: he was always conscious of his body, his walk, feeling as though he trod in sand. So he believed that he really did not like flowers.

Mrs Powers paused at intervals, sniffing, tasting dew upon buds and blooms then the path passed between violet beds to where against a privet hedge there would soon be lilies. Beside a green iron bench beneath a magnolia she paused again, staring up into the tree. A mockingbird flew out and she said:

"There's one, Joe. See?"

"One what? Bird nest?"

"No, a bloom. Not quite, but in a week or so. Do you know magnolia blooms?"

"Sure: not good for anything if you pick 'em. Touch it, and it turns brown on you. Fades."

"That's true of almost everything, isn't it?"

"Yeh, but how many folks believe it? Reckon the loot does?"

"I dont know. . . . I wonder if he'll have a chance to touch that one?"

"Why should he want to? He's already got one that's turning brown on him."

She looked at him, not comprehending at once. Her black eyes, her red mouth like a pomegranate blossom. Then she said:

"Oh. Magnolia. . . . I'd thought of her as a——something like an orchid. So you think she's a magnolia?"

"Not an orchid, anyways. Find orchids anywhere but you wouldn't hardly find her in Illinoy or Denver, hardly."

"I guess you are right. I wonder if there are any more like her anywhere?"

"I dunno. But if there aint, there's already one too many."

"Lets sit down a while. Where's my cigarette?"

She sat on the bench and he offered her his paper pack. He struck a match for her.

"So you think she wont marry him, Joe?"

"I aint so sure any more. I think I am changing my mind about it. She wont miss a chance to marry what she calls a hero ——if just to keep somebody else from getting him." (Meaning you, he thought)

(Meaning me, she thought) She said: "Not if she knows he's going to die?"

"What does she know about dying? She cant even imagine herself getting old, let alone imagining anybody she is interested in dying. I bet she believes they can even patch him up so it wont show."

"Joe, you are an incurable sentimentalist. You mean you think she'll marry him because she is letting him think she will and because she is a 'good' woman. You are quite a gentle person, Joe."

"I aint!" he retorted with warmth. "I am as hard as they make 'em: I got to be." He saw she was laughing at him and he grinned ruefully. "Well you got me that time, didn't you?" He became suddenly serious. "But it aint her I'm worrying about. Its his old man. Why didn't you tell him how bad off he was?"

She quite feminine and Napoleonic:

"Why did you send me on ahead instead of coming yourself? I told you I'd spoil it." She flipped her cigarette away and put her hand on his arm. "I didn't have the heart to, Joe. If you could have seen his face! and heard him! He was like a child, Joe. He showed me all of Donald's things, you know: pictures, and a sling-shot, and a girl's undie and a hyacinth bulb he carried with him in France. And there was that girl and everything. I just couldn't. Do you blame me?"

"Well, its alright now. It was a kind of rotten trick though, to let him find it all out at once before all them people at the station. We done the best we could, didn't we?"

"Yes we did. I wish we could have done more." Her gaze brooded across the garden where out in the sun beyond the trees bees were already at work. Across the garden, beyond a street and another wall you could see the top of a pear tree like a branching candelabra, closely bloomed, white, white. . . . She stirred crossing her knees. "That girl fainting though. What do you——"

"Oh, I expected that. But here comes Othello, like he was looking for us."

They watched the late conductor of the lawn mower as he shuffled his shapeless shoes along the gravel. He saw them and halted.

"Mr Gillmum, Rev'un say fer you to come to de house."

"Me?"

"You Mist' Gillmum, aint you?"

"Oh, sure." He rose. "Excuse me, ma'am. You coming too?"

"You go and see what he wants. I'll come on after a while."

The negro had turned shuffling on ahead and the lawn mower resumed its chattering song as Gilligan mounted the steps. The rector stood on the verandah, his face was calm but it was evident he had not slept.

"Sorry to trouble you, Mr Gilligan, but Donald is awake and I am not familiar with his clothing as you are. I gave away his civilian things when he——when he——"

"Sure, sir," Gilligan answered in sharp pity for the gray-faced man. He dont know him yet! "I'll help him."

The divine ineffectual would have followed but Gilligan leaped away from him, up the stairs. He saw Mrs Powers coming from the garden and he descended to the lawn, meeting her.

"Good morning, Doctor," she responded to his greeting. "I have been looking at your flowers. I hope you dont mind?"

"Not at all, not at all, my dear madam. An old man is always flattered when his flowers are admired. The young are so beautifully convinced that their emotions are admirable: young girls wear the clothes of their older sisters who require clothes, principally because they do not need them themselves, just 'for fun', or perhaps to pander to an illusion of the male; but as we grow older what we are loses importance, giving place to what we do. And I have never been able to do anything well save raise flowers. And that is, I think, an obscure emotional housewifery in me: I had thought to grow old with my books among my roses: until my eyes became too poor to read longer I would read, after that I would sit in the sun. Now of course, with my son at home again, I must put that by. I am anxious for you to see Donald this morning. You will notice a marked improvement."

"Oh, I'm sure I shall," she answered wanting to put her arms around him. But he was so big and so confident. At the corner of the house was a tree covered with tiny white-bellied leaves like a mist, like a swirl of arrested silver water. The rector offered his arm with heavy gallantry.

"Shall we go in to breakfast?"

Emmy had been before them with narcissi and red roses in a vase repeated the red of strawberries in flat blue bowls. The rector drew her chair.

"When we are alone Emmy sits here but she has a strange reluctance to dining with strangers or when guests are present."

Mrs Powers sat down and Emmy appeared and disappeared for no apparent reason. At last there came slow feet on the staircase slanting across the open door. She saw their legs, then their bodies crossed her vision and the rector rose as they appeared in the door.

"Good morning, Donald," he said. (That my father? Sure, Loot. That's him)

"Good morning, sir."

The divine stood huge and tense and powerless as Gilligan helped Mahon into his seat.

"Here's Mrs Powers too, Loot."

He turned his faltering puzzled gaze upon her. "Good morning," he said but her eyes were on his father's face. She lowered her gaze to her plate feeling hot moisture against her lids. What have I done? she thought, what have I done?

She tried to eat but could not, watching Mahon awkward with his left hand, peering into his plate eating hardly at all and Gilligan's healthy employment of knife and fork, and the rector tasting nothing, watching his son's every move with gray despair.

Emmy appeared again with fresh dishes. Averting her face she set the dishes down awkwardly and was about to flee precipitately when the rector looking up stopped her. She turned in stiff self-conscious fright, hanging her head.

"Here's Emmy, Donald," he said.

Mahon raised his head and looked at his father. Then his puzzled gaze touched Gilligan's face and returned to his plate, and his hand rose slowly to his mouth. Emmy stood for a space and her black eyes became wide and the blood drained from her face slowly. Then she put the back of one red hand against her mouth and fled, blundering into the door.

I cant stand this. Mrs Powers rose unnoticed save by Gilligan and followed Emmy. Upon a table in the kitchen Emmy leaned, bent double almost, her head cradled in her red arms. What a terrible position to cry in, Mrs Powers thought, putting her arms around Emmy. The girl jerked herself erect staring at the other. Her face was wrung with weeping, ugly.

"He didn't speak to me!" she gasped.

"He didn't know his father, Emmy. Dont be silly." She held Emmy's elbows, smelling harsh soap. Emmy clung to her.

"But me, me! He didn't even look at me!" she repeated.

It was on her tongue to say Why should he? but Emmy's blurred sobbing and her awkward wrung body; the very kinship of tears to tears, something to cling to after having been for so long a prop to others. . . .

Outside the window was a trellised morning glory vine with a sparrow in it and clinging to Emmy, holding each other in a recurrent mutual sorrow she tasted warm salt in her throat.

Damn, damn, damn, she said amid her own racking infrequent tears.

4.

In front of the postoffice the rector was the center of an interested circle when Mr Saunders saw him. The gathering was representative embracing the professions with a liberal leaven of those inevitable casuals, cravatless, overalled or unoveralled, who seem to suffer no compulsions whatever, which anything from a captured still to a negro with an epileptic fit or a mouth organ attracts to itself like atoms to a magnet, in any small southern town——or northern or western town, probably.

"Yes, yes, quite a surprise," the rector was saying. "I had no intimation of it, none whatever until a friend with whom he was travelling——he is not yet fully recovered, you see—— preceded him in order to inform me."

(One of them airy-plane fellers)

(S'what I say: if the Lord had intended folks to fly around in the air He'd a give 'em wings)

(Well, he's been closter to the Lord 'n you'll ever git)

This outer kindly curious fringe made way for Mr Saunders.

(Closter 'n that feller'll ever git anyway. This speaker was probably a Baptist. Guffaws)

Mr Saunders extending his hand said:

"Well, Doctor, we are mighty glad to hear the good news."

"Ah, good morning, good morning." The rector took the offered hand in his huge paw. "Yes, quite a surprise. I was hoping to see you. How is Cecily this morning?" he asked in a lower tone. But there was no need, no lack of privacy: there was a general movement into the postoffice. The mail was in and the window had opened and even those who expected no mail, who had received no mail in months, must needs answer one of the most enduring compulsions of the American nation. The rector's news had become stale in the face of the possibility of a stamped personal communication of some sort, of any sort.

Charlestown like numberless other old towns throughout the south had been built around a circle of tethered horses and mules. In the middle of the square was the courthouse—a simple utilitarian edifice of brick and sixteen beautiful Ionic columns stained with generations of casual chewing tobacco. Elms surrounded the courthouse and beneath these trees, on scarred and carved wood benches and chairs the city fathers, progenitors of solid laws and solid citizens who believed in Tom Watson and feared only God and drouth, in black string ties or the faded brushed gray and bronze meaningless medals of the Confederate States of America, no longer having to make any pretense toward labor, slept or whittled away the long drowsy days while their juniors of all ages not yet old enough to frankly slumber in public, played checkers or chewed tobacco and talked. A lawyer, a drug clerk and two nondescripts tossed iron discs back and forth between two holes in the ground. And above all brooded early April sweetly pregnant with noon.

Yet all had a pleasant word for the rector as he and Mr Saunders passed, even the slumberers roused from the light sleep of the aged to ask about Donald. The divine's progress was almost triumphal.

Mr Saunders walked beside him, returning greetings, pre-occupied. Damn these women-folks, he fretted. They passed beneath a stone shaft bearing a confederate soldier shading his marble eyes forever in eternal rigid vigilance and the rector repeated his question.

"She is feeling better this morning. It is too bad she fainted yesterday, but she isn't strong, you know."

"That was to be expected: his unannounced arrival rather startled us all. Even Donald acknowledges that, I am sure. Their attachment also, you see."

Trees arching greenly over the street made a green tunnel of quiet, the sidewalk was checkered with shade. Mr Saunders felt the need of mopping his neck. He took two cigars from his pocket but the rector waved them away. Damn these women! Minnie should have done this.

The rector said: "We have a beautiful town, Mr Saunders. These streets, these trees. . . . This quiet is just the thing for Donald."

"Yes, yes, just the thing for him." (how to begin, how to begin) "Doctor——"

"You and Mrs Saunders must come in this afternoon and see him. I had expected you last night, but remembering that Cecily had been quite overcome——It is well you did not, though. Donald was fatigued and Mrs P—I thought it better to have a doctor—just as a precaution, you see—and he advised Donald to go to bed."

"Yes, yes, we had intended to come but as you say, his condition, his first night at home, and Cecily's condition too——" He could feel his very moral fiber disintegrating. Yet his course had seemed so logical last night after his wife had taken him to task, taking him as a clinching argument, to see his daughter weeping in bed. Damn these women! he repeated for the third time. He puffed his cigar and flung it away, mentally girding himself.

"About this engagement, Doctor——"

"Ah yes, I was thinking of it myself. Do you know, I believe Cecily is the best medicine he can have? Wait," as the other would have interrupted, "it will naturally take her some time to become accustomed to his—to him——" he faced his companion confidentially, "he has a scar, you see, but I am confident this can be removed even though Cecily does become accustomed to it. In fact I am depending on her to make a new man of him in a short time."

Mr Saunders gave it up. Tomorrow, he promised himself. Tomorrow I will do it.

"He is naturally a bit confused now," the divine continued, "but care and attention and, above all, Cecily will remedy that. Do you know," he turned his kind gaze on Mr Saunders again, "do you know, he didn't even know me at first when I went into his room this morning? Merely a temporary condition though, I assure you. Quite to be expected," he added quickly. "Dont you think that was to be expected?"

"I should think so, yes. But what happened to him? how did he manage to turn up like this?"

"He wont talk about it. A friend who came home with him assures me that he doesn't know, cannot remember. But this happens quite often, the young man—a soldier himself—tells me and that it will all come back to him someday. Donald seems to have lost all his papers save only a certificate of discharge from a British hospital. But pardon me: you were saying something about the engagement."

"No, no. It was nothing." The sun was overhead: it was almost noon. Around the horizon were a few fat thick clouds like whipped cream. Rain this afternoon. Suddenly he spoke:

"By the way, Doctor, I wonder if I might stop in and speak to Donald?"

"By all means. Certainly. He will be glad to see an old friend. Stop in by all means."

The clouds were steadily piling higher. They passed beneath the church spire and crossed the lawn, they mounted the steps of the rectory and Mrs Powers sitting with a book raised her eyes. She saw the resemblance immediately: the rector's "Mr Saunders is an old friend of Donald's" was unnecessary. She rose shutting her book on her forefinger.

"Mr Mahon is lying down. Mr Gilligan is with him, I think. Let me call."

"No, no," Mr Saunders objected quickly, "dont disturb him. I will call later."

"After you have come out of your way to speak to him? He will be disappointed if you dont go up. You are an old friend, you know. You said Mr Saunders is an old friend of Donald's, didn't you, Doctor?"

"Yes indeed. He is Cecily's father."

"Then you must come up by all means." She put her hand on his elbow.

"No, no, ma'am. Dont you think it would be better not to disturb him now, Doctor?" he appealed to the rector.

"Well, perhaps so. You and Mrs Saunders are coming this afternoon, then?"

But she was obdurate. "Hush, Doctor. Surely Donald can see Miss Saunders' father at any time." She firmly compelled him through the door and he and the divine followed her up the stairs. To her knock Gilligan's voice replied and she opened the door.

"Here is Cecily's father to see Donald, Joe," she said, standing aside.

The door opened and flooded the narrow passage with light, closing, it reft the passage of light again, and moving through a walled twilight, she descended the stairs again slowly. The lawn mower was long since stilled and beneath a tree she could see the recumbent form and one propped knee of its languid conductor, lapped in slumber. Along the street passed slowly the hourly quota of negro children who seeming to have no arbitrary hours, seemingly free of all compulsions of time or higher learning, went to and from school at any hour of a possible lighted twelve, carrying lunch pails of ex-molasses and -lard tins. Some of them also carried books. The lunch was usually eaten on the way to school, which was conducted by a fattish negro in a lawn tie and an alpaca coat who could take a given line from any book from the telephone directory down and soon have the entire room chanting it after him, like Vachel Lindsay. Then they were off for the day. The clouds had piled higher and thicker taking a lavender tinge, making bits of sky laked among them more blue. The air was becoming sultry, oppressive, and the church spire had lost perspective until now it seemed but two dimensions of metal or card-board.

The leaves hung lifeless and sad, as if life were being recalled from them before it had been fully given, leaving only the ghosts of young leaves. As she lingered near the door she could hear Emmy clashing dishes in the dining room and at last she heard that for which she had waited.

"——expect you and Mrs Saunders this afternoon, then," the rector was saying as they appeared.

"Yes, yes," he answered with detachment. His eyes met Mrs Powers'. How like her he is! she thought, and her heart sank. Have I blundered again? She examined his face fleetingly and sighed with relief.

"How do you think he looks, Mr Saunders?" she asked.

"Fine, considering his long trip: fine."

The rector said happily: "I noticed it myself this morning. Didn't you also, Mrs Powers?" His eyes implored her and she said Yes. "You should have seen him yesterday to discern the amazing improvement in him. Eh, Mrs Powers?"

"Yes indeed, sir. We all commented on it this morning."

Mr Saunders carrying his limp panama hat moved toward the steps.

"Well, Doctor, its fine having the boy home again. We are all glad for our own sakes as well as for yours. If there is any-thing we can do——" he added with neighborly sincerity.

"Thank you, thank you: I will not hesitate. But Donald is in a position to help himself now, provided he gets his medi-cine often enough. We depend on you for this, you know," the rector answered with jovial innuendo.

Mr Saunders added a complement of expected laughter. "As soon as she is herself again we, her mother and I, expect it to be the other way: we expect to be asking you to lend us Cecily occasionally."

"Well, that might be arranged, I imagine—especially with a friend." The rector laughed in turn and Mrs Powers listening exulted. Then she knew a brief misgiving. They are so much alike! Will they change his mind for him, those women? She said:

"I think I'll walk as far as the gate with Mr Saunders, if he doesn't mind."

"Not at all, ma'am. I'll be delighted."

The rector stood in the doorway and beamed upon them as they descended the steps. "Sorry you can not remain to dinner," he said.

"Some other time, Doctor. My missus is waiting for me today."

"Yes, some other time," the rector agreed. He entered the house again, and they crossed grass beneath the imminent heavens. Mr Saunders looked at her sharply. "I dont like this," he stated. "Why doesn't someone tell him the truth about that boy?"

"Neither do I," she answered. "But if they did, would he believe it? Did anyone have to tell you about him?"

"My God, no. Anybody could look at him. . . . It made me sick. But then, I'm chicken livered, anyway," he added with mirthless apology. "What did the doctor say about him?"

"Nothing definite, except he remembers nothing that happened before he was hurt. The man that was wounded is dead and this is another one: a grown child. Its his apathy, his detachment from everything that's so terrible. He doesn't seem to care where he is nor what he does. He must have been passed from hand to hand, like a child."

"I mean, about his recovery."

She shrugged. "Who can tell? There is nothing physically wrong with him that surgeons can remedy, if that's what you mean."

He walked on in silence. "His father should be told, though," he said at last.

"I know, but who is to do it? Besides, he is bound to know some day so why not let him believe as he wishes as long as he can? The shock will be no greater at one time than at another. And he is old, and so big and happy now. And then Donald may recover, you know," she lied.

"Yes, that's right. But do you think he will?"

"Why not? He cant remain forever as he is now." They had

reached the gate. The iron was rough and hot with sun under her hand and there was no blue anywhere in the sky.

Mr Saunders fumbling with his hat said: "But suppose he—he does not recover?"

She gave him a direct look. "Dies, you mean?" she asked brutally.

"Well, yes. Since you put it that way."

"Now that's what I want to discuss with you. It is a question of strengthening his morale, of giving him some reason to—well, buck up. And who could do that better than Miss Saunders?"

"But ma'am, aint you asking a lot, asking me to risk my daughter's happiness on such a poor bet as that?"

"You dont understand. I am not asking that the engagement be insisted upon. I mean, why not let Cecily—Miss Saunders—see him as often as she will, let her be sweethearts with him if necessary until he gets to know her again and will make an effort for himself. Time enough then to talk of engagements. Think, Mr Saunders: suppose he were your son. That wouldn't be very much to ask of a friend, would it?"

He looked at her again in admiration, keenly.

"You've got a head on your shoulders, young lady. So what I'm to do is prevail on her to come and see him, is it?"

"You must do more than that: you must see that she does come, that she acts just as she acted with him before." She gripped his arm. "You must not let her mother dissuade her, you must not. Remember, he might have been your son."

"What makes you think her mother might object?" he asked in amazement.

She smiled faintly with her lips. The smile never reached her eyes. "You forget I'm a woman too," she said. Then her face became serious, imminent. "But you must not let that happen, do you hear?" Her eyes compelled him. "Is that a promise?"

"Yes," he agreed meeting her level glance. He took her firm, proffered hand and felt her clean, muscular clasp.

"A promise, then," she said as warm great drops of rain dissolving from the fat, dull sky splashed heavily. She said Goodbye and fled running across the lawn toward the house before assaulting gray battalions of rain. Her long legs swept her up and onto the verandah as the pursuing rain, foiled, whirled like cavalry with silver lances across the lawn.

5.

Mr Saunders casting an uneasy look at the dissolving sky let himself out the gate and here returning from school was his son, saying:

"Did you see his scar, daddy? Did you see his scar?"

The man stared at this troublesome small miniature of himself and then he knelt suddenly taking his son into his arms, holding him close.

"You seen his scar," young Robert Saunders accused trying to release himself as the rain galloped over them, through the trees.

6.

Emmy's eyes were black and shallow as a toy animal's and her hair was a sun-burned shock of no particular color. There was something wild in Emmy's face: you knew that she outran, outfought, outclimbed her brothers, you could imagine her developing like a small but sturdy greenness on a dunghill. Not a flower. But not dung either.

Her father was a house painter, with the house painter's inevitable penchant for alcohol and he used to beat his wife. She fortunately failed to survive the birth of Emmy's fourth brother, whereupon her father desisted from the bottle long enough to woo and wed an angular shrew who serving as an instrument of retribution, beat him soundly with stove wood in her lighter moments.

"Dont never marry a woman, Emmy," her father maudlin and affectionate advised her. "If I had it to do all over again I'd take a man every time."

"I wont never marry nobody," Emmy had promised herself passionately, especially after Donald had gone to the war and her laboriously worded letters to him had gone unanswered. (And now he dont even know me, she thought dully)

"I wont never marry nobody," she repeated, putting dinner on the table. "I think I'll just die," she said staring through a streaming window into the rain, watching the gusty rain surge like a gray yet silver ship across her vision, nursing a final plate between her hands. She broke her revery and putting the plate on the table she went and stood without the study door where they were sitting watching the streaming window panes, hearing the gray rain like a million little feet across the roof and in the trees.

"Alright, uncle Joe," she said fleeing kitchenward.

Before they were half through lunch the downpour had ceased, the ships of rain had surged on drawing before the wind, leaving only a whisper in the wet green waves of leaves, with an occasional gust running in long white lines like elves holding hands across the grass. But Emmy would not appear with dessert.

"Emmy!" called the rector again.

Mrs Powers rose. "I'll go see," she said.

The kitchen was empty. "Emmy?" she called quietly. There was no reply and she was on the point of leaving when impulse bade her look behind the open door. She swung it away from the wall and Emmy stared at her dumbly.

"Emmy, what is it?" she asked.

But Emmy wordless, marched from her hiding place and taking a tray she placed the prepared dessert on it and handed it to Mrs Powers.

"This is silly, Emmy, acting this way. You must give him time to get used to us again."

But Emmy only looked at her from beyond the frontiers of her inarticulate despair and the other woman carried the tray in to the table. "Emmy's not feeling well," she explained.

"I am afraid Emmy works too hard," the rector said. "She was always a hard worker, dont you remember, Donald?"

Mahon raised his puzzled gaze to his father's face.

"Emmy?" he repeated.

"Dont you remember Emmy?"

"Yes, sir," he repeated tonelessly.

7.

The window panes had cleared though it yet rained. She sat after the men had left the table and at last Emmy peered through the door, then entered. She rose and together the two of them cleared the table over Emmy's mild protest and carried the broken meal to the kitchen. Mrs Powers turned back her sleeves briskly.

"No, no, lemme do it," Emmy objected. "You'll spot up your dress."

"Its an old one: no matter if I do."

"It dont look old to me. I think its right pretty. But this is my work: you go on and lemme do it."

"I know, but I've got to do something or I'll go wild. Dont you worry about this dress: I dont."

"You are rich: you dont have to, I guess," Emmy answered coldly, examining the dress.

"Do you like it?"

Emmy made no reply.

"I think clothes of this sort suit people of your and my type, dont you?"

"I dunno. I never thought about it," splashing water in the sink.

"I tell you what," said Mrs Powers watching Emmy's firm sturdy back. "I have a new dress in my trunk that doesn't suit me for some reason. When we get through suppose you come up with me and we'll try it on you. I can sew a little and we can make it fit you exactly. What about it?"

Emmy thawed imperceptibly. "What use would I have for it? I dont go anywhere and I got clothes good enough to wash and sweep and cook in."

"I know, but its always well to have some dress-up things. I will lend you stockings and things to go with it, and a hat too."

Emmy slid dishes into hot water and steam rose about her reddened arms. "Where's your husband?" she asked irrelevantly.

"He was killed in the war, Emmy."

"Oh," she said. Then after a while: "and you so young, too." She gave Mrs Powers a quick kind glance: sisters in sorrow. (My Donald was killed too)

Mrs Powers rose quickly. "Where's a cup towel? Lets get done so we can try that dress."

Emmy drew her hands from the water and dried them on her apron. "Wait, lemme get one for you, too."

A bedraggled sparrow eyed her from the limp glistening morning glory vine and Emmy dropped the apron over her head and knotted the cords at the back. Steam rose again about Emmy's forearms, wreathing her head, and the china was warm and smooth and sensuous to the touch; glass gleamed under Mrs Powers' towelling and a dull parade of silver took the light mutely, hushing it as like two priestesses they repeated the orisons of Clothes.

As they passed the study door they saw the rector and his son gazing quietly into a rain-perplexed tree and Gilligan sprawled on his back on a battered divan, smoking and reading.

8.

Emmy outfitted from head to heel thanked her awkwardly.

"How good the rain smells!" Mrs Powers interrupted her. "Sit down a while, wont you?"

Emmy admiring her finery came suddenly from out her cinderella dream. "I cant. I got some mending to do. I nearly clean forgot it."

"Bring your mending in here, then, so we can talk. I haven't had a woman to talk to in months, it seems like. Bring it in here and let me help you."

Emmy flattered said: "Why do you want to do my work?"

"I told you if I dont have something to do I'll be a crazy woman in two days. Please, Emmy, as a favor. Wont you?"

"Alright. Lemme get it." She gathered up her garments and leaving the room she returned with a heaped basket and they sat on either side of it.

"His poor huge socks," Mrs Powers raised her encased hand. "Like chair covers, aren't they?"

Emmy laughed happily above her needle, and beneath swooning gusts of rain across the roof the pile of neatly folded and mended garments grew steadily.

"Emmy," Mrs Powers said after a time, "what was Donald like before? You knew him a long time, didn't you?"

Emmy's needle continued its mute tiny flashing and after a while Mrs Powers leaned across the basket and putting her hand under Emmy's chin raised her bent face. Emmy twisted her head aside and bent again over her needle. Mrs Powers rose and drew the shades, darkening the room against the rain-combed afternoon. Emmy continued to peer blindly at her darning until the other woman took it from her hand, then she raised her head and stared at her new friend with beast-like unresisting hopelessness.

Mrs Powers took Emmy's arms and drew her erect. "Come, Emmy," she said feeling the bones in Emmy's hard muscular arms. Mrs Powers knew that lacking a bed any reclining inti-macy was conducive to confidence, so she drew Emmy down beside her in an ancient obese armchair. And with heedless rain filling the room with hushed monotonous sound, Emmy told her brief story.

"We was in school together—when he was there at all. He never came, mostly. They couldn't make him. He'd just go off, into the country by himself and not come back for two or three days. And nights too. It was one night when he—— when he——"

Her voice died away and Mrs Powers said: "When he what, Emmy? Aren't you going too fast?"

"Sometimes he used to walk home from school with me. He wouldn't never have a hat or a coat and his face was like——it was like he ought to live in the woods. You know: not like he ought to went to school or had to dress up. And so you never did know when you'd see him. He'd come in school almost any time and folks would see him way out in the country at night. Sometimes he'd sleep in folks' houses in the country and sometimes niggers would find him asleep in sand ditches. Everybody knowed him. And then one night——"

"How old were you then?"

"I was sixteen and he was nineteen. And then one night——"

"But you are going too fast. Tell me about you and him before that. Did you like him?"

"I liked him better than anybody. When we was both younger we dammed up a place in a creek and built a swim-ming hole and we used to go in everyday. And then we'd lie in a old blanket we had and sleep until time to get up and dress and go home. And in summer we was together nearly all the time. Then one day he'd just disappear and nobody wouldn't know where he was. And then he'd be outside our house some morning, calling me.

"The trouble was that I always lied to pappy where I had been and I hated that. Donald always told his father: he never lied about nothing he ever did. But he was braver than me, I reckon.

"And then when I was fourteen pappy found out about how I liked Donald and so he took me out of school and kept me home all the time, so I didn't hardly ever get to see Donald. Pappy made me promise I wouldn't go around with him any more. He had come for me once or twice and I told him I couldn't go, and then one day he come and pappy was at home.

"Pappy run out to the gate and told him not to come fooling around there no more but Donald stood right up to him. Not acting bad, but just like pappy was a fly or something. And so pappy come in the house mad and said he wasn't going to have any such goings-on with his girls and he hit me and then he was sorry and cried (he was drunk, you see) and made me swear I wouldn't never see Donald again. And I had to. But I thought of how much fun we used to have and I wanted to die.

"And so I didn't see Donald for a long time. Then folks said that he was going to marry that—that——her. I knew Donald didn't care much about me: he never cared about anybody, so knowing he never liked nobody at all was something. But when I heard that he was going to marry her——

"Anyway, I didn't sleep much at night and so I'd sit on the porch after I'd undressed lots of times, thinking about him and watching the moon getting bigger every night. And then one night, when the moon was almost full and you could see like day almost, I saw somebody walk up to our gate and stop there. And I knew it was Donald and he knew I was there because he said:

" 'Come here, Emmy.'

"And I went to him, and it was like old times because I forgot all about him marrying her, because he still liked me, to come after so long, and he took my hand and we walked down the road not talking at all. After a while we came to the place where you turn off the road to go to our swimming hole and when we crawled through the fence my nightie got hung and he said Take it off. And I did and we put it in a plum bush and went on.

"The water looked so soft in the moonlight you couldn't tell where the water was hardly, and so we swam a while and then Donald hid his clothes too and we went on up on top of a hill. Everything was so kind of pretty and the grass felt so good to your feet and all of a sudden Donald ran on ahead of me. I can keep up with Donald when I want to but for some reason tonight I didn't want to, and so I sat down. I could see him running along the top of the hill, all shiny in the moonlight, then he ran back down the hill toward the creek.

"And so I laid down. I couldn't see anything except the sky and I dont know how long it was when all of a sudden there his head was against the sky, over me, and he was wet again and I could see the moonlight kind of running on his wet shoulders and arms, and he looked at me. I couldn't see his eyes, but I could feel them somehow like things touching me. When he looks at you——you feel like a bird, kind of: like you was going swooping right away from the ground or something. But now there was something different too. I could hear him panting from running and I could feel something inside me panting too. I was afraid and I wasn't afraid. It was like everything was dead except us. And then he said:

"'Emmy. Emmy.' kind of like that.

"And then——and then——"

"Yes. And then he made love to you."

Emmy turned suddenly and the other held her close.

"And now he dont know me, he dont even know me!" she wailed.

Mrs Powers held her and at last Emmy raised her hand and pushed her hair from her face.

"And then?" Mrs Powers prompted.

"And afterwards we laid there and held each other and I felt so quiet, so good, and some cows came up and looked at us and went away. And I could feel his hand going right slow from my shoulder along my side as far as he could reach and then back again, slow, slow. We didn't talk at all, just his hand going up and down my side, so smooth and quiet. And after a while I was asleep.

"Then I waked up. It was getting dawn and I was cramped and wet and cold and he was gone, but I knew he would come back. And sure enough he did, with some blackberries. We ate 'em and watched it getting light in the east. Then when the blackberries were gone I could feel the cold wet grass under me again and see the sky all yellow and chilly behind his head.

"After a while we went back by the swimming hole and he put on his clothes and we got my nightie and I put it on. It was getting light fast and he wanted to go all the way home with me, only I wouldn't let him: I didn't care what happened now. And when I went through the gate there was pappy standing on the porch."

She was silent. Her story seemed to be finished. She breathed regularly as a child against the other's shoulder.

"And what then, Emmy?" Mrs Powers prompted again.

"Well, when I came to the porch I stopped and he said 'Where have you been?' and I said 'None of your business' and he said 'You whore, I'll beat you to death' and I said 'Touch me.' But he didn't. I think I would have killed him if he had. He went in the house and I went in and dressed and bundled up my clothes and left. And I haven't been back, either."

"What did you do then?"

"I got a job doing rough sewing for Mrs Miller (she's a dress-maker) and she let me sleep in her shop until I could earn some money. I hadn't been there but three days when one day Mr Mahon walked in. He said that Donald had told him about us and that Donald had gone off to the war, and that he had come for me. So I have been here ever since. So I didn't see Donald anymore. And now he dont know me at all."

"You poor child," Mrs Powers said. She raised Emmy's face: it was calm, purged. She no longer felt superior to the girl. Suddenly Emmy sprang to her feet and gathered up the mended clothes.

"Wait, Emmy," she called. But Emmy was gone.

She lit a cigarette and sat smoking slowly in her great dim room with its heterogeneous collection of furniture. After a while she rose to draw aside the curtains. The rain had ceased and long lances of sunlight pierced the washed immaculate air, striking sparks amid the dripping trees.

She crushed out her cigarette and descending the stairs she saw a strange retreating back and the rector turning from the door said hopelessly, staring at her:

"He doesn't give us much hope for Donald's sight."

"But he's only a general practitioner. We'll get a specialist from Atlanta," she encouraged him, touching his sleeve.

And here was Miss Cecily Saunders tapping her delicate way up the fast-drying walk, between the fresh-sparkled grass.

9.

Cecily sat in her room in pale satin knickers and a thin orange colored sweater, with her slim legs elevated to the arm of another chair, reading when her father opened the door. He stood in the door and stared at her in silent disapproval, she met his gaze for a time and then lowered her legs.

"Do nice girls sit around half-naked like this?" he asked coldly.

She laid her book aside and rose.

"Maybe I'm not a nice girl," she said flippantly. He watched her as she enveloped her narrow body in a flimsy diaphanous robe.

"I suppose you consider that an improvement, do you?"

"You shouldn't come in my room without knocking, daddy," she told him fretfully.

"No more I will, if that's the way you sit in it." He knew he was creating an unfortunate atmosphere in which to say what he wanted to but he felt compelled to continue. "Can you imagine your mother sitting in her room half undressed like this?"

"I hadn't thought about it." She leaned against the mantel, combatively respectful. "But I can if she wanted to."

He sat down. "I want to talk to you, Sis." His tone was changed and she sank onto the foot of the bed curling her legs under her, regarding him hostilely.

How clumsy I am, he thought, clearing his throat. "Its about young Mahon."

She looked at him.

"I saw him this noon, you know." She was forcing him to do all the talking. Dammit, what an amazing ability children have for making parental admonition hard to achieve. Even Bob was developing it.

Cecily's eyes were green and fathomless. She extended her arm taking a nail file from her dressing table. The downpour had ceased and the rain was only a whisper in the wet leaves. Cecily bent her face above the graceful slender gesturing of her hands.

"I say, I saw young Mahon today," her father repeated with rising choler.

"You did? How did he look, daddy?" Her tone was so soft, so innocent that he sighed with relief. He glanced at her sharply but her face was lowered sweetly and demurely: he could see only her hair filled with warm reddish lights and the shallow plane of her cheek and her soft unemphatic chin.

"That boy's in bad shape, Sis."

"His poor father," she commiserated above her busy hands. "It is so hard on him, isn't it?"

"His father doesn't know."

She looked quickly up and her eyes became gray and dark, darker still. He saw that she didn't know either.

"Doesn't know?" she repeated. "How can he help seeing that scar?" Her face blanched and her hand touched her breast delicately. "Do you mean——"

"No, no," he said hastily. "I mean his father thinks that he——his father doesn't think——I mean his father forgets that his journey has tired him, you see," he finished awkwardly. He continued swiftly: "That's what I wanted to talk to you about."

"About being engaged to him? How can I, with that scar? How can I?"

"No, no, not engaged to him if you dont want to be. We wont think about the engagement at all now. But just keep on seeing him until he gets well, you see."

"But, daddy, I cant. I just cant."

"Why, Sis?"

"Oh, his face: I cant bear it anymore." Her own face was wrung with the recollection of a passed anguish. "Dont you see I cant? I would if I could."

"But you'll get used to it. And I expect a good doctor can patch him up and hide it. Doctors can do anything these days.

Why, Sis, you are the one who can do more for him right now than any doctor."

She lowered her head to her arms folded upon the footrail of the bed and her father stood beside her putting his arms around her slim, nervous body.

"Cant you do that much, Sis? Just drop in and see him occasionally?"

"I just cant," she moaned. "I just cant."

"Well, then, I guess you cant see that Farr boy anymore, either."

She raised her head quickly and her body became taut under his arm.

"Who says I cant?"

"I say so, Sis," he replied gently and firmly.

Her eyes became blue with anger, almost black.

"You cant prevent it. You know you cant." She thrust herself back against his arm trying to evade it. He held her and she twisted her head aside straining from him.

"Look at me," he said quietly, putting his other hand under her cheek. She resisted, he felt her warm breath on his hand, but he forced her face around. Her eyes blazed at him.

"If you cant occasionally see the man you are engaged to, and a sick man to boot, I'm damned if I'll have you running around with anybody else."

There were red prints where his fingers were on her cheek and her eyes filled slowly.

"You are hurting me," she said and feeling her soft vague chin in his palm and her fragile body against his arm he knew a sudden access of contrition. He picked her up bodily and sat again in a chair, holding her on his lap.

"Now, now," he whispered rocking, holding her face against his shoulder, "I didn't mean to be so rough about it."

She lay against him limply weeping and the rain filled the interval whispering across the roof, among the leaves of trees. After a long space in which they could hear dripping eaves and the happy sound of gutters and a small ivory clock in the room, she moved and still holding her face against his coat, she clasped her father about the neck.

"We wont think about it anymore," he told her kissing her cheek. She clasped him again tightly, then slipping from his lap she stood at her dressing table, dabbing powder upon her face. He rose and in the mirror across her shoulder he saw her blurred face and the deft nervousness of her hands. "We wont think about it anymore," he repeated opening the door. The orange sweater was a hushed incandescence under the formal illusion of her robe, molding her narrow back as he closed the door after him.

As he passed his wife's room she called to him:

"What were you scolding Cecily for, Robert?"

But he stumped on down the stairs ignoring her. Soon she heard him cursing Tobe from the back porch.

Mrs Saunders entered her daughter's room and found her swiftly dressing. The sun broke suddenly through the rain and long lances of sunlight pierced the washed immaculate air, striking the burnished trees to sparks of falling water.

"Where are you going, Cecily?" she asked.

"To see Donald," Cecily replied drawing on her stockings, twisting them skillfully and deftly at the knees.

10.

Januarius Jones lounging through the wet grass circled the house and peering through the kitchen window saw Emmy's back and one angled arm sawing across her body. He mounted the steps quietly and entered. Emmy's stare above her poised iron was impersonally combative. Jones' yellow eyes unabashed took her and the ironing board and the otherwise empty kitchen boldly. Jones said:

"Well, Cinderella."

"My name is Emmy," she told him icily.

"That's right," he agreed equably, "so it is. Emmy, Emmeline, Emmylune, Lune——'La lune ne grade aucune rancune' But does it? Or perhaps you prefer 'noir sur la lune?' or do you make finer or less fine distinctions than this? It might be jazzed a bit, you know. Aelia thought so, quite successfully, but then she had a casement in which to lean at dusk and harp her sorrow on her golden hair. You dont seem to have any golden hair, but, then, you might jazz your hair up a little, too. Ah, this restless young generation! Wanting to jazz up everything, not only their complexes, but the shapes of their behinds as well."

She turned her back on him indifferently and again her arm sawed the iron steadily along a stretched fabric. He became so still that after a while she turned to see what had become of him. He was so close behind her that her hair brushed his face. Still clutching the iron she shrieked.

"Hah, my proud beauty!" hissed Jones in accepted style putting his arms around her.

"Let me go," she said glaring at him.

"Your speech is wrong," Jones informed her helpfully. " 'Release me, villain, or it will be the worse for you,' is what you should say."

"Let me go," she repeated.

"Not till you divulge them papers," he answered fat and solemn, his yellow eyes expressionless as a dead man's.

"Lemme go, or I'll burn you," she cried hotly, brandishing the iron. They stared at one another. Emmy's black eyes were fiercely implacable and Jones said at last:

"Dam'f I dont believe you would."

"See if I dont," she said with anger. But he released her and sprang away in time. Her red hand brushed her hair from her hot face and her eyes blazed at him. "Get out, now," she ordered and Jones sauntering easily toward the door remarked plaintively:

"What's the matter with you women here, anyway? Wildcats, wildcats. By the way, how is the dying hero today?"

"Go on now," she repeated gesturing with the iron. He passed through the door and closed it behind him. Then he opened it again and making her a deep fattish bow from the threshold he withdrew.

In the dark hallway he halted, listening. Light from the front door fell directly in his face: he could see only edged indications of sparse furniture. He paused listening. No, she isn't here, he decided. Not enough talk going on for her to be here. That femme hates silence like a cat does water. Cecily and silence: oil and water. And she'll be on top of it, too. Damn little bitch, wonder what she meant by that yesterday. And Georgie, too. She's such a fast worker I guess it takes a whole string to keep her busy. Oh well, there's always tomorrow. Especially when today aint over yet. Go in and pull the Great Dane's leg a while.

At the study door he met Gilligan. He didn't recognise him at first.

"Bless my soul," he said at last. "Has the army disbanded already? What will Pershing do now, without any soldiers to salute him? We had scarcely enough men to fight a war with, but with a long peace ahead of us—man, we are helpless."

Gilligan said coldly: "Whatcher want?"

"Why, nothing, thank you. Thank you so much. I merely came to call upon our young friend in the kitchen and to incidentally inquire after Mercury's brother."

"Whose brother?"

"Young Mr Mahon, in a manner of speaking, then."

"Doctor's with him," Gilligan replied curtly. "You cant go in now." He turned on his heel.

"Not at all," murmured Jones after the other's departing back. "Not at all, my dear fellow."

Yawning he strolled up the hall. He stood in the entrance, speculative, filling his pipe. He yawned again openly. At his right was an open door and he entered a stuffily formal room. Here was a convenient window-sill upon which to put spent matches and sitting beside it he elevated his feet to another chair.

The room was depressingly hung with glum portraits of someone's forebears between which the principal strain of kinship appeared to be some sort of stomach trouble. Or perhaps they were portraits of the Ancient Mariner at different ages before he wore out his albatross. (Not even a dead fish could make a man look like that, thought Jones, refusing the dyspeptic gambit of their fretful painted eyes. No wonder the parson believes in hell) A piano had not been opened in years, and opened would probably sound like the faces looked. Jones rose and from a bookcase he got a copy of 'Paradise Lost' (cheerful thing to face a sinner with, he thought) and returned to his chair. The chair was hard, but Jones was not. He elevated his feet again.

The rector and a stranger came into his vision, pausing at the front door in conversation. The stranger departed and that black woman appeared. She and the rector exchanged a few words, Jones remarked with slow, lustful approval her firm free carriage and

And here came Miss Cecily Saunders in pale lilac with a green ribbon at her waist tapping her delicate way up the fast drying gravel path between fresh sparkled grass.

"Uncle Joe!" she called but the rector had already withdrawn to his study. Mrs Powers met her and she said:

"Oh. How do you do? May I see Donald?"

She entered the hall beneath the dim lovely fanlight and her roving glance remarked one sitting with his back to a window. She said Donald and sailed into the room like a bird. One hand covered her eyes and the other was outstretched as she ran with quick tapping steps and sank before him at his feet burying her face in his lap.

"Donald, Donald! I will try to get used to it, I will try! Oh, Donald, Donald! Your poor face! But I will, I will," she repeated hysterically. Her fumbling hand touched his sleeve and slipping down his arm she drew his hand under her cheek, clasping it. "I didn't mean to, yesterday. I wouldn't hurt you for anything, Donald. I couldn't help it, but I love you, Donald, my precious, my own." She burrowed deeper into his lap.

"Put your arms around me, Donald, until I get used to you again."

He complied drawing her upward. Suddenly struck with something familiar about the coat she raised her head. It was Januarius Jones.

She sprang to her feet.

"You beast, why didn't you tell me?"

"My dear ma'am, who am I to refuse what the gods send?"

But she did not wait to hear him. At the door Mrs Powers stood watching with interest. Now she's laughing at me! Cecily thought furiously. Her glance was a blue dagger and her voice was like dripped honey.

"How silly of me, not to have looked," she said sweetly. "Seeing you, I thought at once that Donald would be nearby. I am sure if I were a man I'd always be as near you as possible. But I didn't know you and Mr——Mr Smith were such good friends. Though they say fat men are really awfully attractive. May I see Donald——now? Do you mind?"

Her anger lent her fortitude. When she entered the study she looked at Mahon without a qualm, scar and all. She greeted the rector kissing him, then she turned swift and graceful to

Mahon, averting her eyes from his brow. He sat quietly, watching her without emotion.

You have caused me to look foolish, she told him with whispered smooth fury, sweetly kissing his mouth.

Jones ignored followed down the hall and stood without the closed study door, listening, hearing her throaty rapid speech beyond the bland panel. Then stooping he peered through the keyhole. But he could see nothing and feeling his creased waist-line constricting his breathing, feeling his braces cutting into his stooped fleshy shoulders he rose under Gilligan's detached contemplative stare. Jones' own yellow eyes became quietly empty and he walked around Gilligan's immovable belligerence and on toward the front door, whistling casually.

II.

Cecily Saunders returned home nursing the yet uncooled embers of her anger. From beyond the turn of the verandah her mother called her name and she found her parents sitting together.

"How is Donald?" her mother asked and not waiting for a reply she said: "George Farr 'phoned again after you left. I wish you'd leave some message for him. It keeps Tobe forever stopping whatever he is doing to answer the 'phone."

Cecily making no reply would have passed on to a french window opening upon the porch but her father caught her hand stopping her.

"How is Donald looking today?" he said, repeating his wife.

Her unrelaxed hand tried to withdraw from his. "I dont know and I dont care," she said sharply.

"Why, didn't you go there?" her mother's voice was faintly laced with surprise. "I thought you were going there?"

"Let me go, daddy," she wrenched her hand nervously. "I want to change my dress."

He could feel her rigid delicate bones. "Please," she implored and he said:

"Come here, Sis."

"Now, Robert," his wife interposed. "You promised me to let her alone."

"Come here, Sis," he repeated and her hand becoming lax she allowed herself to be drawn to the arm of his chair. She sat nervously, impatient, and he put his arm around her.

"Why didn't you go there?"

"Now, Robert, you promised," his wife parroted futilely.

"Let me go, daddy." She was rigid beneath her thin, pale dress. He held her and she said: "I did go there."

"Did you see Donald?"

"Oh yes. That black ugly woman finally——condescended to let me see him a few minutes. In her presence, of course."

"What black ugly woman, darling?" asked Mrs Saunders with interest.

"Black woman? Oh, you mean Mrs Whats-her-name. Why, Sis, I thought you and she would like each other. She has got a good level head, I thought."

"I dont doubt it. Only——"

"What black woman, Cecily?"

"——Only you'd better not let Donald see that you are smitten with her."

"Now, now, Sis. What are you talking about?"

"Oh, its well enough to talk that way," she said taut and passionate, "but haven't I eyes of my own? Haven't I seen? Why did she come all the way from Chicago or wherever it was with him? And yet you expect me——"

"Who came from where? What woman, Cecily? What woman, Robert?" They ignored her.

"Now, Sis, you aint just to her. You're just excited."

His arm held her fragile rigidity.

"I tell you, it isn't that—just her. I had forgiven that because he is sick and because of how he used to be about—about girls. You know, before the war. But he has humiliated me in public: this afternoon he——he—— Let me go, daddy," she repeated imploring, trying to thrust herself away from him.

"But what woman, Cecily? What is all this about a woman?" Her mother's voice was fretted.

"Sis, honey, remember he's sick. And I know more about Mrs—er—Mrs Powers than you do." He removed his arm yet still held her wrist. "Now, you think——"

"Robert, who is this woman?"

"——about it tonight and we'll talk it over in the morning."

"No, I am through with him, I tell you. He has humiliated me before her." Her hand came free and she sprang toward the window.

"Cecily!" her mother called after the slim swirl of her vanishing dress, "are you going to call George Farr?"

"No! Not if he was the last man in the world. I hate men." The swift staccato of her feet died away on the stairs, and then a door slammed. Mrs Saunders sank creaking into her chair.

"Now, Robert." So he told her.

12.

Cecily did not appear at breakfast. Her father mounted to her room and knocked, this time.

"Yes?" Her voice penetrated the wood, muffled thinly.

"Its me, Sis. Can I come in?"

There was no reply so he entered. She had not even bathed her face and upon the pillow she was flushed, childish with sleep. The room was permeated with her body's intimate repose: it was in his nostrils like an odor and he felt ill at ease, cumbersome and awkward. He sat on the edge of the bed and took her surrendered hand diffidently. It was unresponsive:

"How do you feel this morning?"

She made no reply, lazily feeling her ascendency and he continued with assumed lightness:

"Do you feel any better about poor young Mahon this morning?"

"I've put him out of my mind. He doesn't need me anymore."

"Course he does," heartily, "we expect you to be his best medicine."

"How can I?"

"How? What do you mean?"

"He brought his own medicine with him."

Her calmness, her exasperating calmness. He must flog himself into yesterday's rage. That was the only way to do anything with 'em, damn 'em.

"Did it ever occur to you that I, in my limited way, may know more about this than you?"

She withdrew her hand and slid it beneath the covers, making no reply, not even looking at him.

He continued: "You are acting like a fool, Cecily. What did the man do to you yesterday?"

"He simply insulted me before another woman. But I dont care to discuss it."

"But listen, Sis. Are you refusing to see him even when seeing him means getting him well again?"

"He's got that black woman. If she cant cure him with all her experience, I certainly cant."

Her father's face slowly suffused. She glanced at him impersonally, then turned her head on the pillow, staring out the window.

"So you refuse to see him anymore?"

"What else can I do? He very evidently does not want me to bother him any longer. Do you want me to go where I'm not wanted?"

He swallowed his anger, trying to speak calmly, trying to match her calm.

"Dont you see that I'm not trying to make you do anything? that I am only trying to help that boy get on his feet again? Suppose he was Bob, suppose Bob was lying there like he is."

"Then you'd better get engaged to him yourself. I'm not."

"Look at me," he said with such quiet, such repression that she lay motionless, holding her breath. He put a rough hand on her shoulder.

"You dont have to man-handle me," she told him calmly turning her head.

"Listen to me. You are not to see that Farr boy anymore. Understand?"

Her eyes were unfathomable as sea water.

"Do you understand me?" he repeated.

"Yes, I hear you."

He rose. They were amazingly alike. He turned at the door meeting her stubborn impersonal gaze. "I mean it, Sis."

Her eyes clouded suddenly. "I am sick and tired of men. Do you think I care?"

The door closed behind him. She lay staring at its inscrutable painted surface, running her fingers lightly over her breasts, across her belly, drawing concentric circles upon her body, beneath the covers wondering how it would feel to have a baby, hating that inevitable time when she'd have to have one, blurring her slim epicenity, blurring her body with pain. . . .

13.

Miss Cecily Saunders in pale blue linen entered a neighbor's house, gushing, paying a morning call. Women did not like her, and she knew it. Yet she had a way with them, a way of charming them temporarily with her conventional perfection, insincere though she might be. Her tact and graceful deference were such that they discussed her disparagingly only behind her back. None of them could long resist her. She always seemed to enjoy other people's gossip. It was not until later you found that she had gossiped none herself. And this indeed requires tact.

She chatted briefly while her hostess pottered among tubbed flowers then asking and receiving permission she entered the house to use the telephone.

14.

Mr George Farr lurking casually within the courthouse portals saw her unmistakable approaching figure far down the shady street, remarking her quick nervous stride. He gloated, fondling her in his eyes with a slow sensuousness. That's the way to treat 'em: make 'em come to you. Forgetting that he had phoned her vainly five times in thirty hours. But her surprise was so perfect, her greeting so impersonal that he began to doubt his own ears.

"My God, I thought I'd never get you over the phone."

"Yes?" She paused creating an unpleasant illusion of arrested haste.

"Been sick?"

"Yes, sort of. Well," moving on, "I'm awfully glad to have seen you. Call me again sometime, when I'm in, wont you?"

"But say, Cecily——"

She paused again and looked at him over her shoulder with courteous patience. "Yes?"

"Where are you going?"

"Oh, I'm running errands today. Buying some things for mamma. Goodbye." She moved again, her blue linen shaping delicate and crisp to her stride. A negro driving a wagon passed between them interminable as Time: he thought the wagon would never pass. He darted around it and caught up with her.

"Be careful," she said quickly. "Daddy's down town. I am not supposed to see you anymore. My folks are down on you."

"Why?" he asked in startled vacuity.

"I dont know. Perhaps he has heard of your running around with women and thinks you will ruin me. That's it, probably."

Flattered he said: "Aw, come on."

They walked beneath awnings. Wagons tethered to slumbering mules and horses were motionless in the square. They were lapped, surrounded, submerged by the frank odor of unwashed negroes, most of whom wore at least one ex-garment of the army O.D.; and their slow unemphatic voices and their careless ready laughter which has also somewhere beneath it something elemental and sorrowful and unresisted, lay drowsily upon the noon.

At the corner was a drug store having in each window an identical globe containing liquids once red and green respectively but faded now to a weak similar brown by the suns of many summers. She stayed him with her hand.

"You mustn't come any farther, George, please."

"Oh, come on, Cecily."

"No, no. Goodbye." Her slim hand stopped him dead in his tracks.

"Come in and have a drink."

"No, I cant. I have so many things to do. I'm sorry."

"Well, after you get through then," he suggested as a last resort.

"I cant tell. But if you want to, you can wait here for me and I'll come back if I have time. If you want to, you know."

"Alright. I'll wait here for you. Please come, Cecily."

"I cant promise. Goodbye."

He was forced to watch her retreating from him, mincing

and graceful, diminishing. Hell, she wont come, he told himself. But he daren't leave for fear she might. He watched her as long as he could see her, watching her head among other heads, sometimes seeing her whole body, delicate and unmistakable. He lit a cigarette and lounged into the drug store.

After a while the clock on the courthouse struck twelve and he threw away his fifth cigarette. God damn her, she wont have another chance to stand me up, he swore. Cursing her he felt better and pushed open the screen door.

He sprang suddenly back into the store and stepped swiftly out of sight and the soda clerk glassy-haired and white-jacketed said "Whatcher dodging?" with interest. She passed walking and talking gaily with a young married man who clerked in a department store. She looked in as they passed, without seeing him.

He waited, wrung and bitter with anger and jealousy, until he knew she had turned the corner. Then he swung the door outward furiously. He cursed her again, blindly, and someone behind him saying "Mist' George Mist' George" monotonously drew up beside him. He whirled upon a negro boy.

"What in hell you want?" he snapped.

"Letter fer you," replied the negro equably, shaming him with better breeding. He took it and gave the boy a coin. It was written on a scrap of wrapping paper and it read: Come tonight after they have gone to bed. I may not get out. But come——if you want to.

He read and re-read it, he stared at her spidery nervous script until the words themselves ceased to mean anything to his mind. He was sick with relief. Everything, the ancient slumbering courthouse, the elms, the hitched somnolent horses and mules, the stolid coagulation of negroes and the slow unemphasis of their talk and laughter, all seemed someway different, lovely and beautiful under the indolent noon.

He drew a long breath.

Chapter Four.

I.

Mr George Farr considered himself quite a man. I wonder if it shows in my face? he thought, keenly examining the faces of men whom he passed trying to fancy that he did see something in some faces that other faces had not. But he had to admit that he could see nothing, and he knew a slight depression, a disappointment. Strange. If that didn't show in your face what could you do for things to show in your face? It would be fine if (George Farr was a gentleman) if without talking men who had women could somehow know each other on sight—some sort of involuntary sign: an automatic masonry. Of course women were no new thing to him. But not like this. Then the pleasing thought occurred to him that he was unique in the world, that nothing like this had happened to any other man, that no one else could know it from his face because nobody else had ever thought of such a thing. Anyway I know it. He gloated over a secret thought like a pleasant taste in the mouth.

When he remembered (remember? had he thought of anything else?) how she had run into the dark house in her night gown, weeping, he felt quite masculine and superior and gentle. She's alright now though, I guess they all do that.

His Jove-like calm was slightly shaken however after he had tried twice unsuccessfully to get her over the phone and it was completely shattered when late in the afternoon she drove serenely by him in a car with a girl friend, utterly ignoring him. She didn't see me. (You know she did) She didn't see me! (You know damn well she did)

By nightfall he was on the verge of his possible mild unemphatic insanity. Then this cooled away as the sun cooled from the sky. He felt nothing yet like an unattached ghost he felt compelled to linger around the corner which she would pass if she did come down town. Suddenly he knew terror. What if I were to see her with another man? It would be worse than death he knew, trying to make himself leave, to hide somewhere like a wounded beast. But his body would not go.

He saw her time after time and when it turned out to be someone else he did not know what he felt. And so when she did turn the corner he did not believe his eyes at first. It was her brother that he first recognised, then he saw her and all his life went into his eyes leaving his body but an awkward ugly gesture in unquicked clay. He could not have said how long it was that he was unconscious of the stone base of the monument on which he sat while she and her brother moved slowly and implacably across his vision, then his life flowed completely, emptying his eyes and filling his body again giving him dominion over his arms and legs and temporarily sight-less he sprang after her.

"Hi, George," young Robert greeted him casually, as an equal. "Goin' to the show?"

She looked at him swiftly, delicately, with terror and something like loathing.

"Cecily——" he said.

Her eyes were dark, black, and she averted her head and hurried on.

"Cecily," he implored touching her arm.

At his touch she shuddered, shrinking from him. "Dont, dont touch me," she said piteously. Her face was blanched, colorless, and he stood watching her frail dress flowing to the fragile articulation of her body as she and her brother passed on, leaving him. And he too partook of her pain and terror, not knowing what it was.

2.

Donald Mahon's home coming, poor fellow, was hardly a nine days' wonder even. Curious kindly neighbors came in ——men who stood or sat jovially respectable, cheerful: solid business men interested now in the Ku Klux Klan more than in war, and interested in war only as a matter of dollars and cents, while their wives chatted about clothes to each other across Mahon's scarred oblivious brow; a few of the rector's more casual acquaintances democratically uncravated, hush-ing their tobacco into a bulged cheek, diffidently but firmly refusing to surrender their hats; girls that he had known, had danced with or courted of summer nights come now to look once upon his face and then quickly aside in hushed nausea, not coming anymore unless his face happened to be hidden on the first visit (upon which they finally found opportunity to see it); boys come to go away fretted because he wouldn't tell any war stories——all this going on about him while Gilligan, his glum major-domo, handled them all with impartial discouraging efficiency.

"Beat it, now," he repeated to young Robert Saunders who with sundry contemporaries to whom he had promised something good in the way of damaged soldiers, had called.

"He's going to marry my sister. I'd like to know why I cant see him," young Robert protested. He was in the uncomfortable position of one who has inveigled his friends into a gold mine and then cannot produce the mine. They jeered at him and he justified his position hotly, appealing to Gilligan.

"G'wan now, beat it. Show's over. G'wan now." Gilligan shut the door on him. Mrs Powers descending the stairs said: "What is it, Joe?"

"That damn Saunders hellion brought his whole gang around to see his scar. We got to stop this," he stated with exasperation, "cant have these damn folks in and out of here all day long, staring at him."

"Well, it is about over," she told him, "they have all called by now. Even their funny little paper has appeared. 'War Hero Returns' you know—that sort of thing."

"I hope so," he answered without hope. "God knows they've all been here once. Do you know, while I was living and eating and sleeping with men all the time I never thought much of them, but since I got civilized again and seen all these women around here saying Aint his face terrible, poor boy, and Will she marry him? and Did you see her down town yesterday almost nekkid? why, I think a little better of men after all. You'll notice them soldiers dont bother him, specially the ones that was overseas. They just kind of call the whole thing off. He just had hard luck and whatcher going to do about it? is the way they figure. Some didn't and some did, the way they think of it."

They stood together looking out the window upon the sleepy street. Women quite palpably 'dressed' went steadily beneath parasols in one direction. "Ladies' Aid," murmured Gilligan. "W.C.T.U. maybe."

"I think you are becoming misanthropic, Joe."

Gilligan glanced at her smooth contemplative profile almost on a level with his own.

"About women? When I say soldiers I dont mean me. I wasn't no soldier anymore than a man that fixes watches is a watch maker. And when I say women I dont mean you."

She put her arm over his shoulder. It was firm, latent with strength, comforting. He knew that he could embrace her in the same way, that if he wished she would kiss him, frankly and firmly, that her eyelids would never veil her eyes at the touch of his mouth. What man is for her? he wondered knowing that after all no man was for her, knowing that she would go through with all physical intimacies, that she would undress to a (lover?) with this same impersonal efficiency. (He should be a——a—— he should be a gladiator or a statesman or a victorious general: someone hard and ruthless who would expect nothing from her, of whom she would expect nothing. Like two gods exchanging golden baubles. And I, I am no gladiator nor statesman nor general: I am nothing. Perhaps that's why I want so much from her) He put his arm over her shoulders.

Niggers and mules. Afternoon lay in a coma in the street, like a woman recently loved. Quiet and warm: nothing now that the lover has gone away. Leaves were like a green liquid arrested in mid-flow, flattened and spread; leaves were as though cut with scissors from green paper and pasted flat on the afternoon: someone dreamed them and then forgot his dream. Niggers and mules.

Monotonous wagons drawn by long-eared beasts crawled past. Negroes humped with sleep, portentous upon each wagon and in the wagon bed itself sat other negroes upon chairs: a pagan catafalque under the afternoon. Rigid, as though carved in Egypt ten thousand years ago. Slow dust rising veiled their passing, like Time; the necks of mules limber as rubber hose swayed their heads from side to side, looking behind them always. But the mules were asleep also. "Ketch me sleep, he kill me. But I got mule blood in me: when he sleep, I sleep; when he wake, I wake."

In the study where Donald sat his father wrote steadily on tomorrow's sermon. The afternoon slept without.

The Town:

War Hero Returns. . . .

His face . . . the way that girl goes on with that Farr boy. . . .

Young Robert Saunders:

I just want to see his scar. . . .

Cecily:

And now I'm not a good woman anymore. Oh, well, it had to be sometime, I guess. . . .

George Farr:

Yes! Yes! she was a virgin! But if she wont see me, it means somebody else. Her body in another's arms. . . . Why must you? Why must you? What do you want? Tell me: I will do anything, anything. . . .

Margaret:

Can nothing at all move me again? Nothing to desire? Nothing to stir me, to move me save pity? . . .

Gilligan:

Margaret, tell me what you want. I will do it. Tell me, Margaret. . . .

The rector wrote 'The Lord is my shepherd: I shall not want.'

Donald Mahon knowing Time as only something which was taking from him a world he did not particularly mind losing stared out a window into green and motionless leaves: a motionless blur.

The afternoon dreamed on toward sunset. Niggers and mules. . . . At last Gilligan broke the silence.

"That old fat one is going to send her car to take him riding."

Mrs Powers made no reply.

3.

San Francisco, Cal
April 5, 1919

Dear Margaret—

Well I am at home again I got here this after noon. As soon as I got away from mother I am sitting down to write to you. Home seems pretty good after you have been doing a pretty risky thing like lots of them cracked up at. Its boreing all these

girls how they go on over a flying man if you ever experri-
anced it isnt it. There was a couple of janes on the train I met.
Well anyway they saw my hat band and they gave me the eye
they were society girls they said but I am not so dumb any
way they was nice kids and they might of been society girls.
Anyway I got there phone numbers and I am going to give
them a call. Just kidding them see there is only one woman
for me Margaret you know it. Well we rode on into San Francisco talking and laughing in there stateroom so Iam going to
take the best looking of them out this week I made a date with
her exept she wants me to bring a fellow for her friend so I
guess I will poor kids they probly havent had much fun dureing the war like a man can have dureing the war. But I am just
kidding them Margaret you mustent be jealous like I am not
jealous over Lieut Mahon. Well mother is dragging me out to
tea I had rather ~~take a kick in~~ I had rather be shot than go
exept she insists. Give my reguards to Joe.

With love
Julian.

Mrs Powers and Gilligan met the specialist from Atlanta at
the station. In the cab he listened to her attentively.

"But, my dear madam," he objected when she had finished,
"you are asking me to commit an ethical violation."

"But surely, Doctor, it isn't a violation of professional ethics
to let his father believe as he wishes to believe, is it?"

"No, it is a violation of my personal ethics."

"Then, you tell me and let me tell his father."

"Yes, I will do that. But pardon me, may I ask what exactly
is your relation to him?"

"We are to be married," she answered looking at him
steadily.

"Oh. Then that is quite alright. I will promise not to say
anything before his father that can disturb him."

He kept his promise. After lunch he joined her where she
sat on the shaded quiet verandah. She put aside her embroidery frame and he took a chair, puffing furiously at his cigar
until it burned evenly.

"What is he waiting for?" he asked suddenly.

"Waiting for?" she repeated.

He flashed her a keen gray glance. "There is no ultimate hope for him, you know."

"For his sight, you mean?"

"That's practically gone now. I mean for him."

"I know. That's what Mr Gilligan said two weeks ago."

"H'm. Is Mr Gilligan a doctor?"

"No. But it doesn't take a doctor to see that, does it?"

"Not necessarily. But I think Mr Gilligan rather over-shot himself, making a public statement like that."

She rocked gently. He veiled his head in smoke, watching the evenly burning ash at the cigar tip. She said:

"You think that there is no hope for him, then?"

"Frankly, I do not." He tilted the ash carefully over the balustrade. "He is practically a dead man now. More than that, he should have been dead these three months were it not for the fact that he seems to be waiting for something. Something he has begun but has not completed, something he has carried from his former life that he does not remember consciously. That is his only hold on life that I can see." He gave her another keen glance. "How does he regard you now? He remembers nothing of his life before he was injured."

She met his sharp kind gaze a moment then she suddenly decided to tell him the truth. He watched her intently until she had finished.

"So you are meddling with providence, are you?"

"Wouldn't you have done the same?" she defended herself.

"I never speculate on what I would have done," he answered shortly. "There can be no If in my profession. I work in tissue in bone, not in circumstance."

"Well, its done now. I am in it too far to withdraw. So you think he may go at any time?"

"You are asking me to speculate again. What I said was that he will go whenever that final spark somewhere in him is no longer fed. His body is already dead. Further than that I cannot say."

"An operation?" she suggested.

"He would not survive it. And in the second place the human machine can only be patched and parts replaced up to a certain point. And all that has been done for him, or he would have never been released from any hospital."

Afternoon drew on. They sat quietly talking while sunlight becoming lateral broke through the screening leaves and sprinkled the porch with flecks of yellow, like mica in a stream. The same negro in the same undershirt droned up and down the lawn with his mower, an occasional vehicle passed slumberous and creaking behind twitching mules, or moving more swiftly, leaving a fretful odor of gasoline to die beneath the afternoon.

The rector joined them after a while.

"Then there's nothing to do except let him build himself up, eh Doctor?" he asked.

"Yes, that is my advice. Attention, rest and quiet, let him resume old habits. About his sight though——"

The rector looked up slowly. "Yes, I realize his sight must go. But there are compensations. He is engaged to be married to a very charming lady. Dont you think that will give him incentive to help himself?"

"Yes, that should if anything can."

"What do you think? Shall we hurry the marriage along?"

"We—ll——" the doctor hesitated: he was not exactly accustomed to giving advice on this subject.

Mrs Powers came to his rescue. "I think we had better not hurry him at all," she said quickly. "Let him accustom himself leisurely, you see. Dont you think so, Doctor Baird?"

"Yes, Reverend, you let Mrs Powers here advise you about that. I have every confidence in her judgment. You let her take charge of this thing. Women always more capable than we are, you know."

"That's quite true. We are already under measureless obligations to Mrs Powers."

"Nonsense. I have almost adopted Donald myself."

The cab came at last and Gilligan appeared with the doctor's things. They rose and Mrs Powers slipped her arm through the rector's. She squeezed his arm and released him. As she and Gilligan flanking the doctor descended the steps the rector said again, timidly:

"You are sure, Doctor, that there is nothing to be done immediately? We are naturally anxious, you know," he ended apologetically.

"No, no," the doctor replied testily, "he can help himself more than we can help him."

The rector stood watching until the cab turned the corner. Looking back she could see him in the door, staring after them. Then the house was out of sight.

As the train drew into the station the doctor said, taking her hand:

"You've let yourself in for something that is going to be unpleasant, young lady."

She gave him a straight glance in return.

"I'll take the risk," she said shaking his hand firmly.

"Well. Goodbye then, and good luck."

"Goodbye sir," she answered. "And thank you."

He turned to Gilligan offering his hand.

"And the same to you, Doctor Gilligan," he said with faint sarcasm. They saw his neat gray back disappear and Gilligan turning to her asked:

"What'd he call me Doctor for?"

"Come on, Joe," she said not replying to his question, "lets walk back. I want to walk through the woods again."

4.

The air was sweet with fresh-sawed lumber and they walked through a pale yellow city of symmetrical stacked planks. A continuous line of negroes carried boards up a cleated incline like a chicken run into a freight car and flung them clashing to the floor, under the eye of an informally clad white man who reclined easily upon a lumber pile, chewing indolent tobacco. He watched them with interest as they passed following the faint wagon road.

They crossed grass-grown steel rails and trees obscured the lumber yard but until they reached the bottom of the hill the voices of the negroes raised in bursts of meaningless laughter or snatches of song in a sorrowful minor came to them, and the slow reverberations of the cast boards smote at measured intervals. Quietly under the spell of the still late afternoon woods they descended a loamy hill following the faint downward winding of the road. At the foot of the hill a dogwood tree spread flat palm-like branches in invocation among dense green, like a white nun.

"Niggers cut them for fire wood because they are easy to chop," she said breaking the silence. "Shame, isn't it?"

"Do they?" he murmured without interest. With the soft sandy soil giving easily under their feet they came upon water. It ran somberly from out massed honeysuckle vines and crossed the dim road into another impenetrable thicket, murmuring. She stopped and bending slightly they could see their heads and their two fore-shortened bodies repeating themselves.

"Do we look that funny to people, I wonder?" she said. Then she stepped quickly across. "Come on, Joe."

The road passed from the dim greenness into sunlight again. It was still sandy and the going was harder, exasperating.

"You'll have to pull me, Joe." She took his arm, feeling her heels sink and slip treacherously at each step. Her unevenly distributed weight made his own progress more difficult and he disengaged his arm and put his hand against her back.

"That's better," she said leaning against his firm hand. The road circled the foot of a hill and trees descending the hill were halted by the curving road's green canyon as though waiting to step across when they had passed. Sun was in the trees like an arrested lateral rain and ahead where circling the green track of the stream approached the road again they heard young voices and a sound of water.

They walked slowly through the shifting sand and the voices beyond a screen of thick leaves became louder. She squeezed his arm for silence and they left the road and parted leaves cautiously upon glinted disturbed water taking and giving the sun in a flashing barter of gold for gold, dazzling the eyes. Two wet matted heads spread opening fans of water like muskrats and on a limb, balanced precariously to dive, stood a third swimmer. His body was the color of old paper, beautiful as a young animal's.

They stepped into view and Gilligan said:

"Hi, Colonel."

The diver took one quick terrified look and releasing his hold he fell like a stone into the water. The other two shocked and motionless stared at the intruders, then when the diver reappeared above the surface they whooped at him in merciless derision. He swam like an eel across the pool and took refuge beneath the over-hanging bank, out of sight. His companions still squalled at him in inarticulate mirth. She raised her voice above the din.

"Come on, Joe. We've spoiled their fun."

They left the noise behind and again in the road, she remarked:

"We shouldn't have done that. Poor boy, they'll tease him to death now. What makes men so silly, Joe?"

"Dam'f I know. But they sure are. Do you know who that was?"

"No. Who was it?"

"Her brother."

"Her——?"

"Young Saunders."

"Oh, was it? Poor boy, I'm sorry I shocked him."

And well she might have been could she have seen his malevolent face watching her retreating figure as he swiftly donned his clothes. I'll fix you! he swore, almost crying.

The road wound through a depression between two small ridges. The sun was yet in the tops of trees and here were cedars unsunned and solemn, a green quiet nave. A thrush sang and they stopped as one, listening to its four notes, watching the fading patches of sun on the top of the ridge.

"Lets sit down and have a cigarette," she suggested.

She lowered herself easily and he sat beside her as young Robert Saunders panting up the hill behind them saw them and fell flat, creeping as near as he dared. Gilligan reclining on his elbow watched her pallid face. Her head was lowered and she dug in the earth with a stick. Her unconscious profile was in relief against a dark cedar and she said, feeling his eyes on her:

"Joe, we have got to do something about that girl. We cant expect Doctor Mahon to take sickness as an excuse much longer. I hoped her father would make her come, but they are so much alike. . . ."

"Whatcher want to do? Want me to go and drag her up by the hair?"

"I expect that would be the best way, after all." Her twig broke and casting it aside she searched for another one.

"Sure it would——if you got to fool with her kind at all."

"Unluckily though, this is a civilised age and you cant do that."

"So called," muttered Gilligan. He sucked at his cigarette then watched the spun white arc of its flight. The thrush sang again filling the interval liquidly and young Robert thinking Is it Sis they're talking about? felt fire on his leg and brushed from it an ant almost half an inch long. Drag her by the hair, huh? he muttered. I'd like to see 'em. Ow, but he stings! rubbing his leg, which did not help it any.

"What are we going to do, Joe? Tell me. You know about people."

Gilligan shifted his weight and his corrugated elbow tingled under his other hand.

"We've been thinking of them ever since we met. Lets think about you and me for a while," he said roughly.

She looked at him quickly. Her black hair and her mouth like a pomegranate blossom. Her eyes were black and they became quite gentle as she said:

"Please, Joe."

"Oh, I aint going to propose. I just want you to talk to me about yourself for a while."

"What do you want me to tell you?"

"Nothing you dont want to. Just quit thinking about the loot for a while. Just talk to me."

"So you are surprised to find a woman doing something without some obvious material end in view. Aren't you?" He was silent, nursing his knees, staring between them at the ground. "Joe, you think I'm in love with him, dont you?" (Uhuh! Stealing Sis' feller. Young Robert Saunders squirming nearer, taking sand into his bosom) "Dont you, Joe?"

"I dont know," he replied sullenly and she asked:

"What kind of women have you known, Joe?"

"The wrong kind, I guess. Leastways none of 'em ever made me lose a night's sleep until I saw you."

"It isn't me that made you lose a night's sleep. I just happened to be the first woman you ever knew doing something you thought only a man would do. You had nice fixed ideas about women and I upset them. Wasn't that it?"

She looked at his averted face, at his reliable homely face. (Are they going to talk all night? thought young Robert Saunders. Hunger was in his belly and he was gritty and uncomfortable with sand)

The sun was almost down. Only the tips of trees were yet dipped in fading light and where they sat the shadow became a violet substance in which the thrush sang and then fell still.

"Margaret," said Gilligan at last, "were you in love with your husband?"

Her face in the dusk was a smooth pallor, and after a while:

"I dont know, Joe. I dont think I was. You see, I lived in a small town and I had got kind of sick lazing around home all morning and dressing up just to walk down town in the afternoon and spending the evenings messing around with men, so after we got in the war I persuaded some friends of my mother's to get me a position in New York. Then I got into the Red Cross——you know, helping in canteens, dancing with those poor country boys on leave, lost as sheep, trying to have a good time. And nothing in the world is harder to do in New York.

"And one night Dick (my husband) came in. I didn't notice him at first, but after we had danced together and I saw he was—well—impressed, I asked him about himself. He was in an officers' training camp.

"Then I started getting letters from him and at last he wrote that he would be in New York until he sailed. I had got in the habit of Dick by that time and when I saw him again all spic and span and soldiers saluting him I thought he was grand. You remember how it was then—everybody excited and hysterical, like a big circus.

"So every night we went out to dinner and to dance and after we would sit in my room and smoke and talk until all hours, till daylight. You know how it was: all soldiers talking of dying gloriously in battle without really believing it or knowing very much about it, and how women kind of got the same idea, like the 'flu——that what you did today would not matter tomorrow, that there really wasn't a tomorrow at all.

"You see, I think we both had agreed that we were not in love with each other for always but we were both young and so we might as well get all the fun we could. And then, three days before he sailed he suggested that we get married. I had had proposals from nearly every soldier I had been at all kind to, just as all the other girls did, and so I wasn't surprised much. I told him I had other men friends and I knew that he knew other women, but neither of us bothered about that. He told me he expected to know women in France and that he didn't expect me to be a hermit while he was gone. And so we met the next morning and got married and I went to work.

"He called for me at the canteen while I was dancing with some boys on leave and the other girls all congratulated us (lots of them had done the same thing) only some of them teased me about being a highbrow and marrying an officer. You see, we all got so many proposals we hardly listened to them. And I dont think they listened to us either.

"He called for me and we went to his hotel. You see, Joe, it was like when you are a child in the dark and you keep on saying It isn't dark, It isn't dark. We were together three days and then his boat sailed. I missed him like the devil at first. I moped around without anybody to feel sorry for me: so many of my friends were in the same fix, with no sympathy to waste. Then I got dreadfully afraid I might be going to have a baby and I almost hated Dick. But when I was sure I wasn't I went back to the canteen, and after a while I hardly thought of Dick at all.

"I got more proposals of course, and I didn't have such a bad time. Sometimes at night I'd wake up wanting Dick but after a time he got to be a shadowy sort of person, like George Washington. And at last I didn't even miss him anymore.

"Then I began to get letters from him, addressed to his dear little wife and telling me how he missed me and so forth. Well, that brought it all back again and I'd write him everyday for a time. And then I found that writing bored me, that I no longer looked forward to getting one of those dreadful flimsy envelopes that had already been opened by a censor.

"I didn't write anymore. And one day I got a letter saying that he didn't know when he'd be able to write again but it would be as soon as he could. That was when he was going up to the front, I guess. I thought about it for a day or two and then I made up my mind that the best thing for both of us was just to call the whole thing off. So I sat down and wrote him, wishing him good luck and asking him to wish me the same.

"And then, before my letter reached him I received an official notice that he had been killed in action. He never got my letter at all. He died believing that everything was the same between us."

She brooded in the imminent twilight. "You see, I feel someway that I wasn't square with him. And so I guess I am trying to make it up to him in some way."

Gilligan felt impersonal, weary. He took her hand and rubbed his cheek against it. Her hand turned in his and patted his cheek, withdrawing. (Holding hands! gloated young Robert Saunders) She leaned down peering into Gilligan's face. He sat motionless, taut. Take her in my arms, he debated, overcome her with my own passion. Feeling this she withdrew from him, though her body had not moved.

"That wouldn't do any good, Joe. Dont you know it wouldn't?" she asked.

"Yes, I know it," he said. "Lets go."

"I'm sorry, Joe," she told him in a low voice, rising. He rose and helped her to her feet. She brushed her skirt and walked on beside him. The sun was completely gone and they walked through a violet silence soft as milk. "I wish I could, Joe," she added.

He made no reply and she said: "Dont you believe me?"

He strode on and she grasped his arm, stopping. He faced her and in her firm sexless embrace he stood staring at the blur of her face almost on a level with his own in longing and despair. (Uhuh, kissing! crowed young Robert Saunders, releasing his cramped limbs, trailing them like an Indian)

Then they turned and walked on, out of his sight. Night was almost come: only the footprint of day, only the odor of day, only a rumor, a ghost of light among the trees.

5.

He burst into his sister's room. She was fixing her hair and she saw him in the mirror, panting and regrettably soiled.

"Get out, you little beast," she said.

Undaunted he gave his news: "Say, she's in love with Donald, that other one says, and I seen them kissing."

Her arrested hands bloomed delicately in her hair.

"Who is?"

"That other lady at Donald's house."

"Saw her kissing Donald?"

"Naw, kissing that soldier feller that aint got no scar."

"Did she say she was in love with Donald?" she turned trying to grasp her brother's arm.

"Naw, but that soldier said she is and she never said nothing. So I guess she is, dont you?"

"The cat! I'll fix her."

"That's right," he commended. "That's what I told her when she sneaked up on me nekkid. I knowed you wouldn't let no woman beat you out of Donald."

6.

Emmy put supper on the table. The house was quiet and dark. No lights yet. She went to the study door. Mahon and his father sat in the dusk quietly watching the darkness come slow and soundless as a measured respiration. Donald's head was in silhouette against a fading window and Emmy saw it and felt her heart contract as she remembered that head above her against the sky, on a night long, long ago.

But now the back of it was toward her and he no longer remembered her. She entered the room silently as the twilight itself and standing beside his chair, looking down upon his thin worn hair that had once been so wild, so soft, she drew his unresisting head against her hard little hip. His face was quiet under her slow hand and as she gazed out into the twilight upon which they two gazed she tasted the bitter ashes of an old sorrow and she bent suddenly over his devastated head, moaning against it, making no sound.

The rector stirred heavily in the dusk. "That you, Emmy?"

"Supper's ready," she said quietly. Mrs Powers and Gilligan mounted the steps onto the verandah.

7.

Doctor Gary could waltz with a level glass of water on his head, without spilling a drop. He did not care for the more modern dances, the nervous ones. "All jumping around—like monkeys. Why try to do something a beast can do so much better?" he was wont to say. "But a waltz now. Can a dog waltz, or a cow?" He was a smallish man, bald and dapper, and women liked him. Such a nice bedside manner. Doctor Gary was much in demand both professionally and socially. He had also served in a French hospital in '14, '15, and '16. "Like hell," he described it. "Long alleys of excrement and red paint."

Doctor Gary followed by Gilligan descended nattily from Donald's room, smoothing the set of his coat, dusting his hands with a silk handkerchief. The rector appeared hugely from his study saying: "Well, Doctor?"

Doctor Gary rolled a slender cigarette from a cloth sack, returning the sack to its lair in his cuff. When carried in his pocket it made a bulge in the cloth. He struck a match.

"Who feeds him at table?"

The rector surprised answered: "Emmy has been giving him his meals—helping him, that is," he qualified.

"Put it in his mouth for him?"

"No, no. She merely guides his hand. Why do you ask?"

"Who dresses and undresses him?"

"Mr Gilligan here assists him. But why——"

"Have to dress and undress him like a baby, dont you?" he turned sharply to Gilligan.

"Kind of," Gilligan admitted. Mrs Powers came out of the study and Doctor Gary nodded briefly to her. The rector said: "But why do you ask, Doctor?"

The doctor looked at him sharply. "Why? why?" he turned to Gilligan. "Tell him," he snapped.

The rector gazed at Gilligan. Dont say it, his eyes seemed to plead. Gilligan's glance fell. He stood dumbly gazing at his feet and the doctor said abruptly: "Boy's blind. Been blind three or four days. How you didn't know it I cant see." He settled his coat and took his derby hat. "Why didn't you tell?" he asked Gilligan. "You knew, didn't you? Well, no matter. I'll look in again tomorrow. Goodday, madam. Goodday."

Mrs Powers took the rector's arm. "I hate that man," she said. "Damn little snob. But dont you mind, uncle Joe. Remember, that Atlanta doctor told us he would lose his sight. But doctors dont know everything: who knows, perhaps when he gets strong and well he can have his sight restored."

"Yes, yes," the rector agreed clinging to straws. "Lets get him well and then we can see."

He turned heavily and reentered his study. She and Gilligan looked at one another a long moment.

"I could weep for him, Joe."

"So could I—if it would do any good," he answered somberly. "But for God's sake, keep people out today."

"I intend to. But its hard to refuse them: they mean so well, so kind and neighborly."

"Kind, hell. They are just like that Saunders brat: come to see his scar. Come in and mill around and ask him how he got it and if it hurt. As if he knowed or cared."

"Yes. But they shan't come in and stare at his poor head anymore. We wont let them in, Joe. Tell them he is not well, tell them anything."

She entered the study. The rector sat at his desk, a pen poised above an immaculate sheet but he was not writing. His face was propped on one great fist and his gaze brooded darkly upon the opposite wall.

She stood beside him, then she touched him. He started like a goaded beast before he recognised her.

"This had to come, you know," she told him quietly.

"Yes, yes. I have expected it. We all have, have we not?"

"Yes, we all have," she agreed.

"Poor Cecily. I was just thinking of her. It will be a blow to her, I am afraid. But she really cares for Donald, thank God. Her affection for him is quite pretty. You have noticed it, haven't you?"

"Yes, yes."

"Its too bad she is not strong enough to come everyday. But she is quite delicate, as you know, dont you?"

"Yes, yes. I'm sure she will come when she can."

"So am I. Thank God, there is one thing which has not failed him."

His hands were clasped loosely upon the paper before him.

"Oh, you are writing a sermon and I have interrupted you. I didn't know," she apologised, withdrawing.

"Not at all. Dont go, I can do this later."

"No, you do it now. I will go and sit with Donald. Mr Gilligan is going to fix a chair for him on the lawn today, it is so nice out."

"Yes, yes. I will finish my sermon and join you."

From the door she looked back. But he was not writing. His face was propped on one great fist and his gaze brooded darkly upon the opposite wall.

Mahon sat in a deck chair. He wore blue glasses and a soft limp hat concealed his brow. He liked to be read to though no one could tell whether or not the words meant anything to him. Perhaps it was the sound of the voice that he liked. This time it was Gibbons' History of Rome and Gilligan wallowed atrociously among polysyllabic words when Mrs Powers joined them. He had brought a chair for her and she sat neither hearing nor not hearing, letting Gilligan's droning voice soothe her as it did Mahon. The leaves above her head stirred faintly, agitated upon the ineffable sky, dappling her dress with shadow. Clover was again thrusting above the recently mown grass and bees broke it: bees were humming golden arrows tipped or untipped with honey and from the church spire pigeons were remote and unemphatic as sleep.

A noise aroused her and Gilligan ceased reading. Mahon sat motionless, hopeless as Time as across the grass came an old negro woman followed by a strapping young negro in a private's uniform. They came straight toward the sitting group and the woman's voice rose upon the slumberous afternoon.

"Hush yo' mouf, Loosh," she was saying, "it'll be a po' day in de mawnin' when my baby dont wanter see his ole Cal'line. Donald, Mist' Donald honey, here Callie come ter you, honey; here yo' mammy come ter you." She completed the last steps in a shuffling lope. Gilligan rose intercepting her.

"Hold up, Aunty. He's asleep. Dont bother him."

"Naw, suh! He dont wanter sleep when his own folks comes ter see him." Her voice rose again and Donald moved in his chair. "Whut I tell you? he wake: look at 'im. Mist' Donald, honey!"

Gilligan held her withered arm while she strained like a leashed hound.

"Bless de Lawd, done sont you back ter yo' mammy. Yes, Jesus! Ev'yday I prayed, and de Lawd heard me." She turned to Gilligan. "Lemme go, please suh."

"Let her go, Joe," Mrs Powers seconded and Gilligan released her. She knelt beside Donald's chair putting her hands on his face. Loosh stood diffidently in the background.

"Donald, baby, look at me. Dont you know who dis is? Dis yo' Callie whut use ter put you ter bed, honey. Look here at me. Lawd, de white folks done ruint you, but nummine, yo' mammy gwine look after her baby. You, Loosh!" still kneeling she turned and called to her grand-son. "Come up here and speak ter Mist' Donald. Here, whar he kin see you. Donald, honey, here dis triflin' nigger talkin' ter you. Look at him, in dem soldier clothes."

Loosh took two paces and came smartly to attention, saluting. "If de lootenant please, Co'pul Nelson glad ter see—— Co'pul Nelson glad ter see de lootenant lookin' so well."

"Dont you stand dar wavin' yo' arm at yo' Mist' Donald, nigger boy. Come up here and speak ter him like you been raised to."

Loosh lost his military bearing and he became again that same boy who had known Mahon long ago, before the world went crazy. He came up diffidently and took Mahon's hand in his kind rough black one. "Mist' Donald?" he said.

"Dat's it," his grandmother commended. "Mist' Donald, dat Loosh talkin' ter you. Mist' Donald?"

Mahon stirred in his chair and Gilligan forcibly lifted the old woman to her feet. "Now, Aunty. That's enough for one time. You come back tomorrow."

"Lawd! ter hear de day when white man tell me Mist' Donald dont wanter see me!"

"He's sick, Aunty," Mrs Powers explained. "Of course he wants to see you. When he is better you and Loosh must come everyday."

"Yes ma'am! Dey aint enough water in de sevum seas to keep me from my baby. I'm comin' back, honey. I gwine look after you."

"Get her away, Loosh," Mrs Powers whispered to the negro. "He's sick, you know."

"Yessum. He one sick man in dis world. Ef you wants me fer anything, any black man kin tell you whar I'm at, ma'am." He took his grandmother's arm. "Come on here, mammy. Us got to be goin'."

"I'm a-comin' back, Donald honey. I aint gwine leave you." They retreated and her voice died away. Mahon said:

"Joe."

"Whatcher say, Loot?"

"When am I going to get out?"

"Out of what, Loot?"

But he was silent, and Gilligan and Mrs Powers stared at each other tensely. At last he spoke again:

"I've got to go home, Joe." He raised his hand fumbling, striking his glasses and they fell from his face. Gilligan replaced them.

"Whatcher wanta go home for, Loot?"

But he had lost his thought. Then:

"Who was that talking, Joe?"

Gilligan told him and he sat slowly plaiting the corner of his jacket (the suit Gilligan had got for him) in his fingers. Then he said: "Carry on, Joe."

Gilligan picked up the book again and soon his voice resumed its soporific drone. Mahon became still in his chair. After a while Gilligan ceased, Mahon did not move and he rose and peered over the blue glasses.

"You never can tell when he's asleep and when he aint," he said fretfully.

Chapter Five.

I.

Captain Green who raised the company had got a captain's commission from the governor of the state thereby. But Captain Green was dead. He might have been a good officer, he might have been anything: certainly he remembered his friends. Two subaltern's commissions had been given away politically in spite of him, so the best he could do was to make his friend Madden First Sergeant. Which he did.

And so here was Green in bars and shiny puttees, here was Madden trying to acquire the habit of saying Sir to him, here was Tom and Dick and Harry with whom both Green and Madden had gambled and drunk whiskey trying to learn to remember that there was a difference not only between them and Green and Madden but that there was also a difference between Madden and Green.

"Oh well," they said in American camps, "he's working hard: let him get used to it. Its only on parade, hey, Sergeant?"

"Sure," Sergeant Madden replied. "The Colonel is giving us hell about our appearance. Cant we do better than this?"

But at Brest:

"What in hell does he think he is? Pershing?" they asked Sergeant Madden.

"Come on, come on, snap into it. If I hear another word out of a man he goes before the Captain." Sergeant Madden also had changed.

In wartime one lives in today. Yesterday is past and tomorrow may never come. Wait till we get into action, they told each other, we'll kill the son of a bitch. "Not Madden?" asked one horrified. They only looked at him. "For Christ's sake," remarked someone at last.

But Fate using the war department as an instrument circumvented them. When Sergeant Madden reported to his present captain and his erstwhile friend Green said:

"Sit down, dammit. Nobody's coming in. I know what you're going to say. I am moving anyhow: should get my papers tonight. Wait," he added as Madden would have interrupted, "if I want to hold my commission I have got to work. These goddam training camps turn out officers trained. But I wasn't. And so I am going to school for a while. Christ. At my age. I wish to God somebody else had gotten up this damn outfit. Do you know where I would like to be now? Out yonder with them, calling somebody else a son of a bitch, as they are calling me now. Do you think I get any fun out of this?"

"Ah, hell, let 'em talk. What do you expect?"

"Nothing. Only I had to promise the mother of every goddam one of them that I'd look out for him and not get him hurt. And now there's not a bastard one wouldn't shoot me in the back if he got a chance."

"But what do you expect from them? What do you want? This is no picnic, you know."

They sat silent across a table from each other. Their faces were ridged and sharp, cavernous in the unshaded glare of light while they sat thinking of home, of quiet elm shaded streets along which wagons creaked and crawled through the dusty day and along which girls and boys walked in the evening to and from the picture show or to sip sweet chilled liquid in drug stores; of peace and quiet and all homely things, of a time when there was no war.

They thought of young days not so far behind them, of the faint unease of complete physical satisfaction, of youth and lust like icing on a cake, making the cake sweeter. . . . Outside was Brittany and mud, an equivocal city, temporary and twice foreign, lust in a foreign tongue. Tomorrow we die.

At last Captain Green said diffidently:

"You are alright?"

"Hell yes. They wanted to reduce me at one time, but I am alright now."

Green opened his mouth twice, like a fish, and Madden said quickly: "I'll look after them. Dont you worry."

"Ah, I'm not. Not about those bastards."

An orderly entered, saluting. Green acknowledged him and the man delivered his message stiffly and withdrew.

"There it is," said the captain.

"You'll go tomorrow, then?"

"Yes. Yes. I hope so," he answered vaguely staring at the sergeant. Madden rose.

"Well. I think I'll run along. I feel tired tonight."

Green rose also and they stared at each other like strangers across the table.

"You'll come in and see me in the morning?"

"I guess so. Sure, I'll come in."

Madden wished to withdraw and Green wanted him to, but they stood awkwardly, silent. At last Green said:

"I am obliged to you."

Madden's light-caverned eyes held a question. Their shadows were monstrous.

"For helping me get by with that dose. Court-martial, you know. . . ."

"What did you expect of me?" No more, Green acknowledged and Madden continued: "Why dont you let those women alone? They are all rotten with it."

"Easy to say." Green laughed mirthlessly. "For you, I mean."

Madden's hand strayed to the pocket of his blouse, then fell to his side again. After a while he repeated: "Well, I'll be going."

The captain moved around the table, extending his hand. "Well, goodbye."

Madden did not take it. "Goodbye?"

"I may not see you again," the other explained lamely.

"Hell. You talk like you are going home. Dont be a fool. Those birds dont mean anything by panning you. It will be the same with anybody."

Green watched his whitening knuckles on the table.

"I didn't mean that. I meant——" He could not say I may be killed. A man simply didn't say a thing like that. "You will get to the front before I do, I expect?"

"Perhaps so. But there is enough for all of us, I reckon."

The rain had ceased for some reason and there came up faintly on the damp air that sound made by battalions and regiments being quiet, an orderly silence louder than a riot. Outside Madden felt mud, knew darkness and damp, he smelled food and excrement and slumber beneath a sky too remote to distinguish between peace and war.

2.

He thought at times of Captain Green as he crossed France
seeing the intermittent silver smugness of rain spaced forever
with poplars like an eternal frieze giving away upon vistas
fallow and fecund, roads and canals and villages shining their
roofs violently; spires and trees; roads, villages, villages, towns,
a city; villages, villages; then cars and troops and cars and
troops at junction points. He saw people going about warfare
in a businesslike way, he saw French soldiers playing croquet
in stained horizon blue, he saw American soldiers watching
them, giving them American cigarettes; he saw American and
British soldiers fighting, saw nobody minding them particularly. Save the M.P.'s. A man must be in a funny frame of mind
to be an M.P. Or a nigger general. The war zone. Business as
usual. The golden age for non-combatants.

He thought at times of Green wondering where he was even
after he had got to know his new company commander. A
man quite different from Green. He had been a college instructor and he could explain to you where Alexander and
Napoleon and Grant made their mistakes. He was mild: his
voice could scarcely be heard on a parade ground and his men
all said: Wait until we get into the lines. We'll fix the son of
a bitch.

Sergeant Madden however got along quite well with his officers, particularly with a lieutenant named Powers. And with
the men too. Even after a training period with dummies in a
miniature sector he got along with them. They had become
accustomed to the sound of far guns (shooting at other
people, however) and the flickering horizon at night, they had
been bombed by aeroplanes while lined up for mess at a field
kitchen while the personnel of a concealed french battery
watched them without interest from a dug-out, they had received much advice from troops that had been in the lines.

At last they were going in themselves after a measureless
space of aimless marching here and there, and the sound of
guns though no nearer seemingly was no longer impersonal.
They tramped by night, feeling their feet sink and hearing
them suck in mud. Then they felt sloping ground and were in
a ditch. It was as if they were burying themselves, descending

to their own graves in the bowels of the wet black earth, into a darkness so dense as to constrict breathing, constrict the heart. They stumbled on in the darkness.

Out of the gratis advice they had received they recalled strongest to drop when a gun went off or when they heard a shell coming, so when a machine gun far to the right stuttered breaking the slow hysteria of decay which buried them someone dropped, someone stumbled over him, then they all went down as one man. The officer cursed them, non-coms kicked them erect again. Then while they stood huddled in the dark smelling death and the slow hysteria of decay the lieutenant ran along the line making them a brief bitter speech.

"Who in hell told you to lie down? The only guns within two miles of you are those things you got in your hands there. Feel it? this thing here—" slapping the rifles— "this is a gun. Sergeants, if another man drops tramp him right into the mud and leave him."

They plowed on, panting and cursing in whispers. Suddenly they were among men and a veteran of four days sensing that effluvia of men new to battle said:

"Why, look at the soldiers come to fight in the war."

"Silence, there!" a non-com's voice, and a sergeant came jumping along saying Where is your officer? Men going out brushed them, passing on in the pitch wet darkness and a voice whispered wickedly Look out for gas. The word Gas passed on from mouth to mouth and Authority raged them into silence again. But the mischief had been done.

Gas. Bullets and death and damnation. But Gas. It looked like mist, they had been told. First thing you know you are in it. And then——Goodnight.

Silence broken by muddy movements of unrest and breathing. Eastward the sky paled impalpably, more like a death than a birth of anything, and they peered out in front of them, seeing nothing. There seemed to be no war here at all though to the right a rumorous guttural of guns rose and fell heavily on the thick weary dawn. Powers, the officer, had passed from man to man. No one must fire: there was a patrol out there somewhere in the darkness. Dawn grew gray and slow, after a while the earth took a vague form and someone seeing a lesser darkness screamed Gas.

Powers and Madden sprang among them as they fought blindly fumbling and tearing at their gas masks, trampling each other, but they were powerless. The lieutenant laid about him with his fists trying to make himself heard and the man who had given the alarm whirled suddenly on the fire-step, his head and shoulders sharp against the sorrowful dawn.

"You got us killed," he shrieked shooting the officer in the face at point-blank range.

3.

Sergeant Madden thought of Green again on a later day as he ran over broken ground at Cantigny saying Come on, you bastards, do you want to live forever? He forgot Green temporarily as he lay beside a boy who had sold him shoes back home, in a shell hole too small for them, feeling a gale whipping his exposed knee and leg and foot as a tufted branch is whipped by a storm. After a while night came and the gale passed away and the man beside him died.

While in hospital he saw Captain Green's name in a published casualty list.

While in hospital he also discovered that he had lost his photograph. He asked hospital orderlies and nurses about it, but no one recalled having seen it among his effects. It was just as well, though. She had in the meantime married a lieutenant on the staff of a college R.O.T.C. unit.

4.

Mrs Burney's black was neat and completely air-proof: she did not believe in air save as a necessary adjunct to breathing. Mr Burney a morose silent man whose occupation was that of languidly sawing boards and then mildly nailing them together again took all his ideas from his wife, so he believed this too.

She toiled neat as a pin along the street, both fretted with and grateful to the heat because of her rheumatism, making a call. When she thought of her destination, of her changed status in the town, above her dull and quenchless sorrow she knew a faint pride: the stroke of fate which robbed her likewise made of her an aristocrat. The Mrs Worthingtons, the

Mrs Saunderses, all spoke to her now as one of them, as if she too rode in a car and bought a half dozen new dresses a year. Her boy had done this for her, his absence accomplishing that which his presence had never done, could never do.

Her black gown drank heat and held it in solution about her, her cotton umbrella became only a delusion. How hot for April, she thought, seeing cars containing pliant women's bodies in cool thin cloth passing her. Other women walking in delicate gay shades nodded to her bent small rotundity, greeting her pleasantly. Her flat 'common sense' shoes carried her steadily and proudly on.

She turned a corner and the sun through maples was directly in her face. She lowered her umbrella to it and remarking after a while a broken drain and feeling an arching thrust of poorly laid concrete she slanted the umbrella back. Pigeons in the spire were coolly remote from the heat, unemphatic as sleep and she passed through an iron gate, following a gravelled path. The rambling façade of the rectory dreamed in the afternoon above a lawn broken by geranium beds and a group of chairs beneath a tree. She crossed grass and the rector rose huge as a rock, black and shapeless, greeting her.

(Oh, the poor man, how bad he looks. And so old, so old we are for this to happen to us. He was not any good, but he was my son. And now Mrs Worthington and Mrs Saunders and Mrs Wardle speak to me, stop in to chat, chatting about this and that while there is my Dewey dead. They hadn't no sons and now his son come back and mine didn't, and how gray his face, poor man)

She panted with heat like a dog, feeling pain in her bones and she hobbled horribly across to the grouped figures. It was because the sun was in her eyes that she couldn't see, sun going down beyond a lattice wall covered with wistaria. Pigeons crooned liquid gutturals from the spire, slanting like smears of paint, and the rector was saying:

"This is Mrs Powers, Mrs Burney, a friend of Donald's. Donald, here is Mrs Burney. You remember Mrs Burney: she is Dewey's mother, you remember."

Mrs Burney took a proffered chair blindly. Her dress held heat, her umbrella tripped her bonelessly then bonelessly avoided her. The rector closed it and Mrs Powers settled her in the chair. She rubbed at her eyes with a black bordered cotton handkerchief.

Donald Mahon waked to voices. Mrs Powers was saying: "How good of you to come. All Donald's old friends have been so nice to him. Especially the ones who had sons in the war. They know, dont they?"

(Oh, the poor man, the poor man. And your scarred face! Madden didn't tell me your face was scarred, Dewey)

Pigeons like slow sleep, afternoon passing away, dying. Mrs Burney in her tight hot black, the rector huge and black and shapeless, Mrs Burney with an unhealed sorrow, Mrs Powers—— (Dick, Dick. How young, how terribly young: tomorrow must never come. Kiss me, kiss me through my hair. Dick, Dick. My body flowing away from me, dividing. How ugly men are, naked. Dont leave me, dont leave me! I know I dont love you, but dont leave me. No, no! we dont love each other! We dont, we dont! Hold me close, close: my body's intimacy is broken, unseeing: thank God my body cannot see. Your body is so ugly, Dick! Dear Dick. Your bones, your mouth hard and shaped as a bone: rigid. My body flows away: you cannot hold it. Why do you sleep, Dick? My body flows on and on: you cannot hold it, for yours is so ugly, dear Dick. . . . 'You may not hear from me for some time. I will write when I can'. . . .)

Donald Mahon hearing voices stirred in his chair. He felt substance he could not see, heard what did not move him at all. "Carry on, Joe."

The afternoon dreamed on, unbroken. A negro informal in an undershirt restrained his mower and stood beneath a tree, talking to a woman across the fence. Mrs Burney in her rigid unbearable black: Mrs Worthington speaks to me, but Dewey is dead. Oh, the poor man, his gray face. My boy is dead but his boy has come home, come home . . . with a woman. What is she doing here? Mrs Mitchell says . . . Mrs Mitchell says. . . . That Saunders girl is engaged to him. She was down town yesterday almost nekkid. With the sun on her. . . . She wiped her eyes again under inevitable spring.

Donald Mahon hearing voices: "Carry on, Joe."

"I come to see how your boy is getting along, what with everything." (Dewey, my boy)

(I miss you like hell, Dick. Someone to sleep with? I dont know. Oh, Dick, Dick. You left no mark on me: nothing. Kiss me through my hair, Dick, with all your ugly body, and lets dont ever see each other again, ever. . . . No we wont, dear ugly Dick)

(Yes, that was Donald. He is dead) "He is much better, thank you. Give him a few weeks' rest and he will be alright again."

"I am so glad, so glad," she answered pitying him, envying him. (My son died, a hero: Mrs Worthington and Mrs Saunders chat with me, about nothing) "Poor boy, dont he remember his friends at all?"

"Yes, yes." (This was Donald, my son) "Donald, dont you remember Mrs Burney? She is Dewey's mother, you know."

(. . . nice, but not forever. I wish you all the luck and love in the world. Wish me luck, dear Dick. . . .)

Donald Mahon hearing voices: "Carry on, Joe."

The way that girl goes on with men! she thought exultantly. Dewey may be dead, but thank God he aint engaged to her. "Your boy is home, he'll be married soon and everything. So nice for you, so nice. . . ."

"There, there," the rector said touching her shoulder kindly, "you must come often to see him."

"Yes, I will come often," she replied through her black bordered cotton handkerchief. "Its so nice he come home safe and well. Some didn't." (Dewey, Dewey)

The sun flamed slowly across the wistaria, seeking interstices. She would see Mrs Worthington down town now, probably. Mrs Worthington would ask her how she was, how her husband was. (My rheumatism, but I am old. Yes, yes. When we get old. . . . You are old too, she would think with comfortable malice, older than me. Old, old, too old for things like this to happen to us. He was so good to me, so big and strong: brave) She rose and someone handed her the cotton umbrella.

"Yes, yes, I will come again to see him." (Poor boy. Poor man, his face: so gray)

The lawnmower chattered slowly, reluctantly breaking the evening. Mrs Burney disturbing bees crossed the grass blindly. One passed her at the gate and remarking an arching thrust of poorly laid concrete and a broken drain she slanted her umbrella backward shielding her neat black-clad air-proof back.

Sucking silver sound of pigeons slanting to and from the spire like smears of soft paint on a cloudless sky. The sun lengthened the shadow of the wistaria covered wall, immersing the grouped chairs in cool shadow. Waiting for sunset.

(Dick, my love that I did not love, Dick, your ugly body breaking into mine, like a burglar, my body flowing away, washing away all trace of yours. . . . Kiss and forget me: remember me only to wish me luck, dear ugly dead Dick. . . .)

(This was my son, Donald. He is dead)

Gilligan crossing the lawn said: "Who was that?"

"Mrs Burney," the rector told him. "Her son was killed. You've probably heard of him in town."

"Yeh, I've heard of him. He was the one under indictment for stealing fifty pounds of sugar, and they let him go to enlist, wasn't he?"

"There were stories. . . ." The rector's voice died away.

Donald Mahon hearing silence: "You stopped, Joe."

Gilligan stood near him settling the colored glasses on his eyes. "Sure, Loot. More Rome?"

The shadow of the wall took them completely and at last he said:

"Carry on, Joe."

5.

She missed Mrs Worthington. She saw the old woman drive smoothly away from Price's in her car, alone in the back seat. The negro driver's head was round as a cannon ball and Mrs Burney watched it draw away, smelling gasoline. The shadow of the courthouse was like thinned tobacco smoke filling one side of the square and standing in the door of a store she saw an acquaintance, a friend of her son's. He had been in Dewey's company, an officer or something but he hadn't got killed, not him! Trust them generals and things.

(No, no! I wont feel like this! He done the best he could. It aint his fault if he wasn't brave enough to get killed, like Dewey was. They are all jealous of Dewey anyway: wont talk about him except that he done what was right. Done what was right! Didn't I know he would? Dewey, Dewey. So young he was, so big and brave. Until that Green man took him off and got him killed)

She felt sorry for the man, felt kindly toward him, pitying him. She stopped beside him. Yes, ma'am, he was alright. Yes, the other boys were alright.

"But then you wasn't killed," she explained. "All soldiers wasn't like Dewey: so brave—foolhardy, almost. . . . I always told him not to let that Green get him——get him——"

"Yes, yes," he agreed looking at her meticulous bent neatness.

"He was alright? He didn't want for nothing?"

"No, no, he was alright," he assured her. Sunset was almost come. Sparrows in a final delirium in the dusty elms, the last wagons going slowly country-ward.

"Men dont know," she said bitterly. "You probably never done for him what you could. That Mr Green . . . I always misdoubted him."

"He is dead too, you know," he reminded her.

(I wont be unjust to him!) "You was an officer or something: seems like you'd have took better care of a boy you knowed."

"We did all we could for him," he told her patiently. The square empty of wagons was quiet. Women went slowly in the last of the sun, meeting husbands, going home to supper. She felt her rheumatism more, now that the air was getting cooler, and she became restive in her fretful black.

"Well. You seen his grave, you say. . . . You are sure he was alright?" So big and strong he was, so good to her.

"Yes, yes. He was alright."

Madden watched her bent neat rotundity going down the street among shadows, beneath metallic awnings. The shadow of the courthouse had taken half the town like a silent victorious army, not firing a shot. The sparrows completed a final dusty delirium and went away, went away across evening into morning, retracing months: a year:

Someone on a fire-step had shouted Gas and the officer leaped among them striking, imploring. Then he saw the officer's face in red and bitter relief as the man on the fire-step, sharp against the sorrowful dawn turned screaming You have got us killed and shot him in the face at point blank range.

6.

San Francisco, Cal
April 14, 1919

Dear Margaret——

I got your letter and I intended to answering it sooner but I have been busy running around. Yes she was not a bad kid she has shown me a good time no she is not so good looking but she takes a good photo she wants to go in the movies. And a director told her she photographed better than any girl he has seen. She has a car and she is a swell dancer but of coarse I just like to play around with with her she is to young for me. To really care for. No I have not gone to work yet. This girl goes to the U. and she is talking about me going there next year. So I may go there next year. Well there is no news I have done a little flying but mostly dancing and running around. I have got to go out on a party now or I would write more. Next time more next time give my reguards to every body I know.

Your sincere friend
Julian Lowe.

7.

Mahon liked music so Mrs Worthington sent her car for them. Mrs Worthington lived in a large beautiful old house which her husband, conveniently dead, had bequeathed with a colorless male cousin who had false teeth and no occupation that anyone knew of to her. The male cousin's articulation was bad: (he had been struck in the mouth with an axe in a dice game in Cuba during the Spanish-American war) perhaps this was why he did nothing.

Mrs Worthington ate too much and suffered from gout and a flouted will. So her church connection was rather trying to the minister and his flock. But she had money—that panacea for all ills of the flesh and spirit. She believed in rights for women, as long as women would let her dictate what was right for them.

One usually ignored the male relation. But sometimes one pitied him.

But she sent her car for them and with Mrs Powers and
Mahon in the rear and Gilligan beside the negro driver they
rolled smoothly beneath elms, seeing stars in a clear sky, smelling growing things, hearing a rhythmic thumping soon to
become music.

8.

This, the spring of 1919, was the day of the Boy, of him who
had been too young for soldiering. For two years he had had
a dry time of it. Of course girls had used him during the
scarcity of men, but always in such a detached impersonal
manner. Like committing fornication with a beautiful woman
who chews gum steadily all the while. O Uniform O Vanity.
They used him but when a uniform showed up he got the air.

Up to that time uniforms could all walk: they were not only
fashionable and romantic but they were also quite keen on
spending what money they had and they were also going too
far away and too immediately to tell on you. Of course it was
silly that some uniforms had to salute others, but it was nice
too. Especially if the uniform you had caught happened to be
a salutee. And heaven only knows how much damage among
feminine hearts a set of pilot's wings was capable of.

And the shows:

Beautiful pure girls (American) in afternoon or evening
gowns (doubtless under Brigade Orders) caught in deserted
fire-trenches by Prussian Hussars (on passes signed by Be-
lasco) in parade uniform; courtesans in Paris frocks demoral-
izing Brigade staffs, having subalterns with arrow collar
profiles and creased breeches, whom the generals all think are
German spies and handsome old generals whom the subalterns all think may be German spies glaring at each other
across her languid body, while corporal comedians entertain
the beautiful-limbed and otherwise idle Red Cross nurses
(American). The French women present are either marquises
or whores or German spies, sometimes both, sometimes all
three. The marquises may be told immediately because they
all wear sabots, having given their shoes with the rest of their
clothing to the French army, retaining only a pair of forty
carat diamond ear-rings. Their sons are all aviators who have

been out on a patrol since the previous Tuesday causing the
marquises to be a trifle distrait. The regular whores patronise
them, while the German spies make love to the generals. A
courtesan (doubtless also under Brigade Orders) later saves
the sector by sex appeal after gunpowder has failed and the
whole thing is wound up with a sort of garden party near a
papier-mâché dugout in which the army sits in 60 lb. packs,
all three smoking cigarettes, while the Prussian Guard gnashes
its teeth at them from an adjacent card-board trench.

A chaplain appears who, to indicate that the soldiers all love
him because he is one of them, achieves innuendoes about
home and mother and fornication. A large new flag is flown
and the enemy fires at it vainly with .22 rifles. The men on our
side cheer, led by the padre.

"What," said a beautiful painted girl, not listening, to James
Dough who had been for two years a corporal-pilot in a
French chasse escadrille, "is the difference between an Amer-
ican Ace and a French or British aviator?"

"About six reels," answered James Dough glumly (such a
dull man! Where did Mrs Wardle get him?) who had shot
down thirteen enemy craft and had himself been crashed twice,
giving him eleven points without allowing for evaporation.

"How nice. Is that so, really? You had movies in France,
too, then?"

"Yes. Gave us something to do in our spare time."

"Yes," she agreed, offering him her oblivious profile. "You
must have had an awfully good time while we poor women
were slaving here rolling bandages and knitting things. I hope
women can fight in the next war: I had much rather march
and shoot guns than knit. Do you think they will let women
fight in the next one?" she asked watching a young man dancing, limber as a worm.

"I expect they'll have to." James Dough shifted his artificial
leg, nursing his festering arm between the bones of which a
tracer bullet had passed. "If they want to have another war."

"Yes." She yearned toward the agile prancing youth. His
body was young in years, his hair was glued smoothly to his
skull. His face under a layer of powder was shaved and pallid,
sophisticated; he and his partner blonde and briefly skirted,
slid and poised and drifted like a dream. The negro cornetist

stayed his sweating crew and the assault arrested withdrew, leaving the walls of silence peopled by the unconquered defenders of talk. Boys of both sexes swayed arm in arm, taking sliding tripping steps, waiting for the music, and the agile youth lounging immaculately said: "Have this dance?"

She said "Hel—lo," sweetly drawling. "Have you met Mr Dough? Mr Rivers, Mr Dough. Mr Dough is a visitor in town."

Mr Rivers patronised Mr Dough easily and repeated: "Dance the next?" Mr Rivers had had one year at Princeton.

"I'm sorry. Mr Dough doesn't dance," answered Miss Cecily Saunders faultlessly. Mr Rivers, well bred, with all the benefit of a year at a cultural center, mooned his blank face at her.

"Aw, come on. You aren't going to sit out all evening, are you? What did you come here for?"

"No, no: later, perhaps. I want to talk to Mr Dough. You hadn't thought of that, had you?"

He stared at her quietly and emptily. At last he mumbled "Sorry" and lounged away.

"Really," began Dough, "not on my account, you know. If you want to dance——"

"Oh, I have to see those—those infants all the time. Really, it is quite a relief to meet someone who knows more than dancing and——and——dancing. But tell me about yourself. Do you like Charlestown? I can see that you are accustomed to large cities but dont you find something charming about these small towns?"

Mr Rivers roved his eye seeing two girls watching him in poised invitation, but he moved on toward a group of men standing and sitting near the steps, managing in some way to create the illusion of being both participants and spectators at the same time. They were all of a kind: there was a kinship like an odor among them, a belligerent self-effacement. Wall flowers. Wall flowers. Good to talk to the hostess and dance with the duds. But even the talkative hostess had given them up now. One or two of them, bolder than the rest but disseminating that same faint identical odor, stood beside girls waiting for the music to start again but the majority of them herded near the steps, touching each other as if for mutual protection. Mr Rivers heard phrases in bad French and he joined them aware of his own fitted dinner jacket revealing his matchless linen.

"May I see you a minute, Madden?"

The man quietly smoking detached himself from the group. He was not big yet there was something big and calm about him: a sense of competent inertia after activity. "Yes?" he said.

"Do me a favor, will you?"

"Yes?" the man repeated courteously noncommittal.

"There's a man here who cant dance, that nephew of Mrs Wardle's that was hurt in the war. Cecily——I mean Miss Saunders——has been with him all evening. She wants to dance."

The other watched him with calm intensity and Mr Rivers suddenly lost his superior air.

"To tell the truth, I want to dance with her. Would you mind sitting with him a while? I'd be awfully obliged if you would."

"Does Miss Saunders want to dance?"

"Sure she does. She said so." The other's gaze was so penetrating that he felt moisture and drew his handkerchief and wiped his powdered brow, lightly, not to disarrange his hair. "God damn it," he burst out, "you soldiers think you own things, dont you?"

Columns, imitation Doric, supported a remote small balcony, high and obscure. Couples strolled in awaiting the music, talk and laughter and movement distorted by a lax transparency of curtains inside the house. Along the balustrade of the verandah red eyes of cigarettes glowed; a girl stooping ostrich-like drew up her stocking and light from a window found her young shapeless leg. The negro cornetist having learned in his thirty years a century of the white man's lust blinked his dispassionate eye, leading his crew in a fresh assault. Couples erupted in, clasped and danced; vague blurs locked together on the lawn, beyond the light.

'. . . Uncle Joe, Sister Kate, all shimmy like jelly on a plate . . .'

Mr Rivers felt like a chip in a current: he knew a sharp puerile anger. Then as they turned the angle of the porch he saw Cecily delicate in a silver frock fragile as spun glass. She carried a green feather fan and her slim animated turned body, her nervous prettiness filled him with speculation. The light falling diffidently on her felt her arm, her short body, suavely indicated her long virginal legs.

'. . . Uncle Bud, ninety-two, shook his cane and shimmied too . . .'

Dr Gary danced by without his glass of water: they avoided him and Cecily looked up breaking her speech.

"Oh, Mr Madden! How do you do?" She gave him her hand and presented him to Mr Dough. "I'm awfully flattered that you decided to speak to me——or did Lee have to drag you over? Ah, that's how it was. You were going to ignore me, I know you were. Of course we cant hope to compete with French women——"

Madden protested conventionally and she made room for him beside her.

"Sit down. Mr Dough was a soldier too, you know."

Mr Rivers said heavily: "Mr Dough will excuse you. How about a dance? Time to go home, soon."

She civilly ignored him and James Dough shifted his leg. "Really, Miss Saunders, please dance. I wouldn't spoil your evening for anything."

"Do you hear that, Mr Madden? The man is driving me away. Would you do that?" she tilted her eyes at him effectively. Then she turned to Dough with restrained graceful impulsiveness. "I still call him Mr Madden, though we have known each other all our lives. But then he was in the war, and I wasn't. He is so—so experienced, you see. And I am only a girl. If I had been a boy like Lee here I'd have gone and been a lieutenant in shiny boots or a general or something by now. Wouldn't I?" Her turning body was graceful, impulsive: a fragile spontaneity. "I cannot call you mister anymore. Do you mind?"

"Lets dance." Mr Rivers tapping his foot to the music watched this with sophisticated boredom. He yawned openly. "Lets dance."

"Rufus, ma'am," said Madden.

"Rufus. And you mustn't say ma'am to me any longer. You wont, will you?"

"No ma—I mean, no."

"Oh, you nearly forgot then——"

"Lets dance," repeated Mr Rivers.

"—but you wont forget anymore. You wont, will you?"

"No, no."

"Dont you let him forget, Mr Dough. I am depending on you."

"Good, good. But you go and dance with Mr Smith here."

She rose. "He is sending me away," she stated with mock humility. Then she shrugged narrowly, nervously. "I know we aren't as attractive as French women, but you must make the best of us. Poor Lee here doesn't know any French women, so we can please him. But you soldiers dont like us anymore, I'm afraid."

"Not at all: we give you up to Mr Lee only on condition that you come back to us."

"Now that's better. But you are saying that just to be polite," she accused.

"No, no, if you dont dance with Mr Lee here you will be impolite. He has asked you several times."

She shrugged again nervously. "So I guess I must dance, Lee. Unless you have changed your mind too, and dont want me?"

He took her hand. "Hell, come on."

Restraining him, she turned to the other two, who had risen also. "You will wait for me?" They assured her and she released them. Dough's creaking artificial knee was drowned by the music, and she gave herself to Mr Rivers' embrace. They took the syncopation, he felt her shallow breast and her knees briefly, and said: "What you doing to him?" slipping his arm further around her feeling the swell of her hip under his hand.

"Doing to him?"

"Ah, lets dance."

Locked together they poised and slid and poised, feeling the beat of the music, toying with it, eluding it, seeking it again, drifting like a broken dream.

9.

George Farr from the outer darkness glowered at her watching her slim body cut by a masculine arm, watching her head beside another head, seeing her limbs beneath her silver dress anticipating her partner's limbs, seeing the luminous plane of her arm across his black shoulders, her fan drooping from her arched wrist like a willow at evening. He heard the rhythmic troubling obscenities of saxophones, he saw vague shapes in the darkness and smelled earth and things growing in it. A couple passed them and a girl said "Hello, George. Coming in?" No, he told her, wallowing in all the passionate despairs of spring and youth and jealousy, getting of them an exquisite bliss.

His friend beside him, a soda-clerk, spat his cigarette. "Lets have another drink."

The bottle was a combination of alcohol and sweet syrup purloined from the drug store. It was temporarily hot to the throat but this passed away leaving a sweet inner fire, a courage.

"To hell with them," he said.

"You aint going in, are you?" his friend asked. They had another drink. The music beat on among youthful leaves, into the darkness, beneath the gold and mute cacophony of stars. The light from the verandah mounting was lost, the house loomed huge against the sky: a rock against which waves of trees broke and breaking were forever arrested, and the stars were golden unicorns neighing unheard through blue meadows spurning them with hooves sharp and scintillant as ice. The sky so remote, so sad, spurned by the unicorns of gold that neighing soundlessly from dusk to dawn had seen them, had seen her, her taut body prone and naked as a narrow pool, sweetly dividing: two silver streams from a single source. . . .

"I'm not going in," he answered moving away. They crossed the lawn and in the shadow of a crepe-myrtle one with the sound of parted breath became two and they walked quickly on, averting their eyes.

"Hell no," he repeated. "I'm not going in."

10.

This was the day of the Boy, male and female.

"Look at them, Joe," Mrs Powers said, "sitting there like lost souls waiting to get in hell."

The car had stopped broad-side on where they could get a good view.

"They dont look like they're sitting to me," Gilligan answered with enthusiasm. "Look at them two, look where he's got his hand. This is what they call polite dancing, is it? I never learned it: I would of got throwed out of anywhere I ever danced doing that. But I had a unfortunate youth: I never danced with nice people."

Through two heavy identical magnolias the lighted porch was like a stage. The dancers moved locked two and two, taking the changing light, eluding it. . . .

'. . . shake and break it, dont let it fall . . .'

Along the balustrade they sat like birds, effacingly belligerent. Wall flowers.

"No, no, I mean those ex-soldiers there. Look at them. Sitting there, talking their army French, kidding themselves. Why did they come, Joe?"

"Same reason we come. Like a show, aint it? But how do you know they're soldiers? . . . Look at them two there," he crowed suddenly with childish intentness. The couple slid and poised, losing the syncopation deliberately, seeking and finding it, losing it again. . . . Her limbs eluded his, anticipated his: the breath of a touch and an escape which he too was quick to assist. Touch and retreat: no satiety. "Wow, if that tune ever stops! . . ."

"Dont be silly, Joe. I know them: I have seen their kind too often at the canteen, acting just that way: poor kind dull boys going to war and because they were going girls were nice to them. But now there is no war for them to go to. And look how the girls treat them."

"What was you saying?" asked Gilligan with detachment. He tore his eyes from the couple. "Wow, if the loot could see this it'd sure wake him up, wouldn't it?"

Mahon sat quietly beside Mrs Powers. Gilligan turning in his seat beside the negro driver looked at his quiet shape. The syncopation pulsed about them a reiteration of wind and strings warm and troubling as water. She leaned toward him.

"Like it, Donald?"

He stirred, raising his hand to his glasses.

"Come on, Loot," said Gilligan quickly, "dont knock 'em off. We might lose 'em here."

Mahon lowered his hand obediently.

"Music's pretty good, aint it?"

"Pretty good, Joe," he agreed.

Gilligan looked at the dancers again. "Pretty good aint the half of it. Look at 'em."

'. . . oh, oh, I wonder where my easy rider's gone . . .'

He turned suddenly to Mrs Powers. "You know who that is there?"

Mrs Powers saw Dr Gary without his glass of water, she saw a feather fan like a willow at evening and the luminous plane of a bare arm across conventional black. She saw two heads as one head, cheek to cheek expressionless and fixed as a ritual above a slow synchronization of limbs.

"That Saunders lady," Gilligan explained.

She watched the girl's graceful motion, a restrained delicate abandon and Gilligan continued:

"I think I'll go closer, with them birds sitting there. I got to see this."

They greeted him with the effusiveness of people who are brought together by invitation yet are not quite certain of themselves and of the spirit of the invitation; in this case the eternal country boys of one national mental state lost in the comparative metropolitan atmosphere of one diametrically opposed to it. To feel provincial: finding that a certain conventional state of behavior has become inexplicably obsolete over night.

Most of them Gilligan knew by name and he sat also upon the balustrade. He was offered and accepted a cigarette and he perched among them while they talked loudly, drowning the intimation of dancers they could not emulate, of girls who once waited upon their favors and who now ignored them—the hang-over of warfare in a society tired of warfare. Puzzled and lost, poor devils. Once Society drank war, brought them into manhood with a cultivated taste for war, but now Society seemed to have found something else for a beverage while they were not yet accustomed to two and seventy five percent.

"Look at those kids that grew up while we were away," one advised him with passion. "The girls dont like it. But what can they do? We cant do them dances. It aint just going through them motions. You could learn that, I guess. Its—its——"

he sought vainly for words. He gave it up and continued: "Funny, too. I learned things from French women. . . . Say, the girls dont like it, do they? They haven't changed that much, you know."

"Naw, they dont like it," Gilligan answered. "Look at them two."

"Sure, they dont like it. These are nice girls: they will be the mothers of the next generation. Of course they dont like it."

"Somebody sure does, though," Gilligan replied. Dr Gary passed dancing smoothly, efficiently, quite decorous yet enjoying himself. His partner was young and briefly skirted, you could see that she danced with him because it was the thing to dance with Dr Gary—nobody knew why exactly. She was conscious of physical freedom, of her young uncorseted body flat as a boy's and like a boy's pleasuring in freedom and motion, as though freedom and motion were water, pleasuring her flesh to the interrupted teasing of silk. Her glance followed over Dr Gary's shoulder (it was masculine because it was drably conventional in black) an arrested seeking for a lost rhythm, lost deliberately. Dr Gary's partner skilfully following him watched the other couple, ignoring the girl. (If there's justice in heaven, I'll get him next time)

"Dancing with you," said Dr Gary, "is like a poem by a minor poet named Swinburne." Dr Gary preferred Milton: he had the passages all designated, like a play.

"Swinburne?" she smiled vaguely, watching the other couple, not losing the rhythm, not cracking her paint. Her face was smooth, as skilfully done and as artificial as an orchid. "Did he write poems, too?" (Is he thinking of Ella Wilcox or Irene Castle? He is a grand dancer: takes a good dancer to get along with Cecily) "I think Kipling is awfully cute, dont you?" (What a funny dress Cecily's got on)

Gilligan watching the dancers said: "What?"

The other repeated defensively: "He was in a French base. Sure he was. Two or three years. Good fellow." He added: "Even if he can dance like they do." Light, motion, sound: no solidity, a turgid compulsion passionate and evanescent. And outside spring like a young girl reft of happiness, incapable of sorrow.

". . . throw it on the wall. Oh, oh, oh, oh . . ." "——wont

never forget his expression when he said Jack, mine's got syph. Had her . . . shake it and break it, shake it. . . . First night in Paris . . . then the other one . . . dont let it fall . . . with a gun . . . twenty dollars in gold pinned to my . . . I wonder where my easy, easy rider's. . . ."

"Sure," Gilligan agreed. He wondered where Madden whom he liked was and not expecting an answer he was informed. (There she is again) Her feather fan like a willow at evening and her arm crossing conventional black a slim warm plane. Jove would have said How virginal her legs are but Gilligan not being Jove said For Christ's sake, wishing Donald Mahon were her partner or failing this, being glad he couldn't see her.

The music stopped. The dancers stood waiting its renewal. The hostess talking interminably appeared and as before a plague of people scattered before her passage. Gilligan caught, submerged beneath waves of talk suffered her, watching couples pass from the verandah onto the vague lawn. How soft their bodies look, their little backs and hips, he thought saying Yes ma'am and No ma'am. At last he walked away and left her talking, and in a swing he saw Madden and a stranger.

"This is Mr Dough," Madden said greeting him. "How's Mahon?"

Gilligan shook hands. "He's outside there, now, with Mrs Powers."

"He is? Mahon was with the British," he explained to his companion. "Aviation."

He betrayed a faint interest. "R.A.F.?"

"I guess so," Gilligan replied. "We brought him over to hear the music a while."

"Brought him?"

"Got his in the head. Dont remember much," Madden informed the other. "Did you say Mrs Powers is with him?" he asked Gilligan.

"Yeh, she came. Why not come out and speak to 'em?"

Madden looked at his companion. Dough shifted his cork leg. "I think not," he said. "I'll wait for you."

Madden rose.

"Come on," said Gilligan, "she'll be glad to see you. She aint a bad sort, as Madden can tell you."

"No, I'll wait here, thanks. But come back, will you?"

Madden looked at him reading his unexpressed thought. "She's dancing now. I'll be back before then."

They left him lighting a cigarette. The negro cornetist had restrained his men and removed them temporarily. The porch was deserted save for the group sitting on the balustrade. These the hostess with a renascence of optimism had run to earth and captured.

Gilligan and Madden crossed grass leaving lights behind. "Mrs Powers, you remember Mr Madden," Gilligan informed her formally. He was not big yet there was something big and calm about him, a sense of competent inertia after activity. He saw her colorless face against the canopied darkness of the car, her black eyes and her mouth like a scar. Beside her Mahon sat motionless and remote, waiting for the music which you could not tell whether or not he heard.

"Good evening, ma'am," he said enveloping her firm, slow hand, remembering a figure sharp against the sky screaming You have got us killed and firing point blank into another man's face red and bitter in a relief of transient flame against a sorrowful dawn.

II.

Jones challenging the competition danced with her twice, once for six feet and then for nine feet. She could not dance with the muscular facility of some of the other girls. Perhaps this was the reason she was in such demand. Dancing with the more skilled ones was too much like dancing with agile boys. Anyway, men all seemed to want to dance with her, to touch her.

Jones foiled the second time became yellowy speculative: tactical; then watching his chance he cut in upon glued hair and a dinner coat. The man raised his empty ironed face fretfully but Jones skilfully cut her out of the prancing herd and into the angle made by the corner of the balustrade. Here only his back could be assailed.

He knew his advantage was but temporary so he spoke quickly.

"Friend of yours here tonight."

Her feather fan drew softly across his neck. He sought her knee with his and she eluded him with efficiency, trying vainly to manoeuver from the corner. One importuned him from behind desiring to cut in, and she said with exasperation:

"Do you dance, Mr Jones? They have a good floor here. Suppose we try it."

"Your friend Donald dances. Ask him for one," he told her feeling her shallow breast and her nervous effort to evade him. One importuned him from behind and she raised her pretty un-pretty face. Her hair was soft and fine, carelessly caught about her head and her painted mouth purple in this light said:

"Here? Dancing?"

"With his two Niobes. I saw the female one and I imagine the male one is there too."

"Niobes?"

"That Mrs Powers, or whatever her name is."

She held her head back to see his face.

"You are lying."

"No, I'm not. They are here."

She stared at him, he could feel her fan drooping from her arched wrist on his cheek softly and one importuned him from behind. "Sitting out now, in a car," he added.

"With Mrs Powers?"

"Watch your step, sister, or she'll have him."

She slipped from him suddenly. "If you aren't going to dance. . . ."

One importuning him from behind repeated tirelessly May I cut in?   and she evaded Jones' arm.

"Oh, Lee. Mr Jones doesn't dance."

"M'I've this dance," mumbled the conventional one conventionally, already encircling her. Jones stood baggy and yellow, yellowly watching her fan upon her partner's coat like a hushed splash of water, her arching neck and her arm crossing a black shoulder, with luminous warmth, the indicated silver evasion of her limbs anticipating her partner's like a broken dream.

"Got a match?" Jones pausing asked abruptly of a man sitting alone in a swing. He lit his pipe and lounged in slow and fat belligerence among a group sitting upon the balustrade near the steps, like birds. The negro cornetist spurred his men to fiercer endeavor, the brass died and a plaintive minor of hushed voices carried the rhythm until the brass suspiring again, took it. Jones sucked his pipe, thrusting his hands in his jacket and a slim arm slid suddenly beneath his tweed sleeve.

"Wait for me, Lee." Jones looking around remarked her fan and the glass-like fragility of her dress. "I must see some people in a car."

The boy's ironed face was a fretted fatuity above his immaculate linen.

"Let me go with you."

"No, no. You wait for me. Mr Jones will take me: you dont even know them. You dance until I come back. Promise?"

"But, say——"

Her hand flashed slimly staying him. "No, no. Please. Promise?"

He promised and stood to stare at them as they descended the steps passing on beneath the two magnolias and so on into darkness where her dress became a substanceless articulation beside the man's shapeless tweed. After a while he turned and walked down the emptying verandah. Where'd that slob come from? he wondered, seeing two girls watching him in poised invitation. Do they let anybody in here? As he hesitated, the hostess appeared talking interminably, but he circumvented her with skill of long practice. Beyond a shadowed corner in the half-darkness of a swing a man sat alone. He approached and before he could make his request the man extended a box of matches.

"Thanks," he murmured without surprise, lighting his cigarette. He strolled away and the owner of the matches fingered the small crisp wood box, wondering mildly who the third one would be.

12.

"No, no, lets go to them first." She arrested their progress and after a time succeeded in releasing her arm. As they stood a couple passed them and the girl leaning to her whispered: "See right through you. Stay out of the light."

They passed on and she looked after them watching the other girl. Cat! What a queer dress she has on. Funny ankles. Funny. Poor girl.

But she had little time for impersonal speculation, being attached temporarily to Jones. "No, no," she repeated twisting the hand he held, drawing him in the direction of the car. Mrs Powers looking over Madden's head saw them.

Jones released the fragile writhing of her fingers and she sped delicately over the damp grass. He followed fatly and she put her hands on the door of the car, her narrow nervous hands between which the green fan splashed graciously.

"Oh, how do you do? I didn't have any idea you were coming! If I had I would have arranged for partners for you. I'm sure you dance awfully well. But then, as soon as the men see you here you wont lack for partners, I know."

(What does she want with him now? Watching me: doesn't trust me with him)

"Awfully nice dance. And Mr Gilligan!" (What's she wanta come worrying him now for? She bothers about him damn little while he's sitting home there) "Of course one simply does not see Donald without Mr Gilligan. It must be nice to have Mr Gilligan fond of you like that. Dont you think so, Mrs Powers?" Her braced straightening arms supported a pliant slow curve backward from her hips.

"And Rufus." (Yes, she is pretty. And silly. But—but pretty) "You deserted me for another woman! Dont say you didn't. I tried to make him dance with me, Mrs Powers, but he wouldn't do it. Perhaps you had better luck?" A dropped knee molded the glass-like fragility of her silver dress. "Ah, you needn't say anything: we know how attractive Mrs Powers is, dont we, Mr Jones?" (See your behind, the shape of it. And your whole leg, when you stand like that. Knows it, too)

Her eyes became hard, black. "You told me they were dancing," she accused.

"He cant dance, you know," Mrs Powers said. "We brought him so he could hear the music."

"Mr Jones told me you and he were dancing. And I believed him: I seem to know so much less than other people about him. But, of course, he is sick, he does not——remember his old friends, now that he has made new ones."

(Is she going to cry? It would be just like her. The fool, the little fool) "I think you are not fair to him. But wont you get in and sit down? Mr Madden, will you——?"

Madden had already opened the door.

"No, no: if he likes the music I'd only disturb him. He had much rather sit with Mrs Powers, I know."

(Yes, she's going to make a scene) "Please, just a moment. He hasn't seen you today, you know."

She hesitated, then Jones regarded the dividing soft curve of her thighs and the fleeting exposure of a stocking and borrowed a match from Gilligan. The music had ceased and through the identical magnolias the porch was like an empty stage. The negro driver's head was round as a capped cannon ball: perhaps he slept. She mounted and sank in the dark seat beside Mahon sitting still and resigned and Mrs Powers suddenly spoke:

"You dance, dont you, Mr Madden?"

"Yes, a little," he admitted. She descended from the car and turning met Cecily's startled shallow face.

"I'll leave you to visit with Donald while I have a dance or two with Mr Madden, shall I?" She took Madden's arm. "Dont you want to come in, too, Joe?"

"I guess not. Competition'll be too much for me. I'll get you to learn me in private sometime, so I can be a credit to you."

Cecily in exasperation saw the other woman stealing part of her audience. But here were still Jones and Gilligan. Jones climbed heavily into the vacated seat, uninvited. Cecily gave him a fierce glance and turned her back to him feeling his arm against her side.

"Donald, sweetheart," she said putting her arm around him. From here she could not see the scar so she drew his face to hers with her hand, laying her cheek against it. Feeling her touch, hearing voices, he stirred. "Its Cecily, Donald," she said sweetly.

"Cecily," he parroted.

"Yes. Put your arm around me like you used to, Donald, dear heart." She moved nervously but the length of Jones' arm remained against her closely as though attached by suction, like an octopus' tentacle. Trying to avoid him her arm about Mahon tightened convulsively and he raised his hand touching her face, fumbling at his glasses. "Easy there, Loot," Gilligan warned quickly and he lowered his hand.

Cecily kissed his cheek swiftly and sat up, releasing him. "Oh, there goes the music again, and I have this dance." She stood up in the car, looking about. One lounging immaculately, smoking, strolled past. "Oh, Lee," she called in happy relief, "here I am."

She opened the door and sprang out as the conventional one approached. Jones descended fatly, baggily, and stood dragging his jacket across his thick heavy hips staring yellowly at Mr. Rivers. Her turning body poised again and she said to Gilligan:

"You aren't dancing tonight?"

"Not like that," he replied. "No ma'am. Where I come from folks'd have to buy a license to dance that way."

Her laugh was in three notes and she was like a swept tree. Her eyes beneath lowered lids, her teeth between her purple lips glittered briefly.

"I think that's awfully clever. And Mr Jones doesn't dance, so all I have left is Lee."

Lee—Mr Rivers——stood waiting and Jones said heavily: "This is my dance."

"I'm sorry. I promised Lee," she answered swiftly. "But you cut in, wont you?" Her hand was briefly on his sleeve and Jones contemplating Mr Rivers yellowly repeated:

"This is my dance."

Mr Rivers looked at him and then looked quickly away. "Oh, beg pardon. Your dance?"

"Lee!" she said sharply reaching her hand again. Mr Rivers met Jones' stare once more. "Beg pardon," he muttered, "I'll cut in." He lounged onward. Cecily let her glance follow him, then she shrugged and turned to Jones: her neck, her arm took faint light warmly, smoothly. She took Jones' tweed sleeve.

"Say," Gilligan murmured watching them retreat, "you can see right through her."

"Dat's de war," said the negro driver sleeping again immediately.

13.

Jones dragged her resisting among shadows. A crepe-myrtle bush obscured the house from sight.

"Let me go!" she said struggling.

"What's the matter with you? You kissed me once, didn't you?"

"Let me go," she repeated.

"What for? For that goddamned dead man? What does he care about you?" He held her until her nervous energy deserting her left her fragile as a captured bird. He stared at the white blur which was her face and she was aware of the shapeless looming bulk of his body in the darkness, smelling wool and tobacco.

"Let me go," she said piteously and finding herself suddenly free she fled across grass, knowing dew upon her thin shoes, seeing gratefully a row of men sitting like birds on the balustrade. Mr Rivers' ironed face above his immaculate linen met her. She grasped his arm.

"Lets dance, Lee," she said thinly, striking her body sharply against him, taking the broken suggestion of saxophones.

14.

Mrs Powers had a small triumph: the rail-birds had given her a 'rush.'

"Say," they had nudged each other, "look who Rufe's got."

And while the hostess stood in effusive volubility beside her straight dark dress two of them whispering together beckoned Madden aside.

"Powers?" they said when he joined them. But he hushed them.

"Yes, that was him. But that's not for talk, you know. Dont tell them, see." His glance swept the group along the rail. "Wont do any good, you know."

"Hell, no," they assured him. Powers!

And so they danced with her, one or two at first, then having watched her firm capable performance all of them that danced at all were soon involved in a jolly competition, following her as she danced with one of their number, importuning her between dances: some of them even went so far as to seek out other partners whom they knew at all.

Madden after a time merely looked on, but his two friends were assiduous, tireless, seeing that she did not dance too long with the poor dancers, fetching her cups of insipid punch, kind and a little tactless.

Her popularity brought the expected harvest of feminine speculation. Her clothes were criticised, her 'nerve' in coming to a dance in a street dress, in coming at all. Living in a house with two young men, one of them a stranger. No other woman there . . . except a servant. And there had been something funny about that girl, years ago. Mrs Wardle spoke to her, though. But she speaks to every one who cant avoid her. And Cecily Saunders stopped between dances, holding her arm, chatting in her coarse, nervous, rushing speech, rolling her eyes about at all the inevitable men, talking all the time. . . . The negro cornetist unleashed his indefatigable pack anew and the verandah broke again into clasped couples.

Mrs Powers catching Madden's eye signalled him.

"I must go," she said. "If I have to drink another cup of that punch——"

They threaded their way among the dancers followed by her protesting train. But she was firm and they told her goodnight with regret and gratitude, shaking her hand.

"It was like old times," one of them diffidently phrased it and her slow friendly unsmiling glance took them all.

"Wasn't it? Again soon, I hope. Goodbye, goodbye." They watched her until her dark dress merged with shadow beyond the zone of light. The music swept on, the brass swooned away and the rhythm was carried by a hushed plaintive minor of voices until the brass recovered.

"Say, you could see right through her," Gilligan remarked with interest as they came up. Madden opened the door and helped her in, needlessly.

"I'm tired, Joe. Lets go."

The negro driver's head was round as a capped cannon ball and he was not asleep. Madden stood aside, hearing the spitting engine merge into a meshed whine of gears, watching them rolling smoothly down the drive.

Powers . . . a man jumping along a trench of demoralized troops caught in a pointless hysteria. Powers. A face briefly spitted on the flame of a rifle: a white moth beneath a reluctant and sorrowful dawn.

15.

George Farr and his friend the soda clerk walked beneath trees that in reverse motion swam backward above their heads, saw houses huge and dark or else faintly luminous shapes of flat lesser dark where no trees were. People were asleep in them, people lapped in slumber, temporarily freed of the flesh. Other people elsewhere dancing under the spring sky: girls dancing with boys while other boys whose bodies had known all intimacies with the bodies of girls walked dark streets alone, alone. . . .

"Well," his friend remarked, "we got two more good drinks left."

He drank fiercely, feeling the fire in his throat become an inner grateful fire pleasuring in it like a passionate muscular ecstasy. (Her body prone and naked as a narrow pool, flowing away like two silver streams from a single source) Dr Gary would dance with her, would put his arm around her, anyone could touch her. (Except you: she doesn't even speak to you who have seen her prone and silver . . . moonlight on her like sweetly dividing water, marbled and slender and unblemished by any shadow, the sweet passion of her constricting arms that constricting hid her body beyond the obscuring prehensileness of her mouth——) Oh, God, oh, God.

"Say, whatcher say we go back to the store and mix some more?"

He did not answer and his friend repeated the suggestion.

"Let me alone," he said suddenly, savagely.

"Goddam you, I'm not hurting you!" the other answered with justifiable heat.

They stopped at a corner where another street stretched away beneath trees into obscurity in uncomfortable intimacy. (I'm sorry: I am a fool. I'm sorry I flew out at you who are not at all to blame) He turned heavily.

"Well, I guess I'll go in. Dont feel so good tonight. See you in the morning."

His friend accepted his unspoken apology.

"Sure. See you tomorrow."

The other's coatless figure faded and after a while his footsteps died away. And he had the town, the earth, the world to himself and his sorrow. Music came faint as a troubling rumor beneath the spring night, sweetened by distance: a longing knowing no ease. (Oh, God, oh, God)

Chapter Six.

At last George Farr gave up trying to see her. He had phoned vainly and time after time—at last the telephone became the end in place of the means: he had forgotten what he wanted to see her for. Finally he told himself that he hated her, that he would go away; finally he was taking as much pains to avoid her as he had formerly taken to see her. So he slunk about the streets like a criminal avoiding her, feeling his very heart stop when he did occasionally see her unmistakable body from a distance. And at night he lay writhing, sleepless, thinking of her; then to rise, don a few garments and walk past her dark house to gaze in slow misery at the room where he knew she lay soft and warm in intimate slumber, then to return home and to bed, dreaming of her brokenly.

When her note came at last he knew relief sharp and bitter as the pain had been. When he took the square white paper from the postoffice, when he saw her nervous spidery script sprawled thinly across it, he felt something like a shocking silent concussion at the base of his brain. I wont go, he told himself, knowing that he would, and he re-read it wondering if he could bear to see her, if he could speak to her, touch her again.

He was ahead of the appointed time, sitting hidden from view at a turn of the stairs leading up to the balcony. The stairs were enclosed by a solid wooden balustrade and from the foot of the steps the long tunnel of the drug store swept toward light and the entrance, a tunnel filled with the mingled scents of carbolic and sweet syrups: a medicated, a synthetic purity.

He saw her as she entered the door and rising he saw her pause on seeing him, then as in a dream, silhouetted against the door and with light toying with her white dress giving it a shallow nimbus she came tap-tapping on her high heels toward him. He sat back trembling and heard her mount the steps. He saw her dress and feeling his breath catch he raised his eyes to her face as without pausing she sank into his arms like a settling bird.

"Cecily, oh, Cecily," he said brokenly taking her kiss. He withdrew his mouth. "You damn near killed me."

She drew his face quickly back to hers, murmuring against his cheek. He held her close and they sat for a long time. At last he whispered: "You'll ruin your dress sitting here." But she only shook her head, clinging to him. Finally she sat up.

"Is this my drink?" she asked, picking up one of the glassed, sweetish liquids beside him. She put the other glass in his hand. He closed his fingers on it, still looking at her.

"Now we'll have to get married," he said fatuously.

"Yes?" sipping her drink.

"Well, wont we?" he asked in surprise.

"You've got it backward. Now we dont have to get married." She gave him a quick glance, and seeing his face she laughed. Her occasional coarseness so out of keeping with her innate and utter delicacy always shocked him. But then George Farr like most men was by nature a prude. He eyed her with disapproval, silent. She set her glass down and leaned her breast against him.

"George?" she said.

He thawed putting his arm about her, but she refused her mouth. She thrust herself away from him and he, feeling that he had conquered, released her.

"But aren't you going to marry me?"

"Darling, aren't we already married now? Do you doubt me, or is it only a marriage license will keep you true to me?"

"You know it isn't." He couldn't tell her that it was jealousy, that he didn't trust her. "Its only that——"

"Only what?"

"Only that if you wont marry me, you dont love me."

She moved from him. Her eyes became dark blue. "Can you say that?" She looked away, and her movement was half shiver, half shrug. "I might have known it, though. Well, I've been a fool, I guess. You were just——just passing the time with me, then?"

"Cecily——" trying to take her in his arms again. She evaded him and rose.

"I dont blame you. I suppose that's what any man would have done in your place. That's all men ever want of me, anyway. So it might as well have been you as anyone. . . . Only, I'm sorry you didn't tell me before——sooner, George.

I thought you were different." She gave him her narrow back. How little, how——how helpless she is! And I have hurt her, he thought in sharp pain, rising and putting his arm around her, careless of who might see.

"Dont, dont," she whispered quickly turning. Her eyes were quite green again. "Someone will see! Sit down!"

"Not till you take that back."

"Sit down, sit down, please, George! Please, please!"

"Take that back, then."

Her eyes were dark again and he read terror in her face and released her, sitting down again.

"Promise me not to ever, ever, ever do that again."

He promised dully and she sat beside him. She slid her hand into his and he looked up.

"Why do you treat me like this?"

"Like what?" he asked.

"Saying I dont love you. What other proof do you want? what other proof can I give you? What do you consider proof? Tell me: I'll try to do it." She looked at him in delicate humility.

"I'm sorry: forgive me," he said abjectly.

"I've already forgiven you. Its forgetting it I cant promise. I dont doubt you, George, or I couldn't have. . . ." Her voice died away and she clutched his hand convulsively, then released it. She rose.

"I must go."

He caught her hand. It was unresponsive. "May I see you this afternoon?"

"Oh no. I cant come back this afternoon. I have some sewing to do."

"Oh, come on, put it off. Dont treat me again like you did. I nearly went crazy, I swear I did."

"Sweetheart, I cant, I simply cant. Dont you know I want to see you as badly as you want to see me; that I would come if I could?"

"Let me come down there, then."

"I believe you are crazy," she told him with contemplation. "Dont you know I'm not supposed to see you at all?"

"Then I'm coming tonight."

"Hush!" she whispered quickly, descending the steps.

"But I am," he repeated stubbornly. She looked hurriedly about the store and her heart turned to water. Here sitting at a table in the alcove made by the ascending stairs was that fat man, with a half empty glass before him.

She knew dreadful terror and she stared at his round bent head while all her blood drained from her icy heart. She put her hand on the railing lest she fall. Then this gave way to anger. The man was a nemesis: everytime she had seen him since that first day at luncheon at uncle Joe's he had flouted her, had injured her with diabolic ingenuity. And now, if he had heard——

George had risen following her but at her frantic gesture, her terror stricken face, he retreated again. Then she changed her expression as readily as you would a hat. She descended the steps.

"Good morning, Mr Jones."

Jones looked up with his customary phlegmatic calm then he rose lazily courteous. She watched him narrowly with the terror-sharpened cunning of an animal, but his face and manner told nothing.

"Good morning, Miss Saunders."

"You have the morning coca-cola habit too, I see. Why didn't you come up and join me?"

"I am still cursing myself for missing that pleasure. You see, I didn't know you were alone." His yellow bodiless stare was as impersonal as the jars of yellowish liquid in the windows and her heart sank.

"I didn't see nor hear you come in, or I would have called you."

He was noncommittal. "Thank you. The misfortune is mine, however."

She said suddenly:

"I wonder if you'll do me a favor? I have a thousand million things to do this morning. Will you go with me and help me remember them——do you mind?" Her eyes held a desperate coquetry.

Jones' eyes were fathomless, slowly yellow. "I'll be delighted."

"Finish your drink, then." George Farr's good-looking face wrung and jealous peered down at them. She made no sign yet there was such pitiful terror in her whole attitude that even George's dull and jealous intelligence took her meaning. His face sank again from view. Jones said:

"Let the drink go. I dont know why I keep on trying the things. Make myself think I have a high-ball, perhaps."

She laughed in three notes. "You cant expect to satisfy tastes like that in this place. In Atlanta now——"

"Yes, you can do lots of things in Atlanta you cant do here."

She laughed again, flatteringly, and they moved up the antiseptic tunnel of the drug store, toward the entrance. She could laugh in such a way as to lend the most innocent remark a double entendre: you immediately accepted the fact that you had said something clever, without recalling what it was at all. Jones' yellow idol's stare remarked her body's articulation, her pretty nervous face, while George Farr in a sick dull rage watched them in silhouette flatly. Then they reassumed depth and she fragile as a Tanagra and he slouching and shapeless and tweeded disappeared.

2.

"Say," said young Robert Saunders, "are you a soldier too?"

Jones lunching to a slow completion, heavily courteous, deferentially conversational, had already won Mrs Saunders. Of Mr Saunders he was not so sure. Nor did he care. Finding that the guest knew practically nothing about money or crops or politics Mr Saunders soon let him be, to gossip trivially with Mrs Saunders. Cecily was perfect: pleasantly tactful, letting him talk. Young Robert though was bent on a seduction of his own.

"Say," he repeated for the third time, watching Jones' every move with admiration, "was you a soldier too?"

"Were, Robert," corrected his mother.

"Yessum. Was you a soldier in the war?"

"Robert. Let Mr Jones alone, now."

"Sure, old fellow," Jones answered. "I fought some."

"Oh, did you?" asked Mrs Saunders. "How interesting," she commented without interest. Then: "I suppose you never happened to run across Donald Mahon in France, did you?"

"No. I had very little time in which to meet people, you

see," replied Jones with gravity, who had never seen the statue of Liberty——even from behind.

"What did you do?" asked young Robert, indefatigable.

"I suppose so." Mrs Saunders sighed with repletion and rang a bell. "The war was so big. Shall we go?"

Jones drew her chair and young Robert repeated tirelessly: "What did you do in the war? Did you kill folks?"

The older people passed on to the verandah. Cecily with a gesture of her head indicated a room and Jones entered followed by young Robert still importunate. The scent of Mr Saunders' cigar wafted down the hall, into the room where they sat and young Robert refraining his litany caught Jones' yellow fathomless eye, like a snake's, and young Robert's spine knew an abrupt faint chill. Watching Jones cautiously he moved nearer his sister.

"Run along, Bobby. Dont you see that real soldiers never like to talk about themselves?"

He was nothing loath. He suddenly desired to be in the warm sun. This room had got cold. Still watching Jones he sidled past him to the door. "Well, I guess I'll be going," he remarked.

"What did you do to him?" she asked when he had gone.

"I? Nothing. Why?"

"You scared him, some way. Didn't you see how he watched you?"

"No, I didn't notice it." He filled his pipe slowly.

"I suppose not. But then you frighten lots of people, dont you?"

"Not as many as you'd think. Lots of them I'd like to frighten can take care of themselves too well."

"Yes? But why frighten them?"

"Sometimes that's the only way to get what you want from people."

"Oh . . . they have a name for that, haven't they? Blackmail, isn't it?"

"I dont know. Is it?"

She shrugged with assumed indifference. "Why do you ask me about it?"

His yellow stare became unbearable and she looked away. How quiet it is outside, under the spell of noon. Trees shaded the house, the room was dark and cool. Furniture was slow unemphatic gleams of lesser dusk and young Robert Saunders at the age of sixty-five was framed and indistinct above the mantel: her grandfather.

She wished for George. He should be here to help her. But what could he do? she reconsidered with that vast tolerance of their men which women must gain by giving their bodies (else how do they continue to live with them?) that knowledge that the conquering male is after all no better than a clumsy tactless child. She examined Jones with desperate speculation. If he were not so fat! Like a worm.

She repeated: "Why do you ask me?"

"I dont know. You never have been frightened by anyone, have you?"

She watched him, not replying.

"Perhaps that's because you have never done anything to be afraid of?"

She sat on a divan, her hands palm-up on either side, watching him. He rose suddenly and she as suddenly shed her careless laxness, becoming defensive, watchful. But he only scratched a match on the iron grate screen. He sucked it into his pipe bowl while she watched the fleshy concavity of his cheeks and the golden pulsations of the flame in his eyes. He pushed the match through the screen and resumed his seat. But she did not relax.

"When are you to be married?" he asked suddenly.

"Married?"

"Yes. Isn't it all arranged?"

She felt slow, slow blood in her throat and wrists, in her palms: her blood seemed to mark-away an interval that would never pass. Jones watching the light in her fine hair; lazy and yellow as an idol Jones released her at last.

"He expects it, you know."

Her blood liquefied again and became cold. She could feel the skin all over her body. She said:

"What makes you think he does? He is too sick to expect anything now."

"He?"

"You said Donald expects it."

"My dear girl, I said. . . ."

He could see the nimbus of light in her hair and the shape of her, but her face he could not see. He rose. She did not move as he sat beside her. The divan sank luxuriously beneath his weight sensuously enfolding him. She did not move, her hand lay palm-up between them but he ignored it.

"Why dont you ask me how much I heard?"

"Heard? When?" Her whole attitude expressed ingenuous interest.

He knew that in her examination of his face there was calm speculation and probably contempt. He considered moving beyond her so that she must face the light and leave his own face in shadow. . . . The light in her hair, caressing the shape of her cheek. Her hand between them naked and palm-upward grew to a monstrous size: it was the symbol of her body. His hand a masculine body for hers to curl inside. Browning, is it? seeing noon becoming afternoon, becoming gold and slightly wearied among leaves like the limp hands of women. Her hand was a frail impersonal barrier, restraining him.

"You attach a lot of importance to a kiss, dont you?" she asked at length. He shaped her unresponsive hand to his and she continued lightly: "That's funny, in you."

"Why, in me?"

"You've had lots of girls crazy about you, haven't you?"

"What makes you think that?"

"I dont know. The way you——everything about you." She could never decide exactly about him. The feminine predominated so in him, and the rest of him was feline: a woman with a man's body and a cat's nature.

"I expect you are right. You are an authority regarding your own species yourself." He released her hand saying Excuse me and lit his pipe again. Her hand remained lax, impersonal between them: it might have been a handkerchief. He pushed the dead match through the screen and said:

"What makes you think I attach so much importance to a kiss?"

Light in her hair was the thumbed rim of a silver coin, the divan embraced her quietly and light quietly followed the long slope of her limbs. A wind came among the leaves without the window, stroking them together. Noon was past.

"I mean, you think that whenever a woman kisses a man or tells him something that she means something by it."

"She does mean something by it. Of course it never is what the poor devil thinks she means, but she means something."

"Then you certainly dont blame the woman if the man chooses to think she meant something she didn't at all mean, do you?"

"Why not? It would be the devil of a chaotic world if you never could count on whether or not people mean what they say. You knew damn well what I meant when you let me kiss you that day."

"But I dont know that you meant anything, anymore than I did. You are the one who——"

"Like hell you didn't," Jones interrupted roughly. "You knew what I meant by it."

"I think we are getting personal," she told him with faint distaste.

Jones sucked his pipe. "Certainly we are. What else are we interested in except you and me?"

She crossed her knees. "Never in my life——"

"In God's name, dont say it. I have heard that from so many women. I had expected better of someone as vain as I am."

He would be fairly decent looking, she thought, if he were not so fat—and could dye his eyes another color. After a while she spoke.

"What do you think I mean when I do either of them?"

"I couldn't begin to say. You are a fast worker, too fast for me. I doubt if I could keep up with the men you kiss and lie to, let alone with what you mean in each case. I dont think you can yourself."

"So you cannot imagine letting people make love to you and saying things to them without meaning anything by it?"

"I cannot. I always mean something by what I say or do."

"For instance?" Her voice was faintly interested, ironical.

Again he considered moving, so that her face would be in light and his in shadow. But then he would no longer be beside her. He said roughly:

"I meant by that kiss that someday I intend to have your body."

"Oh," she said sweetly, "its all arranged then? How nice. I

can now understand your success with us. Just a question of will power, isn't it? Look the beast in the eye and he——I mean she——is yours. That must save you a lot of your valuable time and trouble, I imagine?"

Jones' stare was calm: bold and contemplative, obscene as a goat's. "You dont believe I can?" he asked.

She shrugged delicately, nervously, and her lax hand between them grew again like a flower: it was as if her whole body became her hand. The symbol of a delicate bodyless lust. Her hand seemed to melt into his yet remain without volition, her hand unawaked in his and her body was also yet sleeping softly crushed about with her fragile clothing. Her long legs not for locomotion but for the studied completion of a rhythm carried to its nth: compulsion of progress, movement; her body created for all men to dream after. A poplar vain and pliant, trying attitude after attitude, gesture after gesture—— 'a girl trying gown after gown, perplexed but in pleasure'. Her unseen face nimbused with light and her body which was no body crumpling a dress that had been dreamed. Not for maternity, not even for love: a thing for the eye and the mind. Epicene, he thought, feeling her slim bones, the bitter nervousness latent in her flesh.

"If I really held you close you'd pass right through me like a ghost, I am afraid," he said and his clasp was loosely about her.

"Quite a job," she said coarsely. "Why are you so fat?"

"Hush," he told her, "you'll spoil it."

His embrace but touched her and she with amazing tact suffered him. Her skin was neither warm nor cool, her body in the divan's embrace was nothing, her limbs only an indication of crushed texture. He refused to hear her breathing as he refused to feel a bodily substance in his arms. Not an ivory carving: this would have body, rigidity; not an animal that eats and digests——this is the heart's desire purged of flesh. "Be quiet," he told himself as much as her, "dont spoil it."

The trumpets in his blood, the symphony of living, died away. The golden sand of hours bowled by day ran through the narrow neck of time into the corresponding globe of night, to be inverted and so flow back again. Jones felt the slow black sand of time marking his life away. "Hush," he said, "dont spoil it."

The sentries in her blood lay down, but they lay down near the ramparts with their arms in their hands, waiting the alarm, the inevitable 'stand-to'. And they sat clasped in the vaguely gleamed twilight of the room, Jones a fat Mirandola in a chaste Platonic nympholepsy, a religio-sentimental orgy in gray tweed shaping an insincere fleeting articulation of damp clay to an old imperishable desire, building himself a papier-mâché Virgin: and Cecily Saunders wondering what, how much, he had heard, frightened and determined. What manner of man is this? she thought alertly, wanting George to be there and put an end to this situation, how she did not know; wondering if the fact of his absence were significant.

Outside the window leaves stirred and cried soundlessly: Noon was past. And under the bowled pale sky trees and grass, hills and valleys, somewhere the sea, regretted him with relief.

No, no, he thought with awakened despair, dont spoil it. But she had moved and her hair brushed his face. Hair. Everyone, anyone, has hair. (To hold it, to hold it) But it was hair and here was a body in his arms, fragile and delicate it might be, but still a body, a woman: something to answer the call of his flesh, to retreat pausing, touching him tentatively teasing, retreating yet still answering the call of his flesh. Impalpable and dominating. He removed his arm.

"You little fool, dont you know you had me?"

Her position had not changed. The divan embraced her in its impersonal clasp. Light like the thumbed rim of a coin about her indistinct face, her long legs crushed to her dress. Her hand released lay slim and lax between them. But he ignored it.

"Tell me what you heard," she said.

He rose.

"Goodbye," he said. "Thanks for lunch, or dinner, or whatever you call it."

"Dinner," she told him. "We are common people." She rose also and studiedly leaned her hip against the arm of a chair. His yellow eyes washed over her warm and clear as urine and he said God damn you. She sat down again, leaning back into the corner of the divan and as he sat beside her seemingly without moving she came to him.

"Tell me what you heard."

He embraced her, silent and morose. She moved slightly and he knew she was offering her mouth.

"How do you prefer a proposal?" he asked.

"How?"

"Yes. What form do you like it in? You have had two or three in the last few days, haven't you?"

"Are you proposing?"

"That was my humble intention. Sorry I'm dull. That was why I asked for information."

"So when you cant get your women any other way you marry them, then?"

"Dammit, do you think all a man wants of you is your body?" She was silent and he continued: "I am not going to tell on you, you know." Her tense body, her silence was a question. "What I heard, I mean."

"Do you think I care? You have told me yourself that women say one thing and mean another. So I dont have to worry about what you heard. You said so yourself." Her body became a direct challenge yet she had not moved. "Didn't you?"

"Dont do that," he said sharply. "What makes you so beautiful and disturbing and so goddamned dull?"

"What do you mean? I am not used——"

"Oh, I give up. I cant explain to you. And you wouldn't understand anyway. I know I am temporarily a fool, and so if you tell me I am I'll kill you."

"Who knows? I may like that." Her soft coarse voice was quiet.

Light in her hair, her mouth speaking, and the vague crushed shape of her body. "Atthis," he said.

"What did you call me?"

He told her. " 'For a moment, an aeon I pause plunging Above the narrow precipice of thy breast' and on and on and on. Do you know how falcons make love? They embrace at an enormous height and fall locked beak to beak, plunging: an unbearable ecstasy. While we have got to assume all sorts of ludicrous postures, knowing our own sweat. The falcon breaks his clasp and swoops away swift and proud and lonely, while man must rise and take his hat and walk out."

She was not listening, hadn't heard him. "Tell me what you heard," she repeated. Where she touched him was a cool fire, he moved from her but she followed like water. "Tell me what you heard."

"What difference does it make, what I heard? I dont care anything about your jelly beans. You can have all the Georges and Donalds you want. Take them all for lovers if you like. I dont want your body. If you can just get that through your beautiful thick head, if you will just let me alone I will never want it again."

"But you have proposed to me. What do you want of me?"

"You wont understand, if I tried to tell you."

"Then, if I did marry you, how would I know how to act toward you? I think you are crazy."

"That's what I have been trying to tell you," Jones answered in a calm fury. "You wont have to act anyway toward me. I will do that. Act with your Donalds and Georges, I tell you."

She was like a light bulb from which the current has been shut. "I think you're crazy," she repeated.

"I know I am." He rose abruptly. "Goodbye. Shall I see your mother or will you thank her for lunch for me?"

Without moving she said: "Come here."

In the hall, he could hear Mrs Saunders' chair as it creaked to her rocking, through the front door he saw trees, the lawn and the street. She said Come here again. Her body was a vague white shape as he entered the room again and light was the thumbed rim of a coin about her head. He said:

"If I come back, you know what it means."

"But I cant marry you. I am engaged."

"I wasn't talking about that."

"Then what do you mean?"

"Goodbye," he repeated. At the front door he could hear Mr and Mrs Saunders talking, but from the room he had left came a soft movement louder than any other sound. He thought she was following him. But the door remained empty and when he looked into the room again she sat as he had left her. He could not even tell if she were looking at him.

"I thought you had gone," she remarked.

After a time he said: "Men have lied to you a lot, haven't they?"

"What makes you say that?"

He looked at her a long moment. Then he turned to the door again.

"Come here," she repeated quickly.

She made no movement save to slightly avert her face as he embraced her. "I'm not going to kiss you," he told her.

"I'm not so sure of that." Yet his clasp was impersonal.

"Listen. You are a shallow fool, but at least you can do as you are told. And that is, let me alone about what I heard. Do you understand? You've got that much sense, haven't you? I'm not going to hurt you: I dont even want to see you again. So just let me alone about it. If I heard anything I have already forgotten it—and its damn seldom I do anything this decent. Do you hear?"

She was cool and pliant as a young tree, in his arms and against his jaw she said: "Tell me what you heard?"

"Alright, then," he said savagely. His hand cupped her shoulder holding her powerless and his other hand ruthlessly brought her face around. She resisted, twisting her face from his fat palm.

"No, no, tell me first."

He dragged her face up brutally and she said in a smothered whisper: "You are hurting me!"

"I dont give a damn. That might go with George, but not with me."

He saw her eyes go dark, saw the red print of his fingers on her cheek and chin. He held her face where the light fell on it, examining it with sybaritish anticipation. She exclaimed quickly, staring at him:

"Here comes daddy! Stop!"

But it was Mrs Saunders in the door and Jones was calm, circumspect, lazy and remote as an idol.

"Why, its quite cool in here, isn't it? But so dark. How do you keep awake?" said Mrs Saunders, entering. "I nearly went to sleep several times on the porch. But the glare is so bad on the porch. Robert went off to school without his hat: I dont know what he will do."

"Perhaps they haven't a porch at the school house," murmured Jones.

"Why, I dont recall. But our school is quite modern. It was built in—when was it built, Cecily?"

"I dont know, mamma."

"Yes. But it is quite new. Was it last year or the year before, darling?"

"I dont know, mamma."

"I told him to wear his hat because of the glare, but of course, he didn't. Boys are so hard to manage. Were you hard to manage when you were a child, Mr Jones?"

"No, ma'am," answered Jones who had no mother that he could name and who might have claimed any number of possible fathers, "I never gave my parents much trouble. I am of a quiet nature, you see. In fact until I reached my eleventh year the only time I ever knew passion was one day when I discovered beneath the imminent shadow of our annual picnic that my Sunday School card was missing. At our church they gave prizes for attendance and knowing the lesson and my card bore forty one stars when it disappeared." Jones grew up in a Catholic orphanage, but like Henry James, he attained verisimilitude by means of tediousness.

"How dreadful. And did you find it again?"

"Oh yes. I found it in time for the picnic. My father had used it to enter a one dollar bet on a race horse. When I went to my father's place of business to prevail on him to return home, as was my custom, just as I passed through the swinging doors, one of his business associates there was saying Whose card is this? I recognised my forty one stars immediately and claimed it, collecting twenty two dollars, by the way. Since then I have been a firm believer in christianity."

"How interesting," Mrs Saunders commented, without having heard him. "I wish Robert liked Sunday School as much as that."

"Perhaps he would, at twenty two to one."

"Pardon me?" she said. Cecily rose and Mrs Saunders said: "Darling, if Mr Jones is going, perhaps you had better lie down. You look tired. Dont you think she looks tired, Mr Jones?"

"Yes indeed. I had just commented on it."

"Now, mamma," said Cecily.

"Thank you for lunch." Jones moved doorward and Mrs

Saunders replied conventionally, wondering why he did not try to reduce. (But perhaps he is trying, she added with belated tolerance) Cecily followed him.

"Do come again," she told him staring at his face. "How much did you hear?" she whispered with fierce desperation. "You MUST tell me."

Jones bowed fatly to Mrs Saunders and again bathed the girl in his fathomless yellow stare. She stood beside him in the door and the afternoon fell full upon her slender fragility. Jones said:

"I am coming tonight."

She said What? And he repeated.

"You heard that?" her mouth shaped the words against her blanched face. "You heard that?"

"I say that."

Blood came beneath her skin again and her eyes became opaque, cloudy. "No you aren't," she told him. He looked at her calmly and her knuckles whitened on his sleeve. "Please," she said with utter sincerity. He made no answer and she added: "Suppose I tell daddy?"

"Come in again, Mr Jones," Mrs Saunders said. Jones' mouth shaped You dont dare. Cecily stared at him in hatred and bitter desperation, in helpless terror and despair. "So glad to have you," Mrs Saunders was saying. "Cecily, you had better lie down: you dont look at all well. Cecily is not very strong, Mr Jones."

"Yes indeed. One can easily see she isn't strong," Jones agreed politely. The screen door severed them and Cecily's mouth elastic and mobile as red rubber shaped Dont.

But Jones made no reply. He descended wooden steps and walked beneath locust trees in which bees were busy. Roses were slashed upon green bushes, roses red as the mouths of courtesans, red as Cecily's mouth shaping Dont come.

She watched his fat lazy tweed back until he reached the gate and street, then she turned to where her mother stood in impatient anticipation of her freed stout body. The light was behind her and the older woman could not see her face, but there was something in her attitude, in the relaxed hopeless tension of her body that caused the other to look at her in quick alarm.

"Cecily?"

The girl touched her and Mrs Saunders put her arm around her daughter. The older woman had eaten too much, as usual, and she breathed heavily knowing her corsets, counting the minutes until she would be free of them.

"Cecily?"

"Where is daddy, mamma?"

"Why, he's gone to town. What is it, baby?" she asked quickly, "what's the matter?"

Cecily clung to her mother. The other was like a rock, a panting rock: something imperishable, impervious to passion and fear. And heartless.

"I must see him," she answered. "I have just got to see him."

The other said: "There, there. Go to your room and lie down a while." She sighed heavily. "No wonder you dont feel well. Those new potatoes at dinner! will I learn when to stop eating? But if it isn't one thing its another, isn't it? Darling, would you mind coming in and unlacing me? I think I'll lie down a while before I dress to go to Mrs Coleman's."

"Yes, mamma. Of course," she answered, wanting her father, George, anyone to help her.

3.

George Farr lurking along a street climbed a fence swiftly when the exodus from the picture show came along. Despite himself he simply could not act as though he were out for a casual stroll but must drift aimlessly and noticeably back and forth along the street with a sort of skulking frankness. He was too nervous to go somewhere else and time his return; he was too nervous to conceal himself and stay there. So he gave up and became frankly skulking, climbing a fence smartly when the exodus from the picture show began.

Nine thirty.

People sat on porches rocking and talking in low tones, enjoying the warmth of April, people passing beneath dark trees along the street, old and young, men and women, making comfortable unintelligible sounds like cattle going to barn and bed. Tiny red eyes passed along at mouth-height and burning tobacco lingered behind, sweet and pungent. Spitting arc lights at street corners revealed them temporarily, dogging them with elastic shadows. Cars passed under the lights and he recognised friends: young men and the inevitable girls with whom they were 'going'——coiffed or bobbed hair and slim young hands fluttering forever about it, keeping it in place. . . . The cars passed on into darkness, into another light, into darkness again.

Ten.

Dew on the grass, dew on small unpickable roses, making them sweeter, giving them an odor. Otherwise they had no odor except that of youth and growth, as young girls have no particular attributes save the kinship of youth and growth. Dew on the grass, the grass assumed a faint luminousness as if it had stolen light from day and the moisture of night were releasing it, giving it back to the world again. Tree frogs shrilled in the trees, insects droned in the grass. Tree frogs are poison, negroes had told him. If they spit on you, you'll die. When he moved they fell silent (getting ready to spit, perhaps) when he became still again they released the liquid flute-like monotony swelling in their throats, filling the night with the imminence of summer. Spring like a girl losing her girdle. . . . People passed in belated ones and twos. Words reached him in meaningless snatches. Fireflies had not yet come.

Ten thirty.

Rocking blurs on porches rose and went indoors, entering rooms, and lights flashed off here and on there, beyond smoothly descending shades. George Farr stole across a deserted lawn to a magnolia tree. Beneath it fumbling in a darkness so inky that the rest of the world seemed quite visible in comparison he found a water tap: water gushed filling his incautious shoe and a mockingbird flew darkly and suddenly out. He drank, wetting his dry hot mouth and returned to his post. When he was still again the frogs and insects teased at silence gently, not to break it completely. As the small odorless roses unfolded under the dew their scent grew as though they too were growing, doubling in size.

Eleven.

Solemnly the clock on the courthouse, staring its four bland faces across the town like a kind and sleepless god, dropped eleven measured golden bells of sound. Silence carried them away, silence and dark that passing along the street like a watchman snatched scraps of light from windows, palming them as a pickpocket palms handkerchiefs. A belated car passed swiftly. Nice girls must be home by eleven. The street, the town, the world, was empty for him.

He lay on his back in a slow consciousness of relaxing muscles, feeling his back and thighs and legs luxuriously. It became so quiet that he dared to smoke, though being careful not to expose the match unduly. Then he lay down again, stretching, feeling the gracious earth through his clothing. After a while his cigarette burned down and he spun it from two fingers and sickling his knee he reached his ankle, scratching. Life of some sort had also got down his neck, or it felt like it, which was just as bad. He writhed his back against the earth and the irritation ceased. . . . It must be eleven thirty by now. He waited for what he judged to be five minutes then he held his watch this way and that, trying to read it. But it only tantalised him: he could have sworn to almost any hour or minute you could name. So he cupped another cautious match. It was eleven fourteen. Hell.

He lay back again, cradling his head in his clasped arms. From this position the sky became a flat plane, flat as the brass-studded lid of a dark blue box. Then as he watched it assumed depth again, it was as if he lay on the bottom of the sea while sea-weed clotting blackly lifted surface-ward, unshaken by any current, motionless; it was as if he lay on his stomach staring downward into water through which his gorgon's hair clotting blackly sank straight and black and motionless. Eleven thirty.

He had lost his body, he could not feel it at all. It was as though vision was a bodiless eye suspended in dark blue space, an Eye without Thought, regarding without surprise an antic world, where wanton stars galloped neighing like unicorns in blue meadows. . . . After a while the Eye having nothing in or by which to close itself, ceased to see; and he waked thinking that he was being tortured, that his arms were being crushed and wrung from his body. He dreamed that he had screamed and finding that to move his arms from beneath his head was an agony equalled only by that of letting them stay there he rolled writhing, chewing his lip. His whole blood took fire: his pain became a swooning ecstasy that swooned away. Yet they still felt like somebody else's arms, even after the pain had gone. He could not even take out his watch, he was afraid he would not be able to climb the fence.

But he achieved this, knowing it was midnight because the street lamps had been turned off; and in the personal imminent desertion of the street he slunk feeling, though there was none to see him, more like a criminal than ever, now that his enterprise was really under way. He walked on trying to bolster his moral courage, trying not to look like a sneaking nigger, but in spite of him it seemed that every dark quiet house stared at him, watching him with blank and lightless eyes, making his back itch after he had passed. What if they do see me? What am I doing that anyone shouldn't do? Walking along a deserted street after midnight. That's all. But this did not stop the prickling of hair on the back of his neck.

His gait faltered, not quite stopping altogether: near the trunk of a tree he thought he discerned movement, a thicker darkness. His first impulse was to turn back, then he cursed himself for an excitable fool. Suppose it were someone. He had as much right to the street as the other had—more, if the other were concealing himself. He strode on no longer skulking, feeling on the contrary quite righteous. As he passed the tree the thicker darkness shifted slowly. Whoever it was did not wish to be seen. The other evidently feared him more than he did the other, so he passed on boldly. He looked back once or twice, but saw nothing.

Her house was dark but remembering the shadow behind the tree and for the sake of general precaution he passed steadily on. After a block or so he halted, straining his ears. Nothing save the peaceful unemphatic night sounds. He crossed the street and stopped again. Nothing. Frogs and crickets and that was all. He walked in the grass beside the pavement, stealing quiet as a shadow to the corner of her lawn. He climbed the fence and crouching he stole along beside a hedge until he was opposite the house, where he stopped again. The house was still, unlighted, bulking huge and square in slumber and he sped swiftly from the shadow of the hedge to the shadow of the verandah at the place where a french window gave upon it. He sat down in a flower bed leaning his back against the wall.

The turned flower bed filled the darkness with the smell of fresh earth, something friendly and personal in a world of enormous vague formless shapes of greater and lesser darkness. The night, the silence, was complete and profound: a formless region filled with the smell of fresh earth and the measured ticking of the watch in his pocket. After a time he felt soft damp earth through his trousers upon his thighs and he sat in a slow physical content, a oneness with the earth, waiting for a sound from the dark house at his back. He heard a sound after a while, but it was from the street. He sat still and calm: with the inconsistency of his kind he felt safer here where he had no business being than he had on the street where he had every right. The sound approached, becoming two vague figures and Tobe and the cook passed along the drive, murmuring softly to each other, toward their quarters. . . . Soon the night was again vague and vast and empty.

Again he became one with earth, with dark and silence, with his own body . . . with her body like a little silver water sweetly dividing . . . turned earth and hyacinths along a verandah, swinging soundless bells. . . . How can breasts be small as yours, and yet be breasts . . . the dull gleam of her eyes beneath lowered lids, of her teeth beneath her lips, her arms rising like two sweet wings of a dream. . . . Her body like——

He took breath into himself, holding it. Something came slow and shapeless across the lawn toward him, pausing opposite. He breathed again, held his breath again. The thing moved and came directly toward him and he sat motionless until it had almost reached the flower bed in which he sat. Then he sprang to his feet and before the other could raise a hand he fell upon the intruder, raging silently. The man accepted battle and they fell clawing and panting, making no outcry. They were at such close quarters, it was so dark, that they could not damage each other, and intent on battle they were oblivious of their surroundings until Jones hissed suddenly beneath George Farr's armpit:

"Look out! Somebody's coming!"

They mutually paused and sat clasping each other like the first position of a sedentary dance. A light had appeared suddenly in a lower window and with one accord they rose and hurled themselves into the shadow of the porch, plunging into the flower bed as Mr Saunders stepped through the window. Crushing themselves against the brick wall they lay clasped and involved as two worms, in a mutual passion for concealment, hearing Mr Saunders' feet on the floor above their heads. They held their breath, closing their eyes like ostriches and the man came to the edge of the verandah and standing directly over them he shook cigar ashes upon them and spat across their prone bodies . . . after years had passed he turned and went away.

After a while Jones heaved and George Farr released his cramped body. The light was off again and the house bulked huge and square, sleeping among trees. They rose and stole across the lawn, after they had passed the frogs and crickets resumed their mild monotonies.

"What——" began George Farr, once they were on the street again.

"Shut up," Jones interrupted. "Wait until we are further away."

They walked side by side and George Farr seething decided what he thought was a safe distance. Stopping he faced the other.

"What in hell were you doing there?" he burst out.

Jones had dirt on his face and his collar had burst. George Farr's tie was like a hangman's knot under his ear and he wiped his face with his handkerchief.

"What were you doing there?" Jones countered.

"None of your damn business," he answered hotly. "What I ask is, What in hell do you mean, hanging around that house?"

"Maybe she asked me to. What do you think of that?"

"You lie," said George Farr, springing upon him. They fought again in the darkness, beneath the arching silence of elms. Jones was like a bear and George Farr feeling his soft enveloping hug kicked his leg from beneath him. They fell

Jones uppermost and George lay gasping with the wind driven from his lungs while Jones held him upon his back.

"How about it?" Jones asked thinking of his shin. "Got enough?"

For reply George heaved and struggled but the other held him down, thumping his head rhythmically upon the hard earth.

"Come on, come on, dont act like a child. What do we want to fight for?"

"Take back what you said about her, then," he panted. Then he lay still and cursed Jones. Jones unmoved said:

"Got enough? Promise?"

He arched his back, writhing, trying vainly to cast off Jones' fat enveloping bulk. At last he promised in weak rage, almost weeping, and Jones removed his soft weight. George Farr sat up.

"You better go home," Jones advised him. He rose to his feet. "Come on, get up." He took George's arm and tugged at it.

"Let go, you bastard!"

"Funny how things get around," remarked Jones mildly, releasing him. George got slowly to his feet and Jones continued: "Run along now. You have been out late enough. Had a fight and everything."

George Farr panting rearranged his clothing. Jones bulked vaguely beside him.

"Goodnight," Jones said at last.

"Goodnight."

They faced each other and after a time Jones repeated:

"Goodnight, I said."

"I heard you."

"What's the matter? Not going now?"

"Hell, no."

"Well I am." He turned away. "See you again."

George followed him doggedly. Jones slow and fat, shapeless in the darkness: "Do you live down this way now? You've moved recently, haven't you?"

"I live wherever you do tonight," George Farr told him stubbornly.

"Thanks awfully. But I have only one bed and I dont like to sleep double. So I cant ask you in. Some other time."

They walked slowly beneath dark trees, in dogged intimacy. The clock from the courthouse struck one and the stroke died away into silence. After a while Jones stopped again.

"Look here, what are you following me for?"

"She didn't ask you to come there tonight."

"How do you know? If she asked you she would ask me."

"Listen," said George Farr, "if you dont let her alone, I'll kill you. I swear I will."

"Salut," murmured Jones. "Ave, Caesar. . . . Why dont you tell her father that? Perhaps he'll let you set up a tent on the lawn to protect her. Now, you go on and let me alone, do you hear?" George held his ground stubbornly. "You want me to beat hell out of you again?" Jones suggested.

"Try it," he whispered with dry passion. Jones said:

"Well, we've both wasted this night, anyway. Its too late now——"

"I'll kill you! She never told you to come at all. You just followed me: I saw you behind that tree. You let her alone, do you hear?"

"In God's name, man. Dont you see that all I want now is sleep? Lets go home, for heaven's sake."

"You swear you are going home?"

"Yes, yes. I swear. Goodnight."

George Farr watched the other's shapeless fading figure, soon it became but a thicker shadow among shadows. Then he turned homeward himself in cooled anger and bitter disappointment, and desire. That blundering idiot had interfered, perhaps he would interfere everytime. Or perhaps she would change her mind, perhaps, since he had failed her tonight. . . . Even Fate envied him this happiness, this unbearable happiness, he thought bitterly. Beneath trees arching the quiet sky, spring loosing her girdle languorous . . . her body like a narrow pool sweetly. . . . I thought I had lost you, I found you again, and now he. . . . He paused struck sharply by a thought, an intuition, and turned and sped swiftly back.

He stood near a tree at the corner of the lawn and after a short time he saw something moving shapeless and slow across the faint grass, along a hedge. He strode out boldly and the other saw him and paused, then that one too stood erect and came boldly to meet him. Jones joined him murmuring Oh hell and they stood in static dejection, side by side.

"Well?" challenged George Farr at last.

Jones sat down heavily on the sidewalk. "Lets smoke a while," he suggested in that impersonal tone which people sitting up with corpses use.

George Farr sat down beside him and Jones held a match to his cigarette, then lit his own pipe. He sighed, clouding his head with an unseen pungency of tobacco. George Farr sighed, resting his back against a tree. The stars swam on like the mast-head lights of squadrons and squadrons on a dark river, going on and on. Darkness and silence and a world turning through darkness toward another day . . . the bark of the tree was rough, the ground was hard. He wished vaguely that he were fat like Jones, temporarily. . . .

. . . Then, waking, it was about to be dawn. He no longer felt the earth and the tree save when he moved. It seemed to him that his thighs must be flattened like a table-top and that his back had cogs in to which the projections of the tree trunk fitted like the locked rims of wheels.

There was a rumor of light eastward, somewhere beyond her house and the room where she lay in the soft familiar intimacy of sleep, like a faintly blown trumpet; soon perspective returned to a mysterious world and instead of being a huge portentous shadow among lesser shadows Jones became only a fat young man in baggy tweed, white and pathetic and snoring on his back.

George Farr waking saw him so, saw earth stains on him and a faint incandescence of dew. George Farr bore stains himself and his tie was a hangman's noose beneath his ear. The wheel of the world slowing through the hours of darkness passed the dead center point and gained momentum. After a while Jones opened his eyes, groaning. He rose stiffly, stretching and spitting, yawning.

"Good time to go in, I think," he said. George Farr tasting his sour mouth moved and felt little pains like tiny red ants running over him. He too rose. They stood side by side. They yawned again.

Jones turned fatly, limping a little.

"Goodnight," he said.

"Goodnight."

The east grew yellow, then red, and day had really come into the world, breaking the slumber of sparrows.

4.

But Cecily Saunders was not asleep. Lying on her back in bed, in her dark room she too listened to the hushed sounds of night, smelling the sweet scents of spring and dark and growing things: the earth, watching the wheel of the world with the terrible calm inevitability of life turning through the hours of darkness passing its dead center point and, turning faster, drawing the waters of dawn up from the hushed cistern of the east, breaking the slumber of sparrows.

5.

"May I see him?" she pled hysterically, "may I? Oh, may I, please?"

Mrs Powers seeing her face said: "Why, child! What is it? What is it, darling?"

"Alone, alone. Please. May I? May I?"

"Of course. What——"

"Thank you, thank you." She sped down the hall and crossed the study like a bird.

"Donald, Donald! Its Cecily, sweetheart. Cecily. Dont you know Cecily?"

"Cecily," he repeated mildly. Then she stopped his mouth with hers, clinging to him.

"I will marry you, I will, I will. Donald, look at me. But you cannot, you cannot see me, can you? But I will marry you, today, anytime: Cecily will marry you, Donald. You cannot see me, can you, Donald? Cecily? Cecily?"

"Cecily," he repeated.

"Oh, your poor, poor face, your blind scarred face! But I will marry you. They said I wouldn't, I mustn't, but yes, yes, Donald, my dear love!"

Mrs Powers following her raised her to her feet, removing her arms.

"You might hurt him, you know," she said.

Chapter Seven.

1.

"Joe."

"Whatcher say, Loot?"

"I'm going to get married, Joe."

"Sure you are, Loot. Some day—" tapping himself on the chest.

"What's that, Joe?"

"I say, Good luck. You got a fine girl."

"Cecily. . . . Joe?"

"Hello?"

"She'll get used to my face."

"You damn right. Your face is alright. But easy there, dont knock 'em off. Attaboy," as the other lowered his fumbling hand.

"What do I have to wear 'em for, Joe? Get married as well without 'em, cant I?"

"I'll be damned if I know why they make you wear 'em. I'll ask Margaret. Here, lemme have 'em," he said suddenly removing the glasses. "Damn shame, making you keep 'em on. How's that? Better?"

"Carry on, Joe."

2.

San Francisco, Cal
April 24, 1919

Margaret dearest——

I miss you so much. If I could only see each other and talk to each other. I sit in my room and I think you are the only woman for me. Girls are not like you they are so young and dumb you cant trust them. I hope you are lonely for me like I am just to know you are sweetheart. When I kissed you that day I know you are the only woman for me Margaret. You cannot trust them. I told her hes just kidding her he wont get her in the movies. So i sit in my room and outside life goes on just the same though we are thousand miles apart wanting to see you like hell I think of how happy we will be. I havent told my mother yet because we have been waiting we ought to tell her I think if you think so. And she will invite you out here and we can be together all day riding and swimming and dancing and talking to each other. If I can arrange busness afairs I will come for you soon as I can. It is hell without you I miss you and love you like hell.

J.

3.

It had rained the night before but this morning was soft as a breeze. Birds across the lawn parabolic from tree to tree mocked him as he passed lounging and slovenly in his careless unpressed tweeds, and a tree near the corner of the verandah turning upward its ceaseless white-bellied leaves was a swirling silver veil stood on end, a fountain arrested forever: carven water.

He saw the black woman in the garden among roses, blowing smoke upon them from her pursed mouth, bending over them sniffing, and he joined her with slow anticipated malice, mentally slipping her straight dark unemphatic dress downward from her straight back, over her firm quiet thighs. Hearing his feet on the gravel she looked over her shoulder without surprise. Her poised cigarette balanced on its tip a wavering plume of vapor and Jones said:

"I have come to weep with you."

She met his stare, saying nothing. Her other hand blanched upon a solid mosaic of red and green, her repose absorbed all motion from her immediate atmosphere so that the plume of her cigarette became rigid as a pencil flowering its tip into nothingness.

"I mean your hard luck, losing your intended," he explained.

She raised her cigarette and expelled smoke. He lounged nearer, his expensive jacket, which had evidently had no attention since he bought it, sagging to the thrust of his heavy hands, shaping his fat thighs. His eyes were bold and lazy, clear as a goat's. She got of him an impression of aped intelligence imposed on an innate viciousness: the cat that walks by himself.

"Who are your people, Mr Jones?" she asked after a while.

"I am the world's little brother. I probably have a bar sinister in my 'scutcheon. In spite of me, my libido seems to be a complex regarding decency."

What does that mean? she wondered. "What is your escutcheon, then?"

"One newspaper-wrapped bundle, couchant and rampant, on a door-step, stone, upon a field noir and damned froid. Device: Quand mangerai-je?"

"Oh. A foundling." She smoked again.

"I believe that is the term. It is too bad we are contemporary: you might have found the thing yourself. I would not have thrown you down."

"Thrown me down?"

"You can never tell just exactly how dead these soldiers are, can you? You think you have him and then the devil reveals as much idiocy as a normal healthy person, doesn't he?"

She skilfully pinched the coal from her cigarette end and flipped the stub in a white twinkling arc, grinding the coal under her toe. "If that was an implied compliment——"

"Only fools imply compliments. The wise man comes right out with it, point blank. Imply criticism——unless the criticised is not in ear-shot."

"It seems to me that's a rather precarious doctrine for a man who——if you will pardon me——seems not exactly a combative sort."

"Combative?"

"Well, a fighting man, then. I cant imagine you lasting very long in an encounter with——say Mr Gilligan."

"Does that imply that you have now taken Mr Gilligan as a ——protector?"

"No more than it implies that I expect compliments from you. For all your intelligence you seem to have acquired next to no skill at all with women."

Jones remote and yellowly unfathomable stared at her mouth. "For instance?"

"For instance, Miss Saunders," she said wickedly. "You seem to have let her get away from you, dont you?"

"Miss Saunders," repeated Jones counterfeiting surprise, admiring the way she had turned the tables on him without reverting to sex, "my dear lady, can you imagine anyone making love to her? Epicene. Of course its different with a man practically dead," he added, "he probably doesn't care much whom he marries, nor whether or not he marries at all."

"No? I understood from your conduct the day I arrived that you had your eye on her. But perhaps I was mistaken, after all."

"Granted I had: you and I seem to be in the same fix now, dont we?"

She pinched through the stem of a rose, feeling him quite near her. Without looking at him she said:

"You have forgotten what I told you already, haven't you?" He did not reply. She released her rose and moved slightly away from him. "That you have no skill in seduction. Dont you know I can see what you are leading up to—that you and I should console one another? That's too childish, even for you. I have had to play at too many of these sexual acrostics with poor boys whom I respected even when I didn't like them." The rose splashed redly against the front of her dark dress, she secured it with a pin. "Let me give you some advice," she continued sharply. "The next time you try to seduce anyone, dont do it with talk, with words. Women know more about words than men ever will. And they know how little they can ever possibly mean."

Jones removed his yellow stare. His next move was quite feminine: he turned and lounged away without a word. For he had seen Emmy beyond the garden hanging washed clothes upon a line. Mrs Powers followed his slouching figure, then she said Oh. She had just remarked Emmy raising garments to a line with formal gestures, like a Greek masque.

She watched Jones approach Emmy, saw Emmy when she heard his step, poise a half-raised cloth in a formal arrested gesture, turning her head across her reverted body. Damn the beast, Mrs Powers thought, wondering whether or not to follow and interfere. But what good would it do? he'll only come back later. And playing Cerberus to Emmy. . . . She removed her gaze from them and saw Gilligan approaching her. He blurted:

"Damn that girl. Do you know what I think? I think she——"
"What girl?"

"Whats-her-name, Saunders. I think she's scared of something. She acts like she might have got herself into a jam of some kind and is trying to get out of it by taking the loot right quick. Scared. Flopping around like a fish."

"Why dont you like her, Joe? You dont want her to marry him."

"No it aint that. It just frets me to see her change her mind every twenty minutes." He offered her a cigarette which she refused and lit one himself. "I'm jealous, I guess," he said after a time, "seeing the loot getting married when neither of 'em want to specially, while I cant get my girl a tall. . . ."

"What, Joe? You married?"

He looked at her steadily. "Dont talk like that. You know what I mean."

"Oh, Lord. Twice in one hour." His gaze was so steady, so serious that she looked quickly away.

"What's that?" he asked. She took the rose from her dress and slipped it into his lapel.

"Joe, what is that beast hanging around here for?"

"Who? What beast?" He followed her glance. "Oh. That damn feller. I'm going to beat hell out of him on principle, some day. I dont like him."

"Neither do I. Hope I'm there to see you do it."

"Has he been bothering you?" he asked quickly.

She gave him her steady gaze. "Do you think he could?"

"That's right," he admitted. He looked at Jones and Emmy again. "That's another thing. That Saunders girl lets him fool around her. I dont like anybody that will stand for him."

"Dont be silly, Joe. She's just young and more or less of a fool about men."

"If that's your polite way of putting it, I agree with you." His eyes touched her smooth cheek blackly winged by her hair. "If you had let a man think you was going to marry him you wouldn't blow hot and cold like that."

She stared away across the garden and he repeated: "Would you, Margaret?"

"You are a fool yourself, Joe. Only you are a nice fool." She met his intent gaze and he said Margaret?

She put her swift strong hand on his arm. "Dont, Joe. Please."

He rammed his hands into his pockets, turning away. They walked on in silence.

4.

Spring, a soft breeze was in the rector's fringe of hair as with upflung head he tramped the porch like an old warhorse who hears again a trumpet after he had long thought all wars were done. Birds in the wind across the lawn, parabolic from tree to tree and a tree at the corner of the house turning upward its white-bellied leaves in a passionate arrested rush: it and the rector faced each other in ecstasy. A friend came morosely along the path from the kitchen door.

"Good morning, Mr Jones," the rector boomed, scattering sparrows from the screening vine. The tree to his voice took a more unbearable ecstasy, its twinkling leaves swirled in a never escaping silver skyward rush.

Jones nursing his hand replied Good morning in slow obese anger. He mounted the steps and the rector bathed him in hearty exuberance:

"Come 'round to congratulate us on the good news, eh? Fine, my boy; fine, fine. Yes, everything is arranged at last. Come in, come——"

Emmy flopped onto the verandah belligerently. "Uncle Joe," she said, shooting at Jones a hot exulting glance. Jones nursing his hand glowered at her. (Goddam you, you'll suffer for this!)

"Eh? What is it, Emmy?"

"Mr Saunders is on the phone; he wants to know if you'll see him this morning." (I showed you! Teach you to fool with me!)

"Ah yes. Mr Saunders coming to discuss plans for the wedding, Mr Jones."

"Yes, sir." (I'll fix you!)

"What'll I tell him?" (Do it, if you think you can. You never have come off very well yet. You fat worm)

"Tell him, By all means. That I had intended calling upon him myself. Yes, indeed. Ah, Mr Jones, we are all to be congratulated this morning."

"Yes, sir." (You little slut)

"Tell him By all means, Emmy."

"Alright." (I told you I'd do it! I told you you cant fool with me. Didn't I, now?)

"And Emmy, Mr Jones will be with us for dinner. A celebration is in order, eh, Mr Jones?"

"Without doubt. We all have something to celebrate over." (That's what makes me so damn mad: you said you would, and I let you do it. Slam a door on my hand! Damn you to hell)

"Alright. He can stay if he wants to." (Damn YOU to hell) Emmy arrowed him another hot exulting glance and slammed the door as a parting shot.

The rector tramped heavily, happily, like a boy. "Ah, Mr Jones, to be young as he is, to have your live circumscribed, moved hither and yonder at the vacillations of such delightful pests. Women, women! How charming never to know exactly what you want! While we men are always so sure we do. Dullness, dullness, Mr Jones. Perhaps that's why we like them, yet cannot stand very much of them. What do you think?"

Jones glumly silent, nursing his hand, said after a while: "I dont know. But it seems to me your son has had extraordinarily good luck with his women."

"Yes?" the rector said with interest, "how so?"

"Well (I think you told me he was once involved with Emmy?) well, he no longer remembers Emmy (damn her soul: slam a door on me) and now he is about to become involved with another whom he will not even have to look at. What more could one ask than that?"

The rector looked at him keenly and kindly a moment. "You have retained several of your youthful characteristics, Mr Jones."

"What do you mean?" asked Jones with defensive belligerence. A car drew up to the gate and after Mr Saunders had descended, drove away.

"One in particular: that of being unnecessarily and pettily brutal about rather insignificant things. Ah," he added looking up, "here is Mr Saunders. Excuse me, will you? You will probably find Mrs Powers and Mr Gilligan in the garden," he said over his shoulder, greeting his caller.

Jones in a vindictive rage saw them shake hands. They ignored him and he lounged viciously past them seeking his pipe. It eluded him and he cursed it slowly, beating at his various pockets.

"I had intended calling upon you today." The rector took his caller affectionately by the elbow. "Come in, come in."

Mr Saunders allowed himself to be propelled across the verandah, murmuring a conventional response. The rector herded him heartily beneath the fanlight, down the dark hall and into the study without noticing the caller's air of uncomfortable reserve. He moved a chair for the guest and took his own seat at the desk. Through the window he could see a shallow section of the tree that unseen but suggested swirled upward in an ecstasy of never escaping silver-bellied leaves.

The rector's swivel chair protested, tilting. "Ah, yes, you smoke cigars, I recall. Matches at your elbow."

Mr Saunders rolled his cigar slowly in his fingers. At last he made up his mind and lit it.

"Well, the young people have at last taken things out of our hands, eh?" The rector spoke around his pipe. "I will say now that I have long desired it and frankly, I expected it. Though I would not have insisted, knowing Donald's condition. But as Cecily herself desires it——"

"Yes, yes," agreed Mr Saunders slowly. The rector did not notice.

"You, I know, have been a stanch advocate of it all along. Mrs Powers repeated your conversation to me."

"Yes, that's right."

"And do you know, I look for this marriage to be better than a medicine for him. Not my own idea," he added in swift explanation. "Frankly, I was sceptical but Mrs Powers and Joe—Mr Gilligan—advanced it first, and the surgeon from Atlanta convinced us all. He assured us that Cecily could do as much if not more for him than anyone. These were his very words, if I recall correctly. And now, since she desires it so much, since you and her mother support her. . . . Do you know," he slapped his caller upon the shoulder, "do you know, were I a betting man I would wager that we will not know the boy in a year's time!"

Mr Saunders had trouble getting his cigar to burn. He bit the end from it savagely then wreathing his head in smoke he blurted:

"Mrs Saunders seems to have a few doubts yet." He fanned the smoke away and saw the rector's huge face gone gray and quiet. "Not objections, exactly, you understand," he added hurriedly, apologetically. Damn the woman, why couldn't she have come herself instead of sending him?

The divine made a clicking sound. "This is bad. I had not expected this."

"Oh, I am sure we can convince her, you and I. Especially with Sis on our side." He had forgotten his own scruples, forgotten that he did not want his daughter to marry anyone.

"This is bad," the rector repeated hopelessly.

"She will not refuse her consent," Mr Saunders lied hastily. "It is only that she is not convinced as to its soundness, considering Do—Cecily's—Cecily's youth, you see," he finished with inspiration. "On the contrary, in fact. I only brought it up so that we could have a clear understanding. Dont you think it is best to know all the facts?"

"Yes, yes." The rector was having trouble with his own tobacco. He put his pipe aside, pushing it away. He rose and tramped heavily along the worn path across the rug.

"I am sorry," said Mr Saunders.

(This was Donald, my son. He is dead)

"But come, come, we are making mountains out of mole hills," the rector exclaimed at last, but without conviction, "as you say, if the girl wants to marry Donald I am sure her mother will not refuse her consent. What do you think? shall we call on her? Perhaps she does not understand the situation, that—that they care for each other so much. She has not seen Donald since he returned, and you know how rumors get about. . . ." (This was Donald, my son. He is dead)

He paused mountainous and shapeless in his casual black, yearning upon the other. Mr Saunders rose from his chair and the rector took his arm lest he escape.

"Yes, that is best. We will see her together and talk it over thoroughly before we make a definite decision. Yes, yes," the rector repeated to flog his own failing conviction, spurring it. "This afternoon, then?"

"This afternoon," Mr Saunders agreed.

"Yes, that is our proper course. I'm sure she does not understand. You dont think she fully understands?"

(This was Donald, my son. He is dead)

"Yes, yes," Mr Saunders agreed in his turn.

Jones found his pipe at last and nursing his bruised hand he filled and lit it.

5.

She had just met Mrs Worthington in a store and they had discussed putting up plums. Then Mrs Worthington saying Goodbye waddled away slowly to her car. The negro driver helped her in with efficient detachment and shut the door.

I'm spryer than her, thought Mrs Burney exultantly, watching the other's gouty painful movements. Spite of she's rich and got a car, she added feeling better through malice, suppressing her own bone-aches, walking spryer than the rich one. Spite of she's got money. And here approaching was that strange woman staying at parson Mahon's, the one that come here with him and that other man, getting herself talked about, and right. The one everybody expected to marry him and that he had throwed down for that boy-chasing Saunders girl.

"Well," she remarked with comfortable curiosity, peering up into the white calm face of the tall dark woman in her dark dress with immaculate cuffs and collar, "I hear you are going to have a marriage up at your house. That's so nice for Donald. He's quite sweet on her, aint he?"

"Yes. They were engaged a long time, you know."

"Yes, they was. But folks never thought she'd wait for him, let alone take him sick and scratched up like he is. She's had lots of chances since."

"Folks think lots of things that aren't true," Mrs Powers reminded her. But Mrs Burney was intent on her own words.

"Yes, she's had lots of chances. But then Donald has too, aint he?" she asked cunningly.

"I dont know. You see, I haven't known him very long."

"Oh, you aint? Folks all thought you and him was old friends, like."

Mrs Powers looked down at her neat cramped figure in its air-proof black without replying.

Mrs Burney sighed. "Well, marriages is nice. My boy never married. Like's not he would by now: girls was all crazy about him, only he went to war so young." Her peering salacious curiosity suddenly left her. "You heard about my boy?" she asked, yearning.

"Yes, they told me, Dr Mahon did. He was a good soldier, wasn't he?"

"Yes. And them folks got him killed with just a lot of men around: nobody to do nothing for him. Seems like they might of took him into a house where women-folks could of eased him. Them others come back, spry and bragging much as you please. Trust them officers and things not to get hurt!" Her washed blue eyes brooded across the quiet square. After a time she said:

"You never lost no one you loved in the war, did you?"

"No," Mrs Powers answered gently.

"I never thought so," the other stated fretfully. "You dont look like it, so tall and pretty. But then, most didn't. He was so young," she explained, "so brave. . . ." She fumbled with her umbrella. Then she said briskly:

"Mahon's boy come back, anyway. That's something. Specially as he's taking a bride." She became curious again, obscene: "He's alright, aint he?"

"Alright?"

"I mean, for marriage. He aint——its just——I mean a man aint no right to palm himself off on a woman if he aint——"

"Goodmorning," said Mrs Powers curtly, leaving her cramped and neat in her meticulous airproof black, holding her cotton umbrella like a flag, stubborn, refusing to surrender.

6.

"You fool, you idiot, marrying a blind man; a man with nothing, practically dead."

"He is not! He is not!"

"What do you call him then? Aunt Callie Nelson was here the other day saying that the white folks had killed him."

"You know nigger talk doesn't mean anything. They probably wouldn't let her worry him, so she says he——"

"Nonsense. Aunt Callie has raised more children than I can
count. If she says he is sick, he is."

"I dont care. I am going to marry him."

Mrs Saunders sighed, creaking. Cecily stood before her
flushed and obstinate. "Listen, honey. If you marry him you
are throwing yourself away, all your chances, all your youth
and prettiness; all the men that like you: men who are good
matches."

"I dont care," she repeated stubbornly.

"Think. There are so many you can have for the taking, so
much you can have: a big wedding in Atlanta with all your
friends for brides-maids, clothes, a wedding trip. . . . And
then to throw yourself away. After your father and I have done
so much for you."

"I dont care. I am going to marry him."

"But why? Do you love him?"

"Yes, yes!"

"That scar too?"

Cecily's face blanched as she stared at her mother. Her eyes
became dark and she half raised her hand, delicately. Mrs
Saunders took her hand and drew her resisting onto her lap.
Cecily protested tautly but her mother held her, drawing her
head to her shoulder, smoothing her hair. "I'm sorry, baby. I
didn't mean to say that. But tell me what it is."

Her mother would not fight fair. She knew this with anger
but the older woman's tactics scattered her defenses: she knew
she was about to cry. Then it would be all up.

"Let me go," she said struggling, hating her mother's un-
fairness.

"Hush, hush. There, lie here and tell me what it is. You
must have some reason."

She ceased to struggle, becoming completely lax. "I haven't.
I just want to marry him. Let me go. Please, mamma."

"Cecily, did your father put this idea in your head?"

She shook her head and her mother turned her face up.
"Look at me."

They stared at each other and Mrs Saunders repeated: "Tell
me what your reason is."

"I cant."

"You mean you wont?"

"I cant tell you." She slipped suddenly from her mother's lap but Mrs Saunders held her kneeling against her knee. "I wont," she cried struggling. The other held her tightly. "You are hurting me!"

"Tell me."

Cecily wrenched herself free and stood. "I cant tell you. I have just got to marry him."

"Got to marry him? What do you mean?" She stared at her daughter, gradually remembering old rumors about Mahon, gossip she had forgot. "Got to marry him? Do you mean that you——that my daughter——a daughter of mine?——a blind man, a man who has nothing, a pauper——?"

Cecily stared at her mother and her face flamed. "You think—you said that to—— Oh, you're not my mother: you are somebody else." Suddenly she cried like a child, wide-mouthed, not even hiding her face. She whirled running. "Dont ever speak to me again," she gasped and fled wailing up the stairs. And a door slammed.

Mrs Saunders sat thinking, tapping her teeth monotonously with a finger nail. After a while she rose and telephoned to her husband down town.

7.

Voices: The Town:

I wonder what that woman that came home with him thinks about it, now he's taken another one. If I were that Saunders girl I wouldn't take a man that brought another woman with him right up to my door, you might say. And that new one, what'll she do now? Go away and get another man, I reckon. Hope she'll learn enough to get a well one this time . . . . Funny goings-on in that house. And a preacher of the gospel, too. Even if he is a Episcopal. If he wasn't such a nice man. . . .

George Farr:

It isn't true, Cecily, darling, sweetheart. You cant, you cant. After your body prone and narrow as a pool, dividing——

The Town:

I hear that boy of Mahon's, that hurt fellow, and that girl of Saunders' are going to get married. My wife said they never would, but I said all the time——

Mrs Burney:

Men dont know. They should of looked out for him better. Saying he never wanted for nothing. . . .

George Farr:

Cecily, Cecily. . . . Is this death?

The Town:

There's that soldier that came with Mahon. I guess that woman will take him now. But maybe she dont have to. He might have been saving time, himself.

Well, wouldn't you, if you was him?

Sergeant Madden:

Powers. Powers. . . . A man's face spitted like a moth on a lance of flame. Powers. . . . Rotten luck for her.

Mrs Burney:

Dewey, my boy. . . .

Sergeant Madden:

No, ma'am. He was alright. We did all we could——

Cecily Saunders:

Yes, yes, Donald; I will, I will! I will get used to your poor face, Donald! George, my dear love; take me away, George!

Sergeant Madden:

Yes, yes, he was alright. . . . A man on a fire-step, screaming with fear.

George Farr:

Cecily, how could you, how could you?

The Town:

That girl . . . time she was took in hand by somebody. Running around town nearly nekkid. Good thing he's blind, aint it?

Guess she hopes he'll stay blind, too.

Margaret Powers:

No, no, goodbye, dear dead Dick, ugly dead Dick. . . .

Joe Gilligan:

He is dying, he gets the woman he doesn't even want, while I am not dying. . . . Margaret, what shall I do? What can I say?

Emmy:

Come here, Emmy? Ah, come to me, Donald. But he is dead.

Cecily Saunders:

George, my lover, my poor dear. . . . What have we done?

Mrs Burney:

Dewey, Dewey, so brave, so young. . . .

(This was Donald, my son. He is dead)

8.

Mrs Powers mounted the stairs under Mrs Saunders' curious eyes. The older woman had been cold, almost rude, but Mrs Powers had won her point and choosing Cecily's door from her mother's directions she knocked. . . . After a while she knocked again and called:

"Miss Saunders."

Silence was again a hushed tense interval then Cecily's muffled voice:

"Go away."

"Please," she insisted. "I want to see you a moment."

"No, no. Go away."

"But I must see you." There was no reply and she added: "I have just talked to your mother, and to Dr Mahon. Let me come in, wont you?"

She heard movement, a bed; then another interval. Fool, taking time to powder her face. But you would too, she told herself. The door opened under her hand.

Powder only made the traces of tears more visible and Cecily turned her back as Mrs Powers entered the room. She could see the indentation of a body on the bed, and a crumpled pillow. Mrs Powers not being offered a chair sat on the foot of the bed and Cecily across the room, leaning in a window and staring out, said ungraciously: "What do you want?"

How like her this room is! thought the caller observing pale maple and a triple mirrored dressing table bearing a collection of fragile crystal, and careless delicate clothing about on chairs, on the floor. On a chest of drawers was a small camera picture, framed.

"May I look?" she asked knowing instinctively who it was. Cecily stubbornly presenting her back in a thin formless

garment through which light from the window passed revealing her narrow torso, made no reply. Mrs Powers approached
and saw Donald Mahon bareheaded, in a shabby unbuttoned tunic standing before a corrugated iron wall, carrying
a small resigned dog casually by the scruff of the neck, like a
hand-bag.

"That's so typical of him, isn't it?" she commented and
Cecily said rudely:

"What do you want with me?"

"That's exactly what your mother asked me, you know. She
seemed to think I was interfering too."

"Well, aren't you? Nobody asked you to come here." Cecily
turned leaning her thigh against the window ledge.

"I dont think its interference when its warranted, though.
Do you?"

"Warranted? Who asked you to interfere? Did Donald do
it, or are you trying to scare me off? You needn't tell me
Donald asked you to get him out of it: it will be a lie."

"But I'm not: I dont intend to. I'm trying to help you
both."

"Oh, you are against me. Everybody's against me except
Donald. And you keep him shut up like a——a prisoner." She
turned quickly and leaned her head against the window.

Mrs Powers sat quietly examining her, her frail indicated
body under the silly garment she wore, a webby cloying thing
worse than nothing and a fit complement to the single be-
laced garment it revealed above the long hushed gleams of her
stockings. . . . If Cellini had been a hermit-priest he might
have imagined her body, Mrs Powers thought, mildly wishing she could see her naked. At last she rose from the bed
and crossed to the window. Cecily kept her head stubbornly
averted and expecting tears she touched the girl's shoulder.

"Cecily," she said quietly.

Her green eyes were dry, stony, and she moved swiftly
across the room with her delicate narrow stride. She stood
holding the door open. Mrs Powers at the window did not
accept. Did she ever, ever forget herself? she wondered, observing the studied grace of the girl's body turned on the laxed
ball of a thigh. Cecily met her gaze with one of haughty commanding scorn.

"Wont you even leave the room when you are asked?" she said making her swift coarse voice sound measured and cold.

Mrs Powers thinking Oh hell, what's the use? moved so as to lean her thigh against the bed. Cecily without changing her posture moved the door for emphasis. Standing quietly, watching her studied fragility (her legs are rather sweet, she admitted, but why all this posing for me? I'm not a man) Mrs Powers ran her palm slowly along the smooth wood. Suddenly the other slammed the door and returned to the window. Mrs Powers followed.

"Cecily, why cant we talk about it sensibly?" The girl made no reply, ignoring her, crumpling the curtain in her fingers. "Miss Saunders?"

"Why cant you go away and leave me alone?" Cecily flared suddenly, flaming out at her. "I dont want to talk to you about it. I dont want to talk to anyone about it. Why do you come to me?" Her eyes darkened: they were no longer hard. "If you want him, take him then. You have every chance you could want, keeping him shut up there so that even I cant see him!"

"But I dont want him. I am trying to straighten things out for him. Dont you know that if I had wanted him I would have married him before I brought him home?"

"You tried, and couldn't. That's why you didn't. Oh, dont say it wasn't," she rushed on as the other would have spoken. "I saw it that first day. That you were after him. And if you aren't, why do you keep on staying here?"

"You know that's a lie," Mrs Powers replied calmly.

"Then what makes you so interested in him, if you aren't in love with him?"

(This is hopeless) She put her hand on the other's arm, Cecily shrank quickly away and she returned to lean again against the bed. She said:

"Your mother is against this, and Donald's father expects it. But what chance will you have against your mother?" (Against yourself?)

"I certainly dont need any advice from you." Cecily turned her head, her haughtiness, her anger, were gone and in their place was a thin hopeless despair. Even her voice, her whole attitude, had changed. "Dont you see how miserable I am?" she said pitifully. "I didn't mean to be rude to you, but I dont know what to do, I dont know. . . . I am in so much trouble: something terrible has happened to me. Please!"

Mrs Powers seeing her face went to her quickly, putting her arm about the girl's narrow shoulders. Cecily avoided her. "Please, please go!"

"Tell me what it is."

"No, no, I cant. Please——"

They paused listening. Footsteps approaching stopped beyond the door. A knock and her father's voice called her name.

"Yes?"

"Dr Mahon is downstairs. Can you come down?"

The two women stared at each other.

"Come," said Mrs Powers.

Cecily's eyes went dark again and she whispered No, No, No! trembling.

"Sis," her father repeated.

"Say Yes," Mrs Powers whispered.

"Yes, daddy. I'm coming."

"Alright." The footsteps retreated and Mrs Powers drew Cecily toward the door. The girl resisted.

"I cant go like this," she said hysterically.

"Yes you can. Its alright. Come."

Mrs Saunders sitting militant, formal and erect upon her chair was saying as they entered:

"May I ask what this—this woman has to do with it?"

Her husband chewed a cigar. Light falling upon the rector's face held it like a gray bitten mask. Cecily ran to him. "Uncle Joe!" she cried.

"Cecily!" her mother said sharply.

"What do you mean, coming down like that?"

The rector rose huge and black, embracing her.

"Uncle Joe!" she repeated, clinging to him.

"Now, Robert——" Mrs Saunders began. But the rector interrupted her.

"Cecily," he said raising her face. She twisted her chin and hid her face against his coat.

"Robert," said Mrs Saunders.

The rector spoke grayly. "Cecily, we have talked it over together, and we think——your mother and father——"

She moved in her silly revealing garment. "Daddy?" she exclaimed staring at her father. He would not meet her gaze but sat slowly twisting his cigar. The rector's voice continued:

"We think that you will only——that you—— They say that Donald is going to die, Cecily," he finished.

Lithe as a sapling she thrust herself backward against his arm, bending, to see his face, staring at him. "Oh, uncle Joe! Have you gone back on me, too?" she cried passionately.

9.

George Farr had been quite drunk for a week. His friend the drug clerk thought that he was going crazy. He had become a local landmark, a tradition: even the town soaks began to look upon him with respect, calling him by his first name, swearing undying devotion to him.

In the intervals of belligerent or rollicking or maudlin inebriation he knew periods of devastating despair like a monstrous bliss, like that of a caged animal, of a man being slowly tortured to death: a minor monotony of pain. As a rule though, he managed to stay fairly drunk: Her narrow body, sweetly dividing, naked . . . have another drink. . . . I'll kill you if you keep on fooling around her . . . my girl, my girl. . . . Her narrow . . . 'nother drink. . . . Oh, God, oh, God . . . sweetly dividing for another . . . have drink: what hell I care? Oh, God, oh Godohgod. . . .

Though 'nice' people no longer spoke to him on the streets he was, after a fashion, cared for and protected by casual acquaintances and friends both black and white, as is the manner of small towns particularly and of the 'inferior' classes anywhere.

He sat glassy-eyed among fried smells, among noises, at an oilcloth covered table.

'Clu—hoverrrr blarrr—sums, clo——ver blarrr—sum-mmmssss' sang a nasal voice terribly, the melody ticked off at spaced intervals with a small monotonous sound, like a clock-bomb going off. Like this: Clo(tick)ver(tick)rrr(tick) (tick) bl(tick)ars(tick)ummm(tick)msss. Beside him sat two of his new companions quarrelling, spitting, holding hands and weeping over the cracked interminability of the phonograph record. 'Clo——verrrr blar——sums' it repeated with sac-charine passion; when it ran down they repaired to a filthy alley behind a filthier kitchen to drink of George Farr's whis-key. Then they returned and played the record through again, clutching hands while frank tears slid down their other-wise unwashed cheeks. 'Clooooover blaaaaaarsummmm-mzzz. . . .' Truly, vice is a dull and decorous thing: no life in the world is as hard, requiring as much sheer physical and moral strength as the so-called 'primrose path.' Being 'good' is much less trouble. 'Clo——ver blar——sums. . . .'

. . . After a time his attention was called to the fact that someone had been annoying him for some time. Focusing his eyes he at last recognised the proprietor in an apron on which he must have wiped his dishes for weeks. "What'n'ell y'want?" he asked with feeble liquid belligerence and the man finally ex-plained to him that he was wanted on the telephone in a neighboring drug store. He rose, pulling himself together. 'Clu——hooooover blar——sums. . . .'

After a few years he languished from a telephone mouth-piece, holding himself erect, watching without interest a light globe over the prescription desk describing slow concentric circles.

"George?" There was something in the unknown voice, such anguish, as to almost shock him sober. "George!"

"This George . . . hello. . . ."

"George, its Cecily. Cecily. . . ."

Drunkenness left him like a retreating wave. He could feel his heart stop then surge, deafening him, blinding him with his own blood.

"George . . . do you hear me?"

(Ah, George, to have been drunk now!) (Cecily, oh Cecily!) "Yes! Yes!" gripping the instrument as though this would keep her against escape. "Yes, Cecily? Cecily! Its George. . . ."

"Come to me, now; at once."

"Yes, yes. Now?"

"Come, George, darling. Hurry, hurry. . . ."

"Yes!" he cried again. "Hello, hello!" The line made no re-sponse. He waited, but it was dead. His heart pounded and pounded, hotly: he could taste his own hot bitter blood in his throat. (Cecily! oh Cecily!)

He plunged down the length of the store and while a middle-aged clerk filling a prescription poised his bottle to watch in dull amazement George Farr tore his shirt open at the throat and thrust his whole head beneath a gushing water tap in a frenzy of activity.

(Cecily, oh Cecily!)

10.

He seemed so old, so tired as he sat at the head of the table toying with his food, as if the very fiber of him had lost all resilience. Gilligan ate with his usual informal appetite and Donald and Emmy sat side by side, so that Emmy could help him. Emmy enjoyed mothering him, now that she could never have him again for a lover, she objected with passionate ardor when Mrs Powers offered to relieve her. The Donald she had known was dead: this one was but a sorry substitute, but Emmy was going to make the best of it, as women will. She had even got accustomed to taking her food after it had cooled.

Mrs Powers sat watching them. Emmy's shock of no-particular-color hair was near his worn head in intent devotion, her labor-worried hand seemed to have an eye of its own, so quick, so tender it was to anticipate him and guide his hand with the food she had prepared for him. Mrs Powers wondered which Donald Emmy loved the more, wondering if she had not perhaps forgotten the former one completely save as a symbol of sorrow. Then the amazing logical thought occurred to her that here was the woman for Donald to marry.

Of course she was. Why had no one thought of that before? Then she told herself that no one had done very much thinking during the whole affair, that it had got on without any particular drain on any intelligence. Why did we all take it for granted that he must marry Cecily and no other? Yet we all accepted it as an arbitrary fact and off we went with our eyes closed and our mouths open, like hounds in full cry.

But would Emmy take him? Wouldn't she be so frightened at the prospect that she'd be too self-conscious with him afterward to care for him as skilfully as she does now; wouldn't it cause her to confuse in her mind to his detriment two separate Donalds——a lover and an invalid? I wonder what Joe will think about it.

She looked at Emmy impersonal as Omnipotence, helping Donald with self-effacing skill, seeming to envelope him yet never touching him. Anyway, I'll ask her, she thought sipping her tea.

Night was come. Tree frogs remembering last night's rain resumed their monotonous molding of liquid beads of sound; grass blades and leaves losing shapes of solidity gained shapes of sound—the still suspire of the earth, of ground preparing for slumber; flowers by day spikes of bloom became with night spikes of scent; the silver tree at the corner of the house hushed its never still, never escaping ecstasy. Already toads hopped along concrete pavement drinking prisoned heat through their dragging bellies.

Suddenly the rector started from his dream. "Tut, tut. We are making mountains out of mole hills, as usual. If she wants to marry Donald, I am sure her people will not withhold their consent always. Why should they object to their daughter marrying him? Do you know——"

"Hush!" she said. He looked up at her startled, then seeing her warning glance touch Mahon's oblivious head he understood. She saw Emmy's wide shocked eyes on her, and rose at her place. "You are through, aren't you?" she said to the rector. "Suppose we go to the study."

Mahon sat quiet, chewing. She could not tell whether or not he had heard. She passed behind Emmy and leaning to her whispered "I want to speak to you. Dont say anything to Donald."

The rector preceding her fumbled the light on in the study.

"You must be careful," she told him, "how you talk before him, how you tell him."

"Yes," he agreed apologetically. "I was so deep in thought. . . ."

"I know you were. I dont think it is necessary to tell him at all, until he asks."

"And that will never be. She loves Donald: she will not let her people prevent her marrying him. I am not customarily in favor of such a procedure as instigating a young woman to marry against her parents' wishes, but in this case. . . . You do not think that I am inconsistent, that I am partial because my son is involved?"

"No, no, of course not."

"Dont you agree with me, that she will insist on the wedding?"

"Yes indeed." What else could she say?

Gilligan and Mahon had gone and Emmy was clearing the table when she returned. Emmy whirled upon her:

"She aint going to take him? What was uncle Joe saying?"

"Her people dont like the idea. That's all. She hasn't refused. But I think we had better stop it now, Emmy. She changes her mind so often, nobody can tell what she'll do."

Emmy turned back to the table, lowering her head, scraping a plate. Mrs Powers watched her busy elbow, hearing the little clashing noises of china and silver. A bowl of white roses shattered slowly upon the center of the table.

"What do you think, Emmy?"

"I dont know," Emmy replied sullenly. "She aint my kind. I dont know nothing about it."

Mrs Powers approached the table.

"Emmy," she said. The other did not raise her head, made no reply. She turned the girl gently by the shoulder. "Would you marry him, Emmy?"

Emmy straightened hotly, clutching a plate and a fork.

"Me? Me marry him? Me take another's leavings? (Donald, Donald) And her leavings at that, her that's run after every boy in town, dressed up in her silk clothes?"

Mrs Powers moved back to the door and Emmy scraped dishes fiercely. This plate became blurred, Emmy blinked and saw something splash on it. She shant see me cry! she whispered passionately, bending her head lower, waiting for Mrs Powers to ask her again. (Donald, Donald. . . .)

When she was young, going to school along streets in the spring, having to wear coarse dresses and shoes while other girls wore silk and thin leather; being not pretty at all while other girls were pretty——

Walking home, to where work awaited her while other girls were riding in cars or having ice cream or talking to boys and dancing with them, with boys that had no use for her, sometimes he would step out beside her, so still, so quick, all of a sudden——and she didn't mind not having silk.

And when they swam and fished and roamed the woods together she forgot she wasn't pretty, even. Because he was beautiful, with his body all brown and quick, so still—— making her feel beautiful too.

And when he said Come here, Emmy she went to him and wet grass and dew under her and over her his head with the whole sky for a crown, and the moon running on them like a water that wasn't wet and that you couldn't feel. . . .

Marry him? Yes! Yes! Let him be sick: she would cure him; let him be a Donald that had forgotten her——she had not forgotten: she could remember enough for both of them. Yes! Yes! she cried soundlessly, stacking dishes, waiting for Mrs Powers to ask her again. Her red hands were blind, tears splashed fatly on her wrists. Yes! Yes! trying to think it so loudly that the other must hear. She shant see me cry! she whispered again. But the other woman only stood in the door watching her busy back, so she gathered up the dishes slowly, there being no reason to linger any longer. Keeping her head averted she carried the dishes to the pantry door, slowly, waiting for the other to speak again. But the other woman said nothing and Emmy left the room, her pride forbidding her to let the other see her tears.

II.

The study was dark when she passed but she could see the rector's head in dim silhouette against the more spacious darkness outside the window. She passed slowly onto the verandah. Leaning her quiet tall body against a column in the darkness beyond the fan of light from the door she listened to the hushed myriad life of night-things, to the slow voices of people passing unseen along an unseen street, watching the hurried staring twin eyes of motor cars like restless insects. A car slowing drew up to the corner and after a while a dark figure came along the pale gravel of the path, hurried yet diffident. It paused and screamed delicately in midpath, then sped on toward the steps where it stopped again and Mrs Powers stepped forward from beside her post.

"Oh," gasped Miss Cecily Saunders, starting back, lifting her hand slimly against her dark dress. "Mrs Powers?"

"Yes. Come in, wont you?"

Cecily ran with nervous grace up the steps. "It was a f-frog," she explained between her quick respirations, "I nearly stepped——uhhh!" She shuddered, a slim muted flame hushed darkly in dark clothing. "Is uncle Joe here? May I——" her voice died away diffidently.

"He is in his study," she answered. What has happened to her? she thought. Cecily stood so that light from the door fell full on her: there was in her face a thin nervous despair, a hopeless recklessness, and she stared into the other woman's shadowed face for a long moment.

Then she said Thank you, thank you, suddenly, hysterically, and ran quickly into the house. Mrs Powers looked after her, then following saw her dark dress. She is going away, Mrs Powers thought with conviction.

Cecily flew on ahead like a slim dark bird, into the unlighted study. "Uncle Joe?" she said poised, touching either side of the door-frame. The rector's chair creaked suddenly.

"Eh?" he said and the girl sailed across the room like a bat, dark in the darkness, sinking at his feet, clutching his knees. He tried to raise her but she clung to his legs the tighter, burrowing her head into his lap.

"Uncle Joe, forgive me, forgive me!"

"Yes, yes. I knew you would come to us. I told them——"

"No, no, I——I——You have always been so good, so sweet to me, that I couldn't. . . ." She clutched him again fiercely.

"Cecily, what is it? Now, now, you mustn't cry about it. Come now, what is it?" Knowing a sharp premonition he raised her face trying to see it. But it was only a formless soft blur warmly in his hands.

"Say you forgive me first, dear uncle Joe. Wont you? Say it, say it. If you wont forgive me, I dont know what'll become of me." His hands slipping down felt her delicate tense shoulders and he said:

"Of course I forgive you."

"Thank you. Oh, thank you. You are so kind——" she caught his hand holding it against her mouth.

"What is it, Cecily?" he asked quietly, trying to soothe her. She raised her head. "I am going away."

"Then you aren't going to marry Donald?"

She lowered her head to his knees again, clutching his hand in her long nervous fingers, holding it against her face.

"I cannot, I cannot. I am a—I am not a good woman anymore, dear uncle Joe. Forgive me. Forgive me. . . ."

He withdrew his hand and she let herself be raised to her feet feeling his arms, his huge kind body. "There, there," patting her back with his gentle heavy hand. "Dont cry."

"I must go," she said at last, moving slimly and darkly against his bulk. He released her. She clutched his hand again, sharply, letting it go. "Goodbye," she whispered, and fled swift and dark as a bird, graceful to a delicate tapping of heels, as she had come. She passed Mrs Powers on the porch without seeing her and sped down the steps, and the other woman watched her slim dark figure disappear. . . . After an interval the car that had stopped at the corner of the lawn flashed its lights on again and drove away. . . .

She pressed the light switch and entered the study. The rector stared at her as she approached the desk, quiet and hopeless.

"Cecily has broken the engagement, Margaret. So the wedding is off."

"Nonsense," she told him sharply, touching him with her firm hand. "I'm going to marry him myself. I intended to all the time. Didn't you suspect?"

12.

San Francisco, Cal
April 25, 1919

Darling Margaret——

I told mother last night and of coarse she thinks we are too young. But I explained to her how times have changed since the war how the war makes you older than they used to. I see these birds my age that did not serve specially flying which is an education and they seem like kids to me because I have at last found the woman I want and my kid days are over. After knowing so many women to found you so far away when I did not expect it. Mother says for me to go in business and make money if I expect a woman to marry me so I am going to start in tomorrow I already have got the place. So it will not be long till I see you and take you in my arms at last and all ways. How can I tell you how much I love you you are so diferent from them. Loving you has all ready made me a serious man reelizing responsabilities. They are all so silly compared with you talking of jazz and going some place where all the time I have been invited on parties but I refuse because I rather sit in my room thinking of you putting my thoughts down on paper let them have there silly fun. I think of you all ways and if it did not make you so unhappy I would wish you thought of me always. But dont I would not make you unhappy at all my own dearest. So think of me and remember I love you only and willlove you only will love you all ways.

Forever yours
Julian.

13.

The Baptist minister, a young dervish in a white lawn tie, being most available came and did his duty and went away. He was young and fearfully conscientious and kindhearted, upright and passionately desirous of doing good: so much so that he was a bore. But he had soldiered after a fashion and he liked and respected Dr Mahon, refusing to believe that, simply because Dr Mahon was Episcopal, he was going to hell as soon as he died.

He wished them luck and fled busily away, answering his own obscure compulsions. They watched his busy energetic backside until he was out of sight. Then Gilligan silently helped Mahon down the steps and across the lawn to his favorite seat beneath the tree. The new Mrs Mahon walked beside them, silent also. Silence was her wont, but not Gilligan's. Yet he had spoken no word to her. Walking near him she put out her hand and touched Gilligan's arm: he turned to her a face so bleak, so reft that she knew a sharp revulsion, a sickness with everything. (Dick, Dick! How well you got out of this mess) She looked quickly away, across the garden, beyond the spire where pigeons crooned the afternoon away, unemphatic as sleep, biting her lip. Married, and she had never felt so alone.

Gilligan settled Mahon in his chair with his impersonal half-reckless care. Mahon said:

"Well, Joe, I'm married at last."

"Yes," answered Gilligan. His careless spontaneity was gone. Even Mahon noticed it in his dim oblivious way.

"I say, Joe."

"What is it, Loot?"

Mahon sat silent and his wife took her customary chair, leaning back and staring up into the tree. He said at last:

"Carry on, Joe."

"Not now, Loot. I dont feel so many. Think I'll take a walk," he answered feeling Mrs Mahon's eyes on him. He met her gaze harshly, combatively.

"Joe," she said quietly, bitterly.

Gilligan saw her pallid face, her dark unhappy eyes, her mouth like a tired scar and he knew shame. His own bleak face softened.

"Alright, Loot," he said quietly, matching her tone, with a trace of his old ambiguous unseriousness, "what'll it be? bust up a few more minor empires, huh?"

Just a trace, but it was there. Mrs Mahon looked at him again with gratitude and that old grave happiness which he knew so well, unsmiling but content, which had been missing for so long, so long, and it was as though she had laid her firm strong hand on him. He looked quickly away from her face, sad and happy, not bitter any more.

"Carry on, Joe."

Chapter Eight.

San Francisco, Cal
April 27, 1919

My dearest sweetheart—

Just a line to let you know that I have gone into business into the banking business making money for you. To give ourselves the position in the world you deserve and a home of our own. The work is congenyal talking to other people in the business that dont know anything about aviation. All they think about is going out to dance with men. Everyday means one day less for us to be with you forever. All my love.

yours forever
Julian

Nine day, or ninety day, or nine hundred day sensations have a happy faculty for passing away, into oblivion whence pass sooner or later all of man's inventions. Keeps from getting the world all cluttered up. You say right off that this is God's work, but it must be a woman: no man could be so utilitarian. But then, women preserve only those things which can or might be used again, so this theory is also exploded.

After a while there were no more of the local curious to call; after a while those who had said I told you so when Miss Cecily Saunders let it be known that she would marry the parson's son and who said I told you so when she did not marry the parson's son forgot about it. There were other things to think and talk of: this was the lying-in period of the K.K.K. and the lying-out of Mr Wilson, a democratish gentleman living in Washington, D.C.

Besides, it was all legal now. Miss Cecily Saunders was safely married——though nobody knows where they was from the time they drove out of town in George Farr's car until they was properly married by a priest in Atlanta the next day (but then I always told you about that girl). They all hoped for the worst. And that Mrs Whats-her-name, that tall black-headed woman at Mahon's had at last married somebody, putting an end to that equivocal situation.

And so April became May. There were fair days when the sun becoming warmer and warmer rising drank off the dew and flowers bloomed like girls ready for a ball, then drooped in the languorous fulsome heat like girls after a ball; when earth like a fat woman recklessly trying giddy hat after hat, trying a trimming of apple and pear and peach: threw it away, tried narcissus and jonquil and flag: threw it away——so early flowers passed and later flowers bloomed to fade and fall, giving place to yet later ones. Fruit blossoms were gone, pear was forgotten: what were once tall candle sticks, silvery with white bloom were now tall jade candle sticks of leaves beneath the blue cathedral of sky across which in hushed processional went clouds like choir boys slow and surpliced.

Leaves grew larger and greener until all rumor of azure and silver and pink had gone from them; birds sang and made love and married and built houses in them and in the tree at the corner of the house that yet swirled its white-bellied leaves in neverescaping skying ecstasies; bees broke clover upon the lawn, interrupted at intervals by the lawn-mower and its informal languid conductor.

Their mode of life had not changed. The rector neither happy nor unhappy, neither resigned nor protesting, occasionally entered some dream within himself. He conducted services in the dim oaked tunnel of the church while his flock hissed softly among themselves or slept between the responses, while pigeons held their own crooning rituals of audible slumber in the spire which arcing across motionless young clouds seemed slow and imminent with ruin; he married two people and buried one: Gilligan finding this ominous said so aloud; Mrs Mahon finding this silly said so aloud.

Mrs Worthington sent her car at times and they drove into the country regretting the dogwood, the three of them (two of them did, that is. Mahon had forgot what dogwood was); the three of them sat beneath the tree while one of them wallowed manfully among polysyllabics and another of them sat motionless, neither asleep nor awake. They could never tell whether or not he had heard. Nor could they ever tell whether or not he knew whom he had married. Perhaps he didn't care.

Emmy efficient and gentle, mothering him, was a trifle subdued. Gilligan still slept on his cot at the foot of Mahon's bed, lest he be needed.

"You two are the ones who should have married him," his wife remarked with quiet wit.

3.

Mrs Mahon and Gilligan had resumed their old status of companionship and quiet pleasure in each other's company. Now that he no longer hoped to marry her she could be freer with him.

"Perhaps this is what we needed, Joe. Anyway, I never knew anyone I liked half this much."

They walked slowly in the garden along the avenue of roses which passed beneath two oaks beyond which against a wall poplars in a restless formal row were like columns of a temple.

"You're easy pleased then," Gilligan answered with sour assumed moroseness. He didn't have to tell her how much he liked her.

"Poor Joe," she said. "Cigarette, please."

"Poor you," he retorted giving her one. "I'm alright. I aint married."

"You cant escape forever, though. You are too nice: safe for the family, will stand hitched."

"Is that a bargain?" he asked.

"Sufficient unto the day, Joe. . . ."

After a while he stayed her with his hand. "Listen."

They halted and she stared at him intently. "What?"

"There's that damn mockingbird again. Hear him? What's he got to sing about, you reckon?"

"He's got plenty to sing about. April's got to be May, and still spring isn't half over. Listen. . . ."

4.

Emmy had become an obsession with Januarius Jones, such an obsession that it had got completely out of the realm of sex into that of mathematics, like a paranoia. He manufactured chances to see her, only to be repulsed: he lay in wait for her like a highwayman, he begged, he threatened, he tried physical strength; and he was repulsed. It had got to where had she acceded suddenly he would have been completely reft of one of his motivating impulses, of his elemental impulse to live: he might have died. Yet he knew that if he didn't get her soon he would become crazy, an imbecile.

After a time it assumed the magic of numbers. He had failed twice: this time success must be his or the whole cosmic scheme would crumble hurling him screaming into blackness where no blackness was, death where death was not. Januarius Jones by nature and inclination a Turk, was also becoming an oriental. He felt that his number must come: the fact that it would not was making an idiot of him.

He dreamed of her at night, he mistook other women for her, other voices for hers; he hung skulking about the rectory at all hours too wrought up to come in where he might have to converse sanely with sane people. Sometimes the rector tramping huge and oblivious in his dream flushed him in out-of-the-way corners of concealment, flushed him without surprise.

"Ah, Mr Jones," he would say, starting like a goaded elephant, "good morning."

"Good morning, sir," Jones would reply, his eyes glued on the house.

"You are out for a walk?"

"Yes, sir. Yes, sir." And he would walk hurriedly away in an opposite direction as the rector entering his dream again, resumed his own.

Emmy told Mrs Mahon of this with scornful contempt.

"Why dont you tell Joe, or let me tell him?" she asked.

Emmy sniffed with capable independence. "About that worm? I can take care of him, all right. I do my own fighting."

"And I bet you are good at it, too."

And Emmy said: "I guess I am."

5.

April had become May.

Fair days, and wet days in which rain ran with silver lances over the lawn, in which rain dripped leaf to leaf while birds still sang in the hushed damp greenness under the trees, and made love and married and built houses and still sang; in which rain grew soft as the grief of a young girl grieving for the sake of grief.

Mahon hardly ever rose now. They had got him a movable bed and upon this he lay sometimes in the house, sometimes on the verandah where the wistaria inverted its cool lilac flame, while Gilligan read to him. They had done with Rome and they now swam through the tedious charm of Rousseau's "Confessions" to Gilligan's hushed childish delight. Kind neighbors came to inquire; the specialist from Atlanta came once by request and once on his own initiative, making a friendly call and addressing Gilligan meticulously as "Doctor," spent the afternoon chatting with them, and went away. Mrs Mahon and he liked each other immensely. Dr Gary called once or twice and insulted them all and went away nattily smoking his slender rolled cigarettes. Mrs Mahon and he did not like each other at all. The rector grew grayer and quieter, neither unhappy nor happy, neither protesting nor resigned.

"Wait until next month. He will be stronger then. This is a trying month for invalids. Dont you think so?" he asked his daughter-in-law.

"Yes," she would tell him, looking out at the green world, the sweet sweet spring, "yes, yes."

6.

It was a postcard. You buy them for a penny, stamp and all. The postoffice furnishes writing materials free.

'Got your letter. Will write later. Remember me to Gilligan and Lieut. Mahon. Julian L.'

7.

Mahon was asleep on the verandah and the other three sat beneath the tree on the lawn, watching the sun go down. At last the reddened edge of the disc was sliced like a cheese by the wistaria-covered lattice wall and the neutral buds were a pale agitation against the dead afternoon. Soon the evening star would be there above the poplar tip, perplexing it, immaculate and ineffable, and the poplar was vain as a girl darkly in arrested passionate ecstasy. Half of the moon was a pale broken coin near the zenith and at the end of the lawn the first fireflies were like lazily blown sparks from cool fires. A negro woman passing crooned a religious song, mellow and passionless and sad.

They sat talking quietly. The grass was becoming gray with dew and she felt dew on her thin shoes. Suddenly Emmy came around the corner of the house running and darted up the steps and through the entrance, swift in the dusk.

"What in the world——" began Mrs Mahon, then they saw Jones like a fat satyr leaping after her, hopelessly distanced. When he saw them he slowed immediately and lounged up to them slovenly as ever. His yellow eyes were calmly opaque but she could see the heave of his breathing. Convulsed with laughter, she at last found her voice.

"Good evening, Mr Jones."

"Say," Gilligan said with interest, "what was you——"

"Hush, Joe," Mrs Mahon told him. Jones' eyes, clear and yellow, obscene and old in sin as a goat's, roved between them.

"Good evening, Mr Jones." The rector became abruptly aware of his presence. "Walking again, eh?"

"Running," Gilligan corrected and the rector repeated Eh? looking from Jones to Gilligan.

Mrs Mahon indicated a chair. "Sit down, Mr Jones. You must be rather fatigued, I imagine."

Jones stared toward the house, tore his eyes away and sat down. The canvas sagged under him and he rose and spun his chair so as to face the dreaming façade of the rectory. He sat again.

"Say," Gilligan asked him, "what was you doing, anyway?"

Jones eyed him briefly, heavily. "Running," he snapped, turning his eyes again to the dark house.

"Running?" the divine repeated.

"I know: I seen that much from here. What was you running for, I asked."

"Reducing, perhaps," Mrs Mahon remarked with quiet malice.

Jones turned his yellow stare upon her. Twilight was gathering swiftly. He was a fat and shapeless mass palely tweeded.

"Reducing, yes. But not to marriage."

"I wouldn't be so sure of that, if I were you," she told him. "A courtship like that will soon reduce you to anything, almost."

"Yeh," Gilligan amended, "if that's the only way you got to get a wife you'd better pick out another one besides Emmy. You'll be a shadow time you catch her. That is," he added, "if you aim to do your courting on foot."

"What's this?" the rector asked.

"Perhaps Mr Jones was merely preparing to write a poem. Living it first, you know," Mrs Mahon offered. He looked at her sharply. "Atalanta," she suggested in the dusk.

"Atlanta?" said Gilligan, "what's—"

"Try an apple next time, Mr Jones," she advised.

"Or a handful of salt, Mr Jones," added Gilligan in a thin falsetto. Then in his natural voice: "But what's Atlanta got to——"

"Or a cherry, Mr Gilligan," said Jones viciously. "But then, I am not God, you know."

"Shut your mouth, fellow," Gilligan told him roughly.

"What's this?" the rector repeated.

Jones turned to him heavily explanatory:

"It means, sir, that Mr Gilligan is under the impression that his wit is of as much importance to me as my actions are to him."

"Not me," denied Gilligan with warmth. "You and me dont have the same thoughts about anything, fellow."

"Why shouldn't they be?" the rector asked. "It is but natural to believe that one's actions and thoughts are as important to others as they are to oneself, is it not?"

Gilligan gave this his entire attention. It was getting above his head, beyond his depth. But Jones was something tangible and he had already chosen Jones for his own.

"Naturally," agreed Jones with patronage. "There is a kinship between the human instruments of all action and thought and emotion: Napoleon thinks his actions are important, Swift thinks his emotions are important, Savonarola thinks his beliefs are important. And they were. But we are discussing Mr Gilligan."

"Say——" began Gilligan.

"Very apt, Mr Jones," murmured Mrs Mahon above the suggested triangle of her cuffs and collar, "a soldier, a priest and a dyspeptic."

"Say," Gilligan repeated, "who's swift, anyway? I kind of got bogged up back there."

"Mr Jones is, according to his analogy. You are Napoleon, Joe."

"Him? Not quite swift enough to catch himself a girl, though. The way he was gaining on Emmy——You ought to have a bicycle," he suggested.

"There's your answer, Mr Jones," the rector told him. Jones looked toward Gilligan's fading figure in disgust, like that of a swordsman who has been disarmed by a peasant with a pitchfork.

"That's what association with the clergy does for you," he said crassly.

"What is it?" Gilligan asked. "What did I say wrong?"

Mrs Mahon leaned over and squeezed his arm. "You didn't say anything wrong, Joe. You were grand."

Jones glowered sullenly in the dusk.

"By the way," he said suddenly, "how is your husband today?"

"Just the same, thank you."

"Stands wedded life as well as can be expected, does he?" She ignored this. Gilligan watched him in leashed antici- pation. He continued: "That's too bad. You had expected great things from marriage, hadn't you? Sort of a miraculous rejuvenation?"

"Shut up, fellow," Gilligan told him. "Whatcher mean, anyway?"

"Nothing, Mr Galahad, nothing at all. I merely made a civil enquiry. . . . . Shows you that when a man marries his troubles continue, doesn't it?"

"Then you oughtn't to have no worries about your trou- bles," Gilligan told him savagely.

"What?"

"I mean if you dont have no better luck than you have twice that I know of——"

"He has a good excuse for one failure, Joe," Mrs Mahon said.

They both looked toward her voice. The sky was bowled with a still disseminated light that cast no shadow and branches of trees were rigid as coral in a mellow tideless sea.

"Mr Jones says that to make love to Miss Saunders would be epicene."

"Epicene? What's that?"

"Shall I tell him, Mr Jones? or will you?"

"Certainly. You intend to, anyway, dont you?"

"Epicene is something you want but cant get, Joe."

Jones rose viciously. "If you will allow me, I'll retire, I think," he said savagely. "Good evening."

"Sure," agreed Gilligan with alacrity rising also. "I'll see Mr Jones to the gate. He might get mixed up and head for the kitchen by mistake. Emmy might be one of them epicenes, too."

Without seeming to hurry Jones faded briskly away. Gilligan sprang after him. Jones sensing him whirled in the dusk and Gilligan leaped upon him.

"For the good of your soul," Gilligan told him joyously. "You might say that's what running with preachers does for you, mightn't you?" he panted as they went down.

They rolled in dew and an elbow struck him smartly under the chin. Jones was up immediately and Gilligan tasting his bitten tongue sprang in pursuit, but Jones retained his lead. "He has sure learned to run from somebody," Gilligan grunted. "Practicing on Emmy so much, I guess. Wisht I was Emmy, now—until I catch him."

Jones doubled the house and plunged into the dreaming garden. Gilligan turning the corner of the house saw the hushed expanse where his enemy was, but his enemy, himself, was out of sight. Roses bloomed quietly under the imminence of night, hyacinths swung pale bells, waiting for another day. Dusk was a dream of arrested time, the mockingbird rippled it tentatively, and everywhere blooms slept passionately, waiting for tomorrow. But Jones was gone.

He stopped to listen upon the paling gravel, between the slow unpickable passion of roses, seeing the pale broken coin of the moon attain a richer luster against the unemphatic sky. Gilligan stilled his heaving lungs to listen, but he heard nothing. Then he began to systematically beat the firefly-starred scented dusk of the garden, beating all available cover, leaving not a blade of grass unturned. But Jones had got away clean; the slow hands of dusk had removed him as cleanly as the prestidigitator rieves a rabbit from an immaculate hat.

He stood in the center of the garden and cursed Jones thoroughly on the off chance that he might be within hearing, then Gilligan slowly retraced his steps, retracing the course of the race through the palpable violet dusk. He passed the unlighted house where Emmy went somewhere about her duties, where at the corner of the verandah near the silver tree's twilight-musicked ecstasy Mahon slept on his movable bed and on across the lawn, while evening, like a ship with twilight-colored sails, dreamed on down the world. The chairs were formless blurs beneath the tree and Mrs Mahon's presence was indicated principally by her white collar and cuffs. As he approached, he could see dimly the rector reclined in slumber and the woman's dark dress shaped her against the dull white of her canvas chair. Her face was pallid, winged either side by her hair. She raised her hand as he drew near.

"He's asleep," she whispered as he sat beside her.

"He got away, damn him," he told her in exasperation.

"Too bad. Better luck next time."

"You bet. And there'll be a next time soon as I see him again."

Night was almost come. Light, all light passed from the world, from the earth, and leaves were still. Night was almost come, but not quite; day was almost gone, but not quite. Her shoes were quite soaked with dew.

"How long he has slept." She broke the silence diffidently. "We'll have to wake him soon for supper."

Gilligan stirred in his chair and almost as she spoke the rector sat hugely and suddenly up.

"Wait, Donald," he said lumbering to his feet. With elephantine swiftness he hurried across the lawn toward the darkly dreaming house.

"Did he call?" they spoke together in a dark foreboding. They half rose and stared toward the house, then at each other's indistinct white face. "Did you——?" the question hung poised in the dusk between them. And here was the evening star bloomed miraculously at the poplar's tip and the slender tree was a leafed and passionate Atalanta poising her golden apple.

"No, did you?" he replied.

But they had heard nothing.

"He dreamed," she said.

"Yes," Gilligan agreed. "He dreamed."

8.

Donald Mahon lay quietly conscious of unseen forgotten spring, of greenness neither recalled nor forgot. After a time the nothingness in which he lived took him wholly again, but restlessly. It was like a sea into which he could neither completely pass nor completely go away from. Day became afternoon, became dusk and imminent evening: evening like a ship, with twilight-colored sails, dreamed down the world darkly toward darkness. And suddenly he found that he was passing from the dark world in which he had lived for a time he could not remember, again into a day that had long passed, that had already been spent by those who lived and wept and died, and so remembering it, this day was his alone: the one trophy he had reft from Time and Space. Per ardua ad astra.

I never knew I could carry this much petrol, he thought in unsurprised ubiquity, leaving a darkness he did not remember for a day he had long forgot, finding that the day, his own familiar day, was approaching noon. It must be about ten oclock, for the sun was getting overhead and a few degrees behind him, because he could see the shadow of his head bisecting in an old familiarity the hand upon the control column and the shadow of the cockpit rim across his flanks, filling his lap, while the sun fell almost directly downward upon his other hand lying idly on the edge of the fuselage. Even the staggered lower wing was partly shadowed by the upper one.

Yes, it is about ten, he thought with a sense of familiarity. Soon he would look at the time and make sure, but now. . . . With the quick skill of practice and habit he swept the horizon with a brief observing glance, casting a look above, banking slightly to see behind. All clear. The only craft in sight were far away to the left: a cumbersome observation 'plane doing artillery work. A brief glance divulged a pair of scouts high above it; and above these he knew were probably two more.

Might have a look, he thought, knowing instinctively that

they were Huns, calculating whether or not he could reach the spotter before the protecting scouts saw him. No, I guess not, he decided. Better get on home. Fuel's low. He settled his swinging compass needle.

Ahead of him and to the right, far away, what was once Ypres was like the cracked scab on an ancient festering sore; beneath him were other shining sores lividly on a corpse that would not be let to die. . . . He passed on, lonely and remote as a gull.

Then suddenly it was as if a cold wind had blown upon him. What is it? he thought. It was that the sun had been suddenly blotted from him. The empty world, the sky, were yet filled with lazy spring sunlight but the sun that had been full upon him had been brushed away as by a hand. In the moment of realizing this, cursing his stupidity he dived steeply slipping to the left. Five threads of vapor passed between the upper and lower planes, each one nearer his body, then he felt two distinct shocks at the base of his skull and vision was reft from him as if a button somewhere had been pressed. His trained hand nosed the machine up smartly and finding the Vickers release in the darkness he fired into the bland morning marbled and imminent with March.

Sight flickered on again like a poorly made electrical contact, he watched holes pitting into the fabric near him like a miraculous small-pox and as he hung poised firing into the sky a dial on his instrument board exploded with a small sound. Then he felt his hand, saw his glove burst, saw his bared bones. Then sight flashed off again, he felt himself lurch falling until his belt caught him sharply across the abdomen and heard something gnawing through his frontal bone, like mice. You'll break your damn teeth there, he told them opening his eyes.

His father's heavy face hung over him in the dusk, like a murdered Caesar's.

He knew sight again and an imminent nothingness more profound than any yet, while evening, like a ship with twilight-colored sails, drew down the world, putting calmly out to an immeasurable sea. "That's how it happened," he said, staring at him.

Chapter Nine.

I.

Sex and death: the front door and the back door of the world. How indissolubly are they associated in us! In youth they lift us out of the flesh, in old age they reduce us again to the flesh; one to fatten us, the other to flay us, for the worm. When are sexual compulsions more readily answered than in war and famine and flood and fire?

Jones lurking across the street saw the coast clear at last.

(First marched a uniformed self constituted guard led by a subaltern with three silver V's on his sleeve, and a Boy Scout bugler furnished by the young Baptist minister, a fiery-eyed dervish who had served in the Y.M.C.A.)

And then, fatly arrogant as a cat, Jones let himself through the iron gate.

(The last motor car trailed slowly up the street and the casuals gathered through curiosity—the town should raise a monument to Donald Mahon, with effigies of Margaret Mahon-Powers and Joe Gilligan for caryatides—and the little blackguard boys both black and white and including young Robert Saunders, come to envy the boy bugler, drifted away)

And still cat-like Jones mounted the steps and entered the deserted house. His yellow goat's eyes became empty as he paused listening. Then he moved quietly toward the kitchen.

(The procession moved slowly across the square. Country people in town to trade turned to stare vacuously, merchant and doctor and lawyer came to door and window to look; the city fathers drowsing in the courthouse yard having success-fully circumvented sex, having reached the point where death would look after them instead of they after death, waked and looked and slept again. Into a street among and between horses and mules tethered to wagons it passed, into a street bordered by shabby negro stores and shops, and here was Loosh standing stiffly at salute as it passed. "Who dat, Loosh?" "Mist' Donald Mahon." "Well, Jesus! We all gwine dat way some day. All roads leads to de graveyard.")

Emmy sat at the kitchen table, her head between her hard

elbows and her hands clasping behind her head, in her hair. How long she had sat there she did not know, but she had heard them clumsily carrying him from the house and she had put her hands over her ears, not to hear. But it seemed as if she could hear in spite of her closed ears, those horrible blundering utterly useless sounds, the hushed scraping of timid foot-steps, the muted thumping of wood against wood that passing leaves behind an unbearable unchastity of stale flowers as though flowers themselves getting a rumor of death became corrupt——all the excruciating ceremony for disposing of human carrion. So she had not heard Mrs Mahon until the other touched her shoulder. (I would have cured him! If they had just let me marry him instead of her!) At the touch Emmy raised her swollen blurred face, swollen because she couldn't seem to cry. (If I could just cry——You are prettier'n me, with your black hair and your painted mouth. That's the reason)

"Come, Emmy," Mrs Mahon said.

"Let me alone! Go away!" she said fiercely. "You got him killed: now bury him yourself."

"He would have wanted you to come, Emmy," the other woman said gently.

"Go away, let me alone, I tell you!" She dropped her head to the table again, bumping her forehead. . . .

There was no sound in the kitchen save a clock. Life. death. life. death. life. death. forever and ever. (If I could only cry!) She could hear the dusty sound of sparrows and she imagined she could see the shadows growing longer across the grass. Soon it will be night, she thought, remembering that night long, long ago, the last time she had seen Donald, her Donald: not that one! and he had said Come here, Emmy, and she had gone to him. Her Donald was dead long long ago. . . . The clock went life. death. life. death. There was something frozen in her chest, like a dish-cloth in winter.

(The procession moved beneath arching iron letters. Rest in Peace in cast repetition: Our motto is one for every cemetery, a cemetery for everyone throughout the land. Away following where fingers of sunlight pointed among cedars, doves were cool, throatily unemphatic among the dead)

"Go away," Emmy repeated to another touch on her shoulder, thinking she had dreamed. It was a dream! she thought and the frozen dish-rag in her chest melted with unbearable relief, becoming tears. It was Jones who had touched her but anyone would have been the same, and she turned in a passion of weeping, clinging to him.

(I am the resurrection and the life, Saith the Lord. . . .)

Jones' yellow stare enveloped her like amber, remarking her sun-burned hair and her foreshortened thigh wrung by her turning body into high relief.

(Whosoever believeth in Me, Though he were dead. . . .)

My God, when will she get done weeping? First she wets my pants, then my coat. But this time she'll dry it for me, or I'll know the reason why.

(yet shall he live, And whoseoever liveth and believeth in Me, shall never die. . . .)

Emmy's sobbing died away: she knew no sensation save that of warmth and languorous contentment, emptiness, not even when Jones raised her face and kissed her. "Come, Emmy," he said raising her by the arm-pits. She rose obediently, leaning against him warm and empty, and he led her through the house up the stairs and into her room. Outside the window the afternoon became abruptly rain, without warning, with no flapping of pennons nor sound of trumpet to herald it.

(The sun had gone, had been recalled as quickly as a usurer's note and the doves fell silent or went away. The Baptist dervish's Boy Scout lipped his bugle, sounding taps)

2.

"Hi, Bob," called a familiar voice, that of a compatriot. "Le's gwup to Miller's. They're playin' ball up there."

He looked at his friend, making no reply to the greeting, and his expression was so strange that the other said: "Whatcher look so funny about? You aint sick, are you?"

"I dont haf to play ball if I dont want to, do I?" he replied with sudden heat. He walked on while the other boy stood watching him with open mouth. After a while he too turned and went on, stopping once or twice to look again at his friend become suddenly strange and queer. Then he passed whooping from sight, forgetting him.

How strange everything looked! This street, these familiar

trees——was this his home here, where his mother and father were, where Sis lived, where he ate and slept, lapped closely around with safety and solidity, where darkness was kind and sweet for sleeping? He mounted the steps and entered, wanting his mother. But of course she hadn't got back from——He found himself suddenly running through the hall toward a voice raised in crooning comforting song. Here was a friend mountainous in blue calico, her elephantine thighs undulating gracious as the wake of a river boat as she moved between table and stove.

She broke off her mellow passionless song, exclaiming: "Bless yo' heart, honey, what is it?"

But he did not know. He only clung to her comforting voluminous skirt in a gust of uncontrollable sorrow while she wiped biscuit dough from her hands on a towel. Then she picked him up and sat upon a stiff backed chair rocking back and forth and holding him against her balloon-like breast until his fit of weeping shuddered away.

Outside the window afternoon became abruptly rain, without warning, with no flapping of pennons nor sound of trumpet to herald it.

3.

There was nothing harsh about this rain. It was gray and quiet as a benediction. The birds did not even cease to sing and the west was already thinning to a moist and imminent gold.

The rector bareheaded walked slowly, unconscious of the rain and the dripping trees, beside his daughter-in-law across the lawn, houseward, and they mounted the steps together passing beneath the dim and unwashed fanlight. Within the hall he stood while water ran down his face and dripped from his clothing in a series of small sounds. She took his arm and led him into the study and to his chair. He sat obediently and she took his handkerchief from the breast of his coat and wiped the rain from his temples and face. He submitted, fumbling for his pipe.

She watched him as he sprinkled tobacco liberally over the desk-top, trying to fill the bowl, then she quietly took it from his hand. "Try this. It is much simpler," she told him taking a cigarette from her jacket pocket and putting it in his mouth. "You have never smoked one, have you?"

"Eh? Oh, thank you. Never too old to learn, eh?"

She lit it for him and quickly fetched a glass from the pantry. Kneeling beside the desk she drew out drawer after drawer until she found the bottle of whiskey. He seemed to have forgotten her until she put the glass in his hand.

Then he looked up at her from a bottomless grateful anguish and she sat suddenly on the arm of his chair, drawing his head against her breast. His untasted drink in one hand and his slowly burning cigarette lifting an unshaken plume of vapor from the other; and after a while the rain passed away and the dripping eaves but added to the freshened silence, measuring it, spacing it off, and the sun breaking through the west took a last look at the earth before going down.

"So you will not stay," he said at last, repeating her unspoken decision.

"No," she said, holding him.

4.

Before her descending, the hill crossed with fire-flies. At its foot among dark trees was unseen water and Emmy walked slowly on feeling the tall wet grass sopping her to the knees, draggling her skirt.

She walked on and soon was among trees that as she moved, moved overhead like dark ships parting the star-filled river of the sky, letting the parted waters join again behind them with never a ripple. The pool lay darkly in the dark: sky and trees above it, trees and sky beneath it. She sat down on the wet earth, seeing through the trees the moon becoming steadily brighter in the darkening sky. A dog saw it also and bayed: a mellow long sound that slid immaculately down a hill of silence, yet at the same time seemed to linger about her like a rumor of a far despair.

Tree trunks taking light from the moon, streaks of moonlight in the water——she could almost imagine she saw him standing there across the pool with her beside him; leaning above the water she could almost see them darting keen and swift and naked, flashing in the moon.

She could feel earth strike through her clothes against legs and belly and elbows . . . the dog bayed again, hopeless and sorrowful, dying, dying away.

. . . After a while she rose slowly, feeling her damp clothes, thinking of the long walk home. Tomorrow was wash day.

5.

"Damn!" said Mrs Mahon staring at the bulletin board. Gilligan setting down her smart leather bags against the station wall remarked briefly:

"Late?"

"Thirty minutes. What beastly luck."

"Well, cant be helped. Wanta go back to the house and wait?"

"No, I dont. I dont like these abortive departures. Get my ticket, please." She gave him her purse and standing on tiptoe to see her reflection in a raised window she did a few deft things to her hat, then sauntered along the platform to the admiration of those casuals always to be found around small railway stations anywhere in these United States. And yet Continentals labor under the delusion that we spend all our time working!

Freedom comes with the decision: it does not wait for the act. She felt freer, more at peace with herself than she had felt in months. But I wont think about that, she decided deliberately. It is best just to be free, not even to know you are free, not to let it into the conscious mind. To be consciously anything argues a comparison, a bond with antithesis. Live in your dream, do not attain it, else comes satiety ——or sorrow. Which is worse, I wonder? Dr Mahon and his dream: reft, restored, reft again. Funny for someone, I guess. And Donald with his scar and his stiffened hand quiet in the warm earth, in the warmth and the dark, where the one cannot hurt him and the other he will not need. No dream for him! The ones with whom he now sleeps dont care what his face looks like. Per ardua ad astra. . . . And Jones, what dream is his? "Nightmare, I hope," she said aloud viciously and one collarless and spitting tobacco said Ma'am? with interest.

Gilligan reappeared with her ticket.

"You're a nice boy, Joe," she told him receiving her purse. He ignored her thanks. "Come on, lets walk a ways."

"Will my bags be alright there, do you think?"

"Sure." He looked about, then beckoned to a negro youth reclining miraculously on a steel cable that angled up to a telephone pole. "Here, son."

The negro said Suh? without moving. "Git up dar, boy. Dat white man talkin' to you," said a companion squatting on his heels against the wall. The lad rose and a coin spun arcing from Gilligan's hand.

"Keep your eye on them bags till I come back, will you?"

"Awright, cap'm." The boy slouched over to the bags and became restfully and easily static beside them. He went to sleep immediately, like a horse.

"Damn 'em, they do what you say, but they make you feel so——so——"

"Immature, dont they?" she suggested.

"That's it: like you was a kid or something and they'd look after you even if you dont know exactly what you want."

"You're a funny sort, Joe. And nice. Too nice to waste."

Her profile was sharp, pallid against a doorway darkly opened. "I'm giving you a chance not to waste me."

"Come on, lets walk a bit." She took his arm and moved slowly along the track, conscious that her ankles were being examined. The two threads of steel ran narrowing and curving away beyond trees. If you could see them as far as you can see, further than you can see. . . .

"Huh?" asked Gilligan walking moodily beside her.

"Look at the spring, Joe. See, in the trees: summer is almost here, Joe."

"Yeh, summer is almost here. Funny, aint it? I'm always kind of surprised to find that things get on about the same, spite of us. I guess old nature does too much of a wholesale business to ever be surprised at us, let alone worrying if we aint quite the fellows we think we ought to of been."

Holding his arm, walking a rail:

"What kind of fellows do we think we are, Joe?"

"I dont know what kind of a fel—girl you think you are and I dont know what kind of a fellow I think I am, but I do know you and I fooled around trying to help nature make a good job out of a poor one without having no luck at it."

Flat leaves cupped each a drop of sunlight and the trees seemed coolly on fire with evening. Here was a wooden foot-bridge crossing a stream and a footpath mounting a hill. "Lets sit on the rail of the bridge," she suggested guiding him toward it. Before he could help her she had turned her back to the rail and her straightening arms raised her easily. She hooked her heels over a lower rail and he mounted beside her. "Lets have a cigarette."

She produced a pack from her hand bag and he accepted one, scraping a match. "Who has had any luck in this business?" she asked.

"The loot has."

"No he hasn't. When you are married you are either lucky or unlucky, but when you are dead you aren't either: you aren't anything."

"That's right. He dont have to bother about his luck anymore. . . . The padre's lucky, though."

"How?"

"Well, if you have hard luck and your hard luck passes, aint you lucky?"

"I dont know. You are too much for me now, Joe."

"And how about that girl? Fellow's got money, I hear, and no particular brains. She's lucky."

"Do you think she's satisfied?"

Gilligan gazed at her attentively, not replying.

"Think how much fun she could have got out of being so romantically widowed, and so young. I'll bet she's cursing her luck this minute."

He regarded her with admiration. "I always thought I'd like to be a buzzard," he remarked, "but now I think I'd like to be a woman."

"Good gracious, Joe, why in the world?"

"Now, long as you're being one of them sybils, tell me about this bird Jones. He's lucky."

"How lucky?"

"Well, he gets what he wants, dont he?"

"Not the women he wants?"

"Not exactly. Certainly he dont get all the women he wants. He failed twice to my knowledge. But failure dont seem to worry him. That's what I mean by lucky." Their cigarettes arced together into the stream, hissing. "I guess brass gets along about as well as anything else with women."

"You mean stupidity."

"No, I dont. Stupidity. That's the reason I cant get the one I want."

She put her hand on his arm. "You aren't stupid, Joe. And you aren't bold, either."

"Yes I am. Can you imagine me considering anybody's feelings when they's something I want?"

"I cant imagine you doing anything without considering somebody else's feelings."

Offended he became impersonal. " 'Course you are entitled to your own opinion. I know I aint bold like the man in that story. You remember? accosted a woman on the street and her husband was with her and knocked him down. When he got up brushing himself off a man says: 'For heaven's sake, friend, do you do that often?' and the bird says: 'Sure. Of course I get knocked down occasionally, but you'd be surprised.' I guess he just charged the beatings to overhead," he finished with his old sardonic humor.

She laughed out. Then she said: "Why dont you try that, Joe?"

He looked at her quietly for a time. She met his gaze unwavering and he slipped to his feet and facing her put his arm around her. "What does that mean, Margaret?"

She made no reply and he lifted her down. She put her arms over his shoulders. "You dont mean anything by it," he told her quietly, touching her mouth with his. His clasp became lax.

"Not like that, Joe."

"Not like what?" he asked stupidly.

For answer she drew his face down to hers and kissed him with slow fire. Then they knew that after all they were strangers to each other. He hastened to fill an uncomfortable interval. "Does that mean you will?"

"I cant, Joe," she answered standing easily in his arms.

"But why not, Margaret? You never give me any reasons."

She was silent in profile against sun-shot green. "If I didn't like you so damn much, I wouldn't tell you. But its your name, Joe. I couldn't marry a man named Gilligan."

He was really hurt. "I'm sorry," he said dully. She laid her cheek against his. On the crest of the hill tree trunks were a barred grate beyond which the fires of evening were dying away. "I could change it," he suggested.

Across the evening came a long sound. "There's your train," he said.

She thrust herself slightly from him, to see his face. "Joe, forgive me. I didn't mean that—"

"That's alright," he interrupted patting her back with awkward gentleness. "Come on, lets get back."

The locomotive appeared blackly at the curve, plumed with steam like a sinister squat knight and grew larger without seeming to progress. But it was moving and roared past the station in its own good time bearing the puny controller of its destiny like a goggled greasy excrescence in its cab. The train jarred to a stop and an eruption of white jacketed porters.

She put her arms around him again, to the edification of the by-standers. "Joe, I didn't mean that. But dont you see, I have been married twice already, with damn little luck either time, and I just haven't the courage to risk it again. But if I could marry anyone, dont you know it would be you? Kiss me, Joe."

He complied. "Bless your heart, darling. If I married you you'd be dead in a year, Joe. All the men that marry me die, you know."

"I'll take the risk," he told her.

"But I wont. I'm too young to bury three husbands." People got off, passed them, other people got on. And above all like at obbligato the vocal competition of cab-men. "Joe, does it really hurt you for me to go?"

He looked at her dumbly.

"Joe!" she exclaimed and a party passed them. It was Mr and Mrs George Farr: they saw Cecily's stricken face as she melted graceful and fragile and weeping into her father's arms. And here was Mr George Farr morose and thunderous behind her, ignored.

"What did I tell you?" Mrs Mahon said clutching Gilligan's arm.

"You're right," he answered from his own despair. "Its a sweet honeymoon he's had, poor devil."

The party passed on around the station and she looked at Gilligan again.

"Joe, come with me."

"To a minister?" he asked with resurgent hope.

"No, just as we are. Then when we get fed up all we need do is wish each other luck and go our ways."

He stared at her, shocked.

"Damn your presbyterian soul, Joe. Now you think I'm a bad woman."

"No, I dont, ma'am. But I cant do that."

"Why not?"

"I dunno: I just cant."

"But what difference does it make?"

"Why, none, if it was just your body I wanted. But I want ——I want——"

"What do you want, Joe?"

"Hell. Come on, lets get aboard."

"You are coming, then?"

"You know I aint. You knew you was safe when you said that."

He picked up her bags, a porter ravished them skilfully from him, and he helped her into the car. She sat upon green plush and he removed his hat awkwardly, extending his hand. "Well, goodbye."

Her face pallid and calm beneath her small white and black hat, above her immaculate collar. She ignored his hand.

"Look at me, Joe. Have I ever told you a lie?"

"No," he admitted.

"Then dont you know I am not lying to you now? I meant what I said. Sit down here."

"No, no, I cant do it that way. You know I cant."

"Yes. I cant even seduce you, Joe. I'm sorry. I'd like to make you happy for a short time, if I could. But I guess it isn't in the cards, is it?" She raised her face. He kissed her.

"Goodbye."

"Goodbye, Joe."

But why not, he thought with cinders under his feet, why not take her this way? I could persuade her in time, perhaps before we reach Atlanta. He turned and sprang back on board the train. He hadn't much time and when he saw that her seat was empty he rushed through the car in a mounting excitement. She was not in the next car either.

Have I forgotten which car she is in? he thought. But no, that was where he had left her for there was the negro youth still motionless opposite the window. He hurried back to take another look at her place. Yes, there were her bags. He ran blundering into other passengers, the whole length of the train. She was not there.

She has changed her mind and got off looking for me, he thought in an agony of futile endeavor. He slammed open a vestibule and leaped to the ground as the train began to move. Careless of how he must look to the station loungers he leaped toward the waiting room. It was empty, a hurried glance up and down the platform did not discover her and he turned despairing to the moving train.

She must be on it! he thought furiously, cursing himself because he had not stayed on board until she reappeared. For now the train was moving too swiftly and all the vestibules were closed. Then the last car slid smoothly past and he saw her standing on the rear platform where she had gone in order to see him again and where he had not thought of looking for her.

"Margaret!" he cried after the arrogant steel thing, running vainly down the track after it, seeing it smoothly distancing him. "Margaret!" he cried again, stretching his arms to her, to the vocal support of the loungers.

"Whup up a little, mister," a voice advised.

"Ten to one on the train," a sporting one offered. There were no takers.

He stopped at last, actually weeping with anger and despair, watching her figure in its dark straight dress and white collar and cuffs become smaller and smaller with the diminishing train that left behind a derisive whistle blast and a trailing fading vapor like an insult, moving along twin threads of steel out of his sight and his life.

. . . At last he left the track at right angles and climbed a wire fence into woods where spring becoming languorous with summer turned sweetly nightward, though summer had not quite come.

6.

Deep in a thicket from which the evening was slowly dissolving a thrush sang four liquid notes. Like the shape of her mouth, he thought, feeling the heat of his pain become cool with the cooling of sunset. The small stream murmured busily like a faint incantation and repeated alder shoots leaned over it Narcissus-like. The thrush disturbed flashed a modest streak of brown deeper into the woods, and sang again. Mosquitoes spun about him, unresisted: he seemed to get ease from their sharp irritation. Something else to think about.

I could have made it up to her. I would make up to her for everything that ever hurt her, so that when she remembered things that once hurt her she'd say Was this I? If I could just have told her! Only I couldn't seem to think of what to say. Me, that talks all the time, being stuck for words. . . . Aimlessly he followed the stream. Soon it ran among violet shadows, among willows and he heard a louder water. Parting the willows he came upon an old mill-race and a small lake calmly repeating the calm sky and the opposite dark trees. He saw fish gleaming dully upon the earth, and the buttocks of a man.

"Lost something?" he asked, watching ripples spreading from the man's submerged arm. The other heaved himself to his hands and knees, looking up over his shoulder.

"Dropped my terbaccer," he replied in an unemphatic drawl. "Dont happen to have none on you, do you?"

"Got a cigarette, if that'll do you any good." Gilligan offered his pack and the other squatting on his heels took one.

"Much obliged. Feller likes a little smoke once in a while, dont he?"

"Fellow likes a lot of little things in this world, once in a while."

The other guffawed not comprehending but suspecting a reference to sex. "Well, I aint got none o' that, but I got the next thing to it." He rose lean as a hound and from beneath a willow clump he extracted a gallon jug. With awkward formality he tendered it. "Allers take a mite with me when I go fishin'," he explained. "Seems to make the fish bite more'n the muskeeters less."

Gilligan took the jug awkwardly. What in hell did you do with it?

"Here, lemme show you," his host said, relieving him of it. Crooking his first finger in the handle the man raised the jug with a round back-handed sweep to his horizontal upper arm, craning his neck until his mouth met the mouth of the vessel. Gilligan could see his pumping adam's apple against the pale sky. He lowered the jug and drew the back of his hand across his mouth. "That's how she's done," he said handing the thing to Gilligan.

Gilligan tried it with inferior success, feeling the stuff chill upon his chin, sopping the front of his waistcoat. But in his throat it was like fire: it seemed to explode pleasantly as soon as it touched his stomach. He lowered the vessel, coughing.

"Good God, what is it?"

The other laughed hoarsely, slapping his thighs. "Never drunk no corn before, haint you? But how does she feel inside? Better'n out, dont she?"

Gilligan admitted that she did. He could feel all his nerves like electric filaments in a bulb: he was conscious of nothing else. Then it became a warmth and an exhilaration. He raised the jug again and did better.

I'll go to Atlanta tomorrow and find her, catch her before she takes a train out of there, he promised himself. I will find her: she cannot escape me forever. The other drank again and Gilligan lit a cigarette. He, too, knew a sense of freedom, of being master of his own destiny. I'll go to Atlanta tomorrow, find her, make her marry me, he repeated. Why did I let her go?

But why not tonight? Sure, why not tonight? I can find her! I know I can. Even in New York. Funny I never thought of that before. His legs and arms had no sensation, his cigarette slipped from his nerveless fingers and reaching for the tiny coal he wavered, finding that he could no longer control his body. Hell, I aint that drunk, he thought, but was forced to admit that he was.

"Say, what was that stuff, anyway? I can hardly stand up."

The other guffawed again, flattered. "Aint she though? Make her myself, and she's good. You'll git used to it though. Take another." He drank it like water, with unction.

"Dam'f I do. I got to get to town."

"Take a little sup. I'll put you on the road alright."

If two drinks make me feel this good, I'll scream if I take another, he thought. But his friend insisted and he drank again. "Lets go," he said returning the jug.

The man carrying "her" circled the lake. Gilligan blundered behind him, among cypress knees, in occasional mud. After a time he regained some control over his body and they came to a break in the willows and a road slashed in the red sandy soil.

"Here you be, friend. Jest keep right to the road. 'Taint over a mile."

"Alright. Much obliged to you. You've sure got a son of a gun of a drink there."

"She's alright, aint she?" the other agreed.

"Well, goodnight." Gilligan extended his hand and the other grasped it formally and limply and pumped it once, from a rigid elbow. "Take keer of yo'self."

"I'll try to," Gilligan promised. The other's gangling malaria-ridden figure faded again among the willows. The road gashed across the land stretched silent and empty before him, below the east was a rumorous promise of moonlight. He trod in dust between dark trees like spilled ink upon the pale clear page of the sky, and soon the moon was more than a promise. He saw the rim of it sharpening the tips of trees, saw soon the whole disc bland as a saucer. Whip-poor-wills were like lost coins among the trees and one blundered awkwardly from the dust almost under his feet. The whiskey died away in the loneliness, soon his temporarily mis-laid despair took its place again.

After a while passing beneath crossed skeletoned arms on a pole he crossed the railroad and followed a lane between negro cabins, smelling the intimate odor of negroes. The cabins were dark but from them came soft meaningless laughter and slow unemphatic voices, cheerful, yet somehow filled with all the old despairs of time and breath.

Under the moon, quavering with the passion of spring and flesh, among whitewashed walls papered inwardly with old newspapers, something pagan using the white man's conven-

tions as it used his clothing, hushed and powerful, not knowing its own power:

'Sweet chariot . . . comin' fer to ca'y me home. . . .'

Three young men passed him, shuffling in the dust, aping
their own mute shadows in the dusty road, sharp with the
passed sweat of labor: You may be fas' but you cant las', cause
yo' mommer go' slow you down.

He trod on with the moon in his face, seeing the cupolaed
clock squatting like a benignant god on the courthouse,
against the sky, staring across the town with four faces. He
passed yet more cabins while sweet mellow voices called from
door to door. A dog bayed the moon, clear and sorrowful and
a voice cursed it in soft syllables.

'. . . sweet chariot, comin' fer to ca'y me home . . . yes,
Jesus, comin' fer to ca'y me hoooome. . . .'

The church loomed a black shadow with a silver roof and
he crossed the lawn, passing beneath slumbrous ivied walls.
In the garden the mockingbird that lived in the magnolia rippled the silence, and along the moony wall of the rectory, from
ledge to ledge something crawled shapelessly. What in hell,
thought Gilligan, seeing it pause at Emmy's window.

He leaped flower beds swiftly and noiselessly. Here was a
convenient gutter and Jones did not hear him until he had
almost reached the window to which the other clung. They
regarded each other precariously, the one clinging to the
window, the other to the gutter.

"What are you trying to do?" Gilligan asked.

"Climb up here a little further and I'll show you," Jones told
him, snarling his yellow teeth.

"Come away from there, fellow."

"Damn my soul, if here aint the squire of dames again! We
all hoped you had gone off with that black woman."

"Are you coming down, or am I going to come up there
and throw you down?"

"I dont know: am I? or are you?"

For reply Gilligan heaved himself up grasping the window
ledge. Jones clinging tried to kick him in the face but Gilligan
caught his foot, releasing his grasp on the gutter. For a
moment they swung like a great pendulum against the side of

the house, then Jones' hold on the window was torn loose
and they plunged together into a bed of tulips. Jones was first
on his feet and kicking Gilligan in the side he fled. Gilligan
sprang after him and overtook him smartly.

This time it was hyacinths. Jones fought like a woman, kicking, clawing, biting; but Gilligan hauled him to his feet and
knocked him down. Jones rose again and was felled once
more. This time he crawled and grasping Gilligan's knees
pulled him down. Jones kicked himself free and rising fled
anew. Gilligan sat up contemplating pursuit, but gave it up as
he watched Jones' unwieldy body leaping away through the
moonlight.

Jones doubled the church at good speed and let himself out
the gate. He saw no pursuit so his pace slackened to a walk.
Beneath quiet elms his breath became easier. Branches mo-
tionlessly leafed were still against stars and mopping his face
and neck with his handkerchief he walked along a deserted
street. At a corner he stopped to dip his handkerchief in a
trough for watering horses, bathing his face and hands. The
water reduced the pain of the blows he had received and as he
paced fatly on from shadow to moonlight and then to shadow
again, dogged by his own skulking shapeless shadow, the calm
still night washed his recent tribulation completely from his
mind.

From shadowed porches beyond oaks and maples, elms and
magnolias, from beyond screening vines starred with motionless pallid blossoms came snatches of hushed talk and sweet
broken laughter. . . . Male and female created He them,
young. Jones was young, too. 'Yet ah, that Spring should
vanish with the Rose! That Youth's sweet-scented Manuscript
should close! The Nightingale that in the Branches sang, Ah,
whence, and whither flown again, who knows! . . .' Wish I
had a girl tonight, he sighed.

The moon was serene: 'Ah, Moon of my Delight that
know'st no wane, The Moon of Heav'n is rising once again:
How oft hereafter rising shall she look Through this same
Garden after me—in vain!' But how spring itself is imminent
with autumn, with death: 'As autumn and the moon of death
draw nigh The sad long days of summer herein lie And she
too warm in sorrow 'neath the trees Turns to night and weeps,

and longs to die.' And in the magic of spring and youth and moonlight Jones raised his clear sentimental tenor.

'Sweetheart, sweetheart, sweetheart'

His slow shadow blotted out the pen strokes of iron pickets but when he had passed the pen strokes were still there upon the dark soft grass. Clumps of petunia and cannas broke the smooth stretch of lawn and above the bronze foliage of magnolias the serene columns of a white house rose more beautiful in simplicity than death.

Jones leaned his elbows on a gate, staring at his lumpy shadow at his feet, smelling cape jasmine, hearing a mockingbird somewhere, somewhere. . . .

Jones sighed. It was a sigh of pure ennui.

7.

On the rector's desk was a letter addressed to Mr Julian Lowe, —— st., San Francisco, Cal., telling him of her marriage and of her husband's death. It had been returned by the postoffice department stamped Removed. Present address unknown.

8.

Gilligan sitting in the hyacinth bed watched Jones' flight. He aint so bad for a fat one, he admitted, rising. Emmy'll sure have to sleep single tonight. The mockingbird in the magnolia as though it had waited for hostilities to cease, sang again.

"What in hell have you got to sing about?" Gilligan shook his fist at the tree. The bird ignored him and he brushed dark earth from his clothes. Anyway, he soliloquised, I feel better. Wish I could have held the bastard, though. He passed from the garden with a last look at the ruined hyacinth bed. The rector looming met him at the corner of the house beneath the hushed slumbrous passion of the silver tree.

"That you, Joe? I thought I heard noises in the garden."

"You did. I was trying to beat hell out of that fat one, but I couldn't hold the so—I couldn't hold him. He lit out."

"Fighting? My dear boy!"

"It wasn't no fight: he was too busy getting away. It takes two folks to fight, padre."

"Fighting doesn't settle anything, Joe. I'm sorry you resorted to it. Was anyone hurt?"

"No, worse luck," Gilligan replied ruefully, thinking of his soiled clothes and his abortive vengeance.

"I am glad of that. But boys will fight, eh, Joe? Donald fought in his day."

"You damn right he did, reverend. I bet he was a son-of-a-gun in his day."

The rector's heavy lined face took a flared match, between his cupped hands he sucked at his pipe. He walked slowly in the moonlight across the lawn toward the gate. Gilligan followed. "I feel restless tonight," he explained. "Shall we walk a while?"

They paced slowly beneath arched and moon-bitten trees, scuffing their feet in shadows of leaves. Under the moon lights in houses were yellow futilities.

"Well Joe, things are back to normal again. People come and go, but Emmy and I seem to be like the biblical rocks. What are your plans?"

Gilligan lit a cigarette with ostentatiousness, hiding his embarrassment. "Well, padre, to tell the truth, I aint got any. If its all the same to you I think I'll stay on with you a while longer."

"And welcome, dear boy," the rector answered heartily. Then he stopped and faced the other, keenly. "God bless you, Joe. Was it on my account you decided to stay?"

Gilligan averted his face guiltily. "Well, padre——"

"Not at all. I wont have it. You have already done all you can. This is no place for a young man, Joe."

The rector's bald forehead and his blobby nose were intersecting planes in the moonlight, his eyes were cavernous. Gilligan knew suddenly all the old sorrows of the race, black or yellow or white, and he found himself telling the rector all about her.

"Tut, tut," the divine said, "this is bad, Joe." He lowered himself hugely to the edge of the sidewalk and Gilligan sat beside him. "Circumstance moves in marvellous ways, Joe."

"I thought you'd a said God, reverend."

"God is circumstance, Joe. God is in this life. We know nothing about the next. That will take care of itself in good time. 'The kingdom of God is in man's own heart,' the Book says."

"Aint that a kind of funny doctrine for a parson to get off?"

"Remember, I am an old man, Joe. Too old for bickering or bitterness. We make our own heaven or hell in this world. Who knows; perhaps when we die we may not be required to go anywhere nor do anything at all. That would be heaven."

"Or other people make it for us."

The divine put his heavy arm across Gilligan's shoulder. "You are suffering from disappointment. But this will pass away. The saddest thing about love, Joe, is that not only the love cannot last forever, but even the heart-break is soon forgotten. How does it go? 'Men have died and worms have eaten them, but not for love' No, no," as Gilligan would have interrupted, "I know that is an unbearable belief, but all truth is unbearable. Do we not both suffer at this moment from the facts of division and death?"

Gilligan knew shame. Bothering him now, me with a fancied disappointment! The rector spoke again. "I think it would be a good idea for you to stay, after all, until you make your future plans. So lets consider it closed, eh? Suppose we walk further——unless you are tired?"

Gilligan rose in effusive negation. After a while the quiet tree-tunnelled street became a winding road, and leaving the town behind them they descended and then mounted a hill. Cresting the hill beneath the moon, seeing the world breaking away from them into dark, moon-silvered ridges above valleys where mist hung slumberous, they passed a small house, sleeping among climbing roses. Beyond it an orchard slept the night away in symmetrical rows, squatting and pregnant. "Willard has good fruit," the divine murmured.

The road dropped on again descending between reddish gashes and across a level moon-lit space broken by a clump of saplings came a pure quavering chord of music, wordless and far away.

"They are holding services. Negroes," the rector explained. They walked on in the dust passing neat tidy houses dark with slumber. An occasional group of negroes passed them, bearing lighted lanterns that jetted vain little flames futilely in the moonlight. "No one knows why they do that," the divine replied to Gilligan's question. "Perhaps it is to light their churches with."

The singing drew nearer and nearer, at last crouching among a clump of trees beside the road they saw the shabby church with its canting travesty of a spire. Within it was a soft glow of kerosene serving only to make the darkness and the heat thicker, making thicker the imminence of sex after harsh labor along the mooned land; and from it welled the crooning submerged passion of the dark race. It was nothing, it was everything; then it swelled to an ecstasy, taking the white man's words as readily as it took his remote God and made a personal Father of him.

Feed Thy sheep O Jesus. All the longing of mankind for a Oneness with Something, somewhere. Feed Thy sheep O Jesus. . . . The rector and Gilligan stood side by side in the dusty road. The road went on under the moon, vaguely dissolving without perspective. Worn-out red-gutted fields were now alternate splashes of soft black and silver; trees had each a silver nimbus save those moonward from them, which were sharp as bronze.

Feed Thy sheep O Jesus. The voices rose full and soft. There was no organ: no organ was needed as above the harmonic passion of base and baritone, soaring, a clear soprano of women's voices like a flight of gold and heavenly birds. They stood together in the dust, the rector in his shapeless black and Gilligan in his new hard serge listening, seeing the shabby church become beautiful with mellow longing, passionate and sad.

Then the singing died, fading away along the mooned land inevitable with tomorrow and sweat, with sex and death and damnation; and they turned townward under the moon, feeling dust in their shoes.

(end)

MOSQUITOES

To Helen, Beautiful and Wise

CONTENTS

PROLOGUE 261

THE FIRST DAY 298

THE SECOND DAY 336

THE THIRD DAY 389

THE FOURTH DAY 449

EPILOGUE 496

In spring, the sweet young spring, decked out with little green, necklaced braceleted with the song of idiotic birds, spurious and sweet and tawdry as a shopgirl in her cheap finery, like an idiot with money and no taste, they were little and young and trusting: you could kill them sometimes. But now, as August like a languorous replete bird winged slowly through the pale summer toward the moon of decay and death they were bigger, vicious; ubiquitous as undertakers, cunning as pawnbrokers, confident and unavoidable as politicians. They came cityward lustful as country-boys, as passionately integral as a college football squad, pervading and monstrous but without majesty: a biblical plague seen through the wrong end of a binocular: the majesty of Fate become contemptuous through ubiquity and sheer repetition

Prologue

"THE sex instinct," repeated Mr Talliaferro in his careful cockney, with that smug complacence with which you plead guilty to a characteristic which you privately consider a virtue, "is quite strong in me. Frankness, without which there can be no friendship, without which two people cannot really ever 'get' one another, as you artists say; frankness as I was saying, I believe——"

"Yes," his host agreed. "Would you mind moving a little?"

He complied with obsequious courtesy, remarking the thin fretful flashing of a chisel beneath a rhythmic maul. Wood scented gratefully slid from its mute flashing, and slapping vainly about him with his handkerchief he moved in a Bluebeard's closet of blonde hair in severed clots, examining with concern a faint even powdering of dust upon his neat small patentleather shoes. Yes, one must pay a price for art. . . . Watching the rhythmic power of the other's back and arm he speculated briefly upon which was more to be desired—— muscularity and an undershirt, or his own symmetrical sleeve, and reassured he continued:

"—frankness compels me to admit that the sex instinct is perhaps my most dominating compulsion." Mr Talliaferro believed that Conversation—not talk: Conversation—with an intellectual equal consisted of admitting as many socalled unpublishable facts as possible about oneself: Mr Talliaferro often mused with regret on the degree of intimacy he might have established with his artistic acquaintances had he but acquired the habit of masturbation in his youth. But he had not even done this.

"Yes," his host agreed again, thrusting a hard hip into him. Not at all, murmured Mr Talliaferro quickly. A harsh wall restored his equilibrium roughly and hearing a friction of cloth and plaster he rebounded with repressed alacrity.

"Pardon me," he chattered. His entire sleeve indicated his arm in gritty white and regarding his coat with consternation he moved out of range and sat upon an upturned wooden block. Brushing did no good and the ungracious surface on which he sat recalling his trousers, he rose to spread his handkerchief upon it. Whenever he came here he invariably soiled his clothes, but under that spell put on us by those we admire doing something we ourselves cannot do, he always returned.

The chisel bit steadily beneath the slow arc of the maul. His host ignored him. Mr Talliaferro slapped viciously and vainly at the back of his hand as he sat in lukewarm shadow while light came across roofs and chimneypots, passing through a dingy skylight, becoming weary. His host labored on in the tired light while the guest sat on his hard block regretting his sleeve, watching the other's hard body in stained trousers and undershirt, watching the curling vigor of his hair.

Outside the window New Orleans, the vieux carré, brooded in a faintly tarnished languor like an aging yet still beautiful courtesan in a smokefilled room, avid yet weary too of ardent ways. Above the city summer was hushed warmly into the bowled weary passion of the sky. Spring and the cruellest months were gone, the cruel months, the wantons that break the fat hybernatant dullness and comfort of Time; August was on the wing, and September——a month of languorous days regretful as woodsmoke. But Mr Talliaferro's youth, or lack of it, troubled him no longer. Thank God.

No youth to trouble the individual in this room at all. What this room troubled was something eternal in the race, something immortal. And youth is not deathless. Thank God. This unevenly boarded floor, these rough stained walls broken by high small practically useless windows beautifully set, crouching lintels cutting the immaculate ruined pitch of walls which had housed slaves long ago, slaves long dead and dust with the age that had produced them and which they had served with a kind and gracious dignity—shades of servants and masters now in a more gracious region, lending dignity to eternity. After all, only a few chosen can accept service with dignity: it is man's impulse to do for himself. It rests with the servant to lend dignity to an unnatural proceeding. And outside, above rooftops becoming slowly violet, summer lay supine, unchaste with decay.

As you entered the room the thing drew your eye: you turned sharply as to a sound, expecting movement. But it was marble, it could not move. And when you tore your eyes away and turned your back on it at last, you got again untarnished and high and clean that sense of swiftness, of space encompassed; but on looking again it was as before: motionless and passionately eternal—the virginal breastless torso of a girl, headless armless legless, in marble temporarily caught and hushed yet passionate still for escape, passionate and simple and eternal in the equivocal derisive darkness of the world. Nothing to trouble your youth or lack of it: rather something to trouble the very fibrous integrity of your being. Mr Talliaferro slapped his neck savagely.

The manipulator of the chisel and maul ceased his labor and straightened up, flexing his arms and shoulder muscles. And as though it had graciously waited for him to get done, the light faded quietly and abruptly: the room was like a bathtub after the drain has been opened. Mr Talliaferro rose also and his host turned upon him a face like that of a heavy hawk, breaking his dream. Mr Talliaferro regretted his sleeve again and said briskly:

"Then I may tell Mrs Maurier that you will come?"

"What?" the other asked sharply, staring at him. "Oh. Hell, I have work to do. Sorry. Tell her I am sorry."

Mr Talliaferro's disappointment was tinged faintly with exasperation as he watched the other cross the darkening room to a rough wood bench and raise a cheap enamelware water pitcher, gulping from it. "But, I say," said Mr Talliaferro fretfully.

"No, no," the other repeated brusquely, wiping his beard on his upper arm. "Some other time, perhaps. I am too busy to bother with her now. Sorry." He swung to the open door and from a hook screwed into it he took down a thin coat and a battered tweed cap. Mr Talliaferro watched his muscles bulge the thin cloth with envious distaste, recalling anew the unmuscled emphasis of his own pressed flannel. The other was palpably on the verge of abrupt departure and Mr Talliaferro to whom solitude, particularly dingy solitude, was unbearable, took his stiff straw hat from the bench where it flaunted its wanton gay band above the slim yellow gleam of his straight malacca stick.

"Wait," he said, "and I'll join you."

"The other paused, looking back. "I'm going out," he stated belligerently.

Mr Talliaferro at a momentary loss said fatuously: "Why— ah, I thought——I should——" The hawk's face brooded above him in the dusk remotely and he added quickly: "I could return, however."

"Sure its no trouble?"

"Not at all, my dear fellow, not at all! Only call on me: I will be only too glad to return."

"Well, if you're sure its no trouble, suppose you fetch me a bottle of milk from the grocer on the corner. You know the place, dont you? Here's the empty one."

With one of his characteristic plunging movements the other passed through the door and Mr Talliaferro stood in a dapper fretted surprise, clutching a coin in one hand and an unwashed milk bottle in the other. On the stairs, watching the other's shape descending into the welled darkness, he stopped again and standing on one leg like a crane he clasped the bottle under his arm and slapped at his ankle, viciously and vainly.

2.

Descending a final stair and turning into a darkling corridor he passed two people indistinguishably kissing, and he hastened on toward the street door. He paused here in active indecision, opening his coat. The bottle had become clammy in his hand: he contemplated it through his sense of touch with acute repugnance. Unseen, it seemed to have become unbearably dirty. He desired something, vaguely—a newspaper perhaps; but before striking a match he looked quickly over his shoulder. They were gone, hushing their chimed footsteps up the dark curve of the stair: their locked tread was like a physical embrace. His match flared a puny fledged gold that followed his clasped gleaming stick as if it were a train of gunpowder, but the passage was empty, swept with chill stone, imminent with weary moisture . . . the match burned down to the even polished temper of his fingernails and plunged him back into darkness more intense.

He opened the street door. Twilight ran in like a quiet violet dog and nursing his bottle he peered out across an

undimensional feathered square, across stencilled palms and
Andrew Jackson in childish effigy bestriding the terrific arrested plunge of his curly balanced horse, toward the long
unemphasis of the Pontalba building and three spires of a
cathedral graduated by perspective, pure and slumberous beneath the decadent languor of August and evening. Mr Talliaferro thrust his head modestly forth, looking both ways along
the street. Then he withdrew his head and closed the door
again.

He employed his immaculate linen handkerchief reluctantly
before thrusting the bottle beneath his coat. It bulged dis-
tressingly under his exploring hand and he removed the bottle
in a mounting desperation. He struck another match, setting
the bottle down at his feet to do so, but there was nothing in
which he might wrap, conceal the thing. His impulse was to
grasp it and hurl it against the wall: he already pleasured in its
anticipated glassy crash. But Mr Talliaferro was quite honorable: he had passed his word. Or he might return to his
friend's room and get a bit of paper. He stood in hot indecision until feet on the stairs descending decided for him. He
bent and fumbled for the bottle, struck it and heard its disconsolate empty flight, captured it at last and opening the
street door anew, rushed hurriedly forth.

The violet dusk held in soft suspension lights slow as bell-
strokes, Jackson Square was now a green and quiet lake in
which abode lights round as jellyfish, feathering with silver
mimosa and pomegranate and hibiscus beneath which lantana
and cannas bled and bled. Pontalba and cathedral were cut
from black paper and pasted flat on a green sky; above them
taller palms were fixed in black and soundless explosions. The
street was empty but from Royal street there came the hum
of a trolley that rose to a staggering clatter, passed on and
away, leaving an interval filled with the gracious sound of in-
flated rubber on asphalt, like a tearing of endless silk. Clasping his accursed bottle, feeling like a criminal, Mr Talliaferro
hurried on.

He walked swiftly beside a dark wall, passing small indiscriminate shops dimly lighted with gas, smelling food of all
kinds, fulsome, slightly overripe. The proprietors and their
families sat before them in tilted chairs, women nursing babies

into slumber spoke in soft south European syllables one to another, children scurried about and before him, ignoring him or becoming aware of him and crouching in shadow like animals, defensive passive and motionless. He turned the corner. Royal street sprang in two directions and he darted into a grocery store on the corner, passing the proprietor in the door sitting with his legs spread for comfort, nursing the Italian balloon of his belly on his lap. The proprietor removed his short terrific pipe and belched, rising to follow. Mr Talliaferro set his bottle down hastily.

The grocer belched again, frankly. "Good afternoon," he said in a broad West End accent much nearer the real thing than Mr Talliaferro's. "Meelk, hay?"

Mr Talliaferro extended the coin, murmuring, watching the man's thick reluctant thighs as he picked up the bottle without repugnance and slid it into a pigeonholed box and opening a refrigerator, took therefrom a fresh one. Mr Talliaferro recoiled.

"Haven't you a bit of paper to wrap it in?" he asked diffidently.

"Why, sure," the other agreed affably. "Make her in a parcel, hay?" He complied with exasperating deliberation, and breathing freer but still oppressed Mr Talliaferro took his purchase and glancing hurriedly about, stepped into the street. And paused, stricken.

She was under full sail and convoyed by a slimmer one when she saw him, but she tacked at once and came about in a hushed swishing of silk and an expensive clashing of impedimenta—handbag and chains and beads. Her hand bloomed fatly through a bracelet, ringed and manicured, and her hothouse face wore an expression of infantile trusting astonishment.

"Mister Talliaferro! What a surprise!" she exclaimed, accenting the first word of each phrase, as was her manner. And she really was surprised. Mrs Maurier went through the world continually amazed at chance, whether or not she had instigated it. Mr Talliaferro shifted his parcel quickly behind him, to its imminent destruction, being forced to accept her hand without removing his hat. He rectified this as soon as possible. "I would never have expected to see you in this part of town at this hour. But you have been calling on some of your artist friends, I suppose?"

The slim one had stopped also and stood examining Mr Talliaferro with cool uninterest. The older woman turned to her. "Mr Talliaferro knows all the interesting people in the Quarter, darling. All the people who are—who are creating—creating things. Beautiful things. Beauty, you know." Mrs Maurier waved her glittering hand vaguely in the direction of Rampart street. Or it may have been toward the sky, in which stars had begun to flower like pale and tarnished gardenias. "Oh, do excuse me, Mr Talliaferro——This is my niece, Miss Robyn, of whom you have heard me speak. She and her brother have come to comfort a lonely old woman——" her glance held a decayed coquetry and taking his cue Mr Talliaferro said:

"Nonsense, dear lady. It is we, your unhappy admirers, who need comforting. Perhaps Miss Robyn will take pity on us also?" He bowed toward the niece with calculated formality. The niece was not enthusiastic.

"Now, darling," Mrs Maurier turned to her niece with rapture. "Here is an example of the chivalry of our southern men. Can you imagine a man in Chicago saying that?"

"Not hardly," the niece agreed.

Her aunt rushed on: "That is why I have been so anxious for Pat to visit me, so she can meet men who are—who are— My niece is named for me, you see, Mr Talliaferro. Isn't that nice?" She pressed Mr Talliaferro with recurrent happy astonishment.

Mr Talliaferro bowed again, came within an ace of dropping the bottle, darted the hand which clutched his hat and stick behind him to steady it. "Charming, charming," he agreed, perspiring under his hair.

"But, really, I am so surprised to find you here at this hour. And I suppose you are as surprised to find us here, aren't you? But I have just found the most won—derful thing! Do look at it, Mr Talliaferro: I do so want your opinion." She extended a dull lead plaque from which in dim bas-relief of faded red and blue simpered a Madonna with an expression of infantile astonishment identical with that of Mrs Maurier, and a Child somehow smug and complacent looking as an old man. Mr

Talliaferro, feeling the poised precariousness of the bottle, dared not release his hand. He bent over the extended object. "Do take it, so you can examine it under the light," its owner insisted. Mr Talliaferro perspired again mildly and the niece spoke suddenly:

"I'll hold your package."

She moved with young swiftness and before he could demur she had taken the bottle from his hand. "Ow," she exclaimed, almost dropping it herself, and her aunt gushed:

"Oh, you have discovered something also, haven't you? Now I've gone and shown you my treasure and all the while you were concealing something much, much nicer." She waggled her hands to indicate dejection. "You will consider mine trash, I know you will," she went on with heavy assumed displeasure. "Oh, to be a man, so I could poke around in shops all day and really discover things! Do show us what you have, Mr Talliaferro."

"Its a bottle of milk," remarked the niece, examining Mr Talliaferro with interest.

Her aunt shrieked. Her breast heaved with repression, glinting her pins and beads. "A bottle of milk? Have you turned artist, too?"

For the first and last time in his life Mr Talliaferro wished a lady dead. But he was a gentleman: he only seethed inwardly. He laughed with abortive heartiness.

"An artist? You flatter me, dear lady. I'm afraid my soul does not aspire so high. I am content to be merely a—"

"Milkman," suggested the young female devil.

"——Mæcenas alone. If I might so style myself."

Mrs Maurier sighed with disappointment and surprise. "Ah, Mr Talliaferro, I am dreadfully disappointed. I had hoped for a moment that some of your artist friends had at last prevailed on you to give something to the world of Art. No, no: dont say you cannot: I am sure you are capable of it, what with your——your delicacy of soul, your——" she waved her hand again vaguely toward the sky above Rampart street. "Ah, to be a man, with no ties save those of the soul. To create, to create." She returned easily to Royal street. "But, really, a bottle of milk, Mr Talliaferro?"

"Merely for my friend Gordon. I looked in on him this

afternoon and found him quite busy. So I ran out to fetch him milk for his supper. These artists!" Mr Talliaferro shrugged. "You know how they live."

"Yes, indeed. Genius. A hard taskmaster, isn't it? Perhaps you are wise in not giving your life to it. It is a long lonely road. But how is Mr Gordon? I am so continually occupied with things—unavoidable duties, which my conscience will not permit me to evade (I am very conscientious, you know) that I simply haven't the time to see as much of the Quarter as I should like. I had promised Mr Gordon faithfully to call, and to have him to dinner soon. I am sure he thinks I have forgotten him. Please make my peace with him, wont you? Assure him that I have not forgotten him."

"I am sure he realizes how many calls you have on your time," Mr Talliaferro assured her gallantly. "Dont let that distress you at all."

"Yes, I really dont know how I get anything done: I am always surprised when I find I have a spare moment for my own pleasure." She turned her expression of happy astonishment on him again. The niece spun slowly and slimly on one high heel; the sweet young curve of her shanks straight and brittle as the legs of a bird, ending in the pointed inky splashes of her narrow slippers, entranced him. Her hat was a small brilliant bell about her face and she wore her clothing with a rakish casualness, as though she had opened her wardrobe and said Lets go down town. Her aunt was saying:

"But what about our yachting party? You gave Mr Gordon my invitation?"

Mr Talliaferro was troubled. "We—ll, you see, he is quite busy now. He—— He has a commission which will admit of no delay," he concluded with inspiration.

"Ah, Mr Talliaferro! You haven't told him he is invited. Shame on you! Then I must tell him myself, since you have failed me."

"No: really——"

She interrupted. "Forgive me, dear Mr Talliaferro. I didn't mean to be unjust. I am glad you didn't invite him. It will be better for me to do it, so I can overcome any scruples he may have. He is quite shy, you know. Oh, quite, I assure you. Artistic temperament, you understand: so spirituel. . . ."

"Yes," agreed Mr Talliaferro covertly watching the niece, who ceased her spinning and got her seemingly boneless body into an undimensional angular flatness pure as an Egyptian carving.

"So I shall attend to it myself. I shall call him tonight: we sail at noon tomorrow, you know. That will allow him sufficient time, dont you think. He's one of these artists who never have much, lucky people." Mrs Maurier looked at her watch. "Heavens above, seven thirty. We must fly. Come, darling. Cant we drop you somewhere, Mr Talliaferro?"

"Thank you, no. I must take Gordon's milk to him, and then I am engaged for the evening."

"Ah, Mr Talliaferro! Its a woman, I know." She rolled her eyes roguishly. "What a terrible man you are." She lowered her voice and tapped him on the sleeve. "Do be careful what you say before this child. My instincts are all bohemian, but she . . . unsophisticated . . ." her voice bathed him warmly and Mr Talliaferro bridled: had he had a moustache he would have stroked it. Mrs Maurier jangled and glittered again: her expression became one of pure delight. "But, of course! We will drive you to Mr Gordon's and then I can run in and invite him on our party. The very thing! How fortunate to have thought of it. Come, darling."

Without stopping the niece angled her leg upward and outward, scratching her ankle. Mr Talliaferro recalled the milk bottle and assented gratefully, falling in on the curbside with meticulous thoughtfulness. A short distance up the street Mrs Maurier's car squatted gleaming expensively. The negro driver descended and opened the door and Mr Talliaferro sank into gracious upholstery, nursing his bottle, smelling flowers cut and delicately vased, promising himself a car next year.

3.

They rolled smoothly, passing beneath spaced lights and around narrow corners, while Mrs Maurier talked steadily of her and Mr Talliaferro's and Gordon's souls. The niece sat quietly. Mr Talliaferro was conscious of the clean young odor of her, like that of young trees; and when they passed beneath lights he could see her slim shape, the impersonal revelation of her legs and her bare sexless knees. Mr Talliaferro luxuriated, clutching his bottle of milk, wishing the ride need not end. But the car drew up to the curb again, and he must get out, no matter with what reluctance.

"I'll run up and bring him down to you," he suggested with premonitory tact.

"No, no: lets all go up," Mrs Maurier objected. "I want Patricia to see how genius looks at home."

"Gee, Aunty, I've seen these dives before," the niece said. "They're everywhere. I'll wait for you." She jackknifed her body effortlessly, scratching her ankles with her brown hands.

"Its so interesting to see how they live, darling. You'll simply love it." Mr. Talliaferro demurred again, but Mrs Maurier overrode him with sheer words. So against his better judgment he struck matches for them, leading the way up the dark torturous stairs, while their three shadows aped them, rising and falling monstrously upon the ancient wall. Long before they reached the final stage Mrs Maurier was puffing and panting: Mr Talliaferro took a puerile vengeful glee from hearing her labored breath. But he was a gentleman and he put this from him, rebuking himself. He knocked on a door, was bidden, opened it:

"Back, are you?" Gordon sat in his single chair, munching a thick sandwich, clutching a book. The unshaded light glared savagely upon his undershirt.

"You have callers." Mr Talliaferro offered his belated warning but the other looking up had already seen beyond his shoulder Mrs Maurier's interested face. He rose and cursed Mr Talliaferro, who had begun immediately his unhappy explanation: "Mrs Maurier insisted on dropping in——"

Mrs Maurier vanquished him anew. "Mister Gordon!" She sailed into the room, bearing her expression of happy astonishment like a round platter stood on edge. "How *do* you do? Can you ever, ever forgive us for intruding like this?" she went on in her gushing italics. "We just met Mr Talliaferro on the street with your milk, and we decided to brave the lion in his den. How do you do?" She forced her effusive hand upon him, staring about in happy curiosity. "So this is where genius labors. How charming: so—so original. And that——" she indicated a corner screened off by a draggled length of green rep "—is your bedroom, isn't it? How delightful! Ah, Mr Gordon, how I envy you this freedom. And a view—you have a view, also, haven't you?" She held his hand and stared entranced at a high useless window framing two tired-looking stars of the fourth magnitude.

"I would have if I were eight feet tall," he corrected. She looked at him quickly, happily. Mr Talliaferro laughed nervously.

"That would be delightful," she agreed readily. "I was so anxious to have my niece see a real studio, Mr Gordon, where a real artist works. Darling——" she paused, still holding captive his hand, looking over her shoulder fatly "—darling, let me present you to a real sculptor, one from whom we expect great things. . . . Darling," she repeated in a louder tone. The niece, untroubled by the stairs, had drifted in after them and she now stood before the single marble. "Come and speak to Mr Gordon, darling." Beneath her aunt's saccharine modulation was a faint trace of something not so sweet after all. The niece turned her head and nodded slightly without looking at him. Gordon released his hand.

"Mr Talliaferro tells me you have a commission." Mrs Maurier's voice was again a happy astonished honey. "May we see it? I know artists dont like to exhibit an incomplete work, but just among friends, you see. . . . You both know how sensitive to beauty I am, though I have been denied the creative impulse myself."

"Yes," agreed Gordon, watching the niece.

"I have long intended visiting your studio, as I promised, you remember. So I shall take this opportunity of looking about—Do you mind?"

"Help yourself: Talliaferro can show you things. Pardon me." He lurched characteristically between them and Mrs Maurier chanted:

"Yes, indeed. Mr Talliaferro, like myself, is sensitive to the beautiful in Art. Ah, Mr Talliaferro, why were you and I given a love for the beautiful yet denied the ability to create it from stone and wood and clay. . . ."

Her body in its brief simple dress was motionless when he came over to her. After a time he said:

"Like it?"

Her jaw in profile was heavy: there was something masculine about it. But in full face it was not heavy, only quiet. Her mouth was full and colorless, unpainted, and her eyes were opaque as smoke. She met his gaze, remarking the icy blueness of his eyes (like a surgeon's, she thought) and looked at the marble again.

"I dont know," she answered slowly. Then: "Its like me."

"How like you?" he asked gravely.

She didn't answer. Then she said: "Can I touch it?"

"If you like," he replied, examining the line of her jaw, her firm brief nose. She made no move and he added: "Aren't you going to touch it?"

"I've changed my mind," she told him calmly. Gordon glanced over his shoulder to where Mrs Maurier pored volubly over something. Mr Talliaferro yea'd her with restrained passion.

"Why is it like you?" he repeated.

She said irrelevantly: "Why hasn't she anything here?" Her brown hand flashed slimly across the high unemphasis of the marble's breast, and withdrew.

"You haven't much there yourself." She met his steady gaze steadily. "Why should it have anything there?" he asked.

"You're right," she agreed with the judicial complaisance of an equal. "I see now. Of course she shouldn't. I didn't quite——quite get it for a moment."

Gordon examined with growing interest her flat breast and belly, her boy's body which the poise of it and the thinness of her arms belied. Sexless, yet somehow vaguely troubling. Perhaps just young, like a calf or a colt. "How old are you?" he asked abruptly.

"Eighteen, if its any of your business," she replied without rancor, staring at the marble. Suddenly she looked up at him again. "I wish I could have it," she said with sudden sincerity and longing, quite like a four year old.

"Thanks," said Gordon. "That was quite sincere, too, wasn't it? Of course you cant have it, though. You see that, dont you?"

She was silent. He knew she could see no reason why she shouldn't have it.

"I guess so," she agreed at last. "I just thought I'd see, though."

"Not to overlook any bets?"

"Oh, well, by tomorrow I probably wont want it, anyway. . . . And if I still do, I can get something just as good."

"You mean," he amended, "that if you still want it tomorrow, you can get it. Dont you?"

Her hand as if it were a separate organism reached out slowly stroking the marble. "Why are you so black?" she asked.

"Black?"

"Not your hair and beard. I like your red hair and beard. But you. You are black. I mean. . . ." her voice fell and he suggested Soul? "I dont know what that is," she stated quietly.

"Neither do I. You might ask your aunt, though. She seems familiar with souls."

She glanced over her shoulder, showing him her other unequal profile. "Ask her yourself. Here she comes."

Mrs Maurier surged her scented upholstered bulk between them. "Wonderful, wonderful," she was exclaiming in sincere astonishment. "And this . . ." her voice died away and she gazed at the marble, dazed. Mr Talliaferro echoed her immaculately, taking to himself the showman's credit.

"Do you see what he has caught?" he bugled melodiously. "Do you see? The spirit of youth, of something fine and hard and clean in the world: something we all desire until our mouths are stopped with dust." Desire with Mr Talliaferro had long since become an unfulfilled habit requiring no longer any particular object at all.

"Yes," agreed Mrs Maurier. "How beautiful. What—what does it signify, Mr Gordon?"

"Nothing, Aunt Pat," the niece snapped. "It doesn't have to."

"But, really——"

"What do you want it to signify? Suppose it signified a—a dog, or an icecream soda, what difference would it make? Isn't it all right like it is?"

"Yes indeed, Mrs Maurier," Mr Talliaferro agreed with soothing haste, "it is not necessary that it have objective significance. We must accept it for what it is: pure form untrammelled by any relation to a familiar or utilitarian object."

"Oh, yes: untrammelled." Here was a word Mrs Maurier knew. "The untrammelled spirit: freedom like the eagle's."

"Shut up, Aunty," the niece told her. "Dont be a fool."

"But it has what Talliaferro calls objective significance," Gordon interrupted brutally. "This is my feminine ideal: a virgin with no legs to leave me, no arms to hold me, no head to talk to me."

"Mister Gordon!" Mrs Maurier stared at him over her compressed breast. Then she thought of something that did possess objective significance. "I had almost forgotten our reason for calling so late. Not," she added quickly, "that we needed any other reason to—to—Mr Talliaferro, how was it those old people used to put it, about pausing on Life's busy highroad to kneel for a moment at the Master's feet. . . ?" Mrs Maurier's voice faded and her face assumed an expression of mild concern. "Or is it the bible of which I am thinking? Well, no matter. We dropped in to invite you for a yachting party, a few days on the lake——"

"Yes. Talliaferro told me about it. Sorry, but I shall be unable to come."

Mrs Maurier's eyes became quite round. She turned to Mr Talliaferro. "Mister Talliaferro! You told me you hadn't mentioned it to him!"

Mr Talliaferro writhed acutely. "Do forgive me, if I left you under that impression. It was quite unintentional. I only desired that you speak to him yourself and make him reconsider. The party will not be complete without him, will it?"

"Not at all. Really, Mr Gordon, wont you reconsider? Surely you wont disappoint us." She stooped creaking and slapped at her ankle. "Pardon me."

"No. Sorry. I have work to do."

Mrs Maurier transferred her expression of astonishment and dejection to Mr Talliaferro. "It cant be that he doesn't want to go. There must be some other reason. Do say something to him, Mr Talliaferro. We simply must have him. Mr Fairchild is going, and Eva and Dorothy: we simply must have a sculptor. Do convince him, Mr Talliaferro."

"I'm sure his decision is not final: I am sure he will not deprive us of his company. A few days on the water will do him no end of good——freshen him up like a tonic. Eh, Gordon?"

Gordon's hawk's face brooded above them remote and insufferable with arrogance. The niece had turned away, drifting slowly about the room, grave and quiet and curious, straight as a poplar. Mrs Maurier implored him with her eyes, doglike, temporarily silent. Suddenly she had an inspiration.

"Come, people, lets all go to my house for dinner. Then we can discuss it at our ease."

Mr Talliaferro demurred. "I am engaged this evening, you know," he reminded her.

"Oh, Mr Talliaferro." She put her hand on his sleeve. "Dont you fail me too. I always depend on you when people fail me. Cant you defer your engagement?"

"Really, I am afraid not. Not in this case," Mr Talliaferro replied smugly. "Though I am distressed. . . ."

Mrs Maurier sighed. "These women! Mr Talliaferro is perfectly terrible with women," she informed Gordon. "But you will come, wont you?"

The niece had drifted up to them and stood rubbing the calf of one leg against the other shin. Gordon turned to her. "Will you be there?"

Damn their little souls she whispered on a sucked breath. She yawned. "Oh yes. I eat. But I'm going to bed darn soon." She yawned again, patting the broad pale oval of her mouth with brown fingers.

"Patricia!" exclaimed her aunt in shocked amazement. "Of course you will do nothing of the kind. The very idea! Come, Mr Gordon."

"No, thanks. I am engaged myself," he answered stiffly. "Some other time, perhaps."

"I simply wont take No for an answer. Do help me, Mr Talliaferro. He simply must come."

"Do you want him to come as he is?" the niece asked.

Her aunt glanced briefly at the undershirt, and shuddered. But she said bravely: "Of course, if he wishes. What are clothes, compared with this?" she described an arc with her hand: diamonds glittered on its orbit. "So you cannot evade it, Mr Gordon. You must come."

Her hand poised above his arm, pouncing. He eluded it brusquely. "Excuse me." Mr Talliaferro avoided his sudden movement just in time and the niece said wickedly:

"There's a shirt behind the door, if that's what you are looking for. You wont need a tie, with that beard."

He picked her up by the elbows, as you would a high narrow table, and set her aside. Then his tall controlled body filled and emptied the door and disappeared in the darkness of the hallway. The niece gazed after him. Mrs Maurier stared at the door, then to Mr Talliaferro in quiet amazement. "What in the world——" Her hands clashed vainly among her various festooned belongings. "Where is he going?" she said at last.

The niece said suddenly: "I like him." She too gazed at the door through which passing he seemed to have emptied the room. "I bet he doesn't come back," she remarked.

Her aunt shrieked. "Doesn't come back?"

"Well, I wouldn't if I were him." She returned to the marble, stroking it with slow desire. Mrs Maurier gazed helplessly at Mr Talliaferro. "Where——" she began.

"I'll go see," he offered, breaking his own trance. The two women regarded his vanishing neat back.

"Never in my life——Patricia, what did you mean by being so rude to him? Of course he is offended. Dont you know how sensitive artists are? After I have worked so hard to cultivate him, too!"

"Nonsense. It'll do him good. He thinks just a little too well of himself as it is."

"But to insult the man in his own house. I cant understand you young people at all. Why, if I'd said a thing like that to a gentleman, and a stranger——I cant imagine what your father can mean, letting you grow up like this. He certainly knows better than this——"

"I'm not to blame for the way he acted. You are the one, yourself. Suppose you'd been sitting in your room in your shimmy and a couple of men you hardly knew had walked in on you and tried to persuade you to go somewhere you didn't want to, what would you have done?"

"These people are different," her aunt told her coldly. "You dont understand them. Artists dont require privacy as we do— it means nothing whatever to them. But anyone, artist or no, would object——"

"Oh, haul in your sheet. You're jibing," the niece interrupted coarsely.

Mr Talliaferro reappeared panting with delicate repression. "Gordon was called hurriedly away. He asked me to make his excuses and to express his disappointment over having to leave so unceremoniously."

"Then he's not coming to dinner." Mrs Maurier sighed, feeling her age, the imminence of dark and death. She seemed not only unable to get new men anymore, but to hold to the old ones, even . . . Mr Talliaferro, too . . . age, age. . . . She sighed again. "Come, darling," she said in a strangely chastened tone, quieter, pitiable in a way. The niece put both her firm tanned hands on the marble, hard hard. O beautiful she whispered in salutation and farewell, turning quickly away.

"Lets go," she said, "I'm starving."

Mr Talliaferro had lost his box of matches: he was desolated. So they were forced to feel their way down the stairs, disturbing years and years of dust upon the rail. The stone corridor was cool and dank and filled with a suppressed minor humming. They hurried on.

Night was fully come and the car squatted at the curb in patient silhouette; the negro driver sat within with all the windows closed. Within its friendly familiarity Mrs Maurier's spirits rose again. She gave Mr Talliaferro her hand, sugaring her voice again with a decayed coquetry. "You will call me, then? But dont promise: I know how completely your time is taken up——" she leaned forward, tapping him on the cheek "——Don Juan!"

He laughed deprecatingly, with pleasure. The niece from her corner said:

"Good evening, Mr Tarver."

Mr Talliaferro stood slightly inclined from the hips, frozen. He closed his eyes like a dog awaiting the fall of the stick, while time passed and passed . . . he opened his eyes again, after how long he knew not. But Mrs Maurier's fingers were but leaving his cheek and the niece was invisible in her corner: a bodiless evil. Then he straightened up, feeling his cold entrails resume their proper place. The car drew away and he watched it, thinking of the girl's youngness, her hard clean youngness, with fear and a troubling unhappy desire like an old sorrow. Were children really like dogs, could they penetrate one's concealment, know one instinctively?

Mrs Maurier settled back comfortably. "Mr Talliaferro is perfectly terrible with women," she informed her niece.

"I bet he is," the niece agreed, "perfectly terrible."

4.

Mr Talliaferro had been married while quite young by a rather plainfaced girl whom he was trying to seduce. But now, at thirty eight, he was a widower these eight years. He was the final result of some rather casual biological research conducted by two people who, like the great majority, had no business producing children at all. The family originated in northern Alabama and drifted slowly westward ever after, thus proving that a certain racial impulse, which one Horace Greeley summed up in a slogan so excruciatingly apt that he didn't have to observe it himself, has not yet died away. His brothers were various and they attained their several milieus principally by chance; milieus ranging from an untimely heaven via someone else's horse and a rope and a Texas cottonwood, through a classical chair in a small Kansas college, to a state legislature via someone else's votes. This one got as far as California. They never did know what became of Mr Talliaferro's sister.

Mr Talliaferro had got what is known as a careful raising: he had been forced while yet young and pliable to do all the things to which his natural impulses objected and to forego all the things he could possibly have had any fun doing. After a while nature gave up and this became habit with him. Nature surrendered him without a qualm: even disease germs seemed to ignore him.

His marriage had driven him into work as drouth drives the fish down stream into the larger waters, and things had gone hard with them during the years during which he had shifted from position to position, correspondence course to correspondence course until he had an incorrect and impractical smattering of information regarding every possible genteel method of gaining money, before finally and inevitably gravitating into the women's clothing section of a large department store.

Here he felt that he had at last come into his own (he always got along much better with women than with men) and his restored faith in himself enabled him to rise with comfortable ease to the coveted position of wholesale buyer. He knew women's clothes and interested in women, it was his belief that knowledge of the frail intimate things they preferred gave him an insight which no other man had into the psychology of women. But he merely speculated upon this, for he remained faithful to his wife, though she was bedridden: an invalid.

And then, when success was in his grasp and life had become smooth at last for them, his wife died. He had become habituated to marriage, sincerely attached to her, and readjustment came slowly. Yet in time he became accustomed to the novelty of mature liberty. He had been married so young that freedom was an unexplored field to him. He took pleasure in his snug bachelor quarters in the proper neighborhood, in his solitary routine of days: of walking home in the dusk for the sake of his figure, examining the soft bodies of girls on the street, knowing that if he cared to take one of them, there was none save the girls themselves to say him nay; to his dinners alone or in company with an available literary friend.

Mr Talliaferro did Europe in forty one days, gained thereby a worldly air and a smattering of aesthetics and a precious accent, and returned to New Orleans feeling that he was Complete. His only alarm was his thinning hair, his only worry the fact that he had been born Tarver, not Talliaferro.

But long since celibacy had begun to oppress him.

5.

Handling his stick smartly, he turned into Broussard's. As he had hoped, here was Dawson Fairchild, the novelist, resembling a benevolent walrus too recently out of bed to have made a toilet, dining in company with three men. Mr Talliaferro paused diffidently in the doorway and a rosycheeked waiter resembling a studious Harvard undergraduate in an actor's dinner coat, assailed him courteously. At last he caught Fairchild's eye and the other greeted him across the small room, then said something to his three companions that caused them to halfturn in their chairs to watch his approach. Mr Talliaferro, to whom entering a restaurant alone and securing a table was an excruciating process, joined them with relief. The cherubic waiter spun a chair from an adjoining table deftly against Mr Talliaferro's knees as he shook Fairchild's hand.

"You're just in time," Fairchild told him, propping his fist and a clutched fork on the table. "This is Mr Hooper. You know these other folks, I think."

Mr Talliaferro ducked his head to a man with iron gray hair and an orotund humorless face like that of a thwarted Sunday school superintendent, who insisted on shaking his hand, then his glance took in the other two members of the party—a tall ghostly young man with a thin evaporation of fair hair and a pale prehensile mouth, and a bald semitic man with a pasty loosejowled face and sad quizzical eyes.

"We were discussing," began Fairchild when the stranger interrupted with a bland and utterly unselfconscious rudeness.

"What did you say the name was?" he asked, fixing Mr Talliaferro with his eye. Mr Talliaferro met the eye and knew immediately a faint unease. He answered the question but the other brushed the reply aside. "I mean your given name. I didn't catch it today."

"Why, Ernest," Mr Talliaferro told him with alarm.

"Ah yes: Ernest. You must pardon me, but travelling, meeting new faces each Tuesday, as I do——" he interrupted himself with the same bland unconsciousness. "What are your impressions of the get-together today?" Ere Mr Talliaferro could reply he interrupted himself again. "You have a splendid organization here," he informed them generally, compelling them with his glance, "and a city that is worthy of it. Except for this southern laziness of yours. You folks need more northern blood to bring out your possibilities. Still, I wont complain: you boys have treated me pretty well." He put some food in his mouth and chewed it down hurriedly, forestalling anyone else who might have hoped to speak. "I was glad that my itinerary brought me here, to see the city and be with the boys today, and that one of your reporters afforded me the opportunity to see something of your bohemian life by directing me to Mr Fairchild here, who, I understand, is an author." He met Mr Talliaferro's expression of courteous amazement again. "I am glad to see how you boys are carrying on the good work; I might say, the Master's work, for it is only by taking the Lord into our daily lives——" He stared at Mr Talliaferro once more. "What did you say the name was?"

"Ernest," suggested Fairchild mildly.

"——Ernest. People, the man in the street, the breadwinner—he on whom the heavy burden of life rests, does he know what we stand for, what we can give him in spite of himself—forgetfulness of the trials of day by day. He knows nothing of our ideals of service, of the benefits to ourselves, to each other, to you——" he met Fairchild's burly quizzical gaze "——to himself. And, by the way," he added coming to earth again, "there are a few points on this subject I am going to take up with your secretary tomorrow." He transfixed Mr Talliaferro again. "What were your impressions of my remarks today?"

"I beg pardon?"

"What did you think of my idea for getting a hundred percent church attendance by keeping them afraid they'd miss something good by staying away?"

Mr Talliaferro turned his stricken face to the others, one by one. After a while his interrogator said in a tone of cold displeasure: "You dont mean to say you do not recall me?"

Mr Talliaferro cringed. "Really, sir—I am distressed——" The other interrupted heavily.

"You were not at lunch today?"

"No," Mr Talliaferro replied with effusive gratitude, "I take only a glass of buttermilk at noon. I breakfast late, you see." The other stared at him with chill displeasure, and Mr Talliaferro added with inspiration: "You have mistaken me for someone else, I fear."

The stranger regarded Mr Talliaferro for a cold moment. The waiter placed a dish before Mr Talliaferro and he fell upon it in a flurry of acute discomfort. "Do you mean—" began the stranger. Then he put his fork down and turned his disapproval coldly upon Fairchild. "Didn't I understand you to say that this——gentleman was a member of Rotary?"

Mr Talliaferro suspended his fork and he too looked at Fairchild in shocked unbelief. "I? A member of Rotary?" he repeated.

"Why, I kind of got the impression he was," Fairchild admitted. "Hadn't you heard that Talliaferro was a rotarian?" he appealed to the others. They were noncommittal and he continued: "I seem to recall somebody telling me you were a rotarian. But then, you know how rumors get around. Maybe it was because of your prominence in the business life of our city. Talliaferro is a member of one of our largest ladies' clothing houses," he explained. "He is just the man to help you figure out some way to get God into the mercantile business, teach him the meaning of Service. Hey, Talliaferro?"

"No: really, I——" Mr Talliaferro objected with alarm.

The stranger interrupted again. "Well, there is nothing better on God's green earth than Rotary. Mr Fairchild had given me to understand that you were a member," he accused with a recurrence of cold suspicion. Mr Talliaferro squirmed with unhappy negation. The other stared him down, then he took out his watch. "Well, well. I must run along. I run my day to schedule. You'd be astonished to learn how much time can be saved by cutting off a minute here and a minute there," he informed them. "And——"

"What do you do with them?" Fairchild asked.

"I beg pardon?"

"When you've cut off enough minutes here and there to make up a sizable mess, what do you do with them?"

"——and setting a time limit to everything you do makes a man get more punch into it, makes him take the hills on high, you might say." A drop of nicotine on the end of your tongue will kill a dog thought Fairchild, chuckling to himself.

"Our forefathers reduced the process of gain to proverbs, but we have beaten them: we have reduced the whole of existence to fetiches," he said aloud.

"To words of one syllable that look well in large red type," the semitic man corrected.

The stranger ignored them. He was halfturned in his chair. He gestured at the waiter's back, then he snapped his fingers until he had attracted the waiter's attention. "Trouble with these small second rate places," he told them, "no pep, no efficiency in handling trade. Check, please," he directed briskly. The cherubic waiter bent over them.

"You found the dinner nice?" he suggested.

"Sure, sure, all right. Bring the bill, will you, George?"

The waiter looked at the others, hesitating.

"Never mind, Mr Broussard," Fairchild said quickly. "We wont go right now. Mr Hooper here has got to catch a train. You are my guest," he explained to the stranger. The other protested conventionally: he offered to match coins for it, but Fairchild repeated: "You are my guest tonight. Too bad you must hurry away."

"Yes. But I haven't got the leisure you New Orleans fellows have. Got to keep on the jump, myself." He rose and shook hands all around. "Glad to've met you boys," he said to each in turn. He clasped Mr Talliaferro's elbow with his left hand while their hands were engaged. The waiter fetched his hat and he gave the man a half dollar with a flourish. "If you're ever in the little city," he paused to reassure Fairchild.

"Sure, sure," Fairchild agreed heartily, and they sat down again. The late guest paused at the street door a moment, then he darted forth shouting Taxi! Taxi! The cab took him to the Monteleone hotel, three blocks away, where he purchased two tomorrow's papers and he sat in the lobby for an hour, dozing over them. Then he went up to his room and lay in bed staring at them until he had harried his mind into unconsciousness by the sheer idiocy of print.

6.

"Now," said Fairchild, "let that be a lesson to you young men. That's what you'll come to by joining things—getting the habit of it. As soon as a man begins to join clubs and lodges, his spiritual fibre begins to disintegrate. When you are young, you join things because they profess high ideals. You believe in ideals at that age, you know. Which is all right—as long as you just believe in them as ideals and not as criterions of conduct. But after a while, you join more things, you are getting older and more sedate and 'sensible'—believing in ideals is too much trouble, so you begin to live up to them with your outward life, in your contacts with other people. And when you've made a form of behavior out of an ideal its not an ideal any longer, and you become a public nuisance."

"Its a man's own fault if the fetichmen annoy him," the

semitic man said. "Nowadays there are enough things for everyone to belong to something."

"That's a rather stiff price to pay for immunity, though," Fairchild objected.

"That need not bother you," the other told him. "You have already paid it."

Mr Talliaferro laid aside his fork. "I do hope he's not offended," he murmured. Fairchild chuckled.

"At what?" the semitic man asked. He and Fairchild regarded Mr Talliaferro kindly.

"At Fairchild's little joke," Mr Talliaferro explained.

Fairchild laughed. "I'm afraid we disappointed him. He probably not only does not believe that we are bohemians, but doubts that we are even artistic. Probably the least he expected was to be taken to dinner at the studio of two people who are not married to each other, and to be offered hashish instead of food."

"And to be seduced by a girl in an orange smock and no stockings," the ghostly young man added in a sepulchral tone.

"Yes," Fairchild said. "But he wouldn't have succumbed, though."

"No," the semitic man agreed. "But, like any christian, he would have liked the opportunity to refuse."

"Yes, that's right," Fairchild admitted. He said: "I guess he thinks that if you dont stay up all night and get drunk and ravish some body there's no use in being an artist."

"Which is worse?" murmured the semitic man.

"God knows," Fairchild answered. "I've never been ravished. . . ." He sucked at his coffee. "But he's not the first man that ever hoped to be ravished and was disappointed. I've spent a lot of time in different places laying myself open, and always come off undefiled. Hey, Talliaferro?"

Mr Talliaferro squirmed again, diffidently. Fairchild lit a cigarette. "Well, both of them are vices, and we've all seen tonight what an uncontrolled vice will lead a man into—— defining a vice as any natural impulse which rides you, like the gregarious instinct in Hooper." He ceased a while. Then he chuckled again. "God must look about our American scene with a good deal of consternation, watching the antics of these volunteers who are trying to help Him."

"Or entertainment," the semitic man amended. "But why American scene?"

"Because our doings are so much more comical. Other nations seem to be able to entertain the possibility that God may not be a rotarian or an elk or a boy scout after all. We dont. And convictions are always alarming, unless you are looking at them from behind."

The waiter approached with a box of cigars. The semitic man took one. Mr Talliaferro finished his dinner with decorous expedition. The semitic man said:

"My people produced Jesus, your people christianized him. And ever since you have been trying to get Him out of your church. And now that you have practically succeeded, look at what is filling the vacuum of His departure. Do you think that your new ideal of willynilly Service without request or recourse is better than your old ideal of humility? No, no—" as Fairchild would have spoken "—I dont mean as far as results go. The only ones who ever gain by the spiritual machinations of mankind are the small minority who gain emotional or mental or physical exercise from the activity itself, never the passive majority for whom the crusade is set afoot."

"Katharsis by peristalsis," murmured the blond young man, who was nurturing a reputation for cleverness. Fairchild said:

"Are you opposed to religion, then—in its general sense, I mean."

"Certainly not," the semitic man answered. "The only sense in which religion is general is when it benefits the greatest number in the same way. And the universal benefit of religion is that it gets the children out of the house on Sunday morning."

"But education gets them out of the house five days a week," Fairchild pointed out.

"That's true, too, but I am not at home myself on those days: education has already got me out of the house six days a week." The waiter brought Mr Talliaferro's coffee. Fairchild lit another cigarette.

"So you believe that the sole accomplishment of education is that it keeps us away from home?"

"What other general result can you name? It doesn't make us all brave or healthy or happy or wise, it doesn't even keep us married. In fact, to take an education by the modern process is like marrying in haste and spending the rest of your life making the best of it. But, understand me: I have no quarrel with education. I dont think it hurts you much, except to make you unhappy and unfit for work, for which man was cursed by the gods before they had learned about education. And if it were not education, it would be something else just as bad, and perhaps worse. Man must fill his time some way, you know."

"But to go back to religion——" "the spirit protestant eternal," murmured the blond young man hoarsely. "——do you mean any particular religion, or just the general teaching of Christ?"

"What has Christ to do with it?"

"Well, its generally accepted that he instigated a certain branch of it, whatever his motives really were."

"It is generally accepted that first you must have an effect to discern a cause. And it is a human trait to foist the blunders of the age and race upon someone or something too remote or heedless or weak to resist. But when you say religion, you have a particular sect in mind, haven't you?"

"Yes," Fairchild admitted. "I always think of the protestant religion."

"The worst of all," the semitic man said. "To raise children in, I mean. For some reason one can be a catholic or a jew, and be religious at home. But a protestant at home is only a protestant. It seems to me that the protestant faith was invented for the sole purpose of filling our jails and morgues and houses of detention. I speak now of its more rabid manifestations, particularly of its machinations in smaller settlements. How do young protestant boys in small towns spend Sunday afternoons, with baseball and all such natural muscular vents denied them? They kill, they slay and steal and burn. Have you ever noticed how many juvenile firearm accidents occur on Sunday, how many fires in barns and outhouses happen on Sunday afternoon?" He ceased and shook the ash from his cigar carefully into his coffee cup. Mr Talliaferro, seeing an opening, coughed and spoke.

"By the way, I saw Gordon today. Tried to persuade him for our yachting party tomorrow. He doesn't enthuse, so to speak, though I assured him how much we'd all like to have him."

"Oh, he'll come, I guess," Fairchild said. "He'd be a fool not to let her feed him for a few days."

"He'd pay a fairly high price for his food," the semitic man remarked drily. Fairchild looked at him and he added: "Gordon hasn't served his apprenticeship yet, you know. You've got through yours."

"Oh." Fairchild grinned. "Well, yes, I did kind of play out on her, I reckon." He turned to Mr Talliaferro. "Has she been to him in person to sell him the trip, yet?"

Mr Talliaferro hid his mild retrospective discomfort behind a lighted match. "Yes, she stopped in this afternoon. I was with him at the time."

"Good for her," the semitic man applauded and Fairchild said with interest:

"She did? What did Gordon do?"

"He left," Mr Talliaferro admitted mildly.

"Walked out on her, did he?" Fairchild glanced briefly at the semitic man. He laughed. "You are right," he agreed. He laughed again, and Mr Talliaferro said:

"He really should come, you know. I thought perhaps—" diffidently "—that you'd help me persuade him. The fact that you will be with us, and your—er—assured position in the creative world. . . ."

"No, I guess not," Fairchild decided. "I'm not much of a hand for changing folks' opinions. I guess I wont meddle in it."

"But, really," Mr Talliaferro persisted, "the trip would benefit the man's work. Besides," he added with inspiration, "he will round out our party. A novelist, a painter—"

"I am invited, too," the blond young man put in sepulchrally. Mr Talliaferro accepted him with apologetic effusion. "By all means, a poet. I was about to mention you, my dear fellow. Two poets, in fact, with Eva W——" "I am the best poet in New Orleans," the other interrupted, with sepulchral belligerence. "Yes, yes," Mr Talliaferro agreed quickly, "——and a sculptor——you see?" he appealed to the semitic man. The semitic man met Mr Talliaferro's importunate gaze kindly, without reply. Fairchild turned to him.

"We—ll," he began. Then: "What do you think?"

The semitic man glanced briefly at him. "I think we'll need Gordon by all means." Fairchild grinned again and agreed.

"Yes, I guess you're right."

7.

The waiter brought Fairchild his change and stood courteously beside them as they rose. Mr Talliaferro caught Fairchild's eye and leaned nearer, diffidently, lowering his tone.

"Eh?" Fairchild said in his burly jovial voice, not lowering it.

"Would like a moment, if you've time. Your advice—"

"Not tonight?" Fairchild asked in alarm.

"Why, yes." Mr Talliaferro was faintly apologetic. "Just a few moments, if you are alone——" he gestured meaningly with his head toward the other two.

"No, not tonight. Julius and I are spending the evening together." Mr Talliaferro's face fell and Fairchild added kindly, "Some other time, perhaps."

"Yes, of course," Mr Talliaferro agreed faultlessly, "some other time."

8.

Fairchild stopped at the corner of Bourbon street to laugh. Mr Talliaferro and the blond young man retreated toward Royal street, Mr Talliaferro pacing sedately yet intently beside the other's tall ghostly figure. Soon they turned the corner, passing from view. Fairchild, carrying his limp panama hat, chuckled heavily. The semitic man slapped the back of his neck.

"The race," said Fairchild, "is playing out. Once we did things with muscle. Then we found out that all creatures didn't have the same kind of muscle, so we invented ways of doing things with sticks and stones. Then somebody invented a way of using shiny trinkets to make the stick-and-stone people do what they wanted them to. And now the stick-and-stone people are about to get all the shiny trinkets, and so all we have left is words. And that's the last resort. When someone invents a way to produce words without mental process, where will we wordusers be?"

"Whoever invented American politics has already done that," the semitic man said.

"American politics aint universal though," Fairchild answered. "No other nation could afford it. But if the world's awe and belief in words ever does falter. . . ."

"That will be an unfortunate day for you, anyway," the semitic man said.

"Yes?" remarked Fairchild.

"You'll have to go to work."

"Well, I dont object to work."

"Nobody does. On the contrary, in fact. That's the reason you people are so dissatisfied in your perversion. The laborer curses his job; on Saturday night he tells the world that he is through until Monday. But did you ever know a writer to admit that he was not either planning or writing a novel constantly? Or two or three, even?"

Fairchild pondered a while. "Yes, you're right. We do have to say we are writing a new novel whether we are or not."

"Of course you do. Art is against nature: those who choose it are perverts, and in choosing it they cast all things behind them. So to admit that you are not working on something constantly is an admission that your life is temporarily pointless, and so unbearable."

"Yes," repeated Fairchild. ". . . . But why perversion?"

"Perversion?"

"You dont think its natural for man to spend his life making little crooked marks on paper, do you? Doing things with colors, or stringing sounds together, now, I grant you. . . ." The semitic man slapped his neck again.

"God knows," said Fairchild.

9.

The car swept sibilantly up the drive and on around the house. There was a light on the veranda vaguely beyond vines; they descended and Mrs Maurier crossed the veranda and passed clashing and jangling through a french window. The niece turned the corner and followed the veranda where, beyond a nook spaced with wicker and chintz and magazines gaily on a table, her brother sat coatless on a divan beneath a walllamp. There was a faint litter of shavings about his feet and clinging to his trousers, and at the moment he bent with a carpenter's saw over something in his lap. The saw scraped fretfully, monotonously, and she stopped beside him and stood scratching her knee. Presently he raised his head.

"Hello," he remarked without enthusiasm. "Go to the library and get me a cigarette."

"I've got one on me, somewhere." She searched the pockets of her linen dress, but without success. "Where——" she said. She mused a moment, spreading her pocket with her hand, staring into it. Then she said Oh yes and took off her hat. From the crown of it she produced one limp cigarette. "I ought to have another," she mused aloud, searching the hat again. "I guess that's all, though. You can have it: I dont want one, anyway." She extended the cigarette and skirled her hat onto the lounge beside.

"Look out," he said quickly, "dont put it there. I need all this space. Put it somewhere else, cant you?" He pushed the hat off the divan, onto the floor, and accepted the cigarette. The tobacco was partially shredded from it and it was limp, like a worm. "Whatcher been doing to it? How long've you had it, anyway?" She sat beside him and he raked a match across his thigh.

"How's it coming, Josh?" she asked, extending her hand toward the object on his lap. It was a cylinder of wood larger than a silver dollar and about three inches long. He fended her off with the hand which held the lighted match, thrusting her elbow beneath her chin.

"Let it alone, I tell you."

"Oh, all right. Keep your shirt on." She moved slightly away and he took up the saw again, putting the burning cigarette on the wicker lounge between them. A thin pencil of smoke rose from it into the windless air, and soon a faint smell of burning. She picked up the cigarette, drew once at it and replaced it so it would not scorch the wicker. The saw grated jerkily and thinly; outside, beyond the vines, insects scraped monotonously one to another in the heavy swooning darkness. A moth, having evaded the wire screen, gyrated idiotically beneath and about the light. She raised her skirt to stare at a small feverish spot on her brown knee. . . . The saw grated

jerkily, ceased, and he laid it aside again. The cylinder was in
two sections, fitted one into another and she drew one foot
beneath the other knee, bending nearer to watch him, breathing against his neck. He moved restively and she said at last:

"Say, Gus, how long will it take you to get it finished?"

He raised his face, suspending his knife blade. They were
twins: just as there was something masculine about her jaw,
so was there something feminine about his.

"For God's sake," he exclaimed, "let me alone, cant you? Go
away and pull your clothes down. Dont you ever get tired of
waving your legs around?"

A yellow negro in a starched jacket stepped silently around
the corner. When they looked up he turned without speaking.
"All right, Walter," she said. But he was gone. They followed,
leaving the cigarette to lift its unwavering plume and a thin
smell of burning wicker into the somnolent air.

                               10.

     fool fool you have work to do o cursed of god cursed and
forgotten form shapes cunningly sweated cunning to simplicity shapes out of chaos more satisfactory than bread to
the belly form by a madmans dream gat on the body of chaos
le garçon vierge of the soul horned by utility o cuckold of
derision

The warehouse, the dock, was a formal rectangle without
perspective. Flat as cardboard, and projecting at a faint motionless angle above it, against a lighter spaciousness and a sky
not quite so imminent and weary, masts of a freighter lying
against the dock. Form and utility, Gordon repeated to himself. Or form and chance. Or chance and utility. Beneath,
within the somber gloom of the warehouse where men had
sweated and labored, across the empty floor lately thunderous
with trucks, amid the rich overripe odors of the ends of
earth—coffee and resin and tow and fruit—he walked surrounded by ghosts, passing on.

The hull of the freighter bulked, forecastle and poop soaring darkly sharp, solid, cutting off vision, soaring its superstructure on the sky. The river unseen continued a ceaseless
sound against the hull, lulling it with a simulation of the sea,

and about the piles of the wharf. The shore and the river curved away like the bodies of two dark sleepers embracing, curved one to another in slumber; and far away opposite the Point, banked lights flickered like a pile of yet living ashes in a wind. Gordon paused, leaning over the edge of the wharf, staring down into the water.

stars in my hair in my hair and beard i am crowned with stars christ by his own hand an autogethsemane carved darkly out of pure space but not rigid no no an unmuscled wallowing fecund and foul the placid tragic body of a woman who conceives without pleasure bears without pain

what would i say to her fool fool you have work to do you have nothing accursed intolerant and unclean too warm your damn bones then whiskey will do as well or a chisel and maul any damn squirrel keeps warm in a cage go on go on then israfel revolted surprised behind a haycock by a male relation fortitude become a matchflame snuffed by a small white belly where was it i once saw a dogwood tree not white but tan tan as cream what will you say to her bitter and new as a sunburned flame bitter and new those two little silken snails somewhere under her dress horned pinkly yet reluctant o israfel ay wax your wings with the thin odorless moisture of her thighs strangle your heart with hair fool fool cursed and forgotten of god

He flung back his head and laughed a huge laugh in the loneliness. His voice surged like a dark billow against the wall behind him, then ebbing outward over the dim formless river it died slowly away . . . then from the other shore a mirthless echo mocked him, and it too died away. He went on, treading the dark resinscented wharf.

Presently he came to a break in the black depthless monotony of the wall, and the wall again assumed a pure and inevitable formal significance sharp against the glow of the city. He turned his back to the river and soon was among freight cars black and angular, looming; and down the tracks, much further away than it appeared, an engine glared and panted while filaments of steel radiating from it toward and about his feet were like incandescent veins in a dark leaf.

There was a moon, low in the sky and worn, thumbed partly away like an old coin; and he went on. Above banana and palm the cathedral spires soared without perspective on the hot sky. Looking through the tall pickets into Jackson park was like looking into an aquarium—a moist and motionless absinthecloudy green of all shades from ink-black to a thin and rigid feathering of silver on pomegranate and mimosa like coral in a tideless sea, amid which globular lights hung dull and unstraying as jellyfish, incandescent yet without seeming to emanate light; and in the center of it Andrew's baroque plunging stasis nimbused about with thin gleams as though he too were recently wetted.

He crossed the street into shadow, following the wall. Two figures stood indistinguishably at his door. "Pardon me," he said touching the nearer man peremptorily, and as he did so the other man turned.

"Why, here he is now," this one said. "Hello, Gordon. Julius and I were looking for you."

"Yes?" Gordon loomed above the two shorter men, staring down at them, remote and arrogant. Fairchild removed his hat, mopping his face. Then he flipped his handkerchief viciously about his head.

"I dont mind the heat," he explained fretfully. "I like it, in fact. Like an old race horse, you know. He's willing enough, you know, but in the cool weather when his muscles are stiff and his bones ache, the young ones all show him up. But about Fourth of July, when the sun gets hot and his muscles loosen up and his old bones dont complain any more, then he's good as any of 'em."

"Yes?" repeated Gordon looking above them into shadow. The semitic man removed his cigar.

"It will be better on the water tomorrow," he said.

Gordon brooded above them. Then he remembered himself. "Come up," he directed abruptly, elbowing the semitic man aside and extending his latchkey.

"No, no," Fairchild demurred quickly. "We wont stop. Julius just reminded me: we came to see if you'd change your mind and come with us on Mrs Maurier's boat tomorrow. We saw T——"

"I have," Gordon interrupted him. "I'm coming."

"That's good," Fairchild agreed heartily. "You probably wont regret it much. He may enjoy it, Julius," he added.

"Besides, you'll be wise to go on and get it over with, then she'll let you alone. After all, you cant afford to ignore people that own food and automobiles, you know. Can he, Julius?"

The semitic man agreed. "When he clutters himself up with people—which he can't avoid doing—by all means let it be with people who own food and whiskey and motorcars. The less intelligent the better." He struck a match to his cigar. "But he wont last very long with her, anyway. He'll last even a shorter time than you did," he told Fairchild.

"Yes, I guess you're right. But he ought to keep a line on her, anyhow. If you can neither ride nor drive the beast yourself, its a good idea to keep it in a pasture nearby: you may someday be able to swap it for something, you know."

"A ford, for instance, or a radio," the semitic man suggested. "But you've got your simile backward."

"Backward?" repeated the other.

"You were speaking from the point of view of the rider," he explained.

"Oh," Fairchild remarked. He emitted a disparaging sound. " 'Ford' is good," he said heavily.

"I think 'radio' is pretty good, myself," the other said complacently.

"Oh, dry up." Fairchild replaced his hat. "So you are coming with us, then," he said to Gordon.

"Yes, I'm coming. But wont you come up?"

"No, no: not tonight. I know your place, you see." Gordon made no reply, brooding his tall head in the shadow. "Well, I'll phone her and have her send a car for you tomorrow," Fairchild added. "Come on, Julius, lets go. Glad you changed your mind," he added belatedly. "Goodnight. Come on, Julius."

They crossed the street and entered the square. Once within the gates they were assailed, waylaid from behind every blade and leaf with a silent, vicious delight. "Good Lord," exclaimed Fairchild, flipping his handkerchief madly about, "lets go over to the docks. Maybe there aint any nautical ones." He hurried on, the semitic man ambling beside him, clamping his dead cigar.

"He's a funny chap," the semitic man remarked. They waited for a trolley to pass, then crossed the street. The wharf, the warehouse, was a formal rectangle with two slender masts projecting above it at a faint angle. They went on between two dark buildings and halted again while a switch engine drew an interminable monotony of cars up the track.

"He ought to get out of himself more," Fairchild commented. "You cant be an artist all the time. You'll go crazy."

"You couldn't," the other corrected. "But then, you are not an artist. There is somewhere within you a bewildered stenographer with a gift for people, but outwardly you might be anything. You are an artist only when you are telling about people, while Gordon is not an artist only when he is cutting at a piece of wood or stone. And its very difficult for a man like that to establish workable relations with people. Other artists are too busy playing with their own egos, workaday people will not or cannot bother with him, so his alternatives are misanthropy or an endless gabbling of aesthetic fostersisters of both sexes. Particularly if his lot is cast outside of New York city."

"There you go: disparaging our latin quarter again. Where's your civic pride? where's your common courtesy, even? Even the dog wont bite the hand that holds the bread."

"Corn belt," the other said shortly, "Indiana talking. You people are born with the booster complex up there, aren't you? Or do you acquire it with sunburned necks?"

"Oh well, we nordics are at a disadvantage," Fairchild replied. His tone was unctuous, the other detected something falsely frank in it. "We've got to fix our ideas on a terrestrial place; though we know its secondrate, that's the best we can do. But your people have got all heaven for your old home town, you know."

"I could forgive everything except the unpardonable clumsiness of that," the other told him. "Your idea is not bad. Why dont you give it to Mark Frost——roughly, you know—and let him untangle it for you? You and he could both use it then—if you are quick enough, that is."

Fairchild laughed. "Now, you lay off our New Orleans bohemian life—stay away from us if you dont like it. I like it, myself: there is a kind of charming futility about it, like——"

"Like a country club where they play croquet instead of golf," the other supplied for him.

"Well, yes," Fairchild agreed, "something like that." The warehouse loomed above them. They passed into it and amid the ghosts of the ends of the earth. "A croquet player may not be much of a go getter, but what do you think of a man that just sits around and criticises croquet?"

"Well, I'm like the rest of you immortals: I've got to pass the time in some way in order to gain some idea of how to pass eternity," the semitic man answered. They passed through the warehouse and onto the dock. It was cooler here, quieter. Two ferry boats passed and repassed like a pair of golden swans in a barren cycle of courtship. The shore and the river curved away in a dark embracing slumber to where a bank of tiny lights flickered and trembled, bodiless and far away. It was much cooler here and they removed their hats. The semitic man unclamped his dead cigar and cast it outward. Silence, water, night, absorbed it without a sound.

The First Day.

Ten Oclock.

THE Nausikaa lay in the basin—a nice thing, with her white matronly hull and mahogany-and-brass superstructure and the Yacht club flag at the peak. A firm steady wind blew in from the lake and Mrs Maurier, having already got a taste of the sea, had donned her yachting cap and clashed and jangled in a happy pointless ecstasy. Her two cars had made several trips and would make several more, creeping and jouncing along the inferior macadam road upon and beside which the spoor of coca cola and almond bar betrayed the lair of the hot dog and the less-than-one-percent. All the jollity of departure under a perfect day, heatridden city behind, and a breeze too steady for the darn things to light on you. Her guests each with his or her jar of almond cream and sunburn lotion came aboard in bright babbling surges, calling Ship ahoy everyone, and other suitable nautical cries, while various casuals gathered along the quay, looked on with morose interest. Mrs Maurier clashed and jangled in a happy and senseless excitement.

On the upper deck, where the steward broke out chairs for them, her guests in their colored clothing gathered, dressed for deep water in batik and flowing ties and open collars, informal and colorful with the exception of Mark Frost, the ghostly young man, a poet who produced an occasional cerebral and obscure poem in four or seven lines reminding one somehow of the function of evacuation excruciatingly and incompletely performed. He wore ironed serge and a high starched collar and he borrowed a cigarette of the steward and lay immediately at full length on something, as was his way. Mrs Wiseman and Miss Jameson, flanking Mr Talliaferro, sat with cigarettes also. Fairchild, accompanied by Gordon, the semitic man and a florid stranger in heavy tweeds, and carrying among them several weighty looking suitcases, had gone directly below.

"Are we all here? Are we all here?" Mrs Maurier chanted beneath her yachting cap, roving her eyes among her guests.

Her niece stood at the afterrail beside a soft blonde girl in a slightlysoiled green dress. They both gazed shoreward where at the end of the gangplank a flashy youth lounged in a sort of skulking belligerence, smoking cigarettes. The niece said, without turning her gaze, "What's the matter with him? Why doesn't he come aboard?" The youth's attention seemed to be anywhere else save on the boat, yet he was so obviously there, in the eye, belligerent and skulking. The niece called Hey. Then she said:

"What's his name? You better tell him to come on, hadn't you?"

The blonde girl hissed "Pete!" in a repressed tone. The youth moved his slanted stiff straw hat an inch and the blonde girl beckoned to him. He slanted the hat to the back of his head: his whole attitude gave the impression that he was some distance away. "Aint you coming with us?" the blonde girl asked in that surreptitious tone.

"Whatcher say?" he replied loudly, so that everybody looked at him——even the reclining poet raised his head.

"Come on aboard, Pete," the niece called. "Be yourself."

The youth took another cigarette from his pack. He buttoned his narrow coat. "Well, I guess I will," he agreed in his carrying tone. Mrs Maurier held her expression of infantile astonishment up to him as he crossed the gangplank. He evaded her politely, climbing the rail with that fluid agility of the young.

"Are you the new steward?" she asked doubtfully, blinking at him.

"Sure, lady," he agreed courteously, putting his cigarette in his mouth. The other guests stared at him from their deck chairs and slanting his hat forward he ran the gauntlet of their eyes, passing aft to join the two girls. Mrs Maurier gazed after his high vented coat in astonishment. Then she remarked the blonde girl beside her niece. She blinked again.

"Why——" she began. Then she said: "Patricia, who——"

"Oh yes," the niece said, "this is——" She turned to the blonde girl. "What's your name, Jenny? I forgot."

"Genevieve Steinbauer," the blonde girl submitted.

"——Miss Steinbauer. And this one is Pete Something. I met them downtown. They want to go, too."

Mrs Maurier transferred her astonishment from Jenny's vague ripe prettiness to Pete's bold uncomfortable face. "Why, he's the new steward, isn't he?"

"I dont know." The niece looked at Jenny again. "Is he?" she asked. Jenny didn't know either. Pete himself was uncomfortably noncommittal.

"I dunno," he answered. "You told me to come," he accused the niece.

"She means," the niece explained, "did you come to work on the boat?"

"Not me," Pete answered quickly. "I aint a sailor. If she expects me to run this ferry for her, me and Jenny are going back to town."

"You dont have to run it. She's got regular men for that. There's your steward, anyway, Aunt Pat," the niece said. "Pete just wanted to come with Jenny. That's all."

Mrs Maurier looked. Yes, there was the steward, descending the companionway with a load of luggage. She looked again at Pete and Jenny, but at that moment voices came aft, breaking her amazement. The Captain wished to know if he should cast off: the message was relayed by all present.

"Are we all here?" Mrs Maurier chanted anew, forgetting Jenny and Pete. "Mr Fairchild——Where is he?" She roved her round frantic face, trying to count noses. "Where is Mr Fairchild?" she repeated in panic. Her car was backing and filling to turn around and she ran to the rail, screaming at the driver. He stopped the car, completely blocking the road, and hung his head out with resignation. Mrs Wiseman said:

"He's here: he came with Ernest, didn't he?"

Mr Talliaferro corroborated her and Mrs Maurier roved her frantic gaze anew, trying to count them. A sailor sprang ashore and cast off the head- and sternlines under the morose regard of the casuals. The helmsman thrust his head from the wheel house and he and the deck hand bawled at each other. The sailor sprang aboard and the Nausikaa moved slightly in the water, like a soundless awakening sigh. The steward drew in the gangplank and the engineroom telegraph rang remotely. The Nausikaa waked further, quivering a little, and as a gap of water grew between quay and boat without any sensation of motion whatever, Mrs Maurier's second car came jouncing into view, honking madly, and the niece sitting flat on the deck and stripping off her stockings, said:

"Here comes Josh."

Mrs Maurier shrieked. The car stopped and her nephew descended without haste. The steward, coiling the sternline down, gathered it up and flung it outward across the growing gap of water. The telegraph rang again. The Nausikaa sighed and went back to sleep, rocking sedately. "Shake it up, Josh," his sister called. Mrs Maurier shrieked again and two of the loungers caught the line and dug their heels as the nephew, coatless and hatless, approached without haste and climbed aboard, carrying a new carpenter's saw.

"I had to go down town and buy one," he explained casually. "Walter wouldn't let me bring yours."

Eleven Oclock.

At last Mrs Maurier succeeded in cornering her niece. New Orleans, the basin, the Yacht club, were far behind. The Nausikaa sped youthfully and gaily under a blue and drowsy day, beneath her forefoot a small bow wave spread its sedate fading fan. Mrs Maurier's people could not escape her now. They had settled themselves comfortably on deck: there was nothing to look at save one another, nothing to do save wait for lunch. All, that is, except Jenny and Pete. Pete holding his hat on stood yet at the afterrail with Jenny beside him. Her air was that of a soft and futile cajolery, to which Pete was smoldering and impervious. Mrs Maurier breathed a sigh of temporary relief and astonishment and ran her niece to earth in the after companionway.

"Patricia," she demanded, "what on earth did you invite those two——young people for?"

"God knows," the niece answered, looking past her aunt's yachting cap to Pete belligerent and uncomfortable beside Jenny's bovine white placidity. "God knows. If you want to turn around and take 'em back, dont let me stand in your way."

"But why did you ask them?"

"Well, I couldn't tell that they were going to turn out to be so wet, could I? And you said yourself there were not enough women coming. You said so yourself last night."

"Yes, but why ask those two? Who are they? Where did you ever meet such people?"

"I met Jenny downtown. She——"

"I know: but where did you come to know her? How long have you known her?"

"I met her downtown this morning, I tell you, in Holmes' while I was buying a bathing suit. She said she'd like to come, but the other one was waiting outside on the street for her and he put his foot down: said she couldn't go without him. He's her heavy, I gather."

Mrs Maurier's astonishment was sincere now. "Do you mean to tell me," she said in shocked unbelief, "that you never saw these people before? that you invited two people you never saw before to come on a party on my boat?"

"I just asked Jenny," the niece explained patiently. "The other one had to come so she could come. I didn't want him specially. How could I know her when I never saw her before? If I had, you can bet I wouldn't have asked her. She's a complete washout, far as I'm concerned. But I couldn't see that this morning. I thought she was all right then. Gabriel's pants, look at 'em." They both looked back at Jenny in her flimsy green dress, at Pete holding his hat on. "Well, I got 'em here: I guess I'll have to keep 'em from getting stepped on. I think I'll get Pete a piece of string to tie his hat down with, anyway." She swung herself easily up the companionway: Mrs Maurier saw with horrified surprise that she wore neither shoes nor stockings.

"Patricia!" she shrieked. The niece paused, looking over her shoulder. Her aunt pointed mutely at her bare legs.

"Haul in your sheet, Aunt Pat," the niece replied brusquely, "you're jibing."

ONE OCLOCK.

Lunch was spread on deck, on collapsible cardtables set end to end. When she appeared her guests all regarded her brightly, a trifle curiously. Mrs Maurier, oblivious, herded them toward it. "Sit anywhere, people," she repeated in singsong. "Girls will be at a premium this voyage. To the winner belongs the fair lady, remember." This sounded a little strange to her, so she repeated: "Sit anywhere, people; the gentlemen must make. . . ." She looked about upon her guests and her voice died away. Her party consisted of Mrs Wiseman, Miss Jameson, herself, Jenny and Pete clotting unhappily behind her niece, Mr Talliaferro and her nephew who had already seated himself. "Where are the gentlemen?" she asked at large.

"Jumped overboard," muttered Pete darkly, unheard, clutching his hat. The others stood, watching her brightly.

"Where are the gentlemen?" Mrs Maurier repeated.

"If you'd stop talking a minute you wouldn't have to ask," her nephew told her. He had already seated himself and he now spooned into a grapefruit with preoccupied celerity.

"Theodore!" his aunt exclaimed.

From below there came an indistinguishable mixture of sound somehow vaguely convivial. "Whooping it up," the nephew added looking up at his aunt, at her expression of reproof. "In a hurry," he explained. "Got to get done. Cant wait on those birds." He remarked his sister's guests for the first time. "Who're your friends, Gus?" he asked without interest. Then he fell anew upon his grapefruit.

"Theodore!" his aunt exclaimed again. The indistinguishable convivial sound welled, becoming laughter. Mrs Maurier roved her astonished eyes. "What can they be doing?"

Mr Talliaferro moved deferentially, tactfully. "If you wish——"

"Oh, Mr Talliaferro, if you would be so kind," Mrs Maurier accepted with emotion.

"Let the steward go, Aunt Pat. Lets eat," the niece said, thrusting Jenny forward. "Come on, Pete. Gimme your hat," she added, offering to take it. Pete refused to surrender it.

"Wait," the nephew interjected, "I'll get 'em up." He picked up the thick plate and flipping the grapefruit hull overboard he turned sideways in his chair and hammered a brisk staccato on the deck with the dish.

"Theodore!" his aunt exclaimed for the third time. "Mr Talliaferro, will you——" Mr Talliaferro sped toward the companionway, vanished.

"Aw, let the steward go, Aunt Pat," the niece repeated. "Come on, lets sit down. Let up, Josh, for God's sake."

"Yes, Mrs Maurier, lets dont wait for them," Mrs Wiseman abetted, seating herself also. The others followed suit. Mrs Maurier roved her fretted eyes. "Well," she submitted at last. Then she remarked Pete, still clutching his hat. "I'll take your hat," she offered, extending her hand. Pete foiled her quickly.

"Look out," he said, "I've got it." He moved beyond Jenny, putting his hat behind him in his chair. At this moment the gentlemen appeared from below, talking loudly.

"Ah, wretches," began the hostess with flaccid coquetry, shaking her finger at them. Fairchild was in the lead, burly and jovial, a shade unsteady as to gait. Mr Talliaferro brought up the rear: he too had now a temporarily emancipated air.

"I guess you thought we'd jumped the ship," Fairchild suggested, happily apologetic. Mrs Maurier sought Mr Talliaferro's evasive eye. "We were helping Major Ayers find his teeth," Fairchild added.

"Lost 'em in that little rabbit hutch where we were," explained the florid man. "Couldn't find 'em right off. No teeth, no tiffin, y'know. If you dont mind?" he murmured politely, seating himself next Mrs Wiseman. "Ah, grapefruit." He raised his voice again. "How jolly: seen no grapefruit since we left New Orleans, eh, Julius?"

"Lost his teeth?" repeated Mrs Maurier, dazed. The niece and her brother regarded the florid man with interest.

"They fell out of his mouth," Fairchild elaborated, taking the seat next Miss Jameson. "He was laughing at something Julius said, and they fell out of his mouth and somebody kicked 'em under the bunk, you see. What was it you said, Julius?"

Mr Talliaferro essayed to seat himself beside the florid man. Mrs Maurier again sought his eye, forced him, and vanquished him with bright implacable command. He rose and went to the chair next to her, and she leaned toward him, sniffing. "Ah, Mr Talliaferro," she murmured with playful implacability, "Naughty, naughty." "Just a nip——they were rather insistent," Mr Talliaferro apologized. "You men, you naughty men. I'll forgive you, however, this once," she answered. "Do ring, please."

The semitic man's flaccid face and dark compassionate eyes

presided at the head of the table. Gordon stood for a time after the others were seated, then he came and took the seat between Mrs Maurier and her niece, with abrupt arrogance. The niece looked up briefly. "Hello, Blackbeard." Mrs Maurier smiled at him automatically. She said:

"Listen, people. Mr Talliaferro is going to make an announcement. About promptness," she added to Mr Talliaferro, putting her hand on his sleeve.

"Ah yes. I say, you chaps almost missed lunch. We were not going to wait on you. The lunch hour is half after twelve, hereafter, and everyone must be present promptly. Ship's discipline, you know. Eh, Commodore?"

The hostess corroborated. "You must be good children," she added with playful relief, looking about her table. Her worried expression returned. "Why, there's an empty place. Who isn't here?" She roved her eyes in growing alarm. "Someone isn't here," she repeated. She had a brief and dreadful vision of having to put back short one guest, of inquest and reporters and headlines, and of floating inert buttocks in some lonely reach of the lake, that would later wash ashore with that mute inopportune implacability of the drowned. The guests stared at one another, then at the vacant place, then at one another again. Mrs Maurier tried to call a mental roll, staring at each in turn. Presently Miss Jameson said:

"Why, its Mark, isn't it?"

It was Mark. They had forgot him. Mrs Maurier dispatched the steward, who found the ghostly poet still at full length on the upper deck. He appeared in his ironed serge, bathing them briefly in his pale gaze.

"You gave us rather a turn, my dear fellow," Mr Talliaferro informed him in reproof, taking upon himself the duties of host.

"I wondered how long it would be before some one saw fit to notify me that lunch was ready," the poet replied with cold dignity, taking his place.

Fairchild, watching him, said abruptly: "Say, Julius, Mark's the very man for Major Ayers, aint he? Say, Major, here's a man to take your first bottle. Tell him about your scheme."

The florid man regarded the poet affably. "Ah yes. Its a salts, you see. You spoon a bit of it into your——"

"A what?" asked the poet, poising his spoon and staring at the florid man. The others all poised their tools and stared at the florid man.

"A salts," he explained, "like our salts at home, y'know——"

"A——?" repeated Mrs Maurier. Mr Talliaferro's eyes popped mildly.

"All Americans are constipated," the florid man continued blithely, "do with a bit of salts in a tumbler of water in the morning. Now, my scheme is——"

"Mr Talliaferro!" Mrs Maurier implored. Mr Talliaferro girded himself anew.

"My dear sir," he began.

"——is to put the salts up in a tweaky phial, a phial that will look well on one's nighttable: a jolly design of some sort. All Americans will buy it. Now, the population of your country is several millions, I fancy, and when you take into consideration the fact that all Americans are con—"

"My dear sir," said Mr Talliaferro, louder.

"Eh?" said the florid man, looking at him.

"What kind of a jar will you put 'em in?" asked the nephew, his mind taking fire.

"Some tweaky sort of thing, that all Americans will buy——"

"The American flag and a couple of doves holding dollar marks in their bills, and a handle that when you pull it out, its a corkscrew," suggested Fairchild. The florid man glared at him with interest and calculation.

"Or," the semitic man suggested, "a small condensed table for calculating interest on one side and a good recipe for beer on the other." The florid man glared at him with interest.

"That's just for men," Mrs Wiseman said. "How about the women's trade?"

"A bit of mirror would do for them, dont you think?" the florid man offered, "surrounded by a design in colors, eh?" Mrs Wiseman gave him a murderous glance and the poet added:

"And a formula for preventing conception and a secret place for hairpins."

The hostess moaned Mr Talliaferro! Mrs Wiseman said savagely:

"I have a better idea than that, for both sexes: your photograph on one side and the golden rule on the other." The florid man glared at her with interest. The nephew broke in once more:

"I mean, have you invented a jar yet? some way to get the stuff out of the jar?"

"Oh yes. I've done that. You spoon it out, you know."

"But tell 'em how you know all Americans are constipated," Fairchild suggested. Mrs Maurier rang the service bell furiously and at length. The steward appeared and as he removed the plates and replaced them with others, the florid man leaned nearer Mrs Wiseman.

"What's that chap?" he asked indicating Mr Talliaferro.

"What is he?" Mrs Wiseman repeated. "Why——I think he sells things downtown. Doesn't he, Julius?" she appealed to her brother.

"I mean, what—ah—race does he belong to?"

"Oh. You'd noticed his accent, then?"

"Yes. I noticed he doesn't talk like Americans. Thought perhaps he is one of your natives."

"One of our——?" She stared at him.

"Your red Indians, y'know," he explained.

Mrs Maurier rang her little bell again, sort of chattering to herself.

Two Oclock.

Mrs Maurier put an end to that luncheon as soon as she decently could. If I can only break them up, get them into a bridge game, she thought in an agony. It had got to where every time one of the gentlemen made the precursory sound of speech Mrs Maurier flinched and cringed nearer Mr Talliaferro. At least she could depend on him, provided. . . . But she was going to do the providing in his case. They had discussed Major Ayers' salts throughout the meal. Eva Wiseman had turned renegade and abetted them, despite the atmosphere of reproof Mrs Maurier had tried to foster and support. And, on top of all this the strange young man had the queerest manner of using knife and fork. Mr Fairchild's way was—well, uncouth, but after all, one must pay a price for Art. Jenny, on the other hand, had an undeniable style, feeding herself with her little finger at a rigid and elegant angle from her hand. And now Fairchild was saying:

"Now here's a clear case of poetic justice for you. A hundred odd years ago Major Ayers' grandpa wants to come to New Orleans, but our grandfathers stop him down yonder in those Chalmette swamps and lick hell out of him. And now Major Ayers comes into the city itself and conquers it with a laxative, a laxative so mild that, as he says, you dont even notice it. Hey, Julius?"

"It also confounds all the old convictions regarding the irreconciliability of science and art," the semitic man suggested.

"Huh?" said Fairchild. "Oh, sure. That's right. Say, he certainly ought to make Al Jackson a present of a bottle, oughtn't he?"

The thin poet groaned sepulchrally. Major Ayers repeated "Al Jackson?"

The steward removed the cloth. The table was formed of a number of cardtables; by Mrs Maurier's direction he did not remove these. She called him to her, whispered to him: he went below.

"Why, didn't you ever hear of Al Jackson?" asked Fairchild in unctuous surprise. "He's a funny man, a direct descendant of Old Hickory that licked you folks in 1812, he claims. He's quite a character in New Orleans." The other guests all listened to Fairchild with a sort of noncommittal attention. "You can always tell him because he wears congress boots all the time——"

"Congress boots?" murmured Major Ayers, staring at him.

Fairchild explained, raising his foot above the level of the table to demonstrate. "Sure. On the street, at formal gatherings, even in evening dress he wears 'em. He even wears 'em in bathing."

"In bathing? I say." Major Ayers stared at the narrator with his round chinablue eyes.

"Sure. Wont let anyone see him barefoot. A family deformity, you see. Old Hickory himself had it: that's the reason he outfought the British in those swamps. He'd never have whipped 'em otherwise. When you get to town, go down to Jackson square and look at that statue of the old fellow. He's got on congress boots." He turned to the semitic man. "By the way, Julius, you remember about Old Hickory's cavalry, dont you?" The semitic man was noncommittal and Fairchild continued:

"Well, the old general bought a place in Florida, a stock farm, they told him it was, and he gathered up a bunch of mountaineers from his Tennessee place and sent 'em down there with a herd of horses. Well sir, when they got there they found the place was pretty near all swamp. But they were hardy folks, so they lit right in to make the best of it. In the meantime——"

"Doing what?" asked the nephew.

"Huh?" said Fairchild.

"What were they going to do in Florida? That's what we all want to know," Mrs Wiseman said.

"Selling real estate to the Indians," the semitic man suggested. Major Ayers stared at him with his little blue eyes.

"No, they were going to run a dude ranch for the big hotels at Palm Beach," Fairchild told them. "And in the meantime some of these horses strayed off into the swamps and in some way the breed got crossed with alligators. And so, when Old Hickory found he was going to have to fight his battle down there in those Chalmette swamps, he sent over to his Florida place and had 'em round up as many of those half horse-half alligators as they could, and he mounted some of his infantry on 'em and the British couldn't stop 'em at all. The British didn't know Florida——"

"That's true," the semitic man put in, "there were no excursions then."

"——and they didn't even know what the things were, you see."

Major Ayers and Mrs Maurier stared at Fairchild in quiet childlike astonishment. "Go on," said Major Ayers at last, "you're pulling my leg."

"No, no: ask Julius. But then, it is kind of hard for a foreigner to get us. We're a simple people, we Americans, kind of childlike and hearty. And you've got to be both to cross a horse on an alligator and then find some use for him, you know. That's part of our national temperament, Major. You'll understand it better when you've been among us longer. Wont he, Julius?"

"Yes, he'll be able to get us all right when he's been in America long enough to acquire our customs. Its the custom that makes the man, you know."

"Ah yes," said Major Ayers, blinking at him. "But there's one of your customs I'll not be able to acquire: your habit of eating apple tarts. We dont have apple tarts at home, y'know. No Englishman nor Welshman nor Scot will eat an apple tart."

"You dont?" repeated Fairchild. "Why, I seem to remember——"

"But not apple tarts, old lad. We have other sorts, but no apple tarts. You see, years ago it was a custom at Eton for the young lads to pop out at all hours and buy apple tarts. And one day a chap, a cabinet member's son, died of a surfeit of apple tarts whereupon his father had parliament put through a bill that no minor should be able to purchase an apple tart in the British Dominions. So this generation grew up without them; the former generation died off, and now the present generation never heard of apple tarts." He turned to the semitic man. "Custom, as you just remarked."

The ghostly poet, waiting his chance, murmured "Secretary of the Interior," but this was ignored. Mrs Maurier stared at Major Ayers, and Fairchild and the others all stared at Major Ayers' florid bland face, and there was an interval of silence during which the hostess glanced about hopelessly among her guests. The steward reappeared and she hailed him with utter relief, ringing her little bell again commandingly. The others looked toward her and she passed her gaze from face to face.

"Now, people, at four oclock we will be in good bathing water. Until then, what do you say to a nice game of bridge? Of course, those who really must have a siesta will be excused, but I'm sure no one will wish to remain below on such a day as this," she added brightly. "Let me see—Mr Fairchild, Mrs Wiseman, Patricia and Julius, will be table number one. Major Ayers, Miss Jameson, Mr——Talliaferro——" her gaze came to rest on Jenny. "Do you play bridge, Miss——child?"

Fairchild had risen in some trepidation. "Say, Julius, Major Ayers had better lie down a while, dont you think? Being new to our hot climate, you know. And Gordon too. Hey, Gordon, dont you reckon we better lie down a while?"

"Right you are," Major Ayers agreed with alacrity, rising also. "If the ladies will excuse us, that is. Might get a touch of sun, you know," he added, glancing briefly at the awning overhead.

"But really," said Mrs Maurier helplessly. The gentlemen, clotting, moved toward the companionway.

"Coming, Gordon?" Fairchild called.

Mrs Maurier turned to Gordon. "Surely, Mr Gordon, you'll not desert us?"

Gordon looked at the niece. She met his harsh arrogant stare calmly, and he turned away. "Yes. Dont play cards," he answered shortly.

"But really," repeated Mrs Maurier. Mr Talliaferro and Pete remained. The nephew had already taken himself off to his new carpenter's saw. Mrs Maurier looked at Pete. Then she looked away. Not even necessary to ask Pete. "You wont play at all?" she called after the departing gentlemen, hopelessly.

"Sure, we'll come back later," Fairchild assured her, herding his watch below. They descended noisily.

Mrs Maurier looked about on her depleted party with astonished despair. The niece gazed at the emptied companionway a moment, then she looked about at the remainder of the party grouped about the superfluous cardtables. "And you said you didn't have enough women to go around," she remarked.

"But we can have one table, anyway." Mrs Maurier brightened suddenly. "There's Eva, Dorothy, Mr Talliaferro and m—— Why, here's Mark," she exclaimed. They had forgot him again. "Mark, of course. I'll cut out this hand."

Mr Talliaferro demurred. "By no means. I'll cut out. You take the hand: I insist."

Mrs Maurier refused. Mr Talliaferro became insistent and she examined him with cold speculation. Mr Talliaferro at last averted his eyes and Mrs Maurier glanced briefly toward the companionway. She was firm.

* * * * *

"Poor Talliaferro," the semitic man said. Fairchild led the way along the passage, pausing at his door while his gang trod his heels. "Did you see his face? She'll keep him under her thumb from now on."

"I dont feel sorry for him," Fairchild said. "I think he kind of likes it: he's always a little uncomfortable with men, you know. Being among a bunch of women seems to restore his confidence in himself, gives him a sense of superiority which his contacts with men seem to have pretty well hammered out of him. I guess the world does seem a kind of crude place to a man that spends eight hours a day surrounded by lace-trimmed crêpe-de-chine," he added, fumbling at the door. "Besides, he cant come to me for advice about how to seduce somebody. He's a fairly intelligent man, more sensitive than most, and yet he too labors under the illusion that Art is just a valid camouflage for rutting." He opened the door at last and they entered and sat variously while he knelt and dragged from beneath the bunk a heavy suitcase.

"She's quite wealthy, isn't she?" Major Ayers asked from the bunk. The semitic man, as was his way, had already preempted the single chair. Gordon leaned his back against the wall, tall and shabby and arrogant.

"Rotten with it," Fairchild answered. He got a bottle from the suitcase and rose to his feet and held the bottle against the light, gloating. "She owns plantations or something, dont she, Julius? First family, or something like that?"

"Something like that," the semitic man agreed. "She is a northerner, herself. Married it. I think that explains her, myself."

"Explains her?" Fairchild repeated, passing glasses among them.

"Its a long story. I'll tell it to you some day."

"It'll take a long story to explain her," Fairchild rejoined. "Say, she'd be a better bet for Major Ayers than the laxative business, wouldn't she? I'd rather own plantations than a patent medicine plant, any day."

"He'd have to remove Talliaferro, somehow," the semitic man remarked.

"Talliaferro's not thinking seriously of her, is he?"

"He'd better be," the other answered. "I wouldn't say he's got intentions on her, exactly," he corrected. "He's just there without knowing it: a natural hazard as regards anyone else's prospects."

"Freedom, and the laxative business, or plantations and Mrs

Maurier," Fairchild mused aloud. "Well, I dont know——
What do you think, Gordon?"

Gordon stood against the wall, aloof, not listening to them
hardly, watching within the bitter and arrogant loneliness of
his heart a shape strange and new as fire swirling, headless
armless legless but when his name was spoken he stirred. . . .
"Lets have a drink."

Fairchild filled the glasses: the muscles at the bases of their
noses tightened. "That's a pretty good rejoinder to every
emergency life may offer—like Squire Western's hollo," the
semitic man said.

"Yes, but freedom——" began Fairchild.

"Drink your whiskey," the other told him. "Take what little
freedom you'll ever get while you can. Freedom from the
police is the greatest freedom man can demand or expect."

"Freedom," said Major Ayers, "the only freedom is in war-
time. Everyone too busy fighting or getting ribbons or a snug
berth to annoy you. Samurai or headhunters—take your
choice. Mud and glory, or a bit of ribbon on a clean tunic.
Mud and abnegation and dear whiskey and England full of
your beastly expeditionary forces. You were better than Cana-
dians, though," he admitted, "not so damned many of you. It
was a priceless war, eh? . . . I like a bit of red, myself," he confided. "Staff tabs worth two on the breast: only see the breast
from one side. Ribbon's good in peacetime, however."

"But even peace cant last forever, can it?" the semitic man
added.

"It'll last a while—this one. Cant have another war right
off. Too many would stop away. Regulars all jump in and get
all the cushy jobs right off: learned in the last one, y'know;
and the others would all get their backs up and refuse to go
again." He mused for a moment. "The last one made war so
damned unpopular with the proletariat. They overdid it: like
the showman who fills his stage so full chaps can see through
into the wings."

"You folks were pretty good at war bunk yourselves,
weren't you?" Fairchild said. War bunk? repeated Major
Ayers. Fairchild explained.

"We didn't pay money for it, though," Major Ayers answered. "We only gave ribbons. . . . Pretty good whiskey, eh?"

*   *   *   *   *

"If you want me to," Jenny said, "I'll put it away in my room somewheres."

Pete crammed it down on his head, holding his head rigidly tilted a little to windward. The wind was eating his cigarette right out of his mouth: he held his hand as a shield, smoking behind his hand.

"Its all right," he answered. "Where'd you put it, anyway?"

". . . Somewheres. I'd just kind of put it away somewheres." The wind was in her dress, molding it, and clasping her hands about the rail she let herself swing backward to the full stretch of her arms while the wind molded her thighs. Pete's coat, buttoned, ballooned its vented flaring skirts.

"Yes," he said, "I can just kind of put it away myself, when I want. . . . Look out, kid." Jenny had drawn herself up to the rail again. The rail was breast high to her, but by hooking her legs over the lower rail she could draw herself upward, and by creasing her flat young belly over the top one she leaned far out over the water. The water sheared away creaming: a white fading through milky jade to blue again, and a thin spray whipped from it, scuttering like small shot. "Come on, get back on the boat. We are not riding the blinds this trip."

"Gee," said Jenny, creasing her young belly, hanging out over the water, while wind molded and flipped her little skirts, revealing the pink backs of her knees above her stockings. The helmsman thrust his head out and yelled at her, and Jenny craned her neck to look back at him, swinging her blown drowsy hair.

"Keep your shirt on, brother," Pete shouted back at the helmsman, for form's sake. "What'd I tell you, dumbness?" he hissed at Jenny, pulling her down. "Come on, now, its their boat. Try to act like somebody."

"I wasn't hurting it," Jenny answered placidly. "I guess I can do this, cant I?" She let her body swing back again at the stretch of her arms. ". . . Say, there he is with that saw again. I wonder what he's making?"

"Whatever it is he probably dont need any help from us," Pete answered. ". . . Say, how long did she say this was going to last?"

"I dont know . . . maybe they'll dance or something after a

while. This is kind of funny, aint it? They are not going anywhere, and they dont do anything . . . kind of like a movie or
something." Jenny brooded softly, gazing at the nephew where
he sat with his saw in the lee of the wheelhouse, immersed and
oblivious. "If I was rich, I'd stay where I could spend it. Not
like this, where there's not even anything to look at."

"Yeh. If you were rich you'd buy a lot of clothes and jewelry and an automobile. And then what'd you do? wear your
clothes out sitting in the automobile, huh?"

"I guess so. . . . I wouldn't buy a boat, anyway. . . . I think
he's kind of goodlooking. Not very snappy looking, though.
I wonder what he's making."

"Better go ask him," Pete answered shortly. "I dont know."

"I dont want to know, anyhow. I was just kind of wondering." She swung herself slowly at arms' length, against the
wind, slowly until she swung herself over beside Pete, leaning
her back against him.

"Go on and ask him," Pete insisted, his elbows hooked over
the rail, ignoring Jenny's soft weight, "a pretty boy like him
wont bite you."

"I dont mind being bit," Jenny replied placidly.
". . . Pete. . . ?"

"Get away, kid: I'm respectable," Pete told her. "Try your
pretty boy—see if you can compete with that saw."

"I like peppy looking men," Jenny remarked. She sighed.
"Gee, I wish there was a movie to go to or something." (I
wonder what he's making)

                    *   *   *   *   *

"What horsepower does she develop?" the nephew asked,
raising his voice above the deep vibration of the engine, staring at it entranced. It was clean as a watch, nickled and redleaded—a latent and brooding power beneath a thin film of
golden lubricating oil like the film of moisture on a splendid
animal functioning, physical with perfection. The captain in a
once white cap with a tarnished emblem above the visor, and
a thin undershirt stained with grease, told him how much
horsepower she developed.

He stood in a confined atmosphere, oppressive with energy: an ecstatic tingling that penetrated to the core of his
body, giving to his entrails a slightly unpleasant sensation of

lightness, staring at the engine with rapture. It was as beautiful as a racehorse and in a way terrifying since with all its implacable soulless power there was no motion to be seen save a trivial nervous flickering of rockerarms: a thin bright clicking that rode just above the remote contemplative thunder of it. The keelplates shook with it, the very bulkheads trembled with it, as though a moment were approaching when it would burst the steel as a cocoon is burst and soar upward and outward on dreadful and splendid wings of energy and flame . . . but the engine was bolted down with huge bolts, clean and firm and neatly redleaded, bolts nothing could break, firmly fixed as the nethermost foundations of the world. Across the engine, above the flicking rockerarms, the captain's soiled cap appeared and vanished. The nephew moved carefully around the engine, following.

There was a port at the height of his eyes and he saw beyond it sky bisected by a rigid curving sweep of water stiff with a fading energy like bronze. The captain was busy with a wisp of cotton waste, hovering about the engine, dabbing at its immaculate anatomy with needless maternal infatuation. The nephew watched with interest. The captain leaned nearer, wiped his waste through a small accumulation of grease at the base of a pushrod, raised it to the light. The nephew approached, peering over the captain's shoulder. It was a tiny speck, quite dead.

"What is it, Josh?" his sister said, breathing against his neck. The nephew turned sharply.

"Gabriel's pants," he said. "What are you doing down here? Who told you to come down here?"

"I wanted to come, too," she answered crowding against him. "What is it, Captain? What've you and Gus got?"

"Here," her brother thrust at her, "get on back on deck where you belong. You haven't got any business down here."

"What is it, Captain?" she repeated, ignoring him. The captain extended his rag. "Did the engine kill it?" she asked. "Gee, I wish we could get all of 'em down here and lock the door for a while, dont you?" She stared at the engine, at the flicking rockerarms. She squealed. "Look! Look how fast they're going. Its going awfully fast, isn't it, Captain?"

"Yes ma'am," the captain replied. "Pretty fast."

"What's her bore and stroke?" the nephew asked. The captain examined a dial. Then he turned a valve slightly. Then he examined the dial again. The nephew repeated his question, and the captain told him.

"She revs up pretty well, dont she?" the nephew suggested after a while.

"Yes, sir," the captain answered. He was busy doing something with two small wrenches. The nephew offered to help. His sister followed, curious and intent.

"I expect you better let me do it alone," the captain said, courteous and firm. "I know her better than you, I expect. . . . Suppose you and the young lady stand over there just a little."

"You sure do keep her clean, captain," the niece said. "Clean enough to eat off of, isn't she?"

The captain thawed. "She's worth keeping clean. Best marine engine made. German. She cost twelve thousand dollars."

"Gee," the niece remarked in a hushed tone. Her brother turned upon her, pushing her before him from the room.

"Look here," he said fiercely, his voice shaking, when they were again in the passage. "What are you doing, following me around? What did I tell you I was going to do if you followed me any more?"

"I wasn't following you. I——"

"Yes, you were," he interrupted, shaking her, "following me. You——"

"I just wanted to come, too. Besides its Aunt Pat's boat: its not yours. I've got as much right down there as you have."

"Aw, get on up on deck. And if I catch you trailing around behind me again . . ." his voice merged into a dire and nameless threat. The niece turned toward the companionway.

"Oh, haul in your sheet: you're jibing."

Four Oclock.

They sat at their bridge game on deck, shuffling, dealing, speaking in sparse monosyllables. The Nausikaa surged sedately onward under the blue drowsing afternoon. Far away on the horizon, the lazy smudge of the Mandeville ferry.

Mrs Maurier on the outskirt of the game, gazed at intervals abstractedly into space. From below there came an indistinguishable sound, welling at intervals, and falling, and Mr Talliaferro grew restive. The sound died away at intervals, swelled again. The Nausikaa paced sedately on.

They played their hands, dealt and shuffled again. Mr Talliaferro was becoming distrait. Every once in a while his attention strayed and returning found Mrs Maurier's eyes upon him, coldly contemplative, and he bent anew over his cards. . . . The indistinguishable sound swelled once more. Mr Talliaferro trumped his partner's queen and the gentlemen in their bathing suits surged up the stairs.

They completely ignored the card players, passing aft in a body and talking loudly——something about a wager. They paused at the rail upon which the steward leaned at the moment; here they clotted momentarily, then Major Ayers detached himself from the group and flung himself briskly and awkwardly overboard. "Hurray," roared Fairchild. "He wins!" Mrs Maurier had raised her face when they passed, she had spoken to them and had watched them when they halted, and she saw Major Ayers leap overboard with a shocked and dreadful doubt of her own eyesight. Then she screamed.

The steward stripped off his jacket, detached and flung a lifebelt, then followed himself, diving outward and away from the screw. "Two of 'em," Fairchild howled with joy. "Pick you up when we come back," he megaphoned through his hands.

Major Ayers came up in the wake of the yacht, swimming strongly. The Nausikaa circled, the telegraph rang. Major Ayers and the steward had reached the lifebelt together and before the Nausikaa lost way completely the helmsman and the deckhand had swung the tender overside completely and soon they hauled Major Ayers savagely into the small boat.

The Nausikaa was hove to. Mrs Maurier was helped below to her cabin, where her irate captain attended her presently. Meanwhile the other gentlemen plunged in and began to cajole the ladies, so the rest of the party went below and donned their bathing suits.

Jenny didn't have one: her sole preparation for the voyage had consisted of the purchase of a lipstick and a comb. The niece loaned Jenny hers, and in this borrowed suit which fit her a shade too well, Jenny clung to the gunwale of the tender,

clutching Pete's hand and floating her pink-and-white face like
a toy balloon unwetted above the water, while Pete sat in the
boat fully dressed even to his hat, glowering.

Mr Talliaferro's bathing suit was red, giving him a bizarre
desiccated look like a recently extracted tooth. He wore also
a red rubber cap and he let himself gingerly into the water feet
first from the stern of the tender, and here he clung beside the
placid Jenny, trying to engage her in small talk beneath Pete's
thunderous regard. The ghostly poet in his ironed serge——
he didn't swim——lay again at full length on four chairs, craning his pale prehensile face above the bathers.

Fairchild looked more like a walrus than ever, a deceptively
sedate walrus of middleage suddenly evincing a streak of de-
moniac puerility. He wallowed and splashed, heavily playful,
and seconded by Major Ayers, annoyed the ladies by pinching them under water and by splashing them, wetting Pete liberally where he sat smoldering with Jenny clinging to his hand
and squealing, trying to protect her makeup. The semitic man
paddled around with that rather ludicrous intentness of a fat
man swimming. Gordon sat on the rail, looking on. Fairchild
and Major Ayers at last succeeded in driving the ladies back
into the tender, about which they splashed and yapped with
the tactless playfulness of dogs, while Pete refraining Look out
goddam you lookout christ whatcher doing look out struck at
their fingers with one of his discarded and sopping shoes.

Above this onesided merriment the niece appeared poised
upon the top of the wheel house, unseen by those below. They
were aware first of a white arrow arcing down the sky. The
water took it lazily and while they stared at the slow green
vortex where it had entered there was a commotion behind
Fairchild, and as he opened his mouth his gaping surprise
vanished beneath the surface. In its place the niece balanced
momentarily on something under the water, then she fell
plunging in the direction of Major Ayers' yet passive astonishment. The ladies screamed with delight. Major Ayers also
vanished, the niece plunged on and Fairchild appeared
presently, coughing and gasping and climbed briskly into the
tender where Mr Talliaferro with admirable presence of mind
already was, having deserted Jenny without a qualm. "I've got
enough," Fairchild said when he could speak.

Major Ayers, however, accepted the challenge. The niece
trod water and awaited him. "Drown him, Pat!" the ladies
shrieked. Just before he reached her, her dark wet head vanished and for a while Major Ayers plunged about in a kind of
active resignation. Then he vanished again and the niece, clad
in a suit of her brother's underwear——a knitted sleeveless
jersey and short narrow trunks—surged out of the water and
stood erect on his shoulders. Then she put her foot on the top
of his head and thrust him deeper yet. Then she plunged on
and trod water again. Major Ayers reappeared at last, already
headed for the boat. He had enough also, and the gentlemen
dragged him aboard and they dripped across the deck and
passed below, to the derision of the ladies.

The ladies got aboard themselves. Pete standing erect in the
tender, was trying to haul Jenny out of the water. She hung
like an expensive doll confection from his hands, raising at lax
intervals a white lovely leg, while Mr Talliaferro, kneeling,
pawed at her shoulders. "Come on, come on," Pete hissed at
her. The niece swam up and thrust at Jenny's sweet thighs
until Jenny tumbled at last into the tender in a soft blonde
abandon: a charming awkwardness. The niece held the tender
steady while they boarded the yacht, then she slid skilfully out
of the water, sleek and dripping as a seal; and as she swung
her short coarse hair back from her face she saw hands, and
Gordon's voice said:

"Give me your hands."

She clasped his hard wrists and felt herself flying. The setting sun came level into his beard and upon all his tall lean
body, and dripping water on the deck she stood and looked
at him with admiration. "Gee, you're hard," she said. She
touched his forearms again, then she struck him with her fist
on his hard high chest. "Do it again, will you?"

"Swing you again?" he asked. But she was already in the
tender, extending her arms while sunset was a moist gold
sheathing her. Again that sensation of flying, of space and
motion and his hard hands coming into it; and for an instant
she stopped in midflight, hand to hand and arm braced to arm,
high above the deck while water dripping from her turned
to gold as it fell. Sunset was in his eyes: a glory, he could not
see; and her taut simple body, almost breastless and with the

fleeting hips of a boy, was an ecstasy in golden marble, and in her face the passionate ecstasy of a child.

At last her feet touched the deck again and she turned. She sped toward the companionway and as she flashed downward the last of the sun slid upon her and over her with joy. Then she was gone, and Gordon stood looking at the wet and simple prints of her naked feet on the deck.

Six Oclock.

They had raised land just about the time Major Ayers won his wager, and while the last of day drained out of the world the Nausikaa at halfspeed forged slowly into a sluggish river mouth, broaching a timeless violet twilight between solemn bearded cypresses motionless as bronze. You might, by listening, have heard a slow requiem in this tall nave, might have heard here the chanted orisons of the dark heart of the world turning toward slumber. The world was becoming dimensionless, the tall bearded cypresses drew nearer one to another across the wallowing river with the soulless implacability of pagan gods, gazing down upon this mahogany-and-brass intruder with inscrutable unalarm. The water was like oil and the Nausikaa forged onward without any sensation of motion through a corridor without ceiling or floor.

Mr Talliaferro stood at the sternrail beside Jenny and her morose hatted duenna. In the dusk Jenny's white troubling placidity bloomed like a heavy flower, pervading and rife like an odor lazier, heavier than that of lilies. Pete loomed beyond her: the last light in the world was concentrated in the implacable glaze of his hat, leaving the atmosphere about them darker still; and in the weary passion of August and nightfall Mr Talliaferro's dry interminable voice fell lower and lower and finally ceased altogether; and abruptly becoming aware of an old mislaid sorrow Mr Talliaferro slapped suddenly at the back of his hand, with consternation, remarking at the same time that Pete was also restive and that Jenny was agitating herself as though she were rubbing her body against her clothing from within. Then, as if at a signal, they were all about them, unseen, with a dreadful bucolic intentness, unlike their urban cousins, making no sound. Jenny and Pete and Mr

Talliaferro evacuated the deck. At the companionway the ghostly poet joined them hurriedly, flapping his handkerchief about his face and neck and the top of his unnurtured evaporating head. At that instant Mrs Maurier's voice rose from somewhere in astonished adjuration, and presently the Nausikaa put about and felt her way back to open water, and stood out to sea. And not at halfspeed, either.

SEVEN OCLOCK.

Years ago Mrs Maurier had learned that unadulterated fruit juice was salutary, nay, necessary to a nautical life. A piece of information strange, irrelevant at first draught, yet on second thought quite possible, not to mention pleasant in contemplation, so she had accepted it, taking it unto herself and making of it an undeviating marine conviction. Hence there was grapefruit again for dinner: she was going to inoculate them first, then take chances.

Fairchild's gang was ultimately started from its lair in his quarters. The other guests were already seated and they regarded the newcomers with interest and trepidation and, on Mrs Maurier's part, with actual alarm.

"Here comes the dogwatch," Mrs Wiseman remarked brightly. "Its the gentlemen, isn't it? We haven't seen any gentlemen since we left New Orleans, hey, Dorothy?"

Her brother grinned at her sadly. "How about Mark and Talliaferro?"

"Oh, Mark's a poet. That lets him out. And Ernest isn't a poet. So that lets him out, too," she replied with airy feminine logic. "Isn't that right, Mark?"

"I'm the best poet in New Orleans," the ghostly young man said heavily, mooning his pale prehensile face at her.

"We were kind of wondering where you were, Mark," Fairchild told the best poet in New Orleans. "We got the idea you were supposed to be on the boat with us. Too bad you couldn't come," he continued tediously.

"Maybe Mark couldn't find himself in time," the semitic man suggested, taking his seat.

"He's found his appetite, though," Fairchild replied. "Maybe he'll find the rest of himself laying around somewhere nearby." He seated himself and stared at the plate before him. He murmured Well Well with abstraction. His companions found seats. Major Ayers stared at his plate. He murmured Well Well also. Mrs Maurier chewed her lip nervously, putting her hand on Mr Talliaferro's sleeve. Major Ayers murmured: "It does look familiar, doesn't it?" and Fairchild said: "Why, its grapefruit: I can tell every time." He looked at Major Ayers. "I'm not going to eat mine, now. I'm going to put it away and save it."

"Right you are," agreed Major Ayers readily. "Save 'em, by all means." He set his grapefruit carefully to one side. "Advise you people to do the same," he added at large.

"Save them?" Mrs Maurier repeated in astonishment. "Why, there are more of them. We have several crates."

Fairchild wagged his head at her. "I cant risk it. They might be lost overboard or something, and us miles from land. I'm going to save mine."

Major Ayers offered a suggestion. "Save the rind, anyway. Might need 'em. Never tell what might happen at sea, y'know," he said owlishly.

"Sure," Fairchild agreed. "Might need 'em in a pinch to prevent constipation." Mrs Maurier clasped Mr Talliaferro's arm again.

"Mr Talliaferro," she whispered imploringly. Mr Talliaferro sprang to the breach.

"Now that we are all together at last," he began, clearing his throat, "the Commodore wishes us to choose our first port of call. In other words, people, where shall we go tomorrow?" He looked from face to face about the table.

"Why, nowhere," answered Fairchild with surprise. "We just came from somewhere yesterday, didn't we?"

"You mean today," Mrs Wiseman told him. "We left New Orleans this morning."

"Oh, did we? Well, well. It takes a long time to spend the afternoon, dont it? But we dont want to go anywhere, do we?"

"Oh yes," Mr Talliaferro contradicted him smoothly. "Tomorrow we are going up the Tchufuncta river and spend the day fishing. Our plan was to go up the river and spend the night, but this was found impossible. So we shall go up tomorrow. Is this unanimous? or shall we call for a ballot?"

"Gabriel's pants," the niece said to Jenny, "I itch just to think about that, dont you?"

Fairchild brightened. "Up the Tchufuncta?" he repeated. "Why, that's where the Jackson place is. Maybe Al's at home. Major Ayers must meet Al Jackson, Julius."

"Al Jackson?" Major Ayers repeated. The best poet in New Orleans groaned and Mrs Wiseman said: "Good Lord, Dawson."

"Sure. The one I was telling about at lunch, you know."

"Ah yes: the alligator chap, eh?"

Mrs Maurier exclaimed Mr Talliaferro again.

"Very well," Mr Talliaferro said loudly. "That's settled, then. Fishing has it. And in the meantime, the Commodore invites you all to a dancing party on deck immediately after dinner. So finish your dinner, people. Fairchild, you are to lead the grand march."

"Sure," Fairchild agreed again. "Yes, that's the one. His father has a fish ranch up here. That's where Al got his start, and now he's the biggest fisherd in the world——"

"Did you see the sunset this evening, Major Ayers?" Mrs Wiseman asked loudly. "Deliciously messy, wasn't it?"

"Nature getting even with Turner," the poet suggested.

"That will take years and years," Mrs Wiseman answered. Mrs Maurier sailed in, gushing.

"Our southern sunsets, Major Ayers——" But Major Ayers was staring at Fairchild.

—"Fisherd?" he murmured.

"Sure. Like the old cattle ranches out west, you know. But instead of a cattle ranch, Al Jackson as got a fish ranch out in the wide open spaces of the Gulf of Mexico——"

"Where men are sharks," put in Mrs Wiseman. "Dont leave that out." Major Ayers stared at her.

"Sure. Where men are men. That's where this beautiful blonde girl comes in. Like Jenny yonder. Maybe Jenny's the one. Are you the girl, Jenny?" Major Ayers now stared at Jenny.

Jenny was gazing at the narrator, her blue ineffable eyes quite round, holding a piece of bread in her hand. "Sir?" she said at last.

"Are you the girl that lives on that Jackson fish ranch out in the Gulf of Mexico?"

"I live on Esplanade," Jenny said after a while, tentatively.

"Mr Fairchild!" Mrs Maurier exclaimed. Mr Talliaferro said: "My dear sir."

"No, I reckon you are not the one, or you'd know it. I dont imagine that even Claude Jackson could live on a fish ranch in the Gulf of Mexico and not know it. This girl is from Brooklyn, anyway—a society girl. She went down there to find her brother. Her brother had just graduated from reform school and so his old man sent him down there for the Jacksons to make a fisherd out of him. He hadn't shown any aptitude for anything else, you see, and his old man knew it didn't take much intelligence to herd a fish. His sister——"

"But, I say," Major Ayers interrupted, "why do they herd their fish?"

"They round 'em up and brand 'em, you see. Al Jackson brands——"

"Brand 'em?"

"Sure: marks 'em so he can tell his fish from ordinary wild fish—mavericks, they call 'em. And now he owns nearly all the fish in the world—a fish millionaire, even if he is fish-poor right now. Wherever you see a marked fish, its one of Al Jackson's."

"Marks his fish, eh?"

"Sure: notches their tails."

"Mr Fairchild," Mrs Maurier said.

"But our fish at home have notched tails," Major Ayers objected.

"Well, they are Jackson fish that have strayed off the range, then."

"Why doesn't he establish a European agent?" the ghostly poet asked viciously.

Major Ayers stared about from face to face. "I say," he began. He stuck there. The hostess rose decisively.

"Come, people, lets go on deck."

"No, no," the niece said quickly, "go on: tell us some more." Mrs Wiseman rose also.

"Dawson," she said firmly, "shut up. We simply cannot stand any more. This afternoon has been too trying. Come on, lets go up," she said, herding the ladies firmly out of the room, taking Mr Talliaferro along also.

NINE OCLOCK.

He needed a bit of wire. He had reached that impasse familiar to all creators, where he could not decide which of a number of things to do next. His object had attained that stage of completion in which the simplicity of the initial impulse dissolves into a number of trivial necessary details; and lying on his bunk in the cabin he and Mr Talliaferro shared, his saw at hand and a thin litter of sawdust and shavings well impermeating the bedclothing, he held his wooden cylinder to the small inadequate light and decided that he could do with a bit of stiff wire or something of that nature.

He swung his legs out of the berth and flowed to the floor in a single beautiful motion, and crossing the room on his bare feet he searched Mr Talliaferro's effects without success, so he passed from the cabin and opened the door of the opposite room, without knocking. It was one of the women's rooms, but as it happened there was nobody in it and on the dressing table among a scented frail litter of fabric and delicate objects of crystal and porcelain he found a package of cigarettes lightly dusted over with pinkish powder. He took two of them.

Still in his bare feet he went on along the passage, and opening another door he let subdued light from the passage into a room filled with snoring, discerning vaguely the sleeper and, on a peg in the wall, a stained white cap. Captain's room he decided leaving the door open and traversing the room silently to another door.

There was a dim small light in this room, gleaming dully on the viscid anatomy of the now motionless engine, but he ignored the engine now, going about his search with businesslike expedition. There was a wood cabinet against the wall: some of the drawers were locked. He rummaged through the others, pausing at times to raise certain objects to the light for a closer inspection, discarding them again. He closed the last drawer and stood with his hand on the cabinet, examining the room.

A piece of wire would do, a short piece of stiff wire . . . there were wires on one wall, passing among and between switches. But these were electric wires and probably indispensable. Electric wires . . . battery room. It must be there, beyond that small door.

It was there—a shadowfilled cubbyhole smelling of acids, of decomposition: a verdigris of decay. Plenty of wires here, but no loose ones. . . . He stared around, and presently he saw something upright and gleaming dully. It was a piece of mechanism, steel, smooth and odorless and rather comforting in this tomb of smells, and he examined it curiously, striking matches. And there, attached to it, was exactly what he needed—a small straight steel rod.

I wonder what it does he thought. It looked . . . a winch of some kind, maybe. But what would they want with a winch down here? Something they dont use much, evidently, he assured himself. Too clean. Cleaner than the engine. Not greased all over like the engine. They mustn't hardly ever use it. . . . Or a pump. A pump, that's what it is. They wont need a pump once a year: not any bilge in a boat kept up like a grand piano. Anyhow, they couldn't possibly need it before tomorrow, and I'll be through with it then. Chances are they wouldn't miss it if I kept it altogether.

The rod came off easily. Plenty of wrenches in the cabinet, and he just unscrewed the nuts at each end of the rod and lifted it out. He paused again, holding the rod in his hand. . . . Suppose he were to injure the rod some way. He hadn't considered that and he stood turning the rod this way and that in his fingers, watching dull gleams of light on its slender polished length. It was so exactly what he needed. Steel, too, good steel: it cost twelve thousand dollars. And if you cant get good steel for that. . . . He put his tongue on it. It tasted principally of machine oil, but it must be good hard steel, costing twelve thousand dollars. I guess I cant hurt anything that cost twelve thousand dollars, especially by just using it one time. . . . "If they need it tomorrow I'll be through with it, anyway," he said aloud.

He replaced the wrenches. His mouth tasted of machine oil and he spat. The Captain yet snored and he passed through the Captain's room on his bare feet, closing the door thoughtfully so the light from the passage wouldn't disturb the sleeper. He slipped the rod into his pocket. His hands were greasy and so he wiped them on the seat of his trousers.

He paused again at the galley door, where the steward was still busy over the sink. The steward stopped long enough to find a candle for him, then he returned to his room. He lit the candle, drew Mr Talliaferro's suitcase from beneath the bunk and dripping a bit of hot wax onto it, he fixed the candle upright. Then he got Mr Talliaferro's pigskin enclosed shaving kit and propped the rod upon it with the end of the rod in the candle flame. His mouth still tasted of machine oil and so he climbed onto his berth and spat through the port, discovering as he did so that the port was screened. It'll dry, though.

He touched the rod. It was getting warm. But he wanted it red hot. His mouth yet tasted of machine oil and he remembered the other cigarette. It was in the same pocket in which he had had the rod, and it too was slightly reminiscent of machinery, but the burning tobacco would soon kill that.

The rod was getting pretty hot, so he fetched the wooden cylinder from the bunk, and laying the cigarette on the edge of the suitcase he picked up the rod and held its heated end firmly against the selected spot on the cylinder, and soon a thin thread of smoke rose curling into the windless air. The smoke had a faint odor like that of scorching leather in it, also. Machine oil, probably.

TEN OCLOCK.

Its being an artist Mrs Maurier said to herself with helpless despondence. Mrs Wiseman, Miss Jameson, Mark and Mr Talliaferro sat at bridge. She herself did not feel like playing: the strain of her party kept her too nervous and wrought up. "You simply cannot tell what they're going to do," she said aloud in her exasperation, seeing again Major Ayers' vanishing awkward shape and Fairchild leaning over the rail and howling after him like a bullvoiced Druid priest at a sacrifice.

"Yes," Mrs Wiseman agreed, "its like an excursion, isn't it?——all drunkenness and trampling around," she added, attempting to finesse. "Damn you, Mark."

"Its worse than that," the niece corrected pausing to watch the hissing fall of cards, "its like a cattle boat—all trampling around."

Mrs Maurier sighed. "What ever it is . . ." her sentence died stillborn. The niece drifted away, and a tall shape appeared from shadow and joined her, and they went on down the dark deck and from her sight. It was that queer shabby Mr Gordon, and she knew a sudden sharp stab of conscience, of having failed in her duty as a hostess. She had barely exchanged a word with him since they came aboard. Its that terrible Mr Fairchild, she told herself. But who could have known that a middleaged man, and a successful novelist, could or would conduct himself so?

The moon was getting up, spreading a silver flare of moonlight on the water. The Nausikaa swung gently at her cables, motionless but never still, sleeping but not dead, as is the manner of ships on the seas of the world, cradled like a silver dreaming gull on the water . . . her yacht. Her party, people whom she had invited together for their mutual pleasure. . . . Maybe they think I ought to get drunk with them, she thought.

She roused herself, creating conversation. The cardplayers shuffled and dealt interminably, replying Mmmm to her remarks, irrelevant and detached, or pausing to answer sensibly with a patient deference. Mrs Maurier rose briskly.

"Come, people, I know you are tired of cards. Lets have some music and dance a while."

"I'd rather play bridge with Mark than dance with him," Mrs Wiseman said. ". . . Whose trick was that?"

"There'll be plenty of men when the music starts," Mrs Maurier said.

"Mmmm," replied Mrs Wiseman. . . . "It'll take more than a victrola record to get any men on this party. . . . You'll need extradition papers. . . . Three without and three aces. How much is that, Ernest?"

"Wouldn't you like to dance, Mr Talliaferro?" Mrs Maurier persisted.

"Whatever you wish, dear lady," Mr Talliaferro answered with courteous detachment, busy with his pencil. "That makes——" He totted up a column of his neat figures, then he raised his head. "I beg your pardon: did you say something?"

"Dont bother," Mrs Maurier said. "I'll put on a record myself: I'm sure our party will gather when they hear it."

She wound up the portable victrola, put on a record. "You finish your rubber, and I'll look about and see whom I can find," she added. Mmmm they replied.

The victrola raised its teasing rhythms of saxophones and drums, and Mrs Maurier prowled around, peering into the shadows. She found the steward first, whom she dispatched to the gentlemen with a command couched in the form of an invitation. Then, further along, she discovered Gordon, and her niece sitting on the rail with her legs locked about a stanchion.

"Do be careful," she said, "you might fall. We are going to dance a while," she added happily.

"Not me," her niece answered quickly. "Not tonight, anyway. You have to dance enough in this world on dry land."

"You will certainly not prevent Mr Gordon's dancing, however. Come, Mr Gordon, we need you."

"I dont dance," Gordon answered shortly.

"You dont dance?" Mrs Maurier repeated. "You really dont dance at all?"

"Run along, Aunt Pat," the niece answered for him. "We're talking about art."

Mrs Maurier sighed. "Where's Theodore?" she asked at last. "Perhaps he will help us out."

"He's in bed. He went to bed right after dinner. But you might go down and ask him if he wants to get up and dance."

Mrs Maurier stared helplessly at Gordon. Then she turned away. The steward met her: the gentlemen were sorry, but they had all gone to bed. They were tired after such a strenuous day. She sighed again, and passed on to the companionway. There seemed to be nothing else she could do for them. I've certainly tried, she told herself taking this thin satisfaction, and stopped again while something shapeless in the dark companionway unblent, becoming two, and after a while Pete said from the darkness:

"Its me and Jenny."

Jenny made a soft meaningless sound and Mrs Maurier bent forward suspiciously. Mrs Wiseman's remark about excursion boats recurred to her.

"You are enjoying the moon, I suppose?" she remarked.

"Yessum," Jenny answered, "we're just sitting here."

"Dont you children want to dance? They have started the victrola," Mrs Maurier said in a resurgence of optimism.

"Yessum," said Jenny again, after a while. But they made no further move, and Mrs Maurier sniffed. Quite genteelly, and she said icily:

"Excuse me, please."

They made room for her to pass, and she descended without looking back again, and found her door. She snapped the light switch viciously. Then she sighed again.

Its being an artist, she told herself again, helplessly.

*   *   *   *   *

"Damn, damn, damn," said Mrs Wiseman slapping her cards on the table. The victrola record had played itself through and into an endless monotonous rasping. "Mark, stop that thing, as you love God. I'm far enough behind, without being jinxed." The ghostly poet rose obediently and Mrs Wiseman swept her hand amid the cards on the table, scattering them. "I'm not going to spend any more of my life putting little spotted squares of paper in orderly sequence for three dull people——tonight, anyway. Gimme a cigarette, someone." She thrust her chair back and Mr Talliaferro opened his case to her. She took one and lifted her foot to the other knee and scratched a match on the sole of her slipper. "Lets talk a while instead."

"Where on earth did you get those garters?" Miss Jameson asked curiously.

"These?" She flipped her skirt down. "Why? Dont you like 'em?"

"They are a trifle out of the picture, on you."

"What kind would you suggest for me? Pieces of colored string?"

"You ought to have black ones clasped with natural size red roses," Mark Frost told her. "That's what one would expect to find on you."

"Wrrrong, me good man," Mrs Wiseman answered dramatically, "you have wronged me foully. . . . Where's Mrs Maurier, I wonder?"

"She must have caught somebody. That Gordon man, perhaps," Miss Jameson replied. "I saw him at the rail yonder a while ago."

"Ah, Mr Talliaferro!" exclaimed Mrs Wiseman. "Look out for yourself. Widders and artists, you know. You see how susceptible I am, myself. Wasn't there ever a fortune teller to warn you of a tall red stranger in your destiny?"

"You are a widow only by courtesy," the poet rejoined, "like the servingmaids in sixteenth century literature."

"So are some of the artists, my boy," Mrs Wiseman replied. "But all the men on board are not even artists. What, Ernest?"

Mr Talliaferro bridled smugly through the smoke of his cigarette. Mrs Wiseman consumed hers in an unbroken series of deep draughts and flipped it railward: a twinkling scarlet coal. "I said talk," she reminded them, "not a few mild disjointed beans of gossip." She rose. "Come on, lets go to bed, Dorothy."

Miss Jameson sat, a humorless inertia. "And leave that moon?"

Mrs Wiseman yawned, stretching her arms. The moon spread her silver ceaseless hand on the dark water. Mrs Wiseman turned, spreading her arms in a flamboyant gesture in silhouette against it. "Ah, Moon, poor weary one. . . . By yon black moon," she apostrophised.

"No wonder it looks tired," the poet remarked hollowly. "Think of how much adultery its had to look upon."

"Or assume the blame for," Mrs Wiseman amended. She dropped her arms. "I wish I were in love," she said. "Why aren't you and Ernest more . . . more. . . . Come on, Dorothy. Lets go to bed."

"Have I got to move?" Miss Jameson said. She rose, however. The men rose also, and the two women departed. When they had gone Mr Talliaferro gathered up the cards Mrs Wiseman had scattered. Some of them had fallen to the deck.

Eleven Oclock.

Mr Talliaferro tapped diffidently at the door of Fairchild's room, was bidden, and opening it he saw the semitic man sitting in the lone chair and Major Ayers and Fairchild on the bunk, holding glasses. "Come in," Fairchild repeated. "How did you escape? Push her overboard and run?"

Mr Talliaferro grinned with deprecation, regarding the bottle sitting on a small table, rubbing his hands together with anticipation.

"The human body can stand anything, cant it?" the semitic man remarked. "But I imagine Talliaferro is just about at the end of his rope, without outside aid," he added. Major Ayers glared at him affably with his chinablue eyes.

"Yes, Talliaferro's sure earned a drink," Fairchild agreed. "Where's Gordon? Was he on deck?"

"I think so," Mr Talliaferro replied. "I believe he's with Miss Robyn."

"Well, more power to him," Fairchild said. "Hope she wont handle him as roughly as she did us, hey, Major?"

"You and Major Ayers deserved exactly what you got," the semitic man rejoined. "You cant complain."

"I guess so. But I dont like to see a human being arrogating to himself the privileges and pleasures of providence. Quelling nuisances is God's job."

"How about instruments of providence?"

"Oh, take another drink," Fairchild told him. "Stop talking so Talliaferro can have one, anyway. Then we better get up on deck. The ladies might begin to wonder what has become of us."

"Why should they?" the semitic man asked innocently. Fairchild heaved himself off the bunk and got Mr Talliaferro a tumbler. Mr Talliaferro drank it slowly, unctuously; and pressed, accepted another.

Fairchild regarded him brightly. "No maidenheads popping yet, I suppose?"

Mr Talliaferro emptied his glass with a slight flourish. He grimaced slightly. "What is it that makes artists so coarse of speech, Major Ayers? When you rob a pleasure of surreptitiousness, you rob it of half its charm, dont you think?"

The semitic man agreed with him. Major Ayers, though, was loyal. "Oh, artists are all right. I like artists," he said. They had another drink and Fairchild put the bottle away.

"Lets go up a while," he suggested, prodding them to their feet and herding them toward the door. Mr Talliaferro allowed the others to precede him. Lingering, he touched Fairchild's arm. The other glanced at his meaningful expression, and paused.

"I want your advice," Mr Talliaferro explained. Major Ayers and the semitic man halted in the passage, waiting.

"Go on, you fellows," Fairchild told them. "I'll be along in a moment." He turned to Mr Talliaferro. "Who's the lucky girl this time?"

Mr Talliaferro whispered a name. "Now, this is my plan of campaign. What do you think——"

"Wait," Fairchild interrupted, "lets have a drink on it." Mr Talliaferro closed the door again, carefully.

*   *   *   *   *

Fairchild swung the door open.

"And you think it will work?" Mr Talliaferro repeated, quitting the room.

"Sure, sure; I think its airtight: that she might just as well make up her mind to the inevitable."

"No, really: I want your candid opinion. I have more faith in your judgment of people than anyone I know."

"Sure, sure," Fairchild repeated solemnly. "She cant resist you. No chance, no chance at all. To tell the truth, I kind of hate to think of women and young girls going around exposed to a man like you."

Mr Talliaferro glanced over his shoulder at Fairchild, quickly, doubtfully. But the other's face was solemn, without guile. Mr Talliaferro went on again. "Well, wish me luck," he said.

"Sure. The admiral expects every man to do his duty, you know," Fairchild replied solemnly, following Mr Talliaferro's dapper figure up the stairs.

*   *   *   *   *

Major Ayers and the semitic man awaited them. There were no ladies. Nobody at all, in fact. The deck was deserted.

"Are you sure?" Fairchild insisted. "Have you looked good? I kind of wanted to dance some. Come on, lets look again."

At the door of the wheelhouse they came upon the helmsman. He wore only an undershirt above his trousers and he was gazing into the sky. "Fine night," Fairchild greeted him.

"Fine now," the helmsman agreed. "Bad weather off there, though." He extended his arm toward the southwest. "Lake may be running pretty high by morning. We're on a lee shore, too." He stared again into the sky.

"Ah, I guess not," Fairchild replied with large optimism. "Hardly on a clear night like this, do you reckon?"

The helmsman stared into the sky, making no answer. They passed on.

"I forgot to tell you the ladies had retired," Mr Talliaferro remarked.

"That's funny," Fairchild said. "I wonder if they thought we were not coming back?"

"Perhaps they were afraid we were," the semitic man suggested.

"Huh," said Fairchild. . . . "What time is it, anyway?"

It was twelve oclock, and the sky toward the zenith was hazed over, obscuring the stars. But the moon was still undimmed, bland and chill, affable and bloodless as a successful procuress, bathing the yacht in quiet silver; and across the southern sky went a procession of small clouds like silver dolphins on a rigid ultramarine wave, like an ancient geographical woodcut.

The Second Day.

B Y three oclock the storm had blown itself out across the lake and by dawn, when the helmsman waked the captain, the lake, as he had predicted, was running pretty high. The trend was directly inshore, waves came up in endless battalions under a cloudless sky, curling and creaming along the hull, dying fading as the water shoaled astern of the yacht to a thin white smother against a dark impenetrable band of trees. The Nausikaa rose and fell, bows on, dragging at her taut cables. The helmsman roused the captain and returned swiftly to the wheelhouse.

The deckhand got the anchors up, and the helmsman rang the telegraph. The Nausikaa shivered awake, coming to life again, and pausing for a moment between two waves like a swimmer, she surged ahead. She paid off a little and the helmsman spun the wheel. But she didn't respond, falling off steadily and gaining speed; and as the helmsman put the wheel down hard the Nausikaa fell broadside on into the trough of the waves. The helmsman rang the telegraph again and shouted to the deckhand to let go the anchors.

By seven oclock the Nausikaa, dragging her anchors, had touched bottom with a faint jar. She considered a moment then freed herself and crawling a bit further up the shoaling sand she turned herself a little, and with a barely perceptible list she sat down like a plump bather waistdeep in the water, taking the waves on her beam.

* * * * *

Dorothy Jameson had a bold humorless style. She preferred portraits, though she occasionally painted stilllife—harsh implacable fruit and flowers in dimensionless bowls upon tables without depth. Her teeth were large and white in the pale revelation of her gums, and her gray eyes were coldly effective. Her body was long, loosely articulated and frail, and while spending in Greenwich village the two years she had considered necessary for the assimilation of American tendencies in painting, she had taken a lover although she was still a virgin.

She took the lover principally because he owed her money

which he had borrowed from her in order to pay a debt to another woman. The lover ultimately eloped to Paris with a wealthy Pittsburgh lady, pawning her—Dorothy's—fur coat on the way to the dock and mailing the ticket back to her from shipboard. The lover himself was a musician. He was quite advanced: what is known as a radical, and in the intervals of experimenting with the conventional tonal scale he served as part of the orchestra in an uptown dancing place. It was here that he met the Pittsburgh lady.

But this episode was complete, almost out of her memory even; and she had had a year abroad and had returned to New Orleans where she settled down to a moderate allowance which permitted her a studio in the Vieux Carré and her name several times on the police docket for reckless driving and a humorless and reasonably pleasant cultivation of her individuality, with no more than a mild occasional nagging at the hands of her family like a sound of rain heard beyond a closed window.

She had always had trouble with her men. Principally through habit since that almost forgotten episode she had always tried for artists, but sooner or later they inevitably ran out on her. With the exception of Mark Frost, that is. And in his case, she realized, it was sheer inertia more than anything else. And she admitted with a remote perspicuity, who cared one way or the other whether or not they kept Mark Frost? No one ever cared long for an artist who did nothing save create art, and very little of that.

But other men, men she recognised as having potentialities, all passed through a violent but temporary period of interest which ceased as abruptly as it began, without leaving even the lingering threads of mutual remembered incidence, like those brief thunderstorms of August that threaten and dissolve for no apparent reason, without producing any rain.

At times she speculated with almost masculine detachment on the reason for this. She always tried to keep their relations on the plane which the men themselves seemed to prefer—certainly no woman would, and few women could, demand less of their men than she did. She never made arbitrary demands on their time, never caused them to wait for her nor to see her home at inconvenient hours, never made them fetch and carry for her; she fed them and she flattered herself that she was a good listener. And yet. . . . She thought of the women she knew: how all of them had at least one obviously entranced male; she thought of the women she had observed: of how they seemed to acquire a man at will, and if he failed to stay acquired, how readily they replaced him.

She thought of the people on board, briefly reviewing them. Eva Wiseman. She had had one husband, practically discarded him. Men liked her. Fairchild, for instance: a man of undisputed ability and accomplishment. Yet this might be due to his friendship with her brother. But no, Fairchild was not that sort: social obligations rested too lightly upon him. It was because he was attracted to her. Because of kindred tastes? But I create too, she reminded herself.

Then she thought of the two young girls. Of the niece Patricia, with her frank curiosity in things, her childish delight in strenuous physical motion, of her hard unsentimentality and no interest whatever in the function of creating art (I'll bet she doesn't even read) and Gordon aloof and insufferably arrogant, yet intrigued. And Fairchild also interested in his impersonal way. Even Pete, probably.

Pete, and Jenny. Jenny with her soft placidity, her sheer passive appeal to the senses, and Mr Talliaferro braving Mrs Maurier's displeasure to dangle about her, fawning almost. Even she felt Jenny's appeal—an utterly mindless rifeness of young pink flesh, a supine potential fecundity lovely to look upon: a doll awaiting quickening and challenging it with neither joy nor sorrow. She had brought one man with her. . . . No, not brought, even: he had followed in her blonde troubling orbit as a tide follows the moon, without volition, against his inclination, perhaps. Two women who had no interest whatever in the arts, yet who without effort drew to themselves men, artistic men. Opposites, antitheses . . . perhaps, she thought, I have been trying for the wrong kind of men, perhaps the artistic man is not my type.

Seven Oclock.

"No, ma'am," the nephew replied courteously, "its a pipe."
"Oh," she murmured, "a pipe."

He bent over his wooden cylinder, paring at it with a knife, delicately, with care. It was much cooler today. The sun had risen from out a serrated miniature sea, into a cloudless sky. For a while the yacht had had a perceptible motion—it was this motion which had roused her—but now it had ceased, although sizable waves yet came in from the lake, creaming whitely along the hull, and spent themselves shoaling up the beach toward a dark cliff of trees. She'd had no idea last night that they were so close to land, either. But distances always confused her by night.

She wished she'd brought a coat: had she anticipated such a cool spell in August. . . . She stood huddling her scarf about her shoulders, watching his brown intent forearms and his coarse cropped head exactly like his sister's, mildly desiring breakfast. I wonder if he's hungry, she thought. She remarked: "Aren't you rather chilly this morning without a coat?"

He carved at his object with a rapt maternal absorption, and after a while she said, louder:

"Wouldn't it be simpler to buy one?"

"I hope so," he murmured . . . then he raised his head and the sun shone full into his opaque yellowflecked eyes. "What'd you say?"

"I should think you'd wait until we got ashore and buy one instead of trying to make one."

"You cant buy one like this. They dont make 'em."

The cylinder came in two sections, carved and fitted cunningly. He raised one piece, squinting at it, and carved an infinitesimal sliver from it. Then he returned it to its husband. Then he broke them apart again and carved an infinitesimal sliver from the other piece, fitted them together again. Miss Jameson watched him.

"Do you carry the design in your head?" she asked.

He raised his head again. "Huh?" he said in a dazed tone.

"The design you're carving. Are you just carving from memory, or what?"

"Design?" he repeated. "What design?"

It was much cooler today.

*   *   *   *   *

There was in Pete's face a kind of active alarm not quite yet dispersed, and clutching his sheet of newspaper he rose with belated politeness, but she said: "No, no: I'll get it. Keep your seat." So he stood acutely, clutching his paper while she fetched a chair and drew it up beside his. "Its quite chilly this morning, isn't it?"

"Sure is," he agreed. "When I woke up this morning and felt all that cold wind and the boat going up and down, I didn't know what we were in to. I didn't feel so good this morning anyway, and with the boat going up and down like it was. . . . Its still now, though. Looks like they went in closer to the bank and parked it this time."

"Yes, it seems to me we're closer than we were last night." When she was settled, he sat also and presently he forgot and put his feet back on the rail. Then he remembered and removed them.

"Why, how did you manage to get a paper this morning? Did we put in shore somewhere last night?" she asked, raising her feet to the rail.

For some reason he felt uncomfortable about his paper. "Its just an old piece," he explained lamely. "I found it down stairs somewhere. It kind of kept my mind off of how bad I felt." He made a gesture, repudiating it.

"Dont throw it away," she said quickly, "go on—dont let me interrupt if you found something interesting in it. I'm sorry you aren't feeling well. Perhaps you'll feel better after breakfast."

"Maybe so," he agreed without conviction. "I dont feel much like breakfast, waking up like I did and feeling kind of bad, and the boat going up and down, too."

"You'll get over that, I'm sure." She leaned nearer to see the paper. It was a single sheet of a Sunday magazine section: a depressing looking article in small print about Romanesque architecture, interspersed with blurred indistinguishable photographs. "Are you interested in architecture?" she asked intensely.

"I guess not," he replied. "I was just looking it over until they get up." He slanted his hat anew: under cover of this movement he raised his feet to the rail, settling down on his spine. She said:

"So many people waste their time over things like architecture and such. Its much better to be a part of life, dont you think? Much better to be in it yourself and make your own mistakes and enjoy making them and suffering for them, than to make your life barren through dedicating it to an improbable and ungrateful posterity. Dont you think so?"

"I hadn't thought about it," Pete said cautiously. He lit a cigarette. "Breakfast is late today."

"Of course you hadn't. That's what I admire about a man like you. You know life so well that you aren't afraid of what it might do to you. You dont spend your time thinking about life, do you?"

"Not much," he agreed. "A man dont want to be a fish, though."

"You'll never be a fish, Pete (everyone calls you Pete, dont they——do you mind?) I think the serious things really are the things that make for happiness—people and things that are compatible, love. . . . So many people are content just to sit around and talk about them instead of getting out and attaining them. As if life were a joke of some kind. . . . May I have a cigarette? Thanks. You smoke these too, I see. A m——Thanks. I like your hat: it just suits the shape of your face. You have an extremely interesting face—do you know it? And your eyes. I never saw eyes exactly the color of yours. But I suppose lots of women have told you that, haven't they?"

"I guess so," Pete answered. "They'll tell you anything." He snapped the match into flame with his thumbnail.

"Is that what love has meant to you, Pete—deception?" she leaned to the match, staring at him with the humorless invitation of her eyes. "Is that your opinion of us?"

"Aw, they dont mean nothing by it," Pete said in something like alarm. "What time do they have breakfast on this line?" He rose. "I guess I better run down stairs before its ready. It oughtn't to be long," he added. Miss Jameson was gazing quietly out across the water. She wore a thin scarf about her shoulders: a webbed brilliant thing that lent her a bloodless fragility, as did the faint bridge of freckles (relict of a single afternoon of sunlight) across her nose. She now sat suddenly quiet, poising the cigarette in her long delicate fingers, and Pete stood beside her, acutely uncomfortable, why he knew not. "I guess I'll go down stairs before breakfast," he repeated.

"Say"—he extended his newspaper—"why dont you look it over while I'm gone?"

Then she looked at him again, and took the paper. "Ah, Pete, you dont know much about us—for all your experience."

"Sure," he replied. "I'll see you again, see?" and he went away. I'm glad I had a clean collar yesterday, he thought turning into the companionway. This trip sure ought to be over in a couple of years. . . . Just as he began the descent he looked back at her. The newspaper lay across her lap, but she wasn't looking at it. And she had thrown the cigarette away, too. My God Pete said to himself. Then he was struck by a thought. Pete, my boy, he told himself, its going to be a hard trip. He descended into the narrow passage. It swept forward on either hand, broken smugly by spaced mute doors with brass knobs. He slowed momentarily, counting doors to find his own, and while he paused the door at his hand opened suddenly and the niece appeared clutching a raincoat about her.

"Hello," she said.

"Dont mention it," Pete replied, raising his hat slightly. "Jenny up, too?"

"Say, I dreamed you lost that thing," the niece told him. "Yes, she'll be out soon, I guess."

"That's good. I was afraid she was going to lay there and starve to death."

"No, she'll be out pretty soon." They stood facing each other in the narrow passage, blocking it completely, and the niece said: "Get on, Pete. I feel too tired to climb over you this morning."

He stood aside for her and watching her retreat he called after her: "Losing your pants."

She stopped and dragged at her hips as a shapeless fabric descending from beneath the raincoat wadded slow and lethargic about her feet. She stood on one leg and kicked at the mass, then stooping she picked from amid its folds a man's frayed and shapeless necktie. "Damn that string," she said, kicking out of the garment and picking it up.

Pete turned in the narrow corridor, counting discrete identical doors. He smelled coffee and he added to himself A hard trip, and, with unction: I'll tell the world it is.

Eight Oclock.

"Its the steering gear," Mrs Maurier explained at the breakfast table. "Some——"

"I know," Mrs Wiseman exclaimed immediately above her grapefruit, "German spies."

Mrs Maurier stared at her with patient astonishment. She said How cute. "It worked perfectly yesterday. The Captain said it worked perfectly yesterday. But this morning, when the storm came up . . . anyway, we're aground, and they are sending someone to get a tug to pull us off. They are trying to find the trouble this morning, but I dont know. . . ."

Mrs Wiseman leaned toward her, patting her fumbling ringed hand. "There, there, dont you feel badly about it: it wasn't your fault. They'll get us off soon, and we can have just as much fun here as we would sailing around. More, perhaps: motion seems to have had a bad effect on the party. I wonder. . . ." Fairchild and his people had not yet arrived: before each vacant place its grapefruit, innocent and profound. Surely just the prospect of more grapefruit couldn't have driven them. . . .

Mrs Maurier followed her gaze. "Perhaps its just as well," she murmured.

"Anyway, I've always wanted to be shipwrecked," Mrs Wiseman went on. "What do they call it? scuttled the ship, isn't it? But surely Dawson and Julius couldn't have thought of this, though." Mrs Maurier brooding above her plate, raised her eyes, cringing. "No, no," the other answered herself hastily. "Of course not: that's silly. It just happened, as things do. But let this be a lesson to you children never to lay yourselves open to suspicion," she added looking from the niece to the nephew. The steward appeared with coffee. Mrs Maurier directed him to leave the gentlemen's fruit until it suited their pleasure to come for it.

"They couldn't have done it if they'd wanted to," the niece replied. "They dont know anything about machinery. Josh could have done it. He knows all about automobile motors. I bet you could fix it for 'em if you wanted to, couldn't you, Gus?"

He didn't seem to have heard her at all. He finished his breakfast, eating with a steady and complete preoccupation, then thrusting his chair back he asked generally for a cigarette. His sister produced a package from somewhere. It bore yet faint traces of pinkish scented powder and Miss Jameson said sharply:

"I wondered who took my cigarettes. It was you, was it?"

"I thought you'd forgot 'em and so I brought 'em up with me." She and her brother took one each, and she slid the package across the table. Miss Jameson picked it up, stared into it a moment, then put it in her handbag. The nephew had a patent lighter. They all watched with interest, and after a while Mr Talliaferro with facetious intent offered him a match. But it took fire finally, and he lit his cigarette and snapped the cap down. "Gimme a light too, Gus," his sister said quickly and from the pocket of his shirt he took two matches, laid them beside her plate. He rose.

He whistled four bars of Sleepytime Gal monotonously, ending on a prolonged excruciating note, and from the bedclothing at the foot of his bunk he got the steel rod and stood squinting his eyes against the smoke of his cigarette, examining it. One end of it was kind of blackened and pinching the cloth of his trouserleg about it, he shuttled it swiftly back and forth. Then he examined it again. It was still kind of black. The smoke of his cigarette was making his eyes water, so he spat it out and ground his heel on it.

After a time he found a toothbrush and crossing the passage to a lavatory he scrubbed the rod. A little of the black came off, onto the brush, and he dried the rod on his shirt and scrubbed the brush against the screen in a port, then against a redleaded water pipe, and then against the back of his hand. He sniffed at it . . . a kind of machinery smell yet, but you wont notice it with tooth paste on it. He returned and replaced the brush among Mr Talliaferro's things.

He whistled four bars of Sleepytime Gal monotonously. The engine room was deserted. But he was making no effort toward concealment, anyway. He found the wrenches again and went to the battery room and restored the rod without haste, whistling with monotonous preoccupation. He replaced the wrenches and stood for a while examining the slumbering engine with rapture. Then still without haste he quitted the room.

The Captain, the steward and the deckhand sat at breakfast in the saloon. He paused in the door.

"Broke down, have we?" he asked.

"Yes, sir," the Captain answered shortly. They went on with their breakfast.

"What's the trouble?" No reply, and after a time he suggested: "Engine play out?"

"Steering gear," the Captain answered shortly.

"You ought to could fix that. . . . Where is the steering gear?"

"Engine room," the Captain replied.

The nephew turned away. "Well, I haven't touched anything in the engine room."

The Captain bent above his plate, chewing. Then his jaws ceased and he raised his head sharply, staring after the nephew retreating down the passage.

Ten Oclock.

"The trouble with you, Talliaferro, is that you aint bold enough with women. That's your trouble."

"But I——" Fairchild wouldn't let him finish.

"I dont mean with words. They dont care anything about words except as little things to pass the time with. You cant be bold with them with words: you cant even shock them with words. Though the reason may be that half the time they are not listening to you. They aint interested in what you're going to say: they are interested in what you're going to do."

"Yes, but—— How do you mean, be bold? What must I do to be bold?"

"How do they do it everywhere? Aint every paper you pick up full of accounts of men being caught in Kansas City or Omaha under compromising conditions with young girls who've been missing from Indianapolis and Peoria and even Chicago for days and days? Surely if a man can get as far as Kansas City with a Chicago girl, without her shooting him through chance or affection or sheer exuberance of spirits or something, he can pretty safely risk a New Orleans girl."

"But why should Talliaferro want to take a New Orleans girl, or any other girl, to Kansas City?" the semitic man asked. They ignored him.

"I know," Mr Talliaferro rejoined. "But these men have always just robbed a cigar store. I couldn't do that, you know."

"Well, maybe New Orleans girls wont require that: maybe they haven't got that sophisticated yet. They may not be aware that their favors are worth as high as a cigar store. But I dont know: there are moving pictures, and some of 'em probably even read newspapers too, so I'd advise you to get busy right away. The word may have already got around that if they just hold off another day or so, they can get a cigar store for practically nothing. And there aint very many cigar stores in New Orleans, you know."

"But," the semitic man put in again, "Talliaferro doesn't want a girl and a cigar store both, you know."

"That's right," Fairchild agreed. "You aint looking for tobacco, are you, Talliaferro?"

Eleven Oclock.

"No, sir," the nephew answered patiently, "its a pipe."

"A pipe?" Fairchild drew nearer, interested. "What's the idea? will it smoke longer than an ordinary pipe? Holds more tobacco, eh?"

"Smokes cooler," the nephew corrected, carving minutely at his cylinders. "Wont burn your tongue. Smoke the tobacco down to the last grain, and it wont burn your tongue. You change gears on it, kind of, like a car."

"Well, I'm damned. How does it work?" Fairchild dragged up a chair, and the nephew showed him how it worked. "Well I'm damned," he repeated, taking fire. "Say, you ought to make a pile of money out of it, if you make it work, you know."

"It works," the nephew answered, joining his cylinders again. "Made a little one out of pine. Smoked pretty good for a pine pipe. It'll work all right."

"What kind of wood are you using now?"

"Cherry." He carved and fitted intently, bending his coarse dark head above his work. Fairchild watched him. "Well, I'm damned," he said again in a sort of heavy astonishment. "Funny nobody thought of it before. Say, we might form a stock company, you know, with Julius and Major Ayers. He's trying to get rich right away at something that dont require work, and this pipe is a lot better idea than the one he's got, for I cant imagine even Americans spending much money for something that dont do anything except keep your bowels open. That's too sensible for us, even though we will buy anything. . . . Your sister tells me you and she are going to Yale college next month."

"I am," he corrected, without raising his head. "She just thinks she's going too, that's all. She kept on worrying dad until he said she could go. She'll be wanting to do something else by then."

"What does she do?" Fairchild asked. "I mean, does she have a string of beaux and run around dancing and buying things like most girls like her do?"

"Naw," the nephew answered, "she spends most of her time and mine too tagging around after me. Oh, she's all right, I guess," he added tolerantly, "but she hasn't got much sense." He unfitted the cylinders, squinting at them.

"That's where she changes gear, is it?" Fairchild leaned nearer again. "Yes, she's a pretty nice sort of a kid. Kind of like a racehorse colt, you know. . . . So you're going up to Yale. I used to want to go to Yale, myself, once. Only I had to go where I could. I guess there comes a time in the life of every young American, of the class that wants scholastic learning or that accepts the inevitability of education, when he wants to go to Yale or Harvard. Maybe that's the value of Yale or Harvard to our American life: a kind of illusion of an intellectual Nirvana that makes the ones that cant go there work like hell where they do go, so as not to show up so poorly alongside of the anointed. Still, ninety nine out of a hundred Yale and Harvard turn out are reasonably bearable to live with, if they aint anything else. And that's something to say for any manufactory, I guess. But I'd like to have gone there. . . ." The nephew was not listening particularly. He shaved and trimmed solicitously at his cylinder. Fairchild said:

"It was a kind of funny college I went to. A denominational college, you know, where they turned out preachers. I was working in a mowing machinery factory in Indiana, and the owner of the factory was an alumnus and a trustee of this college. He was a sanctimonious old fellow with a beard like a goat, and every year he offered a half scholarship to be competed for by young men working for him. You won it, you know, and he found you a job near the college to pay your board but not enough to do anything else—to keep you from fleshly temptations, you know—and he had a monthly report on your progress sent to him. And I won it, that year.

"It was just for one year, so I tried to take every thing I could. I had about six or seven lectures every day, besides the work I had to do to earn my board. But I kind of got interested in learning things: I learned in spite of the instructors we had. They were a bunch of broken down preachers: head full of dogma and intolerance and a belly full of big meaningless words. English literature course whittled down Shakespeare because he wrote about whores without pointing a moral and one instructor always insisted that the head devil in Paradise Lost was an inspired prophetic portrait of Darwin, and they wouldn't touch Byron with a ten foot pole. And Swinburne was reduced to his mother and his old standby, the ocean. And I guess they'd have cut this out had they worn one piece bathing suits in those days. But in spite of it, I kind of got interested in learning things. I would like to have looked inside my mind, after that year was up. . . ." He gazed out over the water, over the snoring waves, steady and wind frothed. He laughed. "And I joined a fraternity, too, almost."

The nephew bent over his pipe. Fairchild produced a package of cigarettes. The nephew accepted one with abstraction. He accepted a light, also. "I guess you've got your eye on a fraternity, haven't you?" he suggested.

"Senior club," the nephew corrected shortly. "If I can make it."

"Senior club," Fairchild repeated. "That means you wont join for three years, eh? That's a good idea. I like that idea. But I had to do everything in one year, you see. I couldn't wait. I never had much time to mix with the other students. Six hours a day at lectures, and the rest of the time working and studying for next day. But I couldn't help but hear something about it, about rushing and pledges and so on, and how so and so were after this fellow or that, because he made the football team or something.

"There was a fellow at my boarding house: a kind of handsome tall fellow he was, always talking about the big athletes and such in school. He knew them all by their first names, and he always had some yarn about girls and he was always showing you a pink envelope or something——a kind of gentlemanly innuendo, protecting their good names. He was a senior, he told me, and he was the first one to talk to me about fraternities. He said he had belonged to one a long time, though he didn't wear a badge. He had given his badge to a girl, who wouldn't return it. . . . You see," Fairchild explained again, "I had to work so much—you know: getting into a rut of work for bread and meat, where chance couldn't touch me much. Chance and information. That's what they mean by wisdom, horsesense, you know. . . .

"He was the one that told me he could get me in this fraternity, if I wanted to." He drew at his cigarette, flipped it away. "Its young people who put life into ritual by making conventions a living part of life: only old people destroy life by making it a ritual. And I wanted to get all I could out of being in a college. The boy that belongs to a secret pirates' gang and who dreams of defending an abstraction with his blood, hasn't quite died out before twenty one, you know. But I didn't have any money.

"Then he suggested that I get more work temporarily. He pointed out to me other men who belonged to it, or who were going to join—baseball players, and captains of teams, and prize scholars and such. So I got more work. He told me not to mention it to anybody, that that was the way they did it. I didn't know anybody much, you see," he explained. "I had to work pretty steady all day: no chance to get to know anybody well enough to talk to 'em." He mused upon the ceaseless fading battalions of waves. "So I got some more work to do. This had to be night work, so I got a job helping to fire the college power plant. I could take my books along with me and study while the steam was up, only it cut into my sleep some, and sometimes I would get too drowsy to study. So I had to give up one of my lecture courses, though the instructor finally agreed to let me try to make it up during the

Christmas vacation. But I learned how to sleep in a cinder pile or a coal bunker, anyway." The nephew was interested now. His knife was idle in his hand, his cylinder reposed, forgetting the agony of wood.

"It would take twenty five dollars, but working overtime as I was, I figured it wouldn't be any actual cost to me at all, except the loss of sleep. And a young fellow can stand that if he has to. I was used to work, you know, and it seemed to me that this was just like finding twenty five dollars.

"I had been working about a month when this fellow came to me and told me that something had happened and that the fraternity would have to initiate right away, and he asked me how much I had earned. I lacked a little of having twenty five dollars, so he said he would loan me the difference to make it up; and I went to the power house manager and told him I had to have some money to pay a dentist with, and got my money and gave it to this fellow, and he told me where to be the following night——behind the library at a certain hour. So I did: I was there, like he said." Fairchild laughed again.

"What'd the bird do?" the nephew asked. "Gyp you?"

"It was cold, that night. Late November, and a cold wind came right out of the north, whistling around that building, among the bare trees. Just a few dead leaves on the trees that made a kind of sad dry sound. We had won a football game that afternoon and I could hear yelling occasionally, and see lights in the dormitories where the ones that could afford to lived, warm and jolly looking, with the bare trees swaying and waving across the windows. Still celebrating the game we had won.

"So I walked back and forth, stamping my feet, and after a while I went around the corner of the library where it wasn't so cold and I could stick out my head occasionally in case they came looking for me. From this side of the building I could see the hall where the girls lived. It was all lighted up, as if for a party, and I could see shadows coming and going upon the drawn shades, where they were dressing up and fixing their hair and all; and pretty soon I heard a crowd coming across the campus and I thought here they come at last. But they passed on, going toward the girls' hall, where the party was.

"I walked up and down some more, stamping my feet. Pretty soon I heard a clock striking nine. In a half an hour I'd have to be back at the power house. They were playing music at the party: I could hear it even in spite of the closed windows, and I thought maybe I'd go closer. But the wind was colder: and there was a little snow in it, and besides I was afraid they'd come for me and I wouldn't be there. So I stamped my feet, walking up and down. Pretty soon I knew it must be nine thirty, but I stayed a while longer, and soon it was snowing hard—a blizzard. It was the first snow of the year, and somebody came to the door of the party and saw it, and then they all came out to look, yelling: I could hear the girls' voices, kind of high and excited and fresh, and the music was louder. Then they went back, and the music was faint again, and then the clock struck ten. So I went on back to the power house. I was already late." He ceased, musing on the glittering battalions of waves and hands of wind slapping them whitely. He laughed again. "But I nearly joined one, though."

"How about the bird," the nephew asked. "Didn't you hunt him up the next day?"

"He was gone. I never saw him again. I found out later he wasn't even in college. I never did know what became of him." Fairchild rose. "Well, you get it finished, and we'll form a company and get rich."

The nephew sat, clutching his knife and his cylinder, gazing after Fairchild's stocky back until the other passed from view. "You poor prune," he said, resuming his work again.

Two Oclock.

It was that interval so unbearable to young active people: directly after lunch on a summer day. Everyone else was dozing somewhere, no one to talk to and nothing to do. It was warmer than in the forenoon though the sky was still clear, and waves yet came in before a steady wind, slapping the Nausikaa on her comfortable beam and creaming on past to fade and die frothing up the shoaling beach and its still palisade of trees.

The niece hung over the bows, watching the waves. They were diminishing, by sunset there would be none at all, but occasionally one came in large enough to send up a thin exhilarating spray. Her dress whipped about her bare legs and she gazed downward into the restless water, trying to make up her mind to get her bathing suit. But if I go in now I'll get tired and then when the others go in later I wont have anything to do. She gazed down into the water, watching it surge and shift and change, watching the slack anchor cables severing the incoming waves, feeling the wind against her back.

Then the wind blew upon her face and she idled along the deck and paused again at the wheelhouse, yawning. Nobody there. But that's so, the helmsman went off early to get word for a tug. She entered the room, examining the control fixtures with interest. She touched the wheel, tentatively. It turned all right: they must have fixed it, whatever was broken about it. She removed her hand and examined the room again, hopefully, and her eyes came upon a binocular suspended from a nail in the wall.

Through the binocular she saw a blur in two colors, but presently under her fingers the blur became trees startlingly distinct and separate leaf from leaf and bough from bough and pendants of rusty green moss were beards of contemplative goats ruminating among the trees above a yellow strip of beach and a smother of foam in which the sun hung little fleeting rainbows. She watched this for a time, entranced, then swinging the glass slowly, waves slid past at armslength, curling and creaming; and swinging the glass further, the rail leapt monstrously into view and upon the rail a nameless object emitting at that instant a number of circular yellow basins. The yellow things fell into the water, seemingly so near, yet without any sound, and swinging the glass again, the thing that had emitted them was gone, and in its place the back of a man, close enough for her to touch him by extending her hand.

She lowered the glass and the man's back sprang away, becoming that of the steward carrying a garbage pail, and she knew what the yellow basins were. She raised the glass again and again the steward sprang suddenly and silently within reach of her arm. She called Hey! and when he paused and turned his face was plain as plain. She waved her hand to him, but he only looked at her a moment. Then he went on around a corner.

She hung the binocular back on its nail and followed along the deck where he had disappeared. Inside the companionway and obliquely through the galley door, she could see him moving about, washing the luncheon dishes, and she sat on the top step of the stairs. There was a round small window beside her, and he bent over the sink while light fell directly upon his brown head. She watched him quietly, intently but without rudeness, as a child would, until he looked up and remarked her tanned serious face framed roundly in the port. "Hello," she said.

"Hello," he answered as gravely.

"You have to work all the time, dont you?" she asked. "Say, I liked the way you went over after that man, yesterday. With your clothes on, too. Not many have sense enough to dive away from the propeller. What's your name?"

David West, he told her, scraping a stew pan and sloshing water into it. Steam rose from the water and about it bobbed a cake of thick implacable looking yellow soap. The niece sat bent forward to see through the window, rubbing her palms on her bare calves. "Its too bad you have to work whether we are aground or not," she remarked. "The Captain and the rest of them dont have anything to do now, except just lie around. They can have more fun than us, now. Aunt Pat's kind of terrible," she explained. "Have you been with her long?"

"No, ma'am. This is my first trip. But I dont mind light work like this. Aint much to do, when you get settled down to it. Aint nothing to what I have done."

"Oh. You dont. . . . You are not a regular cook, are you?"

"No, ma'am, not regular," he admitted. "It was Mr Fairchild got me this job with Mrs——with her."

"He did? Gee, he knows everybody almost, dont he?"

"Does he?"

She gazed through the round window, watching a blackened kettle brighten beneath his brush. Soap frothed, piled like summer clouds, floated in the sink like small reflections of clouds. "Have you known him long?" she asked. "Mr Fairchild, I mean?"

"I didn't know him any until a couple of days ago. I was in that park where that statue is, down close to the docks, and he came by and we were talking and I wasn't working then and so he got me this job. I can do any kind of work," he added with quiet pride.

"You can? You dont live in New Orleans, do you?"

"Indiana," he told her. "I'm just travelling around."

"Gee," the niece said, "I wish I were a man, like that. I bet its all right, going around wherever you want to. I guess I'd work on ships. That's what I'd do."

"Yes," he agreed. "That's where I learned to cook—on a ship."

"Not——?"

"Yes'm, to the Mediterranean ports, last trip."

"Gee," she said again. "You've seen lots, haven't you? What would you do, when you got to places? You didn't just stay on the ship, did you?"

"No'm. I went to a lot of towns. Away from the coast."

"To Paris, I bet?"

"No'm," he admitted, with just a trace of sheepishness, "I never seemed to get to Paris. But next——"

"I knew you wouldn't," she said quickly. "Say, men just go to Europe because they say European women are fast, dont they? Are European women like that? Promiscuous, like they say?"

"I dont know," he said. "I nev——"

"I bet you never had time to fool with them, did you? That's what I'd do: I wouldn't waste my time on women, if I went to Europe. They make me sick: these little college boys with their balloon pants, and colored stickers all over their suitcases, bringing empty cognac bottles back with 'em and snickering about french girls, and trying to make love to you in french. Say, I bet where you went you could see a lot of mountains and little cute towns on the side of 'em, and old gray walls and ruined castles on the mountains, couldn't you?"

"Yes'm. And one place was high over a lake. It was blue as . . . blue like. . . . Washing water," he said finally. "Water with bluing in it. They put bluing in water when they wash clothes, country folks do," he explained.

"I know," she said impatiently. "Were there mountains around it?"

"The Alps mountains, and little white boats on it no bigger

than bugs. You couldn't see 'em moving: you only could see the water kind of spreading out to each side. The water would keep on spreading out until it pretty near touched both shores whenever a boat passed. And you could lay on your back on the mountain where I was and watch eagles flying around way up above the water, until sunset. Then the eagles all went back to the mountains." David gazed through the port, past her sober tanned face mooned there by the round window, not even seeing it any longer, seeing instead his washingpowder colored lake and his lonely mountains and eagles against the blue. "And then the sun would go down, and sometimes the mountains would look like they were on fire all over. That was the ice and snow on 'em. It was pretty at night too," he added simply, scrubbing again at his pots.

"Gee," she said with hushed young longing. "And that's what you get for being a woman. I guess I'll have to get married and have a bunch of kids." She watched him with her grave opaque eyes. "No, I'm not, either," she said fiercely. "I'm going to make Hank let me go there next summer. Cant you go back then, too? Say, you fix it up to go back there then, and I'll go home and see Hank about it and then I'll come over. Josh'll want to come too, most likely, and you'll know where the places are. Cant you do that?"

"I guess I could," he answered slowly. "Only——"

"Only what?"

"Nothing," he said at last.

"Well, you fix it up to go, then. I'll give you my address and you can write me when to start and where to meet you. . . . I guess I couldn't go over on the same boat you'll be on, could I?"

"I'm afraid not," he answered.

"Well, it'll be all right, anyway. Gee, David, I wish we could go tomorrow, dont you? I wonder if they let people swim in that lake? But I dont know—maybe its nicer to be way up there where you were, looking down at it. Next summer. . . ." Her unseeing eyes rested upon his brown busy head while her spirit lay on its belly above Maggiore, watching little white boats no bigger than water beetles, and the lonely arrogant eagles aloft in blue sunshot space surrounded and enclosed by mountains cloudbrooded, taller than God.

David dried his pots and pans and hung them along the bulkhead in a burnished row. He washed out his dishcloths and hung them to dry upon the wall. The niece watched him.

"Its too bad you have to work all the time," she said with polite regret.

"I'm all done now."

"Lets go swimming, then. It ought to be good now. I've just been waiting for somebody to go in with me."

"I cant," he answered. "I've got a little more work I better do now."

"I thought you were through. Will it take you very long? If it wont, lets go in then: I'll wait."

"Well, you see I dont go in during the day. I go in early in the morning, before you are up."

"Say, I hadn't thought of that. I bet its fine, then, isn't it? How about calling me in the morning, when you are ready to go in? Wont you?" He hesitated again and she added, watching him with her sober opaque eyes: "Is it because you dont like to go swimming with girls? That's all right: I wont bother you. I swim pretty well. You wont have to keep me from drowning."

"It aint that," he answered lamely. "You see, I . . . I haven't got a bathing suit," he blurted.

"Oh, is that all? I'll get my brother's for you. It'll be kind of tight, but I guess you can wear it. I'll get it for you now, if you'll go in."

"I cant," he repeated. "I've still got some cleaning up to do."

"Well——" She got to her feet. "If you wont, then. But in the morning? you promised, you know."

"All right," he agreed.

"I'll try to be awake. But you just knock at the door—the second one to the right, you know." She turned on her silent bare feet. She paused again. "Dont forget you promised," she called back. Then her flat boy's body was gone, and David turned again to his work.

The niece went on up the deck and turned the corner of the deckhouse on her silent feet just in time to see Jenny rout and disperse an attack by Mr Talliaferro. She stepped back beyond the corner, unseen.

*   *   *   *   *

Boldness. But Fairchild had said you cant be bold with words. How, then, to be bold? To try to do anything without words, it seemed to him, was like trying to grow grain without seed. Still, Fairchild had said . . . who knew people, women . . . Mr Talliaferro prowled restlessly having the boat to himself practically, and presently he found Jenny sleeping placidly in a chair in the shade of the deckhouse. Blonde and pink and soft in sleep was Jenny: a passive soft abandon fitting like water to the sagging embrace of the canvas chair. Mr Talliaferro envied that chair with a surge of fire like an adolescent's in his dry bones, and while he stood regarding the sprawled awkwardness of Jenny's sweet thighs and legs and one little soiled hand dangling across her hip, that surge of imminence and fire and desolation seemed to lightly distend all his organs, leaving a thin salty taste on his tongue. Mr Talliaferro glanced quickly about the deck.

He glanced quickly about the deck, then feeling rather foolish but strangely and exuberantly young, he came near and bending he traced lightly with his hand the heavy laxity of Jenny's body through the canvas which supported her. Then he thought terribly that some one was watching him and he sprang erect with an alarm like nausea, staring at Jenny's closed eyes. But her eyelids lay shadowed, a faint transparent blue upon her cheeks and her breath was a little regular wind come recently from off fresh milk. But he still felt eyes upon him and he stood acutely, trying to think of something to do, some casual gesture to perform. A cigarette, his chaotic brain supplied at last. But he had none, and still spurred by this need, he darted quickly away and to his cabin.

The nephew slept yet in his berth and breathing rather fast Mr Talliaferro got his cigarettes and then he stood before the mirror, examining his face, seeking wildness, recklessness there. But it bore its customary expression of polite faint alarm and he smoothed his hair, thinking of the sweet passive sag of that deckchair . . . yes, almost directly over his head. . . . He rushed back on deck in a surge of fear that she had waked and risen, gone away. He restrained himself by an effort to a more sedate pace, reconnoitering the deck. All was well.

He smoked his cigarette in short nervous puffs, hearing his heart, tasting that warm salt. Yes, his hand was actually trembling, and he stood in a casual attitude, looking about at water and sky and shore. Then he moved and still with casualness he strolled back to where Jenny slept, unchanged her supine abandon, soft and oblivious and terrifying.

Mr Talliaferro bent over her. Then he got on one knee, then on both knees. Jenny slept ineffably, breathing her sweet regular breath upon his face . . . he wondered if he could rise quickly enough, in an emergency. . . . He rose and looked about, then tiptoed across the deck and still on tiptoe he fetched another chair and set it beside Jenny's, and sat down. But it was for reclining, so he tried sitting on the edge of it. Too high, and amid his other chaotic emotions was a harried despair, of futility and an implacable passing of Opportunity, while all the time it was as though he stood nearby yet aloof, watching his own antics. He lit another cigarette with hands that trembled, took three puffs that he did not taste, and cast it away.

Hard this floor his old knees yes Yes Jenny her breath Yes Yes her red soft mouth where little teeth but showed parted blondness a golden pink swirl kaleidoscopic a single blue eye not come fully awake her breath yes Yes He felt eyes again, knew they were there but he cast all things away, and sprawled nuzzling for Jenny's mouth as she came awake.

"Wake sleeping Princess kiss," Mr Talliaferro jabbered in a dry falsetto.

Jenny squealed, moving her head a little. Then she came fully awake and got her hand under Mr Talliaferro's chin. "Wake Princess with kiss," Mr Talliaferro repeated, laughing a thin hysterical laugh, obsessed with an utter and dreadful need to complete the gesture.

Jenny heaved herself up, thrusting Mr Talliaferro back on his heels. "Whatcher doing, you old——" Jenny glared at him and seeking about in that vague pinkish region which was her mind she brought forth finally an expression such as a steamboat mate or a railroad flagman, heated with wine, might apply to his temporary Saturday night Phillida, who would charge him for it by the letter—like a cable gram.

She watched Mr Talliaferro's dapper dispersion with soft blonde indignation. When he had disappeared she flopped back in the chair again. She snorted, a soft indignant sound, and turned again onto her side. Once more she expelled her breath with righteous indignation, and soon thereafter she drowsed again and slept.

NINE OCLOCK.

It was a sleazy scrap of slightly soiled applegreen crêpe and its principal purpose seemed to be that of indicating vaguely the shape of Jenny's behind, as she danced caressing the twin soft points of her thighs with the lingering sterility of an aged lover. It looked as if she might have slept in it recently, and there was also a small hat of pale straw, of no particular shape, ribboned. Jenny slid about in Mr Talliaferro's embrace with placid skill. She and Pete had just quarrelled bitterly. Pete had, that is. Jenny's bovine troubling placidity had merely dissolved into tears, causing her eyes to be more ineffable than ever, and she had gone calmly about what she had intended all the time: to have as much fun as she could, as long as she was here. Pete couldn't walk out on her: all he could do would be to fuss and sulk, or maybe hit her. He had done that once, thereby voluntarily making himself her bond slave. She had rather liked it. . . .

Beyond lights, beyond the sound of the victrola, water was a minor ceaseless sound in the darkness; above, vague drowsy stars. Jenny danced on placidly, untroubled by Mr Talliaferro's endless flow of soft words against her neck, hardly conscious of his hand sliding a small concentric circle at the small of her back.

"She looks kind of nice, dont she?" Fairchild said to his companion as they stood at the head of the companionway, come up for air. "Kind of soft and stupid and young, you know. Passive, and at the same time troubling, challenging." He watched them for a time, then he added: "Now there goes the Great Illusion par excellence."

"What's Talliaferro's trouble?" asked the semitic man.

"The illusion that you can seduce women. Which you can't: they just elect you."

"And then, God help you," the other added.

"And with words at that," Fairchild continued. "With words," he repeated savagely.

"Well, why not with words? One thing gets along with women as well as another. And you are a funny sort to disparage words; you, a member of that species all of whose actions are controlled by words. Its the word that overturns thrones and political parties and instigates vice crusades, not things: the Thing is merely the symbol for the Word. And more than that, think what a devil of a fix you and I'd be in were it not for words, were we to lose our faith in words. I'd have nothing to do all day long, and you'd have to work or starve to death." He was silent for a while. Jenny yet slid and poised, pleasuring her young soft placidity. "And after all, his illusion is just as nourishing as yours. Or mine, either."

"I know: but yours or mine aint quite so ridiculous as his is."

"How do you know they aren't?" Fairchild had no reply and the other continued: "After all, it doesn't make any difference what you believe. Man is not only nourished by convictions, he is nourished by any conviction. Whatever you believe, you'll always annoy someone else, but you yourself will follow and bleed and die for it in the face of law, hell or high water. And those who die for causes will perish for any cause, the more tawdry it is the quicker they flock to it. And be quite happy at it, too. Its a provision of providence to keep their time occupied." He sucked at his cigar, but it was dead. "Do you know who is the happiest man in the world today? Mussolini, of course. And do you know who is next? The poor fools he will get killed with his Caesar illusion. Dont pity them however: were it not Mussolini and his illusion it would be someone else and his cause. I believe it is some grand cosmic scheme for fertilizing the earth. . . . And it could be so much worse," he added. "Who knows, they might all migrate to America and fall into the hands of Henry Ford.

"So dont you go around feeling superior to Talliaferro. I think his present illusion and its object are rather charming, almost as charming as the consummation of it would be—which is more than you can say for yours." He held a match to his cigar. His sucking intent face came abruptly out of the darkness, and as abruptly vanished again. He flipped the match toward the rail. "And so do you, you poor emotional eunuch; so do you, despite that bastard of a surgeon and a stenographer which you call your soul, so do you remember with regret kissing in the dark and all the tender and sweet stupidity of young flesh."

"Hell," said Fairchild. "Lets get another drink."

His friend was too kind, too tactful to say I told you so.

* * * * *

Mrs Maurier captured them as they reached the stairs. "Here you are," she exclaimed brightly, prisoning their arms. "Come: lets all dance a while. We need men. Eva has taken Mark away from Dorothy, and she has no partner. Come, Mr Fairchild, Julius."

"We're coming back," Fairchild answered. "We're going now to hunt up Gordon and the Major, and we'll all come right back."

"No, no," she said soothingly. "We'll send the steward for them. Come, now."

"I think we better go," Fairchild objected quickly. "The steward has been working hard all day: he's tired out, I expect. And Gordon's kind of timid—he might not come if you send a servant for him."

She released them doubtfully, staring at them with her round astonished face. "You will. . . ? do come back, Mr Fairchild."

"Sure, sure," Fairchild replied, descending hastily.

"Julius," Mrs Maurier called after them helplessly.

"I'll bring them up in ten minutes," the semitic man promised, following. Mrs Maurier watched them until they had passed from view, then she turned away. Jenny and Mr Talliaferro were still dancing, as were Mrs Wiseman and the ghostly poet. Miss Jameson, partnerless, sat at the cardtable playing solitaire. Mrs Maurier looked on until the record played itself out, then she said firmly:

"I think we'd better change partners among ourselves until the men come up."

Mr Talliaferro released Jenny obediently, and Jenny, released, stood around a while, then drifted away down the deck, passing that tall ugly man leaning alone at the rail, and further along the niece spoke from the shadow:

"Going to bed?"

Jenny paused and turning her head toward the voice she saw the faint glint of Pete's hat. She went on. "Uhuh," she replied.

The moon was getting up, rising out of the dark water: a tarnished implacable Venus.

*   *   *   *   *

Her aunt came along soon, prowling, peering fretfully into shadowy chairs and obscure corners, implacable and tactless as a minor disease.

"My Lord, what've we got to do now?" the niece moaned. She sighed. "She sure makes life real and earnest for everybody, that woman does."

"Dance, I guess," Pete answered. The vicious serrated rim of his hat, where the moon fell upon it, glittered dully like a row of filed teeth; like the gaping lithograph of a charging shark.

"Guess so. Say, I'm going to fade out. Stall her off some way, or run yourself, would be better." The niece rose hurriedly. "So long. See you t—— Oh, you coming too?"

They stepped behind the companionway housing and flattened themselves against it, listening to Mrs Maurier's fretful prowling, and clutching Pete's hand for caution the niece craned her head around the corner. "There's Dorothy, too," she whispered and she withdrew her head and they flattened themselves closer yet, clutching hands, while the two searchers passed, pausing to peer into every obscurity. But they went on, finally, passing from sight. The niece wriggled her fingers free and moved, and moving found that she had turned into Pete's arm, against his dark shape and the reckless angle of his hat topping it.

An interval like that between two fencers ere they engage, Pete's arm moved with confidence and his other arm came about her shoulders with a technique that was forcing her face up. She was so still that he stopped again in a momentary flagging of confidence, and out of this lull a hard elbow came without force but steadily under his chin.

"Try it on your saxophone, Pete," she told him without alarm. His hand moved again and caught her wrist, but she held her elbow jammed against his windpipe, increasing the pressure as he tried to remove her arm, their bodies taut against each other and without motion. Someone approached again and he released her, but before they could dodge again around the corner Miss Jameson saw them.

"Who is that?" she said in her high humorless voice. She drew nearer, peering. "Oh, I recognise Pete's hat. Mrs Maurier wants you." She peered at them suspiciously. "What are you folks doing here?"

"Hiding from Aunt Pat," the niece answered. "What's she going to make us do, now?"

"Why—nothing. She—we ought to be more sociable. Dont you think so? We never are all together, you know. Anyway, she wants to see Pete. Aren't you coming, too?"

"I'm going to bed. Pete can go if he wants to risk it, though." She turned away. Miss Jameson put her hand on Pete's sleeve.

"You dont mind if I take Pete, then?" she persisted intensely.

"I dont if he dont," the niece replied. She went on. "Goodnight."

"That child ought to be spanked," Miss Jameson said viciously. She slid her hand through Pete's elbow. "Come on, Pete."

*   *   *   *   *

The niece stood and rubbed one bare sole against the other shin, hearing their footsteps retreating toward the lights and the fatuous reiteration of the victrola. She rubbed her foot rhythmically up and down her shin, gazing out upon the water where the moon had begun to spread her pallid and boneless hand . . . her foot ceased its motion and she remained motionless for a space. Then she stood on one leg and raised the other one. Under her fingers was a small hard bump, slightly feverish. Gabriel's pants, she whispered. They've found us again. But there was nothing for it except to wait until the tug came. "And finds a lot of picked bones," she added aloud. She went on across the deck; at the stairs she stopped again.

It was David, standing there at the rail, his shirt blanching in the level moonlight, against the dark shoreline. She went over beside him, silent on her bare feet. "Hello, David," she said quietly, putting her elbows on the rail beside his and hunching her shoulders and crossing her legs as his were. "This would be a good night to be on our mountain, looking down at the lake and the little boats all lighted up, wouldn't it? I guess this time next summer we'll be there, wont we? And lots of other places, where you went to. You know nice things,

dont you? When we come back, I'll know nice things, too."
She gazed downward into the dark ceaseless water. It was
never still, never the same, and on it moonlight was broken
into little fleeting silver wings rising and falling and changing.

"Wish I were in it," she said. "Swimming around in the
moonlight. . . . You wont forget about in the morning, will
you?" No, he told her, watching her crossed thin arms and
the cropped crown of her head. "Say," she looked up at him,
"I tell you what: lets go in tonight."

"Now?"

"When the moon gets up more. Aunt Pat wouldn't let me
go now, anyway. But about twelve, when they've gone to bed.
What do you say?" He looked at her, looked at her in such a
strange fashion that she said sharply: "What's the matter?"

"Nothing," he answered at last.

"Well, I'll meet you about twelve oclock, then. I'll get Gus'
bathing suit for you. Dont forget, now."

"No," he repeated, and when she reached the stairs and
looked back at him he was still watching her in that strange
manner. But she didn't puzzle over it long.

TEN OCLOCK.

Jenny had the cabin to herself. Mrs—that one whose name
she always forgot, was still on deck. She could hear them talking, and Mr Fairchild's jolly laugh came from somewhere,
though he hadn't been upstairs when she left, and the muted
nasal sound of the victrola and thumping feet just over her
head. Still dancing. Should she go back? She sat holding a
handglass, staring into it, but the handglass was bland, reminding her that after all this was one night she didn't have
to dance any more. And you have to dance so many nights.
Tomorrow night perhaps, it said. But I dont have to dance tomorrow night, she thought . . . staring into the glass and sitting utterly motionless. . . . Its thin whine rose keening to an
ecstatic point and in the glass she saw it mar her throat with
a small gray speck. . . . She slapped savagely. It eluded her
with a weary practised skill, hanging fuzzily between her and
the unshaded light.

My Lord, why do you want to go to Mandeville? she said.

Her palms flashed, smacking cleanly, and Jenny examined her hand with distaste. Where do they carry so much blood? she wondered, rubbing her palm on the back of her stocking. And so young, too. I hope that's the last one. It must have been, for there was no sound save a small lapping whisper of water and a troubling faraway suggestion of brass broken by a monotonous thumping of feet over her head. Dancing still. You really dont have to dance at all thought Jenny, yawning into the glass, examining with interest the pink and seemingly endless curve of her gullet, when the door opened and the girl Patricia entered the room. She wore a raincoat over her pajamas and Jenny saw her reflected face in the mirror.

"Hello," she said.

"Hello," the niece replied. "I thought you'd have stayed up there prancing around with 'em."

"Lord," Jenny said, "you dont have to dance all your life, do you? You dont seem to be there."

The niece thrust her hands into the raincoat pockets and stared about the small room. "Dont you close that window when you undress?" she asked. "Standing wide open like that. . . ."

Jenny put the mirror down. "That window? I dont guess there's anybody out there this time of night."

The niece went to the port and saw a pale sky bisected laterally by a dark rigidity of water. The moon spread her silver hand on it—a broadening path of silver, and in the path the water came alive ceaselessly, no longer rigid. "I guess not," she murmured. "The only man who could walk on water is dead. . . . Which one is yours?" She threw off the raincoat and turned toward the two berths. The lower garment of her pajamas was tied about her waist with a man's frayed necktie.

"Is he?" Jenny murmured with detachment. "That one," she answered vaguely, twisting her body to examine the back of one reverted leg. After a while she looked up. "That aint mine. That's Mrs Whats-her-name's you are in."

"Well, it dont make any difference." The niece lay flat, spreading her arms and legs luxuriously. "Gimme a cigarette. Have you got any?"

"I haven't got any. I dont smoke." Jenny's leg was satisfactory, so she unwrithed herself.

"You dont smoke? Why dont you?"

"I dont know," Jenny replied. "I just dont."

"Look around and see if Eva's got some somewhere." The niece raised her head. "Go on: look in her things, she wont mind."

Jenny hunted for cigarettes in a soft blonde futility. "Pete's got some," she remarked after a time. "He bought twenty packages just before we left town, to bring on the boat."

"Twenty packages? Good Lord, where'd he think we were going? He must have been scared of shipwreck or something."

"I guess so."

"Gabriel's pants," said the niece. "That's all he brought, was it? Just cigarettes? What did you bring?"

"I brought a comb." Jenny dragged her little soiled dress over her head. Her voice was muffled. "And some rouge." She shook out her drowsy gold hair and let the dress fall to the floor. "Pete's got some, though," she repeated, thrusting the dress beneath the dressing table with her foot.

"I know," the niece rejoined, "and so has Mr Fairchild. And so has the steward, if Mark Frost hasn't borrowed 'em all. And I saw the Captain smoking one, too. But that's not doing me any good."

"No," agreed Jenny placidly. Her undergarment was quite pink, enveloping her from shoulder to knee with ribbons and furbelows. She loosened a few of these and stepped sweetly and rosily out of it, casting it also under the table.

"You aren't going to leave 'em there, are you?" the niece asked. "Why dont you put 'em on the chair?"

"Mrs—Mrs Wiseman puts hers on the chair."

"Well, you got here first: Why dont you take it? Or hang 'em on those hooks behind the door?"

"Hooks?" Jenny looked at the door. "Oh. . . . They'll be all right there, I guess." She stripped off her stockings and laid them on the dressing table. Then she turned to the mirror again, picking up her comb. The comb passed through her fair soft hair with a faint sound, as of silk, and her hair lent to Jenny's divine body a halo like that of an angel. The remote victrola, measured feet, a lapping of water, came into the room.

"You've got a funny figure," the niece remarked after a while, calmly, watching her.

"Funny?" repeated Jenny, looking up softly belligerent. "Its no funnier than yours. At least my legs dont look like birds' legs."

"Neither do mine," the other replied with complacence, flat on her back. "Your legs are all right. I mean, you are kind of thick through the middle for your legs, kind of big behind for them."

"Well, why not? I didn't make it like that, did I?"

"Oh, sure. I guess its all right if you like it to be that way."

Without apparent effort Jenny dislocated her hip, starring downward over her shoulder. Then she turned sideways and accepted the mute proffering of the mirror. Reassured she said: "Sure its all right. I expect to be bigger than that in front, some day."

"So do I . . . when I have to. But what do you want one for?"

"Lord," said Jenny, "I guess I'll have a whole litter of 'em. Besides, I think they are kind of cute. Dont you?"

The sound of the victrola came down, melodious and nasal, and measured feet marked away the lapping of waves. The light was small and inadequate, sunk into the ceiling, and Jenny and the niece agreed that their behinds were kind of cute and pink. Jenny was quite palpably on the point of coming to bed and the other said:

"Dont you wear any nightclothes?"

"I cant wear that thing Mrs Whats-her-name lent me. You said you were going to lend me something, only you didn't. If I'd depended on you on this trip, I guess I'd be about ten miles back yonder, trying to swim home."

"That's right. But it doesn't make any difference what you sleep in, does it? . . . Turn off the light." Light followed Jenny rosily as she crossed the room, it slid rosily upon her as she turned obediently toward the switch beside the door. The niece lay flat on her back, gazing at the unshaded globe. Jenny's angelic nakedness went beyond her vision and suddenly she stared at nothingness with a vague orifice vaguely in the center of it, and beyond the orifice a pale moonfilled sky.

Jenny's bare feet hissed just a little on the uncarpeted floor and she came breathing softly in the dark, and her hand came out of the dark. The niece moved over against the wall. The

round orifice in the center of the dark was obscured, then it
reappeared, and breathing with a soft blonde intentness Jenny
climbed gingerly into the berth. But she bumped her head
anyway, lightly, and she said Ow with placid surprise. The
bunk heaved monstrously, creaking, the porthole vanished
again, then the berth became still and Jenny sighed with a soft
explosive sound.

Then she changed her position again and the other said: "Be
still, can't you?" thrusting at Jenny's boneless naked abandon
with her elbow.

"I'm not fixed yet," Jenny replied without rancor.

"Well, get in then and quit flopping around."

Jenny became lax. "I'm fixed now," she said at last. She
sighed again, a frank yawning sound.

Those slightly dulled feet thudthudded monotonously overhead. Outside, in the pale darkness, water lapped at the hull
of the yacht. The close cabin emptied slowly of heat; heat
ebbed steadily away now that the light was off, and in it was
no sound save that of their breathing. No other sound at all.
"I hope that was the last one, the one I killed," Jenny murmured. "God, yes," the niece agreed. "This party is wearing
enough with just people on it. . . . Say, how'd you like to be
on a party with a boatful of Mr Talliaferros?"

"Which one is he?"

"Why, dont you remember him? You sure ought to. He's
that funny talking little man that puts his hands on you—that
dreadful polite one. I dont see how you could forget a man as
polite as him."

"Oh yes," said Jenny remembering, and the other said:

"Say, Jenny, how about Pete?"

Jenny became utterly still for a moment. Then she said innocently: "What about him?"

"He's mad at you about Mr Talliaferro, isn't he?"

"Pete's all right, I guess."

"You keep yourself all cluttered up with men, dont you?"
the other asked curiously.

"Well, you got to do something," Jenny defended herself.

"Bunk," the niece said roughly, "bunk. You like petting.
That's the reason. Dont you?"

"Well, I dont mind," Jenny answered. "I've kind of got used

to it," she explained. The niece expelled her breath in a thin snorting sound and Jenny repeated: "You've got to do something, haven't you?"

"Oh, sweet attar of bunk," the niece said. In the darkness she made a gesture of disgust. "You women! That's the way Dorothy Jameson thinks about it too, I bet. You better look out: I think she's trying to take Pete away from you."

"Oh, Pete's all right," Jenny repeated placidly. She lay perfectly still again. The water was a cool dim sound. Jenny spoke, suddenly confidential. "Say, you know what she wants Pete to do?"

"No: What?" asked the niece quickly.

"Well—— Say, what kind of a girl is she? Do you know her very good?"

"What does she want Pete to do?" the other insisted.

Jenny was silent. Then she blurted in a prim disapproval: "She wants Pete to let her paint him."

"Yes? and then what?"

"That's it. She wants Pete to let her paint him in a picture."

"Well, that's the way she usually goes about getting men, I guess. What's wrong with it?"

"Well, its the wrong way to go about getting Pete. Pete's not used to that," Jenny replied in that prim tone.

"I dont blame him for not wanting to waste his time that way. But what makes you and Pete so surprised at the idea of it? Pete wont catch lead poisoning just from having his portrait painted."

"Well, it may be all right for folks like you all. But Pete says he wouldn't let any strange woman see him without any clothes on. He's not used to things like that."

"Oh," remarked the niece. Then: "So that's the way she wants to paint him, is it?"

"Why, that's the way they always do it, aint it? in the nude?" Jenny pronounced it nood.

"Good Lord, didn't you ever see a picture of anybody with clothes on? Where'd you get that idea from? From the movies?"

Jenny didn't reply. Then she said suddenly: "Besides, the ones with clothes on are all old ladies, or mayors or something. Anyway, I thought. . . ."

"Thought what?"

"Nothing," Jenny answered and the other said:

"Pete can get that idea right out of his head. Chances are she wants to paint him all regular and respectable: not to shock his modesty at all. I'll tell him so tomorrow."

"Never mind," Jenny said quickly. "I'll tell him. You needn't bother about it."

"All right, whatever you like. . . . Wish I had a cigarette." They lay quiet for a time. Outside water whispered against the hull. The victrola was hushed temporarily and the dancers had ceased. Jenny moved again, onto her side facing the other in the darkness.

"Say," she asked. "What's your brother making?"

"Gus? Why dont you ask him yourself?"

"I did, only. . . ."

"What?"

"Only he didn't tell me. At least, I dont remember."

"What did he say when you asked him?"

Jenny mused briefly. "He kissed me. Before I knew it, and he kind of patted me back here and told me to call again later, that he was in conference or something like that."

"Gabriel's pants," the niece murmured. Then she said sharply: "Look here, you let Josh alone, you hear? Haven't you got enough with Pete and Mr Talliaferro, without fooling with children?"

"I'm not going to fool with any children."

"Well, please dont. Let Josh alone, anyway." She moved her arm, arching her elbow against Jenny's soft nakedness. "Move over some. Gee, woman, you sure do feel indecent. Get over on your side a little, can't you?"

Jenny moved away, rolling onto her back again. They lay quiet, side by side in the dark. "Say," remarked Jenny presently, "Mr——that polite man——" "Talliaferro?" the other prompted. "——Talliaferro. I wonder if he's got a car?"

"I dont know. You better ask him. What do you keep on asking me what people are making or what they've got, for?"

"Taxicabbers are best, I think," Jenny continued, unruffled. "Sometimes when they have cars they dont have anything else. They just take you riding."

"I dont know," the niece repeated. "Say," she said suddenly. "What was that you said to him this afternoon?"

Jenny said Oh. She breathed placidly and regularly for a while. Then she remarked: "I thought you were there, behind that corner."

"Yes. What was it? Say it again." Jenny said it again. The niece repeated after her. "What does it mean?"

"I dont know. I just happened to remember it. I dont know what it means."

"It sounds good," the other said. "You didn't think it up yourself, did you?"

"No. It was a fellow told it to me. There was two couples of us at the Market one night, getting coffee: me and Pete and a girl friend of mine and another fellow. We had been to Mandeville on the boat that day, swimming and dancing. Say, there was a man drownded at Mandeville that day. Pete and Thelma, my girl friend, and Roy, this girl friend of mine's fellow, saw it. I didn't see it because I wasn't with them. I didn't go in bathing with them: it was too sunny. I dont think blondes ought to expose themselves to hot sun like brunettes, do you?"

"Why not? But what about——"

"Oh yes. Anyway, I didn't go in where the man got drownded. I was waiting for them and I got to talking to a funny man. A little kind of black man——"

"A nigger?"

"No, no. He was a white man, except he was awful sunburned and kind of shabby dressed—no necktie and hat. Say, he said some funny things to me. He said I had the best digestion he ever saw and he said if the straps of my dress was to break I'd devastate the country. He said he was a liar by profession and he made good money at it, enough to own a ford as soon as he got it paid out. I think he was crazy. Not dangerous: just crazy."

The niece lay quiet. She said, contemplatively: "You do look like they fed you on bread and milk and put you to bed at sunset everyday. . . . What was his name? Did he tell you?" she asked suddenly.

"Yes, it was——" Jenny pondered a while. "I remember it because he was such a funny kind of man. It was. . . . Walker or Foster or something."

"Walker or Foster? Well, which one was it?"

"It must be Foster because I remembered it by it began with a F like my girl friend's middle name—Frances. Thelma Frances, only she dont use both of them. Only I dont think it was Foster, because—"

"You dont remember it, then."

"Yes I do. Wait. . . . Oh yes: I remember——Faulkner, that was it."

"Faulkner?" The niece pondered in her turn. "Never heard of him," she said at last, with finality. "And he was the one that told you that thing?"

"No. It was after that, when we had come back to N.O. That crazy man was on the boat coming back. He got to talking to Pete and Roy while me and Thelma was fixing up downstairs, and he danced with Thelma. He wouldn't dance with me because he said he didn't dance very well and so he had to keep his mind on the music while he danced. He said he could dance with either Roy or Thelma or Pete but he couldn't dance with me. I think he was crazy. Dont you?"

"It all sounds crazy, the way you tell it. But what about the one that said that to you?"

"Oh yes. Well, we was at the Market. There was a big crowd there because it was Sunday night, see, and these other fellows were there. One of them was a snappy looking fellow and I kind of looked at him. Pete had stopped in a place to get some cigarettes and me and Thelma and Roy was crowded in with a lot of folks, having coffee. So I kind of looked at this good looking fellow."

"Yes. You kind of looked at him. Go on."

"All right. And so the good looking fellow crowded in behind me and started talking to me. There was a man in between me and Roy and this fellow that was talking to me said Is he with you? meaning the man sitting next to me and I said No, I didn't know who he was. And this fellow said How about coming out with him because he had his car parked outside. . . . Pete's brother has a lot of cars. One of them is the same as Pete's. . . . And then. . . . Oh yes, and I said Where will we go because my old man didn't like for me to go out with strangers and the fellow said He wasn't a stranger, that

anybody could tell me who some name was: I forgot what it
was he said his name was. And I said he'd better ask Pete if I
could go and he said Who is Pete? Well, there was a big man
standing near where we was. He was big as a stevedore and
just then this big man happened to look at me again. He
looked at me a minute and I kind of knew that he'd look at
me again pretty soon, so I told this fellow talking to me that
he was Pete, and when the big man looked somewheres else
a minute this fellow said that to me. And then the big man
looked at me again, and the fellow kind of went away. So I
got up and went to where Thelma and Roy was, and pretty
soon Pete came back. And that's how I learned it."

"Well, it sure sounds good. I wonder. . . . Say, let me use it
some, will you?"

"All right," Jenny agreed. "You can have it. Say, what's that
you keep telling your aunt? Something about pulling up the
sheet or something?" The niece told her. "That sounds good,
too," Jenny said magnanimously.

"Does it? I tell you what: you let me use yours sometimes,
and you can take mine. How about it?"

"All right," Jenny agreed again. "Its a trade."

Water lapped and whispered ceaselessly in the pale darkness.
The curve of the low ceiling directly over the berth lent a faint
sense of oppression to the cabin, but this sense of oppression
faded out into the comparatively greater spaciousness of the
room, of the darkness with a round orifice vaguely in the center
of it. The moon was higher and the lower curve of the brass
rim of the port was now a thin silver sickle, like a new moon.

Jenny moved again, turning against the other's side, breathing ineffably across the niece's face. The niece lay with Jenny's
passive nakedness against her arm, and moving her arm outward from the elbow she slowly stroked the back of her hand
along the swell of Jenny's thigh. Slowly, back and forth, while
Jenny lay supine and receptive as a cat. Slowly, back and forth
and back. . . . "I like flesh," the niece murmured. "Warm and
smooth. Wish I'd lived in Rome . . . oiled gladiators . . .
Jenny," she said abruptly, "are you a virgin?"

"Of course I am," Jenny answered immediately in a startled
tone. She lay for a moment in lax astonishment. "I mean," she

said, "I——yes. I mean yes. Of course I am." She brooded in passive surprise, then her body lost its laxness. "Say——"

"Well," the niece agreed judicially, "I guess that's about what I'd have said, myself."

"Say," demanded Jenny, thoroughly aroused. "What'd you ask me that for?"

"Just to see what you'd say. It doesn't make any difference, you know, whether you are or not. I know lots of girls that say they're not. I dont think all of 'em are lying, either."

"Maybe it dont to some folks," Jenny rejoined primly, "but I dont approve of it. I think a girl loses a man's respect by pom—prom——I dont approve of it, that's all. And I dont think you had any right to ask me."

"Good Lord, you sound like a girl Scout or something. Dont Pete ever try to persuade you otherwise?"

"Say, what're you asking me questions like that for?"

"I just wanted to see what you'd say. I dont think its anything to tear your shirt over. You're too easily shocked, Jenny," the niece informed her.

"Well, who wouldn't be? If you want to know what folks say when you ask 'em things like that, why dont you ask 'em to yourself? Did anybody ever ask you if you were one?"

"Not that I know of. But I wou——"

"Well, are you?"

The niece lay perfectly still a moment. "Am I what?"

"Are you a virgin?"

"Why, of course I am," she answered sharply. She raised herself on her elbow. "I mean——Say, look here—"

"Well, that's what I'd a said, myself," Jenny responded with placid malice from the darkness.

The niece poised on her tense elbow above Jenny's sweet regular breathing. "Anyway, what bus——I mean—You asked me so quick," she rushed on. "I wasn't even thinking about being asked something like that."

"Neither was I. You asked me quicker than I asked you."

"But it was different. We were talking about you being one. We were not even thinking about me being one. You asked it so quick I had to say that. It wasn't fair."

"So did I have to say what I said. It was as fair for you as it was for me."

"No, it was different. I had to say I wasn't: quick, like that."

"Well, I'll ask it when you're not surprised, then. Are you?"

The niece lay quiet for a time. "You mean, sure enough?"

"Yes." Jenny breathed her warm intent breath across the other's face.

The niece lay silent again. After a time she said: "Hell." and then: "Yes, I am. Its not worth lying about."

"That's what I think," Jenny agreed smugly. She became placidly silent in the darkness. The other waited a moment, then said sharply: "Well? Are you one?"

"Sure I am."

"I mean, sure enough. You said sure enough, didn't you?"

"Sure I am," Jenny repeated.

"You're not playing fair," the niece accused. "I told you."

"Well, I told you, too."

"Honest? You swear?"

"Sure I am," Jenny said again with her glib and devastating placidity.

The niece said: "Hell." She snorted thinly.

They lay quiet, side by side. They were quiet on deck too, but it seemed as though there still lingered in the darkness a thin stubborn ghost of syncopation and thudding tireless feet. Jenny wiggled her free toes with pleasure. Presently she said: "You're mad, aint you?" No reply. "You've got a good figure, too," Jenny offered, conciliatory. "I think you've got a right sweet little shape."

But the other refused to be cajoled. Jenny sighed again ineffably, her milk-and-honey breath. She said: "Your brother's a college boy, aint he? I know some college boys. Tulane. I think college boys are cute. They dont dress as well as Pete . . . sloppy. . . ." She mused for a time. "I wore a frat pin once, for a couple of days. I guess your brother belongs to it, dont he?"

"Gus? Belong to one of these jerkwater clubs? I guess not. He's a Yale man—he will be next month, that is. I'm going with him. They dont take every Tom Dick and Harry that show up in, up there. You have to wait until sophomore year. But Gus is going to work for a senior society, anyhow. He dont think much of fraternities. Gee, you'd sure give him a laugh if he could hear you."

"Well, I didn't know. It seems to me one thing you join is about like another. What's he going to get by joining the one he's going to join?"

"You dont get anything, stupid. You just join it."

Jenny pondered this a while. "And you have to work to join it?"

"Three years. And only a few make it, then."

"And if you do make it, you dont get anything except a little button or something? Good Lord. . . . Say, you know what I'm going to tell him tomorrow? I'm going to tell him he better hold up the sheet: he's——he's——What's the rest of it?"

"Oh, shut up and get over on your side," the niece said sharply, turning her back. "You dont understand anything about it."

"I sure dont," Jenny agreed, rolling away onto her other side, and they lay with their backs to each other and their behinds just touching, as children do. . . . "Three years. . . . Good Lord."

*   *   *   *   *

Fairchild had not returned. But she had known they would not: she was not even surprised, and so once more her party had evolved into interminable cards. Mrs Wiseman, herself, Mr Talliaferro and Mark. By craning her neck she could see Dorothy Jameson's frail humorless intentness and the tawdry sophistication of Jenny's young man where they swung their legs from the roof of the wheelhouse. The moon was getting up and Pete's straw hat was a dull implacable gleam slanted above the red eye of his eternal cigarette. And, yes, there was that queer shy shabby Mr Gordon, mooning alone as usual; and again she felt a stab of reproof, for having neglected him. At least the others seemed to be enjoying the voyage, however trying they might be to each other. But what could she do for him? He was so difficult, so ill at ease whenever she extended herself for him. . . . Mrs Maurier rose.

"For a while," she explained, "Mr Gordon . . . the trials of a hostess, you know. You might play dummy until I——no: wait." She called Dorothy with saccharine insistence and presently Miss Jameson responded. "Wont you take my hand for a short time? I'm sure the young gentleman will excuse you."

"I'm sorry," Miss Jameson called back. "I have a headache. Please excuse me."

"Go on, Mrs Maurier," Mrs Wiseman said. "We can pass the time until you come back: we've got used to sitting around."

Mrs Maurier roved her helpless astonishment.

"Yes, do," Mr Talliaferro added, "we understand."

Mrs Maurier looked over where Gordon still leaned his tall body upon the rail. "I really must," she explained again. . . . "Its such a comfort to have a few on whom I can depend."

"Yes, do," Mr Talliaferro repeated.

When she had gone Mrs Wiseman said: "Lets play red dog for pennies. I've got a few dollars left."

* * * * *

She joined him quietly. He glanced his gaunt face at her, glanced away. "How quiet, how peaceful it is," she began, undeterred, leaning beside him and gazing also out across the restless slumber of water upon which the worn moon spread her ceaseless peacock's tail like a train of silver sequins. In the yet level rays of the moon the man's face was spare and cavernous, haughty and inhuman, almost. He doesn't get enough to eat she knew suddenly and infallibly. Its like a silver faun's face she thought. But he is so difficult, shy. . . . "So few of us take time to look inward and contemplate ourselves, dont you think? Its the life we lead, I suppose. Only he who creates has not lost the art of this: of making his life complete by living within himself. Dont you think so, Mr Gordon?"

"Yes," he answered shortly. Beyond the dimensionless curve of deck on which he stood he could see, forward and downward, the stem of the yacht:—a pure triangle of sheer white with small waves lapping at its horizontal leg, breaking and flashing each with its particle of shattered moonlight, making a ceaseless small whispering. Mrs Maurier moved her hands in a gesture: moonlight smoldered greenly amid her rings.

"To live within yourself, to be sufficient unto yourself. There is so much unhappiness in the world . . ." she sighed again with astonishment. "To go through life, keeping yourself from becoming involved in it, to gather inspiration for your Work——Ah, Mr Gordon, how lucky you who create are. As for we others, the best we can hope is that sometime, somewhere, somehow we may be fortunate enough to furnish the inspiration, or the setting for it, at least. But, after all, that would be an end in itself, I think. To know that one had given her mite to Art, no matter how humble the mite or the giver . . . the humble laborer, Mr Gordon: she too has her place in the scheme of things, she too has given something to the world, she too has walked where gods have trod. And I do so hope that you will find on this voyage something to compensate you for having been taken away from your Work."

"Yes," said Gordon again, staring at her with his arrogant uncomfortable stare. The man looks positively uncanny she thought with a queer cold feeling within her. Like an animal, a beast of some sort. Her own gaze fluttered away and despite herself she glanced quickly over her shoulder to the reassuring group at the card table. Dorothy's and Jenny's young man's legs swung innocent and rhythmic from the top of the wheelhouse, and as she looked Pete snapped his cigarette outward and into the dark water, twinkling.

"But to be a world in oneself, to regard the antics of man as one would a puppet show——Ah, Mr Gordon, how happy you must be."

"Yes," he repeated. Sufficient unto himself in the city of his arrogance, in the marble tower of his loneliness and pride, and. . . . She coming into the dark sky of his life like a star, like a flame O bitter and new. . . . Somewhere within him was a far dreadful laughter, unheard; his whole life was become toothed with jeering laughter, and he faced the old woman again putting his hand on her and turning her face upward and into the moonlight. Mrs Maurier knew utter fear. Not fright, fear: a passive and tragic condition like a dream. She whispered Mr Gordon, but made no sound.

"I'm not going to hurt you," he said harshly, staring at her face as a surgeon might. "Tell me about her," he commanded. "Why aren't you her mother, so you could tell me how conceiving her must have been, how carrying her in your loins must have been?"

Mr Gordon! she implored through her dry lips, without making a sound. His hand moved over her face, learning the bones of her forehead and eyesockets and nose, through her flesh.

"There is something in your face, something behind all this silliness," he went on in his cold level voice while an interval of frozen time refused to pass. His hand pinched the loose sag of flesh around her mouth, slid along the fading line of her cheek and jaw. "I suppose you've had what you call your sorrow, too, haven't you?"

"Mr Gordon!" she said at last, finding her voice. He released her as abruptly and stood over her, gaunt and ill-nourished and arrogant in the moonlight while she believed she was going to faint, hoping vaguely that he would make some effort to catch her when she did, knowing that he would not do so. But she didn't faint, and the moon spread her silver and boneless hand on the water, and the water lapped and lapped at the pure dreaming hull of the Nausikaa, with a faint whispering sound.

Eleven Oclock.

"Do you know," said Mrs Wiseman rising and speaking across her chair, "what I'm going to do if this lasts another night? I'm going to ask Julius to exchange with me and let me get drunk with Dawson and Major Ayers in his place. And so, to one and all, goodnight."

"Aren't you going to wait for Dorothy?" Mark Frost asked.

She glanced toward the wheelhouse. "No, I guess Pete can look out for himself," she replied, and left them.

The moon cast a deep shadow on the western side of the deck, and near the companionway someone lay in a chair. She slowed, passing. "Mrs Maurier?" she said. "We wondered what had become of you. Been asleep?"

Mrs Maurier sat up slowly, as a very old person moves. The younger woman bent down to her, quickly solicitous. "You dont feel well, do you?"

"Is it time to go below?" Mrs Maurier asked, raising herself more briskly. "Our bridge game. . . ."

"You all had beat us too badly. But cant I——"

"No, no," Mrs Maurier objected quickly, a trifle testily. "Its nothing: I was just sitting here enjoying the moonlight."

"We thought Mr Gordon was with you." Mrs Maurier shuddered.

"These terrible men," she said with an attempt at lightness. "These artists!"

"Gordon, too? I thought he had escaped Dawson and Julius."

"Gordon, too," Mrs Maurier replied. She rose. "Come: I think we'd better go to bed." She shuddered again, as with cold: her flesh seemed to shake despite her, and she took the younger woman's arm, clinging to it. "I do feel a little tired," she confessed. "The first few days are always trying, dont you think? But we have a very nice party, dont you think so?"

"An awfully nice party," the other agreed without irony. "But we are all tired: we'll all feel better tomorrow, I know."

Mrs Maurier descended the stairs slowly, heavily. The other steadied her with her strong hand, and opening Mrs Maurier's door she reached in and found the light button. "There. Would you like anything before you go to bed?"

"No, no," Mrs Maurier answered, entering and averting her face quickly. She crossed the room and busied herself at the dressingtable, keeping her back to the other. "Thank you, nothing. I shall go to sleep at once, I think. I always sleep well on the water. Goodnight."

Mrs Wiseman closed the door. I wonder what it is she thought, I wonder what happened to her? She went on along the passage to her own door. Something did, something happened to her she repeated, putting her hand on the door and turning the knob.

*   *   *   *   *

No motion was anywhere, and no sound. The lazy intermittent voices from the deck had long ceased, and after a time the niece turned over, facing Jenny again in the darkness, gazing out into the more spacious darkness of the cabin across Jenny's vaguely curving shape. "Hello, Jenny," she murmured drowsily. No reply, and she put her hand upon Jenny's body, stroking it lightly and slowly along her side and her swelling hip falling away again. Jenny sighed her soft ineffable sigh and she turned also, breathing against the other's face. She made a soft wet sound with her mouth and put her arm across the niece's body. The niece raised herself slightly on her elbow, stroking her hand along Jenny's side. As the niece raised herself Jenny's arm slid further down her body, then it tightened, and Jenny spoke an indistinguishable word that wasn't Pete. The niece bent over Jenny in the dark. Her moving hand ceased in the valley beneath the swell of Jenny's thigh and she was quite motionless a moment. Then she laid her sober broad mouth against Jenny's cheek.

Jenny made again her drowsy moaning sound, and without seeming to move at all she came to the other with a boneless enveloping movement, turning her head until their mouths touched. Immediately Jenny went lax, yet she still seemed to envelope the other, holding their bodies together with her mouth. . . . Abruptly the niece jerked her mouth away and sprawling her hard body sharply across Jenny's breast she leaned out of the berth, spitting.

"Ugh!" She made a harsh shuddering sound. "Good Lord, who ever taught you to kiss that way? Ugh!" she exclaimed, spitting again.

Jenny came fully awake. "Oh," she cried, "you're hurting me!"

The niece rolled back into the berth, thrusting at her. "Come on, now, untangle your legs. Who taught you to kiss that way?" she repeated.

Jenny was panting. She lay muscleless while the other thrust her lax body away. "It was your fault," she moaned. "You started it!"

"I didn't do any such thing. You did it yourself. I was just rubbing my hand on you. What's the matter? were you dreaming?"

"I couldn't help it," Jenny moaned futilely. "You started it."

"Well, I didn't know you were going to act that way. Kissing like that! Ugh!" Jenny lay passive, whimpering and panting. "What'd you do it for?"

"I dont know. That's how everybody does it, I thought."

"I dont," the niece told her sharply, "not that way. Nobody but common people kiss that way."

"I didn't know," Jenny repeated.

"Well, dont cry about it." The niece flopped down again. The bunk protested, then ceased. Jenny's whimpering died away. Her breathing became again regular, and after a while she asked:

"How do nice people do it, then?"

The niece raised herself again. "You promise to not——to be careful, this time?"

"All right," Jenny agreed, "I promise."

The niece approached Jenny's unseen face with hers and again without seeming to move Jenny came to her, softly enveloping. The niece stopped warily for a second, then with a sudden movement she touched Jenny's nose with her mouth. Jenny moved her head obediently, but before their mouths found each other the niece paused again, utterly motionless above Jenny while Jenny's mouth made a soft tentative seeking movement in the dark. There was a sound at the door, the niece raised her head and paused again, and almost immediately the door swung open revealing the lighted passage and after an interval in which there was no movement the light in the room clicked on and Mrs Wiseman stood in the doorway, staring at them with a dark intent speculation.

Twelve Oclock.

The moon had got higher, that worn and bloodless one, old and a little weary and shedding her tired silver on yacht and water and shore, and the yacht, the deck and its fixtures were passionless as a dream upon the shifting silvered wings of water when she appeared in her bathing suit. She stood for a moment in the doorway until she saw movement and his white shirt where he half turned on the coil of rope where he sat. Her lifted hand blanched slimly in the hushed treachery of the moon: a gesture, and her bare feet made no sound on the deck.

"Hello, David. I'm on time, like I said. Where's your bathing suit?"

"I didn't think you would come," he said, looking up at her. "I didn't think you meant it."

"Why not?" she asked. "Good Lord, what'd I want to tell you I was, if I wasn't, for?"

"I dont know. I just thought. . . . You sure are brown, seeing it in the moonlight."

"Yes, I've got a good one," she agreed. "Where's your bathing suit? Why haven't you got it on?"

"You were going to get one for me, you said."

She stared at his face in consternation. "That's right: I sure was. I forgot it. Wait, maybe I can wake Josh up and get it. It wont take long. You wait here."

He stopped her. "It'll be all right. Dont bother about it tonight. I'll get it some other time."

"No, I'll get it. I want somebody to go in with me. You wait."

"No, never mind: I'll row the boat for you."

"Say, you still dont believe I meant it, do you?" She examined him curiously. "All right, then. I guess I'll have to go in by myself. You can row the boat, anyway. Come on."

He fetched the oars and they got in the tender and cast off. "Only I wish you had a bathing suit," she repeated from the stern. "I'd rather have somebody to go in with me. Couldn't you go in in your clothes or something? Say, I'll turn my back, and you take off your clothes and jump in: how about that?"

"I guess not," he answered in alarm. "I guess I better not do that."

"Shucks, I wanted somebody to go swimming with me. Its not any fun by myself. . . . Take off your shirt and pants, then, and go in in your underclothes. That's almost like a bathing suit: I went in yesterday in Josh's."

"I'll row the boat for you while you go in," he repeated.

The niece said Shucks again. David pulled steadily on upon the mooned and shifting water. Little waves slapped the bottom of the boat lightly as it rose and fell, and behind them the yacht was pure and passionless as a dream against the dark trees.

"I just love tonight," the niece said. "Its like we owned everything." She lay flat on her back on the stern seat, propping her heels against the gunwale. David pulled rhythmically, the motion of the boat was a rhythm that lent to the moon and stars swinging up and down beyond the tapering simplicity of her propped knees a motion slow and soothing as a huge tree in a wind.

"How far do you want to go?" he asked presently.

"I dont care," she answered, gazing into the sky. He rowed on, the oarlocks thumping and measured and she turned onto her belly, dragging her arm in the water while small bubbles of silver fire clung to her arm, broke away reluctantly and swam slowly to the surface, disappeared. . . . Little casual swells slapped the bottom of the boat, lightly, slid on along the hull, mooned with bubbled fire. She slid her legs over and swung from the stern of the boat, dragging through the water. He pulled on a few strokes.

"I cant row with you hanging there," he said. Her two hands vanished from the gunwale, her dark head vanished but when he slewed the boat sharply and half rose she reappeared, whipping a faint shower of silvered drops from her hair. The moon slid and ran on her alternate arms and before her spread a fan of silver lines, shifting and spreading and fading.

"Gee," she said. Her voice came low along the water, not loud, but still distinct: little waves lapped at it. "Its grand: warm as warm. You better come in." Her head vanished again, he saw her sickling legs as they vanished, and once more she rayed shattered silver from her flung head. She swam up to the boat. "Come on in, David," she insisted, "take off your shirt and pants and jump in. I'll swim out and wait for you. Come on, now," she commanded.

So he removed his outer garments, sitting in the bottom of the boat, and slid quickly and modestly into the water. "Isn't it grand?" she called to him. "Come on out here."

"We better not get too far from the boat," he said cautiously, "she aint got any anchor, you know."

"We can catch it. It wont drift fast. Come on out here, and I'll race you back to it."

He swam out to where her dark wet head awaited him. "I bet I beat you," she challenged. "Are you ready? One—Two—Three—Go!" and she did beat him and with a single unceasing motion she slid upward and into the tender, and stood erect for the moonlight to slide over her in hushed silver. "I'll plunge for distance with you," she now challenged. David hung by his hands, submerged to his neck. She waited for him to get into the skiff, then she said: "You can dive, cant you?" But he still clung to the gunwale, looking up at her. "Come on, David," she said sharply. "Are you timid, or what? I'm not going to look at you, if you dont want me to." So he got into the boat, modestly keeping his back to her. But even his wet curious garment could not make ridiculous the young lean splendor of him.

"I dont see what you are ashamed of. You've got a good physique," she told him. "Tall and hard looking. . . . Are you ready? One—Two—Three—Go!"

But soon she was content to float on her back and regain breath, while he trod water beside her. Little hands of water lapped at her, in her hair and upon her face, and she breathed deeply, closing her eyes against the bland waning moon. "I'll hold you up a while," he offered, putting his hand under the small of her back. "You sure can," she said, holding herself motionless. "Is it hard to do? Let me see if I can hold you up. This water is different from seawater: you dont hardly sink in seawater if you want to." She let her legs sink and he lay obediently on his back. "I can hold you up, can't I? Say, can you carry somebody in the water, like life savers?"

"A little," he admitted and she rolled again onto her back and he showed her how it was done. Then she must try it herself, and he submitted with dubious resignation. Her hard young arm gripped him chokingly across his throat, jamming against his windpipe, and she plunged violently forward, threshing her legs. He jerked up his arms to remove her strangling elbow and his head went under, openmouthed. He fought free of her, and reappeared, gasping. Her concerned face came to him and she tried to hold him up, unnecessarily.

"I'm so sorry: I didn't mean to duck you."

"Its all right," he said, coughing and strangling.

"I didn't do it right, did I? Are you all right, now?" She watched him anxiously, trying to support him.

"I'm all right," he repeated. "You had the wrong hold," he explained, treading water. "You had me around the neck."

"Gee, I thought I was doing it right. I'll do it right this time."

"I guess we better wait and practise it in shallow water, sometime," he demurred quickly.

"Why. . . . All right," she agreed. "I think I know how, now. I guess I had better learn good first though. I'm awful sorry I strangled you."

"It dont hurt any more. I dont notice it."

"But it was such a dumb thing to do. I'll learn it good next time."

"You know how now, all right. You just got the wrong hold that time. Try it again: see if you dont know it."

"You dont mind?" she said with quick joy. "I wont catch you wrong this time. . . . No, no, I might duck you again. I'd better learn it first."

"Sure you wont," he said. "You know how, now. You wont hurt me. Try it." He turned onto his back.

"Gee, David," she said. She slid her arm carefully across his chest and beneath his opposite arm. "That's right? Now, I'm going."

She held him carefully, intent on doing it correctly, while he encouraged her. But their progress was maddeningly slow: the boat seemed miles away, and so much of her effort was needed to keep her own head above water. Soon she was breathing faster, gulping air and then closing her mouth against the water her thrusting arm swirled up against her face. I will do it, I will do it she told herself, but it was so much harder than it had looked. The skiff rose and fell against the stars, and the mooned water bubbled about her. It would take more effort, or she'd have to give up. And she'd drown before that.

The arm that held him was numb, and she swam harder, shifting her grip and again her hard elbow shut with strangling force upon his windpipe. But he was expecting it and without moving his body he twisted his head aside and filling his lungs he shut his mouth and eyes. . . . Soon she ceased swimming and her arm slid down again, holding him up, and he filled his lungs and opened his eyes to remark the gunwale of the tender rising and falling against the sky above his head.

"I did make it," she gasped, "I did make it. Are you all right?" she asked, panting. "I sure did it, David. I knew I could." She clung to the skiff, resting her head upon her hands, panting. "I thought for a while, when I had to change my hold, that I was doing it wrong again. But I did it right, didn't I?" The remote chill stars swung over them, and the decaying disc of the moon, over the empty world in which they clung by their hands, side by side. "I'm pretty near all in," she admitted.

"Its pretty hard," he agreed, "until you've practised it a lot. I'll hold you up until you get your breath." He put his arm around her, under the water.

"I'm not all the way winded," she protested, but by degrees she relaxed until he supported her whole weight feeling her

heart thumping against his palm, while she clung to the gunwale resting her bowed head upon her hands; and it was like
he had been in a dark room, and all of a sudden the lights had
come on: simple, like that.

It was like one morning when he was in a bunch of hoboes
riding a freight into San Francisco and the bulls had jumped
them and they had had to walk in. Along the water front it
was, and there were a lot of boats in the water, kind of rocking back and forth at anchor: he could see reflections of boats
and of the piles of the wharves in the water, wavering back
and forth; and after a while dawn had come up out of the
smoke of the city, like a sound you couldn't hear, and a lot of
yellow and pink had come onto the water where the boats
were rocking, and around the piles of the wharf little yellow
lines seemed to come right up out of the water; and pretty
soon there were gulls looking like they had pink and yellow
feathers, slanting and wheeling around.

And it was like there was a street in a city, a street with a
lot of trash in it, but pretty soon he was out of the street and
in a place where trees were. It must be spring, because the
trees were not exactly bare, and yet they didn't exactly have
leaves on them, and there was a wind coming through the
trees and he stopped and heard music somewhere; it was like
he had just waked up, and a wind with music in it was coming
across green hills brave in a clean dawn. Simple, like that.

She moved at last against his arm. "Maybe I can climb in,
now. You better gimme a push, I guess." His hand found her
knee, slid down, and she raised her foot to his palm. He saw
her flat boy's body against the stars rising, and she was in the
boat, leaning down to him. "Catch my hands," she said, extending them, but for a time he didn't move at all, but only
clung to the gunwale and looked up at her with an utter longing, like a dog.

*   *   *   *   *

Mrs Maurier lay in bed in her darkened room. There was
a port just above the bed, and a long pencil of moonlight
came slanting through it, shattering upon the floor and
filling the room with a cold disseminated radiance. Upon the
chair, vaguely, her clothes: shapeless, familiar mass, comforting; and about her the intimate familiarity of her own

possessions—her toilet things, her clothing, her very particular odor with which she had grown so familiar that she no longer noticed it at all.

She lay in bed—her bed, especially built, was the most comfortable one on board—surrounded, lapped in security and easeful things, walled and secure within the bland hushed planes of the bulkheads. A faint happy sound came in to her: little tongues of water lapping ceaselessly along side the yacht, against her yacht—that island of security that was always waiting to transport her comfortably beyond the rumors of the world and its sorrows; and beyond the yacht, space: water and sky and darkness and silence, a worn cold moon neither merry nor sad. . . . Mrs Maurier lay in her easy bed, within her comfortable room, weeping long shuddering sobs: a passive terrible hysteria without a sound.

The Third Day.

THIS morning waked in a quiet fathomless mist. It was upon the world of water unstirred, soon the first faint wind of morning would thin it away; but now it was about the Nausikaa timelessly: the yacht was a thick jewel swaddled in soft gray wool, while in the wool some where dawn was like a suspended breath. The first morning of Time might well be beyond this mist, and trumpets preliminary to a golden flourish, and held in suspension in it might be heard yet the voices of the Far Gods on the first morning saying It is well: let there be light. A short distance away, a shadow, a rumor, a more palpable thickness: this was the shore. The water, fading out of the mist, became as a dark metal in which the Nausikaa was rigidly fixed, and the yacht was motionless, swaddled in mist like a fat jewel.

FIVE OCLOCK.

Up from the darkness of the companionway the niece came, naked and silent as a ghost. She stood for a space, but there was no sound from anywhere, and she crossed the deck and stopped again at the rail, breathing the soft chill mist into her lungs, feeling the mist swaddling her firm simple body with a faint lingering chilliness. Her legs and arms were so tan that naked she appeared to wear a bathing suit of a startling white. She climbed the rail, the tender rocked a little under her, causing the black motionless water to come alive, making faint sounds. Then she slid over the stern and swam out into the mist.

The water divided with oily reluctance, closing behind her again with scarce a ripple. Here, at the water level, she could see nothing save a grayness and flaccid disturbed tongues of water lapping into it, leaving small fleeting gaps between mist and water before the mist filled them again silently as settling wings. The hull of the yacht was a vague thing, a thing felt, known, rather than seen. She swam slowly circling the place where she knew it should be.

She swam slowly and steadily, trying to keep her approximate distance by instinct. But, consciously, this was hard to do; consciously in this vague restricted immensity, this limitless vagueness whose center was herself, the yacht could be in any direction from her. She paused and trod water, while little tongues of water kissed her face, lapping against her lips. Its on my right she told herself. Its on my right, over there. Not fear: merely a faint unease, an exasperation; but to reassure herself she swam a few strokes in that direction. The mist neither thickened nor thinned. She trod water again and water licked at her face soundlessly. Damn your fool soul she whispered, and at that moment a round huge thing like a dead lidless eye watched her suddenly from the mist and there came a faint sound from somewhere in the mist above her head. In two strokes she touched the hull of the yacht: a vindication. She knew a faint pride and a touch of relief and she swam along the hull and circled the stern. She grasped the gunwale of the tender and hung there for a while, getting her wind back.

That faint sound came again from the deck: a movement, and she spoke into the mist: "David?" The mist took the word sweeping it lightly against the hull, then it rebounded again and the mist absorbed it. But he heard and he appeared vaguely above her at the rail, looking down at her where she hung in the water. "Go away, so I can get out," she said. He didn't move and she added: "I haven't got on any bathing suit. Go away a minute, David."

But he didn't move. He leaned over the rail, looking at her with a dumb and utter longing and after a while she slid quickly and easily into the tender; and still he remained motionless, making no move to help her as her grave simple body came swiftly aboard the yacht. "Be back in a minute," she said over her shoulder and her startling white bathing suit sped across the deck and out of the ken of his dog's eyes. The mist without thinning was filling with light, an imminence of dawn like a glory, a splendor of trumpets unheard.

Her minute was three minutes. She reappeared in her little colored linen dress, her dark coarse hair still damp, carrying her shoes and stockings in her hand. He hadn't moved at all. "Well, lets get going," she said. She looked at him impatiently. "Aren't you ready yet?"

He stirred at last, watching her with the passive abjection of a dog. "Come on," she said sharply. "Haven't you got the stuff for breakfast yet? What's the matter with you, David? Snap out of your trance." She examined him again, with a sober impersonality. "You didn't believe I was going to do it—is that it? Or are you backing out yourself? Come on: say so now, if you want to call it off." She came nearer, examining his face with her grave opaque eyes. She extended her hand. "David?"

He took her hand slowly, looking at her, and she grasped his hand and shook his arm sharply. "Wake up. Say, you haven't—— Come on, lets get some stuff for breakfast, and beat it. We haven't got all day."

He followed her and in the galley she switched on the light and chose a flat box of bacon and a loaf of bread, putting them on the table and delving again among boxes and lockers and shelves. "Have you got matches? a knife?" she asked over her shoulder. "And——where are oranges? Lets take some oranges. I love oranges, dont you?" She turned her head to look at him. His hand was just touching her sleeve, so diffidently that she had not felt it. She turned suddenly, putting the oranges down, and put her arms about him, hard and firm and sexless, drawing his cheek down to her sober moist kiss. She could feel his hammering erratic heart against her breast, could hear it surging in the silence almost as though it were in her own body. His arms tightened and he moved his head, seeing her mouth, but she evaded him with a quick movement, without reproof. "No, no, not that. Everybody does that." She strained him against her hard body again, then released him. "Come on, now. Have you got everything?" She examined the shelves again, finding at last a small basket. It was filled with damp lettuce but she dumped the lettuce out and put her things in it. "You take my shoes. They'll go in your pocket, won't they?" She crumpled her limp blonde stockings into her slippers and gave them to him. Then she picked up the basket and snapped off the light.

Day was a nearer thing yet, thought it was not quite come. Though the mist had not thinned, the yacht was visible from stem to stern, asleep like a gull with folded wings; and against her hull the water sighed a long awaking sigh. The shoreline was darker, a more palpable vagueness in the mist.

"Say," she remarked, stopping suddenly, "how are we going to get ashore? I forgot that. We dont want to take the tender."

"Swim," he suggested. Her dark damp head came just to his chin and she mused for a time in a sober consternation.

"Isn't there some way we can go in the tender and then pull it back to the yacht with a rope?"

"I. . . . Yes. Yes, we can do that."

"Well, you get a rope then. Snap into it."

When he returned with a coiled line she was already in the tender with the oars, and she watched with interest while he passed the rope around a stanchion and brought both ends into the boat with him and made one of the ends fast to the ringbolt in the stem of the skiff. Then she caught the idea and she sat and paid out the line while he pulled away for shore. Soon they beached and she sprang ashore, still holding the free end of the rope. "How're we going to keep the tender from pulling the rope back around that post and getting aloose?" she asked.

"I'll show you," he answered, and she watched him while he tied the oars and the rowlocks together with the free end of the line and wedged them beneath the thwarts. "That'll hold, I guess. Somebody'll be sure to see her pretty soon," he added, and prepared to draw the skiff back to the yacht.

"Wait a minute," she said. She mused gravely, gazing at the dim shadowy yacht, then she borrowed matches from him, and sitting on the gunwale of the tender she tore a strip of paper from the bacon box and with a charred match printed Going to   She looked up. "Where are we going?" He looked at her and she added quickly: "I mean, what town? We'll have to go to a town somewhere, you know, to get back to New Orleans so I can get some clothes and my seventeen dollars. What's the name of a town?"

After a while he said: "I dont know. I never——"

"That's right. You never were over here before, either, were you? Well, what's that town the ferries go to? the one Jenny's always talking about you have fun at?" She stared again at the vague shape of the Nausikaa, then she suddenly printed Mandeville. "That's the name of it—Mandeville. Which way is Mandeville from here?" He didn't know and she added: "No matter: we'll find it, I guess." She signed the note and laid it on the sternseat, weighting it with a small rock. "Now, pull her off," she commanded, and soon there came back to them across the motionless water a faint thud. "Now, throw the oar as far as you can. Somebody'll see the rope and pull it in."

He threw the oar like a javelin, easily. "Good throw," she commended. "Goodbye, Nausikaa," she said. "Wait," she added, "I better put my shoes on, I guess." He gave her her slippers and she sat flat on the narrow beach and put them on, returning the crumpled stockings to him. "Wait" she said again, taking the stockings again and flipping them out. She slid one of them over her brown arm and withdrew a crumpled wad—the money she had been able to rake up by ransacking her aunt's and Mrs Wiseman's and Miss Jameson's things. She reached her hand and he drew her to her feet. "You'd better carry the money," she said, giving it to him. "Now for breakfast," she said clutching his hand.

Six Oclock.

Trees heavy and ancient with moss loomed out of it hugely and grayly: the mist might have been a sluggish growth between and among them. No, this mist might have been the first prehistoric morning itself; it might have been the very substance in which the seed of the beginning of things fecundated, and these huge and silent trees might have been the first living things, too recently born to know either fear or astonishment, dragging their sluggish umbilical cords from out the old miasmic womb of a nothingness latent and dreadful. She crowded against him, suddenly quiet and subdued, trembling a little like a puppy against the reassurance of his arm. "Gee," she said in a small voice.

That small sound did not die away. It merely dissolved into the moist gray surrounding them, and it was as if at a movement of any sort the word might repeat itself somewhere between sky and ground as a pebble is shaken out of cotton batting. He put his arm across her shoulders and at his touch she turned quickly beneath his armpit, hiding her face. "I'm hungry," she said at last, in that small voice. "That's what's the matter with me," she added with more assurance. "I want something to eat."

"Want me to build a fire?" he asked of the coarse dark crown of her head.

"No, no," she answered quickly, holding to him. "Besides, we are too close to the lake here. Somebody might see it. We ought to get further from the shore." She clung to him, inside his arm. "I guess we'd better wait here until the fog goes away, though. A piece of bread will do." She reached her brown hand. "Lets sit down somewhere. We'll sit down and eat some bread," she decided. "And when the fog goes away we can find the road. Come on, lets find a log or something."

She drew him by the hand and they sat at the foot of a huge tree, on the damp ground, while she delved into the basket. She broke a bit from the loaf and gave it to him, and a fragment for herself. Then she slid further down against her propped heels until her back rested against him, and bit from her bread. She sighed contentedly. "There now. Dont you just love this?" She raised her grave chewing face to look at him. "All gray and lonesome. Makes you feel kind of cold on the outside and warm inside, doesn't it?——say, you aren't eating your bread. Eat your bread, David. I love bread, dont you?" She moved again, inward upon herself: in some way she seemed to get herself yet closer against him.

The mist was already beginning to thin, breaking with a heavy reluctance before a rumor of motion too faint to be called wind. The mist broke raggedly and drifted in sluggish wraiths that seemed to devour all sound, swaying and swinging like huge spectral apes from tree to tree, rising and falling, revealing sombre patriarchs of trees, hiding them again. From far far back in the swamp there came a hoarse homely sound— an alligator's lovesong. "Chicago," she murmured. "Didn't know we were so near home." Soon the sun; and she sprawled against him, contentedly munching her bread.

SEVEN OCLOCK.

They hadn't found the road, but they had reached a safe distance from the lake. She had discovered a butterfly larger than her two hands clinging to a spotlight of sun on the ancient trunk of a tree, moving its damp lovely wings like laboring ex-

posed lungs of glass or silk; and while he gathered firewood—
a difficult feat, since neither of them had thought of a hatchet—
she paused at the edge of a black stream to harry a sluggish
thick serpent with a small switch. A huge gaudy bird came up
and cursed her, and the snake ignored her with a sort of tired
unillusion and plopped heavily into the thick water. Then,
looking around, she saw a thin fire in the sombre equivocal
twilight of the trees.

They ate again: the oranges, they broiled bacon, scorched
it, dropped it on the ground, retrieved and wiped it and
chewed it down; and the rest of the loaf. "Dont you just love
camping?" She sat crosslegged and wiped a strip of bacon on
her skirt. "Lets always do this, David: lets dont ever have a
house where you've always got to stay in one place. We'll just
go around like this, camping. . . . David?" She raised the strip
of bacon and met his dumb yearning eyes. She poised her
bacon. "Dont look at me like that," she told him sharply.
Then, more gently: "Dont ever look at anybody like that.
You'll never get anybody to run away with you if you look at
'em like that, David." She extended her hand. His hand came
out, slowly and diffidently, but her grip was hard; actual. She
shook his arm for emphasis.

"How was I looking at you?" he asked after a while, in a
voice that didn't seem to him to be his voice at all. "How do
you want me to look at you?"

"Oh——You know how. Not like that, though. Like that,
you look at me just like a——a man, that's all. Or a dog. Not
like David." She writhed her hand free, and ate her strip of
bacon. Then she wiped her fingers on her dress. "Gimme a
cigarette."

The mist had gone, and the sun came already sinister and
hot among the trees, upon the miasmic earth. She sat on her
crossed ankles, replete, smoking. Abruptly she poised the cigarette in a tense cessation of all movement. Then she moved
her head quickly, staring at him in consternation. She moved
again, suddenly slapping her bare leg.

"What is it?" he asked.

For reply she extended her flat tan palm. In the center of
it was a dark speck and a tiny splash of crimson. "Good
Lord, gimme my stockings," she exclaimed. "We'll have to

move. Gee, I'd forgotten about them," she said, drawing her stockings over her straightening legs. She sprang to her feet. "We'll soon be out, though. David, stop looking at me that way. Look like you were having a good time, at least. Cheer up, David. A man would think you were losing your nerve already. Buck up: I think its grand, running off like this. Dont you think its grand?" She turned her head and saw again that diffident still gesture of his hand touching her dress. Across the hot morning there came the high screech of the Nausikaa's whistle.

Eight Oclock.

"No, sir," the nephew answered patiently, "its a pipe."

"A pipe, eh?" repeated Major Ayers, glaring at him with his hard affable little eyes. "You make pipes, eh?"

"I'm making this one," the nephew replied with preoccupation.

"Came away and left your own ashore, perhaps?" Major Ayers suggested after a time.

"Naw. I dont smoke 'em. I'm just making a new kind."

"Ah, I see. For the market." Major Ayers' mind slowly took fire. "Money in it, eh? Americans would buy a new kind of pipe, too. You've made arrangements for the marketing of it, of course?"

"No, I'm just making it. For fun," the nephew explained in that patient tone you use with obtuse children. Major Ayers glared at his bent preoccupied head.

"Yes," he agreed. "Best to say nothing about it until you've completed all your computations regarding the cost of production. Dont blame you, at all. . . ." Major Ayers brooded with calculation. He said: "Americans really would buy a new sort of pipe. Strange no one had thought of that." The nephew carved minutely at his cylinder. Major Ayers said, secretly: "No, I dont blame you at all. But when you've done, you'll require capital: that sort of thing, you know. And then . . . a word to your friends at the proper time, eh?" The nephew looked up.

"A word to my friends?" he repeated. "Say, I'm just making a pipe, I tell you. A pipe. Just to be making it. For fun."

"Right you are," Major Ayers agreed suavely. "No offense, dear lad. I dont blame you, dont blame you at all. Experienced the same situation myself."

Nine Oclock.

They found the road at last—two faint scars and a powder of unbearable dust upon a raised levee traversing the swamp. But between them and the road was a foul sluggish width of water and vegetation and biology. Huge cypress roots thrust up like weathered bones out of a green scum and a quaking neither earth nor water, and always those bearded eternal trees like gods regarding without alarm this puny desecration of a silence of air and earth and water ancient when hoary old Time himself was a pink and dreadful miracle in his mother's arms.

It was she who found the fallen tree, she who first essayed its oozy treacherous bark and first stood in the empty road stretching monotonously in either direction between battalioned patriarchs of trees. She was panting a little, whipping a broken green branch about her body, watching him as he inched his way across the fallen trunk. "Come on, David," she called impatiently. "Here's the road: we're all right now." He was across the ditch and he now struggled up the rank reluctant levee bank. She leaned down and reached her hand to him. But he would not take it, so she leaned further and clutched his shirt. "Now, which way is Mandeville?"

"That way," he answered immediately, pointing.

"You said you never were over here before," she accused.

"No. But we were west of Mandeville when we went aground, and the lake is back yonder. So Mandeville must be that way."

"I dont think so. Its this way: see, the swamp isn't so thick this way. Besides, I just know its this way."

He looked at her a moment. "All right," he agreed. "I guess you are right."

"But dont you know which way it is? Isn't there any way you can tell?" She bent and whipped her legs with the broken branch.

"Well, the lake is over yonder, and we were west of Mandeville last night, and——"

"You're just guessing," she interrupted harshly.

"Yes," he answered. "I guess you are right."

"Well, we've got to go somewhere. We can't stand here." She twitched her shoulders, writhing her body beneath her dress. "Which way, then?"

"Well, we w——"

She turned abruptly in the direction she had chosen. "Come on: I'll die here." She strode on ahead.

TEN OCLOCK.

She was trying to explain it to Pete. The sun had risen sinister and hot, climbing into a drowsy haze, and up from a low vague region neither water nor sky, clouds like fat little girls in starched frocks marched solemnly.

"Its a thing they join at that place he's going to. Only they have to work to join it, and sometimes you dont even get to join it then. And the ones that do join it dont get anything except a little button or something."

"Pipe down and try again," Pete told her, leaning with his elbows and one heel hooked backward on the rail, his hat slanted across his reckless dark face, squinting his eyes against the smoke of his cigarette. "What're you talking about?"

"There's something in the water," Jenny remarked with placid astonishment, creasing her belly over the rail and staring downward into the faintly rippled water while the land breeze molded her little green dress. "It must of fell off the boat. . . . I'm talking about that college he's going to. You work to join things there. You work three years, she says. And then maybe——"

"What college?"

"I forgot. Its the one where they have big football games in the papers every year. He's——"

"Yale and Harvard?"

"Uhuh. That's the one she said. He's——"

"Which one? Yale, or Harvard?"

"Uhuh. And so he——"

"Come on, baby. You're talking about two colleges. Was it Yale she said? or Harvard? or Sing Sing, or what?"

"Oh," Jenny said. "It was Yale. Yes, that's the one she said.

And he'll have to work three years to join it. And even then maybe he cant."

"Well, what about it? Suppose he does work three years, what about it?"

"Why, if he does, he wont get anything except a little button or something; even if he does join it, I mean." Jenny brooded softly, creasing herself upon the rail. "He's going to have to work for it," she recurred again in a dull soft amazement. "He'll have to work three years for it, and even then he may not——"

"Dont be dumb all your life, kid," Pete told her.

Wind and sun were in Jenny's drowsing hair. The deck swept trimly forward, deserted. The others were gathered on the deck above. Occasionally they could hear voices, and a pair of masculine feet were crossed innocently upon the rail directly over Pete's head. A halfsmoked cigarette spun in a small twinkling arc astern. Jenny watched it drop lightly onto the water, where it floated amid the other rubbish that had caught her attention. Pete spun his own cigarette backward over his shoulder, but this one sank immediately, to her placid surprise.

"Let the boy join his club, if he wants," Pete added. "What kind of a club is it? what do they do?"

"I dont know. They just join it. You work for it three years," she said. "Three years. . . . Gee, by that time you'd be too old to do anything if you got to join it. . . . Three years. My Lord."

"Sit down, and give your wooden leg a rest," Pete said. "Dont be a dumbbell forever." He examined the deck narrowly a moment, then without changing his position against the rail he turned his head toward Jenny. "Give papa a kiss."

Jenny glanced briefly up the deck. Then she came with a sort of wary docility, raising her ineffable face . . . presently Pete withdrew his face. "What's the matter?" he asked.

"The matter with what?" said Jenny innocently.

Pete unhooked his heel. He put his arm around Jenny. Their faces merged again and Jenny became an impersonal softness against his mouth and a single blue eye and a drowsing aura of hair. Again Pete raised his head. "Say, what's the matter with you, anyway?"

Jenny released herself with a boneless blonde motion. "I dont kiss that way anymore," she stated primly, patting her hair with her small dirty fingers. "Its not refined."

Pete hooked his heel again over the rail, violently. "Yeh, that's the trouble with this whole boat. Refined. Refined," said Pete again with a slow bitter contempt. "Hell yes. Damn near refined me out of my girl. Refined! Jesus Christ." He got out another cigarette and struck three matches viciously and vainly.

"Well, it aint. I'm not going to kiss like that anymore, neither."

"All right, all right. I'm not asking you to. There are other janes on this boat that aint so damn refined," he said ominously. Jenny bent again over the rail. "Yes, I'll get along being refined as well as you will," he added, glancing at her and catching her watching him from the corner of one ineffable speculative eye. He flung his cigarette away. "No, listen, baby, I was just talking," he said quickly. "I was just kidding, see? I didn't mean that." Jenny removed the eye, giving him only the sunshot aureole of her angelic head. Pete put his hand on her arm. "I was just kidding about that jane. Christ, do you think I'd fool around with that old bat?" Her arm was utterly passive under his hand. "Look here, kid." Jenny didn't stir and Pete dragged at her roughly, pulling her around until she looked at him. Her face was quite bland, blank. "Look here," Pete said. "I've been watching you fooling around with that old bird. You watch your step: see?" He shook her.

"Ow," Jenny said. "You're hurting my arm. Who're you talking about? Mr Fairchild, or that fat old jew?"

"That's all right who I'm talking about." Pete bent his bold reckless face over her blonde and innocent mask. "I'm watching you. Watch your step, see?"

"Oh, you mean Gramma," said Jenny with bland comprehension. Without seeming to move at all she came to him, tentatively and warily. She paused a moment and drew her head back slightly. "Do it refined, Pete". . . . "Like this?" . . . . "Mmmmmm". . . . After a while Pete raised his head. "I guess I can stand being refined for a day or two," he said.

"Mmmmm" Jenny agreed. The Nausikaa lay motionless on the scarce rippled water: her pennon dropped languidly against the languorous sky. . . . "Gimme a kiss, sweetness."

ELEVEN OCLOCK.

The swamp did not seem to end, ever. On either side of the road it brooded, fetid and timeless, sombre and hushed and dreadful. The road went on and on through a bearded tunnel, beneath the sinister brass sky. The dew was long departed and dust puffed listlessly to her fierce striding. David tramped behind her, watching two splotches of dead blood on her stockings. Abruptly there were three of them and he drew abreast of her. She looked over her shoulder, showing him her wrung face. "Dont come near me!" she cried. "Dont you see you make 'em worse?"

He dropped behind again and she stopped suddenly, dropping the broken branch and extending her arms. "David," she said. He went to her, awkwardly, and she clung to him, whimpering. She raised her face, staring at him. "Cant you do something? They hurt me, David." But he only looked at her with his unutterable dumb longing. She tightened her arms, released him quickly. "We'll be out soon," she said picking up the branch again. "It'll be different then. Look! there's another big butterfly." Her squeal of delight became again a thin whimpering sound. She strode on.

* * * * *

Jenny found Mrs Wiseman in their room, changing her dress.

"Mr Tal—Talliaferro," Jenny began. Then she said: "He's an awful refined man, I guess. Dont you think so?"

"Refined?" the other repeated. "Exactly that. Ernest invented that word."

"He did?" Jenny went to the mirror and looked at herself a while. "Her brother's refined too, aint he?"

"Whose brother, honey?" Mrs Wiseman paused and watched Jenny curiously.

"The one with that saw."

"Oh. Yes, fairly so. He seems to be too busy to be anything else. Why?"

"And that popeyed man. All Englishmen are refined, though. There was one in a movie I saw. He was awful refined." Jenny looked at her reflected face, timelessly and completely entertained. Mrs Wiseman gazed at Jenny's fine minted hair, at her sleazy little dress revealing the divine inevitability of her soft body.

"Come here, Jenny," she said.

Twelve Oclock.

When he reached her she sat huddled in the road, crouching bonelessly upon herself, huddling her head in her crossed thin arms. He stood beside her, and presently he spoke her name. She rocked back and forth, then wrung her body in an ecstasy. "They hurt me, they hurt me," she wailed, crouching again in that impossible spasm of agony. David knelt beside her and spoke her name again. She sat up.

"Look," she said wildly, "on my legs—look, look," staring with a sort of fascination at a score of great gray specks hovering about her bloodflecked stockings, making no effort to brush them away. She raised her wild face again. "Do you see them? They are everywhere on me—my back, my back, where I cant reach." She lay suddenly flat, writhing her back in the dust, clutching his hand. Then she sat up again and against his knees she turned, wringing her body from the hips, trying to draw her bloody legs beneath her brief skirt. He held her while she writhed in his grasp, staring her wild bloodless face up at him. "I must get in water," she panted. "I must get in water. Mud, anything. I'm dying, I tell you."

"Yes, yes: I'll get you some water. You wait here. Will you wait here?"

"You'll get me some water? You will? You promise?"

"Yes, yes," he repeated. "I'll get you some. You wait here. You wait here, see?" he repeated idiotically. She bent again inward upon herself, moaning, writhing in the dust, and he plunged down the bank, stripping his shirt off, and dipped it into the foul warm ditch. She had dragged her dress up about her shoulders, revealing her startling white bathing suit between her knickers and the satin band binding her breasts. "On my back," she moaned, bending forward again, "quick, quick!"

He laid the wet shirt on her back. She caught the ends of it and drew it around her, and presently she leaned back against his knees with a long shuddering sigh. "I want a drink. Cant I have a drink, David?"

"Soon," he promised with despair. "You can have one soon as we get out of the swamp."

She moaned again, a long whimpering sound, lowering her head between her arms. They crouched together in the dusty road. The road went on shimmering before them, endless beneath bearded watching trees, crossing the implacable swamp with a puerile bravado like a thin voice cursing in a cathedral. Needles of fire darted about them, about his bare shoulders and arms. After a while she said: "Wet it again, please, David."

He did so, and returned, scrambling up the steep rank levee side. "Now, bathe my face, David." She raised her face and closed her eyes, and he bathed her face and throat and brushed her damp coarse hair back from her brow.

"Lets put the shirt on you," he suggested.

"No," she demurred against his arm without opening her eyes, drowsily. "They'll eat you alive without it."

"They dont bother me like they do you. Come on, put it on." She demurred again and he tried awkwardly to draw the shirt over her head. "I dont need it," he repeated.

"No. . . . Keep it, David. . . . You ought to keep it. Besides, I'd rather have it underneath. . . . Oooo, it feels so good. You're sure you dont need it?" She opened her eyes, watching him with that sober gravity of hers. He insisted and she sat up and slipped her dress over her head. He helped her to don the shirt, then she slipped her dress on again. "I wouldn't take it, only they hurt me so damn bad. I'll do something for you someday, David. I swear I will."

"Sure," he repeated. "I dont need it."

He rose, and she came to her feet in a single motion, before he could offer to help her. "I swear I wouldn't take it if they didn't hurt me so much, David," she persisted, putting her hand on his shoulder, raising her tanned serious face.

"Sure, I know."

"I'll pay you back somehow. Come on: lets get out of here."

ONE OCLOCK.

Mrs Wiseman and Miss Jameson drove Mrs Maurier, moaning and wringing her hands, from the galley and prepared lunch. Grapefruit again, disguised thinly.

"We have so many of them," the hostess apologised help-lessly. "And the steward gone. . . . We are aground too, you see," she explained.

"Oh, we can stand a little hardship, I guess," Fairchild re-assured her jovially. "The race hasn't degenerated that far. In a book, now, it would be kind of terrible; if you forced char-acters in a book to eat as much grapefruit as we do, both the art boys and the humanitarians would stand on their hind legs and howl. But in real life—— In life, anything might happen; in actual life people will do anything. Its only in books that people must function according to arbitrary rules of conduct and probability; its only in books that events must never flout credulity."

"That's true," Mrs Wiseman agreed. "People's characters, when writers delineate them by revealing their likings and dis-likings, always appear so perfect, so inevitably consistent, but in li——"

"That's why literature is art and biology isn't," her brother interrupted. "A character in a book must be consistent in all things, while man is consistent in one thing only: he is consistently vain. Its his vanity alone which keeps his par-ticles damp and adhering one to another, instead of like any other handful of dust which any wind that passes can disseminate."

"In other words, he is consistently inconsistent," Mark Frost recapitulated.

"I guess so," the semitic man replied. "Whatever that means. . . . But what were you saying, Eva?"

"I was thinking of how book people, when you find them in real life, have such a perverse and disconcerting way of liking and disliking the wrong things. For instance, Dorothy here. Suppose you were drawing Dorothy's character in a novel, Dawson. Any writer would give her a liking for blue jewelry: white gold and platinum, and sapphires in dull silver—you know. Wouldn't you do that?"

"Why, yes, so I would," Fairchild agreed with interest. "She would like blue things, sure enough."

"And then," the other continued, "music. You'd say she would like Grieg, and those other cold mad northern people with icewater in their veins, wouldn't you?"

"Yes," Fairchild agreed again, thinking immediately of Ibsen and the Peer Gynt legend and remembering a sonnet of Siegfried Sassoon's about Sibelius that he had once read in a magazine. "That's what she would like."

"Should like," Mrs Wiseman corrected, "for the sake of esthetic consistency. But I bet you are wrong. Isn't he, Dorothy?"

"Why, yes," Miss Jameson replied. "I always liked Chopin."

Mrs Wiseman shrugged: a graceful dark gesture. "And there you are. That's what makes art so discouraging. You come to expect anything associated with and dependent on the actions of man to be discouraging. But it always shocks me to learn that art also depends on population, on the herd instinct, just as much as manufacturing automobiles or stockings does——"

"Only they can't advertise art by means of women's legs yet," Mark Frost interrupted.

"Dont be silly, Mark," Mrs Wiseman said sharply. "That's exactly how art came to the attention of the ninety nine who dont produce it and so have any possible reason for buying it——postcards and lithographs barely esoteric enough to escape police persecution. Ask any man on the street what he understands by the word art: he'll tell you it means a picture. Wont he?" she appealed to Fairchild.

"That's so," he agreed. "And its a wrong impression. Art means anything consciously done well, to my notion. Living, or building a good lawn mower or playing poker. I dont like this modern idea of restricting the word to painting at all."

"The art of Life, of a beautiful and complete existence of the Soul," Mrs Maurier put in. "Dont you think that is Art's greatest function, Mr Gordon?"

"Of course you dont, child," Mrs Wiseman told Fairchild, ignoring Mrs Maurier. "As rabidly American as you are, you cant stick that, can you? And there's the seat of your bewilderment, Dawson;—your belief that the function of creating art depends on geography."

"It does. You cant grow corn without something to plant it in."

"But you dont plant corn in geography: you plant it in soil. It not only does not matter where that soil is, you can even move the soil from one place to another—around the world, if you like—and it will still grow corn."

"You'd have a different kind of corn though—Russian corn, or Latin or Anglo-saxon corn."

"All corn is the same to the belly," the semitic man said.

"Julius!" exclaimed Mrs Maurier. "The Soul's hunger: that is the true purpose of Art. There are so many things to satisfy the grosser appetites. Dont you think so, Mr Talliaferro?"

"Yes." Mrs Wiseman took her brother up. "Dawson clings to his conviction for the old reason: Its good enough to live with and comfortable to die with—like a belief in immortality. Insurance against doubt or alarm."

"And laziness," her brother added. Mrs Maurier exclaimed Julius! again. "Clinging spiritually to one little spot of the earth's surface, so much of his labor is performed for him. Details of dress and habit and speech which entail no hardship in the assimilation and which, piled one on another, become quite as imposing as any single startling stroke of originality, as trivialities in quantity will. Dont you agree? But then, I suppose that all poets in their hearts consider prosewriters shirkers, dont they?"

"Yes," his sister agreed. "We do think they are lazy—just a little. Not mentally, but that their . . . not hearts—" "Souls?" her brother suggested. "I hate that word, but its the nearest thing. . . ." She met her brother's sad quizzical eyes and exclaimed: "Oh, Julius! I could kill you, at times. He's laughing at me, Dawson."

"He's laughing at us both," Fairchild said. "But let him have his fun, poor fellow." He chuckled, and lit a cigarette. "Let him laugh. I always did want to be one of those old time eunuchs, for one night. They must have just laughed themselves to death when those sultans and things would come visiting."

"Mister Fairchild! Whatever in the world!" exclaimed Mrs Maurier.

"Its a good thing there's some one to see something amusing in that process," the other rejoined. "The husbands, the active participants, never seem to."

"That's a provision of nature's for racial survival," Fairchild said. "If the husbands ever saw the comic aspect of it. . . . But they never do, even when they have the opportunity, no matter how white and delicate the hand that decorates their brows."

"Its not lovely ladies nor dashing strangers," the semitic man said, "its the marriage ceremony that disfigures our foreheads."

Fairchild grunted. Then he chuckled again. "There'd sure be a decline in population if a man were twins and had to stand around and watch himself making love."

"How about women," asked Mrs Wiseman.

"Oh well, there wouldn't be so much of them in sight. And anyway, its your backside that's ridiculous, that gives you away, you know."

Mrs Maurier made an indistinguishable shrill sound. Mark Frost said: "But population need not suffer. Someone would invent a mechanical contrivance to do the work."

"Well, well, Mark! That's an idea. You should copyright it at once, get Ted yonder to make you one, and have Major Ayers to exploit it. Yes sir, that's the trick," Fairchild continued, "an instrument, a small one they could carry in their vanity cases, eh?"

"Mr Fairchild!"

"But not too small," he added and Mrs Wiseman said Dawson commandingly.

"No," the semitic man said judicially, "that'll never be necessary. It'll take more than ridicule to make unpopular a form of conduct of such long usage and proven worth."

"Yes, I guess so," Fairchild agreed. "There'll always be somebody who will prefer the old way. Some hidebound reactionary, you know," he added. "Reactionary," he repeated, pleased with the term. "I hope so, anyway. I for one will always vote for the old way (and we'll always put things to a vote, in this country. That's the only general pastime we have, now that practically everybody is a christian, and all the Indians are dead). Yes sir, I'll always vote for the old orthodox way: what was good enough for my fathers is good enough for me. Hey, Talliaferro? And I bet——"

"Shut up, Dawson," Mrs Wiseman said again, "I want to talk some."

"——bet we'd all vote for it, too——"

"Mister Fairchild!"

"Chopin," Mrs Wiseman interrupted. "Really, Dorothy,

I'm disappointed in you." She shrugged again, flashing her hands. Mrs Maurier said with relief:

"How much Chopin has meant to me in my sorrows——" she looked about in a tragic confiding astonishment "——no one will ever know."

"Surely," agreed Mrs Wiseman, "he always does." She turned to Miss Jameson. "Just think how much better Dawson would have done you than God did. With all deference to Mrs Maurier, so many people find comfort in Chopin. Its like having a pain that aspirin will cure, you know. I could have forgiven you even Verdi, but Chopin! Chopin," she repeated, then with happy inspiration: "Snow rotting under a dead moon."

Mark Frost sat staring at his hands on his lap, beneath the edge of the table, moving his lips slightly. Fairchild said:

"What music do you like, Eva?"

"Oh—De Bussy, George Gershwin, Berlioz perhaps—— why not?"

"Berlioz," repeated Miss Jameson mimicking the other's tone: "Swedenborg on a French holiday." Mark Frost stared at his hands on his lap, moving his lips slightly.

"Forget your notebook, Mark?" Fairchild asked quizzically.

"Its very sad," the semitic man said. "Man gets along quite well until that unhappy day on which someone else discovers him thinking. After that, God help him: he doesn't dare leave home without a notebook. Its very sad."

"Mark's not such an accomplished buccaneer as you and Dawson," his sister answered quickly. "At least he requires a notebook."

"My dear girl," the semitic man murmured in his lazy voice. "You flatter yourself."

"So do I," Fairchild said. "I always——"

"Which?" the semitic man asked. "Yourself, or me?"

"What?" said Fairchild, staring at him.

"Nothing. Excuse me: you were saying——?"

"I was saying that I always carry my portfolio with me because its the only comfortable thing I ever found to sit on."

* * * * *

Talk, talk, talk: the utter and heartbreaking stupidity of words. It seemed endless, as though it might go on forever.

Ideas, thoughts, become mere sounds to be bandied about until they were dead.

Noon was oppressive as a hand, as the ceaseless blow of a brass hand: a brass blow neither struck nor withheld; brass rushing wings that would not pass. The deck blistered with it, the rail was too hot to touch and the patches of shadow about the deck were heavy and heatsoaked as sodden blankets. The water was an unbearable glitter, the forest was a bronze wall cast at a fearful heat and not yet cooled, and no breeze was anywhere under the world's heaven.

But the unbearable hiatus of noon passed at last, and the soundless brazen wings rushed westward. The deck was deserted as it had been on that first afternoon when he had caught her in midflight like a damp swallow, a swallow hard and passionate with flight; and it was as though he yet saw upon the deck the wet and simple prints of her naked feet, and he seemed to feel about him like an odor, that young hard graveness of hers. No wonder she was gone out of it; she, who here was as a flame among stale ashes, a little tanned flame; who gone, was as a pipe blown thinly and far away, as a remembered surf on a rocky coast at dawn . . . ay ay strangle your heart o israfel winged with loneliness feathered bitter with pride

*   *   *   *   *

Dust spun from their feet, swirling sluggish and lazy in the brooding dreadful noon. Beside them always and always those eternal bearded trees, bearded and brooding, older and stiller than eternity. The road ran on like a hypnotism: a dull and endless progression from which there was no escape.

After a while he missed her from her position at his shoulder and he stopped and looked back. She was kneeling beside the foul ditch. He watched stupidly, then he suddenly realized what she was about and he ran back to her, grasping her by the shoulders. "Here, you cant do that! That stuff is poison: you cant drink it!"

"I cant help it! I've got to have some water, I've got to!" She strained against his hands. "Please, David. Just one mouthful. Please, David. Please David."

He got his hands under her arms, but his feet slid in the rank sloping grass and he went up to his knees in thick reluctant water. She twisted in his hands. "Please, Oh please! Just enough to wet my mouth. Look at my mouth." She raised her face: her broad pale lips were parched, rough. "Please, David."

But he held her. "Put your feet in it, like mine. That'll help some," he said through his own dry harsh throat. "Here, let me take off your shoes."

She sat whimpering like a dog while he removed her slippers. Then she slid her legs into the water and moaned with partial relief. The sunlight was beginning to slant at last, slanting westward like a rushing of unheard golden wings across the sky, though the sombre twilight under the trees was unchanged—sombre and soundless, brooding, and filled with a vicious darting of invisible fire.

"I must have water," she said at last. "You'll have to find me some water, David."

"Yes." He climbed heavily out of the hot ooze, out of the mud and slime. He bent and slid his hands under her arms. "Get up. We must go on."

TWO OCLOCK.

Jenny yawned, frankly, then she did something to the front of her dress, drawing it away from her to peer down into her bosom. It seemed to be all right, and she settled her dress again with a preening motion, lifting her shoulders and smoothing it over her hips. She went upstairs and presently she saw them, sitting around like always. Mrs Maurier wasn't there.

She drifted over to the rail and laxed herself against it and stood there, placidly waiting until Mr Talliaferro became aware of her presence. "I was watching these things in the water," she said when he came to her like a tack to a magnet, volitionless and verbose.

"Where?" He also stared overside.

"That stuff there," she answered, looking forward to the group of chairs.

"Why, that's just refuse from the galley," Mr Talliaferro said with surprise.

"Is it? Its kind of funny looking. . . . There's some more of it down here a ways." Mr Talliaferro followed her, intrigued and curious. She stopped and glanced back over her shoulder and beyond him: Mr Talliaferro aped her but saw no living thing except Mark Frost on the edge of the group. The others were out of sight beyond the deckhouse. "Its farther on," Jenny said.

Further along she stopped again and again she looked forward. "Where?" Mr Talliaferro asked.

"Here." Jenny stared at the lake a moment. Then she examined the deck again. Mr Talliaferro was thoroughly puzzled now, even a trifle alarmed. "It was right here, that funny thing I saw. I guess its gone, though."

"What was it you saw?"

"Some kind of a funny thing," she answered with detachment. . . . "The sun is hot here." Jenny moved away and went to where an angle of the deckhouse wall formed a shallow niche. Mr Talliaferro followed her in amazement. Again Jenny peered around him, examining that part of the deck which was in sight and the immediate approaches to it; then she became utterly static beside him, and without moving at all she seemed to envelop him, giving him to think of himself surrounded enclosed by the sweet cloudy fire of her thighs, as young girls can.

Mr Talliaferro saw her as through a blonde mist. A lightness was moving down his members, a lightness so exquisite as to be almost unbearable, while above it all he listened to the dry interminable incoherence of his own voice. That unbearable lightness moved down his arms to his hands, and down his legs reaching his feet at last, and Mr Talliaferro fled.

Jenny looked after him. She sighed.

*   *   *   *   *

After a while the white dusty road left the swamp behind. It ran now through a country vaguely upland: sand and pines and a crisp thick undergrowth sunburnt and sibilant.

"We're out of it at last," she called back to him. Her pace quickened and she called over her shoulder: "It cant be much further now. Come on, lets run a while." He shouted to her, but she trotted on, drawing away from him. He followed her splotched flashing legs at a slower pace, steadily losing distance.

Her legs twinkled on ahead in the shimmering forgotten road. Heat wavered and shimmered above the road and the sky was a metallic intolerable bowl and the tall pines in the windless afternoon exuded a thin exhilarating odor of resin and heat, casting sparse patches of shade upon the shimmering endless ribbon of the road. Lizards scuttled in the dust before them, hissing abruptly amid the dusty brittle undergrowth beside the road. The road went on and on, endless and shimmering ahead of them. He called to her again, but she trotted on, unheeding.

Without faltering in her pace she turned and ran from the road, and when he reached her she leaned against a tree, panting. "I ran too much," she gasped through her pale open mouth. "I feel funny—all gone. Better hold me up," she said, staring at him. "No: let me lie down." She slumped against him. "My heart's going too fast. Feel how its going." He felt her heart leaping against his hand. "Its too fast, isn't it? What'll I do now?" she asked soberly. "Do something quick, David," she told him, staring at him, and he lowered her awkwardly and knelt beside her and drew her upper body across his legs, supporting her head. She closed her eyes against the implacable sky, but opened them immediately and struggled to rise. "No, no: I mustn't stay here. I want to get up again. Help me up."

He did so, and had to hold her on her feet. "I must go on," she repeated. "Make me go on, David. I dont want to die here. Make me go on, I tell you." Her face was flushed: he could see blood pumping in her throat, and holding her so he knew sharp and utter terror. "What must I do?" she was saying. "You ought to know. Dont you know what to do? I'm sick, I tell you. They've given me hydrophobia or something." She closed her eyes and all her muscles relaxed at once and she slipped to the ground and he knelt again beside her in terror and despair. "Raise my head a little," she muttered and he sat and again drew her across his legs and raised her head against his breast, smoothing her damp hair from her forehead. "That's right." She opened her eyes. "Cheer up, David. . . . I told you once about looking at me like that." Then she closed her eyes again.

Three Oclock.

"If we were only afloat," Mrs Maurier moaned for the twelfth time. "They cant be further than Mandeville: I know they cant. What will Henry say to me!"

"Why dont they start her up and try to get off again?" Fairchild asked. "Maybe the sand has settled or something by now," he added vaguely.

"The Captain says they cant, that we'll have to wait for the tug. They sent for a tug yesterday, and it hasn't come yet," she added in a sort of stubborn astonishment. She rose and went to the rail and stared up the lake toward Mandeville.

"You wouldn't think it 'ud take a tug to pull us off," Fairchild remarked. "She aint such a big boat, you know. Seems like any sort of a boat would pull us off. I've seen little launches hauling bigger boats than this around. And a river tug can haul six or eight of these steel barges, upstream, too."

Mrs Maurier returned hopefully. "It really doesn't seem necessary to have a tug to move this yacht, does it? You'd think that sailors could think of some thing, some way, something with ropes and things," she added, also vaguely.

"What would they stand on while they pulled the ropes?" Mark Frost wanted to know. "They couldn't pull from the shore. That isn't the way we want to go."

"They might row out in the tender and anchor," the semitic man offered as his mite.

"Why, yes," Mrs Maurier agreed, brightening. "If they could just anchor the tender securely, they might . . . if there were something to pull the rope with. The men themselves. . . . Do you suppose the sailors themselves could move a boat like this by hand?"

"I've seen a single river tug not much bigger than a ford hauling a whole string of loaded steel barges up the river," Fairchild repeated. He sat and stared from one to another of his companions and a strange light came into his eyes. "Say," he said suddenly, "I bet that if all of us were to. . . ."

The semitic man and Mark Frost groaned in simultaneous alarm, and Pete sitting on the outskirt of the group rose hastily and unostentatiously and headed for the companionway. He ducked into his room and stood listening. Yes, they were

really going to try it. He could hear Fairchild's burly voice calling for all the men, and also one or two voices raised in protest; and above all of them the voice of the old woman in an
indistinguishable senseless excitement. Jesus Christ Pete whispered, clutching his hat.

People descending the stairs alarmed him and he sprang
behind the open door. It was Fairchild and the fat jew, but
they passed his door and entered the room next to his, from
which he heard immediately sounds of activity that culminated
in a thin concussion of glass and glass.

"My God, man——" the fat jew's voice——"what have you
done? Do you really think we can move this boat?"

"Naw. I just want to stir 'em up a little. Life's getting altogether too tame on this boat: nothing's happened at all today.
I did it principally to see Talliaferro and Mark Frost sweat
some." Fairchild laughed. His laughter died into chuckles,
heavily. "But I have seen a little river tug no bigger than a ford
hauling a st——"

"Good Lord," the other man said again. "Finish your drink.
O immaculate cherubim," he said, going on down the passage.
Fairchild followed. Pete heard their feet on the stairs, then
crossing the deck, and he returned to the port.

Yes sir, they were going to try it, sure as hell. They were
now embarking in the tender: he could hear them, thumping
and banging around and talking; a thin shriek of momentary
alarm. Women, too (Damn to hell, I bet Jenny's with 'em,
Pete whispered to himself). And somebody that didn't want
to go at all.

Voices without; alarums and excursions, etc:

Come on, Mark, you've got to go: all the men will be needed,
hey, Mrs Maurier?
Yes indeed; indeed yes. All the men must help.
Sure: all you brave strong men have got to go.
I'm a poet, not an oarsman. I cant——
So is Eva: look at her. She's going.
Shelley could row a boat.
Yes, and remember what happened to him, too.
I'm going to keep you all from drowning Jenny. That's—
(Damn to hell, Pete whispered) why I'm going.

Aw, come on, Mark; earn your board and keep.

Ooo, hold the boat still, Dawson.

Come on, come on. Say, where's Pete?

Pete!

Pete! (Feet on the deck)

Pete! Oh, Pete! (At the companionway)

Pete! (Jesus Christ, Pete whispered, making no sound)

Never mind, Eva. We've got a boatload now. If anybody else comes, they'll have to walk.

There's somebody missing yet. Who is it?

Ah, we've got enough. Come on.

But somebody aint here. I dont guess he fell overboard while we were not looking, do you?

Oh, come on and lets go. Shove off, you Talliaferro (A scream) Look out, there: catch her! Y'all right, Jenny? Lets go, then. Careful now.

Ooooooo!

"Damn to hell, she's with 'em," Pete whispered again, trying to see through the port. More thumping, and presently the tender came jerkily and lethargically into sight, loaded to the gunwales like a nigger excursion. Yes, Jenny was in it, and Mrs Wiseman and five men, including Mr Talliaferro. Mrs Maurier leaned over the rail above Pete's head, waving her handkerchief and shrieking at them as the tender drew uncertainly away, trailing a rope behind it. Almost everyone had an oar: the small boat bristled with oars beating the water vainly, so that it resembled a tarantula with palsy and no kneejoints. But they finally began to get the knack of it and gradually the boat began to assume something like a definite direction. As Pete watched it there came again feet on the stairs, and a voice said guardedly:

"Ed."

An indistinguishable response from the Captain's room and the voice added mysteriously: "Come up on deck a minute." Then the footsteps withdrew, accompanied.

*   *   *   *   *

The tender evinced a maddening inclination to progress in any fashion save that for which she was built. Fairchild turned his head and glanced comprehensively about his small congested island enclosed with an unrhythmic clashing of blades.

The oars clashed against each other, jabbing and scuttering at the tortured water until the tender resembled an ancient stiffjointed horse in a state of mad unreasoning alarm.

"We've got too many rowers," Fairchild decided. Mark Frost drew in his oar immediately, striking the semitic man across the knuckles with it. "No, no: not you," Fairchild said. "Julius, you quit: you aint doing any good, anyhow: you're the one that's holding us back. Gordon, and Mark, and Talliaferro and me——"

"I want to row," Mrs Wiseman said. "Let me have Julius' oar. Ernest will have to help Jenny watch the rope."

"Take mine," Mark Frost offered quickly, extending his oar and clashing it against someone else's. The boat rocked alarmingly. Jenny squealed. "Look out," Fairchild exclaimed. "Do you want to have us all in the water? Julius, pass your oar along——that's it. Now, you folks sit still back there. Dammit, Mark, if you hit anybody else with that thing we'll throw you out. Shelley could swim, too, you know."

Mrs Wiseman got fixed at last with her oar, and at last the tender became comparatively docile. Jenny and Mr Talliaferro sat in the stern, paying out the line. "Now," Fairchild glanced about at his crew and gave the command: "Lets go."

"Give way, all," Mrs Wiseman corrected with inspiration. They dipped their oars anew. Mark Frost drew his oar in once more, clashing it against Gordon's.

"Let me get my handkerchief," he said. "My hands are tender."

"That's what I want, too," Mrs Wiseman decided. "Gimme yours, Ernest."

Mark Frost released his oar and it lept quickly overboard. "Catch that paddle!" Fairchild shouted. Mr Talliaferro and Mrs Wiseman both reached for it and Gordon and the semitic man trimmed the boat at the ultimate instant. It became stable presently and Jenny closed her mouth upon her soundless scream. The oar swam away and stopped just beyond reach, rising and falling on the faint swells. "We'll have to row over and get it," Mrs Wiseman said. So they did, but just before they reached it the oar swam on again, slowly, maddeningly. The rowers clashed and churned. Mr Talliaferro sat in taut diffident alarm.

"I really think," he said, "we'd better return to the yacht. The ladies, you know."

But they didn't heed him. "Now, Ernest," Mrs Wiseman directed sharply, "reach out and grab it."

But it eluded them again and Fairchild said: "Lets let the damn thing go. We've got enough left to row with, anyway." But at that moment the oar, rocking sedately, swung slowly around and swam docilely up alongside. "Grab it, grab it!" Mrs Wiseman cried. "I really think——" Mr Talliaferro offered again. Mark Frost grabbed it and it came meekly and unresistingly out of the water. "I've got it," he said, and as he spoke it lept viciously at him and struck him on the mouth. Then it became docile again.

They got started again, finally; and after a few false attempts they acquired a vague sort of rhythm; though Mark Frost, favoring his hands, caught a crab at every stroke for a while, liberally wetting Jenny and Mr Talliaferro where they sat tensely in the stern. Jenny's eyes were quite round and her mouth was a small red O: a continuous soundless squeal. Mr Talliaferro's expression was that of a haggard anticipatory alarm. He said again: "I really think——"

"I suspect we had better try to go another way," the semitic man suggested without emphasis from the bow, "or we'll be aground ourselves."

They all scuttered their oars upon the water, craning their necks. The shore was only a few yards away and immediately, as though they had heard the semitic man speak, needles of fire assailed the crew with fierce joy. They bent again to their oars, flapping their spare frantic hands about their heads, and after a few minutes of violent commotion the tender acquiesced and crept slowly and terrifically seaward again. But their presence was now known, the original scouting party was reinforced, and offing could not help them.

"I really think," Mr Talliaferro said, "for the ladies' sake, that we'd better return."

"So do I," Mark Frost abetted quickly.

"Dont lose your nerve, Mark," Mrs Wiseman told him. "Just a little more and we can take a nice long boatride this afternoon."

"Sure," Fairchild said. "We've come too far to quit now."

"I've had enough boat riding in the last half hour to do me a long time," the poet answered. "Lets go back. How about it, you fellows back there? How about it, Jenny? Dont you want to go back?"

Jenny answered "Yes Sir" in a small frightened voice, clutching the seat with both hands. Her green dress was splotched and stained with water from Mark Frost's oar. Mrs Wiseman released one hand and patted Jenny's knee.

"Shut up, Mark. Jenny's all right. Aren't you, darling? It'll be such a good joke if we really were to get the boat afloat. Look sharp, Ernest. Isn't that rope almost tight?"

It was nearly taut, sliding away into the water in a lovely slender arc and rising again to the bow of the yacht. Mrs Maurier stood at the rail, waving her handkerchief at intervals. On the further rail sat three people in attitudes studiedly casual: the Captain, the helmsman and the deckhand.

"Now," Fairchild said, "lets all get started at the same time. Talliaferro, you keep the rope straight; and Julius——" he glanced over his shoulder, sweating, marshalling his crew. "Durn that shore," he exclaimed in an annoyed tone, "there it is again." They were nearly ashore a second time. Commotion, and more sweat and a virulent invisible fire; and after a while the tender acquiesced reluctantly and again they attained the necessary offing.

"Give way, all!" Mrs Wiseman cried. They dug their oars anew.

"Mine hurts my hands," Mark Frost complained. "Is it moving, Ernest?"

The tender was off the yacht's quarter: the bows of the yacht pointed inshore of them. Mr Talliaferro rose cautiously and knelt on the seat, putting his hand on Jenny's shoulder to steady himself.

"Not yet," he replied.

"Pull all you know, men," Fairchild panted, releasing one hand momentarily and batting it madly about his face. The crew pulled and sweated, goaded unto madness with invisible needles of fire, clashing one another's fingers with their oars, and presently the tender acquired a motion reminiscent of the rocking horses of childhood.

"The rope's becoming loose," Mr Talliaferro called in a warning tone.

"Pull," Fairchild urged them, gritting his teeth. Mark Frost groaned dismally, releasing one hand to fan it across his face.

"Its still loose," Mr Talliaferro said after a time.

"She must be moving, then," Fairchild panted.

"Maybe its because we aren't singing," Mrs Wiseman suggested presently, resting on her oar: "Dont you know any deepsea chanteys, Dawson?"

"Let Julius sing: he aint doing anything," Fairchild answered. "Pull, you devils!"

Mr Talliaferro shrieked suddenly: "She's moving! She's moving!"

They all ceased rowing to stare at the yacht. Sure enough, she was swinging slowly across their stern. "She's moving!" Mr Talliaferro screamed again, waving his arms. Mrs Maurier responded from the deck of the yacht with her handkerchief; beyond her the three men sat motionless and casual. "Why dont the fools start the engine?" Fairchild gasped. "Pull!" he roared.

They dipped their oars with new life, flailing the water like mad. The yacht swung slowly: soon she was pointing her prow seaward of them, and continued to swing slowly around. "She's coming off, she's coming off," Mr Talliaferro chanted in a thin falsetto, his voice breaking, fairly dancing up and down. Mrs Maurier was shrieking also, waving her handkerchief. "She's coming off," Mr Talliaferro chanted, standing erect and clutching Jenny's shoulder. "Pull, pull!"

"All together," Fairchild gasped, and the crew repeated it, flailing the water. The yacht was almost broadside to them now. "She's coming," Mr Talliaferro screamed in an ecstasy. "She's co——"

A faint abrupt shock. The tender stopped immediately. They saw the sweet blonde entirety of Jenny's legs and the pink seat of her ribboned undergarment, as with a wild despairing cry Mr Talliaferro plunged overboard, taking Jenny with him, and vanished beneath the waves.

All but his buttocks, that is. They didn't quite vanish, and presently all of Mr Talliaferro rose in eighteen inches of water and stared in shocked amazement at the branch of a tree directly over his head. Jenny yet prone in the water, was an indistinguishable turmoil of blondeness and green crêpe and fright. She rose, slipped and fell again. The semitic man stepped into the water and picked her up bodily and set her in the boat where she sat and gazed at them with abject beseeching eyes, strangling.

Only Mrs Wiseman had presence of mind to thump her between the shoulders, and after a dreadful trancelike interval during which they sat clutching their oars and gazing at her while she beseeched them with her eyes, she caught her breath, wailing. Mrs Wiseman mothered her, holding her draggled unhappy wetness while Jenny wept dreadfully. "He——he sc— scared me so bad," Jenny gasped after a time, shuddering and crying again, utterly abject, making no effort to hide her face.

Mrs Wiseman made meaningless comforting sounds, holding Jenny in her arms. She borrowed a handkerchief and wiped Jenny's streaming face. Mr Talliaferro stood in the lake and dripped disconsolately, peering his harried face across Mrs Wiseman's shoulder. The others sat motionless, holding their oars.

Jenny raised her little wet hands futilely about her face. Then she remarked her hand and she held it before her face, gazing at it. On it was a thinly spreading crimson stain that grew as she watched it, and Jenny wept again with utter and hopeless misery.

"Oh, you've cut your poor hand! Dawson," Mrs Wiseman said, "you are the most consummate idiot unleashed. You take us right back to that yacht. Dont try to row back: we'll never get there. Cant you pull us back with the rope?"

They could, and Mrs Wiseman helped Jenny into the bow and the men took their places again. Mr Talliaferro flitted about in the water with his despairing face. "Jump in," Fairchild told him. "We aint going to maroon you."

They pulled the tender back to the yacht with chastened expedition. Mrs Maurier met them at the rail, shrieking with alarm and astonishment. Pete was beside her. The sailors had discretely vanished.

"What is it? What is it?" Mrs Maurier chanted, mooning her round alarmed face above them. They brought the tender alongside and held it steady while Mrs Wiseman helped Jenny across thwarts and to the rail. Mr Talliaferro flitted about in a harried distraction, but Jenny shrank from him. "You scared me so bad," she repeated.

Pete leaned over the rail, reaching his hands, while Mr Talliaferro flitted about his victim. The tender rocked, scraping against the hull of the yacht. Pete caught Jenny's hands.

"Hold the boat still, you old fool," he told Mr Talliaferro fiercely.

*   *   *   *   *

His legs were completely numb beneath her weight, but he would not move. He swished the broken branch about her. At intervals he whipped it across his own back. Her face wasn't so flushed and he laid his hand again above her heart.

At his touch she opened her eyes. "Hello, David. I dreamed about water. . . . Where've you been all these years?" She closed her eyes again. "I feel better," she said after a while. "What time is it?" He looked at the sun and guessed. "We must go on," she said. "Help me up."

She sat up and a million red ants scurried through the arteries of his legs. She stood, dizzy and swaying, holding to him. "Gee, I'm not worth a damn. Next time you elope you'd better make her stand a physical examination, David. Do you hear? . . . But we must go on: come on, make me walk." She took a few unsteady steps and clutched him again, closing her eyes. "Jesus H, if I ever get out of this alive. . . . " She stopped again. "What must we do?" she asked.

"I'll carry you a ways," he said.

"Can you? I mean, aren't you too tired?"

"I'll carry you a ways, until we get somewhere," he repeated.

"I guess you'll have to. . . . But if you were me, I'd leave you flat. That's what I'd do."

He squatted before her and reached back and slid his hands under her knees, and as he straightened up she leaned forward onto his back and put her arms around his neck, clasping the broken branch against his chest. He rose slowly, hitching her legs further around his hips as the constriction of her skirt lessened. "You're awful nice to me, David," she murmured against his neck, limp upon his back.

*   *   *   *   *

Mrs Wiseman washed and bound Jenny's hand, interestingly; then she scrubbed Jenny's little soft wormlike fingers and cleaned her fingernails while Jenny, naked, dried rosily in the cabined air. Underthings were not difficult, and stockings were simple also. But Jenny's feet were short rather than small, and shoes were a problem. Though Jenny insisted that Mrs Wiseman's shoes were quite comfortable.

But she was clothed at last, and Mrs Wiseman gathered up the two wet garments gingerly, and went to lean her hip against the bunk. The dress Jenny now wore belonged to the girl Patricia, and Jenny stood before the mirror, bulging it divinely, examining herself in the mirror, smoothing the dress over her hips with a slow preening motion.

I had no idea there was that much difference between them the other thought. Its far more exciting than a bathing suit. . . . "Jenny," she said, "I think——really, I—— Darling, you simply must not go where men can see you, like that. For Mrs Maurier's sake, you know: she's having enough trouble as it is, without any rioting."

"Dont it look all right? It feels all right," Jenny answered, trying to see as much of herself as possible in a twelve inch glass.

"I dont doubt it. You must be able to feel every stitch in it. But we'll have to get something else for you to wear. Slip it off, darling."

Jenny obeyed. "It feels all right to me," she repeated. "It dont feel funny."

"It doesn't look funny, not at all. On the contrary, in fact. That's the trouble with it," the other answered delving busily in her bag.

"I always thought I had the kind of figure that you could wear anything," Jenny persisted, holding the dress regretfully in her hands.

"You have," the other told her, "exactly that kind. Terribly like that. Simple and inevitable. Devastating."

"Devastating," Jenny repeated with interest. . . . "There was a kind of funny little man at Mandeville that day. . . ." She turned to the mirror again, trying to see as much of herself as possible. "I been told I have a figure like Dorothy Mackaill's, only not too thin. . . . I think a little flesh is becoming to a girl, dont you?"

"Devastating," the other agreed again. She rose and held a dark colored dress between her hands. You'll look worse than ever in this . . . terrible as a young widow. . . ." She went to Jenny and held the dress against her, contemplative, then still holding the dress between her hands she put her arms around Jenny. "A little flesh is worse than a little dynamite, Jenny," she said soberly, looking at Jenny with her dark sad eyes. . . . "Does your hand still hurt?"

"Its all right, now," Jenny craned her neck, peering downward along her flank. "Its a little long, aint it?"

"Yours will dry soon." She raised Jenny's face and kissed her on the mouth. "Slip it on, and we'll hang your things in the sun."

Four Oclock.

He strode on in the dust, along the endless shimmering road, between pines like fixed explosions on the afternoon. The afternoon was an endless unbearable brightness. Their shapeless merged shadow moved on; two steps more and he would tread upon it and through it as he did the sparse shadows of pines, but it moved on just ahead of him between the faded forgotten ruts, keeping its distance effortlessly in the uneven dust. The dust was fine as powder and unbroken; only an occasional hoofprint, a fading ghost of a forgotten passage. Above, the metallic implacable sky resting upon his bowed neck and her lax, damp weight upon his back and her cheek against his neck, rubbing monotonously against it. Thin fire darted upon him constantly. He strode on.

The dusty road swam into his vision, passed beneath his feet and so behind like an endless ribbon. He found that his mouth was open, drooling though no moisture came, and his gums took a thin dry texture like cigarette paper. He closed his mouth, trying to moisten his gums.

Trees without tops passed him, marched up abreast of him, topless, and fell behind; the rank roadside grass approaching, became monstrous and separate blade from blade: lizards hissed in it sibilantly, ere it faded behind him. Thin unseen fire darted upon him, but he didn't even feel it, for in his shoulders and arms there was no longer any sensation at all save that of her lax weight upon his back and the brass sky resting against his neck and her moist cheek rubbing against his neck monotonously. He found that his mouth was open again, and he closed it.

"That's far enough," she said presently rousing. "Let me down." Their merged shadow blended at intervals with the shadows of the tall topless trees, but beyond the shadow of the trees their blended shadow appeared again, two paces ahead of him. And the road went on ahead of him shimmering and blistered and whiter than salt. "Put me down, David," she repeated.

"No," he said between his dry rough teeth, above the remote imperturbable tramping of his heart. "Not tired." His heart made a remote sound. Each beat seemed to be somewhere in his head, just behind his eyes; each beat was a red tide that temporarily obscured his vision. But it always ebbed, then another dull surge blinded him for a moment. But remote, like a tramping of soldiers in red uniforms stepping endlessly across the door of a room where he was, where he crouched trying to look out the door. It was a dull heavy sound, like a steamer's engines, and he found that he was thinking of water, of a blue monotony of seas. It was a red sound, just back of his eyes.

The road came on, an endless blistering ribbon between worn ruts where nothing had passed for a long time. The sea makes a swishing sound in your ears. Regular. Swish. Swish. Not against your eyes, though. Not against the backs of your eyes. The shadow came out of a blotch of larger shadows cast by trees that had no tops. Two steps more. No, three steps now. Three steps. Getting to be afternoon, getting to be later than it was once. Three steps, then. All right. Man walks on his hind legs; a man can take three steps, a monkey can take three steps, but there is water in a monkey's cage, in a pan. Three steps. All right. One. Two. Three. Gone. Gone. Gone. Its a red sound. Not behind your eyes. Sea. See. Sea. See. You're in a cave, you're in a cave of dark sound, the sound of the sea is outside the cave. Sea. See. See. See. Not when they keep stepping in front of the door.

There was another sound in his ears, now: a faint annoying sound, and the weight on his back was shifting of its own volition, thrusting him downward toward the blistering blanched dust in which he walked, took three steps a man can take three steps and he staggered, trying to shift his numb arms and get a new grip. His mouth was open again and when he tried to shut it, it made a dry hissing sound. One. Two. Three. One. Two. Three.

"Let me down, I tell you," she repeated, thrusting herself backward. "Look! there's a signboard. Let me down, I tell you. I can walk now." She thrust herself away from him, twisting her legs from his grasp and forcing him down, and he stumbled and went to his knees. Her feet touched the ground and still astride of his body she braced herself and held him partially up by his shoulders. He stopped at last, on all fours like a beast, his head hanging between his shoulders; and kneeling beside him in the dust she slid her hand under his forehead to lessen the tension on his neck and raised her eyes to the signboard. Mandeville. 14 miles, and a crude finger pointing in the direction from which they had come. The front of her dress was damp, blotched darkly with his sweat.

* * * * *

After the women had hovered Jenny's draggled helplessness below decks, Fairchild removed his hat and mopped his face, looking about upon his fatuous Frankenstein with a sort of childlike astonishment. Then his gaze came to rest on Mr Talliaferro's haggard damp despair, and he laughed and laughed.

"Laugh you may," the semitic man told him, "but much more of this sort of humor and you'll be doing your laughing ashore. I think now, Mr Talliaferro'd start an active protest with you as its immediate object, that we'd all be inclined to support him." Mr Talliaferro dripped forlornly: an utter hopeless dejection. The semitic man looked at him, then he too looked about at the others and upon the now peaceful scene of their recent activities. "One certainly pays a price for art," he murmured. "One really does."

"Talliaferro's the only one who has suffered any actual damage," Fairchild protested. "And I'm just going to buy him off now. Come on, Talliaferro, we can fix you up."

"That wont be sufficient," the semitic man said, still ominous. "The rest of us have been assailed enough in our vanities to rise from principle."

"Well then, if I have to, I'll buy you all off," Fairchild answered. He led the way toward the stairs. But he halted again and looked back at them. "Where's Gordon?" he asked. Nobody knew. "Well, no matter. He knows where to come." He went on. "After all," he said, "there are compensations for art, aint there?"

The semitic man admitted that there were. "Though," he added, "its a high price to pay for whiskey." He descended in his turn. "Yes, we really must get something out of it. We spend enough time on it and suffer enough moral and mental turmoil because of it."

"Sure," Fairchild agreed. "The ones that produce it get a lot from it. They get the boon of keeping their time pretty well filled. And that's a whole lot to expect in this world," he said profoundly, fumbling at his door. It opened at last and he said: "Oh, here you are. Say, you just missed it."

Major Ayers, his neglected tumbler beside him and clutching a book, came up for air when they entered, festooned yet with a kind of affable bewilderment. "Missed what?" he repeated.

They all began to tell him about it at once, producing Mr Talliaferro as evidence from where he lurked unhappily in their midst, for Major Ayers' inspection and commiseration; and still telling him about it they found seats while Fairchild again assumed the ritual of his hidden suitcase. Major Ayers already had the chair, but the semitic man attempted the book anyway. "What have you got there?" he asked.

Major Ayers' hearty bewilderment descended upon him again. "I was passing the time," he explained quickly. He stared at the book. "Its quite strange," he said. Then he added: "I mean, the way. . . . The way they get their books up nowadays. I like the way they get their books up. Jolly, with colors, y'know. But I——" he considered a moment. "I rather lost the habit of reading at Sandhurst," he explained in a burst of confidence. "And then, on active service constantly. . . ."

"War is bad," the semitic man agreed. "What were you reading?"

"I rather lost the habit of reading at Sandhurst," Major Ayers explained again. He raised the book again, and as he read he mouthed the words over to himself. The semitic man, intrigued, read over Major Ayers' shoulder. Major Ayers looked up again. "It seems to have something to do with syphilis," he explained apologetically.

"Maybe its just constipation," Fairchild suggested. Fairchild opened a fresh bottle. "Somebody'll have to dig up some more glasses. Mark, see if you can slip back to the kitchen and get one or two more. Lets see the book," he said reaching his hand.

The semitic man forestalled him. "You go ahead and give us some whiskey. I'd rather forget my grief that way, just now."

"But look," Fairchild insisted. The other fended him off.

"Give us some whiskey, I tell you," he repeated. "Here's Mark with the glasses. What we need, in this country, is protection from artists. They even want to annoy us with one another's stuff."

"Go ahead," Fairchild replied equably, "have your joke. You know my opinion of smartness." He passed glasses among them.

"He cant mean that," the semitic man said. "Just because the New Republic gives him hell——"

"But the Dial once bought a story from him," Mark Frost said with hollow envy.

"And what a fate for a man in all the lusty pride of his Ohio valley masculinity: immolation in a home for Old Young Ladies of either sex. . . . That atmosphere was too rare for him. Eh, Dawson?"

Fairchild laughed. "Well, I aint much of an Alpinist. What do you want to be in there for, Mark?"

"It would suit Mark exactly, that vague polite fury of the intellect in which they function. What I cant see is how Mark has managed to stay out of it. . . . But then, if you'll look close enough, you'll find an occasional grain of truth in these remarks which Mark and I make and which you consider merely smart. But you utter things not quite clever enough to be untrue, and while we are marvelling at your profundity, you lose courage and flatly contradict yourself the next moment. Why, only that tactless and wellmeaning God of yours alone knows. Why anyone should worry enough about the temporary meaning or construction of words to contradict himself

consciously or to feel annoyed when he has done it unconsciously, is beyond me."

"Well, it is a kind of sterility—Words," Fairchild admitted. "You begin to substitute words for things and deeds, like
the withered cuckold husband that took the Decameron to
bed with him everynight, and pretty soon the thing or the
deed becomes just a kind of shadow of a certain sound you
make by shaping your mouth a certain way. But you have a
confusion, too. I dont claim that words have life in themselves. But words brought into a happy conjunction produce
something that lives, just as soil and climate and an acorn in
proper conjunction will produce a tree. Words are like acorns,
you know. Every one of 'em wont make a tree, but if you just
have enough of 'em, you're bound to get a tree sooner or later."

"If you just talk long enough, you're bound to say the right
thing some day. Is that what you mean?" the semitic man
asked.

"Let me show you what I mean." Fairchild reached again
for the book.

"For heaven's sake," the other exclaimed, "let us have this
one drink in peace. We'll admit your contention, if that's what
you want. Isn't that what you say, Major?"

"No: really," Major Ayers protested. "I enjoyed the book.
Though I rather lost the habit of reading at Sa——"

"I like the book myself," Mark Frost said. "My only criticism is that it got published."

"You cant avoid that," Fairchild told him. "Its inevitable: it
happens to everyone who will take the risk of writing down a
thousand coherent consecutive words."

"And sooner than that," the semitic man added, "if you've
murdered your husband, or won a golf championship."

"Yes," Fairchild agreed. "Cold print. Your stuff looks so different in cold print. It lends a kind of impersonal authority,
even to stupidity."

"That's backward," the other said. "Stupidity lends a kind
of impersonal authority even to cold print."

Fairchild stared at him. "Say, what did you just tell me
about contradicting myself?"

"I can afford to," the semitic man answered. "I never authen-
ticate mine." He drained his glass. "But as for art and artists,

I prefer artists: I dont even object to paying my pro rata to feed them, so long as I am not compelled to listen to them."

"It seems to me," Fairchild rejoined, "that you spend a lot of time listening to them, for a man who professes to dislike it and who dont have to."

"That's because I'd have to listen to somebody—an artist or a shoeclerk. And the artist is more entertaining because he knows less about what he is trying to do. . . . And besides, I talk a little, myself. I wonder what became of Gordon?"

FIVE OCLOCK.

Evening came sad as horns among the trees. The road had dropped downward again into the swamp where amid rank impenetrable jungle dark streams wallowed aimless and obscene, and against the hidden flame of the west huge trees brooded bearded and ancient as prophets out of Genesis. David lay at full length at the roadside. He had lain there a long time, but at last he sat up and looked about for her.

She stood beside a cypress, up to her knees in thick water, her arms crossed against the tree trunk and her face hidden in her arms, utterly motionless. About them, a moist green twilight filled with unseen fire.

"David?" Her voice was muffled by her arms, and after it, there was no sound in this fecund timeless twilight of trees. He sat beside the road, and presently she spoke again. "Its a mess, David. I didn't know it was going to be like this." He made a harsh awkward sound, as though it were someone else's voice he was trying to speak with. "Hush," she said: "Its my fault: I got you into this. I'm sorry, David."

These trees were thicker, huger, more ancient than any yet, amid the brooding twilight of their beards. "What must we do now, David?" After a while she raised her head and looked at him and repeated the question.

He answered slowly: "Whatever you want to do."

She said: "Come here, David." And he got slowly to his feet and stepped into the black, thick water and went to her, and for a while she looked at him soberly, without moving. Then she turned from the tree and came nearer, and they stood in the foul black water, embracing. Suddenly she clasped him fiercely. "Cant you do something about it? Cant you make it different? Must it be like this?"

"What do you want me to do?" he asked slowly in that voice which was not his. She loosed her arms and he repeated as though prompted: "You do whatever you want to."

"I'm damn sorry, David, for getting you into this. Josh is right: I'm just a fool." She writhed her body beneath her dress, whimpering again. "They hurt me so damn bad," she moaned.

"We must get out of this," he said. "You tell me what you want to do."

"It will be all right, if I do what I think is best?" she asked quickly, staring at him with her grave opaque eyes. "You swear it will?"

"Yes," he answered with utter weariness. "You do whatever you want to."

She became at once passive, a submissive docility in his embrace. But he stood holding her loosely, not even looking at her. As abruptly her passiveness faded and she said: "You're all right, David. I'd like to do something for you. Pay you back, some way." She looked at him again and found that he was looking at her. "David! why, David! Dont feel that way about it!" But he continued to look at her with his quiet utter yearning. "David, I'm sorry, sorry, sorry. What can I do about it? Tell me: I'll do it. Anything, just anything."

"Its all right," he said.

"But it isn't. I want to make it up to you, some way, for getting you into this." His head was averted: he seemed to be listening. Then the sound came again across the afternoon, among the patriarchal trees—a faint, fretful sound.

"There's a boat. We are close to the lake."

"Yes," she agreed. "I heard it a while ago. I think its coming in near here." She moved and he released her. She listened again, touching his shoulder lightly. "Yes, its coming this way. You'd better take your shirt again. Turn your back, please, David."

Six Oclock.

"Sure, I know where your boat is——seen her hove to when I come along. In mighty shaller water, too. Aint more'n three miles down the lake," the man told them, setting a galvanized pail of water on the edge of the veranda. His house stood on piles driven into the moist earth at the edge of the jungle. Before it a dark broad stream was seemingly without any movement at all between rigid palisades of trees.

The man stood on the veranda and watched her while she poured dippersful of heavenly water on her head. The water ran through her hair and dripped down her face, sopping her dress while the man stood and watched her. His blue collarless shirt was fastened at the throat by a brass collarbutton, his sweatstained suspenders drew his faded cotton trousers snugly over his paunch. His loose jowls moved rhythmically and he spat brownly upon the earth at their feet, barely averting his head.

"You folks been wandering around in the swamp all day?" he asked, staring at her with his pale heavy eyes, roving his gaze slowly up her muddy stockings and her stained dress. "What you want to go back fer, now? Feller got enough, huh?" He spat again, and made a heavy sound of disparagement and disgust. "Aint no such thing as enough. Git a real man, next time." He looked at David and asked him a question, using an unprintable verb.

Anger, automatic and despite his weariness, fired him slowly, but she forestalled him. "Lets get back to the boat, first," she said to him. She looked at the man again, meeting his pale heavy stare. "How much?" she asked briskly.

"Five dollars." He glanced at David again. "In advance."

David put his hand to his waist. "With my money," she said quickly, watching him as he dug into his watchpocket and extracted a single bill, neatly folded. "No, no: with mine," she insisted peremptorily, staying his hand. "Where's mine?" she asked, and he drew from his trousers her crumpled mass of notes and she took it.

The man accepted the bill and spat again. He descended heavily from the porch and led the way down to the water where his launch was moored. They got in and he cast off, thrust the boat away from the shore and bent heavily over the engine. "Yes, sir, that's the way with these town fellers. No guts. Next time, come over to this side and git you a real man. I kin git off most any day. And I wont be honing to git home by sundown, neither," he added looking back over his shoulder.

"Shut your mouth," she told him sharply. "Make him shut up, David."

The man paused, staring at her with his pale sleepy eyes. "Now, look a here," he began heavily.

"Shut up and start your flivver," she repeated. "You've got your money, so lets go if we are going."

"Well, that's all right, too. I like 'em to have a little git-up-and-git to 'em." He stared at her with his lazy dropping eyes, chewing rhythmically. Then he called her a name.

David rose from his seat, but she restrained him with one hand, and cursed the man fluently and glibly. "Now, get started," she finished. "If he opens his head again, David, just knock him right out of the boat."

The man snarled his yellow teeth at them, then he bent again over the engine. Its fretful clamor rose soon and the boat slid away, circling, cutting the black motionless water. Ahead, soon, there was a glint of space beyond the trees, a glint of water; and soon they had passed from the bronze nave of the river out onto the lake beneath the rushing soundless wings of sunset and a dying glory of day under the cooling brass bowl of the sky.

*   *   *   *   *

The Nausikaa was more like a rosy gull than ever in the sunset, squatting sedately upon the darkening indigo of the water, against the black metallic trees. The man shut off his fussy engine and the launch slid up alongside and the man caught the rail and held his boat stationary, watching her muddy legs as she climbed aboard the yacht.

No one was in sight. They stood at the rail, looking down upon his thick backside while he spun the flywheel again. The engine caught at last and the launch circled away from the yacht and headed again into the sunset while the fussy engine desecrated the calm of water and sky and trees. Soon the boat was only a speck in the fading path of the sunset.

"David?" she said, when it had gone. She turned and put her firm tanned hand on his breast and he turned his head also and looked at her with his beastlike longing.

"Its all right," he said after a time. She put her arms around him again, sexless and hard, drawing his cheek down to her sober moist kiss. This time he did not move his head.

"I'm sorry, David."

"Its all right," he repeated. She laid her hands flat on his chest and he released her. For a time they gazed at each other. Then she left him and crossed the deck and descended the companionway without looking back, and so left him and the evening from which the sun had gone suddenly and into which night was as suddenly come, and across which the fretful thin sound of the launch came yet faintly along the dreaming water, beneath the tarnished sky where stars were already pricking like a hushed magical blooming of flowers.

* * * * *

She found the others at dinner in the saloon, since what breeze there was was still offshore and the saloon was screened. They greeted her with various surprise, but she ignored them, and her aunt's round suffused face, going haughtily to her place.

"Patricia," Mrs Maurier said at last, "where have you been?"

"Walking," the niece snapped. In her hand she carried a small crumpled mass and she put this on the table, separating the notes and smoothing them into three flat sheaves.

"Patricia," said Mrs Maurier again.

"I owe you six dollars," she told Miss Jameson, putting one of the sheaves beside her plate. "You only had a dollar," she informed Mrs Wiseman, passing a single note across the table to her. "I'll pay you the rest of yours when we get home," she told her aunt, reaching across Mr Talliaferro's shoulder with the third sheaf. She met her aunt's apoplectic face again. "I brought your steward back, too. So you haven't got anything to kick about."

"Patricia," Mrs Maurier said. She said, chokingly: "Mr Gordon: didn't he come back with you?"

"He wasn't with me. What would I want to take him along for? I already had one man."

Mrs Maurier's face became dreadful, and as the blood died swooning in her heart she had again that brief vision of floating inert buttocks, later to wash ashore with that inopportune and terrible implacability of the drowned. "Patricia,—" she said dreadfully.

"Oh, haul in your sheet," the niece interrupted wearily. "You're jibing. Gosh, I'm hungry." She sat down and met her brother's cold gaze. "And you too, Josh," she added, taking a piece of bread.

The nephew glanced briefly at his aunt's wrung face. "You ought to beat hell out of her," he said calmly, going on with his dinner.

NINE OCLOCK.

"But I saw him about four oclock," Fairchild argued. "He was in the boat with us. Didn't you see him, Major? but that's so: you were not with us. You saw him, Mark, didn't you?"

"He was in the boat when we started. I remember that. But I dont remember seeing him after Ernest fell out."

"Well I do. I know I saw him on deck right after we got back. But I cant remember seeing him in the boat after Jenny and Talliaferro. . . . Ah, he's all right, though. He'll show up soon. He aint the sort to get drowned."

"Dont be too sure of that," Major Ayers said. "There are no other women missing, you know."

Fairchild laughed his burly appreciative laugh. Then he met Major Ayers' glassy solemn stare, and ceased. Then he laughed once more, somewhat after the manner of one feeling his way into a dark room, and ceased again, turning on Major Ayers his trustful baffled expression. Major Ayers said:

"This place to which these young people went today——"
"Mandeville," the semitic man supplied. "——what sort of a place is it?" They told him. "Ah yes. They have facilities for this sort of thing, eh?"

"Well, not more so than usual," the semitic man answered and Fairchild said, still watching Major Ayers with a sort of cautious bafflement:

"Not any more than you can carry along with you. We Americans always carry our own facilities with us. Its living high tension, gogetting lives like we do in this country, you see."

Major Ayers glared at him politely. "Somewhat like the continent," he suggested after a time.

"Not exactly," the semitic man said. "In America you often

find an H in caste." Fairchild and Major Ayers stared at the semitic man.

"As well as a cast in chaste," Mark Frost put in. Fairchild and Major Ayers now stared at him, watching him while he lit a fresh cigarette from the stub of his present one and left his chair and went to lie at full length on the deck.

"Why not?" the semitic man took him up. "Love itself is stone blind."

"It has to be," Mark Frost answered. Major Ayers stared from one to the other for a while. He said:

"This Mandeville, now. It is a convention, eh? A local convention?"

"Convention?" Fairchild repeated.

"I mean, like our Gretna Green. You ask a lady there, and immediately there is an understanding: saves unnecessary explanations and all that."

"I thought Gretna Green was a place where they used to go to get marriage licenses in a hurry," Fairchild said suspiciously.

"It was, once," Major Ayers agreed. "But during the great fire all the registrars' and parsons' homes were destroyed. And in those days communication was so poor that word didn't get about until a fortnight or so later. In the meantime quite a few young people had gone there in all sincerity, y'know, and were forced to return the next day without benefit of clergy. Of course the young ladies durst not tell until matters were remedied, which, during those unsettled times, might be anytime up to a month or so. But by that time, of course, the police had heard of it——London police always hear of things in time, you know."

"And so, when you go to Gretna Green now, you get a policeman," the semitic man said.

"You've Yokohama in mind," Major Ayers answered as gravely. "Of course, they are native policemen," he added.

"Like whitebait," the semitic man suggested.

"Or sardines," Mark Frost corrected.

"Or sardines," Major Ayers agreed suavely. He sucked violently at his cold pipe while Fairchild stared at him with intrigued bewilderment. "But this young lady, the one who popped off with the steward. And came back the same day. . . . Is this customary with your young girls? I ask for information," he added quickly. "Our young girls dont do that, y'know; with us, only decayed countesses do that—cut off to Italy with chauffeurs and second footmen. And they never return before nightfall. But our young girls. . . ."

"Art," the semitic man explained succinctly. Mark Frost elaborated:

"In Europe, being an artist is a form of behavior; in America, its an excuse for a form of behavior."

"Yes. But, I say——" Major Ayers mused again. He sucked violently at his cold pipe. Then: "She's not the one who did that tweaky little book, is she? The syphilis book?"

"No. That was Julius' sister: the one named Eva," Fairchild said. "This one that eloped and then came back aint an artist at all. Its just the artistic atmosphere of this boat, I guess."

"Oh," said Major Ayers. "Strange," he remarked. He rose and thumped his pipe against his palm. Then he blew through the stem and put it in his pocket. "I think I shall go below and have a whiskey. Who'll come along?"

"I guess I wont, right now," Fairchild decided. The semitic man said Later on. Major Ayers turned to the prone poet.

"And you, old thing?"

"Bring it up to us," Mark Frost suggested. But Fairchild vetoed this. The semitic man supported him and Major Ayers departed.

"I wish I had a drink," Mark Frost said.

"Go down and have one, then," Fairchild told him. The poet groaned.

The semitic man lighted his cigar again and Fairchild spoke from his tentative bewilderment.

"That was interesting, about Gretna Green, wasn't it? I didn't know about that. Never read it anywhere, I mean. But I guess there's lots of grand things in the annals of all people that never get into the history books." The semitic man chuckled. Fairchild tried to see his face in the obscurity. Then he said:

"Englishmen are funny folks: always kidding you at the wrong time. Things just on the verge of improbability, and just when you have made up your mind to take it one way, you find they meant it the other." He mused a while in the darkness. "It was kind of nice, wasn't it? Young people, young men and girls caught in that strange hushed magic of sex and the mystery of intimate clothing and functions and all, and of lying side by side in the darkness, telling each other things——that's the charm of virginity: telling each other things: virginity dont make any difference as far as the body's concerned—young people running away together in a flurry of secrecy and caution and desire, and getting there to find. . . ." Again he turned his kind baffled face toward his friend. He continued after a while.

"Of course the girls would be persuaded, after they'd come that far, wouldn't they? You know—strange surroundings, a strange room like an island in an uncharted sea full of monsters like landlords and strangers and such, the sheer business of caring for the body and getting it from place to place, feeding it and caring for it; and your young man thwarted and lustful and probably fearful that you'd change your mind and back out altogether, and a strange room all secret and locked and far away from familiar things and you young and soft and nice to look at and knowing it, too. . . . Of course they'd be persuaded.

"And of course, when they got back home, they wouldn't tell, not until another parson turned up and everything was all regular again. And maybe not then. Maybe they'd whisper it to a friend someday, after they'd been married long enough to prefer talking to other women to talking to their husbands, while they were discussing the things women talk about. But they wouldn't tell the young unmarried ones, though. And if they, even a year later, ever got wind of another one being seen going there or coming away. . . . They are such practical creatures, you know: only men hold to conventions for moral reasons."

"Or from habit," the semitic man added.

"Yes," Fairchild agreed. . . . "I wonder what became of Gordon."

*　*　*　*　*

Jenny remarked his legs, tweeded. How can he stand them heavy clothes in this weather she thought with placid wonder, calling him soundlessly as he passed. His purposeful stride faltered and he came over beside her.

"Enjoying the evening, eh?" he suggested affably, glaring

down at her in the darkness. Inside her borrowed clothes she was rife as whipped cream, blonde and perishable as an expensive pastry.

"Kind of," she admitted. Major Ayers leaned his elbows on the rail.

"I was on my way below," he told her.

"Yes, sir," Jenny agreed, passive in the darkness, like an erotic lightning bug projecting that sense of himself surrounded enclosed by the sweet cloudy fire of her thighs, as young girls will. Major Ayers looked down at her vague soft head. Then he jerked his head sharply, glaring about.

"Enjoying the evening, eh?" he asked again.

"Yes, sir," Jenny repeated. She bloomed like a cloying heavy flower. Major Ayers moved restively. Again he jerked his head as if he had heard his name spoken. Then he looked at Jenny again.

"Are you a native of New Orleans?"

"Yes, sir. Esplanade."

"I beg pardon?"

"Esplanade. Where I live in New Orleans," she explained. "Its a street," she added after a while.

"Oh," Major Ayers murmured. . . . "Do you like living there?"

"I dont know. I always lived there." After a time she added: "Its not far."

"Not far, eh?"

"No, sir." She stood motionless beside him and for the third time Major Ayers turned his head quickly, as though someone were trying to attract his attention.

"I was on my way below . . ." he repeated. Jenny waited a while. Then she murmured:

"Its a fine night for courting."

"Courting?" Major Ayers repeated.

"With dates." Major Ayers stared down upon her hushed-soft hair. "When boys come to see you," she explained. "When you go out with boys."

"Go out with boys," Major Ayers repeated. "To Mandeville, perhaps?"

"Sometimes," she agreed. "I been there."

"Do you go often?"

"Why . . . sometimes," she repeated.

"With boys, eh? With men, too, hey?"

"Yes, sir," Jenny answered with mild surprise. "I dont guess anybody would just go there by herself."

Major Ayers calculated heavily. Jenny stood docile and rife, projecting her little enticing aura, doing her best. "I say," he said presently, "suppose we pop down there tomorrow, you and I?"

"Tomorrow?" Jenny repeated with soft astonishment.

"Tonight, then," he amended. "What d'ye say?"

"Tonight   ? Can we get there tonight? Its kind of late, aint it? How'll we get there?"

"Like those people who went this morning did. There's a tram or a bus, isn't there? Or a train at the nearest village?"

"I dont know. They come back in a boat."

"Oh, a boat." Major Ayers considered a moment. "Well, no matter: we'll wait until tomorrow, then. We'll go tomorrow, eh?"

"Yes, sir," Jenny repeated tirelessly, passive and rife, projecting her emanation. Once more Major Ayers looked about him. Then he moved his hand from the rail and as Jenny, seeing the movement, turned to him with a slow unreluctance, he chucked her under the chin.

"Right, then," he said briskly, moving away. "Tomorrow it is." Jenny gazed after him in passive astonishment and he turned and came back to her, and giving her an intimate inviting glare he chucked her again under her soft surprised chin. Then he departed permanently. Jenny gazed after his tweed-clad dissolving shape, watching him out of sight. He sure is a foreigner she told herself. She sighed.

* * * * *

The water lapped at the hull with little sounds, little hushed sounds like boneless hands, and she leaned again over the rail, gazing downward into the dark water.

He would be refined as anybody she mused to herself. Being her brother. . . . More refined, because she had been away all day with that waiter in the dining room. . . . But maybe the waiter was refined too. Except I never found many boys that . . . I guess her aunt must have jumped on her. I wonder what she'd done when they come back, if we'd got the boat

started and went away . . . and now that redheaded man
and . . . She says he's drowned. . . .

Jenny gazed into the dark water, thinking of death, of being
helpless in that terrible suffocating resilience of water, feeling again that utter and dreadful helplessness of terror and
fear. So when Mr Talliaferro was suddenly and silently beside
her, touching her, she recognised him by instinct; and feeling again her world become unstable and shifting beneath
her, feeling all familiar solid things fall away from under her,
seeing familiar faces and objects arc swooping away from her
as she plunged from glaring sunlight through a timeless interval into Fear like a green lambence straying to receive her,
she was stark and tranced. But at last she could move again,
screaming.

"You scared me so bad," she gasped piteously, shrinking
away from him. She turned and ran, ran toward light, toward
the security of walls.

* * * * *

The room was dark: no sound within it, and after the dim
spaciousness of the deck it seemed close and hot. But here
were comfortable walls, and Jenny snapped on the light and
entered, entered into an atmosphere of familiarity:—a vague
ghost of the scent she liked and with which she had happily
been impregnated when she came aboard and which had not
yet completely died away, and the thin sharp odor of lilacs
which she had come to associate with Mrs Wiseman and
which lingered also in the room; and the other's clothing,
and her own comb on the dressing table and the bright metal
cylinder of her lip stick beside it.

Jenny looked at her face in the mirror for a while, then she
removed a garment and returned to gaze at her stainless pink-
and-whiteness, ineffable, unmarred by any thought at all.
Then she removed the rest of her clothes, and again before the
glass she passed her comb through the drowsing miniature
Golconda of her hair. Then she got her naked body placidly
into bed, as was her habit since three nights. But she didn't
turn out the light.

She lay in her berth, gazing up at the smug glare of light
upon the painted unbroken sweep of ceiling. Time passed
while she lay rosy and motionless, measured away by the small

boneless hands of water lapping against the hull beyond the port; and she could hear feet also, and people moving about and making sounds. She didn't know what it was she wanted, except it was something. So she lay on her back rosy and quiet beneath the unshaded glare of the inadequate light, until after a while she thought that maybe she was going to cry. Maybe that was it, so she lay naked and rosy and passive on her back, waiting to begin.

She could still hear people moving about: voices and feet, and she kept waiting for that first taste of crying that comes into your throat before you really get started: that feeling like there were two little salty canals just under your ears when you feel sorry for yourself, and that other kind of feeling you have at the base of your nose. Only my nose dont get red when I cry she thought in a placid imminent misery of sadness and meaningless despair, waiting passive and still and without dread for it to begin. But before it began, Mrs Wiseman entered the room.

She came over to Jenny and Jenny looked up and saw the other's dark small head, like a deer's head, against the light, and that dark intent way the other had of looking at her, and presently Mrs Wiseman said:

"What is it, Jenny? What's the matter?"

But she had forgotten what it was, almost: all she could remember now was that there had been something, but now that the other had come, Jenny couldn't hardly remember that she had forgotten anything even, and so she just lay and looked up at the other's dark slender head against the unshaded light.

"Poor child, you have had a hard day of it, haven't you?" She put her hand on Jenny's brow, smoothing back the fine hushed gold of Jenny's hair, stroking her hand along Jenny's cheek. Jenny lay quiet under the hand, drowsing her eyes like a stroked kitten, and then she knew she could cry all right, whenever she wanted to. Only it was almost as much fun just lying here and knowing you could whenever you got ready to, as the crying would be. She opened her blue ineffable eyes.

"Do you suppose he's really drownded?" she asked. Mrs Wiseman's hand stroked Jenny's cheek, pushing her hair upward and away from her brow.

"I dont know, darling," she answered soberly. "He's a luck-less man. And anything may happen to a luckless man. But dont you think about that anymore. Do you hear?" She leaned her face down to Jenny's. "Do you hear?" she said again.

*   *   *   *   *

"No," Fairchild said, "he aint the sort to get drowned. Some people just aint the sort. . . . I wonder," he broke off suddenly and gazed at his companions. "Say, do you suppose he went off because he thought that girl was gone for good?"

"Drowned himself for love?" Mark Frost said. "Not in this day and time. People suicide because of money and disease: not for love."

"I dont know about that," Fairchild objected. "They used to die because of love. And human nature dont change. Its actions achieve different results under different conditions, but human nature dont change."

"Mark is right," the semitic man said. "People in the old books died of heartbreak, also, which was probably merely some ailment that any modern surgeon or veterinarian could cure out of hand. But people do not die of love. That's the reason love and death in conjunction have such an undying appeal in books: they are never very closely associated any-where else.

"But as for a broken heart in this day of general literacy and facilities for disseminating the printed word——" he made a sound of disparagement. "Lucky he who believes his heart is broken: he can immediately write a book and so take revenge (what is more terrible than the knowledge that the man you just knocked down discovered a coin in the gutter while get-ting up?) on him or her who damaged his or her ventricles. Besides cleaning up in the movies and the magazines. No, no," he repeated. "You dont commit suicide when you are disap-pointed in love. You write a book."

"I dont know about that," repeated Fairchild stubbornly. "People will do anything. But I suppose it takes a fool to be-lieve that and act on that principle." Beyond the eastern hori-zon was a rumor of pale silver, pallid and chill and faint, and they sat for a while in silence, thinking of love and death. The red eye of a cigarette twelve inches from the deck: this was Mark Frost. Fairchild broke the silence.

"The way she went off with Da—with the steward. It was kind of nice, wasn't it? And came back. No excuses, no explanation——'think no evil' you know. That's what these postwar young folks have taught us. Only old people like Julius and me would ever see evil in what people, young folks, do. But then, I guess folks growing up into the manner of looking at life that we inherited, would find evil in anything where inclination wasn't subservient to duty. We were taught to believe that duty was infallible, or it wouldn't be duty, and if it were just unpleasant enough, you got a mark in heaven, sure. . . . But maybe it aint so different, taken one generation by another. Most of our sins are vicarious, anyhow. I guess when you are young you have too much fun just being, to sin very much. But its kind of nice, being young in this generation."

"Surely. We all think that when our arteries begin to harden," the semitic man rejoined. "Not only are most of our sins vicarious, but most of our pleasures are, too. Look at our books, our stage, our movies. Who supports 'em? Not the young folks. They'd rather walk around or just sit and hold each other's hands."

"Its a substitute," Fairchild said. "Dont you see?"

"Substitute for what? When you are young, and in love yesterday and out today and in again tomorrow, do you know anything about love? Is it anything to you except a rather dreadful mixture of jealousy and thwarted desires and interference with that man's world which, after all we all prefer, and nagging and maybe a little pleasure like a drug? Its not the women you sleep with that you remember, you know."

"No, thank God," Fairchild said. The other continued:

"Its the old problem of the aristocracy over and over: a natural envy of that minority which is at liberty to commit all the sins which the majority cannot stop earning a living long enough to commit." He lit his cigar again. "Young people always shape their lives as the preceding generation requires of them. I dont mean exactly that they go to church when they are told to, for instance, because their elders expect it of them—though God only knows what other reason they could possibly have for going to church as it is conducted nowadays, with a warden to patrol the building in urban localities and in the rural districts squads of K.K.K.'s beating the surrounding copses and all those traditional retreats that in the olden days enabled the church to produce a soul for everyone it saved. But youth in general lives unquestioningly according to the arbitrary precepts of its elders.

"For instance, a generation ago higher education was not considered so essential, and young people grew up at home into the convention that the thing to do was to get married at twenty one and go to work immediately, regardless of one's equipment or inclination or aptitude. But now they grow up into the convention that youth, that being under thirty years of age, is a protracted sophomore course without lectures, in which one must spend one's entire time dressed like a caricature, drinking homemade booze and pawing at the opposite sex in the intervals of being arrested by traffic policemen. A few years ago a socalled commercial artist (groan, damn you) named John Held began to caricature college life, cloistered and otherwise, in the magazines: ever since then college life, cloistered and otherwise, has been busy caricaturing John Held. It is expected of them by their elders, you see. And the young people humor them: young people are far more tolerant of the inexplicable and dangerous vagaries of their elders than the elders ever were or ever will be of the natural and harmless foibles of their children. . . . But perhaps they both enjoy it."

"I dont know," Fairchild said. "Not even the old folks would like to be surrounded by people making such a drama of existence. And the young folks wouldn't like it, either: young people have so many other things to do, you know. I think. . . ." His voice ceased, died into darkness and a faint lapping sound of water. The moon had swum up out of the east again, that waning moon of decay, worn and affable and cold. It was a magic on the water, a magic of pallid and fleshless things. The red eye of Mark Frost's cigarette arced slow and lateral in his invisible hand, returned to its station twelve inches above the deck, and glowed and faded like a pulse. "You see," Fairchild added like an apology, "I believe in young love in the spring, and things like that. I guess I'm a hopeless sentimentalist."

The semitic man grunted. Mark Frost said: "Virtue through abjectness and falsification: immolation of insincerity." Fairchild ignored him, wrapped in this dream of his own.

"When youth goes out of you, you get out of it. Out of life, I mean. Up to that time you just live; after that, you are aware of living: living becomes a conscious process. Like thinking does in time, you know. You become conscious of thinking, and then you start right off to think in words. And first thing you know, you dont have thoughts in your mind at all: you just have words in it. But when you are young, you just be. Then you reach a stage in which you do. Then a stage in which you think, and last of all, where you just remember. Or try to."

"Sex and death," said Mark Frost sepulchrally, arcing the red eye of his cigarette. "A blank wall on which sex casts a shadow; the shadow is life."

The semitic man grunted again, immersed in one of his rare periods of uncommunicativeness. The moon climbed higher, the pallid unmuscled belly of the moon, and the Nausikaa dreamed like a silver gull on the dark restless water.

"I dont know," Fairchild said again. "I never found anything shadowy about life, people. Least of all, about my own doings. But it may be that there are shadowy people in the world, people to whom life is a kind of antic shadow. But people like that make no impression on me at all, I cant seem to get them at all. But this may be because I have a kind of firm belief that life is all right." Mark Frost had cast away his final cigarette and was now a long prone shadow. The semitic man was motionless also, holding his dead cigar.

"I was spending the summer with my grandfather, in Indiana. In the country. I was a boy then, and it was a kind of family reunion, with aunts and cousins that hadn't seen each other in years. Children, too, all sizes.

"There was a girl that I remember, about my age, I reckon. She had blue eyes and a lot of long prim golden curls. This girl, Jenny, must have looked like her, when she was about twelve. I didn't know the other children very well, and besides I was used to furnishing my own diversion anyway; so I just kind of hung around and watched them doing the things children do. I didn't know how to go about getting acquainted with them. I'd seen how the other newcomers would do it, and I'd kind of plan to myself how I'd go about it: what I'd say when I went up to them. . . ." He ceased and mused for a time in a kind of hushed surprise. "Just like Talliaferro," he said at last, quietly. "I hadn't thought of that before." He mused for a time. Then he spoke again.

"I was kind of like a dog going among strange dogs. Scared, kind of, but acting haughty and aloof. But I watched them. The way she made up to them, for instance. The day after she came, she was the leader, always telling them what to do next. She had blue dresses, mostly." Mark Frost snored in the silence. The Nausikaa dreamed like a gull on the dark water.

"This was before the day of water works and sewage systems in country homes, and this one had the usual outhouse. It was down a path from the house. In the late summer there were tall burdocks on either side of the path, taller than a twelve-year-old boy by late August. The outhouse was a small square frame box kind of a thing, with a partition separating the men from the women inside.

"It was a hot day, in the middle of the afternoon. The others were down in the orchard, under the trees. From where I had been, in a big tree in the yard, I could see them, and the girls' colored dresses in the shade; and when I climbed down from the tree and went across the back yard and through the gate and along the path toward the privy I could still see them occasionally through gaps in the burdocks. They were sitting around in the shade, playing some game, or maybe just talking. I went on down the path and went inside, and when I turned to shut the door to the men's side, I looked back. And I saw her blue dress kind of shining, coming along the path between the tall weeds. I couldn't tell if she had seen me or not, but I knew that if I went back I'd have to pass her, and I was ashamed to do this. It would have been different if I'd already been there and was coming away: or it seemed to me that it would have. Boys are that way, you know," he added uncertainly, turning his bewilderment again toward his friend. The other grunted. Mark Frost snored in his shadow.

"So I shut the door quick and stood right quiet, and soon I heard her enter the other side. I didn't know yet if she'd seen me, but I was going to stay quiet as I could until she went away. I just had to do that, it seemed to me.

"Children are much more psychic than adults. More of a child's life goes on in its mind than people believe. A child can distill the whole gamut of experiences it has never actually known, into a single instant. Anthropology explains a little of it. But not much, because the gaps in human knowledge that have to be bridged by speculation are too large. The first thing a child is taught is the infallibility and necessity of precept; and by the time a child is old enough to add anything to our knowledge of the mind, it has forgotten. The soul sheds every year, like snakes do, I believe. You cant recall the emotions you felt last year: you remember only that an emotion was associated with some physical fact of experience. But all you have of it now is a kind of ghost of happiness and a vague and meaningless regret. Experience: why should we be expected to learn wisdom from experience? Muscles only remember, and it takes repetition and repetition to teach a muscle anything. . . ."

Arcturus, Orion swinging head downward by his knees; in the southern sky an electric lobster fading as the moon rose. Water lapped at the hull of the Nausikaa with little sounds.

"So I tiptoed across to the seat. It was hot in there, with the sun beating down on it: I could smell hot resin even above the smell of the place itself. In a corner of the ceiling there was a dirt dobber's nest—a hard lump of clay with holes in it stuck to the ceiling, and big green flies made a steady droning sound. I remember how hot it was in there, and that feeling places like that give you—a kind of letting down of the bars of pretence, you know; a kind of submerging of civilized strictures before the grand implacability of nature and the physical body. And I stood there, feeling this feeling, and the heat, and hearing the drone of those big flies, holding my breath and listening for a sound from beyond the partition. But there wasn't any sound from beyond it, so I put my head down through the seat. Do you know what I saw?"

Mark Frost snored. The moon, the pallid belly of the moon, inundating the world with a tarnished magic not of living things, laying her silver fleshless hand on the water, tipping with silver the little hands of water that whispered and lapped against the hull of the yacht. The semitic man clutched his dead cigar and he and Fairchild sat in the implacable laxing of muscles and softening tissue of their forty odd years, seeing two wide curious blue eyes into which an inverted surprise came clear as water, and long golden curls swinging downward above the ordure, and they sat in silence, remembering youth and love, and time and death.

Eleven Oclock.

Mark Frost had roused and with a ghostly epigram had taken himself off to bed. Later the semitic man rose and departed, leaving him with a cigar; and Fairchild sat with his stockinged feet on the rail, puffing at the unfamiliar weed. He could see the whole deck in the pallid moonlight, and presently he remarked someone sitting near the afterrail. How long this person had been there Fairchild could not have told, but he was there now, alone and quite motionless, and there was something about his attitude that unleashed Fairchild's curiosity, and at last he rose from his chair.

It was David, the steward. He sat on a coiled rope, holding something in his hands, between his knees. When Fairchild stopped beside him, David raised his head slowly into the moonlight and gazed at the older man, making no effort to conceal that which he held. Fairchild leaned nearer to see. It was a slipper, a single slipper cracked and stained with dried mud and disreputable, yet seeming still to hold in its mute shape something of that hard and sexless graveness of hers.

After a while David looked away, gazing again out across the dark water and its path of shifting silver, holding the slipper between his hands; and without speaking Fairchild turned and went quietly away.

The Fourth Day.

F AIRCHILD waked and lay for a while luxuriously on his back. After a time he turned onto his side to doze again, and when he turned he noticed the square of paper lying on the floor, as though it had been thrust under his door. He lay watching it for a while, then he came fully awake, and he rose and crossed the room and picked it up.

"Dear Mr Fairchild I am leaving the boat to day I have got a better job I have got 2 days comeing to me I will not clame it be cause I am leaveing the boat be fore the trip finished tell Mrs More I have got a better job ask her she will pay you $5 dollars of it you loned me yours truly

"David West"

He reread the note, brooding over it, then he folded it and put it in the pocket of his pajama jacket, and poured himself a drink. The semitic man in his berth snored, profound, defenseless on his back.

Fairchild sat again in his berth, his drink untasted beside him, and he unfolded the note and read it through again, remembering youth, thinking of age and slackening flesh like an old thin sorrow everywhere in the world.

EIGHT O'CLOCK.

"Now dont you worry at all," they reassured Mrs Maurier. "We can do just as we did yesterday: it will be more fun than ever, that way. Dorothy and I can open cans and warm things. We can get along just as well without a steward as with one, cant we, Dorothy?"

"It will be like a picnic," Miss Jameson agreed. "Of course, the men will have to help too," she added, looking at Pete with her pale humorless eyes.

Mrs Maurier submitted, dogging them with her moaning fatuousness while Mrs Wiseman and Miss Jameson and the niece opened cans and heated things, smearing dreadfully about the galley with grease and juices and blood from the niece's thumb; opening, at Mark Frost's instigation, a can labelled Beans, which turned out to be green string beans.

But they got coffee made at last, and breakfast was finally not very late. As they had said, it was like a picnic, though there were no ants, as the semitic man pointed out just before he was ejected from the kitchen.

"We'll open a can of them for you," his sister offered briskly. Besides, there was still plenty of grapefruit.

EIGHT THIRTY.

At breakfast:

Fairchild—But I saw him after we got back to the yacht. I know I did.

Mark—No, he wasn't in the boat when we came back: I remember now. I never saw him after we changed places, just after Jenny and Ernest fell out.

Julius—That's so. . . . Was he in the boat with us, at all? Does anybody remember seeing him in the boat at all?

Fairchild—Sure he was: dont you remember how Mark kept hitting him with his oar? I tell you I saw——

Mark—He was in the boat at first. But after Je——

Fairchild—Sure he was. Dont you remember seeing him after we got back, Eva?

Eva—I dont know. My back was toward all of you while we were rowing. And after Ernest threw Jenny out, I dont remember who was there and who wasn't.

Fairchild—Talliaferro was facing us. Didn't you see him, Talliaferro? And Jenny: Jenny ought to remember. Dont you remember seeing him, Jenny?

Mr Talliaferro—I was watching the rope, you know.

Fairchild—How about you, Jenny? Dont you remember?

Eva—Now dont you bother Jenny about it. How could she be expected to remember anything about it? How could anybody be expected to or want to remember anything about such an idiotic—idiotic——

Fairchild—Well, I do. Dont you all remember him going below with us, after we got back?

Mrs Maurier wrung her hands—Doesn't someone know anything about it? Its terrible. I dont know what to do: you people dont seem to realize what a position it puts me in, such a dreadful thing hanging over me. You people have nothing to lose, but I live here, I have a certain. . . . And now a thing like this—

Fairchild—Ah, he aint drowned. He'll turn up soon: you watch what I say.

The niece—And if he's drowned, we'll find him all right. The water isn't very deep between here and the shore.

(Her aunt gazed at her dreadfully.)

The nephew—Besides, a dead body always floats after forty eight hours. All we have to do is wait right here until tomorrow morning: chances are he'll be bumping alongside, ready to be hauled back on board.

(Mrs Maurier screamed. Her scream shuddered and died among her chins and she gazed about at her party in abject despair.)

Fairchild—Aw, he aint drowned. I tell you I saw——

The niece—Sure. Cheer up, Aunt Pat. We'll get him back, even if he is. Its not like losing him altogether, you know. If you send his body back, maybe his folks wont even claim your boat or anything.

Eva—Shut up, you children.

Fairchild—But I tell you I saw——

NINE OCLOCK.

Forward, Jenny, the niece, her brother come temporarily out of his scientific shell, and Pete stood in a group; Pete in his straw hat, the nephew with his lean young body, and the two girls in their little scanty dresses and awkward with a sort of terrible grace;—so flagrantly young they were that it served as a barrier between them and the others, causing even Mr Talliaferro to lurk nearby without the courage to join them.

"These young girls," Fairchild said. He watched the group, watched the niece and Jenny as they clung to the rail and swung aimlessly back and forth, pivoting on their heels in a sheer wantonness of young muscles. "They scare me," he admitted. "Not a possible or probable chastity, you know. Chastity aint. . . ."

"A bodiless illusion multiplied by lack of opportunity," Mark Frost said.

"Waat?" he asked, looking at the poet. "Well, maybe so." He resumed his own tenuous thought. "Maybe we all have different ideas of sex, like all races do. . . . Maybe us three sitting here are racially unrelated to each other, as regards sex. Like a Frenchman and an Anglo-Saxon and a Mongol, for instance."

"Sex," said the semitic man, "to an Italian is something like a firecracker at a children's party; to a Frenchman, a business the relaxation from which is making money; to an Englishman, a nuisance; to an American, a horserace. Now, which are you?"

Fairchild laughed. He watched the group forward a while. "Their strange sexless shapes, you know," he went on. "We, you and I, grew up expecting something beneath a woman's dress. Something satisfying in the way of breasts and hips and such. But now. . . . Do you remember the pictures you used to get in cigarettes, or that you saw in magazines in barber shops? Anna Held and Eva Tanguay with shapes like elegant parlor lamp chimneys? Where are they now? Now, on the street, what do you see? creatures with the uncomplex awkwardness of calves or colts, with two little knobs for breasts and indicated buttocks that, except for their soft look, might well belong to a boy of fifteen. Not satisfying anymore: just exciting. And monotonous. And mostly monotonous.

"Where," he continued, "are the soft bulging rabbit-like things women used to have inside their clothes? Gone, with the poor Indian and ten cent beer and cambric drawers. But still, they are kind of nice, these young girls: kind of like a thin monotonous flute music or something."

"Shrill and stupid," the semitic man agreed. He too gazed at the group forward for a time. "Who was the fool who said that our clothing, our customs in dress, does not affect the shape of our bodies and our behavior?"

"Not stupid," the other objected. "Women are never stupid. Their mental equipment is too sublimely sufficient to do what little directing their bodies require. And when your mentality is sufficient to your bodily needs, where there is such a perfect mating of capability and necessity, there cant be any stupidity. When women have more intelligence than that, they become nuisances sooner or later. All they need is enough intelligence to move and eat and observe the cardinal precautions of existence——"

"And recognise the current mode in time to standardize themselves," Mark Frost put in.

"Well, yes. And I dont object to that, either," Fairchild said. "As a purely lay brother to the human race, I mean. After all, they are merely articulated genital organs with a kind of aptitude for spending whatever money you have; so when they get themselves up to look exactly like all the other ones, you can give all your attention to their bodies."

"How about the exceptions?" Mark Frost asked. "The ones that dont paint or bob their hair?"

"Poor things," Fairchild answered and the semitic man said: "Perhaps there is a heaven, after all."

"You believe they have souls, then?" Fairchild asked.

"Certainly. If they are not born with them, its a poor creature indeed who cannot get one from some fool man by the time she's eleven years old."

"That's right," Fairchild agreed. He watched the group forward for a time. Then he rose. "I think I'll go over and hear what they're talking about."

* * * * *

Mrs Wiseman came up and borrowed a cigarette of Mark Frost, and they watched Fairchild's burly retreating back. The semitic man said: "There's a man of undoubted talent, despite his fumbling bewilderment in the presence of sophisticated emotions."

"Despite his lack of self assurance, you mean," Mark Frost corrected.

"No, it isn't that," Mrs Wiseman put in. "You mean the same thing that Julius does:—that, having been born an American and of a provincial middle western lower middle class family, he has inherited all the lower middle class's awe of Education with a capital E, an awe which the very fact of his own difficulty in getting to college and staying there, has increased."

"Yes," her brother agreed. "And the reaction which sheer accumulated years and human experience has brought about in him has swung him to the opposite extreme without destroying that ingrained awe or offering him anything to replace it with at all. His writing seems fumbling, not because life is unclear to him, but because of his innate humorless belief that, though it bewilder him at times, life at bottom is sound and admirable and fine; and because hovering over this American scene into which he has been thrust, the ghosts of the Emersons and Lowells and Greelys and other exemplifiers of Education with a capital E, who 'seated on chairs in handsomely carpeted parlors' and surrounded by an atmosphere of halfcalf and security, dominated American letters in its most healthy American phase, 'without heat or vulgarity,' simper yet in a sort of ubiquitous watchfulness. A sort of puerile bravado in flouting while he fears," he explained.

"But," his sister said, "for a man like Dawson there is no better American tradition than theirs—if he but knew it. They may have sat among their objects, transcribing their Greek and Latin and holding correspondences across the Atlantic, but they still found time to put out of their New England ports with the Word of God in one hand and a belaying pin in the other and all sails drawing aloft; and whatever they fell foul of was American. And, by God, it was American. And is yet."

"Yes," her brother agreed again. "But he lacks what they had at command among their shelves of discrete books and their dearth of heat and vulgarity:—a standard of literature that is international. No, not a standard, exactly: a belief, a conviction that his talent need not be restricted to delineating things which his conscious mind assures him are American reactions."

"Freedom?" suggested Mark Frost hollowly.

"No. No one needs freedom. We cannot bear it. He need only let himself go, let himself forget all this fetich of culture and education which his upbringing and the ghosts of those whom circumstance permitted to reside longer at colleges than himself, and whom despite himself he regards with awe, assure him that he lacks. For by getting himself and his own bewilderment and inhibitions out of the way and by describing, in a manner that even translation cannot injure (as Balzac did) American life as American life is, it will become eternal and timeless despite him. Life everywhere is the same, you know. Manners of living it may be different—are they not different between adjoining villages? family names, profits on a single field or orchard, work influences—but man's old compulsions, duty and inclination: the axis and the circumference of his squirrel cage, they do not change. Details do not matter, details only entertain us. And nothing that merely entertains us can matter because the things that entertain us are purely speculative: prospective pleasures which we probably will not achieve. The other things only surprise us. And he who has stood the surprise of birth, can stand anything."

TEN OCLOCK.

"Gabriel's pants," the nephew said, raising his head. "I've already told you once what I'm making, haven't I?"

He had repaired to his retreat in the lee of the wheelhouse, where he would be less liable to interruption. Or so he thought.

Jenny stood beside his chair and looked at him placidly. "I wasn't going to ask you again," she replied without rancor. "I just happened to be walking by here." Then she examined the visible deck space with a brief comprehensive glance. "This is a fine place for courting," she remarked.

"Is, huh?" the nephew said. "What's the matter with Pete?" His knife ceased and he raised his head again. Jenny answered something vaguely. She moved her head again and stood without exactly looking at him, placid and rife, giving him to think of himself surrounded enclosed by the sweet cloudy fire of her thighs, as young girls do. The nephew laid his pipe and his knife aside.

"Where'm I going to sit?" Jenny said, so he moved over in his canvas chair, making room, and she came with slow unreluctance and squirmed into the sagging chair. "Its a kind of tight fit," she remarked.

. . . . Presently the nephew raised his head. "You dont put much pep into your petting," he remarked. So Jenny placidly put more pep into it. . . . After a time the nephew raised his head and gazed out over the water. "Gabriel's pants," he murmured in a tone of hushed detachment, stroking his hand slowly over the placid points of Jenny's thighs, "Gabriel's pants" . . . . After a while he raised his head. "Say," he said abruptly, "where's Pete?"

"Back yonder, somewheres," Jenny answered. "I saw him just before you stopped me."

The nephew craned his neck, looking aft along the deck. Then he uncraned it. After a while he raised his head. "I guess that's enough," he said. He pushed at Jenny's blonde abandon. "Get up, now. I got my work to do. Beat it, now."

"Gimme time to," Jenny said placidly, struggling out of the chair. It was a kind of tight fit, but she stood erect finally, smoothing at her clothes. The nephew resumed his tools, and so after a while Jenny went away.

Eleven Oclock.

It was a thin volume bound in dark blue boards and a narrow orange arabesque of esoteric design unbroken across front and back near the top, and the title, in orange: 'Satyricon in Starlight'.

"Now, here," said Fairchild, flattening a page under his hand, his heavy hornrimmed spectacles riding his blobby benign face jauntily, "is the Major's syphilis poem. After all, poetry has accomplished something when it causes a man like the Major to mull over it for a while. Poets lack business judgment. Now, if I——"

"Perhaps that's what makes one a poet," the semitic man suggested. "Being able to sustain a fine obliviousness of the world and its compulsions."

"You're thinking of oyster fishermen," Mrs Wiseman said. "Being a successful poet is being just glittering and obscure and imminent enough in your public life to excuse whatever you might do privately."

"If I were a poet——" Fairchild attempted.

"That's right," the semitic man said. "Nowadays the gentle art has attained that state of perfection where you dont have to know anything about literature at all to be a poet; and the time is coming when you wont even have to write to be one. But that day hasn't quite arrived yet: you still have to write something occasionally; not very often, of course, but still occasionally. And if its obscure enough every one is satisfied and you have vindicated yourself and are immediately forgotten and are again at perfect liberty to dine with whoever will invite you."

"But, listen," repeated Fairchild. "If I were a poet, you know what I'd do? I'd——"

"You'd capture an unattached but ardent wealthy female. Or, lacking that, some other and more fortunate poet would divide a weekend or so with you: there seems to be a noblesse oblige among them," the other answered. "Gentlemen poets, that is," he added.

"No," said Fairchild, indefatigable. "I'd intersperse my book with photographs and art studies of ineffable morons in bathing suits or clutching imitation lace window curtains across their middles. That's what I'd do."

"That would damn it as Art," Mark Frost objected.

"You are confusing Art with Studio Life, Mark," Mrs Wiseman told him. She forestalled him and accepted a cigarette. "I'm all out, myself. Sorry. Thanks."

"Why not?" Mark Frost responded. "If studio life costs you enough, it becomes art. You've got to have a good reason to give to your people back home in Ohio or Indiana or somewhere."

"But everybody wasn't born in the Ohio valley, thank God," the semitic man said. Fairchild stared at him, kind and puzzled, a trifle belligerent. "I speak for those of us who read books instead of writing them," he explained. "Its bad enough to grow into the conviction after you reach the age of discretion that you are to spend the rest of your life writing books, but to have your very infancy darkened by the possibility that you may have to write the Great American Novel. . . ."

"Oh," Fairchild said. "Well, maybe you are like me: prefer a live poet to the writings of any man."

"Make it a dead poet, and I'll agree."

"Well. . . ." He settled his spectacles. "Listen to this:" Mark Frost groaned, rising, and departed. Fairchild read implacably:

" 'On rose and peach their droppings bled,
Love a sacrifice has lain,
Beneath his hand his mouth is slain,
Beneath his hand his mouth is dead——'

"No: wait." He skipped back up the page. Mrs Wiseman listened restively, her brother with his customary quizzical phlegm.

> " 'The Raven bleak and Philomel
> Amid the bleeding trees were fixed,
> His hoarse cry and hers were mixed
> And through the dark their droppings fell
>
> Upon the red erupted rose,
> Upon the broken branch of peach
> Blurred with scented mouths, that each
> To another sing, and close——' "

He read the entire poem through. "What do you make of it?" he asked.

"Mostly words," the semitic man answered promptly. "A sort of cocktail of words. I imagine you get quite a jolt from it, if your taste is educated to cocktails."

"Well, why not?" Mrs Wiseman said, with fierce protectiveness. "Only fools require ideas in verse."

"Perhaps so," her brother admitted. "But there's no nourishment in electricity, as you poets nowadays seem to believe."

"Well, what would you have them write about, then?" she demanded. "There's only one possible subject to write anything about. What is there worth the effort and despair of writing about, except love and death?"

"That's the feminine of it. You'd better let art alone and stick to artists, as is your nature."

"But women have done some good things," Fairchild objected. "I've read——"

"They bear geniuses. But do you think they care anything about the pictures and music their children produce? that they have any other emotion than a fierce tolerance toward the vagaries of the child? Do you think Shakespeare's mother was any prouder of him than, say, Tom o' Bedlam's?"

"Certainly she was," Mrs Wiseman said. "Shakespeare made money."

"You made a bad choice for comparison," Fairchild said. "All artists are kind of insane. Dont you think so?" he asked Mrs Wiseman.

"Yes," she snapped. "Almost as insane as the ones that sit around and talk about them."

"Well——" Fairchild stared again at the page under his hand. He said, slowly: "Its a kind of dark thing. Its kind of like somebody brings you to a dark door. Will you enter that room, or not?"

"But the old fellows got you into the room first," the semitic man said. "Then they asked you if you wanted to go out or not."

"I dont know. There are rooms, dark rooms, that they didn't know anything about at all. Freud and these other Germans——"

"Discovered them just in time to supply our shelterless literati with free sleeping quarters. But you and Eva just agreed that subject, substance, doesn't signify in verse, that the best poetry is just words."

"Yes . . . infatuation with words," Fairchild agreed. "That's when you hammer out good poetry, great poetry. A kind of singing rhythm in the world that you get into without knowing it, like a swimmer gets into a current. Words . . . I had it once."

"Shut up, Dawson," Mrs Wiseman said. "Julius can afford to be a fool."

"Words," repeated Fairchild. "But its gone out of me now. That first infatuation, I mean; that sheer infatuation with and marvelling over the beauty and power of words. That has gone out of me. Used up, I guess. So I cant write poetry anymore. It takes me too long to say things, now."

"We all wrote poetry, when we were young," the semitic man said. "Some of us even put it down on paper. But all of us wrote it."

"Yes," repeated Fairchild, turning slowly onward through the volume. "Listen:

> " 'o spring o wanton o cruel
> baring to the curved and hungry hand
> of march your white unsubtle thighs'

and listen:" He turned onward. Mrs Wiseman was gazing aft where Jenny and Mr Talliaferro had come into view and now leaned together upon the rail. The semitic man listened with weary courtesy.

" 'above unsapped convolvulæ of hills
april a bee sipping perplexed with pleasure'

Its a kind of childlike faith in the efficacy of words, you see; a kind of belief that circumstance somewhere will invest the veriest platitude with magic. And darn it, it does happen at times, let it be historically or grammatically or physically incorrect and impossible; let it even be trite: there comes a time when it will be invested with a something not of this life, this world, at all. Its a kind of fire, you know. . . ." He fumbled himself among words, staring at them, at the semitic man's sad quizzical eyes and Mrs Wiseman's averted face. "Somebody, some drug clerk or something, has shredded the tender—and do you know what I believe? I believe he's always writing it for some woman, that he fondly believes he's stealing a march on some brute bigger or richer or handsomer than he is; I believe that every word a writing man writes is put down with the ultimate intention of impressing some woman that probably dont care anything at all for literature, as is the nature of women. Well, maybe she aint always a flesh and blood creature: she might be only the symbol of a desire. But she is feminine. Fame is only a byproduct. . . . Do you remember, the old boys never even bothered to sign their things. . . . But I dont know. I suppose nobody ever knows a man's reasons for what he does: you can only generalize from results.

"He very seldom knows his reasons, himself," the other said. "And by the time he has recovered from his astonishment at the unforeseen result he got, he has forgotten what reason he once believed he had. . . . But how can you generalize from a poem? what result does a poem have? You say that substance doesn't matter, has no proper place in a poem. You have," the semitic man continued with curious speculation, "the strangest habit of contradicting yourself, fumbling around and then turning tail and beating your listener to the refutation. . . . But, God knows, there is plenty of room for speculation in modern verse. Fumbling, too, though the poets themselves do most of this. Dont you agree, Eva?"

His sister answered "What?" turning upon him her dark preoccupied gaze. He repeated the question. Fairchild interrupted in full career:

"The trouble with modern verse is, that to comprehend it you must have recently passed through an emotional experience identical with that through which the poet himself has recently passed. The poetry of modern poets is like a pair of shoes that only those whose feet are shaped like the cobbler's feet, can wear; while the old boys turned out shoes that anybody who can walk at all, can wear——"

"Like overshoes," the other suggested.

"Like overshoes," Fairchild agreed. "But then, I aint disparaging. Perhaps the few the shoes fit can go a lot further than a whole herd of people shod alike could go."

"Interesting, anyway," the semitic man said, "to reduce the spiritual progress of the race to terms of an emotional migration—aesthetic Israelites crossing unwetted a pink sea of dullness and security. What about it, Eva?"

Mrs Wiseman, thinking of Jenny's soft body, came out of her dream. "I think you are both not only silly, but dull." She rose. "I want to bum another cigarette, Dawson."

He gave her one, and a match, and she left them. Fairchild turned a few pages. "Its kind of difficult for me to reconcile her with this book," he said slowly. "Does it strike you that way?"

"Not so much that she wrote this," the other answered, "but that she wrote anything at all. That anybody should. But there's no puzzle about the book itself. Not to me, that is. But you, straying trustfully about this park of dark and rootless trees which Dr Ellis and your Germans have recently thrown open to the public. . . . You'll always be a babe in that wood, you know. Bewildered, and slightly annoyed; restive, like Ashur-banipal's stallion when his master mounted him."

"Emotional bisexuality," Fairchild said.

"Yes. But you are trying to reconcile the book and the author. A book is the writer's secret life, the dark twin of a man: you cant reconcile them. And with you, when the inevitable clash comes, the author's actual character is the one that goes down, for you are of those for whom fact and fallacy gain verisimilitude by being in cold print."

"Perhaps so," Fairchild said, with detachment, brooding again on a page. "Listen:

> " 'Lips that of thy weary all seem weariest
> Seem wearier for the curled and pallid sly
> Still riddle of thy secret face, and thy
> Sick despair of its own ill obsessed;
>
> Lay not to heart thy boy's hand to protest
> That smiling leaves thy tired mouth reconciled,
> For swearing so keeps thee but ill beguiled
> With secret joy of thine own woman's breast.
>
> Weary thy mouth with smiling: canst thou bride
> Thyself with thee, or thine own kissing slake?
> Thy virgin's waking doth itself deride
> With sleep's sharp absence, coming so awake;
> And near thy mouth thy twinned heart's grief doth hide
> For there's no breast between: it cannot break.'

"Hermaphroditus," he said. "That's what its about. Its a kind of dark perversion. Like a fire that dont need any fuel, that lives on its own heat. I mean, all modern verse is a kind of perversion. Like the day for healthy poetry is over and done with, that modern people were not born to write poetry anymore. Other things, I grant. But not poetry. Kind of like men nowadays are not masculine and lusty enough to tamper with something that borders so close to the unnatural. A kind of sterile race: women too masculine to conceive, men too feminine to beget. . . ." He closed the book and removed his spectacles slowly. "You and me sitting here, right now, this is one of the most insidious things poetry has to combat. General education has made it too easy for everybody to have an opinion on it. On everything else, too. The only people who should be allowed an opinion on poetry should be poets. But as it is. . . . But then, all artists have to suffer it, though: oblivion and scorn and indignation and, what is worse, the adulation of fools."

"And," added the semitic man, "what is still worse: talk."

Twelve Oclock.

"You must get rather tired of bothering about it," Fairchild suggested as they descended toward lunch. (There was an off-shore breeze and the saloon was screened. And besides, it was near the galley.) "Why dont you leave it in your stateroom? Major Ayers is pretty trustworthy, I guess."

"It'll be all right," Pete replied. "I've got used to it. I'd miss it, see?"

"Yes," the other agreed. "New one, eh?"

"I've had it a while." Pete removed it and Fairchild remarked its wanton gay band and the heavy plaiting of the straw.

"I like a panama myself," he murmured. "A soft hat. . . . This must have cost five or six dollars, didn't it?"

"Yeh," Pete agreed. "But I guess I can look out for it."

"Its a nice hat," the semitic man said. "Not everybody can wear a stiff straw. But it rather suits the shape of Pete's face, dont you think?"

"Yes, that's so," Fairchild agreed. "Pete has a kind of humorless reckless face that a stiff hat just suits. A man with a humorous face should never wear a stiff hat. But then, only a humorless man would dare buy one."

Pete preceded them into the saloon. The man's intent was kindly, anyway. Funny old bird. Easy. Easy. Somebody's gutting. Anybody's. Fairchild spoke to him again with a kind of tactful persistence:

"Look here: here's a good place to leave it while you eat. You hadn't seen this place, I reckon. Slip it under here, see? it'll be safe as a church under here until you want it again. Look, Julius, this place was made for a stiff straw hat, wasn't it?" This place was a collapsible serving table of two shelves that let shallowly into the bulkhead: it operated by a spring and anything placed on the lower shelf would be inviolate until someone came along and lowered the shelves again.

"It dont bother me any," Pete said.

"All right," the other answered. "But you might as well leave it here: its such a grand place to leave a hat. Lots better than the places in theaters. I kind of wish I had a hat to leave there. Dont you, Julius?"

"I can hold it all right," Pete said again.

"Sure," Fairchild agreed readily, "but just try it a moment." Pete did so, and the other two watched with interest. "It just fits, dont it? Why not leave it there, just for a trial?"

"I guess not. I guess I'll hold onto it," Pete decided. He took his hat again and when he had taken his seat he slid it into its usual place between the chairback and himself.

Mrs Maurier was chanting: "Sit down, people," in an apologetic, hopeless tone. "You must excuse things. I had hoped to have lunch on deck, but with the wind blowing from the shore. . . ."

"They've found where we are and that we are good to eat, so it doesn't make any difference where the wind blows from," Mrs Wiseman said, businesslike with her tray.

"And with the steward gone, and things so unsettled," the hostess resumed in antistrophe, roving her unhappy gaze. "And Mr Gordon—"

"Oh, he's all right," Fairchild said, heavily helpful, taking his seat. "He'll show up all right."

"Dont be a fool, Aunt Pat," the niece added. "What would he want to get drowned for?"

"I'm so unlucky," Mrs Maurier moaned. "Things—things happen to me, you see," she explained, haunted with that vision of a pale implacability of water and sodden pants, and a red beard straying amid the slanting green regions of the sea in a dreadful simulation of life.

"Aw shucks," the niece protested. "Ugly like he is, and so full of himself. . . . He's got too many good reasons for getting drowned. Its the ones that dont have any excuse for it, that get drowned and run down by taxis and things."

"But you never can tell what people will do," Mrs Maurier rejoined, becoming profound through the sheer disintegration of comfortable things. "People will do anything."

"Well, if he is drowned, I guess he wanted to be," the niece said bloodlessly. "He certainly cant expect us to fool around here waiting on him, anyway. I never heard of anybody fading out without leaving a note of some kind. Did you, Jenny?"

Jenny sat in a soft anticipatory dread. "Did he get drownded?" she asked. "One day at Mandeville, I saw. . . ." Into Jenny's heavenly eyes there welled momentarily a selfless emotion, temporarily pure and clean. Mrs Wiseman looked at her, compelling her with her eyes. She said:

"Oh, forget about Gordon for a while. If he's drowned (which I dont believe) he's drowned; if he isn't, he'll show up again, just as Dawson says."

"That's what I say," the niece supported her quickly. "Only he'd better show up soon, if he wants to go back with us. We've got to get back home."

"You have?" her aunt said with heavy astonished irony. "How are you going, pray?"

"Perhaps her brother will make us a boat with his saw," Mark Frost suggested.

"That's an idea," Fairchild agreed. "Say, Josh, haven't you got a tool of some sort that'll get us off again?" The nephew regarded Fairchild solemnly.

"Whittle it off," he said. "Lend you my knife, if you'll bring it back right away." He resumed his meal.

"Well, we've got to get back," his sister repeated. "You folks can stay around here if you want to, but me and Josh have got to get back to New Orleans."

"Going by Mandeville?" Mark Frost asked.

"But the tug should be here at any time," Mrs Maurier insisted, reverting again to her hopeless amaze. The niece gave Mark Frost a grave speculative stare.

"You're smart, aren't you?"

"I've got to be," Mark Frost answered equably, "or I'd——"

"——have to work, huh? It takes a smart man to sponge off of Aunt Pat, dont it?"

"Patricia!" her aunt exclaimed.

"Well, we have got to get back. We've got to get ready to go up to New Haven next month."

Her brother came again out of his dream. "We have?" he repeated heavily.

"I'm going, too," she answered quickly. "Hank said I could."

"Look here," her brother said. "Are you going to follow me around all your life?"

"I'm going to Yale," she repeated stubbornly. "Hank said I could go."

"Hank?" Fairchild repeated, watching the niece with interest.

"Its what she calls her father," her aunt explained. "Patricia——"

"Well, you cant go," her brother answered violently. "Dam'f I'm going to have you tracking around behind me forever. I cant move, for you. You ought to be a bill collector."

"I dont care: I'm going," she repeated stubbornly. Her aunt said vainly:

"Theodore!"

"Well, I cant do anything, for her," he complained bitterly. "I cant move, for her. And now she's talking about going—— She worried Hank until he had to say she could go. God knows, I'd a said that too: I wouldn't want her around me all the time."

"Shut your goddam mouth," his sister told him. Mrs Maurier chanted Patricia Patricia. "I'm going, I'm going, I'm going!"

"What'll you do up there?" Fairchild asked. The niece whirled, viciously belligerent. Then she said:

"What'd you say?"

"I mean, what'll you do to pass the time, while he's at classes and things? Are you going to take some work, too?"

"Oh, I'll just go around with balloon pants. Night clubs and things. I wont bother him: I wont hardly see him: he's such a damn crum."

"Like hell you will," her brother interrupted, "you're not going, I tell you."

"Yes I am. Hank said I could go. He said I could. I——"

"Well, you wont ever see me: I'm not going to have you tagging around after me up there."

"Are you the only one in the world that's going up there next year? Are you the only one that'll be there? I'm not going up there to waste my time hanging around the entrance to Dwight or Osborne hall just to see you. You wont catch me sitting on the rail of the Green with freshmen. I'll be going to places that maybe you'll get in in three years, if you dont bust out or something. Dont you worry about me. Who was it," she rushed on, "got invited up for prom week last year, except Hank wouldn't let me go? who was it saw the Game last fall, while you were perched up on the top row with a bunch of newspaper reporters, in the rain?"

"You didn't go to prom week."

"Because Hank wouldn't let me. But I'll be there next year, and you can haul out the family sock on it."

"Oh, shut up for a while," her brother said wearily. "Maybe some of these ladies want to talk some."

Two Oclock.

And there was the tug squatting at her cables, breaking the southern horizon with an effect of abrupt magic, like a stereopticon slide flashed on the screen while you had turned your head for a moment.

"Look at that boat," said Mark Frost, broaching. Mrs Maurier directly behind him, shrieked:

"Its the tug!" She turned and screamed down the companionway: "Its the tug: the tug has come!" The others all chanted "The Tug! the tug!" Major Ayers exclaimed dramatically and opportunely: "Ha. Gone away!"

"It has come at last," Mrs Maurier shrieked. "It came while we were at lunch. Has anyone——" she roved her eyes about. "The captain—— Has he been notified? Mr Talliaferro——?"

"Surely," Mr Talliaferro agreed with polite alacrity, mounting the stairs and disintegrating his members with expedition, "I'll summon the captain."

So he rushed forward and the others came on deck and stared at the tug; and a gentle breeze blew offshore and they slapped intermittently at their exposed surfaces. Mr Talliaferro shouted "Captain! oh, Captain!" about the deck: he screamed it into the empty wheelhouse and returned. "He must be asleep," he told them.

"We are off at last," Mrs Maurier intoned. "We can get off at last. The tug has come: I sent for it days and days ago. But we can get off now. But the captain. . . . Where is the captain? He shouldn't be asleep, at this time. Of all times for the captain to be asleep—Mr Talliaferro——"

"But Gordon," Mark Frost said. "How about——"

Miss Jameson clutched his arm. "Lets get off first," she said.

"I called him," Mr Talliaferro reminded them. "He must be asleep in his room."

"He must be asleep," Mrs Maurier repeated. "Will some gentleman——"

Mr Talliaferro took his cue. "I'll go," he said.

"If you will be so kind," Mrs Maurier screamed after him. She stared again at the tug. "He should have been here, so we could be all ready to start," she said fretfully. She waved her handkerchief at the tug: it ignored her.

"We might be getting everything ready, though," Fairchild suggested. "We ought to have everything ready when they pull us off."

"That's so," Mark Frost agreed. "We better run down and pack, hadn't we?"

"Ah, we aint going back home yet. We've just started the cruise. Are we, folks?"

They all looked at the hostess. She roved her stricken eyes, but she said at last, bravely: "Why no. No, of course not, if you dont want to. . . . But the captain: we ought to be ready," she repeated.

"Well, lets get ready," Mrs Wiseman said.

"Nobody knows anything about boats except Fairchild," Mark Frost said. Mr Talliaferro returned, barren.

"Me?" Fairchild repeated. "Talliaferro's been across the whole ocean. And there's Major Ayers. All Britishers cut their teeth on anchor chains and marlinspikes."

"And draw their toys with lubbers' lines," Mrs Wiseman chanted. "Its almost a poem. Finish it, someone."

Mr Talliaferro made a sound of alarm. "No: really, I—" Mrs Maurier turned to Fairchild. "Will you assume charge until the captain appears, Mr Fairchild?"

"Mr Fairchild," Mr Talliaferro parroted. "Mr Fairchild is temporary commodore, people. The captain doesn't seem to be on board," he whispered to Mrs Maurier.

Fairchild glanced about with a sort of ludicrous helplessness. "What am I supposed to do?" he asked. "Jump overboard with a shovel and shovel the sand away?"

"A man who has reiterated his superiority as much as you have for the last week should never be at a loss for what to do," Mrs Wiseman told him. "We ladies had already thought of that. You are the one to think of something else."

"Well, I've already thought of not jumping overboard and shoveling her off," Fairchild answered. "But that dont seem to help much, does it?"

"You ought to coil ropes or something like that," Miss Jameson suggested. "That's what they were always doing on all the ships I ever read about."

"All right," Fairchild agreed equably. "We'll coil ropes, then. Where are the ropes?"

"That's your trouble," Mrs Wiseman said. "You're captain now."

"Well, we'll find some ropes and coil 'em." He addressed Mrs Maurier. "We have your permission to coil ropes?"

"No: really," Mrs Maurier said in her helpless astonished voice. "Isn't there something we can do? Cant we signal to them with a sheet? They may not know this is the right boat."

"Oh, they know, I guess. Anyway, we'll coil ropes and be ready for them. Come on here, you men." He named over his depleted watch and herded it forward. He herded it down to his cabin and nourished it with stimulants.

"We may coil the right rope, at that," the semitic man suggested. "Major Ayers ought to know something about boats: it should be in his British blood."

Major Ayers didn't think so. "American boats have amphibious traits that are lacking in ours," he explained. "Half the voyage on land, y'know," he explained tediously.

"Sure," Fairchild agreed. He brought his watch above again and forward, where instinct told him the ropes should be. "I wonder where the captain is. Surely he aint drowned, do you reckon?"

"I guess not," the semitic man answered. "He gets paid for this. . . . There comes a boat."

The boat came from the tug, and soon it came alongside and the captain came over the rail. A stranger followed him and they went below without haste, leaving Mrs Maurier's words like vain unmated birds in the air. "Lets get ready, then," Fairchild ordered his crew. "Lets tie a rope to something."

So they tied a rope to something, knotting it intricately, then Major Ayers discovered that they had tied it to a winch handle which fitted loosely into a socket and would probably come out quite easily, once a strain came on the rope. So they untied it and found something attached firmly to the deck, and they tied the rope to this, and after a while the captain and the stranger, clutching a short evil pipe, came back on deck and stood and watched them. "We've got the right rope," Fairchild told his watch in undertone, and they knotted the rope intricately and straightened up. "How's that, Cap?" Fairchild asked.

"All right," the captain answered. "Can we trouble you for a match?"

Fairchild gave them a match. The stranger fired his pipe and they got back into the tender and departed. They hadn't got far when the one called Walter came out and called to them, and they put about and returned for him. Then they went back to the tug. Fairchild's watch had all ceased work, and it gazed after the tender. After a time Fairchild said: "He said that was the right rope. So I guess we can quit."

So they did, and went aft to where the ladies were, and presently the tender came bobbing back across the water. It came alongside again and a negro, sweating gently and regularly, held it steady while the one called Walter and yet another stranger got aboard, bringing a rope that trailed away into the water behind them.

Everybody watched with interest while Walter and his companion made the line fast in the bows, after having removed Fairchild's rope. Then Walter and his friend went below.

"Say," said Fairchild suddenly, "do you reckon they've found our whiskey?"

"I guess not," the semitic man reassured him. "I hope not," he amended; and they all returned in a body to stare down into the tender where the negro sat without selfconsciousness eating of a large grayish object. While they watched the negro Walter and his companion returned and the stranger bawled at the tug through his hands. A reply at last, and the other end of the line which they had recently brought aboard the yacht and made fast, slid down from the deck of the tug and plopped heavily into the water; and Walter and his companion drew it aboard the yacht and coiled it down, wet and dripping. Then they elbowed themselves to the rail, cast the rope into the tender and got in themselves and the negro stowed his strange edible object temporarily away and rowed back to the tug.

"You guessed wrong again," Mark Frost said with sepulchral irony. He bent and scratched his ankles. "Try another rope."

"You wait," Fairchild retorted. "Wait ten minutes, then talk. We'll be under full steam in ten minutes. . . . Where did that boat come from?"

This boat was a skiff, come when and from where they knew not; and beneath the drowsy afternoon there came faintly from somewhere up the lake the fretful sound of a motor boat engine. The skiff drew alongside, manned by a malaria ridden man wearing a woman's dilapidated hat of black straw that lent him a vaguely bereaved air.

"Whar's the drownded feller?" he asked, grasping the rail.

"We dont know," Fairchild answered. "We missed him somewhere between here and the shore." He extended his arm. The newcomer followed his gesture sadly.

"Any reward?"

"Reward?" repeated Fairchild.

"Reward?" Mrs Maurier chimed in, breathlessly. "Yes, there is a reward: I offer a reward."

"How much?"

"You find him first," the semitic man put in. "There'll be a reward, all right."

The man clung yet to the rail. "Have you drug fer him yet?"

"No, we've just started hunting," Fairchild answered. "You go on and look around, and we'll get our boat and come out and help you. There'll be a reward."

The man pushed his skiff clear and engaged his oars. The sound of the motor boat grew clearer steadily: soon it came into view, with two men in it, and changed its course and bore down on the skiff. The fussy little engine ceased its racket and it slid up to the skiff, pushing a dying ripple under its stem. The two boats clung together for a time, then they parted, and at a short distance from each other they moved slowly onward while their occupants prodded at the lake bottom with their oars.

"Look at them," the semitic man said, "just like buzzards. Probably be a dozen boats out there in the next hour. How do you suppose they learned about it?"

"Lord knows," Fairchild answered. "Lets get our crew and go out and help look. We better get the tug's men."

They shouted in turn for a while, and presently one came to the rail of the tug and gazed apathetically at them, and went away; and after a while the small boat came away from the tug and crossed to them. A consultation, assisted by all hands while the man from the tug moved unhurriedly about the business of making fast another and dirtier rope to the Nausikaa's bows. Then he and Walter went back to the tug, paying out the line behind them while Mrs Maurier's insistence wasted itself upon the somnolent afternoon. The guests looked at one another helplessly. Then Fairchild said with determination:

"Come on: we'll go in our boat." He chose his men and they gathered all the available oars and prepared to embark.

"Here comes the tug's boat again," Mark Frost said.

"They forgot and tied one end of that rope to something," Mrs Wiseman said viciously. The boat came alongside without haste and it and the yacht's tender lay rubbing noses, and Walter's companion asked, without interest:

"Wher's the feller y'all drownded?"

"I'll go along in their boat to show 'em," Fairchild decided. Mark Frost got back aboard the yacht with alacrity. Fairchild stopped him. "You folks come on behind us in this boat. The more to hunt, the better."

Mark Frost groaned and acquiesced. The others took their places and under Fairchild's direction the two tenders retraced the course of yesterday. The first two boats were some distance ahead, moving slowly; and the tenders separated also and the searchers poled along, prodding with their oars at the lake floor. And such is the influence of action on the mind that soon even Fairchild's burly optimism became hushed and uncertain before the imminence of the unknown, and he too was accepting the possible for the probable, unaware.

The sun was hazed, as though wearied of its own implacable heat, and the water, that water which might hold, soon to be revealed, the mute evidence of the ultimate flouting of all man's strife, lapped and plopped at the mechanical fragilities that supported them: a small sound, monotonous and without rancor——it could well wait! They poled slowly on.

Soon the four boats, fanwise, had traversed the course, and they turned and quartered back and forth again, slowly and in silence. Afternoon drew on, drowsing, somnolent. Yacht and tug lay motionless in a blinding shimmer of water and sun. . . .

Again the course of yesterday was covered foot by foot, patiently and silently, and in vain; and the four boats as without volition drew nearer each other, drifting closer together as sheep huddle, while water lapped and plopped beneath their hulls, sinister and untroubled by waiting . . . soon the motor boat drifted up and scraped lightly along the hull in which Fairchild sat and he raised his head, blinking against the glare. After a while he said:

"Are you a ghost, or am I?"

"I was about to ask you that," Gordon sitting in the motor boat replied. They sat and stared at each other. The other boats came up, and presently the one called Walter spoke.

"Is this all you wanted out here?" he asked in a tone of polite disgust, breaking the spell. "Or do you want to row around some more?"

Fairchild went immoderately into hysterical laughter.

Four Oclock.

The malarial man had attached his skiff to the fat man's motor boat and they had puttered away in a morose dejection, rewardless; the tug had whistled a final derisive blast, showed them her squat unpretty stern where the negro leaned eating again of his grayish object, and as dirty a pair of heels as it would ever be their luck to see, and sailed away. The Nausikaa was free once more and she sped quickly onward, gaining offing, and the final sharp concussion of flesh and flesh died away beneath the afternoon.

Mrs Maurier had gazed at him, raising her hands in a fluttering cringing gesture, had cut him dead.

"But I saw you on the boat right after we came back," Fairchild repeated with a sort of stubborn wonder. He opened a fresh bottle.

"You couldn't have," Gordon answered shortly. "I got out of the boat in the middle of Talliaferro's excitement." He waved away the proffered glass. The semitic man said triumphantly, "I told you so," and Fairchild essayed again, stubbornly:

"But I s——"

"If you say that again," the semitic man told him, "I'll kill you." He addressed Gordon. "And you thought Dawson was drowned?"

"Yes. The man who brought me back—I stumbled on his house this morning—he had already heard of it, somehow: it must have spread all up and down the lake. He didn't re-member the name, exactly, and when I named over the party and said Dawson Fairchild, he agreed. Dawson and Gordon—you see? And so I thought——"

Fairchild began to laugh again. He laughed steadily, trying to say something. "And so——and so he comes back and sp— spends——" Again that hysterical note came into his laughter and his hands trembled, clinking the bottle against the glass and sloshing a spoonful of the liquor onto the floor "——and spends. . . . He comes back, you know, and spends half a day looking——looking for his own bububod——"

The semitic man rose and took the bottle and glass from him and half led, half thrust him onto his bunk. "You sit down and drink this."

Fairchild drank the whiskey obediently. The semitic man turned to Gordon again. "What made you come back? Not just because you heard Dawson was drowned, was it?"

Gordon stood against the wall, mudstained and silent. He raised his head, staring at them and through them with his harsh uncomfortable stare. Fairchild touched the semitic man's knee warningly. "That's neither here nor there," he said. "The question is, shall we or shall we not get drunk? I kind of think we've got to, myself."

"Yes," the other agreed. "It looks like its up to us. Gordon ought to celebrate his resurrection, anyway."

"No," Gordon answered. "I dont want any." The semitic man protested, but again Fairchild gripped him silent, and when Gordon turned toward the door he rose and followed him into the passage.

"She came back too, you know," he said.

Gordon looked down at the shorter man with his lean bearded face, his lonely hawk's face arrogant with shyness and pride. "I know it," he answered (Your name is like a little golden bell hung in my heart). "The man who brought me back was the same one who brought them back yesterday."

"He was?" said Fairchild. "He's doing a landoffice business with deserters, aint he?"

"Yes," Gordon answered. And he went on down the passage with a singing lightness in his heart, a bright silver joy like wings.

*   *   *   *   *

The deck was deserted, as on that other afternoon, but he waited patiently in the hushed happiness of his dream and his arrogant bitter heart was as young as any yet, as forgetful of yesterday and of tomorrow. And soon, as though in answer to it, she came barelegged and molded by the wind of motion, and her grave surprise ebbed and she thrust him a hard tanned hand.

"So you ran away too," she said.

"And so did you," he answered after an interval filled with a thing all silver and clean and fine.

"That's right. . . . We're sure the herrings on this boat, aren't we?"

"Herrings?"

"Guts, you know," she explained. She looked at him gravely from beneath the coarse dark bang of her hair. . . . "But you came back," she accused.

"And so did you," he reminded her from amid his soundless silver wings.

FIVE OCLOCK.

"But we're moving again, at last," Mrs Maurier repeated at intervals, with a detached air, listening to a sound somehow vaguely convivial that welled at intervals up the companionway. Presently Mrs Wiseman remarked the hostess' distrait air, and she too ceased, hearkening.

"Not again?" she said with foreboding.

"I'm afraid so," the other answered unhappily.

Mr Talliaferro hearkened also. "Perhaps I'd better——" he began. Mrs Maurier fixed him with her eye, and Mrs Wiseman said:

"Poor fellows. They have had to stand a great deal in the last few days."

"Boys will be boys," Mr Talliaferro added with docile regret, listening with yearning to that vaguely convivial sound.

Mrs Maurier listened to it, coldly detached and speculative. She said:

"But we are moving again, anyway."

Six Oclock.

The sun was setting across the scudding water: the water was shot goldenly with it, as was the gleaming mahogany-and-brass elegance of the yacht; and the silver wings in his heart were touched with pink and gold, while he stood looking down upon the coarse crown of her head, at her body's grave and sexless replica of his own attitude against the rail: an unconscious aping both comical and heartshaking.

"Do you know," he asked, "what Cyrano said once?" *Once there was a king who possessed all things. All things were his: power, and glory, and wealth, and splendor and ease. And so he sat at dusk in his marble court filled with the sound of water and of birds and surrounded by the fixed gesturing of palms, looking out across the hushed fading domes of his city, and beyond, to the dreaming lilac barriers of his world——*

"No: what?" she asked. But he only looked down upon her with his cavernous uncomfortable eyes. "What did he say?" she repeated. And then: "Was he in love with her?"

"I think so. . . . Yes, he was in love with her. She couldn't leave him, either. Couldn't go away from him at all."

"She couldn't? What'd he done to her? Locked her up?"

"Maybe she didn't want to," he suggested.

"Huh." and then: "She was an awful goof, then. Was he fool enough to believe she didn't want to?"

"He didn't take any chances. He had her locked up. In a book."

"In a book?" she repeated. Then she comprehended. "Oh. . . . That's what you've done, isn't it? With that marble girl without any arms and legs you made? Hadn't you rather have a live one? Say, you haven't got any sweetheart or anything, have you?"

"No," he answered. "How did you know?"

"You look so bad. Shabby. But that's the reason: no woman is going to waste time on a man that's satisfied with a piece of wood or something. You ought to get out of yourself. You'll either bust all of a sudden some day, or just dry up. . . . How old are you?"

"Thirty six," he told her. She said:

"Gabriel's pants. Thirty six years old, and living in a hole with a piece of rock, like a dog with a dry bone. Gabriel's pants. Why dont you get rid of it?" But he only stared down at her. "Give it to me, wont you?"

"No."

"I'll buy it from you, then."

"No."

"Give you——" she looked at him with sober detachment. "Give you seventeen dollars for it. Cash."

"No."

She looked at him with a sort of patient exasperation. "Well, what are you going to do with it? Have you got any reason for keeping it? You didn't steal it, did you? Dont tell me you haven't got any use for seventeen dollars, living like you do. I bet you haven't got five dollars to your name, right now. Bet you came on this party to save food. I'll give you twenty dollars, seventeen in cash." He continued to gaze at her as though he had not heard.——*and the king spoke to a slave crouching at his feet—Halim—Lord?—I possess all things, do I not?—Thou art the son of morning, Lord—Then listen, Halim: I have a desire——*

"Twenty five," she said, shaking his arm.

"No."

"No, no, no, no!" she hammered both brown fists on the rail. "You make me so damn mad! Cant you say anything except No? You—you—" she glared at him with her angry tanned face and her grave opaque eyes, and used that phrase Jenny had traded her. He took her by the elbows, and she became taut, still watching his face: he could feel the small hard muscles in her arms. "What are you going to do?" she asked. He raised her from the floor, and she began to struggle. But he carried her implacably across the deck and sat on a deckchair and turned her face downward across his knees. She clawed and kicked in a silent fury, but he held her, and she ceased to struggle, and set her teeth into his leg through the gritty cloth of his trousers, and clung like a raging puppy while he drew her skirt tight across her thighs and spanked her, spanked her good.

"I meant it!" she cried, raging and tearless, when he had dragged her teeth loose and had set her upright on his lap. There was a small wet oval on his trouserleg. "I meant it!" she repeated, taut and raging.

"I know you meant it. That's why I spanked you. Not because you said it: what you said doesn't mean any thing: you've got the gender backward. I spanked you because you meant it, whether you knew what to say or not."

Suddenly she became lax and wept, and he held her against his breast. But she ceased crying as abruptly, and lay quiet while he moved his hand over her face, slowly and firmly, but lightly.——*It is like a thing heard, not as a music of brass and plucked strings is heard and a pallid voluption of dancing girls among the strings; nay, Halim, it is no pale virgin from Tal with painted fingernails and honey and myrrh cunningly beneath her tongue. Nor is it a scent as of myrrh and roses to soften and make to flow like water the pith in a man's bones, nor yet—Stay, Halim: Once I was . . . once I was? Is not this a true thing? It is dawn, in the high cold hills, dawn is like a wind in the clean hills, and on the wind comes the thin piping of shepherds, and the smell of dawn and of almond trees on the wind. Is not that a true thing?— Ay, Lord. I told thee that. I was there.*

"Are you a petter, as well as a he-man?" she asked, becoming taut again and rolling upward her exposed eye. His hand moved slowly about her cheekbone and jaw, pausing, tracing a muscle, moving on.——*Then hark thee, Halim: I desire a thing that, had I not been at all, becoming aware of it I would awake; that, dead, remembering it I would cling to this world though it be as a beggar in a tattered robe; yea, rather that would I than a king among kings amid the soft and scented sounds of paradise. Find me this, O Halim.* "Say," she said curiously, no longer alarmed, "what are you doing that for?"

"Learning your face."

"Learning my face? Are you going to make me in marble?" she asked quickly, raising herself. "Can you do a marble of my head?"

"Yes."

"Can I have it?" She thrust herself away, watching his face. "Make two of them, then," she suggested. And then: "If you wont do that, give me the other one, the one you've got, and

I'll pose for this one without charging you anything. How about that?"

"Maybe."

"I'd rather do that than to have this one. Have you learned my face good?" She moved again, quickly, returning to her former position and turning her face up. "Learn it good." *Now, this Halim was an old man, so old that he had forgotten much. He had held this king on his first pony, walking patiently beside him through the streets and paths; he had stood between the young prince and all those forms of sudden and complete annihilation which the young prince had engendered after the ingenuous fashion of boys; he had got himself between the young prince and the inevitable parental admonishment which these entailed. And he sat with his gray hands on his thin knees and his gray head bent above his hands while dusk came across the simple immaculate domes of the city and into the court, stilling the sound of birds so that the lilac silence of the court was teased only by the plashing of water, and on among the grave restlessness of the palms. After a while Halim spoke.—Ah, Lord, in the Georgian hills I loved this maid myself, when I was a lad. But that was long ago, and she is dead.* She lay still against his breast while sunset died like brass horns across the water. She said, without moving: "You're a funny man. . . . I wonder if I could sculp? Suppose I learn your face? . . . Well, dont then. I'd just as soon lie still. You're a lot more comfortable to lie on than you look. Only I'd think you'd be getting tired—I'm no humming bird. Aren't you tired of holding me?" she persisted. He moved his head at last, looking again at her with his caverned uncomfortable eyes, and she tried to do something with her eyes, assuming at the same time an attitude, a kind of leering invitation so palpably theatrical and false that it but served to emphasize that grave hard sexlessness of hers.

"What are you trying to do?" he asked quietly, "vamp me?"

She said "Shucks." She sat up, then squirmed off his lap and to her feet. "So you wont give it to me? You just wont?"

"No," he told her soberly. She turned away, but presently she stopped again and looked back at him.

"Give you twenty five dollars for it."

"No."

She said "Shucks" again and she went on on her brown

silent feet, and was gone. (Your name is like a little golden bell hung in my heart, and when I think of you. . . .) The Nausikaa sped on. It was twilight abruptly; soon, a star.

SEVEN OCLOCK.

The place did appear impregnable, but then he had got used to feeling it behind him in his chair, where he knew nothing was going to happen to it. Besides, to change now, after so many days, would be like hedging on a bet. . . . Still, to let that fat jew and that other old bum kid him about it. . . . He paused in the door of the saloon. . . . The others were seated and well into their dinner, but before four vacant places that bland eternal grapefruit, sinister and bland as taxes. Some of them hadn't arrived: he'd have time to run back to his room and leave it. And let one of them drunkards throw it out the window for a joke?

Mrs Wiseman carrying a tray said briskly: "Gangway, Pete" and he crowded against the wall for her to pass, and the niece turning her head called him. "Belly up," she said, and he heard a further trampling drawing near. He hesitated a second, then he thrust his hat into the little cubbyhole between the two shelves. He'd risk it tonight, anyway. He could still sort of keep an eye on it. He took his seat.

Fairchild's watch surged in: a hearty joviality that presently died away into a startled consternation when it saw the grapefruit. "My God," said Fairchild in a hushed tone.

"Sit down, Dawson," Mrs Wiseman ordered sharply. "We've had about all that sort of humor this voyage will stand."

"That's what I think," he agreed readily. "That's what Julius and Major Ayers and me think at every meal. And yet, when we come to the table, what do we see?"

"My first is an Indian princess," said Mark Frost in a hollow lilting tone. "But its a little early to play charades yet, isn't it?"

Major Ayers said "Eh?" looking from Mark Frost to Fairchild. Then he ventured. "Its grapefruit, isn't it?"

"But we have so many of them," Mrs Maurier explained. "You are supposed to never get tired of them."

"That's it," said Fairchild solemnly. "Major Ayers guessed it the first time. I wasn't certain what it was, myself. But you cant fool Major Ayers: you cant fool a man that's travelled as much as he has, with just a grapefruit. I guess you've shot lots of grapefruit in China and India, haven't you, Major?"

"Dawson, sit down," Mrs Wiseman repeated. "Make them sit down, Julius, or go out to the kitchen, if they just want to stand around and talk."

Fairchild sat down quickly. "Never mind," he said. "We can stand it if the ladies can. The human body can stand anything," he added owlishly. "It can get drunk and stay up and dance all night, consume crate after crate of gr——" Mrs Wiseman leaned across his shoulder and swept his grapefruit away. "Here," he exclaimed.

"They dont want 'em," she told Miss Jameson across the table. "Get his, too." So they reft Major Ayers of his also and Mrs Wiseman clashed the plates viciously onto her tray. In passing behind Mrs Maurier she struck the collapsible serving table with her hip and said "Damn!" pausing to release the catch and slam it back into the bulkhead. Pete's hat slid onto the floor and she thrust it against the wall with her toe.

"Yes sir," Fairchild repeated, "the human body can stand lots of things, but if I have to eat another grapefruit——Say, Julius, I was examining my back today, and you know, my skin is getting dry and rough, with a kind of yellowish cast. If it keeps on, first thing I know I wont anymore dare undress in public than Al Jack——"

Mark Frost made a sound of sharp alarm. "Look out, people," he exclaimed, rising. "I'm going to get out of here."

"——Jackson would take off his shoes in public," Fairchild continued unperturbed. Mrs Wiseman returned and stood with her hands on her hips, regarding Fairchild's unkempt head with disgust. Mrs Maurier gazed helplessly at him.

"Everyone's finished," Mrs Wiseman said. "Come on, lets go on deck."

"No," Mrs Maurier protested. She said firmly: "Mr Fairchild."

"Go on," the niece urged him. "What about Al Jackson?"

"Shut up, Pat," Mrs Wiseman commanded. "Come on, you all. Let 'em stay here and drivel to each other. Lets lock 'em in here: what do you say?"

Mrs Maurier asserted herself. She rose. "Mr Fairchild, I

simply will not have—— If you continue in this behavior, I shall leave the room. Dont you see how trying——how difficult——how difficult——" beneath the beseeching helplessness of her eyes her various chins began to quiver a little "——how difficult——"

Mrs Wiseman touched her arm. "Come: its useless to argue with them now. Come, dear." She drew Mrs Maurier's chair aside and the old woman took a step and stopped abruptly, clutching the other's arm.

"I've stepped on something," she said, peering blindly.

Pete rose with a mad inarticulate cry.

*   *   *   *   *

Old Man Jackson—Fairchild continued—claims to be a lineal descendant of Old Hickory. A fine old southern stock, with all a fine old southern family's pride. Al has a lot of that pride himself: that's why he wont take off his shoes in company. I'll tell you the reason later.

Well, Old Man Jackson was a bookkeeper or something, drawing a small salary with a big family to support, and he wanted to better himself with the minimum of labor, like a descendant of any fine old southern family naturally would, and so he thought up the idea of taking up some of this Louisiana swamp land and raising sheep on it. He'd noticed how much ranker vegetation grows on trees in swampy land, so he figured that wool ought to grow the same rank way on a sheep raised in a swamp. So he threw up his bookkeeping job and took up a few hundred acres of Tchufuncta river swamp and stocked it with sheep, using the money his wife's uncle, a member of an old aristocratic Tennessee moonshining family, had left 'em.

But his sheep started right in to get themselves drowned, so he made life belts for 'em out of some small wooden kegs that had been part of the heritage from that Tennessee uncle, so that when the sheep strayed off into deep water they would float until the current washed 'em back to land again. This worked all right, but still his sheep kept on disappearing— the ewes and lambs did, that is. Then he found that the alligators were——

"Yes," murmured Major Ayers, "Old Hickory."

———getting them. So he made some imitation rams' horns out of wood and fastened a pair to each ewe and to every lamb when it was born. And that reduced his losses by alligators to a minimum scarcely worth notice. The rams' flesh seemed to be too rank even for alligators.

After a time the life belts wore out, but the sheep had learned to swim pretty well by then, so Old Man Jackson decided it wasn't worth while to put anymore life belts on 'em. The fact is, the sheep had got to like the water: the first crop of lambs would only come out of the water at feeding time, and when the first shearing time came around, he and his boys had to round up the sheep with boats.

By the next shearing time, those sheep wouldn't even come out of the water to be fed. So he and his boys would go out in the boats and set floating tubs of feed around in the bayous for them. This crop of lambs could dive, too. They never saw one of them on land at all: they'd only see their heads swimming across the bogues and sloughs.

Finally another shearing time came around. Old Man Jackson tried to catch one of them, but the sheep could swim faster than he and his boys could row, and the young ones dived under water and got away. So they finally had to borrow a motor boat. And when they finally tired one of those sheep down and caught it and took it out of the water, they found that only the top of its back had any wool on it. The rest of its body was scaled like a fish. And when they finally caught one of the spring lambs on an alligator hook, they found that its tail had broadened out and flattened like a beaver's, and that it had no legs at all. They didn't hardly know what it was, at first.

"I say," murmured Major Ayers.

Yes sir, completely atrophied away. Time passed, they never saw the next crop of lambs at all. The food they set out the birds ate, and when the next shearing time came they couldn't even catch one with the motor boat. They hadn't even seen one in three weeks. They knew they were still there though, because they could occasionally hear 'em baa-ing at night way back in the swamp. They caught one occasionally on a trotline of shark hooks baited with ears of corn, but not many.

Well sir, the more Old Man Jackson thought about that

swampful of sheep, the madder he got. He'd stamp around the house and swear he'd catch 'em if he had to buy a motor boat that would run fifty miles an hour, and a diving suit for himself and every one of his boys. He had one boy named Claude—Al's brother, you know. Claude was kind of wild: hell after women, a gambler and a drunkard—a kind of handsome humorless fellow with lots of dash. And finally Claude made a trade with his father to have half of every sheep he could catch and he got to work right away. He never bothered with boats or trotlines: he just took off his clothes and went right in the water and grappled for 'em.

"Grappled for 'em?" Major Ayers repeated.

Sure: run one down and hem him up under the bank and drag him out with his bare hands. That was Claude all over. And then they found that this year's lambs didn't have any wool at all, and that its flesh was the best fish eating in Louisiana; being partly cornfed that way giving it a good flavor, you see. So that's where Old Man Jackson quit the sheep business and went to fish ranching on a large scale. He knew he had a snap as long as Claude could catch 'em, so he made arrangements with the New Orleans markets right away, and they began to get rich.

"By jove," Major Ayers whispered tensely, his mind taking fire.

Claude liked the work. It was an adventurous kind of life that just suited him, so he quit everything and gave all his time to it. He quit drinking and gambling and running around at night, and there was a marked decrease in vice in that neighborhood, and the young girls pined for him at the local dances and sat on their front porches of a Sunday evening in vain.

Pretty soon he could outswim the old sheep, and having to dive so much after the young ones he got to where he could stay under water longer and longer at a time. Sometimes he'd stay under for a half hour or more. And pretty soon he got to where he'd stay in the water all day, only coming out to eat and sleep; and then they noticed that Claude's skin was beginning to look funny and that he walked kind of peculiar, like his knees were stiff or something. Soon after that he quit coming out of the water at all, even to eat, so they'd bring his dinner down to the water and leave it, and after a while he'd swim up and get it. Sometimes they wouldn't see Claude for days. But he was still catching those sheep, herding 'em into a pen Old Man Jackson had built in a shallow bayou and fenced off with hog wire, and his half of the money was growing in the bank. Occasionally halfeaten pieces of sheep would float ashore, and Old Man Jackson decided alligators were getting 'em again. But he couldn't put horns on 'em now because no one but Claude could catch 'em, and he hadn't seen Claude in some time.

It had been a couple of weeks since anybody had seen Claude, when one day there was a big commotion in the sheep pen. Old Man Jackson and a couple of his other boys ran down there and when they got there they could see the sheep jumping out of the water every which way, trying to get back on land again; and after a while a big alligator rushed out from among 'em, and Old Man Jackson knew what had scared the sheep.

And then, right behind the alligator he saw Claude. Claude's eyes had kind of shifted around to the side of his head and his mouth had spread back a good way, and his teeth had got longer. And then Old Man Jackson knew what had scared that alligator. But that was the last they ever saw of Claude.

Pretty soon after that, though, there was a shark scare at the bathing beaches along the Gulf coast. It seemed to be a lone shark that kept annoying women bathers, especially blondes; and they knew it was Claude Jackson. He was always hell after blondes.

Fairchild ceased. The niece squealed and jumped up and came to him, patting his back. Jenny's round ineffable eyes were upon him, utterly without thought. The semitic man sat slumped in his chair: he may have slept.

Major Ayers stared at Fairchild a long time. At last he said: "But why does the alligator feller wear congress boots?"

Fairchild mused a moment. Then he said dramatically: "He's got webbed feet."

"Yes," Major Ayers agreed. He mused in turn. "But this chap that got rich——"

The niece squealed again. She sat beside Fairchild and regarded him with admiration. "Go on, go on," she said. "About the one that stole the money, you know."

Fairchild looked at her kindly. Into the silence there came a thin saccharine strain. "There's the victrola," he said. "Lets go up and start a dance."

"The one who stole the money," she insisted. "Please." She put her hand on his shoulder.

"Some other time," he promised, rising. "Lets go up and dance now." The semitic man yet slumped in his chair. Fairchild shook him. "Wake up, Julius. I'm safe now."

The semitic man opened his eyes and Major Ayers said: "How much did they gain with their fish?"

"Not as much as they would have with a patent nice tasting laxative. All Americans dont eat fish, you know. Come on, lets go up and hold that dance they've been worrying us about every night."

NINE OCLOCK.

"Say," the niece said as she and Jenny mounted to the deck. "Remember that thing we swapped for the other night? the one you let me use for the one I let you use?"

"I guess so," Jenny answered. "I remember swapping."

"Have you used it yet?"

"I never can think of it," Jenny confessed. "I never can remember what it was you told me. . . . Besides, I've got another one, now."

"You have? Who told it to you?"

"The popeyed man. That English man."

"Major Ayers?"

"Uhuh. Last night we was talking and he kept on saying for us to go to Mandeville today. He kept on saying it. And so this morning he acted like he thought I meant we was going. He acted like he was mad."

"What was it he said?" Jenny told her—a mixture of pidgin-English and Hindustani that Major Ayers must have picked up along the Singapore waterfront or mayhap at some devious and doubtful place in the Straits, but after Jenny had repeated it it didn't sound like anything at all. "What?" the niece asked. Jenny said it again. "It dont sound like anything, to me," the niece said. "Is that the way he said it?"

"That's what it sounded like to me," Jenny replied.

The niece said curiously: "Men sure do swear at you a lot. They're always cursing you. What do you do to them, any way?"

"I dont do anything to them," Jenny answered. "I am just talking to them."

"Well, they sure do. . . . Say, you can have that one back you loaned me."

"Have you used it on anybody?" Jenny asked with interest.

"I tried it on that redheaded Gordon."

"That drownded man? What'd he say?"

"He beat me." The niece rubbed herself with a tanned retrospective hand. "He just beat hell out of me," she said.

"Gee," said Jenny.

Ten Oclock.

Fairchild gathered his watch, nourished it, brought it on deck again. The ladies hailed its appearance with doubtful pleasure. Mr Talliaferro and Jenny were dancing. The niece and Pete with his damaged hat, were performing together with a skillful and sexless abandon that was almost professional, while the rest of the party sat watching them.

"Whee," Fairchild squealed, watching the niece and Pete with growing childish admiration. At the moment they faced each other at a short distance, their bodies rigid as far as the waist. But below this they were as amazing jointless toys, their legs seemed to fly in every direction at once until their knees seemed to touch the floor. Then they caught hands and whirled sharply together, without a break in that dizzy staccato of heels. "Say, Major, look there! Look there, Julius! Come on, I believe I can do that."

He led his men to the assault. The victrola ran down at the moment: he directed the semitic man to attend it and went at once to where Pete and the niece stood. "Say, you folks are regular professionals. Pete, let me have her this time, will you? I want her to show me how you do that. Will you show me? Pete wont mind."

"All right," the niece agreed. "I'll show you. I owe you something for that yarn at dinner tonight." She put her hand on Pete's arm. "Dont go off, Pete. I'll show him and then he

can practice on the others. Dont you go off: you are all right.
You might take Jenny for a while. She must be tired: he's been
leaning on her for a half an hour. Come on, Dawson. Watch
me now." She had no bones at all.

Major Ayers and the semitic man had partners, though
more sedately. Major Ayers galloped around in a heavy dra-
goonish manner: when the record ended Miss Jameson was
panting. She offered to sit out the next one, but Fairchild
overruled her. He believed he had the knack of it. "We'll put
the old girl's dance over in style," he told them. Major Ayers,
inflamed by Fairchild's example, offered for the niece himself.
Mr Talliaferro, reft of Jenny, acquired Mrs Wiseman, the semitic man was cajoling the hostess. "We'll put her dance over
for her," Fairchild chanted. They were off.

Gordon had come up from somewhere and he stood in
shadow, watching. "Come on, Gordon," Fairchild shouted
to him. "Grab one." When the music ceased Gordon cut in
on Major Ayers. The niece looked up in surprise, and Major
Ayers departed in Jenny's direction. "I didn't know you
danced," she said.

"Why not?" Gordon asked.

"You just dont look like you did. And you told Aunt Pat
you couldn't dance."

"I cant," he answered, staring down at her. "Bitter," he said
slowly. "That's what you are. New. Like bark when the sap is
rising."

"Will you give it to me?" He was silent. She could not see
his face distinctly: only the bearded shape of his tall head.
"Why wont you give it to me?" Still no answer, and his head
was ugly as bronze against the sky. Fairchild started the machine again: a saxophone was a wailing obscenity, and she
raised her arms. "Come on."

                    *   *   *   *   *

When that one was finished Fairchild's watch rushed below
again, and presently Mr Talliaferro saw his chance and followed surreptitiously. Fairchild and Major Ayers were ecstat-
ically voluble: the small room fairly moiled with sound. Then
they rushed back on deck.

"Watch your step, Talliaferro," Fairchild cautioned him as
they ascended. "She's got her eye on you. Have you danced

with her yet?" Mr Talliaferro had not. "Better kind of breathe away from her when you do."

He led his men to the assault. The ladies demurred, but Fairchild was everywhere, cajoling, threatening, keeping life in the party. Putting the old girl's dance over. Mrs Maurier was trying to catch Mr Talliaferro's eye. The niece had peremptorily commandeered Pete again, and again Gordon stood in his shadow, haughty and aloof. They were off.

ELEVEN OCLOCK.

"I say," said Mr Talliaferro, popping briskly and cautiously into the room, accepting his glass, "we'd better slow up a bit, hadn't we?"

"What for?" asked the semitic man, and Fairchild said:

"Ah, its all right. She expects it from us. Somebody's got to be the hoi polloi, you know. Besides, we want to make this cruise memorable in the annals of deep water. Hey, Major? Talliaferro better go easy, though."

"Oh, we'll look out for Talliaferro," the semitic man said.

"No damned fear," Major Ayers assured him. "Have a go, eh?" They all had a go. Then they rushed back on deck.

* * * * *

"What do you do in New Orleans, Pete?" Miss Jameson asked intensely.

"One thing and another," Pete answered cautiously. "I'm in business with my brother," he added.

"You have lots of friends, I imagine? Girls would all like to dance with you. You are one of the best dancers I ever saw— almost a professional. I like dancing."

"Yeh," Pete agreed. He was restive. "I guess—"

"I wonder if you and I couldn't get together some evening and dance again? I dont go to night clubs much, because none of the men I know dance very well. But I'd enjoy it, with you."

"I guess so," Pete answered. "Well, I——"

"I'll give you my phone number and address, and you call me soon, will you? You might come out to dinner, and we'll go out afterward, you know."

"Sure," Pete answered uncomfortably. He removed his hat

and examined the crown. Then he slanted it once more across his dark reckless head. Miss Jameson said:

"Do you ever make dates ahead, Pete?"

"Naw," he answered quickly. "I wouldn't have a date over a day old. I just call 'em up and take 'em out and bring 'em back in time to go to work next day. I wouldn't have one I had to wait until tomorrow on."

"Neither do I. So I tell you what: lets break the rule one time, and make a date for the first night we are ashore—what do you say? You come out to dinner at my house, and we'll go out later to dance. I've got a car."

"I—— Well, you see——"

"We'll just do that," Miss Jameson continued, remorselessly. "We wont forget that: its a promise, isn't it?"

Pete rose. "I guess we——I guess I better not promise. Something might turn up, so I—so we couldn't make it. I guess. . . ." She sat quietly, looking at him. . . . "Maybe it'll be better to wait and fix it up when we get back. I might have to be out of town or something that day, see? Maybe we better wait and see how things shape up." Still she said nothing, and presently she removed her patient humorless eyes and looked out across the darkling water, and Pete stood uncomfortably with his goading urge to keep on saying something. "I guess we better wait and see later, see?" Her head was turned away, so he departed unostentatiously. He paused again and looked back at her. She gazed still out over the water: an uncomplaining abjectness of passivity, quiet in her shadowed chair.

*   *   *   *   *

As he embraced her, Jenny removed his hat slanted viciously upon his reckless head, and examined the broken crown with a recurrence of soft astonishment; and still holding the hat in her hand she came to him with a flowing enveloping movement, without seeming to move at all. Their faces merged and Jenny was immediately utterly boneless, seeming to suspend her merging rifeness by her soft mouth, then she opened her mouth against his . . . after a while Pete raised his head. Jenny's face was a passive drowsing blur rich, ineffably rich in the darkness; and Pete got out his unfresh handkerchief and wiped her mouth, quite gently.

"Got over it without leaving a scar, didn't you?" he said. Without volition they swung in a world unseen and warm as water; unseen and rife and beautiful, strange and hushed and grave beneath that waning moon of decay and death. . . . "Give your old man a kiss, kid. . . ."

* * * * *

The niece entered her aunt's room, without knocking. Mrs Maurier raised her astonished, shrieking face and dragged a garment shapelessly across her recently uncorseted breast, as women do. When she had partially recovered from the shock she ran heavily to the door and locked it.

"Its just me," the niece said. "Say, Aunt Pat——"

Her aunt gasped: her breast and chins billowed unconfined. "Why dont you knock? You should never enter a room like that. Doesn't Henry ever——"

"Sure he does," the niece interrupted. "All the time. Say, Aunt Pat, Pete thinks you ought to pay him for his hat. For stepping on it, you know."

Her aunt stared at her. "What?"

"You stepped through Pete's hat. He and Jenny think you ought to pay for it. Or offer to, anyway. I expect if you'd offer to, he wouldn't take it."

"Thinks I ought to p——" Mrs Maurier's voice faded into a shocked soundless amazement.

"Yes, they think so. . . . I mentioned it because I promised them I would. You dont have to unless you want to, you know."

"Thinks I ought to p——" Again Mrs Maurier's voice failed her, and her amazement became a chaotic thing that filled her round face interestingly. Then it froze into something definite: a coldly determined displeasure, and she recovered her voice.

"I have lodged and fed these people for a week," she said without humor. "I do not feel that I am called upon to clothe them also."

"Well, I just mentioned it because I promised," the niece repeated soothingly.

* * * * *

Mrs Maurier, Jenny and the niece had disappeared, to Mr Talliaferro's mixed relief. They still had two left, however. They took turn about with them.

Major Ayers, Fairchild and the semitic man, rushed below
again, Mr Talliaferro following openly this time, and a trifle
erratically. "How's it coming along?" Fairchild asked, poising
the bottle.

Mr Talliaferro made a wet deprecating sound, glancing at
the other two. They regarded him with kindly interest.

"Oh, they're all right," Fairchild assured him. "They are as
anxious to see you put it over as I am." He set the bottle down
well within reach, and gulped at his glass. "I tell you what, its
boldness does the trick with women, aint it, Major?"

"Right you are. Boldness: dash in: take 'em by storm."

"Sure. That's what you want to do. Have another drink."
He filled Mr Talliaferro's glass.

"That's my plan, exactly. Boldness. Boldness. Boldness." Mr
Talliaferro stared at the other glassily. He tried to wink.
"Didn't you see me dancing with her?"

"Yes, but that aint bold enough. If I were you, if I were
doing it, I'd turn the trick tonight, now. Say, Julius, you know
what I'd do? I'd go right to her room: walk right in. He's been
dancing with her and talking to her: ground already broken,
you see. I bet she's in there right now, waiting for him, hoping
he is bold enough to come in to her. He'll feel pretty cheap
tomorrow when he finds he missed his chance, wont he? You
never have but one chance with a woman, you know. If you
fail her then, she's done with you—the next man that comes
along gets her. It aint the man a woman cares for that reaps
the harvest of passion, you know: its the next man that comes
along after she's lost the other one. I'd sure hate to think I'd
been doing work for somebody else to get the benefit of,
wouldn't you?"

Mr Talliaferro stared at him. He swallowed twice. "But suppose, just suppose, she isn't expecting me."

"Oh, sure. Of course you've got to take that risk. It would
take a bold man, anyway, to walk right in her room, walk right
in without knocking and go straight to the bed. And how
many women would resist? I wouldn't, if I were a woman. If
you were her, Talliaferro, would you resist? I've found," he
went on, "that boldness gets pretty near anything, in this
world, especially women. But it takes a bold man. . . . Say, I
bet Major Ayers would do it."

"Right you are. I'd walk right in, by jove. . . . I say, I think I shall, anyway. Which one is it? not the old one?"

"All right. That is, if Talliaferro dont want to. He has first shot, you know: he's done all the heavy preparatory work. But it takes a bold man."

"Oh, Talliaferro's bold as any man," the semitic man said.

"But really," Mr Talliaferro repeated, "suppose she isn't expecting me. Suppose she were to call out——No, no."

"Yes, Talliaferro aint bold enough. We better let Major Ayers go, after all. No necessity for disappointing the girl, at least."

"Besides," Mr Talliaferro added quickly, "she is in a room with someone else."

"No, she aint. She's in a room to herself, now—that one at the end of this hall."

"That's Mrs Maurier's room," Mr Talliaferro said, staring at him.

"No, no, she changed. That room has a broken screen, so she changed. Julius and I were helping her move this afternoon. Weren't we, Julius? That's how I happen to know Jenny's in there now."

"But, really——" Mr Talliaferro swallowed again. "Are you sure that's her room? This is a serious matter, you know."

"Have another drink," Fairchild said.

Twelve Oclock.

The deck was deserted. Fairchild and Major Ayers halted, gazing about in pained astonishment. The victrola was hooded and mute, smugly inscrutable. They held a hurried council, then they set forth to beat up stragglers. There were no stragglers.

"Put on a record," Fairchild suggested at last. "Maybe that'll get 'em up here. They must have thought we'd gone to bed."

The semitic man started the victrola again, and again Major Ayers and Fairchild combed the deck, vainly. The moon had risen, its bony erstwhile disc was thumbed into the sky like a coin after too much handling.

* * * * *

Mrs Maurier routed out the captain and together they repaired to Fairchild's room. "Find it all," she directed. "Every single one." The captain found it all. "Now, open that window."

She gave the captain further directions, when they had finished, and she returned to her room and sat again on the edge of her bed. Moonlight came into the room level as a lance through the port, like a marble pencil shattering and filling the room with a thin silver dust, as of marble. "It has come, at last," she whispered, aware of her body heavy and soft with years. I should feel happy, I should feel happy she told herself, but her limbs felt chill and strange to her and within her a terrible thing was swelling, a thing terrible and poisonous and released, like water that has been dammed too long: as though there were waking within her comfortable long-familiar body a thing that abode there dormant, which she had harbored unaware.

She sat on the edge of her bed, feeling her strange chill limbs while that swelling thing within her unfolded like an intricate poisonous flower, an intricate slow convolvulæ of petals that grew and faded, died and were replaced by other petals huger and more implacable.

Her limbs were strange and cold: they were trembling. That dark flower of laughter, that secret hideous flower grew and grew until that entire world which was herself was become a slow implacable swirling of hysteria that rose in her throat and shook it as though with a myriad small hands; while from overhead there came a thin saccharine strain spaced off by a heavy thumping of feet where Fairchild was teaching Major Ayers to Charleston.

And soon, another sound: and the Nausikaa trembled and pulsed, girding herself with motion.

*   *   *   *   *

Mr Talliaferro stood in the bows, letting the wind blow upon his face, amid his hair. The worn moon had risen and she spread her boneless hand upon the ceaseless water, and the cold remote stars swung overhead, cold and remote and incurious: what cared they for the haggard despair in his face, for the hushed despair in his heart? They had seen too much human moiling and indecision and astonishment to be concerned over the fact that Mr Talliaferro had got himself engaged to marry again.

. . . . Soon, a sound: and the Nausikaa trembled and pulsed, girding herself with motion.

*   *   *   *   *

Suddenly Fairchild stopped, raising his hand for silence. "What's that?" he asked.

"What's what?" responded Major Ayers, pausing also and staring at him.

"I thought I heard something fall into the water." He crossed to the rail, leaning over it. Major Ayers followed him and they listened. But the dark restless water was untroubled by any foreign sound, the night was calm, islanding the worn bland disc of the moon.

"Steward throwing out grapefruit," Major Ayers suggested at last. They turned away.

"Hope so," Fairchild said. "Start her up again, Julius."

And soon, another sound: and the Nausikaa trembled and pulsed, girding herself with motion.

Epilogue.

SEAWATER had done strange things to Jenny's little green dress. It was roughdried and draggled, and it had kind of sagged here and drawn up there. The skirt in the back, for instance, because now between the gracious miniature ballooning of its hem and the tops of her dingy stockings, you saw pink flesh.

But she was ineffably unaware of this as she stood on Canal street waiting for her car to come along, watching Pete's damaged hat slanting away amid the traffic, clutching the dime he had given her for carfare in her little soiled hand. Soon her car came along and she got on it and gave the conductor her dime and received change and put seven cents in the machine, while men, unshaven men and coatless men and old men and spruce young men and men that smelled of toilet water and bay rum and sweat and men that smelled of just sweat, watched her with the moist abjectness of hounds. Then she went on up the aisle, rife, placidly unreluctant and then the car jolted forward and she sat partly upon a fat man in a derby and a newspaper, who looked up at her and then hunched over to the window and dived again into his newspaper with his derby on.

The car hummed and spurted and jolted and stopped and jolted and hummed and spurted between croaching walls and old iron lovely as dingy lace, and shrieking children from south Europe once removed and wild and soft as animals and cheerful with filth, and old rich foodsmells, smells rich enough to fatten flesh through the lungs; and women screaming from adjacent door to door in bright dirty shawls. Her three pennies had got warm and moist in her hand, so she changed them to the other hand and dried her palm on her thigh.

Soon it was a broader street at right angles: a weary green spaciousness of late August foliage and civilization again in the shape of a filling station; and she descended and passed between houses possessing once and long ago individuality, reserve, but now become somehow vaguely and dingily identical, reaching at last an iron gate through which she went and on up a shallow narrow concrete walk bordered by beds in which flowers for some reason never seemed to grow well, and so across the veranda and into the house.

Her father was on the night force and he now sat in his sock feet and with his galluses down, at his supper of mackerel (it was Friday) and fried potatoes and coffee and an early afternoon edition. He wiped his mustache with two sweeps of the back of his hand.

"Where you been?"

Jenny entered the room removing her hat. She dropped it on the floor and came up in a flanking movement. "On a boat ride," she answered.

Her father drew his feet under his chair to rise and his face suffused slowly with relief and anger.

"And you think you can go off like that, without a word to nobody, and then walk back into this house——" But Jenny captured him and she squirmed onto his rising lap and though he tried to defend himself, kissed him through his mackerelish mustache, and held him speechless while she delved amid that vague pinkish region which was her mind. After a while she remembered it.

"Haul up your sheet," she said. "You're jibing."

2.

Pete was the baby: he was too young to have been aware of it, of course, but that electric sign with the family name on it had marked a climacteric:—the phoenixlike rise of the family fortunes from the dun ashes of respectability and a small restaurant catering to Italian working people, to the final and ultimate Americanization of the family, since this fortune like most American ones, was built on the flouting of a statutory impediment.

Prior to nineteen nineteen you entered a dingy room fecund with the rich and heavy odors of Italian cooking, you sat surrounded by Italian faces and frank Italian eating sounds, at oilcloth of a cheerful red-and-white check and cunningly stained, impermeated with food, where you were presently supplied with more food. Perhaps old lady Ginotta herself came bustling out with soup and one thumb in a thick platter and a brisk word for you, or by Joe, anyway, barearmed and skilful and taciturn; while Mr Ginotta himself in his stained apron stood talking to a table of his intimates. Perhaps if you lingered long enough over your banana or overripe oft-handled grapes you would see Pete in his ragged corduroy knickers and faded clean shirt, with his shock of curly hair and his queer golden eyes, twelve years old and beautiful as only an Italian lad can be.

But now all this was changed. Where was once a dingy foodladen room, wooden floored and not too clean, was now a tiled space cleared and waxed for dancing and enclosed on one side by mirrors and on the other by a row of booths containing each a table and two chairs and lighted each by a discrete table lamp of that surreptitious and unmistakable shade of pink and curtained each with heavy maroon rep. And where you once got food good and Italian and cheap, you now paid so much for it that you were not required to eat it at all: and platters of spaghetti and roasted whole fowls, borne not by Joe barearmed and skillful if taciturn but by dinner coated waiters with faces ironed and older than sin;—platters which served as stage properties for the oldest and weariest comedy in the world, were served you and later removed by the waiters with a sort of clairvoyant ubiquity and returned to the kitchen practically intact. And from the kitchen there came no odor of cooking at all.

Joe's idea, it was. Joe, five and twenty and more American than any of them, had seen the writing on the wall, had argued, prevailed and proven himself right. Mr Ginotta had not stood prosperity. He was afraid of the new floor, to begin with. It was too slick, dangerous for a man of his age and bulk; and to look out of his kitchen, that kitchen into which he no longer dared bring his stained apron, upon a room once crowded with his friends and noisy and cheerful with eating and smells. . . .

But all that was changed now. The very waiters themselves he did not know, and the food they bore back and forth was not food, and the noise now was a turgid pandemonium of saxophones and drums and, riding above it like distracted birds, a shrill and metallic laughter of women, ceaseless and without joy, and the smells a blending of tobacco and alcohol and unchaste scent. And from the kitchen there came no longer any odor of cooking at all: even his range was gone, replaced by an oil stove.

So he died, fairly full of years and with more money to his name in the bank than most Italian princes have. Mrs Ginotta had the flu at the same time. It had settled in her ears and as time passed she became quite deaf; and because of the fact that her old friends now went elsewhere to dine and the people who came now arrived quite late, after she was in bed mostly, and her old man was dead and her sons were such Americans now, busy and rich and taciturn, and because the strange waiters frightened her a little, the old lady had got out of the habit of talking at all. She prepared food for her sons on the new stove of which she was afraid, but they were in and out so much it was hard to anticipate their mealtimes, and her eyes being no longer good enough for sewing, she spent her time puttering about their living quarters overhead, or in a corner of the kitchen where she would be out of the way, preparing vegetables and such—things that didn't require keenness of sight or attention.

The room itself she would not enter, though from her accustomed corner in the kitchen she could on occasion watch the boneless sophistication of the saxophone player and the drummer's flapping elbows, and years ago she had heard the noise they made. But that was long ago and she had forgotten it, and now she accepted their antics as she accepted the other changes, associating no sound with them at all. Joe had several automobiles now: big noticeable ones, and he used to try to persuade her to ride in them. But she refused stubbornly always, though it was a matter of neighborhood comment, how good the Ginotta boys were to the old lady.

But Joe, with his shrewd taciturn face and his thinning hair and his shirt of heavy striped silk smoothly taut across his tight embryonic paunch; Joe standing with his headwaiter at the desk, paused in his occupation to glance down that room with its every modern fixture, its tiled floor and lights and mirrors, with commendable pride. With the quiet joy of ownership his gaze followed its mirrored diminishing tunnel, passing on to the discreetly curtained entrance beneath that electric sign, that ultimate accolade of Americanization flashing his name in golden letters in rain or mist or against the remote insane stars themselves, and to his brother slanting his damaged hat defiantly, turning in beneath it.

Joe held his sheaf of banknotes in one hand and his poised wetted finger over it and watched Pete traverse the mirrored length of the room. "Where in hell you been?" he demanded.

"To the country," Pete answered shortly. "Anything to eat?"

"Eat, hell," his brother exclaimed. "Here I've had to pay a man two days just because you were off helling around somewheres. And now you come in talking about something to eat. Here——" he put aside his sheaf of money and from a drawer he took a pack of small slips of paper and ran through them. The headwaiter counted money undisturbed, methodically. "I promised this stuff to her by noon. You get busy and run it out there—here's the address—and no more fooling, see? Eat, hell." But Pete had brushed past the other without even pausing. His brother followed him. "You get right at it, you hear?" He raised his voice. "You think you can walk out of here and stay as long as you want, huh? You think you can come strolling back after a week, huh? You think you own this place?"

The old lady was waiting inside the kitchen door. She didn't hardly talk at all any more: only made sounds, wet sounds of satisfaction and alarm; and she saw her older son's face and she made these sounds now, looking from one to the other but not offering to touch them. Pete entered the room and his brother stopped at the door, and the old lady shuffled across to the stove and fetched Pete a plate of warmed-over spaghetti and fish and set it before him at a zinc-covered table. His brother stood in the door, glaring at him.

"Get up from there, now, like I told you. Come on, come on, you can eat when you get back."

But the old lady bustled around, getting between them with the stubborn barrier of her deafness, and her alarmed sounds rose again, then fell and became a sort of meaningless crooning while she kept herself between them, pushing Pete's plate nearer, putting his knife and fork into his hands. "Look out," Pete said at last, pushing her hands away. Joe glared from the door, but he humored her as he always did.

"Make it snappy," he said gruffly, turning away. When he had gone the old lady returned to her chair and her discarded bowl of vegetables.

Pete ate hungrily. Sounds came back to him: a broom, and indistinguishable words, and then the street door opened and closed and above a swift tapping of heels he heard a woman's voice. It spoke to his brother at the desk, but the brittle staccato came on without stopping, and as Pete raised his head the girl entered on her high cheap heels and an unbelievable length of pale stocking severed sharply by her skimpy dark frock. Within the small bright bell of her hat, her painted passionate face, and her tawdry shrillness was jointless and poised as a thin tree.

"Where you been?" she asked.

"Off with some women." He resumed his meal.

"More than one?" she asked quickly, watching him.

"Yeh. Five or six. Reason it took me so long."

"Oh," she said. "You're some little poppa, aint you?" He continued to eat and she came over beside him. "Whatcher so glum about? Somebody take your candy away from you?" She removed his hat. "Say, look at your hat." She stared at it, then laid it on the table and sliding her hand into his thickly curling hair she tugged his face up, and his queer golden eyes. "Wipe your mouth off," she said. But she kissed him, anyway, and raised her head again. "You better wipe it off now, sure enough," she said with contemplation. She released his hair. "Well, I got to go." And she turned, but paused again at the old lady's chair and screamed at her in Italian. The old lady looked up, nodding her head, then bent to her beans again.

Pete finished his meal. He could still hear her shrill voice from the other room, and he lit a cigarette and strolled out. The old lady hadn't been watching him, but as soon as he was gone, she got up and removed the plate and washed it and put it away, and then sat down again and picked up her bowl.

"Ready to go, huh?" His brother looked up from the desk. "Here's the address. Snap it up, now: I told her I'd have it out there by noon." The bulk of Joe's business was outside, like this. He had a name for reliability of which he was proud. "Take the Studebaker," he added.

"That old hack?" Pete paused, protesting. "I'll take your Chrysler."

"Damn if you will," his brother rejoined, heating again. "Get on, now, take that Studebaker like I told you," he said violently. "If you dont like it, buy one of your own."

"Ah, shut up." Pete turned away. Within one of the booths, beyond a partly drawn curtain, he saw her facing the mirror, renewing the paint on her mouth. Beside her stood one of the waiters in his shirtsleeves, holding a mop. She made a swift signal with her hand to his reflection in the glass. He slanted his hat again without replying.

She was an old hack, beside the fawn-and-nickel splendor of the new Chrysler, but she would go and she would carry six or seven cases comfortably—the four cases he now had were just peas in a matchbox. He followed the traffic to Canal street, crossed it and fell into the line waiting to turn out St Charles. The line inched forward, stopped, inched forward again when the bell rang. The policeman at the curb held the line again and Pete sat watching the swarming darting news-boys, and loafers and shoppers and promenaders and little coltlike girls with their monotonous blonde legs. The bell rang, but the cop still held them. Pete leaned out, jazzing his idling engine. "Come on, come on, you blue-bellied bastard," he called. "Lets go."

At last the cop lowered his glove and Pete whipped skilfully into St Charles, and presently the street widened and became an avenue picketed with palms, and settling onto his spine and slanting his damaged straw hat to a swaggering slant on his dark reckless head, he began to overhaul the slow ones, pass-ing them up.

3.

Fairchild's splitting head ultimately roused him, and he lay for some time submerged in the dull throbbing misery of his body before he discovered that the boat was stationary again and, after an effort of unparalleled stoicism, that it was eleven oclock. No sound anywhere, yet there was some thing in the atmosphere of his surroundings, something different. But try-ing to decide what it was only made his head pound the worse, so he gave it up and lay back again. The semitic man slumbered in his berth.

After a while Fairchild groaned, and rose and wavered blunderingly across the cabin and drank deeply of water. Then he saw land through the port: a road and a weathered board wall, and beyond it, trees. Mandeville he decided. He tried to rouse the semitic man, but the other cursed him from slumber and rolled over to face the wall.

He hunted again for a bottle, but there were not even any empty ones: who ever did it had made a clean sweep. Well, a cup of coffee, then. So he got into his trousers and crossed the passage to the lavatory and held his head beneath a tap for a while. Then he returned and finished dressing and sallied forth.

Someone slumbered audibly in Major Ayers' room. It was Major Ayers himself, and Fairchild closed the door and went on, struck anew with that strange atmosphere which the yacht seemed to have gained overnight. The saloon was empty also, and a broken meal offended his temporarily refined sensibilities with partially emptied cups and cold soiled plates. But still no sound, no human sound, save Major Ayers and the semitic man in slumber's strophe and antistrophe. He stood in the door of the saloon and groaned again. Then he took his splitting head on deck.

Here he blinked in the light, shutting his eyes against it while hot brass hammers beat against his eyeballs. Three men dangling their legs over the edge of the quay regarded him, and he opened his eyes again and saw the three men.

"Goodmorning," he said. "What's this town? Mandeville?"

The three men looked at him. After a time one said:

"Mandeville? Mandeville what?"

"What town is it, then?" he asked, but as he spoke awareness came to him and looking about he saw a steel bridge and a trolley on the bridge, and further still, a faint mauve smudge on the sky, and in the other direction the flag that floated above the yacht club, languorous in a faint breeze. The three men sat and swung their legs and watched him. Presently one of them said:

"Your party went off and left you."

"Looks like it," Fairchild agreed. "Do you know if they said anything about sending a car back for us?"

"No, she aint going to send back today," the man answered. Fairchild cleared his aching eyes: it was the captain. "Trolley track over yonder a ways," he called after Fairchild as he turned and descended the companionway.

4.

Major Ayers' appointment was for three oclock. His watch corroborated and commended him as he stepped from the elevator into a long cool corridor glassed on either hand by opaque plate from beyond which came a thin tapping of typewriters. Soon he found the right door and he entered it, and across a low barrier he gave his card to a thin scented girl, glaring at her affably, and stood in the ensuing interval gazing out the window across diversified rectangles of masonry toward the river.

The girl returned. "Mr Reichman will see you now," she said across her chewing gum, swinging the gate open for him.

Mr Reichman shook his hand and offered him a chair and a cigar. He asked Major Ayers for his impressions of New Orleans and immediately interrupted the caller's confused staccato response to ask Major Ayers, for whom the war had served as the single possible condition under which he could have returned to England at all, and to whom for certain private reasons London had been interdict since the Armistice, how affairs compared between the two cities. Then he swung back in his patent chair and said:

"Now, Major, just what is your proposition?"

"Ah yes," said Major Ayers, flicking the ash from his cigar. "Its a salts. Now, all Americans are constipated——"

5.

Beneath him, on the ground floor, where a rectangle of light fell outward across the alleyway, a typewriter was being hammered by a heavy and merciless hand. Fairchild sat with a cigar on his balcony just above the unseen but audible typist, enjoying the cool darkness and the shadowed treefilled spaciousness of the cathedral close beneath his balcony. An occasional trolley clanged and crashed up Royal street, but this was but seldom, and when it had died away there was no sound save the monotonous merging clatter of the typewriter. Then he saw and recognised Mr Talliaferro as he turned the corner, and with an exclamation of alarm he sprang to his feet, kicking his chair over backward. Ducking quickly into the room redolent of pennyroyal he snapped off the reading lamp and leaped up on a couch, feigning sleep.

Mr Talliaferro walked dapperly, swinging his stick, his goal in sight. Yes, Fairchild was right——he knew women, the feminine soul   ? No, not soul: they have no souls. Nature, the feminine nature—that substance, that very substance of their beings, impalpable as moonlight, challenging and retreating at the same time, inconsistent, nay, incomprehensible, yet serving their ends with such a devastating practicality. As though the earth, the world, man and his very desires and impulses themselves, had been invented for the sole purpose of hushing their little hungry souls by filling their time through serving their biological ends. . . .

Yes, boldness. And propinquity. And opportunity, that happy conjunction of technique and circumstance, being with the right one in the right place at the proper time. Yes, yes, Opportunity, Opportunity—more important than all, perhaps. Mr Talliaferro put up Opportunity: he called for a ballot. The ayes had it.

He stopped utterly still in the flash of his inspiration. At last he had it, had the trick, the magic Word. It was so simple that he stood in amaze at the fact that it had not occurred to him before. But then he realized that its very simplicity was the explanation. And my nature is complex he told himself, gazing at stars in a hot dark sky, in a path of sky above the open coffin of the street. It was so devastatingly simple that he knew a faint qualm. Was it——was it exactly sporting? Wasn't it like shooting quail on the ground? But no, no: now that he had the key, now that he had found the Word, he dared admit to himself that he had suffered. Not so much in his vanity, not physically—after all, man can do without the pleasures of love: it will not kill him; but because each failure seemed to put years behind him with far more finality than the mere recurrence of natal days. Yes, Mr Talliaferro owed himself reparation, let them suffer who must. And was that not woman's part from time immemorial?

Opportunity, create your Opportunity, prepare the ground by overlooking none of those small important trivialities which mean so much to them, then take advantage of it. And I can do that he told himself. Indifference, perhaps, as though women were no rare thing with me, that there was perhaps another woman I had rather have seen but circumstances over which neither of us had any control intervened. They like a man who has other women, for some reason. Can it be that love to them is half adultery and half jealousy? . . . Yes, I can do that sort of thing, I really can. . . . "She would have one suit of black underthings," Mr Talliaferro said aloud with a sort of exultation.

He struck the pavement with his stick, lightly. "By God, that's it," he exclaimed in a hushed tone, striding on. "Create the opportunity, lead up to it delicately but firmly. Drop a remark about coming tonight only because I'd promised. . . . Yes, they like an honorable man: it increases their latitude. She'll say 'Please take me to dance,' and I'll say 'No, really, I dont care to dance tonight,' and she'll say 'Wont you take me?' leaning against me, eh?—lets see—yes, she'll take my hand. But I shan't respond at once. She'll tease and then I'll put my arm around her and raise her face in the dark cab and kiss her, coldly, and I'll say 'Do you really want to dance tonight?' and then she'll say 'Oh, I dont know. Suppose we just drive around a while . . . ?' Will she say that at this point? Well, should she not. . . . Lets see, what would she say?"

Mr Talliaferro strode on, musing swiftly. Well, anyway, if she says that, if she does say that, then I'll say 'No, lets dance'. Yes, yes, something like that. Though perhaps I'd better kiss her again, not so coldly, perhaps? . . . But should she say something else. . . . But then, I shall be prepared for any contingency, eh? Half the battle. . . . Yes, something like that, delicately but firmly done, so as not to alarm the quarry. Some walls are carried by storm, but all walls are reduced by siege. There is also the fable of the wind and the sun and the man in a cloak. "We'll change the gender, by jove," Mr Talliaferro said aloud, breaking suddenly from his reverie to discover that he had passed Fairchild's door. He retraced his steps, craning his neck to see the dark window.

"Fairchild!"

No reply.

"Oh, Fairchild!"

The two dark windows were inscrutable as two fates. He pressed the bell, then stepped back to complete his aria. Beside the door was another entrance. Light streamed across a half length lattice blind like a saloon door; beyond it a typewriter was being thumped viciously. Mr Talliaferro knocked diffidently upon the blind.

"Hello," a voice boomed above the chattering machine, though the machine itself did not falter. Mr Talliaferro pondered briefly, then he knocked again.

"Come in, damn you." The voice drowned the typewriter temporarily. "Come in: do you think this is a bathroom?" Mr Talliaferro opened the blind and the huge collarless man at the typewriter raised his sweating leonine head, regarding Mr Talliaferro fretfully. "Well?"

"Pardon me: I'm looking for Fairchild."

"Next floor," the other snapped, poising his hands. "Goodnight."

"But he doesn't answer. Do you happen to know if he is in tonight?"

"I do not."

Mr Talliaferro pondered again, diffidently. "I wonder how I might ascertain? I'm pressed for t——"

"How in hell do I know? Go up and see, or stand out there and call him."

"Thanks, I'll go up, if you've no objection."

"Well, go up, then," the big man answered, leaping again upon his typewriter.

Mr Talliaferro watched him for a time. "May I go through this way?" he ventured at last, mildly and politely.

"Yes, yes. Go anywhere. But for God's sake, dont bother me any longer."

Mr Talliaferro murmured Thanks, sidling past the large frenzied man. The whole small room trembled to the man's heavy hands and the typewriter leaped and chattered like a mad thing.

He went on and into a dark corridor filled with a thin vicious humming, and mounted lightless stairs into an acrid region scented with pennyroyal. Fairchild heard him stumble in the darkness, and groaned. I'll have your blood for this! he swore at the thundering oblivious typewriter beneath him. After a time his door opened and the caller hissed Fairchild! into the room. Fairchild swore again under his breath. The couch complained to his movement, and he said:

"Wait there until I turn up the light. You'll break everything I've got, blundering around in the dark."

Mr Talliaferro sighed with relief. "Well, well, I had just about given you up and gone away when that man beneath you kindly let me come in through his place." The light came on under Fairchild's hand. "Oh, you were asleep, weren't you? So sorry to have disturbed you. But I want your advice, as I failed to see you this morning. . . . You got home all right?" he asked with thoughtful tact.

Fairchild answered "Yes" shortly, and Mr Talliaferro laid his hat and stick on a table, knocking therefrom a vase of late summer flowers. With amazing agility he caught the vase before it crashed, though not before its contents had liberally splashed him. "Ah, the devil!" he ejaculated. He replaced the vase and quickly fell to mopping at his sleeves and coat front with his handkerchief. "And this suit fresh from the presser, too," he added with exasperation.

Fairchild watched him with ill suppressed vindictive glee. "Too bad," he commiserated insincerely, lying again on the couch. "But she wont notice it: she'll be too interested in what you're saying to her."

Mr Talliaferro looked up, quickly, a trifle dubiously. He spread his handkerchief across the corner of the table to dry. Then he smoothed his hands over his neat pale hair.

"Do you think so? Really? That's what I stopped in to discuss with you." For a while Mr Talliaferro sat neatly and gazed at his host from beyond a barrier of a polite and hopeless despair. Fairchild remarked his expression with sudden curiosity, but before he could speak Mr Talliaferro reassimilated himself and became again his familiar articulated mild alarm.

"What's the matter?" Fairchild asked.

"I? Nothing. Nothing at all, my dear fellow. Why do you ask?"

"You looked like you had something on your mind, just then."

The guest laughed artificially. "Not at all. You imagined it, really." His hidden dark thing lurked behind his eyes yet, but he vanquished it temporarily. "I will ask a favor, however, before I . . . before I ask your advice. . . . That you dont mention our——conversation. The general trend of it, you know." Fairchild watched him with curiosity. "To any of our mutual women friends," he added further, meeting his host's kind curious gaze. Suddenly Mr Talliaferro put his cards on the table. "I dont want Mrs Maurier to hear of it, for reasons which I shall tell you at the earliest opportunity."

"All right," Fairchild agreed. "I never mention any of the conversations we have on this subject. I dont reckon I'll start now."

"Thank you." Mr Talliaferro was again his polite smug self. "I have a particular reason, this time, which I'll divulge to you as soon as I consider myself. . . . You will be the first to know."

"Sure," said Fairchild again. "What is it to be this time?"

"Ah, yes," said the guest with swift optimism, "I really believe that I have discovered the secret of success with them: create the proper setting before hand, indifference to pique them, then boldness—that is what I have always overlooked. Listen: tonight I shall turn the trick. But I want your advice." Fairchild groaned and lay back. Mr Talliaferro picked his handkerchief from the table and whipped it about his ankles. He continued:

"Now, I shall make her jealous to begin with, by speaking of another woman in—er, quite intimate terms. She will doubtless wish to dance, but I shall pretend indifference, and when she begs me to take her to dance, perhaps I'll kiss her, suddenly, but with detachment——you see?"

"Yes?" murmured the other, cradling his head on his arms and closing his eyes.

"Yes. So we'll go and dance, and I'll pet her a bit, still impersonally, as if I were thinking of someone else. She'll naturally be intrigued and she'll say 'What are you thinking of?' and I'll say 'Why do you want to know?' She'll plead with me, perhaps dancing quite close to me, cajoling; but I'll say 'I'd rather tell you what you are thinking of' and she will say 'What?' immediately, and I'll say 'You are thinking of me.' Now, what do you think of that? What will she say then?"

"Probably tell you you've got a swelled head."

Mr Talliaferro's face fell. "Do you think she'll say that?"

"Dont know. You'll find out soon enough."

"No," Mr Talliaferro said after a while, "I dont believe she will. I rather fancied she'd think I knew a lot about women." He mused deeply for a time. Then he burst out again: "If she does, I'll say 'Perhaps so. But I am tired of this place. Lets go.' She'll not want to leave, but I'll be firm. And then——" Mr Talliaferro became smug, bursting with something he withheld. "No, no: I shan't tell you—its too excruciatingly simple. Why someone else has not. . . ." He sat gloating.

"Scared I'll run out and use it myself before you have a chance?" Fairchild asked.

"No, really; not at all. I——" He considered a moment, then leaned to the other. "Its not that at all, really; I only feel that. . . . Being the discoverer, that sort of thing, eh? I trust you, my dear fellow," he added swiftly in a burst of confidence. "Merely my own scruples——You see?"

"Sure," said Fairchild drily. "I understand."

"You will have so many opportunities, while I. . . ." Again that dark thing came up behind Mr Talliaferro's eyes and peered forth a moment. He drove it back. "And you really think it will work?"

"Sure. Provided that final coup is as deadly as you claim. And provided she acts like she ought to. It might be a good idea to outline the plot to her, though. So she won't slip up herself."

"You are pulling my leg now," Mr Talliaferro bridled slightly. "But dont you think this plan is good?"

"Airtight. You've thought of everything, haven't you?"

"Surely. That's the only way to win battles, you know. Napoleon taught us that."

"Napoleon also said something about the heaviest artillery, too," the other said wickedly. Mr Talliaferro smiled with deprecatory complacence.

"I am as I am," he murmured.

"Especially when it hasn't been used in some time," Fairchild added. Mr Talliaferro looked like a struck beast and the other said quickly: "But are you going to try this scheme tonight, or are you just describing a hypothetical case?"

Mr Talliaferro produced his watch and glanced at it in consternation. "Good gracious, I must run." He sprang to his feet, thrusting his handkerchief into his pocket. "Thanks for advising me. I really think I have the system at last, dont you?"

"Sure," the other agreed. At the door Mr Talliaferro turned and rushed back to shake hands. "Wish me luck," he said turning again. He paused once more. "Our little talk: you'll not mention it?"

"Sure, sure," repeated Fairchild. The door closed upon the caller and his descending feet sounded on the stairs. He stumbled again, then the street door closed behind him, and Fairchild rose and stood on the balcony watching him out of sight. Fairchild returned to the couch and reclined again, laughing. Abruptly he ceased chuckling and lay for a time in an alarmed concern. Then he groaned again and rose and took his hat.

As he stepped into the alley, the semitic man pausing at the entrance, spoke to him. "Where are you going?" he asked.

"I dont know," Fairchild replied. "Somewhere. The Great Illusion has just called," he explained. "He has an entirely new scheme tonight."

"Oh. Slipping out, are you?" the other asked, lowering his voice.

"No, he just dashed away. But I dont dare stay in this evening. He'll be back inside of two hours to tell me why this one didn't work. We'll have to go somewhere else." The semitic man mopped his handkerchief across his bald head. Beyond the lattice blind beside them the typewriter still chattered. Fairchild chuckled again, then he sighed. "I wish Talliaferro could find him a woman. I'm tired of being seduced. . . . Lets go over to Gordon's."

6.

The niece had already yawned elaborately several times at the lone guest: she was prepared and recognised the preliminary symptoms that indicated that her brother was on the point of his customary abrupt and muttered departure from the table. She rose also, with alacrity.

"Well," she said briskly, "I've enjoyed knowing you a lot, Mark. Next summer maybe we'll be back here, and we'll have to do it again, wont we?"

"Patricia," her aunt said, "sit down."

"I'm sorry, Aunt Pat. But Josh wants me to sit with him, tonight. He's going away tomorrow," she explained to the guest.

"Aren't you going too?" Mark Frost asked.

"Yes, but this is our last night here, and Gus wants me to——"

"Not me," her brother denied quickly. "You needn't come away on my account."

"Well, I think I'd better, anyway."

Her aunt repeated "Patricia."

But the niece ignored her. She circled the table and shook the guest's hand briskly, before he could rise. "Goodbye," she repeated. "Til next summer." Her aunt said Patricia again, firmly. She turned again at the door and said politely: "Good night, Aunt Pat."

Her brother had gone on up the stairs. She hurried after him, leaving her aunt saying Patricia! in the dining room, and reached the head of the stairs in time to see his door close behind him. When she tried the knob the door was locked, so she came away and went quietly to her room.

She stripped off her clothes in the darkness and lay on her bed, and after a while she heard him banging and splashing in the connecting bathroom. When these sounds had ceased she rose and entered the bathroom from her side, quietly, and quietly she tried his door. Unlocked.

She snapped on the light and spun the tap of the shower until needles of water drummed viciously into the bath. She thrust her hand beneath it at intervals: soon it was stinging and cold; and she drew breath as for a dive and sprang beneath it, clutching a cake of soap, and cringed shuddering and squealing while the water needled her hard simple body in its startling white bathing suit, matting her coarse hair, stinging and blinding her.

She whirled the tap again and the water ceased its antiseptic miniature thunder, and after towelling herself vigorously she found that she was as hot as ever, though not sticky any longer; so moving more slowly she returned to her room and donned fresh pajamas. This suit had as yet its original cord. Then she went on her bare silent feet and stood again at the door of her brother's room, listening. "Look out, Josh," she called suddenly, flinging open the door, "I'm coming in."

His room was dark, but she could discern his shaped body in bed and she sped across the room and plumped jouncing onto the bed beside him. He jerked himself up sharply.

"Here," he exclaimed. "What do you want to come in here worrying me for?" He raised himself still further: a brief violent struggle, and the niece thudded solidly on the floor. She said Ow in a muffled surprised tone. "Now, get out and stay out," her brother added. "I want to go to sleep."

"Aw, lemme stay a while. I'm not going to bother you."

"Haven't you been staying under my feet for a week, without coming in here where I'm trying to go to sleep? Get out, now."

"Just a little while," she begged. "I'll lie still if you want to go to sleep."

"You wont keep still. You go on, now."

"Please, Gus. I swear I will."

"Well," he agreed at last, grudgingly. "But if you start flopping around——"

"I'll be still," she promised. She slid quickly onto the bed and lay rigidly on her back. Outside, in the hot darkness, insects scraped and rattled and droned. The room, however, was a spacious quiet coolness, and the curtains at the windows stirred in a ghost of a breeze.

"Josh." She lay flat, perfectly still.

"Huh."

"Didn't you do something to that boat?"

After a while he said: "What boat?" She was silent, taut with listening. He said: "Why? what would I want to do anything to a boat for? What makes you think I did?"

"Didn't you, now? Honest?"

"You're crazy. I never hurt—I never was down there except when you came tagging down there, that morning. What would I want to do anything to it, for?" They lay motionless: a kind of tenseness. He said, suddenly: "Did you tell her I did something to it?"

"Aw, dont be a goof. I'm not going to tell on you."

"You're damn right you wont. I never did anything to it."

"All right, all right: I'm not going to tell, if you haven't got guts to. You're yellow, Josh," she told him calmly.

"Look here, I told you that if you wanted to stay in here, you'd have to keep quiet, didn't I? Shut up, then. Or get out."

"Didn't you break that boat, honest?"

"No, I told you. Now, you shut up or get out of here."

They lay quiet for a time. After a while she moved carefully, turning onto her belly by degrees. She lay still again for a time, then she raised her head. He seemed to be asleep, so she lowered her head again, relaxing her muscles, spreading her arms and legs to where the sheet was still cool.

"I'm glad we're going tomorrow," she murmured, as though to herself. "I like to ride on the train. And mountains again. I love mountains, all blue and . . . blue. . . . We'll be seeing mountains day after tomorrow. Little towns on 'em that dont smell like people eating all the time. And mountains. . . ."

"No mountains between here and Chicago," her brother said gruffly. "Shut up."

"Yes there are." She raised herself on her elbows. "There are some. I saw some coming down here."

"That was in Virginia and Tennessee. We dont go through Virginia to Chicago, dumbbell."

"We go through Tennessee, though."

"Not that part of Tennessee. Shut up, I tell you. Here, you get up and go on back to your room."

"No. Please, just a little while longer. I'll lie still. Come on, Gus, dont be so crummy."

"Get out, now," he repeated implacably.

"I'll be still: I wont say a w—"

"No. Outside, now. Go on. Go on, Gus, like I tell you."

She heaved herself over nearer. "Please, Josh. Then I'll go."

"Well. Be quick about it." He turned his face away and she leaned down and took his ear between her teeth, biting it just a little, making a kind of meaningless maternal sound against his ear. "That's enough," he said presently, turning his head and his moistened ear. "Get out, now."

She rose obediently and returned to her room. It seemed to be hotter in here than in his room, so she got up and removed her pajamas and got back in bed, and lay on her back cradling her dark grave head in her arms and gazing into the darkness, and after a while it wasn't so hot and it was like she was on a high place looking away out where mountains faded dreaming and blue, on and on into a purple haze under the slanting and solemn music of the sun. She'd see 'em, day after tomorrow. Mountains. . . .

7.

Fairchild went directly to the marble and stood before it, clasping his hands at his burly back. The semitic man sat immediately on entering the room, preempting the single chair. The host was busy beyond the rep curtain which constituted his bedroom, from where he presently reappeared with a bottle of whiskey. He had removed both shirt and undershirt now, and beneath a faint reddish fuzz his chest gleamed whitely with heat, like an oiled gladiator's.

"I see," Fairchild remarked as the host entered, "that you too have been caught by this modern day fetich of virginity. But you have this advantage over us: yours will remain inviolate without your having to shut your eyes to its goings-on; you dont have to make any effort to keep yours from being otherwise. Very satisfactory. And very unusual. The greatest part of man's immolation of virginity is, I think, composed of an alarm and a suspicion that someone else may be, as the term is, getting it."

"Perhaps Gordon's alarm regarding his own particular illusion of it is, that someone else may not get it of him," the semitic man suggested.

"No, I guess not," Fairchild said. "He dont expect to sell this to anybody, you know. Who would pay out good money for a virginity he couldn't later violate, if only to assure himself it was the genuine thing?"

"Leda clasping her duck between her thighs could yet be carved out of it however," the other pointed out. "It is large enough for that. Or——"

"Swan," corrected Fairchild.

"No, duck," the semitic man insisted. "Americans would

prefer a duck. Or udders and a figleaf might be added to the thing as it stands. Isn't that possible, Gordon?"

"Yes. It might be restored," Gordon admitted drily. He disappeared again beyond the curtain and returned with two heavy tumblers and a shaving mug bearing a name in gothic lettering of faded gilt. He drew up the bench on which his enamel water pitcher rested, and Fairchild came and sat upon it. Gordon took the shaving mug and went to lean his tall body against the wall. His intolerant hawk's face was like bronze in the unshaded glare of the light. The semitic man puffed at his cigar. Fairchild raised his glass, squinting through it.

"Udders, and a fig leaf," he repeated. He drank and set his tumbler down to light a cigarette. "After all, that is the end of art. I mean——"

"We do get something out of art," the semitic man agreed. "We all admit that."

"Yes," said Fairchild. "Art reminds us of our youth, of that age when life dont need to have her face lifted every so often for us to consider her beautiful. That's about all the virtue there is in art: its a kind of Battle Creek, Michigan for the spirit. And when it reminds us of youth, we remember grief and forget time. That's something."

"Something if all man has to do is forget time," the semitic man rejoined. "But one who spends his days trying to forget time is like one who spends his time forgetting death or digestion. That's just another instance of your unshakable faith in words. Its like morphine, language is. A fearful habit to form: you become a bore to all who would otherwise cherish you. Of course, there is the chance that you may be hailed as a genius after you are dead long years. But what is that to you? There will still be high endeavor that ends as always with kissing in the dark, but where are you? Time. Time? why worry about something that takes care of itself so well? You were born with the habit of consuming time. Be satisfied with that. Tom o' Bedlam had the only genius for consuming Time: that is, to be utterly unaware of it. But you speak for artists. I am thinking of the majority of us who are not artists and who need protection from artists, whose time the artists insists on passing for us. We get along quite well with our sleeping and eating and procreation, if you artists only let us alone. But you accursed who are not satisfied with the world as it is and so must try to rebuild the very floor you are standing on, you keep on talking and shouting and gesturing at us until you get us all fidgetty and alarmed. So I believe that if art served any purpose at all, it would at least keep the artists themselves occupied."

Fairchild raised his glass again. "Its more than that," he said. "Its getting into life, getting into it and wrapping it around you, becoming a part of it. Women can do it without art—old biology takes care of that. But men, men. . . . A woman conceives: does she care afterward whose seed it was? Not she. And bears, and all the rest of her life—her young troubling years, that is—is filled. Of course the father can look at it occasionally. But in art, a man can create without any assistance at all: what he does is his. A perversion, I grant you; but a perversion that builds Chartres, and invents Lear, is a pretty good thing." He drank, and set his tumbler down.

"There are women artists, though," the semitic man said. "How do you explain that?"

"Creation, reproduction from within. . . . Is the dominating impulse in the world feminine, after all, as aboriginal peoples believe? I mean, to reproduce? There is a kind of spider or something. The female is the larger and when the male comes to her, he goes to death: she devours him during the very act of conception. And that's man: a kind of voraciousness that makes an artist stand beside himself with a notebook in his hand always, putting down all the charming things that ever happen to him, killing them for the sake of some problematical something he might or might not ever use. Listen," he said, "love, youth, sorrow and hope and despair—they were nothing at all to me until I found later some need for a particular reaction to put in the mouth of some character of whom I wasn't at that time certain, and that I dont yet consider very admirable. But maybe it was because I had to work all the time to earn a living, when I was a young man."

"Perhaps so," the semitic man agreed. "People still believe they have to work to live."

"Sure you have to work to live," Fairchild said quickly.

"You'd naturally say that. If a man has had to deny himself any pleasures during his pleasuring years, he always likes to believe it was necessary. That's where you get your puritans from. We dont like to see anyone violate laws we observe, and get away with it. God knows, heaven is a dry reward for abnegation."

Fairchild rose and went to stand again before the fluid, passionate fixity of the marble. "The end of art," he repeated. "I mean, to the consumer, not to us: we have to do it, they dont. They can take it or leave it. Probably Gordon feels the same way about stories that I do about sculpture, but for me——" he mused upon the marble for a time. "When the statue is completely nude, it has only a coldly formal significance, you know. But when some foreign matter, like a leaf or a fold of drapery (kept there in defiance of gravity by God only knows what) draws the imagination to where the organs of sex are concealed, it lends the statue a warmer, a——a more——"

"Speculative significance," supplied the semitic man.

"——speculative significance which I must admit I require in my sculpture."

"Certainly the moralists agree with you."

"Why shouldn't they? The same food nourishes everybody's convictions alike. And a man that earns his bread in a glue factory must get some sort of pleasure from smelling cattle hooves, or he'd change his job. There's your perversion, I think."

"And," the semitic man said, "if you spend your life worrying over sex, its an added satisfaction to get paid for your time."

"Yes. But if I earned my bread by means of sex, at least I'd have enough pride about it to be a good honest whore." Gordon came over and filled the glasses again. Fairchild returned and got his, and prowled aimlessly about the room, examining things. The semitic man sat with his handkerchief spread upon his bald head. He regarded Gordon's naked torso with envious wonder. "They dont seem to bother you at all," he stated fretfully.

"Look here," Fairchild called suddenly. He had unswaddled a damp cloth from something and he now bent over his find. "Come here, Julius."

The semitic man rose and joined him. It was clay, yet damp, and from out its dull dead grayness Mrs Maurier looked at them. Her chins, harshly, and her flaccid jaw muscles with savage verisimilitude. Her eyes were caverns thumbed with two motions into the dead familiar astonishment of her face; and yet, behind them, somewhere within those empty sockets, behind all her familiar surprise there was something else, something that exposed her face for the mask it was, and still more, a mask unawares. "Well, I'm damned," Fairchild said slowly, staring at it. "I've known her for a year; and Gordon comes along after four days. . . . Well, I'll be damned," he said again.

"I could have told you," the semitic man said. "But I wanted you to get it by yourself. I dont see how you missed it: I dont see how anyone with your faith in your fellow man could believe that anyone could be as silly as she, without reason."

"An explanation for silliness?" Fairchild repeated. "Does her sort of silliness require explanation?"

"It shouts it," the other answered. "Look how Gordon got it, right away."

"That's so," Fairchild admitted. He gazed at the face again. Then he looked at Gordon with envious admiration. "And you got it right away, didn't you?"

Gordon was replenishing the glasses again. "He couldn't have missed it," the semitic man repeated. "I dont see how you missed it. You are reasonably keen about people——sooner or later."

"Well, I guess I missed her." Fairchild returned and extended his tumbler. "But its the usual thing, aint it? Plantations, and things? First family, and all that?"

"Something like that," the semitic man agreed. He returned to his chair. Fairchild sat again beside the water pitcher. "She's a northerner, herself. Married it. Her husband must have been pretty old when they married. That's what explains her, I think."

"What? being a northerner, or marriage? Marriage starts and explains lots of things about us, just like singleness or widowhood does. And I guess the Ohio river can affect your destiny, too. But how does it explain her?"

"The story is, that her people forced her to marry old Maurier. He had been overseer on a big place before the civil war. He disappeared in '63, and when the war was over he turned up again riding a horse with a Union Army cavalry saddle and a hundred thousand dollars in uncut Federal notes for a saddle blanket. Lord knows what the amount really was, or how he got it, but it was enough to establish him. Money. You cant argue against money: you only protest.

"Everybody expected him to splurge about with his money: show up the penniless aristocracy, that sort of thing; work out some of the inhibitions he must have developed during his overseer days. But he didn't. Perhaps he'd got rid of his inhibitions during his sojourn at the war. Anyway, he failed to live up to character, so people decided that he was a moral coward, that he was off somewhere in a hole with his money, like a rat. And this was the general opinion until a rumor got out about several rather raw land deals in which he was assisted by a jew named Julius Kauffman who was acquiring a fortune and an unsavory name during those years immediately following General Butler's assumption of the local purple. And when the smoke finally cleared somewhat, he had more money than ever rumor could compute and he was the proprietor of that plantation on which he had once been a head servant, and within a decade he was landed gentry. I dont doubt but that he had dug up some blueblood émigré ancestry. He was a small shrewd man, a cold and violent man; just the sort to have an unimpeachable genealogy. Humorless and shrewd, but I dont doubt that he sat at times in the halls of his newly adopted fathers, and laughed.

"The story is that her father came to New Orleans on a business trip, with a blessing from Washington. She was young, then; probably a background of an exclusive school and a social future, the taken-for-granted capital letter kind, but all somehow rather precarious——cabbage, and a footman to serve it; a salon in which they sat politely surrounded by objects and spoke good French, probably, and bailiff's men on the veranda and the butcher's bill at the kitchen door——gentility: evening clothes without fresh underwear beneath them. I imagine he——her father—was pretty near at the end of his rope. Some government appointment, I imagine, brought him south: hijacking privileges with official sanction, you know.

"The whole family seemed to have found our climate salubrious, though, what with hibiscus and mimosa on the lawn instead of bailiffs, and our dulcet airs after the rigors of New England; and she cut quite a figure among the jeunesse dorée of the nineties; fell in love with a young chap, penniless but real people, who led cotillions and went without gloves to send her flowers and glacé trifles from the rue Vendôme and sang to a guitar among the hibiscus and mimosa when stars were wont to rise. Old Maurier had made a bid, himself, in the meantime. Maurier was not yet accepted by the noblesse. But you can't ignore money, you know: you can only protest. And tremble. It took my people to teach the world that. . . . And so—" the semitic man drained his glass. He continued:

"You know how it is, how there comes a certain moment in the course of human events during which everything—public attention, circumstance, even destiny itself—is caught at the single possible instant, and the actions of certain people, for no reason at all, become of paramount interest and importance to the rest of the world? That's how it was with these people. There were wagers laid; a famous gambler even made a book on it. And all the time she went about her affairs, her parties and routs and balls, behind that cold Dresden china mask of hers. She was quite beautiful then, they say. People always painting her, you know. Her face in every exhibition, her name a byword in the street and a toast at Antoine's or the St Charles. . . . But then, perhaps nothing went on behind that mask at all."

"Of course there was," said Fairchild quickly. "For the sake of the story, if nothing else."

"Pride, anyway, I guess. She had that." The semitic man reached for the bottle. Gordon came and refilled his mug. "It must have been pretty hard for her, even if there was only pride to suffer. But women can stand anything——"

"And enjoy it," Fairchild put in. "But go on."

"That's all. They were married in the cathedral. She wasn't a catholic—Ireland had yet to migrate in any sizable quantities when her people established themselves in New England. That was another thing, mind you. And her unhorsed Lochinvar was present. Bets had been made that if he stayed away or passed the word, no one would attend at all. Maurier was still regarded . . . well, imagine for yourself a situation like that: a tradition of ease unassailable and unshakable gone to pieces right under you, and out of the wreckage rising a man who once held your stirrup while you mounted. . . . Thirty years is barely the adolescence of bitterness, you know.

"I'd like to have seen her, coming out of the church afterward. They would have had a canopy leading from the door to the carriage: there must have been a canopy, and flowers, heavy ones—Lochinvar would have sent gardenias; and she, decked out in all the pagan trappings of innocence and her beautiful secret face beside that cold, violent man; graying now, but you have remarked how it takes the harlequinade of aristocracy to really reveal peasant blood, haven't you? And her Lochinvar to wish her godspeed, watching her ankles as she got into the carriage.

"They never had any children. Maurier may have been too old; she herself may have been barren. Often that type is. But I dont think so. I believe. . . . But who knows? I dont. Anyway, that explains her, to me. At first you think its just silliness, lack of occupation—a tub of washing, to be exact. But I see something thwarted back of it all, something stifled, yet which wont quite die."

"A virgin," Fairchild said immediately. "That's what it is, exactly. Fooling with sex, kind of dabbing at it like a kitten at a ball of string. She missed something: her body told her so, insisted, forced her to try to remedy it and fill the vacuum. But now her body is old; it no longer remembers that it missed anything, and all she has left is a habit, the ghost of a need to rectify something the lack of which her body has long since forgotten about."

The semitic man lit his cold cigar again. Fairchild gazed at his glass, turning it this way and that slowly in his hand. Gordon stood yet against the wall, looking beyond them and watching something not in this room. The semitic man slapped his other wrist, then wiped his palm on his handkerchief. Fairchild spoke:

"And I missed it, missed it clean," he mused. "And then Gordon. . . . Say," he looked up suddenly, "how did you happen to learn all this?"

"Julius Kauffman was my grandfather," the semitic man replied.

"Oh. . . . Well. Its a good thing you told me about it. I guess I wont have another chance to get anything from her at first hand." He chuckled, without mirth.

"Oh, yes you will," the other told him. "She wont hold this boat party against us. People are far more tolerant of artists than artists are of people." He puffed at his cigar for a time. "The trouble with you," he said, "is that you dont act right at all. You are the most disappointing artist I know. Mark Frost is much nearer the genuine thing than you are. But then, he's got more time to be a genius than you have: you spend too much time writing. And that's where Gordon is going to fall down. You and he typify genius décolleté. And people who own motor cars and food draw the line just at negligé—somewhere about the collar bone. And remind me to give that to Mark tomorrow: it struck me several times these last few days that he needs a new one."

"Speaking of décolleté——" Fairchild mopped his face again. "What is it that makes a man drink whiskey on a night like this, anyway?"

"I dont know," the other answered. "Perhaps its a scheme of nature's to provide for our Italian immigrants. Or of providence. Prohibition for the Latin, politics for the Irish, invented He them."

Fairchild filled his glass again, unsteadily. "Might as well make a good job of it," he said. Gordon yet leaned against the wall, motionless and remote. Fairchild continued: "Italians and Irish. Where do us homegrown Nordics come in? What has He invented for us?"

"Nothing," the semitic man answered. "You invented providence." Fairchild raised his tumbler, gulping, and a part of the liquor ran over thinly and trickled from both corners of his mouth down his chin. Then he set the glass down and stared at the other with a mild astonishment.

"I am afraid," he enunciated carefully, "that that one is going to do the business for me." He wiped his chin unsteadily, and moving he struck his empty glass to the floor. The semitic man groaned.

"Now we'll have to move again, just when I had become inured to them. Or perhaps you'd like to lie down for a while?"

Fairchild sat musing a moment. "No, I dont," he stated thickly. "If I lay down, I wouldn't get up again. Little air, fresh air. I'll go outside." The semitic man rose and helped him to his feet. Fairchild pulled himself together. "Come along, Gordon. I've got to get outside for a while."

Gordon came out of his dream. He came and raised the bottle to the light, and divided it between his mug and the semitic man's tumbler and supporting Fairchild between them, they drank. Then Fairchild must examine the marble again.

"I think its kind of nice." He stood before it, swaying, swallowing the hot salty liquid that continued to fill his throat. "You kind of wish she could talk, dont you? It would be sort of like a wind through trees. . . . No . . . not talk: you'd like to watch her from a distance on a May morning, bathing in a pool where there were a lot of poplar trees. Now, this is the way to forget your grief."

"She is not blonde," Gordon said harshly, holding the empty bottle in his hand. "She is dark, darker than fire. She is more terrible and beautiful than fire." He ceased and stared at them. Then he raised the bottle and hurled it crashing into the huge littered fireplace.

"Not——?" murmured Fairchild, trying to focus his eyes.

"Marble, purity," Gordon said in his harsh intolerant voice. "Pure because they have yet to discover some way to make it unpure. They would if they could. God damn them!" He stared at them for a moment from beneath his caverned bronze brows. His eyes were pale as two bits of steel. "Forget grief," he repeated harshly. "Only an idiot has no grief, and only a fool would forget it. What else is there in this world sharp enough to stick to your guts?"

He took the thin coat from behind the door and put it on over his naked torso, and they helped Fairchild from the room and down the dark stairs, abruptly subdued and quiet.

8.

Mark Frost stood on the corner, frankly exasperated. The street light sprayed his tall ghostly figure with shadows of the bitten leaves of late August, and he stood in indecision, musing fretfully. His evening was spoiled: too late to instigate anything on his own hook or to join anyone else's party, too soon to go home. Mark Frost depended utterly upon other people to get his time passed.

He was annoyed principally with Mrs Maurier. Annoyed and unpleasantly shocked and puzzled. At her strange . . . not coldness: rather, detachment, aloofness . . . callousness. If you were at all artistic, if you had any taint of art in your blood, dining with her filled the evening. But now, tonight——Never saw the old girl so bloodless in the presence of genius he told himself. Didn't seem to give a damn whether I stayed or went. But perhaps she doesn't feel well, after the recent excitement, he added generously. Being a woman, too. . . . He had completely forgotten about the niece, the sepulchral moth of his heart had completely forgotten that temporary flame.

His car (owned and operated by the city) came along presently, and instinct got him aboard. Instinct also took the proper transfer for him, but a crumb of precaution (or laziness) at the transfer point haled him amid automobiles bearing the young enchanted of various ages swiftly toward nowhere or less, to and within a corner drugstore where was a telephone. His number cost him a nickel.

"Hello. . . . Yes, its me. . . . Thought you were going out tonight. . . . Yes, I did. Very stupid party, though. I couldn't stick it. . . . So you decided to stay in, did you? . . . . No, I just thought I'd call you. . . . You're welcome. I have another button off. . . . Thanks. I'll bring it along the next time I am up that way. . . . Tonight? We——ll . . . huh? . . . all right. I'll come on up. G'bye."

His very ghostliness seemed to annihilate space: he invariably arrived after you had forgotten about him and before you expected him. But she had known him for a long time and ere he could ring she appeared in a window overhead and dropped the latchkey, and he retrieved its forlorn clink and let himself into the dark hall. A light gleamed dimly from the stairhead where she leaned to watch the thin evaporation of his hair as he mounted.

"I'm all alone tonight," she remarked. "The folks are gone for the week end. They didn't expect me back until Sunday."

"That's good," he answered. "I dont feel up to talking to your mother tonight."

"Neither do I. Not to anybody, after these last four days. Come in."

It was a vaguely bookish room, in the middle of which a heavy hotlooking champagne shaded piano lamp cast an oasis of light upon a dull blue brocaded divan. Mark Frost went immediately to the divan and lay at full length upon it. Then he moved again and extracted a package of cigarettes from his jacket. Miss Jameson accepted one and he relaxed again and groaned with hollow relief.

"I'm too comfortable," he said. "I'm really ashamed to be so comfortable."

Miss Jameson drew up a chair, just without the oasis of light. "Help yourself," she replied. "There's nobody here but us. The family wont be back until Sunday night."

"Elegant," Mark Frost murmured. He laid his arm across his face, shading his eyes. "Whole house to yourself. You're lucky. Lord, I'm glad to be off that boat. Never again for me."

"Dont mention that boat." Miss Jameson shuddered. "I think it'll be never again for any of that party. From the way Mrs Maurier talked this morning. Not for Dawson and Julius, anyway."

"Did she send a car back for them?"

"No. After yesterday, they could have fallen overboard and she wouldn't even have notified the police. . . . But lets dont talk about that trip anymore," she said wearily. She sat just beyond the radius of light: a vague humorless fragility. Mark Frost lay on his back, smoking his cigarette. She said: "While I think of it: Will you be sure to lock the door after you? I'll be here alone tonight."

"All right," he promised from beneath his arm. His pale prehensile mouth released the cigarette and his hand swung it to where he hoped there was an ashtray. The ashtray wasn't there and his hand made a series of futile dabbing motions until Miss Jameson leaned forward and moved the ashtray into the automatic ellipsis of his hand. After a while she leaned forward again and crushed out her cigarette. A clock somewhere behind him tapped monotonously at silence and she moved restlessly in her chair, and presently she leaned and took another cigarette from his pack. Mark Frost removed his arm long enough to raise the pack to his vision and count the remaining cigarettes. Then he replaced his arm.

"You're quiet tonight," she remarked. He grunted and she leaned forward once more and ground out her halfsmoked cigarette with decision. She rose. "I'm going to take off some clothes and get into something cooler. Nobody here to object. Excuse me a moment."

He grunted again beneath his arm, and she went away from the oasis of light. She opened the door of her bedroom and stood in the darkness just within the door a moment. Then she closed the door audibly, stood for a moment, then opened it again slightly, and pressed the light switch.

She went to her dressing table and switched on two small shaded electric candles there, and returned and switched off the ceiling light. She considered for a while; then she returned to the door and stood with the knob in her hand, then without closing it she went back to the dressing table and turned off one of the lights there. This left the room filled with a soft pinkish glow in which a hushed gleaming of crystal upon the dressing table was the only distinguishable feature. She removed her dress hastily and stood in her underthings with a kind of cringing, passive courage, but there was still no sound of movement beyond the door, and she switched on the other light again and examined herself in the mirror.

She mused again, examining her frail body in its intimate garment. Then she ran swiftly and silently to a chest of drawers and in a locked drawer she sought feverishly among a delicate neat mass of sheer fabric, coming at last upon an embroidered night dress, neatly folded and unworn and scented faintly. Then, standing where the door, should it open, would conceal her for a moment, she slipped the gown over her head and from beneath it she removed the undergarment. Then she took her reckless troubled heart and the fragile and humorless calmness in which it beat back to the dressing table, and sitting before the mirror she assumed a studied pose, combing and combing out her long uninteresting hair.

*   *   *   *   *

Mark Frost lay at length on the divan, as was his habit, shading his eyes with his arm. At intervals he roused himself to light a fresh cigarette, at each time counting the diminishing

few that remained with a static alarm. A clock ticked regularly
somewhere in the room. The soft light from the lamp bathed
him in a champagnecolored and motionless sea. . . . He raised
a fresh cigarette: his pale prehensile mouth wrapped about it
as though his mouth were a separate organism.

But after a while there were no more cigarettes. And roused
temporarily, he remarked his hostess's prolonged absence. But
he lay back again, luxuriating in quiet and the suave surface
on which he rested. But before long he raised the empty
cigarette pack, and groaned dismally, and rose and prowled
quietly about the room, hoping perhaps to find one cigarette
someone had forgotten. But there was none. The couch drew
him and he returned to the oasis of light, where he discovered
and captured the practically whole cigarette which Miss Jameson had discarded. "Snipe," he murmured with sepulchral hu-
morlessness and he fired it, averting his head lest he lose his
eyelashes in doing so, and he lay once more, shading his eyes
with his arm. The clock ticked on in the silence. It seemed to
be directly behind him: if he could just roll his eyes a bit further back into his skull. . . . He'd better look, anyhow, after
a while. After midnight only one trolley to the hour. If he
missed the twelve oclock car. . . .

So after a while he did look, having to move to do so, and
he immediately rose from the divan in a mad jointless haste.
Fortunately he remembered where he had left his hat and he
caught it up and plunged down the stairs and on through the
dark hall. He blundered into a thing or so, but the pale rectangle of the glass door guided him and after a violent struggle he opened it, and leaping forth he crashed it behind him.
It failed to catch and in midflight down the steps he glanced
wildly back at the growing darkness of its gap that revealed
at the top edge a vague gleam from the light at the head of
the stairs.

The corner was not far, and as he ran loosely and frantically
toward it there came among the grave gesturing of tall palms
a worn and bloodless rumor of the dying moon, and the rising
hum of the car crashed among the trees. He saw its lighted
windows halt, heard its hum cease, saw the windows move
again and heard its hum rise swelling and drowning his hoarse
reiterated cries. But the conductor saw him at last and pulled

the cord again, and the car halted once more, humming impatiently; and Mark Frost plunged his long ungovernable legs across the soft slumberous glare of polished asphalt and clawed his panting ghostly body through the opened doors out of which the conductor leaned, calling to him:

"Come on, come on: this aint a taxi."

9.

Three gray softfooted priests had passed on, but in an interval hushed by windowless old walls there lingers yet a thin celibate despair. Beneath a high stone gate with a crest and a device in carven stone a beggar lies, nursing in his hand a crust of bread

(Gordon, Fairchild and the semitic man walked in the dark city. Above them, the sky: a heavy voluptuous night and huge hot stars like wilting gardenias. About them, streets: narrow shallow canyons of shadow rich with decay, laced with delicate ironwork, scarcely seen)

Spring is in the world somewhere, like a blown keen reed, high and fiery cold—he does not yet see it; a shape which he will know—he does not yet see it. The three priests pass on: the walls have hushed their gray and unshod feet

(In a doorway slightly ajar were women. Their faces in the starlight flat and pallid and rife, odorous exciting and unchaste. Gordon hello dempsey loomed hatless above his two companions. He strode on, paying the women no heed. Fairchild lagged, the semitic man perforce also. A woman laughed, rife and hushed and rich in the odorous dark come in boys lots of girls cool you off come in boys   The semitic man drew Fairchild onward, babbling excitedly)

That's it, that's it! You walk along a dark street, in the dark. The dark is close and intimate about you, holding all things, anything——you need only put out your hand to touch life, to feel the beating heart of life. Beauty: a thing unseen, suggested: natural and fecund and foul—you dont stop for it; you pass on

(The semitic man drew him onward after Gordon's tall striding)   I love three things   *Rats like dull and cunning silver,
keen and plump as death, steal out to gnaw the crust held loosely
by the beggar beneath the stone gate. Unreproved they swarm
about his still recumbent shape, exploring his clothing in an obscene silence, dragging their hot bellies over his lean and agechilled
body, sniffing his intimate parts*   I love three things

(He drew Fairchild onward, babbling in an ecstasy) A voice,
a touch, a sound: life going on about you unseen in the close
dark, beyond these walls, these bricks—— (Fairchild stopped,
laying his hand against the heatdrunken wall beside him,
staring at his friend in the starlight. Gordon strode on ahead)
——in this dark room or that dark room. You want to go into
all the streets of all the cities men live in. To look into all the
darkened rooms in the world. Not with curiosity, not with
dread nor doubt nor disapproval. But humbly, gently. As you
would steal to look in upon a sleeping child, not to disturb it

*Then as one rat they flash away, and secure again and still, they
become as a row of cigarettes unwinking at a single level. The
beggar, whose hand yet shapes his stolen crust, sleeps yet beneath
the stone gate*

(Fairchild babbled on. Gordon striding on ahead, turned and
passed through a door. The door swung open, letting a sheet
of light fall outward across the pavement, then the door
swung to, snatching the sheet of light again. The semitic man
grasped Fairchild's arm. Fairchild halted. About him the city
swooned in a voluption of dark and heat: a sleep which was
not sleep; and dark and heat lapped his burly short body about
with the hidden eternal pulse of the world. Above him, above
the shallow serrated canyon of the street, huge hot stars
burned at the heart of things)

*Three more priests, barefoot, in robes the color of silence, appear
from nowhere. They are speeding after the first three, when they
spy the beggar beneath the stone gate. They pause above him: the
walls hush away their gray and sibilant feet. The rats are motionless as a row of cigarettes*   (Gordon reappeared, looming

above the other two in the hushed starlight. He held in his hand a bottle) *The priests draw nearer, touching one another, leaning diffidently above the beggar in the empty street while silence comes slow as a procession of nuns with breathing blent. Above the hushing walls, a thing wild and passionate, remote and sad; shrill as pipes, and yet unheard. Beneath it, soundless shapes amid which, vaguely, a maiden in an ungirdled robe and with a thin bright chain between her ankles, and a sound of far lamenting*

(They went on around a corner and into a darker street. Gordon stopped again, brooding and remote. He raised the bottle against they sky) Yes, bitter and new as fire. Fuelled close now with sleep. Hushed her strange and ardent fire. A chrysalis of fire whitely. Splendid and new as fire (He drank, listening to the measured beat of his wild bitter heart, then he passed the bottle to his companions, brooding his hawk's face above them against the sky. The others drank. They went on through the dark city)

The beggar yet sleeps, shaping his stolen crust, and one of the priests says Do you require aught of man, Brother? Just above the silence, amid the shapes, a young naked boy daubed with vermilion, carrying casually a crown. He moves erratic with senseless laughter; and the headless naked body of a woman carved from ebony, surrounded by women wearing skins of slain beasts and chained one to another, lamenting. The beggar makes no reply, he does not stir; and a second priest leans nearer his pale halfshadowed face. Beneath his high white brow he is not asleep, for his eyes stare quietly past the three priests without remarking them. The third priest leans down, raising his voice. Brother

(They stopped and drank again. Then they went on, the semitic man carrying the bottle, nursing it against his breast) I love three things (Fairchild walked erratically beside him. Above him, among the mad stars, Gordon's bearded head. The night was full and rich, smelling of streets and people, of secret beings and things)

The beggar does not move and the priest's voice is a dark bird seeking its way from out a cage. Above the silence, between it and the antic sky, there grows a sound like that of the sea heard afar off. The

*three priests gaze at one another. The beggar lies motionless beneath
the stone gate. The rats stare their waiting cigarettes upon the scene*

I love three things: gold, marble and purple   *The sound grows.
Amid shadows and echoes it becomes a wind thunderous from hills
with the clashing hooves of centaurs. The headless black woman is
a carven agony beyond the fading placidity of the ungirdled
maiden, and as the shadows and echoes blend the chained women
women raise their voices anew, lamenting thinly*   (They were accosted. Whispers from every doorway, hands unchaste and importunate and rife in the dense wild darkness. Fairchild
wavered beside him, and Gordon stopped again. "I'm going
in here," he said. "Give me some money." The semitic man
gave him a nameless bill)   *The wind rushes on, becoming filled
with leaping figures antic as flames, and a sound of pipes fierycold
carves the dark world darkly out of space. The centaurs' hooves
clash, storming; shrill voices ride the storm like gusty birds, wild
and passionate and sad*   (A door opened in the wall. Gordon
entered and before the door closed again they saw him in a
narrow passageway lift a woman from the shadow, raising her
against the mad stars, smothering her squeal against his tall
kiss)   *Then voices and sound, shadows and echoes change form
swirling, becoming the headless armless legless torso of a girl, motionless and virginal and passionately eternal before the shadows
and echoes whirl away*

(They went on. The semitic man nursed the bottle against his
breast)   I love three things. . . . Dante invented Beatrice, creating himself a maid that life had not time to create, and laid
upon her frail and unbowed shoulders the whole burden of
man's history of his impossible heart's desire. . . . *At last one
priest, becoming bolder, leans yet nearer and slips his hand beneath
the beggar's sorry robe, against his heart. It is cold*   (Suddenly
Fairchild stumbled heavily beside him and would have fallen.
He held Fairchild up and supported him to the wall and
Fairchild leaned against the wall, his head tilted back, hatless,
staring into the sky, listening to the dark and measured beat
of the heart of things. "That's what it is. Genius." He spoke
slowly, distinctly, staring into the sky. "People confuse it so,
you see. They have got it now to where it signifies only an

active state of the mind in which a picture is painted or a poem is written. When it is not that at all. It is that Passion Week of the heart, that instant of timeless beatitude which some never know; which some, I suppose, gain at will; which others gain through an outside agency like alcohol, like tonight;— that passive state of the heart with which the mind, the brain, has nothing to do at all, in which the hackneyed accidents which make up this world—love and life and death and sex and sorrow—brought together by chance in perfect proportions, take on a kind of splendid and timeless beauty. Like Yseult of the White Hands and Tristan and that clean high-hearted dullness of his; like that young Lady Something that some government executed, asking permission and touching with a kind of sober wonder the edge of the knife that was to cut her head off; like a redhaired girl, an idiot, turning in a white dress beneath a wistaria-covered trellis on a late sunny afternoon in May. . . ." He leaned against the wall, staring into the hushed mad sky, hearing the dark and simple heart of things. From beyond a cornice there came at last a cold and bloodless rumor of the dying moon)

(The semitic man nursed the bottle against his breast. "I love three things: gold, marble and purple——") *The priests cross themselves while the nuns of silence blend anew their breath, and pass on: soon the high windowless walls have hushed away their thin celibate despair. The rats are arrogant as cigarettes. After a while they steal forth again, climbing over the beggar, dragging their hot bellies over him, exploring unreproved his private parts. Somewhere above the dark street, above the windcarved hills, beyond the silence; thin pipes, unheard, wild and passionate and sad* ("——form solidity color," he said to his own dark and passionate heart and to Fairchild beside him, leaning against a dark wall, vomiting)

10.

The rectangle of light yet fell outward across the alleyway; beyond the halflength lattice blind the typewriter yet leaped and thundered.

"Fairchild."

The manipulator of the machine felt a vague annoyance, like knowing that someone is trying to waken you from a pleasant dream, knowing that if you resist the dream will be broken.

"Oh, Fairchild."

He concentrated again, trying to exorcise the ravisher of his heart's beatitude by banging the louder at his keyboard. But at last there came a timid knock at the blind.

"Damn!" He surrendered. "Come in!" he bellowed, raising his head. "My God, where did you come from? I just let you in about ten minutes ago, didn't I?" Then he saw his caller's face. "What's the matter, friend?" he asked quickly. "Sick?"

Mr Talliaferro stood blinking in the light. Then he entered slowly and drooped upon a chair. "Worse than that," he answered with utter despondency. The large man wheeled heavily to face him.

"Need a doctor or anything?"

The caller buried his face in his hands. "No, no, a doctor cant help me."

"Well, what do you want, then? I'm busy. What is it?"

"I believe I want a drink of whiskey," Mr Talliaferro said at last. "If its no trouble," he added with his customary polite diffidence. He raised a stricken face for a moment. "A terrible thing happened to me tonight." He lowered his face to his hands again, and the other rose and returned presently with a tumbler half full of liquor. Mr Talliaferro accepted it gratefully. He took a swallow, then lowered the glass shakily. "I simply must talk to someone. A terrible thing happened to me. . . ." He brooded for a moment. "It was my last opportunity, you see," he burst out suddenly. "For Fairchild now, or you, it would be different; but for me. . . ." Mr Talliaferro hid his face in his free hand. "A terrible thing happened to me," he repeated.

"Well, spit it out, then. But be quick about it."

Mr Talliaferro fumbled his handkerchief weakly, mopping his face. The other sat watching him impatiently. "Well, just as I'd planned, I pretended indifference, said that I didn't care to dance tonight. But she said 'Ah, come along: do you think I came out just to sit in the park or something?' like that. And when I put my arm around her——"

"Around who?"

"Around her. And when I tried to kiss her she just put——"

"But where was this?"

"In the cab. I haven't a car, you see. Though I am planning to buy one next year. And she just put her elbow under my chin and choked me until I had to move back to my side of the seat, and she said, 'I never dance in private or without music, mister man.' and then——"

"In God's name, friend, what are you raving about?"

"About J——about that girl I was with this evening. And so we went to dance, and I was petting her a bit, just as I had done on the boat: no more, I assure you; and she told me immediately to stop. She said something about not having lumbago. And yet, all the time we were on the yacht she never objected once!" Mr Talliaferro looked at his host with polite uncomprehending astonishment. Then he sighed, and finished the whiskey and set the glass near his feet.

"Good Lord," the other murmured in a hushed tone.

Mr Talliaferro continued more briskly: "And quite soon I remarked that her attention was engaged by something or someone behind me. She was dodging her head this way and that as we danced and getting out of step and saying 'Pardon me'; but when I tried to see what it was I could discover nothing at all to engage her like that. So I said 'What are you thinking of?' and she said 'Huh?' like that, and I said 'I can tell you what you are thinking of' and she said 'Who? me? What am I thinking of?' still trying to see something behind me, mind you. Then I saw that she was smiling also, and I said 'You are thinking of me' and she said 'Oh. Was I?' "

"Good God," the other murmured.

"Yes," agreed Mr Talliaferro unhappily. He continued briskly, however: "And so I said, as I'd planned, 'I'm tired of this place. Lets go.' She demurred, but I was firm, and so at last she consented and told me to run down and engage a cab and she would join me on the street."

"I should have suspected something then, but I didn't. I ran down and engaged a cab. I gave the driver ten dollars and he agreed to drive out on some unfrequented road and to stop and pretend that he had lost something back along the road, and wait there until I blew the horn for him."

"So I waited and waited. She didn't appear, so at last I ordered the cab to wait and I ran back up stairs. I didn't see her in the anteroom, so I went back to the dance floor." He ceased, and sat for a while in a brooding dejection.

"Well?" the other prompted.

Mr Talliaferro sighed. "I swear, I think I'll give it up: never have anything to do with them anymore. When I returned to the dance floor I looked for her at the table where we had been sitting. She was not there, and for a moment I couldn't find her, but presently I saw her, dancing. With a man I had never seen before. A large man, like you. I didn't know what to think. I decided finally he was a friend of hers with whom she was dancing until I should return, having misunderstood our arrangement about meeting below. Yet she had told me herself to await her on the street. That's what confused me.

"I waited at the door until I caught her eye finally, and signalled to her. She flipped her hand in reply, as though she desired me to wait until the dance was finished. So I stood there. Other people were entering or leaving, but I kept my place near the door, where she could find me without difficulty. But when the music ceased, they went to a table and sat down and called to a waiter. And she didn't even glance toward me again!

"I began to get angry, then. I walked over to them. I didn't want everyone to see that I was angry, so I bowed to them and she looked up at me and said 'Why, hello. I thought you'd left me and so this kind gentleman was kind enough to take me home.' 'You damn right I will,' the man said, popping his eyes at me. 'Who's he?' You see," Mr Talliaferro interpolated, "I'm trying to talk as he did. I cant imitate his execrable speech. You see, it wouldn't have been so—so—I wouldn't have felt so helpless had he spoken proper English. But the way he said things——there seemed to be no possible rejoinder——You see?"

"Go on, go on," the other said.

"And she said 'Why, he's a little friend of mine' and the man said 'Well, its time little boys like him was in bed.' He looked at me, hard, but I ignored him and said firmly: 'Come, Miss Steinbauer, our taxi is waiting.' Then he said 'Herb, you aint trying to take my girl, are you?' I told him that she had come with me, firmly, you know; and then she said 'Run along. You are tired of dancing: I aint. So I'm going to stay and dance with this nice man. Goodnight.'

"She was smiling again: I could see that they were ridiculing me; and then he laughed—like a horse. 'Beat it, brother,' he said 'she's gave you the air. Come back tomorrow.' Well, when I saw his fat red face all full of teeth, I wanted to hit him. But I remembered myself in time—my position in the city and my friends," he explained, "so I just looked at them and turned and walked away. Of course everyone had seen and heard it all: as I went through the door a waiter said 'Hard luck, fellow, but they will do it.' "

Mr Talliaferro mused again in a sort of polite incomprehension, more of bewilderment than anger or even dejection. He sighed again. "And, on top of all that, the taxi driver had gone off with my ten dollars."

The other man looked at Mr Talliaferro with utter admiration. "O Thou above the thunder and above the excursions and alarms, regard Your masterpiece! Balzac, chew thy bitter thumbs! And here I am, wasting my damn life, trying to invent people by means of the written word!" His face became suddenly suffused: he rose, towering. "Get to hell out of here," he roared. "You have made me sick!"

Mr Talliaferro rose obediently. His hopeless dejection invested him again. "But what am I to do?"

"Do? Do? Go to a brothel, if you want a girl. Or if you are afraid someone will come in and take her away from you, get out on the street and pick one up: bring her here, if you like. But in Christ's dear name, dont ever talk to me again. You have already damaged my ego beyond repair. Do you want another drink?"

Mr Talliaferro sighed again and shook his head. "Thanks just the same," he answered. "Whiskey can't help me any." The large man took his arm and kicking the blind outward he helped Mr Talliaferro kindly but firmly into the alleyway. Then the blind swung to again and Mr Talliaferro stood for a time, listening to the frantic typewriter, watching planes of shadow, letting the darkness soothe him. A cat, slinking, regarded him, then flashed in a swift dingy streak across the alley. He followed it with his eyes in a slow misery, with envy.

Love was so simple for cats—mostly noise, success didn't
seem to make much difference. He sighed and walked slowly
on, leaving the thunderous typewriter behind. Presently he
turned a corner and heard it no more. From beyond a cornice
there came at last a cold and bloodless rumor of the dying
moon.

His decorous pace spaced away streets interesting with
darkness and he walked marvelling that he could be inwardly
so despairing, yet outwardly the same as ever. I wonder if it
does show on me? he thought. It is because I am getting old,
that women are not attracted to me. Yet, I know any number
of men of my age and more, who get women easily . . . or say
they do. . . . It is something I do not possess, something I
have never had. . . .

And soon he would be married again. Mr Talliaferro, seeing
freedom and youth deserting him again, had known at first a
clear sharp regret, almost a despair, realizing that marriage this
time would be a climacteric, that after this he would be definitely no longer young; and a final flare of freedom and youth
had surged in him like a dying flame. But now as he walked
dark streets beneath the hot heavy sky and the mad wilting
gardenias of stars, feeling empty and a little tired, hearing his
grumbling skeleton—that smug and dour and unshakable
comrade who loves so well to say 'I told you so'—he found
himself looking forward to marriage with a thin but definite
relief as a solution to his problem. Yes, he told himself, sighing again, chastity is expected of married men. Or, at least they
dont lose caste by it. . . .

But it was unbearable to believe that he had never had the
power to stir women, that he had been always a firearm unloaded and unaware of it. No, its something I can do, or say,
that I have not yet discovered. As he turned into the quiet
street on which he lived he saw two people in a doorway, embracing. He hurried on.

In his rooms at last he slowly removed his coat and hung it
neatly in a closet without being aware that he had performed
the rite at all, then from his bathroom he got a metal machine
with a handpump attached, and he quartered the room methodically with an acrid spraying of pennyroyal. On each
downstroke there was a faint comfortable resistance, though

the plunger came back quite easily. Like breathing, back and forth and back and forth: a rhythm.

Something I can do Something I can say he repeated to the rhythm of his arm. The liquid hissed pungently, dissolving into the atmosphere, permeating it. Something I can say Something I can do There must be There must be Surely a man would not be endowed with an impulse and yet be denied the ability to slake it Something I can say

His arm moved swifter and swifter, spraying the liquid into the air in short hissing jets. He ceased, and felt for his handkerchief before he recalled that it was in his coat. His fingers discovered something, though, and clasping his reeking machine he removed from his hip pocket a small round metal box and he held it in his hand, gazing at it. Agnes Mabel Becky he read, and he laughed a short, mirthless laugh. Then he moved slowly to his chest of drawers and hid the small box carefully away in its usual place and returned to the closet where his coat hung and got his handkerchief, and mopped his brow with it. But must I become an old man before I discover what it is? Old, old, an old man before I have lived at all. . . .

He went slowly to the bathroom and replaced the pump, and returned with a basin of warm water. He set the basin on the floor and went again to the mirror, examining his face. His hair was getting thin, there was no question about that (cant even keep my hair, he thought bitterly) and his thirty eight years showed in his face. He was not fleshily inclined, yet the skin under his jaw was becoming loose, flabby. He sighed and completed his disrobing, putting his clothing neatly and automatically away as he removed it. On the table beside his chair was a box of flavored digestive lozenges and presently he sat with his feet in the warm water, chewing one of the tablets.

The water mounting warmly through his thin body soothed him, the pungent tablet between his slow jaws gave him a temporary surcease. Lets see he mused to his rhythmic mastication, calmly reviewing the evening. Where did I go wrong tonight? My plan was good: Fairchild himself admitted that. Let me think. . . . His jaws ceased and his gaze brooded on a photograph upon the opposite wall. Why is it that they never act as you had calculated? You can allow for every contingency; and yet they will always do something else, something they themselves could not have imagined nor devised beforehand.

. . . . I have been too gentle with them, I have allowed too much leeway for the intervention of their natural perversity and of sheer chance. That has been my mistake every time: giving them dinners and shows right away, allowing them to relegate me to the position of a suitor, of one waiting upon their pleasure. The trick, the only trick, is to bully them, to dominate them from the start—never employ wiles and never allow them the opportunity to employ wiles. The oldest technique in the world: a club. By God, that's it!

He dried his feet swiftly and thrust them into his bedroom slippers, and went to the telephone and gave a number. "That's the trick, exactly," he whispered exultantly, and then in his ear was a sleepy masculine voice.

"Fairchild? So sorry to disturb you, but I have it at last." A muffled inarticulate sound came over the wire, but he rushed on, unheeding. "I learned through a mistake tonight. The trouble is, I haven't been bold enough with them: I have been afraid of frightening them away. Listen: I will bring her here, I will not take No for an answer; I will be cruel and hard, brutal, if necessary, until she begs for my love. What do you think of that? . . . Hello! Fairchild? . . . ."

An interval filled with a remote buzzing. Then a female voice said:

"You tell 'em, big boy; treat 'em rough."

END

FLAGS IN THE DUST

ONE

I.

A S USUAL old man Falls had brought John Sartoris into the room with him, had walked the three miles in from the county Poor Farm, fetching, like an odor, like the clean dusty smell of his faded overalls, the spirit of the dead man into that room where the dead man's son sat and where the two of them, pauper and banker, would sit for a half an hour in the company of him who had passed beyond death and then returned.

Freed as he was of time and flesh, he was a far more palpable presence than either of the two old men who sat shouting periodically into one another's deafness while the business of the bank went forward in the next room and people in the adjoining stores on either side listened to the indistinguishable uproar of their voices coming through the walls. He was far more palpable than the two old men cemented by a common deafness to a dead period and so drawn thin by the slow attenuation of days; even now, although old man Falls had departed to tramp the three miles back to that which he now called home, John Sartoris seemed to loom still in the room, above and about his son, with his bearded, hawklike face, so that as old Bayard sat with his crossed feet propped against the corner of the cold hearth, holding the pipe in his hand, it seemed to him that he could hear his father's breathing even, as though that other were so much more palpable than mere transiently articulated clay as to even penetrate into the uttermost citadel of silence in which his son lived.

The bowl of the pipe was ornately carved and it was charred with much usage, and on the bit were the prints of his father's teeth, where he had left the very print of his ineradicable bones as though in enduring stone, like the creatures of that prehistoric day that were too grandly conceived and executed either to exist very long or to vanish utterly when dead from an earth shaped and furnished for punier things. Old Bayard sat holding the pipe in his hand.

"What are you giving it to me for, after all this time?" he had asked, fingering the pipe, and old man Falls answered.

543

"Well, I reckon I've kept it long as Cunnel aimed for me to," old man Falls answered. "A po' house aint no fitten place for anything of his'n, Bayard. And I'm goin' on ninety-fo' year old."

Later he gathered up his small parcels and left, but still old Bayard sat for some time, the pipe in his hand, rubbing the bowl slowly with his thumb. After a while John Sartoris departed also, withdrawn rather to that place where the peaceful dead contemplate their glamorous frustrations, and old Bayard rose and thrust the pipe into his pocket and took a cigar from the humidor on the mantel. As he struck the match the door across the room opened and a man wearing a green eyeshade entered and approached.

"Simon's here, Colonel," he said in a voice utterly without inflection.

"What?" Old Bayard said across the match.

"Simon's come."

"Oh. All right."

The other turned and went out. Old Bayard flung the match into the grate and put the cigar in his pocket and closed his desk and took his black felt hat from the top of it and followed the other from the room. The man in the eyeshade and the cashier were busy beyond the grille. Old Bayard stalked on through the lobby and passed through the door with its drawn green shade and emerged upon the street, where Simon in a linen duster and an ancient top-hat held the matched geldings glittering in the spring afternoon, at the curb.

There was a hitching-post there, which old Bayard retained with a testy disregard of industrial progress, but Simon never used it. Until the door opened and Bayard emerged from behind the drawn shades bearing the words "Bank Closed" in cracked gold leaf, Simon retained his seat, the reins in his left hand and the thong of the whip caught smartly back in his right and usually the unvarying and seemingly incombustible fragment of a cigar at a swaggering angle in his black face, talking to the shining team in a steady, lover-like flow. He spoiled horses. He admired Sartorises and he had for them a warmly protective tenderness, but he loved horses, and beneath his hands the sorriest beast bloomed and acquired comeliness like a caressed woman, temperament like an opera star.

Old Bayard closed the door behind him and crossed to the carriage with that stiff erectness which, as a countryman once remarked, if he ever stumbled, would meet itself falling down. One or two passers and a merchant or so in the adjacent doorways saluted him with a sort of florid servility, and behind him the shade on one window drew aside upon the disembodied face of the man in the green eye-shade. The book-keeper was a hillman of indeterminate age, a silent man who performed his duties with tedious slow care and who watched Bayard constantly and covertly all the while he was in view.

Nor did Simon dismount even then. With his race's fine feeling for potential theatrics he drew himself up and arranged the limp folds of the duster, communicating by some means the histrionic moment to the horses so that they too flicked their glittering coats and tossed their leashed heads, and into Simon's wizened black face there came an expression indescribably majestical as he touched his whiphand to his hatbrim. Bayard got into the carriage and Simon clucked to the horses, and the onlookers, halted to admire the momentary drama of the departure, fell behind.

There was something different in Simon's air today, in the very shape of his back and the angle of his hat: he appeared to be bursting with something momentous and ill-contained. But he withheld it for the time being, and at a dashing, restrained pace he drove among the tethered wagons about the square and swung into a broad street where what Bayard called paupers sped back and forth in automobiles, and withheld it until the town was behind them and they trotted on across burgeoning countryside cluttered still with gasoline-propelled paupers but at greater intervals, and his employer had settled back for the changing and peaceful monotony of the four-mile drive. Then Simon checked the team to a more sedate pace and turned his head.

His voice was not particularly robust nor resonant, yet somehow he could talk to old Bayard without difficulty. Others must shout in order to penetrate that wall of deafness beyond which Bayard lived; yet Simon could and did hold long, rambling conversations with him in that monotonous, rather high sing-song of his, particularly while in the carriage, the vibration of which helped Bayard's hearing a little.

"Mist' Bayard done got home," Simon remarked in a conversational tone.

Old Bayard sat perfectly and furiously still for a moment while his heart went on, a little too fast and a little too lightly, cursing his grandson for a furious moment; sat so still that Simon looked back and found him gazing quietly out across the land. Simon raised his voice a little.

"He got offen de two oclock train," he continued. "Jumped off de wrong side and lit out th'ough de woods. Section hand seed 'im. Only he aint never come out home yit when I lef'. I thought he wuz wid you, maybe." Dust spun from beneath the horses' feet and moiled in a sluggish cloud behind them. Against the thickening hedgerows their shadow rushed in failing surges, with twinkling spokes and high-stepping legs in a futility of motion without progress. "Wouldn't even git off at de dee-po," Simon continued, with a kind of fretful exasperation. "De dee-po his own folks built. Jumpin' offen de bline side like a hobo. He never even had on no sojer-clothes. Jes a suit, lak a drummer er somethin'. And when I 'members dem shiny boots and dem light yaller pants and dat 'ere double-jinted backin'-up strop he wo' home las' year. . . ." He turned and looked back again. "Cunnel, you reckon dem war folks is done somethin' ter him?"

"What do you mean?" Bayard demanded. "Is he lame?"

"I mean, him sneakin' into his own town. Sneakin' into town, on de ve'y railroad his own gran'pappy built, jes' like he wuz trash. Dem foreign folks done done somethin' ter him, er dey done sot dey po-lice atter him. I kep' a-tellin' him when he fust went off to dat 'ere foreign war him and Mr Johnny neither never had no business at——"

"Drive on," Bayard said. . . . . . . "Drive on, damn your black hide."

Simon clucked to the horses and shook them into a swifter gait. The road went on between hedgerows parallelling them with the senseless terrific antics of their shadow. Beyond the bordering gums and locusts and massed vines, fields newbroken or being broken spread on toward patches of woodland newly green and splashed with dogwood and judas trees. Behind laborious plows viscid shards of new-turned earth glinted damply in the sun.

This was upland country, lying in tilted slopes against the unbroken blue of the hills, but soon the road descended sheerly into a valley of good broad fields richly somnolent in the levelling afternoon, and presently they drove upon Bayard's own land, and from time to time a plowman lifted his hand to the passing carriage. Then the road approached the railroad and crossed it, and at last the house John Sartoris had built and rebuilt stood among locusts and oaks and Simon swung between iron gates and into a curving drive.

There was a bed of salvia where a Yankee patrol had halted on a day long ago. Simon brought up here with a flourish and Bayard descended and Simon clucked to the team again and rolled his cigar to a freer angle, and took the road back to town.

Bayard stood for a while before his house, but the white simplicity of it dreamed unbroken among ancient sunshot trees. Wistaria mounting one end of the veranda had bloomed and fallen, and a faint drift of shattered petals lay palely about the dark roots of it and about the roots of a rose trained onto the same frame. The rose was slowly but steadily choking the other vine, and it bloomed now thickly with buds no bigger than a thumbnail and blown flowers no larger than silver dollars, myriad, odorless and unpickable.

But the house itself was still and serenely benignant, and he mounted to the empty, colonnaded veranda and crossed it and entered the hall. The house was silent, richly desolate of motion or any sound.

"Bayard."

The stairway with its white spindles and red carpet mounted in a tall slender curve into upper gloom. From the center of the ceiling hung a chandelier of crystal prisms and shades, fitted originally for candles but since wired for electricity; to the right of the entrance, beside folding doors rolled back upon a dim room emanating an atmosphere of solemn and seldom violated stateliness and known as the parlor, stood a tall mirror filled with grave obscurity like a still pool of evening water. At the opposite end of the hall checkered sunlight fell in a long slant across the door, and from somewhere beyond the bar of sunlight a voice rose and fell in a steady preoccupied minor, like a chant. The words were not distinguishable, but Bayard could not hear them at all. He raised his voice again.

"Bayard."

The chanting ceased, and as he turned toward the stairs a tall mulatto woman appeared in the slanting sunlight without the back door and came sibilantly into the house. Her faded blue garment was pinned up about her knees and it was darkly and irregularly blotched. Beneath it her shanks were straight and lean as the legs of a tall bird, and her bare feet were pale coffee-splashes on the dark polished floor.

"Wuz you callin' somebody, Cunnel?" she said, raising her voice to penetrate his deafness. Bayard paused with his hand on the walnut newel post and looked down at the woman's pleasant yellow face.

"Has anybody come in this afternoon?" he asked.

"Why, naw, suh," Elnora answered. "Dey aint nobody here a-tall, dat I knows about. Miss Jenny done gone to huh club-meetin' in town dis evenin'," she added. Bayard stood with his foot raised to the step, glowering at her.

"Why in hell cant you niggers tell me the truth about things?" he raged suddenly. "Or not tell me anything at all?"

"Lawd, Cunnel, who'd be comin' out here, lessen you er Miss Jenny sont 'um?" But he had gone on, tramping furiously up the stairs. The woman looked after him, then she raised her voice: "Does you want Isom, er anything?" He did not look back. Perhaps he had not heard her, and she stood and watched him out of sight. "He's gittin' old," she said to herself quietly, and she turned on her sibilant bare feet and returned down the hall whence she had come.

Bayard stopped again in the upper hall. The western windows were closed with latticed blinds, through which sunlight seeped in yellow dissolving bars that but served to increase the gloom. At the opposite end a tall door opened upon a shallow grilled balcony which offered the valley and the cradling semicircle of the eastern hills in panorama. On either side of this door was a narrow window set with leaded panes of vari-colored glass that, with the bearer of them, constituted John Sartoris' mother's deathbed legacy to him, which his youngest sister had brought from Carolina in a straw-filled hamper in '69.

This was Virginia Du Pre, who came to them, two years a wife and seven years a widow at thirty—a slender woman with a delicate replica of the Sartoris nose and that expression of indomitable and utter weariness which all Southern women had learned to wear, bringing with her the clothing in which she stood and a wicker hamper filled with colored glass. It was she who told them of the manner of Bayard Sartoris' death prior to the second battle of Manassas. She had told the story many times since (at eighty she still told it, on occasions usually inopportune) and as she grew older the tale itself grew richer and richer, taking on a mellow splendor like wine; until what had been a hair-brained prank of two heedless and reckless boys wild with their own youth, was become a gallant and finely tragical focal-point to which the history of the race had been raised from out the old miasmic swamps of spiritual sloth by two angels valiantly fallen and strayed, altering the course of human events and purging the souls of men.

That Carolina Bayard had been rather a handful, even for Sartorises. Not so much a black sheep as a nuisance all of whose qualities were positive and unpredictable. His were merry blue eyes, and his rather long hair fell in tawny curls about his temples. His high-colored face wore that expression of frank and high-hearted dullness which you imagine Richard First as wearing before he went crusading, and once he hunted a pack of fox hounds through a rustic tabernacle in which a Methodist revival was being held; and thirty minutes later (having caught the fox) he returned alone and rode his horse into the ensuing indignation meeting. In a spirit of fun purely: he believed too firmly in Providence, as all his actions clearly showed, to have any religious convictions whatever. So when Fort Moultrie fell and the governor refused to surrender it, the Sartorises were privately a little glad, for now Bayard would have something to do.

In Virginia, as an A.D.C. of Jeb Stuart's, he found plenty to do. As the A.D.C. rather, for though Stuart had a large military family, they were soldiers trying to win a war and needing sleep occasionally: Bayard Sartoris alone was willing, nay eager, to defer sleep to that time when monotony should return to the world. But now was a holiday.

The war was also a godsend to Jeb Stuart, and shortly thereafter, against the dark and bloody obscurity of the northern Virginia campaigns, Jeb Stuart at thirty and Bayard Sartoris at twenty-three stood briefly like two flaming stars garlanded with Fame's burgeoning laurel and the myrtle and roses of Death, incalculable and sudden as meteors in General Pope's troubled military sky, thrusting upon him like an unwilling garment that notoriety which his skill as a soldier could never have won him. And still in a spirit of pure fun: neither Jeb Stuart nor Bayard Sartoris, as their actions clearly showed, had any political convictions involved at all.

Aunt Jenny told the story first shortly after she came to them. It was Christmas time and they sat before a hickory fire in the rebuilt library—Aunt Jenny with her sad resolute face and John Sartoris, bearded and hawklike, and his three children and a guest: a Scottish engineer whom John Sartoris had met in Mexico in '45 and who was now helping him to build his railway.

Work on the railroad had ceased for the holiday season and John Sartoris and his engineer had ridden in at dusk from the suspended railhead in the hills to the north, and they now sat after supper in the firelight. The sun had set ruddily, leaving the air brittle as thin glass with frost, and presently Joby came in with an armful of firewood. He put a fresh billet on the fire, and in the dry air the flames crackled and snapped, popping in fading embers outward upon the hearth.

"Chris'mus!" Joby exclaimed with the grave and simple pleasure of his race, prodding at the blazing logs with the Yankee musket-barrel which stood in the chimney corner until sparks swirled upward into the dark maw of the chimney like wild golden veils, "year dat, chilluns?" John Sartoris' eldest daughter was twenty-two and would be married in June, Bayard was twenty, and the younger girl seventeen; and so Aunt Jenny for all her widowhood was one of the chillen too, to Joby. Then he replaced the musket-barrel in its niche and fired a long pine sliver at the hearth in order to light the candles. But Aunt Jenny stayed him, and he was gone—a shambling figure in an old formal coat too large for him, stooped and gray with age; and Aunt Jenny, speaking always of Jeb Stuart as Mister Stuart, told her story.

It had to do with an April evening, and coffee. Or the lack
of it, rather; and Stuart's military family sat in scented darkness beneath a new moon, talking of ladies and dead pleasures and thinking of home. Away in the darkness horses
moved invisibly with restful sounds, and bivouac fires fell to
glowing points like spent fireflies, and somewhere neither
near nor far the General's body servant touched a guitar in
lingering random chords. Thus they sat in the poignance of
spring and youth's immemorial sadness, forgetting travail and
glory, remembering instead other Virginian evenings with
fiddles above the myriad candles and slender grave measures
picked out with light laughter and lighter feet, thinking *When
will this be again? Shall I make one?* until they had talked themselves into a state of savage nostalgia and words grew shorter
and shorter and less and less frequent. Then the General
roused himself and brought them back by speaking of coffee,
or its lack.

This talk of coffee began to end a short time later with a ride
along midnight roads and then through woods black as pitch,
where horses went at a walk and riders rode with sabre or
musket at arm's length before them lest they be swept from
saddle by invisible boughs, and continued until the forest
thinned with dawn-ghosts and the party of twenty was well
within the Federal lines. Then dawn accomplished itself yet
more and all efforts toward concealment were discarded and
they galloped again and crashed through astonished picket-
parties returning placidly to camp, and fatigue parties setting
forth with picks and axes and shovels in the golden sunrise,
and swept yelling up the knoll where General Pope and his
staff sat at breakfast al fresco.

Two men captured a fat staff-major, others pursued the fleeing breakfasters for a short distance into the sanctuary of the
woods, but most of them rushed on to the General's private
commissary tent and emerged presently from the cyclonic
demolition of it, bearing plunder. Stuart and the three officers
with him halted their dancing mounts at the table and one of
them swept up a huge blackened coffee-pot and tendered it to
the General, and while the enemy shouted and fired muskets
among the trees, they toasted each other in sugarless and
creamless scalding coffee, as with a loving cup.

"General Pope, Sir," Stuart said, bowing in his saddle to the captured officer. He drank and extended the pot.

"I'll drink it, Sir," the major replied, "and thank God he is not here to respond in person."

"I had remarked that he appeared to leave hurriedly," Stuart said. "A prior engagement, perhaps?"

"Yes, Sir. With General Halleck," the major agreed drily. "I am sorry we have him for an opponent instead of Lee."

"So am I, Sir," Stuart answered. "I like General Pope in a war." Bugles were shrilling among the trees far and near, sending the alarm in flying echoes from brigade to brigade lying about the forest, and drums were beating wildly to arms and erratic bursts of musketry surged and trickled along the scattered outposts like the dry clatter of an opening fan, for the name 'Stuart' speeding from picket to picket had peopled the blossoming peaceful woods with gray phantoms.

Stuart turned in his saddle and his men came up and sat their horses and watched him alertly, their spare eager faces like mirrors reflecting their leader's constant consuming flame. Then from the flank there came something like a concerted volley, striking the coffee-pot from Bayard Sartoris' hand and clipping and snapping viciously among the dappled branches above their heads.

"Be pleased to mount, Sir," Stuart said to the captive major, and though his tone was exquisitely courteous all levity was gone from it. "Captain Wylie, you have the heaviest mount: will you——?" The captain freed his stirrup and hauled the prisoner up behind him. "Forward!" the General said and whirled rowelling his bay, and with the thunderous coordination of a single centaur they swept down the knoll and crashed into the forest at the point from which the volley had come before it could be repeated. Blue-clad pigmy shapes plunged scattering before and beneath them, and they rushed on among trees vicious with minies like wasps. Stuart now carried his plumed hat in his hand and his long tawny locks, tossing to the rhythm of his speed, appeared as gallant flames smoking with the wild and self-consuming splendor of his daring.

Behind them and on one flank muskets still banged and popped at their flashing phantoms, and from brigade to

brigade lying spaced about the jocund forest bugles shrilled
their importunate alarms. Stuart bore gradually to the left,
bringing all the uproar into his rear. The country became more
open and they swung into column at the gallop. The captured
major bounced and jolted behind Captain Wylie and the General
eral reined back beside the gallant black thundering along beneath
neath its double load.

"I am distressed to inconvenience you thus, Sir," he began
with his exquisite courtesy. "If you will indicate the general
location of your nearest horse picket I shall be most happy to
capture a mount for you."

"Thank you, General," the major replied, "but majors can
be replaced much easier than horses. I shall not trouble you."

"Just as you wish, Sir," Stuart agreed stiffly. He spurred on
to the head of the column again. They now galloped along a
faint trace that was once a road. It wound on between vernal
palisades of undergrowth and they followed it at a rapid controlled
trolled gait and debouched suddenly upon a glade, and a
squadron of Yankee cavalry reined back with shocked amazement,
ment, then hurled forward again.

Without faltering Stuart whirled his party and plunged back
into the forest. Pistol-balls were thinly about their heads and
the flat tossing reports were trivial as snapping twigs above
the converging thunder of hooves. Stuart swerved from the
road and they crashed headlong through undergrowth. The
Federal horsemen came yelling behind them and Stuart led his
party in a tight circle and halted it panting in a dense swampy
copse and they heard the pursuit sweep past.

They pushed on and regained the road and retraced their
former course, silently and utterly alert. To the left the sound
of the immediate pursuit crashed on, dying away. Then they
cantered again. Presently the woods thickened and they were
forced to slow to a trot, then to a walk. Although there was
no more firing and the bugles too had ceased, into the silence,
above the strong and rapid breathing of the horses and the
sound of their own hearts in their ears, was a nameless something—
thing—a tenseness seeping from tree to tree like an invisible
mist, filling the dewy morning woods with portent though
birds flashed swooping from tree to tree, unaware or disregardful
gardful of it.

A gleam of white through the trees ahead; Stuart raised his hand and they halted and sat their horses, watching him quietly and holding their breaths with listening. Then the General advanced again and broke through the undergrowth into another glade and they followed, and before them rose the knoll with the deserted breakfast-table and the rifled commissary tent. They trotted warily across the glade and halted at the table while the General scribbled hastily upon a scrap of paper. The glade dreamed quiet and empty of threat beneath the mounting golden day; laked within it lay a deep and abiding peace like golden wine; yet beneath this solitude and permeating it was that nameless and waiting portent, patient and brooding and sinister.

"Your sword, Sir," Stuart commanded, and the prisoner removed his weapon and Stuart took it and pinned his scribbled note to the table-top with it. The note read:

"General Stuart's compliments to General Pope, and he is sorry to have missed him again. He will call again tomorrow."

Stuart gathered up his reins. "Forward," he said.

They descended the knoll and crossed the empty glade and at an easy canter they took the road they had traversed that dawn—the road that led toward home. Stuart glanced back at his captive, at the gallant black with its double burden. "If you will direct us to the nearest cavalry picket I will provide you with a proper mount," he offered again.

"Will General Stuart, cavalry leader and General Lee's eyes, jeopardise his safety and that of his men and his cause in order to provide for the temporary comfort of a minor prisoner of his sword? This is not bravery: it is the rashness of a heedless and headstrong boy. There are fifteen thousand men within a radius of two miles of this point; even General Stuart cannot conquer that many, though they are Yankees, single-handed."

"Not for the prisoner, Sir," Stuart replied haughtily, "but for the officer suffering the fortune of war. No gentleman would do less."

"No gentleman has any business in this war," the major retorted. "There is no place for him here. He is an anachronism, like anchovies. At least General Stuart did not capture our anchovies," he added tauntingly. "Perhaps he will send Lee for them in person?"

"Anchovies," repeated Bayard Sartoris who galloped nearby, and he whirled his horse. Stuart shouted at him, but he lifted his reckless stubborn hand and flashed on; and as the General would have turned to follow a Yankee picket fired his piece from the roadside and dashed into the woods, shouting the alarm. Immediately other muskets exploded on all sides and from the forest to the right came the sound of a considerable body put suddenly into motion, and behind them in the direction of the invisible knoll, a volley crashed. A third officer spurred up and caught Stuart's bridle.

"Sir, Sir," he exclaimed. "What would you do?"

Stuart held his mount rearing, and another volley rang behind them, dribbling off into single scattered reports, crashed focalized again, and the noise to the right swelled nearer. "Let go, Allan," Stuart said. "He is my friend."

But the other clung on. "It is too late," he said. "Sartoris can only be killed: you would be captured."

"Forward, Sir, I beg," the captive major added. "What is one man, to a paladin out of romance?"

"Think of Lee, for God's sake, General!" the aide implored. "Forward!" he shouted to the troop, spurring his own mount and dragging the General's onward as a body of Federal horse broke from the woods behind them.

"And so," Aunt Jenny finished, "Mister Stuart went on and Bayard rode back after those anchovies, with all Pope's army shooting at him. He rode yelling 'Yaaaiiiih, Yaaaiiiih, come on, boys!' right up the knoll and jumped his horse over the breakfast table and rode it into the wrecked commissary tent, and a cook who was hidden under the mess stuck his arm out and shot Bayard in the back with a derringer.

"Mister Stuart fought his way out and got back home without losing but two men. He always spoke well of Bayard. He said he was a good officer and a fine cavalryman, but that he was too reckless."

They sat quietly for a time, in the firelight. The flames leaped and popped on the hearth and sparks soared in wild swirling plumes up the chimney, and Bayard Sartoris' brief career swept like a shooting star across the dark plain of their mutual remembering and suffering, lighting it with a transient glare like a soundless thunder-clap, leaving a sort of radiance

when it died. The guest, the Scottish engineer, had sat quietly, listening. After a time he spoke.

"When he rode back, he was no actually cer-rtain there
wer-re anchovies, was he?"

"The Yankee major said there were," Aunt Jenny replied.

"Ay." The Scotsman pondered again. "And did Muster-r
Stuart retur-rn next day, as he said in's note?"

"He went back that afternoon," Aunt Jenny answered,
"looking for Bayard." Ashes soft as rosy feathers shaled glowing onto the hearth, and faded to the softest gray. John Sartoris leaned forward into the firelight and punched at the
blazing logs with the Yankee musket-barrel.

"That was the god-damdest army the world ever saw, I
reckon," he said.

"Yes," Aunt Jenny agreed. "And Bayard was the god-
damdest man in it."

"Yes," John Sartoris admitted soberly, "Bayard was wild."
The Scotsman spoke again.

"This Musterr Stuart, who said your brother was reckless:
Who was he?"

"He was the cavalry general Jeb Stuart," Aunt Jenny answered. She brooded for a while upon the fire; her pale indomitable face held for a moment a tranquil tenderness. "He
had a strange sense of humor," she said. "Nothing ever seemed
quite so diverting to him as General Pope in his night-shirt."
She dreamed once more on some far away place beyond the
rosy battlements of the embers. "Poor man," she said. Then
she said quietly: "I danced a valse with him in Baltimore in
'58," and her voice was proud and still as banners in the dust.

.... But the door was closed now, and what light
passed through the colored panes was richly solemn. To his
left was his grandsons' room, the room in which his grandson's wife and her child had died last October. He stood
beside this door for a moment, then he opened it quietly. The
blinds were closed and the room had that breathless tranquillity of unoccupation, and he closed the door and tramped on
with that heavy-footed obliviousness of the deaf and entered
his own bedroom and crashed the door behind him, as was
his way of shutting doors.

He sat down and removed his shoes, the shoes that were made to his measure twice a year by a Saint Louis house, then he rose and went in his stockings to the window and looked down upon his saddle-mare tethered to a mulberry tree in the back yard and a negro lad lean as a hound, richly static beside it. From the kitchen, invisible from this window, Elnora's endless minor ebbed and flowed unheard by him upon the lazy scene.

He crossed to his closet and drew out a pair of scarred riding-boots and stamped into them and took a cigar from the humidor on his night table, and he stood for a time with the cold cigar between his teeth, having forgotten to light it. Through the cloth of his pocket his hand touched the pipe there, and he took it out and looked at it again, and it seemed to him that he could still hear old man Falls' voice in roaring recapitulation: "Cunnel was settin' thar in a cheer, his sock feet propped on the po'ch railin', smokin' this hyer very pipe. Old Louvinia was settin' on the steps, shellin' a bowl of peas fer supper. And a feller was glad to git even peas sometimes, in them days. And you was settin' back agin' the post. They wa'nt nobody else thar 'cep' yo' aunt, the one 'fo' Miss Jenny come. Cunnel had sont them two gals to Memphis to yo' gran'pappy when he fust went to Virginny with that 'ere regiment that turnt right around and voted him outen the colonelcy. Voted 'im out because he wouldn't be Tom, Dick and Harry with ever' skulkin' camp-robber that come along with a salvaged muskit and claimed to be a sojer. You was about half-grown then, I reckon. How old was you then, Bayard?"

"Fourteen."

"Hey?"

"Fourteen. Do I have to tell you that everytime you tell me this damn story?"

"And thar you all was a-settin' when they turned in at the gate and come trottin' up the carriage drive.

"Old Louvinia drapped the bowl of peas and let out one squawk, but Cunnel shet her up and told her to run and git his boots and pistols and have 'em ready at the back do', and you lit out fer the barn to saddle that stallion. And when them Yankees rid up and stopped—they stopped right whar that flower bed is now—they wa'nt nobody in sight but Cunnel, a-settin' thar like he never even heerd tell of no Yankees.

"The Yankees they sot thar on the hosses, talkin' 'mongst theyselves if this was the right house or not, and Cunnel settin' thar with his sock feet on the railin', gawkin' at 'em like a hill-billy. The Yankee officer he tole one man to ride back to the barn and look fer that 'ere stallion, then he says to Cunnel:

" 'Say, Johnny, whar do the rebel, John Sartoris, live?'

" 'Lives down the road a piece,' Cunnel says, not battin' a eye even. ''Bout two mile,' he says. 'But you wont find 'im now. He's away fightin' the Yanks agin.'

" 'Well, I reckon you better come and show us the way, anyhow,' the Yankee officer says.

"So Cunnel he got up slow and tole 'em to let 'im git his shoes and walkin' stick, and limped into the house, leavin' 'em a-settin' thar waitin'.

"Soon's he was out of sight he run. Old Louvinia was waitin' at the back do' with his coat and boots and pistols and a snack of cawn bread. That 'ere other Yankee had rid into the barn, and Cunnel taken the things from Louvinia and wropped 'em up in the coat and started acrost the back yard like he was jest takin' a walk. 'Bout that time the Yankee come to the barn do'.

" 'They aint no stock hyer a-tall,' the Yank says.

" 'I reckon not,' Cunnel says. 'Cap'm says fer you to come on back,' he says, goin' on. He could feel that 'ere Yank a-watchin' 'im, lookin' right 'twixt his shoulder blades, whar the bullet would hit. Cunnel says that was the hardest thing he ever done in his life, walkin' on thar acrost that lot with his back to'ads that Yankee without breakin' into a run. He was aimin' to'ads the corner of the barn, whar he could git the house between 'em, and Cunnel says hit seemed like he'd been a-walkin' a year without gittin' no closer and not darin' to look back. Cunnel says he wa'nt even thinkin' of nothin' 'cep' he was glad the gals wa'nt at home. He says he never give a thought to yo' aunt back thar in the house, because he says she was a full-blood Sartoris and she was a match fer any jest a dozen Yankees.

"Then the Yank hollered at him, but Cunnel kep' right on, not lookin' back nor nothin'. Then the Yank hollered agin and

Cunnel says he could hyear the hoss movin' and he decided hit was time to stir his shanks. He made the corner of the barn jest as the Yank shot the fust time, and by the time the Yank got to the corner, he was in the hawg-lot, a-tearin' through the jimson weeds to'ads the creek whar you was waitin' with the stallion hid in the willers.

"And thar you was a-standin', holdin' the hoss and that 'ere Yankee patrol yellin' up behind, until Cunnel got his boots on. And then he tole you to tell yo' aunt he wouldn't be home fer supper."

"But what are you giving it to me for, after all this time?" he had asked, fingering the pipe, and old man Falls had said a poorhouse was no fit place for it.

"A thing he toted in his pocket and got enjoyment outen, in them days. Hit 'ud be different, I reckon, while we was a-buildin' the railroad. He said often enough in them days we was all goin' to be in the po'house by Sat'd'y night. Only I beat him, thar. I got thar fo' he did. Or the cemetary he meant, mo' likely, him ridin' up and down the survey with a saddle-bag of money night and day, keepin' jest one cross tie ahead of the po'house, like he said. That 'us when hit changed. When he had to start killin' folks. Them two cyarpet baggers stirrin' up niggers, that he walked right into the room whar they was a-settin' behind a table with they pistols layin' on the table, and that robber and that other feller he kilt, all with that same dang der'nger. When a feller has to start killin' folks, he 'most always has to keep on killin' 'em. And when he does, he's already dead hisself."

It showed on John Sartoris' brow, the dark shadow of fatality and doom, that night when he sat beneath the candles in the dining room and turned a wine glass in his fingers while he talked to his son. The railroad was finished, and today he had been elected to the state legislature after a hard and bitter fight, and doom lay on his brow, and weariness.

"And so," he said, "Redlaw'll kill me tomorrow, for I shall be unarmed. I'm tired of killing men. . . . Pass the wine, Bayard."

And the next day he was dead, whereupon, as though he had but waited for that to release him of the clumsy cluttering of bones and breath, by losing the frustration of his own flesh he could now stiffen and shape that which sprang from him into the fatal semblance of his dream; to be evoked like a genie or a deity by an illiterate old man's tedious reminiscing or by a charred pipe from which even the rank smell of burnt tobacco had long since faded away.

Old Bayard roused himself and went and laid the pipe on his chest of drawers. Then he quitted the room and tramped heavily down the stairs and out through the back.

The negro lad waked easily and untethered the mare and held the stirrup. Old Bayard mounted and remembered the cigar at last and fired it. The negro opened the gate into the lot and trotted on ahead and opened the second gate and let the rider into the field beyond. Bayard rode on, trailing his pungent smoke. From somewhere a ticked setter came up and fell in at the mare's heels.

Elnora stood barelegged on the kitchen floor and soused her mop into the pail and thumped it on the floor again.

"Sinner riz fum de moaner's bench,
 Sinner jump to de penance bench;
 When de preacher ax 'im whut de reason why,
 Says 'Preacher got de women jes' de same ez I'.
 Oh, Lawd, Oh Lawd!
 Dat's whut de matter wid de church today."

2.

Simon's destination was a huge brick house set well up onto the street. The lot had been the site of a fine old colonial house which stood among magnolias and oaks and flowering shrubs. But the house had burned and some of the trees had been felled to make room for an architectural garbling so imposingly terrific as to possess a kind of majesty. It was a monument to the frugality (and the mausoleum of the social aspirations of his women) of a hillman who had moved in from a small settlement called Frenchman's Bend and who, as Miss Jenny Du Pre put it, had built the handsomest house in Frenchman's Bend on the most beautiful lot in Jefferson. The hillman had stuck it out for two years during which his women-folks sat about the veranda all morning in lace-trimmed "boudoir caps" and spent the afternoons in colored

silk riding about town in a rubber-tired surrey; then the hillman sold his house to a new-comer to the town and took his
women back to the country and doubtless set them to work
again.

A number of motor-cars ranked along the street lent a formally festive air to the place, and Simon with his tilted cigar
stub wheeled up and drew rein and indulged in a brief colorful altercation with a negro sitting behind the wheel of a car
parked before the hitching-block. "Dont block off no Sartoris
ca'iage, black boy," Simon concluded, when the other had
moved the motor and permitted him access to the post. "Block
off de commonality, ef you wants, but dont intervoke no equipage waitin' on Cunnel er Miss Jenny. Dey wont stan' fer it."

He descended and tethered the horses, and his spirit mol-
lified by the rebuke administered and laved with the beatitude
of having gained his own way, Simon paused and examined
the motor-car with curiosity and no little superciliousness
tinged faintly with respectful envy, and spoke affably with its
conductor. But not for long, for Simon had sisters in the
Lord in this kitchen, and presently he let himself into the yard
and followed the gravel driveway around to the back. He
could hear the party going on as he passed beneath the windows: that sustained unintelligible gabbling with which white
ladies could surround themselves without effort and which
they seemed to consider a necessary (or unavoidable) adjunct
to having a good time. The fact that it was a card party would
have seemed neither paradoxical nor astonishing to Simon,
for time and much absorbing experience had taught him a
fine tolerance of white folks' vagaries and for those of ladies
of any color.

The hillman had built his house so close to the street that
the greater part of the original lawn with its fine old trees lay
behind it. There were once crepe-myrtle and syringa and lilac
and jasmine bushes without order, and massed honeysuckle
on fences and tree trunks; and after the first house had burned
these had taken the place and made of its shaggy formality a
mazed and scented jungle loved of mockingbirds and thrushes,
where boys and girls lingered on spring and summer nights
among drifting fireflies and quiring whip-poor-wills and usually the liquid tremolo of a screech owl. Then the hillman had

bought it and cut some of the trees in order to build his house near the street after the country fashion, and chopped out the jungle and whitewashed the remaining trees and ran his barn- and hog- and chicken-lot fences between their ghostly trunks. He didn't remain long enough to learn of garages.

Some of the antiseptic desolation of his tenancy had faded now, and its present owner had set out more shrubbery—jasmine and mock-orange and verbena—with green iron tables and chairs beneath them and a pool and a tennis court; and Simon passed on with discreet assurance, and on a consonantless drone of female voices he rode into the kitchen where a thin woman in a funereal purple turban and poising a beaten biscuit heaped with mayonnaise, and a mountainous one in the stained apron of her calling and drinking melted ice-cream from a saucer, rolled their eyes at him.

"I seed him on de street yistiddy and he looked bad; he jes' didn't favor hisself," the visitor was saying as Simon entered, but they dropped the theme of conversation and made him welcome.

"Ef it aint Brother Strother," they said in unison. "Come in, Brother Strother. How is you?"

"Po'ly, ladies; po'ly," Simon replied. He doffed his hat and unclamped his cigar stub and stowed it away in the hat-band. "I'se had a right smart mis'ry in de back. Is y'all kep' well?"

"Right well, I thank you, Brother Strother," the visitor replied. Simon drew a chair up to the table, as he was bidden.

"Whut you gwine eat, Brother Strother?" the cook demanded hospitably. "Dey's party fixin's, en dey's some col' greens en a little sof' ice-cream lef' fum dinner."

"I reckon I'll have a little ice-cream en some of dem greens, Sis' Rachel," Simon replied. "My teef aint much on party doin's no mo'." The cook rose with majestic deliberation and waddled across to a pantry and reached down a platter. She was one of the best cooks in Jefferson: no mistress dared protest against the social amenities of Rachel's kitchen.

"Ef you aint de beatin'es' man!" the first guest exclaimed. "Eatin' ice-cream at yo' age!"

"I been eatin' ice-cream sixty years," Simon said. "Whut reason I got fer quittin' now?"

"Dat's right, Brother Strother," the cook agreed, placing the dish before him. "Eat yo' ice-cream when you kin git it. Jes' a minute en I'll——Here, Meloney," she interrupted herself as a young light negress in a smart white apron and cap entered, bearing a tray of plates containing remnants of edible edifices copied from pictures in ladies' magazines and possessing neither volume nor nourishment, with which the party had been dulling its palates against supper, "git Brother Strother a bowl of dat 'ere ice-cream, honey."

The girl clashed the tray into the sink and rinsed a bowl at the water tap while Simon watched her with his still little eyes. She whipped the bowl through a towel with a fine show of derogatory carelessness, and with her chin at a supercilious angle she clattered on her high heels across the kitchen, still under Simon's unwinking regard, and slammed a door behind her. Then Simon turned his head.

"Yes, ma'am," he repeated, "I been eatin' ice-cream too long ter quit at my age."

"Dey wont no vittle hurt you ez long ez you kin stomach 'um," the cook agreed, raising her saucer to her lips again. The girl returned and with her head still averted she set the bowl of viscid liquid before Simon who, under cover of this movement, dropped his hand on her thigh. The girl smacked him sharply on the back of his gray head with her flat palm.

"Miss Rachel, cant you make him keep his hands to hisself?" she said.

"Aint you 'shamed," Rachel demanded, but without rancor. "A ole gray-head man like you, wid a fam'ly of grown chillen and one foot in de graveyard?"

"Hush yo' mouf, woman," Simon said placidly, spooning spinach into his melted ice-cream. "Aint dey erbout breakin' up in yonder yit?"

"I reckon dey's erbout to," the other guest answered, putting another laden biscuit into her mouth with a gesture of elegant gentility. "Seems like dey's talkin' louder."

"Den dey's started playin' again," Simon corrected. "Talkin' jes' eased off whiles dey et. Yes, suh, dey's started playin' again. Dat's white folks. Nigger aint got sense ernough ter play cards wid all dat racket gwine on."

But they were breaking up. Miss Jenny Du Pre had just finished a story which left the three players at her table avoiding one another's eyes a little self-consciously, as was her way. Miss Jenny travelled very little, and in Pullman smoke-rooms not at all, and people wondered where she got her stories; who had told them to her. And she repeated them anywhere and at any time, choosing the wrong moment and the wrong audience with a cold and cheerful audacity. Young people liked her, and she was much in demand as a chaperone for picnic parties.

She now spoke across the room to the hostess. "I'm going home, Belle," she stated. "I think we are all tired of your party. I know I am." The hostess was a plump, youngish woman and her cleverly-rouged face showed now an hysterical immersion that was almost repose, but when Miss Jenny broke into her consciousness with the imminence of departure this faded quickly, and her face resumed its familiar expression of strained and vague dissatisfaction and she protested conventionally but with a petulant sincerity, as a well-bred child might.

But Miss Jenny was adamant and she rose and her slender wrinkled hand brushed invisible crumbs from the bosom of her black silk dress. "If I stay any longer I'll miss Bayard's toddy time," she explained with her usual forthrightness. "Come on, Narcissa, and I'll drive you home."

"I have my car, thank you, Miss Jenny," the young woman to whom she spoke replied in a grave contralto, rising also; and the others got up with sibilant gathering motions above the petulant modulation of the hostess' protestings, and they drifted slowly into the hall and clotted again before various mirrors, colorful and shrill. Miss Jenny pushed steadily on toward the door.

"Come along, come along," she repeated. "Harry Mitchell wont want to run into all this gabble when he comes home from work."

"Then he can sit in the car out in the garage," the hostess rejoined sharply. "I do wish you wouldn't go. Miss Jenny, I dont think I'll ask you again."

But Miss Jenny only said "Goodbye, goodbye" with cold affability, and with her delicate replica of the Sartoris nose and that straight grenadier's back of hers which gave the pas for erectness to only one back in town—that of her nephew

Bayard—she stood at the steps, where Narcissa Benbow joined her, bringing with her like an odor that aura of grave and serene repose in which she dwelt. "Belle meant that, too," Miss Jenny said.

"Meant what, Miss Jenny?"

"About Harry. . . . . . Now, where do you suppose that damn nigger went to?" They descended the steps and from the parked motors along the street came muffled starting explosions, and the two women traversed the brief flower-bordered walk to the street. "Did you see which way my driver went?" Miss Jenny asked of the negro in the nearest car.

"He went to'ds de back, ma'am." The negro opened the door and slid his legs, clad in army o.d. and a pair of linoleum putties, to the ground. "I'll go git 'im."

"Thank you. Well, thank the Lord that's over," she added. "It's too bad folks haven't the sense or courage to send out invitations, then shut up the house and go away. All the fun of parties is in dressing up and getting there." Ladies came in steady shrill groups down the walk and got into cars or departed on foot with bright, not-quite-musical calls to one another. The sun was down behind Belle's house, and when the women passed from the shadow into the level bar of sunlight beyond they became delicately brilliant as paroquets. Narcissa Benbow wore gray and her eyes were violet, and in her face was that tranquil repose of lilies.

"Not children's parties," she protested.

"I'm talking about parties, not about having fun," Miss Jenny said. "Speaking of children: What's the news from Horace?"

"Oh, hadn't I told you?" the other said quickly. "I had a wire yesterday. He landed in New York Wednesday. It was such a mixed-up sort of message, I never could understand what he was trying to tell me, except that he would have to stay in New York for a week or so. It was over fifty words long."

"Was it a straight message?" Miss Jenny asked. The other said Yes, and she added: "Horace must have got rich, like the soldiers say all the Y.M.C.A. did. Well, if it has taught a man like Horace to make money, the war was a pretty good thing, after all."

"Miss Jenny! How can you talk that way, after John's——after——"

"Fiddlesticks," Miss Jenny said. "The war just gave John a good excuse to get himself killed. If it hadn't been that, it would have been some other way that would have been a bother to everybody around."

"Miss Jenny!"

"I know, my dear. I've lived with these bullheaded Sartorises for eighty years, and I'll never give a single ghost of 'em the satisfaction of shedding a tear over him. What did Horace's message say?"

"It was about something he was bringing home with him," the other answered, and her serene face filled with a sort of fond exasperation. "It was such an incoherent message. . . . . . . Horace never could say anything clearly from a distance." She mused again, gazing down the street with its tunnel of oaks and elms through which sunlight fell in spaced tiger bars. "Do you suppose he could have adopted a war-orphan?"

"War-orphan," Miss Jenny repeated. "More likely it's some war-orphan's mamma." Simon appeared at the corner of the house, wiping his mouth on the back of his hand, and crossed the lawn with shuffling celerity. His cigar was not visible.

"No," the other said quickly, with grave concern. "You dont believe he would have done that? No, no, he wouldn't have. Horace wouldn't have done that. He never does anything without telling me about it first. He would have written: I know he would. You really dont think that sounds like Horace, do you? A thing like that?"

"Hmph," Miss Jenny said through her high-bridged Norman nose. "An innocent like Horace straying with that trusting air of his among all those man-starved European women? He wouldn't know it himself, until it was too late; especially in a foreign language. I bet in every town he was in over seven days his landlady or somebody was keeping his supper on the stove when he was late, or holding sugar out on the other men to sweeten his coffee with. Some men are born to always have some woman making a doormat of herself for him, just as some men are born cuckolded. . . . . . . How old are you?"

"I'm still twenty-six, Miss Jenny," the younger woman replied equably. Simon unhitched the horses and he stood now beside the carriage in his Miss Jenny attitude. It differed from the bank one; there was now in it a gallant and protective deference. Miss Jenny examined the still serenity of the other's face.

"Why dont you get married, and let that baby look after himself for a while? Mark my words, it wont be six months before some other woman will be falling all over herself for the privilege of keeping his feet dry, and he wont even miss you."

"I promised mother," the other replied quietly and without offense. . . . . . . "I dont see why he couldn't have sent an intelligible message."

"Well. . . ." Miss Jenny turned to her carriage. "Maybe it's only an orphan, after all," she said with comfortless reassurance.

"I'll know soon, anyway," the other agreed, and she crossed to a small car at the curb and opened the door. Miss Jenny got in her carriage, and Simon mounted and gathered up the reins.

"Let me know when you hear again," she called as the carriage moved forward. "Drive out and get some more flowers when you want 'em."

"Thank you. Goodbye."

"All right, Simon." The carriage moved on again, and again Simon withheld his news until they were out of town.

"Mist' Bayard done got home," he remarked, in his former conversational tone.

"Where is he?" Miss Jenny demanded immediately.

"He aint come out to de place yit," Simon answered. "I 'speck he went to de graveyard."

"Nonsense," Miss Jenny snapped. "No Sartoris ever goes to the cemetery but once. . . . Does Colonel know he's home?"

"Yessum, I tole him, but he dont ack like he believed I wuz tellin' him de troof."

"You mean, nobody's seen him but you?"

"I aint seed 'im neither," Simon disclaimed. "Section han' seed 'im jump off de train and tole me——"

"You damn fool nigger!" Miss Jenny stormed. "And you went and blurted a fool thing like that to Bayard? Haven't you got any more sense than that?"

"Section han' seed 'im," Simon repeated stubbornly. "I reckon he knowed Mist' Bayard when he seed 'im."

"Well, where is he, then?"

"He mought have gone out to de graveyard," Simon suggested.

"Drive on!"

Miss Jenny found her nephew with two bird-dogs in his office. The room was lined with bookcases containing rows of heavy legal tomes bound in dun calf and emanating an atmosphere of dusty and undisturbed meditation, and a miscellany of fiction of the historical-romantic school (all Dumas was there, and the steady progression of the volumes now constituted Bayard's entire reading, and one volume lay always on the night-table beside his bed) and a collection of indiscriminate objects—small packets of seed, old rusted spurs and bits and harness buckles, brochures on animal and vegetable diseases, ornate tobacco containers which people had given him on various occasions and anniversaries and which he had never used, inexplicable bits of rock and desiccated roots and grain pods—all collected one at a time and for reasons which had long since escaped his memory, yet preserved just the same. The room contained an enormous closet with a padlocked door, and a big table littered with yet more casual objects, and a locked roll-top desk (keys and locks were an obsession with him) and a sofa and three big leather chairs. This room was always referred to as the office, and Bayard now sat here with his hat on and still in his riding boots, transferring bourbon whisky from a small rotund keg to a silver stoppered decanter while the two dogs watched him with majestic gravity.

One of the dogs was quite old and nearly blind. It spent most of the day lying in the sun in the back yard, or during the hot summer days, in the cool dusty obscurity beneath the kitchen. But toward the middle of the afternoon it went around to the front and waited there quietly and gravely until the carriage came up the drive, and when Bayard had descended and entered the house it returned to the back and waited again until Isom led the mare up and Bayard came out and mounted. Then together they spent the afternoon going quietly and unhurriedly about the meadows and fields and woods in their seasonal mutations—the man on his horse and the ticked setter gravely beside him, while the descending evening of their lives drew toward its peaceful close upon the kind land that had bred them both. The young dog was not yet two years old; his net was too hasty for the sedateness of their society overlong, and though at times he set forth with them or came quartering up, splashed and eager, from somewhere to join them in midfield, it was not for long and soon he must dash away with his tongue flapping and the tense delicate feathering of his tail in pursuit of the maddening elusive smells with which the world surrounded him and tempted him from every thicket and copse and ravine.

Bayard's boots were wet to the tops and the soles were caked with mud, and he bent with intense preoccupation above his keg and bottle under the sober curiosity of the dogs. The keg was propped bung-upward in a second chair and he was siphoning the rich brown liquor delicately into the decanter by means of a rubber tube. Miss Jenny entered with her black bonnet still perched on the exact top of her trim white head, and the dogs looked up at her, the older with grave dignity, the younger one more quickly, tapping his tail on the floor with fawning diffidence. But Bayard did not raise his head. Miss Jenny closed the door and stared coldly at his boots.

"Your feet are wet," she stated. Still he didn't look up, but held the tube delicately in the bottle-neck, while the liquor mounted steadily in the decanter. At times his deafness was very convenient, more convenient than actual, perhaps; but who could know certainly? "You go up stairs and get those boots off," Miss Jenny commanded, raising her voice. "I'll fill the decanter."

But within the walled serene tower of his deafness his imperturbability did not falter until the decanter was full and he pinched the tube and raised it and drained it back into the keg. The older dog had not moved, but the younger one had retreated beyond Bayard, where it lay motionless and alert, its head on its crossed forepaws, watching Miss Jenny with one melting unwinking eye. Bayard drew the tube from the keg and looked at her for the first time. "What did you say?"

But Miss Jenny returned to the door and opened it and shouted into the hall, eliciting an alarmed response from the kitchen, followed presently by Simon in the flesh. "Go up and get Colonel's slippers," she directed. When she turned into the room again neither Bayard nor the keg was visible, but from the open closet door there protruded the young dog's interested hind quarters and the tense feathering of his barometric tail; then Bayard thrust the dog out of the closet with his foot and emerged himself and locked the door behind him.

"Has Simon come in, yet?" he asked.

"He's coming now," she answered. "I just called him. Sit down and get those wet boots off." At that moment Simon entered, with the slippers, and Bayard sat obediently and Simon knelt and drew his boots off under Miss Jenny's martinet eye. "Are his socks dry?" she asked.

"No'm, dey aint wet," Simon answered. But she bent and felt them herself.

"Here," Bayard said testily, but Miss Jenny ran her hand over both his feet with brusque imperturbability.

"Precious little fault of his if they aint," she said across the topless wall of his deafness. "And then you have to come along with that fool yarn of yours."

"Section han' seed 'im," Simon repeated stubbornly, thrusting the slippers onto Bayard's feet. "I aint never said I seed him." He looked up and rubbed his hands on his thighs.

Bayard stamped into the slippers. "Bring the toddy fixings, Simon." Then to his aunt, in a tone which he contrived to make casual: "Simon says Bayard got off the train this afternoon." But Miss Jenny was storming at Simon again.

"Come back here and get these boots and set 'em behind the stove," she said. Simon returned and sidled swiftly to the hearth and gathered up the boots. "And take these dogs out of here, too," she added. "Thank the Lord he hasn't thought about bringing his horse in with him." Immediately the old dog came to his feet, and followed by the younger one's diffident alacrity, departed with that same assumed deliberation with which both Bayard and Simon obeyed Miss Jenny's brisk implacability.

"Simon says——" Bayard repeated.

"Simon says fiddlesticks," Miss Jenny snapped. "Have you lived with Simon sixty years without learning that he dont know the truth when he sees it?" And she followed Simon from the room and on to the kitchen, and while Simon's tall yellow daughter bent over her biscuit-board and Simon filled a glass pitcher with fresh water and sliced lemons and set them and a sugar bowl and two tall glasses on a tray, Miss Jenny stood in the doorway and curled Simon's grizzled remaining hair to tighter kinks yet. She had a fine command of language at all times, but when her ire was aroused she soared without effort to sublime heights. Hers was a forceful clarity and a colorful simplicity and a bold use of metaphor that Demosthenes would have envied and which even mules comprehended and of whose intent the most obtuse persons remained not long in doubt; and beneath it Simon's head bobbed lower and lower and the fine assumption of detached preoccupation moulted like feathers from about him, until he caught up the tray and ducked from the room. Miss Jenny's voice followed him, descending easily with a sweeping comprehensiveness that included a warning and a suggestion for future conduct for Simon and Elnora and all their descendants, actual and problematical, for some years.

"And the next time," she concluded, "you or any section hand or brakeman or delivery boy either sees or hears anything you think will be of interest to Colonel, you tell me about it first: I'll do all the telling after that." She gave Elnora another glare for good measure and returned to the office, where her nephew was stirring sugar and water carefully in the two glasses.

Simon in a white jacket officiated as butler—doubled in brass, you might say, only it was not brass, but silver so fine and soft that some of the spoons were worn now almost to paper thinness where fingers in their generations had held them; silver which Simon's grandfather Joby had buried on a time beneath the ammoniac barn floor while Simon, aged three in a single filthy garment, had looked on with a child's grave interest in the curious game.

An effluvium of his primary calling clung about him always, however, even when he was swept and garnished for church and a little shapeless in a discarded Prince Albert coat of Bayard's; and his every advent into the dining room with dishes brought with him, and the easy attitudes into which he fell near the sideboard while answering Miss Jenny's abrupt questions or while pursuing some fragmentary conversation which he and Bayard had been engaged in earlier in the day, disseminated, and his exits left behind him a faint nostalgia of the stables. But tonight he brought dishes in and set them down and scuttled immediately back to the kitchen: Simon realized that again he had talked too much.

Miss Jenny with a shawl of white wool about her shoulders against the evening's coolness, was doing the talking tonight, immersing herself and her nephew in a wealth of trivialities—petty doings and sayings and gossip—a behavior which was not like Miss Jenny at all. She had opinions, and a pithy, savagely humorous way of stating them, but it was very seldom that she descended to gossip. Meanwhile Bayard had shut himself up in that walled tower of his deafness and raised the drawbridge and clashed the portcullis to, where you never knew whether he heard you or no, while his corporeal self ate its supper steadily. Presently they had done and Miss Jenny rang the little silver bell at her hand and Simon opened the pantry door and received again the cold broadside of her displeasure, and shut the door and lurked behind it until they had left the room.

Bayard lit his cigar in the office and Miss Jenny followed him there and drew her chair up to the table beneath the lamp and opened the daily Memphis newspaper. She enjoyed humanity in its more colorful mutations, preferring lively romance to the most impeccable of dun fact, so she took in the more lurid afternoon paper even though it was yesterday's when it reached her, and read with cold avidity accounts of arson and murder and violent dissolution and adultery; in good time and soon the American scene was to furnish her with diversion in the form of bootleggers' wars, but this was not yet. Her nephew sat without the mellow downward pool of the lamp, with his feet braced against the corner of the hearth from which his boot-soles and the boot-soles of John Sartoris before him had long since worn the varnish away, puffing his cigar. He was not reading, and at intervals Miss Jenny glanced above her glasses and across the top of the paper toward him. Then she read again, and there as no sound in the room save the sporadic rustling of the page.

After a time he rose, with one of his characteristic plunging movements, and she watched him as he crossed the room and passed through the door and banged it to behind him. She read on for a while longer, but her attention had followed the heavy tramp of his feet up the hall, and when this ceased she rose and laid the paper aside and followed him to the front door.

The moon had gotten up beyond the dark eastern wall of the hills and it lay without emphasis upon the valley, mounting like a child's balloon behind the oaks and locusts along the drive. Bayard sat with his feet on the veranda rail, in the moonlight. His cigar glowed at spaced intervals, and a shrill monotone of crickets rose from the immediate grass, and further away, from among the trees, a fairy-like piping of young frogs like endless silver small bubbles rising, and a thin sourceless odor of locust drifted up intangible as fading tobacco-wraiths, and from the rear of the house, up the dark hall, Elnora's voice floated in meaningless minor suspense.

Miss Jenny groped in the darkness beside the door and from beside the yawning lesser obscurity of the mirror she took Bayard's hat from the hook, and carried it out to him and put it in his hand. "Dont sit out here too long, now. It aint summer yet."

He grunted indistinguishably, but he put the hat on and she turned and went back to the office and finished the paper and folded it and laid it on the table. She snapped the light off and mounted the dark stairs to her room. The moon shone above the trees at this height and it fell in broad silver bars through the eastern windows.

Before turning up the light she crossed to the southern wall and raised a window there, upon the crickets and frogs and somewhere a mockingbird. Outside the window was a magnolia tree, but it was not to bloom yet, nor had the honeysuckle massed along the garden fence flowered. But this would be soon, and from here she could overlook the garden, could look down upon cape jasmine and syringa and callacanthus where the moon lay upon their bronze and yet unflowered sleep, and upon those other shoots and graftings from the far-away Carolina gardens she had known as a girl.

Just beyond the corner from the invisible kitchen, Elnora's voice welled in mellow falling suspense. *All folks talkin' 'bout heaven aint gwine dar* Elnora sang, and presently she and Simon emerged into the moonlight and took the path to Simon's cabin below the barn. Simon had fired his cigar at last, and the evil smoke of it trailed behind him, fading; but when they had gone the rank pungency of it seemed still to linger within the sound of the crickets and of the frogs upon the silver air, mingled and blended inextricably with the dying fall of Elnora's voice.

All folks talkin' 'bout heaven aint gwine dar

His cigar was cold, and he moved and dug a match from his waistcoat and relit it and braced his feet again upon the railing, and again the drifting sharpness of tobacco lay along the windless currents of the silver air, straying and fading slowly amid locust-breaths and the ceaseless fairy reiteration of crickets and frogs. There was a mockingbird somewhere down the valley, and after a while another sang from the magnolia at the corner of the garden fence. An automobile passed along the smooth valley road, slowed for the railway crossing, then sped on. Before the sound of it had died away, the whistle of the nine-thirty train drifted down from the hills.

Two long blasts with dissolving echoes, two short following ones; but before it came in sight his cigar was cold again, and he sat holding it in his fingers and watched the locomotive drag its string of yellow windows up the valley and into the hills once more, where after a time it whistled again, arrogant and resonant and sad. John Sartoris had sat so on this veranda and watched his two daily trains emerge from the hills and cross the valley into the hills, with lights and smoke and a noisy simulation of speed. But now his railway belonged to a syndicate and there were more than two trains on it that ran from Chicago to the Gulf, completing his dream, while John Sartoris slept among martial cherubim and the useless vainglory of whatever God he did not scorn to recognise.

Then old Bayard's cigar was cold again and he sat with it dead in his fingers and watched a tall shape emerge from the lilac bushes beside the garden fence and cross the patchy moonlight toward the veranda. His grandson wore no hat and he came on and mounted the steps and stood with the moonlight bringing the hawk-like planes of his face into high relief while his grandfather sat with his dead cigar and looked at him.

"Bayard, son?" old Bayard said. Young Bayard stood in the moonlight. His eyesockets were cavernous shadows.

"I tried to keep him from going up there on that goddam little popgun," he said at last with brooding savageness. Then he moved again and old Bayard lowered his feet, but his grandson only dragged a chair violently up beside him and flung himself into it. His motions were abrupt also, like his grandfather's, but controlled and flowing for all their violence.

"Why in hell didn't you let me know you were coming?" old Bayard demanded. "What do you mean, straggling in here like this?"

"I didn't let anybody know." Young Bayard dug a cigarette from his pocket and raked a match on his shoe.

"What?"

"I didn't tell anybody I was coming," he repeated above the cupped match, raising his voice.

"Simon knew it. Do you inform nigger servants of your movements instead of your own granddaddy?"

"Damn Simon, sir," young Bayard shouted. "Who set him to watching me?"

"Dont yell at me, boy," old Bayard shouted in turn. His grandson flung the match away and drew at the cigarette in deep troubled draughts. "Dont wake Jenny," old Bayard added more mildly, striking a match to his cold cigar. "All right, are you?"

"Here," young Bayard said, extending his hand. "Let me hold it. You're going to set your moustache on fire." But old Bayard repulsed him sharply and sucked stubbornly and impotently at the match in his unsteady fingers.

"I said, are you all right?" he repeated.

"Why not?" young Bayard snapped. "Takes damn near as big a fool to get hurt in a war as it does in peacetime. Damn fool, that's what it is." He drew at the cigarette again, then he hurled it not half consumed after the match. "There was one I had to lay for four days to catch him. Had to get Sibleigh in an old crate of an Ak. W. to suck him in for me. Wouldn't look at anything but cold meat, him and his skull and bones. Well, he got it. Stayed on him for six thousand feet, put a whole belt right into his cockpit. You could a covered 'em all with your hat. But the bastard just wouldn't burn." His voice rose again as he talked on. Locust drifted up in sweet gusts, and the crickets and frogs were clear and monotonous as pipes blown drowsily by an idiot boy. From her silver casement the moon looked down upon the valley dissolving in opaline tranquillity into the serene mysterious infinitude of the hills, and young Bayard's voice went on and on, recounting violence and speed and death.

"Hush," old Bayard said again. "You'll wake Jenny," and his grandson's voice sank obediently; but soon it rose again, and after a time Miss Jenny emerged with her white woolen shawl over her night-dress and came and kissed him.

"I reckon you're all right," she said, "or you wouldn't be in such a bad humor. Tell us about Johnny."

"He was drunk," young Bayard answered harshly. "Or a fool. I tried to keep him from going up there, on that damn Camel. You couldn't see your hand, that morning. Air all full of hunks of cloud and any fool could a known that on their side it'd be full of Fokkers that could reach twenty-five thousand, and him on a damn Camel. But he was hell-bent on going up there, damn near to Lille. I couldn't keep him from it. He shot at me," young Bayard said; "I tried to drive him back, but he gave me a burst. He was already high as he could get, but they must have been five thousand feet above us. They flew all over him. Hemmed him up like a damn calf in a pen while one of them sat right on his tail until he took fire and jumped. Then they streaked for home." Locust drifted and drifted on the still air, and the silver rippling of the tree frogs. In the magnolia at the corner of the house the mockingbird sang. Down the valley another one replied.

"Streaked for home, with the rest of his gang," young Bayard said. "Him and his skull and bones. It was Ploeckner," he added, and for the moment his voice was still and untroubled with vindicated pride. "He was one of the best they had. Pupil of Richthofen's."

"Well, that's something," Miss Jenny agreed, stroking his head.

"I tried to keep him from going up there on that goddam little popgun," he burst out again.

"What did you expect, after the way you raised him?" Miss Jenny asked. "You're the oldest. . . . . . . You've been to the cemetery, haven't you?"

"Yessum," he answered quietly.

"What's that?" old Bayard demanded.

"That old fool Simon said that's where you were. . . . You come on and eat your supper," she said briskly and firmly, entering his life again without a by-your-leave, taking up the snarled threads of it after her brisk and capable fashion, and he rose obediently.

"What's that?" old Bayard repeated.

"And you come on in, too." Miss Jenny swept him also into the orbit of her will as you gather a garment from a chair in passing. "Time you were in bed." They followed her to the kitchen and stood while she delved into the ice box and set food on the table, and a pitcher of milk, and drew up a chair.

"Fix him a toddy, Jenny," old Bayard suggested. But Miss Jenny vetoed this immediately.

"Milk's what he wants. I reckon he had to drink enough whisky during that war to last him for a while. Bayard used to never come home from his, without wanting to ride his horse up the front steps and into the house. Come on, now," and she drove old Bayard firmly out of the kitchen and up the stairs. "You go on to bed, you hear? Let him alone for a while." She saw his door shut and entered young Bayard's room and prepared his bed, and after a while from her own room she heard him mount the stairs.

His room was treacherously illumined by the moon, and without turning on the light he went and sat on the bed. Outside the windows the interminable crickets and frogs, as though the moon's rays were thin glass impacting among the trees and shrubs and shattering in brittle musical rain upon the ground, and above this and with a deep timbrous quality, the measured respirations of the pump in the electric plant beyond the barn.

He dug another cigarette from his pocket and lit it. But he took only two draughts before he flung it away. And then he sat quietly in the room which he and John had shared in the young masculine violence of their twinship, on the bed where he and his wife had lain the last night of his leave, the night before he went back to England and thence out to the Front again, where John already was. Beside him on the pillow the wild bronze swirling of her hair was hushed now in the darkness, and she lay holding his arm with both hands against her breast while they talked quietly, soberly at last.

He had not been thinking of her then. When he thought of her who lay rigid in the dark beside him, holding his arm tightly to her breasts, it was only to be a little savagely ashamed of the heedless thing he had done to her. He was thinking of his brother whom he had not seen in over a year, thinking that in a month they would see one another again.

Nor was he thinking of her now, although the walls held, like a withered flower in a casket, something of that magical chaos in which they had lived for two months, tragic and transient as a blooming of honeysuckle and sharp as the odor of mint. He was thinking of his dead brother; the spirit of their violent complementing days lay like a dust everywhere in the room, obliterating that other presence, stopping his breathing, and he went to the window and flung the sash crashing upward and leaned there, gulping air into his lungs like a man who has been submerged and who still cannot believe that he has reached the surface again.

Later, lying naked between the sheets, he waked himself with his own groaning. The room was filled now with a gray light, sourceless and chill, and he turned his head and saw Miss Jenny, the woolen shawl about her shoulders, sitting in a chair beside the bed.

"What's the matter?" he said.

"That's what I want to know," Miss Jenny answered. "You make more noise than that water pump."

"I want a drink."

Miss Jenny leaned over and raised a glass from the floor beside her. Bayard had risen to his elbow and he took the glass. His hand stopped before the glass reached his mouth and he hunched on his elbow, the glass beneath his nose.

"Hell," he said. "I said a drink."

"You drink that milk, boy," Miss Jenny commanded. "You think I'm going to sit up all night just to feed you whisky? Drink it, now."

He emptied the glass obediently and lay back. Miss Jenny set the glass on the floor.

"What time is it?"

"Hush," she said. She laid her hand on his brow. "Go to sleep."

He rolled his head on the pillow, but he could not evade her hand.

"Get away," he said. "Let me alone."

"Hush," Miss Jenny said. "Go to sleep."

TWO

1.

SIMON said: "You aint never yit planted nothin' whar hit ought ter be planted." He sat on the bottom step, whetting the blade of his hoe with a file. Miss Jenny stood with her caller at the edge of the veranda above him, in a man's felt hat and heavy gloves. A pair of shears dangled below her waist, glinting in the morning sunlight.

"And whose business is that?" she demanded. "Yours, or Colonel's? Either one of you can loaf on this porch and tell me where a plant will grow best or look best, but if either of you ever grew as much as a weed out of the ground yourselves, I'd like to see it. I dont give two whoops in the bad place where you or Colonel either thinks a flower ought to be planted; I plant my flowers just exactly where I want 'em to be planted."

"And den dares 'um not ter come up," Simon added. "Dat's de way you en Isom gyardens. Thank de Lawd Isom aint got to make his livin' wid de sort of gyardenin' he learns in dat place." Still whetting at the hoe blade he jerked his head toward the corner of the house.

He wore a disreputable hat, of a fabric these many years anonymous. Miss Jenny stared coldly down upon this hat.

"Isom made his living by being born black," Miss Jenny snapped. "Suppose you quit scraping at that hoe and see if you cant dare some of the grass in that salvia bed to come up."

"I got to git a aidge on dis curry-comb," Simon said. "You go'n out dar to yo' gyarden: I'll git dis bed cleaned up." He scraped steadily at the hoe-blade.

"You've been at that long enough to find out that you cant possibly wear that blade down to the handle with just a file. You've been at it ever since breakfast. I heard you. You get on out there where folks passing will think you're working, anyhow."

Simon groaned dismally and spent a half minute laying the file aside. He laid it on a step, then he picked it up and moved it to another step. Then he laid it against the step behind him.

Then he ran his thumb along the blade, examining it with morose hopefulness.

"Hit mought do now," he said. "But hit'll be jes' like weedin' wid a curry-c——"

"You try it, anyway," Miss Jenny said. "Maybe the weeds'll think it's a hoe. You go give 'em a chance to, anyhow."

"Ise gwine, Ise gwine," Simon answered pettishly, rising and hobbling away. "You go'n see erbout dat place o' yo'n; I'll 'tend ter dis."

Miss Jenny and the caller descended the steps and went on around the corner of the house.

"Why he'd rather sit there and rasp at that new hoe with a file instead of grubbing up a dozen blades of grass in that salvia bed, I cant see," Miss Jenny said. "But he'll do it. He'd sit there and scrape at that hoe until it looked like a saw blade, if I'd let him. Bayard bought a lawn mower three or four years ago—God knows what for—and turned it over to Simon. The folks that made it guaranteed it for a year. They didn't know Simon, though. I often thought, reading about those devastations and things in the papers last year, what a good time Simon would have had in the war. He could have shown 'em things about devastation they never thought of. Isom!" she shouted.

They entered the garden and Miss Jenny paused at the gate. "You, Isom!"

This time there was a reply, and Miss Jenny went on with her caller and Isom lounged up from somewhere and clicked the gate after him.

"Why didn't you——" Miss Jenny looked back over her shoulder, then she stopped and regarded Isom's suddenly military figure with brief, cold astonishment. He now wore khaki, with a divisional emblem on his shoulder and a tarnished service stripe on his cuff. His lean sixteen-year-old neck rose from the slovenly collar's limp, overlarge embrace, and a surprising amount of wrist was visible below the cuffs. The breeches bagged hopelessly into the unskillful wrapping of the putties which, with either a fine sense for the unique or a bland disregard of military usage, he had donned prior to his shoes, and the soiled overseas cap came down regrettably on his bullet head.

"Where did you get those clothes?" The sunlight glinted on Miss Jenny's shears, and Miss Benbow in a white dress and a soft straw hat turned also and looked at him with a strange expression.

"Dey's Caspey's," Isom answered. "I jes' bor'd 'um."

"Caspey?" Miss Jenny repeated. "Is he home?"

"Yessum. He got in las' night on de nine-thirty."

"Last night, did he? Where is he now? Asleep, I reckon?"

"Yessum. Dat's whar he wuz when I lef' home."

"And I reckon that's how you borrowed his uniform," Miss Jenny said tartly. "Well, let him sleep this morning. Give him one day to get over the war. But if it made a fool out of him like it did Bayard, he'd better put that thing on again and go back to it. I'll declare, men cant seem to stand anything." She went on, the guest in her straight white dress following.

"You are awfully hard on men, not to have a husband to bother with, Miss Jenny," she said. "Besides, you're judging all men by your Sartorises."

"They aint my Sartorises," Miss Jenny disclaimed promptly. "I just inherited 'em. But you just wait: you'll have one of your own to bother with soon; you just wait until Horace gets home, then see how long it takes him to get over it. Men cant stand anything," she repeated. "Cant even stand helling around with no worry and no responsibility and no limit to all of the meanness they can think about wanting to do. Do you think a man could sit day after day and month after month in a house miles from nowhere and spend the time between casualty lists tearing up bedclothes and window curtains and table linen to make lint and watching sugar and flour and meat dwindling away and using pine knots for light because there aren't any candles and no candlesticks to put 'em in, if there were, and hiding in nigger cabins while drunken Yankee generals set fire to the house your great-great-great-grandfather built and you and all your folks were born in? Dont talk to me about men suffering in war." Miss Jenny snipped larkspur savagely. "Just you wait until Horace comes home; then you'll see. Just a good excuse for 'em to make nuisances of themselves and stay in the way while the women-folks are trying to clean up the mess they left with their fighting. John at least had consideration enough, after he'd gone and gotten himself into something where he had no business, not to come back and worry everybody to distraction. But Bayard now, coming back in the middle of it and having everybody thinking he was settled down at last, teaching at that Memphis flying school, and then marrying that fool girl."

"Miss Jenny!"

"Well, I dont mean that, but she ought to've been spanked, hard. I know: didn't I do the same thing, myself? It was all that harness Bayard wore. Talk about men being taken in by a uniform!" She clipped larkspur. "Dragging me up there to the wedding, mind you, with a church full of rented swords and some of Bayard's pupils trying to drop roses on 'em when they came out. I reckon some of 'em were not his pupils, because one of 'em finally did drop a handful that missed everything and fell in the street." She snipped larkspur savagely. "I had dinner with 'em one night. Sat in the hotel an hour until they remembered to come for me. Then we stopped at a delicatessen and Bayard and Caroline got out and went in and came back with about a bushel of packages and dumped 'em into the car where they leaked grease on my new stockings. That was the dinner I'd been invited to, mind you; there wasn't a sign of anything that looked or smelt like a stove in the whole place. I didn't offer to help 'em. I told Caroline I didn't know anything about that sort of house-keeping, because my folks were old-fashioned enough to cook food.

"Then the others came in—some of Bayard's soldier friends, and a drove of other folks' wives, near as I could gather. Young women that ought to've been at home, seeing about supper, gabbling and screeching in that silly way young married women have when they're doing something they hope their husbands won't like. They were all unwrapping bottles—about two dozen, I reckon, and Bayard and Caroline came in with that silver I gave 'em and monogrammed napkins and that delicatessen fodder that tasted like swamp grass, on paper plates. We ate it there, sitting on the floor or standing up or just wherever you happened to be.

"That was Caroline's idea of keeping house. She said they'd settle down when they got old, if the war was over by then. About thirty-five, I suppose she meant. Thin as a rail; there wouldn't have been much to spank. But she'd ought to've had it, just the same. Soon as she found out about the baby, she named it. Named it nine months before it was born and told everybody about it. Used to talk about it like it was her grandfather or something. Always saying Bayard wont let me do this or that or the other."

Miss Jenny continued to clip larkspur, the caller tall in a white dress beside her. The fine and huge simplicity of the house rose among thickening trees, the garden lay in sunlight bright with bloom, myriad with scent and with a drowsy humming of bees—a steady golden sound, as of sunlight become audible—all the impalpable veil of the immediate, the familiar; just beyond it a girl with a bronze skirling of hair and a small, supple body in a constant epicene unrepose, a dynamic fixation like that of carven sexless figures caught in moments of action, striving, a mechanism all of whose members must move in performing the most trivial action, her wild hands not accusing but passionate still beyond the veil impalpable but sufficient.

Miss Jenny stooped over the flowerbed, her narrow back, though stooping, erect still, indomitable. A thrush flashed modestly across the bright air and into the magnolia tree in a dying parabola. "And then, when he had to go back to the war, of course he brought her out here and left her on my hands." The caller stood motionless in her white dress, and Miss Jenny said: "No, I dont mean that." She snipped larkspur.

"Poor women," she said. "I reckon we do have to take our revenge wherever and whenever we can get it. Only she ought to've taken it out on Bayard."

"When she died," Narcissa said, "and he couldn't know about it; couldn't have come to her if he had? And you can say that?"

"Bayard love anybody, that cold devil?" Miss Jenny clipped larkspur. "He never cared a snap of his fingers for anybody in his life except Johnny." She snipped larkspur savagely. "Swelling around here like it was our fault, like we made 'em go to that war. And now he's got to have an automobile, got to go all the way to Memphis to buy one. An automobile in Bayard Sartoris' barn, mind you; him that wont even lend the bank's money to a man that owns one. . . . . . . Do you want some sweet peas?"

"Yes, please," Narcissa answered. Miss Jenny straightened up, then she stopped utterly still.

"Just look yonder, will you?" she pointed with the shears. "That's how they suffer from war, poor things." Beyond a frame of sweet peas Isom in his khaki strode solemnly back and forth. Upon his right shoulder was a hoe and on his face an expression of rapt absorption, and as he reversed at the end of his beat, he murmured to himself in measured singsong. "You, Isom!" Miss Jenny shouted.

He halted in midstride, still at shoulder arms. "Ma'am?" he said mildly. Miss Jenny continued to glare at him, and his military bearing faded and he lowered his piece and executed a sort of effacing movement within his martial shroud.

"Put that hoe down and bring that basket over here. That's the first time in your life you ever picked up a garden tool of your own free will. I wish I could discover the kind of uniform that would make you dig in the ground with it; I'd certainly buy you one."

"Yessum."

"If you want to play soldier, you go off somewhere with Bayard and do it. I can raise flowers without any help from the army," she added, turning to the guest with her handful of larkspur. "And what are you laughing at?" she demanded.

"You both looked so funny," the younger woman explained. "You looked so much more like a soldier than poor Isom, for all his uniform." She touched her eyes with her fingertips. "I'm sorry: please forgive me for laughing."

"Hmph," Miss Jenny sniffed. She put the larkspur into the basket and went on to the sweet pea frame and snipped again, viciously. The guest followed, as did Isom with the basket; and presently Miss Jenny was done with sweet peas and she moved on again with her train, pausing to cut a rose here and there, and stopped before a bed where tulips lifted their bright inverted bells. She and Isom had guessed happily, this time; the various colors formed an orderly pattern.

"When we dug 'em up last fall," she told her guest, "I'd put a red one in Isom's right hand and a yellow one in his left, and then I'd say 'All right, Isom, give me the red one.' He'd never fail to hold out his left hand, and if I just looked at him long enough, he'd hold out both hands. 'Didn't I tell you to hold that red one in your right hand?' I'd say. 'Yessum, here 'tis.' And out would come his left hand again. 'That aint your right hand, stupid,' I'd say. 'Dat's de one you said wuz my right hand a while ago,' Mr Isom says. Aint that so, nigger?" Miss Jenny glared at Isom, who again performed his deprecatory effacing movement behind the slow equanimity of his grin.

"Yessum, I 'speck it is."

"You'd better," Miss Jenny rejoined warningly. "Now, how can anybody have a decent garden, with a fool like that? I expect every spring to find corn or lespedeza coming up in the hyacinth beds or something." She examined the tulips again, weighing the balanced colors one against another in her mind. "No, you dont want any tulips," she decided, moving on.

"No, Miss Jenny," the guest agreed demurely. They went on to the gate, and Miss Jenny stopped and took the basket from Isom.

"And you go home and take that thing off, you hear?"

"Yessum."

"And I want to look out that window in a few minutes and see you in the garden with that hoe again," she added. "And I want to see both of your right hands on it and I want to see it moving, too. You hear me?"

"Yessum."

"And tell Caspey to be ready to go to work in the morning. Even niggers that eat here have got to work some." But Isom was gone, and they went on and mounted to the veranda. "Dont he sound like that's exactly what he's going to do?" she confided as they entered the hall. "He knows as well as I do that I wont dare look out that window, after what I said. Come in," she added, opening the parlor doors.

This room was opened but seldom now, though in John Sartoris' day it had been constantly in use. He was always giving dinners, and balls too on occasion, with the folding doors between it and the dining room thrown open and three negroes with stringed instruments on the stairway and all the candles burning, surrounding himself with a pageantry of color and scent and music against which he moved with his bluff and jovial arrogance. He lay also overnight in this room in his gray regimentals and so brought to a conclusion the colorful, if not always untarnished, pageant of his own career, contemplating for the last time his own apotheosis from the jocund mellowness of his generous hearth.

But during his son's time it fell less and less into use, and slowly and imperceptibly it lost its jovial but stately masculinity, becoming by mutual agreement a place for his wife and his son John's wife and Miss Jenny to clean thoroughly twice a year and in which, preceded by a ritualistic unswaddling of brown holland, they entertained their more formal callers. This was its status at the birth of his grandsons and it continued thus until the death of their parents, and later, to that of his wife. After that Miss Jenny bothered with formal callers but little and with the parlor not at all. She said it gave her the creeps.

And so it stayed closed nearly all the time and slowly acquired an atmosphere of solemn and macabre fustiness. Occasionally young Bayard or John would open the door and peer into the solemn obscurity in which the shrouded furniture loomed with a sort of ghostly benignance, like albino mastodons. But they did not enter; already in their minds the room was associated with death, an idea which even the holly and tinsel of Christmas tide could not completely obscure. They were away at school by the time they reached party age, but even during vacations, though they had filled the house with the polite bedlam of their contemporaries, the room would be opened only on Christmas eve, when the tree was set up and a fire lighted, and a bowl of eggnog on the table in the center of the hearth. And after they went to England in '16 it was opened twice a year to be cleaned after the ancient ritual that even Simon had inherited from his forefathers, and to have the piano tuned or when Miss Jenny and Narcissa spent a forenoon or afternoon there, and formally not at all.

The furniture loomed shapelessly in its dun shrouds; the piano alone was uncovered, and Narcissa drew the bench out and removed her hat and dropped it beside her. Miss Jenny set the basket down and from the gloom back of the instrument she drew a straight, hard chair, uncovered also, and sat down and removed her felt hat from her trim white head. Light came through the open door, but the windows were shuttered behind heavy maroon curtains, and it served only to enhance the obscurity and to render more shapeless the hooded anonymous furniture.

But behind these dun bulks and in all the corners of the room there waited, as actors stand within the wings beside the waiting stage, figures in crinoline and hooped muslin and silk; in stocks and flowing coats; in gray too, with crimson sashes and sabres in gallant sheathed repose;—Jeb Stuart himself perhaps, on his glittering garlanded bay or with his sunny hair falling upon fine broadcloth beneath the mistletoe and holly boughs of Baltimore in '58. Miss Jenny sat with her uncompromising grenadier's back and held her hat upon her knees and fixed herself to look on as her guest touched chords from the keyboard and wove them together and rolled the curtain back upon the scene.

In the kitchen Caspey was having breakfast while Simon his father, and Elnora his sister, and Isom his nephew (in uniform) watched him. He had been Simon's understudy in the stables and general handy-man about the place, doing all the work that Simon managed, through the specious excuse of decrepitude and filial gratitude, to slough off onto his shoulders and that Miss Jenny could devise for him and which he could not evade. Old Bayard also employed him in the fields occasionally. Then the draft had got him and bore him to France and the St Sulpice docks as one of a labor battalion, where he did what work corporals and sergeants managed to slough off onto his unmilitary shoulders and that white officers could devise for him and which he could not evade.

Thus all the labor about the place devolved upon Simon and Isom, but Miss Jenny kept Isom piddling about the house so much of the time that Simon was soon as bitter against the War Lords as any professional Democrat. Meanwhile Caspey was working a little and trifling with continental life in its martial phases rather to his future detriment, for at last the tumult died and the captains departed and left a vacuum filled with the usual bitter bickering of Armageddon's heirs-at-law; and Caspey returned to his native land a total loss, sociologically speaking, with a definite disinclination toward labor, honest or otherwise, and two honorable wounds incurred in a razor-hedged crap game. But return he did, to his father's querulous satisfaction and Elnora's and Isom's admiration, and he now sat in the kitchen, telling them about the war.

"I dont take nothin' fum no white folks no mo'," he was saying. "War done changed all dat. If us cullud folks is good enough ter save France fum de Germans, den us is good enough ter have de same rights de Germans is. French folks thinks so, anyhow, and ef America dont, dey's ways of learnin' 'um. Yes, suh, it wuz de cullud soldier saved France and America bofe. Black regiments kilt mo' Germans dan all de white armies put together, let 'lone unloadin' steamboats all day long fer a dollar a day."

"War aint hurt dat big mouf o' yo'n, anyhow," Simon said.

"War unloosed de black man's mouf," Caspey corrected. "Give him de right to talk. Kill Germans, den do yo' oratin', dey tole us. Well, us done it."

"How many you kilt, Unc' Caspey?" Isom asked deferentially.

"I aint never bothered to count 'um up. Been times I kilt mo in one mawnin' dan dey's folks on dis whole place. One time we wuz down in de cellar of a steamboat tied up to de bank, and one of dese submareems sailed up and stopped, and all de white officers run up on de bank and hid. Us boys downstairs didn't know dey wuz anything wrong 'twell folks started clambin' down de ladder. We never had no guns wid us at de time, so when we seed dem green legs comin' down de ladder we crope up behin' 'um, and ez dey come down one of de boys would hit 'um over de haid wid a piece of scantlin' and another would drag 'um outen de way and cut dey th'oat wid a meat-plow. Dey wuz about thirty of 'um. . . . . . . Elnora, is dey any mo' of dat coffee lef'?"

"Sho," Simon murmured. Isom's eyes popped quietly and Elnora lifted the coffee-pot from the stove and refilled Caspey's cup.

Caspey drank coffee for a while. "And another time me and a boy wuz gwine along a road. We got tired unloadin' dem steamboats all day long, so one day de Captain's dog-robber foun' whar he kep' dese here unloaded passes and he tuck a han'ful of 'um, and me and him wuz on de road to town when a truck come along and de boy axed us did us want a lif'. He wuz a school boy, so he writ on three of de passes whenever we come to a place dat mought be M.P. invested, and we got along fine, ridin' about de country on dat private truck, 'twell one mawnin' we looked out whar de truck wuz and dey wuz a M.P. settin' on it whilst de truck boy wuz tryin' to explain to him. So we turned de other way and lit out walkin'. After dat we had to dodge de M.P. towns, 'case me and de other boy couldn't write on de passes.

"One day we wuz gwine along a road. It wuz a busted-up road and it didn't look much like no M.P. country, but dey wuz some of 'em in de las' town we dodged, so we didn't know we wuz so close to whar de fightin' wuz gwine on 'twell we walked onto a bridge and come right onto a whole regiment of Germans, swimmin' in de river. Dey seed us about de same time we seed dem and div under de water, and me and de other boy grabbed up two machine guns settin' dar and we sot on de bridge rail, and ev'y time a German stuck his haid up fer a new breaf, us shot 'im. It wuz jes' like shootin' turkles in a slough. I reckon dey wuz clost to a hun'ed us kilt 'fo' de machine guns run dry. Dat's whut dey gimme dis fer." He drew from his pocket a florid plated medal of Porto Rican origin, and Isom came quietly up to see it.

"Umumuh," Simon said. He sat with his hands on his knees, watching his son with rapt astonishment. Elnora came up also, her arms daubed with flour.

"Whut does dey look like?" she asked. "Like folks?"

"Dey's big," Caspey answered. "Sort of pink lookin' and about eight foot tall. Only folks in de whole American war dat could handle 'um wuz de cullud regiments." Isom returned to his corner beside the woodbox.

"Aint you got some gyardenin' to do, boy?" Simon asked him.

"Naw, suh," Isom answered, his enraptured gaze still on his uncle. "Miss Jenny say us done caught up dis mawnin'."

"Well, dont you come whinin' ter me when she jumps on you," Simon warned him. "Whar'd you kill de nex' lot?" he asked his son.

"Us didn't kill no mo' after dat," Caspey said. "We decided dat wuz enough and dat we better leave de rest of 'um fer de boys dat wuz gittin' paid fer killin' 'um. We went on 'twell de road played out in a field. Dey wuz some ditches and ole

wire fences and holes in de field, wid folks livin' in 'um. De
folks wuz white American soldiers and dey egvised us to pick
us out a hole and stay dar fer a while, ef us wanted de peace
and comfort of de war. So we picked us out a dry hole and
moved in. Dey wasn't nothin' to do all day long but lay in de
shade and watch de air balloons and listen to de shootin' about
fo' miles up de road. De white boy wid me claimed it wuz
rabbit hunters, but I knowed better. De white boys could
write, so dey fixed up de passes and we tuck time about gwine
up to whar de army wuz and gittin' grub. When de passes
give out we foun' whar a French army wid some cannons wuz
livin' over in de woods a ways, so we went over whar dey wuz
and et.

"Dat went on fer a long time, 'twell one day de balloons
wuz gone and de white boys says it wuz time to move again.
But me and de other boy didn't see no use in gwine nowhar
else, so we stayed. Dat evenin' we went over to whar de
French army wuz fer some grub, but dey wuz gone too. De
boy wid me says maybe de Germans done caught 'um, but we
didn't know; hadn't heard no big racket since yistiddy. So we
went back to de cave. Dey wasn't no grub, so we crawled in
and went to bed and slep' dat night, and early de nex' mawnin'
somebody come into de hole and tromped on us and woke us
up. It wuz one of dese army upliftin' ladies huntin' German
bayonets and belt-buckles. She say 'Who dat in here?' and de
other boy says 'Us shock troops'. So we got out, but we hadn't
gone no piece 'fo' here come a wagon-load of M.P.s. And de
passes had done give out."

"Whut you do den?" Simon asked. Isom's eyes bulged quietly in the gloom behind the woodbox.

"Dey tuck us and shut us up in de jail-house fer a while. But
de war wuz mos' thu and dey needed us to load dem steamboats back up, so dey sont us to a town name' Bres'. . . . . . .
I dont take nothin' offen no white man, M.P. er not," Caspey
stated again. "Us boys wuz in a room one night, shootin' dice.
De bugle had done already played de lights out tune, but we
wuz in de army, whar a man kin do whut he wants es long es
dey'll let 'im, so when de M.P. come along and says 'Put out
dat light', one of de boys says 'Come in here, and we'll put
yo'n out'. Dey wuz two of de M.P.s and dey kicked de do' in

and started shootin', and somebody knocked de light over and we run. Dey foun' one of de M.P.s de nex' mawnin' widout nothin' to hole his collar on, and two of de boys wuz daid, too. But dey couldn't fin' who de res' of us wuz. And den we come home."

Caspey emptied his cup. "I dont take nothin' offen no white man no mo', lootenant ner captain ner M.P. War showed de white folks dey cant git along widout de cullud man. Tromple him in de dus', but when de trouble bust loose, hit's 'Please, suh, Mr Cullud Man; right dis way whar de bugle blowin', Mr Cullud Man; you is de savior of de country.' And now de cullud race gwine reap de benefits of de war, and dat soon."

"Sho," murmured Simon.

"Yes, suh. And de women, too. I got my white in France, and I'm gwine git it here, too."

"Lemme tell you somethin', nigger," Simon said. "De good Lawd done took keer of you fer a long time now, but He aint gwine bother wid you always."

"Den I reckon I'll git along widout Him," Caspey retorted. He rose and stretched. "Reckon I'll go down to de big road and ketch a ride into town. Gimme dem clothes, Isom."

Miss Jenny and her guest stood on the veranda when he passed along beside the house and crossed toward the drive.

"There goes your gardener," Narcissa said. Miss Jenny looked.

"That's Caspey," she corrected. "Now, where do you reckon he's headed? Town, I'll bet a dollar," she added, watching his lounging khaki back, by means of which he contrived to disseminate in some way a sort of lazy insolence. "You, Caspey!" she called.

He slowed in passing Narcissa's small car and examined it with a disparagement too lazy to sneer even, then he slouched on.

"You, Caspey!" Miss Jenny repeated, raising her voice. But he went steadily on down the drive, insolent and slouching and unhurried. "He heard me," she said ominously. "We'll see about this when he comes back. Who was the fool anyway, who thought of putting niggers into the same uniform with white men? Mr Vardaman knew better; he told those fools at Washington at the time that it wouldn't do. But politicians!"

She invested the innocent word with an utter and blasting derogation. "If I ever get tired of associating with gentlefolks, I know what I'll do: I'll run for Congress. . . . Listen at me! tiradin' again. I declare, at times I believe these Sartorises and all their possessions just set out to plague and worry me. Thank the Lord, I wont have to associate with 'em after I'm dead. I dont know where they'll be, but no Sartoris is going to stay in heaven any longer than he can help."

The other laughed. "You seem very sure of your own destination, Miss Jenny."

"Why shouldn't I be? Haven't I been laying up crowns and harps for a long time?" She shaded her eyes with her hand and gazed down the drive. Caspey had reached the gate and he now stood beside the road, waiting for a wagon to pass. "Dont you stop for him, you hear?" she said suddenly. "Why wont you stay for dinner?"

"No," the other answered. "I must get on home. Aunt Sally's not well today. . . . . . ." She stood for a moment in the sunlight, her hat and her basket of flowers on her arm, musing. Then with a sudden decision she drew a folded paper from the front of her dress.

"Got another one, did you?" Miss Jenny asked, watching her. "Lemme see it." She took the paper and opened it and stepped back out of the sun. Her nose glasses hung on a slender silk cord that rolled onto a spring in a small gold case pinned to her bosom. She snapped the cord out and set the glasses on her high-bridged nose, and behind them her gray eyes were cold and piercing as a surgeon's.

The paper was a single sheet of foolscap; it bore writing in a frank, open script that at first glance divulged no individuality whatever; a hand youthful yet at the same time so blandly and neatly unsecretive that presently you wondered a little.

"You did not answere mine of 25th. I did not expect you answer it yet. You will answer soon I can wait. I will not harm you I am square and honest you will lern when our ways come to gether. I do not expect you answer Yet. But you know where you make a sign."

Miss Jenny refolded the paper with a gesture of fine and delicate distaste. "I'd burn this thing, if it wasn't the only thing we have to catch him with. I'll give it to Bayard tonight."

"No, no," the other protested quickly, extending her hand. "Please dont. Let me have it and tear it up."

"It's our only evidence, child—this and the other one. We'll get a detective."

"No, no; please! I dont want anybody else to know about it. Please, Miss Jenny." She reached her hand again.

"You want to keep it," Miss Jenny accused coldly. "Just like a young fool woman, to be flattered by a thing like this."

"I'll tear it up," the other repeated. "I would have sooner, but I wanted to tell someone. It—it—I thought I wouldn't feel so filthy, after I had shown it to someone else. Let me have it, please."

"Fiddlesticks. Why should you feel filthy? You haven't encouraged it, have you?"

"Please, Miss Jenny."

But Miss Jenny still held on to it. "Dont be a fool," she snapped. "How can this thing make you feel filthy? Any young woman is liable to get an anonymous letter. And a lot of 'em like it. We all are convinced that men feel that way about us, and we cant help but admire one that's got the courage to tell us, no matter who he is."

"If he'd just signed his name. I wouldn't mind who it was. But like this. . . . . . Please, Miss Jenny."

"Dont be a fool," Miss Jenny repeated. "How can we find who it is, if you destroy the evidence?"

"I dont want to know." Miss Jenny released the paper and Narcissa tore it into bits and cast them over the rail and rubbed her hands on her dress. "I dont want to know. I want to forget all about it."

"Nonsense. You're dying to know, right now. I bet you look at every man you pass and wonder if it's him. And as long as you dont do something about it, it'll go on. Get worse, probably. You better let me tell Bayard."

"No, no. I'd hate for him to know, to think that I would—— might have. . . . . . . It's all right: I'll just burn them up after this, without opening them. . . . I must really go."

"Of course: you'll throw 'em right into the stove," Miss Jenny agreed with cold irony. Narcissa descended the steps and Miss Jenny came forward into the sunlight again, letting her glasses whip back into the case. "It's your business, of course. But I'd not stand for it, if 'twas me. But then, I aint twenty-six years old. . . . Well, come out again when you get another one, or you want some more flowers."

"Yes, I will. Thank you for these."

"And let me know what you hear from Horace. Thank the Lord, it's just a glass-blowing machine, and not a war widow."

"Yes, I will. Goodbye." She went on through the dappled shade in her straight white dress and her basket of flowers stippled upon it, and got in her car. The top was back and she put her hat on and started the engine, and looked back again and waved her hand. "Goodbye."

The negro had moved down the road, slowly, and had stopped again, and he was watching her covertly as she approached. As she passed he looked full at her and she knew he was about to hail her. She opened the throttle and passed him with increasing speed and drove swiftly on to town, where she lived in a brick house among cedars on a hill.

She was arranging the larkspur in a dull lemon urn on the piano. Aunt Sally Wyatt rocked steadily in her chair beside the window, clapping her feet flatly on the floor at each stroke. Her work basket sat on the window ledge between the gentle billowing of the curtains, her ebony walking-stick leaned beside it.

"And you were out there two hours," she said, "and never saw him at all?"

"He wasn't there," Narcissa answered. "He's gone to Memphis."

Aunt Sally rocked steadily. "If I was them, I'd make him stay there. I wouldn't have that boy around me, blood or no blood. . . . . . What did he go to Memphis for? I thought that aeroplane what-do-you-call-it was broke up."

"He went on business, I suppose."

"What business has he got in Memphis? Bayard Sartoris has got more sense than to turn over any business to that hair-brained fool."

"I dont know," Narcissa answered, arranging the larkspur. "He'll be back soon, I suppose. You can ask him then."

"Me ask him? I never said two words to him in his life. And I dont intend to. I been used to associating with gentlefolks."

Narcissa broke some of the stems, arranging the blooms in a pattern. "What's he done that a gentleman doesn't do, Aunt Sally?"

"Why, jumping off water tanks and going up in balloons just to scare folks. You think I'd have that boy around me? I'd have him locked up in the insane asylum, if I was Bayard and Jenny."

"He didn't jump off of the tank. He just swung off of it on a rope and dived into the swimming pool. And it was John that went up in the balloon."

"That wasn't what I heard. I heard he jumped off that tank, across a whole row of freight cars and lumber piles and didn't miss the edge of the pool an inch."

"No he didn't. He swung on a rope from the top of a house and then dived into the pool. The rope was tied to the tank."

"Well, didn't he have to jump over a lot of lumber and freight cars? And couldn't he have broken his neck just as easy that way as jumping off the tank?"

"Yes," Narcissa answered.

"There! What'd I tell you? And what was the use of it?"

"I dont know."

"Of course you dont. That was the reason he did it." Aunt Sally rocked triumphantly for a while. Narcissa put the last touches to the blue pattern of the larkspur. A tortoise-shell cat bunched suddenly and silently in the window beside the work basket, with an effect as of sleight-of-hand. Still crouching it blinked into the room for a moment, then it sank to its belly and with arched neck fell to grooming its shoulder with a narrow pink tongue. Narcissa moved to the window and laid her hand on the creature's sleek back.

"And then, going up in that balloon, when——"

"That wasn't Bayard," Narcissa repeated. "That was John."

"That wasn't what I heard. I heard it was the other one and that Bayard and Jenny were both begging him with tears in their eyes not to do it. I heard——"

"Neither one of them were there. Bayard wasn't even there. It was John did it. He did it because the man that came with the balloon got sick. John went up in it so the country people wouldn't be disappointed. I was there."

"Stood there and let him do it, did you, when you could a telephoned Jenny or walked across the square to the bank and got Bayard? You stood there and never opened your mouth, did you?"

"Yes," Narcissa answered. Stood there beside Horace in the slow, intent ring of country people, watching the globe swelling and tugging at its ropes, watched John Sartoris in a faded flannel shirt and corduroy breeches, while the carnival man explained the rip-cord and the parachute to him; stood there feeling her breath going out faster than she could draw it in again and watched the thing lurch into the air with John sitting on a frail trapeze bar swinging beneath it, with eyes she could not close, saw the balloon and people and all swirl slowly upward and then found herself clinging to Horace behind the shelter of a wagon, trying to get her breath.

He landed three miles away in a brier thicket and disengaged the parachute and regained the road and hailed a passing negro in a wagon. A mile from town they met old Bayard driving furiously in the carriage and the two vehicles stopped side to side in the road while old Bayard in the one exhausted the accumulate fury of his rage and in the other his grandson sat in his shredded clothes and on his scratched face that look of one who has gained for an instant a desire so fine that its escape was a purifaction, not a loss.

The next day, as she was passing a store, he emerged with that abrupt violence which he had in common with his brother, pulling short up to avoid a collision with her.

"Oh, ex—— Why, hello," he said. Beneath the crisscrosses of tape his face was merry and bold and wild, and he wore no hat. For a moment she gazed at him with wide, hopeless eyes, then she clapped her hand to her mouth and went swiftly on, almost running.

Then he was gone, with his brother, shut away by the war as two noisy dogs are penned in a kennel far away. Miss Jenny gave her news of them, of the dull, dutiful letters they sent home at sparse intervals; then he was dead. But away beyond seas, and there was no body to be returned clumsily to earth, and so to her he seemed still to be laughing at that word as he had laughed at all the other mouthsounds that stood for repose, who had not waited for Time and its furniture to teach him that the end of wisdom is to dream high enough not to lose the dream in the seeking of it.

Aunt Sally rocked steadily in her chair.

"Well, it dont matter which one it was. One's bad as the other. But I reckon it aint their fault, raised like they were. Rotten spoiled, both of 'em. Lucy Sartoris wouldn't let anybody control 'em while she lived. If they'd been mine, now. . . ." She rocked on. "Beat it out of 'em, I would. Raising two wild Indians like that. But those folks, thinking there wasn't anybody quite as good as a Sartoris. Even Lucy Cranston, come from as good people as there are in the state, acting like it was divine providence that let her marry one Sartoris and be the mother of two more. Pride, false pride."

She rocked steadily in her chair. Beneath Narcissa's hand the cat purred with lazy arrogance.

"It was a judgment on 'em, taking John instead of that other one. John at least tipped his hat to a lady on the street, but that other boy. . . . . . ." She rocked monotonously, clapping her feet flatly against the floor. "You better stay away from that boy. He'll be killing you same as he did that poor little wife of his."

"At least, give me benefit of clergy first, Aunt Sally," Narcissa said. Beneath her hand, beneath the cat's sleek hide, muscles flowed suddenly into tight knots, like wire, and the animal's body seemed to elongate like rubber as it whipped from beneath her hand and flashed out of sight across the veranda.

"Oh," Narcissa cried. Then she whirled and caught up Aunt Sally's stick and ran from the room.

"What—" Aunt Sally said. "You bring my stick back here," she said. She sat staring at the door, hearing the swift clatter of the other's heels in the hall and then on the veranda. She rose and leaned in the window. "You bring my stick back here," she shouted.

Narcissa sped on across the porch and to the ground. In the canna bed beside the veranda the cat, crouching, jerked its head around and its yellow unwinking eyes. Narcissa rushed at it, the stick raised.

"Put it down!" she cried. "Drop it!" For another second the yellow eyes glared at her, then the animal ducked its head and leaped away in a long fluid bound, the bird between its jaws.

"Oh-h-h, damn you! Damn you! You——you Sartoris!"

and she hurled the stick after the final tortoise flash as the cat
flicked around the corner of the house.

"You get my stick and bring it right back this minute!" Aunt
Sally shouted from the window.

She had seen Bayard once from a distance. He appeared as
usual at the time—a lean figure in casual easy clothes unpressed and a little comfortably shabby, and with his air of
smoldering abrupt violence. He and his brother had both had
this, but Bayard's was a cold, arrogant sort of leashed violence,
while in John it was a warmer thing, spontaneous and merry
and wild. It was Bayard who had attached a rope to a ninety
foot water tank and, from the roof of an adjoining building,
swung himself across the intervening fifty yards of piled
lumber and freight cars and released the rope and dived into
a narrow concrete swimming pool while upturned faces gaped
and screamed—a cold nicety of judgment and unnecessary
cruel skill; John who, one County Fair day, made the balloon
ascension, the aeronaut having been stricken with ptomaine
poisoning, that the county people might not be disappointed,
and landed three miles away in a brier thicket, losing most of
his clothing and skin and returning to town cheerful and babbling in the wagon of a passing negro.

But both of these were utterly beyond her; it was not in her
nature to differentiate between motives whose results were the
same, and on occasions when she had seen them conducting
themselves as civilized beings, had been in the same polite
room with them, she found herself watching them with
shrinking and fearful curiosity, as she might have looked upon
wild beasts with a temporary semblance of men and engaged
in human activities, morally acknowledging the security of the
cage but spiritually unreassured.

But she had not seen them often. They were either away at
school, or if at home they passed their headlong days in the
country, coming into town at rare intervals and then on horseback, in stained corduroy and flannel shirts. Yet rumors of
their doings came in to her from time to time, causing always
in her that shrinking, fascinated distaste, that blending of curiosity and dread, as if a raw wind had blown into that garden
wherein she dwelt. Then they would be gone again, and she

would think of them only to remember Horace and his fine and electric delicacy, and to thank her gods he was not as they.

Then the war, and she learned without any surprise whatever that they had gone to it. That was exactly what they would do, and her nature drowsed again beneath the serene belief that they had been removed from her life for good and always; to her the war had been brought about for the sole purpose of removing them from her life as noisy dogs are shut up in a kennel afar off. Thus her days. Man became amphibious and lived in mud and filth and died and was buried in it; the world looked on in hysterical amazement. But she, within her walled and windless garden, thought of them only with a sober and pointless pity, like a flower's exhalation, and like the flower, uncaring if the scent be sensed or not. She gave clothing and money to funds, and she knitted things also, but she did not know where Saloniki was and was incurious as to how Rheims or Przemysl were pronounced.

Then Horace departed, with his Snopes, and the war became abruptly personal. But it was still not the same war to which the Sartoris boys had gone; and soon she was readjusted again, with Aunt Sally Wyatt in the house and the steady unemphasis of their feminine days. She joined the Red Cross and various other welfare organizations, and she knitted harsh wool with intense brooding skill and performed other labors while other women talked of their menfolks into her grave receptivity.

There was a family of country people moved recently to town—a young man and his pregnant wife and two infant children. They abode in a rejuvenated rented cabin on the edge of town, where the woman did her own housework, while the man was employed by the local distributor for an oil company, laboring all day with a sort of eager fury of willingness and a desire to get on. He was a steady, exemplary sort, willing and unfailingly goodnatured and reliable, so he was drafted immediately and denied exemption and ravished celeritously overseas. His family accompanied him to the station in an automobile supplied by the charity of an old lady of the town and they watched him out of their lives with that tearless uncomplaining gravity of primitive creatures. The Red Cross took charge of the family, but Narcissa Benbow adopted them. She was present when the baby was born two weeks later, she superintended the household—meals and clothing—until the woman was about again, and for the next twelve months she wrote a monthly letter to the husband and father who, having no particular aptitude for it save his unflagging even temper and a ready willingness to do as he was told, was now a company cook in the S.O.S.

This occupation too was just a grave centering of her days; there was no hysteria in it, no conviction that she was helping to slay the biblical Beast, or laying up treasure in heaven. Horace was away too; she was waiting for him to return, marking time, as it were. Then Bayard Sartoris had returned home, with a wife. She sensed the romantic glamor of this with interest and grave approval, as of a dramatic scene, but that was all; Bayard Sartoris went away again. Narcissa met his wife now and then, and always with a little curiosity, as though, voluntarily associating so intimately with a Sartoris, she too must be an animal with the temporary semblance of a human being. There was no common ground between them, between Narcissa with her constancy, her serenity which the other considered provincial and a little dull, and the other with her sexless vivid unrepose and the brittle daring of her speech and actions.

She had learned of John Sartoris' death without any emotion whatever except a faint sense of vindication, a sort of I-told-you-so feeling, which recurred (blended now with a sense of pitying outrage, blaming this too on Bayard) when Bayard's wife died in childbirth in October of the same year, even though she stood with old Bayard's deaf and arrogant back and Miss Jenny's trim indomitability amid sad trees and streaming marble shapes beneath a dissolving afternoon. Then November, and bells and whistles and revolvers. Horace would be coming home soon now, she thought at the time. Before Christmas, perhaps. But before he did so she had seen Bayard once on the street, and later, while she and Miss Jenny were sitting in Miss Jenny's dim parlor. The doors were ajar as usual, and young Bayard appeared suddenly between them and stood looking at her.

"It's Bayard," Miss Jenny said. "Come in here and speak to Narcissa, sonny."

He said Hello vaguely and she turned on the piano bench, and shrank a little against the instrument. "Who is it?" he said, and he came into the room, bringing with him that cold leashed violence which she remembered.

"It's Narcissa," Miss Jenny said testily. "Go on and speak to her and stop acting like you dont know who she is."

Narcissa gave him her hand and he stood holding it loosely, but he was not looking at her. She withdrew her hand, and he looked at her again, then away, and he loomed above them and stood rubbing his hand through his hair.

"I want a drink," he said. "I cant find the key to the desk."

"Stop and talk to us a few minutes, and you can have one."

He stood for a moment above them, then he moved abruptly and before Miss Jenny could speak he had dragged the holland envelope from another chair.

"Let that alone, you Indian!" Miss Jenny exclaimed. She rose. "Here, take my chair, if you're too weak to stand up. I'll be back in a minute," she added to Narcissa; "I'll have to get my keys."

He sat laxly in the chair, rubbing his hand over his head, his gaze brooding somewhere about his booted feet. Narcissa sat utterly quiet, shrunk back against the piano. She spoke at last:

"I am so sorry about your wife . . . John. I asked Miss Jenny to tell you when she. . . . . . ."

He sat rubbing his head slowly, in the brooding violence of his temporary repose.

"You aren't married yourself, are you?" he asked. She sat perfectly still. "Ought to try it," he added. "Everybody ought to get married once, like everybody ought to go to one war."

Miss Jenny returned with the keys, and he got his long abrupt body erect and left them.

"You can go on, now," she said. "He wont bother us again."

"No, I must go." Narcissa rose quickly and took her hat from the top of the piano.

"Why, you haven't been here any time, yet."

"I must go," Narcissa repeated. Miss Jenny rose.

"Well, if you must. I'll cut you some flowers. Wont take a minute."

"No, some other time; I—I have—I'll come out soon and

get some. Goodbye." At the door she glanced swiftly down
the hall; then she went on. Miss Jenny followed to the veranda.
The other had descended the steps and she now went swiftly
on toward her car.

"Come back again soon," Miss Jenny called.

"Yes. Soon," Narcissa answered. "Goodbye."

2.

Young Bayard came back from Memphis in his car. Memphis was seventy-five miles away and the trip had taken an
hour and forty minutes because some of the road was clay
country road. The car was long and low and gray; the four
cylinder engine had sixteen valves and eight spark-plugs, and
the people had guaranteed that it would run eighty miles an
hour, although there was a strip of paper pasted to the windshield, to which he payed no attention whatever, asking him
in red letters not to do so for the first five hundred miles.

He came up the drive and stopped before the house, where
his grandfather sat with his feet on the veranda railing and
Miss Jenny stood trim in her black dress beside a post. She descended the steps and examined it, and opened the door and
got in to try the seat. Simon came to the door and gave it a
brief derogatory look and retired, and Isom appeared around
the corner and circled the car quietly with an utter and yearning admiration. But old Bayard just looked down at the long,
dusty thing, his cigar in his fingers, and grunted.

"Why, it's as comfortable as a rocking-chair," Miss Jenny
said. "Come here and try it," she called to him. But he grunted
again, and sat with his feet on the rail and watched young
Bayard slide in under the wheel. The engine raced experimentally, ceased. Isom stood like a leashed hound beside it.
Young Bayard glanced at him.

"You can go next time," he said.

"Why cant he go now?" Miss Jenny said. "Jump in, Isom."

Isom jumped in, and old Bayard watched them move
soundlessly down the drive and watched the car pass from
sight down the valley. Presently above the trees a cloud of dust
rose into the azure afternoon and hung rosily fading in the
sun, and a sound as of remote thunder died muttering behind

it. Old Bayard puffed his cigar again. Simon appeared again in the door and stood there.

"Now whar you reckon dey gwine right here at supper-time?" he said. Bayard grunted, and Simon stood in the door, mumbling to himself.

Twenty minutes later the car slid up the drive and came to a halt almost in its former tracks. In the back seat Isom's face was like an open piano. Miss Jenny had worn no hat, and she held her hair with both hands, and when the car stopped she sat for a moment so. Then she drew a long breath.

"I wish I smoked cigarettes," she said, and then: "Is that as fast as it'll go?"

Isom got out and opened the door for her. She descended a little stiffly, but her eyes were shining and her dry old cheeks were flushed.

"How fer y'all been?" Simon asked from the door.

"We've been to town," she answered proudly, and her voice was clear as a girl's. Town was four miles away.

After that the significance grew slowly. He received intimations of it from various sources. But because of his deafness, these intimations came slowly since they must come directly to him and not through overheard talk. The actual evidence, the convincing evidence, came from old man Falls. Eight or ten times a year he walked in from the county farm, always stopping in at the bank.

One day a week later old man Falls came in to town and found old Bayard in his office. The office was also the directors' room. It was a large room containing a long table lined with chairs, and a tall cabinet where blank banking forms were kept, and old Bayard's roll-top desk and swivel chair and a sofa on which he napped for an hour each noon.

The desk, like the one at home, was cluttered with a variety of objects which bore no relation whatever to the banking business, and the mantel above the fireplace bore still more objects of an agricultural nature, as well as a dusty assortment of pipes and three or four jars of tobacco which furnished solace for the entire banking force from president to janitor and for a respectable portion of the bank's clientele. Weather permitting, old Bayard spent most of the day in a tilted chair in the street door, and when these patrons found him there, they went on back to the office and filled their pipes from the jars. It was a sort of unspoken convention not to take more than a pipeful at a time. Here old man Falls and old Bayard retired on the old man's monthly visits and shouted at one another (they were both deaf) for a half hour or so. You could hear them plainly from the street and in the adjoining store on either side.

Old man Falls' eyes were blue and innocent as a boy's and his first act was to open the parcel which old Bayard had for him and take out a plug of chewing tobacco, cut off a chew and put it in his mouth, replace the plug and tie the parcel neatly again. Twice a year the parcel contained an entire outfit of clothing, on the other occasions tobacco and a small sack of peppermint candy. He would never cut the string, but always untied it with his stiff, gnarled fingers and tied it back again. He would not accept money.

He sat now in his clean, faded overalls, with the parcel on his knees, telling Bayard about the automobile that had passed him on the road that morning. Everyone had seen or heard of young Bayard's low gray car, but old man Falls was the first to tell his grandfather how he drove it. Old Bayard sat quite still, watching him with his fierce old eyes until he had finished.

"Are you sure who it was?" he asked.

"Hit passed me too fast fer me to tell whether they was anybody in hit a-tall or not. I asked when I fetched town who 'twas. Seems like ever'body knows how fast he runs hit except you."

Old Bayard sat quietly for a time. Then he raised his voice: "Byron."

The door opened quietly and the book-keeper entered—a thin, youngish man with hairy hands and covert close eyes that looked always as though he were just blinking them, though you never saw them closed.

"Yes, sir, Colonel," he said in a slow, nasal voice without inflection.

" 'Phone out to my house and tell my grandson not to touch that car until I come home."

"Yes, sir, Colonel." And he was gone as silently as he appeared.

Bayard slammed around in his swivel chair again and old man Falls leaned forward, peering at his face.

"What's that 'ere wen you got on yo' face, Bayard?" he asked.

"What?" Bayard demanded, then he raised his hand to a small spot which the suffusion of his face had brought into relief. "Here? I dont know what it is. It's been there about a week. Why?"

"Is it gittin' bigger?" the other asked. He rose and laid his parcel down and extended his hand. Old Bayard drew his head back.

"It's nothing," he said testily. "Let it alone." But old man Falls put the other's hand aside and touched the spot with his fingers.

"H'm," he said. "Hard's a rock. Hit'll git bigger, too. I'll watch hit, and when hit's right, I'll take hit off. 'Taint ripe, yit." The book-keeper appeared suddenly and without noise beside them.

"Yo' cook says him and Miss Jenny is off car-ridin' somewheres. I left yo' message."

"Jenny's with him, you say?" old Bayard asked.

"That's what yo' cook says," the book-keeper repeated in his inflectionless voice.

"Well. All right."

The book-keeper withdrew and old man Falls picked up his parcel. "I'll be gittin' on too," he said. "I'll come in next week and take a look at hit. You better let hit alone till I git back." He followed the book-keeper from the room, and presently old Bayard rose and stalked through the lobby and tilted his chair in the door.

That afternoon when he arrived home, the car was not in sight, nor did his aunt answer his call. He mounted to his room and put on his riding-boots and lit a cigar, but when he looked down from his window into the back yard, neither Isom nor the saddled mare were visible. The old setter sat looking up at his window. When old Bayard's head appeared there the dog rose and went to the kitchen door and stood there; then it looked up at his window again. Old Bayard tramped down the stairs and on through the house and entered the kitchen, where Caspey sat at the table, eating and talking to Isom and Elnora.

"And one mo' time me and another boy——" Caspey was saying. Then Isom saw Bayard, and rose from his seat in the woodbox corner and his eyes rolled whitely in his bullet head. Elnora paused also with her broom, but Caspey turned his head without rising, and still chewing steadily he blinked his eyes at old Bayard in the door.

"I sent you word a week ago to come on out here at once, or not to come at all," Bayard said. "Did you get it?" Caspey mumbled something, still chewing, and old Bayard came into the room. "Get up from there and saddle my horse."

Caspey turned his back deliberately and raised his glass of buttermilk. "Git on, Caspey," Elnora hissed at him.

"I aint workin' here," he answered, just beneath Bayard's deafness. He turned to Isom. "Whyn't you go'n git his hoss fer him? Aint you workin' here?"

"Caspey, fer Lawd's sake!" Elnora implored. "Yes, suh, Cunnel; he's gwine," she said loudly.

"Who, me?" Caspey said. "Does I look like it?" He raised the glass steadily to his mouth, then Bayard moved again and Caspey lost his nerve and rose quickly before the other reached him, and crossed the kitchen toward the door, but with sullen insolence in the very shape of his back. As he fumbled with the door Bayard overtook him.

"Are you going to saddle that mare?" he demanded.

"Aint gwine skip it, big boy," Caspey answered, just below Bayard's deafness.

"What?"

"Oh, Lawd, Caspey!" Elnora moaned. Isom crouched into his corner. Caspey raised his eyes swiftly to Bayard's face and opened the screen door.

"I says, I aint gwine skip it," he repeated, raising his voice. Simon stood at the foot of the steps beside the setter, gaping his toothless mouth up at them, and old Bayard reached a stick of stove wood from the box at his hand and knocked Caspey through the opening door and down the steps at his father's feet.

"Now, you go saddle that mare," he said.

Simon helped his son to rise and led him away toward the barn while the setter watched them, gravely interested. "I kep' tellin' you dem new-fangled war notions of yo'n wa'nt gwine ter work on dis place," he said angrily. "And you better thank de good Lawd fer makin' yo' haid hard ez hit is. You go'n git dat mare, en save dat nigger freedom talk fer town-folks: dey mought stomach it. Whut us niggers want ter be free fer, anyhow? Aint we got ez many white folks now ez we kin suppo't?"

That night at supper, old Bayard looked at his grandson across the roast of mutton. "Will Falls told me you passed him on the Poor House hill running forty miles an hour today."

"Forty fiddlesticks," Miss Jenny answered promptly, "it was fifty four. I was watching the—what do you call it, Bayard? speedometer."

Old Bayard sat with his head bent a little, watching his hands trembling on the carving knife and fork; hearing beneath the napkin tucked into his waistcoat, his heart a little too light and a little too fast; feeling Miss Jenny's eyes upon his face.

"Bayard," she said sharply, "what's that on your cheek?" He rose so suddenly that his chair tipped over backward with a crash, and he tramped blindly from the room.

3.

"I know what you want me to do," Miss Jenny told old Bayard across her newspaper. "You want me to let my house-keeping go to the dogs and spend all my time in that car, that's what you want. Well, I'm not going to do it. I dont mind riding with him now and then, but I've got too much to do with my time to spend it keeping him from running that car fast. Neck, too," she added. She rattled the paper crisply.

She said: "Besides, you aint foolish enough to believe he'll drive slow just because there's somebody with him, are you? If you do think so, you'd better send Simon along. Lord knows Simon can spare the time. Since you quit using the carriage, if he does anything at all, I dont know it." She read the paper again.

Old Bayard's cigar smoked in his still hand.

"I might send Isom," he said.

Miss Jenny's paper rattled sharply and she stared at her nephew for a long moment. "God in heaven, man, why dont you put a block and chain on him and have done with it?"

"Well, didn't you suggest sending Simon with him, yourself? Simon has his work to do, but all Isom ever does is saddle my horse once a day, and I can do that myself."

"I was trying to be ironical," Miss Jenny said. "God knows, I should have learned better by this time. But if you've got to invent something new for the niggers to do, you let it be Simon. I need Isom to keep a roof over your head and something to eat on the table." She rattled the paper. "Why dont you come right out and tell him not to drive fast? A man that has to spend eight hours a day sitting in a chair in that bank door ought not to have to spend the rest of the afternoon helling around the country in an automobile if he dont want to."

"Do you think it would do any good to ask him? There was never a damned one of 'em ever paid any attention to my wishes yet."

"Ask, the devil," Miss Jenny said. "Who said anything about ask? Tell him not to. Tell him that if you hear again of his going fast in it, that you'll frail the life out of him. I believe anyway that you like to ride in that car, only you wont admit it, and you just dont want him to ride in it when you cant go too." But old Bayard had slammed his feet to the floor and risen, and he tramped from the room.

Instead of mounting the stairs however Miss Jenny heard his footsteps die away down the hall, and presently she rose and followed to the back porch, where he stood in the darkness there. The night was dark, myriad with drifting odors of the spring and with insects. Dark upon lesser dark, the barn loomed against the sky.

"He hasn't come in yet," she said impatiently, touching his arm. "I could have told you. Go on up and go to bed, now; dont you know he'll let you know when he comes in? You're going to think him into a ditch somewhere, with these fool notions of yours." Then more gently: "You're too childish about that car. It's no more dangerous at night than it is in daytime. Come on, now."

He shook her hand off, but he turned obediently and entered the house. This time he mounted the stairs and she could hear him in his bedroom, thumping about. Presently he ceased slamming doors and drawers and lay beneath the reading lamp with his Dumas. After a time the door opened and young Bayard entered and came into the radius of the light with his bleak eyes.

His grandfather did not remark his presence and he touched his arm. Old Bayard looked up, and when he did so young Bayard turned and quitted the room.

After the shades on the windows were drawn at three oclock old Bayard retired to the office. Inside the grille the cashier and the book-keeper could hear him clattering and banging around beyond the door. The cashier paused, a stack of silver clipped neatly in his fingers.

"Hear 'im?" he said. "Something on his mind here, lately. Used to be he was quiet as a mouse back there until they come for him, but last few days he tromples and thumps around back there like he was fighting hornets."

The book-keeper said nothing. The cashier set the stack of silver aside, built up another one.

"Something on his mind, lately. That examiner must a put a bug in his ear, I reckon."

The book-keeper said nothing. He swung the adding machine to his desk and clicked the lever over. In the back room old Bayard moved audibly about. The cashier stacked the remaining silver neatly and rolled a cigarette. The book-keeper bent above the steady clicking of the machine, and the cashier sealed his cigarette and lit it and waddled to the window and lifted the curtain.

"Simon's brought the carriage, today," he said. "That boy finally wrecked that car, I reckon. Better call Colonel."

The book-keeper slid from his stool and went back to the door and opened it. Old Bayard glanced up from his desk, with his hat on.

"All right, Byron," he said. The book-keeper returned to his desk.

Old Bayard stalked through the bank and opened the street door and stopped utterly, the doorknob in his hand.

"Where's Bayard?" he said.

"He aint comin'," Simon answered. Old Bayard crossed to the carriage.

"What? Where is he?"

"Him en Isom off somewhar in dat cyar," Simon said. "Lawd knows whar dey is by now. Takin' dat boy away fum his work in de middle of de day, cyar-ridin'." Old Bayard laid his hand on the stanchion, the spot on his face coming again into white relief. "Atter all de time I spent tryin' to git some sense inter Isom's haid," Simon continued. He held the horses' heads up, waiting for his employer to enter. "Cyar-ridin'," he said. "Cyar-ridin'."

Old Bayard got in and sank heavily into the seat.

"I'll be damned," he said, "if I haven't got the triflingest set of folks to make a living for God ever made. There's just one thing about it: when I finally have to go to the poorhouse, every damned one of you'll be there when I come."

"Now, here you quoilin' too," Simon said. "Miss Jenny yellin' at me twell I wuz plumb out de gate, and now you already started at dis en'. But ef Mist' Bayard dont leave dat boy alone, he aint gwine ter be no better'n a town nigger spite of all I kin do."

"Jenny's already ruined him," old Bayard said. "Even Bayard cant hurt him much."

"You sho' tole de troof den," Simon agreed. He shook the reins. "Come up, dar."

"Here, Simon," old Bayard said. "Hold up a minute."

Simon reined the horses back. "Whut you want now?"

The spot on old Bayard's cheek had resumed its normal appearance. "Go back to my office and get me a cigar out of that jar on the mantel," he said.

Two days later, as he and Simon tooled sedately homeward through the afternoon, simultaneously almost with the warning thunder of it the car burst upon him on a curve, slewed into the ditch and on to the road again and rushed on; and in the flashing instant he and Simon saw the whites of Isom's eyes and the ivory cropping of his teeth behind the steering wheel. When the car returned home that afternoon Simon conducted Isom to the barn and whipped him with a harness strap.

That night they sat in the office after supper. Old Bayard held his cigar unlighted in his fingers. Miss Jenny read the paper. Faint airs blew in, laden with spring.

Suddenly old Bayard said: "Maybe he'll get tired of it after a while."

Miss Jenny raised her head.

"And when he does," Miss Jenny said, "dont you know what he'll get then? When he finds that car wont go fast enough?" she demanded, staring at him across the paper. He sat with his unlighted cigar, his head bent a little, not looking at her. "He'll buy an aeroplane." She rattled the paper and turned a page. "He ought to have a wife," she added, reading again. "Let him get a son, then he can break his neck as soon and as often as he pleases. Providence doesn't seem to have any judgment at all," she said, thinking of the two of them, of his dead brother. She said: "But Lord knows, I'd hate to see any girl I was fond of, married to him." She rattled the paper again, turned another page. "I dont know what else you expect of him. Of any Sartoris. You dont waste your afternoons riding with him just because you think it'll keep him from turning that car over: you go because when it does happen, you want to be in it, too. So do you think you've got any more consideration for folks than he has?" He held his cigar, his face still averted. Miss Jenny was watching him again across the paper.

"I'm coming down town in the morning, and we're going and have the doctor look at that bump on your face, you hear?"

In his room, as he removed his collar and tie before his chest of drawers, his eye fell upon the pipe which he had laid there four weeks ago, and he put the collar and tie down and picked up the pipe and held it in his hand, rubbing the charred bowl slowly with his thumb.

Then with sudden decision he quitted the room and tramped down the hall. At the end of the hall a stair mounted into the darkness. He fumbled the light switch beside it and mounted, following the cramped turnings cautiously in the dark, to a door set at a difficult angle, and opened it upon a broad, low room with a pitched ceiling, smelling of dust and silence and ancient disused things.

The room was cluttered with indiscriminate furniture—chairs and sofas like patient ghosts holding lightly in dry and rigid embrace yet other ghosts—a fitting place for dead Sartorises to gather and speak among themselves of glamorous and old disastrous days. The unshaded light swung on a single cord from the center of the ceiling. He unknotted it and drew it across to a nail in the wall above a cedar chest. He fastened it here and drew a chair across to the chest and sat down.

The chest had not been opened since 1901, when his son John had succumbed to yellow fever and an old Spanish bullet-wound. There had been two occasions since, in July and in October of last year, but the other grandson still possessed quickness and all the incalculable portent of his heritage. So he had forborne for the time being, expecting to be able to kill two birds with one stone, as it were.

Thus each opening was in a way ceremonial, commemorating the violent finis to some phase of his family's history, and while he struggled with the stiff lock it seemed to him that a legion of ghosts breathed quietly at his shoulder, and he pictured a double line of them with their arrogant identical faces waiting just beyond a portal and stretching away toward the invisible dais where Something sat waiting the latest arrival among them; thought of them chafing a little and a little bewildered, thought and desire being denied them, in a place where, immortal, there were no opportunities for vainglorious swashbuckling. Denied that Sartoris heaven in which they could spend eternity dying deaths of needless and magnificent violence while spectators doomed to immortality looked eternally on. The Valhalla which John Sartoris, turning the wine glass in his big, well-shaped hand that night at the supper table, had seen in its chaste and fragile bubble.

The lock was stiff, and he struggled patiently with it for some time. Rust shaled off, rubbed off onto his hands, and he desisted and rose and rummaged about and returned to the chest with a heavy, cast-iron candlestick and hammered the lock free and removed it and raised the lid. From the chest there rose a thin exhilarating odor of cedar, and something else: a scent drily and muskily nostalgic, as of old ashes. The first object was a garment. The brocade was richly hushed, and the fall of fine Mechlin was dustily yellow, pale and texture-less as February sunlight. He lifted the garment carefully out. The lace cascaded mellow and pale as spilled wine upon his hands, and he laid it aside and lifted out next a rapier. It was a Toledo, a blade delicate and fine as the prolonged stroke of a violin bow, in a velvet sheath. The sheath was elegant and flamboyant and soiled, and the seams had cracked drily.

Old Bayard held the rapier upon his hands for a while, feel-ing the balance of it. It was just such an implement as a Sar-toris would consider the proper equipment for raising tobacco in a virgin wilderness; it and the scarlet heels and the ruffled wristbands in which he broke the earth and fought his stealthy and simple neighbors. And old Bayard held it upon his two hands, seeing in its stained fine blade and shabby elegant sheath the symbol of his race; that too in the tradition: the thing itself fine and clear enough, only the instrument had become a little tarnished in its very aptitude for shaping cir-cumstance to its arrogant ends.

He laid it aside. Next came a heavy cavalry sabre, and a rose-wood case containing two duelling pistols with silver mount-ings and the lean, deceptive delicacy of race horses, and what old man Falls had called "that 'ere dang der'nger." It was a stubby, evil looking thing with its three barrels; viciously and coldly utilitarian, and between the other two weapons it lay like a cold and deadly insect between two flowers.

He removed next the blue army forage-cap of the 'forties and a small pottery vessel and a Mexican machete, and a long-necked oil can such as locomotive drivers use. It was of silver, and engraved upon it was the picture of a locomotive with a huge bell-shaped funnel and surrounded by an ornate wreath. Beneath it, the name, "Virginia" and the date, "August 9, 1873."

He put these aside and with sudden purposefulness he re-moved the other objects—a frogged and braided coat of Con-federate gray and a gown of sprigged muslin scented faintly of lavender and evocative of old formal minuets and drifting honeysuckle among steady candle flames—and came upon a conglomeration of yellowed papers neatly bound in packets, and at last upon a huge, brass-bound bible. He lifted this to the edge of the chest and opened it. The paper was brown and mellow with years, and it had a texture like that of slightly-moist wood ashes, as though each page were held intact by its archaic and fading print. He turned the pages carefully back to the fly leaves. Beginning near the bottom of the final blank page, a column of names and dates rose in stark, fading simplicity, growing fainter and fainter where time had lain upon them. At the top they were still legible, as they were at the foot of the preceding page. But halfway up this page they ceased, and from there on the sheet was blank save for the faint soft mottlings of time and an occasional brownish penstroke significant but without meaning.

Bayard sat for a long time, regarding the stark dissolving apotheosis of his name. Sartorises had derided Time, but Time was not vindictive, being longer than Sartorises. And probably unaware of them. But it was a good gesture, anyway.

"In the nineteenth century," John Sartoris said, "genealogy is poppycock. Particularly in America, where only what a man takes and keeps has any significance, and where all of us have a common ancestry and the only house from which we can claim descent with any assurance, is the Old Bailey. Yet the man who professes to care nothing about his forbears is only a little less vain than he who bases all his actions on blood precedent. And I reckon a Sartoris can have a little vanity and poppycock, if he wants it."

Yes, it was a good gesture, and Bayard sat and mused quietly on the tense he had unwittingly used. Was. Fatality: the augury of a man's destiny peeping out at him from the roadside hedge, if he but recognise it; and again he ran panting through undergrowth while the fading thunder of the smoke-colored stallion swept on in the dusk and the Yankee patrol crashed behind him, crashed fainter and fainter until he crouched with spent, laboring lungs in a brier thicket and heard the pursuit rush on. Then he crawled forth and went to a spring he knew that flowed from the roots of a beech; and as he leaned down to it the final light of day was reflected onto his face, bringing into sharp relief forehead and nose above the cavernous sockets of his eyes and the panting snarl of his teeth, and from the still water there stared back at him for a sudden moment, a skull.

The unturned corners of man's destiny. Well, heaven, that crowded place, lay just beyond one of them, they claimed;

heaven, filled with every man's illusion of himself and with the conflicting illusions of him that parade through the minds of other illusions. . . . He stirred and sighed quietly, and took out his fountain pen. At the foot of the column he wrote:

"John Sartoris. July 5, 1918."

and beneath that:

"Caroline White Sartoris and son. October 27, 1918."

When the ink was dry he closed the book and replaced it and took the pipe from his pocket and put it in the rosewood case with the duelling pistols and the derringer and replaced the other things and closed the chest and locked it.

Miss Jenny found old Bayard in his tilted chair in the door, and he looked up at her with a fine assumption of surprise and his deafness seemed more pronounced than ordinary. But she got him up with cold implacability and led him still grumbling down the street, where merchants and others spoke to her as to a martial queen, old Bayard stalking along beside her with sullen reluctance.

They turned presently and mounted a narrow stairway debouching between two stores, beneath an array of dingy professional signs. At the top was a dark corridor with doors. The nearest door was of pine, its gray paint scarred at the bottom as though it had been kicked repeatedly at the same height and with the same force. In the door itself two holes an inch apart bore mute witness to the missing hasp, and from a staple in the jamb depended the hasp itself, fixed there by a huge rusty lock of an ancient pattern. Bayard offered to stop here, but Miss Jenny led him firmly on to a door across the hall.

This door was freshly painted and grained to represent walnut. Into the top half of it was let a pane of thick, opaque glass bearing a name in raised gilt letters, and two embracing office hours. Miss Jenny opened this door and Bayard followed her into a small cubbyhole of a room of spartan but suave asepsis. The walls were an immaculate new gray, with a reproduction of a Corot and two spidery dry-points in narrow frames, and it contained a new rug in warm buff tones and a bare table and four chairs in fumed oak—all impersonal and clean and inexpensive, but revealing at a glance the proprietor's soul; a soul hampered now by material strictures, but destined and determined to someday function amid Persian rugs and mahogany or teak, and a single irreproachable print on the chaste walls. A young woman in a starched white dress rose from a smaller table on which a telephone sat, and patted her hair.

"Good morning, Myrtle," Miss Jenny said. "Tell Dr Alford we'd like to see him, please."

"You have an appointment?" the girl said in a voice without any inflection at all.

"We'll make one now, then," Miss Jenny replied. "You dont mean to say Dr Alford dont come to work before ten oclock, do you?"

"Dr Alford dont—doesn't see anyone without an appointment," the girl parrotted, gazing at a point above Miss Jenny's head. "If you have no appointment, you'll have to have an ap—"

"Tut, tut," Miss Jenny interrupted briskly, "you run and tell Dr Alford Colonel Sartoris wants to see him, there's a good girl."

"Yessum, Miss Jenny," the girl said obediently and she crossed the room, but at the other door she paused again and again her voice became parrot-like. "Wont you sit down? I'll see if the doctor is engaged."

"You go and tell Dr Alford we're here," Miss Jenny repeated affably. "Tell him I've got some shopping to do this morning."

"Yessum, Miss Jenny," the girl agreed, and disappeared, and after a dignified interval she returned, once more clothed faultlessly in her professional manner. "The doctor will see you now. Come in, please." She held the door open and stood aside.

"Thank you, honey," Miss Jenny replied. "Is your mamma still in bed?"

"No'm, she's sitting up now, thank you."

"That's good," Miss Jenny agreed. "Come on, Bayard."

This room was smaller than the other, and brutally carbolized. There was a white enamelled cabinet filled with vicious nickel gleams, and a metal operating table and an array of electric furnaces and ovens and sterilizers. The doctor in a white linen jacket bent above a small desk, and for a while he proffered them his sleek oblivious profile. Then he glanced up, and rose.

He was in the youthful indeterminate thirties; a newcomer to the town and nephew of an old resident. He had made a fine record in medical school and was of a personable exterior, but there was a sort of preoccupied dignity, a sort of erudite and cold unillusion regarding mankind, about him that precluded the easy intimacy of the small town and caused even those who remembered him as a visiting boy to address him as doctor or mister. He had a small moustache and a face like a mask—a comforting face, but cold; and while Bayard sat restively the doctor probed delicately with dry, scrubbed fingers at the wen on his face. Miss Jenny asked him a question, but he continued his exploration raptly, as though he had not heard, as though she had not even spoken; inserting a small electric bulb which he first sterilized, into Bayard's mouth and snapping its ruby glow on and off within his cheek. Then he removed it and sterilized it again and returned it to the cabinet.

"Well?" Miss Jenny said impatiently. The doctor shut the cabinet carefully and washed and dried his hands and came and stood over them, and with his thumbs hooked in his jacket pockets he became solemnly and unctuously technical, rolling the harsh words from his tongue with an epicurean deliberation.

"It should be removed at once," he concluded. "It should be removed while in its early stage; that is why I advise an immediate operation."

"You mean, it might develop into cancer?" Miss Jenny asked.

"No question about it at all, madam. Course of time. Neglect it, and I can promise you nothing; have it out now, and he need never worry about it again." He looked at Bayard again with lingering and chill contemplation. "It will be very simple. I'll remove it as easily as that." And he made a short gesture with his hand.

"What's that?" Bayard demanded.

"I say, I can take that growth off so easily you wont know it, Colonel Sartoris."

"I'll be damned if you do!" Bayard rose with one of his characteristic plunging movements.

"Sit down, Bayard," Miss Jenny ordered. "Nobody's going

to cut on you without your knowing it. Should it be done right away?" she asked.

"Yes, ma'am. I wouldn't have that thing on my face overnight. Otherwise, it is only fair to warn you that no doctor can assume responsibility for what might ensue. . . . I could remove it in two minutes," he added, looking at Bayard's face again with cold speculation. Then he half turned his head and stopped in a listening attitude, and beyond the thin walls a voice in the other room boomed in rich rolling waves.

"Mawnin', sister," it said. "Didn't I hear Bayard Sartoris cussin' in here?" The doctor and Miss Jenny held their arrested attitudes, then the door surged open and the fattest man in Yocona county filled it. He wore a shiny alpaca coat over waistcoat and trousers of baggy black broadcloth; above a plaited shirt the fatty rolls of his dewlap practically hid his low collar and a black string tie. His Roman senator's head was thatched with a vigorous curling of silvery hair. "What the devil's the matter with you?" he boomed, then he sidled into the room, filling it completely, dwarfing its occupants and its furnishings.

This was Doctor Lucius Quintus Peabody, eighty-seven years old and weighing three hundred and ten pounds and possessing a digestive tract like a horse. He had practiced medicine in Yocona county when a doctor's equipment consisted of a saw and a gallon of whisky and a satchel of calomel; he had been John Sartoris' regimental surgeon, and up to the day of the automobile he would start out at any hour of the twenty-four in any weather and for any distance, over practically impassable roads in a lopsided buckboard to visit anyone, white or black, who sent for him; accepting for fee usually a meal of corn pone and coffee or perhaps a small measure of corn or fruit, or a few flower bulbs or graftings. When he was young and hasty he had kept a daybook, kept it meticulously until these hypothetical assets totalled $10,000.00. But that was forty years ago, and since then he hadn't bothered with a record at all; and now from time to time a countryman enters his shabby office and discharges an obligation, commemorating sometimes the payor's entry into the world, incurred by his father or grandfather and which Dr Peabody himself had long since forgotten about. Every one in the county knew him and sent him hams and wild game at Christmas, and it was said that he could spend the balance of his days driving about the county in the buckboard he still used, with never a thought for board and lodging and without the expenditure of a penny for either. He filled the room with his bluff and homely humanity, and as he crossed the floor and patted Miss Jenny's back with one flail-like hand the whole building trembled to his tread.

"Mawnin', Jenny," he said. "Havin' Bayard measured for insurance?"

"This damn butcher wants to cut on me," Bayard said querulously. "You come on and make 'em let me alone, Loosh."

"Ten A.M.'s mighty early in the day to start carvin' white folks," Dr Peabody boomed. "Nigger's different. Chop up a nigger any time after midnight. What's the matter with him, son?" he asked of Dr Alford.

"I dont believe it's anything but a wart," Miss Jenny said. "But I'm tired of looking at it."

"It's no wart," Dr Alford corrected stiffly. He recapitulated his diagnosis in technical terms while Dr Peabody enveloped them all in the rubicund benevolence of his presence.

"Sounds pretty bad, dont it?" he agreed, and he shook the floor again and pushed Bayard firmly into the chair with one huge hand, and with the other he dragged his face up to the light. Then he dug a pair of iron-bowed spectacles from the pocket of his coat and examined Bayard's wen through them. "Think it ought to come off, do you?"

"I do," Dr Alford answered coldly. "I think it is imperative that it be removed. Unnecessary there. Cancer."

"Folks got along with cancer a long time befo' they invented knives," Dr Peabody said drily. "Hold still, Bayard."

And people like you are one of the reasons, was on the tip of the younger man's tongue. But he forbore and said instead: "I can remove that growth in two minutes, Colonel Sartoris."

"Damned if you do," Bayard rejoined violently, trying to rise. "Get away, Loosh."

"Sit still," Dr Peabody said equably, holding him down while he probed at the wen. "Does it hurt any?"

"No. I never said it did. And I'll be damned—"

"You'll probably be damned anyway," Dr Peabody told

him. "You'd be about as well off dead, anyhow. I dont know anybody that gets less fun out of living than you do."

"You told the truth for once," Miss Jenny agreed. "He's the oldest person I ever knew in my life."

"And so," Dr Peabody continued blandly, "I wouldn't worry about it. Let it stay there. Nobody cares what your face looks like. If you were a young fellow, now, out sparkin' the gals every night——"

"If Dr Peabody is permitted to interfere with impunity——" Dr Alford began.

"Will Falls says he can cure it," Bayard said.

"With that salve of his?" Dr Peabody asked quickly.

"Salve?" Dr Alford repeated. "Colonel Sartoris, if you permit any quack that comes along to treat that growth with home-made or patent remedies, you'll be dead in six months. Dr Peabody even will bear me out," he added with fine irony.

"I dont know," Dr Peabody replied slowly. "Will has done some curious things with that salve of his."

"I must protest against this," Dr Alford said. "Mrs Du Pre, I protest against a member of my profession sanctioning even negatively such a procedure."

"Pshaw, boy," Dr Peabody answered, "we aint goin' to let Will put his dope on Bayard's wart. It's all right for niggers and livestock, but Bayard dont need it. We'll just let this thing alone, long as it dont hurt him."

"If that growth is not removed immediately, I wash my hands of all responsibility," Dr Alford stated. "To neglect it will be as fatal as Mr Falls' salve. Mrs Du Pre, I ask you to witness that this consultation has taken this unethical turn through no fault of mine and over my protest."

"Pshaw, boy," Dr Peabody said again. "This aint hardly worth the trouble of cuttin' out. We'll save you an arm or a leg as soon as that fool grandson of his turns that automobile over with 'em. Come on with me, Bayard."

"Mrs Du Pre——" Dr Alford essayed.

"Bayard can come back, if he wants to." Dr Peabody patted the younger man's shoulder with his heavy hand. "I'm going to take him to my office and talk to him a while. Jenny can bring him back if she wants to. Come on, Bayard." And he led Bayard from the room. Miss Jenny rose also.

"That Loosh Peabody is as big a fogy as old Will Falls," she said. "Old people just fret me to death. You wait: I'll bring him right back here, and we'll finish this business." Dr Alford held the door open for her and she sailed in a stiff silk-clad rage from the room and followed her nephew across the corridor and through the scarred door with its rusty lock, and into a room resembling a miniature cyclonic devastation mellowed peacefully over with dust ancient and undisturbed.

"You, Loosh Peabody," Miss Jenny said.

"Sit down, Jenny," Dr Peabody told her, "and be quiet. Unfasten your shirt, Bayard."

"What?" Bayard said belligerently. The other thrust him into a chair.

"Want to see your chest," he explained. He crossed to an ancient rolltop desk and rummaged through the dusty litter upon it. There was litter and dust everywhere in the huge room. Its four windows gave upon the square, but the elms and sycamores ranged along the sides of the square shaded these first floor offices, so that light entered them but tempered, like light beneath water. In the corners of the ceiling were spider webs thick and heavy as Spanish moss and dingy as old lace; and the once-white walls were an even and unemphatic drab save for a paler rectangle here and there where an outdated calendar had hung and been removed. Besides the desk the room contained three or four miscellaneous chairs in various stages of decrepitude, a rusty stove in a sawdust filled box, and a leather sofa holding mutely amid its broken springs the outline of Dr Peabody's recumbent shape; beside it and slowly gathering successive layers of dust, was a stack of lurid paper covered nickel novels. This was Dr Peabody's library, and on this sofa he passed his office hours, reading them over and over. Other books there were none.

But the waste basket beside the desk and the desk itself and the mantel above the trash-filled fireplace, and the window-ledges too were cluttered with circular mail matter and mail order catalogues and government bulletins of all kinds. In one corner, on an upended packing-box, sat a water cooler of stained oxidized glass; in another corner leaned a clump of cane fishing poles warping slowly of their own weight; and on every horizontal surface rested a collection of objects

not to be found outside of a second-hand store—old garments, bottles, a kerosene lamp, a wooden box of tins of axle
grease, lacking one, a clock in the shape of a bland china
morning-glory supported by four garlanded maidens who
had suffered sundry astonishing anatomical mishaps, and here
and there among their dusty indiscrimination various instruments pertaining to the occupant's profession. It was one of
these that Dr Peabody sought now, in the littered desk on
which sat a single photograph in a wooden frame, and though
Miss Jenny said again, "You, Loosh Peabody, you listen
to me," he continued to seek it with bland and unhurried
equanimity.

"You fasten your clothes and we'll go back to that doctor,"
Miss Jenny said to her nephew. "Neither you nor I can waste
any more time with a doddering old fool."

"Sit down, Jenny," Dr Peabody repeated, and he drew out
a drawer and removed from it a box of cigars and a handful
of faded artificial trout flies and a soiled collar and lastly a
stethescope, then he tumbled the other things back into the
drawer and shut it with his knee.

Miss Jenny sat trim and outraged, fuming while he listened
to Bayard's heart.

"Well," she snapped, "does it tell you how to take that wart
off his face? Will Falls didn't need any telephone to find that
out."

"It tells more than that," Dr Peabody answered. "It tells
how Bayard'll get rid of all his troubles, if he keeps on riding
in that hellion's automobile."

"Fiddlesticks," Miss Jenny said. "Bayard's a good driver. I
never rode with a better one."

"It'll take more'n a good driver to keep this—" he tapped
Bayard's chest with his blunt finger—"goin', time that boy
whirls that thing around another curve or two like I've seen
him do."

"Did you ever hear of a Sartoris dying from a natural cause,
like anybody else?" Miss Jenny demanded. "Dont you know
that heart aint going to take Bayard off before his time? You
get up from there, and come on with me," she added to her
nephew. Bayard buttoned his shirt, and Dr Peabody sat on the
sofa and watched him quietly.

"Bayard," he said suddenly, "why dont you stay out of that damn thing?"

"What?"

"If you dont keep out of that car, you aint goin' to need me nor Will Falls, nor that boy in yonder with all his hand-boiled razors, neither."

"What business is it of yours?" Bayard demanded. "By God, cant I break my neck in peace if I want to?" He rose. He was trembling, fumbling at his waistcoat buttons, and Miss Jenny rose also and made to help him, but he put her roughly aside. Dr Peabody sat quietly, thumping his fat fingers on one fat knee. "I have already outlived my time," Bayard continued more mildly. "I am the first of my name to see sixty years that I know of. I reckon Old Marster is keeping me for a reliable witness to the extinction of it."

"Now," Miss Jenny said icily, "you've made your speech, and Loosh Peabody has wasted the morning for you, so I reckon we can leave now and let Loosh go out and doctor mules for a while, and you can sit around the rest of the day, being a Sartoris and feeling sorry for yourself. Good morning, Loosh."

"Make him let that place alone, Jenny," Dr Peabody said.

"Aint you and Will Falls going to cure it for him?"

"You keep him from letting Will Falls put anything on it," Dr Peabody repeated equably. "It's all right. Just let it alone."

"We're going to a doctor, that's what we're going to do," Miss Jenny replied. "Come on here."

When the door had closed he sat motionless and heard them quarrelling beyond it. Then the sound of their voices moved on down the corridor toward the stairs, and still quarrelling loudly and on Bayard's part with profane emphasis, the voices died away. Then Dr Peabody lay back on the sofa shaped already to the bulk of him, and with random deliberation he reached a nickel thriller blindly from the stack at the head of the couch.

4.

As they neared the bank Narcissa Benbow came along from the opposite direction, and they met at the door, where he made her a ponderous compliment on her appearance while she stood in her pale dress and shouted her grave voice into his deafness. Then he took his tilted chair, and Miss Jenny followed her into the bank and to the window. There was no one behind the grille at the moment save the book-keeper. He looked at them briefly and covertly across his shoulder, then slid from his stool and crossed to the window, but without raising his eyes again.

He took Narcissa's check, and while she listened to Miss Jenny's recapitulation of Bayard's and Loosh Peabody's stubborn masculine stupidity, she remarked the reddish hair which clothed his arms down to the second joints of his fingers; and remarked with a faint yet distinct distaste, and a little curiosity, since it was not particularly warm, the fact that his hands and arms were beaded with perspiration.

Then she made her eyes blank again and took the notes which he pushed under the grille to her and opened her bag. From its blue satin maw the corner of an envelope and some of its superscription peeped suddenly, but she crumpled it quickly from sight and put the money in and closed the bag. They turned away, Miss Jenny still talking, and she paused at the door again, clothed in her still aura of quietness, while Bayard twitted her heavily on imaginary affairs of the heart which furnished the sole theme of conversation between them, shouting serenely at him in return. Then she went on, surrounded by tranquillity like a visible presence or an odor or a sound.

As long as she was in sight, the book-keeper stood at the window. His head was bent and his hand made a series of neat, meaningless figures on the pad beneath it. Then she went on and passed from sight. He moved, and in doing so he found that the pad had adhered to his damp wrist, so that when he removed his arm it came also, then its own weight freed it and it fell to the floor.

He finished the forenoon stooped on his high stool at his high desk beneath the green-shaded light, penning his neat figures into ledgers and writing words into them in the flowing spencerian hand he had been taught in a Memphis business college. At times he slid from the stool and crossed to the window with his covert evasive eyes and served a client, then returned to his stool and picked up his pen. The cashier, a rotund man with bristling hair and lapping jowls like a Berkshire hog, returned presently, accompanied by a director, who followed him inside the grille. They ordered coca-colas from a neighboring drug store by telephone and stood talking until the refreshment arrived by negro boy. Snopes had been included and he descended again and took his glass. The other two sipped theirs; he spooned the ice from his into a spittoon and emptied it at a draught and replaced the glass on the tray and spoke a general and ignored thanks in his sober country idiom and returned to his desk.

Noon came. Old Bayard rose crashing from his tilted chair and stalked back to his office, where he would eat his frugal cold lunch and then sleep for an hour, and banged the door behind him. The cashier took his hat and departed also: for an hour Snopes would have the bank to himself. Outside the square lay motionless beneath noon; the dinnerward exodus of lawyers and merchants and clerks did not disturb its atmosphere of abiding and timeless fixation; in the elms surrounding the courthouse no leaf stirred in the May sunlight. Across the bank windows an occasional shadow passed, but none turned into the door, and presently the square was motionless as a theatre drop.

Snopes drew a sheet of paper from a drawer and laid it beneath the light and wrote slowly upon it, pausing at intervals, drawing his pen through a sentence or a word, writing again. Someone entered; without looking up he slid the paper beneath a ledger, crossed to the window and served the customer, returned and wrote again. The clock on the wall ticked into the silence and into the slow, mouse-like scratching of the pen. The pen ceased at last, but the clock ticked on like a measured dropping of small shot.

He re-read the first draught, slowly. Then he drew out a second sheet and made a careful copy. When this was done he re-read it also, comparing the two; then he folded the copy again and again until it was a small square thickness, and stowed it away in the fob-pocket of his trousers. The original he carried across to the cuspidor, and holding it above the receptacle he struck a match to it and held it in his fingers until the final moment. Then he dropped it into the spittoon and when it was completely consumed, he crushed the charred thing to powder. Quarter to one. He returned to his stool and opened his ledgers again.

At one the cashier with a toothpick appeared at the door talking to someone, then he entered and went to old Bayard's office and opened the door. "One oclock, Colonel," he shouted into the room, and old Bayard's heels thumped heavily on the floor. As Snopes took his hat and emerged from the grille old Bayard stalked forth again and tramped on ahead and took the tilted chair in the doorway.

There is in Jefferson a boarding house known as the Beard hotel. It is a rectangular frame building with a double veranda, just off the square, and it is conducted theoretically by a countryman, but in reality by his wife. Beard is a mild, bleached man of indeterminate age and of less than medium size, dressed always in a collarless shirt and a black evil pipe. He also owns the grist mill near the square, and he may be found either at the mill, or on the outskirts of the checker-game in the courthouse yard, or sitting in his stocking feet on the veranda of his hostelry. He is supposed to suffer from some obscure ailment puzzling to physicians, which prevents him exerting himself physically. His wife is a woman in a soiled apron, with straggling, damp grayish hair and an air of spent but indomitable capability. They have one son, a pale, quiet boy of twelve or so, who is always on the monthly honor roll at school; he may be seen on spring mornings schoolward bound with a bouquet of flowers. His rating among his contemporaries is not high.

Men only patronize the Beard hotel. Itinerant horse- and cattle-traders; countrymen in town overnight during court or the holiday season or arrested perhaps by inclement weather, stop there; and juries during court week——twelve good men and true marching in or out in column of twos, or aligned in chairs and spitting across the veranda rail with solemn and awesome decorum; and two of the town young bloods keep a room there, in which it is rumored dice and cards progress Sundays and drinking is done. But no women. If a skirt (other than Mrs Beard's gray apron) so much as flashes in the vicinity of its celibate portals, the city fathers investigate immediately, and woe to the peripatetic Semiramis if she be run to earth. Here, in company with a number of other bachelors—clerks, mechanics and such—the book-keeper Snopes lives.

And here he repaired when the bank day was finished. The afternoon was a replica of the morning. Then at three oclock the green shades were drawn upon door and windows, and Snopes and the cashier went about striking a daily balance. At 3:30 young Bayard arrived in his car and old Bayard stalked forth and got in it and was driven away. Presently thereafter the janitor, an ancient, practically incapacitated negro called Doctor Jones, came in and doddered futilely with a broom. By 4:30 he was done, and the cashier locked the vault and switched on the light above it, and he and the book-keeper emerged and locked the front door, and the cashier shook it experimentally.

After the bank closed that afternoon Snopes crossed the square and entered a street and approached a square frame building with a double veranda, from which the mournful cacophony of a cheap talking-machine came upon the afternoon. He entered. The music came from the room to the right and as he passed the door he saw a man in a collarless shirt sitting in a chair with his sock feet on another chair, smoking a pipe, the evil reek of which followed him down the hall. The hall smelled of damp, harsh soap, and the linoleum carpet gleamed, still wet. He followed it and approached a sound of steady, savage activity, and came upon a woman in a shapeless gray garment, who ceased mopping and looked at him across her gray shoulder, sweeping her lank hair from her brow with a reddened forearm.

"Evenin', Miz Beard," Snopes said. "Virgil come home yet?"

"He was through here a minute ago," she answered. "If he aint out front, I reckon his paw sent him on a arr'nd. Mr Beard's taken one of his spells in the hip agin. He might a sent Virgil on a arr'nd." Her hair fell lankly across her face again. Again she brushed it aside with a harsh gesture. "You got some mo' work fer him?"

"Yessum. You dont know which-a-way he went?"

"Ef Mr Beard aint sont him nowheres he mought be in the back yard. He dont usually go fur away." Again she dragged her dank hair aside; shaped so long to labor, her muscles were restive under inaction. She grasped the mop again.

Snopes went on, and stood on the kitchen steps above an enclosed space barren of grass and containing a chicken pen also grassless, in which a few fowls huddled or moved about in forlorn distraction in the dust. On one hand was a small kitchen garden of orderly, tended rows. In the corner of the yard was an outhouse of some sort, of weathered boards.

"Virgil," he said. The yard was desolate with ghosts; ghosts of discouraged weeds, of food in the shape of empty tins, broken boxes and barrels, a pile of stove wood and a chopping block across which lay an axe whose helve had been mended with rusty wire amateurishly wound. He descended the steps, and the chickens raised a discordant clamor, anticipating food.

"Virgil."

Sparrows found sustenance of some sort in the dust among the fowls, but the fowls themselves, perhaps with a foreknowledge of frustration and of doom, huddled back and forth along the wire, discordant and distracted, watching him with predatory importunate eyes. He was about to turn and reenter the kitchen when the boy appeared silently and innocently from the outhouse, with his straw-colored hair and his bland eyes. His mouth was pale and almost sweet, but secretive at the corners. His chin was negligible.

"Hi, Mr Snopes, you calling me?"

"Yes, if you aint doin' anything special," Snopes answered.

"I aint," the boy said. They entered the house and passed the room where the woman labored with drab fury. The reek of the pipe, the lugubrious reiteration of the phonograph, filled the hall, and they mounted stairs carpeted also with linoleum fastened to each step by a treacherous sheet-iron strip treated to resemble brass and scuffed and scarred by heavy feet. The upper hall was lined by two identical rows of doors. They entered one of these. The room contained a bed, a chair, a dressing-table and a washstand with a slop-jar beside it. The floor was covered with straw matting frayed in places. The single light hung unshaded from a greenish-brown cord; upon the wall above the paper-filled fireplace a framed lithograph of an Indian maiden in immaculate buckskin leaned her naked bosom above a formal moonlit pool of Italian marble. She held a guitar and a rose, and dusty sparrows sat on the window ledge and watched them brightly through the dusty screen.

The boy entered politely. His pale eyes took in the room and its contents at a comprehensive glance. He said: "That air gun aint come yet, has it, Mr Snopes?"

"No, it aint," Snopes answered. "It'll be here soon, though."

"You ordered off after it a long time, now."

"That's right. But it'll be here soon. Maybe they haven't got one in stock, right now." He crossed to the dresser and took from a drawer a few sheets of foolscap and laid them on the dresser top, and drew a chair up and dragged his suitcase from beneath the bed and set it on the chair. Then he took his fountain pen from his pocket and uncapped it and laid it beside the paper. "It ought to be here any day, now."

The boy seated himself on the suitcase and took up the pen. "They got 'em at Watts' hardware store," he suggested.

"If the one we ordered dont come soon, we'll git one there," Snopes said. "When did we order it, anyway?"

"Week ago Tuesday," the boy answered glibly. "I wrote it down."

"Well, it'll be here soon. You ready?"

The boy squared himself before the paper. "Yes, sir." Snopes took a folded paper from the top pocket of his trousers and spread it open.

"Code number forty eight. Mister Joe Butler, Saint Louis, Missouri," he read, then he leaned over the boy's shoulder, watching the pen. "That's right: up close to the top," he commended. "Now." The boy dropped down the page about two inches, and as Snopes read, he transcribed in his neat, copybook hand, pausing only occasionally to inquire as to the spelling of a word.

" 'I thought once I would try to forget you. But I cannot forget you because you cannot forget me. I saw my letter in your hand satchel today. Every day I can put my hand out and touch you you do not know it. Just to see you walk down the street To know what I know what you know. Some day we will both know to gether when you got use to it. You kept my letter but you do not anser. That is a good sign you do——' " The boy had reached the foot of the page. Snopes removed it, leaving the next sheet ready. He continued to read in his droning, inflectionless voice:

" '——not forget me you would not keep it. I think of you at night the way you walk down the street like I was dirt. You will get over this I can tell you something you will be surprised I know more than watch you walk down the street with cloths. I will some day you will not be surprised then. You pass me you do not know it I know it. You will know it some day. Be cause I will tell you.' Now," he said, and the boy dropped on to the foot of the page. " 'Yours truly Hal Wagner. Code number twenty one.' " Again he looked over the boy's shoulder. "That's right." He blotted the final sheet and gathered it up also. The boy recapped the pen and thrust the chair back, and Snopes produced a small paper bag from his coat.

The boy took it soberly. "Much obliged, Mr Snopes," he said. He opened it and squinted into it. "It's funny that air gun dont come on."

"It sure is," Snopes agreed. "I dont know why it dont come."

"Maybe it got lost in the postoffice," the boy suggested.

"It may have. I reckon that's about what happened to it. I'll write 'em again, tomorrow."

The boy rose, but he stood yet with his straw-colored hair and his bland, innocent face. He took a piece of candy from the sack and ate it without enthusiasm. "I reckon I better tell papa to go to the postoffice and ask 'em if it got lost."

"No, I wouldn't do that," Snopes said quickly. "You wait; I'll 'tend to it. We'll get it, all right."

"Papa wouldn't mind. He could go over there soon's he comes home and see about it. I could find him right now, and ask him to do it, I bet."

"He couldn't do no good," Snopes answered. "You leave it to me. I'll get that gun, all right."

"I could tell him I been working for you," the boy pursued. "I remember them letters."

"No, no, you wait and let me 'tend to it. I'll see about it first thing tomorrow."

"All right, Mr Snopes." He ate another piece of candy, without enthusiasm. He moved toward the door. "I remember

ever' one of them letters. I bet I could sit down and write 'em
all again. I bet I could. Say, Mr Snopes, who is Hal Wagner?
Does he live in Jefferson?"

"No, no. You never seen him. He dont hardly never come
to town. That's the reason I'm 'tending to his business for
him. I'll see about that air gun, all right."

The boy opened the door, then he paused again. "They got
'em at Watts' hardware store. Good ones. I'd sure like to have
one of 'em. Yes, sir, I sure would."

"Sure, sure," Snopes repeated. "Our'n'll be here tomorrow.
You just wait: I'll see you git that gun."

The boy departed. Snopes locked the door, and for a while
he stood beside it with his head bent, his hands slowly knotting and writhing together. Then he took up the folded sheet
and burned it over the hearth and ground the carbonized ash
to dust under his heel. With his knife he cut the address from
the top of the first sheet, the signature from the bottom of the
second, then he folded them and inserted them in a cheap envelope. He sealed this and stamped it, and took out his pen
and with his left hand he addressed the envelope in labored
printed characters. That night he took it to the station and
mailed it on the train.

The next afternoon Virgil Beard killed a mockingbird. It
was singing in the peach tree that grew in the corner of the
chicken-yard.

5.

At times, as Simon puttered about the place during the day,
he could look out across the lot and into the pasture and see
the carriage horses growing daily shabbier and less prideful
with idleness and the lack of their daily grooming, or he would
pass the carriage motionless in its shed, its tongue propped at
an accusing angle on the wooden mechanism he had invented
for that purpose, and in the harness room the duster and
tophat gathered slow dust on the nail in the wall, holding too
in their mute waiting a patient and questioning uncomplaint.
And at times when he stood shabby and stooped a little with
stubborn bewilderment and age on the veranda with its ancient
roses and wistaria and all its spacious and steadfast serenity

and watched Sartorises come and go in a machine a gentleman of his day would have scorned and which any pauper could own and only a fool would ride in, it seemed to him that John Sartoris stood beside him with his bearded and hawklike face and an expression of haughty and fine contempt.

And as he stood so, with afternoon slanting athwart the southern end of the porch and the heady and myriad odors of the waxing spring and the drowsy hum of insects and the singing of birds steady upon it, Isom within the cool doorway or at the corner of the house would hear his grandfather mumbling in a monotonous singsong in which were incomprehension and petulance and querulousness, and Isom would withdraw to the kitchen where his mother labored steadily with her placid yellow face and her endless crooning song.

"Pappy out dar talkin' to ole Marster agin," Isom told her. "Gimme dem cole 'taters, mammy."

"Aint Miss Jenny got some work fer you dis evenin'?" Elnora demanded, giving him the potatoes.

"No'm. She gone off in de cyar again."

"Hit's de Lawd's blessin' you and her aint bofe gone in it, like you is whenever Mist' Bayard'll let you. You git on outen my kitchen, now. I got dis flo' mopped and I dont want it tracked up."

Quite often these days Isom could hear his grandfather talking to John Sartoris as he labored about the stable or the flower beds or the lawn, mumbling away to that arrogant shade which dominated the house and the life that went on there and the whole scene itself across which the railroad he had built ran punily with distance but distinct with miniature verisimilitude, as though it were a stage set for the diversion of him whose stubborn dream, flouting him so deviously and cunningly while the dream was impure, had shaped itself fine and clear now that the dreamer was purged of the grossness of pride with that of flesh.

"Gent'mun equipage," Simon mumbled. He was busy again with his hoe in the salvia bed at the top of the drive. "Ridin' in dat thing, wid a gent'mun's proper equipage goin' ter rack en ruin in de barn." He wasn't thinking of Miss Jenny. It didn't make much difference what women rode in, their menfolks permitting. They only showed off a gentleman's equipage anyhow; they were but the barometers of his establishment, the glass of his gentility: horses themselves knew it. "Yo' own son, yo' own twin grandson ridin' right up in yo' face in a contraption like dat," he continued, "and you lettin' 'um do it. You bad ez dey is. You jes' got ter lay down de law ter 'um, Marse John; wid all dese foreign wars en sich de young folks is growed away fum de correck behavior; dey dont know how ter conduck deyselfs in de gent'mun way. Whut you reckon folks gwine think when dey sees yo' own folks ridin' in de same kine o' rig trash rides in? You jes' got ter resert yo'self, Marse John. Aint Sartorises sot de quality in dis country since befo' de War? And now jes' look at 'um."

He leaned on his hoe and watched the car swing up the drive and stop before the house. Miss Jenny and young Bayard got out and mounted to the veranda. The engine was still running, a faint shimmer of exhaust drifted upon the bright forenoon. Simon came up with his hoe and peered at the array of dials and knobs on the dash. Bayard turned in the door and spoke his name.

"Cut the switch off, Simon," he ordered.

"Cut de which whut off?" Simon said.

"That little bright lever by the steering wheel there. Turn it down."

"Naw, suh," Simon answered, backing away. "I aint gwine tech it. I aint gwine have it blowin' up in my face."

"It wont hurt you," Bayard said impatiently. "Just put your hand on it and pull it down. That little bright jigger there."

Simon peered doubtfully at the gadgets and things, but without coming any nearer, then he craned his neck further and stared over into the car. "I dont see nothin' but dis yere big lever stickin' up thoo de flo'. Dat aint de one you mentionin', is hit?" Bayard said "Hell." He descended in two strides and leaned across the door and cut the switch under Simon's curious blinking regard. The purr of the engine ceased.

"Well, now," Simon said. "Is dat de one you wuz talkin' erbout?" He stared at the switch for a time, then he straightened up and stared at the hood. "She's quit b'ilin' under dar, aint she? Is dat de way you stops her?" But Bayard had mounted the steps again and entered the house. Simon lingered a while longer, examining the gleaming long thing, dynamic as a

motionless locomotive and little awesome, touching it lightly
with his hand, then rubbing his hand on his thigh. He walked
slowly around it and touched the tires, mumbling to himself
and shaking his head, then he returned to his salvia bed, where
Bayard emerged presently and found him.

"Want to take a ride, Simon?" he said.

Simon's hoe ceased and he straightened up. "Who, me?"

"Sure. Come on. We'll go up the road a piece." Simon stood
with his static hoe rubbing his head slowly. "Come on," Bayard
said, "we'll just go up the road a piece. It wont hurt you."

"Naw, suh," Simon agreed. "I dont reckon hit's gwine ter
hurt me." He allowed himself to be drawn gradually toward
the car, gazing at its various members with slow blinking speculation, now that it was about to become an actual quantity
in his life. At the door and with one foot raised to the running board he made a final stand against the subtle powers of
evil judgment. "You aint gwine run it thoo de bushes like you
en Isom done dat day, is you?"

Bayard reassured him, and he got in slowly, with mumbled
sounds of anticipatory concern, and he sat well forward on the
seat with his feet drawn under him, clutching the door with
one hand and a lump of shirt on his chest with the other as
the car moved down the drive. They passed through the gates
and onto the road and still he sat hunched forward on the seat,
as the car gained speed, and with a sudden convulsive motion
he caught his hat just as it blew off his head.

"I 'speck dis is fur ernough, aint it?" he suggested, raising
his voice. He pulled his hat down on his head, but when he
released it he had to clutch wildly at it again, and he removed
it and clasped it beneath his arm, and again his hand fumbled
at his breast and clutched something beneath his shirt. "I got
to weed dat bed dis mawnin'," he said, louder still. "Please,
suh, Mist' Bayard," he added and his wizened old body sat yet
further forward on the seat and he cast quick covert glances at
the steadily increasing rush of the roadside growth.

Then Bayard leaned forward and Simon watched his forearm tauten, and then they shot forward on a roar of sound
like blurred thunder. Earth, the unbelievable ribbon of the
road, crashed beneath them and away behind into mad dust
convolvulae: a dun moiling nausea of speed, and the roadside

greenery was a tunnel rigid and streaming and unbroken. But he said no word, made no other sound, and when Bayard glanced the lipless cruel derision of his teeth at him presently, Simon knelt in the floor, his old disreputable hat under his arm and his hand clutching a fold of his shirt on his breast. Later the white man glanced at him again, and Simon was watching him and the blurred irises of his eyes were no longer a melting pupilless brown: they were red, and in the blast of wind they were unwinking and in them was that mindless phosphorescence of an animal's. Bayard jammed the throttle down to the floor.

The wagon was moving drowsily and peacefully along the road. It was drawn by two mules and was filled with negro women asleep in chairs. Some of them wore drawers. The mules themselves didn't wake at all, but ambled sedately on with the empty wagon and the overturned chairs, even when the car crashed into the shallow ditch and surged back onto the road again and thundered on without slowing. The thunder ceased, but the car rushed on under its own momentum, and it began to sway from side to side as Bayard tried to drag Simon's hands from the switch. But Simon knelt in the floor with his eyes shut tightly and the air blast toying with the grizzled remnant of his hair, holding the switch off with both hands.

"Turn it loose!" Bayard shouted.

"Dat's de way you stops it, Lawd! Dat's de way you stops it, Lawd!" Simon chanted, keeping the switch covered with his hands while Bayard hammered them with his fist. And he clung to it until the car slowed and stopped. Then he fumbled the door open and climbed out. Bayard called to him, but he went on back down the road at a limping rapid shuffle.

"Simon!" Bayard called again. But Simon went on stiffly, like a man who has been deprived of the use of his legs for a long time. "Simon!" But he neither slowed nor looked back, and Bayard started the car again and drove on until he could turn it. Simon now stood in the ditch beside the road, his head bent above his hands when Bayard overtook him and stopped.

"Come on here and get in," he commanded.

"Naw, suh. I'll walk."

"Jump in, now," Bayard ordered sharply. He opened the

door, but Simon stood in the ditch with his hand thrust inside his shirt, and Bayard could see that he was shaking as with an ague. "Come on, you old fool; I'm not going to hurt you."

"I'll walk home," Simon repeated stubbornly but without heat. "You git on wid dat thing."

"Ah, get in, Simon. I didn't know I'd scared you that bad. I'll drive slow. Come on."

"You git on home," Simon said again. "Dey'll be worried erbout you. You kin tell 'um whar I'm at."

Bayard watched him a moment, but Simon was not looking at him, and presently he slammed the door and drove on. Nor did Simon look up even then, even when the car burst once more into thunder and a soundless dun crash of fading dust. After a while the wagon emerged from the dust, the mules now at a high flop-eared trot, and jingled past him, leaving behind it upon the dusty insect-rasped air a woman's voice in a quavering wordless hysteria, passive and quavering and sustained. This faded slowly down the shimmering reaches of the valley and Simon removed from the breast of his shirt an object slung by a greasy cord about his neck. It was small and of no particular shape and it was covered with soiled napped fur: the first joint of the hind leg of a rabbit, caught supposedly in a graveyard in the dark of the moon, and Simon rubbed it through the sweat on his forehead and on the back of his neck, then he returned it to his bosom. His hands were still trembling, and he put his hat on and got back onto the road and turned toward home through the dusty noon.

Bayard drove on down the valley toward town, passing the iron gates and the serene white house among its old trees, and went on at speed. The sound of the unmuffled engine crashed into the dust and swirled it into lethargic bursting shapes, and faded across the planted land. Just outside of town he came upon another wagon and he held the car upon it until the mules reared, tilting the wagon; then he swerved and whipped past with not an inch to spare, so close that the yelling negro in the wagon could see the lipless and savage derision of his teeth.

He went on. In a mounting swoop like a niggard zoom the cemetery with his great-grandfather in pompous effigy gazing out across the valley and his railroad, flashed past, and he thought of old Simon trudging along the dusty road toward home, clutching his rabbit's foot, and again he felt savage and ashamed.

Town among its trees, its shady streets like green tunnels along which tight lives accomplished their peaceful tragedies, and he closed the muffler and at a sedate pace he approached the square. The clock on the courthouse lifted its four faces above the trees, in glimpses seen between arching vistas of trees. Ten minutes to twelve. At twelve exactly his grandfather would repair to the office in the rear of the bank and drink the pint of buttermilk which he brought in with him in a vacuum bottle every morning, and then sleep for an hour on the sofa there. When Bayard turned onto the square the tilted chair in the bank door was already vacant, and he slowed his car and eased it into the curb before a propped sandwich board. Fresh Catfish Today the board stated in letters of liquefied chalk, and through the screen doors beyond it came a smell of refrigerated food—cheese and pickle and such—with a faint overtone of fried grease.

He stood for a moment on the sidewalk while the noon throng parted and flowed about him. Negroes slow and aimless as figures of a dark placid dream, with an animal odor, murmuring and laughing among themselves. There was in their consonantless murmuring something ready with mirth, in their laughter something grave and sad; country people—men in overalls or corduroy or khaki and without neckties, women in shapeless calico and sunbonnets and snuff-sticks; groups of young girls in stiff mail-order finery, the young heritage of their bodies' grace dulled already by self-consciousness and labor and unaccustomed high heels and soon to be obscured forever by childbearing; youths and young men in cheap tasteless suits and shirts and caps, weather-tanned and clean-limbed as race horses and a little belligerently blatant. Against the wall squatting a blind negro beggar with a guitar and a wire frame holding a mouthorgan to his lips, patterned the background of smells and sounds with a plaintive reiteration of rich monotonous chords, rhythmic as a mathematical formula but without music. He was a man of at least forty and his was that patient resignation of many sightless years, yet he too wore filthy khaki with a corporal's stripes on one sleeve and a crookedly-sewn Boy Scout emblem on the other, and on his breast a button commemorating the fourth Liberty Loan and a small metal brooch bearing two gold stars, obviously intended for female adornment. His weathered derby was encircled by an officer's hat cord, and on the pavement between his feet sat a tin cup containing a dime and three pennies.

Bayard sought a coin in his pocket, and the beggar sensed his approach and his tune became a single repeated chord but without a break in the rhythm until the coin rang into the cup, and still without a break in the rhythm and the meaningless strains of the mouthorgan, his left hand dropped groping a little to the cup and read the coin in a single motion, then once more the guitar and mouthorgan resumed their monotonous pattern. As Bayard turned away someone spoke at his side—a broad squat man with a keen weathered face and gray temples. He wore corduroys and boots, and his body was the supple body of a horseman and his brown still hands were the hands that horses love. MacCallum his name, one of a family of six brothers who lived eighteen miles away in the hills, and with whom Bayard and John hunted foxes and 'coons during their vacations.

"Been hearing about that car of yourn," MacCallum said. "That's her, is it?" He stepped down from the curb and moved easily about the car, examining it, his hands on his hips. "Too much barrel," he said, "and she looks heavy in the withers. Clumsy. Have to use a curb on her, I reckon?"

"I dont," Bayard answered. "Jump in and I'll show you what she'll do."

"No, much obliged," the other answered. He stepped onto the pavement again, among the negroes gathered to stare at the car. The clock on the courthouse struck twelve, and already along the street there came in small groups children going home from school for the noon recess—little girls with colored boxes and skipping-ropes and talking sibilantly among themselves of intense feminine affairs, and boys in various stages of déshabillé shouting and scuffling and jostling the little girls, who shrank together and gave the little boys cold reverted glares. "Going to eat a snack," he explained. He crossed the pavement and opened the screen door. "You ate yet?" he asked, looking back. "Come on in a minute, anyway." And he patted his hip significantly.

The store was half grocery and confectionery and half restaurant. A number of customers stood about the cluttered but clean front section, with sandwiches and bottles of soda water, and the proprietor bobbed his head with flurried, slightly distrait affability above the counter to them. The rear half was filled with tables at which a number of men and a woman or so, mostly country people, sat eating with awkward and solemn decorum. Next to this was the kitchen, filled with frying odors and the brittle hissing of it, where two negroes moved like wraiths in a blue lethargy of smoke. They crossed this room and MacCallum opened a door set in an outthrust angle of the wall and they entered a smaller room, or rather a large closet. There was a small window high in the wall, and a bare table and three or four chairs, and presently the younger of the two negroes followed them.

"Yes, suh, Mr MacCallum and Mr Sartoris." He set two freshly rinsed glasses to which water yet adhered in sliding beads, on the table and stood drying his hands on his apron. He had a broad untroubled face, a reliable sort of face.

"Lemons and sugar and ice," MacCallum said. "You dont want none of that soda pop, do you?" The negro paused with his hand on the door.

"No," Bayard answered. "Rather have a toddy myself."

"Yes, suh," the negro agreed. "Y'all wants a toddy." And he bowed again with grave approval, and turned again and stepped aside as the proprietor in a fresh apron entered at his customary distracted trot and stood rubbing his hands on his thighs.

"Morning, morning," he said. "How're you, Rafe? Bayard, I saw Miss Jenny and the old Colonel going up to Doc Peabody's office the other day. Aint nothing wrong, is there?" His head was like an inverted egg; his hair curled meticulously away from the part in the center into two careful reddish-brown wings, like a toupée, and his eyes were a melting passionate brown.

"Come in here and shut that door," MacCallum ordered, drawing the other into the room. He produced from beneath his coat a bottle of astonishing proportions and set it on the table. It contained a delicate amber liquid and the proprietor rubbed his hands on his thighs and his hot mild gaze gloated upon it.

"Great Savior," he said, "where'd you have that demijohn hid? in your pants leg?" MacCallum uncorked the bottle and extended it and the proprietor leaned forward and sniffed it, his eyes closed. He sighed.

"Henry's," MacCallum said. "Best run he's made in six months. Reckon you'd take a drink if Bayard and me was to hold you?" The other cackled loudly, unctuously.

"Aint he a comical feller, now?" he asked Bayard. "Some joker, aint he?" He glanced at the table. "You aint got but two gl——" Someone tapped at the door: the proprietor leaned his conical head to it and waggled his hand at them. MacCallum concealed the bottle without haste as the other opened the door. It was the negro, with another glass, and lemons and sugar and a cracked bowl of ice. The proprietor admitted him.

"If they want me up front, tell 'em I've stepped out but I'll be back in a minute, Houston."

"Yes, suh," the negro replied, setting his burden on the table. MacCallum produced the bottle again.

"What do you keep on telling your customers that old lie, for?" he asked. "Everybody knows what you are doing."

The proprietor cackled again, gloating upon the bottle. "Yes, sir," he repeated, "he's sure some joker. Well, you boys have got plenty of time, but I got to get on back and keep things running."

"Go ahead," MacCallum told him, and the proprietor made himself a toddy. He raised the glass, stirring it and sniffing it alternately while the others followed suit. Then he removed his spoon and laid it on the table.

"Well, I hate to hurry a good thing mighty bad," he said, "but business dont wait on pleasure, you know."

"Work does interfere with a man's drinking," MacCallum agreed.

"Yes, sir, it sure does," the other replied. He raised his glass. "Your father's good health," he said. He drank. "I dont see the old gentleman in town much, now a days."

"No," MacCallum answered. "He aint never got over Buddy being in the Yankee army. Claims he aint coming to town again until the Democratic party denies Woodrow Wilson."

"It'll be the best thing they ever done, if they was to recall him and elect a man like Debs or Senator Vardaman president," the proprietor agreed sagely. "Well, that sure was fine. Henry's sure a wonder, aint he?" He set his glass down and turned to the door. "Well, you boys make yourselves at home. If you want anything, just call Houston." And he bustled out at his distracted trot.

"Sit down," MacCallum said. He drew up a chair, and Bayard drew another up opposite across the table. "Deacon sure ought to know good whisky. He's drunk enough of it to float his counters right on out the front door." He filled his glass and pushed the bottle across to Bayard, and they drank again, quietly.

"You look bad, son," MacCallum said suddenly, and Bayard raised his head and found the other examining him with his keen steady eyes. "Overtrained," he added, and Bayard made an abrupt gesture of negation and raised his glass again, but he could still feel the other watching him steadily. "Well, you haven't forgot how to drink good whisky, anyhow. . . . Why dont you come out and take a hunt with us? Got an old red we been saving for you. Been running him off and on for two years, now, with the young dogs. Aint put old General on him yet, because the old feller'll nose him out, and we wanted to save him for you boys. John would have enjoyed that fox. You remember that night Johnny cut across down to Samson's bridge ahead of the dogs, and when we got there, here come him and the fox floating down the river on that drift log, the fox on one end and Johnny on the other, singing that fool song as loud as he could yell? John would have enjoyed this here fox. He outsmarts them young dogs every time. But old General'll get him."

Bayard sat turning his glass in his hand. He reached a packet of cigarettes from his jacket and shook a few of them onto the table at his hand and flipped the packet across to the other. MacCallum drank his toddy steadily and refilled his glass. Bayard lit a cigarette and emptied his glass and reached for the bottle. "You look like hell, boy," MacCallum repeated.

"Dry, I reckon," Bayard answered in a voice as level as the

other's. He made himself another toddy, his cigarette smoking on the table edge. He raised the glass, but instead of drinking he held it for a moment to his nose while the muscles at the base of his nostrils tautened whitely, then he swung the glass from him and with a steady hand he emptied it onto the floor. The other watched him quietly while he poured his glass half full of raw liquor and sloshed a little water into it and tilted it down his throat. "I've been good too damn long," he said aloud, and he fell to talking of the war. Not of combat, but rather of a life peopled by young men like fallen angels, and of a meteoric violence like that of fallen angels, beyond heaven or hell and partaking of both: doomed immortality and immortal doom.

MacCallum sat and listened quietly, drinking his whisky steadily and slowly and without appreciable effect, as though it were milk he drank; and Bayard talked on and presently found himself without surprise eating food. The bottle was now less than half full. The negro Houston had brought the food in and had his drink, taking it neat and without batting an eye. "Ef I had a cow dat give dat, de calf wouldn't git no milk a-tall," he said, "and I wouldn't never churn. Thanky, Mr MacCallum, suh."

Then he was out, and Bayard's voice went on, filling the cubby-hole of a room, surmounting the odor of cheap food too quickly cooked and of sharp spilt whisky, with ghosts of a thing high-pitched as a hysteria, like a glare of fallen meteors on the dark retina of the world. Again a light tap at the door, and the proprietor's egg-shaped head and his hot diffident eyes.

"You gentlemen got everything you want?" he asked, rubbing his hands on his thighs.

"Come and get it," MacCallum said, jerking his head toward the bottle, and the other made himself a toddy in his stale glass and drank it while Bayard finished his tale of himself and an Australian major and two ladies in the Leicester lounge one evening (the Leicester lounge being out of bounds, and the Anzac lost two teeth and his girl, and Bayard himself got a black eye), watching the narrator with round melting astonishment.

"Great Savior," he said, "them av'aytors was sure some hell-raisers, wadn't they? Well, I reckon they're wanting me up front again. You got to keep on the jump to make a living, these days." And he scuttled out again.

"I've been good too goddam long," Bayard repeated harshly, watching MacCallum fill the two glasses. "That's the only thing Johnny was ever good for. Kept me from getting in a rut. Bloody rut, with a couple of old women nagging at me, and nothing to do except scare niggers." He drank his whisky and set the glass down, still clutching it. "Damn ham-handed hun," he said. "He never could fly anyway. I kept trying to keep him from going up there on that goddam popgun," and he cursed his dead brother savagely. Then he raised his glass again, but halted it halfway to his mouth. "Where in hell did my drink go?"

MacCallum emptied the bottle into Bayard's glass, and he drank again and banged the thick tumbler on the table and rose and lurched back against the wall. His chair crashed over backward, and he braced himself, staring at the other. "I kept on trying to keep him from going up there, with that Camel. But he gave me a burst. Right across my nose."

MacCallum rose also. "Come on here," he said quietly, and he offered to take Bayard's arm, but Bayard evaded him and they passed through the kitchen and traversed the long tunnel of the store. Bayard walked steadily enough, and the proprietor bobbed his head at them across the counter.

"Call again, gentlemen," he said. "Call again."

"All right, Deacon," MacCallum answered. Bayard strode on. As they passed the soda-fountain a young lawyer standing beside a stranger, addressed him.

"Captain Sartoris, shake hands with Mr Gratton here. Gratton was up on the British front last spring." The stranger turned and extended his hand, but Bayard stared at him bleakly and strode so steadily on that the other involuntarily gave back in order not to be overborne.

"Why, God damn his soul," he said to Bayard's back. The lawyer grasped his arm.

"He's drunk," he whispered quickly, "he's drunk."

"I dont give a damn," the other exclaimed loudly. "Because he was a goddam shave-tail he thinks——"

"Shhhh, shhhh," the lawyer hissed. The proprietor came to the corner of his candy case, and peered out with hot round alarm.

"Gentlemen, gentlemen!" he exclaimed. The stranger made another violent movement, and Bayard stopped.

"Wait a minute while I bash his face in," he told MacCallum, turning. The stranger thrust the lawyer aside and stepped forward.

"You never saw the day—" he began. MacCallum took Bayard's arm firmly and easily.

"Come on here, boy."

"I'll bash his bloody face in," Bayard stated, looking bleakly at the angry stranger. The lawyer grasped his companion's arm again.

"Get away," the stranger said, flinging him off. "Just let him try it. Come on, you limey——"

"Gentlemen! Gentlemen!" the proprietor wailed.

"Come on here, boy," MacCallum said. "I've got to look at a horse."

"A horse?" Bayard repeated. He turned obediently, then he stopped and looked back. "Cant bash your face in now," he told the stranger. "Sorry. Got to look at a horse. Call for you later at the hotel." But the stranger's back was turned, and behind it the lawyer grimaced and waggled his hand at MacCallum.

"Get him away, MacCallum, for God's sake."

"Bash his face in later," Bayard repeated. "Cant bash yours, though, Eustace," he told the lawyer. "Taught us in ground-school never seduce a fool nor hit a cripple."

"Come on, here," MacCallum repeated, leading him on. At the door Bayard must stop again to light a cigarette; then they went on. It was three oclock and again they walked among school children in released surges. Bayard strode steadily enough, and a little belligerently, and soon MacCallum turned into a side street and they went on, passing negro stores, and between a busy grist mill and a silent cotton gin they turned into a lane filled with tethered horses and mules. From the end of the lane an anvil clanged. They passed the ruby glow of it and a patient horse standing on three legs in the blacksmith's doorway and the squatting overalled men along the shady wall, and came then to a high barred gate backing a long dun-colored brick tunnel smelling of ammonia. A few men sat on the top of the gate, others leaned their crossed arms upon it, and from the paddock itself came voices, then through the slatted gate gleamed a haughty motionless shape of burnished flame.

The stallion stood against the yawning cavern of the livery stable door like a motionless bronze flame, and along its burnished coat ran at intervals little tremors of paler flame, little tongues of nervousness and pride. But its eye was quiet and arrogant, and occasionally and with a kingly air its gaze swept along the group at the gate with a fine disdain, without seeing them as individuals at all, and again little tongues of paler flame rippled flicking along its coat. About its head was a rope hackamore; it was tethered to a door post, and in the background a white man moved about at a respectful distance with a proprietorial air: beside him, a negro hostler with a tow sack tied about his middle with a string. MacCallum and Bayard halted at the gate, and the white man circled the stallion's haughty immobility and crossed to them. The negro hostler came forth also, with a soft dirty cloth and chanting in a mellow singsong. The stallion permitted him to approach and suffered him to erase with his rag the licking nervous little flames that ran in renewed ripples under its skin.

"Aint he a picture, now?" the white man demanded of Mac-Callum, leaning his elbow on the gate. A cheap nickel watch was attached to his suspender loop by a length of raw hide lace leather worn black and soft with age, and his shaven beard was heaviest from the corners of his mouth to his chin; he looked always as though he were chewing tobacco with his mouth open. He was a horse trader by profession, and he was constantly engaged in litigation with the railroad company over the violent demise of his stock by its agency. "Look at that nigger, now," he added. "He'll let Tobe handle him like a baby. I wouldn't get within ten foot of him, myself. Dam'f I know how Tobe does it. Must be some kin between a nigger and a animal, I always claim."

"I reckon he's afraid you'll be crossing the railroad with him some day about the time 39 is due," MacCallum said drily.

"Yes, I reckon I have the hardest luck of any feller in this county," the other agreed. "But they got to settle this time: I got 'em dead to rights this time."

"Yes," MacCallum said. "The railroad company ought to

furnish that stock of yourn with time tables." The other onlookers guffawed.

"Ah, the company's got plenty of money," the trader rejoined. Then he said: "You talk like I might have druv them
mules in front of that train. Lemme tell you how it come
about—"

"I reckon you wont never drive him in front of no train."
MacCallum jerked his head toward the stallion. The negro
burnished its shimmering coat, crooning to it in a monotonous singsong. The trader laughed.

"I reckon not," he admitted. "Not less'n Tobe goes, too.
Just look at him, now. I wouldn't no more walk up to that
animal than I'd fly."

"I'm going to ride that horse," Bayard said suddenly.

"What hoss?" the trader demanded, and the other onlookers watched Bayard climb the gate and vault over into the lot.
"You let that hoss alone, young feller," the trader said. But
Bayard paid him no heed. He went on; the stallion swept its
regal regard upon him and away. "You let that hoss alone,"
the trader shouted, "or I'll have the law on you."

"Let him be," MacCallum said.

"And let him damage a fifteen hundred dollar stallion? That
hoss'll kill him. You, Sartoris!"

From his hip pocket MacCallum drew a wad of bills enclosed by a rubber band. "Let him be," he repeated. "That's
what he wants."

The trader glanced at the roll of money with quick calculation. "I take you gentlemen to witness——" he began loudly,
then he ceased and they watched tensely as Bayard approached
the stallion. The beast swept its haughty glowing eye upon
him again and lifted its head without alarm and snorted. The
negro glanced over his shoulder and crouched against the
animal, and his crooning chant rose to a swifter beat. "Go
back, white folks," he said. The beast snorted again and swept
its head up, snapping the rope like a gossamer thread, and the
negro grasped at the flying rope-end.

"Git away, white folks," he cried. "Git away, quick."

But the stallion eluded his hand. It cropped its teeth in a
vicious arc and the negro leaped sprawling as the animal
soared like a bronze explosion. Bayard had dodged beneath

the sabering hooves and as the horse swirled in a myriad flicking like fire, the spectators saw that the man had contrived
to take a turn with the rope-end about its jaws, then they saw
the animal rear again, dragging the man from the ground
and whipping his body like a rag upon its flashing arc. Then
it stopped trembling as Bayard closed its nostrils with the
twisted rope, and suddenly he was upon its back while it stood
with lowered head and rolling eyes, rippling its coat into quivering tongues before exploding again.

The beast burst like bronze unfolding wings: a fluid desperation; the onlookers tumbled away from the gate and
hurled themselves to safety as the gate splintered to match-
wood beneath its soaring volcanic thunder. Bayard crouched
on its shoulders and dragged its mad head around and they
swept down the lane, spreading pandemonium among the
horses and mules tethered and patient about the blacksmith
shop and among the wagons there. Where the lane debouched
into the street a group of negroes scattered before them, and
without a break in its stride the stallion soared over a small
negro child clutching a stick of striped candy directly in its
path. A wagon drawn by mules was just turning into the lane:
these reared madly before the wild slack-jawed face of the
white man in the wagon, and again Bayard sawed his thun-
derbolt around and headed it away from the square. Down
the lane behind him the spectators ran, shouting through the
dust, the trader among them, and Rafe MacCallum still clutching his roll of money.

The stallion moved beneath him like a tremendous mad
music, uncontrolled, splendidly uncontrollable. The rope
served only to curb its direction, not its speed, and among
shouts from the pavement on either hand he swung the animal
into another street. This was a quieter street; soon they would
be in the country and the stallion could exhaust its rage without the added hazards of motors and pedestrians. Voices faded
behind him in his own thunder: "Runaway! Runaway!" but
the street was deserted save for a small automobile going in
the same direction, and further along beneath the green
tunnel, bright small spots of color scuttled out of the street.
Children. Hope they stay there, he said to himself. His eyes
were streaming a little; beneath him the surging lift and fall;

in his nostrils a sharpness of rage and energy and violated pride like smoke from the animal's body, and he swept past the motor car, remarking in a flashing second a woman's face and a mouth partly open and two eyes round with tranquil astonishment. But the face flashed away without registering on his mind and he saw the children huddled on one side of the street, and on the opposite side a negro playing a hose on the sidewalk, and beside him a second negro with a pitchfork.

Someone screamed from a veranda, and the huddle of children broke, shrieking; a small figure in a white shirt and diminutive pale blue pants darted into the street, and Bayard leaned forward and wrapped the rope about his hand and swerved the beast toward the opposite sidewalk, where the two negroes stood gapemouthed. The small figure came on, flashed safely behind, then a narrow band of rushing green; a tree trunk like a wheel spoke in reverse, and the stallion struck clashing fire from wet concrete. It slid, clashed, fighting for balance, lunged and crashed down; and for Bayard, a red shock, then blackness. The horse scrambled up and whirled and poised and struck viciously at the prone man with its hooves, but the negro with the pitchfork drove it away and it trotted stiffly and with tossing head up the street and passed the halted motor car. At the end of the street it stood trembling and snorting and permitted the negro hostler to touch it. Rafe MacCallum still clutched his roll of bills.

6.

They gathered him up and brought him to town in a commandeered motor car and roused Dr Peabody from slumber. Dr Peabody profanely bandaged Bayard's head and gave him a drink from the bottle which resided in the cluttered waste basket and threatened to telephone Miss Jenny if he didn't go straight home. Rafe MacCallum promised to see that he did so, and the owner of the impressed automobile offered to drive him out. It was a ford body with, in place of a tonneau, a miniature one room cabin of sheet iron and larger than a dog kennel, in each painted window of which a painted housewife simpered across a painted sewing machine, and in it an actual sewing machine neatly fitted, borne thus about the countryside by the agent. The agent's name was V. K. Suratt and he now sat with his shrewd plausible face behind the wheel. Bayard with his humming head sat beside him, and to the fender clung a youth with brown forearms and a slanted extremely new straw hat, who let his limber body absorb the jolts with negligent ease as they rattled sedately out of town on the valley road.

The drink Dr Peabody had given him, instead of quieting his jangled nerves, rolled sluggishly and hotly in his stomach and served only to nauseate him a little, and against his closed eyelids red antic shapes coiled in throbbing and tedious cycles. He watched them dully and without astonishment as they emerged from blackness and swirled sluggishly and consumed themselves and reappeared, each time a little fainter as his mind cleared. And yet, somewhere blended with them, yet at the same time apart and beyond them with a tranquil aloofness and steadfast among their senseless convolutions, was a face. It seemed to have some relation to the instant itself as it culminated in crashing blackness; at the same time it seemed, for all its aloofness, to be a part of the whirling ensuing chaos; a part of it, yet bringing into the red vortex a sort of constant coolness like a faint, shady breeze. So it remained, aloof and not quite distinct, while the coiling shapes faded into a dull unease of physical pain from the jolting of the car, leaving about him like an echo that cool serenity and something else— a sense of shrinking yet fascinated distaste, of which he or something he had done, was the object.

Evening was coming. On either hand cotton and corn thrust green spears above the rich, dark soil, and in the patches of woodland where the sun slanted among violet shadows doves called moodily. After a time Suratt turned from the highway into a faint, rutted wagon road between a field and a patch of woods and they drove straight into the sun, and Bayard removed his hat and held it before his face.

"Sun hurt yo' haid?" Suratt asked. " 'Taint long, now." The road wound presently into the woods where the sun was intermittent, and it rose to a gradual, sandy crest. Beyond this the land fell away in ragged, ill-tended fields and beyond them in a clump of sorry fruit trees and a stunted grove of silver poplar shrubs pale as absinthe and twinkling ceaselessly with no wind, a weathered small house squatted. Beyond it and much larger loomed a barn gray and gaunt with age. The road forked here. One faint arm curved sandily away toward the house; the other went on between rank weeds toward the barn. The youth on the fender leaned his head into the car. "Drive on to the barn," he directed.

Suratt obeyed. Beyond the bordering weeds a fence straggled in limp dilapidation, and from the weeds beside it the handles of a plow stood at a gaunt angle while its shard rusted peacefully in the undergrowth, and other implements rusted half concealed there—skeletons of labor healed over by the earth they were to have violated, kinder than they. The fence turned at an angle and Suratt stopped the car and the youth stepped down and opened the warped wooden gate and Suratt drove on into the barnyard where stood a wagon with drunken wheels and a home-made bed, and the rusting skeleton of a ford car. Low down upon its domed and bald radiator the two lamps gave it an expression of beetling patient astonishment, like a skull, and a lean cow ruminated and watched them with moody eyes.

The barn doors sagged drunkenly from broken hinges, held to the posts with twists of rusty wire; beyond, the cavern of the hallway yawned in stale desolation—a travesty of earth's garnered fullness and its rich inferences. Bayard sat on the fender and leaned his bandaged head against the side of the car and watched Suratt and the youth enter the barn and mount slowly on invisible ladder rungs. The cow chewed in slow dejection, and upon the yellow surface of a pond enclosed by banks of trodden and sun-cracked clay, geese drifted like small muddy clouds. The sun fell in a long slant upon their rumps and upon their suave necks and upon the cow's gaunt rhythmically twitching flank, ridging her visible ribs with dingy gold. Presently Suratt's legs fumbled into view, followed by his cautious body, and after him the youth slid easily down the ladder in one-handed swoops.

He emerged carrying an earthen jug close against his leg. Suratt followed in his neat tieless blue shirt and jerked his head at Bayard, and they turned the corner of the barn among waist-high jimson weeds. Bayard overtook them as the youth with his jug slid with a single motion between two lax strands of barbed wire. Suratt stooped through more sedately and held the top strand taut and set his foot on the lower one until Bayard was through. Behind the barn the ground descended into shadow toward a junglish growth of willow and elder, against which a huge beech and a clump of saplings stood like mottled ghosts, and from which a cool dankness rose like a breath to meet them. The spring welled from the roots of the beech into a wooden frame sunk to its top in white sand that quivered ceaselessly and delicately beneath the water's limpid unrest, and went on into the willow and elder growth.

The earth about the spring was trampled smooth and packed as an earthen floor. Near the spring a blackened iron pot sat on four bricks, beneath it was a heap of pale wood-ashes and a litter of extinct brands and charred fagot-ends. Against the pot leaned a scrubbing board with a ridged metal face, and a rusty tin cup hung from a nail in the tree above the spring. The youth set the jug down and he and Suratt squatted beside it.

"I dont know if we aint a-goin' to git in trouble, givin' Mr Bayard whisky, Hub," Suratt said. "Still, Doc Peabody give him one dram hisself, so I reckon we kin give him one mo'. Aint that right, Mr Bayard?" Squatting he looked up at Bayard with his shrewd affable face. Hub twisted the corn cob stopper from the jug and passed it to Suratt, who tendered it to Bayard. "I been knowin' Mr Bayard ever since he was a chap in knee pants," Suratt confided to Hub, "but this is the first time me and him ever taken a drink together. Aint that so, Mr Bayard? . . . . I reckon you'll want a drinkin' cup, wont you?" But Bayard was already drinking, with the jug tilted across his horizontal forearm and the mouth held to his lips by the same hand, as it should be done. "He knows how to drink outen a jug, dont he?" Suratt added. "I knowed he was all right," he said in a tone of confidential vindication. Bayard lowered the jug and returned it to Suratt, who tendered it formally to Hub.

"Go ahead," Hub said. "Hit it." Suratt did so, with measured pistonings of his adam's apple. Above the stream gnats whirled and spun in a levelling ray of sunlight like erratic golden chaff. Suratt lowered the jug and passed it to Hub and wiped his mouth on the back of his hand.

"How you feel now, Mr Bayard?" he asked. Then he said heavily: "You'll have to excuse me. I reckon I ought to said Cap'm Sartoris, oughtn't I?"

"What for?" Bayard asked. He squatted also on his heels, against the bole of the beech tree. The rising slope of ground behind them hid the barn and the house, and the three of them squatted in a small bowl of peacefulness remote from the world and time, and filled with the cool and limpid breathing of the spring and a seeping of sunlight among the elders and willows like a thinly diffused wine. On the surface of the spring the sky lay reflected, stippled over with windless beech leaves. Hub squatted leanly with his brown forearms clasped about his knees, smoking a cigarette beneath the tilt of his hat. Suratt was across the spring from him. He wore a faded blue shirt, and in contrast to it his hands and his face were a rich even brown, like mahogany. The jug sat rotundly, benignantly between them.

"Yes, sir," Suratt repeated, "I always find the best cure fer a wound is plenty of whisky. Doctors, these here fancy young doctors, 'll tell a feller different, but old Doc Peabody hisself cut off my granpappy's laig while granpappy laid back on the kitchen table with a demijohn in his hand and a mattress and a cheer acrost his laigs and fo' men a-holdin' him down, and him cussin' and singin' so scandalous the women-folks and the chillen went down to the pasture behind the barn and waited. Take some mo'," he said, and he reached the jug across the spring and Bayard drank again. "Reckon you're beginnin' to feel pretty fair, aint you?"

"Damned if I know," Bayard answered. "It's dynamite, boys."

Suratt poised the jug and guffawed, then he lipped it and his adam's apple pumped again in relief against the wall of elder and willow. The elder would soon flower, with pale clumps of tiny blooms. Miss Jenny made a little wine of it every year. Good wine, if you knew how and had the patience. Elder flower wine. Like a ritual for a children's game; a game played by little girls in small pale dresses, between supper and twilight. Above the bowl where sunlight yet came in a level-ling beam, gnats whirled and spun like dust-motes in a still, disused room. Suratt's voice went on affably, ceaselessly re-capitulant, in polite admiration of the hardness of Bayard's head and the fact that this was the first time he and Bayard had ever taken a drink together. They drank again, and Hub began to borrow cigarettes of Bayard and he too became a little profanely and robustly anecdotal in his country idiom, about whisky and girls and dice; and presently he and Suratt were arguing amicably about work. They appeared to be able to sit tirelessly and without discomfort on their heels, but Bayard's legs had soon grown numb and he straightened them, tingling with released blood, and he now sat with his back against the tree and his long legs straight before him, hearing Suratt's voice without listening to it.

His head was now no more than a sort of taut discomfort; at times it seemed to float away from his shoulders and hang against the green wall like a transparent balloon within which or beyond which that face that would neither emerge completely nor yet fade completely away, lingered with shadowy exasperation—two eyes round with a grave shocked astonishment, two lifted hands flashing behind little white shirt and blue pants swerving into a lifting rush plunging clatter crash blackness. . . . . . .

Suratt's slow plausible voice went on steadily, but without any irritant quality. It seemed to fit easily into the still scene, speaking of earthy things. "Way I learnt to chop cotton," he was saying, "my oldest brother taken and put me in the same row ahead of him. Started me off, and soon's I taken a lick or two, here he come behind me. And ever' time my hoe chopped once I could year his'n chop twice. I never had no shoes in them days, neither," he added drily. "So I had to learn to chop fast, with that 'ere hoe of his'n cuttin' at my bare heels. But I swo' then, come what mought, that I wouldn't never plant nothin' in the ground, soon's I could he'p myself. It's all right fer folks that owns the land, but folks like my folks was dont never own no land, and ever' time we made a furrow, we was scratchin' dirt fer somebody else." The gnats danced and whirled more madly yet in the sun above the secret places of the stream, and the sun's light was taking on a rich copper tinge. Suratt rose. "Well, boys, I got to git on back to'ds town, myself." He looked at Bayard again with his shrewd kind face. "I reckon Mr Bayard's clean fergot that knock he taken, aint he?"

"Dammit," Bayard said. "Quit calling me Mr Bayard."

Suratt picked up the jug. "I knowed he was all right, when you got to know him," he told Hub. "I been knowin' him since he was knee-high to a grasshopper, but me and him jest aint been throwed together like this. I was raised a pore boy, fellers, while Mr Bayard's folks has lived on that 'ere big place with plenty of money in the bank and niggers to wait on 'em. But he's all right," he repeated. "He aint goin' to say nothin' about who give him this here whisky."

"Let him tell, if he wants," Hub answered. "I dont give a damn."

They drank again. The sun was almost gone and from the secret marshy places of the stream came a fairy-like piping of young frogs. The gaunt invisible cow lowed barnward, and Hub replaced the corn cob in the jug and drove it home with a blow of his palm and they mounted the hill and crawled through the fence. The cow stood in the barn door and watched them approach and lowed again, moody and mournful, and the geese had left the pond and they now paraded sedately across the barnyard toward the house, in the door of which, framed by two crepe-myrtle bushes, a woman stood.

"Hub," she said in a flat country voice.

"Goin' to town," Hub answered shortly. "Sue'll have to milk."

The woman stood quietly in the door. Hub carried the jug into the barn and the cow followed him, and he heard her and turned and gave her a resounding kick in her gaunt ribs and cursed her without heat. Presently he reappeared and went on to the gate and opened it and Suratt drove through. Then he closed it and wired it to again and swung onto the fender. Bayard moved over and prevailed on Hub to get inside. The woman stood yet in the door, watching them quietly. About the doorstep the geese surged erratically with discordant cries, their necks undulant and suave as formal gestures in a pantomime.

The shadow of the fruit trees fell long across the untidy fields, and the car pushed its elongated shadow before it like the shadow of a huge humpshouldered bird. They mounted the sandy hill in the last of the sun and dropped downward out of sunlight and into violet dusk. The road was soundless with sand and the car lurched in the worn and shifting ruts and on to the highroad again.

The waxing moon stood overhead. As yet it gave off no light though, and they drove on toward town, passing an occasional country wagon homeward bound; these Suratt, who knew nearly every soul in the county, greeted with a grave gesture of his brown hand, and presently where the road crossed a wooden bridge among more willow and elder where dusk was yet denser and more palpable, Suratt stopped the car and climbed out over the door. "You fellers set still," he said. "I wont be but a minute. Got to fill that 'ere radiator." They heard him at the rear of the car, then he reappeared with a tin bucket and let himself gingerly down the roadside bank beside the bridge. Water chuckled and murmured beneath the bridge, invisible with twilight, its murmur burdened with the voice of cricket and frog. Above the willows that marked the course of the stream gnats still spun and whirled, for bullbats appeared from nowhere in long swoops, in midswoop vanished, then appeared again against the serene sky swooping, silent as drops of water on a window-pane; swift and noiseless and intent as though their wings were feathered with twilight and with silence.

Suratt scrambled up the bank, with his pail, and removed the cap and tilted the bucket above the radiator. The moon stood without emphasis overhead, yet a faint shadow of Suratt's head and shoulders fell upon the hood of the car and upon the pallid planking of the bridge the leaning willow fronds were faintly and delicately pencilled in shadow. The last of the water gurgled with faint rumblings into the engine's interior and Suratt replaced the pail and climbed over the blind door. The lights operated from a generator; he switched these on now. While the car was in low speed the lights glared to crescendo, but when he let the clutch in they dropped to a wavering glow no more than a luminous shadow.

Night was fully come when they reached town. Across the land the lights on the courthouse clock were like yellow beads above the trees, and upon the green afterglow a column of smoke stood like a balanced plume. Suratt put them out at the restaurant and drove on, and they entered and the proprietor raised his conical head and his round melting eyes from behind the soda fountain.

"Great Savior, boy," he exclaimed. "Aint you gone home yet? Doc Peabody's been huntin' you ever since four oclock, and Miss Jenny drove to town in the carriage, lookin' for you. You'll kill yourself."

"Get to hell on back yonder, Deacon," Bayard answered, "and bring me and Hub about two dollars' worth of ham and eggs."

Later they returned for the jug in Bayard's car, Bayard and Hub and a third young man, freight agent at the railway station, with three negroes and a bull fiddle in the rear seat. But they drove no further than the edge of the field above the house and stopped there while Hub went on afoot down the sandy road toward the barn. The moon stood pale and cold overhead, and on all sides insects shrilled in the dusty undergrowth. In the rear seat the negroes murmured among themselves.

"Fine night," Mitch, the freight agent, suggested. Bayard made no reply. He smoked moodily, his head closely helmeted in its white bandage. Moon and insects were one, audible and visible, dimensionless and unsourced.

After a while Hub materialized against the dissolving vagueness of the road, crowned by the silver slant of his hat, and he came up and swung the jug onto the door and removed the stopper. Mitch passed it to Bayard.

"Drink," Bayard said, and Mitch did so, then the others drank.

"We aint got nothin' for the niggers to drink out of," Hub said.

"That's so," Mitch agreed. He turned in his seat. "Aint one of you boys got a cup or something?" The negroes murmured again, questioning one another in mellow consternation.

"Wait," Bayard said. He got out and lifted the hood and removed the cap from the breather-pipe. "It'll taste a little like oil for a drink or two, but you boys wont notice it after that."

"Naw, suh," the negroes agreed in chorus. One took the cup and wiped it out with the corner of his coat, and they too drank in turn, with smacking expulsions of breath. Bayard replaced the cap and got in the car.

"Anybody want another right now?" Hub asked, poising the corn cob.

"Give Mitch another," Bayard directed. "He'll have to catch up."

Mitch drank again. Then Bayard took the jug and tilted it. The others watched him respectfully.

"Dam'f he dont drink it," Mitch murmured. "I'd be afraid to hit it so often, if I was you."

"It's my damned head." Bayard lowered the jug and passed it to Hub. "I keep thinking another drink will ease it off some."

"Doc put that bandage on too tight," Hub said. "Want it loosened some?"

"I dont know." Bayard lit another cigarette and threw the match away. "I believe I'll take it off. It's been on there long enough." He raised his hands and fumbled at the bandage.

"You better let it alone," Mitch warned him. But he continued to fumble at the fastening, then he slid his fingers beneath a turn of the cloth and tugged at it savagely. One of the negroes leaned forward with a pocket knife and severed it, and they watched him as he stripped it off and flung it away.

"You ought not to done that," Mitch told him.

"Ah, let him take it off, if he wants," Hub said. "He's all right." He got in and stowed the jug away between his knees. Bayard backed the car around. The sandy road hissed beneath the broad tires of it and rose shaling into the woods again where the dappled moonlight was intermittent, treacherous with dissolving vistas. Invisible and sourceless among the shifting patterns of light and shade whip-poor-wills were like flutes tongued liquidly. The road passed out of the woods and descended, with sand in shifting and silent lurches, and they turned on to the valley road and away from town.

The car went on, on the dry hissing of the closed muffler. The negroes murmured among themselves with mellow snatches of laughter whipped like scraps of torn paper away behind. They passed the iron gates and Bayard's home serenely in the moonlight among its trees, and the silent boxlike flag station and the metal-roofed cotton gin on the railroad siding. The road rose at last into hills. It was smooth and empty and winding, and the negroes fell silent as Bayard increased speed.

But still it was not anything like what they had anticipated of him. Twice more they stopped and drank, and then from an ultimate hilltop they looked down upon another cluster of lights like a clotting of beads upon the pale gash where the railroad ran. Hub produced the breather cap and they drank again.

Through streets identical with those at home they moved slowly, toward an identical square. People on the square turned and looked after them curiously. They crossed the square and followed another street and went on between broad lawns and shaded windows, and presently beyond an iron fence and well back among black and silver trees, lighted windows hung in ordered tiers like rectangular lanterns strung among the branches.

They stopped here in shadow. The negroes descended and lifted the bass viol out, and a guitar. The third one held a slender tube frosted over with keys upon which the intermittent moon glinted in pale points, and they stood with their heads together, murmuring among themselves and touching plaintive muted chords from the strings. Then the one with the clarinet raised it to his lips.

The tunes were old tunes. Some of them were sophisticated tunes and formally intricate, but in the rendition this was lost and all of them were imbued instead with a plaintive similarity, a slurred and rhythmic simplicity, and they drifted in rich plaintive chords upon the silver air fading, dying in minor reiterations along the treacherous vistas of the moon. They played again, an old waltz. The college Cerberus came across the dappled lawn to the fence and leaned his arms upon it, a lumped listening shadow among other shadows. Across the street, in the shadows there, other listeners stood; a car approached and slowed into the curb and shut off engine and lights, and in the tiered windows heads leaned, aureoled against the lighted rooms behind, without individuality, feminine, distant, delicately and divinely young.

They played "Home, Sweet Home" and when the rich minor died away, across to them came a soft clapping of slender palms. Then Mitch sang "Goodnight, Ladies" in his true, oversweet tenor, and the young hands were more importunate; and as they drove away the slender heads leaned aureoled with bright hair in the lighted windows and the soft clapping drifted after them for a long while, fainter and fainter in the silver silence and the moon's infinitude.

At the top of the first hill out of town they stopped and Hub removed the breather cap. Behind them random lights among the trees, and it was as though there came yet to them across the hushed world that sound of young palms like flung delicate flowers before their masculinity and their youth, and they drank without speaking, lapped yet in the fading magic of the lost moment. Mitch sang to himself softly; the car slid purring on again. The road dropped curving smoothly, empty and blanched. Bayard spoke, his voice harsh, abrupt.

"Cut out, Hub," he said. Hub bent forward and reached under the dash and the car swept on with a steady leashed muttering like waking thunderous wings, then the road flattened in a long swoop toward another rise and the muttering leaped to crescendo and the car shot forward with neck-snapping violence. The negroes had stopped talking; one of them raised a wailing shout.

"Reno lost his hat," Hub said, looking back.

"He dont need it," Bayard replied. The car roared up this hill and rushed across the crest of it and flashed around a tight curve.

"Oh, Lawd," the negro wailed. "Mr Bayard!" The air-blast stripped his words away like leaves. "Lemme out, Mr Bayard!"

"Jump out, then," Bayard answered. The road fell from beneath them like a tilting floor and away across a valley, straight now as a string. The negroes clutched their instruments and held to one another. The speedometer showed 55 and 60 and turned gradually on. Sparse houses flashed slumbering away, and fields and patches of woodland like tunnels.

The road went on across the black and silver land. Whippoor-wills called on either side, one to another in quiring liquid reiterations; now and then as the headlights swept in the road's abrupt windings two spots of pale fire blinked in the dust before the bird blundered awkwardly somewhere beneath the radiator. The ridge rose steadily, with wooded slopes falling away on either hand. Sparse negro cabins squatted on the slopes or beside the road, dappled with shadow and lightless and profound with slumber; beneath trees before them wagons stood or warped farm implements leaned, shelterless, after the shiftless fashion of negroes.

The road dipped, then rose again in a long slant broken by another dip; then it stood directly before them like a wall. The car shot upward and over the dip, left the road completely, then swooped dreadfully on, and the negroes' concerted wail whipped forlornly away. Then the ridge attained its crest and the car's thunder ceased and it rolled to a stop. The negroes now sat in the bottom of the tonneau.

"Is dis heaven?" one murmured after a time.

"Dey wouldn't let you in heaven, wid licker on yo' breaf and no hat, feller," another said.

"Ef de Lawd dont take no better keer of me dan He done of dat hat, I dont wanter go dar, noways," the first rejoined.

"Mmmmmmm," the second agreed. "When us come down dat 'ere las' hill, dis yere cla'inet almos' blowed clean outen my han', let 'lone my hat."

"And when us jumped over dat 'ere lawg er whutever it wuz back dar," the third one added, "I thought fer a minute dis whole auto'bile done blowed outen my han'."

They drank again. It was high here, and the air moved with grave coolness. On either hand lay a valley filled with silver mist and with whip-poor-wills; beyond these valleys the silver earth rolled on into the sky. Across it, mournful and far, a dog howled. Bayard's head was as cool and clear as a clapperless bell, within it that face emerged clearly at last: those two eyes round with grave astonishment, winged serenely by two dark wings of hair. It was that Benbow girl, he said to himself, and he sat for a while, gazing into the sky. The lights on the town clock were steadfast and yellow and unwinking in the dissolving distance, but in all other directions the world rolled away in slumberous ridges, milkily opaline.

All of her instincts were antipathetic toward him, toward his violence and his brutally obtuse disregard of all the qualities which composed her being. His idea was like a trampling of heavy feet in those cool corridors of hers, in that grave serenity in which her days accomplished themselves; at the very syllables of his name her instincts brought her upstanding and under arms against him, thus increasing, doubling the

sense of violation by the act of repulsing him and by the necessity for it. And yet, despite her armed sentinels, he still
crashed with that hot violence of his through the bastions and
thundered at the very inmost citadel of her being. Even chance
seemed to abet him, lending to his brutal course a sort of theatrical glamor, a tawdry simulation of the virtues which the
reasons (if he had reasons) for his actions outwardly ridiculed.
That mad flaming beast he rode almost over her car and then
swerved it with an utter disregard of consequences to himself
onto a wet sidewalk in order to avoid a frightened child; the
pallid, suddenly dreaming calm of his bloody face from which
violence had been temporarily wiped as with a damp cloth,
leaving it still with that fine bold austerity of Roman statuary,
beautiful as a flame shaped in bronze and cooled: the outward
form of its energy but without its heat.

Her appetite was gone at supper, and Aunt Sally Wyatt
mouthed her prepared soft food and mumbled querulously at
her because she wouldn't eat.

"My mother saw to it that I drank a good cup of bark tea
when I come sulking to the table and wouldn't eat," Aunt
Sally stated, "but folks nowadays think the good Lord's going
to keep 'em well and them lifting no finger."

"I'm all right," Narcissa insisted. "I just dont want any
supper."

"That's what you say. Let yourself get down, and Lord
knows, I aint strong enough to wait on you. In my day young
folks had more consideration for their elders." She mouthed
her food unprettily, querulously and monotonously retrospective, while Narcissa toyed restively with the food she
could not eat.

Later Aunt Sally continued her monologue while she rocked
with her interminable fancy-work on her lap. She would never
divulge what it was to be when completed, nor for whom, and
she had been working on it for fifteen years, carrying about
with her a shapeless bag of dingy threadbare brocade containing odds and ends of colored fabric in all possible shapes.
She could never bring herself to trim any of them to any pattern, so she shifted and fitted and mused and fitted and shifted
them like pieces of a patient puzzle picture, trying to fit them
to a pattern or to create a pattern about them without using

her scissors, smoothing her colored scraps with flaccid, putty-colored fingers, shifting and shifting them. From the bosom of her dress the needle Narcissa had threaded for her dangled its spidery skein.

Across the room Narcissa sat, with a book. Aunt Sally's voice droned on with querulous interminability while Narcissa read. Suddenly she rose and laid the book down and crossed the room and entered the alcove where her piano sat. But she had not played four bars before her hands crashed in discord, and she shut the piano and went to the telephone.

Miss Jenny thanked her for her solicitude tartly, and dared to say that Bayard was all right, still an active member of the so-called human race, that is, since they had received no official word from the coroner. No, she had heard nothing of him since Loosh Peabody had phoned her at four oclock that Bayard was on his way home with a broken head. The broken head she readily believed, but the other part of the message she had put no credence in whatever, having lived with those damn Sartorises eighty years and knowing that home would be the last place in the world a Sartoris with a broken head would ever consider going. No, she was not even interested in his present whereabouts, and she hoped he hadn't injured the horse? Horses were valuable animals.

Narcissa returned to the living room and explained to Aunt Sally whom she had been talking to and why, and drew a low chair to the lamp and took up her book.

"Well," Aunt Sally said after a time, "if you aint going to talk any. . . ." She fumbled her scraps together and crammed them into the bag. "I thank the Lord sometimes you and Horace aint any blood of mine, the way you all go on. But if you'd drink it, I dont know who's to get sassafras for you: I aint able to, and you wouldn't know it from dog fennel or mullein, yourself."

"I'm all right," Narcissa protested.

"Go ahead," Aunt Sally repeated, "get flat on your back, with me and that trifling nigger to take care of you. She aint wiped off a picture frame in six months, to my certain knowledge. And I've done everything but beg and pray."

She rose and said goodnight and hobbled from the room. Narcissa sat and turned the pages on, hearing the other mount the stairs with measured laborious tappings of her stick, and for a while longer she sat and turned the pages of her book. But presently she flung the book away and went to the piano again, but Aunt Sally thumped on the floor overhead with her stick, and she desisted and returned to her book. So it was with actual pleasure that she greeted Dr Alford a moment later.

"I was passing and heard your piano," he explained. "You haven't stopped?"

She explained that Aunt Sally had gone to bed, and he sat formally and talked to her in his stiff pedantic way on cold and erudite subjects for two hours. Then he departed and she stood in the door and watched him down the drive. The moon stood overhead; along the drive cedars in a rigid curve were pointed against the pale, faintly spangled sky.

She returned to the living room and got her book and turned out the lights and mounted the stairs. Across the hall Aunt Sally snored with genteel placidity, and Narcissa stood for a moment, listening to the homely noise. I will be glad when Horry gets home, she thought, going on.

She turned on her light and undressed and took her book to bed, where she again held her consciousness submerged deliberately as you hold a puppy under water until its struggles cease. And after a time her mind surrendered to the book and she read on, pausing from time to time to think warmly of sleep, reading again. And so when the negroes first blended their instruments beneath the window, she paid them only the most perfunctory notice. Why in the world are those jellybeans serenading me? she thought with faint amusement, visioning immediately Aunt Sally in her night-cap leaning from a window and shouting them away. And she lay with the book open, seeing upon the spread page the picture she had created while the plaintive rhythm of the strings and clarinet drifted into the open window.

Then she sat bolt upright, with a sharp and utter certainty, and clapped the book shut and slipped from bed. From the adjoining room she looked down.

The negroes were grouped on the lawn: the frosted clarinet, the guitar, the sober comic bulk of the viol. At the street entrance to the drive a motor car stood in shadow. The musicians

played once, then a voice called from the car, and they retreated across the lawn and the car moved away, without
lights. She was certain, then: no one else would play one tune
beneath a lady's window, just enough to waken her from
sleep, then go away.

She returned to her room. The book lay face down upon
the bed, but she went to the window and stood there, between
the parted curtains, looking out upon the black and silver
world and the peaceful night. The air moved upon her face
and amid the fallen dark wings of her hair with grave coolness. . . . "The beast, the beast," she whispered to herself. She
let the curtains fall and on her silent feet she descended the
stairs again and found the telephone in the darkness, muffling
its bell when she rang.

Miss Jenny's voice came out of the night with its usual brisk
and cold asperity, and without surprise or curiosity. No, he
had not returned home, for he was by now safely locked up
in jail, she believed, unless the city officers were too corrupt
to obey a lady's request. Serenading? Fiddlesticks. What
would he want to go serenading for? he couldn't injure himself serenading, unless someone killed him with a flat iron or
an alarm clock. And why was she concerned about him?

Narcissa hung up, and for a moment she stood in the darkness, beating her fists on the telephone's unresponsive box.
The beast, the beast.

She received three callers that night. One came formally, the
second came informally, the third came anonymously. The
garage which sheltered her car was a small brick building surrounded by evergreens. One side of it was a continuation of
the garden wall. Beyond the wall a grass-grown lane led back
to another street. The garage was about fifteen yards from the
house and its roof rose to the level of the first-floor windows:
Narcissa's bedroom windows looked out upon the slate roof
of it.

This third caller entered by the lane and mounted onto the
wall and thence onto the garage roof, where he now lay in the
shadow of a cedar, sheltered so from the moon. He had lain
there for a long time. The room facing him was dark when he
arrived, but he had lain in his fastness quiet as an animal and

with an animal's patience, without movement save to occasionally raise his head and reconnoiter the immediate scene with covert dartings of his eyes.

But the room facing him remained dark while an hour passed. In the meantime a car entered the drive (he recognised it; he knew every car in town) and a man entered the house. The second hour passed and the room was still dark and the car stood yet in the drive. Then the man emerged and drove away, and a moment later the lights downstairs went out, and then the window facing him glowed and through the sheer curtains he saw her moving about the room, watched the shadowy motions of her disrobing. Then she passed out of his vision. But the light still burned and he lay with a still and infinite patience, lay so while another hour passed and another car stopped before the house and three men carrying an awkwardly shaped burden came up the drive and stood in the moonlight beneath the window; lay so until they played once and went away. When they had gone she came to the window and parted the curtains and stood for a while in the dark fallen wings of her hair, looking directly into his hidden eyes.

Then the curtains fell again, and once more she was a shadowy movement beyond them. Then the light went off, and he lay face down on the steep pitch of the roof, utterly motionless for a long time, darting from beneath his hidden face covert ceaseless glances, quick and darting and all-embracing as those of an animal.

To Narcissa's house they came finally. They had visited the dark homes of all the other unmarried girls one by one and sat in the car while the negroes stood on the lawn with their blended instruments. Heads had appeared at darkened windows, sometimes lights went up; once they were invited in, but Hub and Mitch hung diffidently back, once refreshment was sent out to them, once they were heartily cursed by a young man who happened to be sitting with the young lady on the dark veranda. In the meantime they had lost the breather cap, and as they moved from house to house all six of them drank fraternally from the jug, turn and turn about. At last they reached the Benbows' and played once beneath the cedars. There was a light yet in one window, but none came to it.

The moon stood well down the sky. Its light was now a cold silver upon things, spent and a little wearied, and the world was empty as they rolled without lights along a street lifeless and fixed in black and silver as any street in the moon itself. Beneath stippled intermittent shadows they went, passed quiet intersections dissolving away, occasionally a car motionless at the curb before a house. A dog crossed the street ahead of them trotting, and went on across a lawn and so from sight, but saving this there was no movement anywhere. The square opened spaciously about the absinthe-cloudy mass of elms that surrounded the courthouse. Among them the round spaced globes were more like huge pallid grapes than ever. Above the exposed vault in each bank burned a single bulb; inside the hotel lobby, before which a row of cars was aligned, another burned. Other lights there were none.

They circled the courthouse, and a shadow moved near the hotel door and detached itself from shadow and came to the curb, a white shirt glinting within a spread coat, and as the slow car swung away toward another street, the man hailed them. Bayard stopped and the man came through the blanched dust and laid his hand on the door.

"Hi, Buck," Mitch said. "You're up pretty late, aint you?"

The man had a sober, good-natured horse's face and he wore a metal star on his unbuttoned waistcoat. His coat humped slightly on his hip.

"What you boys doin'?" he asked. "Been to a dance?"

"Serenading," Bayard answered. "Want a drink, Buck?"

"No, much obliged." He stood with his hand on the door, gravely and goodnaturedly serious. "Aint you fellers out kind of late, yourselves?"

"It is gettin' on," Mitch agreed. The marshal lifted his foot to the running board. Beneath his hat his eyes were in shadow. "We're going in now," Mitch said. The other pondered quietly, and Bayard added:

"Sure; we're on our way home now."

The marshal moved his head slightly and spoke to the negroes.

"I reckon you boys are about ready to turn in, aint you?"

"Yes, suh," the negroes answered, and they got out and lifted the viol out. Bayard gave Reno a bill and they thanked him and said goodnight and picked up the viol and departed quietly down a side street. The marshal turned his head again.

"Aint that yo' car in front of Rogers' café, Mitch?" he asked.

"Reckon so. That's where I left it."

"Well, suppose you run Hub out home, lessen he's goin' to stay in town tonight. Bayard better come with me."

"Aw, hell, Buck," Mitch protested.

"What for?" Bayard demanded.

"His folks are worried about him," the other answered. "They aint seen hide nor hair of him since that stallion throwed him. Where's yo' bandage, Bayard?"

"Took it off," he answered shortly. "See here, Buck, we're going to put Mitch out and then Hub and me are going straight home."

"You been on yo' way home ever since fo' oclock, Bayard," the marshal replied soberly, "but you dont seem to git no nearer there. I reckon you better come with me tonight, like yo' aunt said."

"Did Aunt Jenny tell you to arrest me?"

"They was worried about you, son. Miss Jenny just 'phoned and asked me to kind of see if you was all right until mawnin'. So I reckon we better. You ought to went on home this evenin'."

"Aw, have a heart, Buck," Mitch protested.

"I ruther make Bayard mad than Miss Jenny," the other answered patiently. "You boys go on, and Bayard better come with me."

Mitch and Hub got out and Hub lifted out his jug and they said goodnight and went on to where Mitch's ford stood before the restaurant. The marshal got in beside Bayard. The jail was not far. It loomed presently above its walled court, square and implacable, its slitted upper windows brutal as sabre blows. They turned into an alley and the marshal descended and opened a gate. Bayard drove into the grassless littered compound and stopped while the other went on ahead to a small garage in which stood a ford. He backed this out and motioned Bayard forward. The garage was built to the ford's dimensions, and about a third of Bayard's car stuck out the door of it.

"Better'n nothin', though," the marshal said. "Come on." They entered through the kitchen, into the jailkeeper's living quarters, and Bayard waited in a dark passage until the other found a light. Then they entered a bleak neat room, containing spare conglomerate furnishings and a few scattered articles of masculine apparel.

"Say," Bayard objected. "Aren't you giving me your bed?"

"Wont need it befo' mawnin'," the other answered. "You'll be gone, then. Want me to he'p you off with yo' clothes?"

"No. I'm all right." Then, more graciously: "Goodnight, Buck, and much obliged."

"Goodnight," the marshal answered. He closed the door behind him and Bayard removed his coat and shoes and his tie and snapped the light off and lay on the bed. Moonlight seeped into the room impalpably, refracted and sourceless; the night was without any sound. Beyond the window a cornice rose in a succession of shallow steps against the opaline and dimensionless sky. His head was clear and cold. The whisky he had drunk was completely dead. Or rather, it was as though his head were one Bayard who watched curiously and impersonally that other Bayard who lay in a strange bed and whose alcohol-dulled nerves radiated like threads of ice through that body which he must drag forever about a bleak and barren world with him. "Hell," he said, lying on his back, staring out the window where nothing was to be seen, waiting for sleep, not knowing if it would come or not, not caring a particular damn either way. Nothing to be seen, and the long long span of a man's natural life. Three score and ten years, to drag a stubborn body about the world and cozen its insistent demands. Three score and ten, the bible said. Seventy years. And he was only twenty-six. Not much more than a third through it. Hell.

THREE

HORACE BENBOW in his clean, wretchedly-fitting khaki
which but served to accentuate his air of fine and delicate futility, and laden with an astonishing impedimenta of
knapsacks and kitbags and paper-wrapped parcels, got off the
two-thirty train. Across the tight clotting of descending and
ascending passengers the sound of his spoken name reached
him, and he roved his distraught gaze like a somnambulist
rousing to avoid traffic, about the agglomerate faces. "Hello,
hello," he said, then he thrust himself clear and laid his bags
and parcels on the edge of the platform and moved with intent
haste up the train toward the baggage car.

"Horace!" his sister called again, running after him. The station agent emerged from his office and stopped him and held
him like a finely-bred restive horse and shook his hand, and
thus his sister overtook him. He turned at her voice and came
completely from out his distraction and swept her up in his
arms until her feet were off the ground, and kissed her on the
mouth.

"Dear old Narcy," he said, kissing her again. Then he set
her down and stroked his hands on her face, as a child would.
"Dear old Narcy," he repeated, touching her face with his fine
spatulate hands, gazing at her as though he were drinking that
constant serenity of hers through his eyes. He continued to
say Dear old Narcy, stroking his hands on her face, utterly
oblivious of his surroundings until she recalled him.

"Where in the world are you going, up this way?"

Then he remembered, and released her and rushed on, she
following, and stopped again at the door of the baggage car,
from which the station porter and a trainhand were taking
trunks and boxes as the baggage clerk tilted them out.

"Cant you send down for it?" she asked. But he stood peering into the car, oblivious of her again. The two negroes returned and he stepped aside, still looking into the car with
peering, bird-like motions of his head. "Let's send back for it,"
his sister said again.

"What? Oh. I've seen it every time I changed cars," he told her, completely forgetting the sense of her words. "It'd be rotten luck to have it go astray right at my doorstep, wouldn't it?" Again the negroes moved away with a trunk, and he stepped forward again and peered into the car. "That's just about what happened to it; some clerk forgot to put it on the train at M—— There it is," he interrupted himself. "Easy now, cap," he called in the country idiom, in a fever of alarm as the clerk slammed into the door a box of foreign shape stencilled with a military address. "She's got glass in her."

"All right, colonel," the baggage clerk agreed. "We aint hurt her none, I reckon. If we have, all you got to do is sue us." The two negroes backed up to the door and Horace laid his hands on the box as the clerk tilted it outward. "Easy now, boys," he repeated nervously, and he trotted beside them as they crossed to the platform. "Set it down easy, now. Here, sis, lend a hand, will you?"

"We got it all right, cap'm," the station porter said. "We aint gwine drop it." But Horace continued to dab at it with his hands, and as they set it down he leaned his head to it. "She's all right, aint she?" the station porter asked.

"It's all right," the train porter assured him. He turned away. "Le's go," he called.

"I think it's all right," Horace agreed, his ear against the box. "I dont hear anything. It's packed pretty well." The engine whistled and Horace sprang erect, digging in his pocket, and ran to the moving cars. The porter was closing the vestibule, but he leaned down to Horace's hand and straightened up and touched his cap. Horace returned to his box and gave another coin to the second negro. "Put it in the house for me, careful, now," he directed. "I'll be back for it in a few minutes."

"Yes, suh, Mr Benbow. I'll look out fer it."

"I thought it was lost, once," he confided, slipping his arm inside his sister's, and they moved toward the car. "It was delayed at Brest and didn't come until the next boat. I had the first outfit I bought—a small one—with me, and I pretty near lost that one, too. I was blowing a small one in my cabin on the boat one day, when the whole thing, cabin and all, took fire. The captain decided that I'd better not try it again until we got ashore, what with all the men on board. The vase turned out pretty well, though," he babbled. "Lovely little thing. I'm catching on; I really am. Venice. A voluptuous dream, a little sinister. Must take you there, some day." Then he squeezed her arm and fell to repeating Dear old Narcy, as though the homely sound of the nickname on his tongue was a taste he loved and had not forgotten. A few people still lingered about the station. Some of them spoke to him and he stopped to shake their hands, and a marine private with the Second Division Indian head on his shoulder remarked the triangle on Horace's sleeve and made a vulgar sound of derogation through his pursed lips.

"Howdy, buddy," Horace said, turning upon him his shy startled gaze.

"Evenin', general," the marine answered. He spat, not exactly at Horace's feet, and not exactly anywhere else. Narcissa clamped her brother's arm against her side.

"Do come on home and get into some decent clothes," she said in a lower tone, hurrying him along.

"Get out of uniform?" he said. "I rather fancied myself in khaki," he added, a little hurt. "You really think I am ridiculous in this?"

"Of course not," she answered immediately, squeezing his hand. "Of course not. I'm sorry I said that. You wear it just as long as you want to."

"It's a good uniform," he said soberly. "I dont mean this," he said, gesturing toward the symbol on his arm. They went on. "People will realize that in about ten years, when noncombatants' hysteria has worn itself out and the individual soldiers realize that the A.E.F. didn't invent disillusion."

"What did it invent?" she asked, holding his arm against her, surrounding him with the fond, inattentive serenity of her affection.

"God knows. . . . . . Dear old Narcy," he said again, and they crossed the platform toward her car. "So you have dulled your palate for khaki."

"Of course not," she repeated, shaking his arm a little as she released it. "You wear it just as long as you want to." She opened the car door. Someone called after them and they looked back and saw the porter trotting after them with

Horace's hand-luggage, which he had walked off and left lying on the platform.

"Oh, Lord," he exclaimed, "I worry with it for four thousand miles, then lose it on my own doorstep. Much obliged, Sol." The porter stowed the things in the car. "That's the first outfit I got," Horace added to his sister. "And the vase I blew on shipboard. I'll show it to you when we get home."

His sister got in under the wheel. "Where are your clothes? In the box?"

"Haven't any. Had to throw most of 'em away to make room for the other things. No room for anything else."

Narcissa sat and looked at him for a moment with fond exasperation. "What's the matter?" he asked innocently. "Forget something yourself?"

"No. Get in. Aunt Sally's waiting to see you."

They drove on and mounted the shady gradual hill toward the square, and Horace looked about happily upon familiar scenes. Sidings with freight cars; the platform which in the fall would be laden with cotton bales in serried rotund ranks; the town power plant, a brick building from which there came a steady, unbroken humming and about which in the spring gnarled heaven-trees swung ragged lilac bloom against the harsh ocher and Indian red of a clay cut-bank. Then a street of lesser residences, mostly new. Same tight little houses with a minimum of lawn—homes built by country-bred people and set close to the street after the country fashion; occasionally a house going up on a lot which had been vacant sixteen months ago when he went away. Then other streets opened away beneath arcades of green, shadier, with houses a little older and more imposing as they got away from the station's vicinity; and pedestrians, usually dawdling negro boys at this hour or old men bound townward after their naps, to spend the afternoon in sober futile absorptions.

The hill flattened away into the plateau on which the town proper had been built these hundred and more years ago, and the street became definitely urban presently with garages and small new shops with merchants in shirt-sleeves and customers; the picture show with its lobby plastered with life episodic in colored lithographic mutations. Then the square, with its unbroken low skyline of old weathered brick and fading dead names stubborn yet beneath scaling paint, and drifting negroes in casual and careless o.d. garments worn by both sexes and country people in occasional khaki too; and the brisker urbanites weaving among their placid chewing unhaste and among the men in tilted chairs before certain stores.

The courthouse was of brick too, with stone arches rising among elms, and among the trees the monument of the confederate soldier stood, his musket at order arms, shading his carven eyes with his stone hand. Beneath the porticoes of the courthouse and upon benches about the green, the city fathers sat and talked and drowsed, in uniform too, here and there. But it was the gray of Old Jack and Beauregard and Joe Johnston, and they sat in a grave sedateness of minor political sinecures, smoking and spitting about unhurried checkerboards. When the weather was bad they moved inside to the circuit clerk's office.

It was here that the young men loafed also, pitching dollars or tossing baseballs back and forth or lying on the grass until the young girls in their little colored dresses and cheap nostalgic perfume should come trooping down town through the late afternoon to the drug store. When the weather was bad the young men loafed in the drug stores or in the barber shop.

"Lots of uniforms yet," Horace remarked. "All be home by June. Have the Sartoris boys come home yet?"

"John is dead," his sister answered. "Didn't you know?"

"No," he answered quickly, with swift concern. "Poor old Bayard. Rotten luck they have. Funny family. Always going to wars, and always getting killed. And young Bayard's wife died, you wrote me."

"Yes. But he's here. He's got a racing automobile and he spends all his time tearing around the country. We are expecting every day to hear he's killed himself in it."

"Poor devil," Horace said, and again: "Poor old Colonel. He used to hate an automobile like a snake. Wonder what he thinks about it."

"He goes with him."

"What? Old Bayard in a motor car?"

"Yes. Miss Jenny says it's to keep Bayard from turning it over. But she says Colonel Sartoris doesn't know it, but that

Bayard would just as soon break both their necks. That he probably will before he's done." She drove on across the square, among tethered wagons and cars parked casually and without order. "I hate Bayard Sartoris," she said with sudden vehemence. "I hate all men." Horace looked at her quickly.

"What's the matter? What's Bayard done to you? No, that's backward. What have you done to Bayard?" But she didn't answer. She turned into another street bordered by negro stores of one story and shaded by metal awnings beneath which negroes lounged, skinning bananas or small florid cartons of sweet biscuits; and then a grist mill driven by a spasmodic gasoline engine. It oozed chaff and a sifting dust mote-like in the sun, and above the door a tediously hand-lettered sign: W. C. Beards Mill. Between it and a shuttered and silent gin draped with feathery soiled festoons of lint, an anvil clanged at the end of a short lane filled with wagons and horses and mules, and shaded by mulberry trees beneath which countrymen in overalls squatted. "He ought to have more consideration for the old fellow than that," Horace said fretfully. "Still, they've just gone through with an experience that pretty well shook the verities and the humanities, and whether they know it or not, they've got another one ahead of 'em that'll pretty well finish the business. Give him a little time. . . . . . . But I personally cant see why he shouldn't be allowed to kill himself, if that's what he thinks he wants. Sorry for Miss Jenny, though."

"Yes," his sister agreed, quietly again. "They're worried about Colonel Sartoris' heart, too. Everybody except him and Bayard, that is. I'm glad I have you instead of one of those Sartorises, Horry." She laid her hand quickly and lightly on his thin knee.

"Dear old Narcy," he said, then his face clouded again. "Damn scoundrel," he said. "Well, it's their trouble. How's Aunt Sally been?"

"All right." And then: "I *am* glad you're home, Horry."

The shabby small shops were behind, and now the street opened away between old shady lawns, spacious and quiet. These homes were quite old, in appearance at least, and, set well back from the street and its dust, they emanated a gracious and benign peace, steadfast as a windless afternoon in a world without motion or sound. Horace looked about him and drew a long breath.

"Perhaps this is the reason for wars," he said. "The meaning of peace."

The meaning of peace. They turned into an intersecting street narrower but more shady and even quieter, with a golden Arcadian drowse, and turned through a gate in a honeysuckle-covered fence of iron pickets. From the gate the cinder-packed drive rose in a grave curve between cedars. The cedars had been set out by an English architect of the '40s, who had built the house (with the minor concession of a veranda) in the funereal light tudor which the young Victoria had sanctioned; and beneath and among them, even on the brightest days, lay a resinous exhilarating gloom. Mockingbirds loved them, and catbirds, and thrushes demurely mellifluous in the late afternoon; but the grass beneath them was sparse or nonexistent and there were no insects save fireflies in the dusk.

The drive ascended to the house and curved before it and descended again to the street in an unbroken arc of cedars. Within the arc rose a lone oak, broad and huge and low; around its trunk ran a wooden bench. About this halfmoon of lawn and without the arc of the drive, were bridal wreath and crepe-myrtle bushes old as time, and huge as age, would make them. Big as trees they were, and in one fence corner was an astonishing clump of stunted banana palms and in the other a lantana with its clotted wounds, which Francis Benbow had brought home from Barbados in a tophat-box in '71.

About the oak and from the funereal scimitar of the drive descending, lawn flowed streetward with good sward broken by random clumps of jonquil and narcissus and gladiolus. Originally the lawn was in terraces and the flowers a formal bed on the first terrace. Then Will Benbow, Horace's and Narcissa's father, had had the terraces obliterated. It was done with plows and scrapers and seeded anew with grass, and he had supposed the flower bed destroyed. But the next spring the scattered bulbs sprouted again, and now every year the lawn was stippled with bloom in yellow, white and pink without order. A certain few young girls asked and received permission to pick some of them each spring, and neighbors' children played quietly among them and beneath the cedars. At the top of the drive, where it curved away descending again, sat the brick doll's house in which Horace and Narcissa lived, surrounded always by that cool, faintly-stringent odor of cedar trees.

It was trimmed with white and it had mullioned casements brought out from England; along the veranda eaves and above the door grew a wistaria vine like heavy tarred rope and thicker than a man's wrist. The lower casements stood open upon gently billowing curtains; upon the sill you expected to see a scrubbed wooden bowl, or at least an immaculate and super-cilious cat. But the window sill held only a wicker work-basket from which, like a drooping poinsettia, spilled an end of patchwork in crimson and white; and in the doorway Aunt Sally, a potty little woman in a lace cap, leaned upon a gold-headed ebony walking stick.

Just as it should be, and Horace turned and looked back at his sister crossing the drive with the parcels he had forgotten again. The meaning of peace.

He banged and splashed happily in his bathroom, shouting through the door to his sister where she sat on his bed. His discarded khaki lay upon a chair, holding yet through long as-sociation, in its harsh drab folds something of that taut and delicate futility of his. On the marble-topped dresser lay the crucible and tubes of his glass-blowing outfit, the first one he had bought, and beside it the vase he had blown on ship-board—a small chaste shape in clear glass not four inches tall, fragile as a silver lily and incomplete.

"They work in caves," he was shouting through the door, "down flights of stairs underground. You feel water seeping under your foot while you're reaching for the next step, and when you put your hand out to steady yourself against the wall, it's wet when you take it away. It feels just like blood."

"Horace!"

"Yes, magnificent. And way ahead you see the glow. All of a sudden the tunnel comes glimmering out of nothing, then you see the furnace, with things rising and falling before it, shutting the light off, and the walls go glimmering again. At first they're just shapeless things hunching about. Antic, with shadows on the bloody walls, red shadows; a glare, and black shapes like paper dolls weaving and rising and falling in front of it like a magic lantern shutter. And then a face comes out, blowing, and other faces sort of swell out of the red dark like painted balloons.

"And the things themselves! Sheerly and tragically beautiful. Like preserved flowers, you know. Macabre and inviolate; purged and purified as bronze, yet fragile as soap bubbles. Sound of pipes crystallized. Flutes and oboes, but mostly reeds. Oaten reeds. Damn it, they bloom like flowers right before your eyes. Midsummer night's dream to a salamander." His voice became unintelligible, soaring into measured phrases which she did not recognise, but which from the pitch of his voice she knew were Milton's archangels in their sonorous plunging ruin.

He emerged at last, in a white shirt and serge trousers but still borne aloft on his flaming verbal wings, and while his voice chanted in measured syllables she fetched a pair of shoes from the closet, and while she stood holding the shoes in her hands, he ceased chanting and touched her face again with his hands after that fashion of a child.

At supper Aunt Sally broke into his staccato babbling.

"Did you bring your Snopes back with you?" she asked. This Snopes was a young man, member of a seemingly inexhaustible family which for the last ten years had been moving to town in driblets from a small settlement known as Frenchman's Bend. Flem, the first Snopes, had appeared unheralded one day behind the counter of a small restaurant on a side street, patronized by country folk. With this foothold and like Abraham of old, he brought his blood and legal kin household by household, individual by individual, into town and established them where they could gain money. Flem himself was presently manager of the city light and water plant, and for the following few years he was a sort of handyman to the municipal government; and three years ago, to old Bayard's profane astonishment and unconcealed annoyance, he became vice-president of the Sartoris bank, where already a relation of his was a book-keeper.

He still retained the restaurant, and the canvas tent in the rear of it in which he and his wife and baby had passed the

first few months of their residence in town, and it served as
an alighting-place for incoming Snopeses, from which they
spread to small third-rate businesses of various kinds—grocery stores, barber shops (there was one, an invalid of some
sort, who operated a second-hand peanut parcher)—where
they multiplied and flourished. The older residents, from their
Jeffersonian houses and genteel stores and offices, looked on
with amusement at first. But this was long since become something like consternation.

The Snopes to which Aunt Sally referred was named Mont-
gomery Ward, and just before the draft law went into operation in '17 he applied to a recruiting officer in Memphis and
was turned down because of his heart. Later, to everyone's
surprise, particularly that of Horace Benbow's friends, he departed with Horace to a position in the Y.M.C.A. Later still
it was told of him that he had travelled all the way to Memphis on that day when he had offered for service, with a plug
of chewing tobacco beneath his left armpit. But he and his
patron were already departed when that story got out.

"Did you bring your Snopes back with you?" Aunt Sally
asked.

"No," he answered, and his thin, nerve-sick face clouded
over with a fine cold distaste. "I was very much disappointed
in him. I dont even care to talk about it."

"Anybody could have told you that when you left." Aunt
Sally chewed slowly and steadily above her plate. Horace
brooded for a moment, his thin hand tightened slowly about
his fork.

"It's individuals like that, parasites——" he began, but his
sister interrupted.

"Who cares about an old Snopes, anyway? Besides, it's too
late at night to talk about the horrors of war." Aunt Sally
made a moist sound through her food, a sound of vindicated
superiority.

"It's the generals they have nowadays," she said. "General
Johnston or General Forrest wouldn't have took a Snopes in
his army at all." Aunt Sally was no relation whatever. She lived
next door but one with two maiden sisters, one younger and
one older than she. She had been in and out of the house ever
since Horace and Narcissa could remember, having arrogated

to herself certain rights in their lives before they could walk; privileges which were never definitely expressed and which she never availed herself of, yet the mutual admission of whose existence she never permitted to fall into desuetude. She would walk into any room in the house unannounced, and she liked to talk tediously and a little tactlessly of Horace's and Narcissa's infantile ailments. It was said that she had once 'made eyes' at Will Benbow although she was a woman of thirty four or five when Will married; and she still spoke of him with a faintly disparaging possessiveness, and of his wife she always spoke pleasantly, too. "Julia was a right sweet-natured girl," she would say.

So when Horace went off to the war Aunt Sally moved over to keep Narcissa company: no other arrangement had ever occurred to any of the three of them; the fact that Narcissa must have Aunt Sally in the house for an indefinite year or two or three appeared as unavoidable as the fact that Horace must go to the war. Aunt Sally was a good old soul, but she lived much in the past, shutting her mind with a bland finality to anything which had occurred since 1901. For her, time had gone out drawn by horses, and into her stubborn and placid vacuum the squealing of automobile brakes had never penetrated. She had a lot of the crudities which old people are entitled to. She liked the sound of her own voice and she didn't like to be alone at any time, and as she had never got accustomed to the false teeth which she had bought twelve years ago and so never touched them other than to change weekly the water in which they reposed, she ate unprettily of unprepossessing but easily malleable foods. Narcissa reached her hand beneath the table and touched her brother's knee again.

"I *am* glad you're home, Horry."

He looked at her quickly, and the cloud faded from his face as suddenly as it had come, and his spirit slipped, like a swimmer into a tideless sea, into the serene constancy of her affection again.

He was a lawyer, principally through a sense of duty to the family tradition, and though he had no particular affinity to it other than a love for printed words, for the dwelling-places of books, he contemplated returning to his musty office with a glow of . . . not eagerness: no: of deep and abiding unreluctance, almost of pleasure. The meaning of peace. Old unchanging days; unwinged, perhaps, but undisastrous, too. You dont see it, feel it, save with perspective. Fireflies had not yet come, and the cedars flowed unbroken on either hand down to the street, like a curving ebony wave with rigid unbreaking crests pointed on the sky. Light fell outward from the window, across the porch and upon a bed of cannas, hardy, bronze-like—none of your flower-like fragility, theirs; and within the room Aunt Sally's quavering monotone. Narcissa was there too, beside the lamp with a book, filling the room with her still and constant presence like the odor of jasmine, watching the door through which he had passed; and Horace stood on the veranda with his cold pipe, surrounded by that cool astringency of cedars like another presence. The meaning of peace, he said to himself once more, releasing the grave words one by one within the cool bell of silence into which he had come at last again, hearing them linger with a dying fall pure as silver and crystal struck lightly together.

"How's Belle?" he asked on the evening of his arrival.

"They're all right," his sister answered. "They have a new car."

"Dare say," Horace agreed with detachment. "The war should certainly have accomplished that much." Aunt Sally had left them at last and tapped her slow bedward way. Horace stretched his serge legs luxuriously and for a while he ceased striking matches to his stubborn pipe and sat watching his sister's dark head bent above the magazine upon her knees, lost from lesser and inconstant things. Her hair was smoother than any reposing wings, sweeping with burnished unrebellion to a simple knot low on her neck. "Belle's a rotten correspondent," he said. "Like all women."

She turned a page, without looking up. "Did you write to her often?"

"It's because they realize that letters are only good to bridge intervals between actions, like the interludes in Shakespeare's plays," he went on, oblivious. "And did you ever know a woman who read Shakespeare without skipping the interludes? Shakespeare himself knew that, so he didn't put any women in the interludes. Let the men bombast to one another's echoes while the ladies were backstage washing the dinner dishes or putting the children to bed."

"I never knew a woman that read Shakespeare at all," Narcissa corrected. "He talks too much."

Horace rose and stood above her and patted her dark head.

"O profundity," he said, "you have reduced all wisdom to a phrase, and measured your sex by the stature of a star."

"Well, they dont," she repeated, raising her face.

"No? why dont they?" He struck another match to his pipe, watching her across his cupped hands as gravely and with poised eagerness, like a striking bird. "Your Arlens and Sabatinis talk a lot, and nobody ever had more to say and more trouble saying it than old Dreiser."

"But they have secrets," she explained. "Shakespeare doesn't have any secrets. He tells everything."

"I see. Shakespeare had no sense of discrimination and no instinct for reticence. In other words, he wasn't a gentleman," he suggested.

"Yes. . . . . . That's what I mean."

"And so, to be a gentleman, you must have secrets."

"Oh, you make me tired." She returned to her magazine and he sat beside her on the couch and took her hand in his and stroked it upon his cheek and upon the fine devastation of his hair.

"It's like walking through a twilit garden," he said. "The flowers you know are all there, in their shifts and with their hair combed out for the night, but you know all of them. So you dont bother 'em, you just walk on and sort of stop and turn over a leaf occasionally, a leaf you didn't notice before; perhaps you find a violet under it, or a bluebell or a lightning bug; perhaps only another leaf or a blade of grass. But there's always a drop of dew on it." He continued to stroke her hand upon his face. With her other hand she turned the magazine slowly on, listening to him with fond and serene detachment.

"Did you write to Belle often?" she repeated. "What did you say to her?"

"I wrote what she wanted to read. What all women want in letters. People are really entitled to half of what they think they should have."

"What did you tell her?" Narcissa persisted, turning the pages slowly, her passive hand in his, following the stroking movement of his.

"I told her I was unhappy. Perhaps I was," he added. His sister freed her hand quietly and laid it on the page. He said: "I admire Belle. She's so cannily stupid. Once I feared her. Perhaps. . . . . . No, I dont. I am immune to destruction: I have a magic. Which is a good sign that I am due for it, say the sages," he added. "But then, acquired wisdom is a dry thing; it has a way of crumbling to dust where a sheer and blind coursing of stupid sap is impervious." He sat without touching her, in a rapt and instantaneous repose. "Not like yours, O Serene," he said, waking again. Then he fell to saying Dear old Narcy, and again he took her hand. It did not withdraw; neither did it wholly surrender.

"I dont think you ought to say I'm dull so often, Horry," she said.

"Neither do I," he agreed. "But I must take some sort of revenge on perfection."

Later she lay in her dark room. Across the corridor Aunt Sally snored with placid regularity; in the adjoining room Horace lay while that wild fantastic futility of his voyaged in lonely regions of its own beyond the moon, about meadows nailed with firmamented stars to the ultimate roof of things, where unicorns filled the neighing air with galloping, or grazed or lay supine in golden-hooved repose.

Horace was seven when she was born. In the background of her sober babyhood were three beings whose lives and conduct she had adopted with rapt intensity—a lad with a wild thin face and an unflagging aptitude for tribulation; a darkly gallant shape romantic with smuggled edibles and with strong hard hands that smelled always of a certain thrilling carbolic soap—a being something like Omnipotence but without awesomeness; and lastly, a gentle figure without legs or any inference of locomotion whatever, like a minor shrine, surrounded always by an aura of gentle melancholy and an endless and delicate manipulation of colored silken thread. This last figure was constant with a gentle and melancholy unassertion; the second revolved in an orbit which bore it at regular intervals into outer space, then returned it with its strong and

jolly virility into her intense world again; but the first she had
made her own by a sober and maternal perseverance. And so
by the time she was five or six, people coerced Horace by
threatening to tell Narcissa on him.

Julia Benbow died genteelly when Narcissa was seven, had
been removed from their lives as a small sachet of lavender
might be removed from a chest of linen, leaving a delicate lingering impalpability; and slept now amid pointed cedars and
doves and serene marble shapes. Thus Narcissa acquired two
masculine destinies to control and shape, and through the intense maturity of seven and eight and nine she cajoled and
threatened and commanded and (very occasionally) stormed
them into concurrence. And so through fourteen and fifteen
and sixteen, while Horace was first at Sewanee and later at
Oxford. Then Will Benbow's time came, and he joined his
wife Julia among the marbles and the cedars and the doves,
and the current of her maternalism had now but a single channel. For a time this current was dammed by a stupid mischancing of human affairs, but now Horace was home again
and lay now beneath the same roof and the same recurrence
of days, and the channel was undammed again.

"Why dont you marry, and let that baby look after himself
for a while?" Miss Jenny Du Pre had demanded once, in her
cold, abrupt way. Perhaps when she too was eighty, all men
would be Sartorises to her, also. But that was a long time
away. Sartorises. She thought of Bayard, but briefly, and without any tremor at all. He was now no more than the shadow
of a hawk's flight mirrored fleetingly by the windless surface
of a pool, and gone; where, the pool knew and cared not, leaving no stain.

2.

He was settled soon and easily into the routine of days
between his office and his home. The musty, solemn familiarity of calf-bound and never-violated volumes on whose dusty
bindings prints of Will Benbow's dead fingers might probably yet be found; a little tennis in the afternoons, usually on
Harry Mitchell's fine court; cards in the evenings, also with
Belle and Harry as a general thing, or again and better still,

with the ever accessible and never-failing magic of printed
pages, while his sister sat across the table from him or played
softly to herself in the darkened room across the hall. Occasionally men called on her; Horace received them with unfailing courtesy and a little exasperation, and departed soon to
tramp about the streets or to read in bed. Dr Alford came
stiffly once or twice a week, and Horace, being somewhat of
an amateur casuist, amused himself by blunting delicately
feathered metaphysical darts upon the doctor's bland scientific
hide for an hour or so; it would not be until then that they
realized that Narcissa had not spoken a word for sixty or seventy or eighty minutes. "That's why they come to see you,"
Horace told her—"for an emotional mud-bath."

Aunt Sally had returned home, with her bag of colored
scraps and her false teeth, leaving behind her a fixed impalpability of a nebulous but definite obligation discharged at some
personal sacrifice, and a faint odor of old female flesh which
faded from the premises slowly, lingering yet in unexpected
places, so that at times Narcissa, waking and lying for a while
in the darkness, in the sensuous pleasure of having Horace
home again, imagined that she could hear yet in the dark
myriad silence of the house Aunt Sally's genteel and placid
snores.

At times it would be so distinct that she would pause suddenly and speak Aunt Sally's name into an empty room. And
sometimes Aunt Sally replied, having availed herself again of
her prerogative of coming in at any hour the notion took her,
unannounced, to see how they were getting along and to complain querulously of her own household. She was old, too old
to react easily to change, and it was hard for her to readjust
herself to her sisters' ways again after her long sojourn in a
household where everyone gave in to her regarding all domestic affairs. At home her elder sister ran things in a capable
shrewish fashion; she and the third sister persisted in treating
Aunt Sally like the child she had been sixty five years ago,
whose diet and clothing and hours must be rigorously and
pettishly supervised.

"I cant even go to the bathroom in peace," she complained
querulously. "I'm a good mind to pack up and move back
over here, and let 'em get along the best they can." She rocked

fretfully in the chair which by unspoken agreement was never disputed her, looking about the room with bleared protesting old eyes. "That nigger dont half clean up, since I left. That furniture, now . . . . a damp cloth. . . . . . ."

"I wish you would take her back," Miss Sophia, the elder sister, told Narcissa. "She's got so crotchety since she's been with you that there's no living with her. What's this I hear Horace has taken up? making glassware?"

His proper crucibles and retorts had arrived intact. At first he had insisted on using the cellar, clearing out the lawn mower and the garden tools and all the accumulate impedimenta, and walling up the windows so as to make a dungeon of it. But Narcissa had finally persuaded him upon the upper floor of the garage and here he had set up his furnace and had set fire to the building once and had had four mishaps and produced one almost perfect vase of clear amber, larger, more richly and chastely serene and which he kept always on his night table and called by his sister's name in the intervals of apostrophising both of them impartially in his moments of rhapsody over the realization of the meaning of peace and the unblemished attainment of it, as Thou still unravished bride of quietude.

At times he found himself suddenly quiet, a little humble in the presence of the happiness of his winged and solitary cage. For a cage it was, barring him from freedom with trivial compulsions; but he desired a cage. A topless cage, of course, that his spirit might wing on short excursions into the blue, but far afield his spirit did not desire to go: its direction was always upward plummeting, for a plummeting fall.

Still unchanging days. They were doomed days; he knew it, yet for the time being his devious and uncontrollable impulses had become one with the rhythm of things as a swimmer's counter muscles become one with a current, and cage and all his life grew suave with motion, oblivious of destination. During this period not only did his immediate days become starkly inevitable, but the dead thwarted ones with all the spent and ludicrous disasters which his nature had incurred upon him, grew lustrous in retrospect and without regret, and those to come seemed as undeviating and logical as mathematical formulae beyond an incurious golden veil.

At Sewanee, where he had gone as his father before him, he had been an honor man in his class. As a Rhodes Scholar he had gone to Oxford, there to pursue the verities and humanities with that waiting law office in a Mississippi country town like a gate in the remote background through which he must someday pass, thinking of it not often and with no immediate perspective, accepting it with neither pleasure nor regret. Here, amid the mellow benignance of these walls, was a perfect life, a life accomplishing itself placidly in a region remote from time and into which the world's noises came only from afar and with only that glamorous remote significance of a parade passing along a street far away, with inferences of brass and tinsel fading beyond far walls, into the changeless sky. Here he developed a reasonably fine discrimination in alcohol and a brilliant tennis game, after his erratic electric fashion; but save for an occasional half sophomoric, half travelling-salesmanish sabbatical to the Continent in company with fellow-countrymen, his life was a golden and purposeless dream, without palpable intent or future with the exception of that law office to which he was reconciled by the sheer and youthful insuperability of distance and time.

There had come a day on which he stood in that mild pleasurable perplexity in which we regard our belongings and the seemingly inadequate volume of possible packing space, coatless among his chaotic possessions, slowly rubbing the fine unruly devastation of his head. About the bedroom bags and boxes gaped, and on the bed, on chairs, on the floor, were spread his clothes—jackets and trousers of all kinds and all individual as old friends. A servant moved about in the next room and he entered, but the man ignored him with silent and deft efficiency, and he went on to the window. The thin curtains stirred to a faint troubling exhalation of late spring. He put their gentle billowing aside and lit a cigarette and idly watched the match fall, its initial outward impulse fading into a wavering reluctance, as though space itself were languid in violation. Someone crossing the quad called up to him indistinguishably. He waved his hand vaguely in reply and sat on the window sill.

Outward, above and beyond buildings peaceful and gray and old, within and beyond trees in an untarnished and

gracious resurgence of green, afternoon was like a blonde
woman going slowly in a windless garden; afternoon and June
were like blonde sisters in a windless garden-close, approaching without regret the fall of day. Walking a little slower,
perhaps; perhaps looking backward, but without sadness, untroubled as cows. Horace sat in the window while the servant
methodically reduced the chaos of his possessions to the boxes
and bags, gazing out across ancient gray roofs, and trees which
he had seen in all their seasonal moods, in all moods matching his own. Had he been younger he would have said goodbye to them secretively or defiantly; older, he would have felt
neither the desire to nor the impulse to suppress it. So he sat
quietly in his window for the last time while the curtains
stirred delicately against his hair, brooding upon their dreaming vistas where twilight was slowly finding itself and where,
beyond dissolving spires, lingered grave evening shapes; and
he knew a place where, had he felt like walking, he could hear
a cuckoo, that symbol of sweet and timeless mischief, that
augur of the fever renewed again.

All he wanted anyway was quiet and dull peace and a few
women, preferably young and good looking and fair tennis
players, with whom to indulge in harmless and lazy intrigue.
So his mind was made up, and on the homeward boat he
framed the words with which he should tell his father that he
was going to be an Episcopal minister. But when he reached
New York the wire waited him saying that Will Benbow was
ill, and all thoughts of his future fled his mind during the journey home and during the two subsequent days that his father
lived. Then Will Benbow was buried beside his wife, and Aunt
Sally Wyatt was sombrely ubiquitous about the house and
talked with steady macabre complacence of Will at meals and
snored placidly by night in the guest room. The next day but
one Horace opened his father's law office again.

His practice, what there was of it, consisted of polite interminable litigation that progressed decorously and pleasantly
from conference to conference, the greater part of which were
given to discussions of the world's mutations as exemplified by
men or by printed words; conferences conducted as often as
not across pleasant dinner tables or upon golf links or, if the
conferee were active enough, upon tennis courts—conferences

which wended their endless courses without threat of consummation or of advantage or detriment to anyone involved.

There reposed also in a fire-proof cabinet in his office—the one concession Will Benbow had ever made to progress—a number of wills which Horace had inherited and never read, the testators of which accomplished their lives in black silk and lace caps and an atmosphere of formal and timeless desuetude in stately, high ceiled rooms screened from the ceaseless world by flowering shrubs and old creeping vines; existences circumscribed by church affairs and so-called literary clubs and a conscientious, slightly contemptuous preoccupation with the welfare of remote and obtusely ungrateful heathen peoples. They did not interest themselves in civic affairs. To interfere in the lives or conduct of people whom you saw daily or who served you in various ways or to whose families you occasionally sent food and cast-off clothing, was not genteel. Besides, the heathen was far enough removed for his willy nilly elevation to annoy no one save his yet benighted brethren. Clients upon whom he called at rare intervals by formal and unnecessary request and who bade fair to outlive him as they had outlived his father and to be heired in turn by some yet uncorporeal successor to him. As if God, Circumstance, looking down upon the gracious if faintly niggard completeness of their lives, found not the heart to remove them from surroundings tempered so peacefully to their requirements, to any other of lesser decorum and charm.

The meaning of peace; one of those instants in a man's life, a neap tide in his affairs, when, as though with a premonition of disaster, the moment takes on a sort of fixed clarity in which his actions and desires stand boldly forth unshadowed and rhythmic one with another like two steeds drawing a single chariot along a smooth empty road, and during which the I in him stands like a tranquil deciduated tree above the sere and ludicrous disasters of his days.

3.

Narcissa had failed to call at the office for him and he walked home and changed to flannels and the blue jacket with his Oxford club insignia embroidered upon the breast pocket, and removed his racket from its press. In trees and flower beds spring was accomplishing itself more and more with the accumulating days, and he walked on with the sunset slanting into his hair, toward Belle's. He strode on, chanting to himself, walking a little faster until the majestic monstrosity of the house came into view.

Someone piped thinly to him from beyond the adjoining fence; it was Belle's eight year old daughter, her dress of delicate yellow a single note of a chord of other small colored garments engaged in the intense and grave preoccupations of little girls. Horace waved his racket at her and went on, turning into the drive. The gravel slipped with short sibilance beneath his rubber soles. He did not approach the entrance to the house but continued instead along the drive toward the rear, where already against the further sunshot green of old trees and flowering shrubs he saw a figure in white tautly antic with motion in a single overarching sweep. They were playing already, someone. Belle would be there, already ensconced, Ahenobarbus' vestal, proprietorial and inattentive, preeningly dictatorial; removed from the dust and the heat and the blood; disdainful and the principal actor in the piece. O thou grave myrtle shapes amid which petulant Death.

But Belle was the sort of watcher he preferred, engaged as she would be in that outwardly faultless immersion, in the unflagging theatrics of her own part in the picture, surrounding him as she would with that atmosphere of surreptitious domesticity. Belle didn't play tennis herself: her legs were not good, and Belle knew it; but sat instead in a tea gown of delicate and irreproachable lines at a table advantageously placed and laden with books and magazines and the temporarily discarded impedimenta of her more Atalanta-esque sisters. There was usually a group around Belle's chair—other young women or a young man or so inactive between sets, with an occasional older woman come to see just exactly what was going on or what Belle wore at the time; watching Belle's pretty regal airs with the young men. "Like a moving picture," Aunt Sally Wyatt said once, with cold and curious interest.

And presently Meloney would bring tea out and lay it on the table at Belle's side. Between the two of them, Belle with her semblance of a peahen suave and preening and petulant

upon clipped sward, before marble urns and formal balus-
trades, and Meloney in her starched cap and apron and her
lean shining legs, they made a rite of the most casual gathering; lending a sort of stiffness to it which Meloney seemed to
bring in on her tray and beneath which the calling ladies grew
more and more reserved and coldly watchful and against
which Belle flowered like a hot-house bloom, brilliant and
petulant and perverse.

It had taken Belle some time to overcome Jefferson's prej-
udice against a formal meal between dinner and supper and to
educate the group in which she moved to tea as a function in
itself and not as something to give invalids or as an adjunct to
a party of some sort. But Horace had assisted her, unwittingly
and without self-consciousness; and there had been a youth,
son of a carpenter, of whom Belle had made a poet and sent
to New Orleans and who, being a conscientious objector, had
narrowly escaped prison during the war and who now served
in a reportorial capacity on a Texas newspaper, holding the
position relinquished by a besotted young man who had enlisted in the Marine Corps early in '17.

Bareheaded, in flannels and a blue jacket with his Oxford
club insignia embroidered on the pocket and his racket under
his arm, Horace passed on around the house and the court
came into view with its two occupants in fluid violent action.
Beneath an arcade of white pilasters and vine-hung beams
Belle, surrounded by the fragile, harmonious impedimenta of
the moment, was like a butterfly. Two sat with her, in bright
relief against the dark foliage of a crepe-myrtle not yet in
flower. The other woman (the third member of the group was
a young girl in white and with a grave molasses bang and a
tennis racket across her knees) spoke to him, and Belle greeted
him with a sort of languid possessive desolation. Her hand
was warm, prehensile, like mercury in his palm exploring
softly with delicate bones and petulant scented flesh. Her eyes
were like hothouse grapes and her mouth was redly mobile,
rich with discontent; but waked now from its rouged repose,
this was temporarily lost. She had lost Meloney, she told
him.

"Meloney saw through your gentility," Horace said. "You
grew careless, probably. Your elegance is much inferior to

Meloney's. You surely didn't expect to always deceive anyone who can lend as much rigid discomfort to the function of eating and drinking as Meloney could, did you? Or has she got married some more?"

"She's gone in business," Belle answered fretfully. "A beauty shop. And why, I cant for the life of me see. Those things never do last, here. Can you imagine Jefferson women supporting a beauty shop, with the exception of us three? Mrs Marders and I might; I'm sure we need it, but what use has Frankie for one?"

"What seems curious to me," the other woman said, "is where the money came from. People thought that perhaps you had given it to her, Belle."

"Since when have I been a public benefactor?" Belle said coldly. Horace grinned faintly. Mrs Marders said:

"Now, Belle, we all know how kindhearted you are; dont be modest."

"I said a public benefactor," Belle repeated. Horace said quickly:

"Well, Harry would swap a handmaiden for an ox, any day. At least, he can save a lot of wear and tear on his cellar, not having to counteract your tea in a lot of casual masculine tummies. I suppose there'll be no more tea out here, will there?" he added.

"Dont be silly," Belle said.

Horace said: "I realise now that it is not tennis that I come here for, but for the incalculable amount of uncomfortable superiority I always feel when Meloney . . . serves me tea. . . . I saw your daughter as I came along."

"She's somewhere around, I suppose," Belle agreed indifferently. "You haven't had your hair cut yet," she stated. "Why is it that men have no sense about barbers?" she said generally. The older woman watched Belle and Horace brightly, coldly across her two flaccid chins. The young girl sat quietly in her simple virginal white, her racket on her lap and one brown hand lying upon it like a sleeping tan puppy. She was watching Horace with sober interest but without rudeness, as children do. "They either wont go to the barber at all, or they insist on having their heads all gummed up with pomade and things," Belle added.

"Horace is a poet," the other woman said. Her flesh draped loosely from her cheek-bones like rich, slightly-soiled velvet; her eyes were like the eyes of an old turkey, predatory and un-winking; a little obscene. "Poets must be excused for what they do. You should remember that, Belle." Horace bowed toward her.

"Your race never fails in tact, Belle," he said. "Mrs Marders is one of the few people I know who give the law profession its true evaluation."

"It's like any other business, I suppose," Belle said. "You're late today. Why didn't Narcissa come?"

"I mean, dubbing me a poet," Horace explained. "The law, like poetry, is the final resort of the lame, the halt, the imbe-cile and the blind. I dare say Caesar invented the law business to protect himself against poets."

"You're so clever," Belle said. The young girl spoke suddenly:

"Why do you bother about what men put on their hair, Miss Belle? Mr Mitchell's bald."

The other woman laughed, unctuously, steadily, watching them with her lidless unlaughing eyes. She watched Belle and Horace and still laughed steadily, brightly and cold. " 'Out of the mouths of babes——' " she said. The young girl glanced from one to another with her clear sober eyes. She rose.

"I guess I'll see if I cant get a set now," she said.

Horace moved also. "Let's you and I——" he began. With-out turning her head Belle touched him with her hand.

"Sit down, Frankie," she commanded. "They haven't fin-ished the game yet. You shouldn't laugh so much on an empty stomach," she told Mrs Marders. "Do sit down, Horace."

The girl stood yet with slim and awkward grace, holding her racket. She looked at Belle a moment, then she turned her face to the court again. Horace took the chair beyond Belle; her hand dropped hidden into his, with that secret movement, then it grew passive; it was as though she had turned a cur-rent off somewhere. Like one entering a dark room in search of something, finding it and pressing the light off again.

"Dont you like poets?" Horace spoke across Belle's body. The girl did not turn her head.

"They cant dance," she answered. "I guess they are all right, though. They went to the war, the good ones did. There was one was a good tennis player, that got killed. I've seen his picture, but I dont remember his name."

"Oh, dont start talking about the war, for heaven's sake," Belle said. Her hand stirred in Horace's. "I had to listen to Harry for two years. Explaining why he couldn't go. As if I cared whether he did or not."

"He had a family to support," Mrs Marders suggested brightly. Belle half reclined, her head against the chair-back, her hidden hand moving slowly in Horace's, exploring, turning, ceaselessly like a separate volition curious but without warmth.

"Some of them were aviators," the girl continued. She stood with one little unemphatic hip braced against the table, her racket clasped beneath her arm, turning the pages of a magazine. Then she closed the magazine and again she watched the two figures leanly antic upon the court. "I danced with one of those Sartoris boys once. I was too scared to know which one it was. I wasn't anything but a baby, then."

"Were they poets?" Horace asked. "I mean, the one that got back. I know the other one, the dead one, was."

"He sure can drive that car of his," she answered, still watching the players, her straight hair (hers was the first bobbed head in town) not brown not gold, her brief nose in profile, her brown still hands clasping her racket. Belle stirred and freed her hand.

"Do go on and play, you all," she said. "You make me nervous, both of you." Horace rose with alacrity.

"Come on, Frankie. Let's you and I take 'em on for a set."

The girl looked at him. "I'm not so hot," she said soberly. "I hope you wont get mad."

"Why? If we get beat?" They moved together toward the court where the two players were now exchanging sides. "Do you know what the finest sensation of all is?" Her straight brown head moved just at his shoulder. It's her dress that makes her arms and hands so brown, he thought. Little. He could not remember her at all sixteen months back, when he had gone away. They grow up so quickly, though, after a certain age. Go away again and return, and find her with a baby, probably.

"Good music?" she suggested tentatively, after a time.

"No. It's to finish a day and say to yourself: Here's one day during which I have accomplished nothing and hurt no one and had a whale of a good time. How does it go? 'Count that day lost whose low descending sun——'? Well, they've got it exactly backward."

"I dont know. I learned it in school, I guess," she answered indifferently. "But I dont remember it now. D'you reckon they'll let me play? I'm not so hot," she repeated.

"Of course they will," Horace assured her. And soon they were aligned: the two players, the book-keeper in the local department store and a youth who had been recently expelled from the state university for a practical joke (he had removed the red lantern from the barrier about a street excavation and hung it above the door of the girls' dormitory) against Horace and the girl. Horace was an exceptional player, electric and brilliant. One who knew tennis and who had patience and a cool head could have defeated him out of hand by letting him beat himself. But not these. The points see-sawed back and forth, but usually Horace managed to retrieve the advantage with stroking or strategy so audacious as to obscure the faultiness of his tactics.

Meanwhile he could watch her; her taut earnestness, her unflagging determination not to let him down, her awkward virginal grace. From the back line he outguessed their opponents with detached and impersonal skill, keeping the point in abeyance and playing the ball so as to bring her young intent body into motion as he might pull a puppet's strings. Hers was an awkward speed that cost them points, but from the base line Horace retrieved her errors when he could, pleasuring in the skimpy ballooning of her little dress moulded and dragged by her arms and legs, watching the taut revelations of her speeding body in a sort of ecstasy. Girlwhite and all thy little   Oh. Not pink, no. For a moment I thought she'd no. Disgraceful, her mamma would call it. Or any other older woman. Belle's are pink O muchly "Oaten reed above the lyre," Horace chanted, catching the ball at his shoe-tops with a full swing, watching it duck viciously beyond the net. Oaten reed above the lyre. And Belle like a harped gesture, not sonorous. Piano, perhaps. Blended chords, anyway. Unchaste   ? Knowledgeable better. Knowingly wearied.

Weariedly knowing. Yes, piano. Fugue. Fugue of discontent.
O moon rotting waxed overlong too long

Last point. Game and set. She made it with savage awkwardness; and turned at the net and stood with lowered racket
as he approached. Beneath the simple molasses of her hair she
was perspiring a little. "I kept on letting 'em get my alley," she
explained. "You never bawled me out a single time. What
ought I to do, to break myself of that?"

"You ought to run in a cheese-cloth shimmy on hills under
a new moon," Horace told her. "With chained ankles, of course.
But a slack chain. No, not the moon; but in a dawn like pipes.
Green and gold, and maybe a little pink. Would you risk a
little pink?" She watched him with grave curious eyes as he
stood before her lean in his flannels and with his sick brilliant
face and his wild hair. "No," he corrected himself again. "On
sand. Blanched sand, with dead ripples. Ghosts of dead motion
waved into the sand. Do you know how cold the sea can be
just before dawn, with a falling tide? Like lying in a dead world,
upon the dead respirations of the earth. She's too big to die
all at once. Like elephants. . . . . . How old are you?" Now
all at once her eyes became secretive, and she looked away.
"Now what?" he demanded. "What did you start to say then?"

"There's Mr Mitchell," she said. Harry Mitchell had come
out, in tight flannels and a white silk shirt and new ornate sport
shoes that cost twenty dollars per pair. With a new racket in a
patent case and press, standing with his squat legs and his bald
bullet head and his undershot jaw of rotting teeth beside the
studied picture of his wife. Presently when he had been made
to drink a cup of tea he would gather up all the men present
and lead them through the house to his bathroom and give
them whisky, pouring out a glass and fetching it down to
Rachel. He would give you the shirt off his back. He was a
cotton speculator and a good one; he was ugly as sin and kindhearted and dogmatic and talkative, and he called Belle "little
mother" until she broke him of it. Belle lay yet in her chair;
she was watching them as they turned together from the court.

"What was it?" Horace persisted.

"Sir?"

"What you started to say just then."

"Nothing," she answered. "I wasn't going to say anything."

"Oh, that's too feminine," Horace said. "I didn't expect that of you, after the way you play tennis." They moved on under the veiled contemplation of Belle's gaze.

"Feminine?" Then she added: "I hope I can get another set soon. I'm not a bit tired, are you?"

"Yes. Any woman might have said that. But maybe you're not old enough to be a woman."

"Horace," Belle said.

"I'm seventeen," the girl answered. "Miss Belle likes you, dont she?"

Belle spoke his name again, mellifluously, lazily peremptory. Mrs Marders sat now with her slack chins in a raised teacup. The girl turned to him with polite finality. "Thanks for playing with me," she said. "I'll be better some day, I hope. We beat 'em," she said generally.

"You and the little lady gave 'em the works, hey, big boy?" Harry Mitchell said, showing his discolored teeth. His heavy prognathous jaw narrowed delicately down, then nipped abruptly off into bewildered pugnacity.

"Mr Benbow did," the girl corrected in her clear voice, and she took the chair next Belle. "I kept on letting 'em get my alley."

"Horace," Belle said, "your tea is getting cold."

It had been fetched out by the combination gardener-stableman-chauffeur, temporarily impressed in a white jacket and smelling of vulcanized rubber and ammonia. Mrs Marders removed her chins from her cup. "Horace plays too well," she said, "really too well. The other men cant compare with him. You were lucky to have him for a partner, child."

"Yessum," the girl agreed. "I guess he wont risk me again."

"Nonsense," Mrs Marders rejoined. "Horace enjoyed playing with you, with a young, fresh girl. Didn't you notice it, Belle?"

Belle made no reply. She poured Horace's tea, and at this moment her daughter came across the lawn in her crocus-yellow dress. Her eyes were like stars, more soft and melting than any deer's, and she gave Horace a swift shining glance.

"Well, Titania?" he said.

Belle half turned her head, with the teapot poised above the cup, and Harry set his cup on the table and went and knelt on one knee in her path, as though he were cajoling a puppy. The child came up, still watching Horace with radiant and melting diffidence, and permitted her father to embrace her and fondle her with his short, heavy hands. "Daddy's gal," Harry said. She submitted to having her prim little dress mussed, pleasurably but a little restively; her eyes flew shining again.

"Dont muss your dress, sister," Belle said, and the child evaded her father's hands with a prim movement. "What is it now?" Belle asked. "Why aren't you playing?"

"Nothing. I just came home." She came and stood diffidently beside her mother's chair.

"Speak to the company," Belle said. "Dont you know better than to come where older people are, without speaking to them?" The little girl did so, shyly and faultlessly, greeting them in rotation, and her mother turned and pulled and patted at her straight soft hair. "Now, go on and play. Why do you always want to come around where grown people are? You're not interested in what we're doing."

"Ah, let her stay, mother," Harry said. "She wants to watch her daddy and Horace play tennis."

"Run along, now," Belle repeated with a final pat. "And do keep your dress clean."

"Yessum," the child agreed, and she turned obediently, giving Horace another quick shining look. He watched her and saw Rachel open the kitchen door and speak to her as she passed, saw her turn and mount the steps into the kitchen.

"What a beautifully mannered child," Mrs Marders said.

"They're so hard to do anything with," Belle said. "She has some of her father's traits. Drink your tea, Harry."

Harry took his cup from the table and sucked its lukewarm contents into himself noisily and dutifully. "Well, big boy, how about a set? These squirrels think they can beat us."

"Frankie wants to play again," Belle interposed. "Let the child have the court for a little while, Harry." Harry was busy uncasing his racket. He paused and raised his savage undershot face and his dull kind eyes.

"No, no," the girl protested quickly. "I've had enough. I'd rather look on a while."

"Dont be silly," Belle said. "They can play any time. Make them let her play, Harry."

"Sure the little lady can play," Harry said. "Help yourself;

play as long as you want to." He bent again and returned his racket to its intricate casing, twisting nuts here and there; his back was sullen, with a boy's sullenness.

"Please, Mr Mitchell," the girl said.

"Go ahead," Harry repeated. "Here, you jelly-beans, how about fixing up a set with the little lady?"

"Dont mind him," Belle told the girl. "He and Horace can play some other time. He'll have to make a fourth, anyway."

The two players stood now, politely waiting.

"Sure, Mr Harry, come on. Me and Frankie'll play you and Joe," one of them said.

"You folks go ahead and play a set," Harry repeated. "I've got a little business to talk over with Horace. You all go ahead." He overrode their polite protests and they took the court. Then he jerked his head significantly at Horace.

"Go on with him," Belle said. "The baby." Without looking at him, without touching him, she enveloped him with rich and smoldering promise. Mrs Marders sat across the table from them, curious and bright and cold with her teacup. "Unless you want to play with that silly child again."

"Silly?" Horace repeated. "She's too young to be unconsciously silly yet."

"Run along," Belle told him. "And hurry back. Mrs Marders and I are tired of one another."

Horace followed his host into the house, followed his short rolling gait and the bald indomitability of his head. From the kitchen, as they passed, little Belle's voice came steadily, recounting some astonishment of the day, with an occasional mellow ejaculation from Rachel for antistrophe. In the bathroom Harry got a bottle from a cabinet, and preceded by labored heavy footsteps mounting, Rachel entered without knocking, bearing a pitcher of ice water. "Whyn't y'all g'awn and play, ef you wants?" she demanded. "Whut you let that 'oman treat you and that baby like she do, anyhow?" she demanded of Harry. "You ought to take and lay her out wid a stick of wood. Messin' up my kitchen at fo' oclock in de evenin'. And you aint helpin' none, neither," she told Horace. "Gimme a dram, Mr Harry, please, suh."

She held her glass out and Harry filled it, and waddled heavily from the room; they heard her descend the stairs slowly and heavily on her fallen arches. "Belle couldn't get along without Rachel," Harry said. He rinsed two glasses with ice water and set them on the lavatory. "She talks too much, like all niggers." He poured into the two tumblers, set the bottle down. "To listen to her you'd think Belle was some kind of a wild animal. A dam tiger or something. But Belle and I understand each other. You've got to make allowances for women, anyhow. Different from men. Born contrary; complain when you dont please 'em and complain when you do." He added a little water to his glass; then he said, with astonishing irrelevance: "I'd kill the man that tried to wreck my home like I would a dam snake. Well, let's take one, big boy."

Presently he sloshed water into his empty glass and gulped that, too, and he reverted to his former grievance.

"Cant get to play on my own dam court," he said. "Belle gets all these dam people here every day. What I want is a court where I can come home from work and get in a couple of fast sets every afternoon. Appetizer before supper. But every dam day I get home from work and find a bunch of young girls and jelly-beans, using it like it was a public court in a dam park." Horace drank his more moderately, and Harry lit a cigarette and threw the match onto the floor and hung his leg across the lavatory. "I reckon I'll have to build another court for my own use and put a hogwire fence around it with a yale lock, so Belle cant give picnics on it. There's plenty of room down there by the lot fence. No trees, too. Put it out in the dam sun, and I reckon Belle'll let me use it now and then. Well, suppose we get on back."

He led the way through his bedroom and stopped to show Horace a new repeating rifle he had just bought, and to press upon him a package of cigarettes which he imported from South America, and they descended and emerged into afternoon become later. The sun was level now across the court where three players leaped and sped with soft quick slapping of rubber soles, following the fleeting impact of the ball. Mrs Marders sat yet with her ceaseless chins, although she was speaking of departure when they came up. Belle turned her head against the chair-back, but Harry led Horace on.

"We're going to look over a location for a tennis court. I think I'll take up tennis myself," he told Mrs Marders with heavy irony. It was later still when they returned. Mrs Marders was gone and Belle sat alone, with a magazine. A youth in a battered ford had called for the girl Frankie, but another young man had dropped in, and when Horace and Harry came up the three youths clamored politely for Harry to join them.

Horace halted in his loose, worn flannels, with his thin face brilliant and sick with nerves, smoking his host's cigarettes and watching his hopeless indomitable head and his intent, faintly comical body as he paced off dimensions and talked steadily in his harsh voice; paced back and forth and planned and calculated with something of a boy's fine ability for fabling, for shaping the incontrovertible present to a desire which he will presently lose in a recenter one and so forget.

"Take Horace here," Harry said, obviously pleased. "He'll give you a run for your money." But Horace demurred and the three continued to importune Harry. "Lemme get my racket, then," he said finally, and Horace followed the heavy scuttling of his backside across the court. Belle looked briefly up.

"Did you find a place?"

"Yes," Harry answered, uncasing his racket again. "Where I can play myself, sometimes. A place too far from the street for everybody that comes along to see it and stop." But Belle was reading again. Harry unscrewed his racket press and removed it. "I'll go in one set, then you and I can get in a fast one before dark," he told Horace.

"Yes," Horace agreed. He sat down and watched Harry stride heavily onto the court and take his position, watched the first serve. Then Belle's magazine rustled and slapped onto the table.

"Come," she said, rising. Horace rose, and Belle preceded him and they crossed the lawn and entered the house. Rachel moved about in the kitchen, and they went on through the house, where all noises were remote and the furniture gleamed peacefully indistinct in the dying evening light. Belle slid her hand into his, clutching his hand against her silken thigh, and led him on through a dusky passage and into her music room. This room was quiet too and empty and she stopped against him half turning, and they kissed. But she freed her mouth presently and moved again and he drew the piano bench out and they sat on opposite sides of it and kissed again. "You haven't told me you love me," Belle said, touching his face with her fingertips, and the fine devastation of his hair. "Not in a long time."

"Not since yesterday," Horace agreed, but he told her, she leaning her breast against him and listening with a sort of rapt voluptuous inattention, like a great still cat; and when he had done and sat touching her face and her hair with his delicate wild hands, she removed her breast and opened the piano and touched the keys. Saccharine melodies she played, from memory and in the current mode, that you might hear on any vaudeville stage, and with shallow skill, a feeling for their over-sweet nuances. They sat thus for sometime while the light faded, Belle in another temporary vacuum of discontent, building for herself a world in which she moved romantically, finely and a little tragical; with Horace sitting beside her and watching both Belle in her self-imposed and tragic rôle, and himself performing his part like the old actor whose hair is thin and whose profile is escaping him via his chin, but who can play to any cue at a moment's notice while the younger men chew their bitter thumbs in the wings.

Presently the rapid heavy concussions of Harry's feet thumped again on the stairs mounting, and the harsh word-less uproar of his voice as he led someone else in the back way and up to his bathroom. Belle stopped her hands and leaned against him and kissed him again, clinging. "This is intolera-ble," she said, freeing her mouth with a movement of her head. For a moment she resisted against his arm, then her hands crashed discordantly upon the keys and slid through Horace's hair and down his cheeks tightening. She freed her mouth again. "Now, sit over there."

He obeyed; she on the piano bench was in half shadow. Twilight was almost accomplished; only the line of her bent head and her back, tragic and still, making him feel young again. We do turn corners upon ourselves, like suspicious old ladies spying on servants, Horace thought. No, like boys trying to head off a parade. "There's always divorce," he said.

"To marry again?" Her hands trailed off into chords; merged, faded again into a minor in one hand. Overhead Harry moved with his heavy staccato tread, shaking the house. "You'd make a rotten husband."

"I wont as long as I'm not married," Horace answered.

She said, "Come here," and he went to her, and in the dusk she was again tragic and young and familiar, with a haunting sense of loss, and he knew the sad fecundity of the world, and time's hopeful unillusion that fools itself. "I want to have your child, Horace," she said, and then her own child came up the hall and stood diffidently in the door.

For a moment Belle was an animal awkward and mad with fear. She surged away from him in a mad spurning movement; her hands crashed on the keys as she controlled her instinctive violent escape that left in the dusk a mindless protective antagonism, pervading, in steady cumulate waves, directed at Horace as well.

"Come in, Titania," Horace said.

The little girl stood diffidently in silhouette. Belle's voice was sharp with relief. "Well, what do you want? Sit over there," she hissed at Horace. "What do you want, Belle?" Horace drew away a little, but without rising.

"I've got a new story to tell you, soon," he said. But little Belle stood yet, as though she had not heard, and her mother said:

"Go on and play, Belle. Why did you come in the house? It isn't supper time, yet."

"Everybody's gone home," she answered. "I haven't got anybody to play with."

"Go to the kitchen and talk to Rachel then," Belle said. She struck the keys again, harshly. "You worry me to death, hanging around the house." The little girl stood for a moment longer; then she turned obediently and went away. "Sit over there," Belle repeated. Horace resumed his chair and Belle played again, loudly and swiftly, with cold hysterical skill. Overhead Harry thumped again across the floor; they descended the stairs. Harry was still talking; the voices passed on toward the rear, ceased. Belle continued to play; still about him in the darkening room that blind protective antagonism like a muscular contraction that remains after the impulse of fright has died. Without turning her head she said:

"Are you going to stay for supper?"

He was not, he answered, waking suddenly. She did not rise with him, did not turn her head, and he let himself out the

front door and into the late spring twilight, where was already
a faint star above the windless trees. On the drive just without the garage Harry's new car stood. At the moment he was
doing something to the engine of it while the house-yard-
stable boy held a patent trouble-lamp above the beetling crag
of his head and his daughter and Rachel, holding tools or detached sections of the car's vitals, leaned their intent dissimilar faces across his bent back and into the soft bluish glare of
the light. Horace went on homeward. Twilight, evening, came
swiftly. Before he reached the corner where he turned, the
street lamps sputtered and failed, then glared above the intersections, beneath the arching trees.

4.

"General William Booth has gotten a leprechaun on Uriah's
wife," Horace told himself, and gravely presented the flowers
he had brought, and received in return the starry incense of
her flying eyes. Mrs Marders was among the group of Belle's
more intimate familiars in this room, affable and brightly cold,
a little detached and volubly easy; she admired little Belle's
gifts one by one with impeccable patience. Belle's voice came
from the adjoining room where the piano was bowered for
the occasion by potted palms and banked pots and jars of
bloom, and where yet more ladies were sibilantly crescendic
with an occasional soberly clad male on the outer fringe
of their colorful chattering like rocks dumbly imponderable
about the cauldron where seethed an hysterical tideflux. These
men spoke to one another from the sides of their mouths and,
when addressed by the ladies, with bleak and swift affability,
from the teeth outward. Harry's bald bullet head moved
among his guests, borne hither and yon upon the harsh uproar
of his voice; presently, when the recital would have gotten un-
derway and the ladies engaged, he would begin to lead the
men one by one and on tiptoe from the room and up the back
stairs to his apartments.

But now the guests stood and drifted and chattered, anticipatory and unceasing, and every minute or two Harry gravi-
tated again to the dining room, on the table of which his
daughter's gifts and flowers were arrayed and beside which

little Belle in her pale lilac dress stood in a shining-eyed and breathless ecstasy.

"Daddy's gal," Harry, in his tight, silver-gray gabardine suit and his bright tie with the diamond stud, chortled, putting his short thick hands on her; then together they examined the latest addition to the array of gifts with utter if dissimilar sincerity—little Belle with quiet and shining diffidence, her father stridently, tactlessly overloud. Harry was smoking his cigarettes steadily, scattering ash; he had receptacles of them open on every available flat surface throughout the lighted rooms. "How's the boy?" he added, shaking Horace's hand.

"Will you look at that sumptuous bouquet Horace has brought your daughter," Mrs Marders said. "Horace, it's really a shame. She'd have appreciated a toy or a doll much more, wouldn't you honey? Are you trying to make Belle jealous?"

Little Belle gave Horace her flying stars again. Harry squatted before her.

"Did Horace bring daddy's gal some flowers?" he brayed. "Just look at the flowers Horace brought her." He put his hands on her again. Mrs Marders said quickly:

"You'll burn her dress with that cigarette, Harry."

"Daddy's gal dont care," Harry answered. "Buy her a new dress tomorrow." But little Belle freed herself, craning her soft brown head in alarm, trying to see the back of her frock, and then Belle entered in pink beneath a dark blue frothing of tulle, and the rich bloody auburn of her hair. Little Belle showed her Horace's bouquet, and she knelt and fingered and patted little Belle's hair, and smoothed her dress.

"Did you thank him?" she asked. "I know you didn't."

"Of course she did," Horace interposed. "Just as you thank providence for breath every time you breathe." Little Belle looked up at him with her grave ecstatic shining. "We think girls should always have flowers when they play music and dance," he explained, gravely too. "Dont we?"

"Yes," little Belle agreed breathlessly.

"Yes, sir," Belle corrected fretfully. Patting and pulling at her daughter's delicate wisp of dress, with its tiny embroidered flowers at the yoke. Belle kneeling in a soft swishing of silk, with her rich and smoldering unrepose. Harry stood with his squat, tightly-clothed body, looking at Horace with the friendly, blood-shot bewilderment of his eyes.

"Yes, sir," little Belle piped obediently.

Belle rose, swishing again. "Come on, sister. It's time to begin. And dont forget and start pulling at your clothes."

The indiscriminate furniture—dining-room chairs, rockers, sofas and all—were ranged in semicircular rows facing the corner where the piano was placed. Beside the piano and above little Belle's soft brown head and her little sheer frock and the tense, impotent dangling of her legs, the music teacher, a thin passionate spinster with cold thwarted eyes behind nose glasses, stood. The men clung stubbornly to the rear row of chairs, their sober decorum splotched sparsely among the cacophonous hues of the women's dresses. With the exception of Harry, that is, who now sat with the light full on his bald crag. Just beyond him and between him and Mrs Marders, Horace could see Narcissa's dark burnished head. Belle sat on the front row at the end, turned sideways in her chair. The other ladies were still now, temporarily, in a sort of sibilant vacuum of sound into which the tedious labored tinkling of little Belle's playing fell like a fairy fountain.

The music tinkled and faltered, hesitated, corrected itself to the intent nodding of little Belle's head and the strained meagre gestures of the teacher, tinkled monotonously and tunelessly on while the assembled guests sat in a sort of bland, waiting inattention; and Horace speculated on that persevering and senseless urge of parents (and of all adults) for making children a little ridiculous in their own eyes and in the eyes of other children. The clothes they make them wear, the stupid mature things they make them do. And he found himself wondering if to be cultured did not mean to be purged of all taste; civilized, to be robbed of all fineness of objective judgment regarding oneself. Then he remembered that little Belle also had been born a woman.

The music tinkled thinly, ceased; the teacher leaned forward with a passionate movement and removed the sheet from the rack, and the room swelled with a polite adulation of bored palms. Horace too; and little Belle turned on the bench, with her flying eyes, and Horace grinned faintly at his own masculine vanity. Sympathy here, when she was answering one of the oldest compulsions of her sex, a compulsion that taste nor culture nor anything else would ever cause to appear ridiculous to her. Then the teacher spoke to her and she turned on the bench again, with her rapt laborious fingers and the brown, intent nodding of her head.

Belle sat sideways in her chair. Her head was bent and her hands lay idle upon her lap and she sat brooding and remote. Horace watched her, the line of her neck, the lustrous stillness of her arm; trying to project himself into that region of rich and smoldering immobility into which she had withdrawn for the while. But he could not; she did not seem to be aware of him at all; the corridors where he sought her were empty, and he moved quietly in his seat beneath the thin tinkling of the music and looked about at the other politely attentive heads and beyond them, in the doorway, Harry making significant covert signs in his direction. Harry jerked his thumb toward his mouth and moved his head meaningly, but Horace flipped his hand briefly in reply, without moving. When he looked doorward again Harry was gone.

Little Belle ceased again. When the clapping died the heavy thump-thump-thump of Harry's heels sounded on the ceiling above. Ridiculous, like the innocent defenseless backside of a small boy caught delving into an apple barrel, and a few of the guests cast their eyes upward in polite astonishment. Belle raised her head sharply, with an indescribable gesture, then she looked at Horace with cold and blazing irritation, enveloping, savage, disdainful of who might see. The thumping ceased, became a cautious clumsy tipping, and Belle's anger faded, though her gaze was still full upon him. Little Belle played again and Horace looked away from the cold fixity of Belle's gaze, a little uncomfortably, and so saw Harry and one of the men guests enter surreptitiously and seat themselves; he turned his head again. Beneath the heavy shadow of her hair Belle still watched him, and he shaped three words with his lips. But Belle's mouth did not change its sullen repose, nor her eyes, and then he realized that she was not looking at him at all, perhaps had never been.

Later Belle herself went to the piano and played a trite saccharine waltz and little Belle danced to it with studied, meaningless gestures too thinly conceived and too airily executed
to be quite laughable, and stood with her diffident shining
among the smug palms. She would have danced again, but
Belle rose from the piano, and the guests rose also with
prompt unanimity and surrounded her in laudatory sibilance.
Belle stood moodily beside her daughter in the center of it,
and little Belle pleasurably. Horace rose also. Above the gabbling of the women he could hear Harry again overhead:
thump-thump-thump, and he knew that Belle was also listening although she responded faultlessly to the shrill indistinguishable compliments of her guests. Beside little Belle
the teacher stood, with her cold, sad eyes, proprietorial and
deprecatory, touching little Belle's hair with a meagre passionate hand.

Then they drifted doorward, with their shrill polite uproar.
Little Belle slid from among them and came, a little drunk
with all the furore and her central figuring in it, and took
Horace's hand. "What do you think was the best," she asked.
"When I played, or when I danced?"

"I think they both were," he answered.

"I know. But what do you *think* was the best?"

"Well, I think the dancing was, because your mamma was
playing for you."

"So do I," little Belle agreed. "They could see all of me when
I was dancing, couldn't they? When you are playing, they cant
see but your back."

"Yes," Horace agreed. He moved toward the door, little
Belle still clinging to his hand.

"I wish they wouldn't go. Why do they have to go now?
Cant you stay a while?"

"I must take Narcissa home. She cant go home by herself,
you know."

"Yes," little Belle agreed. "Daddy could take her home in
our car."

"I expect I'd better do it. But I'll be coming back soon."

"Well, all right, then." Little Belle sighed with weary contentment. "I certainly do like parties; I certainly do. I wish we
had one every night." The guests clotted at the door, evacu-

ating with politely trailing phrases into the darkness. Belle stood responding to their recapitulations with smoldering patience. Narcissa stood slightly aside, waiting for him, and Harry was among them again, strident and affable.

"Daddy's gal," he said. "Did Horace see her playing the piano and dancing? Want to go up and take one before you leave?" he asked Horace in a jarring undertone.

"No, thanks. Narcissa's waiting for me. Some other time."

"Sure, sure," Harry agreed, and Horace was aware of Belle beside him, speaking to little Belle, but when he turned his head she was moving away with her silken swishing and her heavy, faint scent. Harry was still talking. "How about a couple of sets tomorrow? Let's get over early, before Belle's gang comes, and get in a couple of fast ones, then let 'em have the court."

"All right," Horace agreed, as he always did to this arrangement, wondering as usual if that boy's optimism of Harry's really permitted him to believe that they could or would follow it out, or if he had just said the phrase so many times that the juxtaposition of the words no longer had any meaning in his liquor-fuddled brain. Then Narcissa was beside him, and they were saying Goodnight, and the door closed upon little Belle, and Harry's glazed squat dome and upon Belle's smoldering and sullen rage. She had said no word to him all evening.

It was the evening of little Belle's recital, the climacteric of her musical year. During the whole evening Belle had not looked at him, had said no word to him, even when, in the departing crush at the door and while Harry was trying to persuade him upstairs for a night-cap, he felt her beside him for an instant, smelled the heavy scent she used. But she said no word to him even then, and he put Harry aside at last and the door closed on little Belle and on Harry's glazed dome, and Horace turned into the darkness and found that Narcissa hadn't waited. She was halfway to the street. "If you're going my way, I'll walk along with you," he called to her. She made no reply, neither did she slacken her pace nor increase it when he joined her.

"Why is it," he began, "that grown people will go to so much trouble to make children do ridiculous things, do you suppose? Belle had a house full of people she doesn't care any-thing about and most of whom dont approve of her, and kept little Belle up three hours past her bedtime; and the result is Harry's about half tight, and Belle is in a bad humor, and little Belle is too excited to go to sleep, and you and I wish we were home and are sorry we didn't stay there."

"Why do you go there, then?" Narcissa asked. Horace was suddenly stilled. They walked on through the darkness, toward the next street light. Against it branches hung like black coral in a yellow sea.

"Oh," Horace said. Then: "I saw that old cat talking with you."

"Why do you call Mrs Marders an old cat? Because she told me something that concerns me and that everybody else seems to know already?"

"So that's who told you, is it? I wondered. . . . . . ." He slid his arm within her unresponsive one. "Dear old Narcy." They passed through the dappled shadows beneath the light, went on into darkness again.

"Is it true?" she asked.

"You forget that lying is a struggle for survival," he said. "Little puny man's way of dragging circumstance about to fit his preconception of himself as a figure in the world. Revenge on the sinister gods."

"Is it true?" she persisted. They walked on, arm in arm, she gravely insistent and waiting; he shaping and discarding phrases in his mind, finding time to be amused at his own fan-tastic impotence in the presence of her constancy.

"People dont usually lie about things that dont concern them," he answered wearily. "They are impervious to the world, even if they aren't to life. Not when the actuality is so much more diverting than their imaginings could be," he added. She freed her arm with grave finality.

"Narcy——"

"Dont," she said. "Dont call me that." The next corner, be-neath the next light, was theirs; they would turn there. Above the arched canyon of the street the sinister gods stared down with pale, unwinking eyes. Horace thrust his hands into his jacket, and for a space he was stilled again while his fingers learned the unfamiliar object they had found in his pocket.

Then he drew it forth: a sheet of heavy notepaper, folded twice and impregnated with a fading heavy scent. A familiar scent, yet baffling for the moment, like a face watching him from an arras. He knew the face would emerge in a moment, but as he held the note in his fingers and sought the face through the corridors of his present distraction, his sister spoke suddenly and hard at his side.

"You've got the smell of her all over you. Oh, Horry, she's dirty!"

"I know," he answered unhappily, and the face emerged clearly, and he was suddenly empty and cold and sad. "I know." It was like a road stretching on through darkness, into nothingness and so away; a road lined with black motionless trees O thou grave myrtle shapes amid which Death. A road along which he and Narcissa walked like two children drawn apart one from the other to opposite sides of it; strangers, yet not daring to separate and go in opposite ways, while the sinister gods watched them with cold unwinking eyes. And somewhere, everywhere, behind and before and about them pervading, the dark warm cave of Belle's rich discontent and the tiger-reek of it.

But the world was opening out before him fearsome and sad and richly moribund, as though he were again an adolescent, and filled with shadowy shapes of dread and of delight not to be denied: he must go on, though the other footsteps sounded fainter and fainter in the darkness behind him and then not at all. Perhaps they had ceased, or turned into a byway.

This byway led her back to Miss Jenny. It was now well into June, and the scent of Miss Jenny's transplanted jasmine drifted steadily into the house and filled it with constant cumulate waves like a fading resonance of viols. The earlier flowers were gone, and the birds had finished eating the strawberries and now sat about the fig bushes all day, waiting for them to ripen; zinnia and delphinium bloomed without any assistance from Isom who, since Caspey had more or less returned to normalcy and laying-by time was yet a while away, might be found on the shady side of the privet hedge along the garden fence, trimming the leaves one by one from a single twig with a pair of mule shears until Miss Jenny returned to the house; whereupon he retreated himself and lay on the creek-bank for the rest of the afternoon, his hat over his eyes and a cane fishing pole propped between his toes. Old Simon pottered querulously about the place. His linen duster and tophat gathered chaff and dust on the nail in the harness room and the horses waxed fat and lazy and insolent in the pasture. The duster and hat came down from the nail and the horses were harnessed to the carriage but once a week, now—on Sundays, to drive in to town to church. Miss Jenny said she was too far along to jeopardize salvation by driving to church at fifty miles an hour; that she had as many sins as her ordinary behavior could take care of, particularly as she had old Bayard's soul to get into heaven somehow, also, what with him and young Bayard tearing around the country every afternoon at the imminent risk of their necks. About young Bayard's soul Miss Jenny did not alarm herself at all: he had no soul.

Meanwhile he rode about the farm and harried the negro tenants in his cold fashion, and in two dollar khaki breeches and a pair of field boots that had cost fourteen guineas he tinkered with farming machinery and with the tractor he had persuaded old Bayard to buy: for the time being he had become almost civilized again. He went to town only occasionally now, and often on horseback, and all in all his days had become so usefully innocuous that both his aunt and his grandfather were growing a little nervously anticipatory.

"Mark my words," Miss Jenny told Narcissa on the day she drove out again. "He's storing up devilment that's going to burst loose all at once, someday, and then there'll be hell to pay. Lord knows what it'll be—maybe he and Isom will take his car and that tractor and hold a steeple chase with 'em. . . . What did you come out for? Got another letter?"

"I've got several more," Narcissa answered lightly. "I'm saving them until I get enough for a book, then I'll bring them all out for you to read." Miss Jenny sat opposite her, erect as a crack guardsman, with that cold briskness of hers that caused agents and strangers to stumble through their errands with premonitions of failure ere they began. The guest sat motionless, her limp straw hat on her knees. "I just came to see

you," she added, and for a moment her face held such grave
and still despair that Miss Jenny sat more erect yet and stared
at her guest with her piercing gray eyes.

"Why, what is it, child? Did the man walk into your house?"

"No, no." The look was gone, but still Miss Jenny watched
her with those keen old eyes that seemed to see so much more
than you thought—or wished. "Shall I play a while? It's been
a long time, hasn't it?"

"Well," Miss Jenny agreed, "if you want to."

There was dust on the piano; Narcissa opened it with a fine
gesture. "If you'll let me get a cloth——"

"Here, lemme dust it," Miss Jenny said, and she caught up
her skirt by the hem and mopped the keyboard violently.
"There, that'll do." Then she drew her chair from behind the
instrument and seated herself. She still watched the other's
profile with speculation and a little curiosity, but presently
the old tunes stirred her memory again, and in a while her
eyes softened and the other and the trouble that had shown
momentarily in her face, were lost in Miss Jenny's own vanquished and abiding dead days, and it was some time before
she realized that Narcissa was weeping quietly while she
played.

Miss Jenny leaned forward and touched her arm. "Now,
you tell me what it is," she commanded. And Narcissa told
her in her grave contralto, still weeping quietly.

"Hmph," Miss Jenny said. "That's to be expected of a man
that hasn't any more to do than Horace. I dont see why you
are so upset over it."

"But that woman," Narcissa wailed suddenly, like a little
girl, burying her face in her hands. "She's so dirty!"

Miss Jenny dug a man's handkerchief from the pocket of her
skirt and gave it to the other:

"What do you mean?" she asked. "Dont she wash often
enough?"

"Not that way. I m-mean she's—she's——" Narcissa turned
suddenly and laid her head on the piano.

"Oh," Miss Jenny said. "All women are, if that's what you
mean." She sat stiffly indomitable, contemplating the other's
shrinking shoulders. "Hmph," she said again. "Horace has
spent so much time being educated that he never has learned

anything. . . . . . . Why didn't you break it up in time? Didn't you see it coming?"

The other wept more quietly now. She sat up and dried her eyes on Miss Jenny's handkerchief. "It started before he went away. Dont you remember?"

"That's so. I do sort of remember a lot of women's gabble. Who told you about it, anyway? Horace?"

"Mrs Marders did. And then Horace did. But I never thought that he'd——I never thought——" again her head dropped to the piano, hidden in her arms. "I wouldn't have treated Horace that way," she wailed.

"Sarah Marders, was it? I might have known. . . . . . I admire strong character, even if it is bad," Miss Jenny stated. "Well, crying wont help any." She rose briskly. "We'll think what to do about it. Only I'd let him go ahead: it'll do him good if she'll just turn around and make a doormat of him. . . . . . . Too bad Harry hasn't got spunk enough to. . . . But I reckon he'll be glad; I know I would—— There, there," she said, at the other's movement of alarm. "I dont reckon Harry'll hurt him. Dry your face, now. You better go to the bathroom and fix up. Bayard'll be coming in soon, and you dont want him to see you've been crying, you know." Narcissa glanced swiftly at the door and dabbed at her face with Miss Jenny's handkerchief.

At times the dark lifted, the black trees were no longer sinister, and then Horace and Narcissa walked the road in sunlight, as of old. Then he would seek her through the house and cross the drive and descend the lawn in the sunny afternoon to where she sat in the white dresses he loved beneath the oak into which a mockingbird came each afternoon and sang, bringing her the result of his latest venture in glass-blowing. He had five now, in different colors and all nearly perfect, and each of them had a name. And as he finished them and before they were scarce cooled, he must bring them across the lawn to where she sat with a book or with a startled caller perhaps, in his stained dishevelled clothes and his sooty hands in which the vase lay demure and fragile as a bubble, and with his face blackened too with smoke and a little mad, passionate and fine and austere.

But then the dark would descend once more, and beyond

the black and motionless trees Belle's sultry imminence was like a presence, like the odor of death. And then he and Narcissa were strangers again, tugging and straining at the shackles of custom and old affection that bound them with slipping bonds.

And then they were no longer even side by side. At times he called back to her through the darkness, making no sound and receiving no reply; at times he hovered distractedly like a dark bird between the two of them. But at last he merged with himself, fused in the fatalism of his nature, and set his face steadily up the road, looking not back again. And then the footsteps behind him ceased.

5.

For a time the earth held him in a hiatus that might have been called contentment. He was up at sunrise, planting things in the ground and watching them grow and tending them; he cursed and harried niggers and mules into motion and kept them there, and put the grist mill into running shape and taught Caspey to drive the tractor, and came in at mealtimes and at night smelling of machine oil and of stables and of the earth and went to bed with grateful muscles and with the sober rhythms of the earth in his body, and so to sleep. But he still waked at times in the peaceful darkness of his room and without previous warning, tense and sweating with old terror. Then, momentarily, the world was laid away and he was a trapped beast in the high blue, mad for life, trapped in the very cunning fabric that had betrayed him who had dared chance too much, and he thought again if, when the bullet found you, you could only crash upward, burst; anything but earth. Not death, no: it was the crash you had to live through so many times before you struck that filled your throat with vomit.

But his days were filled, at least, and he discovered pride again. Nowadays he drove the car into town to fetch his grandfather from habit alone, and though he still considered forty five miles an hour merely cruising speed, he no longer took cold and fiendish pleasure in turning curves on two wheels or in detaching mules from wagons by striking the whiffle-trees

with his bumper in passing. Old Bayard still insisted on riding
with him when he must ride, but with freer breath; and once
he aired to Miss Jenny his growing belief that at last young
Bayard had outworn his seeking for violent destruction.

Miss Jenny, being a true optimist—that is, expecting the
worst at all times and so being daily agreeably surprised—
promptly disillusioned him. Meanwhile she made young
Bayard drink plenty of milk and otherwise superintended his
diet and hours in her martinettish way, and at times she entered his room at night and sat for a while beside the bed
where he slept.

Nevertheless, young Bayard improved in his ways. Without
being aware of the progress of it, he had become submerged
in a monotony of days, had been snared by a rhythm of activities repeated and repeated until his muscles grew so familiar with them as to get his body through the days without
assistance from him at all. He had been so neatly tricked by
earth, that ancient Delilah, that he was not aware that his locks
were shorn, was not aware that Miss Jenny and old Bayard
were wondering how long it would be before they grew out
again. He needs a wife, was Miss Jenny's thought. Then
maybe he'll stay sheared. "A young person to worry with
him," she said to herself. "Bayard's too old, and I've got too
much to do, to worry with the long devil."

He saw Narcissa about the house now and then, sometimes
at the table these days, and he still felt her shrinking and her
distaste, and at times Miss Jenny sat watching the two of them
with a sort of speculation and an exasperation with their seeming obliviousness of one another. He treats her like a dog
would treat a cut-glass pitcher, and she looks at him like a cut-
glass pitcher would look at a dog, she told herself.

Then sowing time was over, and it was summer, and he
found himself with nothing to do. It was like coming dazed
out of sleep, out of the warm, sunny valleys where people lived
into a region where cold peaks of savage despair stood bleakly
above the lost valleys, among black and savage stars.

The road descended in a quiet red curve between pines
through which the hot July winds swelled with a long sound
like a far away passing of trains, descended to a mass of lighter

green of willows, where a creek ran beneath a stone bridge. At the top of the grade the scrubby, rabbitlike mules stopped and the younger negro got down and lifted a gnawed white-oak sapling from the wagon and locked the off rear wheel by wedging the pole between the warped wire-bound spokes of it and across the axle-tree. Then he climbed back into the crazy wagon, where the other negro sat motionless with the rope-spliced reins in his hand and his head tilted creekward. "Whut 'uz dat?" he said.

"Whut wuz whut?" the other asked. His father sat in his attitude of arrested attention, and the younger negro listened also. But there was no further sound save the long sough of the wind among the sober pines and the liquid whistling of a quail somewhere among the green fastnesses of them. "Whut you hear, pappy?" he repeated.

"Somethin' busted down dar. Tree fell, mebbe." He jerked the reins. "Hwup, mules." The mules flapped their jackrabbit ears and lurched the wagon into motion, and they descended among cool dappled shadows, on the jarring scrape of the locked wheel that left behind it a glazed bluish ribbon in the soft red dust. At the foot of the hill the road crossed the bridge and went on mounting again; beneath the bridge the creek rippled and flashed brownly among willows, and beside the bridge and bottom up in the water, a motor car lay. Its front wheels were still spinning and the engine ran at idling speed, trailing a faint shimmer of exhaust. The older negro drove onto the bridge and stopped, and the two of them sat and stared statically down upon the car's long belly. The younger negro spoke suddenly:

"Dar he is! He in de water under hit. I kin see his foots stickin' out."

"He liable ter drown, dar," the other said, with interest and disapproval, and they descended from the wagon. The younger negro slid down the creek bank; the other wrapped the reins deliberately about one of the stakes that held the bed on the frame and thrust his peeled hickory goad beneath the seat and went around and dragged the pole free of the locked wheel and put it in the wagon. Then he also slid gingerly down the bank to where his son squatted, peering at Bayard's submerged legs.

"Dont you git too clost ter dat thing, boy," he commanded. "Hit mought blow up. Dont you year hit still grindin' in dar?"

"We got to git dat man out," the younger one replied. "He gwine drown."

"Dont you tech 'im. White folks be sayin' we done it. We gwine wait right heer 'twell some white man comes erlong."

"He'll drown 'fo' dat," the other said. "Layin' in dat water." He was barefoot, and he stepped into the water and stood again with brown flashing wings of water stemming about his lean black calves.

"You, John Henry!" his father said. "You come 'way fum dat thing."

"We got to git 'im outen dar," the boy repeated, and the one in the water and the other on the bank, they wrangled amicably while the water rippled about Bayard's boot toes. Then the younger negro approached warily and caught Bayard's leg and tugged at it. The body responded, shifted, stopped again, and grunting querulously the older negro sat and removed his shoes and stepped into the water also. "He hung again," John Henry said, squatting in the water with his arm beneath the car. "He hung under de guidin' wheel. His haid aint quite under water, dough. Lemme git de pole."

He mounted the bank and got the sapling from the wagon and returned and joined his father where the other stood in sober, curious disapproval above Bayard's legs, and with the pole they lifted the car enough to drag Bayard out. They lifted him onto the bank and he sprawled there in the sun, with his calm wet face and his matted hair, while water drained out of his boots, and they stood above him on alternate legs and wrung out their overalls.

"Hit's Cunnel Sartorises boy, aint it?" the elder said at last, and he lowered himself stiffly to the sand, groaning and grunting, and donned his shoes.

"Yessuh," the other answered. "Is he daid, pappy?"

"Co'se he is," the other answered pettishly. "Atter dat otto'-bile jumped offen dat bridge wid 'im en den trompled 'im in de creek? Whut you reckon he is, ef he aint daid? And whut you gwine say when de law axes you how come you de onli-est one dat foun' 'im daid? Tell me dat."

"Tell 'um you holp me."

"Hit aint none of my business. I never run dat thing offen dat bridge. Listen at it, dar, mumblin' and grindin' yit. You git on 'fo' hit blows up."

"We better git 'im into town," John Henry said. "Dey mought not nobody else be comin' 'long today." He stooped and lifted Bayard's shoulders and tugged him to a sitting position. "He'p me git 'im up de bank, pappy."

"Hit aint none o' my business," the other repeated, but he stooped and picked up Bayard's legs and they lifted him, and he groaned without waking.

"Dar, now," John Henry exclaimed. "Year dat? He aint daid." But he might well have been, with his long inert body and his head wrung excruciatingly against John Henry's shoulder. They shifted their grips and turned toward the road. "Hah," John Henry exclaimed. "Le's go!"

They struggled up the shaling bank with him and onto the road, where the elder let his end of the burden slip to the ground. "Whuf," he expelled his breath sharply. "He heavy ez a flou' bar'l."

"Come on, pappy," John Henry said. "Le's git 'im in de waggin." The other stooped again, and they raised Bayard with dust caked redly on his wet thighs, and heaved him by grunting stages into the wagon. "He look lak a daid man," John Henry added, "and he sho' do ack lak one. I'll ride back here wid 'im and keep his haid fum bumpin'."

"Git dat brakin' pole you lef' in de creek," his father ordered, and John Henry descended and retrieved the sapling and got in the wagon again and lifted Bayard's head onto his knees, and his father unwrapped the reins and mounted to the sagging seat and picked up his peeled wand.

"I dont lak dis kin' o' traffickin'," he repeated. "Hwup, mules." The mules lurched the wagon into motion once more, and they went on. Behind them the car lay on its back in the creek, its engine still muttering at idling speed.

Its owner lay in the springless wagon, lax and inert with the jolting of it. Thus for some miles, while John Henry held his battered straw hat between the white man's face and the sun. Then the jolting penetrated into that region where Bayard lay, and he groaned again. "Drive slower, pappy," John Henry said. "De joltin' wakin' 'im up."

"I caint he'p dat," the elder replied. "I never run dat otto'-bile offen dat bridge. I got to git on into town en git on back home. Git on dar, mules."

John Henry made to ease him to the jolting, and Bayard groaned again and raised his hand to his chest, and he moved and opened his eyes. But he closed them immediately against the sun and he lay with his head on John Henry's knees, cursing. Then he moved again, trying to sit up. John Henry held him down, and he opened his eyes again, struggling.

"Let go, God damn you!" he said. "I'm hurt."

"Yessuh, captain; ef you'll jes' lay still——"

Bayard heaved himself violently, clutching his side; his teeth glared between his drawn lips and he gripped John Henry's shoulder with a clutch like steel hooks. "Stop," he shouted, glaring wildly at the back of the older negro's head. "Stop him; make him stop! He's driving my damn ribs right through me." He cursed again, trying to get onto his knees, gripping John Henry's shoulder, clutching his side with his other hand. The older negro turned and looked back at him. "Hit him with something," Bayard shouted. "Make him stop. I'm hurt, God damn it!"

The wagon stopped. Bayard was now on all fours, his head hanging and swaying from side to side like a wounded beast. The two negroes watched him quietly, and still clutching his side he moved and essayed to climb out of the wagon. John Henry jumped down and helped him, and he got slowly out and leaned against the wheel, with his sweating, bloodless face and his clenched grin.

"Git back in de waggin, captain," John Henry said, "and le's git to town to de doctor."

The color seemed to have drained from his eyes too. He leaned against the wagon, moistening his lips with his tongue. He moved again and sat down at the roadside, fumbling at the buttons of his shirt. The two negroes watched him.

"Got a knife, son?" he said.

"Yessuh." John Henry produced it, and by Bayard's direction he slit the shirt off. Then with the negro's help Bayard bound it tightly about his body, and he got to his feet.

"Got a cigarette?"

John Henry had not. "Pappy got some chewin' terbacker," he suggested.

"Gimme a chew, then." They gave him a chew and helped him back into the wagon and onto the seat. The other negro took up the lines. They jingled and rattled interminably on in the red dust, from shadow to sunlight, up hill and down. Bayard clutched his chest with his arms and chewed and cursed steadily. On and on, and at every jolt, with every breath, his broken ribs stabbed and probed into his flesh; on and on from shadow to sunlight and into shadow again.

A final hill, and the road emerged from the shade and crossed the flat treeless valley and joined the highway, and here they stopped, the sun blazing downward on his naked shoulders and bare head while he and the old negro wrangled as to whether they should take Bayard home or not. Bayard raged and swore but the other was querulously adamant, whereupon Bayard took the reins from his hands and swung the mules up the valley and with the end of the reins lashed the astonished creatures into mad motion.

This last mile was the worst of all. On all sides of them cultivated fields spread away to the shimmering hills: earth was saturated with heat and broken and turned and saturated again and drunken with it; exuding heat like an alcoholic's breath. The trees along the road were sparse and but half grown, and the mules slowed to a maddening walk in their own dust. He surrendered the reins again, and in a red doze he clung to the seat, conscious only of dreadful thirst, knowing that he was becoming light headed. The negroes too realized that he was going out of his head, and the younger one removed his frayed hat and Bayard put it on.

The mules with their comical, over-large ears assumed fantastic shapes, merged into other shapes without significance; shifted and merged again. At times it seemed to him that they were travelling backward, that they would crawl terrifically past the same tree or telephone pole time after time; and it seemed to him that the three of them and the rattling wagon and the two beasts were caught in a senseless treadmill: a motion without progress, forever and to no escape.

But at last and without his being aware of it, the wagon turned in between the iron gates, and shadow fell upon his naked shoulders, and he opened his eyes and his home swam and floated in a pale mirage. The jolting stopped and the two negroes helped him down and the younger one followed him to the steps, holding his arm. But he flung him off and mounted and crossed the veranda; in the hallway, after the outer glare, he could see nothing for a moment and he stood swaying and a little nauseated, blinking. Then Simon's eyeballs rolled out of the obscurity.

"Whut in de Lawd's name," Simon said, "is you been into now?"

"Simon?" he said. He swayed, staggered for balance, and blundered into something. "Simon?"

Simon moved quickly and touched him. "I kep' tellin' you dat car 'uz gwine kill you; I kep' tellin' you!" Simon slid his arm about Bayard and led him on toward the stairs. But he would not turn here, and they went on down the hall and Simon helped him into the office and he stopped, leaning on a chair.

"Keys," he said thickly. "Aunt Jenny. Get drink."

"Miss Jenny done gone to town wid Miss Benbow," Simon answered. "Dey aint nobody here, aint nobody here a-tall 'cep' de niggers. I kep' tellin' you!" he moaned again, pawing at Bayard. "Dey aint no blood, dough. Come to de sofa and lay down, Mist' Bayard."

Bayard moved again, and Simon supported him, and Bayard lurched around the chair and slumped into it, clutching his chest. "Dey aint no blood," Simon babbled.

"Keys," Bayard repeated. "Get the keys."

"Yessuh, I'll git 'um." But he continued to flap his distracted hands about Bayard until Bayard swore at him and flung him violently off. Still moaning Dey aint no blood, Simon turned and scuttled from the room. Bayard sat forward, clutching his chest, and heard Simon mount the stairs, and cross the floor overhead. Then he was back, and Bayard watched him open the desk and extract the silver stoppered decanter. He set it down and scuttled out again and returned with a glass, to find Bayard beside the desk, drinking from the decanter. Simon helped him back to the chair and poured him a drink into the glass. Then he fetched him a cigarette and hovered futilely and distractedly about him. "Lemme git de doctuh, Mist' Bayard."

"No. Gimme another drink."

Simon obeyed. "Dat's three, already. Lemme go git Miss Jenny en de doctuh, Mist' Bayard, please, suh."

"No. Leave me alone. Get out of here."

He drank that one. The nausea, the mirage shapes, were gone, and he felt better. At every breath his side stabbed him with hot needles, so he was careful to breathe shallowly. If he could only remember that. . . . . . . Yes, he felt much better, so he rose carefully and went to the desk and had another drink. Yes, that was the stuff for a wound, like Suratt had said. Like that time he got that tracer in his belly and nothing would stay on his stomach except gin-and-milk. And this, this wasn't anything: just a few caved slats. Patch up his fuselage with a little piano wire in ten minutes. Not like Johnny. They were all going right into his thighs. Damn butcher wouldn't even raise his sights a little. He must remember to breathe shallowly.

He crossed the room slowly. Simon flitted in the dim hall before him, and he mounted the stairs slowly, holding to the rail while Simon flapped his hands and watched him. He entered his room, the room that had been his and John's, and he stood for a while against the wall until he could breathe shallowly again. Then he crossed to the closet and opened it, and kneeling carefully, with his hand against his side, he opened the chest which was there. There was not much in it: a garment; a small leather-bound book; a shotgun shell to which was attached by a bit of wire a withered bear's paw. It was John's first bear, and the shell with which he had killed it in the river bottom near MacCallum's when he was twelve years old. The book was a new testament; on the flyleaf in faded brown: 'To my son, John, on his seventh birthday, March 16, 1900, from his Mother.' He had one exactly like it; that was the year grandfather had arranged for the morning local freight to stop and pick them up and take them in to town to start to school. The garment was a canvas hunting coat, stained and splotched with what had once been blood and scuffed and torn by briers and smelling yet faintly of saltpeter.

Still kneeling, he lifted the objects out one by one and laid them on the floor. He picked up the coat again, and its fading stale acridity drifted in his nostrils with an intimation of life and warmth. "Johnny," he whispered, "Johnny." Suddenly he raised the garment toward his face but halted it as sharply, and with the coat half raised he looked swiftly over his shoulder. But immediately he recovered himself and turned his head and lifted the garment and laid his face against it, defiantly and deliberately, and knelt so for a time.

Then he rose and gathered up the book and the trophy and the coat and crossed to his chest of drawers and took from it a photograph. It was a picture of John's Princeton eating club group, and he gathered this also under his arm and descended the stairs and passed on out the back door. As he emerged Simon was just crossing the yard with the carriage, and as he passed the kitchen Elnora was crooning one of her mellow endless songs.

Behind the smoke-house squatted the black pot and the wooden tubs where Elnora did her washing in fair weather. She had been washing today; the clothes line swung with its damp, limp burden, and beneath the pot smoke yet curled from the soft ashes. He thrust the pot over with his foot and rolled it aside, and from the woodshed he fetched an armful of rich pine and laid it on the ashes. Soon a blaze, pale in the sunny air; and when the wood was burning strongly he laid the coat and the bible and the trophy and the photograph on the flames and prodded them and turned them until they were consumed. In the kitchen Elnora crooned mellowly as she labored; her voice came rich and plaintful and sad along the sunny reaches of the air. He must remember to breathe shallowly.

Simon drove rapidly to town, but he had been forestalled. The two negroes had told a merchant about finding Bayard on the roadside and the news had reached the bank, and old Bayard sent for Dr Peabody. But Dr Peabody was gone fishing, so he took Dr Alford instead, and the two of them in Dr Alford's car passed Simon just on the edge of town. He turned about and followed them, but by the time he arrived home they had young Bayard anaesthetized and temporarily incapable of further harm; and when Miss Jenny and Narcissa drove unsuspectingly up the drive an hour later, he was bandaged and conscious again. They had not heard of it. Miss

Jenny did not recognise Dr Alford's car standing in the drive, but she had one look at the strange motor. "That fool has killed himself at last," she said, and she got out of Narcissa's machine and sailed into the house and up the stairs.

Bayard lay white and still and a little sheepish in his bed. Old Bayard and the doctor were just leaving, and Miss Jenny waited until they were out of the room, then she raged and stormed at him and stroked his hair, while Simon bobbed and bowed in the corner between bed and wall. "Dasso, Miss Jenny, dasso! I kep' a-tellin' 'im!"

She left him then and descended to the veranda where Dr Alford stood in impeccable departure. Old Bayard sat in the car waiting for him, and on Miss Jenny's appearance he became his stiff self again and completed his departing, and he and old Bayard drove away.

Miss Jenny also looked up and down the veranda, then into the hall. "Where—" she said, then she called: "Narcissa." A reply; "Where are you?" she added. The reply came again and Miss Jenny reentered the house and saw Narcissa's white dress in the gloom where she sat on the piano bench. "He's awake," Miss Jenny said. "You can come up and see him." The other rose and turned her face to the light. "Why, what's the matter?" Miss Jenny demanded. "You look lots worse than he does. You're white as a sheet."

"Nothing," the other answered. "I——" She stared at Miss Jenny a moment, clenching her hands at her sides. "I must go," she said, and she emerged into the hall. "It's late, and Horace. . . . . . ."

"You can come up and speak to him, cant you?" Miss Jenny asked, curiously. "There's not any blood, if that's what you are afraid of."

"It isn't that," Narcissa answered. "I'm not afraid."

Miss Jenny approached her, piercing and curious. "Why, all right," she said kindly. "If you'd rather not. I just thought perhaps you'd like to see he's all right, as long as you are here. But dont, if you dont feel like it."

"Yes. Yes. I feel like it. I want to." She passed Miss Jenny and went on. At the foot of the stairs she paused until Miss Jenny came up behind her, then she went on, mounting swiftly and with her face averted.

"What's the matter with you?" Miss Jenny demanded, trying to see the other's face. "What's happened to you? Have you gone and fallen in love with him?"

"In love . . . him? Bayard?" She paused, then hurried on, clutching the rail. She began to laugh thinly, and put her hand to her mouth. Miss Jenny mounted beside her, piercing and curious and cold; Narcissa hurried on. At the stair head she stopped again, still with her face averted, and let Miss Jenny pass her; and just without the door she stopped and leaned against it, throttling her laughter and her trembling. Then she entered the room, where Miss Jenny stood beside the bed watching her.

There was a sickish-sweet lingering of ether in the room, and she approached the bed blindly and stood beside it with her hidden clenched hands. Bayard's head was pallid and calm, like a chiseled mask brushed lightly over with his spent violence, and he was watching her, and for a while she gazed at him; and Miss Jenny and the room and all, swam away.

"You beast, you beast," she cried thinly. "Why must you always do these things where I've got to see you?"

"I didn't know you were there," Bayard answered mildly, with weak astonishment.

Every few days, by Miss Jenny's request, she came out and sat beside his bed and read to him. He cared nothing at all about books; it is doubtful if he had ever read a book on his own initiative; but he would lie motionless in his cast while her grave contralto voice went on and on in the quiet room. Sometimes he tried to talk to her, but she ignored his attempts and read on; if he persisted, she went away and left him. So he soon learned to lie, usually with his eyes closed, voyaging alone in the bleak and barren regions of his despair, while her voice flowed on and on above the remoter sounds that came up to them—Miss Jenny scolding Simon or Isom downstairs or in the garden; the twittering of birds in the tree just beyond the window; the ceaseless groaning of the water pump below the barn. At times she would cease and look at him and find that he was peacefully sleeping.

6.

Old man Falls came through the lush green of early June, came into town through the yet horizontal sunlight of morning, and in his dusty neat overalls he now sat opposite old Bayard in immaculate linen and a geranium like a merry wound. The room was cool and still, with the clear morning light and the casual dust of a negro janitor's casual and infrequent disturbing. Now that old Bayard was aging, and what with the deaf tenor of his stiffening ways, he was showing more and more a preference for surrounding himself with things of a like nature; showing an incredible aptitude for choosing servants who shaped their days to his in a sort of pottering and hopeless futility. The janitor, who dubbed old Bayard General and whom old Bayard and the other clients for whom he performed seemingly interminable duties of a slovenly and minor nature, addressed as Dr Jones, was one of these. He was black and stooped with querulousness and age, and he took advantage of everyone who would permit him, and old Bayard swore at him all the time he was around and allowed him to steal his tobacco and the bank's winter supply of coal by the scuttleful and peddle it to other negroes.

The windows behind which old Bayard and his caller sat gave upon a vacant lot of rubbish and dusty weeds. It was bounded by the weathered rears of sundry one storey board buildings within which small businesses—repair- and junk-shops and such—had their lowly and ofttimes anonymous being. The lot itself was used by day by country people as a depot for their teams; already some of these were tethered somnolent and ruminant there, and about the stale ammoniac droppings of their patient generations sparrows swirled in garrulous clouds, or pigeons slanted with sounds like rusty shutters, or strode and preened in burnished and predatory pomposity, crooning among themselves with guttural unemphasis.

Old man Falls sat on the opposite side of the trash-filled fireplace, mopping his face with a clean blue bandanna.

"It's my damned old legs," he roared, faintly apologetic. "Used to be I'd walk twelve-fifteen mile to a picnic or a singin' with less study than what that 'ere little old three mile into town gives me now." He mopped the handkerchief about that face of his browned and cheerful these many years with the simple and abounding earth. "Looks like they're fixin' to give out on me, and I aint but ninety-three, neither." He held his parcel in his other hand, but he continued to mop his face, making no motion to open it.

"Why didn't you wait on the road until a wagon came along?" old Bayard shouted. "Always some damn feller with a field full of weeds coming to town."

"I reckon I mought," the other agreed. "But gittin' here so quick would spile my holiday. I aint like you townfolks. I aint got so much time I kin hurry it." He stowed the handkerchief away and rose and laid his parcel carefully on the mantel, and from his shirt he produced a small object wrapped in a clean frayed rag. Beneath his tedious and unhurried fingers there emerged a tin snuff-box polished long since to the dull soft sheen of silver by handling and age. Old Bayard sat and watched, watched quietly as the other removed the cap of the box and put this, too, carefully aside.

"Now, turn yo' face up to the light," old man Falls directed.

"Loosh Peabody says that stuff will give me blood-poisoning, Will."

The other continued his slow preparations, his blue innocent eyes raptly preoccupied. "Loosh Peabody never said that," he corrected quietly. "One of them young doctors told you that, Bayard. Lean yo' face to the light." Old Bayard sat tautly back in his chair, his hands on the arms of it, watching the other with his piercing old eyes soberly, a little wistful; eyes filled with unnameable things like the eyes of old lions, and intent.

Old man Falls poised a dark gob of his ointment on one finger and set the box carefully on his vacated chair, and put his hand on old Bayard's face. But old Bayard still resisted, though passively, watching him with unutterable things in his eyes. Old man Falls drew his face firmly and gently into the light from the window.

"Come on, here. I aint young enough to waste time hurtin' folks. Hold still, now, so I wont spot yo' face up. My hand aint steady enough to lift a rifle ball offen a hot stove-led no mo'."

Bayard submitted then, and old man Falls patted the salve onto the wen with small deft touches. Then he took the bit of cloth and removed the surplus from Bayard's face and wiped his fingers and dropped the rag onto the hearth and knelt stiffly and touched a match to it. "We allus do that," he explained. "My granny got that 'ere from a Choctaw woman nigh a hundred and thutty year ago. Aint none of us never told what hit air nor left no after trace." He rose stiffly and dusted his knees. He recapped the box with the same unhurried care and put it away and picked up his parcel from the mantel and resumed his chair.

"Hit'll turn black tomorrer, and long's hit's black, hit's workin'. Dont put no water on yo' face befo' mawnin', and I'll come in again in ten days and dose hit again, and on the——" he mused a moment, computing slowly on his gnarled fingers; his lips moved, but with no sound. "——the ninth day of July, hit'll drap off. And dont you let Miss Jenny nor none of them doctors worry you about hit."

He sat with his knees together. The parcel lay on his knees and he now opened it after the ancient laborious ritual, picking patiently at the pink knot until a younger person would have screamed at him. Old Bayard merely lit a cigar and propped his feet against the fireplace, and in good time old man Falls solved the knot and removed the string and laid it across his chair-arm. It fell to the floor and he bent and fumbled it into his blunt fingers and laid it again across the chair-arm and watched it a moment lest it fall again, then he opened the parcel. First was his carton of tobacco, and he removed a plug and sniffed it, turned it about in his hand and sniffed it again. But without biting into it he laid it and its fellows aside and delved further yet. He spread open the throat of the resulting paper bag, and his innocent boy's eyes gloated soberly into it.

"I'll declare," he said. "Sometimes I'm right ashamed for havin' sech a consarned sweet-tooth. Hit dont give me no rest a-tall." Still carefully guarding the other objects on his knees he tilted the sack and shook two or three of the striped, shrimp-like things into his palm, returned all but one, which he put into his mouth. "I'm afeard now I'll be loosin' my teeth someday and I'll have to start gummin' 'em or eatin' soft ones. I never did relish soft candy." His leathery cheek bulged slightly, with slow regularity like a respiration. He peered into the sack again, and he sat weighing it in his hand.

"They was times back in sixty three and fo' when a feller could a bought a section of land and a couple of niggers with this yere bag of candy. Lots of times I mind, with ever'thing goin' agin us like, and sugar and cawfee gone and food scace, eatin' stole cawn when they was any to steal and ditch weeds ef they wa'nt; bivouackin' at night in the rain, more'n like. . . . . . ." His voice trailed away among ancient phantoms of the soul's and body's tribulations, into those regions of glamorous and useless strivings where such ghosts abide. He chuckled and mouthed his peppermint again.

"I mind that day we was a-dodgin' around Grant's army, headin' nawth. Grant was at Grenada then, and Cunnel had rousted us boys out and we taken hoss and jined Van Dorn down that-a-way. That was when Cunnel had that 'ere silver stallion. Grant was still at Grenada, but Van Dorn lit out one day, headin' nawth; why, us boys didn't know. Cunnel mought have knowed, but he never told us. Not that we keered much, long's we was headin' to'ds home.

"So our boys was ridin' along to ourselves, goin' to jine up with the balance of 'em later. Leastways the rest of 'em thought we was goin' to jine 'em. But Cunnel never had no idea of doin' that; his cawn hadn't been laid by yit, and he was goin' home fer a spell. We wasn't runnin' away," he explained. "We knowed Van Dorn could handle 'em all right fer a week or two. He usually done it. He was a putty good man," old man Falls said. "A putty good man."

"They were all pretty good men in those days," old Bayard agreed. "But you damn fellers quit fighting and went home too often."

"Well," old man Falls rejoined defensively, "even ef the hull country's overrun with bears, a feller cant hunt bears all the time. He's got to quit once in a while, ef hit's only to rest up the dawgs and hosses. But I reckon them dogs and hosses could stay on the trail long as any," he added with sober pride. " 'Course ever'body couldn't keep up with that 'ere mist-colored stallion. They wasn't but one animal in the Confedrit army could tech him—that last hoss Zeb Fothergill fotch back outen one of Sherman's cavalry pickets on his last trip into Tennessee.

"Nobody never did know what Zeb done on them trips of

his'n; Cunnel claimed hit was jest to steal hosses. But he never got back with lessen one. One time he come back with seven of the orneriest critters that ever walked, I reckon. He tried to swap 'em fer meat and cawn-meal, but wouldn't nobody have 'em; then he tried to give 'em to the army, but even the army wouldn't have 'em. So he finally turned 'em loose and requisitioned to Joe Johnston's haidquarters fer ten hosses sold to Forrest's cavalry. I dont know ef he ever got air answer. Nate Forrest wouldn't a had them hosses. I doubt ef they'd even a et 'em in Vicksburg. . . . . . . I never did put no big reliabililty in Zeb Fothergill, him comin' and goin' by hisself like he done. But he knowed hosses, and he usually fotch a good 'un home ever' time he went away to'ds the war. But he never got another'n like this befo'."

The bulge was gone from his cheek and he produced his pocket knife and cut a neat segment from his plug of tobacco and lipped it from the knife-blade. Then he rewrapped his parcel and tied the string about it. The ash of old Bayard's cigar trembled delicately about its glowing heart, but did not yet fall.

Old man Falls spat neatly and brownly into the cold fireplace. "That day we was in Calhoun county," he continued. "Hit was as putty a summer mawnin' as you ever see; men and hosses rested and fed and feelin' peart, trottin' along the road through the woods and fields whar birds was a-singin' and young rabbits lopin' acrost the road. Cunnel and Zeb was ridin' along side by side on them two hosses, Cunnel on Jupiter and Zeb on that sorrel two-year-old, and they was a-braggin' as usual. We all knowed Cunnel's Jupiter, but Zeb kep' a-contendin' he wouldn't take no man's dust. The road was putty straight across the bottom to'ds the river and Zeb kep' on a-aggin' the Cunnel fer a race, until Cunnel says All right. He told us boys to come on and him and Zeb would wait fer us at the river bridge 'bout fo' mile ahead, and him and Zeb lined up and lit out.

"Them hosses was the puttiest livin' things I ever seen. They went off together like two hawks, neck and neck. They was outen sight in no time, with dust swirlin' behind, but we could foller 'em fer a ways by the dust they left, watchin' it kind of suckin' on down the road like one of these here ottomobiles was in the middle of it. When they come to whar the road drapped down to the river Cunnel had Zeb beat by about three hundred yards. Thar was a spring-branch jest under the ridge, and when Cunnel sailed over the rise, thar was a comp'ny of Yankee cavalry with their hosses picketed and their muskets stacked, eatin' dinner by the spring. Cunnel says they was a-settin' thar gapin' at the rise when he come over hit, holdin' cups of cawfee and hunks of bread in their hands and their muskets stacked about fo'ty foot away, buggin' their eyes at him.

"It was too late fer him to turn back, anyhow, but I dont reckon he would ef they'd been time. He jest spurred down the ridge and rid in amongst 'em, scatterin' cook-fires and guns and men, shoutin' 'Surround 'em, boys! Ef you move, you air dead men.' One or two of 'em made to break away, but Cunnel drawed his pistols and let 'em off, and they come back and scrouged in amongst the others, and thar they set, still a-holdin' their dinner, when Zeb come up. And that was the way we found 'em when we got thar ten minutes later." Old man Falls spat again, neatly and brownly, and he chuckled. His eyes shone like periwinkles. "That cawfee was sho' mighty fine," he added.

"And thar we was, with a passel of prisoners we didn't have no use fer. We held 'em all that day and et their grub; and when night come we taken and throwed their muskets into the crick and taken their ammunition and the rest of the grub and put a gyard on their hosses, then the rest of us laid down. And all that night we laid thar in them fine Yankee blankets, listenin' to them prisoners sneakin' away one at a time, slippin' down the bank into the crick and wadin' off. Time to time one would slip er make a splash er somethin', then they'd all git right still fer a spell. But putty soon we'd hear 'em at it again, crawlin' through the bushes to'ds the crick, and us layin' thar with blanket aidges held agin our faces. Hit was nigh dawn 'fore the last one had snuck off in a way that suited 'im.

"Then Cunnel from whar he was a-layin' let out a yell them pore critters could hear fer a mile.

" 'Go it, Yank,' he says, 'and look out fer moccasins!'

"Next mawnin' we saddled up and loaded our plunder and ever' man taken him a hoss, and lit out fer home. We'd been home two weeks and Cunnel had his cawn laid by, when we heard 'bout Van Dorn ridin' into Holly Springs and burnin' Grant's sto's. Seems like he never needed no help from us, noways." He chewed his tobacco for a time, quietly retrospective, reliving in the company of men now dust with the dust for which they had, unwittingly perhaps, fought, those gallant, pinch-bellied days into which few who now trod that earth could enter with him.

Old Bayard shook the ash from his cigar. "Will," he said, "what the devil were you folks fighting about, anyhow?"

"Bayard," old man Falls answered. "Be damned ef I ever did know."

After old man Falls had departed with his small parcel and his innocently bulging cheek, old Bayard sat and smoked his cigar. Presently he raised his hand and touched the wen on his face, but lightly, remembering old man Falls' parting stricture; and recalling this, the thought that it might not yet be too late, that he might yet remove the paste with water, followed.

He rose and crossed to the lavatory in the corner of the room. Above it was fixed a small cabinet with a mirror in the door, and in it he examined the black spot on his cheek, touching it again with his fingers, then examining his hand. Yes, it might still come off. . . . . . But be damned if he would; be damned to a man who didn't know his own mind. And Will Falls, too; Will Falls, hale and sane and sound as a dollar; Will Falls who, as he himself had said, was too old to have any reason for injuring anyone. He flung his cigar away and quitted the room and tramped through the lobby toward the door where his chair sat. But before he reached the door he turned about and came up to the cashier's window, behind which the cashier sat in a green eyeshade.

"Res," he said.

The cashier looked up. "Yes, Colonel?"

"Who is that damn boy that hangs around here, looking through that window all day?" Old Bayard lowered his voice within a pitch or so of an ordinary conversational tone.

"What boy, Colonel?" Old Bayard pointed, and the cashier raised himself on his stool and peered over the partition and saw beyond the indicated window a boy of ten or twelve watching him with an innocently casual air. "Oh. That's Will Beard's boy, from up at the boarding house," he shouted. "Friend of Byron's, I think."

"What's he doing around here? Every time I walk through here, there he is looking in that window. What does he want?"

"Maybe he's a bank robber," the cashier suggested.

"What?" Old Bayard cupped his ear fiercely in his palm.

"Maybe he's a bank robber," the other shouted, leaning forward on his stool. Old Bayard snorted and tramped violently on and slammed his chair back against the door. The cashier sat lumped and shapeless on his stool, rumbling deep within his gross body. He said, without turning his head: "Colonel's let Will Falls treat him with that salve." Snopes at his desk made no reply; did not raise his head. After a time the boy moved, and drifted casually and innocently away.

Virgil Beard now possessed a pistol that projected a stream of ammoniac water excruciatingly painful to the eyes, a small magic lantern, and an ex-candy showcase in which he kept birds' eggs and an assortment of insects that had died slowly on pins, and a modest hoard of nickels and dimes. With a child's innocent pleasure he divulged to his parents the source of this beneficence, and his mother took Snopes to her gray heart, fixing him special dishes and performing trifling acts to increase his creature comfort with bleak and awkward gratitude.

At times the boy, already dressed and with his bland shining face, would enter his room and waken him from his troubled sleep and sit on a chair while Snopes donned his clothing, talking politely and vaguely of certain things he aimed to do, and of what he would require to do them successfully with. Or if not this, he was on hand at breakfast while his harried gray mother and the slatternly negress bore dishes back and forth from the kitchen, quiet but proprietorial; blandly and innocently portentous. And all during the banking day (it was summer now, and school was out) Snopes never knew when he would look over his shoulder and find the boy lounging without the plate glass window of the bank, watching him with profound and static patience. Presently he would take himself away, and for a short time Snopes would be able to forget him until, wrapped in his mad unsleeping dream, he mounted the boarding house veranda at supper time and found the boy sitting there and waiting patiently his return; innocent and bland, steadfast and unassertive as a minor but chronic disease. "Got another business letter to write tonight, Mr Snopes?"

And sometimes after he had gone to bed and his light was out, he lay in the mad darkness against which his sleepless desire moiled in obscene images and shapes, and heard presently outside his door secret, ratlike sounds; and lay so tense in the dark, expecting the door to open and, preceded by breathing above him sourceless and invisible: "Going to write another letter, Mr Snopes?" And he waked sweating from dreams in which her image lived and moved and thwarted and mocked him, with the pillow crushed against his mean, half insane face, while the words produced themselves in his ears: "Got air other letter to write yet, Mr Snopes?"

So he changed his boarding house. He gave Mrs Beard an awkward, stumbling explanation; vague, composed of sentences with frayed ends. She was sorry to see him go, but she permitted him to pack his meagre belongings and depart without either anger or complaint, as is the way of country people.

He went to live with a relation, that I.O. Snopes who ran the restaurant—a nimble, wiry little man with a talkative face like a nutcracker, and false merry eyes—in a small frame house painted a sultry prodigious yellow, near the railway station. Snopeses did not trust one another enough to develop any intimate relations, and he was permitted to go and come when he pleased. So he found this better than the boarding house, the single deterrent to complete satisfaction being the hulking but catlike presence of I.O.'s son Clarence. But, what with his secretive nature, it had even been his custom to keep all his possessions under lock and key, so this was but a minor matter. Mrs Snopes was a placid mountain of a woman who swung all day in a faded wrapper, in the porch swing. Not reading, not doing anything: just swinging.

He liked it here. It was more private; no transients appearing at the supper table and tramping up and down the hallways all night; no one to try to engage him in conversation on the veranda after supper. Now, after supper he could sit undisturbed on the tight barren little porch in the growing twilight and watch the motor cars congregating at the station across the way to meet the 7:30 train; could watch the train draw into the station with its rows of lighted windows and the hissing plume from the locomotive, and go on again with bells, trailing its diminishing sound into the distant evening, while he sat on the dark porch with his desperate sleepless lust and his fear. Thus, until one evening after supper he stepped through the front door and found Virgil Beard sitting patiently and blandly on the front steps in the twilight.

So he had been run to earth again, and drawn, and hounded again into flight. Yet outwardly he pursued the even tenor of his days, unchanged, performing his duties with his slow meticulous care. But within him smoldered something of which he himself grew afraid, and at times he found himself gazing at his idle hands on the desk before him as though they were not his hands, wondering dully at them and at what they were capable, nay importunate, to do. And day by day that lust and fear and despair that moiled within him merged, becoming desperation—a thing blind and vicious and hopeless, like that of a cornered rat. And always, if he but raised his head and looked toward the window, there was the boy watching him with bland and innocent eyes beneath the pale straw of his hair. Sometimes he blinked; then the boy was gone; sometimes not. So he could never tell whether the face had been there at all, or whether it was merely another face swum momentarily from out the seething of his mind. In the meanwhile he wrote another letter.

7.

Miss Jenny's exasperation and rage when old Bayard arrived home that afternoon was unbounded. "You stubborn old fool," she stormed. "Cant Bayard kill you fast enough, that you've got to let that old quack of a Will Falls give you blood poisoning? After what Dr Alford told you, when even Loosh Peabody, who thinks a course of quinine or calomel will cure anything from a broken neck to chilblains, agreed with him?

I'll declare, sometimes I just lose all patience with you folks; wonder what crime I seem to be expiating by having to live with you. Soon as Bayard sort of quiets down and I can quit jumping every time the 'phone rings, you have to go and let that old pauper daub your face up with axle grease and lamp black. I'm a good mind to pack up and get out, and start life over in some place where they never heard of a Sartoris." She raged and stormed on; old Bayard raged in reply, with violent words and profane, and their voices swelled and surged through the house until Elnora and Simon in the kitchen moved furtively, with cocked ears. Finally old Bayard tramped from the house and mounted his horse and rode away, leaving Miss Jenny to wear her rage out upon the empty air, and then there was peace for a time.

But at supper the storm brewed and burst again. Behind the swing door of the butler's pantry Simon could hear them and young Bayard too, trying to shout them down. "Let up, let up," he howled, "for God's sake. I can't hear myself chew, even."

"And you're another one," Miss Jenny turned promptly on him. "You're just as trying as he is. You and your stiff-necked, sullen ways. Helling around the country in that car just because you think there may be somebody who cares a whoop whether or not you break your worthless neck, and then coming into the supper table smelling like a stable-hand! Just because you went to a war. Do you think you're the only person in the world that ever went to a war? Do you reckon that when my Bayard came back from The War, he made a nuisance of himself to everybody that had to live with him? But he was a gentleman: he raised the devil like a gentleman, not like you Mississippi country people. Clod-hoppers. Look what he did with just a horse," she added. "He didn't need any flying machine."

"Look at the little two-bit war he went to," young Bayard rejoined, "a war that was so sorry that grandfather wouldn't even stay up there in Virginia where it was."

"And nobody wanted him at it," Miss Jenny retorted. "A man that would get mad just because his men deposed him and elected a better colonel in his place. Got mad and came back to the country to lead a bunch of red-neck brigands."

"Little two-bit war," young Bayard repeated. "And on a horse. Anybody can go to a war on a horse. No chance for him to do anything much."

"At least he got himself decently killed," Miss Jenny snapped. "He did more with a horse than you could do with that aeroplane."

"Sho," Simon breathed against the pantry door. "Aint dey gwine it? Takes white folks to sho' 'nough quoil." And so it surged and ebbed through the succeeding days; wore itself out, then surged again when old Bayard returned home with another application of salve. But by this time Simon was having troubles of his own, troubles which he finally consulted old Bayard about one afternoon. Young Bayard was laid up in bed with his crushed ribs, with Miss Jenny mothering him with savage and cherishing affection, and Miss Benbow to visit with him and read aloud to him; and Simon came into his own again. The tophat and the duster came down from the nail, and old Bayard's cigars depleted daily by one, and the fat matched horses spent their accumulated laziness between home and the bank, before which Simon swung them to a halt each afternoon as of old, with his clamped cigar and smartly-furled whip and all the theatrics of the fine moment. "De ot-tomobile," Simon philosophised, "is all right fer pleasure en excitement, but fer de genu-wine gen'lemun tone, dey aint but one thing: dat's hosses."

Thus Simon's opportunity came ready to his hand, and once they were clear of town and the team had settled into its gait, he took advantage of it.

"Well, Cunnel," he began, "looks lak me en you's got to make some financial 'rangements."

"What?" Old Bayard brought his attention back from where it wandered about the familiar planted fields and blue shining hills beyond.

"I says, it looks lak me en you's got to arrange erbout a little cash money."

"Much obliged, Simon," old Bayard answered, "but I dont need any money right now. Much obliged, though."

Simon laughed heartily. "I declare, Cunnel, you sho' is com-ical. Rich man lak you needin' money!" Again he laughed, with unctuous and abortive heartiness. "Yes, suh, you sho' is comical." Then he ceased laughing and became engrossed with the horses for a moment. Twins they were: Roosevelt and Taft, with sleek hides and broad, comfortable buttocks. "You, Taf', lean on dat collar! Laziness gwine go in on you someday, en kill you, sho'." Old Bayard sat watching his apelike head and the swaggering tilt of the tophat. Simon turned his wizened, plausible face over his shoulder again. "But sho' 'nough, now, we is got to quiet dem niggers somehow."

"What have they done? Cant they find anybody to take their money?"

"Well, suh, hit's lak dis," Simon explained. "Hit's kind of all 'round cu'i's. You see, dey been collectin' buildin' money fer dat church whut burnt down, en ez dey got de money up, dey turnt hit over ter me, whut wid my 'ficial position on de church boa'd en bein' I wuz a member of de bes' fambly 'round here. Dat 'uz erbout las' Chris'mus time, en now dey wants de money back."

"That's strange," old Bayard said.

"Yessuh," Simon agreed readily. "Hit struck me jes' 'zackly dat way."

"Well, if they insist, I reckon you'd better give it back to 'em."

"Now you's gittin' to it." Simon turned his head again; his manner was confidential, and he exploded his bomb in a hushed melodramatic tone: "De money's gone."

"Dammit, I know that," old Bayard answered, his levity suddenly gone. "Where is it?"

"I went and put it out," Simon told him, and his tone was still confidential, with a little pained astonishment at the world's obtuseness. "And now dem niggers 'cusin' me of stealin' it."

"Do you mean to tell me that you took charge of money belonging to other people, and then went and loaned it to somebody else?"

"You does de same thing ev'y day," Simon answered. "Aint lendin' out money yo' main business?"

Old Bayard snorted violently. "You get that money back and give it to those niggers, or you'll be in jail, you hear?"

"You talks jes' lak dem uppity town niggers," Simon told him in a pained tone. "Dat money done been put out, now," he reminded his patron.

"Get it back. Haven't you got collateral for it?"

"Is I got which?"

"Something worth the money, to keep until the money is paid back."

"Yessuh, I got dat." Simon chuckled again, unctuously, a satyrish chuckle rich with complacent innuendo. "Yessuh, I got dat, all right. Only I never heard hit called collateral befo'. Naw, suh, not dat."

"Did you give that money to some nigger wench?" old Bayard demanded.

"Well, suh, hit's lak dis——" Simon began, but the other interrupted him.

"Ah, the devil. And now you expect me to pay it back, do you? How much is it?"

"I dont rightly ricollick. Dem niggers claims hit wuz sevumty er ninety dollars er somethin'. But dont you pay 'um no mind; you jes' give 'um whut ever you think is right: dey'll take it."

"I'm damned if I will. They can take it out of your worthless hide, or send you to jail—whichever they want to, but I'm damned if I'll pay one cent of it."

"Now, Cunnel," Simon said, "you aint gwine let dem town niggers 'cuse a member of yo' fambly of stealin', is you?"

"Drive on!" old Bayard shouted. Simon turned on the seat and clucked to the horses and drove on, his cigar tilted toward his hatbrim, his elbows out and the whip caught smartly back in his hand, glancing now and then at the field niggers laboring among the cotton rows with tolerant and easy scorn.

Old man Falls replaced the cap on his tin of salve, wiped the tin carefully with the bit of rag, then knelt on the cold hearth and held a match to the rag.

"I reckon them doctors air still a-tellin' you hit's gwine to kill you, aint they?" he said.

Old Bayard propped his feet against the hearth, cupping a match to his cigar, cupping two tiny matchflames in his eyes. He flung the match away and grunted.

Old man Falls watched the rag take fire sluggishly, with a pungent pencil of yellowish smoke that broke curling in the

still air. "Ever' now and then a feller has to walk up and spit
in deestruction's face, sort of, fer his own good. He has to
kind of put a aidge on hisself, like he'd hold his axe to the
grindstone," he said, squatting before the pungent curling of
the smoke as though in a pagan ritual in miniature. "Ef a
feller'll show his face to deestruction ever' now and then,
deestruction'll leave 'im be 'twell his time comes. Deestruction
likes to take a feller in the back."

"What?" old Bayard said.

Old man Falls rose and dusted his knees carefully.

"Deestruction's like ary other coward," he roared. "Hit
wont strike a feller that's a-lookin' hit in the eye lessen he
pushes hit too clost. Your paw knowed that. Stood in the do'
of that sto' the day them two cyarpet-baggers brung them niggers in to vote 'em that day in '72. Stood thar in his prince
albert coat and beaver hat, with his arms folded, when ever'-
body else had left, and watched them two Missouri fellers
herdin' them niggers up the road to'ds the sto'; stood right in
the middle of the do' while them two cyarpet-baggers begun
backin' off with their hands in their pockets until they was clar
of the niggers, and cussed him. And him standin' thar jest like
this." He crossed his arms on his breast, his hands in sight,
and for a moment old Bayard saw, as through a cloudy glass,
that arrogant and familiar shape which the old man in shabby
overalls had contrived in some way to immolate and preserve
in the vacuum of his own abnegated self.

"Then, when they was gone on back down the road, Cunnel
reached around inside the do' and taken out the ballot box and
sot hit between his feet.

" 'You niggers come hyer to vote, did you?' he says. 'All
right, come up hyer and vote.'

"When they had broke and scattered he let off that 'ere dang
der'nger over their haids a couple of times, then he loaded hit
agin and marched down the road to Miz Winterbottom's,
whar them two fellers boa'ded.

" 'Madam,' he says, liftin' his beaver, 'I have a small matter
of business to discuss with yo' lodgers. Permit me,' he says,
and he put his hat back on and marched up the stairs steady
as a parade, with Miz Winterbottom gapin' after him with her
mouth open. He walked right into the room whar they was

a-settin' behind a table facin' the do', with their pistols layin' on the table.

"When us boys outside heard the three shots we run in. Thar wuz Miz Winterbottom standin' thar, a-gapin' up the stairs, and in a minute hyer comes Cunnel with his hat cocked over his eye, marchin' down steady as a co't jury, breshin' the front of his coat with his hank'cher. And us standin' thar, a-watchin' him. He stopped in front of Miz Winterbottom and lifted his hat agin.

" 'Madam,' he says, 'I was fo'ced to muss up yo' guest-room right considerable. Pray accept my apologies, and have yo' nigger clean it up and send the bill to me. My apologies agin, madam, fer havin' been put to the necessity of exterminatin' vermin on yo' premises. Gentlemen,' he says to us, 'good mawnin'. And he cocked that 'ere beaver on his head and walked out.

"And, Bayard," old man Falls said, "I sort of envied them two nawthuners, be damned ef I didn't. A feller kin take a wife and live with her fer a long time, but after all they aint no kin. But the feller that brings you into the world or sends you outen hit. . . . . . ."

Lurking behind the pantry door Simon could hear the steady storming of Miss Jenny's and old Bayard's voices; later when they had removed to the office and Elnora and Caspey and Isom sat about the table in the kitchen waiting for him, the concussion of Miss Jenny's raging and old Bayard's rock-like stubbornness came in muffled surges, as of far away surf.

"Whut dey quoilin' erbout now?" Caspey asked. "Is you been and done somethin'?" he demanded of his nephew.

Isom rolled his eyes quietly above his steady jaws. "Naw, suh," he mumbled. "I aint done nothin'."

"Seems like dey'd git wo' out, after a while. Whut's pappy doin', Elnora?"

"Up dar in de hall, listenin'. Go tell 'im to come on and git his supper, so I kin git done, Isom."

Isom slid from his chair, still chewing, and left the kitchen. The steady raging of the two voices increased; where the shapeless figure of his grandfather stood like a disreputable and ancient bird in the dark hallway Isom could distinguish

words: . . . . poison . . . . blood . . . . think you can
cut your head off and cure it? . . . . fool put it on your
foot, but . . . . face, head . . . . dead and good riddance . . . . fool of you dying because of your own
bullheaded folly . . . . you first lying on your back,
though . . . .

"You and that damn doctor are going to worry me to
death." Old Bayard's voice drowned the other temporarily.
"Will Falls wont have a chance to kill me. I cant sit in my chair
in town without that damn squirt sidling around me and looking disappointed because I'm still alive on my feet. And when
I come home to get away from him, you cant even let me eat
supper in peace. Have to show me a lot of damn colored pictures of what some fool thinks a man's insides look like."

"Who gwine die, pappy?" Isom whispered.

Simon turned his head. "Whut you hangin' eround here fer,
boy? Go'n back to dat kitchen, whar you belongs."

"Supper waitin'," Isom said. "Who dyin', pappy?"

"Aint nobody dyin'. Does anybody soun' dead? You git on
outen de house, now."

Together they returned down the hall and entered the
kitchen. Behind them the voices raged and stormed, blurred
a little by walls, but dominant and unequivocal.

"Whut dey fightin' erbout, now?" Caspey, chewing, asked.

"Dat's white folks' bizness," Simon told him. "You tend to
yo'n, and dey'll git erlong all right." He sat down and Elnora
rose and filled a cup from the coffee pot on the stove, and
brought it to him. "White folks got dey troubles same as niggers is. Gimme dat dish o' meat, boy."

In the house the storm ran its nightly course, ceased as
though by mutual consent, both parties still firmly entrenched;
resumed at the supper table the next evening. And so on, day
after day, until the second week in July and six days after
young Bayard had been fetched home with his chest crushed,
Miss Jenny and old Bayard and Dr Alford went to Memphis
to consult a well known authority on blood and glandular diseases with whom Dr Alford, with some difficulty, had made a
formal engagement. Young Bayard lay upstairs in his cast, but
Narcissa Benbow had promised to come out and keep him
company during the day.

Between the two of them they got old Bayard on the early train, still protesting profanely like a stubborn and bewildered ox. There were others who knew them in the car and who remarked Dr Alford's juxtaposition and became curious and solicitous. Old Bayard took these opportunities to assert himself again, with violent rumblings which Miss Jenny ignored.

They took him, like a sullen small boy, to the clinic where the specialist was to meet them, and in a room resembling an easy and informal summer hotel lobby they sat among quiet, waiting people talking in whispers, and an untidy clutter of papers and magazines, waiting for the specialist to arrive. They waited a long time. Meanwhile Dr Alford from time to time assaulted the impregnable affability of the woman at the switchboard, was repulsed and returned and sat stiffly beside his patient, aware that with every minute he was losing ground in Miss Jenny's opinion of him. Old Bayard was cowed too, by now, though occasionally he rumbled hopefully at Miss Jenny. "Oh, stop swearing at me," she interrupted him at last. "You cant walk out now. Here, here's the morning paper— take it and be quiet."

Then the specialist entered briskly and went to the switchboard woman, where Dr Alford saw him and rose and went to him. The specialist turned—a brisk, dapper man, who moved with arrogant jerky motions, as though he were exercising with a small sword, and who in turning, almost stepped on Dr Alford. He gave Dr Alford a glassy, impatient stare; then he shook his hand and broke into a high, desiccated burst of words. "On the dot, I see. Promptness. Promptness. That's good. Patient here? Stood the trip all right, did she?"

"Yes, Doctor, he's——"

"Good; good. Undressed and all ready, eh?"

"The patient is a m——"

"Just a moment." The specialist turned. "Oh, Mrs Smith."

"Yes, Doctor." The woman at the switchboard did not raise her head, and at that moment another specialist of some kind, a large one, with a majestic, surreptitious air like a royal undertaker, entered and addressed him, and for a while the two of them rumbled and rattled at one another while Dr Alford stood ignored nearby, fuming stiffly and politely, feeling himself sinking lower and lower in Miss Jenny's opinion of his professional status. Then the two specialists had done, and Dr Alford led his man toward his patient.

"Got the patient all ready, you say? Good; good; save time. Lunching down town today. Had lunch yourself?"

"No, Doctor. But the patient is a——"

"Daresay not," the specialist agreed. "Plenty of time, though." He turned briskly toward a curtained exit, but Dr Alford took his arm firmly but courteously and halted him. Old Bayard was reading the paper. Miss Jenny was watching them frigidly, her bonnet on the exact top of her head.

"Mrs Du Pre; Colonel Sartoris," Dr Alford said. "This is Dr Brandt. Colonel Sartoris is your p——"

"How d'ye do? How d'ye do? Come along with the patient, eh? Daughter? Grand-daughter?" Old Bayard looked up.

"What?" he said, cupping his ear, and found the specialist staring at his face.

"What's that on your face?" he demanded, jerking his hand forth and touching the blackened excrescence. When he did so, the thing came off in his fingers, leaving on old Bayard's withered but unblemished cheek a round spot of skin rosy and fair as any baby's.

On the train that evening old Bayard, who had sat for a long time in deep thought, spoke suddenly.

"Jenny, what day of the month is this?"

"The ninth," Miss Jenny answered. "Why?"

Old Bayard sat for a while longer. Then he rose. "Think I'll go up and smoke a cigar," he said. "I reckon a little tobacco wont hurt me, will it, Doctor?"

Three weeks later they got a bill from the specialist for fifty dollars. "Now I know why he's so well known," Miss Jenny said acidly. Then to her nephew: "You better thank your stars it wasn't your hat he lifted off."

Toward Dr Alford her manner is fiercely and belligerently protective; to old man Falls she gives the briefest and coldest nod and sails on with her nose in air; but to Loosh Peabody she does not speak at all.

8.

She passed from the fresh, hot morning into the cool hall, where Simon uselessly and importantly proprietorial with a duster, bobbed his head to her. "Dey done gone to Memphis today," he told her. "But Mist' Bayard waitin' fer you. Walk right up, missy."

"Thank you," she answered, and she went on and mounted the stairs and left him busily wafting dust from one surface to another and then back again. She mounted into a steady drift of air that blew through the open doors at the end of the hall; through these doors she could see a segment of blue hills and salt-colored sky. At Bayard's door she stopped and stood there for a time, clasping the book to her breast.

The house, despite Simon's activity in the hall below, was a little portentously quiet, without the reassurance of Miss Jenny's bustling presence. Faint sounds reached her from far away—out-of-doors sounds whose final drowsy reverberations drifted into the house on the vivid July air; sounds too somnolent and remote to die away.

But from the room before her no sound came at all. Perhaps he was asleep; and the initial impulse—her given word, and the fortitude of her desperate heart which had enabled her to come out despite Miss Jenny's absence—having served its purpose and deserted her, she stood just without the door, hoping that he was asleep, that he would sleep all day.

But she would have to enter the room in order to find out if he slept, so she touched her hands to her face, as though by that she would restore to it its wonted serene repose for him to see, and entered.

"Simon?" Bayard said, having felt her presence through that sharpened sixth sense of the sick. He lay on his back, his hands beneath his head, gazing out the window across the room, and she paused again just within the door. At last, roused by her silence, he turned his head and his bleak gaze. "Well, I'm damned. I didn't believe you'd come out today."

"Yes," she answered. "How do you feel?"

"Not after the way you sit with one foot in the hall all the time Aunt Jenny's out of the room," he continued. "Did she make you come anyway?"

"She asked me to come out. She doesn't want you to be alone all day, with just Simon in the house. Do you feel better today?"

"So?" he drawled. "Wont you sit down, then?" She crossed to where her customary chair had been moved into a corner and drew it across the floor. He was watching her as she turned the chair about and seated herself. "What do you think about it?"

"About what?"

"About coming out to keep me company?"

"I've brought a new book," she said. "One H——one I just got. I hope you'll like this one."

"I hope so," he agreed, but without conviction. "Seems like I'd like one after a while, dont it? But what do you think about coming out here today?"

"I dont think a sick person should be left alone with just negroes around," she said, her face lowered over the book. "The name of this one is——"

"Why not send a nurse out, then? No use your coming way out here." She met his gaze at last, with her grave desperate eyes. "Why do you come, when you dont want to?" he persisted.

"I dont mind," she answered. She opened the book. "The name of this one is——"

"Dont," he interrupted. "I'll have to listen to that damn thing all day. Let's talk a while." But her head was bent and her hands were still on the open book. "What makes you afraid to talk to me?"

"Afraid?" she repeated. "Had you rather I'd go?"

"What? No, damn it. I want you to be human for one time and talk to me. Come over here." She would not look at him, and she raised her hands between them as though he did not lie helpless on his back two yards away. "Come over here closer," he commanded. She rose, clutching the book.

"I'm going," she said. "I'll tell Simon to stay where he can hear you call. Goodbye."

"Here," he exclaimed. She went swiftly to the door.

"Goodbye."

"After what you just said, about leaving me alone with just niggers on the place?" She paused at the door, and he added with cold cunning: "After what Aunt Jenny told you? What'll I tell her, tonight? Why are you afraid of a man flat on his back, in a damn cast-iron strait-jacket, anyway?" But she only looked at him with her sober, hopeless eyes. "All right, dammit," he said violently. "Go, then." And he jerked his head on the pillow and stared again out the window while she returned to her chair. He said, mildly: "What's the name of this one?" She told him. "Let her go, then. I reckon I'll be asleep soon, anyway."

She opened the book and began to read, swiftly, as though she were crouching behind the screen of words her voice raised between them. She read steadily on for some time, while he on the bed made no movement, her head bent over the book, aware of time passing, as though she were in a contest with time. She finished a sentence and ceased, without raising her head, but almost immediately he spoke. "Go on; I'm still here. Better luck next time."

The forenoon passed on. Somewhere a clock rang the quarter hours, but saving this there was no other sound in the house. Simon's activity below stairs had ceased long since, but a murmur of voices reached her at intervals from somewhere, murmurously indistinguishable. The leaves on the branch beyond the window did not stir in the hot air, and upon it a myriad noises blended in a drowsy monotone—the negroes' voices, sounds of animals in the barnyard, the rhythmic groaning of the water pump; a sudden cacophony of fowls in the garden beneath the window, interspersed with Isom's meaningless cries as he drove them out.

Bayard was asleep now, and as she realized this she realized also that she did not know just when she had stopped reading. And she sat with the page open upon her knees, a page whose words left no echoes whatever in her mind, looking at his calm face. It was again like a bronze mask, purged by illness of the heat of its violence, yet with the violence still slumbering there and only refined a little. . . . She looked away and sat with the book open, her hands lying motionless upon the page, gazing out the window. The curtains hung without motion. On the branch athwart the window the leaves hung motionless beneath the intermittent fingers of the sun, and she sat also without life, the fabric of her dress unstirred by her imperceptible breathing, thinking that there would be peace for her only in a world where there were no men at all.

The clock rang twelve times. Immediately after, a stertorous breathing and surreptitious sounds as of a huge rat, and yet other furtive ratlike sounds in the hall, Simon thrust his head around the door, like the grandfather of all apes. "Is you 'sleep Mist' Bayard?" he said in a rasping whisper.

"Shhhhhhhh," Narcissa said, lifting her hand. Simon entered on tiptoe, breathing heavily, scraping his feet on the floor. "Hush," Narcissa said quickly, "you'll wake him."

"Dinner ready," Simon said, still in that rasping whisper.

"You can keep his warm until he wakes up, cant you?" Narcissa whispered. "Simon!" she whispered. She rose, but he had already crossed to the table, where he fumbled clumsily at the stack of books and contrived at last to topple it to the floor in a random crash. Bayard opened his eyes.

"Good God," he said, "are you here again?"

"Well, now," Simon exclaimed with ready dismay, "ef me en Miss Benbow aint waked him up."

"Why you cant bear to see anybody lying on their back with their eyes closed, I cant see," Bayard said. "Thank God you were not born in a drove, like mosquitoes."

"Des lissen at 'im!" Simon said. "Go to sleep quoilin' en wake up quoilin'. Elnora got dinner ready fer y'all."

"Why didn't you bring it up, then?" Bayard said. "Miss Benbow's too. Unless you'd rather go down?" he added.

In all his movements Simon was a caricature of himself. He now assumed an attitude of shocked reproof. "Dinin' room de place fer comp'ny," he said.

"No," Narcissa said, "I'll go down. I wont put Simon to that trouble."

" 'Taint no trouble," Simon disclaimed. "Only hit aint no—"

"I'll come down," Narcissa said. "You go on and see to Mr Bayard's tray."

"Yes'm," Simon said. He moved toward the door. "You kin walk right down. Elnora have hit on de table time you git dar." He went out.

"I try to keep—" Narcissa began.

"I know," Bayard interrupted. "He wont let anybody sleep through meal time. And you'd better go and have yours, or he'll carry everything back to the kitchen. And you dont have to hurry back just on my account," he added.

"Dont have to hurry back?" She paused at the door and looked back at him. "What do you mean?"

"I thought you might be tired of reading."

"Oh," she said, and looked away and stood for a moment clothed in her grave despair.

"Look here," he said suddenly. "Are you sick or anything? Had you rather go home?"

"No," she answered. She moved again. "I'll be back soon."

She had her meal in lonely state in the sombre dining room while Simon, having dispatched Bayard's tray by Isom, moved about the table and pressed dishes upon her with bland insistence or leaned against the sideboard and conducted a rambling monologue that seemed to have had no beginning and held no prospect of any end. It still flowed easily behind her as she went up the hall; when she stood in the front door it was still going on, volitionless, as though entranced with its own existence and feeding on its own momentum. Beyond the porch the salvia bed lay in an unbearable glare of white light, in clamorous splashes. Beyond it the drive shimmered with heat until, arched over with locust and oak, it descended in a cool green tunnel to the gates and the sultry ribbon of the highroad. Beyond the road fields spread away shimmering, broken here and there by motionless clumps of wood, on to the hills dissolving bluely in the July haze.

She leaned for a while against the door, in her white dress, her cheek against the cool, smooth plane of the jamb, in a faint draft that came steadily from somewhere, though no leaf stirred. Simon had finished in the dining room and a drowsy murmur of voices came up the hall from the kitchen, borne upon that thin stirring of air too warm to be called a breeze.

At last she heard a movement from above stairs and she remembered Isom with Bayard's tray, and she turned and slid the parlor doors ajar and entered. The shades were drawn closely, and the crack of light that followed her but deepened the gloom. She found the piano and stood beside it for a while, touching its dusty surface and thinking of Miss Jenny erect and indomitable in her chair beside it. She heard Isom descend the stairs; soon his footsteps died away down the hall, and she drew out the bench and sat down and laid her arms along the closed lid.

Simon entered the dining room again, mumbling to himself and followed presently by Elnora, and they clashed dishes and talked with a mellow rise and fall of consonantless and indistinguishable words. Then they went away, but still she sat with her arms along the cool wood, in the dark quiet room where even time stagnated a little.

The clock rang again, and she moved. I've been crying, she thought. "I've been crying," she said in a sad whisper that savored its own loneliness and its sorrow. At the tall mirror beside the parlor door she stood and peered at her dim reflection, touching her eyes with her fingertips. Then she went on, but paused again at the stairs, listening, then she mounted briskly and entered Miss Jenny's room and went on to her bathroom and bathed her face.

Bayard lay as she had left him. He was smoking a cigarette now, between puffs he dabbed it casually at a saucer on the bed beside him. "Well?" he said.

"You're going to set the house on fire that way," she told him, removing the saucer. "You know Miss Jenny wouldn't let you do that."

"I know it," he agreed, a little sheepishly, and she dragged the table up and set the saucer on it.

"Can you reach it now?"

"Yes, thanks. Did they give you enough to eat?"

"Oh, yes. Simon's very insistent, you know. Shall I read some more, or had you rather sleep?"

"Read, if you dont mind. I think I'll stay awake, this time."

"Is that a threat?" He looked at her quickly as she seated herself and picked up the book.

"Say, what happened to you?" he demanded. "You acted like you were all in before dinner. Simon give you a drink, or what?"

"No, not that bad." And she laughed, a little wildly, and opened the book. "I forgot to mark the place," she said, turning the leaves swiftly. "Do you remember——No, you were asleep, weren't you? Shall I go back to where you stopped listening?"

"No, just read anywhere. It's all about alike, I guess. If you'll move a little nearer, I believe I can stay awake."

"Sleep, if you want to. I dont mind."

"Meaning you wont come any nearer?" he asked, watching her with his bleak gaze. She moved her chair nearer and opened the book again and turned the pages on.

"I think it was about here," she said, with indecision. "Yes." She read to herself for a line or two, then she began aloud, read to the end of the page, where her voice trailed off in grave consternation. She turned the next page then flipped it back. "I read this once; I remember it now." She turned the leaves on, her serene brow puckered a little. "I must have been asleep too," she said, and she glanced at him with friendly bewilderment. "I seem to have read pages and pages. . . . . . ."

"Oh, begin anywhere," he repeated.

"No: wait; here it is." She read again and picked up the thread of the story. Once or twice she raised her eyes swiftly and found him watching her, bleakly but quietly. After a while he was no longer watching her, and at last, finding that his eyes were closed, she thought he slept. She finished the chapter and stopped.

"No," he said drowsily. "Not yet." Then, when she failed to resume, he opened his eyes and asked for a cigarette. She laid the book aside and struck the match for him, and picked up the book again.

The afternoon wore away. The negroes had gone, and there was no sound about the house save her voice, and the clock at quarter hour intervals; outside the shadows slanted more and more, peaceful harbingers of evening. He was asleep now, despite his contrary conviction, and after a while she stopped and laid the book away. The long shape of him lay stiffly in its cast beneath the sheet, and she sat and looked at his bold still face and the broken travesty of him and her tranquil sorrow overflowed in pity for him. He was so utterly without any affection for any thing at all; so——so . . . . hard (no, that's not the word—but cold eluded her; she could comprehend hardness, but not coldness. . . .)

Afternoon drew on; evening was finding itself. She sat

musing and still and quiet, gazing out of the window where no wind yet stirred the leaves, as though she were waiting for someone to tell her what to do next, and she had lost all account of time other than as a dark unhurrying stream into which she gazed until the mesmerism of water conjured the water itself away.

He made an indescribable sound, and she turned her head quickly and saw his body straining terrifically in its cast, and his clenched hands and his teeth beneath his lifted lip, and as she sat blanched and incapable of further movement he made the sound again. His breath hissed between his teeth and he screamed, a wordless sound that merged into a rush of profanity; and when she rose at last and stood over him with her hands against her mouth, his body relaxed and from beneath his sweating brow he watched her with wide intent eyes in which terror lurked, and mad, cold fury, and despair.

"He damn near got me, then," he said in a dry, light voice, still watching her from beyond the fading agony in his wide eyes. "There was a sort of loop of 'em around my chest, and every time he fired, he twisted the loop a little tighter. . . . . . ." He fumbled at the sheet and tried to draw it up to his face. "Can you get me a handkerchief? Some in that top drawer there."

"Yes," she said. "Yes," and she went to the chest of drawers and held her shaking body upright by clinging to it, and found a handkerchief and brought it to him. She tried to dry his brow and face, but at last he took the handkerchief from her and did it himself. "You scared me," she moaned. "You scared me so bad. I thought. . . . . . ."

"Sorry," he answered shortly. "I dont do that on purpose. I want a cigarette."

She gave it to him and struck the match, and again he had to grasp her hand to hold the flame steady, and still holding her wrist he drew deeply several times. She tried to free her wrist, but his fingers were like steel, and her trembling body betrayed her and she sank into her chair again, staring at him with terror and dread. He consumed the cigarette in deep, swift draughts, and still holding her wrist, he began talking of his dead brother, without preamble, brutally. It was a brutal tale, without beginning, and crassly and uselessly violent and at times profane and gross, though its very wildness robbed it of offensiveness just as its grossness kept it from obscenity. And beneath it all, the bitter struggling of his false and stubborn pride; and she sitting with her arm taut in his grasp and her other hand pressed against her mouth, watching him with terrified fascination.

"He was zigzagging: that was why I couldn't get on the hun. Every time I got my sights on him, John'd barge in between us again, and then I'd have to hoick away before one of the others got on me. Then he quit zigzagging. Soon as I saw him sideslip I knew it was all over. Then I saw the fire streaking out along his wing, and he was looking back. He wasn't looking at the hun at all; he was looking at me. The hun stopped shooting then, and all of us sort of just sat there for a while. I couldn't tell what John was up to until I saw him swing his feet out. Then he thumbed his nose at me like he was always doing and flipped his hand at the hun and kicked his machine out of the way and jumped. He jumped feet first. You cant fall far feet first, you know, and pretty soon he sprawled out flat. There was a bunch of cloud right under us and he smacked on it right on his belly, like what we used to call gut-busters in swimming. But I never could pick him up below the cloud. I know I got down before he could have come out, because after I was down there his machine came diving out right at me, burning good. I pulled away from it, but the damn thing zoomed past and did a split-turn and came at me again, and I had to dodge. And so I never could pick him up when he came out of the cloud. I went down fast, until I knew I was below him, and looked again. But I couldn't find him and then I thought that maybe I hadn't gone far enough, so I dived again. I saw the machine crash about three miles away, but I never could pick John up again. And then they started shooting at me from the ground——"

He talked on and her hand came away from her mouth and slid down her other arm and tugged at his fingers. "Please," she whispered. "Please!" He ceased and looked at her and his fingers shifted, and just as she thought she was free they clamped again, and now both of her wrists were prisoners. She struggled, staring at him dreadfully, but he grinned his white cruel teeth at her and pressed her crossed arms down upon the bed beside him. "Please, please," she implored, struggling; she could feel the flesh of her wrists, feel the bones turn in it like a loose garment; could see his bleak eyes and the fixed derision of his teeth, and suddenly she swayed forward in her chair and her head dropped between her prisoned arms and she wept with hopeless and dreadful hysteria.

After a while there was no sound in the room again, and he moved his head and looked at the dark crown of her head. He lifted his hand and saw the bruised discolorations where he had gripped her wrists. But she did not stir even then, and he dropped his hand upon her wrists again and lay quietly, and after a while even her shuddering and trembling had ceased. "I'm sorry," he said. "I wont do it again." He could see only the top of her dark head, and her hands lay passive beneath his. "I'm sorry," he repeated. "I wont do it anymore."

"You wont drive that car fast anymore?" she asked, without moving; her voice was muffled.

"What?"

She made no answer, and with infinite small pains and slowly he turned himself, cast and all, by degrees onto his side, chewing his lip and swearing under his breath, and laid his other hand on her hair.

"What are you doing?" she asked, still without raising her head. "You'll break your ribs again."

"Yes," he agreed, stroking her hair awkwardly.

"That's the trouble, right there," she said. "That's the way you act: doing things that—that—You do things to hurt yourself just to worry people. You dont get any fun out of doing them."

"No," he agreed, and he lay with his chest full of hot needles, stroking her dark head with his hard, awkward hand. Far above him now the peak among the black and savage stars, and about him the valleys of tranquillity and of peace. It was later still; already shadows were growing in the room and losing themselves in shadow, and beyond the window sunlight was a diffused radiance, sourceless yet palpable; from somewhere cows lowed one to another, moody and mournful. At last she sat up, touching her face and her hair.

"You're all twisted. You'll never get well, if you dont behave yourself. Turn on your back, now." He obeyed, slowly and painfully, his lip between his teeth and faint beads on his forehead, while she watched him with grave anxiety. "Does it hurt?"

"No," he answered, and his hand shut again on her wrists that made no effort to withdraw. The sun was gone, and twilight, foster-dam of quietude and peace, filled the fading room and evening had found itself.

"And you wont drive that car fast anymore?" she persisted from the dusk.

"No," he answered.

9.

Meanwhile she had received another letter from her anonymous correspondent. Horace when he came in one night, had brought it in to her as she lay in bed with a book; tapped at her door and opened it and stood for a moment diffidently, and for a while they looked at one another across the barrier of their estrangement and their stubborn pride.

"Excuse me for disturbing you," he said stiffly. She lay beneath the shaded light, with the dark splash of her hair upon the pillow, and only her eyes moved as he crossed the room and stood above her where she lay with her lowered book, watching him with sober interrogation.

"What are you reading?" he asked. For reply she shut the book on her finger, with the jacket and its colored legend upward. But he did not look at it. His shirt was open beneath his silk dressing gown and his thin hand moved among the objects on the table beside the bed; picked up another book. "I never knew you to read so much."

"I have more time for reading, now," she answered.

"Yes." His hand still moved about the table, touching things here and there. She lay waiting for him to speak. But he did not, and she said:

"What is it, Horace?"

He came and sat on the edge of the bed. But still her eyes were antagonistic and interrogatory and the shadow of her mouth was stubbornly cold. "Narcy?" he said. She lowered her eyes to the book, and he added: "First, I want to apologise for leaving you alone so often at night."

"Yes?"

He laid his hand on her knee. "Look at me." She raised her face, and the antagonism of her eyes. "I want to apologise for leaving you alone at night," he repeated.

"Does that mean you aren't going to do it anymore, or that you're not coming in at all?"

For a time he sat, brooding upon the wild repose of his hand lying on her covered knee. Then he rose and stood beside the table again, touching the objects there, then he returned and sat on the bed. She was reading again, and he tried to take the book from her hand. She resisted.

"What do you want, Horace?" she asked impatiently.

He mused again while she watched his face. He looked up. "Belle and I are going to be married," he blurted.

"Why tell me? Harry is the one to tell. Unless you and Belle are going to dispense with the formality of divorce."

"Yes," he said. "He knows it." He laid his hand on her knee again, stroking it through the covers. "You aren't even surprised, are you?"

"I'm surprised at you, but not at Belle. Belle has a back-stairs nature."

"Yes," he agreed; then: "Who said that to you? You didn't think of that yourself." She lay with her book half raised, watching him. He took her hand roughly; she tried to free it, but vainly. "Who was it?" he demanded.

"Nobody told me. Dont, Horace."

He released her hand. "I know who it was. It was Mrs Du Pre."

"It wasn't anybody," she repeated. "Go away and leave me alone, Horace." And behind the antagonism her eyes were hopeless and desperate. "Don't you see that talking doesn't help any?"

"Yes," he said wearily, but he sat for a while yet, stroking her knee. Then he rose and thrust his hands into his gown, but turning, he paused again and drew forth an envelope from his pocket. "Here's a letter for you. I forgot it this afternoon. Sorry."

She was reading again. "Put it on the table," she said, without raising her eyes. He laid the letter on the table and quitted the room. At the door he looked back, but her head was bent over her book.

As he removed his clothes it did seem that that heavy fading odor of Belle's body clung to them, and to his hands even after he was in bed; and clinging, shaped in the darkness beside him Belle's rich voluption, until within that warm, not-yet-sleeping region where dwells the mother of dreams, Belle grew palpable in ratio as his own body slipped away from him. And Harry too, with his dogged inarticulateness and his hurt groping which was partly damaged vanity and shock, yet mostly a boy's sincere bewilderment, that freed itself terrifically in the form of movie subtitles. Just before he slept his mind, with the mind's uncanny attribute of irrelevant recapitulation, reproduced with the startling ghostliness of a dictaphone, an incident which at the time he had considered trivial. Belle had freed her mouth, and for a moment, her body still against his, she held his face in her two hands and stared at him with intent questioning eyes. "Have you plenty of money, Horace?" And "Yes," he had answered immediately. "Of course I have." And then Belle again, enveloping him like a rich and fatal drug, like a motionless and cloying sea in which he watched himself drown.

The letter lay on the table that night, forgotten; it was not until the next morning that she discovered it and opened it.

"I am trying to forget you I cannot forget you Your big eyes your black hair how white your black hair make you look. And how you walk I am watching you a smell you give off like a flowr. Your eyes shine with mistry and how you walk makes me sick like a fevver all night thinking how you walk. I could touch you you would not know it Every day. But I can not I must pore out on paper must talk You do not know who. Your lips like cupids bow when the day comes when I will press them to mine like I dreamed like a fevver from heaven to hell. I know what you do I know more than you think I see men visting you with bitter twangs. Be care full I am a desprate man Nothing any more to me now If you unholy love a man I will kill him.

"You do not anser. I know you got it I saw one in your hand bag. You better anser soon I am desprate man eat up with fevver I can not sleep for. I will not hurt you but I am desprate. Do not forget I will not hurt you but I am a desprate man."

Meanwhile the days accumulated. Not sad days nor lonely: they were too feverish to be sorrowful, what with her nature torn in two directions, and the walls of her serene garden cast down, and she herself like a night animal or bird caught in a beam of light and trying vainly to escape. Horace had definitely gone his way; and like two strangers they followed the routine of their physical days, in an unbending estrangement of long affection and similar pride beneath a shallow veneer of trivialities. She sat with Bayard almost every day now, but at a discreet distance of two yards. At first he tried to override her with bluster, then with cajolery. But she was firm and at last he desisted and lay gazing quietly out the window or sleeping while she read. From time to time Miss Jenny would come to the door and look in at them and go away. Her shrinking, her sense of anticipation and dread while with him, was gone now, and at times instead of reading they talked, quietly and impersonally, with the ghost of that other afternoon between them, though neither ever referred to it. Miss Jenny had been a little curious about that day, but Narcissa was gravely and demurely noncommittal about it; nor had Bayard ever talked of it, and so there was another bond between them, but unirksome. Miss Jenny had heard gossip about Horace and Belle, but on this subject also Narcissa had nothing to say.

"Have it your own way," Miss Jenny said tartly. "I can draw my own conclusions. I imagine Belle and Horace can produce quite a mess together. And I'm glad of it. That man is making an old maid out of you. It isn't too late now, but if he'd waited five years later to play the fool, there wouldn't be anything left for you except to give music lessons. But you can get married, now."

"Would you advise me to marry?" Narcissa asked.

"I wouldn't advise anybody to marry. You wont be happy, but then, women haven't got civilized enough yet to be happy unmarried, so you might as well try it. We can stand anything, anyhow. And change is good for folks. They say it is, at least."

But Narcissa didn't believe that. I shall never marry, she told herself. Men . . . . that was where unhappiness lay, getting men into your life. And if I couldn't keep Horace, loving him as I did. . . . . . . Bayard slept. She picked up the book and read on to herself, about antic people in an antic world where things happened as they should. The shadows lengthened eastward. She read on, lost from mutable things.

After a while Bayard waked, and she fetched him a cigarette and a match. "You wont have to do this any more," he said. "I reckon you're sorry."

His cast would come off tomorrow, he meant, and he lay smoking his cigarette and talking of what he would do when he was about again. He would see about getting his car repaired first thing; have to take it to Memphis, probably. And he planned a trip for the three of them—Miss Jenny, Narcissa, and himself—while the car was in the shop. "It'll take about a week," he added. "She must be in pretty bad shape. Hope I didn't hurt her guts any."

"But you aren't going to drive it fast anymore," she reminded him. He lay still, his cigarette burning in his fingers. "You promised," she insisted.

"When did I promise?"

"Don't you remember? That . . . . afternoon, when they were . . . ."

"When I scared you?" She sat watching him with her grave troubled eyes. "Come here," he said. She rose and went to the bed and he took her hand.

"You wont drive it fast again?" she persisted.

"No," he answered. "I promise." And they were still so, her hand in his. The curtains stirred in the breeze, and the leaves on the branch beyond the window twinkled and turned and lisped against one another. Sunset was not far away; it would cease then. He moved.

"Narcissa," he said, and she looked at him. "Lean your face down here."

She looked away, and for a while there was no movement, no sound between them.

"I must go," she said at last, quietly, and he released her hand.

His cast was gone, and he was up and about again, moving a little gingerly, to be sure, but already Miss Jenny was beginning to contemplate him a little anxiously. "If we could just arrange to have one of his minor bones broken every month or so, just enough to keep him in the house. . . ."

"That wont be necessary," Narcissa told her. "He's going to behave from now on."

"How do you know?" Miss Jenny demanded. "What in the world makes you think that?"

"He promised he would."

"He'll promise anything when he's flat on his back," Miss Jenny retorted. "They all will; always have. But what makes you think he'll keep it?"

"He promised me he would," Narcissa replied serenely.

His first act was to see about his car. It had been pulled into town and patched up after a fashion until it would run under its own power, but it would be necessary to take it to Memphis to have the frame straightened and the body repaired. Bayard was all for doing this himself, fresh-knit ribs and all, but Miss Jenny put her foot down and after a furious half hour, he was vanquished. And so the car was driven in to Memphis by a youth who hung around one of the garages in town. "Narcissa'll take you driving in her car, if you must ride," Miss Jenny told him.

"In that little peanut parcher?" Bayard said derisively. "It wont do more than twenty one miles an hour."

"No, thank God," Miss Jenny answered. "And I've written to Memphis and asked 'em to fix yours so it'll run just like that, too."

Bayard stared at her with humorless bleakness. "Did you do any such damn thing as that?"

"Oh, take him away, Narcissa," Miss Jenny exclaimed. "Get him out of my sight. I'm so tired of looking at you."

But he wouldn't ride in Narcissa's car at first. He missed no opportunity to speak of it with heavy, facetious disparagement, but he wouldn't ride in it. Dr Alford had evolved a tight elastic bandage for his chest so that he could ride his horse, but he had developed an astonishing propensity for lounging about the house when Narcissa was there. And Narcissa came quite often. Miss Jenny thought it was on Bayard's account and pinned the guest down in her forthright way; whereupon Narcissa told her about Horace and Belle while Miss Jenny sat indomitably erect on her straight chair beside the piano.

"Poor child," she said, and "Lord, aint they fools?" and then: "Well, you're right; I wouldn't marry one of 'em either."

"I'm not," Narcissa answered. "I wish there weren't any of them in the world."

Miss Jenny said, "Hmph."

And then one afternoon they were in Narcissa's car and Bayard was driving, over her protest at first. But he was behaving himself quite sensibly, and at last she relaxed. They drove down the valley road and turned into the hills and she asked where they were going, but his answer was vague. So she sat quietly beside him and the road mounted presently in long curves among dark pines in the slanting afternoon. The road wound on, with changing sunshot vistas of the valley and the opposite hills at every turn, and always the sombre pines and their faint exhilarating odor. After a time they topped a hill and Bayard slowed the car. Beneath them the road sank, then flattened away toward a line of willows, crossed a stone bridge and rose again curving redly from sight among the dark trees.

"There's the place," he said.

"The place?" she repeated dreamily; then as the car rolled forward again, gaining speed, she roused herself and understood what he meant. "You promised," she cried, but he jerked the throttle down its ratchet and she clutched him and tried to scream. But she could make no sound, nor could she close her eyes as the narrow bridge hurtled dancing toward them. And then her breath stopped and her heart as they flashed with a sharp reverberation like hail on a tin roof, between willows and a crashing glint of water and shot on up the next hill. The small car swayed on the curve, lost its footing and went into the ditch, bounded out and hurled across the road. Then Bayard straightened it out and with diminishing speed it rocked on up the hill, and stopped. She sat beside him, her bloodless mouth open, beseeching him with her wide hopeless eyes. Then she caught her breath, wailing.

"I didn't mean—" he began awkwardly. "I just wanted to see if I could do it," and he put his arms around her and she clung to him, moving her hands crazily about his shoulders. "I didn't mean——" he essayed again, and then her crazed hands were on his face and she was sobbing wildly against his mouth.

10.

Through the morning hours and following his sleepless night, he bent over his desk beneath the green-shaded light, penning his neat, meticulous figures into the ledgers. The routine of the bank went on; old Bayard sat in his tilted chair in the fresh August morning while passers went to and fro, greeting him with florid cheerful gestures and receiving in return his half military salute—people cheerful and happy with their orderly affairs; the cashier served the morning line of depositors and swapped jovial anecdote with them. For this was the summer cool spell and there was a vividness in the air, a presage of the golden days of frost and yellowing persimmons in the wornout fields, and of sweet small grapes in the matted vines along the sandy branches, and the scent of cooking sorghum upon the smoky air. But Snopes crouched over his desk after his sleepless night, with jealousy and thwarted desire and furious impotent rage in his vitals.

His head felt hot and dull, and heavy, and to the cashier's surprise, he offered to buy the coca-colas, ordering two for himself, drank them one after the other and returned to his ledgers. So the morning wore away. His neat figures accumulated slowly in the ruled columns, steadily and with a maddening aloofness from his own turmoil and without a mistake although his mind coiled and coiled upon itself, tormenting him with fleeing obscene images in which she moved with another. He had thought it dreadful when he was not certain that there was another; but now to know it, to find knowledge of it on every tongue . . . . and young Sartoris, at that: a man whom he had hated instinctively with all his sense of inferiority and all the venom of his worm-like nature. Married, married. Adultery, concealed if suspected, he could have borne; but this, boldly, in the world's face, flouting him with his own impotence. . . . . . . He dug a cheap, soiled handkerchief from his hip pocket and wiped the saliva from his jaws.

By changing his position a little he could see old Bayard, could catch a glint of his white suit where he sat oblivious in the door. There was a sort of fascination in the old fellow now, serving as he did as an object upon which Snopes could vent the secret, vicarious rage of his half-insane mind. And all during the morning he watched the other covertly; once old Bayard entered the cage and passed within arms' length of him, and when he moved his hand to wipe his drooling mouth, he found that the page had adhered to his wrist, blotting the last entry he had made. With his knife blade he erased the smear and rewrote it.

All the forenoon he bent over his ledgers, watching his hand pen the neat figures into the ruled columns with a sort of astonishment. After his sleepless night he labored in a kind of stupor, his mind too spent even to contemplate the coiling images of his lust, thwarted now for all time, save with a dull astonishment that the images no longer filled his blood with fury and despair, so that it was some time before his dulled nerves reacted to a fresh threat and caused him to raise his head. Virgil Beard was just entering the door.

He slid hurriedly from his stool and slipped around the corner and darted through the door of old Bayard's office. He crouched within the door, heard the boy ask politely for him, heard the cashier say that he was there a minute ago but that he reckoned he had stepped out; heard the boy say well, he reckoned he'd wait for him. And he crouched within the door, wiping his drooling mouth with his handkerchief.

After a while he opened the door cautiously. The boy squatted patiently and blandly on his heels against the wall, and Snopes stood again with his clenched trembling hands. He did not curse: his desperate fury was beyond words; but his breath came and went with a swift ah-ah-ah sound in his throat and it seemed to him that his eyeballs were being drawn back and back into his skull, turning further and further until the cords that drew them reached the snapping point. He opened the door.

"Hi, Mr Snopes," the boy said genially, rising; but Snopes strode on and entered the grille and approached the cashier.

"Res," he said, in a voice scarcely articulate, "gimme five dollars."

"What?"

"Gimme five dollars," he repeated hoarsely. The cashier did

so, scribbled a notation and speared it on the file at his elbow. The boy had come up to the second window, but Snopes went on and he followed the man back to the office, his bare feet hissing on the linoleum floor.

"I tried to find you last night," he explained. "But you wasn't to home." Then he looked up and saw Snopes' face, and after a moment he screamed and broke his trance and turned to flee. But the man caught him by his overalls, and he writhed and twisted, screaming with utter terror as the man dragged him across the office and opened the door that gave onto the vacant lot. Snopes was trying to say something in his mad, shaking voice, but the boy screamed steadily, hanging limp from the other's hand as he tried to thrust the bill into his pocket. At last he succeeded and the boy, who staggered away, found his legs, and fled.

"What were you whuppin' that boy, for?" the cashier asked curiously, when Snopes returned to his desk.

"For not minding his own business," he snapped, opening his ledger again.

During the hour the cashier was out to lunch Snopes was his outward usual self—uncommunicative but efficient, a little covertly sullen, with his mean, close-set eyes and his stubby features; patrons remarked nothing unusual in his bearing. Nor did the cashier when he returned, sucking a toothpick and belching at intervals. But instead of going home to dinner, Snopes repaired to a street occupied by negro stores and barber shops and inquired from door to door. After a half hour search he found the negro he sought, held a few minutes' conversation with him, then returned across town to his cousin's restaurant and had a platter of hamburger steak and a cup of coffee. At two oclock he was back at his desk.

The afternoon passed. Three oclock came; he went around and touched old Bayard's shoulder and he rose and dragged his chair inside and Snopes closed the doors and drew the green shades upon the windows. Then he totaled his ledgers while the cashier counted the cash. In the meantime Simon drove up to the door and presently old Bayard stalked forth and got in the carriage and was driven off. Snopes and the cashier compared notes and struck a balance, and while the other stacked the money away in receptacles he carried his ledgers one by one into the vault. The cashier followed with the cash and put it away and they emerged as the cashier was about to close the vault, when Snopes stopped him. "Forgot that cash-book," he explained. The cashier returned to his window and Snopes carried the book into the vault and put it away and emerged and clashed the door to, and hiding the dial with his body, he rattled the knob briskly. The cashier had his back turned, rolling a cigarette.

"See it's throwed good," he said. Snopes rattled the knob again, then shook the door.

"That's got it." They took their hats and emerged from the cage and locked it behind them, and passed through the front door, which the cashier closed and shook also. He struck a match to his cigarette.

"See you tomorrow," he said.

"All right," Snopes agreed, and he stood looking after the other's shapeless back in its shabby alpaca coat. He produced his soiled handkerchief and wiped his mouth again.

That evening about eight oclock he was back downtown. He stood for a time with the group that sat nightly in front of the drug store on the corner; stood quietly among them, listening but saying nothing, as was his way. Then he moved on, without being missed, and walked slowly up the street and stopped at the bank door. One or two passers spoke to him while he was finding his key and opening the door; he responded in his flat country idiom and entered and closed the door behind him. A single bulb burned above the vault. He raised the shade on the window beside it and entered the grilled cage and turned on the light above his desk. Here passers could see him, could have watched him for several minutes as he bent over his desk, writing slowly. It was his final letter, in which he poured out his lust and his hatred and his jealousy, and the language was the obscenity which his jealousy and desire had hoarded away in his temporarily half-crazed mind and which the past night and day had liberated. When it was finished he blotted it carefully and folded it and put it in his pocket, and snapped his light off. He entered the directors' room and in the darkness he unlocked the door which gave onto the vacant lot, closed it and left it unlocked.

He returned to the front and drew the shade on the window, and drew the other shades to their full extent, until no crack of light showed at their edges, emerged and locked the door behind him. On the street he looked casually back at the windows. The shades were drawn close; the interior of the bank was invisible from the street.

The group still talked in front of the drug store and he stopped again on the outskirts of it. People passed back and forth along the street and in or out of the drug store; one or two of the group drifted away, and newcomers took their places. An automobile drew up to the curb, was served by a negro lad; drove away. The clock on the courthouse struck nine measured strokes.

Soon, with a noise of starting engines, motor cars began to stream out of a side street and onto the square, and presently a flux of pedestrians appeared. It was the exodus from the picture show, and cars one after another drew up to the curb with young men and girls in them, and other youths and girls in pairs turned into the drug store with talk and shrill laughter and cries one to another, with slender bodies in delicate colored dresses, shrill as apes and awkward, divinely young. Then the more sedate groups—a man with a child or so gazing longingly into the scented and gleaming interior of the store, followed by three or four women—his wife and a neighbor or so—talking sedately among themselves; more children—little girls in prim and sibilant clots, and boys scuffling and darting with changing adolescent shouts. A few of the sitters rose and joined passing groups.

More belated couples came up the street and entered the drug store, and other cars; other couples emerged and strolled on. The night watchman came along presently, with his star on his open vest and a pistol and a flash light in his hip pockets; he too stopped and joined in the slow, unhurried talk. The last couple emerged from the drug store, and the last car drove away. And presently the lights behind them flashed off and the proprietor jingled his keys in the door and rattled it, and stood for a moment among them, then went on. Ten oclock. Snopes rose to his feet.

"Well, I reckon I'll turn in," he said generally.

"Time we all did," another said, and they rose also. "Good night, Buck."

"Good night, gentlemen," the night watchman replied.

As he crossed the now empty square he looked up at the lighted face of the clock. It was ten minutes past eleven. There was no sign of life save the lonely figure of the night marshal in the door of the lighted postoffice lobby.

He left the square and entered a street and went steadily beneath the arc lights, having the street to himself and the regular recapitulation of his striding shadow dogging him out of the darkness, through the pool of the light and into darkness again. He turned a corner and followed a yet quieter street and turned presently from it into a lane between massed banks of honeysuckle higher than his head and sweet on the night air. The lane was dark and he increased his pace. On either hand the upper stories of houses rose above the honeysuckle, with now and then a lighted window among the dark trees. He kept close to the wall and went swiftly on, passing now between back premises. After a while another house loomed, and a serried row of cedars against the paler sky, and he stole beside a stone wall and so came opposite the garage. He stopped here and sought in the lush grass beneath the wall and stooped and picked up a pole, which he leaned against the wall. With the aid of the pole he mounted on to the wall and thence to the garage roof.

But the house was dark, and presently he slid to the ground and stole across the lawn and stopped beneath a window. There was a light somewhere toward the front, but no sound, no movement, and he stood for a time listening, darting his eyes this way and that, covert and ceaseless as a cornered animal.

The screen responded easily to his knife and he raised it and listened again. Then with a single scrambling motion he was in the room, crouching. Still no sound save the thudding of his heart, and the whole house gave off that unmistakable emanation of temporary desertion. He drew out his handkerchief and wiped his mouth.

The light was in the next room, and he went on. The stairs rose from the end of this room and he scuttled silently across it and mounted swiftly into the upper darkness and groped forward until he touched a wall, then a door. The knob turned under his fingers.

It was the right room; he knew that at once: her presence was all about him, and for a time his heart thudded and thudded in his throat and fury and lust and despair shook him. He pulled himself together; he must get out quickly, and he groped his way across to the bed and lay face down upon it, his head buried in the pillows, writhing and making smothered, animal-like moanings. But he must get out, and he got up and groped across the room again. What little light there was was behind him now, and instead of finding the door he blundered into a chest of drawers, and stood there a moment, learning its shape with his hands. Then he opened one of the drawers and fumbled in it. It was filled with a faintly scented fragility of garments, but he could not distinguish one from another with his hands.

He found a match in his pocket and struck it beneath the shelter of his palm, and by its light he chose one of the soft garments, discovering as the match died a packet of letters in the corner of the drawer. He recognised them at once, dropped the dead match to the floor and took the packet from the drawer and put it in his pocket, and placed the letter he had just written in the drawer, and he stood for a time with the garment crushed against his face; remained so for some time, until a sound caused him to jerk his head up, listening. A car was coming up the drive, and as he sprang to the window, its lights swept beneath him and fell full upon the open garage, and he crouched at the window in a panic. Then he sped to the door and stopped again crouching, panting and snarling with indecision.

He ran back to the window. The garage was dark, and two dark figures were approaching the house and he crouched beside the window until they had passed from sight. Then, still clutching the garment, he climbed out the window and swung from the sill a moment by his hands, and closed his eyes and dropped.

A crash of glass and he sprawled numbed by shock amid lesser crashes and a burst of stale, dry dust. He had fallen into a shallow flower pit and he scrambled out and tried to stand

and fell again, while nausea swirled in him. It was his knee, and he lay sick and with drawn, gasping lips while his trouser leg sopped slowly and warmly, clutching the garment and staring at the dark sky with wide, mad eyes. He heard voices in the house, and a light came on behind the window above him and he turned crawling, and at a scrambling hobble he crossed the lawn and plunged into the shadow of the cedars beside the garage, where he lay watching the window in which a man leaned, peering out; and he moaned a little while his blood ran between his clasped fingers. He drove himself onward again and dragged his bleeding leg on up to the wall and dropped into the lane and cast the pole down. A hundred yards further he stopped and drew his torn trousers aside and tried to bandage the gash in his leg. But the handkerchief stained over almost at once, and still blood ran and ran down his leg and into his shoe.

Once in the back room of the bank, he rolled his trouser leg up and removed the handkerchief and bathed the gash at the lavatory. It still bled, and the sight of his own blood sickened him, and he swayed against the wall, watching his blood. Then he removed his shirt and bound it as tightly as he could about his leg. He still felt nausea, and he drank long of the tepid water from the tap. Immediately it welled salinely within him and he clung to the lavatory, sweating, trying not to vomit, until the spell passed. His leg felt numb and dead, and he was weak and he wished to lie down but he dared not.

He entered the grille, his left heel showing yet a red print at each step. The vault door opened soundlessly; without a light he found the key to the cash box and opened it. He took only banknotes, but he took all he could find. Then he closed the vault and locked it, returned to the lavatory and wetted a towel and removed his heel prints from the linoleum floor. Then he passed out the back door, threw the latch so it would lock behind him. The clock on the courthouse rang midnight.

In an alley between two negro stores a man sat in a battered ford, waiting. He gave the negro a bill and the negro cranked the engine and came and stared curiously at the bloody cloth beneath his torn trousers. "Whut happened, boss? Y'aint hurt, is you?"

"Run into some wire," he answered shortly. "She's got plenty gas, aint she?" The negro said yes, and he drove on. As he crossed the square the night marshal, Buck, stood beneath the light before the postoffice, and Snopes cursed him with silent and bitter derision. He drove on and entered another street and passed from view, and presently the sound of his going had died away.

He drove through Frenchman's Bend at two oclock, without stopping. The village was dark; Varner's store, the blacksmith shop (now a garage too, with a gasoline pump), Mrs Littlejohn's huge, unpainted boarding house—all the remembered scenes of his boyhood—were without life; he went on. He drove now along a rutted wagon road, between swampy jungle, at a snail's pace. After a half hour the road mounted a small knoll wooded with scrub oak and indiscriminate saplings, and faded into a barren, sun-baked surface in the middle of which squatted a low, broken backed log house. His lights swept across its gaping front, and a huge gaunt hound descended from the porch and bellowed at him. He stopped and switched the lights off.

His leg was stiff and dead, and when he descended he was forced to cling to the car for a time, moving it back and forth until it would bear his weight. The hound stood ten feet away and thundered at him in a sober conscientious fury until he spoke to it, whereupon it ceased its clamor but stood yet in an attitude of watchful belligerence. He limped toward it, and it recognised him, and together they crossed the barren plot in the soundless dust and mounted the veranda. "Turpin," he called in a guarded voice.

The dog had followed him onto the porch, and it flopped noisily and scratched itself. The house consisted of two wings joined by an open hall; through the hall he could see sky, and another warped roof tree on the slope behind the house. His leg tingled and throbbed as with pins of fire. I got that 'ere bandage too tight, he thought. "Turpin."

A movement from the wing at his left, and into the lesser obscurity of the hall a shape emerged and stood in vague relief against the sky, in a knee-length night-shirt and a shot gun. "Who's thar?" the shape demanded.

"Byron Snopes."

The man leaned the gun against the wall and came onto the porch, and they shook hands limply. "What you doin', this time of night? Thought you was in town."

"On a trip for the bank," Snopes explained. "Just drove in, and I got to git right on. Might be gone some time, and I wanted to see Minnie Sue."

The other rubbed the wild shock of his head, then he scratched his leg. "She's a-sleepin'. Caint you wait till daylight?"

"I got to git on," he repeated. "Got to be pretty nigh Alabama by daybreak."

The man brooded heavily, rubbing his flank. "Well," he said finally. "Ef you caint wait till mawnin'." He padded back into the house and vanished. The hound flopped again at Snopes' feet and sniffed noisily. From the river bottom a mile away an owl hooted with its mournful rising inflection. Snopes thrust his hand into his coat and touched the wadded delicate garment. In his breast pocket the money bulked against his arm.

Another figure stepped soundlessly into the hall, against the lighter sky; a smaller figure and even more shapeless, that stood for a moment, then came out to him. He put his arms around her, feeling her free body beneath the rough garment she had hastily donned. "Byron?" she said. "What is it, Byron?" He was trying to kiss her, and she suffered him readily, but withdrew her face immediately, peering at him. He drew her away from the door.

"Come on," he whispered. His voice was shaking and hoarse, and his body was trembling also. He led her to the steps and tried to draw her on, but she held back a little, peering at him.

"Let's set on the steps," she said. "What's the matter, Byron? You got a chill?"

"I'm all right. Let's git away where we can talk."

She let him draw her forward and down the steps, but as they moved further and further away from the house she began to resist, with curiosity and growing alarm. "Byron," she said again and stopped. His hands were trembling upon her, moving about her body, and his voice was shaking so that she could not understand him.

"You aint got on nothing under here but your nightgown, have you?" he whispered.

"What?" He drew her a little farther, but she stopped firmly and he could not move her; she was as strong as he. "You tell me what it is, now," she commanded. "You aint ready fer our marryin' yet, are you?"

But he made no answer. He was trembling more than ever, pawing at her. They struggled, and at last he succeeded in dragging her to the ground and he sprawled beside her, pawing at her clothing; whereupon she struggled in earnest, and soon she held him helpless while he sprawled with his face against her throat, babbling a name not hers. When he was still she turned and thrust him away, and rose to her feet.

"You come back tomorrer, when you git over this," she said, and she ran silently toward the house, and was gone.

He sat where she had left him for a long time, with his half-insane face between his knees and madness and helpless rage and thwarted desire coiling within him. The owl hooted again from the black river bottom; its cry faded mournfully across the land, beneath the chill stars, and the hound came silently through the dust and sniffed at him, and went away. After a time he rose and limped to the car and started the engine.

FOUR

IT WAS a sunny Sunday afternoon in October. Narcissa and Bayard had driven off soon after dinner, and Miss Jenny and old Bayard were sitting on the sunny end of the veranda when, preceded by Simon, the deputation came solemnly around the corner of the house from the rear. It consisted of six negroes in a catholic variety of Sunday raiment and it was headed by a huge, bull-necked negro in a hind-side-before collar and a prince albert coat, with an orotund air and a wild, compelling eye.

"Yere dey is, Cunnel," Simon said, and without pausing he mounted the steps and turned about, leaving no doubt in any one's mind as to which side he considered himself aligned with. The deputation halted and milled a little, solemnly decorous.

"What's this?" Miss Jenny asked. "That you, uncle Bird?"

"Yessum, Miss Jenny." One of the committee uncovered his grizzled wool and bowed. "How you gittin' on?" The others shuffled their feet, and one by one they removed their hats. The leader clasped his across his chest like a congressman being photographed.

"Here, Simon," old Bayard demanded. "What's this? What did you bring these niggers around here for?"

"Dey come fer dey money," Simon explained.

"What?"

"Money?" Miss Jenny repeated with interest. "What money, Simon?"

"Dey come fer de money you promised 'um," Simon shouted.

"I told you I wasn't going to pay that money," old Bayard said. "Did Simon tell you I was going to pay it?" he demanded of the deputation.

"What money?" Miss Jenny repeated. "What are you talking about, Simon?" The leader of the committee was shaping his face for words, but Simon forestalled him.

"Why, Cunnel, you tole me yo'self to tell dem niggers you wuz gwine pay 'um."

"I didn't do any such thing," old Bayard answered violently. "I told you that if they wanted to put you in jail, to go ahead and do it. That's what I told you."

"Why, Cunnel, you said it des' ez plain. You jes' fergot erbout it. I kin prove it by Miss Jenny you tole me——"

"Not by me," Miss Jenny interrupted. "This is the first I heard about it. Whose money is it, Simon?"

Simon gave her a pained, reproachful look. "He tole me to tell 'um he wuz gwine pay it."

"I'm damned if I did," old Bayard shouted. "I told you I wouldn't pay a damn cent of it. And I told you that if you let 'em worry me about it, I'd skin you alive, sir."

"I aint gwine let 'um worry you," Simon answered soothingly. "Dat's whut I'm fixin' now. You jes' give 'um dey money, en me en you kin fix it up later."

"I'll be eternally damned, if I will; if I let a lazy nigger that aint worth his keep——"

"But somebody got to pay 'um," Simon pointed out patiently. "Aint dat right, Miss Jenny?"

"That's right," Miss Jenny agreed. "But I aint the one."

"Yessuh, dey aint no argument dat somebody got to pay 'um. Ef somebody dont quiet 'um down, dey'll put me in de jail. And den whut'll y'all do, widout nobody to keep dem hosses fed en clean, en to clean de house en wait on de table? Co'se I dont mine gwine to jail, even ef dem stone flo's aint gwine do my mis'ry no good." And he drew a long and affecting picture, of high and grail-like principles, and of patient abnegation. Old Bayard slammed his feet to the floor.

"How much is it?"

The leader swelled within his prince albert. "Brudder Mo'," he said, "will you read out de total emoluments owed to de pupposed Secon' Baptis' church by de late Deacon Strother in his capacity ez treasurer of de church boa'd?"

Brother Moore created a mild disturbance in the rear of the group, emerging presently by the agency of sundry willing hands—a small, reluctant ebon negro in sombre, overlarge black—where the parson majestically made room for him, contriving by some means to focus attention on him. He laid his hat on the ground at his feet and from the right hand pocket of his coat he produced in order, a red bandanna handkerchief;

a shoe horn; a plug of chewing tobacco, and holding these in his free hand he delved again, with an expression of mildly conscientious alarm. Then he replaced the objects, and from his left pocket he produced a pocket knife; a stick on which was wound a length of soiled twine; a short piece of leather strap attached to a rusty and apparently idle buckle, and lastly a greasy, dogeared notebook. He crammed the other things back into his pocket, dropping the strap, which he stooped and recovered, then he and the parson held a brief whispered conversation. He opened the notebook and fumbled at the leaves, fumbled at them until the parson leaned over his shoulder and found the proper page and laid his finger upon it.

"How much is it, reverend?" old Bayard asked impatiently.

"Brudder Mo' will now read out de amount," the parson intoned. Brother Moore looked at the page with his tranced gaze and mumbled something in a practically indistinguishable voice.

"What?" old Bayard demanded, cupping his ear.

"Make 'im talk up," Simon said. "Cant nobody tell whut he sayin'."

"Louder," the parson rumbled, with just a trace of impatience.

"Sixty sevum dollars en fawty cents," Brother Moore enunciated at last. Old Bayard slammed back in his chair and swore for a long minute while Simon watched him with covert anxiety. Then he rose and tramped up the veranda and into the house, still swearing. Simon sighed and relaxed. The deputation milled again, and Brother Moore faded briskly into the rear rank of it. The parson however still retained his former attitude of fateful and impressive profundity.

"What became of that money, Simon?" Miss Jenny asked curiously. "You had it, didn't you?"

"Dat's whut dey claims," Simon answered.

"What did you do with it?"

"Hit's all right," Simon assured her. "I jes' put it out, sort of."

"I bet you did," she agreed drily. "I bet it never even got cool while you had it. They deserve to lose it for ever giving it to you in the first place. Who did you put it out to?"

"Oh, me en Cunnel done fix dat up," Simon said easily.

"Long time ago." Old Bayard tramped in the hall again, and emerged flapping a check in his hand.

"Here," he commanded, and the parson approached the railing and took it and folded it away in his pocket. "And if you folks are fools enough to turn any more money over to him, dont come to me for it, you hear?" He glared at the deputation a moment; then he glared at Simon. "And the next time you steal money and come to me to pay it back, I'm going to have you arrested and prosecute you myself. Get those niggers out of here."

The deputation had already stirred, with a concerted movement, but the parson halted them with a commanding hand. He faced Simon again. "Deacon Strother," he said, "ez awdained minister of de late Fust Baptis' church, en recalled minister of de pupposed Secon' Baptis' church, en chairman of dis committee, I hereby reinfestes you wid yo' fawmer capacity of deacon in de said pupposed Secon' Baptis' church. Amen. Cunnel Sartoris en ma'am, good day." Then he turned and herded his committee from the scene.

"Thank de Lawd, we got dat offen our mind," Simon said, and he came and lowered himself to the top step, groaning pleasurably.

"And you remember what I said," old Bayard warned him. "One more time, now——"

But Simon was craning his head in the direction the church board had taken. "Dar now," he said. "Whut you reckon dey wants now?" For the committee had returned and it now peered diffidently around the corner of the house.

"Well," old Bayard demanded. "What is it now?"

They were trying to thrust Brother Moore forward again, but he won this time. At last the parson spoke.

"You fergot de fawty cents, white folks."

"What?"

"He says you lef' out de extry fawty cents," Simon shouted. Old Bayard exploded; Miss Jenny clapped her hands to her ears and the committee rolled its eyes in fearsome admiration while he soared to magnificent heights, alighting finally upon Simon.

"You give him that forty cents, and get 'em out of here," old Bayard stormed. "And if you ever let 'em come back here again, I'll take a horsewhip to the whole passel of you."

"Lawd, Cunnel, I aint got no fawty cents, en you knows it. Cant dey do widout dat, after gittin' de balance of it?"

"Yes you have, Simon," Miss Jenny said. "You had a half a dollar left after I ordered those shoes for you last night." Again Simon looked at her with pained astonishment.

"Give it to 'em," old Bayard commanded. Slowly Simon reached into his pocket and produced a half dollar and turned it slowly in his palm.

"I mought need dis money, Cunnel," he protested. "Seems like dey mought leave me dis."

"Give 'em that money!" old Bayard thundered. "I reckon you can pay forty cents of it, at least." Simon rose reluctantly, and the parson approached.

"Whar's my dime change?" Simon demanded, nor would he surrender the coin until two nickels were in his hand. Then the committee departed.

"Now," old Bayard said, "I want to know what you did with that money."

"Well, suh," Simon began readily, "it wuz like dis. I put dat money out." Miss Jenny rose.

"My Lord, are you all going over that again?" And she left them. In her room, where she sat in a sunny window, she could still hear them—old Bayard's stormy rage, and Simon's bland and plausible evasion rising and falling on the drowsy Sabbath air.

There was a rose, a single remaining rose. Through the sad, dead days of late summer it had continued to bloom, and now though persimmons had long swung their miniature suns among the caterpillar-festooned branches, and gum and maple and hickory had flaunted two gold-and-scarlet weeks, and the grass, where grandfathers of grasshoppers squatted sluggishly like sullen octogenarians, had been pencilled twice delicately with frost, and the sunny noons were scented with sassafras, it still bloomed. Overripe now, and a little gallantly blowsy, like a fading burlesque star. Miss Jenny worked in a sweater, nowadays, and her trowel glinted in her earthy glove.

"It's like some women I've known," she said. "It just dont know how to give up gracefully and be a grandmamma."

"Let it have the summer out," Narcissa in her dark woolen

dress, protested. She had a trowel too, and she pottered serenely after Miss Jenny's scolding brisk impatience, accomplishing nothing. Worse than nothing, worse than Isom even, because she demoralized Isom, who had immediately given his unspoken allegiance to the Left, or passive, Wing. "It's entitled to its summer."

"Some folks dont know when summer's over," Miss Jenny rejoined. "Indian summer's no excuse for senile adolescence."

"It isn't senility, either."

"All right. You'll see, some day."

"Oh, someday. I'm not quite prepared to be a grandmother, yet."

"You're doing pretty well." Miss Jenny trowelled a tulip bulb carefully and expertly up and removed the clotted earth from its roots. "We seem to have pretty well worn out Bayard, for the time being," she continued. "I reckon we'd better name him John this time."

"Yes?"

"Yes," Miss Jenny repeated. "We'll name him John. You, Isom!"

The gin had been running steadily for a month, now, what with the Sartoris cotton and that of other planters further up the valley, and of smaller croppers with their tilted fields among the hills. The Sartoris place was farmed on shares. Most of the tenants had picked their cotton, and gathered the late corn; and of late afternoons, with Indian summer upon the land and an ancient sadness sharp as woodsmoke on the windless air, Bayard and Narcissa would drive out to where, beside a spring on the edge of the woods, the negroes brought their cane and made their communal winter sorghum molasses. One of the negroes, a sort of patriarch among the tenants, owned the mill and the mule that furnished the motive power. He did the grinding and superintended the cooking of the sap for a tithe, and when Bayard and Narcissa arrived the mule would be plodding in a monotonous and patient circle, its feet rustling in the dried cane-pith, while one of the patriarch's grandsons fed the cane into the crusher.

Round and round the mule went, setting its narrow, deer-like feet delicately down in the hissing cane-pith, its neck bobbing limber as a section of rubber hose in the collar, with its trace-galled flanks and flopping, lifeless ears, and its half-closed eyes drowsing venomously behind pale lids, apparently asleep with the monotony of its own motion. Some Homer of the cotton fields should sing the saga of the mule and of his place in the South. He it was, more than any other one creature or thing, who, steadfast to the land when all else faltered before the hopeless juggernaut of circumstance, impervious to conditions that broke men's hearts because of his venomous and patient preoccupation with the immediate present, won the prone South from beneath the iron heel of Reconstruction and taught it pride again through humility and courage through adversity overcome; who accomplished the well-nigh impossible despite hopeless odds, by sheer and vindictive patience. Father and mother he does not resemble, sons and daughters he will never have; vindictive and patient (it is a known fact that he will labor ten years willingly and patiently for you, for the privilege of kicking you once); solitary but without pride, self-sufficient but without vanity; his voice is his own derision. Outcast and pariah, he has neither friend, wife, mistress nor sweetheart; celibate, he is unscarred, possesses neither pillar nor desert cave, he is not assaulted by temptations nor flagellated by dreams nor assuaged by visions; faith, hope and charity are not his. Misanthropic, he labors six days without reward for one creature whom he hates, bound with chains to another whom he despises, and spends the seventh day kicking or being kicked by his fellows. Misunderstood even by that creature (the nigger who drives him) whose impulses and mental processes most closely resemble his, he performs alien actions among alien surroundings; he finds bread not only for a race, but for an entire form of behavior; meek, his inheritance is cooked away from him along with his soul in a glue factory. Ugly, untiring and perverse, he can be moved neither by reason, flattery, nor promise of reward; he performs his humble monotonous duties without complaint, and his meed is blows. Alive, he is haled through the world, an object of general derision; unwept, unhonored and unsung, he bleaches his awkward, accusing bones among rusting cans and broken crockery and worn-out automobile tires on lonely hillsides, while his flesh soars unawares against the blue in the craws of buzzards.

As they approached, the groaning and creaking of the mill would be the first intimation, unless the wind happened to blow toward them. Then it would be the sharp, subtly exciting odor of fermentation and of boiling molasses. Bayard liked the smell of it, and they would drive up and stop for a time while the boy rolled his eyes covertly at them as he fed cane into the mill, while they watched the patient mule and the old man stooped above the simmering pot. Sometimes Bayard got out and went over and talked to him, leaving Narcissa in the car, lapped in the ripe odors of the failing year and all its rich, vague sadness, her gaze brooding upon Bayard and the old negro—the one lean and tall and fatally young and the other stooped with time, and her spirit went out in serene and steady waves, surrounding him unawares.

Then he would return and get in beside her, and she would touch his rough clothing but so lightly that he was not conscious of it, and they would drive back along the faint uneven road, beside the flaunting woods, and soon, above turning locusts and oaks, the white house simple and huge and steadfast, and the orange disc of the harvest moon getting above the ultimate hills, ripe as cheese.

Sometimes they went back after dark. The mill was still then, its long arm motionless across the firelit scene. The mule was munching in stable, or stamping and nuzzling its empty manger, or asleep standing, boding not of tomorrow; and against the firelight many shadows moved. The negroes had gathered now: old men and women sitting on crackling cushions of cane about the blaze which one of their number fed with pressed stalks until its incense-laden fury swirled licking at the boughs overhead, making more golden still the twinkling golden leaves; and young men and girls, and children squatting and still as animals, staring into the fire. Sometimes they sang—quavering, wordless chords in which plaintive minors blent with mellow bass in immemorial and sad suspense, their grave dark faces bent to the flames and with no motion of lips. But when the white folks arrived the singing ceased, and they sat or lay about the fire on which the blackened pot simmered, talking in broken murmurous overtones ready with sorrowful mirth, while in shadowy beds among the dry whispering cane-stalks youths and girls murmured and giggled.

Always one of them, and sometimes both, stopped in the office where old Bayard and Miss Jenny were. There was a fire of logs on the hearth now, and they would sit in the glow of it—Miss Jenny beneath the light with her lurid daily paper; old Bayard with his slippered feet propped against the fireplace, his head wreathed in smoke and the old setter dreaming fitfully beside his chair, reliving proud and ancient stands perhaps, or further back still, the lean, gawky days of his young doghood, when the world was full of scents that maddened the blood in him and pride had not taught him self-restraint; Narcissa and Bayard between them—Narcissa dreaming too in the firelight, grave and tranquil, and young Bayard smoking his cigarettes in his leashed and moody repose.

At last old Bayard would throw his cigar into the fire and drop his feet to the floor, and the dog would wake and raise its head and blink and yawn with such gaping deliberation that Narcissa, watching him, invariably yawned also. "Well, Jenny?"

Miss Jenny would lay her paper aside and rise. "Let me," Narcissa would say. "Let me go." But Miss Jenny never would, and presently she would return with a tray and three glasses, and old Bayard would unlock his desk and fetch the silver-stoppered decanter and compound three toddies with ritualistic care.

Once Bayard persuaded her into khaki and boots and carried her 'possum hunting. Caspey with a streaked lantern and a cow's horn slung over his shoulder, and Isom with a gunny sack and an axe, and four shadowy, restless hounds waited for them at the lot gate and they set off among ghostly shocks of corn, where every day Bayard kicked up a covey of quail, toward the woods.

"Where we going to start tonight, Caspey?" Bayard asked.

"Back of Unc' Henry's. Dey's one in dat grape vine behine de cotton house. Blue treed 'im down dar las' night."

"How do you know he's there tonight, Caspey?" Narcissa asked.

"He be back," Caspey answered confidently. "He right dar now, watchin' dis lantern wid his eyes scrooched up, listenin' to hear ef de dawgs wid us."

They climbed through a fence and Caspey stooped and set the lantern down. The dogs moiled and tugged about his legs

with sniffings and throaty growls at one another as he unleashed them. "You, Ruby! Stan' still, dar. Hole up here, you
potlickin' fool." They whimpered and surged, their eyes melting in fluid brief gleams, then they faded soundlessly and
swiftly into the darkness. "Give 'um a little time," Caspey said.
"Let 'um see ef he dar yit." From the darkness ahead a dog
yapped three times on a high note. "Dat's dat young dog,"
Caspey said. "Jes' showin' off. He aint smelt nothin'." Overhead the stars swam vaguely in the hazy sky; the air was not
yet chill, the earth still warm to the touch. They stood in a
steady oasis of lantern light in a world of but one dimension,
a vague cistern of darkness filled with meagre light and topped
with an edgeless canopy of ragged stars. The lantern was
smoking and emanating a faint odor of heat. Caspey raised it
and turned the wick down and set it at his feet again. Then
from the darkness there came a single note, resonant and low
and grave.

"Dar he," Isom said.

"Hit's Ruby," Caspey agreed, picking up the lantern. "She
got 'im." The young dog yapped again, with fierce hysteria,
then the single low cry chimed. Narcissa slid her arm through
Bayard's. " 'Taint no rush," Caspey told her. "Dey aint treed
yit. Whooy. H'mawn, dawg." The young dog had ceased its
yapping, but still at intervals the other one bayed her single
timbrous note, and they followed it. "H'mawn, dawg."

They stumbled a little over fading plow-scars, after Caspey's
bobbing lantern, and the darkness went suddenly crescendic
with short steady cries in four keys. "Dey got 'im," Isom said.

"Dat's right," Caspey replied. "Le's go. Hold 'im, dawg!"
They trotted now, Narcissa clinging to Bayard's arm, and
plunged through rank grass and over another fence and so
among trees. Eyes gleamed fleetingly from the darkness ahead,
and another gust of barking interspersed with tense and eager
whimperings, and among stumbling half-lit shadows dogs
surged about them. "He up dar," Caspey said. "Ole Blue sees
'im."

"Dar Unc' Henry's dawg, too," Isom said.

Caspey grunted. "I knowed he'd be here. He cant keep up
wid a 'possum no mo', but jes' let a dog tree whar he kin hear
'im. . . ." He set the lantern upon his head and peered up into

the vine-matted sapling, and Bayard drew a flashlight from his pocket and turned its beam into the tree. The three older hounds and Uncle Henry's ancient, moth-eaten beast sat in a tense circle about the tree, whimpering or barking in short spaced gusts, but the young one yapped steadily in mad, hysterical rushes. "Kick dat puppy still," Caspey commanded.

"You, Ginger, hush yo' mouf," Isom shouted; he laid his axe and sack down and caught the puppy and held it between his knees. Caspey and Bayard moved slowly about the tree, among the eager dogs; Narcissa followed them. "Dem vines is so thick up dar. . . . . . ." Caspey said.

"Here he is," Bayard said suddenly. "I've got 'im." He steadied his light and Caspey moved behind him and looked over his shoulder.

"Where?" Narcissa asked. "Can you see it?"

"Dat's right," Caspey agreed. "Dar he is. Ruby dont lie. When she say he dar, he dar."

"Where is he, Bayard?" Narcissa repeated. He drew her before him and trained the light over her head, into the tree, and presently from the massed vines two reddish points of fire not a match-breadth apart, gleamed at her, winked out, then shone again.

"He movin'," Caspey said. "Young 'possum. Git up dar and shake 'im out, Isom." Bayard held his light on the creature's eyes and Caspey set his lantern down and herded the dogs together at his knees. Isom scrambled up into the tree and vanished in the mass of vine, but they could follow his progress by the shaking branches and his panting ejaculations as he threatened the animal with a mixture of cajolery and adjuration.

"Hah," he grunted. "Aint gwine hurt you. Aint gwine do nothin' ter you but th'ow you in de cook-pot. Look out, mister; I'se comin' up dar." More commotion; it ceased, they could hear him moving the branches cautiously. "Here he," he called suddenly. "Hole dem dawgs, now."

"Little 'un, aint he?" Caspey asked.

"Cant tell. Can't see nothin' but his face. Watch dem dawgs." The upper part of the sapling burst into violent and sustained fury; Isom whooped louder and louder as he shook the branches. "Whooy, here he comes," he shouted, and something dropped sluggishly and reluctantly from branch to invisible branch, stopped, and the dogs set up a straining clamor. The thing fell again, and Bayard's light followed a lumpy object that plumped with a resounding thud to the ground and vanished immediately beneath a swirl of hounds. Caspey and Bayard leaped among them with shouts, and at last succeeded in dragging them clear, and Narcissa saw the creature in the pool of the flashlight, lying on its side in a grinning curve, its eyes closed and its pink, baby-like hands doubled against its breast. She looked at the motionless thing with pity and distinct loathing—such a paradox, its vulpine, skull-like grin and those tiny, human-looking hands, and the long, rat-like tail of it. Isom dropped from the tree, and Caspey turned the three straining clamorous dogs he held over to his nephew and picked up the axe, and while Narcissa watched in shrinking curiosity, he laid the axe across the thing's neck and put his foot on either end of the helve, and grasped the animal's tail. . . . . . . She turned and fled, her hand to her mouth.

But the wall of darkness stopped her and she stood trembling and a little sick, watching them as they moved about the lantern. Then Caspey drove the dogs away, giving Uncle Henry's octogenarian a hearty and resounding kick that sent him homeward with bloodcurdling and astonished wails, and Isom swung the lumpy sack to his shoulder, and Bayard turned and looked for her. "Narcissa?"

"Here," she answered. He came to her.

"That's one. We ought to get a dozen, tonight."

"Oh, no," she shuddered. "No." He peered at her; then he snapped his flashlight full on her face. She lifted her hand and put it aside.

"What's the matter? Not tired already, are you?"

"No." She went on, "I just. . . . Come on; they're leaving us."

Caspey led them on into the woods. They walked now in a dry sibilance of leaves and crackling undergrowth. Trees loomed in to the lantern light; above them, among the thinning branches, stars swam in the hushed, vague sky. The dogs were on ahead, and they went on among the looming tree trunks, sliding down into ditches where sand gleamed in the lantern's pool and where the scissoring shadow of Caspey's legs was enormous, struggled through snatching briers and up the other bank.

"We better head away fum de creek bottom," Caspey suggested. "Dey mought strike a 'coon, and den dey wont git home 'fo' day." He bore away toward the open again; they emerged from the woods and crossed a field of sedge, odorous of sun and dust, in which the lantern was lightly nimbused. "H'mawn, dawg." They entered the woods again. Narcissa was beginning to tire, but Bayard strode on with a fine obliviousness of that possibility, and she followed without complaint. At last, from some distance away, came that single ringing cry. Caspey stopped. "Le's see which way he gwine." They stood in the darkness, in the sad, faintly chill decline of the year, among the dying trees, listening. "Whooy," Caspey shouted mellowly. "Go git 'im."

The dog replied, and they moved again, slowly, pausing at intervals to listen. The hound bayed; there were two voices now, and they seemed to be moving in a circle across their path. "Whooy," Caspey called, his voice ebbing in falling echoes among the trees. They went on. Again the dogs gave tongue, half the circle away from where the first cry had come. "He ca'yin' 'um right back whar he come fum," Caspey said. "We better wait 'twell dey gits 'im straightened out." He set the lantern down and squatted beside it, and Isom sloughed his burden and squatted also, and Bayard sat against a tree trunk and drew Narcissa down beside him. The dogs bayed again, nearer. Caspey stared off into the darkness toward the sound.

"I believe hit's a 'coon dey got," Isom said.

"Mought be. Hill 'coon."

"Headin' fer dat holler tree, aint he?"

"Soun' like it." They listened, motionless. "We have a job, den. Whooy." There was a faint chill in the air now, as the day's sunlight cooled from the ground, and Narcissa moved closer to Bayard. He took a packet of cigarettes from his jacket and gave Caspey one and lit one for himself. Isom squatted on his heels, his eyes rolling whitely in the lantern light.

"Gimme one, please, suh," he said.

"You aint got no business smokin', boy," Caspey told him.

But Bayard gave him one, and he squatted leanly on his haunches, holding the white tube in his black diffident hand. There was a scurrying noise in the leaves behind them and a tense whimpering, and the young dog came into the light and slid with squeaking whimpers, and the diffident, fleeting phosphorous of its eyes against Caspey's leg. "Whut you want?" Caspey said, dropping his hand on its head. "Somethin' skeer you out dar?" The puppy genuflected its gawky young body and nuzzled whimpering at Caspey's hand. "He mus' a foun' a bear down yonder," Caspey said. "Wouldn't dem other dawgs he'p you ketch 'im?"

"Poor little fellow," Narcissa said. "Did he really get scared, Caspey? Come here, puppy."

"De other dawgs jes' went off and lef' 'im," Caspey answered. The puppy moiled diffidently about Caspey's knees; then it scrambled up and licked his face.

"Git down fum here!" Caspey exclaimed, and he flung the puppy away. It flopped awkwardly in the dry leaves and scrambled to its feet, and at that moment the hounds bayed again, mellow and chiming and timbrous in the darkness, and the puppy whirled and sped yapping shrilly toward the sound. The dogs bayed again; Isom and Caspey listened. "Yes, suh," Caspey repeated. "He headin' fer dat down tree."

"You know this country like you do the back yard, dont you, Caspey?" Narcissa said.

"Yessum, I ought to. I been over it a hund'ed times since I wuz bawn. Mist' Bayard do too. He been huntin' it long ez I is, pretty near. Him and Mist' Johnny bofe. Miss Jenny send me wid 'um when dey had dey fust gun; me and dat 'ere single bar'l gun I use ter have ter tie together wid a string. You 'member dat ole single bar'l, Mist' Bayard? But hit would shoot. Many's de fox squir'l we shot in dese woods. Rabbits, too." Bayard was leaning back against the tree. He was gazing off into the treetops and the soft sky beyond, his cigarette burning slowly in his hand. She looked at his bleak profile against the lantern glow, then she moved closer against him. But he did not respond, and she slid her hand into his. But it too was cold, and again he had left her for the lonely heights of his despair. Caspey was speaking again, in his slow, consonantless voice with its overtones of mellow sadness. "Mist'

Johnny, now, he sho' could shoot. You 'member dat time me and you and him wuz——"

Bayard rose. He dropped his cigarette and crushed it carefully with his heel. "Let's go," he said. "They aint going to tree." He drew Narcissa to her feet and turned and went on. Caspey got up and unslung his horn and put it to his lips. The sound swelled about them, grave and clear and prolonged, then it died into echoes and so into silence again, leaving no ripple in the still darkness.

It was near midnight when they left Caspey and Isom at their cabin and followed the lane toward the house. The barn loomed presently beside them, and the house among its thinning trees, against the hazy sky. He opened the gate and she passed through and he followed and closed it, and turning he found her beside him, and stopped. "Bayard?" she whispered, leaning against him, and he put his arms around her and stood so, gazing above her head into the sky. She took his face between her palms and drew it down, but his lips were cold and upon them she tasted fatality and doom, and she clung to him for a time, her head bowed against his chest.

After that she would not go with him again. So he went alone, returning anywhere between midnight and dawn, ripping his clothing off quietly in the darkness and sliding cautiously into bed. But when he was still, she would touch him and speak his name in the dark beside him, and turn to him warm and soft with sleep. And they would lie so, holding to one another in the darkness and the temporary abeyance of his despair and the isolation of that doom he could not escape.

2.

"Well," Miss Jenny said briskly, above the soup. "Your girl's gone and left you, and now you can find time to come out and see your kin folks, cant you?"

Horace grinned a little. "To tell the truth, I came out to get something to eat. I dont think that one woman in ten has any aptitude for keeping house, but my place is certainly not in the home."

"You mean," Miss Jenny corrected, "that not one man in ten has sense enough to marry a decent cook."

"Maybe they have more sense and consideration for others than to spoil decent cooks," he suggested.

"Yes," young Bayard said. "Even a cook'll quit work when she gets married."

"Dat's de troof," Simon, propped in a slightly florid attitude against the sideboard, in a collarless boiled shirt and his Sunday pants (it is Thanksgiving day) and reeking a little of whisky in addition to his normal odors, agreed. "I had to fin' Euphrony fo' new cookin' places de fust two mont' we wuz ma'ied."

Dr Peabody said: "Simon must have married somebody else's cook."

"I'd rather marry somebody else's cook than somebody else's wife," Miss Jenny snapped.

"Miss Jenny!" Narcissa reproved. "You hush."

"I'm sorry," Miss Jenny said immediately. "I wasn't saying that at you, Horace: it just popped into my head. I was talking to you, Loosh Peabody. You think, just because you've eaten off of us Thanksgiving and Christmas for sixty years, that you can come into my own house and laugh at me, dont you?"

"Hush, Miss Jenny!" Narcissa repeated. Horace put down his spoon, and Narcissa's hand found his beneath the table.

"What's that?" Old Bayard, his napkin tucked into his waistcoat, lowered his spoon and cupped his hand to his ear.

"Nothing," young Bayard told him. "Aunt Jenny and Doc fighting again. Come alive, Simon." Simon stirred and removed the soup plates, but laggardly, still giving his interested attention to the altercation.

"Yes," Miss Jenny rushed on. "Just because that old fool of a Will Falls put axle grease on a little bump on his face without killing him dead, you have to go around swelled up like a poisoned dog. What did you have to do with it? You certainly didn't take it off. Maybe you conjured it on his face to begin with?"

"Haven't you got a piece of bread or something Miss Jenny can put in her mouth, Simon?" Dr Peabody asked mildly. Miss Jenny glared at him a moment, then flopped back in her chair.

"You, Simon! Are you dead?" Simon removed the plates and bore them out, and the guests sat avoiding one another's eyes a little, while Miss Jenny behind her barricade of cups and urns and jugs and things, continued to breathe fire and brimstone.

"Will Falls," old Bayard repeated. "Jenny, tell Simon, when he fixes that basket, to come to my office: I've got something to go in it." This something was the pint flask of whisky which he included in old man Falls' Thanksgiving and Christmas basket and which the old fellow divided out in spoonsful as far as it would go among his ancient and homeless cronies on those days; and invariably old Bayard reminded her to tell Simon of something which neither of them had overlooked.

"All right," she returned. Simon reappeared, with a huge silver coffee-urn, set it beside Miss Jenny, and retreated to the kitchen.

"How many of you want coffee now?" she asked generally. "Bayard will no more sit down to a meal without his coffee than he'd fly. Will you, Horace?" He declined, and without looking at Dr Peabody she said: "I reckon you'll have to have some, wont you?"

"If it's no trouble," he answered mildly. He winked at Narcissa and assumed an expression of lugubrious diffidence. Miss Jenny drew two cups, and Simon appeared with a huge platter borne gallantly and precariously aloft and set it before old Bayard with a magnificent flourish.

"My God, Simon," young Bayard said, "where did you get a whale this time of year?"

"Dat's a fish in dis worl', mon," Simon agreed. And it was a fish. It was a yard long and broad as a saddle blanket; it was a jolly red color and it lay gaping on the platter with an air of dashing and rollicking joviality.

"Dammit, Jenny," old Bayard said pettishly, "what did you want to have this thing, for? Who wants to clutter his stomach up with fish, in November, with a kitchen full of 'possum and turkey and squirrel?"

"There are other people to eat here besides you," she retorted. "If you dont want any, dont eat it. We always had a fish course at home," she added. "But you cant wean these Mississippi country folks away from bread and meat to save your life. Here, Simon." Simon set a stack of plates before old

Bayard and he now came with his tray and Miss Jenny put two coffee cups on it, and he served them to old Bayard and Dr Peabody. Miss Jenny drew a cup for herself, and Simon passed sugar and cream. Old Bayard carved the fish, still rumbling heavily.

"I aint ever found anything wrong with fish at any time of year," Dr Peabody said.

"You wouldn't," Miss Jenny snapped. Again he winked heavily at Narcissa.

"Only," he continued, "I like to catch my own, out of my own pond. Mine have mo' food value."

"Still got your pond, Doc?" young Bayard asked.

"Yes. But the fishin' aint been so good, this year. Abe had the flu last winter, and ever since he's been goin' to sleep on me, and I have to sit there and wait until he wakes up and takes the fish off and baits my hook again. But finally I thought about tyin' one end of a cord to his leg and the other end to the bench, and now when I get a bite, I just reach around and give the string a yank and wake 'im up. You'll have to bring yo' wife out, someday, Bayard. She aint never seen my pond."

"You haven't?" Bayard asked Narcissa. She had not. "He's got benches all around it, with footrests, and a railing just high enough to prop your pole on, and a nigger to every fisherman to bait his hook and take the fish off. I dont see why you feed all those niggers, Doc."

"Well, I've had 'em around so long I dont know how to get shut of 'em, 'less I drown 'em. Feedin' 'em is the main trouble, though. Takes every thing I can make. If it wasn't for them, I'd a quit practicin' long ago. That's the reason I dine out whenever I can: every time I get a free meal, it's the same as a half holiday to a workin' man."

"How many have you got, Doctor?" Narcissa asked.

"I dont rightly know," he answered. "I got six or seven registered ones, but I dont know how many scrubs I have. I see a new yearlin' every day or so." Simon was watching him with rapt interest.

"You aint got no extry room out dar, is you, Doctuh?" he asked. "Here I slaves all de livelong day, keepin' 'um in vittles en sech."

"Can you eat cold fish and greens every day?" Dr Peabody asked him solemnly.

"Well, suh," Simon answered doubtfully, "I aint so sho' erbout dat. I burnt out on fish once, when I wuz a young man, en I aint had no right stomach fer it since."

"Well, that's about all we eat, out home."

"All right, Simon," Miss Jenny said. Simon was propped statically against the sideboard, watching Dr Peabody with musing astonishment.

"En you keeps yo' size on cole fish en greens? Gentlemun, I'd be a bone-rack on dem kine o' vittles in two weeks, I sholy would."

"Simon!" Miss Jenny raised her voice sharply. "Why wont you let him alone, Loosh, so he can 'tend to his business?" Simon came abruptly untranced and removed the fish. Beneath the table Narcissa slipped her hand in Horace's again.

"Lay off of Doc, Aunt Jenny," young Bayard said. He touched his grandfather's arm. "Cant you make her let Doc alone?"

"What's he doing, Jenny?" old Bayard asked. "Wont he eat his dinner?"

"None of us'll get to eat anything, if he sits there and talks to Simon about cold fish and greens," Miss Jenny replied.

"I think you're mean, to treat him like you do, Miss Jenny," Narcissa said.

"Well, it gives me something to be thankful for," Dr Peabody answered, "that you never took me when you had the chance. I went and proposed to Jenny once," he told them.

"You old gray-headed liar," Miss Jenny said, "you never did any such a thing!"

"Oh, yes, I did. Only I did it on John Sartoris' account. He said he was havin' mo' trouble than he could stand with politics outside his home. And, do you know——"

"Loosh Peabody, you're the biggest liar in the world!"

"——I pretty near had her persuaded for a while? It was that first spring them weeds she brought out here from Ca'lina bloomed, and there was a moon and we were in the garden and there was a mockin'bird——"

"No such thing!" Miss Jenny shouted. "There never was——"

"Look at her face, if you believe I'm lyin'," Dr Peabody said.

"Look at her face," young Bayard echoed rudely. "She's blushing!"

And she was blushing, but her cheeks were like banners, and her head was still high amid the gibing laughter. Narcissa rose and came to her and laid her arm about her trim erect shoulders. "You all hush this minute," she said. "You'd better consider yourselves lucky that any of us ever marry you, and flattered even when we refuse."

"I am flattered," Dr Peabody rejoined, "or I wouldn't be a widower now."

"Who wouldn't be a widower, the size of a hogshead and living on cold fish and turnip greens?" Miss Jenny said. "Sit down, honey. I aint scared of any man alive."

Narcissa resumed her seat, and Simon appeared again, with Isom in procession now, and for the next few minutes they moved steadily between kitchen and dining room with a roast turkey and a smoked ham and a dish of quail and another of squirrel, and a baked 'possum in a bed of sweet potatoes; and squash and pickled beets, and sweet potatoes and Irish potatoes, and rice and hominy, and hot biscuit and beaten biscuit and delicate long sticks of cornbread, and strawberry and pear preserves, and quince and apple jelly, and stewed cranberries and pickled peaches.

Then they ceased talking for a while and really ate, glancing now and then across the table at one another in a rosy glow of amicability and steamy odors. From time to time Isom entered with hot bread, while Simon stood overlooking the field somewhat as Caesar must have stood looking down into Gaul, once it was well in hand, or the Lord God Himself when He contemplated His latest chemical experiment and saw that it was good.

"After this, Simon," Dr Peabody said, and he sighed a little, "I reckon I can take you on and find you a little side meat now and then."

"I 'speck you kin," Simon agreed, watching them like an eagle-eyed general who rushes reserves to the threatened points, pressing more food upon them as they faltered. But even Dr Peabody allowed himself vanquished after a time, and then Simon brought in pies of three kinds, and a small, deadly

plum pudding, and cake baked cunningly with whisky and
nuts and fruit as ravishing as odors of heaven and treacherous
and fatal as sin; and at last, with an air sibylline and solemnly
profound, a bottle of port. The sun lay hazily in the glowing
west, falling levelly through the windows and upon the silver
arrayed upon the sideboard, dreaming in mellow gleams
among its placid rotundities and upon the colored panes in
the fanlight high in the western wall.

But that was November, the season of hazy, languorous
days, when the first flush of autumn was over and winter beneath the sere horizon breathed yet a spell. November, when
like a shawled matron among her children the earth died
peacefully, without pain and of no disease. Early in December the rains set in and the year turned gray beneath the season
of dissolution and of death. All night and all day it whispered
upon the roof and along the eaves; the trees shed their final
stubborn leaves in it and gestured their black and sorrowful
branches against ceaseless vistas; only a lone hickory at the
foot of the park kept its leaves yet, gleaming like a sodden
flame on the eternal azure; beyond the valley the hills were
hidden by a swaddling of rain.

Almost daily, despite Miss Jenny's strictures and com-
mands and the grave protest in Narcissa's eyes, Bayard went
forth with a shotgun and the two dogs, to return just before dark wet to the skin. And cold; his lips would be chill on
hers, and his eyes bleak and haunted, and in the yellow firelight of their room she would cling to him, or lie crying quietly in the darkness beside his rigid body with a ghost between
them.

"Look here," Miss Jenny said, coming upon her as she sat
brooding before the fire in old Bayard's den. "You spend too
much time this way; you're getting moony. Stop worrying
about him: he's spent half his life soaking wet, yet neither one
of 'em ever had a cold, even, that I can remember."

"Hasn't he?" she answered listlessly. Miss Jenny stood beside her chair, watching her keenly. Then she laid her hand on
Narcissa's head, quite gently, for a Sartoris.

"Are you worrying because maybe he dont love you like you
think he ought to?"

"It isn't that," she answered. "He doesn't love anybody. He wont even love the baby. He doesn't seem to be glad, or sorry, or anything."

"No," Miss Jenny agreed. The fire crackled and leaped among the resinous logs. Beyond the gray window the day dissolved endlessly. "Listen," Miss Jenny said abruptly. "Dont you ride in that car with him any more. You hear?"

"No. It wont make him drive slowly. Nothing will."

"Of course not. Nobody believes it will, not even Bayard. He goes along for the same reason that boy himself does. Sartoris. It's in the blood. Savages, everyone of 'em. No earthly use to anybody." Together they gazed into the leaping flames, Miss Jenny's hand still lying on Narcissa's head. "I'm sorry I got you into this."

"You didn't do it. Nobody got me into it. I did it myself."

"H'm," Miss Jenny said. And then: "Would you do it over again?" The other did not reply, and she repeated the question. "Would you?"

"Yes," Narcissa answered. "Dont you know I would?" Again there was silence between them, in which without words they sealed their hopeless pact with that fine and passive courage of women. Narcissa rose. "I believe I'll go in and spend the day with Horace, if you dont mind," she said.

"All right," Miss Jenny agreed. "I believe I would, too. Horace probably needs a little looking after, by now. He looked sort of gaunt when he was out here last week. Like he wasn't getting proper food."

When she entered the kitchen door Eunice, the cook, turned from the bread board and lifted her daubed hands in a soft dark gesture. "Well, Miss Narcy," she said. "We aint seed you in a mont'. Is you come all de way in de rain?"

"I came in the carriage. It was too wet for the car." She came into the room. Eunice watched her with grave pleasure. "How are you all getting along?"

"He gits enough to eat, all right," Eunice answered. "I sees to dat. But I has to make 'im eat it. He needs you back here."

"I'm here, for the day, anyhow. What have you got for dinner?" Together they lifted lids and peered into the simmering vessels on the stove and in the oven. "Oh, chocolate pie!"

"I has to toll 'im wid dat," Eunice explained. "He'll eat any-thing, ef I jes' makes 'im a chocolate pie," she added proudly.

"I bet he does," Narcissa agreed. "Nobody can make choco-late pies like yours."

"Dis one aint turnt out so well," Eunice said, deprecatory. "I aint so pleased wid it."

"Why, Eunice! It's perfect."

"No'm, it aint up to de mark," Eunice insisted. But she beamed, gravely diffident, and for a few minutes the two of them talked amicably while Narcissa pried into cupboards and boxes.

Then she returned to the house and mounted to her room. The dressing table was bare of its intimate silver and crystal, and the drawers were empty, and the entire room with its air of still and fading desolation, reproached her. Chill, too; there had been no fire in the grate since last spring, and on the table beside the bed, in a blue vase, was a small faded bunch of flow-ers, forgotten and withered and dead. Touching them, they crumbled in her fingers, leaving a stain, and the water in the vase smelled of rank decay. She opened the window and threw them out.

The room was too chill to stop in long, and she decided to ask Eunice to build a fire on the hearth, for the comfort of that part of her which still lingered here, soberly and a little sor-rowful in the chill and reproachful desolation. At her chest of drawers she paused again and remembered those letters, fret-fully and with a little musing alarm, deprecating anew her carelessness in not destroying them. But maybe she had, and so she entered again into the closed circle of her bewilderment and first fear, trying to remember what she had done with them. But she was certain she had left them in the drawer with her underthings, positive that she had put them there. Yet she had never been able to find them, nor had Eunice nor Horace seen them. The day she had missed them was the day before her wedding, when she packed her things. That day she had missed them, finding in their stead one in a different hand-writing, which she did not remember having received. The gist of it was plain enough, although she had not understood some of it literally. But on that day, she read it with tran-quil detachment: it and all it brought to mind was definitely behind her now. And lacking even this, she would not have been shocked if she had comprehended it. Curious a little, perhaps, at some of the words, but that is all.

But what she had done with those other letters she could not remember, and not being able to gave her moments of definite fear when she considered the possibility that people might learn that someone had thought such things about her and put them into words. Well, they were gone; there was nothing to do save hope that she had destroyed them as she had the last one, or if she had not, to trust that they would never be found. Yet that brought back the original distaste and dread: the possibility that the intactness of her deep and heretofore inviolate serenity might be the sport of circumstance; that she must trust to chance against the eventuality of a stranger casually picking a stray bit of paper from the ground. . . . . . .

But she would put this firmly aside, for the time being, at least. This should be Horace's day, and her own too; a surcease from that ghost-ridden dream to which she clung, waking. She descended the stairs. There was a fire in the living room. It had burned down to embers however, and she put coal on it and punched it to a blaze. That would be the first thing he'd see when he entered; perhaps he'd wonder; perhaps he'd know before he entered, having sensed her presence. She considered telephoning him, and she mused indecisively for a moment before the fire; then decided to let it be a surprise. But supposing he didn't come home to dinner because of the rain. She considered this, and pictured him walking along a street in the rain, and immediately and with instinctive foreknowledge, she went to the closet beneath the stairs and opened the door. It was as she had known: his overcoat and raincoat both hung there; the chances were he didn't even have an umbrella, and again irritation and exasperation and untroubled affection welled within her, and it was as it had been of old again, and all that had since come between them, rolled away like clouds.

Heretofore her piano had always been rolled into the living room when cold weather came. But now it stood yet in the smaller alcove. There was a fireplace here, but no fire had been lighted yet, and the room was chilly. Beneath her hands the cold keys gave forth a sluggish chord, accusing, reproving too; and she returned to the fire and stood where she could see through the window the drive beneath its sombre, dripping cedars. The small clock on the mantel behind her chimed twelve, and she went to the window and stood with her nose touching the chill glass and her breath frosting it over. Soon, now: he was erratic in his hours, but never tardy, and every-time an umbrella came into sight, her heart leaped a little. But it was not he, and she followed the bearer's plodding passage until he shifted the umbrella enough for her to recognise him, and so she did not see Horace until he was half way up the drive. His hat was turned down about his face and his coat collar was hunched to his ears, and as she had known, he didn't even have an umbrella.

"Oh, you idiot," she said and ran to the door and through the curtained glass she saw his shadowy shape come leaping up the steps. He flung the door open and entered, whipping his sodden hat against his leg, and so did not see her until she stepped forth. "You idiot," she said. "Where's your raincoat?"

For a moment he stared at her with his wild and diffident unrepose, then he said "Narcy!" and his face lighted and he swept her into his wet arms.

"Dont," she cried. "You're wet!" But he swung her from the floor, against his sopping chest, repeating Narcy, Narcy; then his cold nose was against her face and she tasted rain.

"Narcy," he said again, hugging her, and she ceased resisting and clung to him. Then abruptly he released her and jerked his head up and stared at her with sober intensity.

"Narcy," he said, still staring at her, "has that surly black-guard   ?"

"No, of course not," she answered sharply. "Have you gone crazy?" Then she clung to him again, wet clothes and all, as though she would never let him go. "Oh, Horry," she said, "I've been a beast to you!"

"I was hoping," he said—they had eaten the chocolate pie and Horace now stood before the living room fire, his coffee cup on the mantel, striking matches to his pipe—"That you might have come home for good. That they had sent you back."

"No," she answered. "I wish. . . . . . ."

"What?"

But she only said: "You'll be having somebody, soon." And then: "When is it to be, Horry?"

He sucked intently at his pipe; in his eyes little twin match-flames rose and fell. "I dont know. Next spring, I suppose. Whenever she will."

"You dont want to," she stated quietly. "Not after what it's all got to be now."

"She's in Reno now," he added, puffing at his pipe, his face averted a little. "Little Belle wrote me a letter about mountains."

She said: "Poor Harry." She sat with her chin in her palms, gazing into the fire.

"He'll have little Belle," he reminded her. "He cares more for her than he does for Belle, anyway."

"You dont know," she told him soberly. "You just say that because you want to believe it."

"Dont you think he's well off, rid of a woman who doesn't want him, who doesn't even love his child very much?"

"You dont know," she repeated. "People cant—cant—You cant play fast and loose with the way things ought to go on, after they've started off."

"Oh, people." He raised the cup and drained it, and sat down. "Barging around through a lifetime, clotting for no reason, breaking apart again for no reason still. Chemicals. No need to pity a chemical."

"Chemicals," she mused, her serene face rosy in the firelight. "Chemicals. Maybe that's the reason so many of the things people do smell bad."

"Well, I dont know that I ever thought of it in exactly that way," he answered gravely. "But I daresay you're right, having femininity on your side." He brooded himself, restlessly. "But I suppose it's all sort of messy: living and seething corruption glossed over for a while by smoothly colored flesh; all foul, until the clean and naked bone." He mused again, she quietly beside him. "But it's something there, something you go after; must; driven. Not always swine. A plan somewhere, I suppose, known to Whoever first set the fermentation going. Perhaps it's just too big to be seen, like a locomotive is a porous mongrel substance without edges to the grains of sand that give it traction on wet rails. Or perhaps He has forgotten Himself what the plan was."

"But do you like to think of a woman who'll willingly give up her child in order to marry another man a little sooner?"

"Of course I dont. But neither do I like to remember that I have exchanged you for Belle, or that she has red hair and is going to be fat someday, or that she has lain in another man's arms and has a child that isn't mine, even though she did voluntarily give it up. Yet there are any number of virgins who love children walking the world today, some of whom look a little like you, probably, and a modest number of which I allow myself to believe, without conceit, that I could marry. And yet. . . . . . ." He struck another match to his pipe, but he let it go out again and sat forward in his chair, the pipe held loosely in his joined hands. "That may be the secret, after all. Not any subconscious striving after what we believe will be happiness, contentment; but a sort of gadfly urge after the petty, ignoble impulses which man has tried so vainly to conjure with words out of himself. Nature, perhaps, watching him as he tries to wean himself away from the rank and richly foul old mire that spawned him, biding her time and flouting that illusion of purifaction which he has foisted upon himself and calls his soul. But it's something there, something you— you—" He brooded upon the fire, holding his cold pipe. She put her hand out and touched his, and he clasped it and looked at her with his groping and wide intensity. But she was gazing into the fire, her cheek in her palm, and she drew his hand to her and stroked it on her face.

"Poor Horry," she said.

"Not happiness," he repeated. "I'm happier now than I'll ever be again. You dont find that, when you suddenly swap the part of yourself which you want least, for the half of someone else that he or she doesn't want. Do you? Did you find it?"

But she only said "Poor Horry" again. She stroked his hand slowly against her cheek as she stared into the shaling ruby of the coals. The clock chimed again, with blent small silver bells. She spoke without moving.

"Aren't you going back to the office this afternoon?"

"No." His tone was again the grave, lightly casual one which he employed with her. "I'm taking a holiday. Next time you come, I may have a case and cant."

"You never have cases: you have functions," she answered. "But I dont think you ought to neglect your business," she added with grave reproof.

"Neither do I," he agreed. "But whatever else is business for, then?"

"Dont be silly. . . . . . . Put on some coal, Horry."

But later he reverted again to his groping and tragic pre-monitions. They had spent the afternoon sitting before the re-plenished fire; later she had gone to the kitchen and made tea. The day still dissolved ceaselessly and monotonously without, and they sat and talked in a sober and happy isolation from their acquired ghosts, and again their feet chimed together upon the dark road and, their faces turned inward to one an-other's, the sinister and watchful trees were no longer there. But the road was in reality two roads become parallel for a brief mile and soon to part again, and now and then their feet stumbled.

"It's having been younger once," he said. "Being dragged by time out of a certain day like a kitten from a tow sack, being thrust into another sack with shreds of the first one sticking to your claws. Like the burro that the prospector keeps on loading down with a rock here and a rock there until it drops, leaving him in the middle of his desert, surrounded by wait-ing buzzards," he added, musing in metaphors. "Plunder. That's all it is. If you could just be translated every so often, given a blank, fresh start, with nothing to remember. Dipped in Lethe every decade or so. . . . . . ."

"Or every year," she added. "Or day."

"Yes." The rain dripped and dripped, thickening the twi-light; the room grew shadowy. The fire had burned down again; its steady fading glow fell upon their musing faces and brought the tea things on the low table beside them, out of the obscurity in quiet rotund gleams; and they sat hand in hand in the fitful shadows and the silence, waiting for some-thing. And at last it came: a thundering knock at the door, and they knew then what it was they waited for, and through the window they saw the carriage curtains gleaming in the dusk and the horses stamping and steaming on the drive, in the ceaseless rain.

3.

Horace had seen her on the street twice, his attention caught by the bronze splendor of her hair and by an indefinable something in her air, her carriage. It was not boldness and not arrogance exactly, but a sort of calm, lazy contemptuousness that left him seeking in his mind after an experience lost somewhere within the veils of years that swaddled his dead childhood; an experience so sharply felt at the time that the recollection of it lingered yet somewhere just beneath his consciousness although the motivation of its virginal clarity was lost beyond recall. The wakened ghost of it was so strong that during the rest of the day he roused from periods of abstraction to find that he had been searching for it a little fearfully among the crumbled and long unvisited corridors of his mind, and later as he sat before his fire at home, with a book. Then, as he lay in bed thinking of Belle and waiting for sleep, he remembered it.

He was five years old and his father had taken him to his first circus, and clinging to the man's hard, reassuring hand in a daze of blaring sounds and sharp cries and scents that tightened his small entrails with a sense of fabulous and unimaginable imminence and left him a little sick, he raised his head and found a tiger watching him with yellow and lazy contemplation; and while his whole small body was a tranced and soundless scream, the animal gaped and flicked its lips with an unbelievably pink tongue. It was an old tiger and toothless, and it had doubtless gazed through these same bars at decades and decades of Horaces, yet in him a thing these many generations politely dormant waked shrieking, and again for a red moment he dangled madly by his hands from the lowermost limb of a tree.

That was it, and though that youthful reaction was dulled now by the years, he found himself watching her on the street somewhat as a timorous person is drawn with delicious revulsions to gaze into a window filled with knives. He found himself thinking of her often, wondering who she was. A stranger, he had never seen her in company with anyone who might identify her. She was always alone and always definitely going somewhere; not at all as a transient, a visitor idling about the streets. And always that air of hers, lazy, predatory and coldly contemptuous. The sort of woman men stare after on the street and who does not even do them the honor of ignoring them.

The third time he saw her he was passing a store, a newly-opened department store, just as she emerged at that free, purposeful gait he had come to know. In the center of the door sill was a small iron ridge onto which the double doors locked, and she caught the heel of her slipper on this ridge and emerged stumbling in a cascade of small parcels, and swearing. It was a man's bold swearing, and she caught her balance and stamped her foot and kicked one of her dropped parcels savagely into the gutter. Horace retrieved it and turning saw her stooping for the others, and together they gathered them up and rose, and she glanced at him briefly with level eyes of a thick, dark brown and shot with golden lights somehow paradoxically cold.

"Thanks," she said, without emphasis, taking the packages from him. "They ought to be jailed for having a mantrap like that in the door." Then she looked at him again, a level stare without boldness or rudeness. "You're Horace Benbow, aren't you?" she asked.

"Yes, that is my name. But I dont believe——"

She was counting her packages. "One more yet," she said, glancing about her feet. "Must be in the street." He followed her to the curb, where she had already picked up the other parcel, and she regarded its muddy side and swore again. "Now I'll have to have it rewrapped."

"Yes, too bad, isn't it?" he agreed. "If you'll allow me——"

"I'll have it done at the drug store. Come along, if you're not too busy. I want to talk to you."

She seemed to take it for granted that he would follow, and he did so, with curiosity and that feeling stronger than ever of a timorous person before a window of sharp knives. When he drew abreast of her she looked at him again (she was almost as tall as he) from beneath her level brows. Her face was rather thin, with broad nostrils. Her mouth was flat though full, and there was in the ugly distinction of her face an inde-scribable something; a something boding and leashed, yet un-tamed. Carnivorous, he thought. A lady tiger in a tea gown; and remarking something of his thoughts in his face, she said: "I forgot: of course you dont know who I am. I'm Belle's sister."

"Oh, of course. You're Joan. I should have known."

"How? Nobody yet ever said we look alike. And you never saw me before."

"No," he agreed. "But I've been expecting for the last three months that some of Belle's kinfolks would be coming here to see what sort of animal I am."

"They wouldn't have sent me, though," she replied. "You can be easy on that." They went on along the street. Horace responded to greetings, but she strode on with that feline poise of hers; he was aware that men turned to look after her, but in her air there was neither awareness nor disregard of it, conscious or otherwise. And again he remembered that tiger yawning with bored and lazy contempt while round and static eyes stared down its cavernous pink gullet. "I want to stop here," she said, as they reached the drug store. "Do you have to go back to the store, or whatever it is?"

"Office," he corrected. "Not right away."

"That's right," she agreed, and he swung the door open for her. "You're a dentist, aren't you? Belle told me."

"Then I'm afraid she's deceiving us both," he answered drily. She glanced at him with her level, speculative gaze, and he added: "She's got the names confused and sent you to the wrong man."

"You seem to be clever," she said over her shoulder. "And I despise clever men. Dont you know any better than to waste cleverness on women? Save it for your friends." A youthful clerk in a white jacket approached, staring at her boldly; she asked him with contemptuous politeness to rewrap her parcel. Horace stopped beside her.

"Women friends?" he asked.

"Women what?" She stooped down, peering into a show-case of cosmetics. "Well, maybe so," she said indifferently. "But I never believe 'em, though. Cheap sports." She straight-ened up. "Belle's all right, if that's what you want to ask. It's done her good. She doesn't look so bad-humored and settled down, now. Sort of fat and sullen."

"I'm glad you think that. But what I am wondering is, how you happened to come here. Harry's living at the hotel, isn't he?"

"He's opened the house again, now. He just wanted some-body to talk to. I came to see what you look like," she told him.

"What I look like?"

"Yes, to see the man that could make old Belle kick over the traces." Her eyes were coldly contemplative, a little curious. "What did you do to her? I'll bet you haven't even got any money to speak of."

Horace grinned a little. "I must seem rather thoroughly im-possible to you, then," he suggested.

"Oh, there's no accounting for the men women pick out. I sometimes wonder at myself. Only I've never chosen one I had to nurse, yet." The clerk returned with her package, and she made a trifling purchase and gathered up her effects. "I sup-pose you have to stick around your office all day, dont you?"

"Yes. It's the toothache season now, you know."

"You sound like a college boy now," she said coldly. "I sup-pose Belle's ghost will let you out at night, though?"

"It goes along too," he answered.

"Well, I'm not afraid of ghosts. I carry a few around, myself."

"You mean dripping flesh and bloody bones, dont you?" She looked at him again, with her flecked eyes that should have been warm but were not.

"I imagine you could be quite a nuisance," she told him. He opened the door and she passed through it. And gave him a brief nod, and while he stood on the street with his hat lifted she strode on, without even a conventional Thank you or Goodbye.

That evening while he sat at his lonely supper, she tele-phoned him, and thirty minutes later she came in Harry's car for him. And for the next three hours she drove him about while he sat hunched into his overcoat against the raw air. She wore no coat herself and appeared impervious to the chill, and she carried him on short excursions into the muddy winter countryside, the car sliding and skidding while he sat with tensed anticipatory muscles. But mostly they drove monotonously around town while he felt more and more like a fatted and succulent eating-creature in a suave parading cage. Sometimes she talked, but usually she drove in a lazy preoccupation, seemingly utterly oblivious of him.

Later, when she had begun coming to his house, coming without secrecy and with an unhurried contempt for possible eyes and ears and tongues—a contempt that also disregarded Horace's acute unease on that score, she still fell frequently into those periods of aloof and purring repose. Then, sitting before the fire in his living room, with the bronze and electric disorder of her hair and the firelight glowing in little red points in her unwinking eyes, she was like a sheathed poniard, like Chablis in a tall-stemmed glass. At these times she would utterly ignore him, cold and inaccessible. Then she would rouse and talk brutally of her lovers. Never of herself, other than to give him the salient points in her history that Belle had hinted at with a sort of belligerent prudery. The surface history was brief and simple enough. Married at eighteen to a man three times her age, she had deserted him in Honolulu and fled to Australia with an Englishman, assuming his name; was divorced by her husband, discovered by first hand experience that no Englishman out of his native island has any honor about women; was deserted by him in Bombay, and in Calcutta, she married again. An American, a young man, an employee of the Standard oil company. A year later she divorced him, and since then her career had been devious and a little obscure, due to her restlessness. Her family would know next to nothing of her whereabouts, receiving her brief, infrequent letters from random points half the world apart. Her first husband had made a settlement on her, and from time to time and without warning she returned home and spent a day or a week or a month in the company of her father's bitter reserve and her mother's ready tearful uncomplaint, while neighbors, older people who had known her all her life, girls with whom she had played in pinafores and boys with whom she had sweethearted during the spring and summer of adolescence and newcomers to the town, looked after her on the street.

Forthright and inscrutable and unpredictable: sometimes she stayed an hour motionless before the fire while he sat nearby and did not dare touch her; sometimes she lay beside him while the firelight, fallen to a steady glow of coals, filled his bedroom with looming and motionless shadows until midnight or later, talking about her former lovers with a brutality that caused him hopeless and despairing anger and something of a child's hurt disillusion; speaking of them with that same utter lack of vanity and conventional modesty with which she discussed her body, asking him to tell her again that he thought her body beautiful, asking him if he had ever seen a match for her legs, then taking him with a savage and carnivorous suddenness that left him spent. Yet all the while remote beyond that barrier of cold inscrutability which he was never able to break down, and rising at last, again that other feline and inaccessible self and departing without even the formality of a final kiss or a Goodbye and leaving him to wonder, despite the evidences of her presence, whether he had not dreamed it, after all.

She made but one request of him: that he refrain from talking to her of love. "I'm tired of having to listen to it and talk and act a lot of childish stupidity," she explained. "I dont know anything about it, and I dont care to."

"You dont think there is any such thing?" he asked.

"I've never found it. And if we can get anything from each other worth having, what's the use in talking about it? And it'll take a race of better people than we are to bear it, if there's any such thing. Save that for Belle: you'll probably need it."

One night she did not depart at all. That was the night she revealed another feline trait: that of a prowling curiosity about dark rooms. She had paused at Narcissa's door, and although he tried to draw her onward, she opened the door and found the light switch and pressed it on. "Whose room is this?"

"Narcissa's," he answered shortly. "Come away."

"Oh, your sister's. The one that married that Sartoris." She examined the room quietly. "I'd like to have known that man," she said in a musing tone. "I think I'd be good for him. Marrying women, then leaving them after a month or two. Only one man ever left me," she stated calmly. "I was practically a child, or that wouldn't have. . . . . . . Yes, I'd have been just the thing for him." She entered the room; he followed and took her arm again.

"Come away, Joan."

"But I dont know," she added. "Maybe it's a good thing he's gone, after all. For both of us."

"Yes. Come away."

She turned her head and stared at him with her level inscrutable eyes, beneath the bronze disorder of her hair. "Men are funny animals," she said. "You carry so much junk around with you." There was in her eyes a cold derisive curiosity. "What do you call it? sacrilege? desecration?"

"Come away," he repeated.

Next day, in the gray December forenoon among the musty books in his office, the reaction found him. It was more than reaction: it was revulsion, and he held a spiritual stock-taking with a sort of bleak derision: for a moment, in company with the sinister gods themselves, he looked down upon Horace Benbow as upon an antic and irresponsible worm. It was worse; it was conduct not even becoming a college sophomore—he, who had thought to have put all such these ten years behind him; and he thought of his sister and he felt unclean. On the way home at noon he saw Harry Mitchell approaching, and he ducked into a store and hid—a thing Belle had never caused him to do.

He would not go to his room, where the impact of her presence must yet linger, and Eunice served his meal with her face averted, emanating disapproval and reproach; and he angered slowly and asked her the direct question. "Has Mrs Heppleton gone yet, Eunice?"

"I dont know, suh," Eunice answered, still without looking at him. She turned doorward.

"You dont know when she left?"

"I dont know, suh," Eunice repeated doggedly, and the swing door slapped behind her in dying oscillations.

But he would not mount to his room, and soon he was back down town again. It was a gray, raw day, following the two recent weeks of bright frosty weather. Christmas was not a week away, and already the shop windows bloomed in toy fairylands, with life in its mutations in miniature among cedar branches and cotton batting and dusted over with powdered tinsel, amid which Santa Claus in his myriad avatars simpered in fixed and rosy benignance; and with fruit and cocoanuts and giant sticks of peppermint; and fireworks of all kinds—roman candles and crackers and pinwheels; and about the muddy square fetlock-deep horses stood hitched to wagons laden with berried holly and mistletoe.

He was too restless to remain in one place, and through the short afternoon, on trivial pretexts or on no pretext at all, he descended the stairs and walked along the streets among the slow throngs of black and white in the first throes of the long winter vacation; and at last he realized that he was hoping to see her, realized it with longing and with dread, looking along the street before him for a glimpse of her shapeless marten coat and the curbed wild blaze of her hair, and the lithe and purposeful arrogance of her carriage, ready to flee when he did so.

But by the time he reached home in the early dusk the dread was still there, but it was only the savor of the longing, and without even pausing to remove his hat and coat he went to the telephone in its chill and darkling alcove beneath the stairs. And he stood with the chill receiver to his ear and watching the cloudy irregularity of his breath upon the nickel mouthpiece, waiting until out of the twilight and the chill the lazy purring of her voice should come. After a time he asked central to ring again, with polite impatience. He could hear the other instrument shrill again and he thought of her long body rising from its warm nest in her chair before a fire somewhere in the quiet house, imagined he could hear her feet on stairs nearer and nearer "Now. Now she is lifting her hand to the receiver now Now." But it was Rachel, the cook. Naw, suh, Miz Heppleton aint here. Yes, suh, she gone away. Suh? Naw, suh, she aint comin' back. She went off on de evenin' train. Naw, suh, Rachel didn't know where she was going.

It used to be that he'd fling his coat and hat down and Narcissa would come along presently and hang them up. But already bachelordom was getting him house-broke—accomplishing what affection never had and never would—and he hung his coat, in the pocket of which an unopened letter from Belle lay forgotten, carefully in the closet beneath the stairs, fumbling patiently with his chilled hands until he found a vacant hook. Then he mounted the stairs and opened his door and entered the cold room where between the secret walls she lingered yet in a hundred palpable ways—in the mirror above his chest of drawers, in the bed, the chairs; on the deep rug before the hearth where she had crouched naked and drowsing like a cat. The fire had burned out; the ashes were cold and the room was icy chill: outside, the graying twilight. He built up the fire and drew his chair close to the hearth and sat before it, his thin delicate hands spread to the crackling blaze.

4.

. . . . this time it was a ford car, and Bayard saw its wild skid as the driver tried to jerk it across the treacherous thawing road, and in the flashing moment and with swift amusement, he saw, between the driver's cravatless collar and the woman's stocking bound around his head beneath his hat and tied under his chin, his adam's apple like a scared puppy in a tow sack. This flashed on and behind, and Bayard wrenched the wheel, and the stalled ford swam sickeningly into view again as the big car slewed greasily upon the clay surface, its declutched engine roaring. Then the other car swam from sight again as he wrenched the wheel over and slammed the clutch in for more stability; and once more that sickening, unhurried rush as the car refused to regain its feet and the frosty December world swept laterally across his vision. Old Bayard lurched against him: from the corner of his eye he could see the old fellow's hand clutching at the top of the door. Now they were facing the bluff on which the cemetery lay; directly over them John Sartoris' effigy lifted its florid stone gesture, and from among motionless cedars gazed out upon the valley where for two miles the railroad he had built ran beneath his carven eyes. Bayard wrenched the wheel once more.

On the other side of the road a precipice dropped sheer away, among scrub cedars and corroded ridges skeletoned brittlely with frost and muddy ice where the sun had not yet reached; the rear end of the car hung timelessly over this before it swung again, with the power full on, swung on until its nose pointed down hill again, with never a slackening of its speed. But still it would not come into the ruts again and it had lost the crown of the road, and though they had almost reached the foot of the hill, Bayard saw they would not make it. Just before they slipped off he wrenched the steering wheel over and swung the nose straight over the bank, and the car poised lazily for a moment, as though taking breath. "Hang on," he shouted to his grandfather. Then they plunged.

An interval utterly without sound and in which all sensation of motion was lost. Then scrub cedar burst crackling about them and whipping branches of it exploded upon the radiator and slapped viciously at them as they leaned with braced feet, and the car slewed in a long bounce. Another vacuum-like interval, then a shock that banged the wheel into Bayard's chest and jerked it in his tight hands, wrenching his arm-sockets. Beside him his grandfather lurched forward and he threw out his arm just in time to keep the other from crashing through the windshield. "Hang on," he shouted again. The car had never faltered and he dragged the leaping wheel over and swung it down the ravine and opened the engine again, and with the engine and the momentum of the plunge, they rocked and crashed on down the ditch and turned and heaved up the now shallow bank and onto the road again. Bayard brought it to a stop.

He sat motionless for a moment. "Whew," he said. And then: "Great God in the mountain." His grandfather sat motionless beside him, his hand still clutching the door and his head bent a little. "Think I'll have a cigarette, after that," Bayard added. He dug one from his pocket, and a match; his hands were shaking. "I thought of that damn concrete bridge again, just as she went over," he explained, apologetically. He took a deep draught at his cigarette and glanced at his grandfather. "Y'all right?" Old Bayard made no reply, and with the cigarette poised, Bayard looked at him. He sat as before, his head bent a little and his hand on the door. "Grandfather?" Bayard said sharply. Still old Bayard didn't move, even when his grandson flung the cigarette away and shook him roughly.

5.

Up the last hill the tireless pony bore him, and in the low December sun their shadow fell longly across the ridge and

into the valley beyond, from which the high, shrill yapping of
the dogs came again upon the frosty windless air. Young dogs,
Bayard told himself, and he sat his horse in the faint scar of
the road, listening as the high-pitched hysteria of them swept
echoing across his aural field. Motionless, he could feel frost
in the air. Above him the pines, though there was no wind in
them, made a continuous dry, wild sound, as though the frost
in the air had found voice; above them against the high
evening blue, a shallow V of geese slid. There'll be ice tonight,
he thought, watching them and thinking of black backwaters
where they would come to rest, of rank bayonets of dead
grasses about which water would shrink soon in fixed glassy
ripples in the brittle darkness. Behind him the earth rolled
away ridge on ridge blue as woodsmoke, on into a sky like
thin congealed blood. He turned in his saddle and stared unwinking into the sun that spread like a crimson egg broken
upon the ultimate hills. That meant weather: he snuffed the
still tingling air, hoping he smelled snow.

The pony snorted and tossed his head experimentally, and
found the reins slack and lowered his nose and snorted again
into the dead leaves and the delicate sere needles of pine beneath his feet. "Come up, Perry," Bayard said, jerking the
reins. Perry raised his head and broke into a stiff, jolting trot,
but Bayard lifted him smartly out of it and into his steady foxtrot again. He had not gone far when the dogs broke again
into clamorous uproar to his left, and suddenly near, and as
he reined Perry back and peered ahead along the fading scar
of the road, he saw the fox trotting sedately toward him in the
middle of it. Perry saw it at the same time and laid his fine ears
back and rolled his young eyes. But the animal came on unawares at its steady, unhurried trot, glancing back over its
shoulder from time to time. "Well, I'll be damned," Bayard
whispered, holding Perry rigid between his knees. The fox was
not forty yards away, yet still it came on, seemingly utterly unaware of the horseman. Then Bayard shouted.

The animal glanced at him; the level sun swam redly and
fleetingly in its eyes, then with a single modest flash of brown
it was gone. Bayard expelled his breath: his heart was thumping against his ribs. "Whooy," he yelled. "Come on, dogs!"
The din of them swelled to a shrill pandemonium and the pack

boiled into the road in a chaos of spotted hides and flapping tongues and ears. None of them was more than half grown, and ignoring the horse and rider they surged still clamoring into the undergrowth where the fox had vanished and shrieked frantically on; and as Bayard stood in his stirrups and gazed after them, preceded by yapping in a still higher and more frantic key, two even smaller puppies swarmed out of the woods and galloped past him on their short legs, with whimpering cries and expressions of ludicrous and mad concern. Then the clamor died into hysterical echoes, and so away.

He rode on. On either hand was a ridge: the one darkling like a bronze bastion, upon the other the final rays of the sun lying redly. The air crackled and tingled in his nostrils and seared his lungs with exhilarating needles. The road followed the valley; but half the sun now showed above the western wall, and among intermittent trees, he rode stirrup-deep in shadow like cold water. He would just about reach the house before dark, and he shook Perry up a little. The clamor of the dogs swelled again ahead of him, approaching the road again, and he lifted Perry into a canter.

Presently before him lay a glade—an old field, sedge-grown, its plow scars long healed over. The sun filled it with dying gold, and he pulled Perry short upstanding: there, at the corner of the field beside the road, sat the fox. It sat there on its haunches like a dog, watching the trees across the glade, and Bayard shook Perry forward again. The fox turned its head and looked at him with a covert, fleeting glance, but without alarm, and Bayard halted Perry in intense astonishment. The clamor of the dogs swept nearer through the woods, yet still the fox sat on its haunches, watching the man with covert stolen glances, paying the dogs no heed. It revealed no alarm whatever, not even when the puppies burst yapping madly into the glade. They moiled at the wood's edge for a time while the fox divided its attention between them and the man. At last the largest puppy, evidently the leader, saw the quarry. Immediately they stopped their noise and trotted across the glade and squatted in a circle facing the fox, their tongues lolling. Then with one accord they turned about and faced the darkening woods, from which and nearer and nearer, came that spent, frantic yapping in a higher key. The largest dog barked once; the yapping among the trees swelled with frantic relief and the two smaller puppies appeared and burrowed like moles through the sedge and came up. Then the fox rose and cast another quick, furtive glance at the horseman, and surrounded by the amicable weary calico of the puppies, trotted up the road and vanished among the trees. "Well, I'll be damned," Bayard said, gazing after them. "Come up, Perry."

At last a pale and windless plume of smoke stood above the trees ahead, and he emerged from the woods, and in the rambling wall of the house a window glowed with ruddy invitation across the twilight. Dogs had already set up a resonant, bell-like uproar; above it Bayard could distinguish the clear tenor of puppies and a voice shouting at them, and as he halted Perry in the yard, the fox was vanishing diffidently but without haste beneath the house. A lean figure faced him in the dusk, with an axe in one hand and an armful of wood, and Bayard said:

"What the devil's that thing, Buddy? That fox?"

"That's Ethel," Buddy answered. He put the wood down deliberately, and the axe, and he came and shook Bayard's hand once, limply, in the country fashion, but his hand was hard and firm. "How you?"

"All right," Bayard answered. "I came out to get that old fox Rafe was telling me about."

"Sure," Buddy agreed in his slow, infrequent voice. "We been expectin' you. Git down and lemme take yo' pony."

"No, I'll do it. You take the wood on in; I'll put Perry up." But Buddy was firm, without insistence or rudeness, and Bayard surrendered the horse to him.

"Henry," Buddy shouted at the house. "Henry." A door opened upon jolly leaping flames; a figure stood squatly in it. "Here's Bayard," he said. "Go on in and warm," he added, leading Perry away. Dogs surrounded Bayard; he picked up the wood and the axe and went on toward the house in a ghostly spotted surge of dogs, and the figure stood in the lighted door while he mounted the veranda and leaned the axe against the wall.

"How you?" Henry said, and again the handshake was limp; again the hand was firm and kind, flabbier though than

Buddy's hard young flesh. He relieved Bayard of the wood and they entered the house. The walls were of chinked logs; upon them hung two or three outdated calendars and a patent medicine lithograph in colors. The floor was bare, of hand-trimmed boards scuffed with heavy boots and polished by the pads of generations of dogs; two men could lie side by side in the fireplace. In it now four foot logs blazed against the clay fireback, swirling in wild plumes into the chimney's dark maw, and in silhouette against it, his head haloed by the shaggy silver disorder of his hair, Virginius MacCallum sat. "Hyer's Bayard Sartoris, pappy," Henry said.

The old man turned in his chair with grave, leonine deliberation and extended his hand without rising. In 1861 he was sixteen and he had walked to Lexington, Virginia, and enlisted, served four years in the Stonewall brigade and walked back to Mississippi and built himself a house and got married. His wife's *dot* was a clock and a dressed hog; his own father gave them a mule. His wife was dead these many years, and her successor was dead, but he sat now before the fireplace at which that hog had been cooked, beneath the roof he had built in '66, and on the mantel above him the clock sat, deriding that time whose servant it once had been. "Well, boy?" he said. "You took yo' time about comin'. How's yo' folks?"

"Pretty well, sir," Bayard answered. He looked at the old man's hale ruddy face intently and sharply. No, they hadn't heard yet.

"We been expectin' you ever since Rafe seen you in town last spring. Henry, tell Mandy to put another plate on."

Four dogs had followed him into the room. Three of them watched him gravely with glowing eyes; the other one, a blue-ticked hound with an expression of majestic gravity, came up and touched its cold nose to his hand. "Hi, Gen'ral," he said, rubbing its ears; whereupon the other dogs approached and thrust their noses against his hands.

"Pull up a cheer," Mr MacCallum said. He squared his own chair around and Bayard obeyed, and the dogs followed him, surging with blundering decorum about his knees. "I keep sendin' word in to git yo' granpappy out hyer," the old man continued, "but he's too 'tarnal proud, or too damn lazy to come. Hyer, Gen'ral! Git away from thar. Kick 'em away,

Bayard. Henry!" he shouted. Henry appeared. "Take these hyer damn dawgs out till after supper."

Henry drove the dogs from the room. Mr MacCallum picked up a long pine sliver from the hearth and fired it and lit his pipe, and smothered the sliver in the ashes and laid it on the hearth again. "Rafe and Lee air in town today," he said. "You could have come out in the waggin with them. But I reckon you'd ruther have yo' own hoss."

"Yes, sir," he answered quietly. Then they would know. He stared into the fire for a time, rubbing his hands slowly on his knees, and for an instant he saw the recent months of his life coldly in all their headlong and heedless wastefulness; saw its entirety like the swift unrolling of a film, culminating in that which he had been warned against and that any fool might have foreseen. Well, damn it, suppose it had: was he to blame? had he insisted that his grandfather ride with him? had he given the old fellow a bum heart? And then, coldly: *You were afraid to go home. You made a nigger sneak your horse out to you. You, who deliberately do things your judgment tells you may not be successful, even possible, are afraid to face the consequences of your own acts.* Then again something bitter and deep and sleepless in him blazed out in vindication and justification and accusation; what, he knew not, blazing out at what, Whom, he did not know: *You did it! You caused it all: you killed Johnny.*

Henry had drawn a chair up to the fire, and after a while the old man tapped his clay pipe carefully out against his palm and drew a huge, turnip-shaped silver watch from his corduroy vest. "Half after five," he said. "Aint them boys got in yet?"

"They're here," Henry answered briefly. "Heard 'em takin' out when I put out the dawgs."

"Git the jug, then," his father ordered. Henry rose and departed again, and presently feet clumped heavily on the porch and Bayard turned in his chair and stared bleakly at the door. It opened and Rafe and Lee entered.

"Well, well," Rafe said, and his lean dark face lighted a little. "Got here at last, did you?" He shook Bayard's hand, and Lee followed him. Lee's face, like all of them, was a dark, saturnine mask. He was not so stocky as Rafe, and least talkative of them all. His eyes were black and restless; behind them lurked something wild and sad: he shook Bayard's hand without a word.

But Bayard was watching Rafe. There was nothing in Rafe's face; no coldness, no questioning—Was it possible that he could have been to town, and not heard? Or had Bayard himself dreamed it? But he remembered that unmistakable feel of his grandfather when he had touched him, remembered how he had suddenly slumped as though the very fibre of him, knit so erect and firm for so long by pride and the perverse necessity of his family doom, had given way all at once, letting his skeleton rest at last. Mr MacCallum spoke.

"Did you git to the express office?"

"We never got to town," Rafe answered. "Axle tree broke just this side of Vernon. Had to uncouple the wagon and drive to Vernon and get it patched up. Too late to go in, then. We got our supplies there and come on home."

"Well, hit dont matter. You'll be goin' in next week, for Christmas," the old man said. Bayard drew a long breath and lit a cigarette, and on a draft of vivid darkness Buddy entered and came and squatted leanly in the shadowy chimney corner.

"Got that fox you were telling me about hid out yet?" Bayard asked Rafe.

"Sure. And we'll get 'im, this time. Maybe tomorrow. Weather's changin'."

"Snow?"

"Might be. What's it goin' to do tonight, pappy?"

"Rain," the old man answered. "Tomorrow, too. Scent wont lay good till Wen'sday. Henry!" After a moment he shouted Henry again, and Henry entered, with a blackened kettle trailing a faint plume of vapor and a stoneware jug and a thick tumbler with a metal spoon in it. There was something domestic, womanish, about Henry, with his squat, slightly tubby figure and his mild brown eyes and his capable, unhurried hands. He it was who superintended the kitchen (he was a better cook now than Mandy) and the house, where he could be found most of the time, pottering soberly at some endless task. He visited town almost as infrequently as his father; he cared little for hunting, and his sole relaxation was making whisky, good whisky and for family consumption alone, in a secret fastness known only to his father and to the negro who assisted him, after a recipe handed down from lost generations of his usquebaugh-bred forbears. He set the kettle and the jug and the tumbler on the hearth, and took the clay pipe from his father's hand and put it on the mantel, and reached down a cracked cup of sugar and seven tumblers, each with a spoon in it. The old man leaned forward into the firelight and made the toddies one by one, with tedious and solemn deliberation. When he had made one around, there were two glasses left. "Aint them other boys come in yet?" he asked. Nobody answered, and he corked the jug. Henry set the two extra glasses back on the mantel.

Mandy came to the door presently, filling it with her homely calico expanse. "Y'all kin come on in now," she said, and as she turned waddling Bayard spoke to her and she stopped as the men rose. The old man was straight as an Indian, and with the exception of Buddy's lean and fluid length, he towered above his sons by a head. Mandy waited beside the door and gave Bayard her hand. "You aint been out in a long while, now," she said. "And I bet you aint fergot Mandy, neither."

"Sure I haven't," Bayard answered. But he had. Money, to Mandy, did not compensate for some trinket of no value which John never forgot to bring her when he came. He followed the others into the frosty darkness again. Beneath his feet the ground was already stiffening; overhead the sky was brilliant with stars. He stumbled a little behind the crowding backs until Rafe opened a door into a separate building, and stood aside until they had entered. This room was filled with warmth and a thin blue haze pungent with cooking odors, in which a kerosene lamp burned steadily on a long table. At one end of the table was a single chair; the other three sides were paralleled by backless wooden benches. Against the further wall was the stove, and a huge cupboard of split planks, and a woodbox. Behind the stove two negro men and a half grown boy sat, their faces shining with heat and their eyeballs rolling whitely; about their feet five puppies snarled with mock savageness at one another or chewed damply at the negroes' static ankles or prowled about beneath the stove and the adjacent floor with blundering, aimless inquisitiveness.

"Howdy, boys," Bayard said, calling them by name, and

they bobbed their heads at him with diffident flashes of teeth and polite murmurs.

"Put dem puppies up, Richud," Mandy ordered. The negroes gathered the puppies up one by one and tumbled them into a smaller box behind the stove, where they continued to move about with sundry scratchings and bumpings and an occasional smothered protest. From time to time during the meal a head would appear, staring above the rim of the box with blinking and solemn curiosity, then vanish with an abrupt scuffling thump and more protests, and moiling, infant-like noises rose again. "Hush up dawgs! G'awn to sleep, now," Richard would say, rapping the box with his knuckles. After a while the noise ceased.

The old man took the lone chair, his sons around him, and the guest; some coatless, all collarless, with their dark, saturnine faces stamped all clearly from the same die. They ate. Sausage, and spare ribs, and a dish of hominy and one of fried sweet potatoes, and corn bread and a molasses jug of sorghum, and Mandy poured coffee from a huge enamelware pot. In the middle of the meal the two missing ones came in—Jackson, the eldest, a man of fifty-two, with a broad, high forehead and thick brows and an expression at once dreamy and intense—a sort of shy and impractical Cincinnatus; and Stuart, forty-four and Rafe's twin. Yet although they were twins, there was no closer resemblance between them than between any two of them. As though the die was too firm and made too clean an imprint to be either hurried or altered, even by nature. Stuart had none of Rafe's easy manner (Rafe was the only one of them that, by any stretch of the imagination, could have been called loquacious); on the other hand, he had much of Henry's placidity. He was a good farmer and a canny trader, and he had a respectable bank account of his own. Henry, fifty, was the second son.

They ate with silent and steady decorum, with only the barest essential words, but amicably. Mandy moved back and forth between table and stove.

Before they had finished a sudden bell-like uproar of dogs floated up from the night and seeped through the tight walls, into the room. "Dar, now." The negro Richard cocked his head. Buddy poised his coffee.

"Wher are they, Dick?"

"Right back of de spring-house. Dey got 'im, too." Buddy rose and slid leanly from his corner.

"I'll go with you," Bayard said, rising also. The others ate steadily. Richard got a lantern down from the cupboard top and lit it, and the three of them passed out into the chill darkness across which the baying of the dogs came in musical gusts, ringing as frosty glass. It was chill and dark. The house loomed, its rambling low wall broken only by the ruddy glow of the window. "Ground's about hard already," Bayard remarked.

" 'Twont freeze tonight," Buddy answered. "Will it, Dick?"

"Naw, suh. Gwine rain."

"Go on," Bayard said. "I dont believe it."

"Pappy said so," Buddy replied. "Warmer'n 'twas at sundown."

"Dont feel like it, to me," Bayard insisted. They passed the wagon motionless in the starlight, its tires glinting like satin ribbons, and the long, rambling stable, from which placid munchings came, and an occasional snuffing snort as the lantern passed. Then the lantern twinkled among tree trunks as the path descended; the clamor of the dogs swelled just beneath them and the ghostly shapes of them shifted in the faint glow, and in a sapling just behind the spring house they found the 'possum, curled motionless and with its eyes tightly shut, in a fork not six feet from the ground. Buddy lifted it down by the tail, unresisting. "Hell," Bayard said.

Buddy called the dogs away, and they mounted the path again. In a disused shed behind the kitchen what seemed like at least fifty eyes gleamed in matched red points as Buddy swung the lantern in and flashed it onto a cage screened with chicken wire, from which rose a rank, warm odor and in which grizzled furry bodies moved sluggishly or swung sharp, skull-like faces into the light. He opened the door and dumped his latest capture in among its fellows and gave the lantern to Richard. They emerged. Already the sky was hazed over a little, losing some of its brittle scintillation.

The others sat in a semicircle before the blazing fire; at the old man's feet the blue-ticked hound dozed. They made room for Bayard, and Buddy squatted again in the chimney corner.

"Git 'im?" Mr MacCallum asked.

"Yes, sir," Bayard answered. "Like lifting your hat off a nail in the wall."

The old man puffed again. "We'll give you a sho' 'nough hunt befo' you leave."

Rafe said: "How many you got now, Buddy?"

"Aint got but fo'teen," Buddy answered.

"Fo'teen?" Henry repeated. "We wont never eat fo'teen 'possums."

"Turn 'em 'loose and run 'em again, then," Buddy answered. The old man puffed slowly at his pipe. The others smoked or chewed also, and Bayard produced his cigarettes and offered them to Buddy. Buddy shook his head.

"Buddy aint never started yet," Rafe said.

"You haven't?" Bayard asked. "What's the matter, Buddy?"

"Dont know," Buddy answered, from his shadow. "Just aint had time to learn, I reckon."

The fire crackled and swirled; from time to time Stuart, nearest the box, put another log on. The dog at the old man's feet dreamed, snuffed; soft ashes swirled on the hearth at its nose and it sneezed, waking itself, and raised its head and blinked up at the old man's face, then dozed again. They sat without word and with very little movement, their grave, aquiline faces as though carved by the firelight out of the shadowy darkness, shaped by a single thought and smoothed and colored by the same hand. The old man tapped his pipe carefully out upon his palm and consulted his fat silver watch. Eight oclock.

"We'uns git up at fo' oclock, Bayard," he said. "But you dont have to git up till daylight. Henry, git the jug."

"Four oclock," Bayard repeated, as he and Buddy undressed in the lamplit chill of the lean-to room in which, in a huge wooden bed with a faded patchwork quilt, Buddy slept. "I dont see why you bother to go to bed at all." As he spoke his breath vaporized in the chill air.

"Yes," Buddy agreed, ripping his shirt over his head and kicking his lean, racehorse shanks out of his shabby khaki pants. "Dont take long to spend the night at our house. You're comp'ny, though," he added, and in his voice was just a trace of envy and of longing. Never again after twenty-five will sleep in the morning be so golden. His preparations for sleeping were simple: he removed his boots and pants and shirt and went to bed in his woolen underwear, and he now lay with only his round head in view, watching Bayard who stood in a sleeveless jersey and short thin trunks. "You aint goin' to sleep warm that a way," Buddy said. "You want one o' my heavy 'uns?"

"I'll sleep warm, I guess," Bayard answered. He blew the lamp out and groped his way to the bed, his toes curling away from the icy floor, and got in. The mattress was filled with corn shucks: it rattled beneath him, drily sibilant, and whenever he or Buddy moved at all or took a deep breath even, the shucks shifted with small ticking sounds.

"Git that 'ere quilt tucked in good over thar," Buddy advised from the darkness, expelling his breath in a short explosive sound of relaxation. He yawned, audible but invisible. "Aint seen you in a long while," he suggested.

"That's right. Let's see, when was it? Two—three years, wasn't it?"

"Nineteen fifteen," Buddy answered. "Last time you and him. . . . . . ." Then he added quietly: "I seen in a paper, when it happened. The name. Kind of knowed right off 'twas him. It was a limey paper."

"You did? Where were you?"

"Up there," Buddy answered. "Where them limeys was. Where they sent us. Flat country. Dont see how they ever git it drained enough to make a crop, with all that rain."

"Yes." Bayard's nose was like a lump of ice. He could feel his breath warming his nose a little, could almost see the pale smoke of it as he breathed; could feel the inhalation chilling his nostrils again. It seemed to him that he could feel the planks of the ceiling as they sloped down to the low wall on Buddy's side, could feel the atmosphere packed into the low corner, bitter and chill and thick, too thick for breathing, like invisible slush; and he lay beneath it. . . . He was aware of the dry ticking of shucks beneath him and discovered so that he was breathing in deep troubled draughts and he wished dreadfully to be up, moving, before a fire, light; anywhere, anywhere. Buddy lay beside him in the oppressive, half-congealed solidity of the chill, talking in his slow, inarticulate idiom of the war. It was a vague, dreamy sort of tale, without beginning or end and filled with stumbling references to places wretchedly pronounced—you got an impression of people, creatures without initiation or background or future, caught timelessly in a maze of solitary conflicting preoccupations, like bumping tops, against an imminent but incomprehensible nightmare.

"How'd you like the army, Buddy?" Bayard asked.

"Not much," Buddy answered. "Aint enough to do. Good life for a lazy man." He mused a moment. "They gimme a charm," he added, in a burst of shy, diffident confidence and sober pleasure.

"A charm?" Bayard repeated.

"Uhuh. One of them brass gimcracks on to a colored ribbon. I aimed to show it to you, but I fergot. Do it tomorrow. That 'ere flo's too dang cold to tech till I have to. I'll watch a chance tomorrow when pappy's outen the house."

"Why? Dont he know you got it?"

"He knows," Buddy answered. "Only he dont like it because he claims it's a Yankee charm. Rafe says pappy and Stonewall Jackson aint never surrendered."

"Yes," Bayard repeated. Buddy ceased talking and presently he sighed again, emptying his body for sleep. But Bayard lay rigidly on his back, his eyes wide open. It was like being drunk and whenever you close your eyes, the room starts going round and round, and so you lie rigid in the dark with your eyes wide open, not to get sick. Buddy had ceased talking; presently his breathing became longer, steady and regular, and the shucks shifted with sibilant complaint as Bayard turned slowly onto his side.

Buddy breathed on in the darkness, steadily and peacefully. Bayard could hear his own breathing also, but above it, all around it, enclosing him, that other breathing. As though he were one thing breathing with restrained laboring pants, within himself breathing with Buddy's breathing; using up all the air so that the lesser thing must pant for it. Meanwhile the greater thing breathed deeply and steadily and unawares, asleep, remote; ay, perhaps dead. Perhaps he was dead, and he recalled that morning, relived it again with strained attention

from the time he had seen the first tracer smoke, until from
his steep sideslip he watched the flame burst like the gay flapping of an orange pennon from the nose of John's Camel and
saw his brother's familiar gesture and the sudden awkward
sprawl of his plunging body as it lost equilibrium in midair;
relived it again as you might run over a printed oft-read tale,
trying to remember, feel, a bullet going into his body or head
that might have slain him at the same instant. That would account for it, would explain so much: that he too was dead and
this was hell, through which he moved forever and ever with
an illusion of quickness, seeking his brother who in turn was
somewhere seeking him, never the two to meet. He turned
onto his back again; the shucks whispered beneath him with
dry derision.

The house was full of noises; to his sharpened senses the silence was myriad: the dry agony of wood in the black frost;
the ticking of shucks as he breathed; the very atmosphere itself
like slush ice in the vise of the cold, oppressing his lungs. His
feet were cold, his limbs sweated with it, and about his hot
heart his body was rigid and shivering and he raised his naked
arms above the covers and lay for a time with the cold like a
lead cast about them. And all the while Buddy's steady breathing and his own restrained and panting breath, both sourceless yet involved one with the other.

Beneath the covers again his arms were cold across his chest
and his hands were like ice upon his ribs, and he moved with
infinite caution while the chill croached from his shoulders
downward and the hidden shucks chattered at him, and swung
his legs to the floor. He knew where the door was and he
groped his way to it on curling toes. It was fastened by a
wooden bar, smooth as ice, and fumbling at it he touched
something else beside it, something chill and tubular and upright, and his hand slid down it and he stood for a moment
in the icy pitch darkness with the shotgun in his hands, and
as he stood so, his numb fingers fumbling at the breach, he
remembered the box of shells on the wooden box on which
the lamp sat. A moment longer he stood so, his head bent a
little and the gun in his numb hands; then he leaned it again
in the corner and lifted the wooden bar from its slots carefully
and without noise. The door sagged from the hinges and after

the first jarring scrape, he grasped the edge of it and lifted it back, and stood in the door.

In the sky no star showed, and the sky was the sagging corpse of itself. It lay upon the earth like a deflated balloon; into it the dark shape of the kitchen rose without depth, and the trees beyond, and homely shapes like sad ghosts in the chill corpse-light—the woodpile; a farming tool; a barrel beside the broken stoop at the kitchen door, where he had stumbled, supperward. The gray chill seeped into him like water into sand, with short trickling runs; halting, groping about an obstruction, then on again, trickling at last along his unimpeded bones. He was shaking slowly and steadily with cold; beneath his hands his flesh was rough and without sensation, yet still it jerked and jerked as though something within the dead envelope of him strove to free itself. Above his head, upon the plank roof, there sounded a single light tap, and as though at a signal, the gray silence began to dissolve. He shut the door silently and returned to bed.

In the bed he lay shaking more than ever, to the cold derision of the shucks under him, and he lay quietly on his back, hearing the winter rain whispering on the roof. There was no drumming, as when summer rain falls through the buoyant air, but a whisper of unemphatic sound, as though the atmosphere lying heavily upon the roof dissolved there and dripped sluggishly and steadily from the eaves. His blood ran again, and the covers felt like iron or like ice; but while he lay motionless beneath the rain his blood warmed yet more, until at last his body ceased trembling and he lay presently in something like a tortured and fitful doze, surrounded by coiling images and shapes of stubborn despair and the ceaseless striving for . . . not vindication so much as comprehension, a hand, no matter whose, to touch him out of his black chaos. He would spurn it, of course, but it would restore his cold sufficiency again.

The rain dripped on, dripped and dripped; beside him Buddy breathed placidly and steadily: he had not even changed his position. At times Bayard dozed fitfully: dozing, he was wide awake; waking, he lay in a hazy state filled with improbable moiling and in which there was neither relief nor rest: drop by drop the rain wore the night away, wore time away. But it was so long, so damn long. His spent blood, wearied with struggling, moved through his body in slow beats, like the rain, wearing his flesh away. It comes to all . . . bible . . . some preacher, anyway. Maybe he knew. Peace. It comes to all

At last, from beyond walls, he heard movement. It was indistinguishable, yet he knew it was of human origin, made by people whose names and faces he knew waking again into the world he had not been able even temporarily to lose, people to whom he was . . . and he was comforted. The sounds continued; unmistakably he heard a door, and a voice which with a slight effort of concentration he knew he could name; and best of all, knew that now he could rise and go where they were gathered about a crackling fire where light was, and warmth. And he lay, at ease at last, intending to rise the next moment and go to them, putting it off a little longer while his blood beat slowly through his body and his heart was quieted. Buddy breathed steadily beside him, and his own breath was untroubled now as Buddy's while the human sounds came murmurously into the cold room with grave and homely reassurance. It comes to all, it comes to all his tired heart comforted him, and at last he slept.

He waked in the gray morning, his body weary and heavy and dull: his sleep had not rested him. Buddy was gone, and it still rained, though now it was a definite purposeful sound on the roof and the air was warmer, with a rawness that probed to the very bones of him; and in his stockings and carrying his boots in his hands, he crossed the cold room where Lee and Rafe and Stuart slept, and found Rafe and Jackson before the living room fire.

"We let you sleep," Rafe said, then he said: "Good Lord, boy, you look like a hant. Didn't you sleep last night?"

"Yes, I slept all right," Bayard answered. He sat down and stamped into his boots and buckled the thongs below his knees. Jackson sat at one side of the hearth; in the shadowy corner near his feet a number of small, living creatures moiled silently, and still bent over his boots Bayard said:

"What you got there, Jackson? What sort of puppies are them?"

"New breed I'm tryin'," Jackson answered, and Rafe returned with a half a tumbler of Henry's pale amber whisky.

"Them's Ethel's pups," he said. "Git Jackson to tell you about 'em after you eat. Here, drink this. You look all wore out. Buddy must a kept you awake, talkin'," he added, with dry irony.

Bayard drank the whisky and lit a cigarette. "Mandy's got yo' breakfast on the stove," Rafe said.

"Ethel?" Bayard repeated. "Oh, that fox. I aimed to ask about her, last night. Y'all raise her?"

"Yes. She growed up with last year's batch of puppies. Buddy caught her. And now Jackson aims to revolutionize the huntin' business, with her. Aims to raise a breed of animals with a hound's wind and bottom, and a fox's smartness and speed."

Bayard approached the corner and examined the small creatures with interest and curiosity. "I never saw many fox pups," he said at last, "but I never saw any that looked like them."

"That's what Gen'ral seems to think," Rafe answered.

Jackson spat into the fire and stooped over the creatures. They knew his hands, and the moiling of them became more intense, and Bayard then noticed that they made no sound at all, not even puppy whimperings. "Hit's a experiment," Jackson explained. "The boys makes fun of 'em, but they haint no more'n weaned, yit. You wait and see."

"Dont know what you'll do with 'em," Rafe said brutally. "They wont be big enough fer work stock. Better git yo' breakfast, Bayard."

"You wait and see," Jackson repeated. He touched the scramble of small bodies with his hands, in a gentle, protective gesture. "You cant tell nothin' 'bout a dawg 'twell hit's at least two month old, can you?" he appealed to Bayard, looking up at him with his vague, intense gaze from beneath his shaggy brows.

"Go git yo' breakfast, Bayard," Rafe insisted. "Buddy's done gone and left you."

He bathed his face with icy water in a tin pan on the porch, and ate his breakfast—ham and eggs and flapjacks and sorghum—while Mandy talked to him about his brother. When he returned to the house old Mr MacCallum was there. The puppies moiled inextricably in their corner, and the old man sat with his hands on his knees, watching them with bluff and

ribald enjoyment, while Jackson sat nearby in a sort of hovering concern, like a hen.

"Come hyer, boy," the old man ordered when Bayard appeared. "Hyer, Rafe, git me that 'ere bait line." Rafe went
out, returning presently with a bit of pork rind on the end of
a string. The old man took it and hauled the puppies ungently
into the light, where they crouched abjectly—as strange a
litter as Bayard had ever seen. No two of them looked alike,
and none of them looked like any other living creature—
Neither fox nor hound; partaking of both, yet neither; and
despite their soft infancy, there was about them something
monstrous and contradictory and obscene. Here a fox's keen,
cruel muzzle between the melting, sad eyes of a hound and
its mild ears; there limp ears tried valiantly to stand erect
and failed ignobly in flapping points; and limp brief tails
brushed over with a faint, golden fuzz like the inside of a
chestnut burr. As regards color, they ranged from reddish
brown through an indiscriminate brindle to pure ticked
beneath a faint dun cast; and one of them had, feature for feature, old General's face in comical miniature, even to his expression of sad and dignified disillusion. "Watch 'em, now,"
the old man directed.

He got them all facing forward, then he dangled the meat
directly behind them. Not one became aware of its presence;
he swept it back and forth just above their heads; not one
looked up. Then he swung it directly before their eyes; still
they crouched diffidently on their young, unsteady legs and
gazed at the meat with curiosity but without any personal interest whatever and fell again to moiling soundlessly among
themselves.

"You cant tell nothin' about a dawg——" Jackson began.
His father interrupted him.

"Now, watch." He held the puppies with one hand and with
the other he forced the meat into their mouths. Immediately
they surged clumsily and eagerly over his hand, but he moved
the meat away and at the length of the string he dragged it
along the floor just ahead of them until they had attained a
sort of scrambling lope. Then in midfloor he flicked the meat
slightly aside, but without swerving the puppies blundered
on and into a shadowy corner, where the wall stopped them

and from which there rose presently the patient, voiceless confusion of them. Jackson crossed the floor and picked them up
and brought them back to the fire.

"Now, what do you think of them, fer a pack of huntin'
dawgs?" the old man demanded. "Cant smell, cant bark, and
damn ef I believe they kin see."

"You cant tell nothin' about a dawg——" Jackson essayed
patiently.

"Gen'ral kin," his father interrupted. "Hyer, Rafe, call
Gen'ral in hyer."

Rafe went to the door and called, and presently General entered, his claws hissing a little on the bare floor and his ticked
coat beaded with rain, and he stood and looked into the old
man's face with grave inquiry. "Come hyer," Mr MacCallum
said, and the dog moved again, with slow dignity. At that
moment he saw the puppies beneath Jackson's chair. He
paused in midstride and for a moment he stood looking at
them with fascination and bafflement and a sort of grave
horror, then he gave his master one hurt, reproachful look and
turned and departed, his tail between his legs. Mr MacCallum
sat down and rumbled heavily within himself.

"You cant tell about dawgs——" Jackson repeated. He
stooped and gathered up his charges, and rose.

Mr MacCallum continued to rumble and shake. "Well, I
dont blame the old feller," he said. "Ef I had to look around
on a passel of chaps like them and say to myself Them's my
boys——" But Jackson was gone. The old man sat and rumbled again, with heavy enjoyment. "Yes, suh, I reckon I'd feel
'bout as proud as he does. Rafe, han' me down my pipe."

All that day it rained, and the following day and the one
after that. The dogs lurked about the house all morning, un-
derfoot, or made brief excursions into the weather, returning to sprawl before the fire, drowsing and malodorous and
steaming, until Henry came along and drove them out; twice
from the door Bayard saw the fox, Ethel, fading with brisk
diffidence across the yard. With the exception of Henry and
Jackson, who had a touch of rheumatism, the others were
somewhere out in the rain most of the day. But at mealtimes
they gathered again, shucking their wet outer garments on the

porch and stamping in to thrust their muddy, smoking boots to the fire while Henry fetched the kettle and the jug. And last of all, Buddy, soaking wet.

Buddy had a way of getting his lean length up from his niche beside the chimney at any hour of the day and departing without a word, to return in two hours or six or twelve or forty eight, during which periods and despite the presence of Jackson and Henry and usually Lee, the place had a vague air of desertion, until Bayard realized that the majority of the dogs were absent, also. Hunting, they told him when Buddy had been missing since breakfast.

"Why didn't he let me know?" he demanded.

"Maybe he thought you wouldn't keer to be out in the weather," Jackson suggested.

"Buddy dont mind weather," Henry explained. "One day's like another to him."

"Nothin' aint anything to Buddy," Lee said, in his bitter, passionate voice. He sat brooding in the fire, his womanish hands moving restlessly on his knees. "He'd spend his whole life in that 'ere river bottom, with a hunk of cold cawn bread to eat and a passel of dawgs fer comp'ny." He rose abruptly and quitted the room. Lee was in the late thirties. As a child he had been sickly. He had a good tenor voice and he was much in demand at Sunday singings. He was supposed to be keeping company with a young woman living in the hamlet of Mount Vernon, six miles away. He spent much of his time tramping moodily and alone about the countryside.

Henry spat into the fire and jerked his head after the departing brother. "He been to Vernon lately?"

"Him and Rafe was there two days ago," Jackson answered.

Bayard said: "Well, I wont melt. I wonder if I could catch up with him now?"

They pondered for a while, spitting gravely into the fire. "I misdoubt it," Jackson said at last. "Buddy's liable to be ten mile away by now. You ketch 'im next time 'fo' he starts out."

After that Bayard did so, and he and Buddy tried for birds in the skeletoned fields in the rain, in which the guns made a flat, mournful sound that lingered in the streaming air like a spreading stain, or tried the stagnant backwaters along the river channel for duck and geese; or, accompanied now and then by Rafe, hunted 'coon and wildcat in the bottom. At times and far away, they would hear the shrill yapping of the young dogs in mad career. "Ther goes Ethel," Buddy would remark. Then toward the end of the week the weather cleared, and in a twilight imminent with frost and while the scent lay well upon the wet earth, old General started the red fox that had baffled him so many times.

All through the night the ringing, bell-like tones quavered and swelled and echoed among the hills, and all of them save Henry followed on horseback, guided by the cries of the hounds but mostly by the old man's and Buddy's uncanny and seemingly clairvoyant skill in anticipating the course of the race. Occasionally they stopped while Buddy and his father wrangled about where the quarry would head next, but usually they agreed, apparently anticipating the animal's movements before it knew them itself; and once and again they halted their mounts upon a hill and sat so in the frosty starlight until the dogs' voices welled out of the darkness mournful and chiming, swelled louder and nearer and swept invisibly past not half a mile away; faded diminishing and with a falling suspense, as of bells, into the silence again.

"Thar, now!" the old man exclaimed, shapeless in his overcoat, upon his white horse. "Aint that music fer a man, now?"

"I hope they git 'im this time," Jackson said. "Hit hurts Gen'ral's conceit so much ever' time he fools 'im."

"They wont git 'im," Buddy said. "Soon's he gits tired, he'll hole up in them rocks."

"I reckon we'll have to wait till them pups of Jackson's gits big enough," the old man agreed, "unless they'll refuse to run they own granddaddy. They done refused ever' thing else excep' vittles."

"You jest wait," Jackson repeated, indefatigable. "When them puppies gits old enough to——"

"Listen."

The talking ceased, and again across the silence the dogs' voices rang among the hills. Long, ringing cries fading, falling with a quavering suspense, like touched bells or strings, repeated and sustained by bell-like echoes repeated and dying among the dark hills beneath the stars, lingering yet in the ears crystal-clear, mournful and valiant and a little sad.

"Too bad Johnny aint here," Stuart said quietly. "He'd enjoy this race."

"He was a feller fer huntin', now," Jackson agreed. "He'd keep up with Buddy, even."

"John was a fine boy," the old man said.

"Yes, suh," Jackson repeated, "a right warm-hearted boy. Henry says he never come out hyer withouten he brung Mandy and the boys a little sto'-bought somethin'."

"He never sulled on a hunt," Stuart said. "No matter how cold and wet it was, even when he was a little chap, with that 'ere single bar'l he bought with his own money, that kicked 'im so hard ever' time he shot it. And yit he'd tote it around, instead of that 'ere sixteen old Colonel give 'im, jest because he saved up his own money and bought hit hisself."

"Yes," Jackson agreed. "Ef a feller gits into somethin' on his own accord, he ought to go through with hit cheerful."

"He was sho' a feller fer singin' and shoutin'," Mr MacCallum said. "Skeer all the game in ten mile. I mind that night he up and headed off a race down at Samson's bridge, and next we knowed, here him and the fox come a-floatin' down river on that 'ere drift lawg, and him singin' away loud as he could yell."

"That 'uz Johnny, all over," Jackson agreed. "Gittin' a whoppin' big time outen ever' thing that come up."

"He was a fine boy," Mr MacCallum said again.

"Listen."

Again the hounds gave tongue in the darkness below them. The sound floated up upon the chill air, died into echoes that repeated the sound again until its source was lost and the very earth itself might have found voice, grave and sad and wild with all regret.

Christmas was two days away, and they sat again about the fire after supper; again old General dozed at his master's feet. Tomorrow was Christmas eve and the wagon was going into town, and although, with that grave and unfailing hospitality of theirs, no word had been said to Bayard about his departure, he believed that in all their minds it was taken for granted that he would return home the following day for Christmas; and, since he had not mentioned it himself, a little curiosity and quiet speculation also.

It was cold again, with a vivid chill that caused the blazing logs to pop and crackle with vicious sparks and small embers that leaped out upon the floor, to be crushed out by a lazy boot, and Bayard sat drowsily, his tired muscles relaxed in cumulate waves of heat as in a warm bath, and his stubborn wakeful heart glozed over too, for the time being. Time enough tomorrow to decide whether to go or not. Perhaps he'd just stay on, without even offering that explanation which would never be demanded of him. Then he realized that Rafe, Lee, whoever went, would talk to people, would learn about that which he had not the courage to tell them.

Buddy had come out of his shadowy niche and he now squatted in the center of the semicircle, his back to the fire and his arms around his knees, with his motionless and seemingly tireless ability for sitting timelessly on his heels. He was the baby, twenty years old. His mother had been the old man's second wife, and his hazel eyes and the reddish thatch cropped close to his round head was a noticeable contrast to his brothers' brown eyes and black hair. But the old man had stamped Buddy's face as clearly as ever a one of the other boys', and despite its youth, it too was like the others—aquiline and spare, reserved and grave though a trifle ruddy with his fresh coloring and finer skin.

The others were of medium height or under, ranging from Jackson's faded, vaguely ineffectual lankness, through Henry's placid rotundity and Rafe's (Raphael Semmes he was) and Stuart's poised and stocky muscularity, to Lee's thin and fiery unrepose; but Buddy with his sapling-like leanness stood eye to eye with that father who wore his seventy-seven years as though they were a thin coat. "Long, spindlin' scoundrel," the old man would say, with bluff derogation. "Keeps hisself wore to a shadder totin' around all that 'ere grub he eats." And they would sit in silence, looking at Buddy's jackknifed length with the same identical thought, a thought which each believed peculiar to himself and which none ever divulged—that someday Buddy would marry and perpetuate the name.

Buddy also bore his father's name, though it is doubtful if anyone outside the family and the War Department knew it. He had run away at seventeen and enlisted; at the infantry concentration camp in Arkansas to which he had been sent, a fellow recruit called him Virge and Buddy had fought him steadily and without anger for seven minutes; at the New Jersey embarkation depot another man had done the same thing, and Buddy had fought him, again steadily and thoroughly and without anger. In Europe, still following the deep but uncomplex compulsions of his nature, he had contrived, unwittingly perhaps, to perpetrate something which was later ascertained by authority to have severely annoyed the enemy, for which Buddy had received his charm, as he called it. What it was he did, he could never be brought to say, and the gaud not only failing to placate his father's rage over the fact that a son of his had joined the Federal army, but on the contrary adding fuel to it, the bauble languished among Buddy's sparse effects and his military career was never mentioned in the family circle; and now as usual Buddy squatted among them, his back to the fire and his arms around his knees, while they sat about the hearth with their bed-time toddies, talking of Christmas.

"Turkey," the old man was saying, with fine and rumbling disgust. "With a pen full of 'possums, and a river bottom full of squir'ls and ducks, and a smoke-house full of hawg meat, you damn boys have got to go clean to town and buy a turkey fer Christmas dinner."

"Christmas aint Christmas lessen a feller has a little somethin' different from ever' day," Jackson pointed out mildly.

"You boys jest wants a excuse to git to town and loaf around all day and spend money," the old man retorted. "I've seen a sight mo' Christmases than you have, boy, and ef hit's got to be sto'-bought, hit aint Christmas."

"How 'bout town folks?" Rafe asked. "You aint allowin' them no Christmas a-tall."

"Dont deserve none," the old man snapped. "Livin' on a little two-by-fo' lot, jam right up in the next feller's back do', eatin' outen tin cans."

" 'Sposin' they all broke up in town," Stuart said, "and moved out here and took up land; you'd hear pappy cussin' town then. You couldn't git along without town to keep folks bottled up in, pappy, and you knows it."

"Buyin' turkeys," Mr MacCallum repeated with savage

disgust. "Buyin' 'em. I mind the time when I could take a gun and step out that 'ere do' and git a gobbler in thutty minutes. And a ven'son ham in a hour mo'. Why, you fellers dont know nothin' about Christmas. All you knows is a sto' winder full of cocoanuts and Yankee-made popguns and sich."

"Yes, suh," Rafe said, and he winked at Bayard. "That was the biggest mistake the world ever made, when Lee surrendered. The country aint never got over it."

The old man snorted. "I be damned ef I aint raised the damdest smartest set of boys in the world. Cant tell 'em nothin', cant learn 'em nothin'; cant even set in front of my own fire fer the whole passel of 'em tellin' me how to run the whole damn country. Hyer, you boys, git on to bed."

Next morning Jackson and Rafe and Stuart and Lee left for town at sunup in the wagon. Still none of them had made any sign, expressed any curiosity as to whether they would find him there when they returned that night, or whether it would be another three years before they saw him again. And Bayard stood on the frost-whitened porch, smoking a cigarette in the chill, vivid sunrise, and looked after the wagon with its four muffled figures and wondered if it would be three years again, or ever. The hounds came and nuzzled about him and he dropped his hand among their icy noses and the warm flicking of their tongues, gazing at the trees from beyond which the dry rattling of the wagon came unimpeded upon the clear and soundless morning.

"Ready to go?" Buddy said behind him, and he turned and picked up his shotgun where it leaned against the wall. The hounds surged about them with eager whimperings and frosty breaths and Buddy led them across to their pen and huddled them inside and fastened the door upon their astonished protests. From another kennel he unleashed the young pointer, Dan. Behind them the hounds continued to lift their baffled and mellow expostulations.

Until noon they hunted the ragged, fallow fields and woods-edges in the warming air. The frost was soon gone, and the air warmed to a windless languor; and twice in brier thickets they saw redbirds darting like arrows of scarlet flame. At last Bayard lifted his eyes unwinking into the sun.

"I've got to go back, Buddy," he said. "I'm going home this afternoon."

"All right," Buddy agreed without protest, and he called the dog in. "You come back next month."

Mandy got them some cold food and they ate, and while Buddy was saddling Perry, Bayard went into the house where he found Henry laboriously soling a pair of boots and the old man reading a week-old newspaper through steel-bowed spectacles.

"I reckon yo' folks will be lookin' fer you," Mr MacCallum agreed, removing his spectacles. "We'll be expectin' you back next month, though, to git that 'ere fox. Ef we dont git 'im soon, Gen'ral wont be able to hold up his haid befo' them puppies."

"Yes, sir," Bayard answered. "I will."

"And try to git yo' gran'pappy to come out with you. He kin lay around hyer and eat his haid off well as he kin in town thar."

"Yes, sir, I will."

Buddy led the pony up, and the old man extended his hand without rising, and Henry put aside his cobbling and followed him onto the porch. "Come out again," he said diffidently, giving Bayard's hand a single pump-handle shake; and from a slobbering inquisitive surging of half grown hounds Buddy reached up his hand.

"Be lookin' fer you," he said briefly, and Bayard wheeled away, and when he looked back they lifted their hands gravely. Then Buddy shouted after him and he reined Perry about and returned. Henry had vanished, and he reappeared with a weighted towsack.

"I nigh fergot it," he said. "Jug of cawn pappy's sendin' in to yo' granddaddy. You wont git no better 'n this in Looeyvul ner nowhar else, neither," he added with quiet pride. Bayard thanked him, and Buddy fastened the sack to the pommel, where it lay solidly against his leg.

"There. That'll ride."

"Yes, that'll ride. Much obliged."

"So long."

"So long."

Perry moved on, and he looked back. They still stood there,

quiet and grave and steadfast. Beside the kitchen door the fox, Ethel, sat, watching him covertly; near her the half-grown puppies rolled and played in the sunlight. The sun was an hour high above the western hills; the road wound on into the trees. He looked back again. The house sprawled its rambling length in the wintry afternoon, its smoke like a balanced plume on the windless sky. The door was empty and he shook Perry into his easy, tireless foxtrot, the jug of whisky jouncing a little against his knee.

6.

Where the dim, infrequent road to MacCallum's left the main road, rising, he halted Perry and sat for a while in the sunset. Jefferson, 14 miles. Rafe and the other boys would not be along for some time, yet, what with Christmas eve in town and the slow festive gathering of the county. Still, they may have left town early, so as to get home by dark; might not be an hour away. The sun's rays, slanting, released the chill they had held prisoned in the ground during the perpendicular hours, and it rose slowly about him as he sat Perry in the middle of the road, and slowly his blood cooled with the cessation of Perry's motion. He turned the pony's head away from town and shook him into his foxtrot again.

Darkness overtook him soon, but he rode on beneath the leafless trees, along the pale road in the gathering starlight. Already Perry was thinking of stable and supper and he went on with tentative, inquiring tossings of his head, but obediently and without slackening his gait, knowing not where they were going nor why, save that it was away from home, and a little dubious, though trustfully. The chill grew in the silence and the loneliness and the monotony. Bayard reined Perry to a halt and untied the jug and drank, and fastened it to the saddle again.

The hills rose wild and black about him; no sign of any habitation, no trace of man's hand did they encounter. On all sides the hills rolled blackly away in the starlight, or when the road dipped into valleys where the ruts were already stiffening into iron-like shards that clattered beneath Perry's hooves, they stood darkly towering and sinister overhead, lifting their leafless trees against the spangled sky. Where a stream of winter seepage trickled across the road Perry's feet crackled brittlely in thin ice, and Bayard slacked the reins while the pony snuffed at the water, and drank again from the jug.

He fumbled a match clumsily in his numb fingers and lit a cigarette, and pushed his sleeve back from his wrist. Eleven-thirty. "Well, Perry," his voice sounded loud and sudden in the stillness and the darkness and the cold. "I reckon we better look for a place to hole up till morning." Perry raised his head and snorted, as though he understood the words, as though he would enter the bleak loneliness in which his rider moved, if he could. They went on, mounting again.

The darkness spread away, lessening a little presently where occasional fields lay in the vague starlight, breaking the monotony of trees; and after a time during which he rode with the reins slack on Perry's neck and his hands in his pockets seeking warmth between leather and groin, a cotton house squatted beside the road, its roof dusted over with a frosty sheen as of hushed silver. Not long, he told himself, leaning forward and laying his hand on Perry's neck, feeling the warm, tireless blood there. "House soon, Perry, if we look sharp."

Again Perry whinnied a little, as though he understood, and presently he swerved from the road, and as Bayard reined him up he too saw the faint wagon trail leading away toward a low vague clump of trees. "Good boy, Perry," he said, slackening the reins again.

The house was a cabin. It was dark, but a hound came gauntly from beneath it and bayed at him and continued its uproar while he reined Perry to the door and knocked upon it with his numb hand. From within the house at last a voice, and he shouted "Hello" again. Then he added: "I'm lost. Open the door." The hound bellowed at him indefatigably. After a moment the door cracked upon a dying glow of embers, emitting a rank odor of negroes, and against the crack of warmth, a head.

"You, Jule," the head commanded, "hush yo' mouf." The hound ceased obediently and retired beneath the house, though still growling. "Who dar?"

"I'm lost," Bayard repeated. "Can I stay in your barn tonight?"

"Aint got no barn," the negro answered. "Dey's anudder house down de road a piece."

"I'll pay you." Bayard fumbled in his pocket with his numb hand. "My horse is tired out." The negro's head peered around the door, against the crack of firelight. "Come on, uncle," Bayard added impatiently. "Dont keep a man standing in the cold."

"Who is you, whitefolks?"

"Bayard Sartoris, from Jefferson. Here," and he extended his hand. The negro made no effort to take it.

"Banker Sartorises folks?"

"Yes. Here."

"Wait a minute." The door closed. But Bayard tightened the reins and Perry moved readily and circled the house confidently and went on among frost-stiffened cotton stalks that clattered drily about his knees. As Bayard dismounted onto frozen rutted earth beneath a gaping doorway, a lantern appeared from the cabin, swung low among the bitten stalks and the shadowy scissoring of the man's legs, and the negro came up with a shapeless bundle under his arm and stood with the lantern while Bayard stripped the saddle and bridle off.

"How you manage to git so fur fum home dis time o' night, whitefolks?" he asked curiously.

"Lost," Bayard answered briefly. "Where can I put my horse?"

The negro swung the lantern into a stall. Perry stepped carefully over the sill and turned into the lantern light, his eyes rolling in phosphorescent gleams; Bayard followed and rubbed him down with the dry side of the saddle blanket. The negro vanished and reappeared with a few ears of corn and shucked them into Perry's manger beside the pony's eager nuzzling. "You gwine be keerful about fire, aint you, whitefolks?" he asked.

"Sure. I wont strike any matches at all."

"I got all my stock and tools and feed in here," the negro explained. "I cant affo'd to git burnt out. Insu'ance dont reach dis fur."

"Sure," Bayard repeated. He shut Perry's stall and while the negro watched him he drew the sack forth from where he had set it against the wall, and produced the jug. "Got a cup here?"

The negro vanished again and Bayard could see the lantern through the cracks in the crib in the wall opposite, then he emerged with a rusty can, from which he blew a bursting puff of chaff. They drank. Behind them Perry crunched his corn. The negro showed him the ladder to the loft.

"You wont fergit about dat fire, whitefolks?" he repeated anxiously.

"Sure," Bayard said. "Goodnight." He laid his hand on the ladder, and the negro stopped him and handed him the shapeless bundle he had brought out with him.

"Aint got but one to spare, but hit'll help some. You gwine sleep cole, tonight." It was a quilt, ragged and filthy to the touch, and impregnated with that unmistakable odor of negroes.

"Thanks," Bayard answered. "Much obliged to you. Goodnight."

"Goodnight, whitefolks."

The lantern winked away, to the criss-crossing of the negro's legs, and Bayard mounted into darkness and the dry, pungent scent of hay. Here, in the darkness, he made himself a nest of it and crawled into it and rolled himself into the quilt, filth and odor and all, and thrust his icy hands inside his shirt, against his flinching chest. After a time and slowly his hands began to warm, tingling a little, but still his body lay shivering and jerking with weariness and with cold. Below him Perry munched steadily and peacefully in the darkness, occasionally he stamped, and gradually the jerking of his body ceased. Before he slept he uncovered his arm and looked at the luminous dial on his wrist. One oclock. It was already Christmas.

The sun waked him, falling in red bars through the cracks in the wall, and he lay for a time in his hard bed, with chill bright air on his face like icy water, wondering where he was. Then he remembered, and moving, found that he was stiff with stale cold and that his blood began to move through his limbs in small pellets like bird-shot. He dragged his legs from his odorous bed, but within his boots his feet were dead, and he sat flexing his knees and ankles for some time before his feet waked as with stinging needles. His movements were stiff and awkward, and he descended the ladder slowly and gingerly into the red sun that fell like a blare of trumpets into the hallway. The sun was just above the horizon, huge and red; and housetop, fenceposts, the casual farming tools rusting about the barnyard and the dead cotton stalks where the negro had farmed his land right up to his back door, were dusted over with frost which the sun changed to a scintillant rosy icing like that on a festive cake. Perry thrust his slender muzzle across the stall door and whinnied at his master with vaporous salutation, and Bayard spoke to him and touched his cold nose. Then he untied the sack and drank from the jug. The negro with a milk pail appeared in the door.

"Chris'mus gif', whitefolks," he said, eying the jug. Bayard gave him a drink. "Thanky, suh. You g'awn to de house to de fire. I'll feed yo' hawss. De ole woman got yo' breakfus' ready." Bayard picked up the sack; at the well behind the cabin he drew a pail of icy water and splashed his face.

A fire burned on the broken hearth, amid ashes and charred wood-ends and a litter of cooking vessels. Bayard shut the door behind him, upon the bright cold, and warmth and rich, stale rankness enveloped him like a drug. A woman bent over the hearth replied to his greeting diffidently. Three pickaninnies became utterly still in a corner and watched him with rolling eyes. One of them was a girl, in greasy, nondescript garments, her wool twisted into tight knots of soiled wisps of colored cloth. The second one might have been either or anything. The third one was practically helpless in a garment made from a man's suit of wool underclothes. It was too small to walk and it crawled about the floor in a sort of intense purposelessness, a glazed path running from either nostril to its chin, as though snails had crawled there.

The woman placed a chair before the fire with a dark, effacing gesture. Bayard seated himself and thrust his chilled feet to the fire. "Had your Christmas dram yet, aunty?" he asked.

"Naw, suh. Aint got none, dis year," she answered from somewhere behind him.

He swung the sack toward her voice. "Help yourself. Plenty there." The three children squatted against the wall, watching him steadily, without movement and without sound. "Christmas come yet, chillen?" he asked them. But they only stared at him with the watchful gravity of animals until the woman returned and spoke to them in a chiding tone.

"Show de whitefolks yo' Sandy Claus," she prompted. "Thanky, suh," she added, putting a tin plate on his knees and setting a cracked china cup on the hearth at his feet. "Show 'im," she repeated. "You want folks to think Sandy Claus dont know whar you lives at?"

The children moved then, and from the shadow behind them, where they had hidden them when he entered, they produced a small tin automobile, a string of colored wooden beads, a small mirror and a huge stick of peppermint candy to which trash adhered and which they immediately fell to licking solemnly, turn and turn about. The woman filled the cup from the coffee pot set among the embers, and she uncovered an iron skillet and forked a thick slab of sizzling meat onto his plate, and raked a grayish object from the ashes and broke it in two and dusted it off and put that too on the plate. Bayard ate his side meat and hoecake and drank the thin, tasteless liquid. The children now played quietly with their Christmas, but from time to time he found them watching him steadily and covertly. The man entered with his pail of milk.

"Ole 'oman give you a snack?" he asked.

"Yes. What's the nearest town on the railroad?" The other told him—eight miles away. "Can you drive me over there this morning, and take my horse back to Mr MacCallum's some day this week?"

"My brudder-in-law bor'd my mules," the negro replied readily. "I aint got but de one span, and he done bor'd dem."

"I'll pay you five dollars."

The negro set the pail down, and the woman came and got it. He scratched his head slowly. "Five dollars," Bayard repeated.

"You's in a pow'ful rush, fer Chris'mus, whitefolks."

"Ten dollars," Bayard said impatiently. "Cant you get your mules back from your brother-in-law?"

"I reckon so. I reckon he'll bring 'em back by dinner time. We kin go den."

"Why cant you get 'em now? Take my horse and go get 'em. I want to catch a train."

"I aint had no Chris'mus yit, whitefolks. Feller workin' ev'y day of de year wants a little Chris'mus."

Bayard swore shortly and bleakly, but he said: "All right,

then. Right after dinner. But you see your brother-in-law has
'em back here in plenty of time."

"Dey'll be here: dont you worry about dat."

"All right. You and aunty help yourselves to the jug."

"Thanky, suh."

The stale, airtight room dulled him; the warmth was insidious to his bones wearied and stiff after the chill night. The
negroes moved about the single room, the woman busy at
the hearth with her cooking, the pickaninnies with their frugal
and sorry gewgaws and filthy candy. Bayard sat in his hard
chair and dozed the morning away. Not asleep, but time was
lost in a timeless region where he lingered unawake and into
which he realized after a long while that something was trying
to penetrate; watched its vain attempts with peaceful detachment. But at last it succeeded and reached him: a voice.
"Dinner ready."

The negroes drank with him again, amicably, a little diffidently—two opposed concepts antipathetic by race, blood,
nature and environment, touching for a moment and fused
within an illusion—humankind forgetting its lust and cowardice and greed for a day. "Chris'mus," the woman murmured shyly. "Thanky, suh." Then dinner: 'possum with yams,
more gray ashcake, the dead and tasteless liquid in the coffee
pot; a dozen bananas and jagged shards of cocoanut, the children crawling about his feet like animals scenting food. He realized at last that they were holding back until he had done,
but he overrode them and they dined together; and at last (the
mules having been miraculously returned by a yet uncorporeal brother-in-law) with his depleted jug between his feet in
the wagon bed, he looked once back at the cabin, at the
woman standing in the door and a pale windless drift of smoke
above its chimney.

Against the mules' gaunt ribs the broken harness rattled and
jingled. The air was warm, yet laced too with a thin distilla-
tion of chill that darkness would increase. The road went on
across the bright land. From time to time across the shining
sedge or from beyond brown and leafless woods, came the flat
reports of guns; occasionally they passed other teams or horsemen or pedestrians, who lifted dark restful hands to the negro
buttoned into an army overcoat, with brief covert glances for

the white man on the seat beside him. "Heyo, Chris'mus!" Beyond the yellow sedge and brown ridges the ultimate hills stood bluely against the plumbless sky. "Heyo."

They stopped and drank, and Bayard gave his companion a cigarette. The sun behind them now; no cloud, no wind, no bird in the serene pale cobalt. "Shawt days! Fo' mile mo'. Come up, mules." Between motionless willows, stubbornly green, a dry clatter of loose planks above water in murmurous flashes. The road lifted redly; pines stood against the sky in jagged bastions. They crested this, and a plateau rolled away before them with its pattern of burnished sedge and fallow dark fields and brown woodland, and now and then a house, on into a shimmering azure haze, and low down on the horizon, smoke. "Two mile, now." Behind them the sun was a copper balloon tethered an hour up the sky. They drank again.

It had touched the horizon when they looked down into the final valley where the railroad's shining threads vanished among roofs and trees, and along the air to them distantly came a slow, heavy explosion. "Still celebratin'," the negro said.

Out of the sun they descended into violet shadow where windows gleamed behind wreaths and paper bells, across stoops littered with spent firecrackers. Along the streets children in bright sweaters and jackets sped on shiny coasters and skates and wagons. Again a heavy explosion in the dusk ahead, and they debouched into the square with its Sabbath calm, littered too with shattered scraps of paper. It looked the same way at home, he knew, with men and youths he had known from boyhood lounging the holiday away, drinking a little and shooting fireworks, giving nickels and dimes and quarters to negro lads who shouted Chris'mus gif'! Chris'mus gif'! as they passed. And out home the tree in the parlor and the bowl of eggnog before the fire, and Simon entering his and Johnny's room on tense and clumsy tiptoe and holding his breath above the bed where they lay feigning sleep until his tenseness relaxed, whereupon they both roared "Christmas gift!" at him, to his pained disgust. "Well, I'll de-clare, ef dey aint done caught me ag'in!" But by mid morning he would be recovered, by dinnertime he would be in a state of affable and useless loquacity, and by nightfall completely *hors de combat*, with

Aunt Jenny storming about the house and swearing that never again should it be turned into a barroom for trifling niggers as long as she had her strength, so help her Jupiter. And after dark, somewhere a dance, with holly and mistletoe and paper streamers, and the girls he had always known with their new bracelets and watches and fans amid lights and music and glittering laughter. . . .

A small group stood on a corner, and as the wagon passed and preceded by an abrupt scurrying, yellow flame was stenciled on the twilight and the heavy explosion reverberated in sluggish echoes between the silent walls. The mules quickened against the collars and the wagon rattled on. Through the dusk now, from lighted doorways where bells and wreaths hung, voices called with mellow insistence; children's voices replied, expostulant, reluctantly regretful. Then the station, where a 'bus and four or five cars stood, and Bayard descended and the negro lifted down the sack.

"Much obliged," Bayard said. "Goodbye."

"Goodbye, whitefolks."

In the waiting room a stove glowed red hot and about the room stood cheerful groups, in sleek furs and overcoats, but he did not enter. He set the sack against the wall and tramped up and down the platform, warming his blood again. In both directions along the tracks green switch lights were steady in the dusk; a hands-breadth above the western trees the evening star was like an electric bulb in a glass wall. He tramped back and forth, glancing into the ruddy windows, into the waiting room where the cheerful groups in their furs and overcoats gesticulated with festive though soundless animation, and into the colored waiting room, whose occupants sat patiently and murmurously about the stove in the dingy light. As he turned here a voice spoke diffidently from the shadow beside the door. "Chris'mus gif', boss." He took a coin from his pocket without stopping. Again from the square a firecracker exploded heavily, and above the trees a rocket arced, hung for a moment, then opened like a fist, spreading its golden and fading fingers upon the tranquil indigo sky without a sound.

Then the train came and brought its lighted windows to a jarring halt, and he picked up his sack again. And in the midst of a cheerful throng shouting goodbyes and holiday greetings and messages to absent ones, he got aboard, unshaven, in his scarred boots and stained khaki pants, and his shabby, smoke-colored tweed jacket and his disreputable felt hat, and found a vacant seat and stowed the jug away beneath his legs.

FIVE

". . . and since the essence of spring is loneliness and a little sadness and a sense of mild frustration, I suppose you do get a keener purifaction when a little nostalgia is thrown in for good measure. At home I always found myself remembering apple trees or green lanes or the color of the sea in other places, and I'd be sad that I couldn't be everywhere at once, or that all the spring couldn't be one spring, like Byron's ladies' mouths. But now I seem to be unified and projected upon one single and very definite object, which is something to be said for me, after all." Horace's pen ceased and he gazed at the sheet scrawled over with his practically illegible script, while the words he had just written echoed yet in his mind with a little gallant and whimsical sadness, and for the time being he had quitted the desk and the room and the town and all the crude and blatant newness into which his destiny had brought him, and again that wild and fantastic futility of his roamed unchallenged through the lonely region into which it had at last concentrated its conflicting parts. Already the thick cables along the veranda eaves would be budding into small lilac matchpoints, and with no effort at all he could see the lawn below the cedars, splashed with random narcissi among random jonquils and gladioli waiting to bloom in turn.

But his body sat motionless, its hand with the arrested pen lying upon the scrawled sheet, the paper lying upon the yellow varnished surface of his new desk. The chair in which he sat was new too, as was the room with its dead white walls and imitation oak woodwork. All day long the sun fell upon it, untempered by any shade. In the days of early spring it had been pleasant, falling as it now did through his western window and across the desk where a white hyacinth bloomed in a bowl of glazed maroon pottery. But as he sat musing, gazing out the window where, beyond a tarred roof that drank heat like a sponge and radiated it, against a brick wall a clump of ragged heaven trees lifted shabby, diffident bloom, he dreaded the long hot summer days of sunlight upon the roof directly above him, remembered his dim and musty office at home, in which a breeze seemed always to move, with its serried rows of books dusty and undisturbed that seemed to emanate coolness and quietude even on the hottest days. And thinking of this, he was again lost from the harsh newness in which his body sat. The pen moved again.

"Perhaps fortitude is a sorry imitation of something worth while, after all. To the so many who burrow along like moles in the dark, or like owls, to whom a candle-flame is a surfeit. But not those who carry peace along with them as the candle-flame carries light. I have always been ordered by words, but it seems that I can even restore assurance to my own cowardice by cozening it a little. I dare say you cannot read this as usual, or reading it, it will not mean anything to you. But you will have served your purpose anyway, thou still unravished bride of quietude." Thou wast happier in thy cage, happier? Horace thought, reading the words he had written and in which, as usual, he was washing one woman's linen in the house of another. A thin breeze blew suddenly into the room; there was locust upon it, faintly sweet, and beneath it the paper stirred upon the desk, rousing him; and suddenly, as a man waking, he looked at his watch and replaced it and wrote rapidly:

"We are glad to have little Belle with us. She likes it here: there is a whole family of little girls next door: stair steps of tow pigtails before whom, it must be confessed that little Belle preens just a little; patronizes them, as is her birthright. Children make all the difference in the world about a house. Too bad agents are not wise enough to provide rented houses with them. Particularly one like little Belle, so grave and shining and sort of irrelevantly and intensely mature, you know. But then, you dont know her very well, do you? But we both are very glad to have her with us. I believe that Harry   " The pen ceased, and still poised, he sought the words that so rarely eluded him, realizing as he did so that, though one can lie about others with ready and extemporaneous promptitude, to lie about oneself requires deliberation and a careful choice of expression. Then he glanced again at his watch and crossed that out and wrote: "Belle sends love, O Serene." and blotted it and folded it swiftly into an envelope and addressed and stamped it, and rose and took his hat. By running he could get it on the four oclock train.

Thou wast happier in thy cage, happier. . . . . . . The corridor, with its rubber mat and identical closed doors expensively and importantly discrete; the stairway with its brass-bound steps and at each turning, a heavy brass receptacle in which cigarette butts and scraps of paper reposed upon tobacco-stained sand, all new, all smelling of recent varnish. There was a foyer of imitation oak and imitation marble; the street in an untempered glare of spring sunlight. The building too was new and an imitation of something else, or maybe a skillful and even more durable imitation of that, as was the whole town, the very spirit, the essence of which was crystallized in the courthouse building—an edifice imposing as a theatre drop, flamboyant and cheap and shoddy; obviously built without any definite plan by men without honesty or taste. It was a standing joke that it had cost $60,000, and the people who had paid for it retailed the story without anger, but on the contrary with a little frankly envious admiration.

Ten years ago the town was a hamlet, twelve miles from the railroad. Then a hardwood lumber concern had bought up the cypress swamps nearby and established a factory in the town. It was financed by eastern capital and operated by as plausible and affable a set of brigands as ever stole a county. They robbed the stockholders and the timber owners and one another and spent the money among the local merchants, who promptly caught the enthusiasm, and presently widows and orphans in New York and New England were buying Stutz cars and imported caviar and silk dresses and diamond watches at three prices, and the town bootleggers and the moonshiners in the adjacent swamps waxed rich, and every fourth year the sheriff's office sold at public auction for the price of a Hollywood bungalow. People in the neighboring counties learned of all this and moved there and chopped all the trees down and built themselves mile after mile of identical frame houses with garage to match: the very air smelled of affluence and burning gasoline. Yes, there was money there, how much, no two estimates ever agreed; whose, at any one given time, God Himself could not have said. But it was there, like that afflatus of rank fecundity above a foul and stagnant pool on which bugs dart spawning, die, are replaced in mid-darting; in the air, in men's voices and gestures, seemingly to be had for the taking. That was why Belle had chosen it.

But for the time being Horace was utterly oblivious of its tarnished fury as he walked along the street toward the new, ugly yellow station, carrying his letter the words of which yet echoed derisively in his mind Belle sends love Belle sends love. He had made acquaintances "In spite of yourself," Belle told him harshly. "Thinking you are better than other people." Yes, he had answered. Yes, with a weariness too spent to argue with its own sense of integrity. But he had made a few, some of whom he now passed, was greeted, replied: merchants, another lawyer, his barber; a young man who was trying to sell him an automobile. Naturally Belle would   Belle sends love Belle sends   He still carried his letter in his hand and glancing at the bulletin board on the station wall he saw that the train was a little late, and he went on down the platform to where the mail car would stop and gave the letter to the mail carrier—a lank, goose-necked man with a huge pistol strapped to his thigh Thou wast happier   The express agent came along, dragging his truck   in thy cage, happier   "Got another 'un today?" he asked, greeting Horace.

"What?" Horace said. "Oh, good afternoon."

"Got another 'un today?" the other repeated.

"Yes," Horace answered, watching the other swing the truck skillfully into position beside the rails   Happier   The sun was warm; already there was something of summer's rankness in it—a quality which, at home where among green and ancient trees and graver and more constant surroundings, dwelt quietude and the soul's annealment, it had not even in July. Soon, soon, he said, and again he went voyaging alone from where his body leaned against a strange wall in a brief hiatus of the new harsh compulsions it now suffered. This will not last always: I have made too little effort to change my fellow man's actions and beliefs to have won a place in anyone's plan of infinity   In thy cage, happier?

The locomotive slid past, rousing him: he had not heard it, and the cars on rasping wheels, and from the door of the express car the clerk with a pencil stuck jauntily beneath his cap, flipped his hand at him. "Here you are, Professor," he said, handing down first to the agent a small wooden crate from which moisture dripped. "Smelling a little stout, today, but the fish wont mind that, will they?" Horace approached, his nostrils tightening a little. The clerk in the car door was watching him with friendly curiosity. "Say," he asked, "what kind of city fish you got around here, that have to have mail-order bait?"

"It's shrimp," Horace explained.

"Shrimp?" the other repeated. "Eat 'em yourself, do you?" he asked with interest.

"Yes. My wife's very fond of them."

"Well, I'll be damned," the clerk said heartily, "I thought it was some kind of patent fish-bait you were getting every Tuesday. Well, every man to his taste, I reckon. But I'll take steak, myself. All right, Bud; grab it."

Horace signed the agent's receipt and lifted the crate from the truck, holding it carefully away from himself. The smell invariably roused in him a faint but definite repulsion which he was not able to overcome, though Belle preferred shrimp above all foods. And it always seemed to him for hours afterward that the smell clung about his clothing, despite the fact that he knew better, knew that he had carried the package well clear of himself. He carried it so now, his elbow against his side and his forearm at a slight, tense angle with the dripping weight.

Behind him the bell rang, and with the bitten, deep snorts of starting, the train moved. He looked back and saw the cars slide past, gaining speed, carrying his letter away and the quiet, the intimacy the writing and the touching of it, had brought him. But day after tomorrow he could write again *Belle sends love Belle sends* Ah, well, we all respond to strings. And She would understand, it and the necessity for it, the dreadful need; She in her serene aloofness partaking of gods *Belle sends*

The street from curb to curb was uptorn. It was in the throes of being paved. Along it lines of negroes labored with pick and shovel, swinging their tools in a languid rhythm. Steadily and with a lazy unhaste that seemed to spend itself in snatches of plaintive minor chanting punctuated by short grunting ejaculations which died upon the sunny air and ebbed away from the languid rhythm of picks that struck not; shovels that did not dig. Further up the street a huge misshapen machine like an antediluvian nightmare clattered and groaned. It dominated the scene with its noisy and measured fury, but against this as against a heroic frieze, the negroes labored on, their chanting and their motions more soporific than a measured tolling of far away bells.

His arm was becoming numb, but the first mark—a water plug—where he changed hands for the first time, was still a hundred yards away; and when he reached it and swapped the crate to the other hand, his fingers were dead of all sensation and his biceps was jumping a little within his sleeve. Which goes to prove the fallacy of all theories of physical training. According to that, every succeeding Tuesday he should be able to go a little further without changing, until by Christmas he would be able to carry the package all the way home without changing hands; and by Christmas ten years, all the way back to Gulfport, where they came from. Prize, maybe. More letters behind his name, anyway. C.S. Carrier of Shrimp. H. Benbow, M.A., Ll.D., C.S.　Thou wast happier

The next mark was the corner where he turned, and he went on along the treeless street, between smug rows of houses identical one with another. Cheap frame houses, patently new, each with a garage and a car, usually a car that cost as much again as the house did. He reached the corner and changed hands again and turned into a smaller street, trailing spaced drops of melting ice behind him.

He lived on this street, and it was still open: motors could run on it, and he went on, dripping his trailing moisture along the sidewalk. With a motor car now, he could have Soon; perhaps next year; then things　But naturally Belle would miss her car, after having had one always, a new one every year. Harry, and his passion for shiny wheels . . . . which some would call generosity. . . . . . . "You lied to me. You told me you had plenty of money." Lied Lied took me away from my　Well, it would be better now, with little Belle. And Harry would find . . . who functioned in movie subtitles, harshly: "What else do you want of mine? My dam blood?"

Man's life. No apparent explanation for it save as an opportunity for doing things he'd spend the rest of it not being very proud of. Well, she had her child again, anyway, he told himself, thinking how women never forgive the men who permit them to do the things which they later have any cause to regret; and remembering that day when, with little Belle's awkwardly packed suitcase in the rack overhead and little Belle primly beside him in a state of demure and shining excitement at the prospect of moving suddenly to a new town, he had shrunk into his corner like a felon until the familiar station and that picture of Harry's ugly dogged head and his eyes like those of a stricken ox, were left behind, he wondered if little Belle too would someday. . . . . . . But that last picture of Harry's face had a way of returning. It's only injured vanity, he argued with himself; he's hurt in his own estimation because he couldn't keep the female he had chosen in the world's sight. But still his eyes and their patient bloodshot bewilderment, to be exorcised somehow. He's a fool, anyway, he told himself savagely, And who has time to pity fools? Then he said God help us, God help us all, and then at last humor saved him and he thought with a fine whimsical flash of it that probably Belle would send him to Harry next for a motor car.

Man's very tragedies flout him. He has invented a masque for tragedy, given it the austerity which he believes the spectacle of himself warrants, and the thing makes faces behind his back; dead alone, he is not ridiculous, and even then only in his own eyes   Thou wast happier   A voice piped with thin familiarity from beyond a fence. It was little Belle playing with the little girls next door, to whom she had already divulged with the bland naiveté of children that Horace was not her real daddy: he was just the one that lived with them now, because her real daddy's name was Daddy and he lived in another town. It was a prettier town than this, while the little girls listened with respect coldly concealed: little Belle had gained a sort of grudging cosmopolitanish glamor, what with her uniquely diversified family.

At the next gate he paused, and opened it and entered his rented lawn where his rented garage stared its empty door at him like an accusing eye, and still carrying his package carefully away from him he went on between the two spindling poplars he had set out and approached his rented frame house with its yellow paint and its naked veranda, knowing that from behind a shade somewhere, Belle was watching him. In negligee, the heavy mass of her hair caught up with studied carelessness, and her hot, suspicious eyes and the rich and sullen discontent of her mouth   Lied lied took me away from my husband: what is to keep   The wild bronze flame of her hair   Her   Injury, yes. Inexcusable because of the utter lack of necessity or reason for it. Giving him nothing, taking nothing away from him. Obscene. Yes, obscene: a deliberate breaking of the rhythm of things for no reason; to both Belle and himself an insult; to Narcissa, in her home where her serenity lingered grave and constant and steadfast as a diffused and sourceless light, it was an adolescent scribbling on the walls of a temple. Reason in itself confounded If what parts can so remain. . . . "I didn't lie. I told you; did what she would not have had the cowardice to do." What is to keep   Ay, obscene if you will, but there was about her a sort of gallantry, like a swordsman who asks no quarter and gives none; slays or is slain with a fine gesture or no gesture at all; tragic and austere and fine, with the wild bronze flame of her hair. And he, he not only hadn't made a good battle; he hadn't even made a decent ghost. Thou wast happier in thy cage, happier? Nor oceans and seas. . . . . . .

"She had ghosts in her bed," Horace said, mounting the steps.

2.

In January his aunt received a post card from Bayard mailed at Tampico; a month later, from Mexico City, a wire for money. And that was the last intimation he gave that he contemplated being at any given place long enough for a communication to reach him, although from time to time he indicated by gaudy postals where he had been, after the bleak and brutal way of him. In April the card came from Rio, followed by an interval during which he seemed to have completely vanished and which Miss Jenny and Narcissa passed quietly at home, their days centered placidly about the expected child, which Miss Jenny had already named John. Miss Jenny felt that old Bayard had somehow flouted them all, had committed lese majesty toward his ancestors and the lusty glamor of the family doom by dying, as she put it, practically from the "inside out." Thus he was in something like bad odor with her, and as young Bayard was in more or less abeyance, neither flesh nor fowl, she fell to talking more and more of John. Soon after old Bayard's death, in a sudden burst of rummaging and prowling which she called winter cleaning, she had found among his mother's relics a miniature of John done by a New Orleans painter when John and Bayard were about eight. Miss Jenny remembered that there had been one of each and it seemed to her that she could remember putting them both away together when their mother died. But the other she could not find. So she left Simon to gather up the litter she had made and brought the miniature downstairs to where Narcissa sat in the "office" and together they examined it.

The hair even at that early time was of a rich tawny shade, and rather long. "I remember that first day," Miss Jenny said, "when they came home from school. Bloody as hogs, both of 'em, from fighting other boys who said they looked like girls. Their mother washed 'em and petted 'em, but they were too busy bragging to Simon and Bayard about the slaughter they had done to mind it much. 'You ought to seen the others,' Johnny kept saying. Bayard blew up, of course; said it was a damn shame to send a boy out on the street with curls down his back, and finally he bullied the poor woman into agreeing to let Simon barber 'em. And do you know what? Neither of 'em would let his hair be touched. It seems there were still a few they hadn't licked yet, and they were going to make the whole school admit that they could wear hair down to their heels, if they wanted to. And I reckon they did, because after two or three more bloody days they came home once without any fresh wounds and then they let Simon cut it off while their mother sat behind the piano in the parlor and cried. And that was the last of it as long as they were in school here. I dont know what they kept on fighting folks about after they went away to school, but they found some reason. That was why we finally had to separate 'em while they were at Virginia and send Johnny to Princeton. They shot dice or something to see which one would be expelled, I think, and when Johnny lost they used to meet in New York every month or so. I found some letters in Bayard's desk that the chief of police in New

York wrote to the professors at Princeton and Virginia, asking 'em not to let Bayard and Johnny come back there any more, that the professors sent on to us. And one time Bayard had to pay fifteen hundred dollars for something they did to a policeman or a waiter or something."

Miss Jenny talked on, but Narcissa was not listening. She was examining the painted face in the miniature. It was a child's face that looked at her, and it was Bayard's too, yet there was already in it, not that bleak arrogance she had come to know in Bayard's, but a sort of frank spontaneity, warm and ready and generous; and as Narcissa held the small oval in her hand while the steady blue eyes looked quietly back at her and from the whole face among its tawny curls, with its smooth skin and child's mouth, there shone like a warm radiance something sweet and merry and wild, she realized as she never had before the blind tragedy of human events. And while she sat motionless with the medallion in her hand and Miss Jenny thought she was looking at it, she was cherishing the child under her own heart with all the aroused constancy of her nature: it was as though already she could discern the dark silver shape of that doom which she had incurred, standing beside her chair, waiting and biding its time. No, No she whispered with passionate protest, surrounding her child with wave after wave of that strength which welled so abundantly within her as the days accumulated, manning her walls with invincible garrisons. She was even glad Miss Jenny had shown her the thing: she was now forewarned as well as forearmed.

Meanwhile Miss Jenny continued to talk about the child as Johnny and to recall anecdotes of that other John's childhood, until at last Narcissa realized that Miss Jenny was getting the two confused; and with a sort of shock she knew that Miss Jenny was getting old, that at last even her indomitable old heart was growing a little tired. It was a shock, for she had never associated senility with Miss Jenny, who was so spare and erect and brusque and uncompromising and kind, looking after the place which was not hers and to which she had been transplanted when her own alien roots in a far away place where customs and manners and even the very climate itself, were different, had been severed violently; running it with tireless efficiency and with the assistance of only a doddering old negro as irresponsible as a child.

But run the place she did, just as though old Bayard and young Bayard were there. But at night when they sat before the fire in the office as the year drew on and the night air drifted in heavy again with locust and with the song of mockingbirds and with all the renewed and timeless mischief of spring and at last even Miss Jenny admitted that they no longer needed a fire; when at these times she talked, Narcissa noticed that she no longer talked of her far off girlhood and of Jeb Stuart with his crimson sash and his garlanded bay and his mandolin, but always of a time no further back than Bayard's and John's childhood. As though her life were closing, not into the future, but out of the past, like a spool being rewound.

And Narcissa would sit, serene again behind her forewarned bastions, listening, admiring more than ever that indomitable spirit that, born with a woman's body into a heritage of rash and heedless men and seemingly for the sole purpose of cherishing those men to their early and violent ends, and this over a period of history which had seen brothers and husband slain in the same useless mischancing of human affairs, had seen, as in a nightmare not to be healed by either waking or sleep, the foundations of her life swept away and had her roots torn bodily from that soil where her forefathers slept trusting in the integrity of mankind;—a period at which the men themselves, for all their headlong and scornful rashness, would have quailed had their parts been passive parts and their doom been waiting. And she thought how much finer that gallantry which never lowered blade to foes no sword could find, that uncomplaining steadfastness of those unsung (ay, unwept, too) women than the fustian and useless glamor of the men that obscured it. *And now she is trying to make me one of them; to make of my child just another rocket to glare for a moment in the sky, then die away.*

But she was serene again, and her days centered more and more as her time drew nearer, and Miss Jenny's voice was only a sound, comforting but without significance. Each week she received a whimsical, gallantly humorous letter from Horace: these she read too with tranquil detachment—what she could

decipher, that is. She had always found Horace's writing difficult, and parts that she could decipher meant nothing. But she
knew that he expected that.

Then it was definitely spring again. Miss Jenny's and Isom's
annual vernal altercation began, pursued its violent but harmless course in the garden beneath her window. They brought
the tulip bulbs up from the cellar and set them out, Narcissa
helping, and spaded up the other beds and unswaddled the
roses and the transplanted jasmine. Narcissa drove into town,
saw the first jonquils on the deserted lawn, blooming as
though she and Horace were still there, and she sent Horace
a box of them, and later, the narcissi. But when the gladioli
bloomed she was not going out any more save in the late afternoon or early evening, when with Miss Jenny she walked
in the garden among burgeoning bloom and mockingbirds
and belated thrushes where the long avenues of gloaming twilight reluctant leaned, Miss Jenny still talking of Johnny, confusing the unborn with the dead.

Early in June they received a request for money from Bayard
in San Francisco, where he had at last succeeded in being
robbed. Miss Jenny sent it. "You come on home?" she wired
him, not telling Narcissa. "He'll come home, now," she did
tell her. "You see if he dont. If for nothing else than to worry
us for a while."

But a week later he still had not come home, and Miss Jenny
wired him again, a night letter. But when the wire was dispatched he was in Chicago, and when it reached San Francisco
he was sitting among saxophones and painted ladies and middle aged husbands at a table littered with soiled glasses and
stained with cigarette ash and spilt liquor, accompanied by a
girl and two men. One of the men wore whipcord, with an
army pilot's wings on his breast. The other was a stocky man
in shabby serge, with gray temples and intense, visionary eyes.
The girl was a slim long thing, mostly legs apparently, with a
bold red mouth and cold eyes, in an ultra smart dancing frock,
and when the other two men came across the room and spoke
to Bayard she was cajoling him to drink with thinly-concealed
insistence. She and the aviator now danced together, and from
time to time she looked back to where Bayard sat drinking

steadily while the shabby man talked to him. She was saying: "I'm scared of him."

The shabby man was talking with leashed excitability, using two napkins folded lengthwise into narrow strips to illustrate something, his voice hoarse and importunate against the meaningless pandemonium of horns and drums. For a while Bayard had half listened, staring at the man with his cold eyes, but now he was watching something or some one across the room, letting the man talk on, unheeded. He was drinking whisky and soda steadily, with the bottle beside him. His hand was steady enough, but his face was dead white and he was quite drunk; and looking across at him from time to time, the girl was saying to her partner: "I'm scared, I tell you. God, I didn't know what to do, when you and your friend came over. Promise you wont go and leave us."

"You scared?" the aviator repeated in a jeering tone, but he too glanced back at Bayard's white arrogant face. "I bet you dont even need a horse."

"You dont know him," the girl rejoined, and she clutched his hand and struck her body shivering against his, and though his arm tightened and his hand slid down her back a little, it was under cover of the shuffling throng into which they were wedged, and a little warily, and he said quickly:

"Ease off, Sister: he's looking this way. I saw him knock two teeth out of an Australian captain that just tried to speak to a girl he was with in a London dive two years ago." They moved on until the band was across the floor from them. "What're you scared of? He's not an Indian: he wont hurt you as long as you mind your step. He's all right. I've known him a long time, in places where you had to be good, believe me."

"You dont know," she repeated. "I——" The music crashed to a stop; in the sudden silence the shabby man's voice rose from the nearby table:

"——could just get one of these damn yellow-livered pilots to——" His voice was drowned again in a surge of noise, drunken voices and shrill woman-laughter and scraping chairs, but as they approached the table the shabby man still talked with leashed insistent gestures while Bayard stared across the room at whatever it was he watched, lifting his glass steadily to his lips. The girl clutched her partner's arm.

"You've got to help me pass him out," she begged swiftly. "I'm scared to leave with him, I tell you."

"Pass Sartoris out? The man dont wear hair, nor the woman neither. Run back to kindergarden, Sister." Then, struck with her utter sincerity, he said: "Say, what's he done to you, anyway?"

"I dont know. He'll do anything. He threw an empty bottle at a traffic cop as we were driving out here. You've got——"

"Hush it," he commanded. The shabby man ceased talking and looked up impatiently. Bayard still gazed across the room.

"Brother-in-law over there," he said, speaking slowly and carefully. "Dont speak to family. Mad at us. Beat him out of his wife." They turned and looked.

"Where?" the aviator asked. He beckoned a waiter. "Here, Jack."

"Man with diamond headlight," Bayard said. "Brave man. Cant speak to him, though. Might hit me. Friend with him, anyhow."

The aviator looked again. "Looks like his grandmother," he said. He called the waiter again, then to the girl: "Another cocktail?" He picked up the bottle and filled his glass and Bayard's, and turned to the shabby man. "Where's yours?"

The shabby man waved it impatiently aside. "Look," he picked up the napkins again. "Dihedral increases in ratio to air pressure. By speed up to a certain point, see? Now, what I want to find out——"

"Tell it to the Marines, buddy," the aviator interrupted. "I heard a couple of years ago they got a airyplane. Here, waiter!" Bayard was now watching the shabby man bleakly.

"You aren't drinking," the girl said. She touched the aviator beneath the table.

"No," Bayard agreed. "Why dont you fly his coffin for him, Monaghan?"

"Me?" The aviator set his glass down. "Like hell. My leave comes due next month." He raised his glass again. "Here's to wind-up," he said, "and no heel-taps."

"Yes," Bayard agreed, not touching his glass. His face was pale and rigid, a metal mask again.

"I tell you there's no danger at all, as long as you keep the speed below the point I'll give you," the shabby man said with heat. "I've tested the wings with weights, and proved the lift and checked all my figures; all you have to——"

"Wont you drink with us?" the girl insisted.

"Sure he will," the aviator said. "Say, you remember that night in Amiens when that big Irish devil, Comyn, wrecked the Cloche-Clos by blowing that A.P.M.'s whistle at the door?" The shabby man sat smoothing the folded napkins on the table before him. Then he burst forth again, his voice hoarse and mad with the intensity of his frustrated dream:

"I've worked and slaved, and begged and borrowed, and now when I've got the machine and a government inspector, I cant get a test because you damn yellow-livered pilots wont take it up. A service full of you, drawing flying pay for sitting on hotel roofs, swilling alcohol. You overseas pilots talking about your guts! No wonder the Germans——"

"Shut up," Bayard told him without heat, in his cold, careful voice.

"You're not drinking," the girl repeated. "Wont you?" She picked up his glass and touched her lips to it and extended it to him. Taking it, he caught her hand too and held her so. But again he was staring across the room.

"Not brother-in-law," he said. "Husband-in-law. No. Wife's brother's husband-in-law. Wife used to be wife's brother's girl. Married, now. Fat woman. He's lucky."

"What're you talking about?" the aviator demanded. "Come on, let's have a drink."

The girl leaned away from him at the length of her arm. With her other hand she lifted her glass and smiled at him with brief and terrified coquetry. But he held her wrist in his hard fingers, and while she stared at him wildly he drew her steadily toward him. "Turn me loose," she whispered. "Dont," and she set her glass down and with the other hand she tried to unclasp his fingers. The shabby man was brooding over his folded napkins; the aviator was carefully occupied with his drink. "Dont," she whispered again. Her body was twisted in her chair and she put her hand out quickly, lest she be dragged out of it, and for a moment they stared at one another—she with wide and mute terror; he bleakly with the cold mask of his face. Then he released her and rose and thrust his chair back.

"Come on, you," he said to the shabby man. He drew a wad of bills from his pocket and laid one beside her on the table. "That'll get you home," he said. But she sat nursing the wrist he had held, watching him without a sound. The aviator was discreetly interested in the bottom of his glass. "Come on," Bayard repeated to the shabby man, and the other rose and followed him.

In a small alcove Harry Mitchell sat. On his table too were bottles and glasses, and he now sat slumped in his chair, his eyes closed and his bald head rosy with perspiration in the glow of an electric candle. Beside him was a woman who turned and looked at Bayard with blazing and harried desperation; above them stood a waiter with a head like a monk's, and as Bayard passed he saw that the diamond was missing from Harry's tie and he heard their bitter suppressed voices as their hands struggled over something on the table beyond the discreet shelter of their bodies, and as he and his companion reached the exit the woman's voice rose with a burst of filthy rage into a shrill hysterical scream cut sharply off, as if someone had clapped a hand over her mouth.

The next day Miss Jenny drove into town and wired him again. But when this wire was dispatched, Bayard was sitting in an aeroplane on the tarmac of the government field at Dayton, while the shabby man hovered and darted here and there in a frenzied manner and a group of army pilots stood nearby, soberly noncommittal. The machine looked like any other bi-plane, save that there were no visible cables between the planes, which were braced from within by wires on a system of springs; hence, motionless on the ground, dihedral was negative. The theory was that while in level flight dihedral would be eliminated for speed, and when the machine was banked, side pressure would automatically increase dihedral for manoeuverability. The cockpit was set well back toward the fin. "So you can see the wings when they buckle," the man who lent him a helmet and goggles, said drily. "It's an old pair," he added. Bayard glanced at him, coldly humorless. "Look here, Sartoris," the other said. "Let that crate alone. These birds show up here every week with something that will revolutionize flying, some new kind of mantrap that flies fine—on paper. If the C.O. wont give him a pilot (and you know we try anything here that has a prop on it) you can gamble it's a washout."

But Bayard took the helmet and goggles and went on toward the hangar. The group followed him and stood quietly about with their bleak, wind-gnawed faces while the engine was warming up. But when Bayard got in and settled his goggles, the man who had lent them to him approached and put something in his lap. "Here," he said brusquely. "Take this." It was a woman's garter, and Bayard picked it up and gave it back to him.

"I wont need it," he said. "Thanks just the same."

"Well. You know your own business. But if you ever let her get her nose down, you're going to lose everything but the wheels."

"I know," Bayard answered. "I'll keep her up." The shabby man rushed up again, still talking. "Yes, yes," Bayard replied impatiently. "You told me all that before. Contact." A mechanic spun the propeller over, and as the machine moved out toward midfield the shabby man still clung to the cockpit rim and shouted at him. Soon he was running to keep up and still shouting, and Bayard lifted his hands off the cowling and opened the throttle. But when he reached the end of the field and turned into the wind the man was running toward him and waving his arms. Bayard opened the throttle full and the machine lurched forward and when he passed the shabby man in midfield the tail was high and the plane rushed on in long bounds, and he had a fleeting glimpse of the man's wild arms and his open mouth as the bounding ceased.

From the V strut out each wing tipped and swayed, and he jockeyed the thing carefully on, gaining height. He realized that there was a certain point beyond which his own speed was likely to rob him of lifting surface. He had about two thousand feet now, and he turned, and in doing so he found that aileron pressure utterly negatived the inner plane's dihedral and doubled that of the outer one, and he found himself in the wildest skid he had seen since his hun days. The machine not only skidded: it flung its tail up like a diving whale and the air speed indicator leaped thirty miles past the dead line the inventor had given him. He was headed back toward the field now, in a shallow dive, and he pulled the stick back.

The wingtips buckled sharply; he flung the stick forward just before they ripped completely off, and he knew that only the speed of the dive kept him from falling like an inside out umbrella. And the speed was increasing: already he had overshot the field, under a thousand feet high. He pulled the stick back again; again the wingtips buckled and he slapped the stick over and kicked again into that wild skid, to check his speed. Again the machine swung its tail in a soaring arc, but this time the wings came off and he ducked his head automatically as one of them slapped viciously past it and crashed into the tail, shearing it too away.

3.

That day Narcissa's child was born, and the following day Simon drove Miss Jenny into town and set her down before the telegraph office and held the horses champing and tossing with gallant restiveness by a slight and surreptitious tightening of the reins, while beneath the tophat and the voluminous duster, he contrived by some means to actually strut sitting down. So Dr Peabody found him when he came along the street in the June sunlight, in his slovenly alpaca coat, carrying a newspaper.

"You look like a frog, Simon," he said. "Where's Miss Jenny?"

"Yessuh," Simon agreed. "Yessuh. Dey's swellin' en rejoicin' now. De little marster done arrive'. Yessuh, de little marster done arrive' and de ole times comin' back."

"Where's Miss Jenny?" Dr Peabody repeated impatiently.

"She in dar, tellygraftin' dat boy ter come on back hyer whar he belong at." Dr Peabody turned away and Simon watched him, a little fretted at his apathy in the face of the event. "Takes it jes' like trash," Simon mused aloud, with annoyed disparagement. "Nummine; we gwine wake 'um all up, now. Yessuh, de olden times comin' back ergain, sho'. Like in Mars' John's time, when de Cunnel wuz de young marster en de niggers fum de quawtuhs gethered on de front lawn, wishin' Mistis en de little marster well." And he watched Dr Peabody enter the door and through the plate glass window he saw him approach Miss Jenny as she stood at the counter with her message.

"Come home you fool and see your family or I will have you arrested" the message read in her firm, lucid script. "It's more than ten words," she told the operator, "but that dont matter this time. He'll come now: you watch. Or I'll send the sheriff after him, sure as his name's Sartoris."

"Yes, ma'am," the operator said. He was apparently having trouble reading it, and he looked up after a moment and was about to speak when Miss Jenny remarked his distraction and repeated the message briskly.

"And make it stronger than that, if you want to," she added.

"Yes, ma'am," he said again, and he ducked down behind his desk, and presently and with a little mounting curiosity and impatience Miss Jenny leaned across the counter with a silver dollar in her fingers and watched him count the words three times in a sort of painful flurry.

"What's the matter, young man?" she demanded. "The government dont forbid the mentioning of a day old child in a telegram, does it?"

The operator looked up. "Yes, ma'am, it's all right," he said at last, and she gave him the dollar, and as he sat holding it and Miss Jenny watched him with yet more impatience, Dr Peabody came in and touched her arm.

"Come away, Jenny," he said.

"Good morning," she said, turning at his voice. "Well, it's about time you took notice. This is the first Sartoris you've been a day late on in how many years, Loosh? And soon as I get that fool boy home, it'll be like old times again, as Simon says."

"Yes. Simon told me. Come along here."

"Let me get my change." She turned to the counter, where the operator stood with the message in one hand and the coin in the other. "Well, young man? Aint a dollar enough?"

"Yes, ma'am," he repeated, turning upon Dr Peabody his dumb, distracted eyes. Dr Peabody reached fatly and took the message and the coin from him.

"Come along, Jenny," he said again. Miss Jenny stood motionless for a moment, in her black silk dress and her black bonnet set squarely on her head, staring at him with her piercing old eyes that saw so much and so truly. Then she walked steadily to the door and stepped into the street and waited until he joined her, and her hand was steady too as she took the folded paper he offered. MISSISSIPPI AVIATOR it said in discreet capitals, and she returned it to him immediately and from her waist she took a small sheer handkerchief and wiped her fingers lightly.

"I dont have to read it," she said. "They never get into the papers but one way. And I know that he was somewhere he had no business being, doing something that wasn't any affair of his."

"Yes," Dr Peabody said. He followed her to the carriage and put his hands clumsily upon her as she mounted.

"Dont paw me, Loosh," she snapped. "I'm not a cripple." But he supported her elbow with his huge, gentle hand until she was seated, then he stood with his hat off while Simon laid the linen robe across her knees.

"Here," he said, and extended her the silver dollar and she returned it to her bag and clicked it shut and wiped her fingers again on her handkerchief.

"Well," she said. Then: "Thank God that's the last one. For a while, anyway. Home, Simon."

Simon sat magnificently, but under the occasion he unbent a little. "When you gwine come out en see de young marster, Doctuh?"

"Soon, Simon," he answered, and Simon clucked to the horses and wheeled away with a flourish, his hat tilted and the whip caught smartly back. Dr Peabody stood in the street, a shapeless hogshead of a man in a shabby alpaca coat, his hat in one hand and the folded newspaper and the yellow unsent message in the other, until Miss Jenny's straight slender back and the squarely indomitable angle of her bonnet had passed from sight.

But that was not the last one. One morning a week later, Simon was found in a negro cabin in town, his grizzled head crushed in by a blunt instrument anonymously wielded.

"In whose house?" Miss Jenny demanded into the telephone. In that of a woman named Meloney Harris, the voice

told her. Meloney   Mel   Belle Mitchell's face flashed
before her mind, and she remembered: the mulatto girl whose
smart apron and cap and lean shining shanks had lent such an
air to Belle's parties, and who had quit Belle in order to set up
a beauty parlor. Miss Jenny thanked the voice and hung up
the receiver.

"The old grayheaded reprobate," she said, and she went into
old Bayard's office and sat down. "So that's where that church
money went that he 'put out.' I wondered. . . . . . ." She sat
stiffly and uncompromisingly erect in her chair, her hands idle
on her lap. Well, that *is* the last one of 'em, she thought. But
no, he was hardly a Sartoris: he had at least some shadow of
a reason, while the others. . . . . . "I think," Miss Jenny said,
who had not spent a day in bed since she was forty years old,
"that I'll be sick for a while."

And she did just exactly that. Went to bed, where she lay
propped on pillows in a frivolous lace cap, and would permit
no doctor to see her save Dr Peabody who called once informally and sat sheepishly for thirty minutes while Miss Jenny
vented her invalid's spleen and the recurred anger of the salve
fiasco upon him. And here she held daily councils with Isom
and Elnora, and at the most unexpected moments she would
storm with unimpaired vigor from her window at Isom and
Caspey in the yard beneath.

The child and the placid, gaily turbaned mountain who superintended his hours, spent most of the day in this room, and
presently Narcissa herself; and the three of them would sit for
rapt murmurous hours in a sort of choral debauch of abnegation while the object of it slept digesting, waked, stoked himself anew and slept again.

"He's a Sartoris, all right," Miss Jenny said, "but an improved model. He hasn't got that wild look of 'em. I believe
it was the name. Bayard. We did well to name him Johnny."

"Yes," Narcissa said, watching her sleeping son with grave
and tranquil serenity.

And there Miss Jenny stayed until her while was up. Three
weeks it was. She set the date before she went to bed and
held to it stubbornly, refusing even to rise and attend the
christening. That day fell on Sunday. It was late in June and

jasmine drifted into the house in steady waves. Narcissa and the nurse, in an even more gaudy turban, had brought the baby, bathed and garnished and scented in his ceremonial robes, in to her, and later she heard them drive away in the carriage, and then the house was still again. The curtains stirred peacefully at the windows, and all the peaceful scents of summer came up on the sunny breeze, and sounds—birds, somewhere a Sabbath bell, and Elnora's voice, chastened a little by her recent bereavement but still rich and mellow as she went about getting dinner. She sang sadly and endlessly and without words as she moved about the kitchen, but she broke off short when she looked around and saw Miss Jenny looking a little frail but dressed and erect as ever, in the door.

"Miss Jenny! Whut in de worl'! You git on back to yo' bed. Here, lemme he'p you back." But Miss Jenny came firmly on.

"Where's Isom?" she demanded.

"He at de barn. You come on back to bed. I'm gwine tell Miss Narcissa on you."

"Get away," Miss Jenny said. "I'm tired staying in the house. I'm going to town. Call Isom." Elnora protested still, but Miss Jenny insisted coldly, and Elnora went to the door and called Isom and returned, portentous with pessimistic warnings, and presently Isom entered.

"Here," Miss Jenny said, handing him the keys. "Get the car out." Isom departed and Miss Jenny followed more slowly, and Elnora would have followed too, darkly solicitous, but Miss Jenny sent her back to her kitchen; and she crossed the yard and got in beside Isom. "And you drive this thing careful, boy," she told him, "or I'll get over there and do it myself."

When they reached town, from slender spires rising among trees against the puffy clouds of summer, bells were ringing lazily. At the edge of town Miss Jenny bade Isom turn into a grassy lane and they followed this and stopped presently before the iron gates to the cemetery. "I want to see if they fixed Simon all right," she explained. "I'm not going to church today: I've been shut up between walls long enough." Just from the prospect she got a mild exhilaration, like that of a small boy playing out of school.

The negro ground lay beyond the cemetery proper, and

Isom led her to Simon's grave. Simon's burying society had taken care of him, and after three weeks the mound was still heaped with floral designs from which the blooms had fallen, leaving a rank, lean mass of stems and peacefully rusting wire skeletons. Elnora, someone, had been before her, and the grave was bordered with tedious rows of broken gaudy bits of crockery and of colored glass. "I reckon he'll have to have a headstone, too," Miss Jenny said aloud, and turning, saw Isom hauling his overalled legs into a tree, about which two catbirds whirled and darted in scolding circles. "You, Isom."

"Yessum." Isom dropped obediently to the ground and the birds threatened him with a final burst of hysterical profanity. They entered the whitefolks' section and passed now between marble shapes bearing names that she knew well, and dates in a stark and peaceful simplicity in the impervious stone. Now and then they were surmounted by symbolical urns and doves and surrounded by clipped tended sward green against the blanched marble and the blue, dappled sky and the black cedars from amid which doves crooned endlessly reiterant. Here and there bright unfaded flowers lay in random bursts against the pattern of white and green; and presently John Sartoris lifted his stone back and his fulsome gesture amid a clump of cedars beyond which the bluff sheered sharply away into the valley.

Bayard's grave too was a shapeless mass of withered flowers, and Miss Jenny had Isom clear them off and carry them away. The masons were preparing to lay the curbing around it, and the headstone itself sat nearby beneath a canvas cover. She lifted the canvas and read the clean, new lettering: Bayard Sartoris. March 16, 1893 – June 11, 1920. That was better. Simple: no Sartoris man to invent bombast to put on it. Cant even lie dead in the ground without strutting and swaggering. Beside the grave was a second headstone; like the other save for the inscription. But the Sartoris touch was there, despite the fact that there was no grave to accompany it, and the whole thing was like a boastful voice in an empty church. Yet withal there was something else, as though the merry wild spirit of him who had laughed away so much of his heritage of humorless and fustian vainglory, managed somehow even yet, though his bones lay in an anonymous grave beyond the seas, to soften the arrogant gesture with which they had said him farewell:

> Lieut. John Sartoris, R.A.F.
> Killed in action, July 5, 1918.
> 'I bare him on eagles' wings and brought him unto Me'

A faint breeze soughed in the cedars like a long sigh, and the branches moved gravely in it. Across the spaced tranquillity of the marble shapes the doves crooned their endless rising inflections. Isom returned for another armful of withered flowers and bore it away.

Old Bayard's headstone was simple too, having been born, as he had, too late for one war and too soon for the next, and she thought what a joke They had played on him: forbidding him opportunities for swashbuckling and then denying him the privilege of being buried by men who would have invented vainglory for him. The cedars had almost overgrown his son John's and John's wife's graves. Sunlight reached them only in splashes, dappling the weathered stone with fitful stipplings; only with difficulty could the inscription have been deciphered. But she knew what it would be, what with the virus, the inspiration and the example of that one which dominated them all, which gave to the whole place in which weary people were supposed to be resting, an orotund solemnity having no more to do with mortality than the bindings of books have to do with their characters, and beneath which the headstones of the wives whom they had dragged into their arrogant orbits were, despite their pompous genealogical references, modest and effacing as the song of thrushes beneath the eyrie of an eagle.

He stood on a stone pedestal, in his frock coat and bareheaded, one leg slightly advanced and one hand resting lightly on the stone pylon beside him. His head was lifted a little in that gesture of haughty pride which repeated itself generation after generation with a fateful fidelity, his back to the world and his carven eyes gazing out across the valley where his railroad ran and the blue changeless hills beyond, and beyond that, the ramparts of infinity itself. The pedestal and effigy were mottled with seasons of rain and sun and with drippings

from the cedar branches, and the bold carving of the letters
was bleared with mold, yet still decipherable:

Colonel John Sartoris, C.S.A.
1823   1876
Soldier, Statesman, Citizen of the World
For man's enlightenment he lived
By man's ingratitude he died

Pause here, son of sorrow; remember death.

This inscription had caused some furore on the part of the
slayer's family, and a formal protest had followed. But in com-
plying with popular opinion, old Bayard had had his revenge:
he caused the line 'by man's ingratitude he died' to be chis-
elled crudely out and added beneath it: 'Fell at the hand of——
Redlaw, Sept. 4, 1876.'

Miss Jenny stood for a time, musing, a slender, erect figure
in black silk and a small uncompromising black bonnet. The
wind drew among the cedars in long sighs, and steadily as
pulses the sad hopeless reiteration of the doves came along the
sunny air. Isom returned for the last armful of dead flowers,
and looking out across the marble vistas where shadows of
noon moved, she watched a group of children playing quietly
and a little stiffly in their bright Sunday finery, among the
tranquil dead. Well, it was the last one, at last, gathered in
solemn conclave about the dying reverberation of their arrogant lusts, their dust moldering quietly beneath the pagan
symbols of their vainglory and the carven gestures of it in enduring stone; and she remembered something Narcissa had
said once, about a world without men, and wondered if
therein lay peaceful avenues and dwellings thatched with
quiet; and she didn't know.

Isom returned, and as they moved away Dr Peabody called
her name. He was dressed as usual in his shabby broadcloth
trousers and his shiny alpaca coat and a floppy panama hat,
and his son was with him.

"Well, boy," Miss Jenny said, giving young Loosh her hand.
His face was big-boned and roughly molded. He had a thatch
of straight, stiff black hair and his eyes were steady and brown
and his mouth was large; and in all his ugly face there was

reliability and gentleness and humor. He was rawboned and he wore his clothing awkwardly, and his hands were large and bony and with them he performed delicate surgical operations with the deftness of a hunter skinning a squirrel and with the celerity of a prestidigitator. He lived in New York, where he was associated with a surgeon whose name was a household word, and once a year and sometimes twice he rode thirty six hours on the train, spent twenty hours with his father (which they passed walking about town or riding about the countryside in the sagging buckboard all day, and sitting on the veranda or before the fire all night talking) and took the train again and ninety two hours later, was back at his clinic. He was thirty years old, only child of the woman Dr Peabody had courted for fourteen years before he was able to marry her. The courtship was during the days when he physicked and amputated the whole county by buckboard; often after a year's separation he would drive forty miles to see her, to be intercepted on the way and deflected to a childbed or a mangled limb, with only a scribbled message to assuage the interval of another year. "So you're home again, are you?" Miss Jenny asked.

"Yes, ma'am. And find you as spry and handsome as ever."

"Jenny's too bad-tempered to ever do anything but dry up and blow away," Dr Peabody said.

"You'll remember I never let you wait on me, when I'm not well," she retorted. "I reckon you'll be tearing off again on the next train, wont you?" she asked young Loosh.

"Yessum, I'm afraid so. My vacation hasn't come due, yet."

"Well, at this rate you'll spend it at an old men's home somewhere. Why dont you all come out and have dinner, so he can see the boy?"

"I'd like to," young Loosh answered, "but I dont have time to do all the things I want to, so I just make up my mind not to do any of 'em. Besides, I'll have to spend this afternoon fishing," he added.

"Yes," his father put in, "and choppin' up good fish with a pocket knife just to see what makes 'em go. Lemme tell you what he did this mawnin': he grabbed up that dawg that Abe shot last winter and laid its leg open and untangled them ligaments so quick that Abe not only didn't know what he was up to, but even the dawg didn't know it till it was too late to holler. Only you forgot to dig a little further for his soul," he added to his son.

"You dont know if he hasn't got one," young Loosh said, unruffled. "Dr Straud has been experimenting with electricity; he says he believes the soul——"

"Fiddlesticks," Miss Jenny interrupted. "You'd better get him a jar of Will Falls' salve to carry back to his doctor, Loosh. Well——" she glanced at the sun "—I'd better be going. If you wont come out to dinner——?"

"Thank you, ma'am," young Loosh answered. His father said:

"I brought him in to show him that collection of yours. We didn't know we looked that underfed."

"Help yourself," Miss Jenny answered. She went on, and they stood and watched her trim back until she passed out of sight beyond the cedars.

"And now there's another one," young Loosh said musingly. "Another one to grow up and keep his folks in a stew until he finally succeeds in doing what they all expect him to do. Well, maybe that Benbow blood will sort of hold him down. They're quiet folks, that girl; and Horace sort of . . . . and just women to raise him. . . . . . ."

His father grunted. "He's got Sartoris blood in him, too."

All of Narcissa's instincts had been antipathetic to him; his idea was a threat and his presence a violation of the very depths of her nature: in the headlong violence of him she had been like a lily in a gale which rocked it to its roots in a sort of vacuum, without any actual laying-on of hands. And now the gale had gone on; the lily had forgotten it as its fury died away into fading vibrations of old terrors and dreads, and the stalk recovered and the bell itself was untarnished save by the friction of its own petals. The gale is gone, and though the lily is sad a little vibration of ancient fears, it is not sorry.

Miss Jenny had arrived home, looking a little spent, and Narcissa had scolded her and at last prevailed on her to lie down after dinner. And here she had dozed while the drowsy afternoon wore away, and waked to lengthening shadows and a sound of piano keys touched softly below stairs. I've slept all afternoon, she told herself in a sort of consternation; yet she lay for a time yet while the curtains stirred faintly at the windows and the sound of the piano came up mingled with the jasmine from the garden and with the garrulous evensong of sparrows from the mulberry trees in the back yard. She rose and crossed the hall and entered Narcissa's room, where the child slept in its crib; beside him the nurse dozed placidly. Miss Jenny tiptoed out and descended the stairs and entered the parlor and drew her chair out from behind the piano. Narcissa stopped playing.

"Do you feel rested?" she asked. "You shouldn't have done that this morning."

"Fiddlesticks," Miss Jenny rejoined. "It always does me good to see all those fool pompous men lying there with their marble mottoes and things. Thank the Lord, none of 'em will have a chance at me. I reckon the Lord knows His business, but I declare, sometimes. . . . . . . Play something." Narcissa obeyed, touching the keys softly, and Miss Jenny sat listening for a while. The evening drew subtly onward; the shadows in the room grew more and more palpable. Outside the sparrows gossiped in shrill clouds. From the garden jasmine came in to them steady as breathing, and presently Miss Jenny roused and began to talk of the child. Narcissa played quietly on, her white dress with its black ribbon at the waist vaguely luminous in the dusk, with a hushed sheen like wax. Jasmine drifted and drifted; the sparrows were still now, and Miss Jenny talked on in the twilight about little Johnny while Narcissa played with rapt inattention, as though she were not listening. Then, without ceasing and without turning her head, she said:

"He isn't John. He's Benbow Sartoris."

"What?"

"His name is Benbow Sartoris," she repeated.

Miss Jenny sat quite still for a moment. In the next room Elnora moved about, laying the table for supper. "And do you think that'll do any good?" Miss Jenny demanded. "Do you think you can change one of 'em with a name?"

The music went on in the dusk softly; the dusk was peopled with ghosts of glamorous and old disastrous things. And if they were just glamorous enough, there was sure to be a

Sartoris in them, and then they were sure to be disastrous. Pawns. But the Player and the game He plays .... He must have a name for His pawns, though, but perhaps Sartoris is the game itself—a game outmoded and played with pawns shaped too late and to an old dead pattern, and of which the Player Himself is a little wearied. For there is death in the sound of it, and a glamorous fatality, like silver pennons downrushing at sunset, or a dying fall of horns along the road to Roncevaux.

"Do you think," Miss Jenny repeated, "that because his name is Benbow, he'll be any less a Sartoris and a scoundrel and a fool?"

Narcissa played on as though she were not listening. Then she turned her head and without stopping her hands, she smiled at Miss Jenny quietly, a little dreamily, with serene fond detachment. Beyond Miss Jenny's trim fading head the maroon curtains hung motionless; beyond the window evening was a windless lilac dream, foster-dam of quietude and peace.

THE SOUND AND THE FURY

April Seventh, 1928.

THROUGH the fence, between the curling flower spaces, I could see them hitting. They were coming toward where the flag was and I went along the fence. Luster was hunting in the grass by the flower tree. They took the flag out, and they were hitting. Then they put the flag back and they went to the table, and he hit and the other hit. Then they went on, and I went along the fence. Luster came away from the flower tree and we went along the fence and they stopped and we stopped and I looked through the fence while Luster was hunting in the grass.

"Here, caddie." He hit. They went away across the pasture. I held to the fence and watched them going away.

"Listen at you, now." Luster said. "Aint you something, thirty three years old, going on that way. After I done went all the way to town to buy you that cake. Hush up that moaning. Aint you going to help me find that quarter so I can go to the show tonight."

They were hitting little, across the pasture. I went back along the fence to where the flag was. It flapped on the bright grass and the trees.

"Come on." Luster said. "We done looked there. They aint no more coming right now. Les go down to the branch and find that quarter before them niggers finds it."

It was red, flapping on the pasture. Then there was a bird slanting and tilting on it. Luster threw. The flag flapped on the bright grass and the trees. I held to the fence.

"Shut up that moaning." Luster said. "I cant make them come if they aint coming, can I. If you dont hush up, mammy aint going to have no birthday for you. If you dont hush, you know what I going to do. I going to eat that cake all up. Eat them candles, too. Eat all them thirty three candles. Come on, les go down to the branch. I got to find my quarter. Maybe we can find one of they balls. Here. Here they is. Way over yonder. See." He came to the fence and pointed his arm. "See them. They aint coming back here no more. Come on."

We went along the fence and came to the garden fence, where our shadows were. My shadow was higher than Luster's on the fence. We came to the broken place and went through it.

"Wait a minute." Luster said. "You snagged on that nail again. Cant you never crawl through here without snagging on that nail."

Caddy uncaught me and we crawled through. Uncle Maury said to not let anybody see us, so we better stoop over, Caddy said. Stoop over, Benjy. Like this, see. We stooped over and crossed the garden, where the flowers rasped and rattled against us. The ground was hard. We climbed the fence, where the pigs were grunting and snuffing. I expect they're sorry because one of them got killed today, Caddy said. The ground was hard, churned and knotted.

Keep your hands in your pockets, Caddy said. Or they'll get froze. You dont want your hands froze on Christmas, do you.

"It's too cold out there." Versh said. "You dont want to go out doors."

"What is it now." Mother said.

"He want to go out doors." Versh said.

"Let him go." Uncle Maury said.

"It's too cold." Mother said. "He'd better stay in. Benjamin. Stop that, now."

"It wont hurt him." Uncle Maury said.

"You, Benjamin." Mother said. "If you dont be good, you'll have to go to the kitchen."

"Mammy say keep him out the kitchen today." Versh said. "She say she got all that cooking to get done."

"Let him go, Caroline." Uncle Maury said. "You'll worry yourself sick over him."

"I know it." Mother said. "It's a judgment on me. I sometimes wonder."

"I know, I know." Uncle Maury said. "You must keep your strength up. I'll make you a toddy."

"It just upsets me that much more." Mother said. "Dont you know it does."

"You'll feel better." Uncle Maury said. "Wrap him up good, boy, and take him out for a while."

Uncle Maury went away. Versh went away.

"Please hush." Mother said. "We're trying to get you out as fast as we can. I dont want you to get sick."

Versh put my overshoes and overcoat on and we took my cap and went out. Uncle Maury was putting the bottle away in the sideboard in the diningroom.

"Keep him out about half an hour, boy." Uncle Maury said. "Keep him in the yard, now."

"Yes, sir." Versh said. "We dont never let him get off the place."

We went out doors. The sun was cold and bright.

"Where you heading for." Versh said. "You dont think you going to town, does you." We went through the rattling leaves. The gate was cold. "You better keep them hands in your pockets." Versh said. "You get them froze onto that gate, then what you do. Whyn't you wait for them in the house." He put my hands into my pockets. I could hear him rattling in the leaves. I could smell the cold. The gate was cold.

"Here some hickeynuts. Whooey. Git up that tree. Look here at this squirl, Benjy."

I couldn't feel the gate at all, but I could smell the bright cold.

"You better put them hands back in your pockets."

Caddy was walking. Then she was running, her booksatchel swinging and jouncing behind her.

"Hello, Benjy." Caddy said. She opened the gate and came in and stooped down. Caddy smelled like leaves. "Did you come to meet me." she said. "Did you come to meet Caddy. What did you let him get his hands so cold for, Versh."

"I told him to keep them in his pockets." Versh said. "Holding on to that ahun gate."

"Did you come to meet Caddy." she said, rubbing my hands. "What is it. What are you trying to tell Caddy." Caddy smelled like trees and like when she says we were asleep.

What are you moaning about, Luster said. You can watch them again when we get to the branch. Here. Here's you a jimson weed. He gave me the flower. We went through the fence, into the lot.

"What is it." Caddy said. "What are you trying to tell Caddy. Did they send him out, Versh."

"Couldn't keep him in." Versh said. "He kept on until they let him go and he come right straight down here, looking through the gate."

"What is it." Caddy said. "Did you think it would be Christmas when I came home from school. Is that what you thought. Christmas is the day after tomorrow. Santy Claus, Benjy. Santy Claus. Come on, let's run to the house and get warm." She took my hand and we ran through the bright rustling leaves. We ran up the steps and out of the bright cold, into the dark cold. Uncle Maury was putting the bottle back in the sideboard. He called Caddy. Caddy said,

"Take him in to the fire, Versh. Go with Versh." she said. "I'll come in a minute."

We went to the fire. Mother said,

"Is he cold, Versh."

"Nome." Versh said.

"Take his overcoat and overshoes off." Mother said. "How many times do I have to tell you not to bring him into the house with his overshoes on."

"Yessum." Versh said. "Hold still, now." He took my overshoes off and unbuttoned my coat. Caddy said,

"Wait, Versh. Cant he go out again, Mother. I want him to go with me."

"You'd better leave him here." Uncle Maury said. "He's been out enough today."

"I think you'd both better stay in." Mother said. "It's getting colder, Dilsey says."

"Oh, Mother." Caddy said.

"Nonsense." Uncle Maury said. "She's been in school all day. She needs the fresh air. Run along, Candace."

"Let him go, Mother." Caddy said. "Please. You know he'll cry."

"Then why did you mention it before him." Mother said. "Why did you come in here. To give him some excuse to worry me again. You've been out enough today. I think you'd better sit down here and play with him."

"Let them go, Caroline." Uncle Maury said. "A little cold wont hurt them. Remember, you've got to keep your strength up."

"I know." Mother said. "Nobody knows how I dread Christmas. Nobody knows. I am not one of those women who can stand things. I wish for Jason's and the children's sakes I was stronger."

"You must do the best you can and not let them worry you." Uncle Maury said. "Run along, you two. But dont stay out long, now. Your mother will worry."

"Yes, sir." Caddy said. "Come on, Benjy. We're going out doors again." She buttoned my coat and we went toward the door.

"Are you going to take that baby out without his overshoes." Mother said. "Do you want to make him sick, with the house full of company."

"I forgot." Caddy said. "I thought he had them on."

We went back. "You must think." Mother said. *Hold still now* Versh said. He put my overshoes on. "Someday I'll be gone, and you'll have to think for him." *Now stomp* Versh said. "Come here and kiss Mother, Benjamin."

Caddy took me to Mother's chair and Mother took my face in her hands and then she held me against her.

"My poor baby." she said. She let me go. "You and Versh take good care of him, honey."

"Yessum." Caddy said. We went out. Caddy said,

"You needn't go, Versh. I'll keep him for a while."

"All right." Versh said. "I aint going out in that cold for no fun." He went on and we stopped in the hall and Caddy knelt and put her arms around me and her cold bright face against mine. She smelled like trees.

"You're not a poor baby. Are you. Are you. You've got your Caddy. Haven't you got your Caddy."

Cant you shut up that moaning and slobbering, Luster said. Aint you shamed of yourself, making all this racket. We passed the carriage house, where the carriage was. It had a new wheel.

"Git in, now, and set still until your maw come." Dilsey said. She shoved me into the carriage. T. P. held the reins. "Clare I dont see how come Jason wont get a new surrey." Dilsey said. "This thing going to fall to pieces under you all some day. Look at them wheels."

Mother came out, pulling her veil down. She had some flowers.

"Where's Roskus." she said.

"Roskus cant lift his arms, today." Dilsey said. "T. P. can drive all right."

"I'm afraid to." Mother said. "It seems to me you all could

furnish me with a driver for the carriage once a week. It's little enough I ask, Lord knows."

"You know just as well as me that Roskus got the rheumatism too bad to do more than he have to, Miss Cahline." Dilsey said. "You come on and get in, now. T. P. can drive you just as good as Roskus."

"I'm afraid to." Mother said. "With the baby."

Dilsey went up the steps. "You calling that thing a baby." she said. She took Mother's arm. "A man big as T. P. Come on, now, if you going."

"I'm afraid to." Mother said. They came down the steps and Dilsey helped Mother in. "Perhaps it'll be the best thing, for all of us." Mother said.

"Aint you shamed, talking that way." Dilsey said. "Dont you know it'll take more than a eighteen year old nigger to make Queenie run away. She older than him and Benjy put together. And dont you start no projecking with Queenie, you hear me. T. P. If you dont drive to suit Miss Cahline, I going to put Roskus on you. He aint too tied up to do that."

"Yessum." T. P. said.

"I just know something will happen." Mother said. "Stop, Benjamin."

"Give him a flower to hold." Dilsey said. "That what he wanting." She reached her hand in.

"No, no." Mother said. "You'll have them all scattered."

"You hold them." Dilsey said. "I'll get him one out." She gave me a flower and her hand went away.

"Go on now, fore Quentin see you and have to go too." Dilsey said.

"Where is she." Mother said.

"She down to the house playing with Luster." Dilsey said. "Go on, T. P. Drive that surrey like Roskus told you, now."

"Yessum." T. P. said. "Hum up, Queenie."

"Quentin." Mother said. "Dont let   "

"Course I is." Dilsey said.

The carriage jolted and crunched on the drive. "I'm afraid to go and leave Quentin." Mother said. "I'd better not go. T. P." We went through the gate, where it didn't jolt anymore. T. P. hit Queenie with the whip.

"You, T. P." Mother said.

"Got to get her going." T. P. said. "Keep her wake up till we get back to the barn."

"Turn around." Mother said. "I'm afraid to go and leave Quentin."

"Cant turn here." T. P. said. Then it was broader.

"Cant you turn here." Mother said.

"All right." T. P. said. We began to turn.

"You, T. P." Mother said, clutching me.

"I got to turn around some how." T. P. said. "Whoa, Queenie." We stopped.

"You'll turn us over." Mother said.

"What you want to do, then." T. P. said.

"I'm afraid for you to try to turn around." Mother said.

"Get up, Queenie." T. P. said. We went on.

"I just know Dilsey will let something happen to Quentin while I'm gone." Mother said. "We must hurry back."

"Hum up, there." T. P. said. He hit Queenie with the whip.

"You, T. P." Mother said, clutching me. I could hear Queenie's feet and the bright shapes went smooth and steady on both sides, the shadows of them flowing across Queenie's back. They went on like the bright tops of wheels. Then those on one side stopped at the tall white post where the soldier was. But on the other side they went on smooth and steady, but a little slower.

"What do you want." Jason said. He had his hands in his pockets and a pencil behind his ear.

"We're going to the cemetery." Mother said.

"All right." Jason said. "I dont aim to stop you, do I. Was that all you wanted with me, just to tell me that."

"I know you wont come." Mother said. "I'd feel safer if you would."

"Safe from what." Jason said. "Father and Quentin cant hurt you."

Mother put her handkerchief under her veil. "Stop it, Mother." Jason said. "Do you want to get that damn looney to bawling in the middle of the square. Drive on, T. P."

"Hum up, Queenie." T. P. said.

"It's a judgment on me." Mother said. "But I'll be gone too, soon."

"Here." Jason said.

"Whoa." T. P. said. Jason said,

"Uncle Maury's drawing on you for fifty. What do you want to do about it."

"Why ask me." Mother said. "I dont have any say so. I try not to worry you and Dilsey. I'll be gone soon, and then you   "

"Go on, T. P." Jason said.

"Hum up, Queenie." T. P. said. The shapes flowed on. The ones on the other side began again, bright and fast and smooth, like when Caddy says we are going to sleep.

Cry baby, Luster said. Aint you shamed. We went through the barn. The stalls were all open. You aint got no spotted pony to ride now, Luster said. The floor was dry and dusty. The roof was falling. The slanting holes were full of spinning yellow. What do you want to go that way, for. You want to get your head knocked off with one of them balls.

"Keep your hands in your pockets." Caddy said. "Or they'll be froze. You dont want your hands froze on Christmas, do you."

We went around the barn. The big cow and the little one were standing in the door, and we could hear Prince and Queenie and Fancy stomping inside the barn. "If it wasn't so cold, we'd ride Fancy." Caddy said. "But it's too cold to hold on today." Then we could see the branch, where the smoke was blowing. "That's where they are killing the pig." Caddy said. "We can come back by there and see them." We went down the hill.

"You want to carry the letter." Caddy said. "You can carry it." She took the letter out of her pocket and put it in mine. "It's a Christmas present." Caddy said. "Uncle Maury is going to surprise Mrs Patterson with it. We got to give it to her without letting anybody see it. Keep your hands in your pockets good, now." We came to the branch.

"It's froze." Caddy said. "Look." She broke the top of the water and held a piece of it against my face. "Ice. That means how cold it is." She helped me across and we went up the hill. "We cant even tell Mother and Father. You know what I think it is. I think it's a surprise for Mother and Father and Mr Patterson both, because Mr Patterson sent you some candy. Do you remember when Mr Patterson sent you some candy last summer."

There was a fence. The vine was dry, and the wind rattled in it.

"Only I dont see why Uncle Maury didn't send Versh." Caddy said. "Versh wont tell." Mrs Patterson was looking out the window. "You wait here." Caddy said. "Wait right here, now. I'll be back in a minute. Give me the letter." She took the letter out of my pocket. "Keep your hands in your pockets." She climbed the fence with the letter in her hand and went through the brown, rattling flowers. Mrs Patterson came to the door and opened it and stood there.

Mr Patterson was chopping in the green flowers. He stopped chopping and looked at me. Mrs Patterson came across the garden, running. When I saw her eyes I began to cry. You idiot, Mrs Patterson said, I told him never to send you alone again. Give it to me. Quick. Mr Patterson came fast, with the hoe. Mrs Patterson leaned across the fence, reaching her hand. She was trying to climb the fence. Give it to me, she said, Give it to me. Mr Patterson climbed the fence. He took the letter. Mrs Patterson's dress was caught on the fence. I saw her eyes again and I ran down the hill.

"They aint nothing over yonder but houses." Luster said. "We going down to the branch."

They were washing down at the branch. One of them was singing. I could smell the clothes flapping, and the smoke blowing across the branch.

"You stay down here." Luster said. "You aint got no business up yonder. Them folks hit you, sho."

"What he want to do."

"He dont know what he want to do." Luster said. "He think he want to go up yonder where they knocking that ball. You sit down here and play with your jimson weed. Look at them chillen playing in the branch, if you got to look at something. How come you cant behave yourself like folks." I sat down on the bank, where they were washing, and the smoke blowing blue.

"Is you all seen anything of a quarter down here." Luster said.

"What quarter."

"The one I had here this morning." Luster said. "I lost it somewhere. It fell through this here hole in my pocket. If I dont find it I cant go to the show tonight."

"Where'd you get a quarter, boy. Find it in white folks' pocket while they aint looking."

"Got it at the getting place." Luster said. "Plenty more where that one come from. Only I got to find that one. Is you all found it yet."

"I aint studying no quarter. I got my own business to tend to."

"Come on here." Luster said. "Help me look for it."

"He wouldn't know a quarter if he was to see it, would he."

"He can help look just the same." Luster said. "You all going to the show tonight."

"Dont talk to me about no show. Time I get done over this here tub I be too tired to lift my hand to do nothing."

"I bet you be there." Luster said. "I bet you was there last night. I bet you all be right there when that tent open."

"Be enough niggers there without me. Was last night."

"Nigger's money good as white folks, I reckon."

"White folks gives nigger money because know first white man comes along with a band going to get it all back, so nigger can go to work for some more."

"Aint nobody going make you go to that show."

"Aint yet. Aint thought of it, I reckon."

"What you got against white folks."

"Aint got nothing against them. I goes my way and lets white folks go theirs. I aint studying that show."

"Got a man in it can play a tune on a saw. Play it like a banjo."

"You go last night." Luster said. "I going tonight. If I can find where I lost that quarter."

"You going take him with you, I reckon."

"Me." Luster said. "You reckon I be found anywhere with him, time he start bellering."

"What does you do when he start bellering."

"I whips him." Luster said. He sat down and rolled up his overalls. They played in the branch.

"You all found any balls yet." Luster said.

"Aint you talking biggity. I bet you better not let your grandmammy hear you talking like that."

Luster got into the branch, where they were playing. He hunted in the water, along the bank.

"I had it when we was down here this morning." Luster said.

"Where bouts you lose it."

"Right out this here hole in my pocket." Luster said. They hunted in the branch. Then they all stood up quick and stopped, then they splashed and fought in the branch. Luster got it and they squatted in the water, looking up the hill through the bushes.

"Where is they." Luster said.

"Aint in sight yet."

Luster put it in his pocket. They came down the hill.

"Did a ball come down here."

"It ought to be in the water. Didn't any of you boys see it or hear it."

"Aint heard nothing come down here." Luster said. "Heard something hit that tree up yonder. Dont know which way it went."

They looked in the branch.

"Hell. Look along the branch. It came down here. I saw it."

They looked along the branch. Then they went back up the hill.

"Have you got that ball." the boy said.

"What I want with it." Luster said. "I aint seen no ball."

The boy got in the water. He went on. He turned and looked at Luster again. He went on down the branch.

The man said "Caddie" up the hill. The boy got out of the water and went up the hill.

"Now, just listen at you." Luster said. "Hush up."

"What he moaning about now."

"Lawd knows." Luster said. "He just starts like that. He been at it all morning. Cause it his birthday, I reckon."

"How old he."

"He thirty three." Luster said. "Thirty three this morning."

"You mean, he been three years old thirty years."

"I going by what mammy say." Luster said. "I dont know. We going to have thirty three candles on a cake, anyway. Little cake. Wont hardly hold them. Hush up. Come on back here." He came and caught my arm. "You old looney." he said. "You want me to whip you."

"I bet you will."

"I is done it. Hush, now." Luster said. "Aint I told you you cant go up there. They'll knock your head clean off with one of them balls. Come on, here." He pulled me back. "Sit down." I sat down and he took off my shoes and rolled up my trousers. "Now, git in that water and play and see can you stop that slobbering and moaning."

I hushed and got in the water *and Roskus came and said to come to supper and Caddy said,*

It's not supper time yet. I'm not going.

She was wet. We were playing in the branch and Caddy squatted down and got her dress wet and Versh said,

"Your mommer going to whip you for getting your dress wet."

"She's not going to do any such thing." Caddy said.

"How do you know." Quentin said.

"That's all right how I know." Caddy said. "How do you know."

"She said she was." Quentin said. "Besides, I'm older than you."

"I'm seven years old." Caddy said. "I guess I know."

"I'm older than that." Quentin said. "I go to school. Dont I, Versh."

"I'm going to school next year." Caddy said. "When it comes. Aint I, Versh."

"You know she whip you when you get your dress wet." Versh said.

"It's not wet." Caddy said. She stood up in the water and looked at her dress. "I'll take it off." she said. "Then it'll dry."

"I bet you wont." Quentin said.

"I bet I will." Caddy said.

"I bet you better not." Quentin said.

Caddy came to Versh and me and turned her back.

"Unbutton it, Versh." she said.

"Dont you do it, Versh." Quentin said.

"Taint none of my dress." Versh said.

"You unbutton it, Versh." Caddy said. "Or I'll tell Dilsey what you did yesterday." So Versh unbuttoned it.

"You just take your dress off." Quentin said. Caddy took her dress off and threw it on the bank. Then she didn't have on anything but her bodice and drawers, and Quentin slapped her and she slipped and fell down in the water. When she got up she began to splash water on Quentin, and Quentin splashed water on Caddy. Some of it splashed on Versh and me and Versh picked me up and put me on the bank. He said he was going to tell on Caddy and Quentin, and then Quentin and Caddy began to splash water at Versh. He got behind a bush.

"I'm going to tell mammy on you all." Versh said.

Quentin climbed up the bank and tried to catch Versh, but Versh ran away and Quentin couldn't. When Quentin came back Versh stopped and hollered that he was going to tell. Caddy told him that if he wouldn't tell, they'd let him come back. So Versh said he wouldn't, and they let him.

"Now I guess you're satisfied." Quentin said. "We'll both get whipped now."

"I dont care." Caddy said. "I'll run away."

"Yes you will." Quentin said.

"I'll run away and never come back." Caddy said. I began to cry. Caddy turned around and said "Hush" So I hushed. Then they played in the branch. Jason was playing too. He was by himself further down the branch. Versh came around the bush and lifted me down into the water again. Caddy was all wet and muddy behind, and I started to cry and she came and squatted in the water.

"Hush now." she said. "I'm not going to run away." So I hushed. Caddy smelled like trees in the rain.

What is the matter with you, Luster said. Cant you get done with that moaning and play in the branch like folks.

Whyn't you take him on home. Didn't they told you not to take him off the place.

He still think they own this pasture, Luster said. Cant nobody see down here from the house, noways.

We can. And folks dont like to look at a looney. Taint no luck in it.

Roskus came and said to come to supper and Caddy said it wasn't supper time yet.

"Yes tis." Roskus said. "Dilsey say for you all to come on to the house. Bring them on, Versh." He went up the hill, where the cow was lowing.

"Maybe we'll be dry by the time we get to the house." Quentin said.

"It was all your fault." Caddy said. "I hope we do get whipped." She put her dress on and Versh buttoned it.

"They wont know you got wet." Versh said. "It dont show on you. Less me and Jason tells."

"Are you going to tell, Jason." Caddy said.

"Tell on who." Jason said.

"He wont tell." Quentin said. "Will you, Jason."

"I bet he does tell." Caddy said. "He'll tell Damuddy."

"He cant tell her." Quentin said. "She's sick. If we walk slow it'll be too dark for them to see."

"I dont care whether they see or not." Caddy said. "I'm going to tell, myself. You carry him up the hill, Versh."

"Jason wont tell." Quentin said. "You remember that bow and arrow I made you, Jason."

"It's broke now." Jason said.

"Let him tell." Caddy said. "I dont give a cuss. Carry Maury up the hill, Versh." Versh squatted and I got on his back.

See you all at the show tonight, Luster said. Come on, here. We got to find that quarter.

"If we go slow, it'll be dark when we get there." Quentin said.

"I'm not going slow." Caddy said. We went up the hill, but Quentin didn't come. He was down at the branch when we got to where we could smell the pigs. They were grunting and snuffing in the trough in the corner. Jason came behind us, with his hands in his pockets. Roskus was milking the cow in the barn door.

The cows came jumping out of the barn.

"Go on." T. P. said. "Holler again. I going to holler myself. Whooey." Quentin kicked T. P. again. He kicked T. P. into the trough where the pigs ate and T. P. lay there. "Hot dog." T. P. said. "Didn't he get me then. You see that white man kick me that time. Whooey."

I wasn't crying, but I couldn't stop. I wasn't crying, but the ground wasn't still, and then I was crying. The ground kept sloping up and the cows ran up the hill. T. P. tried to get up. He fell down again and the cows ran down the hill. Quentin held my arm and we went toward the barn. Then the barn wasn't there and we had to wait until it came back. I didn't see it come back. It came behind us and Quentin set me down in the trough where the cows ate. I held on to it. It was going away too, and I held to it. The cows ran down the hill again, across the door. I couldn't stop. Quentin and T. P. came up the hill, fighting. T. P. was falling down the hill and Quentin dragged him up the hill. Quentin hit T. P. I couldn't stop.

"Stand up." Quentin said. "You stay right here. Dont you go away until I get back."

"Me and Benjy going back to the wedding." T. P. said. "Whooey."

Quentin hit T. P. again. Then he began to thump T. P. against the wall. T. P. was laughing. Every time Quentin thumped him against the wall he tried to say Whooey, but he couldn't say it for laughing. I quit crying, but I couldn't stop. T. P. fell on me and the barn door went away. It went down the hill and T. P. was fighting by himself and he fell down again. He was still laughing, and I couldn't stop, and I tried to get up and I fell down, and I couldn't stop. Versh said,

"You sho done it now. I'll declare if you aint. Shut up that yelling."

T. P. was still laughing. He flopped on the door and laughed. "Whooey." he said. "Me and Benjy going back to the wedding. Sassprilluh." T. P. said.

"Hush." Versh said. "Where you get it."

"Out the cellar." T. P. said. "Whooey."

"Hush up." Versh said. "Where bouts in the cellar."

"Anywhere." T. P. said. He laughed some more. "Moren a hundred bottles lef. Moren a million. Look out, nigger, I going to holler."

Quentin said, "Lift him up."

Versh lifted me up.

"Drink this, Benjy." Quentin said. The glass was hot. "Hush, now." Quentin said. "Drink it."

"Sassprilluh." T. P. said. "Lemme drink it, Mr Quentin."

"You shut your mouth." Versh said. "Mr Quentin wear you out."

"Hold him, Versh." Quentin said.

They held me. It was hot on my chin and on my shirt. "Drink." Quentin said. They held my head. It was hot inside me, and I began again. I was crying now, and something was happening inside me and I cried more, and they held me until it stopped happening. Then I hushed. It was still going around, and then the shapes began. Open the crib, Versh. They were going slow. Spread those empty sacks on the floor. They were going faster, almost fast enough. Now. Pick up his feet. They went on, smooth and bright. I could hear T. P. laughing. I went on with them, up the bright hill.

At the top of the hill Versh put me down. "Come on here, Quentin." he called, looking back down the hill. Quentin was still standing there by the branch. He was chunking into the shadows where the branch was.

"Let the old skizzard stay there." Caddy said. She took my hand and we went on past the barn and through the gate. There was a frog on the brick walk, squatting in the middle of it. Caddy stepped over it and pulled me on.

"Come on, Maury." she said. It still squatted there until Jason poked at it with his toe.

"He'll make a wart on you." Versh said. The frog hopped away.

"Come on, Maury." Caddy said.

"They got company tonight." Versh said.

"How do you know." Caddy said.

"With all them lights on." Versh said. "Light in every window."

"I reckon we can turn all the lights on without company, if we want to." Caddy said.

"I bet it's company." Versh said. "You all better go in the back and slip upstairs."

"I dont care." Caddy said. "I'll walk right in the parlor where they are."

"I bet your pappy whip you if you do." Versh said.

"I dont care." Caddy said. "I'll walk right in the parlor. I'll walk right in the dining room and eat supper."

"Where you sit." Versh said.

"I'd sit in Damuddy's chair." Caddy said. "She eats in bed."

"I'm hungry." Jason said. He passed us and ran on up the walk. He had his hands in his pockets and he fell down. Versh went and picked him up.

"If you keep them hands out your pockets, you could stay on your feet." Versh said. "You cant never get them out in time to catch yourself, fat as you is."

Father was standing by the kitchen steps.

"Where's Quentin." he said.

"He coming up the walk." Versh said. Quentin was coming slow. His shirt was a white blur.

"Oh." Father said. Light fell down the steps, on him.

"Caddy and Quentin threw water on each other." Jason said. We waited.

"They did." Father said. Quentin came, and Father said, "You can eat supper in the kitchen tonight." He stooped and took me up, and the light came tumbling down the steps on me too, and I could look down at Caddy and Jason and Quentin and Versh. Father turned toward the steps. "You must be quiet, though." he said.

"Why must we be quiet, Father." Caddy said. "Have we got company."

"Yes." Father said.

"I told you they was company." Versh said.

"You did not." Caddy said. "I was the one that said there was. I said I would   "

"Hush." Father said. They hushed and Father opened the door and we crossed the back porch and went in to the kitchen. Dilsey was there, and Father put me in the chair and closed the apron down and pushed it to the table, where supper was. It was steaming up.

"You mind Dilsey, now." Father said. "Dont let them make any more noise than they can help, Dilsey."

"Yes, sir." Dilsey said. Father went away.

"Remember to mind Dilsey, now." he said behind us. I leaned my face over where the supper was. It steamed up on my face.

"Let them mind me tonight, Father." Caddy said.

"I wont." Jason said. "I'm going to mind Dilsey."

"You'll have to, if Father says so." Caddy said. "Let them mind me, Father."

"I wont." Jason said. "I wont mind you."

"Hush." Father said. "You all mind Caddy, then. When they are done, bring them up the back stairs, Dilsey."

"Yes, sir." Dilsey said.

"There." Caddy said. "Now I guess you'll mind me."

"You all hush, now." Dilsey said. "You got to be quiet tonight."

"Why do we have to be quiet tonight." Caddy whispered.

"Never you mind." Dilsey said. "You'll know in the Lawd's own time." She brought my bowl. The steam from it came and tickled my face. "Come here, Versh." Dilsey said.

"When is the Lawd's own time, Dilsey." Caddy said.

"It's Sunday." Quentin said. "Dont you know anything."

"Shhhhhh." Dilsey said. "Didn't Mr Jason say for you all to be quiet. Eat your supper, now. Here, Versh. Git his spoon." Versh's hand came with the spoon, into the bowl. The spoon came up to my mouth. The steam tickled into my mouth. Then we quit eating and we looked at each other and we were quiet, and then we heard it again and I began to cry.

"What was that." Caddy said. She put her hand on my hand.

"That was Mother." Quentin said. The spoon came up and I ate, then I cried again.

"Hush." Caddy said. But I didn't hush and she came and put her arms around me. Dilsey went and closed both the doors and then we couldn't hear it.

"Hush, now." Caddy said. I hushed and ate. Quentin wasn't eating, but Jason was.

"That was Mother." Quentin said. He got up.

"You set right down." Dilsey said. "They got company in there, and you in them muddy clothes. You set down too, Caddy, and get done eating."

"She was crying." Quentin said.

"It was somebody singing." Caddy said. "Wasn't it, Dilsey."

"You all eat your supper, now, like Mr Jason said." Dilsey said. "You'll know in the Lawd's own time." Caddy went back to her chair.

"I told you it was a party." she said.

Versh said, "He done et all that."

"Bring his bowl here." Dilsey said. The bowl went away.

"Dilsey." Caddy said. "Quentin's not eating his supper. Hasn't he got to mind me."

"Eat your supper, Quentin." Dilsey said. "You all got to get done and get out of my kitchen."

"I dont want any more supper." Quentin said.

"You've got to eat if I say you have." Caddy said. "Hasn't he, Dilsey."

The bowl steamed up to my face, and Versh's hand dipped the spoon in it and the steam tickled into my mouth.

"I dont want any more." Quentin said. "How can they have a party when Damuddy's sick."

"They'll have it down stairs." Caddy said. "She can come to the landing and see it. That's what I'm going to do when I get my nightie on."

"Mother was crying." Quentin said. "Wasn't she crying, Dilsey."

"Dont you come pestering at me, boy." Dilsey said. "I got to get supper for all them folks soon as you all get done eating."

After a while even Jason was through eating, and he began to cry.

"Now you got to tune up." Dilsey said.

"He does it every night since Damuddy was sick and he cant sleep with her." Caddy said. "Cry baby."

"I'm going to tell on you." Jason said.

He was crying. "You've already told." Caddy said. "There's not anything else you can tell, now."

"You all needs to go to bed." Dilsey said. She came and lifted me down and wiped my face and hands with a warm cloth. "Versh, can you get them up the back stairs quiet. You, Jason, shut up that crying."

"It's too early to go to bed now." Caddy said. "We dont ever have to go to bed this early."

"You is tonight." Dilsey said. "Your paw say for you to come right on up stairs when you et supper. You heard him."

"He said to mind me." Caddy said.

"I'm not going to mind you." Jason said.

"You have to." Caddy said. "Come on, now. You have to do like I say."

"Make them be quiet, Versh." Dilsey said. "You all going to be quiet, aint you."

"What do we have to be so quiet for, tonight." Caddy said.

"Your mommer aint feeling well." Dilsey said. "You all go on with Versh, now."

"I told you Mother was crying." Quentin said. Versh took me up and opened the door onto the back porch. We went out and Versh closed the door black. I could smell Versh and feel him. You all be quiet, now. We're not going up stairs yet. Mr Jason said for you to come right up stairs. He said to mind me. I'm not going to mind you. But he said for all of us to. Didn't he, Quentin. I could feel Versh's head. I could hear us. Didn't he, Versh. Yes, that right. Then I say for us to go out doors a while. Come on. Versh opened the door and we went out.

We went down the steps.

"I expect we'd better go down to Versh's house, so we'll be quiet." Caddy said. Versh put me down and Caddy took my hand and we went down the brick walk.

"Come on." Caddy said. "That frog's gone. He's hopped way over to the garden, by now. Maybe we'll see another one." Roskus came with the milk buckets. He went on. Quentin wasn't coming with us. He was sitting on the kitchen steps. We went down to Versh's house. I liked to smell Versh's house. *There was a fire in it and T. P. squatting in his shirt tail in front of it, chunking it into a blaze.*

Then I got up and T. P. dressed me and we went to the kitchen and ate. Dilsey was singing and I began to cry and she stopped.

"Keep him away from the house, now." Dilsey said.

"We cant go that way." T. P. said.

We played in the branch.

"We cant go around yonder." T. P. said. "Dont you know mammy say we cant."

Dilsey was singing in the kitchen and I began to cry.

"Hush." T. P. said. "Come on. Les go down to the barn."

Roskus was milking at the barn. He was milking with one hand, and groaning. Some birds sat on the barn door and watched him. One of them came down and ate with the cows. I watched Roskus milk while T. P. was feeding Queenie and Prince. The calf was in the pig pen. It nuzzled at the wire, bawling.

"T. P." Roskus said. T. P. said Sir, in the barn. Fancy held her head over the door, because T. P. hadn't fed her yet. "Git done there." Roskus said. "You got to do this milking. I cant use my right hand no more."

T. P. came and milked.

"Whyn't you get the doctor." T. P. said.

"Doctor cant do no good." Roskus said. "Not on this place."

"What wrong with this place." T. P. said.

"Taint no luck on this place." Roskus said. "Turn that calf in if you done."

Taint no luck on this place, Roskus said. The fire rose and fell behind him and Versh, sliding on his and Versh's face. Dilsey finished putting me to bed. The bed smelled like T. P.   I liked it.

"What you know about it." Dilsey said. "What trance you been in."

"Dont need no trance." Roskus said. "Aint the sign of it laying right there on that bed. Aint the sign of it been here for folks to see fifteen years now."

"Spose it is." Dilsey said. "It aint hurt none of you and yourn, is it. Versh working and Frony married off your hands and T. P. getting big enough to take your place when rheumatism finish getting you."

"They been two, now." Roskus said. "Going to be one more. I seen the sign, and you is too."

"I heard a squinch owl that night." T. P. said. "Dan wouldn't come and get his supper, neither. Wouldn't come no closer than the barn. Begun howling right after dark. Versh heard him."

"Going to be more than one more." Dilsey said. "Show me the man what aint going to die, bless Jesus."

"Dying aint all." Roskus said.

"I knows what you thinking." Dilsey said. "And they aint going to be no luck in saying that name, lessen you going to set up with him while he cries."

"They aint no luck on this place." Roskus said. "I seen it at first but when they changed his name I knowed it."

"Hush your mouth." Dilsey said. She pulled the covers up. It smelled like T. P. "You all shut up now, till he get to sleep."

"I seen the sign." Roskus said.

"Sign T. P. got to do all your work for you." Dilsey said. *Take him and Quentin down to the house and let them play with Luster, where Frony can watch them, T. P., and go and help your paw.*

We finished eating. T. P. took Quentin up and we went down to T. P.'s house. Luster was playing in the dirt. T. P. put Quentin down and she played in the dirt too. Luster had some spools and he and Quentin fought and Quentin had the spools. Luster cried and Frony came and gave Luster a tin can to play with, and then I had the spools and Quentin fought me and I cried.

"Hush." Frony said. "Aint you shamed of yourself. Taking a baby's play pretty." She took the spools from me and gave them back to Quentin.

"Hush, now." Frony said. "Hush, I tell you."

"Hush up." Frony said. "You needs whipping, that's what you needs." She took Luster and Quentin up. "Come on here." she said. We went to the barn. T. P. was milking the cow. Roskus was sitting on the box.

"What's the matter with him now." Roskus said.

"You have to keep him down here." Frony said. "He fighting these babies again. Taking they play things. Stay here with T. P. now, and see can you hush a while."

"Clean that udder good now." Roskus said. "You milked that young cow dry last winter. If you milk this one dry, they aint going to be no more milk."

Dilsey was singing.

"Not around yonder." T. P. said. "Dont you know mammy say you cant go around there."

They were singing.

"Come on." T. P. said. "Les go play with Quentin and Luster. Come on."

Quentin and Luster were playing in the dirt in front of T. P.'s house. There was a fire in the house, rising and falling, with Roskus sitting black against it.

"That's three, thank the Lawd." Roskus said. "I told you two years ago. They aint no luck on this place."

"Whyn't you get out, then." Dilsey said. She was undressing me. "Your bad luck talk got them Memphis notions into Versh. That ought to satisfy you."

"If that all the bad luck Versh have." Roskus said.

Frony came in.

"You all done." Dilsey said.

"T. P. finishing up." Frony said. "Miss Cahline want you to put Quentin to bed."

"I'm coming just as fast as I can." Dilsey said. "She ought to know by this time I aint got no wings."

"That's what I tell you." Roskus said. "They aint no luck going be on no place where one of they own chillen's name aint never spoke."

"Hush." Dilsey said. "Do you want to get him started."

"Raising a child not to know its own mammy's name." Roskus said.

"Dont you bother your head about her." Dilsey said. "I raised all of them and I reckon I can raise one more. Hush, now. Let him get to sleep if he will."

"Saying a name." Frony said. "He dont know nobody's name."

"You just say it and see if he dont." Dilsey said. "You say it to him while he sleeping and I bet he hear you."

"He know lot more than folks thinks." Roskus said. "He knowed they time was coming, like that pointer done. He could tell you when hisn coming, if he could talk. Or yours. Or mine."

"You take Luster outen that bed, mammy." Frony said. "That boy conjure him."

"Hush your mouth." Dilsey said. "Aint you got no better sense than that. What you want to listen to Roskus for, anyway. Get in, Benjy."

Dilsey pushed me and I got in the bed, where Luster already was. He was asleep. Dilsey took a long piece of wood and laid it between Luster and me. "Stay on your side now." Dilsey said. "Luster little, and you dont want to hurt him."

You cant go yet, T. P. said. Wait.

We looked around the corner of the house and watched the carriages go away.

"Now." T. P. said. He took Quentin up and we ran down to the corner of the fence and watched them pass. "There he go." T. P. said. "See that one with the glass in it. Look at him. He laying in there. See him."

Come on, Luster said, I going to take this here ball down home, where I wont lose it. Naw, sir, you cant have it. If them men sees you with it, they'll say you stole it. Hush up, now. You cant have it. What business you got with it. You cant play no ball.

Frony and T. P. were playing in the dirt by the door. T. P. had lightning bugs in a bottle.

"How did you all get back out." Frony said.

"We've got company." Caddy said. "Father said for us to mind me tonight. I expect you and T. P. will have to mind me too."

"I'm not going to mind you." Jason said. "Frony and T. P. dont have to either."

"They will if I say so." Caddy said. "Maybe I wont say for them to."

"T. P. dont mind nobody." Frony said. "Is they started the funeral yet."

"What's a funeral." Jason said.

"Didn't mammy tell you not to tell them." Versh said.

"Where they moans." Frony said. "They moaned two days on Sis Beulah Clay."

They moaned at Dilsey's house. Dilsey was moaning. When Dilsey moaned Luster said, Hush, and we hushed, and then I began to cry and Blue howled under the kitchen steps. Then Dilsey stopped and we stopped.

"Oh." Caddy said. "That's niggers. White folks dont have funerals."

"Mammy said us not to tell them, Frony." Versh said.

"Tell them what." Caddy said.

Dilsey moaned, and when it got to the place I began to cry and Blue howled under the steps. Luster, Frony said in the window. Take them down to the barn. I cant get no cooking done with all that racket. That hound too. Get them outen here.

I aint going down there, Luster said. I might meet pappy down there. I seen him last night, waving his arms in the barn.

"I like to know why not." Frony said. "White folks dies too. Your grandmammy dead as any nigger can get, I reckon."

"Dogs are dead." Caddy said. "And when Nancy fell in the ditch and Roskus shot her and the buzzards came and undressed her."

The bones rounded out of the ditch, where the dark vines were in the black ditch, into the moonlight, like some of the shapes had stopped. Then they all stopped and it was dark, and when I stopped to start again I could hear Mother, and feet walking fast away, and I could smell it. Then the room came, but my eyes went shut. I didn't stop. I could smell it. T. P. unpinned the bed clothes.

"Hush." he said. "Shhhhhhhh."

But I could smell it. T. P. pulled me up and he put on my clothes fast.

"Hush, Benjy." he said. "We going down to our house. You want to go down to our house, where Frony is. Hush. Shhhhh."

He laced my shoes and put my cap on and we went out. There was a light in the hall. Across the hall we could hear Mother.

"Shhhhhh, Benjy." T. P. said. "We'll be out in a minute."

A door opened and I could smell it more than ever, and a head came out. It wasn't Father. Father was sick there.

"Can you take him out of the house."

"That's where we going." T. P. said. Dilsey came up the stairs.

"Hush." she said. "Hush. Take him down home, T. P. Frony fixing him a bed. You all look after him, now. Hush, Benjy. Go on with T. P."

She went where we could hear Mother.

"Better keep him there." It wasn't Father. He shut the door, but I could still smell it.

We went down stairs. The stairs went down into the dark and T. P. took my hand, and we went out the door, out of the dark. Dan was sitting in the back yard, howling.

"He smell it." T. P. said. "Is that the way you found it out."

We went down the steps, where our shadows were.

"I forgot your coat." T. P. said. "You ought to had it. But I aint going back."

Dan howled.

"Hush now." T. P. said. Our shadows moved, but Dan's shadow didn't move except to howl when he did.

"I cant take you down home, bellering like you is." T. P. said. "You was bad enough before you got that bullfrog voice. Come on."

We went along the brick walk, with our shadows. The pig pen smelled like pigs. The cow stood in the lot, chewing at us. Dan howled.

"You going to wake the whole town up." T. P. said. "Cant you hush."

We saw Fancy, eating by the branch. The moon shone on the water when we got there.

"Naw, sir." T. P. said. "This too close. We cant stop here.
Come on. Now, just look at you. Got your whole leg wet.
Come on, here." Dan howled.

The ditch came up out of the buzzing grass. The bones
rounded out of the black vines.

"Now." T. P. said. "Beller your head off if you want to. You
got the whole night and a twenty acre pasture to beller in."

T. P. lay down in the ditch and I sat down, watching the
bones where the buzzards ate Nancy, flapping black and slow
and heavy out of the ditch.

*I had it when we was down here before, Luster said. I showed it
to you. Didn't you see it. I took it out of my pocket right here and
showed it to you.*

"Do you think buzzards are going to undress Damuddy."
Caddy said. "You're crazy."

"You're a skizzard." Jason said. He began to cry.

"You're a knobnot." Caddy said. Jason cried. His hands
were in his pockets.

"Jason going to be rich man." Versh said. "He holding his
money all the time."

Jason cried.

"Now you've got him started." Caddy said. "Hush up,
Jason. How can buzzards get in where Damuddy is. Father
wouldn't let them. Would you let a buzzard undress you.
Hush up, now."

Jason hushed. "Frony said it was a funeral." he said.

"Well it's not." Caddy said. "It's a party. Frony dont know
anything about it. He wants your lightning bugs, T. P. Let
him hold it a while."

T. P. gave me the bottle of lightning bugs.

"I bet if we go around to the parlor window we can see
something." Caddy said. "Then you'll believe me."

"I already knows." Frony said. "I dont need to see."

"You better hush your mouth, Frony." Versh said. "Mammy
going whip you."

"What is it." Caddy said.

"I knows what I knows." Frony said.

"Come on." Caddy said. "Let's go around to the front."

We started to go.

"T. P. wants his lightning bugs." Frony said.

"Let him hold it a while longer, T. P." Caddy said. "We'll bring it back."

"You all never caught them." Frony said.

"If I say you and T. P. can come too, will you let him hold it." Caddy said.

"Aint nobody said me and T. P. got to mind you." Frony said.

"If I say you dont have to, will you let him hold it." Caddy said.

"All right." Frony said. "Let him hold it, T. P. We going to watch them moaning."

"They aint moaning." Caddy said. "I tell you it's a party. Are they moaning, Versh."

"We aint going to know what they doing, standing here." Versh said.

"Come on." Caddy said. "Frony and T. P. dont have to mind me. But the rest of us do. You better carry him, Versh. It's getting dark."

Versh took me up and we went on around the kitchen.

When we looked around the corner we could see the lights coming up the drive. T. P. went back to the cellar door and opened it.

You know what's down there, T. P. said. Soda water. I seen Mr Jason come up with both hands full of them. Wait here a minute.

T. P. went and looked in the kitchen door. Dilsey said, What are you peeping in here for. Where's Benjy.

He out here, T. P. said.

Go on and watch him, Dilsey said. Keep him out the house now.

Yessum, T. P. said. Is they started yet.

You go on and keep that boy out of sight, Dilsey said. I got all I can tend to.

A snake crawled out from under the house. Jason said he wasn't afraid of snakes and Caddy said he was but she wasn't and Versh said they both were and Caddy said to be quiet, like Father said.

You aint got to start bellering now, T. P. said. You want some this sassprilluh.

It tickled my nose and eyes.

If you aint going to drink it, let me get to it, T. P. said. All right, here tis. We better get another bottle while aint nobody bothering us. You be quiet, now.

We stopped under the tree by the parlor window. Versh set me down in the wet grass. It was cold. There were lights in all the windows.

"That's where Damuddy is." Caddy said. "She's sick every day now. When she gets well we're going to have a picnic."

"I knows what I knows." Frony said.

The trees were buzzing, and the grass.

"The one next to it is where we have the measles." Caddy said. "Where do you and T. P. have the measles, Frony."

"Has them just wherever we is, I reckon." Frony said.

"They haven't started yet." Caddy said.

They getting ready to start, T. P. said. You stand right here now while I get that box so we can see in the window. Here, les finish drinking this here sassprilluh. It make me feel just like a squinch owl inside.

We drank the sassprilluh and T. P. pushed the bottle through the lattice, under the house, and went away. I could hear them in the parlor and I clawed my hands against the wall. T. P. dragged the box. He fell down, and he began to laugh. He lay there, laughing into the grass. He got up and dragged the box under the window, trying not to laugh.

"I skeered I going to holler." T. P. said. "Git on the box and see is they started."

"They haven't started because the band hasn't come yet." Caddy said.

"They aint going to have no band." Frony said.

"How do you know." Caddy said.

"I knows what I knows." Frony said.

"You dont know anything." Caddy said. She went to the tree. "Push me up, Versh."

"Your paw told you to stay out that tree." Versh said.

"That was a long time ago." Caddy said. "I expect he's forgotten about it. Besides, he said to mind me tonight. Didn't he didn't he say to mind me tonight."

"I'm not going to mind you." Jason said. "Frony and T. P. are not going to either."

"Push me up, Versh." Caddy said.

"All right." Versh said. "You the one going to get whipped. I aint." He went and pushed Caddy up into the tree to the first limb. We watched the muddy bottom of her drawers. Then we couldn't see her. We could hear the tree thrashing.

"Mr Jason said if you break that tree he whip you." Versh said.

"I'm going to tell on her too." Jason said.

The tree quit thrashing. We looked up into the still branches.

"What you seeing." Frony whispered.

I saw them. Then I saw Caddy, with flowers in her hair, and a long veil like shining wind. Caddy Caddy

"Hush." T. P. said. "They going to hear you. Get down quick." He pulled me. Caddy. I clawed my hands against the wall Caddy. T. P. pulled me. "Hush." he said. "Hush. Come on here quick." He pulled me on. Caddy "Hush up, Benjy. You want them to hear you. Come on, les drink some more sassprilluh, then we can come back if you hush. We better get one more bottle or we both be hollering. We can say Dan drunk it. Mr Quentin always saying he so smart, we can say he sassprilluh dog, too."

The moonlight came down the cellar stairs. We drank some more sassprilluh.

"You know what I wish." T. P. said. "I wish a bear would walk in that cellar door. You know what I do. I walk right up to him and spit in he eye. Gimme that bottle to stop my mouth before I holler."

T. P. fell down. He began to laugh, and the cellar door and the moonlight jumped away and something hit me.

"Hush up." T. P. said, trying not to laugh. "Lawd, they'll all hear us. Get up." T. P. said. "Get up, Benjy, quick." He was thrashing about and laughing and I tried to get up. The cellar steps ran up the hill in the moonlight and T. P. fell up the hill, into the moonlight, and I ran against the fence and T. P. ran behind me saying "Hush up hush up." Then he fell into the flowers, laughing, and I ran into the box. But when I tried to climb onto it it jumped away and hit me on the back of the head and my throat made a sound. It made the sound again and I stopped trying to get up, and it made the sound again and I began to cry. But my throat kept on making the sound while T. P. was pulling me. It kept on making it and I couldn't tell if I was crying or not, and T. P. fell down on top of me, laughing, and it kept on making the sound and Quentin kicked T. P. and Caddy put her arms around me, and her shining veil, and I couldn't smell trees anymore and I began to cry.

Benjy, Caddy said, Benjy. She put her arms around me again, but I went away. "What is it, Benjy." she said. "Is it this hat." She took her hat off and came again, and I went away.

"Benjy." she said. "What is it, Benjy. What has Caddy done."

"He dont like that prissy dress." Jason said. "You think you're grown up, dont you. You think you're better than anybody else, dont you. Prissy."

"You shut your mouth." Caddy said. "You dirty little beast. Benjy."

"Just because you are fourteen, you think you're grown up, dont you." Jason said. "You think you're something. Dont you."

"Hush, Benjy." Caddy said. "You'll disturb Mother. Hush."

But I didn't hush, and when she went away I followed, and she stopped on the stairs and waited and I stopped too.

"What is it, Benjy." Caddy said. "Tell Caddy. She'll do it. Try."

"Candace." Mother said.

"Yessum." Caddy said.

"Why are you teasing him." Mother said. "Bring him here."

We went to Mother's room, where she was lying with the sickness on a cloth on her head.

"What is the matter now." Mother said. "Benjamin."

"Benjy." Caddy said. She came again, but I went away.

"You must have done something to him." Mother said. "Why wont you let him alone, so I can have some peace. Give him the box and please go on and let him alone."

Caddy got the box and set it on the floor and opened it. It was full of stars. When I was still, they were still. When I moved, they glinted and sparkled. I hushed.

Then I heard Caddy walking and I began again.

"Benjamin." Mother said. "Come here." I went to the door. "You, Benjamin." Mother said.

"What is it now." Father said. "Where are you going."

"Take him downstairs and get someone to watch him, Jason." Mother said. "You know I'm ill, yet you   "

Father shut the door behind us.

"T. P." he said.

"Sir." T. P. said downstairs.

"Benjy's coming down." Father said. "Go with T. P."

I went to the bathroom door. I could hear the water.

"Benjy." T. P. said downstairs.

I could hear the water. I listened to it.

"Benjy." T. P. said downstairs.

I listened to the water.

I couldn't hear the water, and Caddy opened the door.

"Why, Benjy." she said. She looked at me and I went and she put her arms around me. "Did you find Caddy again." she said. "Did you think Caddy had run away." Caddy smelled like trees.

We went to Caddy's room. She sat down at the mirror. She stopped her hands and looked at me.

"Why, Benjy. What is it." she said. "You mustn't cry. Caddy's not going away. See here." she said. She took up the bottle and took the stopper out and held it to my nose. "Sweet. Smell. Good."

I went away and I didn't hush, and she held the bottle in her hand, looking at me.

"Oh." she said. She put the bottle down and came and put her arms around me. "So that was it. And you were trying to tell Caddy and you couldn't tell her. You wanted to, but you couldn't, could you. Of course Caddy wont. Of course Caddy wont. Just wait till I dress."

Caddy dressed and took up the bottle again and we went down to the kitchen.

"Dilsey." Caddy said. "Benjy's got a present for you." She stooped down and put the bottle in my hand. "Hold it out to Dilsey, now." Caddy held my hand out and Dilsey took the bottle.

"Well I'll declare." Dilsey said. "If my baby aint give Dilsey a bottle of perfume. Just look here, Roskus."

Caddy smelled like trees. "We dont like perfume ourselves." Caddy said.

She smelled like trees.

"Come on, now." Dilsey said. "You too big to sleep with folks. You a big boy now. Thirteen years old. Big enough to sleep by yourself in Uncle Maury's room." Dilsey said.

Uncle Maury was sick. His eye was sick, and his mouth. Versh took his supper up to him on the tray.

"Maury says he's going to shoot the scoundrel." Father said. "I told him he'd better not mention it to Patterson before hand." He drank.

"Jason." Mother said.

"Shoot who, Father." Quentin said. "What's Uncle Maury going to shoot him for."

"Because he couldn't take a little joke." Father said.

"Jason." Mother said. "How can you. You'd sit right there and see Maury shot down in ambush, and laugh."

"Then Maury'd better stay out of ambush." Father said.

"Shoot who, Father." Quentin said. "Who's Uncle Maury going to shoot."

"Nobody." Father said. "I dont own a pistol."

Mother began to cry. "If you begrudge Maury your food, why aren't you man enough to say so to his face. To ridicule him before the children, behind his back."

"Of course I dont." Father said. "I admire Maury. He is invaluable to my own sense of racial superiority. I wouldn't swap Maury for a matched team. And do you know why, Quentin."

"No, sir." Quentin said.

"*Et ego in arcadia* I have forgotten the latin for hay." Father said. "There, there." he said. "I was just joking." He drank and set the glass down and went and put his hand on Mother's shoulder.

"It's no joke." Mother said. "My people are every bit as well born as yours. Just because Maury's health is bad."

"Of course." Father said. "Bad health is the primary reason for all life. Created by disease, within putrefaction, into decay. Versh."

"Sir." Versh said behind my chair.

"Take the decanter and fill it."

"And tell Dilsey to come and take Benjamin up to bed." Mother said.

"You a big boy." Dilsey said. "Caddy tired sleeping with you. Hush now, so you can go to sleep." The room went away, but I didn't hush, and the room came back and Dilsey came and sat on the bed, looking at me.

"Aint you going to be a good boy and hush." Dilsey said. "You aint, is you. See can you wait a minute, then."

She went away. There wasn't anything in the door. Then Caddy was in it.

"Hush." Caddy said. "I'm coming."

I hushed and Dilsey turned back the spread and Caddy got in between the spread and the blanket. She didn't take off her bathrobe.

"Now." she said. "Here I am." Dilsey came with a blanket and spread it over her and tucked it around her.

"He be gone in a minute." Dilsey said. "I leave the light on in your room."

"All right." Caddy said. She snuggled her head beside mine on the pillow. "Goodnight, Dilsey."

"Goodnight, honey." Dilsey said. The room went black. *Caddy smelled like trees.*

We looked up into the tree where she was.

"What she seeing, Versh." Frony whispered.

"Shhhhhhh." Caddy said in the tree. Dilsey said,

"You come on here." She came around the corner of the house. "Whyn't you all go on up stairs, like your paw said, stead of slipping out behind my back. Where's Caddy and Quentin."

"I told her not to climb up that tree." Jason said. "I'm going to tell on her."

"Who in what tree." Dilsey said. She came and looked up into the tree. "Caddy." Dilsey said. The branches began to shake again.

"You, Satan." Dilsey said. "Come down from there."

"Hush." Caddy said. "Dont you know Father said to be quiet." Her legs came in sight and Dilsey reached up and lifted her out of the tree.

"Aint you got any better sense than to let them come around here." Dilsey said.

"I couldn't do nothing with her." Versh said.

"What you all doing here." Dilsey said. "Who told you to come up to the house."

"She did." Frony said. "She told us to come."

"Who told you you got to do what she say." Dilsey said. "Get on home, now." Frony and T. P. went on. We couldn't see them when they were still going away.

"Out here in the middle of the night." Dilsey said. She took me up and we went to the kitchen.

"Slipping out behind my back." Dilsey said. "When you knowed it's past your bedtime."

"Shhhh, Dilsey." Caddy said. "Dont talk so loud. We've got to be quiet."

"You hush your mouth and get quiet, then." Dilsey said. "Where's Quentin."

"Quentin's mad because we had to mind me tonight." Caddy said. "He's still got T. P.'s bottle of lightning bugs."

"I reckon T. P. can get along without it." Dilsey said. "You go and find Quentin, Versh. Roskus say he seen him going towards the barn." Versh went on. We couldn't see him.

"They're not doing anything in there." Caddy said. "Just sitting in chairs and looking."

"They dont need no help from you all to do that." Dilsey said. We went around the kitchen.

Where you want to go now, Luster said. You going back to watch them knocking ball again. We done looked for it over there. Here. Wait a minute. You wait right here while I go back and get that ball. I done thought of something.

The kitchen was dark. The trees were black on the sky. Dan came waddling out from under the steps and chewed my ankle. I went around the kitchen, where the moon was. Dan came scuffling along, into the moon.

"Benjy." T. P. said in the house.

The flower tree by the parlor window wasn't dark, but the thick trees were. The grass was buzzing in the moonlight where my shadow walked on the grass.

"You, Benjy." T. P. said in the house. "Where you hiding. You slipping off. I knows it."

Luster came back. Wait, he said. Here. Dont go over there. Miss Quentin and her beau in the swing yonder. You come on this way. Come back here, Benjy.

It was dark under the trees. Dan wouldn't come. He stayed in the moonlight. Then I could see the swing and I began to cry.

Come away from there, Benjy, Luster said. You know Miss Quentin going to get mad.

It was two now, and then one in the swing. Caddy came fast, white in the darkness.

"Benjy." she said. "How did you slip out. Where's Versh."

She put her arms around me and I hushed and held to her dress and tried to pull her away.

"Why, Benjy." she said. "What is it. T. P." she called.

The one in the swing got up and came, and I cried and pulled Caddy's dress.

"Benjy." Caddy said. "It's just Charlie. Dont you know Charlie."

"Where's his nigger." Charlie said. "What do they let him run around loose for."

"Hush, Benjy." Caddy said. "Go away, Charlie. He doesn't like you." Charlie went away and I hushed. I pulled at Caddy's dress.

"Why, Benjy." Caddy said. "Aren't you going to let me stay here and talk to Charlie a while."

"Call that nigger." Charlie said. He came back. I cried louder and pulled at Caddy's dress.

"Go away, Charlie." Caddy said. Charlie came and put his hands on Caddy and I cried more. I cried loud.

"No, no." Caddy said. "No. No."

"He cant talk." Charlie said. "Caddy."

"Are you crazy." Caddy said. She began to breathe fast. "He can see. Dont. Dont." Caddy fought. They both breathed fast. "Please. Please." Caddy whispered.

"Send him away." Charlie said.

"I will." Caddy said. "Let me go."

"Will you send him away." Charlie said.

"Yes." Caddy said. "Let me go." Charlie went away. "Hush." Caddy said. "He's gone." I hushed. I could hear her and feel her chest going.

"I'll have to take him to the house." she said. She took my hand. "I'm coming." she whispered.

"Wait." Charlie said. "Call the nigger."

"No." Caddy said. "I'll come back. Come on, Benjy."

"Caddy." Charlie whispered, loud. We went on. "You better come back. Are you coming back." Caddy and I were running. "Caddy." Charlie said. We ran out into the moonlight, toward the kitchen.

"Caddy." Charlie said.

Caddy and I ran. We ran up the kitchen steps, onto the porch, and Caddy knelt down in the dark and held me. I could hear her and feel her chest. "I wont." she said. "I wont anymore, ever. Benjy. Benjy." Then she was crying, and I cried, and we held each other. "Hush." she said. "Hush. I wont anymore." So I hushed and Caddy got up and we went into the kitchen and turned the light on and Caddy took the kitchen soap and washed her mouth at the sink, hard. Caddy smelled like trees.

I kept a telling you to stay away from there, Luster said. They sat up in the swing, quick. Quentin had her hands on her hair. He had a red tie.

You old crazy loon, Quentin said. I'm going to tell Dilsey about the way you let him follow everywhere I go. I'm going to make her whip you good.

"I couldn't stop him." Luster said. "Come on here, Benjy."

"Yes you could." Quentin said. "You didn't try. You were both snooping around after me. Did Grandmother send you all out here to spy on me." She jumped out of the swing. "If you dont take him right away this minute and keep him away, I'm going to make Jason whip you."

"I cant do nothing with him." Luster said. "You try it if you think you can."

"Shut your mouth." Quentin said. "Are you going to get him away."

"Ah, let him stay." he said. He had a red tie. The sun was red on it. "Look here, Jack." He struck a match and put it in his mouth. Then he took the match out of his mouth. It was still burning. "Want to try it." he said. I went over there. "Open your mouth." he said. I opened my mouth. Quentin hit the match with her hand and it went away.

"Goddam you." Quentin said. "Do you want to get him started. Dont you know he'll beller all day. I'm going to tell Dilsey on you." She went away running.

"Here, kid." he said. "Hey. Come on back. I aint going to fool with him."

Quentin ran on to the house. She went around the kitchen.

"You played hell then, Jack." he said. "Aint you."

"He cant tell what you saying." Luster said. "He deef and dumb."

"Is." he said. "How long's he been that way."

"Been that way thirty three years today." Luster said. "Born looney. Is you one of them show folks."

"Why." he said.

"I dont ricklick seeing you around here before." Luster said.

"Well, what about it." he said.

"Nothing." Luster said. "I going tonight."

He looked at me.

"You aint the one can play a tune on that saw, is you." Luster said.

"It'll cost you a quarter to find that out." he said. He looked at me. "Why dont they lock him up." he said. "What'd you bring him out here for."

"You aint talking to me." Luster said. "I cant do nothing with him. I just come over here looking for a quarter I lost so I can go to the show tonight. Look like now I aint going to get to go." Luster looked on the ground. "You aint got no extra quarter, is you." Luster said.

"No." he said. "I aint."

"I reckon I just have to find that other one, then." Luster said. He put his hand in his pocket. "You dont want to buy no golf ball neither, does you." Luster said.

"What kind of ball." he said.

"Golf ball." Luster said. "I dont want but a quarter."

"What for." he said. "What do I want with it."

"I didn't think you did." Luster said. "Come on here, mulehead." he said. "Come on here and watch them knocking that ball. Here. Here something you can play with along with that jimson weed." Luster picked it up and gave it to me. It was bright.

"Where'd you get that." he said. His tie was red in the sun, walking.

"Found it under this here bush." Luster said. "I thought for a minute it was that quarter I lost."

He came and took it.

"Hush." Luster said. "He going to give it back when he done looking at it."

"Agnes Mabel Becky." he said. He looked toward the house.

"Hush." Luster said. "He fixing to give it back."

He gave it to me and I hushed.

"Who come to see her last night." he said.

"I dont know." Luster said. "They comes every night she can climb down that tree. I dont keep no track of them."

"Damn if one of them didn't leave a track." he said. He looked at the house. Then he went and lay down in the swing. "Go away." he said. "Dont bother me."

"Come on here." Luster said. "You done played hell now. Time Miss Quentin get done telling on you."

We went to the fence and looked through the curling flower spaces. Luster hunted in the grass.

"I had it right here." he said. I saw the flag flapping, and the sun slanting on the broad grass.

"They'll be some along soon." Luster said. "There some now, but they going away. Come on and help me look for it."

We went along the fence.

"Hush." Luster said. "How can I make them come over here, if they aint coming. Wait. They'll be some in a minute. Look yonder. Here they come."

I went along the fence, to the gate, where the girls passed with their booksatchels. "You, Benjy." Luster said. "Come back here."

You cant do no good looking through the gate, T. P. said. Miss Caddy done gone long ways away. Done got married and left you. You cant do no good, holding to the gate and crying. She cant hear you.

What is it he wants, T. P. Mother said. Cant you play with him and keep him quiet.

He want to go down yonder and look through the gate, T. P. said.

Well, he cannot do it, Mother said. It's raining. You will just have to play with him and keep him quiet. You, Benjamin.

Aint nothing going to quiet him, T. P. said. He think if he down to the gate, Miss Caddy come back.

Nonsense, Mother said.

I could hear them talking. I went out the door and I couldn't hear them, and I went down to the gate, where the girls passed with their booksatchels. They looked at me, walking fast, with their heads turned. I tried to say, but they went on, and I went along the fence, trying to say, and they went faster. Then they were running and I came to the corner of the fence and I couldn't go any further, and I held to the fence, looking after them and trying to say.

"You, Benjy." T. P. said. "What you doing, slipping out. Dont you know Dilsey whip you."

"You cant do no good, moaning and slobbering through the fence." T. P. said. "You done skeered them chillen. Look at them, walking on the other side of the street."

How did he get out, Father said. Did you leave the gate un-latched when you came in, Jason.

Of course not, Jason said. Dont you know I've got better sense than to do that. Do you think I wanted anything like this to happen. This family is bad enough, God knows. I could have told you, all the time. I reckon you'll send him to Jackson, now. If Mr Burgess dont shoot him first.

Hush, Father said.

I could have told you, all the time, Jason said.

It was open when I touched it, and I held to it in the twilight. I wasn't crying, and I tried to stop, watching the girls coming along in the twilight. I wasn't crying.

"There he is."

They stopped.

"He cant get out. He wont hurt anybody, anyway. Come on."

"I'm scared to. I'm scared. I'm going to cross the street."

"He cant get out."

I wasn't crying.

"Dont be a fraid cat. Come on."

They came on in the twilight. I wasn't crying, and I held to the gate. They came slow.

"I'm scared."

"He wont hurt you. I pass here every day. He just runs along the fence."

They came on. I opened the gate and they stopped, turning. I was trying to say, and I caught her, trying to say, and she screamed and I was trying to say and trying and the bright shapes began to stop and I tried to get out. I tried to get it off of my face, but the bright shapes were going again. They were going up the hill to where it fell away and I tried to cry. But when I breathed in, I couldn't breathe out again to cry, and I tried to keep from falling off the hill and I fell off the hill into the bright, whirling shapes.

Here, looney, Luster said. Here come some. Hush your slobbering and moaning, now.

They came to the flag. He took it out and they hit, then he put the flag back.

"Mister." Luster said.

He looked around. "What." he said.

"Want to buy a golf ball." Luster said.

"Let's see it." he said. He came to the fence and Luster reached the ball through.

"Where'd you get it." he said.

"Found it." Luster said.

"I know that." he said. "Where. In somebody's golf bag."

"I found it laying over here in the yard." Luster said. "I'll take a quarter for it."

"What makes you think it's yours." he said.

"I found it." Luster said.

"Then find yourself another one." he said. He put it in his pocket and went away.

"I got to go to that show tonight." Luster said.

"That so." he said. He went to the table. "Fore caddie." he said. He hit.

"I'll declare." Luster said. "You fusses when you dont see them and you fusses when you does. Why cant you hush. Dont you reckon folks gets tired of listening to you all the time. Here. You dropped your jimson weed." He picked it up and gave it back to me. "You needs a new one. You bout wore that one out." We stood at the fence and watched them.

"That white man hard to get along with." Luster said. "You see him take my ball." They went on. We went on along the fence. We came to the garden and we couldn't go any further. I held to the fence and looked through the flower spaces. They went away.

"Now you aint got nothing to moan about." Luster said. "Hush up. I the one got something to moan over, you aint. Here. Whyn't you hold on to that weed. You be bellering about it next." He gave me the flower. "Where you heading now."

Our shadows were on the grass. They got to the trees before we did. Mine got there first. Then we got there, and then the shadows were gone. There was a flower in the bottle. I put the other flower in it.

"Aint you a grown man, now." Luster said. "Playing with two weeds in a bottle. You know what they going to do with you when Miss Cahline die. They going to send you to Jackson, where you belong. Mr Jason say so. Where you can hold the bars all day long with the rest of the looneys and slobber. How you like that."

Luster knocked the flowers over with his hand. "That's what they'll do to you at Jackson when you starts bellering."

I tried to pick up the flowers. Luster picked them up, and they went away. I began to cry.

"Beller." Luster said. "Beller. You want something to beller about. All right, then. Caddy." he whispered. "Caddy. Beller now. Caddy."

"Luster." Dilsey said from the kitchen.

The flowers came back.

"Hush." Luster said. "Here they is. Look. It's fixed back just like it was at first. Hush, now."

"You, Luster." Dilsey said.

"Yessum." Luster said. "We coming. You done played hell. Get up." He jerked my arm and I got up. We went out of the trees. Our shadows were gone.

"Hush." Luster said. "Look at all them folks watching you. Hush."

"You bring him on here." Dilsey said. She came down the steps.

"What you done to him now." she said.

"Aint done nothing to him." Luster said. "He just started bellering."

"Yes you is." Dilsey said. "You done something to him. Where you been."

"Over yonder under them cedars." Luster said.

"Getting Quentin all riled up." Dilsey said. "Why cant you keep him away from her. Dont you know she dont like him where she at."

"Got as much time for him as I is." Luster said. "He aint none of my uncle."

"Dont you sass me, nigger boy." Dilsey said.

"I aint done nothing to him." Luster said. "He was playing there, and all of a sudden he started bellering."

"Is you been projecking with his graveyard." Dilsey said.

"I aint touched his graveyard." Luster said.

"Dont lie to me, boy." Dilsey said. We went up the steps and into the kitchen. Dilsey opened the firedoor and drew a chair up in front of it and I sat down. I hushed.

What you want to get her started for, Dilsey said. Whyn't you keep him out of there.

He was just looking at the fire, Caddy said. Mother was telling him his new name. We didn't mean to get her started.

I knows you didn't, Dilsey said. Him at one end of the house and her at the other. You let my things alone, now. Dont you touch nothing till I get back.

"Aint you shamed of yourself." Dilsey said. "Teasing him." She set the cake on the table.

"I aint been teasing him." Luster said. "He was playing with that bottle full of dogfennel and all of a sudden he started up bellering. You heard him."

"You aint done nothing to his flowers." Dilsey said.

"I aint touched his graveyard." Luster said. "What I want with his truck. I was just hunting for that quarter."

"You lost it, did you." Dilsey said. She lit the candles on the cake. Some of them were little ones. Some were big ones cut into little pieces. "I told you to go put it away. Now I reckon you want me to get you another one from Frony."

"I got to go to that show, Benjy or no Benjy." Luster said. "I aint going to follow him around day and night both."

"You going to do just what he want you to, nigger boy." Dilsey said. "You hear me."

"Aint I always done it." Luster said. "Dont I always does what he wants. Dont I, Benjy."

"Then you keep it up." Dilsey said. "Bringing him in here, bawling and getting her started too. You all go ahead and eat this cake, now, before Jason come. I dont want him jumping on me about a cake I bought with my own money. Me baking a cake here, with him counting every egg that comes into this kitchen. See can you let him alone now, less you dont want to go to that show tonight."

Dilsey went away.

"You cant blow out no candles." Luster said. "Watch me blow them out." He leaned down and puffed his face. The candles went away. I began to cry. "Hush." Luster said. "Here. Look at the fire whiles I cuts this cake."

I could hear the clock, and I could hear Caddy standing behind me, and I could hear the roof. It's still raining, Caddy said. I hate rain. I hate everything. And then her head came into my lap and she was crying, holding me, and I began to cry. Then I looked at the fire again and the bright, smooth shapes went again. I could hear the clock and the roof and Caddy.

I ate some cake. Luster's hand came and took another piece. I could hear him eating. I looked at the fire.

A long piece of wire came across my shoulder. It went to the door, and then the fire went away. I began to cry.

"What you howling for now." Luster said. "Look there." The fire was there. I hushed. "Cant you set and look at the fire and be quiet like mammy told you." Luster said. "You ought to be ashamed of yourself. Here. Here's you some more cake."

"What you done to him now." Dilsey said. "Cant you never let him alone."

"I was just trying to get him to hush up and not sturb Miss Cahline." Luster said. "Something got him started again."

"And I know what that something name." Dilsey said. "I'm going to get Versh to take a stick to you when he comes home. You just trying yourself. You been doing it all day. Did you take him down to the branch."

"Nome." Luster said. "We been right here in this yard all day, like you said."

His hand came for another piece of cake. Dilsey hit his hand. "Reach it again, and I chop it right off with this here butcher knife." Dilsey said. "I bet he aint had one piece of it."

"Yes he is." Luster said. "He already had twice as much as me. Ask him if he aint."

"Reach hit one more time." Dilsey said. "Just reach it."

That's right, Dilsey said. I reckon it'll be my time to cry next. Reckon Maury going to let me cry on him a while, too.

His name's Benjy now, Caddy said.

How come it is, Dilsey said. He aint wore out the name he was born with yet, is he.

Benjamin came out of the bible, Caddy said. It's a better name for him than Maury was.

How come it is, Dilsey said.

Mother says it is, Caddy said.

Huh, Dilsey said. Name aint going to help him. Hurt him, neither. Folks dont have no luck, changing names. My name been Dilsey since fore I could remember and it be Dilsey when they's long forgot me.

How will they know it's Dilsey, when it's long forgot, Dilsey, Caddy said.

It'll be in the Book, honey, Dilsey said. Writ out.

Can you read it, Caddy said.

Wont have to, Dilsey said. They'll read it for me. All I got to do is say Ise here.

The long wire came across my shoulder, and the fire went away. I began to cry.

Dilsey and Luster fought.

"I seen you." Dilsey said. "Oho, I seen you." She dragged Luster out of the corner, shaking him. "Wasn't nothing bothering him, was they. You just wait till your pappy come home. I wish I was young like I use to be, I'd tear them years right off your head. I good mind to lock you up in that cellar and not let you go to that show tonight, I sho is."

"Ow, mammy." Luster said. "Ow, mammy."

I put my hand out to where the fire had been.

"Catch him." Dilsey said. "Catch him back."

My hand jerked back and I put it in my mouth and Dilsey caught me. I could still hear the clock between my voice. Dilsey reached back and hit Luster on the head. My voice was going loud every time.

"Get that soda." Dilsey said. She took my hand out of my mouth. My voice went louder then and my hand tried to go back to my mouth, but Dilsey held it. My voice went loud. She sprinkled soda on my hand.

"Look in the pantry and tear a piece off of that rag hanging on the nail." she said. "Hush, now. You dont want to make your maw sick again, does you. Here, look at the fire. Dilsey make your hand stop hurting in just a minute. Look at the fire." She opened the fire door. I looked at the fire, but my hand didn't stop and I didn't stop. My hand was trying to go to my mouth, but Dilsey held it.

She wrapped the cloth around it. Mother said,

"What is it now. Cant I even be sick in peace. Do I have to get up out of bed to come down to him, with two grown negroes to take care of him."

"He all right now." Dilsey said. "He going to quit. He just burnt his hand a little."

"With two grown negroes, you must bring him into the house, bawling." Mother said. "You got him started on purpose, because you know I'm sick." She came and stood by me. "Hush." she said. "Right this minute. Did you give him this cake."

"I bought it." Dilsey said. "It never come out of Jason's pantry. I fixed him some birthday."

"Do you want to poison him with that cheap store cake." Mother said. "Is that what you are trying to do. Am I never to have one minute's peace."

"You go on back up stairs and lay down." Dilsey said. "It'll quit smarting him in a minute now, and he'll hush. Come on, now."

"And leave him down here for you all to do something else to." Mother said. "How can I lie there, with him bawling down here. Benjamin. Hush this minute."

"They aint nowhere else to take him." Dilsey said. "We aint got the room we use to have. He cant stay out in the yard, crying where all the neighbors can see him."

"I know, I know." Mother said. "It's all my fault. I'll be gone soon, and you and Jason will both get along better." She began to cry.

"You hush that, now." Dilsey said. "You'll get yourself down again. You come on back up stairs. Luster going to take him to the liberry and play with him till I get his supper done."

Dilsey and Mother went out.

"Hush up." Luster said. "You hush up. You want me to burn your other hand for you. You aint hurt. Hush up."

"Here." Dilsey said. "Stop crying, now." She gave me the slipper, and I hushed. "Take him to the liberry." she said. "And if I hear him again, I going to whip you myself."

We went to the library. Luster turned on the light. The windows went black, and the dark tall place on the wall came and I went and touched it. It was like a door, only it wasn't a door.

The fire came behind me and I went to the fire and sat on the floor, holding the slipper. The fire went higher. It went onto the cushion in Mother's chair.

"Hush up." Luster said. "Cant you never get done for a while. Here I done built you a fire, and you wont even look at it."

Your name is Benjy, Caddy said. Do you hear. Benjy. Benjy.

Dont tell him that, Mother said. Bring him here.

Caddy lifted me under the arms.

Get up, Mau—— I mean Benjy, she said.

Dont try to carry him, Mother said. Cant you lead him over here. Is that too much for you to think of.

I can carry him, Caddy said. "Let me carry him up, Dilsey."

"Go on, Minute." Dilsey said. "You aint big enough to tote a flea. You go on and be quiet, like Mr Jason said."

There was a light at the top of the stairs. Father was there, in his shirt sleeves. The way he looked said Hush. Caddy whispered,

"Is Mother sick."

Versh set me down and we went into Mother's room. There was a fire. It was rising and falling on the walls. There was another fire in the mirror. I could smell the sickness. It was on a cloth folded on Mother's head. Her hair was on the pillow. The fire didn't reach it, but it shone on her hand, where her rings were jumping.

"Come and tell Mother goodnight." Caddy said. We went to the bed. The fire went out of the mirror. Father got up from the bed and lifted me up and Mother put her hand on my head.

"What time is it." Mother said. Her eyes were closed.

"Ten minutes to seven." Father said.

"It's too early for him to go to bed." Mother said. "He'll wake up at daybreak, and I simply cannot bear another day like today."

"There, there." Father said. He touched Mother's face.

"I know I'm nothing but a burden to you." Mother said. "But I'll be gone soon. Then you will be rid of my bothering."

"Hush." Father said. "I'll take him downstairs a while." He took me up. "Come on, old fellow. Let's go down stairs a while. We'll have to be quiet while Quentin is studying, now."

Caddy went and leaned her face over the bed and Mother's hand came into the firelight. Her rings jumped on Caddy's back.

Mother's sick, Father said. Dilsey will put you to bed. Where's Quentin.

Versh getting him, Dilsey said.

Father stood and watched us go past. We could hear Mother in her room. Caddy said "Hush." Jason was still climbing the stairs. He had his hands in his pockets.

"You all must be good tonight." Father said. "And be quiet, so you wont disturb Mother."

"We'll be quiet." Caddy said. "You must be quiet now, Jason." she said. We tiptoed.

We could hear the roof. I could see the fire in the mirror too. Caddy lifted me again.

"Come on, now." she said. "Then you can come back to the fire. Hush, now."

"Candace." Mother said.

"Hush, Benjy." Caddy said. "Mother wants you a minute. Like a good boy. Then you can come back. Benjy."

Caddy let me down, and I hushed.

"Let him stay here, Mother. When he's through looking at the fire, then you can tell him."

"Candace." Mother said. Caddy stooped and lifted me. We staggered. "Candace." Mother said.

"Hush." Caddy said. "You can still see it. Hush."

"Bring him here." Mother said. "He's too big for you to carry. You must stop trying. You'll injure your back. All of our women have prided themselves on their carriage. Do you want to look like a washerwoman."

"He's not too heavy." Caddy said. "I can carry him."

"Well, I dont want him carried, then." Mother said. "A five year old child. No, no. Not in my lap. Let him stand up."

"If you'll hold him, he'll stop." Caddy said. "Hush." she said. "You can go right back. Here. Here's your cushion. See."

"Dont, Candace." Mother said.

"Let him look at it and he'll be quiet." Caddy said. "Hold up just a minute while I slip it out. There, Benjy. Look."

I looked at it and hushed.

"You humor him too much." Mother said. "You and your father both. You dont realise that I am the one who has to pay for it. Damuddy spoiled Jason that way and it took him two years to outgrow it, and I am not strong enough to go through the same thing with Benjamin."

"You dont need to bother with him." Caddy said. "I like to take care of him. Dont I. Benjy."

"Candace." Mother said. "I told you not to call him that. It was bad enough when your father insisted on calling you by that silly nickname, and I will not have him called by one. Nicknames are vulgar. Only common people use them. Benjamin." she said.

"Look at me." Mother said.

"Benjamin." she said. She took my face in her hands and turned it to hers.

"Benjamin." she said. "Take that cushion away, Candace."

"He'll cry." Caddy said.

"Take that cushion away, like I told you." Mother said. "He must learn to mind."

The cushion went away.

"Hush, Benjy." Caddy said.

"You go over there and sit down." Mother said. "Benjamin." She held my face to hers.

"Stop that." she said. "Stop it."

But I didn't stop and Mother caught me in her arms and began to cry, and I cried. Then the cushion came back and Caddy held it above Mother's head. She drew Mother back in the chair and Mother lay crying against the red and yellow cushion.

"Hush, Mother." Caddy said. "You go up stairs and lay down, so you can be sick. I'll go get Dilsey." She led me to the fire and I looked at the bright, smooth shapes. I could hear the fire and the roof.

Father took me up. He smelled like rain.

"Well, Benjy." he said. "Have you been a good boy today."

Caddy and Jason were fighting in the mirror.

"You, Caddy." Father said.

They fought. Jason began to cry.

"Caddy." Father said. Jason was crying. He wasn't fighting anymore, but we could see Caddy fighting in the mirror and Father put me down and went into the mirror and fought too. He lifted Caddy up. She fought. Jason lay on the floor, crying. He had the scissors in his hand. Father held Caddy.

"He cut up all Benjy's dolls." Caddy said. "I'll slit his gizzle."

"Candace." Father said.

"I will." Caddy said. "I will." She fought. Father held her. She kicked at Jason. He rolled into the corner, out of the mirror. Father brought Caddy to the fire. They were all out of the mirror. Only the fire was in it. Like the fire was in a door.

"Stop that." Father said. "Do you want to make Mother sick in her room."

Caddy stopped. "He cut up all the dolls Mau—Benjy and I made." Caddy said. "He did it just for meanness."

"I didn't." Jason said. He was sitting up, crying. "I didn't know they were his. I just thought they were some old papers."

"You couldn't help but know." Caddy said. "You did it just "

"Hush." Father said. "Jason." he said.

"I'll make you some more tomorrow." Caddy said. "We'll make a lot of them. Here, you can look at the cushion, too."

Jason came in.

I kept telling you to hush, Luster said.

What's the matter now, Jason said.

"He just trying hisself." Luster said. "That the way he been going on all day."

"Why dont you let him alone, then." Jason said. "If you cant keep him quiet, you'll have to take him out to the kitchen. The rest of us cant shut ourselves up in a room like Mother does."

"Mammy say keep him out the kitchen till she get supper." Luster said.

"Then play with him and keep him quiet." Jason said. "Do I have to work all day and then come home to a mad house." He opened the paper and read it.

You can look at the fire and the mirror and the cushion too, Caddy said. You wont have to wait until supper to look at the cushion, now. We could hear the roof. We could hear Jason too, crying loud beyond the wall.

Dilsey said, "You come, Jason. You letting him alone, is you."

"Yessum." Luster said.

"Where Quentin." Dilsey said. "Supper near bout ready."

"I dont know'm." Luster said. "I aint seen her."

Dilsey went away. "Quentin." she said in the hall. "Quentin. Supper ready."

We could hear the roof. Quentin smelled like rain, too.

What did Jason do, he said.

He cut up all Benjy's dolls, Caddy said.

Mother said to not call him Benjy, Quentin said. He sat on the rug by us. I wish it wouldn't rain, he said. You cant do anything.

You've been in a fight, Caddy said. Haven't you.

It wasn't much, Quentin said.

You can tell it, Caddy said. Father'll see it.

I dont care, Quentin said. I wish it wouldn't rain.

Quentin said, "Didn't Dilsey say supper was ready."

"Yessum." Luster said. Jason looked at Quentin. Then he read the paper again. Quentin came in. "She say it bout ready." Luster said. Quentin jumped down in Mother's chair. Luster said,

"Mr Jason."

"What." Jason said.

"Let me have two bits." Luster said.

"What for." Jason said.

"To go to the show tonight." Luster said.

"I thought Dilsey was going to get a quarter from Frony for you." Jason said.

"She did." Luster said. "I lost it. Me and Benjy hunted all day for that quarter. You can ask him."

"Then borrow one from him." Jason said. "I have to work for mine." He read the paper. Quentin looked at the fire. The fire was in her eyes and on her mouth. Her mouth was red.

"I tried to keep him away from there." Luster said.

"Shut your mouth." Quentin said. Jason looked at her.

"What did I tell you I was going to do if I saw you with that show fellow again." he said. Quentin looked at the fire. "Did you hear me." Jason said.

"I heard you." Quentin said. "Why dont you do it, then."

"Dont you worry." Jason said.

"I'm not." Quentin said. Jason read the paper again.

I could hear the roof. Father leaned forward and looked at Quentin.

Hello, he said. Who won.

"Nobody." Quentin said. "They stopped us. Teachers."

"Who was it." Father said. "Will you tell."

"It was all right." Quentin said. "He was as big as me."

"That's good." Father said. "Can you tell what it was about."

"It wasn't anything." Quentin said. "He said he would put a frog in her desk and she wouldn't dare to whip him."

"Oh." Father said. "She. And then what."

"Yes, sir." Quentin said. "And then I kind of hit him."

We could hear the roof and the fire, and a snuffling outside the door.

"Where was he going to get a frog in November." Father said.

"I dont know, sir." Quentin said.

We could hear them.

"Jason." Father said. We could hear Jason.

"Jason." Father said. "Come in here and stop that."

We could hear the roof and the fire and Jason.

"Stop that, now." Father said. "Do you want me to whip you again." Father lifted Jason up into the chair by him. Jason snuffled. We could hear the fire and the roof. Jason snuffled a little louder.

"One more time." Father said. We could hear the fire and the roof.

Dilsey said, All right. You all can come on to supper.

Versh smelled like rain. He smelled like a dog, too. We could hear the fire and the roof.

We could hear Caddy walking fast. Father and Mother looked at the door. Caddy passed it, walking fast. She didn't look. She walked fast.

"Candace." Mother said. Caddy stopped walking.

"Yes, Mother." she said.

"Hush, Caroline." Father said.

"Come here." Mother said.

"Hush, Caroline." Father said. "Let her alone."

Caddy came to the door and stood there, looking at Father and Mother. Her eyes flew at me, and away. I began to cry.

It went loud and I got up. Caddy came in and stood with her back to the wall, looking at me. I went toward her, crying, and she shrank against the wall and I saw her eyes and I cried louder and pulled at her dress. She put her hands out but I pulled at her dress. Her eyes ran.

Versh said, Your name Benjamin now. You know how come your name Benjamin now. They making a bluegum out of you. Mammy say in old time your granpaw changed nigger's name, and he turn preacher, and when they look at him, he bluegum too. Didn't use to be bluegum, neither. And when family woman look him in the eye in the full of the moon, chile born bluegum. And one evening, when they was about a dozen them bluegum chillen running around the place, he never come home. Possum hunters found him in the woods, et clean. And you know who et him. Them bluegum chillen did.

We were in the hall. Caddy was still looking at me. Her hand was against her mouth and I saw her eyes and I cried. We went up the stairs. She stopped again, against the wall, looking at me and I cried and she went on and I came on, crying, and she shrank against the wall, looking at me. She opened the door to her room, but I pulled at her dress and we went to the bathroom and she stood against the door, looking at me. Then she put her arm across her face and I pushed at her, crying.

What are you doing to him, Jason said. Why cant you let him alone.

I aint touching him, Luster said. He been doing this way all day long. He needs whipping.

He needs to be sent to Jackson, Quentin said. How can anybody live in a house like this.

If you dont like it, young lady, you'd better get out, Jason said.

I'm going to, Quentin said. Don't you worry.

Versh said, "You move back some, so I can dry my legs off." He shoved me back a little. "Dont you start bellering, now. You can still see it. That's all you have to do. You aint had to be out in the rain like I is. You's born lucky and dont know it." He lay on his back before the fire.

"You know how come your name Benjamin now." Versh said. "Your mamma too proud for you. What mammy say."

"You be still there and let me dry my legs off." Versh said. "Or you know what I'll do. I'll skin your rinktum."

We could hear the fire and the roof and Versh.

Versh got up quick and jerked his legs back. Father said, "All right, Versh."

"I'll feed him tonight." Caddy said. "Sometimes he cries when Versh feeds him."

"Take this tray up." Dilsey said. "And hurry back and feed Benjy."

"Dont you want Caddy to feed you." Caddy said.

Has he got to keep that old dirty slipper on the table, Quentin said. Why dont you feed him in the kitchen. It's like eating with a pig.

If you dont like the way we eat, you'd better not come to the table, Jason said.

Steam came off of Roskus. He was sitting in front of the stove. The oven door was open and Roskus had his feet in it. Steam came off the bowl. Caddy put the spoon into my mouth easy. There was a black spot on the inside of the bowl.

Now, now, Dilsey said. He aint going to bother you no more.

It got down below the mark. Then the bowl was empty. It went away. "He's hungry tonight." Caddy said. The bowl came back. I couldn't see the spot. Then I could. "He's starved, tonight." Caddy said. "Look how much he's eaten."

Yes he will, Quentin said. You all send him out to spy on me. I hate this house. I'm going to run away.

Roskus said, "It going to rain all night."

You've been running a long time, not to've got any further off than mealtime, Jason said.

See if I dont, Quentin said.

"Then I dont know what I going to do." Dilsey said. "It caught me in the hip so bad now I cant scarcely move. Climbing them stairs all evening."

Oh, I wouldn't be surprised, Jason said. I wouldn't be surprised at anything you'd do.

Quentin threw her napkin on the table.

Hush your mouth, Jason, Dilsey said. She went and put her arm around Quentin. Sit down, honey, Dilsey said. He ought to be shamed of hisself, throwing what aint your fault up to you.

"She sulling again, is she." Roskus said.

"Hush your mouth." Dilsey said.

Quentin pushed Dilsey away. She looked at Jason. Her mouth was red. She picked up her glass of water and swung her arm back,

*looking at Jason. Dilsey caught her arm. They fought. The glass
broke on the table, and the water ran into the table. Quentin was
running.*

"Mother's sick again." Caddy said.

"Sho she is." Dilsey said. "Weather like this make anybody
sick. When you going to get done eating, boy."

*Goddam you, Quentin said. Goddam you. We could hear her
running on the stairs. We went to the library.*

Caddy gave me the cushion, and I could look at the cushion and the mirror and the fire.

"We must be quiet while Quentin's studying." Father said.
"What are you doing, Jason."

"Nothing." Jason said.

"Suppose you come over here to do it, then." Father said.
Jason came out of the corner.

"What are you chewing." Father said.

"Nothing." Jason said.

"He's chewing paper again." Caddy said.

"Come here, Jason." Father said.

Jason threw into the fire. It hissed, uncurled, turning black.
Then it was gray. Then it was gone. Caddy and Father and
Jason were in Mother's chair. Jason's eyes were puffed shut
and his mouth moved, like tasting. Caddy's head was on
Father's shoulder. Her hair was like fire, and little points of
fire were in her eyes, and I went and Father lifted me into the
chair too, and Caddy held me. She smelled like trees.

*She smelled like trees. In the corner it was dark, but I could see
the window. I squatted there, holding the slipper. I couldn't see it,
but my hands saw it, and I could hear it getting night, and my
hands saw the slipper but I couldn't see myself, but my hands could
see the slipper, and I squatted there, hearing it getting dark.*

*Here you is, Luster said. Look what I got. He showed it to me.
You know where I got it. Miss Quentin give it to me. I knowed
they couldn't keep me out. What you doing, off in here. I thought
you done slipped back out doors. Aint you done enough moaning
and slobbering today, without hiding off in this here empty room,
mumbling and taking on. Come on here to bed, so I can get up
there before it starts. I cant fool with you all night tonight. Just
let them horns toot the first toot and I done gone.*

We didn't go to our room.

"This is where we have the measles." Caddy said. "Why do we have to sleep in here tonight."

"What you care where you sleep." Dilsey said. She shut the door and sat down and began to undress me. Jason began to cry. "Hush." Dilsey said.

"I want to sleep with Damuddy." Jason said.

"She's sick." Caddy said. "You can sleep with her when she gets well. Cant he, Dilsey."

"Hush, now." Dilsey said. Jason hushed.

"Our nighties are here, and everything." Caddy said. "It's like moving."

"And you better get into them." Dilsey said. "You be unbuttoning Jason."

Caddy unbuttoned Jason. He began to cry.

"You want to get whipped." Dilsey said. Jason hushed.

Quentin, Mother said in the hall.

What, Quentin said beyond the wall. We heard Mother lock the door. She looked in our door and came in and stooped over the bed and kissed me on the forehead.

When you get him to bed, go and ask Dilsey if she objects to my having a hot water bottle, Mother said. Tell her that if she does, I'll try to get along without it. Tell her I just want to know.

Yessum, Luster said. Come on. Get your pants off.

Quentin and Versh came in. Quentin had his face turned away. "What are you crying for." Caddy said.

"Hush." Dilsey said. "You all get undressed, now. You can go on home, Versh."

I got undressed and I looked at myself, and I began to cry. Hush, Luster said. Looking for them aint going to do no good. They're gone. You keep on like this, and we aint going have you no more birthday. He put my gown on. I hushed, and then Luster stopped, his head toward the window. Then he went to the window and looked out. He came back and took my arm. Here she come, he said. Be quiet, now. We went to the window and looked out. It came out of Quentin's window and climbed across into the tree. We watched the tree shaking. The shaking went down the tree, then it came out and we watched it go away across the grass. Then we couldn't see it. Come on, Luster said. There now. Hear them horns. You get in that bed while my foots behaves.

There were two beds. Quentin got in the other one. He

turned his face to the wall. Dilsey put Jason in with him.
Caddy took her dress off.

"Just look at your drawers." Dilsey said. "You better be glad
your maw aint seen you."

"I already told on her." Jason said.

"I bound you would." Dilsey said.

"And see what you got by it." Caddy said. "Tattletale."

"What did I get by it." Jason said.

"Whyn't you get your nightie on." Dilsey said. She went
and helped Caddy take off her bodice and drawers. "Just look
at you." Dilsey said. She wadded the drawers and scrubbed
Caddy behind with them. "It done soaked clean through onto
you." she said. "But you wont get no bath this night. Here."
She put Caddy's nightie on her and Caddy climbed into the
bed and Dilsey went to the door and stood with her hand on
the light. "You all be quiet now, you hear." she said.

"All right." Caddy said. "Mother's not coming in tonight."
she said. "So we still have to mind me."

"Yes." Dilsey said. "Go to sleep, now."

"Mother's sick." Caddy said. "She and Damuddy are both
sick."

"Hush." Dilsey said. "You go to sleep."

The room went black, except the door. Then the door went
black. Caddy said, "Hush, Maury" putting her hand on me.
So I stayed hushed. We could hear us. We could hear the dark.

It went away, and Father looked at us. He looked at
Quentin and Jason, then he came and kissed Caddy and put
his hand on my head.

"Is Mother very sick." Caddy said.

"No." Father said. "Are you going to take good care of
Maury."

"Yes." Caddy said.

Father went to the door and looked at us again. Then the
dark came back, and he stood black in the door, and then the
door turned black again. Caddy held me and I could hear us
all, and the darkness, and something I could smell. And then
I could see the windows, where the trees were buzzing. Then
the dark began to go in smooth, bright shapes, like it always
does, even when Caddy says that I have been asleep.

June Second, 1910.

WHEN the shadow of the sash appeared on the curtains it was between seven and eight oclock and then I was in time again, hearing the watch. It was Grandfather's and when Father gave it to me he said I give you the mausoleum of all hope and desire; it's rather excruciating-ly apt that you will use it to gain the reducto absurdum of all human experience which can fit your individual needs no better than it fitted his or his father's. I give it to you not that you may remember time, but that you might forget it now and then for a moment and not spend all your breath trying to conquer it. Because no battle is ever won he said. They are not even fought. The field only reveals to man his own folly and despair, and victory is an illusion of philosophers and fools.

It was propped against the collar box and I lay listening to it. Hearing it, that is. I dont suppose anybody ever deliberately listens to a watch or a clock. You dont have to. You can be oblivious to the sound for a long while, then in a second of ticking it can create in the mind unbroken the long diminishing parade of time you didn't hear. Like Father said down the long and lonely light-rays you might see Jesus walking, like. And the good Saint Francis that said Little Sister Death, that never had a sister.

Through the wall I heard Shreve's bed-springs and then his slippers on the floor hishing. I got up and went to the dresser and slid my hand along it and touched the watch and turned it face-down and went back to bed. But the shadow of the sash was still there and I had learned to tell almost to the minute, so I'd have to turn my back to it, feeling the eyes animals used to have in the back of their heads when it was on top, itching. It's always the idle habits you acquire which you will regret. Father said that. That Christ was not crucified: he was worn away by a minute clicking of little wheels. That had no sister.

And so as soon as I knew I couldn't see it, I began to wonder what time it was. Father said that constant speculation regarding the position of mechanical hands on an arbitrary dial which is a symptom of mind-function. Excrement Father said like sweating. And I saying All right. Wonder. Go on and wonder.

If it had been cloudy I could have looked at the window, thinking what he said about idle habits. Thinking it would be nice for them down at New London if the weather held up like this. Why shouldn't it? The month of brides, the voice that breathed   *She ran right out of the mirror, out of the banked scent. Roses. Roses. Mr and Mrs Jason Richmond Compson announce the marriage of.* Roses. Not virgins like dogwood, milkweed. I said I have committed incest, Father I said. Roses. Cunning and serene. If you attend Harvard one year, but dont see the boat-race, there should be a refund. Let Jason have it. Give Jason a year at Harvard.

Shreve stood in the door, putting his collar on, his glasses glinting rosily, as though he had washed them with his face. "You taking a cut this morning?"

"Is it that late?"

He looked at his watch. "Bell in two minutes."

"I didn't know it was that late." He was still looking at the watch, his mouth shaping. "I'll have to hustle. I cant stand another cut. The dean told me last week——" He put the watch back into his pocket. Then I quit talking.

"You'd better slip on your pants and run," he said. He went out.

I got up and moved about, listening to him through the wall. He entered the sitting-room, toward the door.

"Aren't you ready yet?"

"Not yet. Run along. I'll make it."

He went out. The door closed. His feet went down the corridor. Then I could hear the watch again. I quit moving around and went to the window and drew the curtains aside and watched them running for chapel, the same ones fighting the same heaving coat-sleeves, the same books and flapping collars flushing past like debris on a flood, and Spoade. Calling Shreve my husband. Ah let him alone, Shreve said, if he's got better sense than to chase after the little dirty sluts, whose business. In the South you are ashamed of being a virgin. Boys. Men. They lie about it. Because it means less to women, Father said. He said it was men invented virginity not women. Father said it's like death: only a state in which the others are

left and I said, But to believe it doesn't matter and he said,
That's what's so sad about anything: not only virginity and I
said, Why couldn't it have been me and not her who is un-
virgin and he said, That's why that's sad too; nothing is even
worth the changing of it, and Shreve said if he's got better
sense than to chase after the little dirty sluts and I said Did
you ever have a sister? Did you? Did you?

Spoade was in the middle of them like a terrapin in a street
full of scuttering dead leaves, his collar about his ears, moving
at his customary unhurried walk. He was from South Carolina, a senior. It was his club's boast that he never ran for
chapel and had never got there on time and had never been
absent in four years and had never made either chapel or first
lecture with a shirt on his back and socks on his feet. About
ten oclock he'd come in Thompson's, get two cups of coffee,
sit down and take his socks out of his pocket and remove his
shoes and put them on while the coffee cooled. About noon
you'd see him with a shirt and collar on, like anybody else.
The others passed him running, but he never increased his
pace at all. After a while the quad was empty.

A sparrow slanted across the sunlight, onto the window
ledge, and cocked his head at me. His eye was round and
bright. First he'd watch me with one eye, then flick! and it
would be the other one, his throat pumping faster than any
pulse. The hour began to strike. The sparrow quit swapping
eyes and watched me steadily with the same one until the
chimes ceased, as if he were listening too. Then he flicked off
the ledge and was gone.

It was a while before the last stroke ceased vibrating. It
stayed in the air, more felt than heard, for a long time. Like
all the bells that ever rang still ringing in the long dying light-
rays and Jesus and Saint Francis talking about his sister. Because if it were just to hell; if that were all of it. Finished. If
things just finished themselves. Nobody else there but her and
me. If we could just have done something so dreadful that
they would have fled hell except us. *I have committed incest I
said Father it was I it was not Dalton Ames*   And when he put
Dalton Ames. Dalton Ames. Dalton Ames. When he put the
pistol in my hand I didn't. That's why I didn't. He would be
there and she would and I would. Dalton Ames. Dalton Ames.

Dalton Ames. If we could have just done something so dreadful and Father said That's sad too people cannot do anything that dreadful they cannot do anything very dreadful at all they cannot even remember tomorrow what seemed dreadful today and I said, You can shirk all things and he said, Ah can you. And I will look down and see my murmuring bones and the deep water like wind, like a roof of wind, and after a long time they cannot distinguish even bones upon the lonely and inviolate sand. Until on the Day when He says Rise only the flat-iron would come floating up. It's not when you realise that nothing can help you—religion, pride, anything—it's when you realise that you dont need any aid. Dalton Ames. Dalton Ames. Dalton Ames. If I could have been his mother lying with open body lifted laughing, holding his father with my hand refraining, seeing, watching him die before he lived. *One minute she was standing in the door*

I went to the dresser and took up the watch, with the face still down. I tapped the crystal on the corner of the dresser and caught the fragments of glass in my hand and put them into the ashtray and twisted the hands off and put them in the tray. The watch ticked on. I turned the face up, the blank dial with little wheels clicking and clicking behind it, not knowing any better. Jesus walking on Galilee and Washington not telling lies. Father brought back a watch-charm from the Saint Louis Fair to Jason: a tiny opera glass into which you squinted with one eye and saw a skyscraper, a ferris wheel all spidery, Niagara Falls on a pinhead. There was a red smear on the dial. When I saw it my thumb began to smart. I put the watch down and went into Shreve's room and got the iodine and painted the cut. I cleaned the rest of the glass out of the rim with a towel.

I laid out two suits of underwear, with socks, shirts, collars and ties, and packed my trunk. I put in everything except my new suit and an old one and two pairs of shoes and two hats, and my books. I carried the books into the sitting-room and stacked them on the table, the ones I had brought from home and the ones *Father said it used to be a gentleman was known by his books; nowadays he is known by the ones he has not returned* and locked the trunk and addressed it. The quarter hour sounded. I stopped and listened to it until the chimes ceased.

I bathed and shaved. The water made my finger smart a little, so I painted it again. I put on my new suit and put my watch on and packed the other suit and the accessories and my razor and brushes in my hand bag, and folded the trunk key into a sheet of paper and put it in an envelope and addressed it to Father, and wrote the two notes and sealed them.

The shadow hadn't quite cleared the stoop. I stopped inside the door, watching the shadow move. It moved almost perceptibly, creeping back inside the door, driving the shadow back into the door. *Only she was running already when I heard it. In the mirror she was running before I knew what it was. That quick her train caught up over her arm she ran out of the mirror like a cloud, her veil swirling in long glints her heels brittle and fast clutching her dress onto her shoulder with the other hand, running out of the mirror the smells roses roses the voice that breathed o'er Eden. Then she was across the porch I couldn't hear her heels then in the moonlight like a cloud, the floating shadow of the veil running across the grass, into the bellowing. She ran out of her dress, clutching her bridal, running into the bellowing where T. P. in the dew Whooey Sassprilluh Benjy under the box bellowing. Father had a V-shaped silver cuirass on his running chest*

Shreve said, "Well, you didn't. . . . . . . Is it a wedding or a wake?"

"I couldn't make it," I said.

"Not with all that primping. What's the matter? You think this was Sunday?"

"I reckon the police wont get me for wearing my new suit one time," I said.

"I was thinking about the Square students. They'll think you go to Harvard. Have you got too proud to attend classes too?"

"I'm going to eat first." The shadow on the stoop was gone. I stepped into sunlight, finding my shadow again. I walked down the steps just ahead of it. The half hour went. Then the chimes ceased and died away.

Deacon wasn't at the postoffice either. I stamped the two envelopes and mailed the one to Father and put Shreve's in my inside pocket, and then I remembered where I had last seen the Deacon. It was on Decoration Day, in a G.A.R. uniform, in the middle of the parade. If you waited long enough on any corner you would see him in whatever parade came along. The one before was on Columbus' or Garibaldi's or somebody's birthday. He was in the Street Sweepers' section, in a stovepipe hat, carrying a two inch Italian flag, smoking a cigar among the brooms and scoops. But the last time was the G.A.R. one, because Shreve said:

"There now. Just look at what your grandpa did to that poor old nigger."

"Yes," I said. "Now he can spend day after day marching in parades. If it hadn't been for my grandfather, he'd have to work like whitefolks."

I didn't see him anywhere. But I never knew even a working nigger that you could find when you wanted him, let alone one that lived off the fat of the land. A car came along. I went over to town and went to Parker's and had a good breakfast. While I was eating I heard a clock strike the hour. But then I suppose it takes at least one hour to lose time in, who has been longer than history getting into the mechanical progression of it.

When I finished breakfast I bought a cigar. The girl said a fifty cent one was the best, so I took one and lit it and went out to the street. I stood there and took a couple of puffs, then I held it in my hand and went on toward the corner. I passed a jeweller's window, but I looked away in time. At the corner two bootblacks caught me, one on either side, shrill and raucous, like blackbirds. I gave the cigar to one of them, and the other one a nickel. Then they let me alone. The one with the cigar was trying to sell it to the other for the nickel.

There was a clock, high up in the sun, and I thought about how, when you dont want to do a thing, your body will try to trick you into doing it, sort of unawares. I could feel the muscles in the back of my neck, and then I could hear my watch ticking away in my pocket and after a while I had all the other sounds shut away, leaving only the watch in my pocket. I turned back up the street, to the window. He was working at the table behind the window. He was going bald. There was a glass in his eye—a metal tube screwed into his face. I went in.

The place was full of ticking, like crickets in September grass, and I could hear a big clock on the wall above his head.

He looked up, his eye big and blurred and rushing beyond the glass. I took mine out and handed it to him.

"I broke my watch."

He flipped it over in his hand. "I should say you have. You must have stepped on it."

"Yes, sir. I knocked it off the dresser and stepped on it in the dark. It's still running though."

He pried the back open and squinted into it. "Seems to be all right. I cant tell until I go over it, though. I'll go into it this afternoon."

"I'll bring it back later," I said. "Would you mind telling me if any of those watches in the window are right?"

He held my watch on his palm and looked up at me with his blurred rushing eye.

"I made a bet with a fellow," I said. "And I forgot my glasses this morning."

"Why, all right," he said. He laid the watch down and half rose on his stool and looked over the barrier. Then he glanced up at the wall. "It's twen——"

"Dont tell me," I said, "please sir. Just tell me if any of them are right."

He looked at me again. He sat back on the stool and pushed the glass up onto his forehead. It left a red circle around his eye and when it was gone his whole face looked naked. "What're you celebrating today?" he said. "That boat race aint until next week, is it?"

"No, sir. This is just a private celebration. Birthday. Are any of them right?"

"No. But they haven't been regulated and set yet. If you're thinking of buying one of them——"

"No, sir. I dont need a watch. We have a clock in our sitting room. I'll have this one fixed when I do." I reached my hand.

"Better leave it now."

"I'll bring it back later." He gave me the watch. I put it in my pocket. I couldn't hear it now, above all the others. "I'm much obliged to you. I hope I haven't taken up your time."

"That's all right. Bring it in when you are ready. And you better put off this celebration until after we win that boat race."

"Yes, sir. I reckon I had."

I went out, shutting the door upon the ticking. I looked back into the window. He was watching me across the barrier. There were about a dozen watches in the window, a dozen different hours and each with the same assertive and contradictory assurance that mine had, without any hands at all. Contradicting one another. I could hear mine, ticking away inside my pocket, even though nobody could see it, even though it could tell nothing if anyone could.

And so I told myself to take that one. Because Father said clocks slay time. He said time is dead as long as it is being clicked off by little wheels; only when the clock stops does time come to life. The hands were extended, slightly off the horizontal at a faint angle, like a gull tilting into the wind. Holding all I used to be sorry about like the new moon holding water, niggers say. The jeweller was working again, bent over his bench, the tube tunnelled into his face. His hair was parted in the center. The part ran up into the bald spot, like a drained marsh in December.

I saw the hardware store from across the street. I didn't know you bought flat-irons by the pound.

"Maybe you want a tailor's goose," the clerk said. "They weigh ten pounds." Only they were bigger than I thought. So I got two six-pound little ones, because they would look like a pair of shoes wrapped up. They felt heavy enough together, but I thought again how Father had said about the reducto absurdum of human experience, thinking how the only opportunity I seemed to have for the application of Harvard. Maybe by next year; thinking maybe it takes two years in school to learn to do that properly.

But they felt heavy enough in the air. A car came. I got on. I didn't see the placard on the front. It was full, mostly prosperous looking people reading newspapers. The only vacant seat was beside a nigger. He wore a derby and shined shoes and he was holding a dead cigar stub. I used to think that a Southerner had to be always conscious of niggers. I thought that Northerners would expect him to. When I first came East I kept thinking You've got to remember to think of them as colored people not niggers, and if it hadn't happened that I wasn't thrown with many of them, I'd have wasted a lot of time and trouble before I learned that the best way to take all people, black or white, is to take them for what they think they are, then leave them alone. That was when I realised that a nigger is not a person so much as a form of behavior; a sort of obverse reflection of the white people he lives among. But I thought at first that I ought to miss having a lot of them around me because I thought that Northerners thought I did, but I didn't know that I really had missed Roskus and Dilsey and them until that morning in Virginia. The train was stopped when I waked and I raised the shade and looked out. The car was blocking a road crossing, where two white fences came down a hill and then sprayed outward and downward like part of the skeleton of a horn, and there was a nigger on a mule in the middle of the stiff ruts, waiting for the train to move. How long he had been there I didn't know, but he sat straddle of the mule, his head wrapped in a piece of blanket, as if they had been built there with the fence and the road, or with the hill, carved out of the hill itself, like a sign put there saying You are home again. He didn't have a saddle and his feet dangled almost to the ground. The mule looked like a rabbit. I raised the window.

"Hey, Uncle," I said. "Is this the way?"

"Suh?" He looked at me, then he loosened the blanket and lifted it away from his ear.

"Christmas gift!" I said.

"Sho comin, boss. You done caught me, aint you."

"I'll let you off this time." I dragged my pants out of the little hammock and got a quarter out. "But look out next time. I'll be coming back through here two days after New Year, and look out then." I threw the quarter out the window. "Buy yourself some Santy Claus."

"Yes, suh," he said. He got down and picked up the quarter and rubbed it on his leg. "Thanky, young marster. Thanky." Then the train began to move. I leaned out the window, into the cold air, looking back. He stood there beside the gaunt rabbit of a mule, the two of them shabby and motionless and unimpatient. The train swung around the curve, the engine puffing with short, heavy blasts, and they passed smoothly from sight that way, with that quality about them of shabby and timeless patience, of static serenity: that blending of child-like and ready incompetence and paradoxical reliability that tends and protects them it loves out of all reason and robs them steadily and evades responsibility and obligations by means too barefaced to be called subterfuge even and is taken in theft or evasion with only that frank and spontaneous admiration for the victor which a gentleman feels for anyone who beats him in a fair contest, and withal a fond and unflagging tolerance for whitefolks' vagaries like that of a grandparent for unpredictable and troublesome children, which I had forgotten. And all that day, while the train wound through rushing gaps and along ledges where movement was only a laboring sound of the exhaust and groaning wheels and the eternal mountains stood fading into the thick sky, I thought of home, of the bleak station and the mud and the niggers and country folks thronging slowly about the square, with toy monkeys and wagons and candy in sacks and roman candles sticking out, and my insides would move like they used to do in school when the bell rang.

I wouldn't begin counting until the clock struck three. Then I would begin, counting to sixty and folding down one finger and thinking of the other fourteen fingers waiting to be folded down, or thirteen or twelve or eight or seven, until all of a sudden I'd realise silence and the unwinking minds, and I'd say "Ma'am?" "Your name is Quentin, isn't it?" Miss Laura would say. Then more silence and the cruel unwinking minds and hands jerking into the silence. "Tell Quentin who discovered the Mississippi River, Henry." "DeSoto." Then the minds would go away, and after a while I'd be afraid I had gotten behind and I'd count fast and fold down another finger, then I'd be afraid I was going too fast and I'd slow up, then I'd get afraid and count fast again. So I never could come out even with the bell, and the released surging of feet moving already, feeling earth in the scuffed floor, and the day like a pane of glass struck a light, sharp blow, and my insides would move, sitting still. *Moving sitting still. My bowels moved for thee. One minute she was standing in the door. Benjy. Bellowing. Benjamin the child of mine old age bellowing. Caddy! Caddy!*

I'm going to run away. He began to cry she went and touched him. Hush. I'm not going to. Hush. He hushed. Dilsey.

He smell what you tell him when he want to. Dont have to listen nor talk.

Can he smell that new name they give him? Can he smell bad luck?

What he want to worry about luck for? Luck cant do him no hurt.

What they change his name for then if aint trying to help his luck?

The car stopped, started, stopped again. Below the window I watched the crowns of people's heads passing beneath new straw hats not yet unbleached. There were women in the car now, with market baskets, and men in work-clothes were beginning to outnumber the shined shoes and collars.

The nigger touched my knee. "Pardon me," he said. I swung my legs out and let him pass. We were going beside a blank wall, the sound clattering back into the car, at the women with market baskets on their knees and a man in a stained hat with a pipe stuck in the band. I could smell water, and in a break in the wall I saw a glint of water and two masts, and a gull motionless in midair, like on an invisible wire between the masts, and I raised my hand and through my coat touched the letters I had written. When the car stopped I got off.

The bridge was open to let a schooner through. She was in tow, the tug nudging along under her quarter, trailing smoke, but the ship herself was like she was moving without visible means. A man naked to the waist was coiling down a line on the fo'c'sle head. His body was burned the color of leaf tobacco. Another man in a straw hat without any crown was at the wheel. The ship went through the bridge, moving under bare poles like a ghost in broad day, with three gulls hovering above the stern like toys on invisible wires.

When it closed I crossed to the other side and leaned on the rail above the boathouses. The float was empty and the doors were closed. Crew just pulled in the late afternoon now, resting up before. The shadow of the bridge, the tiers of railing, my shadow leaning flat upon the water, so easily had I tricked it that would not quit me. At least fifty feet it was, and if I only had something to blot it into the water, holding it until it was drowned, the shadow of the package like two shoes wrapped up lying on the water. Niggers say a drowned man's shadow was watching for him in the water all the time. It twinkled and glinted, like breathing, the float slow like breathing too, and debris half submerged, healing out to the

sea and the caverns and the grottoes of the sea. The displace-
ment of water is equal to the something of something. Reducto absurdum of all human experience, and two six-pound
flat-irons weigh more than one tailor's goose. What a sinful
waste Dilsey would say. Benjy knew it when Damuddy died.
He cried. *He smell hit. He smell hit.*

The tug came back downstream, the water shearing in long
rolling cylinders, rocking the float at last with the echo of passage, the float lurching onto the rolling cylinder with a plop-
ping sound and a long jarring noise as the door rolled back
and two men emerged, carrying a shell. They set it in the water
and a moment later Bland came out, with the sculls. He wore
flannels, a gray jacket and a stiff straw hat. Either he or his
mother had read somewhere that Oxford students pulled in
flannels and stiff hats, so early one March they bought Gerald
a one pair shell and in his flannels and stiff hat he went on the
river. The folks at the boathouse threatened to call a policeman, but he went anyway. His mother came down in a hired
auto, in a fur suit like an arctic explorer's, and saw him off in
a twenty-five mile wind and a steady drove of ice floes like
dirty sheep. Ever since then I have believed that God is not
only a gentleman and a sport; he is a Kentuckian too. When
he sailed away she made a detour and came down to the river
again and drove along parallel with him, the car in low gear.
They said you couldn't have told they'd ever seen one another
before, like a King and Queen, not even looking at one another, just moving side by side across Massachusetts on parallel courses like a couple of planets.

He got in and pulled away. He pulled pretty well now. He
ought to. They said his mother tried to make him give rowing
up and do something else the rest of his class couldn't or
wouldn't do, but for once he was stubborn. If you could call
it stubbornness, sitting in his attitudes of princely boredom,
with his curly yellow hair and his violet eyes and his eyelashes
and his New York clothes, while his mamma was telling us
about Gerald's horses and Gerald's niggers and Gerald's
women. Husbands and fathers in Kentucky must have been
awful glad when she carried Gerald off to Cambridge. She had
an apartment over in town, and Gerald had one there too,
besides his rooms in college. She approved of Gerald associ-

ating with me because I at least revealed a blundering sense of noblesse oblige by getting myself born below Mason and Dixon, and a few others whose Geography met the requirements (minimum). Forgave, at least. Or condoned. But since she met Spoade coming out of chapel one He said she couldn't be a lady no lady would be out at that hour of the night she never had been able to forgive him for having five names, including that of a present English ducal house. I'm sure she solaced herself by being convinced that some misfit Maingault or Mortemar had got mixed up with the lodge-keeper's daughter. Which was quite probable, whether she invented it or not. Spoade was the world's champion sitter-around, no holds barred and gouging discretionary.

The shell was a speck now, the oars catching the sun in spaced glints, as if the hull were winking itself along him along. *Did you ever have a sister? No but they're all bitches. Did you ever have a sister? One minute she was. Bitches. Not bitch one minute she stood in the door* Dalton Ames. Dalton Ames. Dalton Shirts. I thought all the time they were khaki, army issue khaki, until I saw they were of heavy Chinese silk or finest flannel because they made his face so brown his eyes so blue. Dalton Ames. It just missed gentility. Theatrical fixture. Just pâpier-maché, then touch. Oh. Asbestos. Not quite bronze. *But wont see him at the house.*

Caddy's a woman too remember. She must do things for women's reasons too.

Why wont you bring him to the house, Caddy? Why must you do like nigger women do in the pasture the ditches the dark woods hot hidden furious in the dark woods.

And after a while I had been hearing my watch for some time and I could feel the letters crackle through my coat, against the railing, and I leaned on the railing, watching my shadow, how I had tricked it. I moved along the rail, but my suit was dark too and I could wipe my hands, watching my shadow, how I had tricked it. I walked it into the shadow of the quai. Then I went east.

Harvard my Harvard boy Harvard harvard That pimple-faced infant she met at the field-meet with colored ribbons. Skulking along the fence trying to whistle her out like a puppy. Because they couldn't cajole him into the diningroom Mother believed he had some sort of spell he was going to cast on her when he got her alone. Yet any blackguard *He was lying beside the box under the window bellowing* that could drive up in a limousine with a flower in his buttonhole. *Harvard. Quentin this is Herbert. My Harvard boy. Herbert will be a big brother has already promised Jason*

Hearty, celluloid like a drummer. Face full of teeth white but not smiling. *I've heard of him up there.* All teeth but not smiling. *You going to drive?*

Get in Quentin.

You going to drive.

It's her car aren't you proud of your little sister owns first auto in town Herbert his present. Louis has been giving her lessons every morning didn't you get my letter Mr and Mrs Jason Richmond Compson announce the marriage of their daughter Candace to Mr Sydney Herbert Head on the twenty-fifth of April one thousand nine hundred and ten at Jefferson Mississippi. At home after the first of August number Something Something Avenue South Bend Indiana. Shreve said Aren't you even going to open it? *Three days. Times. Mr and Mrs Jason Richmond Compson* Young Lochinvar rode out of the west a little too soon, didn't he?

I'm from the south. You're funny, aren't you.

O yes I knew it was somewhere in the country.

You're funny, aren't you. You ought to join the circus.

I did. That's how I ruined my eyes watering the elephant's fleas. *Three times* These country girls. You cant ever tell about them, can you. Well, anyway Byron never had his wish, thank God. *But not hit a man in glasses* Aren't you even going to open it? *It lay on the table a candle burning at each corner upon the envelope tied in a soiled pink garter two artificial flowers. Not hit a man in glasses.*

Country people poor things they never saw an auto before lots of them honk the horn Candace so *She wouldn't look at me* they'll get out of the way *wouldn't look at me* your father wouldn't like it if you were to injure one of them I'll declare your father will simply have to get an auto now I'm almost sorry you brought it down Herbert I've enjoyed it so much of course there's the carriage but so often when I'd like to go out Mr Compson has the darkies doing something it would be worth my head to interrupt he insists that Roskus is at my call all the time but I know what that means I know how often people make promises just to satisfy their consciences are you going to treat my little baby girl that way Herbert but I know you wont Herbert has spoiled us all to death Quentin did I write you that he is going to take Jason into his bank when Jason finishes high school Jason will make a splendid banker he is the only one of my children with any practical sense you can thank me for that he takes after my people the others are all Compson   *Jason furnished the flour. They made kites on the back porch and sold them for a nickel a piece, he and the Patterson boy. Jason was treasurer.*

There was no nigger in this car, and the hats unbleached as yet flowing past under the window. Going to Harvard. We have sold Benjy's   *He lay on the ground under the window, bellowing. We have sold Benjy's pasture so that Quentin may go to Harvard*   a brother to you. Your little brother.

You should have a car it's done you no end of good dont you think so Quentin I call him Quentin at once you see I have heard so much about him from Candace.

Why shouldn't you I want my boys to be more than friends yes Candace and Quentin more than friends   *Father I have committed*   what a pity you had no brother or sister   *No sister no sister had no sister*   Dont ask Quentin he and Mr Compson both feel a little insulted when I am strong enough to come down to the table I am going on nerve now I'll pay for it after it's all over and you have taken my little daughter away from me   *My little sister had no. If I could say Mother. Mother*

Unless I do what I am tempted to and take you instead I dont think Mr Compson could overtake the car.

Ah Herbert Candace do you hear that   *She wouldn't look at me soft stubborn jaw-angle not back-looking*   You needn't be jealous though it's just an old woman he's flattering a grown married daughter I cant believe it.

Nonsense you look like a girl you are lots younger than Candace color in your cheeks like a girl   *A face reproachful tearful an odor of camphor and of tears a voice weeping steadily and softly beyond the twilit door the twilight-colored smell of honeysuckle. Bringing empty trunks down the attic stairs they sounded like coffins French Lick. Found not death at the salt lick*

Hats not unbleached and not hats. In three years I can not wear a hat. I could not. Was. Will there be hats then since I was not and not Harvard then. Where the best of thought Father said clings like dead ivy vines upon old dead brick. Not Harvard then. Not to me, anyway. Again. Sadder than was. Again. Saddest of all. Again.

Spoade had a shirt on; then it must be. When I can see my shadow again if not careful that I tricked into the water shall tread again upon my impervious shadow. But no sister. I wouldn't have done it. *I wont have my daughter spied on* I wouldn't have.

How can I control any of them when you have always taught them to have no respect for me and my wishes I know you look down on my people but is that any reason for teaching my children my own children I suffered for to have no respect Trampling my shadow's bones into the concrete with hard heels and then I was hearing the watch, and I touched the letters through my coat.

I will not have my daughter spied on by you or Quentin or anybody no matter what you think she has done

At least you agree there is reason for having her watched

I wouldn't have I wouldn't have. *I know you wouldn't I didn't mean to speak so sharply but women have no respect for each other for themselves*

But why did she The chimes began as I stepped on my shadow, but it was the quarter hour. The Deacon wasn't in sight anywhere. *think I would have   could have*

She didn't mean that that's the way women do things it's because she loves Caddy

The street lamps would go down the hill then rise toward town I walked upon the belly of my shadow. I could extend my hand beyond it. *feeling Father behind me beyond the rasping darkness of summer and August the street lamps* Father and I protect women from one another from themselves our women *Women are like that they dont acquire knowledge of people we are for that they are just born with a practical fertility of suspicion that makes a crop every so often and usually right they have an affinity for evil for supplying whatever the evil lacks in itself for drawing it about them instinctively as you do bed-clothing in slumber fertilising the mind for it until the evil has served its purpose whether it ever existed or no*   He was coming along between a couple of freshmen. He hadn't quite recovered from the parade, for he gave me a salute, a very superior-officerish kind.

"I want to see you a minute," I said, stopping.

"See me? All right. See you again, fellows," he said, stopping and turning back; "glad to have chatted with you." That was the Deacon, all over. Talk about your natural psychologists. They said he hadn't missed a train at the beginning of school in forty years, and that he could pick out a Southerner with one glance. He never missed, and once he had heard you speak, he could name your state. He had a regular uniform he met trains in, a sort of Uncle Tom's cabin outfit, patches and all.

"Yes, suh. Right dis way, young marster, hyer we is," taking your bags. "Hyer, boy, come hyer and git dese grips." Whereupon a moving mountain of luggage would edge up, revealing a white boy of about fifteen, and the Deacon would hang another bag on him somehow and drive him off. "Now, den, dont you drap hit. Yes, suh, young marster, jes give de old nigger yo room number, and hit'll be done got cold dar when you arrives."

From then on until he had you completely subjugated he was always in or out of your room, ubiquitous and garrulous, though his manner gradually moved northward as his raiment improved, until at last when he had bled you until you began to learn better he was calling you Quentin or whatever, and when you saw him next he'd be wearing a cast-off Brooks suit and a hat with a Princeton club I forget which band that someone had given him and which he was pleasantly and unshakably convinced was a part of Abe Lincoln's military sash. Someone spread the story years ago, when he first appeared around college from wherever he came from, that he was a graduate of the divinity school. And when he came to understand what it meant he was so taken with it that he began to retail the story himself, until at last he must have come to believe he really had. Anyway he related long pointless anecdotes of his undergraduate days, speaking familiarly of dead and departed professors by their first names, usually incorrect ones. But he had been guide mentor and friend to unnumbered crops of innocent and lonely freshmen, and I suppose that with all his petty chicanery and hypocrisy he stank no higher in heaven's nostrils than any other.

"Haven't seen you in three-four days," he said, staring at me from his still military aura. "You been sick?"

"No. I've been all right. Working, I reckon. I've seen you, though."

"Yes?"

"In the parade the other day."

"Oh, that. Yes, I was there. I dont care nothing about that sort of thing, you understand, but the boys likes to have me with them, the vet'runs does. Ladies wants all the old vet'runs to turn out, you know. So I has to oblige them."

"And on that Wop holiday too," I said. "You were obliging the W.C.T.U. then, I reckon."

"That? I was doing that for my son-in-law. He aims to get a job on the city forces. Street cleaner. I tells him all he wants is a broom to sleep on. You saw me, did you?"

"Both times. Yes."

"I mean, in uniform. How'd I look?"

"You looked fine. You looked better than any of them. They ought to make you a general, Deacon."

He touched my arm, lightly, his hand that worn, gentle quality of niggers' hands. "Listen. This aint for outside talking. I don't mind telling you because you and me's the same folks, come long and short." He leaned a little to me, speaking rapidly, his eyes not looking at me. "I've got strings out, right now. Wait till next year. Just wait. Then see where I'm marching. I wont need to tell you how I'm fixing it; I say, just wait and see, my boy." He looked at me now and clapped me lightly on the shoulder and rocked back on his heels, nodding at me. "Yes, sir. I didn't turn Democrat three years ago for nothing. My son-in-law on the city; me—— Yes, sir. If just turning Democrat'll make that son of a bitch go to work. . . . . . . And me: just you stand on that corner yonder a year from two days ago, and see."

"I hope so. You deserve it, Deacon. And while I think about it——" I took the letter from my pocket. "Take this around to my room tomorrow and give it to Shreve. He'll have something for you. But not till tomorrow, mind."

He took the letter and examined it. "It's sealed up."

"Yes. And it's written inside, Not good until tomorrow."

"H'm," he said. He looked at the envelope, his mouth pursed. "Something for me, you say?"

"Yes. A present I'm making you."

He was looking at me now, the envelope white in his black hand, in the sun. His eyes were soft and irisless and brown, and suddenly I saw Roskus watching me from behind all his whitefolks' claptrap of uniforms and politics and Harvard manner, diffident, secret, inarticulate and sad. "You aint playing a joke on the old nigger, is you?"

"You know I'm not. Did any Southerner ever play a joke on you?"

"You're right. They're fine folks. But you cant live with them."

"Did you ever try?" I said. But Roskus was gone. Once more he was that self he had long since taught himself to wear in the world's eye, pompous, spurious, not quite gross.

"I'll confer to your wishes, my boy."

"Not until tomorrow, remember."

"Sure," he said; "understood, my boy. Well——"

"I hope——" I said. He looked down at me, benignant, profound. Suddenly I held out my hand and we shook, he gravely, from the pompous height of his municipal and military dream. "You're a good fellow, Deacon. I hope. . . . . . . You've helped a lot of young fellows, here and there."

"I've tried to treat all folks right," he said. "I draw no petty social lines. A man to me is a man, wherever I find him."

"I hope you'll always find as many friends as you've made."

"Young fellows. I get along with them. They dont forget me, neither," he said, waving the envelope. He put it into his pocket and buttoned his coat. "Yes, sir," he said. "I've had good friends."

The chimes began again, the half hour. I stood in the belly of my shadow and listened to the strokes spaced and tranquil along the sunlight, among the thin, still little leaves. Spaced and peaceful and serene, with that quality of autumn always in bells even in the month of brides. *Lying on the ground under the window bellowing* He took one look at her and knew. Out of the mouths of babes. *The street lamps* The chimes ceased. I went back to the postoffice, treading my shadow into pavement. *go down the hill then they rise toward town like lanterns hung one above another on a wall.* Father said because she loves Caddy she loves people through their short-comings. Uncle Maury straddling his legs before the fire must remove one hand long enough to drink Christmas. Jason ran on, his hands in his pockets fell down and lay there like a trussed fowl until Versh set him up. *Whyn't you keep them hands outen your pockets when you running you could stand up then* Rolling his head in the cradle rolling it flat across the back. Caddy told Jason and Versh that the reason Uncle Maury didn't work was that he used to roll his head in the cradle when he was little.

Shreve was coming up the walk, shambling, fatly earnest, his glasses glinting beneath the running leaves like little pools.

"I gave Deacon a note for some things. I may not be in this afternoon, so dont you let him have anything until tomorrow, will you?"

"All right." He looked at me. "Say, what're you doing today, anyhow? All dressed up and mooning around like the prologue to a suttee. Did you go to Psychology this morning?"

"I'm not doing anything. Not until tomorrow, now."

"What's that you got there?"

"Nothing. Pair of shoes I had half-soled. Not until tomorrow, you hear?"

"Sure. All right. Oh, by the way, did you get a letter off the table this morning?"

"No."

"It's there. From Semiramis. Chauffeur brought it before ten oclock."

"All right. I'll get it. Wonder what she wants now."

"Another band recital, I guess. Tumpty ta ta Gerald blah. 'A little louder on the drum, Quentin'. God, I'm glad I'm not a gentleman." He went on, nursing a book, a little shapeless, fatly intent. *The street lamps* do you think so because one of our forefathers was a governor and three were generals and Mother's weren't

any live man is better than any dead man but no live or dead man is very much better than any other live or dead man *Done in Mother's mind though. Finished. Finished. Then we were all poisoned* you are confusing sin and morality women dont

do that your mother is thinking of morality whether it be sin
or not has not occurred to her

Jason I must go away you keep the others I'll take Jason and
go where nobody knows us so he'll have a chance to grow up
and forget all this the others dont love me they have never
loved anything with that streak of Compson selfishness and
false pride Jason was the only one my heart went out to without dread

nonsense Jason is all right I was thinking that as soon as you
feel better you and Caddy might go up to French Lick

and leave Jason here with nobody but you and the darkies

she will forget him then all the talk will die away *found not
death at the salt licks*

maybe I could find a husband for her *not death at the salt
licks*

The car came up and stopped. The bells were still ringing
the half hour. I got on and it went on again, blotting the half
hour. No: the three quarters. Then it would be ten minutes
anyway. To leave Harvard *your mother's dream for sold Benjy's
pasture for*

what have I done to have been given children like these Benjamin was punishment enough and now for her to have no
more regard for me her own mother I've suffered for her
dreamed and planned and sacrificed I went down into the
valley yet never since she opened her eyes has she given me
one unselfish thought at times I look at her I wonder if she
can be my child except Jason he has never given me one
moment's sorrow since I first held him in my arms I knew then
that he was to be my joy and my salvation I thought that Benjamin was punishment enough for any sins I have committed
I thought he was my punishment for putting aside my pride
and marrying a man who held himself above me I dont complain I loved him above all of them because of it because my
duty though Jason pulling at my heart all the while but I see
now that I have not suffered enough I see now that I must
pay for your sins as well as mine what have you done what
sins have your high and mighty people visited upon me but
you'll take up for them you always have found excuses for
your own blood only Jason can do wrong because he is more
Bascomb than Compson while your own daughter my little

daughter my baby girl she is she is no better than that when I was a girl I was unfortunate I was only a Bascomb I was taught that there is no halfway ground that a woman is either a lady or not but I never dreamed when I held her in my arms that any daughter of mine could let herself dont you know I can look at her eyes and tell you may think she'd tell you but she doesn't tell things she is secretive you dont know her I know things she's done that I'd die before I'd have you know that's it go on criticise Jason accuse me of setting him to watch her as if it were a crime while your own daughter can I know you dont love him that you wish to believe faults against him you never have yes ridicule him as you always have Maury you cannot hurt me any more than your children already have and then I'll be gone and Jason with no one to love him shield him from this I look at him every day dreading to see this Compson blood beginning to show in him at last with his sister slipping out to see what do you call it then have you ever laid eyes on him will you even let me try to find out who he is it's not for myself I couldn't bear to see him it's for your sake to protect you but who can fight against bad blood you wont let me try we are to sit back with our hands folded while she not only drags your name in the dirt but corrupts the very air your children breathe Jason you must let me go away I cannot stand it let me have Jason and you keep the others they're not my flesh and blood like he is strangers nothing of mine and I am afraid of them I can take Jason and go where we are not known I'll go down on my knees and pray for the absolution of my sins that he may escape this curse try to forget that the others ever were

If that was the three quarters, not over ten minutes now. One car had just left, and people were already waiting for the next one. I asked, but he didn't know whether another one would leave before noon or not because you'd think that interurbans. So the first one was another trolley. I got on. You can feel noon. I wonder if even miners in the bowels of the earth. That's why whistles: because people that sweat, and if just far enough from sweat you wont hear whistles and in eight minutes you should be that far from sweat in Boston. Father said a man is the sum of his misfortunes. One day you'd think misfortune would get tired, but then time is your misfortune

Father said. A gull on an invisible wire attached through space dragged. You carry the symbol of your frustration into eternity. Then the wings are bigger Father said only who can play a harp.

I could hear my watch whenever the car stopped, but not often they were already eating *Who would play a* Eating the business of eating inside of you space too space and time confused Stomach saying noon brain saying eat oclock   All right I wonder what time it is what of it. People were getting out. The trolley didn't stop so often now, emptied by eating.

Then it was past. I got off and stood in my shadow and after a while a car came along and I got on and went back to the interurban station. There was a car ready to leave, and I found a seat next the window and it started and I watched it sort of frazzle out into slack tide flats, and then trees. Now and then I saw the river and I thought how nice it would be for them down at New London if the weather and Gerald's shell going solemnly up the glinting forenoon and I wondered what the old woman would be wanting now, sending me a note before ten oclock in the morning. What picture of Gerald I to be one of the *Dalton Ames   oh asbestos   Quentin has shot* background. Something with girls in it. Women do have *always his voice above the gabble voice that breathed* an affinity for evil, for believing that no woman is to be trusted, but that some men are too innocent to protect themselves. Plain girls. Remote cousins and family friends whom mere acquaintanceship invested with a sort of blood obligation noblesse oblige. And she sitting there telling us before their faces what a shame it was that Gerald should have all the family looks because a man didn't need it, was better off without it but without it a girl was simply lost. Telling us about Gerald's women in a *Quentin has shot Herbert he shot his voice through the floor of Caddy's room* tone of smug approbation. "When he was seventeen I said to him one day 'What a shame that you should have a mouth like that it should be on a girl's face' and can you imagine *the curtains leaning in on the twilight upon the odor of the apple tree her head against the twilight her arms behind her head kimono-winged the voice that breathed o'er eden clothes upon the bed by the nose seen above the apple* what he said? just seventeen, mind. 'Mother' he said 'it often is'." And him sitting there in attitudes regal watching two or three of them through his eyelashes. They gushed like swallows swooping his eyelashes. Shreve said he always had   *Are you going to look after Benjy and Father*

The less you say about Benjy and Father the better when have you ever considered them Caddy

Promise

You needn't worry about them you're getting out in good shape

Promise I'm sick you'll have to promise wondered who invented that joke but then he always had considered Mrs Bland a remarkably preserved woman he said she was grooming Gerald to seduce a duchess sometime. She called Shreve that fat Canadian youth twice she arranged a new room-mate for me without consulting me at all, once for me to move out, once for

He opened the door in the twilight. His face looked like a pumpkin pie.

"Well, I'll say a fond farewell. Cruel fate may part us, but I will never love another. Never."

"What are you talking about?"

"I'm talking about cruel fate in eight yards of apricot silk and more metal pound for pound than a galley slave and the sole owner and proprietor of the unchallenged peripatetic john of the late Confederacy." Then he told me how she had gone to the proctor to have him moved out and how the proctor had revealed enough low stubbornness to insist on consulting Shreve first. Then she suggested that he send for Shreve right off and do it, and he wouldn't do that, so after that she was hardly civil to Shreve. "I make it a point never to speak harshly of females," Shreve said, "but that woman has got more ways like a bitch than any lady in these sovereign states and dominions." and now Letter on the table by hand, command orchid scented colored If she knew I had passed almost beneath the window knowing it there without   My dear Madam I have not yet had an opportunity of receiving your communication but I beg in advance to be excused today or yesterday and tomorrow or when   As I remember that the next one is to be how Gerald throws his nigger downstairs and how the nigger pled to be allowed to matriculate in the divinity school to be near marster marse gerald and How he ran all the way to the station beside the carriage with tears in his eyes when marse gerald rid away I will wait until the day for

the one about the sawmill husband came to the kitchen door
with a shotgun Gerald went down and bit the gun in two and
handed it back and wiped his hands on a silk handkerchief
threw the handkerchief in the stove I've only heard that one
twice

   shot him through the   I saw you come in here so I watched
my chance and came along thought we might get acquainted
have a cigar

Thanks I dont smoke

No things must have changed up there since my day mind if
I light up

Help yourself

Thanks I've heard a lot I guess your mother wont mind if I
put the match behind the screen will she a lot about you Candace talked about you all the time up there at the Licks   I got
pretty jealous I says to myself who is this Quentin anyway I
must see what this animal looks like because I was hit pretty
hard see soon as I saw the little girl I dont mind telling you it
never occurred to me it was her brother she kept talking about
she couldn't have talked about you any more if you'd been the
only man in the world husband wouldn't have been in it you
wont change your mind and have a smoke

I dont smoke

In that case I wont insist even though it is a pretty fair weed
cost me twenty-five bucks a hundred wholesale friend of in
Havana yes I guess there are lots of changes up there I keep
promising myself a visit but I never get around to it been hitting the ball now for ten years I cant get away from the bank
during school fellow's habits change things that seem important to an undergraduate you know tell me about things up
there

I'm not going to tell Father and Mother if that's what you are
getting at

Not going to tell not going to oh that that's what you are talking about is it you understand that I dont give a damn
whether you tell or not understand that a thing like that unfortunate but no police crime I wasn't the first or the last I was
just unlucky you might have been luckier

You lie

Keep your shirt on I'm not trying to make you tell anything

you dont want to meant no offense of course a young fellow
like you would consider a thing of that sort a lot more serious than you will in five years
I dont know but one way to consider cheating I dont think
I'm likely to learn different at Harvard
We're better than a play you must have made the Dramat well
you're right no need to tell them we'll let bygones be bygones
eh no reason why you and I should let a little thing like that
come between us I like you Quentin I like your appearance
you dont look like these other hicks I'm glad we're going to
hit it off like this I've promised your mother to do something
for Jason but I would like to give you a hand too Jason would
be just as well off here but there's no future in a hole like this
for a young fellow like you
Thanks you'd better stick to Jason he'd suit you better than I
would
I'm sorry about that business but a kid like I was then I never
had a mother like yours to teach me the finer points it would
just hurt her unnecessarily to know it yes you're right no need
to that includes Candace of course
I said Mother and Father
Look here take a look at me how long do you think you'd last
with me
I wont have to last long if you learned to fight up at school
too try and see how long I would
You damned little what do you think you're getting at
Try and see
My God the cigar what would your mother say if she found
a blister on her mantel just in time too look here Quentin
we're about to do something we'll both regret I like you liked
you as soon as I saw you I says he must be a damned good
fellow whoever he is or Candace wouldn't be so keen on him
listen I've been out in the world now for ten years things dont
matter so much then you'll find that out let's you and I get together on this thing sons of old Harvard and all I guess I
wouldn't know the place now best place for a young fellow in
the world I'm going to send my sons there give them a better
chance than I had wait dont go yet let's discuss this thing a
young man gets these ideas and I'm all for them does him
good while he's in school forms his character good for tradi-

tion the school but when he gets out into the world he'll have
to get his the best way he can because he'll find that everybody
else is doing the same thing and be damned to here let's shake
hands and let bygones be bygones for your mother's sake remember her health come on give me your hand here look at
it it's just out of convent look not a blemish not even been
creased yet see here
To hell with your money
No no come on I belong to the family now see I know how
it is with a young fellow he has lots of private affairs it's always
pretty hard to get the old man to stump up for I know haven't
I been there and not so long ago either but now I'm getting
married and all specially up there come on dont be a fool listen
when we get a chance for a real talk I want to tell you about
a little widow over in town
I've heard that too keep your damned money
Call it a loan then just shut your eyes a minute and you'll be
fifty
Keep your hands off of me you'd better get that cigar off the
mantel
Tell and be damned then see what it gets you if you were not
a damned fool you'd have seen that I've got them too tight for
any half-baked Galahad of a brother your mother's told me
about your sort with your head swelled up come in oh come
in dear Quentin and I were just getting acquainted talking
about Harvard did you want me cant stay away from the old
man can she
Go out a minute Herbert I want to talk to Quentin
Come in come in let's all have a gabfest and get acquainted I
was just telling Quentin
Go on Herbert go out a while
Well all right then I suppose you and bubber do want to see
one another once more eh
You'd better take that cigar off the mantel
Right as usual my boy then I'll toddle along let them order
you around while they can Quentin after day after tomorrow
it'll be pretty please to the old man wont it dear give us a kiss
honey
Oh stop that save that for day after tomorrow
I'll want interest then dont let Quentin do anything he cant

finish oh by the way did I tell Quentin the story about the man's parrot and what happened to it a sad story remind me of that think of it yourself ta-ta see you in the funnypaper
Well
Well
What are you up to now
Nothing
You're meddling in my business again didn't you get enough of that last summer
Caddy you've got fever   *You're sick how are you sick*
  I'm just sick. I cant ask.
  Shot his voice through the
  Not that blackguard Caddy
  Now and then the river glinted beyond things in sort of swooping glints, across noon and after. Good after now, though we had passed where he was still pulling upstream majestical in the face of god gods. Better. Gods. God would be canaille too in Boston in Massachusetts. Or maybe just not a husband. The wet oars winking him along in bright winks and female palms. Adulant. Adulant if not a husband he'd ignore God. *That blackguard, Caddy*   The river glinted away beyond a swooping curve.
  I'm sick you'll have to promise
  Sick how are you sick
  I'm just sick I cant ask anybody yet promise you will
  If they need any looking after it's because of you how are you sick
Under the window we could hear the car leaving for the station, the 8:10 train. To bring back cousins. Heads. Increasing himself head by head but not barbers. Manicure girls. We had a blood horse once. In the stable yes, but under leather a cur. *Quentin has shot all of their voices through the floor of Caddy's room*
  The car stopped. I got off, into the middle of my shadow. A road crossed the track. There was a wooden marquee with an old man eating something out of a paper bag, and then the car was out of hearing too. The road went into trees, where it would be shady, but June foliage in New England not much thicker than April at home. I could see a smoke stack. I turned my back to it, tramping my shadow into the dust. *There was something terrible in me sometimes at night I could see it grinning*

at me I could see it through them grinning at me through their
faces it's gone now and I'm sick

  Caddy

  Dont touch me just promise

  If you're sick you cant

  Yes I can after that it'll be all right it wont matter dont let them
send him to Jackson promise

  I promise Caddy Caddy

  Dont touch me dont touch me

  What does it look like Caddy

  What

  That that grins at you that thing through them

I could still see the smoke stack. That's where the water
would be, healing out to the sea and the peaceful grottoes.
Tumbling peacefully they would, and when He said Rise only
the flat irons. When Versh and I hunted all day we wouldn't
take any lunch, and at twelve oclock I'd get hungry. I'd stay
hungry until about one, then all of a sudden I'd even forget
that I wasn't hungry anymore. *The street lamps go down the hill*
then heard the car go down the hill. The chair-arm flat cool smooth
under my forehead shaping the chair the apple tree leaning on my
hair above the eden clothes by the nose seen   You've got fever I
felt it yesterday it's like being near a stove.

  Dont touch me.

  Caddy you cant do it if you are sick. That blackguard.

  I've got to marry somebody. *Then they told me the bone would*
have to be broken again

At last I couldn't see the smoke stack. The road went beside
a wall. Trees leaned over the wall, sprayed with sunlight. The
stone was cool. Walking near it you could feel the coolness.
Only our country was not like this country. There was something about just walking through it. A kind of still and violent fecundity that satisfied even bread-hunger like. Flowing
around you, not brooding and nursing every niggard stone.
Like it were put to makeshift for enough green to go around
among the trees and even the blue of distance not that rich
chimaera.   *told me the bone would have to be broken again and*
inside me it began to say Ah Ah Ah and I began to sweat. What
do I care I know what a broken leg is all it is it wont be anything
I'll just have to stay in the house a little longer that's all and my

jaw-muscles getting numb and my mouth saying Wait Wait just
a minute through the sweat ah ah ah behind my teeth and Father
damn that horse damn that horse. Wait it's my fault. He came
along the fence every morning with a basket toward the kitchen
dragging a stick along the fence every morning I dragged myself to
the window cast and all and laid for him with a piece of coal Dilsey
said you goin to ruin yoself aint you got no mo sense than that not
fo days since you bruck hit. Wait I'll get used to it in a minute wait
just a minute I'll get

Even sound seemed to fail in this air, like the air was worn
out with carrying sounds so long. A dog's voice carries further than a train, in the darkness anyway. And some people's.
Niggers. Louis Hatcher never even used his horn carrying it
and that old lantern. I said, "Louis, when was the last time
you cleaned that lantern?"

"I cleant hit a little while back. You member when all dat
flood-watter wash dem folks away up yonder? I cleant hit dat
ve'y day. Old woman and me settin fo de fire dat night and
she say 'Louis, whut you gwine do ef dat flood git out dis fur?'
and I say 'Dat's a fack. I reckon I had better clean dat lantun
up.' So I cleant hit dat night."

"That flood was way up in Pennsylvania," I said. "It couldn't
ever have got down this far."

"Dat's whut you says," Louis said. "Watter kin git des ez
high en wet in Jefferson ez hit kin in Pennsylvaney, I reckon.
Hit's de folks dat says de high watter cant git dis fur dat comes
floatin out on de ridge-pole, too."

"Did you and Martha get out that night?"

"We done jest dat. I cleant dat lantun and me and her sot
de balance of de night on top o dat knoll back de graveyard.
En ef I'd a knowed of aihy one higher, we'd a been on hit instead."

"And you haven't cleaned that lantern since then."

"Whut I want to clean hit when dey aint no need?"

"You mean, until another flood comes along?"

"Hit kep us outen dat un."

"Oh, come on, Uncle Louis," I said.

"Yes, suh. You do yo way en I do mine. Ef all I got to do
to keep outen de high watter is to clean dis yere lantun, I wont
quoil wid no man."

"Unc' Louis wouldn't ketch nothin wid a light he could see by," Versh said.

"I wuz huntin possums in dis country when dey was still drowndin nits in yo pappy's head wid coal oil, boy," Louis said. "Ketchin um, too."

"Dat's de troof," Versh said. "I reckon Unc' Louis done caught mo possums than aihy man in dis country."

"Yes, suh," Louis said. "I got plenty light fer possums to see, all right. I aint heard none o dem complainin. Hush, now. Dar he. Whooey. Hum awn, dawg." And we'd sit in the dry leaves that whispered a little with the slow respiration of our waiting and with the slow breathing of the earth and the windless October, the rank smell of the lantern fouling the brittle air, listening to the dogs and to the echo of Louis' voice dying away. He never raised it, yet on a still night we have heard it from our front porch. When he called the dogs in he sounded just like the horn he carried slung on his shoulder and never used, but clearer, mellower, as though his voice were a part of darkness and silence, coiling out of it, coiling into it again. WhoOoooo. WhoOoooo. WhoOooooooooooooooooo. *Got to marry somebody*

Have there been very many Caddy

I dont know too many will you look after Benjy and Father

You dont know whose it is then does he know

Dont touch me will you look after Benjy and Father

I began to feel the water before I came to the bridge. The bridge was of gray stone, lichened, dappled with slow moisture where the fungus crept. Beneath it the water was clear and still in the shadow, whispering and clucking about the stone in fading swirls of spinning sky. *Caddy that*

I've got to marry somebody Versh told me about a man who mutilated himself. He went into the woods and did it with a razor, sitting in a ditch. A broken razor flinging them backward over his shoulder the same motion complete the jerked skein of blood backward not looping. But that's not it. It's not not having them. It's never to have had them then I could say O That That's Chinese I dont know Chinese. And Father said it's because you are a virgin: dont you see? Women are never virgins. Purity is a negative state and therefore contrary to nature. It's nature is hurting you not Caddy and I said That's just words and he said So is virginity and I said you dont know. You cant know and he said Yes. On the instant when we come to realise that tragedy is second-hand.

Where the shadow of the bridge fell I could see down for a long way, but not as far as the bottom. When you leave a leaf in water a long time after a while the tissue will be gone and the delicate fibers waving slow as the motion of sleep. They dont touch one another, no matter how knotted up they once were, no matter how close they lay once to the bones. And maybe when He says Rise the eyes will come floating up too, out of the deep quiet and the sleep, to look on glory. And after a while the flat irons would come floating up. I hid them under the end of the bridge and went back and leaned on the rail.

I could not see the bottom, but I could see a long way into the motion of the water before the eye gave out, and then I saw a shadow hanging like a fat arrow stemming into the current. Mayflies skimmed in and out of the shadow of the bridge just above the surface. *If it could just be a hell beyond that: the clean flame the two of us more than dead. Then you will have only me then only me then the two of us amid the pointing and the horror beyond the clean flame* The arrow increased without motion, then in a quick swirl the trout lipped a fly beneath the surface with that sort of gigantic delicacy of an elephant picking up a peanut. The fading vortex drifted away down stream and then I saw the arrow again, nose into the current, wavering delicately to the motion of the water above which the May flies slanted and poised. *Only you and me then amid the pointing and the horror walled by the clean flame*

The trout hung, delicate and motionless among the wavering shadows. Three boys with fishing poles came onto the bridge and we leaned on the rail and looked down at the trout. They knew the fish. He was a neighborhood character.

"They've been trying to catch that trout for twenty-five years. There's a store in Boston offers a twenty-five dollar fishing rod to anybody that can catch him."

"Why dont you all catch him, then? Wouldn't you like to have a twenty-five dollar fishing rod?"

"Yes," they said. They leaned on the rail, looking down at the trout. "I sure would," one said.

"I wouldn't take the rod," the second said. "I'd take the money instead."

"Maybe they wouldn't do that," the first said. "I bet he'd make you take the rod."

"Then I'd sell it."

"You couldn't get twenty-five dollars for it."

"I'd take what I could get, then. I can catch just as many fish with this pole as I could with a twenty-five dollar one." Then they talked about what they would do with twenty-five dollars. They all talked at once, their voices insistent and contradictory and impatient, making of unreality a possibility, then a probability, then an incontrovertible fact, as people will when their desires become words.

"I'd buy a horse and wagon," the second said.

"Yes you would," the others said.

"I would. I know where I can buy one for twenty-five dollars. I know the man."

"Who is it?"

"That's all right who it is. I can buy it for twenty-five dollars."

"Yah," the others said. "He dont know any such thing. He's just talking."

"Do you think so?" the boy said. They continued to jeer at him, but he said nothing more. He leaned on the rail, looking down at the trout which he had already spent, and suddenly the acrimony, the conflict, was gone from their voices, as if to them too it was as though he had captured the fish and bought his horse and wagon, they too partaking of that adult trait of being convinced of anything by an assumption of silent superiority. I suppose that people, using themselves and each other so much by words, are at least consistent in attributing wisdom to a still tongue, and for a while I could feel the other two seeking swiftly for some means by which to cope with him, to rob him of his horse and wagon.

"You couldn't get twenty-five dollars for that pole," the first said. "I bet anything you couldn't."

"He hasn't caught that trout yet," the third said suddenly, then they both cried:

"Yah, what'd I tell you? What's the man's name? I dare you to tell. There aint any such man."

"Ah, shut up," the second said. "Look. Here he comes again." They leaned on the rail, motionless, identical, their poles slanting slenderly in the sunlight, also identical. The trout rose without haste, a shadow in faint wavering increase; again the little vortex faded slowly downstream. "Gee," the first one murmured.

"We dont try to catch him anymore," he said. "We just watch Boston folks that come out and try."

"Is he the only fish in this pool?"

"Yes. He ran all the others out. The best place to fish around here is down at the Eddy."

"No it aint," the second said. "It's better at Bigelow's Mill two to one." Then they argued for a while about which was the best fishing and then left off all of a sudden to watch the trout rise again and the broken swirl of water suck down a little of the sky. I asked how far it was to the nearest town. They told me.

"But the closest car line is that way," the second said, pointing back down the road. "Where are you going?"

"Nowhere. Just walking."

"You from the college?"

"Yes. Are there any factories in that town?"

"Factories?" They looked at me.

"No," the second said. "Not there." They looked at my clothes. "You looking for work?"

"How about Bigelow's Mill?" the third said. "That's a factory."

"Factory my eye. He means a sure enough factory."

"One with a whistle," I said. "I haven't heard any one oclock whistles yet."

"Oh," the second said. "There's a clock in the unitarial steeple. You can find out the time from that. Haven't you got a watch on that chain?"

"I broke it this morning." I showed them my watch. They examined it gravely.

"It's still running," the second said. "What does a watch like that cost?"

"It was a present," I said. "My father gave it to me when I graduated from high school."

"Are you a Canadian?" the third said. He had red hair.

"Canadian?"

"He dont talk like them," the second said. "I've heard them talk. He talks like they do in minstrel shows."

"Say," the third said. "Aint you afraid he'll hit you?"

"Hit me?"

"You said he talks like a colored man."

"Ah, dry up," the second said. "You can see the steeple when you get over that hill there."

I thanked them. "I hope you have good luck. Only dont catch that old fellow down there. He deserves to be let alone."

"Cant anybody catch that fish," the first said. They leaned on the rail, looking down into the water, the three poles like three slanting threads of yellow fire in the sun. I walked upon my shadow, tramping it into the dappled shade of trees again. The road curved, mounting away from the water. It crossed the hill, then descended winding, carrying the eye, the mind on ahead beneath a still green tunnel, and the square cupola above the trees and the round eye of the clock but far enough. I sat down at the roadside. The grass was ankle deep, myriad. The shadows on the road were as still as if they had been put there with a stencil, with slanting pencils of sunlight. But it was only a train, and after a while it died away beyond the trees, the long sound, and then I could hear my watch and the train dying away, as though it were running through another month or another summer somewhere, rushing away under the poised gull and all things rushing. Except Gerald. He would be sort of grand too, pulling in lonely state across the noon, rowing himself right out of noon, up the long bright air like an apotheosis, mounting into a drowsing infinity where only he and the gull, the one terrifically motionless, the other in a steady and measured pull and recover that partook of inertia itself, the world punily beneath their shadows on the sun. *Caddy that blackguard that blackguard Caddy*

Their voices came over the hill, and the three slender poles like balanced threads of running fire. They looked at me passing, not slowing.

"Well," I said. "I dont see him."

"We didn't try to catch him," the first said. "You cant catch that fish."

"There's the clock," the second said, pointing. "You can tell the time when you get a little closer."

"Yes," I said. "All right." I got up. "You all going to town?"

"We're going to the Eddy for chub," the first said.

"You cant catch anything at the Eddy," the second said.

"I guess you want to go to the mill, with a lot of fellows splashing and scaring all the fish away."

"You cant catch any fish at the Eddy."

"We wont catch none nowhere if we dont go on," the third said.

"I dont see why you keep on talking about the Eddy," the second said. "You cant catch anything there."

"You dont have to go," the first said. "You're not tied to me."

"Let's go to the mill and go swimming," the third said.

"I'm going to the Eddy and fish," the first said. "You can do as you please."

"Say, how long has it been since you heard of anybody catching a fish at the Eddy?" the second said to the third.

"Let's go to the mill and go swimming," the third said. The cupola sank slowly beyond the trees, with the round face of the clock far enough yet. We went on in the dappled shade. We came to an orchard, pink and white. It was full of bees; already we could hear them.

"Let's go to the mill and go swimming," the third said. A lane turned off beside the orchard. The third boy slowed and halted. The first went on, flecks of sunlight slipping along the pole across his shoulder and down the back of his shirt. "Come on," the third said. The second boy stopped too. *Why must you marry somebody Caddy*

Do you want me to say it do you think that if I say it it wont be

"Let's go up to the mill," he said. "Come on."

The first boy went on. His bare feet made no sound, falling softer than leaves in the thin dust. In the orchard the bees sounded like a wind getting up, a sound caught by a spell just under crescendo and sustained. The lane went along the wall, arched over, shattered with bloom, dissolving into trees. Sunlight slanted into it, sparse and eager. Yellow butterflies flickered along the shade like flecks of sun.

"What do you want to go to the Eddy for?" the second boy said. "You can fish at the mill if you want to."

"Ah, let him go," the third said. They looked after the first boy. Sunlight slid patchily across his walking shoulders, glinting along the pole like yellow ants.

"Kenny," the second said. *Say it to Father will you I will am my fathers Progenitive I invented him created I him Say it to him it will not be for he will say I was not and then you and I since philoprogenitive*

"Ah, come on," the third boy said. "They're already in." They looked after the first boy. "Yah," they said suddenly, "go on then, mamma's boy. If he goes swimming he'll get his head wet and then he'll get a licking." They turned into the lane and went on, the yellow butterflies slanting about them along the shade.

it is because there is nothing else I believe there is something else but there may not be and then I You will find that even injustice is scarcely worthy of what you believe yourself to be He paid me no attention, his jaw set in profile, his face turned a little away beneath his broken hat.

"Why dont you go swimming with them?" I said. *that blackguard Caddy*

Were you trying to pick a fight with him were you

A liar and a scoundrel Caddy was dropped from his club for cheating at cards got sent to Coventry caught cheating at midterm exams and expelled

Well what about it I'm not going to play cards with

"Do you like fishing better than swimming?" I said. The sound of the bees diminished, sustained yet, as though instead of sinking into silence, silence merely increased between us, as water rises. The road curved again and became a street between shady lawns with white houses. *Caddy that blackguard can you think of Benjy and Father and do it not of me*

What else can I think about what else have I thought about The boy turned from the street. He climbed a picket fence without looking back and crossed the lawn to a tree and laid the pole down and climbed into the fork of the tree and sat there, his back to the road and the dappled sun motionless at last upon his white shirt. *else have I thought about I cant even cry I died last year I told you I had but I didn't know then what I meant I didn't know what I was saying* Some days in late August at home are like this, the air thin and eager like this, with something in it sad and nostalgic and familiar. Man the sum of his climatic experiences Father said. Man the sum of what have you. A problem in impure properties carried tediously to an unvarying nil: stalemate of dust and desire. *but now I know I'm dead I tell you*

Then why must you listen we can go away you and Benjy and me where nobody knows us where The buggy was drawn by a white horse, his feet clopping in the thin dust; spidery wheels chattering thin and dry, moving uphill beneath a rippling shawl of leaves. Elm. No: ellum. Ellum.

On what on your school money the money they sold the pasture for so you could go to Harvard dont you see you've got to finish now if you dont finish he'll have nothing

Sold the pasture His white shirt was motionless in the fork, in the flickering shade. The wheels were spidery. Beneath the sag of the buggy the hooves neatly rapid like the motions of a lady doing embroidery, diminishing without progress like a figure on a treadmill being drawn rapidly offstage. The street turned again. I could see the white cupola, the round stupid assertion of the clock. *Sold the pasture*

Father will be dead in a year they say if he doesn't stop drinking and he wont stop he cant stop since I since last summer and then they'll send Benjy to Jackson I cant cry I cant even cry one minute she was standing in the door the next minute he was pulling at her dress and bellowing his voice hammered back and forth between the walls in waves and she shrinking against the wall getting smaller and smaller with her white face her eyes like thumbs dug into it until he pushed her out of the room his voice hammering back and forth as though its own momentum would not let it stop as though there were no place for it in silence bellowing

When you opened the door a bell tinkled, but just once, high and clear and small in the neat obscurity above the door, as though it were gauged and tempered to make that single clear small sound so as not to wear the bell out nor to require the expenditure of too much silence in restoring it when the door opened upon the recent warm scent of baking; a little dirty child with eyes like a toy bear's and two patent-leather pigtails.

"Hello, sister." Her face was like a cup of milk dashed with coffee in the sweet warm emptiness. "Anybody here?"

But she merely watched me until a door opened and the lady came. Above the counter where the ranks of crisp shapes behind the glass her neat gray face her hair tight and sparse from her neat gray skull, spectacles in neat gray rims riding approaching like something on a wire, like a cash box in a store. She looked like a librarian. Something among dusty shelves of ordered certitudes long divorced from reality, desiccating peacefully, as if a breath of that air which sees injustice done

"Two of these, please, ma'am."

From under the counter she produced a square cut from a newspaper and laid it on the counter and lifted the two buns out. The little girl watched them with still and unwinking eyes like two currants floating motionless in a cup of weak coffee Land of the kike home of the wop. Watching the bread, the neat gray hands, a broad gold band on the left forefinger, knuckled there by a blue knuckle.

"Do you do your own baking, ma'am?"

"Sir?" she said. Like that. Sir? Like on the stage. Sir? "Five cents. Was there anything else?"

"No, ma'am. Not for me. This lady wants something." She was not tall enough to see over the case, so she went to the end of the counter and looked at the little girl.

"Did you bring her in here?"

"No, ma'am. She was here when I came."

"You little wretch," she said. She came out around the counter, but she didn't touch the little girl. "Have you got anything in your pockets?"

"She hasn't got any pockets," I said. "She wasn't doing anything. She was just standing here, waiting for you."

"Why didn't the bell ring, then?" She glared at me. She just needed a bunch of switches, a blackboard behind her 2 x 2 e 5. "She'll hide it under her dress and a body'd never know it. You, child. How'd you get in here?"

The little girl said nothing. She looked at the woman, then she gave me a flying black glance and looked at the woman again. "Them foreigners," the woman said. "How'd she get in without the bell ringing?"

"She came in when I opened the door," I said. "It rang once for both of us. She couldn't reach anything from here, anyway.

Besides, I dont think she would. Would you, sister?" The little girl looked at me, secretive, contemplative. "What do you want? bread?"

She extended her fist. It uncurled upon a nickel, moist and dirty, moist dirt ridged into her flesh. The coin was damp and warm. I could smell it, faintly metallic.

"Have you got a five cent loaf, please, ma'am?"

From beneath the counter she produced a square cut from a newspaper sheet and laid it on the counter and wrapped a loaf into it. I laid the coin and another one on the counter. "And another one of those buns, please, ma'am."

She took another bun from the case. "Give me that parcel," she said. I gave it to her and she unwrapped it and put the third bun in and wrapped it and took up the coins and found two coppers in her apron and gave them to me. I handed them to the little girl. Her fingers closed about them, damp and hot, like worms.

"You going to give her that bun?" the woman said.

"Yessum," I said. "I expect your cooking smells as good to her as it does to me."

I took up the two packages and gave the bread to the little girl, the woman all iron-gray behind the counter, watching us with cold certitude. "You wait a minute," she said. She went to the rear. The door opened again and closed. The little girl watched me, holding the bread against her dirty dress.

"What's your name?" I said. She quit looking at me, but she was still motionless. She didn't even seem to breathe. The woman returned. She had a funny looking thing in her hand. She carried it sort of like it might have been a dead pet rat.

"Here," she said. The child looked at her. "Take it," the woman said, jabbing it at the little girl. "It just looks peculiar. I calculate you wont know the difference when you eat it. Here. I cant stand here all day." The child took it, still watching her. The woman rubbed her hands on her apron. "I got to have that bell fixed," she said. She went to the door and jerked it open. The little bell tinkled once, faint and clear and invisible. We moved toward the door and the woman's peering back.

"Thank you for the cake," I said.

"Them foreigners," she said, staring up into the obscurity

where the bell tinkled. "Take my advice and stay clear of them, young man."

"Yessum," I said. "Come on, sister." We went out. "Thank you, ma'am."

She swung the door to, then jerked it open again, making the bell give forth its single small note. "Foreigners," she said, peering up at the bell.

We went on. "Well," I said. "How about some ice cream?" She was eating the gnarled cake. "Do you like ice cream?" She gave me a black still look, chewing. "Come on."

We came to the drugstore and had some ice cream. She wouldn't put the loaf down. "Why not put it down so you can eat better?" I said, offering to take it. But she held to it, chewing the ice cream like it was taffy. The bitten cake lay on the table. She ate the ice cream steadily, then she fell to on the cake again, looking about at the showcases. I finished mine and we went out.

"Which way do you live?" I said.

A buggy, the one with the white horse it was. Only Doc Peabody is fat. Three hundred pounds. You ride with him on the uphill side, holding on. Children. Walking easier than holding uphill. *Seen the doctor yet   have you seen   Caddy*

I dont have to I cant ask now afterward it will be all right it wont matter

Because women so delicate so mysterious Father said. Delicate equilibrium of periodical filth between two moons balanced. Moons he said full and yellow as harvest moons her hips thighs. Outside outside of them always but. Yellow. Feet soles with walking like. Then know that some man that all those mysterious and imperious concealed. With all that inside of them shapes an outward suavity waiting for a touch to. Liquid putrefaction like drowned things floating like pale rubber flabbily filled getting the odor of honeysuckle all mixed up.

"You'd better take your bread on home, hadn't you?"

She looked at me. She chewed quietly and steadily; at regular intervals a small distension passed smoothly down her throat. I opened my package and gave her one of the buns. "Goodbye," I said.

I went on. Then I looked back. She was behind me. "Do you live down this way?" She said nothing. She walked beside me, under my elbow sort of, eating. We went on. It was quiet, hardly anyone about *getting the odor of honeysuckle all mixed She would have told me not to let me sit there on the steps hearing her door twilight slamming hearing Benjy still crying Supper she would have to come down then getting honeysuckle all mixed up in it* We reached the corner.

"Well, I've got to go down this way," I said. "Goodbye." She stopped too. She swallowed the last of the cake, then she began on the bun, watching me across it. "Goodbye," I said. I turned into the street and went on, but I went to the next corner before I stopped.

"Which way do you live?" I said. "This way?" I pointed down the street. She just looked at me. "Do you live over that way? I bet you live close to the station, where the trains are. Dont you?" She just looked at me, serene and secret and chewing. The street was empty both ways, with quiet lawns and houses neat among the trees, but no one at all except back there. We turned and went back. Two men sat in chairs in front of a store.

"Do you all know this little girl? She sort of took up with me and I cant find where she lives."

They quit looking at me and looked at her.

"Must be one of them new Italian families," one said. He wore a rusty frock coat. "I've seen her before. What's your name, little girl?" She looked at them blackly for a while, her jaws moving steadily. She swallowed without ceasing to chew.

"Maybe she cant speak English," the other said.

"They sent her after bread," I said. "She must be able to speak something."

"What's your pa's name?" the first said. "Pete? Joe? name John huh?" She took another bite from the bun.

"What must I do with her?" I said. "She just follows me. I've got to get back to Boston."

"You from the college?"

"Yes, sir. And I've got to get on back."

"You might go up the street and turn her over to Anse. He'll be up at the livery stable. The marshal."

"I reckon that's what I'll have to do," I said. "I've got to do something with her. Much obliged. Come on, sister."

We went up the street, on the shady side, where the shadow

of the broken façade blotted slowly across the road. We came to the livery stable. The marshal wasn't there. A man sitting in a chair tilted in the broad low door, where a dark cool breeze smelling of ammonia blew among the ranked stalls, said to look at the postoffice. He didn't know her either.

"Them furriners. I cant tell one from another. You might take her across the tracks where they live, and maybe somebody'll claim her."

We went to the postoffice. It was back down the street. The man in the frock coat was opening a newspaper.

"Anse just drove out of town," he said. "I guess you'd better go down past the station and walk past them houses by the river. Somebody there'll know her."

"I guess I'll have to," I said. "Come on, sister." She pushed the last piece of the bun into her mouth and swallowed it. "Want another?" I said. She looked at me, chewing, her eyes black and unwinking and friendly. I took the other two buns out and gave her one and bit into the other. I asked a man where the station was and he showed me. "Come on, sister."

We reached the station and crossed the tracks, where the river was. A bridge crossed it, and a street of jumbled frame houses followed the river, backed onto it. A shabby street, but with an air heterogeneous and vivid too. In the center of an untrimmed plot enclosed by a fence of gaping and broken pickets stood an ancient lopsided surrey and a weathered house from an upper window of which hung a garment of vivid pink.

"Does that look like your house?" I said. She looked at me over the bun. "This one?" I said, pointing. She just chewed, but it seemed to me that I discerned something affirmative, acquiescent even if it wasn't eager, in her air. "This one?" I said. "Come on, then." I entered the broken gate. I looked back at her. "Here?" I said. "This look like your house?"

She nodded her head rapidly, looking at me, gnawing into the damp halfmoon of the bread. We went on. A walk of broken random flags, speared by fresh coarse blades of grass, led to the broken stoop. There was no movement about the house at all, and the pink garment hanging in no wind from the upper window. There was a bell pull with a porcelain knob, attached to about six feet of wire when I stopped pulling and knocked. The little girl had the crust edgeways in her chewing mouth.

A woman opened the door. She looked at me, then she spoke rapidly to the little girl in Italian, with a rising inflexion, then a pause, interrogatory. She spoke to her again, the little girl looking at her across the end of the crust, pushing it into her mouth with a dirty hand.

"She says she lives here," I said. "I met her down town. Is this your bread?"

"No spika," the woman said. She spoke to the little girl again. The little girl just looked at her.

"No live here?" I said. I pointed to the girl, then at her, then at the door. The woman shook her head. She spoke rapidly. She came to the edge of the porch and pointed down the road, speaking.

I nodded violently too. "You come show?" I said. I took her arm, waving my other hand toward the road. She spoke swiftly, pointing. "You come show," I said, trying to lead her down the steps.

"Si, si," she said, holding back, showing me whatever it was. I nodded again.

"Thanks. Thanks. Thanks." I went down the steps and walked toward the gate, not running, but pretty fast. I reached the gate and stopped and looked at her for a while. The crust was gone now, and she looked at me with her black, friendly stare. The woman stood on the stoop, watching us.

"Come on, then," I said. "We'll have to find the right one sooner or later."

She moved along just under my elbow. We went on. The houses all seemed empty. Not a soul in sight. A sort of breathlessness that empty houses have. Yet they couldn't all be empty. All the different rooms, if you could just slice the walls away all of a sudden. Madam, your daughter, if you please. No. Madam, for God's sake, your daughter. She moved along just under my elbow, her shiny tight pigtails, and then the last house played out and the road curved out of sight beyond a wall, following the river. The woman was emerging from the broken gate, with a shawl over her head and clutched under her chin. The road curved on, empty. I found a coin and gave it to the little girl. A quarter. "Goodbye, sister," I said. Then I ran.

I ran fast, not looking back. Just before the road curved away I looked back. She stood in the road, a small figure clasping the loaf of bread to her filthy little dress, her eyes still and black and unwinking. I ran on.

A lane turned from the road. I entered it and after a while I slowed to a fast walk. The lane went between back premises—unpainted houses with more of those gay and startling colored garments on lines, a barn broken-backed, decaying quietly among rank orchard trees, unpruned and weed-choked, pink and white and murmurous with sunlight and with bees. I looked back. The entrance to the lane was empty. I slowed still more, my shadow pacing me, dragging its head through the weeds that hid the fence.

The lane went back to a barred gate, became defunctive in grass, a mere path scarred quietly into new grass. I climbed the gate into a woodlot and crossed it and came to another wall and followed that one, my shadow behind me now. There were vines and creepers where at home would be honeysuckle. Coming and coming especially in the dusk when it rained, getting honeysuckle all mixed up in it as though it were not enough without that, not unbearable enough. *What did you let him for kiss kiss*

I didn't let him I made him watching me getting mad What do you think of that? Red print of my hand coming up through her face like turning a light on under your hand her eyes going bright

It's not for kissing I slapped you. Girl's elbows at fifteen Father said you swallow like you had a fishbone in your throat what's the matter with you and Caddy across the table not to look at me. It's for letting it be some darn town squirt I slapped you you will will you now I guess you say calf rope. My red hand coming up out of her face. What do you think of that scouring her head into the. Grass sticks criss-crossed into the flesh tingling scouring her head. Say calf rope say it

I didn't kiss a dirty girl like Natalie anyway The wall went into shadow, and then my shadow, I had tricked it again. I had forgot about the river curving along the road. I climbed the wall. And then she watched me jump down, holding the loaf against her dress.

I stood in the weeds and we looked at one another for a while.

"Why didn't you tell me you lived out this way, sister?" The loaf was wearing slowly out of the paper; already it needed a new one. "Well, come on then and show me the house." *not a dirty girl like Natalie. It was raining we could hear it on the roof, sighing through the high sweet emptiness of the barn.*

There? touching her

Not there

There? not raining hard but we couldn't hear anything but the roof and if it was my blood or her blood

She pushed me down the ladder and ran off and left me Caddy did

Was it there it hurt you when Caddy did ran off was it there

Oh She walked just under my elbow, the top of her patent leather head, the loaf fraying out of the newspaper.

"If you dont get home pretty soon you're going to wear that loaf out. And then what'll your mamma say?" *I bet I can lift you up*

You cant I'm too heavy

Did Caddy go away did she go to the house you cant see the barn from our house did you ever try to see the barn from

It was her fault she pushed me she ran away

I can lift you up see how I can

Oh her blood or my blood Oh We went on in the thin dust, our feet silent as rubber in the thin dust where pencils of sun slanted in the trees. And I could feel water again running swift and peaceful in the secret shade.

"You live a long way, dont you. You're mighty smart to go this far to town by yourself." *It's like dancing sitting down did you ever dance sitting down? We could hear the rain, a rat in the crib, the empty barn vacant with horses. How do you hold to dance do you hold like this*

Oh

I used to hold like this you thought I wasn't strong enough didn't you

Oh Oh Oh Oh

I hold to use like this I mean did you hear what I said I said oh oh oh oh

The road went on, still and empty, the sun slanting more and more. Her stiff little pigtails were bound at the tips with bits of crimson cloth. A corner of the wrapping flapped a little as she walked, the nose of the loaf naked. I stopped.

"Look here. Do you live down this road? We haven't passed a house in a mile, almost."

She looked at me, black and secret and friendly.

"Where do you live, sister? Dont you live back there in town?"

There was a bird somewhere in the woods, beyond the broken and infrequent slanting of sunlight.

"Your papa's going to be worried about you. Dont you reckon you'll get a whipping for not coming straight home with that bread?"

The bird whistled again, invisible, a sound meaningless and profound, inflexionless, ceasing as though cut off with the blow of a knife, and again, and that sense of water swift and peaceful above secret places, felt, not seen not heard.

"Oh, hell, sister." About half the paper hung limp. "That's not doing any good now." I tore it off and dropped it beside the road. "Come on. We'll have to go back to town. We'll go back along the river."

We left the road. Among the moss little pale flowers grew, and the sense of water mute and unseen. *I hold to use like this I mean I use to hold She stood in the door looking at us her hands on her hips*

You pushed me it was your fault it hurt me too

We were dancing sitting down I bet Caddy cant dance sitting down

Stop that stop that

I was just brushing the trash off the back of your dress

You keep your nasty old hands off of me it was your fault you pushed me down I'm mad at you

I dont care she looked at us stay mad she went away We began to hear the shouts, the splashings; I saw a brown body gleam for an instant.

Stay mad. My shirt was getting wet and my hair. Across the roof hearing the roof loud now I could see Natalie going through the garden among the rain. Get wet I hope you catch pneumonia go on home Cowface. I jumped hard as I could into the hogwallow the mud yellowed up to my waist stinking I kept on plunging until I fell down and rolled over in it "Hear them in swimming, sister? I wouldn't mind doing that myself." If I had time. When I have time. I could hear my watch. *mud was warmer than the rain it smelled awful. She had her back turned I went around in front of her. You know what I was doing? She turned her back I went around in front of her the rain creeping into the mud flatting her bodice through her dress it smelled horrible. I was hugging her that's what I was doing. She turned her back I went around in front of her. I was hugging her I tell you.*

I dont give a damn what you were doing

You dont you dont I'll make you I'll make you give a damn. She hit my hands away I smeared mud on her with the other hand I couldn't feel the wet smacking of her hand I wiped mud from my legs smeared it on her wet hard turning body hearing her fingers going into my face but I couldn't feel it even when the rain began to taste sweet on my lips

They saw us from the water first, heads and shoulders. They yelled and one rose squatting and sprang among them. They looked like beavers, the water lipping about their chins, yelling.

"Take that girl away! What did you want to bring a girl here for? Go on away!"

"She wont hurt you. We just want to watch you for a while."

They squatted in the water. Their heads drew into a clump, watching us, then they broke and rushed toward us, hurling water with their hands. We moved quick.

"Look out, boys; she wont hurt you."

"Go on away, Harvard!" It was the second boy, the one that thought the horse and wagon back there at the bridge. "Splash them, fellows!"

"Let's get out and throw them in," another said. "I aint afraid of any girl."

"Splash them! Splash them!" They rushed toward us, hurling water. We moved back. "Go on away!" they yelled. "Go on away!"

We went away. They huddled just under the bank, their slick heads in a row against the bright water. We went on. "That's not for us, is it." The sun slanted through to the moss here and there, leveller. "Poor kid, you're just a girl." Little flowers grew among the moss, littler than I had ever seen. "You're just a girl. Poor kid." There was a path, curving along beside the water. Then the water was still again, dark and still and swift. "Nothing but a girl. Poor sister." *We lay in the wet grass panting the rain like cold shot on my back. Do you care now do you do you*

My Lord we sure are in a mess get up. Where the rain touched my forehead it began to smart my hand came red away streaking off pink in the rain. Does it hurt

Of course it does what do you reckon

I tried to scratch your eyes out my Lord we sure do stink we better try to wash it off in the branch "There's town again, sister. You'll have to go home now. I've got to get back to school. Look how late it's getting. You'll go home now, wont you?" But she just looked at me with her black, secret, friendly gaze, the half-naked loaf clutched to her breast. "It's wet. I thought we jumped back in time." I took my handkerchief and tried to wipe the loaf, but the crust began to come off, so I stopped. "We'll just have to let it dry itself. Hold it like this." She held it like that. It looked kind of like rats had been eating it now. *and the water building and building up the squatting back the sloughed mud stinking surfaceward pocking the pattering surface like grease on a hot stove. I told you I'd make you*

I dont give a goddam what you do

Then we heard the running and we stopped and looked back and saw him coming up the path running, the level shadows flicking upon his legs.

"He's in a hurry. We'd——" then I saw another man, an oldish man running heavily, clutching a stick, and a boy naked from the waist up, clutching his pants as he ran.

"There's Julio," the little girl said, and then I saw his Italian face and his eyes as he sprang upon me. We went down. His hands were jabbing at my face and he was saying something and trying to bite me, I reckon, and then they hauled him off and held him heaving and thrashing and yelling and they held his arms and he tried to kick me until they dragged him back. The little girl was howling, holding the loaf in both arms. The half naked boy was darting and jumping up and down, clutching his trousers and someone pulled me up in time to see another stark naked figure come around the tranquil bend in the path running and change direction in midstride and leap into the woods, a couple of garments rigid as boards behind it. Julio still struggled. The man who had pulled me up said, "Whoa, now. We got you." He wore a vest but no coat. Upon it was a metal shield. In his other hand he clutched a knotted, polished stick.

"You're Anse, aren't you?" I said. "I was looking for you. What's the matter?"

"I warn you that anything you say will be used against you," he said. "You're under arrest."

"I killa heem," Julio said. He struggled. Two men held him. The little girl howled steadily, holding the bread. "You steala my seester," Julio said. "Let go, meesters."

"Steal his sister?" I said. "Why, I've been——"

"Shet up," Anse said. "You can tell that to Squire."

"Steal his sister?" I said. Julio broke from the men and sprang at me again, but the marshal met him and they struggled until the other two pinioned his arms again. Anse released him, panting.

"You durn furriner," he said. "I've a good mind to take you up too, for assault and battery." He turned to me again. "Will you come peaceable, or do I handcuff you?"

"I'll come peaceable," I said. "Anything, just so I can find someone—do something with—— Stole his sister," I said. "Stole his——"

"I've warned you," Anse said. "He aims to charge you with meditated criminal assault. Here, you, make that gal shut up that noise."

"Oh," I said. Then I began to laugh. Two more boys with plastered heads and round eyes came out of the bushes, buttoning shirts that had already dampened onto their shoulders and arms, and I tried to stop the laughter, but I couldn't.

"Watch him, Anse, he's crazy, I believe."

"I'll h-have to qu-quit," I said. "It'll stop in a mu-minute. The other time it said ah ah ah," I said, laughing. "Let me sit down a while." I sat down, they watching me, and the little girl with her streaked face and the gnawed looking loaf, and the water swift and peaceful below the path. After a while the laughter ran out. But my throat wouldn't quit trying to laugh, like retching after your stomach is empty.

"Whoa, now," Anse said. "Get a grip on yourself."

"Yes," I said, tightening my throat. There was another yellow butterfly, like one of the sunflecks had come loose. After a while I didn't have to hold my throat so tight. I got up. "I'm ready. Which way?"

We followed the path, the two others watching Julio and the little girl and the boys somewhere in the rear. The path went along the river to the bridge. We crossed it and the tracks, people coming to the doors to look at us and more boys materialising from somewhere until when we turned into the main street we had quite a procession. Before the drug store stood an auto, a big one, but I didn't recognise them until Mrs Bland said,

"Why, Quentin! Quentin Compson!" Then I saw Gerald, and Spoade in the back seat, sitting on the back of his neck. And Shreve. I didn't know the two girls.

"Quentin Compson!" Mrs Bland said.

"Good afternoon," I said, raising my hat. "I'm under arrest. I'm sorry I didn't get your note. Did Shreve tell you?"

"Under arrest?" Shreve said. "Excuse me," he said. He heaved himself up and climbed over their feet and got out. He had on a pair of my flannel pants, like a glove. I didn't remember forgetting them. I didn't remember how many chins Mrs Bland had, either. The prettiest girl was with Gerald in front, too. They watched me through veils, with a kind of delicate horror. "Who's under arrest?" Shreve said. "What's this, mister?"

"Gerald," Mrs Bland said. "Send these people away. You get in this car, Quentin."

Gerald got out. Spoade hadn't moved.

"What's he done, Cap?" he said. "Robbed a hen house?"

"I warn you," Anse said. "Do you know the prisoner?"

"Know him," Shreve said. "Look here——"

"Then you can come along to the squire's. You're obstructing justice. Come along." He shook my arm.

"Well, good afternoon," I said. "I'm glad to have seen you all. Sorry I couldn't be with you."

"You, Gerald," Mrs Bland said.

"Look here, constable," Gerald said.

"I warn you you're interfering with an officer of the law," Anse said. "If you've anything to say, you can come to the squire's and make cognizance of the prisoner." We went on. Quite a procession now, Anse and I leading. I could hear them telling them what it was, and Spoade asking questions, and then Julio said something violently in Italian and I looked back and saw the little girl standing at the curb, looking at me with her friendly, inscrutable regard.

"Git on home," Julio shouted at her. "I beat hell outa you."

We went down the street and turned into a bit of lawn in which, set back from the street, stood a one storey building of brick trimmed with white. We went up the rock path to the door, where Anse halted everyone except us and made them remain outside. We entered, a bare room smelling of stale tobacco. There was a sheet iron stove in the center of a wooden frame filled with sand, and a faded map on the wall and the dingy plat of a township. Behind a scarred littered table a man with a fierce roach of iron gray hair peered at us over steel spectacles.

"Got him, did ye, Anse?" he said.

"Got him, Squire."

He opened a huge dusty book and drew it to him and dipped a foul pen into an inkwell filled with what looked like coal dust.

"Look here, mister," Shreve said.

"The prisoner's name," the squire said. I told him. He wrote it slowly into the book, the pen scratching with excruciating deliberation.

"Look here, mister," Shreve said. "We know this fellow. We——"

"Order in the court," Anse said.

"Shut up, bud," Spoade said. "Let him do it his way. He's going to anyhow."

"Age," the squire said. I told him. He wrote that, his mouth moving as he wrote. "Occupation." I told him. "Harvard student, hey?" he said. He looked up at me, bowing his neck a little to see over the spectacles. His eyes were clear and cold, like a goat's. "What are you up to, coming out here kidnapping children?"

"They're crazy, Squire," Shreve said. "Whoever says this boy's kidnapping——"

Julio moved violently. "Crazy?" he said. "Dont I catcha heem, eh? Dont I see weetha my own eyes——"

"You're a liar," Shreve said. "You never——"

"Order, order," Anse said, raising his voice.

"You fellers shet up," the squire said. "If they dont stay quiet, turn 'em out, Anse." They got quiet. The squire looked at Shreve, then at Spoade, then at Gerald. "You know this young man?" he said to Spoade.

"Yes, your honor," Spoade said. "He's just a country boy in school up there. He dont mean any harm. I think the marshal'll find it's a mistake. His father's a congregational minister."

"H'm," the squire said. "What was you doing, exactly?" I told him, he watching me with his cold, pale eyes. "How about it, Anse?"

"Might have been," Anse said. "Them durn furriners."

"I American," Julio said. "I gotta da pape'."

"Where's the gal?"

"He sent her home," Anse said.

"Was she scared or anything?"

"Not till Julio there jumped on the prisoner. They were just walking along the river path, towards town. Some boys swimming told us which way they went."

"It's a mistake, Squire," Spoade said. "Children and dogs are always taking up with him like that. He cant help it."

"H'm," the squire said. He looked out of the window for a while. We watched him. I could hear Julio scratching himself. The squire looked back.

"Air you satisfied the gal aint took any hurt, you, there?"

"No hurt now," Julio said sullenly.

"You quit work to hunt for her?"

"Sure I quit. I run. I run like hell. Looka here, looka there, then man tella me he seen him giva her she eat. She go weetha."

"H'm," the squire said. "Well, son, I calculate you owe Julio something for taking him away from his work."

"Yes, sir," I said. "How much?"

"Dollar, I calculate."

I gave Julio a dollar.

"Well," Spoade said. "If that's all——I reckon he's discharged, your honor?"

The squire didn't look at him. "How far'd you run him, Anse?"

"Two miles, at least. It was about two hours before we caught him."

"H'm," the squire said. He mused a while. We watched him, his stiff crest, the spectacles riding low on his nose. The yellow shape of the window grew slowly across the floor, reached the wall, climbing. Dust motes whirled and slanted. "Six dollars."

"Six dollars?" Shreve said. "What's that for?"

"Six dollars," the squire said. He looked at Shreve a moment, then at me again.

"Look here," Shreve said.

"Shut up," Spoade said. "Give it to him, bud, and let's get out of here. The ladies are waiting for us. You got six dollars?"

"Yes," I said. I gave him six dollars.

"Case dismissed," he said.

"You get a receipt," Shreve said. "You get a signed receipt for that money."

The squire looked at Shreve mildly. "Case dismissed," he said without raising his voice.

"I'll be damned——" Shreve said.

"Come on here," Spoade said, taking his arm. "Good afternoon, Judge. Much obliged." As we passed out the door Julio's voice rose again, violent, then ceased. Spoade was looking at me, his brown eyes quizzical, a little cold. "Well, bud, I reckon you'll do your girl chasing in Boston after this."

"You damned fool," Shreve said. "What the hell do you mean anyway, straggling off here, fooling with these damn wops?"

"Come on," Spoade said. "They must be getting impatient."

Mrs Bland was talking to them. They were Miss Holmes and Miss Daingerfield and they quit listening to her and looked at me again with that delicate and curious horror, their veils turned back upon their little white noses and their eyes fleeing and mysterious beneath the veils.

"Quentin Compson," Mrs Bland said. "What would your mother say. A young man naturally gets into scrapes, but to be arrested on foot by a country policeman. What did they think he'd done, Gerald?"

"Nothing," Gerald said.

"Nonsense. What was it, you, Spoade?"

"He was trying to kidnap that little dirty girl, but they caught him in time," Spoade said.

"Nonsense," Mrs Bland said, but her voice sort of died away and she stared at me for a moment, and the girls drew their breaths in with a soft concerted sound. "Fiddlesticks," Mrs Bland said briskly. "If that isn't just like these ignorant low-class Yankees. Get in, Quentin."

Shreve and I sat on two small collapsible seats. Gerald cranked the car and got in and we started.

"Now, Quentin, you tell me what all this foolishness is about," Mrs Bland said. I told them, Shreve hunched and furious on his little seat and Spoade sitting again on the back of his neck beside Miss Daingerfield.

"And the joke is, all the time Quentin had us all fooled," Spoade said. "All the time we thought he was the model youth that anybody could trust a daughter with, until the police showed him up at his nefarious work."

"Hush up, Spoade," Mrs Bland said. We drove down the street and crossed the bridge and passed the house where the pink garment hung in the window. "That's what you get for not reading my note. Why didn't you come and get it? Mr MacKenzie says he told you it was there."

"Yessum. I intended to, but I never went back to the room."

"You'd have let us sit there waiting I dont know how long, if it hadn't been for Mr MacKenzie. When he said you hadn't come back, that left an extra place, so we asked him to come. We're very glad to have you anyway, Mr MacKenzie." Shreve said nothing. His arms were folded and he glared straight ahead past Gerald's cap. It was a cap for motoring in England. Mrs Bland said so. We passed that house, and three others, and another yard where the little girl stood by the gate. She didn't have the bread now, and her face looked like it had been streaked with coaldust. I waved my hand, but she made no reply, only her head turned slowly as the car passed, following us with her unwinking gaze. Then we ran beside the wall, our shadows running along the wall, and after a while we passed a piece of torn newspaper lying beside the road and I began to laugh again. I could feel it in my throat and I looked off into the trees where the afternoon slanted, thinking of afternoon and of the bird and the boys in swimming. But still

I couldn't stop it and then I knew that if I tried too hard to stop it I'd be crying and I thought about how I'd thought about I could not be a virgin, with so many of them walking along in the shadows and whispering with their soft girlvoices lingering in the shadowy places and the words coming out and perfume and eyes you could feel not see, but if it was that simple to do it wouldn't be anything and if it wasn't anything, what was I and then Mrs Bland said, "Quentin? Is he sick, Mr MacKenzie?" and then Shreve's fat hand touched my knee and Spoade began talking and I quit trying to stop it.

"If that hamper is in his way, Mr MacKenzie, move it over on your side. I brought a hamper of wine because I think young gentlemen should drink wine, although my father, Gerald's grandfather" *ever do that Have you ever done that In the gray darkness a little light her hands locked about*

"They do, when they can get it," Spoade said. "Hey, Shreve?" *her knees her face looking at the sky the smell of honeysuckle upon her face and throat*

"Beer, too," Shreve said. His hand touched my knee again. I moved my knee again. *like a thin wash of lilac colored paint talking about him bringing*

"You're not a gentleman," Spoade said. *him between us until the shape of her blurred not with dark*

"No. I'm Canadian," Shreve said. *talking about him the oar blades winking him along winking the Cap made for motoring in England and all time rushing beneath and they two blurred within the other forever more he had been in the army had killed men*

"I adore Canada," Miss Daingerfield said. "I think it's marvellous."

"Did you ever drink perfume?" Spoade said. *with one hand he could lift her to his shoulder and run with her running Running*

"No," Shreve said. *running the beast with two backs and she blurred in the winking oars running the swine of Euboeleus running coupled within how many Caddy*

"Neither did I," Spoade said. *I dont know too many there was something terrible in me terrible in me Father I have committed Have you ever done that   We didnt we didnt do that did we do that*

"and Gerald's grandfather always picked his own mint before breakfast, while the dew was still on it. He wouldn't even

let old Wilkie touch it do you remember Gerald but always
gathered it himself and made his own julep. He was as crotchety about his julep as an old maid, measuring everything by a
recipe in his head. There was only one man he ever gave that
recipe to; that was" *we did how can you not know it if youll just
wait Ill tell you how it was it was a crime we did a terrible crime
it cannot be hid you think it can but wait   Poor Quentin youve
never done that have you   and Ill tell you how it was Ill tell Father
then itll have to be because you love Father then well have to go
away amid the pointing and the horror the clean flame Ill make
you say we did Im stronger than you Ill make you know we did you
thought it was them but it was me listen I fooled you all the time
it was me you thought I was in the house where that damn honeysuckle trying not to think the swing the cedars the secret surges the
breathing locked drinking the wild breath the yes Yes Yes yes*
"never be got to drink wine himself, but he always said that a
hamper what book did you read that in the one where Gerald's
rowing suit of wine was a necessary part of any gentlemen's
picnic basket" *did you love them Caddy did you love them When
they touched me I died*
    one minute she was standing there the next he was yelling
and pulling at her dress they went into the hall and up the
stairs yelling and shoving at her up the stairs to the bathroom
door and stopped her back against the door and her arm across
her face yelling and trying to shove her into the bathroom
when she came in to supper T. P. was feeding him he started
again just whimpering at first until she touched him then he
yelled she stood there her eyes like cornered rats then I was
running in the gray darkness it smelled of rain and all flower
scents the damp warm air released and crickets sawing away
in the grass pacing me with a small travelling island of silence
Fancy watched me across the fence blotchy like a quilt on a
line I thought damn that nigger he forgot to feed her again I
ran down the hill in that vacuum of crickets like a breath travelling across a mirror she was lying in the water her head on
the sand spit the water flowing about her hips there was a little
more light in the water her skirt half saturated flopped along
her flanks to the waters motion in heavy ripples going
nowhere renewed themselves of their own movement I stood
on the bank I could smell the honeysuckle on the water gap

the air seemed to drizzle with honeysuckle and with the rasping of crickets a substance you could feel on the flesh
is Benjy still crying
I dont know yes I dont know
poor Benjy
I sat down on the bank the grass was damp a little then I found
my shoes wet
get out of that water are you crazy
but she didnt move her face was a white blur framed out of
the blur of the sand by her hair
get out now
she sat up then she rose her skirt flopped against her draining
she climbed the bank her clothes flopping sat down
why dont you wring it out do you want to catch cold
yes
the water sucked and gurgled across the sand spit and on in
the dark among the willows across the shallow the water rippled like a piece of cloth holding still a little light as water does
hes crossed all the oceans all around the world
then she talked about him clasping her wet knees her face
tilted back in the gray light the smell of honeysuckle there was
a light in mothers room and in Benjys where T. P. was putting him to bed
do you love him
her hand came out I didnt move it fumbled down my arm and
she held my hand flat against her chest her heart thudding
no no
did he make you then he made you do it let him he was stronger
than you and he tomorrow Ill kill him I swear I will father
neednt know until afterward and then you and I nobody need
ever know we can take my school money we can cancel my
matriculation Caddy you hate him dont you dont you
she held my hand against her chest her heart thudding I turned
and caught her arm
Caddy you hate him dont you
she moved my hand up against her throat her heart was hammering there
poor Quentin
her face looked at the sky it was low so low that all smells and
sounds of night seemed to have been crowded down like

under a slack tent especially the honeysuckle it had got into
my breathing it was on her face and throat like paint her blood
pounded against my hand I was leaning on my other arm it
began to jerk and jump and I had to pant to get any air at all
out of that thick gray honeysuckle
yes I hate him I would die for him Ive already died for him I
die for him over and over again everytime this goes
when I lifted my hand I could still feel crisscrossed twigs and
grass burning into the palm
poor Quentin
she leaned back on her arms her hands locked about her knees
youve never done that have you
what done what
that what I have what I did
yes yes lots of times with lots of girls
then I was crying her hand touched me again and I was crying
against her damp blouse then she lying on her back looking
past my head into the sky I could see a rim of white under her
irises I opened my knife
do you remember the day damuddy died when you sat down
in the water in your drawers
yes
I held the point of the knife at her throat
it wont take but a second just a second then I can do mine I
can do mine then
all right can you do yours by yourself
yes the blades long enough Benjys in bed by now
yes
it wont take but a second Ill try not to hurt
all right
will you close your eyes
no like this youll have to push it harder
touch your hand to it
but she didnt move her eyes were wide open looking past my
head at the sky
Caddy do you remember how Dilsey fussed at you because
your drawers were muddy
dont cry
Im not crying Caddy
push it are you going to

do you want me to
yes push it
touch your hand to it
dont cry poor Quentin
but I couldnt stop she held my head against her damp hard
breast I could hear her heart going firm and slow now not
hammering and the water gurgling among the willows in the
dark and waves of honeysuckle coming up the air my arm and
shoulder were twisted under me
what is it what are you doing
her muscles gathered I sat up
its my knife I dropped it
she sat up
what time is it
I dont know
she rose to her feet I fumbled along the ground
Im going let it go
to the house
I could feel her standing there I could smell her damp clothes
feeling her there
its right here somewhere
let it go you can find it tomorrow come on
wait a minute Ill find it
are you afraid to
here it is it was right here all the time
was it come on
I got up and followed we went up the hill the crickets hushing before us
its funny how you can sit down and drop something and have
to hunt all around for it
the gray it was gray with dew slanting up into the gray sky
then the trees beyond
damn that honeysuckle I wish it would stop
you used to like it
we crossed the crest and went on toward the trees she walked
into me she gave over a little the ditch was a black scar on the
gray grass she walked into me again she looked at me and gave
over we reached the ditch
lets go this way
what for

lets see if you can still see Nancys bones I havent thought to
look in a long time have you
it was matted with vines and briers dark
they were right here you cant tell whether you see them or not
can you
stop Quentin
come on
the ditch narrowed closed she turned toward the trees
stop Quentin
Caddy
I got in front of her again
Caddy
stop it
I held her
Im stronger than you
she was motionless hard unyielding but still
I wont fight stop youd better stop
Caddy dont Caddy
it wont do any good dont you know it wont let me go
the honeysuckle drizzled and drizzled I could hear the crickets watching us in a circle she moved back went around me
on toward the trees
you go on back to the house you neednt come
I went on
why dont you go on back to the house
damn that honeysuckle
we reached the fence she crawled through I crawled through
when I rose from stooping he was coming out of the trees into
the gray toward us coming toward us tall and flat and still even
moving like he was still she went to him
this is Quentin Im wet Im wet all over you dont have to if you
dont want to
their shadows one shadow her head rose it was above his on
the sky higher their two heads
you dont have to if you dont want to
then not two heads the darkness smelled of rain of damp grass
and leaves the gray light drizzling like rain the honeysuckle
coming up in damp waves I could see her face a blur against
his shoulder he held her in one arm like she was no bigger
than a child he extended his hand

glad to know you
we shook hands then we stood there her shadow high against
his shadow one shadow
whatre you going to do Quentin
walk a while I think Ill go through the woods to the road and
come back through town
I turned away going
goodnight
Quentin
I stopped
what do you want
in the woods the tree frogs were going smelling rain in the air
they sounded like toy music boxes that were hard to turn and
the honeysuckle
come here
what do you want
come here Quentin
I went back she touched my shoulder leaning down her
shadow the blur of her face leaning down from his high
shadow I drew back
look out
you go on home
Im not sleepy Im going to take a walk
wait for me at the branch
Im going for a walk
Ill be there soon wait for me you wait
no Im going through the woods
I didnt look back the tree frogs didnt pay me any mind the
gray light like moss in the trees drizzling but still it wouldnt
rain after a while I turned went back to the edge of the woods
as soon as I got there I began to smell honeysuckle again I
could see the lights on the courthouse clock and the glare of
town the square on the sky and the dark willows along the
branch and the light in mothers windows the light still on in
Benjys room and I stooped through the fence and went across
the pasture running I ran in the gray grass among the crickets
the honeysuckle getting stronger and stronger and the smell
of water then I could see the water the color of gray honeysuckle I lay down on the bank with my face close to the
ground so I couldnt smell the honeysuckle I couldnt smell it

then and I lay there feeling the earth going through my clothes
listening to the water and after a while I wasnt breathing so
hard and I lay there thinking that if I didnt move my face I
wouldnt have to breathe hard and smell it and then I wasnt
thinking about anything at all she came along the bank and
stopped I didnt move
its late you go on home
what
you go on home its late
all right
her clothes rustled I didnt move they stopped rustling
are you going in like I told you
I didnt hear anything
Caddy
yes I will if you want me to I will
I sat up she was sitting on the ground her hands clasped about
her knee
go on to the house like I told you
yes Ill do anything you want me to anything yes
she didnt even look at me I caught her shoulder and shook
her hard
you shut up
I shook her
you shut up you shut up
yes
she lifted her face then I saw she wasnt even looking at me at
all I could see that white rim
get up
I pulled her she was limp I lifted her to her feet
go on now
was Benjy still crying when you left
go on
we crossed the branch the roof came in sight then the windows upstairs
hes asleep now
I had to stop and fasten the gate she went on in the gray light
the smell of rain and still it wouldnt rain and honeysuckle beginning to come from the garden fence beginning she went
into the shadow I could hear her feet then
Caddy

I stopped at the steps I couldnt hear her feet
Caddy
I heard her feet then my hand touched her not warm not cool
just still her clothes a little damp still
do you love him now
not breathing except slow like far away breathing
Caddy do you love him now
I dont know
outside the gray light the shadows of things like dead things
in stagnant water
I wish you were dead
do you you coming in now
are you thinking about him now
I dont know
tell me what youre thinking about tell me
stop stop Quentin
you shut up you shut up you hear me you shut up are you
going to shut up
all right I will stop well make too much noise
Ill kill you do you hear
lets go out to the swing theyll hear you here
Im not crying do you say Im crying
no hush now well wake Benjy up
you go on into the house go on now
I am dont cry Im bad anyway you cant help it
theres a curse on us its not our fault is it our fault
hush come on and go to bed now
you cant make me theres a curse on us
finally I saw him he was just going into the barbershop he
looked out I went on and waited
Ive been looking for you two or three days
you wanted to see me
Im going to see you
he rolled the cigarette quickly with about two motions he
struck the match with his thumb
we cant talk here suppose I meet you somewhere
Ill come to your room are you at the hotel
no thats not so good you know that bridge over the creek in
there back of
yes all right

at one oclock right
yes
I turned away
Im obliged to you
look
I stopped looked back
she all right
he looked like he was made out of bronze his khaki shirt
she need me for anything now
Ill be there at one
she heard me tell T. P. to saddle Prince at one oclock she kept
watching me not eating much she came too
what are you going to do
nothing cant I go for a ride if I want to
youre going to do something what is it
none of your business whore whore
T. P. had Prince at the side door
I wont want him Im going to walk
I went down the drive and out the gate I turned into the lane
then I ran before I reached the bridge I saw him leaning on
the rail the horse was hitched in the woods he looked over his
shoulder then he turned his back he didnt look up until I came
onto the bridge and stopped he had a piece of bark in his
hands breaking pieces from it and dropping them over the rail
into the water
I came to tell you to leave town
he broke a piece of bark deliberately dropped it carefully into
the water watched it float away
I said you must leave town
he looked at me
did she send you to me
I say you must go not my father not anybody I say it
listen save this for a while I want to know if shes all right have
they been bothering her up there
thats something you dont need to trouble yourself about
then I heard myself saying Ill give you until sundown to leave
town
he broke a piece of bark and dropped it into the water then
he laid the bark on the rail and rolled a cigarette with those
two swift motions spun the match over the rail

what will you do if I dont leave
Ill kill you dont think that just because I look like a kid to you
the smoke flowed in two jets from his nostrils across his face
how old are you
I began to shake my hands were on the rail I thought if I hid
them hed know why
Ill give you until tonight
listen buddy whats your name Benjys the natural isnt he you
are
Quentin
my mouth said it I didnt say it at all
Ill give you till sundown
Quentin
he raked the cigarette ash carefully off against the rail he did
it slowly and carefully like sharpening a pencil my hands had
quit shaking
listen no good taking it so hard its not your fault kid it would
have been some other fellow
did you ever have a sister did you
no but theyre all bitches
I hit him my open hand beat the impulse to shut it to his face
his hand moved as fast as mine the cigarette went over the rail
I swung with the other hand he caught it too before the cigarette reached the water he held both my wrists in the same
hand his other hand flicked to his armpit under his coat
behind him the sun slanted and a bird singing somewhere
beyond the sun we looked at one another while the bird
singing he turned my hands loose
look here
he took the bark from the rail and dropped it into the water
it bobbed up the current took it floated away his hand lay on
the rail holding the pistol loosely we waited
you cant hit it now
no
it floated on it was quite still in the woods I heard the bird
again and the water afterward the pistol came up he didnt aim
at all the bark disappeared then pieces of it floated up spreading he hit two more of them pieces of bark no bigger than
silver dollars
thats enough I guess

he swung the cylinder out and blew into the barrel a thin wisp of smoke dissolved he reloaded the three chambers shut the cylinder he handed it to me butt first

what for I wont try to beat that

youll need it from what you said Im giving you this one because youve seen what itll do

to hell with your gun

I hit him I was still trying to hit him long after he was holding my wrists but I still tried then it was like I was looking at him through a piece of colored glass I could hear my blood and then I could see the sky again and branches against it and the sun slanting through them and he holding me on my feet

did you hit me

I couldnt hear

what

yes how do you feel

all right let go

he let me go I leaned against the rail

do you feel all right

let me alone Im all right

can you make it home all right

go on let me alone

youd better not try to walk take my horse

no you go on

you can hang the reins on the pommel and turn him loose hell go back to the stable

let me alone you go on and let me alone

I leaned on the rail looking at the water I heard him untie the horse and ride off and after a while I couldnt hear anything but the water and then the bird again I left the bridge and sat down with my back against a tree and leaned my head against the tree and shut my eyes a patch of sun came through and fell across my eyes and I moved a little further around the tree I heard the bird again and the water and then everything sort of rolled away and I didnt feel anything at all I felt almost good after all those days and the nights with honeysuckle coming up out of the darkness into my room where I was trying to sleep even when after a while I knew that he hadnt hit me that he had lied about that for her sake too and that I had just passed out like a girl but even that didnt matter anymore and

I sat there against the tree with little flecks of sunlight brushing across my face like yellow leaves on a twig listening to the water and not thinking about anything at all even when I heard the horse coming fast I sat there with my eyes closed and heard its feet bunch scuttering the hissing sand and feet running and her hard running hands
fool fool are you hurt
I opened my eyes her hands running on my face
I didnt know which way until I heard the pistol I didnt know where I didnt think he and you running off slipping I didnt think he would have
she held my face between her hands bumping my head against the tree
stop stop that
I caught her wrists
quit that quit it
I knew he wouldnt I knew he wouldnt
she tried to bump my head against the tree
I told him never to speak to me again I told him
she tried to break her wrists free
let me go
stop it Im stronger than you stop it now
let me go Ive got to catch him and ask his let me go Quentin please let me go let me go
all at once she quit her wrists went lax
yes I can tell him I can make him believe anytime I can make him
Caddy
she hadnt hitched Prince he was liable to strike out for home if the notion took him
anytime he will believe me
do you love him Caddy
do I what
she looked at me then everything emptied out of her eyes and they looked like the eyes in statues blank and unseeing and serene
put your hand against my throat
she took my hand and held it flat against her throat
now say his name
Dalton Ames

I felt the first surge of blood there it surged in strong acceler-
ating beats
say it again
her face looked off into the trees where the sun slanted and
where the bird
say it again
Dalton Ames
her blood surged steadily beating and beating against my hand

It kept on running for a long time, but my face felt cold and
sort of dead, and my eye, and the cut place on my finger was
smarting again. I could hear Shreve working the pump, then
he came back with the basin and a round blob of twilight wob-
bling in it, with a yellow edge like a fading balloon, then my
reflection. I tried to see my face in it.

"Has it stopped?" Shreve said. "Give me the rag." He tried
to take it from my hand.

"Look out," I said. "I can do it. Yes, it's about stopped
now." I dipped the rag again, breaking the balloon. The rag
stained the water. "I wish I had a clean one."

"You need a piece of beefsteak for that eye," Shreve said.
"Damn if you wont have a shiner tomorrow. The son of a
bitch," he said.

"Did I hurt him any?" I wrung out the handkerchief and
tried to clean the blood off of my vest.

"You cant get that off," Shreve said. "You'll have to send it
to the cleaner's. Come on, hold it on your eye, why dont you."

"I can get some of it off," I said. But I wasn't doing much
good. "What sort of shape is my collar in?"

"I dont know," Shreve said. "Hold it against your eye.
Here."

"Look out," I said. "I can do it. Did I hurt him any?"

"You may have hit him. I may have looked away just then
or blinked or something. He boxed the hell out of you. He
boxed you all over the place. What did you want to fight him
with your fists for? You goddam fool. How do you feel?"

"I feel fine," I said. "I wonder if I can get something to clean
my vest."

"Oh, forget your damn clothes. Does your eye hurt?"

"I feel fine," I said. Everything was sort of violet and still,
the sky green paling into gold beyond the gable of the house

and a plume of smoke rising from the chimney without any wind. I heard the pump again. A man was filling a pail, watching us across his pumping shoulder. A woman crossed the door, but she didn't look out. I could hear a cow lowing somewhere.

"Come on," Shreve said. "Let your clothes alone and put that rag on your eye. I'll send your suit out first thing tomorrow."

"All right. I'm sorry I didn't bleed on him a little, at least."

"Son of a bitch," Shreve said. Spoade came out of the house, talking to the woman I reckon, and crossed the yard. He looked at me with his cold, quizzical eyes.

"Well, bud," he said, looking at me, "I'll be damned if you dont go to a lot of trouble to have your fun. Kidnapping, then fighting. What do you do on your holidays? burn houses?"

"I'm all right," I said. "What did Mrs Bland say?"

"She's giving Gerald hell for bloodying you up. She'll give you hell for letting him, when she sees you. She dont object to the fighting, it's the blood that annoys her. I think you lost caste with her a little by not holding your blood better. How do you feel?"

"Sure," Shreve said. "If you cant be a Bland, the next best thing is to commit adultery with one or get drunk and fight him, as the case may be."

"Quite right," Spoade said. "But I didn't know Quentin was drunk."

"He wasn't," Shreve said. "Do you have to be drunk to want to hit that son of a bitch?"

"Well, I think I'd have to be pretty drunk to try it, after seeing how Quentin came out. Where'd he learn to box?"

"He's been going to Mike's every day, over in town," I said.

"He has?" Spoade said. "Did you know that when you hit him?"

"I dont know," I said. "I guess so. Yes."

"Wet it again," Shreve said. "Want some fresh water?"

"This is all right," I said. I dipped the cloth again and held it to my eye. "Wish I had something to clean my vest." Spoade was still watching me.

"Say," he said. "What did you hit him for? What was it he said?"

"I dont know. I dont know why I did."

"The first I knew was when you jumped up all of a sudden

and said, 'Did you ever have a sister? did you?' and when he said No, you hit him. I noticed you kept on looking at him, but you didn't seem to be paying any attention to what anybody was saying until you jumped up and asked him if he had any sisters."

"Ah, he was blowing off as usual," Shreve said, "about his women. You know: like he does, before girls, so they dont know exactly what he's saying. All his damn innuendo and lying and a lot of stuff that dont make sense even. Telling us about some wench that he made a date with to meet at a dance hall in Atlantic City and stood her up and went to the hotel and went to bed and how he lay there being sorry for her waiting on the pier for him, without him there to give her what she wanted. Talking about the body's beauty and the sorry ends thereof and how tough women have it, without anything else they can do except lie on their backs. Leda lurking in the bushes, whimpering and moaning for the swan, see. The son of a bitch. I'd hit him myself. Only I'd grabbed up her damn hamper of wine and done it if it had been me."

"Oh," Spoade said, "the champion of dames. Bud, you excite not only admiration, but horror." He looked at me, cold and quizzical. "Good God," he said.

"I'm sorry I hit him," I said. "Do I look too bad to go back and get it over with?"

"Apologies, hell," Shreve said. "Let them go to hell. We're going to town."

"He ought to go back so they'll know he fights like a gentleman," Spoade said. "Gets licked like one, I mean."

"Like this?" Shreve said. "With his clothes all over blood?"

"Why, all right," Spoade said. "You know best."

"He cant go around in his undershirt," Shreve said. "He's not a senior yet. Come on, let's go to town."

"You needn't come," I said. "You go on back to the picnic."

"Hell with them," Shreve said. "Come on here."

"What'll I tell them?" Spoade said. "Tell them you and Quentin had a fight too?"

"Tell them nothing," Shreve said. "Tell her her option expired at sunset. Come on, Quentin. I'll ask that woman where the nearest interurban——"

"No," I said. "I'm not going back to town."

Shreve stopped, looking at me. Turning his glasses looked like small yellow moons.

"What are you going to do?"

"I'm not going back to town yet. You go on back to the picnic. Tell them I wouldn't come back because my clothes were spoiled."

"Look here," he said. "What are you up to?"

"Nothing. I'm all right. You and Spoade go on back. I'll see you tomorrow." I went on across the yard, toward the road.

"Do you know where the station is?" Shreve said.

"I'll find it. I'll see you all tomorrow. Tell Mrs Bland I'm sorry I spoiled her party." They stood watching me. I went around the house. A rock path went down to the road. Roses grew on both sides of the path. I went through the gate, onto the road. It dropped downhill, toward the woods, and I could make out the auto beside the road. I went up the hill. The light increased as I mounted, and before I reached the top I heard a car. It sounded far away across the twilight and I stopped and listened to it. I couldn't make out the auto any longer, but Shreve was standing in the road before the house, looking up the hill. Behind him the yellow light lay like a wash of paint on the roof of the house. I lifted my hand and went on over the hill, listening to the car. Then the house was gone and I stopped in the green and yellow light and heard the car growing louder and louder, until just as it began to die away it ceased all together. I waited until I heard it start again. Then I went on.

As I descended the light dwindled slowly, yet at the same time without altering its quality, as if I and not light were changing, decreasing, though even when the road ran into trees you could have read a newspaper. Pretty soon I came to a lane. I turned into it. It was closer and darker than the road, but when it came out at the trolley stop—another wooden marquee—the light was still unchanged. After the lane it seemed brighter, as though I had walked through night in the lane and come out into morning again. Pretty soon the car came. I got on it, they turning to look at my eye, and found a seat on the left side.

The lights were on in the car, so while we ran between trees I couldn't see anything except my own face and a woman across the aisle with a hat sitting right on top of her head, with a broken feather in it, but when we ran out of the trees I could see the twilight again, that quality of light as if time really had stopped for a while, with the sun hanging just under the horizon, and then we passed the marquee where the old man had been eating out of the sack, and the road going on under the twilight, into twilight and the sense of water peaceful and swift beyond. Then the car went on, the draft building steadily up in the open door until it was drawing steadily through the car with the odor of summer and darkness except honeysuckle. Honeysuckle was the saddest odor of all, I think. I remember lots of them. Wistaria was one. On the rainy days when Mother wasn't feeling quite bad enough to stay away from the windows we used to play under it. When Mother stayed in bed Dilsey would put old clothes on us and let us go out in the rain because she said rain never hurt young folks. But if Mother was up we always began by playing on the porch until she said we were making too much noise, then we went out and played under the wistaria frame.

This was where I saw the river for the last time this morning, about here. I could feel water beyond the twilight, smell. When it bloomed in the spring and it rained the smell was everywhere you didn't notice it so much at other times but when it rained the smell began to come into the house at twilight either it would rain more at twilight or there was something in the light itself but it always smelled strongest then until I would lie in bed thinking when will it stop when will it stop. The draft in the door smelled of water, a damp steady breath. Sometimes I could put myself to sleep saying that over and over until after the honeysuckle got all mixed up in it the whole thing came to symbolise night and unrest I seemed to be lying neither asleep nor awake looking down a long corridor of gray halflight where all stable things had become shadowy paradoxical all I had done shadows all I had felt suffered taking visible form antic and perverse mocking without relevance inherent themselves with the denial of the significance they should have affirmed thinking I was I was not who was not was not who.

I could smell the curves of the river beyond the dusk and I saw the last light supine and tranquil upon tideflats like pieces of broken mirror, then beyond them lights began in the pale clear air, trembling a little like butterflies hovering a long way off. Benjamin the child of. How he used to sit before that mirror. Refuge unfailing in which conflict tempered silenced reconciled. Benjamin the child of mine old age held hostage into Egypt. O Benjamin. Dilsey said it was because Mother was too proud for him. They come into white people's lives like that in sudden sharp black trickles that isolate white facts for an instant in unarguable truth like under a microscope; the rest of the time just voices that laugh when you see nothing to laugh at, tears when no reason for tears. They will bet on the odd or even number of mourners at a funeral. A brothel full of them in Memphis went into a religious trance ran naked into the street. It took three policemen to subdue one of them. Yes Jesus O good man Jesus O that good man.

The car stopped. I got out, with them looking at my eye. When the trolley came it was full. I stopped on the back platform.

"Seats up front," the conductor said. I looked into the car. There were no seats on the left side.

"I'm not going far," I said. "I'll just stand here."

We crossed the river. The bridge, that is, arching slow and high into space, between silence and nothingness where lights—yellow and red and green—trembled in the clear air, repeating themselves.

"Better go up front and get a seat," the conductor said.

"I get off pretty soon," I said. "A couple of blocks."

I got off before we reached the postoffice. They'd all be sitting around somewhere by now though, and then I was hearing my watch and I began to listen for the chimes and I touched Shreve's letter through my coat, the bitten shadows of the elms flowing upon my hand. And then as I turned into the quad the chimes did begin and I went on while the notes came up like ripples on a pool and passed me and went on, saying Quarter to what? All right. Quarter to what.

Our windows were dark. The entrance was empty. I walked close to the left wall when I entered, but it was empty: just the stairs curving up into shadows echoes of feet in the sad generations like light dust upon the shadows, my feet waking them like dust, lightly to settle again.

I could see the letter before I turned the light on, propped against a book on the table so I would see it. Calling him my husband. And then Spoade said they were going somewhere, would not be back until late, and Mrs Bland would need another cavalier. But I would have seen him and he cannot get another car for an hour because after six oclock. I took out my watch and listened to it clicking away, not knowing it couldn't even lie. Then I laid it face up on the table and took Mrs Bland's letter and tore it across and dropped the pieces into the waste basket and took off my coat, vest, collar, tie and shirt. The tie was spoiled too, but then niggers. Maybe a pattern of blood he could call that the one Christ was wearing. I found the gasoline in Shreve's room and spread the vest on the table, where it would be flat, and opened the gasoline.

the first car in town a girl Girl that's what Jason couldn't bear smell of gasoline making him sick then got madder than ever because a girl Girl had no sister but Benjamin Benjamin the child of my sorrowful if I'd just had a mother so I could say Mother Mother It took a lot of gasoline, and then I couldn't tell if it was still the stain or just the gasoline. It had started the cut to smarting again so when I went to wash I hung the vest on a chair and lowered the light cord so that the bulb would be drying the splotch. I washed my face and hands, but even then I could smell it within the soap stinging, constricting the nostrils a little. Then I opened the bag and took the shirt and collar and tie out and put the bloody ones in and closed the bag, and dressed. While I was brushing my hair the half hour went. But there was until the three quarters anyway, except suppose *seeing on the rushing darkness only his own face no broken feather unless two of them but not two like that going to Boston the same night then my face his face for an instant across the crashing when out of darkness two lighted windows in rigid fleeing crash gone his face and mine just I see saw did I see not goodbye the marquee empty of eating the road empty in darkness in silence the bridge arching into silence darkness sleep the water peaceful and swift not goodbye*

I turned out the light and went into my bedroom, out of the gasoline but I could still smell it. I stood at the window the curtains moved slow out of the darkness touching my face like someone breathing asleep, breathing slow into the darkness again, leaving the touch. *After they had gone up stairs Mother lay back in her chair, the camphor handkerchief to her mouth. Father hadn't moved he still sat beside her holding her hand the bellowing hammering away like no place for it in silence* When I was little there was a picture in one of our books, a dark place into which a single weak ray of light came slanting upon two faces lifted out of the shadow. *You know what I'd do if I were King?* she never was a queen or a fairy she was always a king or a giant or a general *I'd break that place open and drag them out and I'd whip them good* It was torn out, jagged out. I was glad. I'd have to turn back to it until the dungeon was Mother herself she and Father upward into weak light holding hands and us lost somewhere below even them without even a ray of light. Then the honeysuckle got into it. As soon as I turned off the light and tried to go to sleep it would begin to come into the room in waves building and building up until I would have to pant to get any air at all out of it until I would have to get up and feel my way like when I was a little boy *hands can see touching in the mind shaping unseen door Door now nothing hands can see* My nose could see gasoline, the vest on the table, the door. The corridor was still empty of all the feet in sad generations seeking water. *yet the eyes unseeing clenched like teeth not disbelieving doubting even the absence of pain shin ankle knee the long invisible flowing of the stair-railing where a misstep in the darkness filled with sleeping Mother Father Caddy Jason Maury door I am not afraid only Mother Father Caddy Jason Maury getting so far ahead sleeping I will sleep fast when I door Door door* It was empty too, the pipes, the porcelain, the stained quiet walls, the throne of contemplation. I had forgotten the glass, but I could *hands can see cooling fingers invisible swan-throat where less than Moses rod the glass touch tentative not to drumming lean cool throat drumming cooling the metal the glass full overfull cooling the glass the fingers flushing sleep leaving the taste of dampened sleep in the long silence of the throat* I returned up the corridor, waking the lost feet in whispering battalions in the silence, into the gasoline, the watch telling its furious lie on the dark table. Then the curtains breathing out of the dark upon my face, leaving the breathing upon my face. A quarter hour yet. And then I'll not be. The peacefullest words. Peacefullest words. *Non fui. Sum.*

Fui. Non sum. Somewhere I heard bells once. Mississippi or
Massachusetts. I was. I am not. Massachusetts or Mississippi.
Shreve has a bottle in his trunk. *Aren't you even going to open
it* Mr and Mrs Jason Richmond Compson announce the
Three times. Days. Aren't you even going to open it marriage of
their daughter Candace *that liquor teaches you to confuse the
means with the end* I am. Drink. I was not. Let us sell Benjy's
pasture so that Quentin may go to Harvard and I may knock
my bones together and together. I will be dead in. Was it one
year Caddy said. Shreve has a bottle in his trunk. Sir I will not
need Shreve's I have sold Benjy's pasture and I can be dead in
Harvard Caddy said in the caverns and the grottoes of the sea
tumbling peacefully to the wavering tides because Harvard is
such a fine sound forty acres is no high price for a fine sound.
A fine dead sound we will swap Benjy's pasture for a fine dead
sound. It will last him a long time because he cannot hear it
unless he can smell it *as soon as she came in the door he began
to cry* I thought all the time it was just one of those town
squirts that Father was always teasing her about until. I didn't
notice him any more than any other stranger drummer or
what thought they were army shirts until all of a sudden I
knew he wasn't thinking of me at all as a potential source of
harm but was thinking of her when he looked at me was looking at me through her like through a piece of colored glass
*why must you meddle with me dont you know it wont do any good
I thought you'd have left that for Mother and Jason*
　did Mother set Jason to spy on you I wouldn't have.
　*Women only use other people's codes of honor it's because she loves
Caddy* staying downstairs even when she was sick so Father
couldn't kid Uncle Maury before Jason Father said Uncle
Maury was too poor a classicist to risk the blind immortal boy
in person he should have chosen Jason because Jason would
have made only the same kind of blunder Uncle Maury himself would have made not one to get him a black eye the Patterson boy was smaller than Jason too they sold the kites for
a nickel a piece until the trouble over finances Jason got a new
partner still smaller one small enough anyway because T. P.
said Jason still treasurer but Father said why should Uncle
Maury work if he Father could support five or six niggers that
did nothing at all but sit with their feet in the oven he certainly

could board and lodge Uncle Maury now and then and lend him a little money who kept his Father's belief in the celestial derivation of his own species at such a fine heat then Mother would cry and say that Father believed his people were better than hers that he was ridiculing Uncle Maury to teach us the same thing she couldn't see that Father was teaching us that all men are just accumulations dolls stuffed with sawdust swept up from the trash heaps where all previous dolls had been thrown away the sawdust flowing from what wound in what side that not for me died not. It used to be I thought of death as a man something like Grandfather a friend of his a kind of private and particular friend like we used to think of Grandfather's desk not to touch it not even to talk loud in the room where it was I always thought of them as being together somewhere all the time waiting for old Colonel Sartoris to come down and sit with them waiting on a high place beyond cedar trees Colonel Sartoris was on a still higher place look-ing out across at something and they were waiting for him to get done looking at it and come down Grandfather wore his uniform and we could hear the murmur of their voices from beyond the cedars they were always talking and Grandfather was always right

The three quarters began. The first note sounded, measured and tranquil, serenely peremptory, emptying the unhurried si-lence for the next one and that's it if people could only change one another forever that way merge like a flame swirling up for an instant then blown cleanly out along the cool eternal dark instead of lying there trying not to think of the swing until all cedars came to have that vivid dead smell of perfume that Benjy hated so. Just by imagining the clump it seemed to me that I could hear whispers secret surges smell the beating of hot blood under wild unsecret flesh watching against red eyelids the swine untethered in pairs rushing coupled into the sea and he we must just stay awake and see evil done for a little while its not always and i it doesnt have to be even that long for a man of courage and he do you consider that courage and i yes sir dont you and he every man is the arbiter of his own virtues whether or not you consider it courageous is of more importance than the act itself than any act otherwise you could not be in earnest and i you dont believe i am serious and he i think you are too serious to give me any cause for alarm you wouldnt have felt driven to the expedient of telling me you had committed incest otherwise and i i wasnt lying i wasnt lying and he you wanted to sublimate a piece of natural human folly into a horror and then exorcise it with truth and i it was to isolate her out of the loud world so that it would have to flee us of necessity and then the sound of it would be as though it had never been and he did you try to make her do it and i i was afraid to i was afraid she might and then it wouldnt have done any good but if i could tell you we did it would have been so and then the others wouldnt be so and then the world would roar away and he and now this other you are not lying now either but you are still blind to what is in yourself to that part of general truth the sequence of natural events and their causes which shadows every mans brow even benjys you are not thinking of finitude you are contemplating an apotheosis in which a temporary state of mind will become symmetrical above the flesh and aware both of itself and of the flesh it will not quite discard you will not even be dead and i temporary and he you cannot bear to think that someday it will no longer hurt you like this now were getting at it you seem to regard it merely as an experience that will whiten your hair overnight so to speak without altering your appearance at all you wont do it under these conditions it will be a gamble and the strange thing is that man who is conceived by accident and whose every breath is a fresh cast with dice already loaded against him will not face that final main which he knows before hand he has assuredly to face without essaying expedients ranging all the way from violence to petty chicanery that would not deceive a child until someday in very disgust he risks every-thing on a single blind turn of a card no man ever does that under the first fury of despair or remorse or bereavement he does it only when he has realised that even the despair or re-morse or bereavement is not particularly important to the dark diceman and i temporary and he it is hard believing to think that a love or a sorrow is a bond purchased without design and which matures willynilly and is recalled without warning to be replaced by whatever issue the gods happen to be float-ing at the time no you will not do that until you come to be-lieve that even she was not quite worth despair perhaps and i i will never do that nobody knows what i know and he i think youd better go on up to cambridge right away you might go up into maine for a month you can afford it if you are careful it might be a good thing watching pennies has healed more scars than jesus and i suppose i realise what you believe i will realise up there next week or next month and he then you will remember that for you to go to harvard has been your mothers dream since you were born and no compson has ever disappointed a lady and i temporary it will be better for me for all of us and he every man is the arbiter of his own virtues but let no man prescribe for another mans wellbeing and i temporary and he was the saddest word of all there is nothing else in the world its not despair until time its not even time until it was

The last note sounded. At last it stopped vibrating and the darkness was still again. I entered the sitting room and turned on the light. I put my vest on. The gasoline was faint now, barely noticeable, and in the mirror the stain didn't show. Not like my eye did, anyway. I put on my coat. Shreve's letter crackled through the cloth and I took it out and examined the address, and put it in my side pocket. Then I carried the watch into Shreve's room and put it in his drawer and went to my room and got a fresh handkerchief and went to the door and put my hand on the light switch. Then I remembered I hadn't brushed my teeth, so I had to open the bag again. I found my toothbrush and got some of Shreve's paste and went out and brushed my teeth. I squeezed the brush as dry as I could and put it back in the bag and shut it, and went to the door again. Before I snapped the light out I looked around to see if there was anything else, then I saw that I had forgotten my hat. I'd have to go by the postoffice and I'd be sure to meet some of them, and they'd think I was a Harvard Square student making like he was a senior. I had forgotten to brush it too, but Shreve had a brush, so I didn't have to open the bag any more.

April Sixth, 1928.

ONCE a bitch always a bitch, what I say. I says you're lucky if her playing out of school is all that worries you. I says she ought to be down there in that kitchen right now, instead of up there in her room, gobbing paint on her face and waiting for six niggers that cant even stand up out of a chair unless they've got a pan full of bread and meat to balance them, to fix breakfast for her. And Mother says,

"But to have the school authorities think that I have no control over her, that I cant——"

"Well," I says. "You cant, can you? You never have tried to do anything with her," I says. "How do you expect to begin this late, when she's seventeen years old?"

She thought about that for a while.

"But to have them think that . . . I didn't even know she had a report card. She told me last fall that they had quit using them this year. And now for Professor Junkin to call me on the telephone and tell me if she's absent one more time, she will have to leave school. How does she do it? Where does she go? You're down town all day; you ought to see her if she stays on the streets."

"Yes," I says. "If she stayed on the streets. I dont reckon she'd be playing out of school just to do something she could do in public," I says.

"What do you mean?" she says.

"I dont mean anything," I says. "I just answered your question." Then she begun to cry again, talking about how her own flesh and blood rose up to curse her.

"You asked me," I says.

"I dont mean you," she says. "You are the only one of them that isn't a reproach to me."

"Sure," I says. "I never had time to be. I never had time to go to Harvard or drink myself into the ground. I had to work. But of course if you want me to follow her around and see what she does, I can quit the store and get a job where I can work at night. Then I can watch her during the day and you can use Ben for the night shift."

"I know I'm just a trouble and a burden to you," she says, crying on the pillow.

"I ought to know it," I says. "You've been telling me that for thirty years. Even Ben ought to know it now. Do you want me to say anything to her about it?"

"Do you think it will do any good?" she says.

"Not if you come down there interfering just when I get started," I says. "If you want me to control her, just say so and keep your hands off. Everytime I try to, you come butting in and then she gives both of us the laugh."

"Remember she's your own flesh and blood," she says.

"Sure," I says, "that's just what I'm thinking of—flesh. And a little blood too, if I had my way. When people act like niggers, no matter who they are the only thing to do is treat them like a nigger."

"I'm afraid you'll lose your temper with her," she says.

"Well," I says. "You haven't had much luck with your system. You want me to do anything about it, or not? Say one way or the other; I've got to get on to work."

"I know you have to slave your life away for us," she says. "You know if I had my way, you'd have an office of your own to go to, and hours that became a Bascomb. Because you are a Bascomb, despite your name. I know that if your father could have foreseen——"

"Well," I says, "I reckon he's entitled to guess wrong now and then, like anybody else, even a Smith or a Jones." She begun to cry again.

"To hear you speak bitterly of your dead father," she says.

"All right," I says, "all right. Have it your way. But as I haven't got an office, I'll have to get on to what I have got. Do you want me to say anything to her?"

"I'm afraid you'll lose your temper with her," she says.

"All right," I says. "I wont say anything, then."

"But something must be done," she says. "To have people think I permit her to stay out of school and run about the streets, or that I cant prevent her doing it. . . . Jason, Jason," she says. "How could you. How could you leave me with these burdens."

"Now, now," I says. "You'll make yourself sick. Why dont

you either lock her up all day too, or turn her over to me and quit worrying over her?"

"My own flesh and blood," she says, crying. So I says,

"All right. I'll tend to her. Quit crying, now."

"Dont lose your temper," she says. "She's just a child, remember."

"No," I says. "I wont." I went out, closing the door.

"Jason," she says. I didn't answer. I went down the hall. "Jason," she says beyond the door. I went on down stairs. There wasn't anybody in the diningroom, then I heard her in the kitchen. She was trying to make Dilsey let her have another cup of coffee. I went in.

"I reckon that's your school costume, is it?" I says. "Or maybe today's a holiday?"

"Just a half a cup, Dilsey," she says. "Please."

"No, suh," Dilsey says. "I aint gwine do it. You aint got no business wid mo'n one cup, a seventeen year old gal, let lone whut Miss Cahline say. You go on and git dressed for school, so you kin ride to town wid Jason. You fixin to be late again."

"No she's not," I says. "We're going to fix that right now." She looked at me, the cup in her hand. She brushed her hair back from her face, her kimono slipping off her shoulder. "You put that cup down and come in here a minute," I says.

"What for?" she says.

"Come on," I says. "Put that cup in the sink and come in here."

"What you up to now, Jason?" Dilsey says.

"You may think you can run over me like you do your grandmother and everybody else," I says. "But you'll find out different. I'll give you ten seconds to put that cup down like I told you."

She quit looking at me. She looked at Dilsey. "What time is it, Dilsey?" she says. "When it's ten seconds, you whistle. Just a half a cup, Dilsey, pl——"

I grabbed her by the arm. She dropped the cup. It broke on the floor and she jerked back, looking at me, but I held her arm. Dilsey got up from her chair.

"You, Jason," she says.

"You turn me loose," Quentin says. "I'll slap you."

"You will, will you?" I says. "You will will you?" She slapped at me. I caught that hand too and held her like a wildcat. "You will, will you?" I says. "You think you will?"

"You, Jason!" Dilsey says. I dragged her into the dining-room. Her kimono came unfastened, flapping about her, dam near naked. Dilsey came hobbling along. I turned and kicked the door shut in her face.

"You keep out of here," I says.

Quentin was leaning against the table, fastening her kimono. I looked at her.

"Now," I says. "I want to know what you mean, playing out of school and telling your grandmother lies and forging her name on your report and worrying her sick. What do you mean by it?"

She didn't say anything. She was fastening her kimono up under her chin, pulling it tight around her, looking at me. She hadn't got around to painting herself yet and her face looked like she had polished it with a gun rag. I went and grabbed her wrist. "What do you mean?" I says.

"None of your damn business," she says. "You turn me loose."

Dilsey came in the door. "You, Jason," she says.

"You get out of here, like I told you," I says, not even looking back. "I want to know where you go when you play out of school," I says. "You keep off the streets, or I'd see you. Who do you play out with? Are you hiding out in the woods with one of those dam slick-headed jellybeans? Is that where you go?"

"You—you old goddam!" she says. She fought, but I held her. "You damn old goddam!" she says.

"I'll show you," I says. "You may can scare an old woman off, but I'll show you who's got hold of you now." I held her with one hand, then she quit fighting and watched me, her eyes getting wide and black.

"What are you going to do?" she says.

"You wait until I get this belt out and I'll show you," I says, pulling my belt out. Then Dilsey grabbed my arm.

"Jason," she says. "You, Jason! Aint you shamed of yourself."

"Dilsey," Quentin says. "Dilsey."

"I aint gwine let him," Dilsey says. "Dont you worry, honey." She held to my arm. Then the belt came out and I jerked loose and flung her away. She stumbled into the table. She was so old she couldn't do any more than move hardly. But that's all right: we need somebody in the kitchen to eat up the grub the young ones cant tote off. She came hobbling between us, trying to hold me again. "Hit me, den," she says, "ef nothin else but hittin somebody wont do you. Hit me," she says.

"You think I wont?" I says.

"I dont put no devilment beyond you," she says. Then I heard Mother on the stairs. I might have known she wasn't going to keep out of it. I let go. She stumbled back against the wall, holding her kimono shut.

"All right," I says. "We'll just put this off a while. But dont think you can run it over me. I'm not an old woman, nor an old half dead nigger, either. You dam little slut," I says.

"Dilsey," she says. "Dilsey, I want my mother."

Dilsey went to her. "Now, now," she says. "He aint gwine so much as lay his hand on you while Ise here." Mother came on down the stairs.

"Jason," she says. "Dilsey."

"Now, now," Dilsey says. "I aint gwine let him tech you." She put her hand on Quentin. She knocked it down.

"You damn old nigger," she says. She ran toward the door.

"Dilsey," Mother says on the stairs. Quentin ran up the stairs, passing her. "Quentin," Mother says. "You, Quentin." Quentin ran on. I could hear her when she reached the top, then in the hall. Then the door slammed.

Mother had stopped. Then she came on. "Dilsey," she says.

"All right," Dilsey says. "Ise comin. You go on and git dat car and wait now," she says, "so you kin cahy her to school."

"Dont you worry," I says. "I'll take her to school and I'm going to see that she stays there. I've started this thing, and I'm going through with it."

"Jason," Mother says on the stairs.

"Go on, now," Dilsey says, going toward the door. "You want to git her started too? Ise comin, Miss Cahline."

I went on out. I could hear them on the steps. "You go on back to bed now," Dilsey was saying. "Dont you know you aint feeling well enough to git up yet? Go on back, now. I'm gwine to see she gits to school in time."

I went on out the back to back the car out, then I had to go all the way round to the front before I found them.

"I thought I told you to put that tire on the back of the car," I says.

"I aint had time," Luster says. "Aint nobody to watch him till mammy git done in de kitchen."

"Yes," I says. "I feed a whole dam kitchen full of niggers to follow around after him, but if I want an automobile tire changed, I have to do it myself."

"I aint had nobody to leave him wid," he says. Then he begun moaning and slobbering.

"Take him on round to the back," I says. "What the hell makes you want to keep him around here where people can see him?" I made them go on, before he got started bellowing good. It's bad enough on Sundays, with that dam field full of people that haven't got a side show and six niggers to feed, knocking a dam oversize mothball around. He's going to keep on running up and down that fence and bellowing every time they come in sight until first thing I know they're going to begin charging me golf dues, then Mother and Dilsey'll have to get a couple of china door knobs and a walking stick and work it out, unless I play at night with a lantern. Then they'd send us all to Jackson, maybe. God knows, they'd hold Old Home week when that happened.

I went on back to the garage. There was the tire, leaning against the wall, but be damned if I was going to put it on. I backed out and turned around. She was standing by the drive. I says,

"I know you haven't got any books: I just want to ask you what you did with them, if it's any of my business. Of course I haven't got any right to ask," I says. "I'm just the one that paid $11.65 for them last September."

"Mother buys my books," she says. "There's not a cent of your money on me. I'd starve first."

"Yes?" I says. "You tell your grandmother that and see what she says. You dont look all the way naked," I says, "even if that stuff on your face does hide more of you than anything else you've got on."

"Do you think your money or hers either paid for a cent of this?" she says.

"Ask your grandmother," I says. "Ask her what became of those checks. You saw her burn one of them, as I remember." She wasn't even listening, with her face all gummed up with paint and her eyes hard as a fice dog's.

"Do you know what I'd do if I thought your money or hers either bought one cent of this?" she says, putting her hand on her dress.

"What would you do?" I says. "Wear a barrel?"

"I'd tear it right off and throw it into the street," she says. "Dont you believe me?"

"Sure you would," I says. "You do it every time."

"See if I wouldn't," she says. She grabbed the neck of her dress in both hands and made like she would tear it.

"You tear that dress," I says, "and I'll give you a whipping right here that you'll remember all your life."

"See if I dont," she says. Then I saw that she really was trying to tear it, to tear it right off of her. By the time I got the car stopped and grabbed her hands there was about a dozen people looking. It made me so mad for a minute it kind of blinded me.

"You do a thing like that again and I'll make you sorry you ever drew breath," I says.

"I'm sorry now," she says. She quit, then her eyes turned kind of funny and I says to myself if you cry here in this car, on the street, I'll whip you. I'll wear you out. Lucky for her she didn't, so I turned her wrists loose and drove on. Luckily we were near an alley, where I could turn into the back street and dodge the square. They were already putting the tent up in Beard's lot. Earl had already given me the two passes for our show windows. She sat there with her face turned away, chewing her lip. "I'm sorry now," she says. "I dont see why I was ever born."

"And I know of at least one other person that dont understand all he knows about that," I says. I stopped in front of the school house. The bell had rung, and the last of them were just going in. "You're on time for once, anyway," I says. "Are you going in there and stay there, or am I coming with you and make you?" She got out and banged the door.

"Remember what I say," I says. "I mean it. Let me hear one more time that you are slipping up and down back alleys with one of those dam squirts."

She turned back at that. "I dont slip around," she says. "I dare anybody to know everything I do."

"And they all know it, too," I says. "Everybody in this town knows what you are. But I wont have it anymore, you hear? I dont care what you do, myself," I says. "But I've got a position in this town, and I'm not going to have any member of my family going on like a nigger wench. You hear me?"

"I dont care," she says. "I'm bad and I'm going to hell, and I dont care. I'd rather be in hell than anywhere where you are."

"If I hear one more time that you haven't been to school, you'll wish you were in hell," I says. She turned and ran on across the yard. "One more time, remember," I says. She didn't look back.

I went to the postoffice and got the mail and drove on to the store and parked. Earl looked at me when I came in. I gave him a chance to say something about my being late, but he just said,

"Those cultivators have come. You'd better help Uncle Job put them up."

I went on to the back, where old Job was uncrating them, at the rate of about three bolts to the hour.

"You ought to be working for me," I says. "Every other no-count nigger in town eats in my kitchen."

"I works to suit de man whut pays me Sat'dy night," he says. "When I does dat, it dont leave me a whole lot of time to please other folks." He screwed up a nut. "Aint nobody works much in dis country cep de boll-weevil, noways," he says.

"You'd better be glad you're not a boll-weevil waiting on those cultivators," I says. "You'd work yourself to death before they'd be ready to prevent you."

"Dat's de troof," he says. "Boll-weevil got tough time. Work ev'y day in de week out in de hot sun, rain er shine. Aint got no front porch to set on en watch de watter-milyuns growin and Sat'dy dont mean nothin a-tall to him."

"Saturday wouldn't mean nothing to you, either," I says, "if it depended on me to pay you wages. Get those things out of the crates now and drag them inside."

I opened her letter first and took the check out. Just like a woman. Six days late. Yet they try to make men believe that they're capable of conducting a business. How long would a man that thought the first of the month came on the sixth last in business. And like as not, when they sent the bank statement out, she would want to know why I never deposited my salary until the sixth. Things like that never occur to a woman.

"I had no answer to my letter about Quentin's easter dress. Did it arrive all right? I've had no answer to the last two letters I wrote her, though the check in the second one was cashed with the other check. Is she sick? Let me know at once or I'll come there and see for myself. You promised you would let me know when she needed things. I will expect to hear from you before the 10th. No you'd better wire me at once. You are opening my letters to her. I know that as well as if I were looking at you. You'd better wire me at once about her to this address."

About that time Earl started yelling at Job, so I put them away and went over to try to put some life into him. What this country needs is white labor. Let these dam trifling niggers starve for a couple of years, then they'd see what a soft thing they have.

Along toward ten oclock I went up front. There was a drummer there. It was a couple of minutes to ten, and I invited him up the street to get a dope. We got to talking about crops.

"There's nothing to it," I says. "Cotton is a speculator's crop. They fill the farmer full of hot air and get him to raise a big crop for them to whipsaw on the market, to trim the suckers with. Do you think the farmer gets anything out of it except a red neck and a hump in his back? You think the man that sweats to put it into the ground gets a red cent more than a bare living," I says. "Let him make a big crop and it wont be worth picking; let him make a small crop and he wont have enough to gin. And what for? so a bunch of dam eastern jews I'm not talking about men of the jewish religion," I says. "I've known some jews that were fine citizens. You might be one yourself," I says.

"No," he says. "I'm an American."

"No offense," I says. "I give every man his due, regardless of religion or anything else. I have nothing against jews as an individual," I says. "It's just the race. You'll admit that they produce nothing. They follow the pioneers into a new country and sell them clothes."

"You're thinking of Armenians," he says, "aren't you. A pioneer wouldn't have any use for new clothes."

"No offense," I says. "I dont hold a man's religion against him."

"Sure," he says. "I'm an American. My folks have some French blood, why I have a nose like this. I'm an American, all right."

"So am I," I says. "Not many of us left. What I'm talking about is the fellows that sit up there in New York and trim the sucker gamblers."

"That's right," he says. "Nothing to gambling, for a poor man. There ought to be a law against it."

"Dont you think I'm right?" I says.

"Yes," he says. "I guess you're right. The farmer catches it coming and going."

"I know I'm right," I says. "It's a sucker game, unless a man gets inside information from somebody that knows what's going on. I happen to be associated with some people who're right there on the ground. They have one of the biggest manipulators in New York for an adviser. Way I do it," I says, "I never risk much at a time. It's the fellow that thinks he knows it all and is trying to make a killing with three dollars that they're laying for. That's why they are in the business."

Then it struck ten. I went up to the telegraph office. It opened up a little, just like they said. I went into the corner and took out the telegram again, just to be sure. While I was looking at it a report came in. It was up two points. They were all buying. I could tell that from what they were saying. Getting aboard. Like they didn't know it could go but one way. Like there was a law or something against doing anything but buying. Well, I reckon those eastern jews have got to live too. But I'll be damned if it hasn't come to a pretty pass when any dam foreigner that cant make a living in the country where God put him, can come to this one and take money right

out of an American's pockets. It was up two points more.
Four points. But hell, they were right there and knew what
was going on. And if I wasn't going to take the advice, what
was I paying them ten dollars a month for. I went out, then
I remembered and came back and sent the wire. "All well.
Q writing today."

"Q?" the operator says.

"Yes," I says. "Q. Cant you spell Q?"

"I just asked to be sure," he says.

"You send it like I wrote it and I'll guarantee you to be
sure," I says. "Send it collect."

"What you sending, Jason?" Doc Wright says, looking over
my shoulder. "Is that a code message to buy?"

"That's all right about that," I says. "You boys use your own
judgment. You know more about it than those New York
folks do."

"Well, I ought to," Doc says. "I'd a saved money this year
raising it at two cents a pound."

Another report came in. It was down a point.

"Jason's selling," Hopkins says. "Look at his face."

"That's all right about what I'm doing," I says. "You boys
follow your own judgment. Those rich New York jews have
got to live like everybody else," I says.

I went on back to the store. Earl was busy up front. I went
on back to the desk and read Lorraine's letter. "Dear daddy
wish you were here. No good parties when daddys out of
town I miss my sweet daddy." I reckon she does. Last time I
gave her forty dollars. Gave it to her. I never promise a woman
anything nor let her know what I'm going to give her. That's
the only way to manage them. Always keep them guessing. If
you cant think of any other way to surprise them, give them
a bust in the jaw.

I tore it up and burned it over the spittoon. I make it a rule
never to keep a scrap of paper bearing a woman's hand, and I
never write them at all. Lorraine is always after me to write to
her but I says anything I forgot to tell you will save till I get
to Memphis again but I says I dont mind you writing me now
and then in a plain envelope, but if you ever try to call me up
on the telephone, Memphis wont hold you I says. I says when
I'm up there I'm one of the boys, but I'm not going to have

any woman calling me on the telephone. Here I says, giving her the forty dollars. If you ever get drunk and take a notion to call me on the phone, just remember this and count ten before you do it.

"When'll that be?" she says.

"What?" I says.

"When you're coming back," she says.

"I'll let you know," I says. Then she tried to buy a beer, but I wouldn't let her. "Keep your money," I says. "Buy yourself a dress with it." I gave the maid a five, too. After all, like I say money has no value; it's just the way you spend it. It dont belong to anybody, so why try to hoard it. It just belongs to the man that can get it and keep it. There's a man right here in Jefferson made a lot of money selling rotten goods to niggers, lived in a room over the store about the size of a pigpen, and did his own cooking. About four or five years ago he was taken sick. Scared the hell out of him so that when he was up again he joined the church and bought himself a Chinese missionary, five thousand dollars a year. I often think how mad he'll be if he was to die and find out there's not any heaven, when he thinks about that five thousand a year. Like I say, he'd better go on and die now and save money.

When it was burned good I was just about to shove the others into my coat when all of a sudden something told me to open Quentin's before I went home, but about that time Earl started yelling for me up front, so I put them away and went and waited on the dam redneck while he spent fifteen minutes deciding whether he wanted a twenty cent hame string or a thirty-five cent one.

"You'd better take that good one," I says. "How do you fellows ever expect to get ahead, trying to work with cheap equipment?"

"If this one aint any good," he says, "why have you got it on sale?"

"I didn't say it wasn't any good," I says. "I said it's not as good as that other one."

"How do you know it's not," he says. "You ever use airy one of them?"

"Because they dont ask thirty-five cents for it," I says. "That's how I know it's not as good."

He held the twenty cent one in his hands, drawing it through his fingers. "I reckon I'll take this hyer one," he says. I offered to take it and wrap it, but he rolled it up and put it in his overalls. Then he took out a tobacco sack and finally got it untied and shook some coins out. He handed me a quarter. "That fifteen cents will buy me a snack of dinner," he says.

"All right," I says. "You're the doctor. But dont come complaining to me next year when you have to buy a new outfit."

"I aint makin next year's crop yit," he says. Finally I got rid of him, but every time I took that letter out something would come up. They were all in town for the show, coming in in droves to give their money to something that brought nothing to the town and wouldn't leave anything except what those grafters in the Mayor's office will split among themselves, and Earl chasing back and forth like a hen in a coop, saying "Yes, ma'am, Mr Compson will wait on you. Jason, show this lady a churn or a nickel's worth of screen hooks."

Well, Jason likes work. I says no I never had university advantages because at Harvard they teach you how to go for a swim at night without knowing how to swim and at Sewanee they dont even teach you what water is. I says you might send me to the state University; maybe I'll learn how to stop my clock with a nose spray and then you can send Ben to the Navy I says or to the cavalry anyway, they use geldings in the cavalry. Then when she sent Quentin home for me to feed too I says I guess that's right too, instead of me having to go way up north for a job they sent the job down here to me and then Mother begun to cry and I says it's not that I have any objection to having it here; if it's any satisfaction to you I'll quit work and nurse it myself and let you and Dilsey keep the flour barrel full, or Ben. Rent him out to a sideshow; there must be folks somewhere that would pay a dime to see him, then she cried more and kept saying my poor afflicted baby and I says yes he'll be quite a help to you when he gets his growth not being more than one and a half times as high as me now and she says she'd be dead soon and then we'd all be better off and so I says all right, all right, have it your way. It's your grandchild, which is more than any other grandparents it's got can say for certain. Only I says it's only a question of time. If you believe she'll do what she says and not try to see it, you fool yourself because the first time that was the Mother kept on saying thank God you are not a Compson except in name, because you are all I have left now, you and Maury and I says well I could spare Uncle Maury myself and then they came and said they were ready to start. Mother stopped crying then. She pulled her veil down and we went down stairs. Uncle Maury was coming out of the diningroom, his handkerchief to his mouth. They kind of made a lane and we went out the door just in time to see Dilsey driving Ben and T. P. back around the corner. We went down the steps and got in. Uncle Maury kept saying Poor little sister, poor little sister, talking around his mouth and patting Mother's hand. Talking around whatever it was.

"Have you got your band on?" she says. "Why dont they go on, before Benjamin comes out and makes a spectacle. Poor little boy. He doesn't know. He cant even realise."

"There, there," Uncle Maury says, patting her hand, talking around his mouth. "It's better so. Let him be unaware of bereavement until he has to."

"Other women have their children to support them in times like this," Mother says.

"You have Jason and me," he says.

"It's so terrible to me," she says. "Having the two of them like this, in less than two years."

"There, there," he says. After a while he kind of sneaked his hand to his mouth and dropped them out the window. Then I knew what I had been smelling. Clove stems. I reckon he thought that the least he could do at Father's or maybe the sideboard thought it was still Father and tripped him up when he passed. Like I say, if he had to sell something to send Quentin to Harvard we'd all been a dam sight better off if he'd sold that sideboard and bought himself a one-armed strait jacket with part of the money. I reckon the reason all the Compson gave out before it got to me like Mother says, is that he drank it up. At least I never heard of him offering to sell anything to send me to Harvard.

So he kept on patting her hand and saying "Poor little sister", patting her hand with one of the black gloves that we got the bill for four days later because it was the twenty-sixth because it was the same day one month that Father went up

there and got it and brought it home and wouldn't tell anything about where she was or anything and Mother crying and
saying "And you didn't even see him? You didn't even try to
get him to make any provision for it?" and Father says "No
she shall not touch his money not one cent of it" and Mother
says "He can be forced to by law. He can prove nothing,
unless——Jason Compson," she says. "Were you fool enough
to tell—"

"Hush, Caroline," Father says, then he sent me to help
Dilsey get that old cradle out of the attic and I says,

"Well, they brought my job home tonight" because all the
time we kept hoping they'd get things straightened out and
he'd keep her because Mother kept saying she would at least
have enough regard for the family not to jeopardise my chance
after she and Quentin had had theirs.

"And whar else do she belong?" Dilsey says. "Who else
gwine raise her cep me? Aint I raised ev'y one of y'all?"

"And a dam fine job you made of it," I says. "Anyway it'll
give her something to sure enough worry over now." So we
carried the cradle down and Dilsey started to set it up in her
old room. Then Mother started sure enough.

"Hush, Miss Cahline," Dilsey says. "You gwine wake
her up."

"In there?" Mother says. "To be contaminated by that atmosphere? It'll be hard enough as it is, with the heritage she
already has."

"Hush," Father says. "Dont be silly."

"Why aint she gwine sleep in here," Dilsey says. "In the
same room whar I put her maw to bed ev'y night of her life
since she was big enough to sleep by herself."

"You dont know," Mother says. "To have my own daughter cast off by her husband. Poor little innocent baby," she
says, looking at Quentin. "You will never know the suffering
you've caused."

"Hush, Caroline," Father says.

"What you want to go on like that fo Jason fer?" Dilsey says.

"I've tried to protect him," Mother says. "I've always tried
to protect him from it. At least I can do my best to shield her."

"How sleepin in dis room gwine hurt her, I like to know,"
Dilsey says.

"I cant help it," Mother says. "I know I'm just a trouble-some old woman. But I know that people cannot flout God's laws with impunity."

"Nonsense," Father says. "Fix it in Miss Caroline's room then, Dilsey."

"You can say nonsense," Mother says. "But she must never know. She must never even learn that name. Dilsey, I forbid you ever to speak that name in her hearing. If she could grow up never to know that she had a mother, I would thank God."

"Dont be a fool," Father says.

"I have never interfered with the way you brought them up," Mother says. "But now I cannot stand anymore. We must decide this now, tonight. Either that name is never to be spoken in her hearing, or she must go, or I will go. Take your choice."

"Hush," Father says. "You're just upset. Fix it in here, Dilsey."

"En you's about sick too," Dilsey says. "You looks like a hant. You git in bed and I'll fix you a toddy and see kin you sleep. I bet you aint had a full night's sleep since you lef."

"No," Mother says. "Dont you know what the doctor says? Why must you encourage him to drink? That's what's the matter with him now. Look at me, I suffer too, but I'm not so weak that I must kill myself with whiskey."

"Fiddlesticks," Father says. "What do doctors know? They make their livings advising people to do whatever they are not doing at the time, which is the extent of anyone's knowledge of the degenerate ape. You'll have a minister in to hold my hand next." Then Mother cried, and he went out. Went down stairs, and then I heard the sideboard. I woke up and heard him going down again. Mother had gone to sleep or some-thing, because the house was quiet at last. He was trying to be quiet too, because I couldn't hear him, only the bottom of his nightshirt and his bare legs in front of the sideboard.

Dilsey fixed the cradle and undressed her and put her in it. She never had waked up since he brought her in the house.

"She pretty near too big fer hit," Dilsey says. "Dar now. I gwine spread me a pallet right acrost de hall, so you wont need to git up in de night."

"I wont sleep," Mother says. "You go on home. I wont

mind. I'll be happy to give the rest of my life to her, if I can just prevent——"

"Hush, now," Dilsey says. "We gwine take keer of her. En you go on to bed too," she says to me. "You got to go to school tomorrow."

So I went out, then Mother called me back and cried on me a while.

"You are my only hope," she says. "Every night I thank God for you." While we were waiting there for them to start she says Thank God if he had to be taken too, it is you left me and not Quentin. Thank God you are not a Compson, because all I have left now is you and Maury and I says, Well I could spare Uncle Maury myself. Well, he kept on patting her hand with his black glove, talking away from her. He took them off when his turn with the shovel came. He got up near the first, where they were holding the umbrellas over them, stamping every now and then and trying to kick the mud off their feet and sticking to the shovels so they'd have to knock it off, making a hollow sound when it fell on it, and when I stepped back around the hack I could see him behind a tombstone, taking another one out of a bottle. I thought he never was going to stop because I had on my new suit too, but it happened that there wasn't much mud on the wheels yet, only Mother saw it and says I dont know when you'll ever have another one and Uncle Maury says, "Now, now. Dont you worry at all. You have me to depend on, always."

And we have. Always. The fourth letter was from him. But there wasn't any need to open it. I could have written it myself, or recited it to her from memory, adding ten dollars just to be safe. But I had a hunch about that other letter. I just felt that it was about time she was up to some of her tricks again. She got pretty wise after that first time. She found out pretty quick that I was a different breed of cat from Father. When they begun to get it filled up toward the top Mother started crying sure enough, so Uncle Maury got in with her and drove off. He says You can come in with somebody; they'll be glad to give you a lift. I'll have to take your mother on and I thought about saying, Yes you ought to brought two bottles instead of just one only I thought about where we were, so I let them go on. Little they cared how wet I got, because then Mother could have a whale of a time being afraid I was taking pneumonia.

Well, I got to thinking about that and watching them throwing dirt into it, slapping it on anyway like they were making mortar or something or building a fence, and I began to feel sort of funny and so I decided to walk around a while. I thought that if I went toward town they'd catch up and be trying to make me get in one of them, so I went on back toward the nigger graveyard. I got under some cedars, where the rain didn't come much, only dripping now and then, where I could see when they got through and went away. After a while they were all gone and I waited a minute and came out.

I had to follow the path to keep out of the wet grass so I didn't see her until I was pretty near there, standing there in a black cloak, looking at the flowers. I knew who it was right off, before she turned and looked at me and lifted up her veil.

"Hello, Jason," she says, holding out her hand. We shook hands.

"What are you doing here?" I says. "I thought you promised her you wouldn't come back here. I thought you had more sense than that."

"Yes?" she says. She looked at the flowers again. There must have been fifty dollars' worth. Somebody had put one bunch on Quentin's. "You did?" she says.

"I'm not surprised though," I says. "I wouldn't put anything past you. You dont mind anybody. You dont give a dam about anybody."

"Oh," she says, "that job." She looked at the grave. "I'm sorry about that, Jason."

"I bet you are," I says. "You'll talk mighty meek now. But you needn't have come back. There's not anything left. Ask Uncle Maury, if you dont believe me."

"I dont want anything," she says. She looked at the grave. "Why didn't they let me know?" she says. "I just happened to see it in the paper. On the back page. Just happened to."

I didn't say anything. We stood there, looking at the grave, and then I got to thinking about when we were little and one thing and another and I got to feeling funny again, kind of mad or something, thinking about now we'd have Uncle Maury around the house all the time, running things like the way he left me to come home in the rain by myself. I says,

"A fine lot you care, sneaking in here soon as he's dead. But it wont do you any good. Dont think that you can take advantage of this to come sneaking back. If you cant stay on the horse you've got, you'll have to walk," I says. "We dont even know your name at that house," I says. "Do you know that? We dont even know your name. You'd be better off if you were down there with him and Quentin," I says. "Do you know that?"

"I know it," she says. "Jason," she says, looking at the grave, "if you'll fix it so I can see her a minute I'll give you fifty dollars."

"You haven't got fifty dollars," I says.

"Will you?" she says, not looking at me.

"Let's see it," I says. "I dont believe you've got fifty dollars."

I could see where her hands were moving under her cloak, then she held her hand out. Dam if it wasn't full of money. I could see two or three yellow ones.

"Does he still give you money?" I says. "How much does he send you?"

"I'll give you a hundred," she says. "Will you?"

"Just a minute," I says. "And just like I say. I wouldn't have her know it for a thousand dollars."

"Yes," she says. "Just like you say do it. Just so I see her a minute. I wont beg or do anything. I'll go right on away."

"Give me the money," I says.

"I'll give it to you afterward," she says.

"Dont you trust me?" I says.

"No," she says. "I know you. I grew up with you."

"You're a fine one to talk about trusting people," I says. "Well," I says. "I got to get on out of the rain. Goodbye." I made to go away.

"Jason," she says. I stopped.

"Yes?" I says. "Hurry up. I'm getting wet."

"All right," she says. "Here." There wasn't anybody in sight. I went back and took the money. She still held to it. "You'll do it?" she says, looking at me from under the veil. "You promise?"

"Let go," I says. "You want somebody to come along and see us?"

She let go. I put the money in my pocket. "You'll do it, Jason?" she says. "I wouldn't ask you, if there was any other way."

"You dam right there's no other way," I says. "Sure I'll do it. I said I would, didn't I? Only you'll have to do just like I say, now."

"Yes," she says. "I will." So I told her where to be, and went to the livery stable. I hurried and got there just as they were unhitching the hack. I asked if they had paid for it yet and he said No and I said Mrs Compson forgot something and wanted it again, so they let me take it. Mink was driving. I bought him a cigar, so we drove around until it begun to get dark on the back streets where they wouldn't see him. Then Mink said he'd have to take the team on back and so I said I'd buy him another cigar and so we drove into the lane and I went across the yard to the house. I stopped in the hall until I could hear Mother and Uncle Maury upstairs, then I went on back to the kitchen. She and Ben were there with Dilsey. I said Mother wanted her and I took her into the house. I found Uncle Maury's raincoat and put it around her and picked her up and went back to the lane and got in the hack. I told Mink to drive to the depot. He was afraid to pass the stable, so we had to go the back way and I saw her standing on the corner under the light and I told Mink to drive close to the walk and when I said Go on, to give the team a bat. Then I took the raincoat off of her and held her to the window and Caddy saw her and sort of jumped forward.

"Hit 'em, Mink!" I says, and Mink gave them a cut and we went past her like a fire engine. "Now get on that train like you promised," I says. I could see her running after us through the back window. "Hit 'em again," I says. "Let's get on home." When we turned the corner she was still running.

And so I counted the money again that night and put it away, and I didn't feel so bad. I says I reckon that'll show you. I reckon you'll know now that you cant beat me out of a job and get away with it. It never occurred to me she wouldn't keep her promise and take that train. But I didn't know much about them then; I didn't have any more sense than to believe what they said, because the next morning dam if she didn't walk right into the store, only she had sense enough to wear the veil and not speak to anybody. It was Saturday morning, because I was at the store, and she came right on back to the desk where I was, walking fast.

"Liar," she says. "Liar."

"Are you crazy?" I says. "What do you mean? coming in here like this?" She started in, but I shut her off. I says, "You already cost me one job; do you want me to lose this one too? If you've got anything to say to me, I'll meet you somewhere after dark. What have you got to say to me?" I says. "Didn't I do everything I said? I said see her a minute, didn't I? Well, didn't you?" She just stood there looking at me, shaking like an ague-fit, her hands clenched and kind of jerking. "I did just what I said I would," I says. "You're the one that lied. You promised to take that train. Didn't you? Didn't you promise? If you think you can get that money back, just try it," I says. "If it'd been a thousand dollars, you'd still owe me after the risk I took. And if I see or hear you're still in town after number 17 runs," I says, "I'll tell Mother and Uncle Maury. Then hold your breath until you see her again." She just stood there, looking at me, twisting her hands together.

"Damn you," she says. "Damn you."

"Sure," I says. "That's all right too. Mind what I say, now. After number 17, and I tell them."

After she was gone I felt better. I says I reckon you'll think twice before you deprive me of a job that was promised me. I was a kid then. I believed folks when they said they'd do things. I've learned better since. Besides, like I say I guess I dont need any man's help to get along I can stand on my own feet like I always have. Then all of a sudden I thought of Dilsey and Uncle Maury. I thought how she'd get around Dilsey and that Uncle Maury would do anything for ten dollars. And there I was, couldn't even get away from the store to protect my own Mother. Like she says, if one of you had to be taken, thank God it was you left me I can depend on you and I says well I dont reckon I'll ever get far enough from the store to get out of your reach. Somebody's got to hold on to what little we have left, I reckon.

So as soon as I got home I fixed Dilsey. I told Dilsey she had leprosy and I got the bible and read where a man's flesh rotted off and I told her that if she ever looked at her or Ben or Quentin they'd catch it too. So I thought I had everything all fixed until that day when I came home and found Ben bellowing. Raising hell and nobody could quiet him. Mother said, Well, get him the slipper then. Dilsey made out she didn't hear. Mother said it again and I says I'd go I couldn't stand that dam noise. Like I say I can stand lots of things I dont expect much from them but if I have to work all day long in a dam store dam if I dont think I deserve a little peace and quiet to eat dinner in. So I says I'd go and Dilsey says quick, "Jason!"

Well, like a flash I knew what was up, but just to make sure I went and got the slipper and brought it back, and just like I thought, when he saw it you'd thought we were killing him. So I made Dilsey own up, then I told Mother. We had to take her up to bed then, and after things got quieted down a little I put the fear of God into Dilsey. As much as you can into a nigger, that is. That's the trouble with nigger servants, when they've been with you for a long time they get so full of self importance that they're not worth a dam. Think they run the whole family.

"I like to know whut's de hurt in lettin dat po chile see her own baby," Dilsey says. "If Mr Jason was still here hit ud be different."

"Only Mr Jason's not here," I says. "I know you wont pay me any mind, but I reckon you'll do what Mother says. You keep on worrying her like this until you get her into the graveyard too, then you can fill the whole house full of ragtag and bobtail. But what did you want to let that dam boy see her for?"

"You's a cold man, Jason, if man you is," she says. "I thank de Lawd I got mo heart dan dat, even ef hit is black."

"At least I'm man enough to keep that flour barrel full," I says. "And if you do that again, you wont be eating out of it either."

So the next time I told her that if she tried Dilsey again, Mother was going to fire Dilsey and send Ben to Jackson and take Quentin and go away. She looked at me for a while.

There wasn't any street light close and I couldn't see her face much. But I could feel her looking at me. When we were little when she'd get mad and couldn't do anything about it her upper lip would begin to jump. Everytime it jumped it would leave a little more of her teeth showing, and all the time she'd be as still as a post, not a muscle moving except her lip jerking higher and higher up her teeth. But she didn't say anything. She just said,

"All right. How much?"

"Well, if one look through a hack window was worth a hundred," I says. So after that she behaved pretty well, only one time she asked to see a statement of the bank account.

"I know they have Mother's indorsement on them," she says. "But I want to see the bank statement. I want to see myself where those checks go."

"That's in Mother's private business," I says. "If you think you have any right to pry into her private affairs I'll tell her you believe those checks are being misappropriated and you want an audit because you dont trust her."

She didn't say anything or move. I could hear her whispering Damn you oh damn you oh damn you.

"Say it out," I says. "I dont reckon it's any secret what you and I think of one another. Maybe you want the money back," I says.

"Listen, Jason," she says. "Dont lie to me now. About her. I wont ask to see anything. If that isn't enough, I'll send more each month. Just promise that she'll——that she—You can do that. Things for her. Be kind to her. Little things that I cant, they wont let. . . . But you wont. You never had a drop of warm blood in you. Listen," she says. "If you'll get Mother to let me have her back, I'll give you a thousand dollars."

"You haven't got a thousand dollars," I says. "I know you're lying now."

"Yes I have. I will have. I can get it."

"And I know how you'll get it," I says. "You'll get it the same way you got her. And when she gets big enough——" Then I thought she really was going to hit at me, and then I didn't know what she was going to do. She acted for a minute like some kind of a toy that's wound up too tight and about to burst all to pieces.

"Oh, I'm crazy," she says. "I'm insane. I cant take her. Keep her. What am I thinking of. Jason," she says, grabbing my arm. Her hands were hot as fever. "You'll have to promise to take care of her, to—— She's kin to you; your own flesh and blood. Promise, Jason. You have Father's name: do you think I'd have to ask him twice? once, even?"

"That's so," I says. "He did leave me something. What do you want me to do," I says. "Buy an apron and a go-cart? I never got you into this," I says. "I run more risk than you do, because you haven't got anything at stake. So if you expect——"

"No," she says, then she begun to laugh and to try to hold it back all at the same time. "No. I have nothing at stake," she says, making that noise, putting her hands to her mouth. "Nuh-nuh-nothing," she says.

"Here," I says. "Stop that!"

"I'm tr-trying to," she says, holding her hands over her mouth. "Oh God, oh God."

"I'm going away from here," I says. "I cant be seen here. You get on out of town now, you hear?"

"Wait," she says, catching my arm. "I've stopped. I wont again. You promise, Jason?" she says, and me feeling her eyes almost like they were touching my face. "You promise? Mother —— that money —— if sometimes she needs things —— If I send checks for her to you, other ones besides those, you'll give them to her? You wont tell? You'll see that she has things like other girls?"

"Sure," I says. "As long as you behave and do like I tell you."

And so when Earl came up front with his hat on he says, "I'm going to step up to Rogers' and get a snack. We wont have time to go home to dinner, I reckon."

"What's the matter we wont have time?" I says.

"With this show in town and all," he says. "They're going to give an afternoon performance too, and they'll all want to get done trading in time to go to it. So we'd better just run up to Rogers'."

"All right," I says. "It's your stomach. If you want to make a slave of yourself to your business, it's all right with me."

"I reckon you'll never be a slave to any business," he says.

"Not unless it's Jason Compson's business," I says.

So when I went back and opened it the only thing that surprised me was it was a money order not a check. Yes, sir. You cant trust a one of them. After all the risk I'd taken, risking Mother finding out about her coming down here once or twice a year sometimes, and me having to tell Mother lies about it. That's gratitude for you. And I wouldn't put it past her to try to notify the postoffice not to let anyone except her cash it. Giving a kid like that fifty dollars. Why I never saw fifty dollars until I was twenty-one years old, with all the other boys with the afternoon off and all day Saturday and me working in a store. Like I say, how can they expect anybody to control her, with her giving her money behind our backs. She has the same home you had I says, and the same raising. I reckon Mother is a better judge of what she needs than you are, that haven't even got a home. "If you want to give her money," I says, "you send it to Mother, dont be giving it to her. If I've got to run this risk every few months, you'll have to do like I say, or it's out."

And just about the time I got ready to begin on it because if Earl thought I was going to dash up the street and gobble two bits worth of indigestion on his account he was bad fooled. I may not be sitting with my feet on a mahogany desk but I am being payed for what I do inside this building and if I cant manage to live a civilised life outside of it I'll go where I can. I can stand on my own feet; I dont need any man's mahogany desk to prop me up. So just about the time I got ready to start I'd have to drop everything and run to sell some redneck a dime's worth of nails or something, and Earl up there gobbling a sandwich and half way back already, like as not, and then I found that all the blanks were gone. I remembered then that I had aimed to get some more, but it was too late now, and then I looked up and there she came. In the back door. I heard her asking old Job if I was there. I just had time to stick them in the drawer and close it.

She came around to the desk. I looked at my watch.

"You been to dinner already?" I says. "It's just twelve; I just heard it strike. You must have flown home and back."

"I'm not going home to dinner," she says. "Did I get a letter today?"

"Were you expecting one?" I says. "Have you got a sweetie that can write?"

"From Mother," she says. "Did I get a letter from Mother?" she says, looking at me.

"Mother got one from her," I says. "I haven't opened it. You'll have to wait until she opens it. She'll let you see it, I imagine."

"Please, Jason," she says, not paying any attention. "Did I get one?"

"What's the matter?" I says. "I never knew you to be this anxious about anybody. You must expect some money from her."

"She said she——" she says. "Please, Jason," she says. "Did I?"

"You must have been to school today, after all," I says. "Somewhere where they taught you to say please. Wait a minute, while I wait on that customer."

I went and waited on him. When I turned to come back she was out of sight behind the desk. I ran. I ran around the desk and caught her as she jerked her hand out of the drawer. I took the letter away from her, beating her knuckles on the desk until she let go.

"You would, would you?" I says.

"Give it to me," she says. "You've already opened it. Give it to me. Please, Jason. It's mine. I saw the name."

"I'll take a hame string to you," I says. "That's what I'll give you. Going into my papers."

"Is there some money in it?" she says, reaching for it. "She said she would send me some money. She promised she would. Give it to me."

"What do you want with money?" I says.

"She said she would," she says. "Give it to me. Please, Jason. I wont ever ask you anything again, if you'll give it to me this time."

"I'm going to, if you'll give me time," I says. I took the letter and the money order out and gave her the letter. She reached for the money order, not hardly glancing at the letter. "You'll have to sign it first," I says.

"How much is it?" she says.

"Read the letter," I says. "I reckon it'll say."

She read it fast, in about two looks.

"It dont say," she says, looking up. She dropped the letter to the floor. "How much is it?"

"It's ten dollars," I says.

"Ten dollars?" she says, staring at me.

"And you ought to be dam glad to get that," I says. "A kid like you. What are you in such a rush for money all of a sudden for?"

"Ten dollars?" she says, like she was talking in her sleep. "Just ten dollars?" She made a grab at the money order. "You're lying," she says. "Thief!" she says. "Thief!"

"You would, would you?" I says, holding her off.

"Give it to me!" she says. "It's mine. She sent it to me. I will see it. I will."

"You will?" I says, holding her. "How're you going to do it?"

"Just let me see it, Jason," she says. "Please. I wont ask you for anything again."

"Think I'm lying, do you?" I says. "Just for that you wont see it."

"But just ten dollars," she says. "She told me she——she told me —— Jason, please please please. I've got to have some money. I've just got to. Give it to me, Jason. I'll do anything if you will."

"Tell me what you've got to have money for," I says.

"I've got to have it," she says. She was looking at me. Then all of a sudden she quit looking at me without moving her eyes at all. I knew she was going to lie. "It's some money I owe," she says. "I've got to pay it. I've got to pay it today."

"Who to?" I says. Her hands were sort of twisting. I could watch her trying to think of a lie to tell. "Have you been charging things at stores again?" I says. "You needn't bother to tell me that. If you can find anybody in this town that'll charge anything to you after what I told them, I'll eat it."

"It's a girl," she says. "It's a girl. I borrowed some money from a girl. I've got to pay it back. Jason, give it to me. Please. I'll do anything. I've got to have it. Mother will pay you. I'll write to her to pay you and that I wont ever ask her for anything again. You can see the letter. Please, Jason. I've got to have it."

"Tell me what you want with it, and I'll see about it," I says. "Tell me." She just stood there, with her hands working against her dress. "All right," I says. "If ten dollars is too little for you, I'll just take it home to Mother, and you know what'll happen to it then. Of course, if you're so rich you dont need ten dollars——"

She stood there, looking at the floor, kind of mumbling to herself. "She said she would send me some money. She said she sends money here and you say she dont send any. She said she's sent a lot of money here. She says it's for me. That it's for me to have some of it. And you say we haven't got any money."

"You know as much about that as I do," I says. "You've seen what happens to those checks."

"Yes," she says, looking at the floor. "Ten dollars," she says. "Ten dollars."

"And you'd better thank your stars it's ten dollars," I says. "Here," I says. I put the money order face down on the desk, holding my hand on it. "Sign it."

"Will you let me see it?" she says. "I just want to look at it. Whatever it says, I wont ask for but ten dollars. You can have the rest. I just want to see it."

"Not after the way you've acted," I says. "You've got to learn one thing, and that is that when I tell you to do something, you've got it to do. You sign your name on that line."

She took the pen, but instead of signing it she just stood there with her head bent and the pen shaking in her hand. Just like her mother. "Oh, God," she says, "oh, God."

"Yes," I says. "That's one thing you'll have to learn if you never learn anything else. Sign it now, and get on out of here."

She signed it. "Where's the money?" she says. I took the order and blotted it and put it in my pocket. Then I gave her the ten dollars.

"Now you go on back to school this afternoon, you hear?" I says. She didn't answer. She crumpled the bill up in her hand like it was a rag or something and went on out the front door just as Earl came in. A customer came in with him and they stopped up front. I gathered up the things and put on my hat and went up front.

"Been much busy?" Earl says.

"Not much," I says. He looked out the door.

"That your car over yonder?" he says. "Better not try to go out home to dinner. We'll likely have another rush just before the show opens. Get you a lunch at Rogers' and put a ticket in the drawer."

"Much obliged," I says. "I can still manage to feed myself, I reckon."

And right there he'd stay, watching that door like a hawk until I came through it again. Well, he'd just have to watch it for a while; I was doing the best I could. The time before I says that's the last one now; you'll have to remember to get some more right away. But who can remember anything in all this hurrah. And now this dam show had to come here the one day I'd have to hunt all over town for a blank check, besides all the other things I had to do to keep the house running, and Earl watching the door like a hawk.

I went to the printing shop and told him I wanted to play a joke on a fellow, but he didn't have anything. Then he told me to have a look in the old opera house, where somebody had stored a lot of papers and junk out of the old Merchants' and Farmers' Bank when it failed, so I dodged up a few more alleys so Earl couldn't see me and finally found old man Simmons and got the key from him and went up there and dug around. At last I found a pad on a Saint Louis bank. And of course she'd pick this one time to look at it close. Well, it would have to do. I couldn't waste any more time now.

I went back to the store. "Forgot some papers Mother wants to go to the bank," I says. I went back to the desk and fixed the check. Trying to hurry and all, I says to myself it's a good thing her eyes are giving out, with that little whore in the house, a Christian forbearing woman like Mother. I says you know just as well as I do what she's going to grow up into but I says that's your business, if you want to keep her and raise her in your house just because of Father. Then she would begin to cry and say it was her own flesh and blood so I just says All right. Have it your way. I can stand it if you can.

I fixed the letter up again and glued it back and went out.

"Try not to be gone any longer than you can help," Earl says.

"All right," I says. I went to the telegraph office. The smart boys were all there.

"Any of you boys made your million yet?" I says.

"Who can do anything, with a market like that?" Doc says.

"What's it doing?" I says. I went in and looked. It was three points under the opening. "You boys are not going to let a little thing like the cotton market beat you, are you?" I says. "I thought you were too smart for that."

"Smart, hell," Doc says. "It was down twelve points at twelve oclock. Cleaned me out."

"Twelve points?" I says. "Why the hell didn't somebody let me know? Why didn't you let me know?" I says to the operator.

"I take it as it comes in," he says. "I'm not running a bucket shop."

"You're smart, aren't you?" I says. "Seems to me, with the money I spend with you, you could take time to call me up. Or maybe your dam company's in a conspiracy with those dam eastern sharks."

He didn't say anything. He made like he was busy.

"You're getting a little too big for your pants," I says. "First thing you know you'll be working for a living."

"What's the matter with you?" Doc says. "You're still three points to the good."

"Yes," I says. "If I happened to be selling. I haven't mentioned that yet, I think. You boys all cleaned out?"

"I got caught twice," Doc says. "I switched just in time."

"Well," I. O. Snopes says. "I've picked hit; I reckon taint no more than fair fer hit to pick me once in a while."

So I left them buying and selling among themselves at a nickel a point. I found a nigger and sent him for my car and stood on the corner and waited. I couldn't see Earl looking up and down the street, with one eye on the clock, because I couldn't see the door from here. After about a week he got back with it.

"Where the hell have you been?" I says. "Riding around where the wenches could see you?"

"I come straight as I could," he says. "I had to drive clean around the square, wid all dem wagons."

I never found a nigger yet that didn't have an airtight alibi for whatever he did. But just turn one loose in a car and he's bound to show off. I got in and went on around the square. I caught a glimpse of Earl in the door across the square.

I went straight to the kitchen and told Dilsey to hurry up with dinner.

"Quentin aint come yit," she says.

"What of that?" I says. "You'll be telling me next that Luster's not quite ready to eat yet. Quentin knows when meals are served in this house. Hurry up with it, now."

Mother was in her room. I gave her the letter. She opened it and took the check out and sat holding it in her hand. I went and got the shovel from the corner and gave her a match. "Come on," I says. "Get it over with. You'll be crying in a minute."

She took the match, but she didn't strike it. She sat there, looking at the check. Just like I said it would be.

"I hate to do it," she says. "To increase your burden by adding Quentin. . . . . . ."

"I guess we'll get along," I says. "Come on. Get it over with."

But she just sat there, holding the check.

"This one is on a different bank," she says. "They have been on an Indianapolis bank."

"Yes," I says. "Women are allowed to do that too."

"Do what?" she says.

"Keep money in two different banks," I says.

"Oh," she says. She looked at the check a while. "I'm glad to know she's so . . . . . . she has so much. . . . . . . God sees that I am doing right," she says.

"Come on," I says. "Finish it. Get the fun over."

"Fun?" she says. "When I think——"

"I thought you were burning this two hundred dollars a month for fun," I says. "Come on, now. Want me to strike the match?"

"I could bring myself to accept them," she says. "For my children's sake. I have no pride."

"You'd never be satisfied," I says. "You know you wouldn't. You've settled that once, let it stay settled. We can get along."

"I leave everything to you," she says. "But sometimes I become afraid that in doing this I am depriving you all of what is rightfully yours. Perhaps I shall be punished for it. If you want me to, I will smother my pride and accept them."

"What would be the good in beginning now, when you've been destroying them for fifteen years?" I says. "If you keep on doing it, you have lost nothing, but if you'd begin to take them now, you'll have lost fifty thousand dollars. We've got along so far, haven't we?" I says. "I haven't seen you in the poorhouse yet."

"Yes," she says. "We Bascombs need nobody's charity. Certainly not that of a fallen woman."

She struck the match and lit the check and put it in the shovel, and then the envelope, and watched them burn.

"You dont know what it is," she says. "Thank God you will never know what a mother feels."

"There are lots of women in this world no better than her," I says.

"But they are not my daughters," she says. "It's not myself," she says. "I'd gladly take her back, sins and all, because she is my flesh and blood. It's for Quentin's sake."

Well, I could have said it wasn't much chance of anybody hurting Quentin much, but like I say I dont expect much but I do want to eat and sleep without a couple of women squabbling and crying in the house.

"And yours," she says. "I know how you feel toward her."

"Let her come back," I says, "far as I'm concerned."

"No," she says. "I owe that to your father's memory."

"When he was trying all the time to persuade you to let her come home when Herbert threw her out?" I says.

"You dont understand," she says. "I know you dont intend to make it more difficult for me. But it's my place to suffer for my children," she says. "I can bear it."

"Seems to me you go to a lot of unnecessary trouble doing it," I says. The paper burned out. I carried it to the grate and put it in. "It just seems a shame to me to burn up good money," I says.

"Let me never see the day when my children will have to accept that, the wages of sin," she says. "I'd rather see even you dead in your coffin first."

"Have it your way," I says. "Are we going to have dinner soon?" I says. "Because if we're not, I'll have to go on back. We're pretty busy today." She got up. "I've told her once," I says. "It seems she's waiting on Quentin or Luster or some-

body. Here, I'll call her. Wait." But she went to the head of
the stairs and called.

"Quentin aint come yit," Dilsey says.

"Well, I'll have to get on back," I says. "I can get a sandwich downtown. I dont want to interfere with Dilsey's
arrangements," I says. Well, that got her started again, with
Dilsey hobbling and mumbling back and forth, saying,

"All right, all right, Ise puttin hit on fast as I kin."

"I try to please you all," Mother says. "I try to make things
as easy for you as I can."

"I'm not complaining, am I?" I says. "Have I said a word
except I had to go back to work?"

"I know," she says. "I know you haven't had the chance the
others had, that you've had to bury yourself in a little country store. I wanted you to get ahead. I knew your father would
never realise that you were the only one who had any business
sense, and then when everything else failed I believed that
when she married, and Herbert . . . after his promise——"

"Well, he was probably lying too," I says. "He may not have
even had a bank. And if he had, I dont reckon he'd have to
come all the way to Mississippi to get a man for it."

We ate a while. I could hear Ben in the kitchen, where
Luster was feeding him. Like I say, if we've got to feed another mouth and she wont take that money, why not send him
down to Jackson. He'll be happier there, with people like him.
I says God knows there's little enough room for pride in this
family, but it dont take much pride to not like to see a thirty
year old man playing around the yard with a nigger boy, running up and down the fence and lowing like a cow whenever
they play golf over there. I says if they'd sent him to Jackson
at first we'd all be better off today. I says, you've done your
duty by him; you've done all anybody can expect of you and
more than most folks would do, so why not send him there
and get that much benefit out of the taxes we pay. Then she
says, "I'll be gone soon. I know I'm just a burden to you" and
I says "You've been saying that so long that I'm beginning to
believe you" only I says you'd better be sure and not let me
know you're gone because I'll sure have him on number seventeen that night and I says I think I know a place where
they'll take her too and the name of it's not Milk street and

Honey avenue either. Then she begun to cry and I says All right all right I have as much pride about my kinfolks as anybody even if I dont always know where they come from.

We ate for a while. Mother sent Dilsey to the front to look for Quentin again.

"I keep telling you she's not coming to dinner," I says.

"She knows better than that," Mother says. "She knows I dont permit her to run about the streets and not come home at meal time. Did you look good, Dilsey?"

"Dont let her, then," I says.

"What can I do," she says. "You have all of you flouted me. Always."

"If you wouldn't come interfering, I'd make her mind," I says. "It wouldn't take me but about one day to straighten her out."

"You'd be too brutal with her," she says. "You have your Uncle Maury's temper."

That reminded me of the letter. I took it out and handed it to her. "You wont have to open it," I says. "The bank will let you know how much it is this time."

"It's addressed to you," she says.

"Go on and open it," I says. She opened it and read it and handed it to me.

" 'My dear young nephew', it says,

'You will be glad to learn that I am now in a position to avail myself of an opportunity regarding which, for reasons which I shall make obvious to you, I shall not go into details until I have an opportunity to divulge it to you in a more secure manner. My business experience has taught me to be chary of committing anything of a confidential nature to any more concrete medium than speech, and my extreme precaution in this instance should give you some inkling of its value. Needless to say, I have just completed a most exhaustive examination of all its phases, and I feel no hesitancy in telling you that it is that sort of golden chance that comes but once in a lifetime, and I now see clearly before me that goal toward which I have long and unflaggingly striven: i.e., the ultimate solidification of my affairs by which I may restore to its rightful position that family of which

I have the honor to be the sole remaining male descendant; that family in which I have ever included your lady mother and her children.

'As it so happens, I am not quite in a position to avail myself of this opportunity to the uttermost which it warrants, but rather than go out of the family to do so, I am today drawing upon your Mother's bank for the small sum necessary to complement my own initial investment, for which I herewith enclose, as a matter of formality, my note of hand at eight percent. per annum. Needless to say, this is merely a formality, to secure your Mother in the event of that circumstance of which man is ever the plaything and sport. For naturally I shall employ this sum as though it were my own and so permit your Mother to avail herself of this opportunity which my exhaustive investigation has shown to be a bonanza—if you will permit the vulgarism—of the first water and purest ray serene.

'This is in confidence, you will understand, from one business man to another; we will harvest our own vineyards, eh? And knowing your Mother's delicate health and that timorousness which such delicately nurtured Southern ladies would naturally feel regarding matters of business, and their charming proneness to divulge unwittingly such matters in conversation, I would suggest that you do not mention it to her at all. On second thought, I advise you not to do so. It might be better to simply restore this sum to the bank at some future date, say, in a lump sum with the other small sums for which I am indebted to her, and say nothing about it at all. It is our duty to shield her from the crass material world as much as possible.

'Your affectionate Uncle,
'Maury L. Bascomb.' "

"What do you want to do about it?" I says, flipping it across the table.

"I know you grudge what I give him," she says.

"It's your money," I says. "If you want to throw it to the birds even, it's your business."

"He's my own brother," Mother says. "He's the last Bas-comb. When we are gone there wont be any more of them."

"That'll be hard on somebody, I guess," I says. "All right, all right," I says. "It's your money. Do as you please with it. You want me to tell the bank to pay it?"

"I know you begrudge him," she says. "I realise the burden on your shoulders. When I'm gone it will be easier on you."

"I could make it easier right now," I says. "All right, all right, I wont mention it again. Move all bedlam in here if you want to."

"He's your own brother," she says. "Even if he is afflicted."

"I'll take your bank book," I says. "I'll draw my check today."

"He kept you waiting six days," she says. "Are you sure the business is sound? It seems strange to me that a solvent busi-ness cannot pay its employees promptly."

"He's all right," I says. "Safe as a bank. I tell him not to bother about mine until we get done collecting every month. That's why it's late sometimes."

"I just couldn't bear to have you lose the little I had to invest for you," she says. "I've often thought that Earl is not a good business man. I know he doesn't take you into his confidence to the extent that your investment in the business should war-rant. I'm going to speak to him."

"No, you let him alone," I says. "It's his business."

"You have a thousand dollars in it."

"You let him alone," I says. "I'm watching things. I have your power of attorney. It'll be all right."

"You dont know what a comfort you are to me," she says. "You have always been my pride and joy, but when you came to me of your own accord and insisted on banking your salary each month in my name, I thanked God it was you left me if they had to be taken."

"They were all right," I says. "They did the best they could, I reckon."

"When you talk that way I know you are thinking bitterly of your father's memory," she says. "You have a right to, I suppose. But it breaks my heart to hear you."

I got up. "If you've got any crying to do," I says, "you'll have to do it alone, because I've got to get on back. I'll get the bank book."

"I'll get it," she says.

"Keep still," I says. "I'll get it." I went up stairs and got the bank book out of her desk and went back to town. I went to the bank and deposited the check and the money order and the other ten, and stopped at the telegraph office. It was one point above the opening. I had already lost thirteen points, all because she had to come helling in there at twelve, worrying me about that letter.

"What time did that report come in?" I says.

"About an hour ago," he says.

"An hour ago?" I says. "What are we paying you for?" I says. "Weekly reports? How do you expect a man to do anything? The whole dam top could blow off and we'd not know it."

"I dont expect you to do anything," he says. "They changed that law making folks play the cotton market."

"They have?" I says. "I hadn't heard. They must have sent the news out over the Western Union."

I went back to the store. Thirteen points. Dam if I believe anybody knows anything about the dam thing except the ones that sit back in those New York offices and watch the country suckers come up and beg them to take their money. Well, a man that just calls shows he has no faith in himself, and like I say if you aren't going to take the advice, what's the use in paying money for it. Besides, these people are right up there on the ground; they know everything that's going on. I could feel the telegram in my pocket. I'd just have to prove that they were using the telegraph company to defraud. That would constitute a bucket shop. And I wouldn't hesitate that long, either. Only be damned if it doesn't look like a company as big and rich as the Western Union could get a market report out on time. Half as quick as they'll get a wire to you saying Your account closed out. But what the hell do they care about the people. They're hand in glove with that New York crowd. Anybody could see that.

When I came in Earl looked at his watch. But he didn't say anything until the customer was gone. Then he says,

"You go home to dinner?"

"I had to go to the dentist," I says because it's not any of his business where I eat but I've got to be in the store with him all the afternoon. And with his jaw running off after all

I've stood. You take a little two by four country storekeeper like I say it takes a man with just five hundred dollars to worry about it fifty thousand dollars' worth.

"You might have told me," he says. "I expected you back right away."

"I'll trade you this tooth and give you ten dollars to boot, any time," I says. "Our agreement was an hour for dinner," I says, "and if you dont like the way I do, you know what you can do about it."

"I've known that some time," he says. "If it hadn't been for your mother I'd have done it before now, too. She's a lady I've got a lot of sympathy for, Jason. Too bad some other folks I know cant say as much."

"Then you can keep it," I says. "When we need any sympathy I'll let you know in plenty of time."

"I've protected you about that business a long time, Jason," he says.

"Yes?" I says, letting him go on. Listening to what he would say before I shut him up.

"I believe I know more about where that automobile came from than she does."

"You think so, do you?" I says. "When are you going to spread the news that I stole it from my mother?"

"I dont say anything," he says. "I know you have her power of attorney. And I know she still believes that thousand dollars is in this business."

"All right," I says. "Since you know so much, I'll tell you a little more: go to the bank and ask them whose account I've been depositing a hundred and sixty dollars on the first of every month for twelve years."

"I dont say anything," he says. "I just ask you to be a little more careful after this."

I never said anything more. It doesn't do any good. I've found that when a man gets into a rut the best thing you can do is let him stay there. And when a man gets it in his head that he's got to tell something on you for your own good, goodnight. I'm glad I haven't got the sort of conscience I've got to nurse like a sick puppy all the time. If I'd ever be as careful over anything as he is to keep his little shirt tail full of business from making him more than eight percent. I reckon he thinks they'd get him on the usury law if he netted more than eight percent. What the hell chance has a man got, tied down in a town like this and to a business like this. Why I could take his business in one year and fix him so he'd never have to work again, only he'd give it all away to the church or something. If there's one thing gets under my skin, it's a dam hypocrite. A man that thinks anything he dont understand all about must be crooked and that first chance he gets he's morally bound to tell the third party what's none of his business to tell. Like I say if I thought every time a man did something I didn't know all about he was bound to be a crook, I reckon I wouldn't have any trouble finding something back there on those books that you wouldn't see any use for running and telling somebody I thought ought to know about it, when for all I knew they might know a dam sight more about it now than I did, and if they didn't it was dam little of my business anyway and he says, "My books are open to anybody. Anybody that has any claim or believes she has any claim on this business can go back there and welcome."

"Sure, you wont tell," I says. "You couldn't square your conscience with that. You'll just take her back there and let her find it. You wont tell, yourself."

"I'm not trying to meddle in your business," he says. "I know you missed out on some things like Quentin had. But your mother has had a misfortunate life too, and if she was to come in here and ask me why you quit, I'd have to tell her. It aint that thousand dollars. You know that. It's because a man never gets anywhere if fact and his ledgers dont square. And I'm not going to lie to anybody, for myself or anybody else."

"Well, then," I says. "I reckon that conscience of yours is a more valuable clerk than I am; it dont have to go home at noon to eat. Only dont let it interfere with my appetite," I says, because how the hell can I do anything right, with that dam family and her not making any effort to control her nor any of them like that time when she happened to see one of them kissing Caddy and all next day she went around the house in a black dress and a veil and even Father couldn't get her to say a word except crying and saying her little daughter was dead and Caddy about fifteen then only in three years she'd been wearing haircloth or probably sandpaper at that rate. Do you think I can afford to have her running about the streets with every drummer that comes to town, I says, and them telling the new ones up and down the road where to pick up a hot one when they made Jefferson. I haven't got much pride, I cant afford it with a kitchen full of niggers to feed and robbing the state asylum of its star freshman. Blood, I says, governors and generals. It's a dam good thing we never had any kings and presidents; we'd all be down there at Jackson chasing butterflies. I says it'd be bad enough if it was mine; I'd at least be sure it was a bastard to begin with, and now even the Lord doesn't know that for certain probably.

So after a while I heard the band start up, and then they begun to clear out. Headed for the show, every one of them. Haggling over a twenty cent hame string to save fifteen cents, so they can give it to a bunch of Yankees that come in and pay maybe ten dollars for the privilege. I went on out to the back.

"Well," I says. "If you dont look out, that bolt will grow into your hand. And then I'm going to take an axe and chop it out. What do you reckon the boll-weevils'll eat if you dont get those cultivators in shape to raise them a crop?" I says, "sage grass?"

"Dem folks sho do play dem horns," he says. "Tell me man in dat show kin play a tune on a handsaw. Pick hit like a banjo."

"Listen," I says. "Do you know how much that show'll spend in this town? About ten dollars," I says. "The ten dollars Buck Turpin has in his pocket right now."

"Whut dey give Mr Buck ten dollars fer?" he says.

"For the privilege of showing here," I says. "You can put the balance of what they'll spend in your eye."

"You mean dey pays ten dollars jest to give dey show here?" he says.

"That's all," I says. "And how much do you reckon—"

"Gret day," he says. "You mean to tell me dey chargin um to let um show here? I'd pay ten dollars to see dat man pick dat saw, ef I had to. I figures dat tomorrow mawnin I be still owin um nine dollars and six bits at dat rate."

And then a Yankee will talk your head off about niggers getting ahead. Get them ahead, what I say. Get them so far ahead you cant find one south of Louisville with a blood hound. Because when I told him about how they'd pick up Saturday night and carry off at least a thousand dollars out of the county, he says,

"I dont begridge um. I kin sho afford my two bits."

"Two bits hell," I says. "That dont begin it. How about the dime or fifteen cents you'll spend for a dam two cent box of candy or something. How about the time you're wasting right now, listening to that band."

"Dat's de troof," he says. "Well, ef I lives twell night hit's gwine to be two bits mo dey takin out of town, dat's sho."

"Then you're a fool," I says.

"Well," he says. "I dont spute dat neither. Ef dat uz a crime, all chain-gangs wouldn't be black."

Well, just about that time I happened to look up the alley and saw her. When I stepped back and looked at my watch I didn't notice at the time who he was because I was looking at the watch. It was just two thirty, forty-five minutes before anybody but me expected her to be out. So when I looked around the door the first thing I saw was the red tie he had on and I was thinking what the hell kind of a man would wear a red tie. But she was sneaking along the alley, watching the door, so I wasn't thinking anything about him until they had gone past. I was wondering if she'd have so little respect for me that she'd not only play out of school when I told her not to, but would walk right past the store, daring me not to see her. Only she couldn't see into the door because the sun fell straight into it and it was like trying to see through an automobile searchlight, so I stood there and watched her go on past, with her face painted up like a dam clown's and her hair all gummed and twisted and a dress that if a woman had come out doors even on Gayoso or Beale street when I was a young fellow with no more than that to cover her legs and behind, she'd been thrown in jail. I'll be damned if they dont dress like they were trying to make every man they passed on the street want to reach out and clap his hand on it. And so I was thinking what kind of a dam man would wear a red tie when all of a sudden I knew he was one of those show folks well as if she'd told me. Well, I can stand a lot; if I couldn't dam if I wouldn't be in a hell of a fix, so when they turned the corner I jumped down and followed. Me, without any hat, in the middle of the afternoon, having to chase up and down back alleys because of my mother's good name. Like I say you cant do anything with a woman like that, if she's got it in her. If it's in her blood, you cant do anything with her. The only thing you can do is to get rid of her, let her go on and live with her own sort.

I went on to the street, but they were out of sight. And there I was, without any hat, looking like I was crazy too. Like a man would naturally think, one of them is crazy and another one drowned himself and the other one was turned out into the street by her husband, what's the reason the rest of them are not crazy too. All the time I could see them watching me like a hawk, waiting for a chance to say Well I'm not surprised I expected it all the time the whole family's crazy. Selling land to send him to Harvard and paying taxes to support a state University all the time that I never saw except twice at a baseball game and not letting her daughter's name be spoken on the place until after a while Father wouldn't even come down town anymore but just sat there all day with the decanter I could see the bottom of his nightshirt and his bare legs and hear the decanter clinking until finally T. P. had to pour it for him and she says You have no respect for your Father's memory and I says I dont know why not it sure is preserved well enough to last only if I'm crazy too God knows what I'll do about it just to look at water makes me sick and I'd just as soon swallow gasoline as a glass of whiskey and Lorraine telling them he may not drink but if you dont believe he's a man I can tell you how to find out she says If I catch you fooling with any of these whores you know what I'll do she says I'll whip her grabbing at her I'll whip her as long as I can find her she says and I says if I dont drink that's my business but have you ever found me short I says I'll buy you enough beer to take a bath in if you want it because I've got every respect for a good honest whore because with Mother's health and the position I try to uphold to have her with no more respect for what I try to do for her than to make her name and my name and my Mother's name a byword in the town.

She had dodged out of sight somewhere. Saw me coming and dodged into another alley, running up and down the alleys with a dam show man in a red tie that everybody would look at and think what kind of a dam man would wear a red tie. Well, the boy kept speaking to me and so I took the telegram without knowing I had taken it. I didn't realise what it was until I was signing for it, and I tore it open without even caring much what it was. I knew all the time what it would be, I reckon. That was the only thing else that could happen, especially holding it up until I had already had the check entered on the pass book.

I dont see how a city no bigger than New York can hold enough people to take the money away from us country suckers. Work like hell all day every day, send them your money and get a little piece of paper back, Your account closed at 20.62. Teasing you along, letting you pile up a little paper profit, then bang! Your account closed at 20.62. And if that wasn't enough, paying ten dollars a month to somebody to tell you how to lose it fast, that either dont know anything about it or is in cahoots with the telegraph company. Well, I'm done with them. They've sucked me in for the last time. Any fool except a fellow that hasn't got any more sense than to take a jew's word for anything could tell the market was going up all the time, with the whole dam delta about to be flooded again and the cotton washed right out of the ground like it was last year. Let it wash a man's crop out of the ground year after year, and them up there in Washington spending fifty thousand dollars a day keeping an army in Nicarauga or some place. Of course it'll overflow again, and then cotton'll be worth thirty cents a pound. Well, I just want to hit them one time and get my money back. I dont want a killing; only these small town gamblers are out for that, I just want my money back that these dam jews have gotten with all their guaranteed inside dope. Then I'm through; they can kiss my foot for every other red cent of mine they get.

I went back to the store. It was half past three almost. Dam little time to do anything in, but then I am used to that. I never had to go to Harvard to learn that. The band had quit playing. Got them all inside now, and they wouldn't have to waste any more wind. Earl says,

"He found you, did he? He was in here with it a while ago. I thought you were out back somewhere."

"Yes," I says. "I got it. They couldn't keep it away from me all afternoon. The town's too small. I've got to go out home a minute," I says. "You can dock me if it'll make you feel any better."

"Go ahead," he says. "I can handle it now. No bad news, I hope."

"You'll have to go to the telegraph office and find that out," I says. "They'll have time to tell you. I haven't."

"I just asked," he says. "Your mother knows she can depend on me."

"She'll appreciate it," I says. "I wont be gone any longer than I have to."

"Take your time," he says. "I can handle it now. You go ahead."

I got the car and went home. Once this morning, twice at noon, and now again, with her and having to chase all over town and having to beg them to let me eat a little of the food I am paying for. Sometimes I think what's the use of anything. With the precedent I've been set I must be crazy to keep on. And now I reckon I'll get home just in time to take a nice long drive after a basket of tomatoes or something and then have to go back to town smelling like a camphor factory so my head wont explode right on my shoulders. I keep telling her there's not a dam thing in that aspirin except flour and water for imaginary invalids. I says you dont know what a headache is. I says you think I'd fool with that dam car at all if it depended on me. I says I can get along without one I've learned to get along without lots of things but if you want to risk yourself in that old wornout surrey with a halfgrown nigger boy all right because I says God looks after Ben's kind, God knows He ought to do something for him but if you think I'm going to trust a thousand dollars' worth of delicate machinery to a halfgrown nigger or a grown one either, you'd better buy him one yourself because I says you like to ride in the car and you know you do.

Dilsey said she was in the house. I went on into the hall and listened, but I didn't hear anything. I went up stairs, but just as I passed her door she called me.

"I just wanted to know who it was," she says. "I'm here alone so much that I hear every sound."

"You dont have to stay here," I says. "You could spend the whole day visiting like other women, if you wanted to." She came to the door.

"I thought maybe you were sick," she says. "Having to hurry through your dinner like you did."

"Better luck next time," I says. "What do you want?"

"Is anything wrong?" she says.

"What could be?" I says. "Cant I come home in the middle of the afternoon without upsetting the whole house?"

"Have you seen Quentin?" she says.

"She's in school," I says.

"It's after three," she says. "I heard the clock strike at least a half an hour ago. She ought to be home by now."

"Ought she?" I says. "When have you ever seen her before dark?"

"She ought to be home," she says. "When I was a girl——"

"You had somebody to make you behave yourself," I says. "She hasn't."

"I cant do anything with her," she says. "I've tried and I've tried."

"And you wont let me, for some reason," I says. "So you ought to be satisfied." I went on to my room. I turned the key easy and stood there until the knob turned. Then she says,

"Jason."

"What," I says.

"I just thought something was wrong."

"Not in here," I says. "You've come to the wrong place."

"I dont mean to worry you," she says.

"I'm glad to hear that," I says. "I wasn't sure. I thought I might have been mistaken. Do you want anything?"

After a while she says, "No. Not any thing." Then she went away. I took the box down and counted out the money and hid the box again and unlocked the door and went out. I thought about the camphor, but it would be too late now, anyway. And I'd just have one more round trip. She was at her door, waiting.

"You want anything from town?" I says.

"No," she says. "I dont mean to meddle in your affairs. But I dont know what I'd do if anything happened to you, Jason."

"I'm all right," I says. "Just a headache."

"I wish you'd take some aspirin," she says. "I know you're not going to stop using the car."

"What's the car got to do with it?" I says. "How can a car give a man a headache?"

"You know gasoline always made you sick," she says. "Ever since you were a child. I wish you'd take some aspirin."

"Keep on wishing it," I says. "It wont hurt you."

I got in the car and started back to town. I had just turned onto the street when I saw a ford coming helling toward me. All of a sudden it stopped. I could hear the wheels sliding and it slewed around and backed and whirled and just as I was thinking what the hell they were up to, I saw that red tie. Then I recognised her face looking back through the window. It whirled into the alley. I saw it turn again, but when I got to the back street it was just disappearing, running like hell.

I saw red. When I recognised that red tie, after all I had told her, I forgot about everything. I never thought about my head even until I came to the first forks and had to stop. Yet we spend money and spend money on roads and dam if it isn't like trying to drive over a sheet of corrugated iron roofing. I'd like to know how a man could be expected to keep up with even a wheelbarrow. I think too much of my car; I'm not going to hammer it to pieces like it was a ford. Chances were they had stolen it, anyway, so why should they give a dam. Like I say blood always tells. If you've got blood like that in you, you'll do anything. I says whatever claim you believe she has on you has already been discharged; I says from now on you have only yourself to blame because you know what any sensible person would do. I says if I've got to spend half my time being a dam detective, at least I'll go where I can get paid for it.

So I had to stop there at the forks. Then I remembered it. It felt like somebody was inside with a hammer, beating on it. I says I've tried to keep you from being worried by her; I says far as I'm concerned, let her go to hell as fast as she pleases and the sooner the better. I says what else do you expect except every dam drummer and cheap show that comes to town because even these town jellybeans give her the go-by now. You dont know what goes on I says, you dont hear the talk that I hear and you can just bet I shut them up too. I says my people owned slaves here when you all were running little shirt tail country stores and farming land no nigger would look at on shares.

If they ever farmed it. It's a good thing the Lord did something for this country; the folks that live on it never have. Friday afternoon, and from right here I could see three miles of land that hadn't even been broken, and every able bodied man in the county in town at that show. I might have been a stranger starving to death, and there wasn't a soul in sight to ask which way to town even. And she trying to get me to take aspirin. I says when I eat bread I'll do it at the table. I says you always talking about how much you give up for us when you could buy ten new dresses a year on the money you spend for those dam patent medicines. It's not something to cure it I need it's just an even break not to have to have them but as long as I have to work ten hours a day to support a kitchen full of niggers in the style they're accustomed to and send them to the show where every other nigger in the county, only he was late already. By the time he got there it would be over.

After a while he got up to the car and when I finally got it through his head if two people in a ford had passed him, he said yes. So I went on, and when I came to where the wagon road turned off I could see the tire tracks. Ab Russell was in his lot, but I didn't bother to ask him and I hadn't got out of sight of his barn hardly when I saw the ford. They had tried to hide it. Done about as well at it as she did at everything else she did. Like I say it's not that I object to so much; maybe she cant help that, it's because she hasn't even got enough consideration for her own family to have any discretion. I'm afraid all the time I'll run into them right in the middle of the street or under a wagon on the square, like a couple of dogs.

I parked and got out. And now I'd have to go way around and cross a plowed field, the only one I had seen since I left town, with every step like somebody was walking along behind me, hitting me on the head with a club. I kept thinking that when I got across the field at least I'd have something level to walk on, that wouldn't jolt me every step, but when I got into the woods it was full of underbrush and I had to twist around through it, and then I came to a ditch full of briers. I went along it for a while, but it got thicker and thicker, and all the time Earl probably telephoning home about where I was and getting Mother all upset again.

When I finally got through I had had to wind around so much that I had to stop and figure out just where the car would be. I knew they wouldn't be far from it, just under the closest bush, so I turned and worked back toward the road. Then I couldn't tell just how far I was, so I'd have to stop and listen, and then with my legs not using so much blood, it all would go into my head like it would explode any minute, and the sun getting down just to where it could shine straight into my eyes and my ears ringing so I couldn't hear anything. I went on, trying to move quiet, then I heard a dog or something and I knew that when he scented me he'd have to come helling up, then it would be all off.

I had gotten beggar lice and twigs and stuff all over me, inside my clothes and shoes and all, and then I happened to look around and I had my hand right on a bunch of poison oak. The only thing I couldn't understand was why it was just poison oak and not a snake or something. So I didn't even bother to move it. I just stood there until the dog went away. Then I went on.

I didn't have any idea where the car was now. I couldn't think about anything except my head, and I'd just stand in one place and sort of wonder if I had really seen a ford even, and I didn't even care much whether I had or not. Like I say, let her lay out all day and all night with everthing in town that wears pants, what do I care. I dont owe anything to anybody that has no more consideration for me, that wouldn't be a dam bit above planting that ford there and making me spend a whole afternoon and Earl taking her back there and showing her the books just because he's too dam virtuous for this world. I says you'll have one hell of a time in heaven, without anybody's business to meddle in only dont you ever let me catch you at it I says, I close my eyes to it because of your grandmother, but just you let me catch you doing it one time on this place, where my mother lives. These dam little slick haired squirts, thinking they are raising so much hell, I'll show them something about hell I says, and you too. I'll make him think that dam red tie is the latch string to hell, if he thinks he can run the woods with my niece.

With the sun and all in my eyes and my blood going so I kept thinking every time my head would go on and burst and get it over with, with briers and things grabbing at me, then I came onto the sand ditch where they had been and I recognised the tree where the car was, and just as I got out of the ditch and started running I heard the car start. It went off fast, blowing the horn. They kept on blowing it, like it was saying Yah. Yah. Yaaahhhhhhhhh, going out of sight. I got to the road just in time to see it go out of sight.

By the time I got up to where my car was, they were clean out of sight, the horn still blowing. Well, I never thought anything about it except I was saying Run. Run back to town. Run home and try to convince Mother that I never saw you in that car. Try to make her believe that I dont know who he was. Try to make her believe that I didn't miss ten feet of catching you in that ditch. Try to make her believe you were standing up, too.

It kept on saying Yahhhhh, Yahhhhh, Yaaahhhhhhhhh, getting fainter and fainter. Then it quit, and I could hear a cow lowing up at Russell's barn. And still I never thought. I went up to the door and opened it and raised my foot. I kind of thought then that the car was leaning a little more than the slant of the road would be, but I never found it out until I got in and started off.

Well, I just sat there. It was getting on toward sundown, and town was about five miles. They never even had guts enough to puncture it, to jab a hole in it. They just let the air out. I just stood there for a while, thinking about that kitchen full of niggers and not one of them had time to lift a tire onto the rack and screw up a couple of bolts. It was kind of funny because even she couldn't have seen far enough ahead to take the pump out on purpose, unless she thought about it while he was letting out the air maybe. But what it probably was was somebody took it out and gave it to Ben to play with for a squirt gun because they'd take the whole car to pieces if he wanted it and Dilsey says, Aint nobody teched yo car. What we want to fool with hit fer? and I says You're a nigger. You're lucky, do you know it? I says I'll swap with you any day because it takes a white man not to have anymore sense than to worry about what a little slut of a girl does.

I walked up to Russell's. He had a pump. That was just an oversight on their part, I reckon. Only I still couldn't believe she'd have had the nerve to. I kept thinking that. I dont know why it is I cant seem to learn that a woman'll do anything. I kept thinking, Let's forget for a while how I feel toward you and how you feel toward me: I just wouldn't do you this way. I wouldn't do you this way no matter what you had done to me. Because like I say blood is blood and you cant get around it. It's not playing a joke that any eight year old boy could have thought of, it's letting your own uncle be laughed at by a man that would wear a red tie. They come into town and call us all a bunch of hicks and think it's too small to hold them. Well he doesn't know just how right he is. And her too. If that's the way she feels about it, she'd better keep right on going and a dam good riddance.

I stopped and returned Russell's pump and drove on to town. I went to the drugstore and got a shot and then I went to the telegraph office. It had closed at 20.21, forty points down. Forty times five dollars; buy something with that if you can, and she'll say, I've got to have it I've just got to and I'll say that's too bad you'll have to try somebody else, I haven't got any money; I've been too busy to make any.

I just looked at him.

"I'll tell you some news," I says. "You'll be astonished to learn that I am interested in the cotton market," I says. "That never occurred to you, did it?"

"I did my best to deliver it," he says. "I tried the store twice and called up your house, but they didn't know where you were," he says, digging in the drawer.

"Deliver what?" I says. He handed me a telegram. "What time did this come?" I says.

"About half past three," he says.

"And now it's ten minutes past five," I says.

"I tried to deliver it," he says. "I couldn't find you."

"That's not my fault, is it?" I says. I opened it, just to see what kind of a lie they'd tell me this time. They must be in one hell of a shape if they've got to come all the way to Mississippi to steal ten dollars a month. Sell, it says. The market will be unstable, with a general downward tendency. Do not be alarmed following government report.

"How much would a message like this cost?" I says. He told me.

"They paid it," he says.

"Then I owe them that much," I says. "I already knew this. Send this collect," I says, taking a blank. Buy, I wrote, Market just on point of blowing its head off. Occasional flurries for purpose of hooking a few more country suckers who haven't got in to the telegraph office yet. Do not be alarmed. "Send that collect," I says.

He looked at the message, then he looked at the clock. "Market closed an hour ago," he says.

"Well," I says. "That's not my fault either. I didn't invent it; I just bought a little of it while under the impression that the telegraph company would keep me informed as to what it was doing."

"A report is posted whenever it comes in," he says.

"Yes," I says. "And in Memphis they have it on a blackboard every ten seconds," I says. "I was within sixty-seven miles of there once this afternoon."

He looked at the message. "You want to send this?" he says.

"I still haven't changed my mind," I says. I wrote the other one out and counted the money. "And this one too, if you're sure you can spell b-u-y."

I went back to the store. I could hear the band from down the street. Prohibition's a fine thing. Used to be they'd come in Saturday with just one pair of shoes in the family and him wearing them, and they'd go down to the express office and get his package; now they all go to the show barefooted, with the merchants in the door like a row of tigers or something in a cage, watching them pass. Earl says,

"I hope it wasn't anything serious."

"What?" I says. He looked at his watch. Then he went to the door and looked at the courthouse clock. "You ought to have a dollar watch," I says. "It wont cost you so much to believe it's lying each time."

"What?" he says.

"Nothing," I says. "Hope I haven't inconvenienced you."

"We were not busy much," he says. "They all went to the show. It's all right."

"If it's not all right," I says, "you know what you can do about it."

"I said it was all right," he says.

"I heard you," I says. "And if it's not all right, you know what you can do about it."

"Do you want to quit?" he says.

"It's not my business," I says. "My wishes dont matter. But dont get the idea that you are protecting me by keeping me."

"You'd be a good business man if you'd let yourself, Jason," he says.

"At least I can tend to my own business and let other people's alone," I says.

"I dont know why you are trying to make me fire you," he says. "You know you could quit anytime and there wouldn't be any hard feelings between us."

"Maybe that's why I dont quit," I says. "As long as I tend to my job, that's what you are paying me for." I went on to the back and got a drink of water and went on out to the back door. Job had the cultivators all set up at last. It was quiet there, and pretty soon my head got a little easier. I could hear them singing now, and then the band played again. Well, let them get every quarter and dime in the county; it was no skin off my back. I've done what I could; a man that can live as long as I have and not know when to quit is a fool. Especially as it's no business of mine. If it was my own daughter now it would be different, because she wouldn't have time to; she'd have to work some to feed a few invalids and idiots and niggers, because how could I have the face to bring anybody there. I've too much respect for anybody to do that. I'm a man, I can stand it, it's my own flesh and blood and I'd like to see the color of the man's eyes that would speak disrespectful of any woman that was my friend it's these dam good women that do it I'd like to see the good, church-going woman that's half as square as Lorraine, whore or no whore. Like I say if I was to get married you'd go up like a balloon and you know it and she says I want you to be happy to have a family of your own not to slave your life away for us. But I'll be gone soon and then you can take a wife but you'll never find a woman who is worthy of you and I says yes I could. You'd get right up out of your grave you know you would. I says no thank you I have all the women I can take care of now if I married a wife she'd probably turn out to be a hophead or something. That's all we lack in this family, I says.

The sun was down beyond the Methodist church now, and the pigeons were flying back and forth around the steeple, and when the band stopped I could hear them cooing. It hadn't been four months since Christmas, and yet they were almost as thick as ever. I reckon Parson Walthall was getting a belly full of them now. You'd have thought we were shooting people, with him making speeches and even holding onto a man's gun when they came over. Talking about peace on earth good will toward all and not a sparrow can fall to earth. But what does he care how thick they get, he hasn't got anything to do: what does he care what time it is. He pays no taxes, he doesn't have to see his money going every year to have the courthouse clock cleaned to where it'll run. They had to pay a man forty-five dollars to clean it. I counted over a hundred half-hatched pigeons on the ground. You'd think they'd have sense enough to leave town. It's a good thing I dont have anymore ties than a pigeon, I'll say that.

The band was playing again, a loud fast tune, like they were breaking up. I reckon they'd be satisfied now. Maybe they'd have enough music to entertain them while they drove fourteen or fifteen miles home and unharnessed in the dark and fed the stock and milked. All they'd have to do would be to whistle the music and tell the jokes to the live stock in the barn, and then they could count up how much they'd made by not taking the stock to the show too. They could figure that if a man had five children and seven mules, he cleared a quarter by taking his family to the show. Just like that. Earl came back with a couple of packages.

"Here's some more stuff going out," he says. "Where's Uncle Job?"

"Gone to the show, I imagine," I says. "Unless you watched him."

"He doesn't slip off," he says. "I can depend on him."

"Meaning me by that," I says.

He went to the door and looked out, listening.

"That's a good band," he says. "It's about time they were breaking up, I'd say."

"Unless they're going to spend the night there," I says. The swallows had begun, and I could hear the sparrows beginning to swarm in the trees in the courthouse yard. Every once in a while a bunch of them would come swirling around in sight above the roof, then go away. They are as big a nuisance as the pigeons, to my notion. You cant even sit in the courthouse yard for them. First thing you know, bing. Right on your hat. But it would take a millionaire to afford to shoot them at five cents a shot. If they'd just put a little poison out there in the square, they'd get rid of them in a day, because if a merchant cant keep his stock from running around the square, he'd better try to deal in something besides chickens, something that dont eat, like plows or onions. And if a man dont keep his dogs up, he either dont want it or he hasn't any business with one. Like I say if all the businesses in a town are run like country businesses, you're going to have a country town.

"It wont do you any good if they have broke up," I says. "They'll have to hitch up and take out to get home by midnight as it is."

"Well," he says. "They enjoy it. Let them spend a little money on a show now and then. A hill farmer works pretty hard and gets mighty little for it."

"There's no law making them farm in the hills," I says. "Or anywhere else."

"Where would you and me be, if it wasn't for the farmers?" he says.

"I'd be home right now," I says. "Lying down, with an ice pack on my head."

"You have these headaches too often," he says. "Why dont you have your teeth examined good? Did he go over them all this morning?"

"Did who?" I says.

"You said you went to the dentist this morning."

"Do you object to my having the headache on your time?" I says. "Is that it?" They were crossing the alley now, coming up from the show.

"There they come," he says. "I reckon I better get up front." He went on. It's a curious thing how, no matter what's wrong with you, a man'll tell you to have your teeth examined and a woman'll tell you to get married. It always takes a man that never made much at any thing to tell you how to run your business, though. Like these college professors without a whole pair of socks to his name, telling you how to make a million in ten years, and a woman that couldn't even get a husband can always tell you how to raise a family.

Old man Job came up with the wagon. After a while he got through wrapping the lines around the whip socket.

"Well," I says. "Was it a good show?"

"I aint been yit," he says. "But I kin be arrested in dat tent tonight, dough."

"Like hell you haven't," I says. "You've been away from here since three oclock. Mr Earl was just back here looking for you."

"I been tendin to my business," he says. "Mr Earl knows whar I been."

"You may can fool him," I says. "I wont tell on you."

"Den he's de onliest man here I'd try to fool," he says. "Whut I want to waste my time foolin a man whut I dont keer whether I sees him Sat'dy night er not? I wont try to fool you," he says. "You too smart fer me. Yes, suh," he says, look-ing busy as hell, putting five or six little packages into the wagon. "You's too smart fer me. Aint a man in dis town kin keep up wid you fer smartness. You fools a man whut so smart he cant even keep up wid hisself," he says, getting in the wagon and unwrapping the reins.

"Who's that?" I says.

"Dat's Mr Jason Compson," he says. "Git up dar, Dan!"

One of the wheels was just about to come off. I watched to see if he'd get out of the alley before it did. Just turn any ve-hicle over to a nigger, though. I says that old rattletrap's just an eyesore, yet you'll keep it standing there in the carriage house a hundred years just so that boy can ride to the ceme-tery once a week. I says he's not the first fellow that'll have to do things he doesn't want to. I'd make him ride in that car like a civilised man or stay at home. What does he know about where he goes or what he goes in, and us keeping a carriage and a horse so he can take a ride on Sunday afternoon.

A lot Job cared whether the wheel came off or not, long as he wouldn't have too far to walk back. Like I say the only place for them is in the field, where they'd have to work from sunup to sundown. They cant stand prosperity or an easy job. Let one stay around white people for a while and he's not worth killing. They get so they can outguess you about work before your very eyes, like Roskus the only mistake he ever made was he got careless one day and died. Shirking and stealing and giving you a little more lip and a little more lip until some day you have to lay them out with a scantling or something. Well, it's Earl's business. But I'd hate to have my business advertised over this town by an old doddering nigger and a wagon that you thought every time it turned a corner it would come all to pieces.

The sun was all high up in the air now, and inside it was beginning to get dark. I went up front. The square was empty. Earl was back closing the safe, and then the clock begun to strike.

"You lock the back door?" he says. I went back and locked it and came back. "I suppose you're going to the show to-night," he says. "I gave you those passes yesterday, didn't I?"

"Yes," I says. "You want them back?"

"No, no," he says. "I just forgot whether I gave them to you or not. No sense in wasting them."

He locked the door and said Goodnight and went on. The sparrows were still rattling away in the trees, but the square was empty except for a few cars. There was a ford in front of the drugstore, but I didn't even look at it. I know when I've had enough of anything. I dont mind trying to help her, but I know when I've had enough. I guess I could teach Luster to drive it, then they could chase her all day long if they wanted to, and I could stay home and play with Ben.

I went in and got a couple of cigars. Then I thought I'd have another headache shot for luck, and I stood and talked with them a while.

"Well," Mac says. "I reckon you've got your money on the Yankees this year."

"What for?" I says.

"The Pennant," he says. "Not anything in the league can beat them."

"Like hell there's not," I says. "They're shot," I says. "You think a team can be that lucky forever?"

"I dont call it luck," Mac says.

"I wouldn't bet on any team that fellow Ruth played on," I says. "Even if I knew it was going to win."

"Yes?" Mac says.

"I can name you a dozen men in either league who're more valuable than he is," I says.

"What have you got against Ruth?" Mac says.

"Nothing," I says. "I haven't got any thing against him. I dont even like to look at his picture." I went on out. The lights were coming on, and people going along the streets toward home. Sometimes the sparrows never got still until full dark. The night they turned on the new lights around the court-house it waked them up and they were flying around and blundering into the lights all night long. They kept it up two or three nights, then one morning they were all gone. Then after about two months they all came back again.

I drove on home. There were no lights in the house yet, but they'd all be looking out the windows, and Dilsey jawing away in the kitchen like it was her own food she was having to keep hot until I got there. You'd think to hear her that there wasn't but one supper in the world, and that was the one she had to keep back a few minutes on my account. Well at least I could come home one time without finding Ben and that nigger hanging on the gate like a bear and a monkey in the same cage. Just let it come toward sundown and he'd head for the gate like a cow for the barn, hanging onto it and bobbing his head and sort of moaning to himself. That's a hog for punishment for you. If what had happened to him for fooling with open gates had happened to me, I never would want to see another one. I often wondered what he'd be thinking about, down there at the gate, watching the girls going home from school, trying to want something he couldn't even remember he didn't and couldn't want any longer. And what he'd think when they'd be undressing him and he'd happen to take a look at himself and begin to cry like he'd do. But like I say they never did enough of that. I says I know what you need you need what they did to Ben then you'd behave. And if you dont know what that was I says, ask Dilsey to tell you.

There was a light in Mother's room. I put the car up and went on into the kitchen. Luster and Ben were there.

"Where's Dilsey?" I says. "Putting supper on?"

"She up stairs wid Miss Cahline," Luster says. "Dey been goin hit. Ever since Miss Quentin come home. Mammy up there keepin um fum fightin. Is dat show come, Mr Jason?"

"Yes," I says.

"I thought I heard de band," he says. "Wish I could go," he says. "I could ef I jes had a quarter."

Dilsey came in. "You come, is you?" she says. "Whut you been up to dis evenin? You knows how much work I got to do; whyn't you git here on time?"

"Maybe I went to the show," I says. "Is supper ready?"

"Wish I could go," Luster says. "I could ef I jes had a quarter."

"You aint got no business at no show," Dilsey says. "You go on in de house and set down," she says. "Dont you go up stairs and git um started again, now."

"What's the matter?" I says.

"Quentin come in a while ago and says you been follerin her around all evenin and den Miss Cahline jumped on her. Whyn't you let her alone? Cant you live in de same house wid yo own blood niece widout quoilin?"

"I cant quarrel with her," I says, "because I haven't seen her since this morning. What does she say I've done now? made her go to school? That's pretty bad," I says.

"Well, you tend to yo business and let her lone," Dilsey says. "I'll take keer of her ef you'n Miss Cahline'll let me. Go on in dar now and behave yoself twell I git supper on."

"Ef I jes had a quarter," Luster says, "I could go to dat show."

"En ef you had wings you could fly to heaven," Dilsey says. "I dont want to hear another word about dat show."

"That reminds me," I says. "I've got a couple of tickets they gave me." I took them out of my coat.

"You fixin to use um?" Luster says.

"Not me," I says. "I wouldn't go to it for ten dollars."

"Gimme one of um, Mr Jason," he says.

"I'll sell you one," I says. "How about it?"

"I aint got no money," he says.

"That's too bad," I says. I made to go out.

"Gimme one of um, Mr Jason," he says. "You aint gwine need um bofe."

"Hush yo mouf," Dilsey says. "Dont you know he aint gwine give nothin away?"

"How much you want fer hit?" he says.

"Five cents," I says.

"I aint got dat much," he says.

"How much you got?" I says.

"I aint got nothin," he says.

"All right," I says. I went on.

"Mr Jason," he says.

"Whyn't you hush up?" Dilsey says. "He jes teasin you. He fixin to use dem tickets hisself. Go on, Jason, and let him lone."

"I dont want them," I says. I came back to the stove. "I came in here to burn them up. But if you want to buy one for a nickel?" I says, looking at him and opening the stove lid.

"I aint got dat much," he says.

"All right," I says. I dropped one of them in the stove.

"You, Jason," Dilsey says. "Aint you shamed?"

"Mr Jason," he says. "Please, suh. I'll fix dem tires ev'y day fer a mont."

"I need the cash," I says. "You can have it for a nickel."

"Hush, Luster," Dilsey says. She jerked him back. "Go on," she says. "Drop hit in. Go on. Git hit over with."

"You can have it for a nickel," I says.

"Go on," Dilsey says. "He aint got no nickel. Go on. Drop hit in."

"All right," I says. I dropped it in and Dilsey shut the stove.

"A big growed man like you," she says. "Git on outen my kitchen. Hush," she says to Luster. "Dont you git Benjy started. I'll git you a quarter fum Frony tonight and you kin go tomorrow night. Hush up, now."

I went on into the living room. I couldn't hear anything from upstairs. I opened the paper. After a while Ben and Luster came in. Ben went to the dark place on the wall where the mirror used to be, rubbing his hands on it and slobbering and moaning. Luster begun punching at the fire.

"What're you doing?" I says. "We dont need any fire tonight."

"I tryin to keep him quiet," he says. "Hit always cold Easter," he says.

"Only this is not Easter," I says. "Let it alone."

He put the poker back and got the cushion out of Mother's chair and gave it to Ben, and he hunkered down in front of the fireplace and got quiet.

I read the paper. There hadn't been a sound from upstairs when Dilsey came in and sent Ben and Luster on to the kitchen and said supper was ready.

"All right," I says. She went out. I sat there, reading the paper. After a while I heard Dilsey looking in at the door.

"Whyn't you come on and eat?" she says.

"I'm waiting for supper," I says.

"Hit's on the table," she says. "I done told you."

"Is it?" I says. "Excuse me. I didn't hear anybody come down."

"They aint comin," she says. "You come on and eat, so I can take something up to them."

"Are they sick?" I says. "What did the doctor say it was? Not Smallpox, I hope."

"Come on here, Jason," she says. "So I kin git done."

"All right," I says, raising the paper again. "I'm waiting for supper now."

I could feel her watching me at the door. I read the paper.

"Whut you want to act like this fer?" she says. "When you knows how much bother I has anyway."

"If Mother is any sicker than she was when she came down to dinner, all right," I says. "But as long as I am buying food for people younger than I am, they'll have to come down to the table to eat it. Let me know when supper's ready," I says, reading the paper again. I heard her climbing the stairs, dragging her feet and grunting and groaning like they were straight up and three feet apart. I heard her at Mother's door, then I heard her calling Quentin, like the door was locked, then she went back to Mother's room and then Mother went and talked to Quentin. Then they came down stairs. I read the paper.

Dilsey came back to the door. "Come on," she says, "fo you kin think up some mo devilment. You just tryin yoself tonight."

I went to the diningroom. Quentin was sitting with her head bent. She had painted her face again. Her nose looked like a porcelain insulator.

"I'm glad you feel well enough to come down," I says to Mother.

"It's little enough I can do for you, to come to the table," she says. "No matter how I feel. I realise that when a man works all day he likes to be surrounded by his family at the supper table. I want to please you. I only wish you and Quentin got along better. It would be easier for me."

"We get along all right," I says. "I dont mind her staying locked up in her room all day if she wants to. But I cant have all this whoop-de-do and sulking at mealtimes. I know that's a lot to ask her, but I'm that way in my own house. Your house, I meant to say."

"It's yours," Mother says. "You are the head of it now."

Quentin hadn't looked up. I helped the plates and she begun to eat.

"Did you get a good piece of meat?" I says. "If you didn't, I'll try to find you a better one."

She didn't say anything.

"I say, did you get a good piece of meat?" I says.

"What?" she says. "Yes. It's all right."

"Will you have some more rice?" I says.

"No," she says.

"Better let me give you some more," I says.

"I dont want any more," she says.

"Not at all," I says. "You're welcome."

"Is your headache gone?" Mother says.

"Headache?" I says.

"I was afraid you were developing one," she says. "When you came in this afternoon."

"Oh," I says. "No, it didn't show up. We stayed so busy this afternoon I forgot about it."

"Was that why you were late?" Mother says. I could see Quentin listening. I looked at her. Her knife and fork were still going, but I caught her looking at me, then she looked at her plate again. I says,

"No. I loaned my car to a fellow about three oclock and I had to wait until he got back with it." I ate for a while.

"Who was it?" Mother says.

"It was one of those show men," I says. "It seems his sister's husband was out riding with some town woman, and he was chasing them."

Quentin sat perfectly still, chewing.

"You ought not to lend your car to people like that," Mother says. "You are too generous with it. That's why I never call on you for it if I can help it."

"I was beginning to think that myself, for a while," I says. "But he got back, all right. He says he found what he was looking for."

"Who was the woman?" Mother says.

"I'll tell you later," I says. "I dont like to talk about such things before Quentin."

Quentin had quit eating. Every once in a while she'd take a drink of water, then she'd sit there crumbling a biscuit up, her face bent over her plate.

"Yes," Mother says. "I suppose women who stay shut up like I do have no idea what goes on in this town."

"Yes," I says. "They dont."

"My life has been so different from that," Mother says. "Thank God I dont know about such wickedness. I dont even want to know about it. I'm not like most people."

I didn't say any more. Quentin sat there, crumbling the biscuit until I quit eating. Then she says,

"Can I go now?" without looking at anybody.

"What?" I says. "Sure, you can go. Were you waiting on us?"

She looked at me. She had crumpled all the bread, but her hands still went on like they were crumpling it yet and her eyes looked like they were cornered or something and then she started biting her mouth like it ought to have poisoned her, with all that red lead.

"Grandmother," she says. "Grandmother——"

"Did you want something else to eat?" I says.

"Why does he treat me like this, Grandmother?" she says. "I never hurt him."

"I want you all to get along with one another," Mother says. "You are all that's left now, and I do want you all to get along better."

"It's his fault," she says. "He wont let me alone, and I have to. If he doesn't want me here, why wont he let me go back to——"

"That's enough," I says. "Not another word."

"Then why wont he let me alone?" she says. "He——he just——"

"He is the nearest thing to a father you've ever had," Mother says. "It's his bread you and I eat. It's only right that he should expect obedience from you."

"It's his fault," she says. She jumped up. "He makes me do it. If he would just——" she looked at us, her eyes cornered, kind of jerking her arms against her sides.

"If I would just what?" I says.

"Whatever I do, it's your fault," she says. "If I'm bad, it's because I had to be. You made me. I wish I was dead. I wish we were all dead." Then she ran. We heard her run up the stairs. Then a door slammed.

"That's the first sensible thing she ever said," I says.

"She didn't go to school today," Mother says.

"How do you know?" I says. "Were you down town?"

"I just know," she says. "I wish you could be kinder to her."

"If I did that I'd have to arrange to see her more than once a day," I says. "You'll have to make her come to the table every meal. Then I could give her an extra piece of meat every time."

"There are little things you could do," she says.

"Like not paying any attention when you ask me to see that she goes to school?" I says.

"She didn't go to school today," she says. "I just know she didn't. She says she went for a car ride with one of the boys this afternoon and you followed her."

"How could I," I says. "When somebody had my car all afternoon? Whether or not she was in school today is already past," I says. "If you've got to worry about it, worry about next Monday."

"I wanted you and she to get along with one another," she says. "But she has inherited all of the headstrong traits. Quentin's too. I thought at the time, with the heritage she would already have, to give her that name, too. Sometimes I think she is the judgment of both of them upon me."

"Good Lord," I says. "You've got a fine mind. No wonder you keep yourself sick all the time."

"What?" she says. "I dont understand."

"I hope not," I says. "A good woman misses a lot she's better off without knowing."

"They were both that way," she says. "They would make interest with your father against me when I tried to correct them. He was always saying they didn't need controlling, that they already knew what cleanliness and honesty were, which was all that anyone could hope to be taught. And now I hope he's satisfied."

"You've got Ben to depend on," I says. "Cheer up."

"They deliberately shut me out of their lives," she says. "It was always her and Quentin. They were always conspiring against me. Against you too, though you were too young to realise it. They always looked on you and me as outsiders, like they did your Uncle Maury. I always told your father that they were allowed too much freedom, to be together too much. When Quentin started to school we had to let her go the next year, so she could be with him. She couldn't bear for any of you to do anything she couldn't. It was vanity in her, vanity and false pride. And then when her troubles began I knew that Quentin would feel that he had to do something just as bad. But I didn't believe that he would have been so selfish as to——I didn't dream that he——"

"Maybe he knew it was going to be a girl," I says. "And that one more of them would be more than he could stand."

"He could have controlled her," she says. "He seemed to be the only person she had any consideration for. But that is a part of the judgment too, I suppose."

"Yes," I says. "Too bad it wasn't me instead of him. You'd be a lot better off."

"You say things like that to hurt me," she says. "I deserve it though. When they began to sell the land to send Quentin to Harvard I told your father that he must make an equal provision for you. Then when Herbert offered to take you into the bank I said, Jason is provided for now, and when all the expense began to pile up and I was forced to sell our furniture and the rest of the pasture, I wrote her at once because I said she will realise that she and Quentin have had their share and part of Jason's too and that it depends on her now to compensate him. I said she will do that out of respect for her father. I believed that, then. But I'm just a poor old woman; I was raised to believe that people would deny themselves for their own flesh and blood. It's my fault. You were right to reproach me."

"Do you think I need any man's help to stand on my feet?"

I says. "Let alone a woman that cant name the father of her own child."

"Jason," she says.

"All right," I says. "I didn't mean that. Of course not."

"If I believed that were possible, after all my suffering."

"Of course it's not," I says. "I didn't mean it."

"I hope that at least is spared me," she says.

"Sure it is," I says. "She's too much like both of them to doubt that."

"I couldn't bear that," she says.

"Then quit thinking about it," I says. "Has she been worrying you any more about getting out at night?"

"No. I made her realise that it was for her own good and that she'd thank me for it some day. She takes her books with her and studies after I lock the door. I see the light on as late as eleven oclock some nights."

"How do you know she's studying?" I says.

"I dont know what else she'd do in there alone," she says. "She never did read any."

"No," I says. "You wouldn't know. And you can thank your stars for that," I says. Only what would be the use in saying it aloud. It would just have her crying on me again.

I heard her go up stairs. Then she called Quentin and Quentin says What? through the door. "Goodnight," Mother says. Then I heard the key in the lock, and Mother went back to her room.

When I finished my cigar and went up, the light was still on. I could see the empty keyhole, but I couldn't hear a sound. She studied quiet. Maybe she learned that in school. I told Mother goodnight and went on to my room and got the box out and counted it again. I could hear the Great American Gelding snoring away like a planing mill. I read somewhere they'd fix men that way to give them women's voices. But maybe he didn't know what they'd done to him. I dont reckon he even knew what he had been trying to do, or why Mr Burgess knocked him out with the fence picket. And if they'd just sent him on to Jackson while he was under the ether, he'd never have known the difference. But that would have been too simple for a Compson to think of. Not half complex enough. Having to wait to do it at all until he broke out and tried to run a little girl down on the street with her own father looking at him. Well, like I say they never started soon enough with their cutting, and they quit too quick. I know at least two more that needed something like that, and one of them not over a mile away, either. But then I dont reckon even that would do any good. Like I say once a bitch always a bitch. And just let me have twenty-four hours without any dam New York jew to advise me what it's going to do. I dont want to make a killing; save that to suck in the smart gamblers with. I just want an even chance to get my money back. And once I've done that they can bring all Beale street and all bedlam in here and two of them can sleep in my bed and another one can have my place at the table too.

April Eighth, 1928.

THE day dawned bleak and chill, a moving wall of gray light out of the northeast which, instead of dissolving into moisture, seemed to disintegrate into minute and venomous particles, like dust that, when Dilsey opened the door of the cabin and emerged, needled laterally into her flesh, precipitating not so much a moisture as a substance partaking of the quality of thin, not quite congealed oil. She wore a stiff black straw hat perched upon her turban, and a maroon velvet cape with a border of mangy and anonymous fur above a dress of purple silk, and she stood in the door for a while with her myriad and sunken face lifted to the weather, and one gaunt hand flac-soled as the belly of a fish, then she moved the cape aside and examined the bosom of her gown.

The gown fell gauntly from her shoulders, across her fallen breasts, then tightened upon her paunch and fell again, ballooning a little above the nether garments which she would remove layer by layer as the spring accomplished and the warm days, in color regal and moribund. She had been a big woman once but now her skeleton rose, draped loosely in unpadded skin that tightened again upon a paunch almost dropsical, as though muscle and tissue had been courage or fortitude which the days or the years had consumed until only the indomitable skeleton was left rising like a ruin or a landmark above the somnolent and impervious guts, and above that the collapsed face that gave the impression of the bones themselves being outside the flesh, lifted into the driving day with an expression at once fatalistic and of a child's astonished disappointment, until she turned and entered the house again and closed the door.

The earth immediately about the door was bare. It had a patina, as though from the soles of bare feet in generations, like old silver or the walls of Mexican houses which have been plastered by hand. Beside the house, shading it in summer, stood three mulberry trees, the fledged leaves that would later be broad and placid as the palms of hands streaming flatly undulant upon the driving air. A pair of jaybirds came up from nowhere, whirled up on the blast like gaudy scraps of cloth or paper and lodged in the mulberries, where they swung in raucous tilt and recover, screaming into the wind that ripped their harsh cries onward and away like scraps of paper or of cloth in turn. Then three more joined them and they swung and tilted in the wrung branches for a time, screaming. The door of the cabin opened and Dilsey emerged once more, this time in a man's felt hat and an army overcoat, beneath the frayed skirts of which her blue gingham dress fell in uneven balloonings, streaming too about her as she crossed the yard and mounted the steps to the kitchen door.

A moment later she emerged, carrying an open umbrella now, which she slanted ahead into the wind, and crossed to the woodpile and laid the umbrella down, still open. Immediately she caught at it and arrested it and held to it for a while, looking about her. Then she closed it and laid it down and stacked stovewood into her crooked arm, against her breast, and picked up the umbrella and got it open at last and returned to the steps and held the wood precariously balanced while she contrived to close the umbrella, which she propped in the corner just within the door. She dumped the wood into the box behind the stove. Then she removed the overcoat and hat and took a soiled apron down from the wall and put it on and built a fire in the stove. While she was doing so, rattling the grate bars and clattering the lids, Mrs Compson began to call her from the head of the stairs.

She wore a dressing gown of quilted black satin, holding it close under her chin. In the other hand she held a red rubber hot water bottle and she stood at the head of the back stairway, calling "Dilsey" at steady and inflectionless intervals into the quiet stairwell that descended into complete darkness, then opened again where a gray window fell across it. "Dilsey," she called, without inflection or emphasis or haste, as though she were not listening for a reply at all. "Dilsey."

Dilsey answered and ceased clattering the stove, but before she could cross the kitchen Mrs Compson called her again, and before she crossed the diningroom and brought her head into relief against the gray splash of the window, still again.

"All right," Dilsey said. "All right, here I is. I'll fill hit soon ez I git some hot water." She gathered up her skirts and mounted the stairs, wholly blotting the gray light. "Put hit down dar en g'awn back to bed."

"I couldn't understand what was the matter," Mrs Compson said. "I've been lying awake for an hour at least, without hearing a sound from the kitchen."

"You put hit down and g'awn back to bed," Dilsey said. She toiled painfully up the steps, shapeless, breathing heavily. "I'll have de fire gwine in a minute, en de water hot in two mo."

"I've been lying there for an hour, at least," Mrs Compson said. "I thought maybe you were waiting for me to come down and start the fire."

Dilsey reached the top of the stairs and took the water bottle. "I'll fix hit in a minute," she said. "Luster overslep dis mawnin, up half de night at dat show. I gwine build de fire myself. Go on now, so you wont wake de others twell I ready."

"If you permit Luster to do things that interfere with his work, you'll have to suffer for it yourself," Mrs Compson said. "Jason wont like this if he hears about it. You know he wont."

" 'Twusn't none of Jason's money he went on," Dilsey said. "Dat's one thing sho." She went on down the stairs. Mrs Compson returned to her room. As she got into bed again she could hear Dilsey yet descending the stairs with a sort of painful and terrific slowness that would have become maddening had it not presently ceased beyond the flapping diminishment of the pantry door.

She entered the kitchen and built up the fire and began to prepare breakfast. In the midst of this she ceased and went to the window and looked out toward her cabin, then she went to the door and opened it and shouted into the driving weather.

"Luster!" she shouted, standing to listen, tilting her face from the wind. "You, Luster!" She listened, then as she prepared to shout again Luster appeared around the corner of the kitchen.

"Ma'am?" he said innocently, so innocently that Dilsey looked down at him, for a moment motionless, with something more than mere surprise.

"Whar you at?" she said.

"Nowhere," he said. "Jes in de cellar."

"Whut you doin in de cellar?" she said. "Dont stand dar in de rain, fool," she said.

"Aint doin nothin," he said. He came up the steps.

"Dont you dare come in dis do widout a armful of wood," she said. "Here I done had to tote yo wood en build yo fire bofe. Didn't I tole you not to leave dis place last night befo dat woodbox wus full to de top?"

"I did," Luster said. "I filled hit."

"Whar hit gone to, den?"

"I dont know'm. I aint teched hit."

"Well, you git hit full up now," she said. "And git on up dar en see bout Benjy."

She shut the door. Luster went to the woodpile. The five jaybirds whirled over the house, screaming, and into the mulberries again. He watched them. He picked up a rock and threw it. "Whoo," he said. "Git on back to hell, whar you belong at. 'Taint Monday yit."

He loaded himself mountainously with stove wood. He could not see over it, and he staggered to the steps and up them and blundered crashing against the door, shedding billets. Then Dilsey came and opened the door for him and he blundered across the kitchen. "You, Luster!" she shouted, but he had already hurled the wood into the box with a thunderous crash. "Hah!" he said.

"Is you tryin to wake up de whole house?" Dilsey said. She hit him on the back of his head with the flat of her hand. "Go on up dar and git Benjy dressed, now."

"Yessum," he said. He went toward the outer door.

"Whar you gwine?" Dilsey said.

"I thought I better go round de house en in by de front, so I wont wake up Miss Cahline en dem."

"You go on up dem back stairs like I tole you en git Benjy's clothes on him," Dilsey said. "Go on, now."

"Yessum," Luster said. He returned and left by the diningroom door. After a while it ceased to flap. Dilsey prepared to make biscuit. As she ground the sifter steadily above the bread board, she sang, to herself at first, something without particular tune or words, repetitive, mournful and plaintive, austere, as she ground a faint, steady snowing of flour onto the bread board. The stove had begun to heat the room and to fill it with murmurous minors of the fire, and presently she was singing louder, as if her voice too had been thawed out by the growing warmth, and then Mrs Compson called her name again from within the house. Dilsey raised her face as if her eyes could and did penetrate the walls and ceiling and saw the old woman in her quilted dressing gown at the head of the stairs, calling her name with machinelike regularity.

"Oh, Lawd," Dilsey said. She set the sifter down and swept up the hem of her apron and wiped her hands and caught up the bottle from the chair on which she had laid it and gathered her apron about the handle of the kettle which was now jetting faintly. "Jes a minute," she called. "De water jes dis minute got hot."

It was not the bottle which Mrs Compson wanted, however, and clutching it by the neck like a dead hen Dilsey went to the foot of the stairs and looked upward.

"Aint Luster up dar wid him?" she said.

"Luster hasn't been in the house. I've been lying here listening for him. I knew he would be late, but I did hope he'd come in time to keep Benjamin from disturbing Jason on Jason's one day in the week to sleep in the morning."

"I dont see how you expect anybody to sleep, wid you standin in de hall, holl'in at folks fum de crack of dawn," Dilsey said. She began to mount the stairs, toiling heavily. "I sont dat boy up dar half an hour ago."

Mrs Compson watched her, holding the dressing gown under her chin. "What are you going to do?" she said.

"Gwine git Benjy dressed en bring him down to de kitchen, whar he wont wake Jason en Quentin," Dilsey said.

"Haven't you started breakfast yet?"

"I'll tend to dat too," Dilsey said. "You better git back in bed twell Luster make yo fire. Hit cold dis mawnin."

"I know it," Mrs Compson said. "My feet are like ice. They were so cold they waked me up." She watched Dilsey mount the stairs. It took her a long while. "You know how it frets Jason when breakfast is late," Mrs Compson said.

"I cant do but one thing at a time," Dilsey said. "You git on back to bed, fo I has you on my hands dis mawnin too."

"If you're going to drop everything to dress Benjamin, I'd better come down and get breakfast. You know as well as I do how Jason acts when it's late."

"En who gwine eat yo messin?" Dilsey said. "Tell me dat. Go on now," she said, toiling upward. Mrs Compson stood watching her as she mounted, steadying herself against the wall with one hand, holding her skirts up with the other.

"Are you going to wake him up just to dress him?" she said.

Dilsey stopped. With her foot lifted to the next step she stood there, her hand against the wall and the gray splash of the window behind her, motionless and shapeless she loomed.

"He aint awake den?" she said.

"He wasn't when I looked in," Mrs Compson said. "But it's past his time. He never does sleep after half past seven. You know he doesn't."

Dilsey said nothing. She made no further move, but though she could not see her save as a blobby shape without depth, Mrs Compson knew that she had lowered her face a little and that she stood now like cows do in the rain, holding the empty water bottle by its neck.

"You're not the one who has to bear it," Mrs Compson said. "It's not your responsibility. You can go away. You dont have to bear the brunt of it day in and day out. You owe nothing to them, to Mr Compson's memory. I know you have never had any tenderness for Jason. You've never tried to conceal it."

Dilsey said nothing. She turned slowly and descended, lowering her body from step to step, as a small child does, her hand against the wall. "You go on and let him alone," she said. "Dont go in dar no mo, now. I'll send Luster up soon as I find him. Let him alone, now."

She returned to the kitchen. She looked into the stove, then she drew her apron over her head and donned the overcoat and opened the outer door and looked up and down the yard. The weather drove upon her flesh, harsh and minute, but the scene was empty of all else that moved. She descended the steps, gingerly, as if for silence, and went around the corner of the kitchen. As she did so Luster emerged quickly and innocently from the cellar door.

Dilsey stopped. "Whut you up to?" she said.

"Nothin," Luster said. "Mr Jason say fer me to find out whar dat water leak in de cellar fum."

"En when wus hit he say fer you to do dat?" Dilsey said. "Last New Year's day, wasn't hit?"

"I thought I jes be lookin whiles dey sleep," Luster said. Dilsey went to the cellar door. He stood aside and she peered down into the obscurity odorous of dank earth and mold and rubber.

"Huh," Dilsey said. She looked at Luster again. He met her gaze blandly, innocent and open. "I dont know whut you up to, but you aint got no business doin hit. You jes tryin me too dis mawnin cause de others is, aint you? You git on up dar en see to Benjy, you hear?"

"Yessum," Luster said. He went on toward the kitchen steps, swiftly.

"Here," Dilsey said. "You git me another armful of wood while I got you."

"Yessum," he said. He passed her on the steps and went to the woodpile. When he blundered again at the door a moment later, again invisible and blind within and beyond his wooden avatar, Dilsey opened the door and guided him across the kitchen with a firm hand.

"Jes thow hit at dat box again," she said. "Jes thow hit."

"I got to," Luster said, panting. "I cant put hit down no other way."

"Den you stand dar en hold hit a while," Dilsey said. She unloaded him a stick at a time. "Whut got into you dis mawnin? Here I sont you fer wood en you aint never brought mo'n six sticks at a time to save yo life twell today. Whut you fixin to ax me kin you do now? Aint dat show lef town yit?"

"Yessum. Hit done gone."

She put the last stick into the box. "Now you go on up dar wid Benjy, like I tole you befo," she said. "And I dont want nobody else yellin down dem stairs at me twell I rings de bell. You hear me."

"Yessum," Luster said. He vanished through the swing door. Dilsey put some more wood in the stove and returned to the bread board. Presently she began to sing again.

The room grew warmer. Soon Dilsey's skin had taken on a rich, lustrous quality as compared with that as of a faint dusting of wood ashes which both it and Luster's had worn as she moved about the kitchen, gathering about her the raw materials of food, coordinating the meal. On the wall above a cupboard, invisible save at night, by lamp light and even then evincing an enigmatic profundity because it had but one hand, a cabinet clock ticked, then with a preliminary sound as if it had cleared its throat, struck five times.

"Eight oclock," Dilsey said. She ceased and tilted her head upward, listening. But there was no sound save the clock and the fire. She opened the oven and looked at the pan of bread, then stooping she paused while someone descended the stairs. She heard the feet cross the diningroom, then the swing door opened and Luster entered, followed by a big man who appeared to have been shaped of some substance whose particles would not or did not cohere to one another or to the frame which supported it. His skin was dead looking and hairless; dropsical too, he moved with a shambling gait like a trained bear. His hair was pale and fine. It had been brushed smoothly down upon his brow like that of children in daguerrotypes. His eyes were clear, of the pale sweet blue of cornflowers, his thick mouth hung open, drooling a little.

"Is he cold?" Dilsey said. She wiped her hands on her apron and touched his hand.

"Ef he aint, I is," Luster said. "Always cold Easter. Aint never seen hit fail. Miss Cahline say ef you aint got time to fix her hot water bottle to never mind about hit."

"Oh, Lawd," Dilsey said. She drew a chair into the corner between the woodbox and the stove. The man went obediently and sat in it. "Look in de dinin room and see whar I laid dat bottle down," Dilsey said. Luster fetched the bottle from the diningroom and Dilsey filled it and gave it to him. "Hurry up, now," she said. "See ef Jason wake now. Tell em hit's all ready."

Luster went out. Ben sat beside the stove. He sat loosely, utterly motionless save for his head, which made a continual bobbing sort of movement as he watched Dilsey with his sweet vague gaze as she moved about. Luster returned.

"He up," he said. "Miss Cahline say put hit on de table." He came to the stove and spread his hands palm down above the firebox. "He up, too," he said. "Gwine hit wid bofe feet dis mawnin."

"Whut's de matter now?" Dilsey said. "Git away fum dar. How kin I do anything wid you standin over de stove?"

"I cold," Luster said.

"You ought to thought about dat whiles you wus down dar in dat cellar," Dilsey said. "Whut de matter wid Jason?"

"Sayin me en Benjy broke dat winder in his room."

"Is dey one broke?" Dilsey said.

"Dat's whut he sayin," Luster said. "Say I broke hit."

"How could you, when he keep hit locked all day en night?"

"Say I broke hit chunkin rocks at hit," Luster said.

"En did you?"

"Nome," Luster said.

"Dont lie to me, boy," Dilsey said.

"I never done hit," Luster said. "Ask Benjy ef I did. I aint stud'in dat winder."

"Who could a broke hit, den?" Dilsey said. "He jes tryin hisself, to wake Quentin up," she said, taking the pan of biscuits out of the stove.

"Reckin so," Luster said. "Dese funny folks. Glad I aint none of em."

"Aint none of who?" Dilsey said. "Lemme tell you somethin, nigger boy, you got jes es much Compson devilment in you es any of em. Is you right sho you never broke dat window?"

"Whut I want to break hit fur?"

"Whut you do any of yo devilment fur?" Dilsey said. "Watch him now, so he cant burn his hand again twell I git de table set."

She went to the diningroom, where they heard her moving about, then she returned and set a plate at the kitchen table and set food there. Ben watched her, slobbering, making a faint, eager sound.

"All right, honey," she said. "Here yo breakfast. Bring his chair, Luster." Luster moved the chair up and Ben sat down, whimpering and slobbering. Dilsey tied a cloth about his neck and wiped his mouth with the end of it. "And see kin you keep fum messin up his clothes one time," she said, handing Luster a spoon.

Ben ceased whimpering. He watched the spoon as it rose to his mouth. It was as if even eagerness were muscle-bound in him too, and hunger itself inarticulate, not knowing it is hunger. Luster fed him with skill and detachment. Now and then his attention would return long enough to enable him to feint the spoon and cause Ben to close his mouth upon the empty air, but it was apparent that Luster's mind was elsewhere. His other hand lay on the back of the chair and upon that dead surface it moved tentatively, delicately, as if he were picking an inaudible tune out of the dead void, and once he even forgot to tease Ben with the spoon while his fingers teased out of the slain wood a soundless and involved arpeggio until Ben recalled him by whimpering again.

In the diningroom Dilsey moved back and forth. Presently she rang a small clear bell, then in the kitchen Luster heard Mrs Compson and Jason descending, and Jason's voice, and he rolled his eyes whitely with listening.

"Sure, I know they didn't break it," Jason said. "Sure, I know that. Maybe the change of weather broke it."

"I dont see how it could have," Mrs Compson said. "Your room stays locked all day long, just as you leave it when you go to town. None of us ever go in there except Sunday, to clean it. I dont want you to think that I would go where I'm not wanted, or that I would permit anyone else to."

"I never said you broke it, did I?" Jason said.

"I dont want to go in your room," Mrs Compson said. "I respect anybody's private affairs. I wouldn't put my foot over the threshold, even if I had a key."

"Yes," Jason said. "I know your keys wont fit. That's why I had the lock changed. What I want to know is, how that window got broken."

"Luster say he didn't do hit," Dilsey said.

"I knew that without asking him," Jason said. "Where's Quentin?" he said.

"Where she is ev'y Sunday mawnin," Dilsey said. "Whut got into you de last few days, anyhow?"

"Well, we're going to change all that," Jason said. "Go up and tell her breakfast is ready."

"You leave her alone now, Jason," Dilsey said. "She gits up fer breakfast ev'y week mawnin, en Miss Cahline lets her stay in bed ev'y Sunday. You knows dat."

"I cant keep a kitchen full of niggers to wait on her pleasure, much as I'd like to," Jason said. "Go and tell her to come down to breakfast."

"Aint nobody have to wait on her," Dilsey said. "I puts her breakfast in de warmer en she——"

"Did you hear me?" Jason said.

"I hears you," Dilsey said. "All I been hearin, when you in de house. Ef hit aint Quentin er yo maw, hit's Luster en Benjy. Whut you let him go on dat way fer, Miss Cahline?"

"You'd better do as he says," Mrs Compson said. "He's head of the house now. It's his right to require us to respect his wishes. I try to do it, and if I can, you can too."

" 'Taint no sense in him bein so bad tempered he got to make Quentin git up jes to suit him," Dilsey said. "Maybe you think she broke dat window."

"She would, if she happened to think of it," Jason said. "You go and do what I told you."

"En I wouldn't blame her none ef she did," Dilsey said, going toward the stairs. "Wid you naggin at her all de blessed time you in de house."

"Hush, Dilsey," Mrs Compson said. "It's neither your place nor mine to tell Jason what to do. Sometimes I think he is wrong, but I try to obey his wishes for you all's sakes. If I'm strong enough to come to the table, Quentin can too."

Dilsey went out. They heard her mounting the stairs. They heard her a long while on the stairs.

"You've got a prize set of servants," Jason said. He helped his mother and himself to food. "Did you ever have one that was worth killing? You must have had some before I was big enough to remember."

"I have to humor them," Mrs Compson said. "I have to depend on them so completely. It's not as if I were strong. I wish I were. I wish I could do all the house work myself. I could at least take that much off your shoulders."

"And a fine pigsty we'd live in, too," Jason said. "Hurry up, Dilsey," he shouted.

"I know you blame me," Mrs Compson said, "for letting them off to go to church today."

"Go where?" Jason said. "Hasn't that damn show left yet?"

"To church," Mrs Compson said. "The darkies are having a

special Easter service. I promised Dilsey two weeks ago that they could get off."

"Which means we'll eat cold dinner," Jason said, "or none at all."

"I know it's my fault," Mrs Compson said. "I know you blame me."

"For what?" Jason said. "You never resurrected Christ, did you?"

They heard Dilsey mount the final stair, then her slow feet overhead.

"Quentin," she said. When she called the first time Jason laid his knife and fork down and he and his mother appeared to wait across the table from one another in identical attitudes; the one cold and shrewd, with close-thatched brown hair curled into two stubborn hooks, one on either side of his forehead like a bartender in caricature, and hazel eyes with black-ringed irises like marbles, the other cold and querulous, with perfectly white hair and eyes pouched and baffled and so dark as to appear to be all pupil or all iris.

"Quentin," Dilsey said. "Get up, honey. Dey waitin breakfast on you."

"I cant understand how that window got broken," Mrs Compson said. "Are you sure it was done yesterday? It could have been like that a long time, with the warm weather. The upper sash, behind the shade like that."

"I've told you for the last time that it happened yesterday," Jason said. "Dont you reckon I know the room I live in? Do you reckon I could have lived in it a week with a hole in the window you could stick your hand. . . . . . ." his voice ceased, ebbed, left him staring at his mother with eyes that for an instant were quite empty of anything. It was as though his eyes were holding their breath, while his mother looked at him, her face flaccid and querulous, interminable, clairvoyant yet obtuse. As they sat so Dilsey said,

"Quentin. Dont play wid me, honey. Come on to breakfast, honey. Dey waitin fer you."

"I cant understand it," Mrs Compson said. "It's just as if somebody had tried to break into the house——" Jason sprang up. His chair crashed over backward. "What—" Mrs Compson said, staring at him as he ran past her and went jumping up the stairs, where he met Dilsey. His face was now in shadow, and Dilsey said,

"She sullin. Yo maw aint unlocked——" But Jason ran on past her and along the corridor to a door. He didn't call. He grasped the knob and tried it, then he stood with the knob in his hand and his head bent a little, as if he were listening to something much further away than the dimensioned room beyond the door, and which he already heard. His attitude was that of one who goes through the motions of listening in order to deceive himself as to what he already hears. Behind him Mrs Compson mounted the stairs, calling his name. Then she saw Dilsey and she quit calling him and began to call Dilsey instead.

"I told you she aint unlocked dat do yit," Dilsey said.

When she spoke he turned and ran toward her, but his voice was quiet, matter of fact. "She carry the key with her?" he said. "Has she got it now, I mean, or will she have——"

"Dilsey," Mrs Compson said on the stairs.

"Is which?" Dilsey said. "Whyn't you let——"

"The key," Jason said. "To that room. Does she carry it with her all the time. Mother." Then he saw Mrs Compson and he went down the stairs and met her. "Give me the key," he said. He fell to pawing at the pockets of the rusty black dressing sacque she wore. She resisted.

"Jason," she said. "Jason! Are you and Dilsey trying to put me to bed again?" she said, trying to fend him off. "Cant you even let me have Sunday in peace?"

"The key," Jason said, pawing at her. "Give it here." He looked back at the door, as if he expected it to fly open before he could get back to it with the key he did not yet have.

"You, Dilsey!" Mrs Compson said, clutching her sacque about her.

"Give me the key, you old fool!" Jason cried suddenly. From her pocket he tugged a huge bunch of rusted keys on an iron ring like a mediaeval jailer's and ran back up the hall with the two women behind him.

"You, Jason!" Mrs Compson said. "He will never find the right one," she said. "You know I never let anyone take my keys, Dilsey," she said. She began to wail.

"Hush," Dilsey said. "He aint gwine do nothin to her. I aint gwine let him."

"But on Sunday morning, in my own house," Mrs Compson said. "When I've tried so hard to raise them christians. Let me find the right key, Jason," she said. She put her hand on his arm. Then she began to struggle with him, but he flung her aside with a motion of his elbow and looked around at her for a moment, his eyes cold and harried, then he turned to the door again and the unwieldy keys.

"Hush," Dilsey said. "You, Jason!"

"Something terrible has happened," Mrs Compson said, wailing again. "I know it has. You, Jason," she said, grasping at him again. "He wont even let me find the key to a room in my own house!"

"Now, now," Dilsey said. "Whut kin happen? I right here. I aint gwine let him hurt her. Quentin," she said, raising her voice, "dont you be skeered, honey, I'se right here."

The door opened, swung inward. He stood in it for a moment, hiding the room, then he stepped aside. "Go in," he said in a thick, light voice. They went in. It was not a girl's room. It was not anybody's room, and the faint scent of cheap cosmetics and the few feminine objects and the other evidences of crude and hopeless efforts to feminise it but added to its anonymity, giving it that dead and stereotyped transience of rooms in assignation houses. The bed had not been disturbed. On the floor lay a soiled undergarment of cheap silk a little too pink, from a half open bureau drawer dangled a single stocking. The window was open. A pear tree grew there, close against the house. It was in bloom and the branches scraped and rasped against the house and the myriad air, driving in the window, brought into the room the forlorn scent of the blossoms.

"Dar now," Dilsey said. "Didn't I told you she all right?"

"All right?" Mrs Compson said. Dilsey followed her into the room and touched her.

"You come on and lay down, now," she said. "I find her in ten minutes."

Mrs Compson shook her off. "Find the note," she said. "Quentin left a note when he did it."

"All right," Dilsey said. "I'll find hit. You come on to yo room, now."

"I knew the minute they named her Quentin this would

happen," Mrs Compson said. She went to the bureau and began to turn over the scattered objects there—scent bottles, a box of powder, a chewed pencil, a pair of scissors with one broken blade lying upon a darned scarf dusted with powder and stained with rouge. "Find the note," she said.

"I is," Dilsey said. "You come on, now. Me and Jason'll find hit. You come on to yo room."

"Jason," Mrs Compson said. "Where is he?" She went to the door. Dilsey followed her on down the hall, to another door. It was closed. "Jason," she called through the door. There was no answer. She tried the knob, then she called him again. But there was still no answer, for he was hurling things backward out of the closet, garments, shoes, a suitcase. Then he emerged carrying a sawn section of tongue-and-groove planking and laid it down and entered the closet again and emerged with a metal box. He set it on the bed and stood looking at the broken lock while he dug a keyring from his pocket and selected a key, and for a time longer he stood with the selected key in his hand, looking at the broken lock. Then he put the keys back in his pocket and carefully tilted the contents of the box out upon the bed. Still carefully he sorted the papers, taking them up one at a time and shaking them. Then he upended the box and shook it too and slowly replaced the papers and stood again, looking at the broken lock, with the box in his hands and his head bent. Outside the window he heard some jaybirds swirl shrieking past and away, their cries whipping away along the wind, and an automobile passed somewhere and died away also. His mother spoke his name again beyond the door, but he didn't move. He heard Dilsey lead her away up the hall, and then a door closed. Then he replaced the box in the closet and flung the garments back into it and went down stairs to the telephone. While he stood there with the receiver to his ear waiting Dilsey came down the stairs. She looked at him, without stopping, and went on.

The wire opened. "This is Jason Compson," he said, his voice so harsh and thick that he had to repeat himself. "Jason Compson," he said, controlling his voice. "Have a car ready, with a deputy, if you cant go, in ten minutes. I'll be there—— What? —— Robbery. My house. I know who it—— Robbery, I say. Have a car read—— What? Aren't you a paid law enforcement—— Yes, I'll be there in five minutes. Have that car ready to leave at once. If you dont, I'll report it to the governor."

He clapped the receiver back and crossed the diningroom, where the scarce broken meal lay cold now on the table, and entered the kitchen. Dilsey was filling the hot water bottle. Ben sat, tranquil and empty. Beside him Luster looked like a fice dog, brightly watchful. He was eating something. Jason went on across the kitchen.

"Aint you going to eat no breakfast?" Dilsey said. He paid her no attention. "Go on en eat yo breakfast, Jason." He went on. The outer door banged behind him. Luster rose and went to the window and looked out.

"Whoo," he said. "Whut happenin up dar? He been beatin Miss Quentin?"

"You hush yo mouf," Dilsey said. "You git Benjy started now en I beat yo head off. You keep him quiet es you kin twell I git back, now." She screwed the cap on the bottle and went out. They heard her go up the stairs, then they heard Jason pass the house in his car. Then there was no sound in the kitchen save the simmering murmur of the kettle and the clock.

"You know whut I bet?" Luster said. "I bet he beat her. I bet he knock her in de head en now he gone fer de doctor. Dat's whut I bet." The clock tick-tocked, solemn and profound. It might have been the dry pulse of the decaying house itself, after a while it whirred and cleared its throat and struck six times. Ben looked up at it, then he looked at the bulletlike silhouette of Luster's head in the window and he begun to bob his head again, drooling. He whimpered.

"Hush up, looney," Luster said without turning. "Look like we aint gwine git to go to no church today." But Ben sat in the chair, his big soft hands dangling between his knees, moaning faintly. Suddenly he wept, a slow bellowing sound, meaningless and sustained. "Hush," Luster said. He turned and lifted his hand. "You want me to whup you?" But Ben looked at him, bellowing slowly with each expiration. Luster came and shook him. "You hush dis minute!" he shouted. "Here," he said. He hauled Ben out of the chair and dragged the chair around facing the stove and opened the door to the firebox and shoved Ben into the chair. They looked like a tug nudging at a clumsy tanker in a narrow dock. Ben sat down again facing the rosy door. He hushed. Then they heard the clock again, and Dilsey slow on the stairs. When she entered he began to whimper again. Then he lifted his voice.

"Whut you done to him?" Dilsey said. "Why cant you let him lone dis mawnin, of all times?"

"I aint doin nothin to him," Luster said. "Mr Jason skeered him, dat's whut hit is. He aint kilt Miss Quentin, is he?"

"Hush, Benjy," Dilsey said. He hushed. She went to the window and looked out. "Is it quit rainin?" she said.

"Yessum," Luster said. "Quit long time ago."

"Den y'all go out do's a while," she said. "I jes got Miss Cahline quiet now."

"Is we gwine to church?" Luster said.

"I let you know bout dat when de time come. You keep him away fum de house twell I calls you."

"Kin we go to de pastuh?" Luster said.

"All right. Only you keep him away fum de house. I done stood all I kin."

"Yessum," Luster said. "Whar Mr Jason gone, mammy?"

"Dat's some mo of yo business, aint it?" Dilsey said. She began to clear the table. "Hush, Benjy. Luster gwine take you out to play."

"Whut he done to Miss Quentin, mammy?" Luster said.

"Aint done nothin to her. You all git on outen here."

"I bet she aint here," Luster said.

Dilsey looked at him. "How you know she aint here?"

"Me and Benjy seed her clamb out de window last night. Didn't us, Benjy?"

"You did?" Dilsey said, looking at him.

"We sees her doin hit ev'y night," Luster said. "Clamb right down dat pear tree."

"Dont you lie to me, nigger boy," Dilsey said.

"I aint lyin. Ask Benjy ef I is."

"Whyn't you say somethin about it, den?"

" 'Twarn't none o my business," Luster said. "I aint gwine git mixed up in white folks' business. Come on here, Benjy, les go out do's."

They went out. Dilsey stood for a while at the table, then she went and cleared the breakfast things from the diningroom and ate her breakfast and cleaned up the kitchen. Then she removed her apron and hung it up and went to the foot of the stairs and listened for a moment. There was no sound. She donned the overcoat and the hat and went across to her cabin.

The rain had stopped. The air now drove out of the southeast, broken overhead into blue patches. Upon the crest of a hill beyond the trees and roofs and spires of town sunlight lay like a pale scrap of cloth, was blotted away. Upon the air a bell came, then as if at a signal, other bells took up the sound and repeated it.

The cabin door opened and Dilsey emerged, again in the maroon cape and the purple gown, and wearing soiled white elbow-length gloves and minus her headcloth now. She came into the yard and called Luster. She waited a while, then she went to the house and around it to the cellar door, moving close to the wall, and looked into the door. Ben sat on the steps. Before him Luster squatted on the damp floor. He held a saw in his left hand, the blade sprung a little by pressure of his hand, and he was in the act of striking the blade with the worn wooden mallet with which she had been making beaten biscuit for more than thirty years. The saw gave forth a single sluggish twang that ceased with lifeless alacrity, leaving the blade in a thin clean curve between Luster's hand and the floor. Still, inscrutable, it bellied.

"Dat's de way he done hit," Luster said. "I jes aint foun de right thing to hit it wid."

"Dat's whut you doin, is it?" Dilsey said. "Bring me dat mallet," she said.

"I aint hurt hit," Luster said.

"Bring hit here," Dilsey said. "Put dat saw whar you got hit first."

He put the saw away and brought the mallet to her. Then Ben wailed again, hopeless and prolonged. It was nothing. Just sound. It might have been all time and injustice and sorrow become vocal for an instant by a conjunction of planets.

"Listen at him," Luster said. "He been gwine on dat way ev'y since you sont us outen de house. I dont know whut got in to him dis mawnin."

"Bring him here," Dilsey said.

"Come on, Benjy," Luster said. He went back down the steps and took Ben's arm. He came obediently, wailing, that slow hoarse sound that ships make, that seems to begin before the sound itself has started, seems to cease before the sound itself has stopped.

"Run and git his cap," Dilsey said. "Dont make no noise Miss Cahline kin hear. Hurry, now. We already late."

"She gwine hear him anyhow, ef you dont stop him," Luster said.

"He stop when we git off de place," Dilsey said. "He smellin hit. Dat's whut hit is."

"Smell whut, mammy?" Luster said.

"You go git dat cap," Dilsey said. Luster went on. They stood in the cellar door, Ben one step below her. The sky was broken now into scudding patches that dragged their swift shadows up out of the shabby garden, over the broken fence and across the yard. Dilsey stroked Ben's head, slowly and steadily, smoothing the bang upon his brow. He wailed quietly, unhurriedly. "Hush," Dilsey said. "Hush, now. We be gone in a minute. Hush, now." He wailed quietly and steadily.

Luster returned, wearing a stiff new straw hat with a colored band and carrying a cloth cap. The hat seemed to isolate Luster's skull, in the beholder's eye as a spotlight would, in all its individual planes and angles. So peculiarly individual was its shape that at first glance the hat appeared to be on the head of someone standing immediately behind Luster. Dilsey looked at the hat.

"Whyn't you wear yo old hat?" she said.

"Couldn't find hit," Luster said.

"I bet you couldn't. I bet you fixed hit last night so you couldn't find hit. You fixin to ruin dat un."

"Aw, mammy," Luster said. "Hit aint gwine rain."

"How you know? You go git dat old hat en put dat new un away."

"Aw, mammy."

"Den you go git de umbreller."

"Aw, mammy."

"Take yo choice," Dilsey said. "Git yo old hat, er de umbreller. I dont keer which."

Luster went to the cabin. Ben wailed quietly.

"Come on," Dilsey said. "Dey kin ketch up wid us. We gwine to hear de singin." They went around the house, toward the gate. "Hush," Dilsey said from time to time as they went down the drive. They reached the gate. Dilsey opened it. Luster was coming down the drive behind them, carrying the umbrella. A woman was with him. "Here dey come," Dilsey said. They passed out the gate. "Now, den," she said. Ben ceased. Luster and his mother overtook them. Frony wore a dress of bright blue silk and a flowered hat. She was a thin woman, with a flat, pleasant face.

"You got six weeks' work right dar on yo back," Dilsey said. "Whut you gwine do ef hit rain?"

"Git wet, I reckon," Frony said. "I aint never stopped no rain yit."

"Mammy always talkin bout hit gwine rain," Luster said.

"Ef I dont worry bout y'all, I dont know who is," Dilsey said. "Come on, we already late."

"Rev'un Shegog gwine preach today," Frony said.

"Is?" Dilsey said. "Who him?"

"He fum Saint Looey," Frony said. "Dat big preacher."

"Huh," Dilsey said. "Whut dey needs is a man kin put de fear of God into dese here triflin young niggers."

"Rev'un Shegog kin do dat," Frony said. "So dey tells."

They went on along the street. Along its quiet length white people in bright clumps moved churchward, under the windy bells, walking now and then in the random and tentative sun. The wind was gusty, out of the southeast, chill and raw after the warm days.

"I wish you wouldn't keep on bringin him to church, mammy," Frony said. "Folks talkin."

"Whut folks?" Dilsey said.

"I hears em," Frony said.

"And I knows whut kind of folks," Dilsey said. "Trash white folks. Dat's who it is. Thinks he aint good enough fer white church, but nigger church aint good enough fer him."

"Dey talks, jes de same," Frony said.

"Den you send um to me," Dilsey said. "Tell um de good Lawd dont keer whether he bright er not. Dont nobody but white trash keer dat."

A street turned off at right angles, descending, and became a dirt road. On either hand the land dropped more sharply; a broad flat dotted with small cabins whose weathered roofs were on a level with the crown of the road. They were set in small grassless plots littered with broken things, bricks, planks, crockery, things of a once utilitarian value. What growth there was consisted of rank weeds and the trees were mulberries and locusts and sycamores—trees that partook also of the foul desiccation which surrounded the houses; trees whose very burgeoning seemed to be the sad and stubborn remnant of September, as if even spring had passed them by, leaving them to feed upon the rich and unmistakable smell of negroes in which they grew.

From the doors negroes spoke to them as they passed, to Dilsey usually:

"Sis' Gibson! How you dis mawnin?"

"I'm well. Is you well?"

"I'm right well, I thank you."

They emerged from the cabins and struggled up the shaling levee to the road—men in staid, hard brown or black, with gold watch chains and now and then a stick; young men in cheap violent blues or stripes and swaggering hats; women a little stiffly sibilant, and children in garments bought second hand of white people, who looked at Ben with the covertness of nocturnal animals:

"I bet you wont go up en tech him."

"How come I wont?"

"I bet you wont. I bet you skeered to."

"He wont hurt folks. He des a looney."

"How come a looney wont hurt folks?"

"Dat un wont. I teched him."

"I bet you wont now."

"Case Miss Dilsey lookin."

"You wont no ways."

"He dont hurt folks. He des a looney."

And steadily the older people speaking to Dilsey, though, unless they were quite old, Dilsey permitted Frony to respond.

"Mammy aint feelin well dis mawnin."

"Dat's too bad. But Rev'un Shegog'll kyo dat. He'll give her de comfort en de unburdenin."

The road rose again, to a scene like a painted backdrop. Notched into a cut of red clay crowned with oaks the road appeared to stop short off, like a cut ribbon. Beside it a weathered church lifted its crazy steeple like a painted church, and the whole scene was as flat and without perspective as a painted cardboard set upon the ultimate edge of the flat earth, against the windy sunlight of space and April and a midmorning filled with bells. Toward the church they thronged with slow sabbath deliberation, the women and children went on in, the men stopped outside and talked in quiet groups until the bell ceased ringing. Then they too entered.

The church had been decorated, with sparse flowers from kitchen gardens and hedgerows, and with streamers of colored crepe paper. Above the pulpit hung a battered Christmas bell, the accordion sort that collapses. The pulpit was empty, though the choir was already in place, fanning themselves although it was not warm.

Most of the women were gathered on one side of the room. They were talking. Then the bell struck one time and they dispersed to their seats and the congregation sat for an instant, expectant. The bell struck again one time. The choir rose and began to sing and the congregation turned its head as one as six small children—four girls with tight pigtails bound with small scraps of cloth like butterflies, and two boys with close napped heads—entered and marched up the aisle, strung together in a harness of white ribbons and flowers, and followed by two men in single file. The second man was huge, of a light coffee color, imposing in a frock coat and white tie. His head was magisterial and profound, his neck rolled above his collar in rich folds. But he was familiar to them, and so the heads were still reverted when he had passed, and it was not until the choir ceased singing that they realised that the visiting clergyman had already entered, and when they saw the man who had preceded their minister enter the pulpit still ahead of him an indescribable sound went up, a sigh, a sound of astonishment and disappointment.

The visitor was undersized, in a shabby alpaca coat. He had a wizened black face like a small, aged monkey. And all the while that the choir sang again and while the six children rose and sang in thin, frightened, tuneless whispers, they watched the insignificant looking man sitting dwarfed and countrified by the minister's imposing bulk, with something like consternation. They were still looking at him with consternation and unbelief when the minister rose and introduced him in rich, rolling tones whose very unction served to increase the visitor's insignificance.

"En dey brung dat all de way fum Saint Looey," Frony whispered.

"I've knowed de Lawd to use cuiser tools dan dat," Dilsey said. "Hush, now," she said to Ben. "Dey fixin to sing again in a minute."

When the visitor rose to speak he sounded like a white man. His voice was level and cold. It sounded too big to have come from him and they listened at first through curiosity, as they would have to a monkey talking. They began to watch him as they would a man on a tight rope. They even forgot his insignificant appearance in the virtuosity with which he ran and poised and swooped upon the cold inflectionless wire of his voice, so that at last, when with a sort of swooping glide he came to rest again beside the reading desk with one arm resting upon it at shoulder height and his monkey body as reft of all motion as a mummy or an emptied vessel, the congregation sighed as if it waked from a collective dream and moved a little in its seats. Behind the pulpit the choir fanned steadily. Dilsey whispered, "Hush, now. Dey fixin to sing in a minute."

Then a voice said, "Brethren."

The preacher had not moved. His arm lay yet across the desk, and he still held that pose while the voice died in sonorous echoes between the walls. It was as different as day and dark from his former tone, with a sad, timbrous quality like an alto horn, sinking into their hearts and speaking there again when it had ceased in fading and cumulate echoes.

"Brethren and sisteren," it said again. The preacher removed his arm and he began to walk back and forth before the desk, his hands clasped behind him, a meagre figure, hunched over upon itself like that of one long immured in striving with the implacable earth, "I got the recollection and the blood of the Lamb!" He tramped steadily back and forth beneath the twisted paper and the Christmas bell, hunched, his hands clasped behind him. He was like a worn small rock whelmed by the successive waves of his voice. With his body he seemed to feed the voice that, succubus like, had fleshed its teeth in him. And the congregation seemed to watch with its own eyes while the voice consumed him, until he was nothing and they were nothing and there was not even a voice but instead their hearts were speaking to one another in chanting measures beyond the need for words, so that when he came to rest against the reading desk, his monkey face lifted and his whole attitude that of a serene, tortured crucifix that transcended its shabbiness and insignificance and made it of no moment, a long moaning expulsion of breath rose from them, and a woman's single soprano: "Yes, Jesus!"

As the scudding day passed overhead the dingy windows glowed and faded in ghostly retrograde. A car passed along the road outside, laboring in the sand, died away. Dilsey sat bolt upright, her hand on Ben's knee. Two tears slid down her fallen cheeks, in and out of the myriad coruscations of immolation and abnegation and time.

"Brethren," the minister said in a harsh whisper, without moving.

"Yes, Jesus!" the woman's voice said, hushed yet.

"Breddren en sistuhn!" His voice rang again, with the horns. He removed his arm and stood erect and raised his hands. "I got de ricklickshun en de blood of de Lamb!" They did not mark just when his intonation, his pronunciation, became negroid, they just sat swaying a little in their seats as the voice took them into itself.

"When de long, cold—— Oh, I tells you, breddren, when de long, cold. . . . . . . I sees de light en I sees de word, po sinner! Dey passed away in Egypt, de swingin chariots; de generations passed away. Wus a rich man: whar he now, O breddren? Wus a po man: whar he now, O sistuhn? Oh I tells you, ef you aint got de milk en de dew of de old salvation when de long, cold years rolls away!"

"Yes, Jesus!"

"I tells you, breddren, en I tells you, sistuhn, dey'll come a time. Po sinner sayin Let me lay down wid de Lawd, lemme lay down my load. Den whut Jesus gwine say, O breddren? O sistuhn? Is you got de ricklickshun en de Blood of de Lamb? Case I aint gwine load down heaven!"

He fumbled in his coat and took out a handkerchief and mopped his face. A low concerted sound rose from the congregation: "Mmmmmmmmmmmmmm!" The woman's voice said, "Yes, Jesus! Jesus!"

"Breddren! Look at dem little chillen settin dar. Jesus wus like dat once. He mammy suffered de glory en de pangs. Sometime maybe she helt him at de nightfall, whilst de angels singin him to sleep; maybe she look out de do en see de Roman po-lice passin." He tramped back and forth, mopping his face. "Listen, breddren! I sees de day. Ma'y settin in de do wid Jesus on her lap, de little Jesus. Like dem chillen dar, de little Jesus. I hears de angels singin de peaceful songs en de glory; I sees de closin eyes; sees Mary jump up, sees de sojer face: We gwine to kill! We gwine to kill! We gwine to kill yo little Jesus! I hears de weepin en de lamentation of de po mammy widout de salvation en de word of God!"

"Mmmmmmmmmmmmmmmmmm! Jesus! Little Jesus!" and another voice, rising:

"I sees, O Jesus! Oh I sees!" and still another, without words, like bubbles rising in water.

"I sees hit, breddren! I sees hit! Sees de blastin, blindin sight! I sees Calvary, wid de sacred trees, sees de thief en de murderer en de least of dese; I hears de boastin en de braggin: Ef you be Jesus, lif up yo tree en walk! I hears de wailin of women en de evenin lamentations; I hears de weepin en de cryin en de turntaway face of God: dey done kilt Jesus; dey done kilt my Son!"

"Mmmmmmmmmmmmmmmm. Jesus! I sees, O Jesus!"

"O blind sinner! Breddren, I tells you; sistuhn, I says to you, when de Lawd did turn His mighty face, say, Aint gwine overload heaven! I can see de widowed God shet His do; I sees de whelmin flood roll between; I sees de darkness en de death everlastin upon de generations. Den, lo! Breddren! Yes, breddren! Whut I see? Whut I see, O sinner? I sees de resurrection en de light; sees de meek Jesus sayin Dey kilt me dat ye shall live again; I died dat dem whut sees en believes shall never die. Breddren, O breddren! I sees de doom crack en de golden horns shoutin down de glory, en de arisen dead whut got de blood en de ricklickshun of de Lamb!"

In the midst of the voices and the hands Ben sat, rapt in his sweet blue gaze. Dilsey sat bolt upright beside, crying rigidly and quietly in the annealment and the blood of the remembered Lamb.

As they walked through the bright noon, up the sandy road with the dispersing congregation talking easily again group to group, she continued to weep, unmindful of the talk.

"He sho a preacher, mon! He didn't look like much at first, but hush!"

"He seed de power en de glory."

"Yes, suh. He seed hit. Face to face he seed hit."

Dilsey made no sound, her face did not quiver as the tears took their sunken and devious courses, walking with her head up, making no effort to dry them away even.

"Whyn't you quit dat, mammy?" Frony said. "Wid all dese people lookin. We be passin white folks soon."

"I've seed de first en de last," Dilsey said. "Never you mind me."

"First en last whut?" Frony said.

"Never you mind," Dilsey said. "I seed de beginnin, en now I sees de endin."

Before they reached the street though she stopped and lifted her skirt and dried her eyes on the hem of her topmost underskirt. Then they went on. Ben shambled along beside Dilsey, watching Luster who anticked along ahead, the umbrella in his hand and his new straw hat slanted viciously in the sunlight, like a big foolish dog watching a small clever one. They reached the gate and entered. Immediately Ben began to whimper again, and for a while all of them looked up the drive at the square, paintless house with its rotting portico.

"Whut's gwine on up dar today?" Frony said. "Somethin is."

"Nothin," Dilsey said. "You tend to yo business en let de whitefolks tend to deir'n."

"Somethin is," Frony said. "I heard him first thing dis mawnin. 'Taint none of my business, dough."

"En I knows whut, too," Luster said.

"You knows mo dan you got any use fer," Dilsey said. "Aint you jes heard Frony say hit aint none of yo business? You take Benjy on to de back and keep him quiet twell I put dinner on."

"I knows whar Miss Quentin is," Luster said.

"Den jes keep hit," Dilsey said. "Soon es Quentin need any

of yo egvice, I'll let you know. Y'all g'awn en play in de back, now."

"You know whut gwine happen soon es dey start playin dat ball over yonder," Luster said.

"Dey wont start fer a while yit. By dat time T. P. be here to take him ridin. Here, you gimme dat new hat."

Luster gave her the hat and he and Ben went on across the back yard. Ben was still whimpering, though not loud. Dilsey and Frony went to the cabin. After a while Dilsey emerged, again in the faded calico dress, and went to the kitchen. The fire had died down. There was no sound in the house. She put on the apron and went up stairs. There was no sound anywhere. Quentin's room was as they had left it. She entered and picked up the undergarment and put the stocking back in the drawer and closed it. Mrs Compson's door was closed. Dilsey stood beside it for a moment, listening. Then she opened it and entered, entered a pervading reek of camphor. The shades were drawn, the room in halflight, and the bed, so that at first she thought Mrs Compson was asleep and was about to close the door when the other spoke.

"Well?" she said. "What is it?"

"Hit's me," Dilsey said. "You want anything?"

Mrs Compson didn't answer. After a while, without moving her head at all, she said: "Where's Jason?"

"He aint come back yit," Dilsey said. "Whut you want?"

Mrs Compson said nothing. Like so many cold, weak people, when faced at last by the incontrovertible disaster she exhumed from somewhere a sort of fortitude, strength. In her case it was an unshakable conviction regarding the yet unplumbed event. "Well," she said presently. "Did you find it?"

"Find whut? Whut you talkin about?"

"The note. At least she would have enough consideration to leave a note. Even Quentin did that."

"Whut you talkin about?" Dilsey said. "Dont you know she all right? I bet she be walkin right in dis do befo dark."

"Fiddlesticks," Mrs Compson said. "It's in the blood. Like uncle, like niece. Or mother. I dont know which would be worse. I dont seem to care."

"Whut you keep on talkin that way fur?" Dilsey said. "Whut she want to do anything like that fur?"

"I dont know. What reason did Quentin have? Under God's heaven what reason did he have? It cant be simply to flout and hurt me. Whoever God is, He would not permit that. I'm a lady. You might not believe that from my offspring, but I am."

"You des wait en see," Dilsey said. "She be here by night, right dar in her bed." Mrs Compson said nothing. The camphor soaked cloth lay upon her brow. The black robe lay across the foot of the bed. Dilsey stood with her hand on the door knob.

"Well," Mrs Compson said. "What do you want? Are you going to fix some dinner for Jason and Benjamin, or not?"

"Jason aint come yit," Dilsey said. "I gwine fix somethin. You sho you dont want nothin? Yo bottle still hot enough?"

"You might hand me my bible."

"I give hit to you dis mawnin, befo I left."

"You laid it on the edge of the bed. How long did you expect it to stay there?"

Dilsey crossed to the bed and groped among the shadows beneath the edge of it and found the bible, face down. She smoothed the bent pages and laid the book on the bed again. Mrs Compson didn't open her eyes. Her hair and the pillow were the same color, beneath the wimple of the medicated cloth she looked like an old nun praying. "Dont put it there again," she said, without opening her eyes. "That's where you put it before. Do you want me to have to get out of bed to pick it up?"

Dilsey reached the book across her and laid it on the broad side of the bed. "You cant see to read, noways," she said. "You want me to raise de shade a little?"

"No. Let them alone. Go on and fix Jason something to eat."

Dilsey went out. She closed the door and returned to the kitchen. The stove was almost cold. While she stood there the clock above the cupboard struck ten times. "One oclock," she said aloud. "Jason aint comin home. Ise seed de first en de last," she said, looking at the cold stove. "I seed de first en de last." She set out some cold food on a table. As she moved back and forth she sang, a hymn. She sang the first two lines over and over to the complete tune. She arranged the meal and went to the door and called Luster, and after a time Luster and Ben entered. Ben was still moaning a little, as to himself.

"He aint never quit," Luster said.

"Y'all come on en eat," Dilsey said. "Jason aint comin to dinner." They sat down at the table. Ben could manage solid food pretty well for himself, though even now, with cold food before him, Dilsey tied a cloth about his neck. He and Luster ate. Dilsey moved about the kitchen, singing the two lines of the hymn which she remembered. "Y'all kin g'awn en eat," she said. "Jason aint comin home."

He was twenty miles away at that time. When he left the house he drove rapidly to town, overreaching the slow sabbath groups and the peremptory bells along the broken air. He crossed the empty square and turned into a narrow street that was abruptly quieter even yet, and stopped before a frame house and went up the flower bordered walk to the porch.

Beyond the screen door people were talking. As he lifted his hand to knock he heard steps, so he withheld his hand until a big man in black broadcloth trousers and a stiff bosomed white shirt without collar opened the door. He had vigorous untidy iron-gray hair and his gray eyes were round and shiny like a little boy's. He took Jason's hand and drew him into the house, still shaking it.

"Come right in," he said. "Come right in."

"You ready to go now?" Jason said.

"Walk right in," the other said, propelling him by the elbow into a room where a man and a woman sat. "You know Myrtle's husband, dont you? Jason Compson, Vernon."

"Yes," Jason said. He did not even look at the man, and as the sheriff drew a chair across the room the man said,

"We'll go out so you can talk. Come on, Myrtle."

"No, no," the sheriff said. "You folks keep your seat. I reckon it aint that serious, Jason? Have a seat."

"I'll tell you as we go along," Jason said. "Get your hat and coat."

"We'll go out," the man said, rising.

"Keep your seat," the sheriff said. "Me and Jason will go out on the porch."

"You get your hat and coat," Jason said. "They've already got a twelve hour start." The sheriff led the way back to the porch. A man and a woman passing spoke to him. He responded with a hearty florid gesture. Bells were still ringing,

from the direction of the section known as Nigger Hollow.
"Get your hat, Sheriff," Jason said. The sheriff drew up two
chairs.

"Have a seat and tell me what the trouble is."

"I told you over the phone," Jason said, standing. "I did
that to save time. Am I going to have to go to law to compel
you to do your sworn duty?"

"You sit down and tell me about it," the sheriff said. "I'll
take care of you all right."

"Care, hell," Jason said. "Is this what you call taking care
of me?"

"You're the one that's holding us up," the sheriff said. "You
sit down and tell me about it."

Jason told him, his sense of injury and impotence feeding
upon its own sound, so that after a time he forgot his haste in
the violent cumulation of his self justification and his outrage.
The sheriff watched him steadily with his cold shiny eyes.

"But you dont know they done it," he said. "You just
think so."

"Dont know?" Jason said. "When I spent two damn days
chasing her through alleys, trying to keep her away from him,
after I told her what I'd do to her if I ever caught her with
him, and you say I dont know that that little b——"

"Now, then," the sheriff said. "That'll do. That's enough of
that." He looked out across the street, his hands in his pockets.

"And when I come to you, a commissioned officer of the
law," Jason said.

"That show's in Mottson this week," the sheriff said.

"Yes," Jason said. "And if I could find a law officer that gave
a solitary damn about protecting the people that elected him
to office, I'd be there too by now." He repeated his story,
harshly recapitulant, seeming to get an actual pleasure out of
his outrage and impotence. The sheriff did not appear to be
listening at all.

"Jason," he said. "What were you doing with three thousand dollars hid in the house?"

"What?" Jason said. "That's my business where I keep my
money. Your business is to help me get it back."

"Did your mother know you had that much on the place?"

"Look here," Jason said. "My house has been robbed. I

know who did it and I know where they are. I come to you as the commissioned officer of the law, and I ask you once more, are you going to make any effort to recover my property, or not?"

"What do you aim to do with that girl, if you catch them?"

"Nothing," Jason said. "Not anything. I wouldn't lay my hand on her. The bitch that cost me a job, the one chance I ever had to get ahead, that killed my father and is shortening my mother's life every day and made my name a laughing stock in the town. I wont do anything to her," he said. "Not anything."

"You drove that girl into running off, Jason," the sheriff said.

"How I conduct my family is no business of yours," Jason said. "Are you going to help me or not?"

"You drove her away from home," the sheriff said. "And I have some suspicions about who that money belongs to that I dont reckon I'll ever know for certain."

Jason stood, slowly wringing the brim of his hat in his hands. He said quietly: "You're not going to make any effort to catch them for me?"

"That's not any of my business, Jason. If you had any actual proof, I'd have to act. But without that I dont figger it's any of my business."

"That's your answer, is it?" Jason said. "Think well, now."

"That's it, Jason."

"All right," Jason said. He put his hat on. "You'll regret this. I wont be helpless. This is not Russia, where just because he wears a little metal badge, a man is immune to law." He went down the steps and got in his car and started the engine. The sheriff watched him drive away, turn, and rush past the house toward town.

The bells were ringing again, high in the scudding sunlight in bright disorderly tatters of sound. He stopped at a filling station and had his tires examined and the tank filled.

"Gwine on a trip, is you?" the negro asked him. He didn't answer. "Look like hit gwine fair off, after all," the negro said.

"Fair off, hell," Jason said. "It'll be raining like hell by twelve oclock." He looked at the sky, thinking about rain, about the slick clay roads, himself stalled somewhere miles from town. He thought about it with a sort of triumph, of the fact that he was going to miss dinner, that by starting now and so serving his compulsion of haste, he would be at the greatest possible distance from both towns when noon came. It seemed to him that in this circumstance was giving him a break, so he said to the negro:

"What the hell are you doing? Has somebody paid you to keep this car standing here as long as you can?"

"Dis here ti' aint got no air a-tall in hit," the negro said.

"Then get the hell away from there and let me have that tube," Jason said.

"Hit up now," the negro said, rising. "You kin ride now."

Jason got in and started the engine and drove off. He went into second gear, the engine spluttering and gasping, and he raced the engine, jamming the throttle down and snapping the choker in and out savagely. "It's going to rain," he said. "Get me half way there, and rain like hell." And he drove on out of the bells and out of town, thinking of himself slogging through the mud, hunting a team. "And every damn one of them will be at church." He thought of how he'd find a church at last and take a team and of the owner coming out, shouting at him and of himself striking the man down. "I'm Jason Compson. See if you can stop me. See if you can elect a man to office that can stop me," he said, thinking of himself entering the courthouse with a file of soldiers and dragging the sheriff out. "Thinks he can sit with his hands folded and see me lose my job. I'll show him about jobs." Of his niece he did not think at all, nor of the arbitrary valuation of the money. Neither of them had had entity or individuality for him for ten years; together they merely symbolised the job in the bank of which he had been deprived before he ever got it.

The air brightened, the running shadow patches were now the obverse, and it seemed to him that the fact that the day was clearing was another cunning stroke on the part of the foe, the fresh battle toward which he was carrying ancient wounds. From time to time he passed churches, unpainted frame buildings with sheet iron steeples, surrounded by tethered teams and shabby motorcars, and it seemed to him that each of them was a picket-post where the rear guards of Circumstance peeped fleetingly back at him. "And damn You, too," he said. "See if You can stop me," thinking of himself, his file of soldiers with the manacled sheriff in the rear, dragging Omnipotence down from his throne, if necessary; of the embattled legions of both hell and heaven through which he tore his way and put his hands at last on his fleeing niece.

The wind was out of the southeast. It blew steadily upon his cheek. It seemed that he could feel the prolonged blow of it sinking through his skull, and suddenly with an old premonition he clapped the brakes on and stopped and sat perfectly still. Then he lifted his hand to his neck and began to curse, and sat there, cursing in a harsh whisper. When it was necessary for him to drive for any length of time he fortified himself with a handkerchief soaked in camphor, which he would tie about his throat when clear of town, thus inhaling the fumes, and he got out and lifted the seat cushion on the chance that there might be a forgotten one there. He looked beneath both seats and stood again for a while, cursing, seeing himself mocked by his own triumphing. He closed his eyes, leaning on the door. He could return and get the forgotten camphor, or he could go on. In either case, his head would be splitting, but at home he could be sure of finding camphor on Sunday, while if he went on he could not be sure. But if he went back, he would be an hour and a half later in reaching Mottson. "Maybe I can drive slow," he said. "Maybe I can drive slow, thinking of something else. . . . . . ."

He got in and started. "I'll think of something else," he said, so he thought about Lorraine. He imagined himself in bed with her, only he was just lying beside her, pleading with her to help him, then he thought of the money again, and that he had been outwitted by a woman, a girl. If he could just believe it was the man who had robbed him. But to have been robbed of that which was to have compensated him for the lost job, which he had acquired through so much effort and risk, by the very symbol of the lost job itself, and worst of all, by a bitch of a girl. He drove on, shielding his face from the steady wind with the corner of his coat.

He could see the opposed forces of his destiny and his will drawing swiftly together now, toward a junction that would be irrevocable; he became cunning. I cant make a blunder, he told himself. There would be just one right thing, without alternatives: he must do that. He believed that both of them would know him on sight, while he'd have to trust to seeing her first, unless the man still wore the red tie. And the fact that he must depend on that red tie seemed to be the sum of the impending disaster; he could almost smell it, feel it above the throbbing of his head.

He crested the final hill. Smoke lay in the valley, and roofs, a spire or two above trees. He drove down the hill and into the town, slowing, telling himself again of the need for caution, to find where the tent was located first. He could not see very well now, and he knew that it was the disaster which kept telling him to go directly and get something for his head. At a filling station they told him that the tent was not up yet, but that the show cars were on a siding at the station. He drove there.

Two gaudily painted pullman cars stood on the track. He reconnoitred them before he got out. He was trying to breathe shallowly, so that the blood would not beat so in his skull. He got out and went along the station wall, watching the cars. A few garments hung out of the windows, limp and crinkled, as though they had been recently laundered. On the earth beside the steps of one sat three canvas chairs. But he saw no sign of life at all until a man in a dirty apron came to the door and emptied a pan of dishwater with a broad gesture, the sunlight glinting on the metal belly of the pan, then entered the car again.

Now I'll have to take him by surprise, before he can warn them, he thought. It never occurred to him that they might not be there, in the car. That they should not be there, that the whole result should not hinge on whether he saw them first or they saw him first, would be opposed to all nature and contrary to the whole rhythm of events. And more than that: he must see them first, get the money back, then what they did would be of no importance to him, while otherwise the whole world would know that he, Jason Compson, had been robbed by Quentin, his niece, a bitch.

He reconnoitred again. Then he went to the car and mounted the steps, swiftly and quietly, and paused at the door. The galley was dark, rank with stale food. The man was a white blur, singing in a cracked, shaky tenor. An old man, he thought, and not as big as I am. He entered the car as the man looked up.

"Hey?" the man said, stopping his song.

"Where are they?" Jason said. "Quick, now. In the sleeping car?"

"Where's who?" the man said.

"Dont lie to me," Jason said. He blundered on in the cluttered obscurity.

"What's that?" the other said. "Who you calling a liar?" and when Jason grasped his shoulder he exclaimed, "Look out, fellow!"

"Dont lie," Jason said. "Where are they?"

"Why, you bastard," the man said. His arm was frail and thin in Jason's grasp. He tried to wrench free, then he turned and fell to scrabbling on the littered table behind him.

"Come on," Jason said. "Where are they?"

"I'll tell you where they are," the man shrieked. "Lemme find my butcher knife."

"Here," Jason said, trying to hold the other. "I'm just asking you a question."

"You bastard," the other shrieked, scrabbling at the table. Jason tried to grasp him in both arms, trying to prison the puny fury of him. The man's body felt so old, so frail, yet so fatally single-purposed that for the first time Jason saw clear and unshadowed the disaster toward which he rushed.

"Quit it!" he said. "Here. Here! I'll get out. Give me time, and I'll get out."

"Call me a liar," the other wailed. "Lemme go. Lemme go just one minute. I'll show you."

Jason glared wildly about, holding the other. Outside it was now bright and sunny, swift and bright and empty, and he thought of the people soon to be going quietly home to Sunday dinner, decorously festive, and of himself trying to hold the fatal, furious little old man whom he dared not release long enough to turn his back and run.

"Will you quit long enough for me to get out?" he said. "Will you?" But the other still struggled, and Jason freed one hand and struck him on the head. A clumsy, hurried blow, and not hard, but the other slumped immediately and slid clattering among pans and buckets to the floor. Jason stood above him, panting, listening. Then he turned and ran from the car. At the door he restrained himself and descended more slowly and stood there again. His breath made a hah hah hah sound and he stood there trying to repress it, darting his gaze this way and that, when at a scuffling sound behind him he turned in time to see the little old man leaping awkwardly and furiously from the vestibule, a rusty hatchet high in his hand.

He grasped at the hatchet, feeling no shock but knowing that he was falling, thinking So this is how it'll end, and he believed that he was about to die and when something crashed against the back of his head he thought How did he hit me there? Only maybe he hit me a long time ago, he thought, And I just now felt it, and he thought Hurry. Hurry. Get it over with, and then a furious desire not to die seized him and he struggled, hearing the old man wailing and cursing in his cracked voice.

He still struggled when they hauled him to his feet, but they held him and he ceased.

"Am I bleeding much?" he said. "The back of my head. Am I bleeding?" He was still saying that while he felt himself being propelled rapidly away, heard the old man's thin furious voice dying away behind him. "Look at my head," he said. "Wait, I——"

"Wait, hell," the man who held him said. "That damn little wasp'll kill you. Keep going. You aint hurt."

"He hit me," Jason said. "Am I bleeding?"

"Keep going," the other said. He led Jason on around the corner of the station, to the empty platform where an express truck stood, where grass grew rigidly in a plot bordered with rigid flowers and a sign in electric lights: Keep your on Mottson, the gap filled by a human eye with an electric pupil. The man released him.

"Now," he said. "You get on out of here and stay out. What were you trying to do? commit suicide?"

"I was looking for two people," Jason said. "I just asked him where they were."

"Who you looking for?"

"It's a girl," Jason said. "And a man. He had on a red tie in Jefferson yesterday. With this show. They robbed me."

"Oh," the man said. "You're the one, are you. Well, they aint here."

"I reckon so," Jason said. He leaned against the wall and put his hand to the back of his head and looked at his palm. "I thought I was bleeding," he said. "I thought he hit me with that hatchet."

"You hit your head on the rail," the man said. "You better go on. They aint here."

"Yes. He said they were not here. I thought he was lying."

"Do you think I'm lying?" the man said.

"No," Jason said. "I know they're not here."

"I told him to get the hell out of there, both of them," the man said. "I wont have nothing like that in my show. I run a respectable show, with a respectable troupe."

"Yes," Jason said. "You dont know where they went?"

"No. And I dont want to know. No member of my show can pull a stunt like that. You her . . . brother?"

"No," Jason said. "It dont matter. I just wanted to see them. You sure he didn't hit me? No blood, I mean."

"There would have been blood if I hadn't got there when I did. You stay away from here, now. That little bastard'll kill you. That your car yonder?"

"Yes."

"Well, you get in it and go back to Jefferson. If you find them, it wont be in my show. I run a respectable show. You say they robbed you?"

"No," Jason said. "It dont make any difference." He went to the car and got in. What is it I must do? he thought. Then he remembered. He started the engine and drove slowly up the street until he found a drugstore. The door was locked. He stood for a while with his hand on the knob and his head bent a little. Then he turned away and when a man came along after a while he asked if there was a drugstore open anywhere, but there was not. Then he asked when the northbound train ran, and the man told him at two thirty. He crossed the pavement and got in the car again and sat there. After a while two negro lads passed. He called to them.

"Can either of you boys drive a car?"

"Yes, suh."

"What'll you charge to drive me to Jefferson right away?"

They looked at one another, murmuring.

"I'll pay a dollar," Jason said.

They murmured again. "Couldn't go fer dat," one said.

"What will you go for?"

"Kin you go?" one said.

"I cant git off," the other said. "Whyn't you drive him up dar? You aint got nothin to do."

"Yes I is."

"Whut you got to do?"

They murmured again, laughing.

"I'll give you two dollars," Jason said. "Either of you."

"I cant git away neither," the first said.

"All right," Jason said. "Go on."

He sat there for some time. He heard a clock strike the half hour, then people began to pass, in Sunday and easter clothes. Some looked at him as they passed, at the man sitting quietly behind the wheel of a small car, with his invisible life ravelled out about him like a wornout sock, and went on. After a while a negro in overalls came up.

"Is you de one wants to go to Jefferson?" he said.

"Yes," Jason said. "What'll you charge me?"

"Fo dollars."

"Give you two."

"Cant go fer no less'n fo." The man in the car sat quietly. He wasn't even looking at him. The negro said, "You want me er not?"

"All right," Jason said. "Get in."

He moved over and the negro took the wheel. Jason closed his eyes. I can get something for it at Jefferson, he told himself, easing himself to the jolting, I can get something there. They drove on, along the streets where people were turning peacefully into houses and Sunday dinners, and on out of town. He thought that. He wasn't thinking of home, where Ben and Luster were eating cold dinner at the kitchen table. Something—the absence of disaster, threat, in any constant evil—permitted him to forget Jefferson as any place which he had ever seen before, where his life must resume itself.

When Ben and Luster were done Dilsey sent them outdoors.

"And see kin you let him alone twell fo oclock. T. P. be here den."

"Yessum," Luster said. They went out. Dilsey ate her dinner and cleared up the kitchen. Then she went to the foot of the stairs and listened, but there was no sound. She returned through the kitchen and out the outer door and stopped on the steps. Ben and Luster were not in sight, but while she stood there she heard another sluggish twang from the direction of the cellar door and she went to the door and looked down upon a repetition of the morning's scene.

"He done hit jes dat way," Luster said. He contemplated the motionless saw with a kind of hopeful dejection. "I aint got de right thing to hit it wid yit," he said.

"En you aint gwine find hit down here, neither," Dilsey said. "You take him on out in de sun. You bofe get pneumonia down here on dis wet flo."

She waited and watched them cross the yard toward a clump of cedar trees near the fence. Then she went on to her cabin.

"Now, dont you git started," Luster said. "I had enough trouble wid you today." There was a hammock made of barrel staves slatted into woven wires. Luster lay down in the swing, but Ben went on vaguely and purposelessly. He began to whimper again. "Hush, now," Luster said. "I fixin to whup you." He lay back in the swing. Ben had stopped moving, but Luster could hear him whimpering. "Is you gwine hush, er aint you?" Luster said. He got up and followed and came upon Ben squatting before a small mound of earth. At either end of it an empty bottle of blue glass that once contained poison was fixed in the ground. In one was a withered stalk of jimson weed. Ben squatted before it, moaning, a slow, inarticulate sound. Still moaning he sought vaguely about and found a twig and put it in the other bottle. "Whyn't you hush?" Luster said. "You want me to give you somethin to sho nough moan about? Sposin I does dis." He knelt and swept the bottle suddenly up and behind him. Ben ceased moaning. He squatted, looking at the small depression where the bottle had sat, then as he drew his lungs full Luster brought the bottle back into view. "Hush!" he hissed. "Dont you dast to beller! Dont you. Dar hit is. See? Here. You fixin to start ef you stays here. Come on, les go see ef dey started knockin ball yit." He took Ben's arm and drew him up and they went to the fence and stood side by side there, peering between the matted honeysuckle not yet in bloom.

"Dar," Luster said. "Dar come some. See um?"

They watched the foursome play onto the green and out, and move to the tee and drive. Ben watched, whimpering, slobbering. When the foursome went on he followed along the fence, bobbing and moaning. One said,

"Here, caddie. Bring the bag."

"Hush, Benjy," Luster said, but Ben went on at his shambling trot, clinging to the fence, wailing in his hoarse, hopeless voice. The man played and went on, Ben keeping pace with him until the fence turned at right angles, and he clung to the fence, watching the people move on and away.

"Will you hush now?" Luster said. "Will you hush now?" He shook Ben's arm. Ben clung to the fence, wailing steadily and hoarsely. "Aint you gwine stop?" Luster said. "Or is you?" Ben gazed through the fence. "All right, den," Luster said. "You want somethin to beller about?" He looked over his shoulder, toward the house. Then he whispered: "Caddy! Beller now. Caddy! Caddy! Caddy!"

A moment later, in the slow intervals of Ben's voice, Luster heard Dilsey calling. He took Ben by the arm and they crossed the yard toward her.

"I tole you he warn't gwine stay quiet," Luster said.

"You vilyun!" Dilsey said. "Whut you done to him?"

"I aint done nothin. I tole you when dem folks start playin, he git started up."

"You come on here," Dilsey said. "Hush, Benjy. Hush, now." But he wouldn't hush. They crossed the yard quickly and went to the cabin and entered. "Run git dat shoe," Dilsey said. "Dont you sturb Miss Cahline, now. Ef she say anything, tell her I got him. Go on, now; you kin sho do dat right, I reckon." Luster went out. Dilsey led Ben to the bed and drew him down beside her and she held him, rocking back and forth, wiping his drooling mouth upon the hem of her skirt. "Hush, now," she said, stroking his head. "Hush. Dilsey got you." But he bellowed slowly, abjectly, without tears; the grave hopeless sound of all voiceless misery under the sun. Luster returned, carrying a white satin slipper. It was yellow now, and cracked, and soiled, and when they gave it into Ben's hand he hushed for a while. But he still whimpered, and soon he lifted his voice again.

"You reckon you kin find T. P.?" Dilsey said.

"He say yistiddy he gwine out to St John's today. Say he be back at fo.'"

Dilsey rocked back and forth, stroking Ben's head.

"Dis long time, O Jesus," she said. "Dis long time."

"I kin drive dat surrey, mammy," Luster said.

"You kill bofe y'all," Dilsey said. "You do hit fer devilment. I knows you got plenty sense to. But I cant trust you. Hush, now," she said. "Hush. Hush."

"Nome I wont," Luster said. "I drives wid T. P." Dilsey rocked back and forth, holding Ben. "Miss Cahline say ef you cant quiet him, she gwine git up en come down en do hit."

"Hush, honey," Dilsey said, stroking Ben's head. "Luster, honey," she said. "Will you think about yo ole mammy en drive dat surrey right?"

"Yessum," Luster said. "I drive hit jes like T. P."

Dilsey stroked Ben's head, rocking back and forth. "I does de bes I kin," she said. "Lawd knows dat. Go git it, den," she said, rising. Luster scuttled out. Ben held the slipper, crying. "Hush, now. Luster gone to git de surrey en take you to de graveyard. We aint gwine risk gittin yo cap," she said. She went to a closet contrived of a calico curtain hung across a corner of the room and got the felt hat she had worn. "We's down to worse'n dis, ef folks jes knowed," she said. "You's de Lawd's chile, anyway. En I be His'n too, fo long, praise Jesus. Here." She put the hat on his head and buttoned his coat. He wailed steadily. She took the slipper from him and put it away and they went out. Luster came up, with an ancient white horse in a battered and lopsided surrey.

"You gwine be careful, Luster?" she said.

"Yessum," Luster said. She helped Ben into the back seat. He had ceased crying, but now he began to whimper again.

"Hit's his flower," Luster said. "Wait, I'll git him one."

"You set right dar," Dilsey said. She went and took the cheekstrap. "Now, hurry en git him one." Luster ran around the house, toward the garden. He came back with a single narcissus.

"Dat un broke," Dilsey said. "Whyn't you git him a good un?"

"Hit de onliest one I could find," Luster said. "Y'all took all of um Friday to dec'rate de church. Wait, I'll fix hit." So while Dilsey held the horse Luster put a splint on the flower stalk with a twig and two bits of string and gave it to Ben. Then he mounted and took the reins. Dilsey still held the bridle.

"You knows de way now?" she said. "Up de street, round de square, to de graveyard, den straight back home."

"Yessum," Luster said. "Hum up, Queenie."

"You gwine be careful, now?"

"Yessum." Dilsey released the bridle.

"Hum up, Queenie," Luster said.

"Here," Dilsey said. "You han me dat whup."

"Aw, mammy," Luster said.

"Give hit here," Dilsey said, approaching the wheel. Luster gave it to her reluctantly.

"I wont never git Queenie started now."

"Never you mind about dat," Dilsey said. "Queenie know mo bout whar she gwine dan you does. All you got to do es set dar en hold dem reins. You knows de way, now?"

"Yessum. Same way T. P. goes ev'y Sunday."

"Den you do de same thing dis Sunday."

"Cose I is. Aint I drove fer T. P. mo'n a hund'ed times?"

"Den do hit again," Dilsey said. "G'awn, now. En ef you hurts Benjy, nigger boy, I dont know whut I do. You bound fer de chain gang, but I'll send you dar fo even chain gang ready fer you."

"Yessum," Luster said. "Hum up, Queenie."

He flapped the lines on Queenie's broad back and the surrey lurched into motion.

"You, Luster!" Dilsey said.

"Hum up, dar!" Luster said. He flapped the lines again. With subterranean rumblings Queenie jogged slowly down the drive and turned into the street, where Luster exhorted her into a gait resembling a prolonged and suspended fall in a forward direction.

Ben quit whimpering. He sat in the middle of the seat, holding the repaired flower upright in his fist, his eyes serene and ineffable. Directly before him Luster's bullet head turned backward continually until the house passed from view, then he pulled to the side of the street and while Ben watched him he descended and broke a switch from a hedge. Queenie lowered her head and fell to cropping the grass until Luster mounted and hauled her head up and harried her into motion again, then he squared his elbows and with the switch and the reins held high he assumed a swaggering attitude out of all proportion to the sedate clopping of Queenie's hooves and the organlike basso of her internal accompaniment. Motors passed them, and pedestrians; once a group of half grown negroes:

"Dar Luster. Whar you gwine, Luster? To de boneyard?"

"Hi," Luster said. "Aint de same boneyard y'all headed fer. Hum up, elefump."

They approached the square, where the Confederate soldier gazed with empty eyes beneath his marble hand in wind and weather. Luster took still another notch in himself and gave the impervious Queenie a cut with the switch, casting his glance about the square. "Dar Mr Jason car," he said, then he spied another group of negroes. "Les show dem niggers how quality does, Benjy," he said. "Whut you say?" He looked back. Ben sat, holding the flower in his fist, his gaze empty and untroubled. Luster hit Queenie again and swung her to the left at the monument.

For an instant Ben sat in an utter hiatus. Then he bellowed. Bellow on bellow, his voice mounted, with scarce interval for breath. There was more than astonishment in it, it was horror; shock; agony eyeless, tongueless; just sound, and Luster's eyes backrolling for a white instant. "Gret God," he said. "Hush! Hush! Gret God!" He whirled again and struck Queenie with the switch. It broke and he cast it away and with Ben's voice mounting toward its unbelievable crescendo Luster caught up the end of the reins and leaned forward as Jason came jumping across the square and onto the step.

With a backhanded blow he hurled Luster aside and caught the reins and sawed Queenie about and doubled the reins back and slashed her across the hips. He cut her again and again, into a plunging gallop, while Ben's hoarse agony roared about them, and swung her about to the right of the monument. Then he struck Luster over the head with his fist.

"Dont you know any better than to take him to the left?" he said. He reached back and struck Ben, breaking the flower stalk again. "Shut up!" he said. "Shut up!" He jerked Queenie back and jumped down. "Get to hell on home with him. If you ever cross that gate with him again, I'll kill you!"

"Yes, suh!" Luster said. He took the reins and hit Queenie with the end of them. "Git up! Git up, dar! Benjy, fer God's sake!"

Ben's voice roared and roared. Queenie moved again, her feet began to clop-clop steadily again, and at once Ben hushed. Luster looked quickly back over his shoulder, then he drove on. The broken flower drooped over Ben's fist and his eyes were empty and blue and serene again as cornice and façade flowed smoothly once more from left to right, post and tree, window and doorway and signboard each in its ordered place.

COMPSON: 1699–1945

Appendix
Compson: 1699–1945

IKKEMOTUBBE. A dispossessed American king. Called 'Du Homme' by his fosterbrother, a Chevalier of France, who had he not been born too late could have been among the brightest in that glittering galaxy of knightly blackguards who were Napolean's marshals, who thus translated Ikkemotubbe's Chickasaw title meaning "The Man"; which translation Ikkemotubbe, himself a man of wit and imagination as well as a shrewd judge of character, including his own, carried one step further and anglicised it to "Doom." Who granted out of his vast lost domain a solid square mile of virgin north Mississippi dirt as truly angled as the four corners of a cardtable top (forested then because these were the old days before 1833 when the stars fell and Jefferson Mississippi was one long rambling onestorey mudchinked log building housing the Chickasaw Agent and his tradingpost store) to the grandson of a Scottish refugee who had lost his own birthright by casting his lot with a king who himself had been dispossessed. This in partial return for the right to proceed in peace, by whatever means he and his people saw fit, afoot or ahorse provided they were Chickasaw horses, to the wild western land presently to be called Oklahoma: not knowing then about the oil.

JACKSON. A Great White Father with a sword. (An old duellist, a brawling lean fierce mangy durable imperishable old lion who set the wellbeing of the nation above the White House and the health of his new political party above either and above them all set not his wife's honor but the principle that honor must be defended whether it was or not because defended it was whether or not.) Who patented sealed and countersigned the grant with his own hand in his gold tepee in Wassi Town, not knowing about the oil either: so that one day the homeless descendants of the dispossessed would ride supine with drink and splendidly comatose above the dusty allotted harborage of their bones in speciallybuilt scarlet-painted hearses and fire-engines.

These were Compsons:

QUENTIN MACLACHAN.   Son of a Glasgow printer, or-
phaned and raised by his mother's people in the Perth high-
lands. Fled to Carolina from Culloden Moor with a claymore
and the tartan he wore by day and slept under by night, and
little else. At eighty, having fought once against an English
king and lost, he would not make that mistake twice and so
fled again one night in 1779, with his infant grandson and
the tartan (the claymore had vanished, along with his son, the
grandson's father, from one of Tarleton's regiments on a
Georgia battlefield about a year ago) into Kentucky, where
a neighbor named Boon or Boone had already established a
settlement.

CHARLES STUART.   Attainted and proscribed by name and
grade in his British regiment. Left for dead in a Georgia
swamp by his own retreating army and then by the advancing
American one, both of which were wrong. He still had the
claymore even when on his homemade wooden leg he finally
overtook his father and son four years later at Harrodsburg
Kentucky, just in time to bury the father and enter upon a long
period of being a split personality while still trying to be the
schoolteacher which he believed he wanted to be, until he gave
up at last and became the gambler he actually was and which
no Compson seemed to realize they all were provided the
gambit was desperate and the odds long enough. Succeeded
at last in risking not only his neck but the security of his family
and the very integrity of the name he would leave behind
him, by joining the confederation headed by an acquaintance
named Wilkinson (a man of considerable talent and influence
and intellect and power) in a plot to secede the whole Mississippi Valley from the United States and join it to Spain. Fled
in his turn when the bubble burst (as anyone except a Compson schoolteacher should have known it would), himself
unique in being the only one of the plotters who had to flee
the country: this not from the vengeance and retribution of
the government which he had attempted to dismember, but
from the furious revulsion of his late confederates now frantic for their own safety. He was not expelled from the United
States, he talked himself countryless, his expulsion due not to

the treason but to his having been so vocal and vociferant in the conduct of it, burning each bridge vocally behind him before he had even reached the place to build the next one: so that it was no provost marshal nor even a civic agency but his late coplotters themselves who put afoot the movement to evict him from Kentucky and the United States and, if they had caught him, probably from the world too. Fled by night too, running true to family tradition, with his son and the old claymore and the tartan.

JASON LYCURGUS.   Who, driven perhaps by the compulsion of the flamboyant name given him by the sardonic embittered woodenlegged indomitable father who perhaps still believed with his heart that what he wanted to be was a classicist schoolteacher, rode up the Natchez Trace one day in 1811 with a pair of fine pistols and one meagre saddlebag on a small lightwaisted but stronghocked mare which could do the first two furlongs in definitely under the halfminute and the next two in not appreciably more, though that was all. But it was enough: who reached the Chickasaw Agency at Okatoba (which in 1860 was still called Old Jefferson) and went no further. Who within six months was the Agent's clerk and within twelve his partner, officially still the clerk though actually half-owner of what was now a considerable store stocked with the mare's winnings in races against the horses of Ikkemotubbe's young men which he, Compson, was always careful to limit to a quarter or at most three furlongs; and in the next year it was Ikkemotubbe who owned the little mare and Compson owned the solid square mile of land which someday would be almost in the center of the town of Jefferson, forested then and still forested twenty years later though rather a park than a forest by that time, with its slavequarters and stables and kitchengardens and the formal lawns and promenades and pavilions laid out by the same architect who built the columned porticoed house furnished by steamboat from France and New Orleans, and still the same square intact mile in 1840 (with not only the little white village called Jefferson beginning to enclose it but an entire white county about to surround it because in a few years now Ikkemotubbe's descendants and people would be gone, those remaining living

not as warriors and hunters but as white men—as shiftless
farmers or, here and there, the masters of what they too called
plantations and the owners of shiftless slaves, a little dirtier
than the white man, a little lazier, a little crueller—until at
last even the wild blood itself would have vanished, to be seen
only occasionally in the noseshape of a Negro on a cotton-
wagon or a white sawmill hand or trapper or locomotive fire-
man), known as the Compson Domain then, since now it was
fit to breed princes, statesmen and generals and bishops, to
avenge the dispossessed Compsons from Culloden and Carolina and Kentucky, then known as the Governor's house because sure enough in time it did produce or at least spawn a
governor—Quentin MacLachan again, after the Culloden
grandfather—and still known as the Old Governor's even after
it had spawned (1861) a general—(called so by predeter-
mined accord and agreement by the whole town and county,
as though they knew even then and beforehand that the old
governor was the last Compson who would not fail at everything he touched save longevity or suicide)—the Brigadier
Jason Lycurgus II who failed at Shiloh in '62 and failed again
though not so badly at Resaca in '64, who put the first mortgage on the still intact square mile to a New England carpet-
bagger in '66, after the old town had been burned by the
Federal General Smith and the new little town, in time to be
populated mainly by the descendants not of Compsons but of
Snopeses, had begun to encroach and then nibble at and into
it as the failed brigadier spent the next forty years selling fragments of it off to keep up the mortgage on the remainder:
until one day in 1900 he died quietly on an army cot in the
hunting and fishing camp in the Tallahatchie River bottom
where he passed most of the end of his days.

And even the old governor was forgotten now; what was
left of the old square mile was now known merely as the
Compson place—the weedchoked traces of the old ruined
lawns and promenades, the house which had needed painting
too long already, the scaling columns of the portico where
Jason III (bred for a lawyer and indeed kept an office upstairs
above the Square, where entombed in dusty filingcases some
of the oldest names in the county—Holston and Sutpen,
Grenier and Beauchamp and Coldfield—faded year by year

among the bottomless labyrinths of chancery: and who knows what dream in the perennial heart of his father, now completing the third of his three avatars—the one as son of a brilliant and gallant statesman, the second as battleleader of brave and gallant men, the third as a sort of privileged pseudo–Daniel Boone–Robinson Crusoe, who had not returned to juvenility because actually he had never left it—that that lawyer's office might again be the anteroom to the governor's mansion and the old splendor) sat all day long with a decanter of whiskey and a litter of dogeared Horaces and Livys and Catalines, composing (it was said) caustic and satiric eulogies on both his dead and his living fellowtownsmen, who sold the last of the property, except that fragment containing the house and the kitchengarden and the collapsing stables and one servant's cabin in which Dilsey's family lived, to a golfclub for the ready money with which his daughter Candace could have her fine wedding in April and his son Quentin could finish one year at Harvard and commit suicide in the following June of 1910; already known as the Old Compson place even while Compsons were still living in it on that spring dusk in 1928 when the old governor's doomed lost nameless seventeen-year-old greatgreatgranddaughter robbed her last remaining sane male relative's (her uncle Jason IV) secret hoard of money and climbed down a rainpipe and ran off with a pitchman in a travelling streetshow, and still known as the Old Compson place long after all traces of Compsons were gone from it: after the widowed mother died and Jason IV, no longer needing to fear Dilsey now, committed his idiot brother, Benjamin, to the State Asylum in Jackson and sold the house to a countryman who operated it as a boardinghouse for juries and horse- and muletraders, and still known as the Old Compson place even after the boardinghouse (and presently the golfcourse too) had vanished and the old square mile was even intact again in row after row of small crowded jerrybuilt individuallyowned demiurban bungalows.

And these:

QUENTIN III. Who loved not his sister's body but some concept of Compson honor precariously and (he knew well) only temporarily supported by the minute fragile membrane of her maidenhead as a miniature replica of all the whole vast globy earth may be poised on the nose of a trained seal. Who loved not the idea of the incest which he would not commit, but some presbyterian concept of its eternal punishment: he, not God, could by that means cast himself and his sister both into hell, where he could guard her forever and keep her forevermore intact amid the eternal fires. But who loved death above all, who loved only death, loved and lived in a deliberate and almost perverted anticipation of death as a lover loves and deliberately refrains from the waiting willing friendly tender incredible body of his beloved, until he can no longer bear not the refraining but the restraint and so flings, hurls himself, relinquishing, drowning. Committed suicide in Cambridge Massachusetts, June 1910, two months after his sister's wedding, waiting first to complete the current academic year and so get the full value of his paid-in-advance tuition, not because he had his old Culloden and Carolina and Kentucky grandfathers in him but because the remaining piece of the old Compson mile which had been sold to pay for his sister's wedding and his year at Harvard had been the one thing, excepting that same sister and the sight of an open fire, which his youngest brother, born an idiot, had loved.

CANDACE (CADDY).   Doomed and knew it, accepted the doom without either seeking or fleeing it. Loved her brother despite him, loved not only him but loved in him that bitter prophet and inflexible corruptless judge of what he considered the family's honor and its doom, as he thought he loved but really hated in her what he considered the frail doomed vessel of its pride and the foul instrument of its disgrace; not only this, she loved him not only in spite of but because of the fact that he himself was incapable of love, accepting the fact that he must value above all not her but the virginity of which she was custodian and on which she placed no value whatever: the frail physical stricture which to her was no more than a hangnail would have been. Knew the brother loved death best of all and was not jealous, would (and perhaps in the calculation and deliberation of her marriage did) have handed him the hypothetical hemlock. Was two months pregnant with another man's child which regardless of what its sex would be she had already named Quentin after the brother whom they both (she and the brother) knew was already the same as dead, when she married (1910) an extremely eligible young Indianian she and her mother had met while vacationing at French Lick the summer before. Divorced by him 1911. Married 1920 to a minor movingpicture magnate, Hollywood California. Divorced by mutual agreement, Mexico 1925. Vanished in Paris with the German occupation, 1940, still beautiful and probably still wealthy too since she did not look within fifteen years of her actual fortyeight, and was not heard of again. Except there was a woman in Jefferson, the county librarian, a mouse-sized and -colored woman who had never married, who had passed through the city schools in the same class with Candace Compson and then spent the rest of her life trying to keep *Forever Amber* in its orderly overlapping avatars and *Jurgen* and *Tom Jones* out of the hands of the highschool juniors and seniors who could reach them down without even having to tiptoe from the back shelves where she herself would have to stand on a box to hide them. One day in 1943, after a week of distraction bordering on disintegration almost, during which those entering the library would find her always in the act of hurriedly closing her desk drawer and turning the key in it (so that the matrons, wives of the bankers and doctors and lawyers, some of whom had also been in that old high-school class, who came and went in the afternoons with the copies of the *Forever Ambers* and the volumes of Thorne Smith carefully wrapped from view in sheets of Memphis and Jackson newspapers, believed she was on the verge of illness or perhaps even loss of mind), she closed and locked the library in the middle of the afternoon and with her handbag clasped tightly under her arm and two feverish spots of determination in her ordinarily colorless cheeks, she entered the farmers' supply store where Jason IV had started as a clerk and where he now owned his own business as a buyer of and dealer in cotton, striding on through that gloomy cavern which only men ever entered—a cavern cluttered and walled and stalag-mitehung with plows and discs and loops of tracechain and singletrees and mulecollars and sidemeat and cheap shoes and horselinament and flour and molasses, gloomy because the goods it contained were not shown but hidden rather since those who supplied Mississippi farmers or at least Negro Mississippi farmers for a share of the crop did not wish, until that crop was made and its value approximately computable, to show them what they could learn to want but only to supply them on specific demand with what they could not help but need—and strode on back to Jason's particular domain in the rear: a railed enclosure cluttered with shelves and pigeonholes bearing spiked dust-and-lint-gathering gin receipts and ledgers and cottonsamples and rank with the blended smell of cheese and kerosene and harnessoil and the tremendous iron stove against which chewed tobacco had been spat for almost a hundred years, and up to the long high sloping counter behind which Jason stood and, not looking again at the overalled men who had quietly stopped talking and even chewing when she entered, with a kind of fainting desperation she opened the handbag and fumbled something out of it and laid it open on the counter and stood trembling and breathing rapidly while Jason looked down at it—a picture, a photograph in color clipped obviously from a slick magazine—a picture filled with luxury and money and sunlight—a Cannebière backdrop of mountains and palms and cypresses and the sea, an open powerful expensive chromiumtrimmed sports car, the woman's face hatless between a rich scarf and a seal coat, ageless and beautiful, cold serene and damned; beside her a handsome lean man of middleage in the ribbons and tabs of a German staffgeneral—and the mousesized mousecolored spinster trembling and aghast at her own temerity, staring across it at the childless bachelor in whom ended that long line of men who had had something in them of decency and pride even after they had begun to fail at the integrity and the pride had become mostly vanity and selfpity: from the expatriate who had to flee his native land with little else except his life yet who still refused to accept defeat, through the man who gambled his life and his good name twice and lost twice and declined to accept that either, and the one who with only a clever small quarterhorse for tool avenged his dispossessed father and grandfather and gained a principality, and the brilliant and gallant governor and the general who though he failed at leading in battle brave and gallant men at least risked his own life too in the failing, to the cultured dipsomaniac who sold the last of his patrimony not to buy drink but to give one of his descendants at least the best chance in life he could think of.

'It's Caddy!' the librarian whispered. 'We must save her!'

'It's Cad, all right,' Jason said. Then he began to laugh. He stood there laughing above the picture, above the cold beautiful face now creased and dogeared from its week's sojourn in the desk drawer and the handbag. And the librarian knew why he was laughing, who had not called him anything but Mr Compson for thirty-two years now, ever since the day in 1911 when Candace, cast off by her husband, had brought her infant daughter home and left the child and departed by the next train, to return no more, and not only the Negro cook, Dilsey, but the librarian too divined by simple instinct that Jason was somehow using the child's life and its illegitimacy both to blackmail the mother not only into staying away from Jefferson for the rest of her life but into appointing him sole unchallengeable trustee of the money she would send for the child's maintenance, and had refused to speak to him at all since that day in 1928 when the daughter climbed down the rainpipe and ran away with the pitchman.

'Jason!' she cried. 'We must save her! Jason! Jason!'—and still crying it even when he took up the picture between thumb and finger and threw it back across the counter toward her.

'That Candace?' he said. 'Dont make me laugh. This bitch aint thirty yet. The other one's fifty now.'

And the library was still locked all the next day too when at three oclock in the afternoon, footsore and spent yet still unflagging and still clasping the handbag tightly under her arm, she turned into a neat small yard in the Negro residence section of Memphis and mounted the steps of the neat small house and rang the bell and the door opened and a black woman of about her own age looked quietly out at her. 'It's Frony, isn't it?' the librarian said. 'Dont you remember me— Melissa Meek, from Jefferson—'

'Yes,' the Negress said. 'Come in. You want to see Mama.' And she entered the room, the neat yet cluttered bedroom of an old Negro, rank with the smell of old people, old women, old Negroes, where the old woman herself sat in a rocker beside the hearth where even though it was June a fire smoldered—a big woman once, in faded clean calico and an immaculate turban wound round her head above the bleared and now apparently almost sightless eyes—and put the dog-eared clipping into the black hands which, like the women of her race, were still as supple and delicately shaped as they had been when she was thirty or twenty or even seventeen.

'It's Caddy!' the librarian said. 'It is! Dilsey! Dilsey!'

'What did he say?' the old Negress said. And the librarian knew whom she meant by 'he', nor did the librarian marvel, not only that the old Negress would know that she (the librarian) would know whom she meant by the 'he', but that the old Negress would know at once that she had already shown the picture to Jason.

'Dont you know what he said?' she cried. 'When he realised she was in danger, he said it was her, even if I hadn't even had a picture to show him. But as soon as he realised that some-body, anybody, even just me, wanted to save her, would try to save her, he said it wasn't. But it is! Look at it!'

'Look at my eyes,' the old Negress said. 'How can I see that picture?'

'Call Frony!' the librarian cried. 'She will know her!' But al-ready the old Negress was folding the clipping carefully back into its old creases, handing it back.

'My eyes aint any good anymore,' she said. 'I cant see it.'

And that was all. At six oclock she fought her way through the crowded bus terminal, the bag clutched under one arm and the return half of her roundtrip ticket in the other hand, and was swept out onto the roaring platform on the diurnal tide of a few middleaged civilians but mostly soldiers and sailors enroute either to leave or to death and the homeless young women, their companions, who for two years now had lived from day to day in pullmans and hotels when they were lucky and in daycoaches and buses and stations and lobbies and public restrooms when not, pausing only long enough to drop their foals in charity wards or policestations and then move on again, and fought her way into the bus, smaller than any other there so that her feet touched the floor only occa-sionally until a shape (a man in khaki; she couldn't see him at all because she was already crying) rose and picked her up bodily and set her into a seat next to the window, where still

crying quietly she could look out upon the fleeing city as it
streaked past and then was behind and presently now she
would be home again, safe in Jefferson where life lived too
with all its incomprehensible passion and turmoil and grief
and fury and despair, but here at six oclock you could close
the covers on it and even the weightless hand of a child could
put it back among its unfeatured kindred on the quiet eternal
shelves and turn the key upon it for the whole and dreamless
night. *Yes* she thought, crying quietly *that was it she didn't
want to see it know whether it was Caddy or not because she knows
Caddy doesn't want to be saved hasn't anything anymore worth
being saved for nothing worth being lost that she can lose*

JASON IV.   The first sane Compson since before Culloden
and (a childless bachelor) hence the last. Logical rational contained and even a philosopher in the old stoic tradition: thinking nothing whatever of God one way or the other and simply
considering the police and so fearing and respecting only
the Negro woman, his sworn enemy since his birth and his
mortal one since that day in 1911 when she too divined by
simple clairvoyance that he was somehow using his infant
niece's illegitimacy to blackmail its mother, who cooked the
food he ate. Who not only fended off and held his own with
Compsons but competed and held his own with the Snopeses
who took over the little town following the turn of the century as the Compsons and Sartorises and their ilk faded from
it (no Snopes, but Jason Compson himself who as soon as his
mother died—the niece had already climbed down the rainpipe and vanished so Dilsey no longer had either of these clubs
to hold over him—committed his idiot younger brother to the
state and vacated the old house, first chopping up the vast
oncesplendid rooms into what he called apartments and selling the whole thing to a countryman who opened a boardinghouse in it), though this was not difficult since to him all
the rest of the town and the world and the human race too
except himself were Compsons, inexplicable yet quite pre-
dictable in that they were in no sense whatever to be trusted.
Who, all the money from the sale of the pasture having gone
for his sister's wedding and his brother's course at Harvard,
used his own niggard savings out of his meagre wages as a

storeclerk to send himself to a Memphis school where he learned to class and grade cotton, and so established his own business with which, following his dipsomaniac father's death, he assumed the entire burden of the rotting family in the rotting house, supporting his idiot brother because of their mother, sacrificing what pleasures might have been the right and just due and even the necessity of a thirty-year-old bachelor, so that his mother's life might continue as nearly as possible to what it had been; this not because he loved her but (a sane man always) simply because he was afraid of the Negro cook whom he could not even force to leave, even when he tried to stop paying her weekly wages; and who despite all this, still managed to save almost three thousand dollars ($2840.50 as he reported it on the night his niece stole it) in niggard and agonised dimes and quarters and halfdollars, which hoard he kept in no bank because to him a banker too was just one more Compson, but hid in a locked bureau drawer in his bedroom whose bed he made and changed himself since he kept the bedroom door locked all the time save when he was passing through it. Who, following a fumbling abortive attempt by his idiot brother on a passing female child, had himself appointed the idiot's guardian without letting their mother know and so was able to have the creature castrated before the mother even knew it was out of the house, and who following the mother's death in 1933 was able to free himself forever not only from the idiot brother and the house but from the Negro woman too, moving into a pair of offices up a flight of stairs above the supplystore containing his cotton ledgers and samples, which he had converted into a bedroom-kitchen-bath, in and out of which on weekends there would be seen a big plain friendly brazenhaired pleasantfaced woman no longer very young, in round 'picture' hats and (in its season) an imitation fur coat, the two of them, the middleaged cottonbuyer and the woman whom the town called, simply, his friend from Memphis, seen at the local picture show on Saturday night and on Sunday morning mounting the apartment stairs with paper bags from the grocer's containing loaves and eggs and oranges and cans of soup, domestic, uxorious, connubial, until the late afternoon bus carried her back to Memphis. He was emancipated now. He

was free. 'In 1865,' he would say, 'Abe Lincoln freed the niggers from the Compsons. In 1933, Jason Compson freed the
Compsons from the niggers.'

BENJAMIN.   Born Maury, after his mother's only brother:
a handsome flashing swaggering workless bachelor who borrowed money from almost anyone, even Dilsey although she
was a Negro, explaining to her as he withdrew his hand from
his pocket that she was not only in his eyes the same as a
member of his sister's family, she would be considered a born
lady anywhere in any eyes. Who, when at last even his mother
realised what he was and insisted weeping that his name must
be changed, was rechristened Benjamin by his brother Quentin
(Benjamin, our lastborn, sold into Egypt). Who loved three
things: the pasture which was sold to pay for Candace's wedding and to send Quentin to Harvard, his sister Candace, firelight. Who lost none of them because he could not remember
his sister but only the loss of her, and firelight was the same
bright shape as going to sleep, and the pasture was even better
sold than before because now he and TP could not only follow
timeless along the fence the motions which it did not even
matter to him were humanbeings swinging golfsticks, TP
could lead them to clumps of grass or weeds where there
would appear suddenly in TP's hand small white spherules
which competed with and even conquered what he did not
even know was gravity and all the immutable laws when released from the hand toward plank floor or smokehouse wall
or concrete sidewalk. Gelded 1913. Committed to the State
Asylum, Jackson 1933. Lost nothing then either because, as
with his sister, he remembered not the pasture but only its
loss, and firelight was still the same bright shape of sleep.

QUENTIN.   The last. Candace's daughter. Fatherless nine
months before her birth, nameless at birth and already doomed
to be unwed from the instant the dividing egg determined its
sex. Who at seventeen, on the one thousand eight hundred
ninetyfifth anniversary of the day before the resurrection of
Our Lord, swung herself by a rainpipe from the window of
the room in which her uncle had locked her at noon, to the
locked window of his own locked and empty bedroom and

broke a pane and entered the window and with the uncle's fire-
poker burst open the locked bureau drawer and took the
money (it was not $2840.50 either, it was almost seven thou-
sand dollars and this was Jason's rage, the red unbearable fury
which on that night and at intervals recurring with little or no
diminishment for the next five years, made him seriously believe would at some unwarned instant destroy him, kill him
as instantaneously dead as a bullet or a lightningbolt: that although he had been robbed not of a mere petty three thousand dollars but of almost seven thousand he couldn't even
tell anybody; because he had been robbed of seven thousand
dollars instead of just three he could not only never receive
justification—he did not want sympathy—from other men unlucky enough to have one bitch for a sister and another for a
niece, he couldn't even go to the police; because he had lost
four thousand dollars which did not belong to him he couldn't
even recover the three thousand which did since those first
four thousand dollars were not only the legal property of his
niece as a part of the money supplied for her support and
maintenance by her mother over the last sixteen years, they
did not exist at all, having been officially recorded as expended
and consumed in the annual reports he submitted to the
district Chancellor, as required of him as guardian and trustee
by his bondsmen: so that he had been robbed not only of his
thievings but his savings too, and by his own victim; he had
been robbed not only of the four thousand dollars which he
had risked jail to acquire but of the three thousand which
he had hoarded at the price of sacrifice and denial, almost a
nickel and a dime at a time, over a period of almost twenty
years: and this not only by his own victim but by a child who
did it at one blow, without premeditation or plan, not even
knowing or even caring how much she would find when she
broke the drawer open; and now he couldn't even go to the
police for help: he who had considered the police always,
never given them any trouble, had paid the taxes for years
which supported them in parasitic and sadistic idleness; not
only that, he didn't dare pursue the girl himself because he
might catch her and she would talk, so that his only recourse
was a vain dream which kept him tossing and sweating on
nights two and three and even four years after the event, when

he should have forgotten about it: of catching her without warning, springing on her out of the dark, before she had had time to spend all the money, and murder her before she had time to open her mouth) and climbed down the same rain-pipe in the dusk and ran away with the pitchman who was already under sentence for bigamy. And so vanished; whatever occupation overtook her would have arrived in no chromium Mercedes; whatever snapshot would have contained no general of staff.

And that was all. These others were not Compsons. They were black:

TP. Who wore on Memphis's Beale Street the fine bright cheap intransigent clothes manufactured specifically for him by the Jew owners of Chicago and New York sweatshops.

FRONY. Who married a pullman porter and went to St Louis to live and later moved back to Memphis to make a home for her mother since Dilsey refused to go further than that.

LUSTER. A man, aged 14. Who was not only capable of the complete care and security of an idiot twice his age and three times his size, but could keep him entertained.

DILSEY.
They endured.

CHRONOLOGY

NOTE ON THE TEXTS

NOTES

Chronology

1897 Born William Cuthbert Falkner, September 25, in New Albany, northeast Mississippi, first child of Maud Butler Falkner (b. 1871) and Murry Cuthbert Falkner (b. 1870). Father is eldest son of John Wesley Thompson Falkner, eldest son of William Clark Falkner. (Great-grandfather William Clark Falkner, born in Tennessee in 1825, came to Ripley, Mississippi, in his teens and became a lawyer, slave-owning planter, and colonel in the Confederate army. He changed his name, according to family legend, from Faulkner to Falkner to avoid confusion with "some no-account folks," wrote several books, including a successful romance, *The White Rose of Memphis*, was twice acquitted on grounds of self-defense after killing men in quarrels, built a short, narrow-gauge railroad, and was elected to the state legislature. In 1889 he was shot to death by an embittered former partner. Grandfather John Wesley Thompson Falkner, a lawyer and politician, inherited control of the Gulf & Chicago Railroad. Father, Murry Cuthbert Falkner, began working for railroad in 1888 and married Maud Butler in 1896, shortly after becoming general passenger agent for New Albany.)

1898–1901 Father becomes treasurer of railroad in November 1898, and family soon moves to Ripley. Brothers Murry C. Falkner, Jr. (nicknamed "Jack"), born June 26, 1899, and John Wesley Thompson Falkner III ("Johncy") born September 24, 1901. William and Murry are dangerously ill with scarlet fever shortly after John's birth.

1902 Grandfather sells railroad and father loses his job. In September family moves forty miles southwest to Oxford, seat of Lafayette County, where grandfather is influential resident of seventeen years. Father begins series of small business ventures and becomes proprietor of a livery stable in November. Maternal grandmother, Lelia Dean Swift Butler ("Damuddy"), moves into family home. Caroline Barr ("Mammy Callie"), born in slavery around 1840, is hired to take care of children. She tells them stories and takes them on long walks in the woods, teaching them to recognize different birds. The Falkner brothers become close to cousin Sallie Murry Wilkins (b. 1899), daughter of aunt Mary Holland Falkner Wilkins.

1903 Meets and occasionally plays with Lida Estelle Oldham (b. 1896), daughter of Republican attorney Lemuel Oldham, when her family moves to Oxford in fall.

1905 Enters first grade. Enjoys drawing and painting with watercolors.

1906 Skips to third grade. Grandmother Sallie Murry Falkner dies December 21.

1907 Grandmother Lelia Butler dies June 1. Third brother, Dean Swift Falkner, born August 15.

1909–13 Begins working in father's livery stable in June. Athletic activities are curtailed in late 1910 when he is put in a tight canvas brace to correct shoulder stoop. Draws, writes stories and poems, and starts to play hooky. Becomes increasingly attracted to Estelle Oldham and shows her his poems. Reads comic magazine *The Arkansas Traveller*, *Pilgrim's Progress*, *Moby-Dick* (telling his brother Murry, "It's one of the best books ever written"), Mark Twain, Joel Chandler Harris, Shakespeare, Fielding, Conrad, Balzac, and Hugo, among others. Shoots his dog accidentally while hunting rabbits in the fall of 1911 and does not hunt again for several years. Becomes active Boy Scout and begins to play high school football in fall 1913.

1914–15 Shows his poetry to law student Phil Stone, four years his senior. Stone becomes close friend, gives him books to read, including works by Swinburne, Keats, Conrad Aiken, Sherwood Anderson, and introduces him to writer and fellow townsman Stark Young. Helps plan yearbook and does sketches for it. Pitches and plays shortstop on baseball team. Returns to school briefly in fall 1915 to play football, then drops out. Hunts deer and bear at camp of "General" James Stone, Phil's father, near Batesville, in the Mississippi Delta thirty miles west of Oxford.

1916–17 Begins working early in 1916 as clerk at grandfather's bank, the First National, and hates it. Drinks his grandfather's liquor. By end of 1916 spends most of his time on campus of University of Mississippi, where he becomes friends with freshman Ben Wasson. Contributes drawings to university yearbook, *Ole Miss*. Continues to write verse influenced by Swinburne and A. E. Housman.

1918   Estelle Oldham tells Falkner she is "ready to elope" with him, despite her engagement to Cornell Franklin, a University of Mississippi graduate now successfully practicing law in Hawaii who is preferred by her family. Falkner insists on getting the Oldhams' consent, but both families oppose marriage, and Estelle's wedding to Franklin is set for April 18. Joins Phil Stone, then studying law at Yale, in New Haven early in April. Meets poets Stephen Vincent Benét and Robert Hillyer. Reads Yeats. Works as ledger clerk at Winchester Repeating Arms Co., where his name is recorded "Faulkner." Determined to join British forces, he and Stone practice English accents and mannerisms. Accepted by Royal Air Force in mid-June. Visits Oxford before reporting to Toronto Recruits' Depot on July 9, where he lists birthplace as Finchley, Middlesex, England, birthdate as May 25, 1898, and spells his name "Faulkner." Brother Murry, serving in the Marines, is wounded in the Argonne on November 1. Faulkner's service is limited to attending ground school. Discharged in December, returns to Oxford wearing newly purchased officer's uniform and Royal Flying Corps wings and suffering, he claims, from effects of crashing a plane.

1919   Continues to work on poetry. Drinks with friends in gambling houses and brothels in Clarksdale and Charleston, Mississippi, Memphis, and New Orleans. Composes long cycle of poems influenced by classical pastoral tradition and modern poetry, especially T. S. Eliot. Sees Estelle frequently during her four-month visit home from Hawaii with her daughter, Victoria. "L'Après-Midi d'un Faune," 40-line poem, appears in *The New Republic* August 6. Other poems are not accepted. Registers in September as a special student at University of Mississippi, where father is now assistant secretary of university. Studies French, Spanish, and Shakespeare; publishes poems in campus paper, *The Mississippian*, and Oxford *Eagle*. First published story, "Landing in Luck," appears in *The Mississippian* in November. In December, agrees to be initiated into Sigma Alpha Epsilon fraternity because of family tradition. Given nicknames "Count" and "Count No 'Count" by fellow students, who consider him aloof and affected.

1920   Inscribes *The Lilacs*, 36-page hand-lettered giftbook of poems, to Phil Stone on New Year's Day. Translates four poems by Paul Verlaine that are published in *The Mississippian* in February and March. Awarded $10 poetry prize by Professor Calvin S. Brown in June. Does odd jobs and assists with Boy Scout troop. Helps build clay tennis court beside Falkners' university-owned home; becomes a good player. Joins The Marionettes, a new university drama group; finishes one-act play (not produced) and works on stage props and set design. Withdraws from university in November during crackdown on fraternities. Receives commission as honorary second lieutenant in RAF; wears uniform with pips on various occasions. Writes *Marionettes*, an experimental verse play; hand-letters several copies of its 55 pages, adding illustrations influenced by Aubrey Beardsley. Wasson sells five at $5 apiece. The Marionettes decline to produce it.

1921   Favorably reviews *Turns and Movies*, volume of verse by Conrad Aiken, in *The Mississippian*. Paints buildings on campus. Presents Estelle Franklin with 88-page bound typescript volume of poems entitled *Vision in Spring* during her visit home in the summer. Accepts invitation of Stark Young to visit him in New York City in the fall. Revisits New Haven, October–November, then rents rooms in New York City and works as clerk in Lord & Taylor bookstore managed by Stark Young's friend Elizabeth Prall. Returns home in December after Phil Stone and Lemuel Oldham secure him position as postmaster at university post office at salary of $1,500 a year.

1922   Writes while on duty at the post office, neglects customers, is reluctant to sort mail, does not always forward it, and keeps patrons' magazines and periodicals in the office until he and his friends have read them. Praises Edna St. Vincent Millay and Eugene O'Neill in articles published in *The Mississippian*. Grandfather John Wesley Thompson Falkner dies March 13. Faulkner does last drawing for yearbook *Ole Miss*. Plays golf. Writes poems, stories, and criticism. *The Double Dealer*, a New Orleans magazine, publishes his short poem "Portrait." Continues to read widely, including works by Conrad Aiken, Eugene O'Neill, and Elinor Wylie.

1923   Begins driving his own car. Becomes scoutmaster during summer. Submits collection *Orpheus, and Other Poems* to The Four Seas Company of Boston in June. They agree to publish it if Faulkner will pay manufacturing costs; Faulkner declines.

1924   Receives gift of James Joyce's *Ulysses* from Phil Stone. Reads Voltaire and stories by Thomas Beer, a popular magazine writer of the time. In May, Four Seas agrees to publish cycle of pastoral poems, *The Marble Faun*, and Faulkner sends $400 to cover publication costs. Phil Stone writes preface and takes active role in negotiations. Continues to write stories and verse, compiling gift volumes for friends. Removed as scoutmaster after local minister denounces his drinking. Faulkner resigns as postmaster October 31. ("I reckon I'll be at the beck and call of folks with money all my life, but thank God I won't ever again have to be at the beck and call of every son of a bitch who's got two cents to buy a stamp.") Visits Elizabeth Prall in New Orleans and meets her husband, Sherwood Anderson, whose work he admires. *The Marble Faun* published in December.

1925   Leaves for New Orleans in January, intending to earn his passage to Europe. Accepts Elizabeth Prall Anderson's invitation to stay in spare room while Sherwood Anderson is away on a lecture tour, then moves into quarters rented from artist William Spratling. Contributes essays, poems, stories, and sketches to the New Orleans *Times-Picayune* and *The Double Dealer*. Meets Anita Loos. Begins work on novel *Mayday*, which Sherwood Anderson, now a close friend, praises. Anderson recommends Faulkner's novel to publisher Boni & Liveright. Visits Stone's brother and his family at Pascagoula on Gulf Coast in June; falls in love with Helen Baird (b. 1904), a sculptor he had met in New Orleans. Sails as passenger on a freighter from New Orleans to Genoa with William Spratling July 7; throws mass of manuscript overboard en route. Travels through Italy and Switzerland to Paris, settling on Left Bank. Grows beard. Goes to Louvre and various galleries; sees paintings by Cézanne, Matisse, Picasso, and other modernists. Years later, says of James Joyce in Paris: "I would go to some effort to go to the café that he inhabited to look at him. But that was the only literary man that I remember seeing in Europe in those days." Works on articles, poems, and fiction, including two novels, *Mosquito* and *Elmer* (about a young American painter, never finished). Tours France on foot and by train; visits World War I battlefields which still show scars of fighting. Visits England briefly in October, but finds it too expensive and returns to France. Learns in Paris that novel *Mayday* as been accepted for publication by Boni & Liveright and retitled *Soldiers' Pay*; Faulkner likes new title. Sails to the United States in December. Visits his publishers in New York before returning to Oxford.

1926　　Inscribes a hand-lettered, illustrated allegorical tale *Mayday* (the same title originally given novel) to Helen Baird in January. Moves in with Spratling at 632 St. Peter Street, New Orleans, in February, going back to Oxford for brief visits. *Soldiers' Pay* published by Boni & Liveright February 25 in printing of 2,500 copies (sells 2,084 by May). Mother, shocked by sexual material in the novel, says that the best thing he could do is leave the country; father refuses to read it. Reviews are generally favorable. Hand-letters a sequence of poems called *Helen: A Courtship* for Helen Baird in June. Vacations in Pascagoula, where he finishes typescript of novel *Mosquitoes* in early September. Returns to New Orleans in fall. Begins novels *Father Abraham*, about an avaricious Mississippi family named Snopes, and *Flags in the Dust*, depicting four generations of Sartoris family, based on Southern and family lore. Parodies Anderson's style in foreword to *Sherwood Anderson & Other Famous Creoles*, a collection of Spratling's sketches, which they publish themselves in an edition of 400 copies that sells out in a week at $1.50 a copy. Book offends Anderson and causes breach between him and Faulkner. Returns to Oxford at Christmas.

1927　　Sees Estelle, who has returned to Oxford after beginning divorce proceedings against Cornell Franklin. Gives her daughter, Victoria, a 47-page tale, *The Wishing Tree*, typed and bound in varicolored paper, in February as a present for her eighth birthday. Helen Baird marries Guy C. Lyman in March. *Mosquitoes* published April 30. Puts *Father Abraham* aside to concentrate on *Flags in the Dust*. Works on it in Pascagoula during summer, and finishes revised typescript in late September. Horace Liveright rejects *Flags in the Dust* in late November and advises Faulkner not to offer it elsewhere.

1928   Begins "Twilight," story about the Compson family, early in the year. ("One day I seemed to shut a door, between me and all publishers' addresses and book lists. I said to myself, Now I can write.") Centered on Caddie Compson, it becomes *The Sound and the Fury*. ("I loved her so much I couldn't decide to give her life just for the duration of a short story. She deserved more than that. So my novel was created, almost in spite of myself.") Sends *Flags in the Dust*, extensively revised, and group of short stories to Ben Wasson, now New York literary agent. Wasson submits *Flags in the Dust* to eleven publishers, all of whom reject it. Faulkner continues to work on new novel. In September, Wasson shows *Flags in the Dust* to Harrison (Hal) Smith, editor at Harcourt, Brace and Company, who writes favorable report. Alfred Harcourt agrees to publish book on condition that it be cut. Faulkner uses $300 advance to go to New York. Dismayed at the cuts Wasson says are necessary, allows him to do most of the cutting. (" 'The trouble is,' he said, 'is that you had about 6 books in here. You were trying to write them all at once.' ") Tries unsuccessfully to sell short stories. Rents a small furnished flat in Greenwich Village and revises and types manuscript of *The Sound and the Fury*. Finishes in October, drinks heavily, and is found unconscious by friends Eric J. (Jim) Devine and Leon Scales, who take care of him in their apartment. Moves in with painter Owen Crump after recovering. Returns to Oxford in December.

1929   *Sartoris* (the cut and retitled *Flags in the Dust*) published by Harcourt, Brace and Company January 31 in first printing of 1,998. Starts writing *Sanctuary*. *The Sound and the Fury* accepted by new firm of Jonathan Cape and Harrison Smith in February; Faulkner receives $200 advance. Estelle's divorce becomes final on April 29. Faulkner receives $200 advance for new novel from Cape & Smith in early

May. Completes *Sanctuary* in late May; Smith writes him that it is too shocking to publish. Asks Smith for an additional $500 advance so that he can get married. Marries Estelle in Presbyterian Church in nearby College Hill, June 20. Borrows money from cousin Sallie Murry (Wilkins) Williams and her husband to go to Pascagoula, where he and Estelle have troubled honeymoon. Reads proofs of *The Sound and the Fury*, restoring italicized passages changed by Wasson. Returns to Oxford and takes job on night shift at the university power plant. Visits mother daily. *The Sound and the Fury* published October 7 in printing of 1,789. Reviews are enthusiastic, sales disappointing. Writes *As I Lay Dying* while at work, beginning October 25 and finishing December 11. ("I am going to write a book by which, at a pinch, I can stand or fall if I never touch ink again.")

1930   Finishes typescript of *As I Lay Dying* on January 12. Begins publishing stories in national magazines when *Forum* accepts "A Rose for Emily" for its April issue. Achieves mass-market success when *The Saturday Evening Post* accepts "Thrift" (appears September) and *Scribner's* accepts "Dry September" (published January 1931). April, purchases rundown antebellum house (lacks electricity and plumbing) and four acres of land in Oxford for $6,000 at 6% interest, with no money down. Names it Rowanoak (or Rowan Oak), and begins renovation, doing much of the work himself. Moves into it in June with Estelle and her children, Victoria (born 1919) and Malcolm (born 1923). Household staff includes Caroline Barr and Ned ("Uncle Ned") Barnett, former slave who had been servant of great-grandfather William Clark Falkner. Chatto & Windus publishes *Soldiers' Pay*, with introduction by Richard Hughes, June 20, first of Faulkner's works to appear in England. Sells "Red Leaves" and "Lizards in Jamshyd's Courtyard" to *The Saturday Evening Post* for $750 each (more than he had received for any novel). *As I Lay Dying*, where for the first time in print the Mississippi locale is identified as Yoknapatawpha County, published October 6 by Cape & Smith in printing of 2,522 copies. Harrison Smith now thinks *Sanctuary* may make money for ailing publishing firm, and sends galley proofs in November. Though the resetting costs Faulkner $270, he revises extensively. Finishes revision in December.

1931   Daughter Alabama, named for Faulkner's great-aunt Ala-
            bama, is born prematurely on January 11 and dies after
            nine days. *Sanctuary*, published February 9 by Cape &
            Smith, sells 3,519 copies by March 4—more than com-
            bined sales of *The Sound and the Fury* and *As I Lay Dying*;
            elicits high praise and increasing attention for Faulkner
            abroad. Gallimard acquires the rights to publish *As I Lay
            Dying* and *Sanctuary* in French. Many in Oxford are
            shocked by *Sanctuary*; Faulkner's father tells a coed carry-
            ing the book that it isn't fit for a nice girl to read, but his
            mother defends him. Chatto & Windus publishes *The
            Sound and the Fury* in April. "Spotted Horses" appears in
            Scribner's in June. Begins work on novel tentatively titled
            Dark House in August, developing theme used in rejected
            short story "Rose of Lebanon." *These 13*, a collection of
            stories, published by Cape & Smith September 21; sells
            better than any of his works except *Sanctuary*. Attends
            Southern Writers' Conference at University of Virginia in
            Charlottesville on his way to New York in October.
            Drinks heavily. Wooed by publishers Bennett Cerf and
            Donald Klopfer of Random House, Harold Guinzberg
            and George Oppenheimer of Viking, and Alfred A.
            Knopf. To keep him away from other publishers, Harri-
            son Smith has Milton Abernethy take Faulkner on ship
            cruise to Jacksonville, Florida, and back to New York.
            Firm of Cape & Smith is dissolved by Jonathan Cape;
            Faulkner signs with new firm, Harrison Smith, Inc. Meets
            his French translator, Princeton professor Maurice Coin-
            dreau, banker and future secretary of defense Robert
            Lovett, Dorothy Parker, H. L. Mencken, Robert Bench-
            ley, John O'Hara, John Dos Passos, Frank Sullivan, and
            Corey Ford (will continue to see some of them on later
            trips). Spends hours talking and drinking with Dashiell
            Hammett and Lillian Hellman. Meets Nathanael West.
            Works on new novel (now called *Light in August*) and
            stories, one of them—"Turn About"—inspired by war sto-
            ries told by Lovett (finished in Oxford, and published
            in *The Saturday Evening Post*, March 1932). Finishes self-
            deprecatory introduction to Random House's Modern
            Library edition of *Sanctuary* (published 1932). Makes con-
            tacts with film studios and writes film treatments. Earns
            enough money during stay in New York to pay bills at
            home. Drinks heavily; friends contact Estelle. She arrives
            early in December, and they return to Oxford before the

middle of the month. Random House publishes story "Idyll in the Desert" in limited edition of 400 copies.

1932   Finishes manuscript of *Light in August* in February and revised typescript in March. Cape's new partnership, Cape & Ballou, goes into receivership in March, owing Faulkner $4,000 in royalties. Goes to work May 7 at Metro-Goldwyn-Mayer studio in Culver City, California, on six-week, $500-per-week contract. Leaves the studio almost immediately, not returning for a week. Takes a $30-a-month cottage on Jackson Street near studio and works unsuccessfully on series of treatments and scripts. At the end of contract makes plans to return home, but director-producer Howard Hawks hires him as scriptwriter for film *Today We Live*, based on "Turn About," beginning his longest Hollywood association. Father dies of heart attack August 7, and Faulkner returns home as head of family. "Dad left mother solvent for only about 1 year," he writes Ben Wasson. "Then it is me." Agreement with Hawks allows him to work in Oxford. Takes stepson Malcolm on walks through woods and bottoms, teaching him to distinguish dangerous from harmless snakes. Returns to Hollywood in October for three weeks, taking mother and brother Dean with him. *Light in August* published October 6 by new firm of Harrison Smith and Robert Haas. Paramount buys film rights to *Sanctuary* (released as *The Story of Temple Drake*, May 12, 1933). Faulkner receives $6,000 from sale. Continues working for MGM in Oxford. Spends part of Hollywood earnings on renovation of Rowan Oak.

1933   Begins flying lessons with Captain Vernon Omlie in February, and makes first solo flight April 20 after seventeen hours of dual instruction. *Today We Live* premieres in Oxford, April 12. *A Green Bough*, poems, published April 20 by Smith & Haas. Travels to New Orleans in May to work on film *Louisiana Lou* with director Tod Browning, but refuses to return to Hollywood for revisions; studio terminates contract May 13. Buys more land adjoining Rowan Oak. Works on stories and novel, *The Peasants*, which uses Snopes characters. Daughter Jill born June 24. Prepares a marked copy (apparently now lost) for a projected Random House limited edition of *The Sound and the Fury* (never published) that would print the Benjy section in three colors, and writes an introduction. ("I wrote this book and learned to read. . . . I discovered that there is actually something to which the shabby term Art not only can, but must, be applied.") Receives $500 for his work on it. Plans novel *Requiem for a Nun*. Buys Omlie's Waco C cabin biplane in fall. Concerned about brother Dean's future, arranges to have Omlie train Dean as a pilot. Flies with Omlie and Dean to New York to meet with publishers early in November, returning in time to go hunting. Earns pilot's license December 14.

1934   Begins new novel *A Dark House* in February, using material from stories "Evangeline" (written 1931) and "Wash" (written 1933). Flies with Omlie to New Orleans for dedication of Shushan Airport February 15. Participates in Mississippi air shows with Omlie, Dean, and others in spring, billed as "William Faulkner's (Famous Author) Air Circus" on one occasion; Faulkner avoids flying aerobatics. *Doctor Martino and Other Stories* published April 16 by Smith & Haas. Pressed for money, writes "Ambuscade," "Retreat," and "Raid," series of Civil War stories centering on Bayard Sartoris and black companion Ringo, hoping to sell them to *The Saturday Evening Post* (they appear in fall). Goes back to work with Hawks in Hollywood for $1,000 a week, from the end of June to late July. Finishes script *Sutter's Gold* in Oxford. Brother Murry is member of FBI team that kills John Dillinger in Chicago, July 22. Writes Smith in August that new novel, now titled *Absalom, Absalom!*, "is not quite ripe yet." Puts it aside and converts unpublished story "This Kind of Courage" into novel, *Pylon*. Sends first chapter to Harrison Smith in November and finishes it by end of December.

1935   Forms Okatoba Fishing and Hunting Club with R. L. Sullivan and Whitson Cook, receiving hunting and fishing rights to several thousand acres of General Stone's Delta land near Batesville, Mississippi. *Pylon* published by Smith & Haas, March 25. Pressed for money, works intensively at writing stories meant to sell. Returns to *Absalom, Absalom!* Resumes occasional flying, though the Waco now belongs to Dean. Goes to New York September 23 to negotiate a better contract with Smith & Haas and to sell stories to magazines. Returns home October 15, without gaining much from the trip. Brother Dean and his three passengers are killed when the Waco crashes November 10. Faulkner assists undertaker in futile attempt to prepare Dean's body for open-casket funeral. Distraught and guilt-ridden, assumes responsibility for Dean's pregnant wife, Louise, and stays for several weeks with her and his grieving mother, who feels suicidal. On December 10, goes to Hollywood for five-week, $1,000-per-week assignment with Hawks for Twentieth Century–Fox, taking *Absalom, Abaslom!* with him. Works on novel early in the morning before going to the studio. Begins intermittent and sometimes intense fifteen-year affair with Hawks's 28-year-old secretary (later his script supervisor), Mississippi divorcée Meta Doherty Carpenter.

1936   After successful completion of draft of script (*The Road to Glory*), begins to drink heavily. Returns to Oxford on sick leave January 13. Finishes manuscript of *Absalom, Absalom!* January 31. Drinks heavily and is hospitalized in Wright's Sanitarium, small private hospital in Byhalia, Mississippi, fifty miles north of Oxford. Reluctant to delay revision of novel by writing stories to make money, signs new contract with Twentieth Century–Fox, again for $1,000 a week. Returns to Hollywood February 26, moving into the Beverly Hills Hotel. Works on several scripts, sees old friends. Dean, daughter of brother Dean Faulkner, born March 22; Faulkner assumes role of surrogate father. Goes boar hunting on Santa Cruz Island with Nathanael West in April. Returns to Oxford early in June and writes to agent when his stories don't sell: "Since last summer I seem to have got out of the habit of writing trash . . ." Draws map of Yoknapatawpha County for *Absalom, Absalom!* Goes back to Hollywood in mid-July for six-month, $750-per-week contract, taking Estelle, Jill, and two servants with him, and moves into a large house just north of Santa Monica. Captain Omlie dies in crash as passenger on commercial flight August 6. Sees Meta Carpenter, who has decided to marry pianist Wolfgang Rebner. Estelle and Faulkner both drink heavily. *Absalom, Absalom!* published October 26 by Random House (which has absorbed the firm of Smith & Haas); receives some critical praise, though sales are not enough to allow freedom from scriptwriting, and Faulkner is unable to sell film rights (had hoped to receive $50,000 for them). Becomes increasingly unproductive at

Twentieth Century–Fox and is laid off in December after earning almost $20,000 for the year. Proposes to convert Bayard Sartoris–Ringo stories, now six in number, into novel and is encouraged by Bennett Cerf and Robert Haas. Harrison Smith leaves Random House. Makes final payment on Rowan Oak.

1937   Returns to studio from layoff February 26 at salary of $1,000 a week. Family moves closer to studio. Unhappiness at work and home exacerbates Faulkner's drinking. March to June, works on film script for *Drums Along the Mohawk*, directed by John Ford. Estelle and Jill return to Oxford in late May. Maurice Coindreau stays with Faulkner for week in June to discuss French translation of *The Sound and the Fury*. Writes "An Odor of Verbena," concluding episode in Bayard-Ringo series. Returns to Rowan Oak in late August, having earned over $21,000 for the year working for Twentieth Century–Fox. Begins story "The Wild Palms," then starts to expand it into a novel. Goes to New York in mid-October to prepare the Bayard-Ringo stories for publication with new Random House editor, Saxe Commins. Stays at Algonquin Hotel; sees old friends, including Harrison Smith, Joel Sayre, Eric J. Devine, and Meta Rebner. Renews friendship with Sherwood Anderson. Drinks heavily, collapses against steam pipe in hotel room, and suffers palm-sized third-degree burn on his back. Treated by doctor, then cared for by Devine, who accompanies him back to Oxford. Resumes work on novel, *If I Forget Thee, Jerusalem* (to be published as *The Wild Palms* at publisher's insistence); says the theme of the book is: "Between grief and nothing I will take grief." Reads Keats and Housman aloud and does crossword puzzles with stepdaughter Victoria after breakup of her first marriage ("He kept me alive," she later says). Intense pain from burn makes sleeping difficult.

1938   *The Unvanquished*, Bayard-Ringo stories reworked with new material into novel, published February 15 by Random House. MGM buys screen rights for $25,000, of which Faulkner receives $19,000 after payment of commissions. Buys 320-acre farm seventeen miles northeast of Oxford and names it Greenfield Farm; insists on raising mules despite brother John's (who is tenant manager) preference for more profitable cattle (later acquires cattle for farm). Despite infection from skin graft performed at the end of February, continues work on *If I Forget Thee, Jerusalem*. Writes to Haas in July: "To me, it was written just as if I had sat on the one side of a wall and the paper was on the other and my hand with the pen thrust through the wall and writing not only on invisible paper but in pitch darkness too . . ." Goes to New York to read proofs of novel, now titled *The Wild Palms*, in late September. Returns to work on Snopes book *The Peasants* and plots out two more volumes, *Rus in Urbe* and *Ilium Falling*, to form trilogy. Takes Harold Ober as new literary agent.

1939   Elected to National Institute of Arts and Letters in January. *The Wild Palms*, published January 19, reviewed in *Time* cover story, sells more than 1,000 copies a week and tops sales of *Sanctuary* by late March. Raises $6,000 by cashing in life insurance policy and obtaining advance from Random House to save Phil Stone from financial disaster. Writes stories, hoping to earn money, and works on Snopes trilogy, retitling volumes *The Hamlet*, *The Town*, and *The Mansion*. Helps brother John at Greenfield Farm, sometimes serving tenants in commissary. Influential favorable essays on Faulkner published by George Marion O'Donnell and Conrad Aiken. Takes short holidays in New York City in October and December after testifying in Washington, D.C., in plagiarism suit brought against Twentieth Century–Fox by writer who claims (wrongly) to have written *The Road to Glory*. Donates manuscript of *Absalom, Absalom!* to relief fund for Spanish Loyalists. "Barn Burning" wins first O. Henry Memorial Award ($300 prize) for best short story published in an American magazine.

1940   Works on proofs of *The Hamlet*. Caroline Barr, in her mid-nineties, suffers stroke and dies January 31. Faulkner gives eulogy in parlor of Rowan Oak. ("She was born in bondage and with a dark skin and most of her early maturity was passed in a dark and tragic time for the land of her birth. She went through vicissitudes which she had not caused; she assumed cares and griefs which were not even her cares and griefs. She was paid wages for this, but pay is still just money. And she never received very much of that . . .") Writes stories about black families. *The Hamlet*, published by Random House April 1, is reviewed favorably, but sales fall below those of *The Wild Palms*. Faces mounting financial pressure from debts, family obligations, and back taxes, but is reluctant to raise funds by selling property. Appeals to Random House for higher advances against royalties, and proposes to make a novel out of series of stories about related black and white families. Tries to get a job in Hollywood. After unsatisfactory negotiations with Random House, goes to New York late in June to negotiate with Harold Guinzburg of The Viking Press, but Viking cannot substantially improve on the Random House offer. Resumes writing stories (five published in the year).

1941   Wires literary agent Harold Ober on January 16 asking for $100; uses part of it to pay electric bill. Organizes Lafayette County aircraft warning system in late June. Wishing to do more in anticipation of U.S. entry into World War II, thinks about securing military commission and hopes to teach air navigation. "The Bear" accepted by *The Saturday Evening Post* for $1,000 in November. Finishes work on series of stories forming novel *Go Down, Moses* in December.

1942   Goes to Washington, D.C., in unsuccessful attempt to secure military or naval commission. *Go Down, Moses, and Other Stories*, dedicated to Caroline Barr, published by Random House May 11. (Faulkner considers it a novel; "and Other Stories" added by publisher.) Deeply in debt and unable to sell stories, seeks Hollywood work through publishers, agents, and friends. Reports for five-month segment of low-paying ($300 a week), long-term Warner Bros. contract on July 27. Moves into Highland Hotel. Works on film about Charles de Gaulle until project is dropped. Resumes affair with Meta Carpenter (now divorced from Rebner). Sees other old friends, including Ruth Ford (University of Mississippi alumna who had once dated brother Dean), and Clark Gable and Howard Hawks, with whom he goes fishing and hunting. Becomes friends with writers A. I. ("Buzz") Bezzerides and Jo Pagano. Writes two scenes for *Air Force*, directed by Hawks. Gets month's leave to return to Oxford for Christmas while remaining on payroll.

1943   Returns to Warner Bros. January 16 on a 26-week, $350-per-week contract. Begins working with Hawks in March on *Battle Cry*, film depicting various Allied nations' roles in the war. Sends one of his RAF pips to nephew James Faulkner, who is training to become Marine Corps fighter pilot (pip is lost when nephew is forced to ditch his Corsair off Okinawa in 1945). Warner Bros. picks up 52-week option at $400 a week in late June; Faulkner drinks and collapses. Writes and revises lengthy and complex script for *Battle Cry*. When the film is canceled in August due to its high cost, takes leave of absence without pay to return to Oxford. Receives $1,000 advance from producer William Bacher to work at home on film treatment about the Unknown Soldier of World War I. Describes it in letter to Ober as "a fable, an indictment of war perhaps" and writes 51-page synopsis in fall.

1944   Reports back to Warner Bros. February 14, and moves in with Bezzerides family on Saltair Street, just north of Santa Monica. Begins work for Hawks on film version of Ernest Hemingway's *To Have and Have Not*. Estelle and Jill join him in June, and they move to an apartment in East Hollywood. Works with Hawks and screenwriter Leigh Bracket on film of Raymond Chandler's *The Big Sleep*. Depression, drinking, and periods of hospitalization follow departure of Jill and Estelle in September. Critic Malcolm Cowley writes the first of several essays on Faulkner, comparing him to Balzac and noting that all his works except *Sanctuary* are out of print. Works on script for *Mildred Pierce*, directed by Michael Curtiz. Requests leave without pay and returns home December 15, taking with him the script for *The Big Sleep*, which he finishes in Oxford.

1945   Works on the "fable" about the Unknown Soldier, hoping to make it into a novel. Returns to Hollywood and Warner Bros. in June, now at $500 a week. Crowley obtains publishers' approval in August to edit a collection of Faulkner's works for the Viking Portable Library series; Faulkner advises him on selections. Works on scripts for *Stallion Road* and briefly with Jean Renoir on *The Southerner*. Continues work on the "fable," rising at 4:00 A.M. and working until 8:00 A.M. before going to the studio. Hollywood agent William Herndon refuses to release him from agent-client agreement and Warner Bros. refuses to release him from exclusive contract. Writes: "I dont like this damn place any better than I ever did. That is one comfort: at least I cant be any sicker tomorrow for Mississippi than I was yesterday." Refusing to assign Warner Bros. film rights to his own writings (including the "fable"), leaves studio without permission September 18. Returns to Rowan Oak, bringing Lady Go-lightly, the mare Jill rode during her stay in California. Redraws map of Yoknapatawpha County and writes "1699–1945 The Compsons" to go with excerpt from *The Sound and the Fury* in Cowley's *Portable Faulkner*; says, "I should have done this when I wrote the book. Then the whole thing would have fallen into pattern like a jigsaw puzzle when the magician's wand touched it." Takes part in annual hunt in November. Short story, "An Error in Chemistry," wins second prize ($250) in *Ellery Queen's Mystery Magazine* contest in December.

1946   Feels trapped and depressed, drinks heavily. Cerf, Haas, and Ober persuade Jack Warner to give Faulkner leave of absence and release from rights assignment so he can finish his novel. Random House pays immediate advance of $1,000 and $500 a month after that. Faulkner worries that novel will take longer to complete than advances can cover. *The Portable Faulkner* published by Viking April 29. Tells class at University of Mississippi in May that the four greatest influences on his work were the Old Testament, Melville, Dostoevski, and Conrad. European reputation, especially in France, grows as works are translated. Jean-Paul Sartre writes of Faulkner's significance in "American Novelists in French Eyes," in September *Atlantic Monthly*. Sells film rights for stories "Death Drag" and "Honor" to RKO for combined net of $6,600, and "Two Soldiers" to Cagney Productions for $3,750. Random House issues *The Sound and the Fury* (with "1699–1945 The Compsons" retitled "Appendix/Compson: 1699–1945" added as first part) and *As I Lay Dying* together in Modern Library edition in October. Nearly hits trees while landing airplane and does not fly as pilot again. Continues work on "fable." Works secretly, because of exclusive Warner Bros. contract, on film script (unidentified) at home.

1947   Meets in April with six literature classes at University of Mississippi on condition no notes be taken. Ranks

Hemingway among top contemporaries, along with Thomas Wolfe, John Dos Passos, and John Steinbeck, but is quoted in wire-service account as saying that Hemingway "has no courage, has never gone out on a limb. He has never used a word where the reader might check his usage in a dictionary." Hemingway is deeply offended, and Faulkner writes apology. Long-time family servant Ned Barnett dies. In November *Partisan Review* declines excerpt about a horse race from the "fable."

1948   Begins mystery novel in January, based on idea mentioned to Haas in 1940; calls it *Intruder in the Dust*, and finishes it in April. MGM buys film rights for $50,000 before publication. Published by Random House September 27, it is his most commercially successful book, selling over 15,000 copies. Feels free of financial pressure for the first time. Turns down Hamilton Basso's proposal of *New Yorker* profile: "I am working tooth and nail at my lifetime ambition to be the last private individual on earth . . ." Works on short-story collection proposed earlier in the year by Random House. Eager to visit friends, goes to New York for holiday in October and meets Malcolm Cowley for the first time. Collapses after few days and recuperates at Cowley's home in Sherman, Connecticut. Decides to arrange stories in collection by cycles, an idea suggested by Cowley three years earlier. Elected to the American Academy of Arts and Letters November 23.

1949   Director Clarence Brown brings MGM company to Oxford to film *Intruder in the Dust*. Faulkner revises screenplay and helps scout locations, but is not given credit because of legal complications with Warner Bros. Rewrites unpublished 1942 mystery story "Knight's Gambit," expanding it into novella. Buys sloop, which he names *The Ring Dove*, and sails it on Sardis Reservoir, 25 miles northwest of Oxford, during spring and summer. Eudora Welty visits and Faulkner takes her sailing. In August is sought out by 20-year-old Joan Williams, Bard College student and aspiring writer from Memphis, who admires his work. Reluctantly attends world premiere of *Intruder in the Dust* on October 9 at refurbished Lyric Theatre, owned by cousin Sallie Murry Williams and her husband. Event is considered to have caused the most excitement since Union general A. J. Smith burned Oxford in Civil

War. "A Courtship" wins O. Henry Award for 1949. Random House publishes *Knight's Gambit*, volume of mystery stories, November 27.

1950   Writes to Joan Williams in January, offering help as a mentor. Goes to New York for ten days in February, staying at Algonquin; sees publishers, old friends (actress Ruth Ford, Joel Sayre, and others), and Joan Williams. Begins sending her notes for a play he hopes they will write together. Writes letter to Memphis *Commercial Appeal* in March protesting failure of Mississippi jury to give death penalty to a white man convicted of murdering three black children. Receives American Academy's William Dean Howells Medal for Fiction in May; does not attend ceremony. Personal involvement with Joan Williams deepens when she returns to Memphis for summer. Gives her manuscript of *The Sound and the Fury*. She is reluctant to rewrite his material for play *Requiem for a Nun*, and their collaboration becomes increasingly difficult. *Collected Stories of William Faulkner* published August 2 by Random House and adopted by Book-of-the-Month Club as alternate fiction selection, receiving generally good reviews. Informed November 10 he will receive 1949 (delayed until 1950) Nobel Prize for Literature. Reluctant to attend, drinks heavily at annual hunt, contracts bad cold, but finally agrees to go to Stockholm with Jill to receive award on December 10. Meets Else Jonsson, widow of Thorsten Jonsson, one of Faulkner's earliest Swedish translators. Gives widely quoted address ("I believe that man will not merely endure: he will prevail"). Afterward, writes to friend, "I fear that some of my fellow Mississippians will never forgive that 30,000$ that durn foreign country gave me for just sitting on my ass writing stuff that makes my own state ashamed to own me." *The New York Times* reports that 100,000 copies of his books have been sold in Modern Library editions, and that 2.5 million paperback copies are in print.

1951   Takes $5,000 of Nobel Prize money for his own use, establishes "Faulkner Memorial" trust fund with remainder for scholarships and other educational purposes. Goes to Hollywood in February for five weeks scriptwriting on *The Left Hand of God* for Hawks. Earns $14,000, including bonus for finishing script ahead of schedule (Hawks does not direct film, and Faulkner does not receive writing credit when it is released in 1955). Sees Meta Carpenter for last time. The Levee Press of Greenville, Mississippi, publishes horse-race piece as *Notes on a Horsethief* February 10. *Collected Stories* receives National Book Award for Fiction March 6. Releases statement to Memphis *Commercial Appeal* doubting guilt and opposing execution of Willie McGee, a black man convicted of raping a white woman (McGee is later executed). Takes three-week trip in April to New York, England, and France, visiting Verdun battlefield, which figures in his "fable." Finishes manuscript of *Requiem for a Nun* in early June. (Writes in letter to Else Jonsson: "I am really tired of writing, the agony and sweat of it. I'll probably never quit though, until I die. But now I feel like nothing would be as peaceful as to break the pencil, throw it away, admit I dont know why, the answers either.") Hears from Ruth Ford that Lemuel Ayers would like to produce *Requiem for a Nun* on stage, and goes to New York for week in July to work on it. Drives Jill to school at Pine Manor Junior College in Wellesley, Massachusetts, with Estelle. *Requiem for a Nun*, with long prose introductions to its three acts, published by Random House October 2. Works on stage version in Cambridge, Massachusetts, in October and November. Becomes officer in the Legion of Honor of the Republic of France at ceremony at French Consulate in New Orleans October 26.

1952   Works on "fable" and trains horse; has two falls in February and March, injuring his back. Attends ceremony commemorating ninetieth anniversary of battle of Shiloh with novelist Shelby Foote, and walks over battlefield with him. Turns down honorary degree of doctor of letters from Tulane University (later declines all other attempts to award him honorary degrees). Attacks "welfare and other bureaus of economic or industrial regimentation" in address delivered May 15 to Delta Council in Cleveland, Mississippi. Takes one-month trip to Europe, though plans to produce his play during Paris cultural festival had fallen through. Collapses in severe pain in Paris; doctors discover two old spinal compression fractures, possibly riding injuries, and advise surgical fusion. Faulkner refuses and visits Harold Raymond of Chatto & Windus

in England, still suffering severe pain. Treated near Oslo,
Norway, by masseur on advice of Else Jonsson. Returns
home feeling better than he has in years, but is not allowed
to ride. Helps Joan Williams with her writing, but relationship is increasingly troubled. Injures back in boating
accident in August. Hospitalized in Memphis in September for convulsive seizure brought on by drinking and
back pain, and again in October, after fall down stairs.
X-rays reveal three additional old spinal compression
fractures. Wears back brace. Helps Ford Foundation prepare *Omnibus* production of "The Faulkner Story" for television in November. Accepts editor and friend Saxe
Commins' invitation to write at his Princeton home. Depression and drinking precipitate collapse and is admitted
to private hospital in New York. After discharge stays in
New York, working on "fable"; sees Joan Williams. Returns home for Christmas.

1953   Stays in Oxford until Estelle recovers from cataract operation. Returns to New York January 31 for indefinite stay,
hoping to finish the "fable." Medical problems continue;
has extensive physiological and neurological examinations
to determine cause of memory lapses, but nothing new is
discovered. Writes semi-autobiographical essay "Mississippi" for *Holiday* (appears April 1954). Returns to Oxford
with Jill in late April when Estelle is hospitalized for severe
hemorrhage. Goes back to New York May 9, when danger
is over. Estelle accompanies him when he gives com-
mencement address at Jill's graduation from Pine Manor.
Jill attends University of Mexico in fall, and Estelle goes
with her when she leaves in late August. Faulkner stays
at Rowan Oak, working on "fable." Hospitalized in
September in Memphis and in Wright's Sanitarium in
Byhalia. Angered when *Life* magazine publishes two-part
article on him, September 28–October 5. Drives to New
York with Joan Williams in October; they see Dylan
Thomas (whose earlier poetry reading Faulkner had found
moving) shortly before Thomas's death in November, and
attend subsequent memorial service. Finishes *A Fable* at
Commins' house in early November. Leaves for Paris to
work with Hawks and screenwriter Harry Kurnitz on film,
Land of the Pharaohs. Meets 19-year-old admirer, Jean
Stein, in St. Moritz on Christmas Eve. Spends Christmas
holidays in Stockholm and sees Else Jonsson.

1954 Stays with Harold Raymond in Biddenden, Kent, England, in early January, and then goes to Switzerland, Paris, and Rome, visiting friends, seeing Jean Stein, and working on film. Arrives in Cairo in mid-February suffering from alcoholic collapse and is taken to Anglo-American Hospital. Continues working on film, but Hawks and Kurnitz do not use most of what he writes. Joan Williams marries Ezra Bowen on March 6. Leaves Egypt March 29. Stays three weeks in Paris, spending one night in hospital. Returns home in late April, after short stay in New York. Writes preface for *A Fable*, but decides not to use it. Works on farm most of May; sells livestock and then rents it out for a year. *A Fable* published by Random House, August 2. At request of U.S. State Department, attends International Writers' Conference in São Paulo, Brazil, stopping off on the way at Lima, Peru. Enjoys trip and offers his services again on return home. Jill marries Paul D. Summers, Jr., August 21, and moves to Charlottesville, Virginia, where Paul attends law school. Faulkner checks into Algonquin Hotel, New York, September 10; divides time between New York and Oxford for next six months. Makes spoken record for Caedmon Records, works on stories and magazine pieces, and feels reassured of ability to earn money. Sees Jean Stein often.

1955 Writes article on hockey game at Madison Square Garden, "An Innocent at Rinkside," for *Sports Illustrated* (appears January 24). Accepts National Book Award for Fiction for *A Fable*, January 25. Works on script for *The Era of Fear*, ABC television program about McCarthyism, but in March angrily rejects contract which includes morals clause and requires membership in unions ABC deals with. Becomes increasingly involved in civil rights issues; writes letters to editors advocating school integration; receives abusive letters and phone calls, and his position angers his brothers. Gives lecture "On Privacy. The American Dream: What Happened to It" at the University of Oregon and University of Montana in April (published in *Harper's*, May). *A Fable* wins Pulitzer Prize in May. Writes article on eighty-first running of Kentucky Derby for *Sports Illustrated*. Helps publicize *Land of the Pharaohs*. Leaves on State Department trip July 29. Spends three weeks in Japan, visiting Tokyo, Nagano, and Kyoto, and delighting Japanese hosts (remarks from colloquia published as *Faulkner at Nagano*, 1956). Returns to New York by way of Philippines (to visit stepdaughter and family), Italy, France, England, and Iceland, combining State Department appearances and vacation. *Big Woods*, collection of hunting stories with new linking material, illustrated by Edward Shenton, published by Random House, October 14. Rushes to Oxford October 23 when mother, almost eighty-five, suffers cerebral hemorrhage; remains while she recuperates. Speaks against discrimination to integrated audience at Memphis meeting of Southern Historical Association, November 10; receives more threatening letters and phone calls. When Jean Stein visits the South, shows her New Orleans and Gulf Coast; they encounter Helen Baird Lyman on a Pascagoula beach. Begins *The Town*, second Snopes volume, in November.

1956   Columbia Pictures takes option on *The Sound and the Fury* for $3,500 (film is released by Twentieth Century–Fox in 1959), and Universal buys *Pylon* for $50,000 (released in 1958 as *The Tarnished Angels*, directed by Douglas Sirk). Goes to New York February 8 to discuss finances with Ober. Worried about imminent violence, writes two articles urging voluntary integration in South to prevent Northern intervention: "On Fear: The South in Labor" (*Harper's*, June), and "A Letter to the North" (*Life*, March). Increasingly alarmed by rising tensions over court-ordered integration of University of Alabama, agrees to interview with *The Reporter* magazine; desperate and drinking, says if South were pushed too hard there would be civil war. Interviewer quotes him as saying that "if it came to fighting I'd fight for Mississippi against the United States even if it meant . . . shooting Negroes." (Later repudiates the interview: "They are statements which no sober man would make, nor it seems to me, any sane man believe.") Does extensive interview with Jean Stein for *The Paris Review*. On return to Oxford, injures back again when he is thrown by horse. Begins vomiting blood March 18; hospitalized in Memphis. By early April feels well enough to go with Estelle to Charlottesville, Virginia, where first grandson, Paul D. Summers III, is born April 15. Works on *The Town* in Oxford during summer. With P. D. East, starts semi-annual satirical paper for Southern moderates, entitled *The Southern Reposure*. First and only issue appears in mid-summer. Writes essay for *Ebony*, appealing for moderation. Albert Camus' adaptation of *Requiem for a Nun* successfully staged in Paris. Goes to Washington, D.C., for four days in September as chairman of writers' group in Eisenhower Administration's People-to-People Program. Chooses Harvey Breit of *The New York Times* as co-chairman; attends meeting at Breit's home November 29.

1957   Continues chairman's work into early February. Refuses Estelle's offer of a divorce. Depressed by changing relationship with Jean Stein, suffers collapse. Goes to Charlottesville as University of Virginia's first writer-in-residence February 9; moves into house on Rugby Road. Meets professors Frederick L. Gwynn and Joseph Blotner, who assist him in setting schedules. Arrives in Athens March 17 for two-week visit at invitation of State Department; sees Greek adaptation of *Requiem for a Nun*. Cruises four days on private yacht in the Aegean. Accepts Silver Medal from Greek Academy. *The Town*, published May 1 by Random House, receives mixed reviews. Presents National Institute of Arts and Letters Gold Medal for Fiction to John Dos Passos May 22. Concludes successful university semester of classroom and public appearances. Rides with friends and in the Farmington Hunt, and tours Civil War battlefields near Richmond. Returns to Rowan Oak for summer, tends to farm and boat, visits mother. Ignores telegrams from producer Jerry Wald reporting on production of film *The Long Hot Summer*, based on *The Hamlet* (released 1958). Goes to Charlottesville in November, intending to ride and fox-hunt, but falls ill with strep throat. Hunts quail near Oxford in December.

1958   Begins to type first draft of *The Mansion*, third and last of the Snopes trilogy, at Rowan Oak in early January. Returns to Charlottesville for second term as writer-in-residence, January 30, meeting classes and public groups. (Remarks are published in *Faulkner in the University: Class Conferences at the University of Virginia, 1957–58* in 1959.) At one session presents "A Word to Virginians," an appeal to state to take the lead in teaching blacks "the responsibilities of equality." Goes to Princeton for two weeks, March 1, meeting with students individually and in groups. Returns to Oxford in May. Declines, for political reasons, invitation to visit Soviet Union with group of writers. Saxe Commins dies July 17. Gives away niece Dean Faulkner, daughter of brother Dean, at her wedding November 9. Goes to Princeton for another week of student sessions, and then to New York to work on *The Mansion* with Random House editor Albert Erskine. Returns to Charlottesville and rides in the Keswick and Farmington hunts; is described by a fellow rider as "all nerve." Second grandchild, William Cuthbert Faulkner Summers, born December 2.

1959   Works on *The Mansion* and hunts quail in Oxford. *Requiem for a Nun*, version adapted for the stage by Ruth Ford, opens on Broadway January 30 after successful London run; closes after forty-three performances. Though not reappointed as writer-in-residence for the year, takes position as consultant on contemporary literature to Alderman Library at University of Virginia, and is assigned library study and typewriter. Accepted as outside member in Farmington Hunt and continues riding with Keswick Hunt. Fractures collarbone when horse falls at Farmington hunter trials March 14. Rides again in May at Rowan Oak despite slow and painful recovery; another horse fall causes additional injuries, necessitating use of crutches for two weeks. Works with Albert Erskine in New York on *The Mansion*, eliminating some of the discrepancies between it and *The Hamlet*. Writes preface to *The Mansion* explaining others. Completes purchase of Charlottesville home on Rugby Road, August 21. Attends four-day UNESCO conference in Denver late September. Harold Ober, long-time agent and friend, dies October 31. *The Mansion* published by Random House, November 13. Continues riding and hunting, suffering occasional falls.

1960   Divides time between Oxford and Charlottesville. Hospitalized briefly at Byhalia for collapse brought on by bourbon administered for self-diagnosed pleurisy. Accepts appointment as Balch Lecturer in American Literature at University of Virginia with minimal duties (salary $250 a year) in August. Mother suffers cerebral hemorrhage, dies October 16. Sees Charlottesville friends often, including Joseph and Yvonne Blotner. Becomes full member of Farmington Hunt. Establishes William Faulkner Foundation December 28, providing scholarships for black

Mississippians and prize for first novels; bequeaths to it the manuscripts he has deposited in the Alderman Library.

1961 Hunts quail in Oxford in January. Reluctantly leaves on two-week State Department trip to Venezuela April 1. Receives the Order of Andrés Bello, Venezuela's highest civilian award; gives speech expressing gratitude in Spanish. Third grandson, A. Burks Summers, born May 30. Shocked by news of Hemingway's suicide, July 2. Returns to Rowan Oak. Begins writing *The Horse Stealers: A Reminiscence*, conceived years earlier as novel about " a sort of Huck Finn"; enjoys work and finishes first draft August 21. Returns to Charlottesville in mid-October. Novel, retitled *The Reivers*, taken by Book-of-the-Month Club eight months before publication. Checks into Algonquin Hotel to work on book with editor Albert Erskine, November 27. Hospitalized in Charlottesville, December 18, suffering from acute respiratory infection, back trouble, and drinking. Leaves after several days, but soon has relapse and is treated at Tucker Neurological and Psychiatric Hospital in Richmond until December 29.

1962 Injured in fall from horse, January 3. Readmitted to Tucker suffering from chest pain, fever, and drinking, January 8. Goes to Rowan Oak to recuperate in mid-January and hunts with nephew James Faulkner. Returns to Charlottesville in early April; intends to make move permanent. Travels to West Point with Estelle, Jill, and Paul, April 19, and reads from *The Reivers*. Turns down president John F. Kennedy's invitation to attend dinner for American Nobel Prize winners. Accepts Gold Medal for Fiction of National Institute of Arts and Letters, presented by Eudora Welty, May 24. Returns to Oxford. *The Reivers* published by Random House, June 4. Thrown by horse near Rowan Oak, June 17. Endures much pain, but continues to go for walks, and negotiates purchase of Red Acres, 250-acre estate outside Charlottesville, for $200,000. Pain and drinking increase; taken by Estelle and James Faulkner to Wright's Sanitarium at Byhalia, July 5. Dies of heart attack, 1:30 A.M. on July 6. After service at Rowan Oak is buried on July 7 in St. Peter's Cemetery, Oxford, Mississippi.

Note on the Texts

This volume prints the texts of *Soldiers' Pay*, *Mosquitoes*, *Flags in the Dust*, and *The Sound and the Fury* that have been established by Noel Polk. All texts are based upon Faulkner's own typescripts, which have been emended to account for revisions by Faulkner that appeared in the first editions, his typing errors, and certain other errors and inconsistencies that clearly demand correction. The texts presented here are based upon comparisons of all extant forms of these works, published and unpublished, to determine the nature and causes of variants among the texts. The goal of these labors—to discover the forms of these works that Faulkner wanted in print at the time of their original publication—is sometimes elusive. Although thousands of pages of typescript and holograph manuscript are available to the editor, it is not always clear what Faulkner's final intentions were, or even whether Faulkner had any "final" intentions regarding some of the individual components of his novels.

No typescript setting copy, nor any stage of galley-proof or page-proof, is known to be extant for any of the four novels collected in this volume. Without the typescript setting copies or proofs it is difficult to account for the differences between the preliminary ribbon and carbon typescripts and the first printings of the published book versions of the novels. Lacking such evidence, the Polk texts of the novels in this volume are based upon a conflation of the underlying preliminary ribbon or carbon typescripts and the first printings. In deciding between variants, the editor used what he has learned about Faulkner's style and preferences in editing the other volumes of the novels in the Library of America series, while being careful not to impose on the early Faulkner the usages and preferences of the later works. The Polk texts thus incorporate into the texts of the typescripts all of the first-edition variants that can reasonably be attributed to Faulkner, while rejecting changes in the first-edition texts that seem likely to be editorial in origin.

In some ways Faulkner was an extremely consistent writer. He never included apostrophes in the words "dont," "wont," "aint," "cant," or "oclock," and never used a period after the titles "Mr," "Mrs," or "Dr". The editors of the first editions generally, though inconsistently, accepted these practices, but compositors often made mistakes, and many periods and apostrophes slipped in. More serious problems also frequently occurred, mostly attendant upon the editors' and Faulkner's indifferent proofreading and upon the editors' general lack of understanding of what Faulkner was trying to do. As a result, the original editors of the novels in this volume intervened in hundreds of ways that affected the capitalization, punctuation, and wording of the published texts.

Faulkner's attitude toward editorial intervention is neither consistent nor entirely clear. Almost from the beginning of his career, Faulkner was a supremely confident craftsman; he was at the same time aware of the complexity of the demands his work would make not merely on the reader but also on the publisher, editor, and proofreader. His response to Ben Wasson's tampering with the Benjy section of *The Sound and the Fury*—that he would rewrite it if publishing were not grown up enough to publish it as he wanted it—reflects both his flexibility toward the realities of publication and his impatience with those mechanical processes of publication beyond his control that might thwart the accomplishment of his artistic goals. He seems to have been indifferent to some types of editorial changes, and he acquiesced to them; he seems not to have cared whether certain words were spelled consistently or not, whether certain of his archaisms were modernized or not, and he seems to have expected his editor to divine from his typing whether each sentence was punctuated exactly as he wanted it—that is, whether or not a variation from an apparent pattern was in fact a deliberate variation or merely an inadvertency an editor should correct.

With the benefit of decades of intense scholarship, we are now in a better position to understand Faulkner's intentions, although clearly many of the original editorial problems remain. The Polk texts attempt to reproduce the texts of Faulkner's typescripts as he intended them to be originally published, in so far as that intention can be reconstructed from the evidence. They accept only those revisions that Faulkner seems to have initiated himself as a response to his own text; this is a very conservative policy that rejects many first edition variants in favor of his original typescript.

While every effort has been made to preserve Faulkner's idiosyncrasies in spelling and punctuation, certain corrections of the typescripts have been necessary. Unmistakable typing errors and other demonstrable errors have been corrected. Faulkner's punctuation has been regularized in two cases: except for using three hyphens (- - -) to indicate a one-em dash, Faulkner was inconsistent throughout his career in the number of hyphens he typed to indicate a dash longer than one em, and in the number of dots he typed to indicate ellipses; in his early novels, he frequently typed as many as twelve or thirteen hyphens or dots. In the Polk texts, three or four hyphens become a one-em dash, five or more become a two-em dash; up to six dots of ellipses are regularized to three or four according to traditional usage, seven or more become seven. Accent marks have been added to foreign words where appropriate.

In January 1925 Faulkner went to New Orleans with plans to sail for Europe but found the city so appealing that he postponed his departure for six months. During his stay he met the novelist Sherwood Anderson, the painter William Spratling, and other artistic habitués of the Vieux Carré, and he supported himself by writing and selling sketches of French Quarter life to the New Orleans *Times-Picayune*. He apparently began work on his first novel soon after his arrival, using the title "Mayday," and completed a revised typescript during the spring, writing "New Orleans / May 1925" in ink on its final page. After Anderson recommended the novel to Boni & Liveright, Faulkner sent a new typescript, retitled *Soldiers' Pay*, to the firm. (Faulkner then used *Mayday* as the title for an illustrated allegorical tale that he gave in 1926 to Helen Baird, a sculptor he had met in New Orleans.) Boni & Liveright accepted the novel and published it on February 25, 1926. Because the typescript Faulkner sent to Boni & Liveright is not known to be extant, the typescript dated "May 1925" and the first edition are the sources for the conflated Polk text of *Soldiers' Pay*.

Faulkner sailed for Europe on July 7, 1925, and arrived in Paris in mid-August. While in Paris he worked on a novel titled "Mosquito" and on another novel (never completed) about a young painter that was called "Elmer" in one version and "A Portrait of Elmer Hodge" in another. Faulkner returned to the United States in December 1925 and spent the summer of 1926 in Pascagoula, on the Mississippi Gulf Coast, working full time on *Mosquitoes*. In late summer he completed a typescript, writing "Pascagoula, Miss / 1 September 1926" in ink on its final page. Faulkner then made numerous handwritten changes to this typescript, which he had retyped and sent to Boni & Liveright. *Mosquitoes* was published on April 30, 1927. There are many substantive variants between the typescript dated "1 September 1926" and the first edition, including the deletion of four passages dealing with sexual subjects (pp. 289.20–290.30; pp. 380.27–382.16; p. 399.39, beginning "Again Pete raised his head," to p. 400.40; and p. 407.8–38 in this volume). Because the typescript Faulkner sent to Boni & Liveright is not known to be extant, the Polk text of *Mosquitoes* is based on a conflation of the typescript dated "1 September 1926" and the first edition.

In the autumn of 1926 Faulkner began writing *Flags in the Dust*, the first of his novels to be set in what he later called "my own little postage stamp of native soil," and in October 1927 he submitted a typescript to Boni & Liveright. This typescript, dated "Oxford, Miss / 29 September 1927," is a composite of several different typings of portions of the novel, done on more than one typewriter and by at least two different typists. Numerous pages bear two or more page numbers; many pages contain revised versions of passages crossed out on previous pages; and there are numerous revisions made by Faulkner in ink throughout the typescript. The novel was rejected by Horace Liveright, who described it in a letter to Faulkner as "diffuse and non-integral with neither very much plot development nor character development. . . . The story really doesn't get anywhere and has a thousand loose ends." After making further revisions, Faulkner sent *Flags in the Dust* to his friend and agent Ben Wasson, who later said that he showed the novel to 11 publishers before Harcourt, Brace accepted it in September 1928 on the condition that it be shortened to about 110,000 words. Faulkner agreed and traveled to New York, where he worked on *The Sound and the Fury* while Wasson did most, if not all, of the cutting; much of the deleted material was excised from episodes involving Horace and Narcissa Benbow.

Sartoris was published by Harcourt, Brace on January 31, 1929 (the new title was chosen by Harcourt). Neither the typescript Faulkner sent to Wasson in 1928, nor any typescripts or proofs used by Harcourt in the publication of *Sartoris*, are known to survive. In 1973 Random House published an edition of *Flags in the Dust* edited by Douglas Day, who used the typescript dated "29 September 1927" as his text, although he made some editorial alterations and interpolated into his text one passage from *Sartoris*. The Polk text of *Flags in the Dust* is also based on the surviving typescript, but it incorporates several passages from *Sartoris* that do not appear in the typescript and which seem clearly to have been written by Faulkner. The result is a conflated text that aims to be as close as possible to the typescript that Faulkner sent to Wasson in 1928.

Faulkner began writing *The Sound and the Fury* early in 1928, using at first the title "Twilight." In the fall he completed a typescript, dated "New York, N.Y. / October 1928," and apparently kept the carbon copy while sending the ribbon copy to Harrison Smith, the editor at Harcourt, Brace who had recommended publication of *Flags in the Dust* to Alfred Harcourt. Harcourt rejected the novel, but permitted Smith to take it with him when he left the company to join Jonathan Cape in a new publishing venture, and in February 1929 Faulkner signed a contract for its publication with Cape and Smith. In the summer of 1929 Faulkner received galley proofs of the first section of *The Sound and the Fury* and discovered that Ben Wasson, who was now an editor at Cape and Smith, had instructed the printer to ignore Faulkner's extensive use of italics and instead to indicate shifts in time by inserting line spaces between sections. Faulkner wrote to Wasson, instructing him to restore the italics and letting him know that he had marked additional passages in the galleys for italicization. Because none of the proofs for *The Sound and the Fury* are known to have survived, it cannot be determined how closely Wasson followed Faulkner's instructions. *The Sound and the Fury* was published by Jonathan Cape and Harrison Smith on October 7, 1929. In 1984 Random House published a "New, Corrected Edition" of *The Sound and the Fury*, prepared by Noel Polk. The corrected edition reproduces the text of the carbon typescript dated "October 1928" except in cases where there is a compelling reason to accept a reading from the 1929 first edition. The text printed in the present volume is that of the 1984 corrected edition, with the following exceptions, keyed to the page and line numbers of the present volume: "trees" replaces "treees" at 881.31; "didn't. . . . . . ." replaces "didn't. . . ." at 939.22; "pled" replaces "plead" at 958.37; "*away*" is followed by two letter spaces instead of one at 981.30; "against" replaces "aganst" at 984.6; "Quentin. . . . . . ." replaces "Quentin. . . ." at 1045.15; "hand. . . . . . ." replaces "hand. . . ." at 1092.29; "cold. . . . . . ." replaces "cold. . . ." at 1104.29; and "else. . . . . . ." replaces "else. . . ." at 1113.26.

Faulkner wrote "1699–1945 The Compsons" in 1945 for inclusion in *The Portable Faulkner*, edited by Malcolm Cowley, which contained a selection from the fourth section of *The Sound and the Fury*. Under the title "Appendix / Compson: 1699–1945" it appeared in the 1946 Modern Library combined edition of *The Sound and the Fury* and *As I Lay Dying*. In 1992 the Modern Library published the text of the 1984 corrected edition of *The Sound and the Fury* in an issue that contained a new text of "Appendix / Compson: 1699–1945," edited by Polk and based on Faulkner's carbon typescript. The text printed in this volume is taken from the 1992 Modern Library issue of *The Sound and the Fury*.

By preserving Faulkner's spelling, punctuation, and wording, even when inconsistent or irregular, the Polk texts strive to be as faithful to Faulkner's usage as surviving evidence permits. In this volume, the reader has the results of the most detailed scholarly efforts thus far made to establish the texts of *Soldiers' Pay*, *Mosquitoes*, *Flags in the Dust*, and *The Sound and the Fury*.

Notes

In the notes below, the reference numbers denote page and line of this volume (the line count includes chapter headings). No note is made for material included in the eleventh edition of *Merriam-Webster's Collegiate Dictionary*. For more detailed notes, references to other studies, and further biographical background than is contained in the Chronology, see: Joseph Blotner, *Faulkner, A Biography*, 2 vols. (New York: Random House, 1974); Joseph Blotner, *Faulkner, A Biography*, *One-Volume Edition* (New York: Random House, 1984); *Selected Letters of William Faulkner* (New York: Random House, 1977), edited by Joseph Blotner; Calvin S. Brown, *A Glossary of Faulkner's South* (New Haven: Yale University Press, 1976); Edwin T. Arnold, "William Faulkner's *Mosquitoes*: An Introduction and Annotations to the Novel" (Ann Arbor: University Microfilms International, 1978); Stephen Neal Dennis, "The Making of *Sartoris*: A Description and Discussion of the Manuscript and Composite Typescript of William Faulkner's Third Novel" (Ann Arbor: University Microfilms International, 1969); William Faulkner, *Mosquitoes: A Facsimile and Transcription of the University of Virginia Holograph Manuscript*, ed. Thomas L. McHaney with David L. Vander Meulen (Charlottesville: The Bibliographical Society of the University of Virginia and the University of Virginia Library, 1997); George Hayhoe, "A Critical and Textual Study of William Faulkner's *Flags in the Dust*" (Ann Arbor: University Microfilms International, 1979); Noel Polk, *An Editorial Handbook for William Faulkner's* The Sound and the Fury (New York: Garland Publishing, 1985).

SOLDIERS' PAY

3.21   white band]   The band denoted an aviation cadet.

15.34   kee wees]   Flightless birds; here, non-flying members of the air service.

21.22   a ribbon: purple, white, purple,]   The ribbon for the British Distinguished Flying Cross.

35.17   kee wees]   See note 15.34.

43.16–23   "Integer . . . Hydaspes."]   Horace, *Odes*, Book I, 22, lines 1–7: "One whose life is clean and by crimes unblemished / Needs no Moorish javelins, needs no bow and / Load of poisoned arrows to carry, Fuscus, / Crammed in his quiver, / Travel though he may over burning sands of /

Syrtes, or through Caucasus ever savage, / Or to regions washed by the far and fabled / River Hydaspes." (Translated by Charles E. Passage.)

50.38–39   Les Contes Drolatiques] *Droll Tales* (1832) by Honoré de Balzac.

51.34–35   'Shropshire Lad,'] *A Shropshire Lad* (1896) by A. E. Housman.

87.37   Tom Watson] Watson (1856–1922) was a Populist congressman from Georgia, 1891–93, and the Populist candidate for president in 1904 and 1908. In 1911 he founded the *Weekly Jeffersonian* and used it to promote nativism, isolationism, and white supremacy. Watson was elected to the U.S. Senate as a Democrat in 1920 and served until his death.

91.1–2   chanting it after him, like Vachel Lindsay] See Vachel Lindsay, "The Congo" (1914).

105.30   'La lune ne grade aucune rancune'] Cf. T. S. Eliot, "Rhapsody on a Windy Night": "La lune garde aucune rancune" ("the moon holds no grudge").

105.31   'noir sur la lune?'] "Dark on the moon."

158.29–30   Ella Wilcox . . . Irene Castle] Ella Wheeler Wilcox (1850–1919), popular poet who achieved notoriety with *Poems of Passion* (1883), followed by many other collections; Irene Castle (1893–1969), dancer who with her husband Vernon Castle popularized such dances as the "Turkey Trot" and the "Castle Walk."

180.4   Mirandola] Giovanni Pico della Mirandola (1463–1494), Italian Neoplatonist philosopher.

234.18   Per ardua ad astra.] "Through adversity to the stars," the motto of the Royal Air Force.

252.34–37   'Ah, Moon of my Delight . . . after me—in vain!'] Edward Fitzgerald, *Rubáiyát of Omar Khayyám* (1859), quatrain 74.

MOSQUITOES

262.14   vieux carré] The French Quarter of New Orleans.

292.22   le garçon vierge] The virgin boy.

293.15–16   israfel] Angel in Islamic tradition cited by Edgar Allan Poe in his poem "Israfel": "None sing so wildly well / As the angel Israfel."

298.12   less-than-one-percent] The Volstead Act, passed in 1919 to enforce Prohibition, permitted the sale of beer containing one half of one percent alcohol by volume.

308.40   congress boots] Men's ankle-high shoes with elastic sides.

317.36   Mandeville] City across Lake Pontchartrain from New Orleans.

323.37   Tchufuncta]   Stream flowing south into the northernmost part of Lake Pontchartrain.

426.34   Sandhurst]   Site of the British Royal Military College.

428.5   Decameron]   Collection of one hundred tales (1358) by Giovanni Boccaccio.

452.22   Anna Held and Eva Tanguay]   Anna Held (1872–1918), Polish-born music-hall performer who became a star of the Ziegfeld Follies; Eva Tanguay (1878–1947), American vaudeville star known as "The I Don't Care Girl."

461.30   Dr Ellis]   Havelock Ellis (1859–1939), author of many works on sexuality including the six-volume *Studies in the Psychology of Sex* (1897–1910).

462.17   Hermaphroditus]   Son of Hermes and Aphrodite who rejected the nymph Salmacis; she prayed that they be united forever, and the prayer was answered by their being combined in one body; cf. Ovid, *Metamorphoses*.

539.14   Agnes Mabel Becky]   The three "merry widows" depicted on boxes of Merry Widow condoms.

FLAGS IN THE DUST

549.32   Fort Moultrie fell]   The fort, one of a series guarding Charleston harbor, was evacuated on the night of December 26, 1860, by its federal garrison, which then moved to Fort Sumter.

556.9   shaled]   Fell.

569.5   net]   Hunting pattern.

575.38   Ak. W.]   Armstrong-Whitworth F.K.8, a two-seat British biplane bomber and reconnaissance aircraft.

576.18   Camel]   Sopwith Camel, a single-seat British biplane fighter aircraft.

576.20   Fokkers]   German single-seat fighter aircraft, including the DR.I triplane and D.VII biplane.

576.36   Richthofen's]   Captain Manfred von Richthofen (1892–1918), the top German fighter ace of World War I, was credited with 80 aerial victories before his death in combat.

589.36   dog-robber]   Orderly.

601.7   S.O.S.]   Service of Supply.

611.18   quoilin']   Quarreling.

639.3–4   Liberty Loan]   U.S. government bonds sold to finance World War I.

642.4   Senator Vardaman]   James K. Vardaman (1861–1930), a Democrat, served in the Mississippi house of representatives, 1890–96; as governor,

1904–8; and in the U.S. Senate, 1913–19, where he warned that the conscription of African-Americans during World War I would threaten white supremacy.

672.10–11   triangle]   Signifying non-combatant status.

674.2   o.d.]   Olive drab.

679.5   peanut parcher]   Movable appliance for roasting peanuts.

682.11–12   Arlens and Sabatinis]   Popular novelists Michael Arlen (1895–1956), author of *The Green Hat*, and Rafael Sabatini (1875–1950), author of *Scaramouche* and *Captain Blood*.

690.19   Ahenobarbus]   A powerful Roman family whose members included the Emperor Nero.

730.13   Van Dorn]   Earl Van Dorn (1820–1863) was a Confederate general from June 1861 to May 1863, when he was killed by a jealous husband in Tennessee.

761.20   peanut parcher]   See note 679.5.

796.1   toll]   Bribe or entice.

832.9   sulled]   Acted sullen.

833.26   Raphael Semmes]   Semmes (1809–1877), a Confederate naval officer, commanded the commerce raider *Alabama* from 1862 to 1864.

861.6   A.P.M.'s]   Assistant Provost Marshal.

THE SOUND AND THE FURY

884.17   projecking]   Playing.

899.19   squinch owl]   Screech owl.

910.24   *Et ego in arcadia*]   "I too have been in Arcadia."

915.38   "Agnes Mabel Becky."]   See note 539.14.

917.14   *Jackson*]   Site of the Mississippi state insane asylum.

927.7   gizzle]   Gizzard.

930.7   *a bluegum*]   A person possessing supernatural powers.

930.39   rinktum]   Rump.

931.37   sulling]   Acting sullen.

935.22   Little Sister Death]   Cf. St. Francis of Assisi, "Canticle of the Sun": "Our sister, the death of the body, from whom no man escapeth."

939.15–16   *the voice that breathed o'er Eden*]   Cf. John Keble, "Holy Matrimony."

948.21   Young Lochinvar . . . west]   Cf. Sir Walter Scott, *Marmion: A Tale of Flodden Field*, Canto Fifth, stanza XII.

949.40   *French Lick*]   A summer resort in southern Indiana.

990.34   *swine of Euboeleus*]   In Greek mythology, the swine who were swallowed up in the earth when Hades carried Persephone down into the underworld to be queen of the dead.

1081.13   flac-soled]   The etymology of this phrase is unknown.

1084.17   back to hell]   In folklore jaybirds were said to be spies sent by the Devil.

1093.3   sullin]   See note 931.37.

1127.1   *Appendix*]   Faulkner wrote "1699–1945 The Compsons" in 1945 for publication in *The Portable Faulkner* (1946), edited by Malcolm Cowley. It was retitled "Appendix/Compson: 1699–1945" for its inclusion in the 1946 Modern Library combined edition of *The Sound and the Fury* and *As I Lay Dying*.

1127.14   1833]   Choctaw Indians were forcibly removed from Mississippi and sent to the Indian Territory from 1831 to 1833.

1128.4   Culloden Moor]   Site of the battle fought near Inverness on April 16, 1746, in which the Hanoverian army led by the Duke of Cumberland defeated Prince Charles Stuart and ended the Jacobite rebellion of 1745.

1128.10   Tarleton's]   Lieutenant Colonel Banastre Tarleton (1754–1833), a British officer who commanded Loyalist cavalry during the Revolutionary War.

1133.15–16   *Forever Amber . . . Tom Jones*]   *Forever Amber* (1944), romance novel set in Restoration England by Kathleen Windsor; *Jurgen: A Comedy of Justice* (1919), romance by James Branch Cabell; *Tom Jones* (1749), novel by Henry Fielding.

1133.26   Thorne Smith]   An American comic novelist (1892–1934) whose works included *Topper* (1926) and *The Passionate Witch* (published posthumously in 1941).

1134.20   Cannebière]   The main boulevard in Marseilles.

Library of Congress Cataloging-in-Publication Data

Faulkner, William, 1897–1962.
    [Novels. Selections]
    Novels, 1926–1929 / William Faulkner.
        p. cm.—(The Library of America ; 164)
    Includes bibliographical references.
    Contents: Soldiers' pay—Mosquitoes—Flags in the dust—
The sound and the fury.
    ISBN 1-931082-89-8 (alk. paper)
    I. Title: Soldiers pay. II. Title: Mosquitoes III. Title: Flags in the dust
IV. Title: Sound and the fury   V. Title   VI. Series.

PS3511.A86A6 2006
813'.52—dc22   2005049444

THE LIBRARY OF AMERICA SERIES

The Library of America fosters appreciation and pride in America's literary heritage by publishing, and keeping permanently in print, authoritative editions of America's best and most significant writing. An independent nonprofit organization, it was founded in 1979 with seed money from the National Endowment for the Humanities and the Ford Foundation.

 1. Herman Melville, *Typee, Omoo, Mardi* (1982)
 2. Nathaniel Hawthorne, *Tales and Sketches* (1982)
 3. Walt Whitman, *Poetry and Prose* (1982)
 4. Harriet Beecher Stowe, *Three Novels* (1982)
 5. Mark Twain, *Mississippi Writings* (1982)
 6. Jack London, *Novels and Stories* (1982)
 7. Jack London, *Novels and Social Writings* (1982)
 8. William Dean Howells, *Novels 1875–1886* (1982)
 9. Herman Melville, *Redburn, White-Jacket, Moby-Dick* (1983)
10. Nathaniel Hawthorne, *Collected Novels* (1983)
11. Francis Parkman, *France and England in North America*, vol. I (1983)
12. Francis Parkman, *France and England in North America*, vol. II (1983)
13. Henry James, *Novels 1871–1880* (1983)
14. Henry Adams, *Novels, Mont Saint Michel, The Education* (1983)
15. Ralph Waldo Emerson, *Essays and Lectures* (1983)
16. Washington Irving, *History, Tales and Sketches* (1983)
17. Thomas Jefferson, *Writings* (1984)
18. Stephen Crane, *Prose and Poetry* (1984)
19. Edgar Allan Poe, *Poetry and Tales* (1984)
20. Edgar Allan Poe, *Essays and Reviews* (1984)
21. Mark Twain, *The Innocents Abroad, Roughing It* (1984)
22. Henry James, *Literary Criticism: Essays, American & English Writers* (1984)
23. Henry James, *Literary Criticism: European Writers & The Prefaces* (1984)
24. Herman Melville, *Pierre, Israel Potter, The Confidence-Man, Tales & Billy Budd* (1985)
25. William Faulkner, *Novels 1930–1935* (1985)
26. James Fenimore Cooper, *The Leatherstocking Tales*, vol. I (1985)
27. James Fenimore Cooper, *The Leatherstocking Tales*, vol. II (1985)
28. Henry David Thoreau, *A Week, Walden, The Maine Woods, Cape Cod* (1985)
29. Henry James, *Novels 1881–1886* (1985)
30. Edith Wharton, *Novels* (1986)
31. Henry Adams, *History of the U.S. during the Administrations of Jefferson* (1986)
32. Henry Adams, *History of the U.S. during the Administrations of Madison* (1986)
33. Frank Norris, *Novels and Essays* (1986)
34. W.E.B. Du Bois, *Writings* (1986)
35. Willa Cather, *Early Novels and Stories* (1987)
36. Theodore Dreiser, *Sister Carrie, Jennie Gerhardt, Twelve Men* (1987)
37. Benjamin Franklin, *Writings* (1987)
38. William James, *Writings 1902–1910* (1987)
39. Flannery O'Connor, *Collected Works* (1988)
40. Eugene O'Neill, *Complete Plays 1913–1920* (1988)
41. Eugene O'Neill, *Complete Plays 1920–1931* (1988)
42. Eugene O'Neill, *Complete Plays 1932–1943* (1988)
43. Henry James, *Novels 1886–1890* (1989)
44. William Dean Howells, *Novels 1886–1888* (1989)
45. Abraham Lincoln, *Speeches and Writings 1832–1858* (1989)
46. Abraham Lincoln, *Speeches and Writings 1859–1865* (1989)
47. Edith Wharton, *Novellas and Other Writings* (1990)
48. William Faulkner, *Novels 1936–1940* (1990)
49. Willa Cather, *Later Novels* (1990)

50. Ulysses S. Grant, *Memoirs and Selected Letters* (1990)
51. William Tecumseh Sherman, *Memoirs* (1990)
52. Washington Irving, *Bracebridge Hall, Tales of a Traveller, The Alhambra* (1991)
53. Francis Parkman, *The Oregon Trail, The Conspiracy of Pontiac* (1991)
54. James Fenimore Cooper, *Sea Tales: The Pilot, The Red Rover* (1991)
55. Richard Wright, *Early Works* (1991)
56. Richard Wright, *Later Works* (1991)
57. Willa Cather, *Stories, Poems, and Other Writings* (1992)
58. William James, *Writings 1878–1899* (1992)
59. Sinclair Lewis, *Main Street & Babbitt* (1992)
60. Mark Twain, *Collected Tales, Sketches, Speeches, & Essays 1852–1890* (1992)
61. Mark Twain, *Collected Tales, Sketches, Speeches, & Essays 1891–1910* (1992)
62. *The Debate on the Constitution: Part One* (1993)
63. *The Debate on the Constitution: Part Two* (1993)
64. Henry James, *Collected Travel Writings: Great Britain & America* (1993)
65. Henry James, *Collected Travel Writings: The Continent* (1993)
66. *American Poetry: The Nineteenth Century,* Vol. 1 (1993)
67. *American Poetry: The Nineteenth Century,* Vol. 2 (1993)
68. Frederick Douglass, *Autobiographies* (1994)
69. Sarah Orne Jewett, *Novels and Stories* (1994)
70. Ralph Waldo Emerson, *Collected Poems and Translations* (1994)
71. Mark Twain, *Historical Romances* (1994)
72. John Steinbeck, *Novels and Stories 1932–1937* (1994)
73. William Faulkner, *Novels 1942–1954* (1994)
74. Zora Neale Hurston, *Novels and Stories* (1995)
75. Zora Neale Hurston, *Folklore, Memoirs, and Other Writings* (1995)
76. Thomas Paine, *Collected Writings* (1995)
77. *Reporting World War II: American Journalism 1938–1944* (1995)
78. *Reporting World War II: American Journalism 1944–1946* (1995)
79. Raymond Chandler, *Stories and Early Novels* (1995)
80. Raymond Chandler, *Later Novels and Other Writings* (1995)
81. Robert Frost, *Collected Poems, Prose, & Plays* (1995)
82. Henry James, *Complete Stories 1892–1898* (1996)
83. Henry James, *Complete Stories 1898–1910* (1996)
84. William Bartram, *Travels and Other Writings* (1996)
85. John Dos Passos, *U.S.A.* (1996)
86. John Steinbeck, *The Grapes of Wrath and Other Writings 1936–1941* (1996)
87. Vladimir Nabokov, *Novels and Memoirs 1941–1951* (1996)
88. Vladimir Nabokov, *Novels 1955–1962* (1996)
89. Vladimir Nabokov, *Novels 1969–1974* (1996)
90. James Thurber, *Writings and Drawings* (1996)
91. George Washington, *Writings* (1997)
92. John Muir, *Nature Writings* (1997)
93. Nathanael West, *Novels and Other Writings* (1997)
94. *Crime Novels: American Noir of the 1930s and 40s* (1997)
95. *Crime Novels: American Noir of the 1950s* (1997)
96. Wallace Stevens, *Collected Poetry and Prose* (1997)
97. James Baldwin, *Early Novels and Stories* (1998)
98. James Baldwin, *Collected Essays* (1998)
99. Gertrude Stein, *Writings 1903–1932* (1998)
100. Gertrude Stein, *Writings 1932–1946* (1998)
101. Eudora Welty, *Complete Novels* (1998)
102. Eudora Welty, *Stories, Essays, & Memoir* (1998)
103. Charles Brockden Brown, *Three Gothic Novels* (1998)
104. *Reporting Vietnam: American Journalism 1959–1969* (1998)
105. *Reporting Vietnam: American Journalism 1969–1975* (1998)
106. Henry James, *Complete Stories 1874–1884* (1999)

107. Henry James, *Complete Stories 1884–1891* (1999)
108. *American Sermons: The Pilgrims to Martin Luther King Jr.* (1999)
109. James Madison, *Writings* (1999)
110. Dashiell Hammett, *Complete Novels* (1999)
111. Henry James, *Complete Stories 1864–1874* (1999)
112. William Faulkner, *Novels 1957–1962* (1999)
113. John James Audubon, *Writings & Drawings* (1999)
114. *Slave Narratives* (2000)
115. *American Poetry: The Twentieth Century,* Vol. 1 (2000)
116. *American Poetry: The Twentieth Century,* Vol. 2 (2000)
117. F. Scott Fitzgerald, *Novels and Stories 1920–1922* (2000)
118. Henry Wadsworth Longfellow, *Poems and Other Writings* (2000)
119. Tennessee Williams, *Plays 1937–1955* (2000)
120. Tennessee Williams, *Plays 1957–1980* (2000)
121. Edith Wharton, *Collected Stories 1891–1910* (2001)
122. Edith Wharton, *Collected Stories 1911–1937* (2001)
123. *The American Revolution: Writings from the War of Independence* (2001)
124. Henry David Thoreau, *Collected Essays and Poems* (2001)
125. Dashiell Hammett, *Crime Stories and Other Writings* (2001)
126. Dawn Powell, *Novels 1930–1942* (2001)
127. Dawn Powell, *Novels 1944–1962* (2001)
128. Carson McCullers, *Complete Novels* (2001)
129. Alexander Hamilton, *Writings* (2001)
130. Mark Twain, *The Gilded Age and Later Novels* (2002)
131. Charles W. Chesnutt, *Stories, Novels, and Essays* (2002)
132. John Steinbeck, *Novels 1942–1952* (2002)
133. Sinclair Lewis, *Arrowsmith, Elmer Gantry, Dodsworth* (2002)
134. Paul Bowles, *The Sheltering Sky, Let It Come Down, The Spider's House* (2002)
135. Paul Bowles, *Collected Stories & Later Writings* (2002)
136. Kate Chopin, *Complete Novels & Stories* (2002)
137. *Reporting Civil Rights: American Journalism 1941–1963* (2003)
138. *Reporting Civil Rights: American Journalism 1963–1973* (2003)
139. Henry James, *Novels 1896–1899* (2003)
140. Theodore Dreiser, *An American Tragedy* (2003)
141. Saul Bellow, *Novels 1944–1953* (2003)
142. John Dos Passos, *Novels 1920–1925* (2003)
143. John Dos Passos, *Travel Books and Other Writings* (2003)
144. Ezra Pound, *Poems and Translations* (2003)
145. James Weldon Johnson, *Writings* (2004)
146. Washington Irving, *Three Western Narratives* (2004)
147. Alexis de Tocqueville, *Democracy in America* (2004)
148. James T. Farrell, *Studs Lonigan: A Trilogy* (2004)
149. Isaac Bashevis Singer, *Collected Stories I* (2004)
150. Isaac Bashevis Singer, *Collected Stories II* (2004)
151. Isaac Bashevis Singer, *Collected Stories III* (2004)
152. Kaufman & Co., *Broadway Comedies* (2004)
153. Theodore Roosevelt, *Rough Riders, An Autobiography* (2004)
154. Theodore Roosevelt, *Letters and Speeches* (2004)
155. H. P. Lovecraft, *Tales* (2005)
156. Louisa May Alcott, *Little Women, Little Men, Jo's Boys* (2005)
157. Philip Roth, *Novels & Stories 1959–1962* (2005)
158. Philip Roth, *Novels 1967–1972* (2005)
159. James Agee, *Let Us Now Praise Famous Men, A Death in the Family* (2005)
160. James Agee, *Film Writing & Selected Journalism* (2005)
161. Richard Henry Dana, Jr., *Two Years Before the Mast & Other Voyages* (2005)
162. Henry James, *Novels 1901–1902* (2006)
163. Arthur Miller, *Collected Plays 1944–1961* (2006)
164. William Faulkner, *Novels 1926–1929* (2006)

This book is set in 10 point Linotron Galliard,
a face designed for photocomposition by Matthew Carter
and based on the sixteenth-century face Granjon. The paper
is acid-free Domtar Literary Opaque and meets the requirements
for permanence of the American National Standards Institute. The
binding material is Brillianta, a woven rayon cloth made by Van
Heek-Scholco Textielfabrieken, Holland. The composition is by
Publishers' Design and Production Services, Inc. Printing
by Malloy Incorporated. Binding by Dekker Book-
binding. Designed by Bruce Campbell.

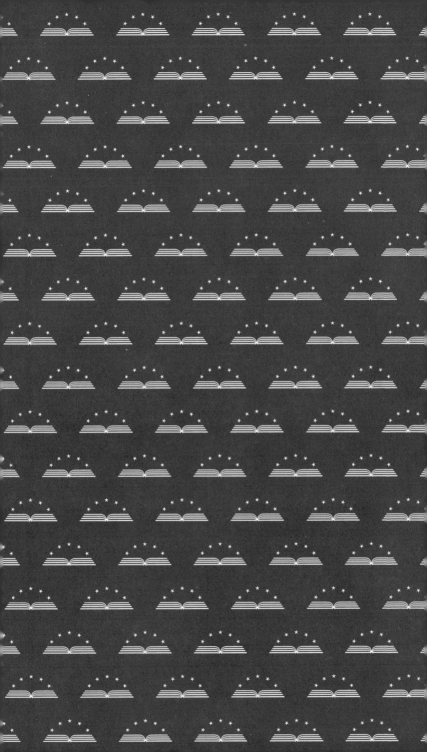